The History of the Tuesday Club

The History of the Ancient and Honorable Tuesday Club

BY DR. ALEXANDER HAMILTON

VOLUME III

Edited by Robert Micklus

PUBLISHED FOR THE INSTITUTE
OF EARLY AMERICAN HISTORY AND CULTURE
WILLIAMSBURG, VIRGINIA

BY THE UNIVERSITY OF NORTH CAROLINA PRESS
CHAPEL HILL AND LONDON

The Institute of Early American History and Culture
is sponsored jointly by the
College of William and Mary and the
Colonial Williamsburg Foundation.

© 1990 The University of North Carolina Press
All rights reserved
Manufactured in the United States of America

The paper in this book meets the guidelines for permanence
and durability of the Committee on Production Guidelines
for Book Longevity of the Council on Library Resources.

Printed in the United States of America

94 93 92 91 90   5 4 3 2 1

Library of Congress Cataloging-in-Publication Data

Hamilton, Alexander, 1712–1756.
    The history of the ancient and honorable Tuesday Club / by
Alexander Hamilton; edited by Robert Micklus.
        p.   cm.
    "Published for the Institute of Early American History and
Culture, Williamsburg, Virginia."
    Includes index.
    ISBN 0-8078-1851-8 (set: alk. paper)
    1. Annapolis (Md.)—History—Colonial period, ca. 1600–1775—
Fiction. 2. Tuesday Club (Annapolis, Md.)—History—18th century—
Fiction. 3. Maryland—History—Colonial period, ca. 1600–1775—
Fiction. I. Micklus, Robert. II. Institute of Early American
History and Culture (Williamsburg, Va.) III. Title.
PS763.H35H57   1990
813'.1—dc20   89-30768
                                                                CIP

Publication of these volumes was made possible by a grant from a fund established by DeWitt Wallace, founder of Reader's Digest.

CONTENTS

List of Music viii

The History of the Ancient and Honorable Tuesday Club, VOLUME III

    Contents 2
    Book XI 7
    Book XII 127
    Book XIII 217
    Book XIV 305

Appendixes 359

Punctuation Changes 379

Substantive Changes 394

Index to Volumes I–III 399

LIST OF MUSIC

Minuet for His Honor 44
Anniversary Ode for 1753 157
    Minuet for the Chancellor 158
    Minuet for His Honor 163
    Gavotte for His Honor 164
    Minuet for Sir John 167
    March for Sir John 167
Minuet for the Poet Laureat 171
Grand Club Jig 172
Overture for His Honor's Entertainment 173
Gavotta Burlesqua for His Honor 174
Minuet for the Attorney General 176
Song of Robin and Jeck 203
The Jurors for the City Bring 346

The History of the Tuesday Club

Volume III

History of The Ancient and Honorable Tuesday Club

From The earliest ages Down to the present times.

Volume III

Autor Noster, Ita describit heroas Clubicos, ut Incertus hæreat Lector, an eruditi magis, fortesve Essent, Corporisque potius aut animi viribus pollerent.

Contents of the History of the Ancient and honorable Tuesday Club

Volume III

Book XI

From the End of the Chancellors rebellion, and Civil wars Concerning the Great Seal, to the Convention of the Grand Committee.

Chapter I.	A Dissertation on the passions of great men, and the passions of Little men, and how they may be raised and depressed, by a propper application of flatulencies in Diet	1
Chapter II.	Celebration of the Seventh Anniversary, with the Anniversary Speech and Ode, libel on his honor the president and Club in the *New York Gazette*	19
Chapter III.	Conclusion of the Seventh Anniversary, with a Second Anniversary Speech by the orator	37
Chapter IV.	The Great Clubical battle of Farce-all-ia fought betwixt Coneïus Pimpeïus Frontinbrass the Great, on one Side, and Mr Secretary Scribble, Mr Protomusicus Neverout, and Laconic Comus Esqr, on the other, with the event of that dreadful Battle, which Compleats the History of Box No 1	56
Chapter V.	The Solem Trial and acquittal of Coneïus Pimpeïus Frontinbrass the Great, Strange Club Hieroglyphics	74
Chapter VI.	Miserable Defects in the Records by the Absence of the Secretary, diminutive duumvirate Club, Letter in Club Latin, yawning oration, Lamentation on the Late Eclipse of the Club by the poet Laureat	104
Chapter VII.	Grand musical Entertainment by Signior Lardini, heroic poem on it by the Poet Laureat	114

Contents

Chapter VIII. Maxims of the ancient & honorable Tuesday Club, Speech of Jonathan Grog Esqr, and other trivial matters 138

Chapter IX. Convention of the Grand Committee, Resolves of the same, examination of Negroe Jeoffry, Heroic Letter of Sir John, the Clubs answer, Irregular proceedings, *Carmen Dolorosum* of the Club. 144a

Book XII

From the Convention of the Grand Committee, to the Trial of Quirpum Comic Esqr.

Chapter I. Concerning Ceremonies, and their great use and Significancy in Civil life and in Clubs 167

Chapter II. An account of the Sneezing trespass by Negroe Peter, a short revival of the Conundrums, Spatterdash Wouldbe Esqr's facetious conversation, Protest of Slyboots pleasant Esqr, election of a Longstanding member 184

Chapter III. The humdrum Sederunt, The Metamorphosis of the bag and Seal, Letter from the Club to his honor the President, with the answer 196

Chapter IV. Celebration of the eight Anniversary, with the Anniversary Ode & Speech, anniversary music 204

Chapter V. Controverted Election of Crinkum Crankum Esqr, musical Composition of Signior Lardini, Learned Speech of Mr Protomusicus 237

Chapter VI. Misbehaviour of the Chancellor, Mr Protomusicus Created attorney General, Tryal of the Chancellor. 244

Chapter VII. Long adjournment of the Club, Speech of the Orator to the Chancellor, Eulogium of Jonathan Grog Esqr on the Club Supper in Verse. 263

Chapter VIII. Petition of Crinkum Crankum Esqr, Creation of Jno: Charlotto Gentleman, Clerk of the Kitchen to the Club, Speech of the Orator. 273

Chapter IX. Confirmation law passed, Accrostic on the Poet Laureat, The Champions departure from the Club, Trial of Quirpum Comic Esqr. 288

Book XIII

From the Forced Club, to the Confirmation of Crinkum Crankum Esqr.

Chapter I.	[introductory essay is missing]	
Chapter II.	The forced Club, δακρυα μελπομενης of the Club, Petition of the Charlestown Club, presented by Mr Broadface round	
Chapter III.	Congratulatory Ode by the poet Laureat, altercation of the president and Chancellor, Learned Club Letter, Second long adjournment of the Club	336
Chapter IV.	Celebration of the 9th Anniversary, anniversary ode & Speech	349
Chapter V.	The Chancellors farewell oration, the attorney Generals Speech against the Late Chancellor, Resolves	369
Chapter VI.	First Tavern Club, held by his honor the President, The Chancellors Poem, Protomusicuses answer to it, Election of a Longstanding member	382
Chapter VII.	Second Tavern Club, Concert of frogs, Critical Epistle by the Secretary, Poem on the Club Tobacco box, by the poet Laureat	401
Chapter VIII.	Speech of Crinkum Crankum Esqr, Confirmation of a Longstanding member, Dr Jaunter's Speech on a Cat's tail	422
Chapter IX.	Tryal of Crinkum Crankum Esqr, Speech of his honor the President	435
Chapter X.	Confirmation of Crinkum Crankum Esqr, Proclamation by his honor's order, Second Speech of Crinkum Crankum Esqr	449

Book XIV

From the Third Tavern Sederunt, to the Celebration of the Tenth Anniversary.

Chapter I.	[introductory essay is missing]	
Chapter II.	Extempore ode of the poet Laureat on his honors Entertainment, Third and 4th Taveren Sederunt, Trial of Crinkum Crankum Esqr	

Contents

Chapter III. Commission of Coll: Comico Butman granted by Coney Pimp Frontinbrass Esqr, Several motions in Club, Speech of the Orator, a new record book ordered, Jonathan Grog Esqr, accused 507

Chapter IV. Mr Attorney Woudbe appears in Club, Trial of Jonathan Grog Esqr, his Condemnation and Sentence, new Song Introduced by his honor the President, Congratulatory Pyndaric Ode by the Poet Laureat 530

Chapter V. Information of Mr Attorney Woudbe, Plea to the Information, Trial of the Attorney General, Historical Sederunt 553

The History of the Ancient and Honorable Tuesday Club

Book XI

From the end of the Chancellor's Rebellion, and Civil wars Concerning the Great Seal, To the Convention of the Grand Committee.

Chapter I

A Dissertation on the Passions of Great men, and the Passions of little men, and how they may be raised and depressed, by a proper application of flatulencies in Diet.

The Subject of the passions has been treated on, by authors of various degrees and abilities, and tho' it affords a large and extensive view, and lays open a Scene of Infinite Variety, yet, there is not a Spot of that vast and Spacious field, that has not been trod over and over again, so that there appears not so much as one pile of Grass, herb or flower, with which a Clubical Author of these our degenerate and threadbare times might bundle up a nosegay, to present as a novelty to the Curious.

In treating of the Passions then, in this Introductory Chapter of the Eleventh book of our history, I do not pretend, (as Indeed I do not know, that I have any where pretended, above once or twice) to produce any thing new upon the Subject, but only to model it out, into a Shape Suitable ‖ to my own fancy and the Capacity and genius of my Readers (if ever I shall have any) which figure, when finished, and exposed to view, if it takes with, or pleases the fancy of any other person, I shall be satisfied, and, if it does not, I shall still be satisfied, being determined before hand, to make myself as easy as an old Shoe, about the matter.

Neither do I propose here, to give a full and Compleat history of the passions, being very Sensible, that it would Require a larger volume, to Comprehend the whole of that Subject, than what would largely Contain all the Transactions of this ponderous and Important Club History which I now write.

The Subject I Intend then to dwell upon, is the passions of Great men, and the passions of little men, what their effects and operations are, in these two different Subjects, and how they may properly be exalted and depressed in either, and regulated in both.

And, if I should, as I go along, in handling this Important Subject, use any Phrazes, Similies, or allusions, not altogether natural or Reconcileable to what is Called Reason or Common Sense, whose places are often assumed by folly and Common nonsense, I hope the Indulgent Reader will pardon me, upon the Credit of the following apology, which I own to have borrowed of that unparallelld, moderen Orator Henly, vizt: "That I use them, because altogether Novell, and what no man ever could think of before," as that Indefatigable Declaimer replied to the person, who taxed him for extolling the Power of Omnipotence, in one of his Ranting extempore prayers, which had extended and spread forth, the mighty *babe of the Universe;*[1] but, that I may avoid the mistakes, which many writers have fallen into, by || neglecting to give Clear and plain definitions of their Subject before they go to work upon it; I shall here define, as Clearly as I am able, what I mean by *Great men,* what by *Little men* and what by *Passions*.

By *great men* then, it is not to be supposed that I mean tall men, or thick men, or fat men, or men of Large Gygantic limbs, neither do I expressly mean, all kings, Emperors, princes, or potentates of any Superior rank or degree to other mortals, or men of Great and Extraordinary Learning and Genius; But what I Intend by the term *Great Man,* is *A mortal wight, who from the Sole merit of some accidental qualities, which fortune has thrown in his way, exalts himself so far above his bretheren of the same Species, that he cannot see them so distinctly, as to discern them to be in the same Scale of nature with himself, but Imagines them to belong to some Inferior Class of Animals, among the brutal tribes.*

By *little men,* I do not mean, your small, dapper, dwarfish, slender, Spider Limb'd fellows, nor your mechanics, beggars or black Guards, or such as are often Called Tag rag and bobtail,[2] nor men of small talents or

---

1. John Henley (1692–1756), or Orator Henley, contributed to the *Spectator* as "Dr. Quir" and published numerous works on oratory, theology, and grammar.
2. "Tag rag and bobtail" refers to the rabble, especially those engaged in unsavory professions.

abilities, nor Ignorant and Simple men, nor such, as for want of the abovenamed fortuitous Qualifications, are of no Note, Credit or account in the world, or, for whom no body cares a farthing, but, by *Small Men*, I mean, *Such as are apt to think, that the aforesaid Great men, who stand much exalted above their heads, are something more than mortal, or a kind of Deities, to be Courted worshiped and adored, and therefore, follow and Cringe upon them, like Spainels, and esteem it even an honor, to be spurned kicked and spit upon by them, for no other Reason, or reward, but that they may be allowed to bask like Sluggish beetles, under the Sunshine of their gracious Countenances.*

By *Passions*, I do not mean these tender and Placid affections of the mind, which have a tendency towards benevolent, || kind, Charitable, heroic, honorable and Grateful actions, and delight the Soul, as it were, with a perpetual Sunshine and State of Serenity, which the aforesaid Specieses of Great and little men never experience, but, I thereby Intend *All these rude, noisy, Contracted, narrow, and Selfish affections, which excite, and blow up perpetual Clouds, fogs, Damps, hurricanes & Storms, in the perturbed minds of the aforesaid great and little men, vizt: Pride, Ambition, Avarice, Envy, Ingratitude and hatred.* [4]

Of these ruling passions then, in the two Classes of great & little men above discribed, I shall treat as Largely as the Compass of this work will allow; and, as great men, in point of modish Ceremony and Civility demand our first notice, I shall pay so much deference to the general accepted Custom & begin with them.

Our Great men then, may be Considered as Automotory machines, which are moved and agitated by a kind of Inherent mechanical Influence, by no means subjected to the guidance of Reason. These great Bodies are Complicated Machines, which when they approach near one another are mutually affected with an attractive and repulsive power, according to the proportion of Size they bear to one another, to the Nature and quality of their Component principles, and most of these Great Bodies have both an attrachent and repellent power Lodged in them, Like the opposite ends of an electrized Glass tube, and of this I am apt to think they participate, from a Certain Subtile penetrating and pervading Substance, much like the electrical fluid, or perhaps the same, which may be evinced, by an easy experiment, vizt: taking one or more of these great bodies into a dark Room in frosty weather, and dusting their Coats well with a Crab tree Cudgel, and rubbing them down very hard with a Curry Comb || and brush, to observe exactly, what quantum of Sparks or fire would emigrate from his bodily mass, and thus, a Judgement must be framed, how much of this attractive and repellent quality, the great man had, or how much, in this respect one [5]

Great man differed from another, that is, how much one Great body excelled the other in quantum of Moderen Merit.

Now, tho' this attrachent and repellant fluid, Lodged in the great Bodies we speak of, has a visible effect of either attracting or repelling, when two or more of these great Bodies encounter one another, yet the operation is not so Strong and vigorous in this case, as when a great body meets with one or more Small bodies, for then it operates most violently either the one way or the other, or both, and sets these Smaller bodies into the most violent agitations and Circumvolutions like the *motor Centralis* in Descartes's vortex.[3]

Thus for Example, when two very great bodies meet in their proper Sphere of action, for example, at court or in the drawing room, or at the Prince's Levée, we can soon perceive how they affect each other, in their attractive power, by that easy smooth, Swimming and placid motion, which they put one another under, expressed in a Genteel tip toe walk, an easy flexure of the body, a wave of the hand, and a pleasant familiar Smile or Grin, on the Countenance, all which wonderful postures and attitudes, of these Immense bodies, are purely mechanical, being not excited by the operations or Influence of any Intelligent mind, again, when two such great Bodies happen to repell each other, the motion is slow and Stately, proportioned to the quantum of matter which it Influences, and appears in the Shape of a haughty Strut, an Indignant frown, and a turn of the two heads a || Contrary way, *en passant,* so, as that each forms as it were a curve line, like the Section of a Parabola, upon the opposite Sides of the way or Street.

But, in Case of the encounter of one Great Body, with one or more little bodies, these phænomena of attraction and repulsion appear in a much more vehement and Surprizing manner, for, like so many Straws, feathers or Grains of dust, at the approach of a large Electrized tube, that are precipitately hurried towards the tube, and adhere to its Surface, in a tremulous Sort of motion, or repell'd from it, as if agitated with a blast of wind, keep their proper distance, and as it were endeavor to get without the Sphere of action of the electrized body, these Small bodies, at the approach of a great one replete with this attracting and repelling fluid, run, rush and fly Confusedly one over the other, Tumble, Jumble and dance about, like so many mad things, and either Cleave to the Surface of the Great body, as it

---

3. Descartes discusses "le centre d'agitation" in numerous letters, but see especially "Descartes à Mersenne," Mar. 2, 1646? "Descartes à Cavendish," Mar. 30, 1646, and "Descartes à Cavendish," June 15, 1646, *Oeuvres de Descartes,* ed. Charles Adam and Paul Tannery (Paris, 1897–1910), IV, 366–371, 379–389, 429–435.

attracts them, or run off precipitately as if the Devil chased them, when it repells.

I believe the truth of what I have here asserted might be made Clear, by many plain experiments, which might daily fall in the way of but a Cursory and Superficial observator; if he will only be at the expence and trowble, of attending for a few days, the two Courts of Versailes and London, or St James's, and get himself introduced once or twice by a friend, to a great Lord's or prime minister's levee, where he will be diverted with numberless examples, of these attractions and repulsions of both Sorts, his whole apparatus of Instruments, to enable him to go thro a Compleat ‖ course of experiments of this kind, are a well dressd wig, a Sword, and a Gentile hired Suit of Cloaths. [7]

Now, the design of this Philosophical, or rather Physical enquiry, which I have but slightly touched upon, is to pave a way to account mechanically for the passions of great men, and the passions of little men, which I believe, I may affirm, without deviating from truth, proceed altogether, from this Subtile automotory fluid, and provided, any Ingenious Gentleman, will undertake to prove, that they, in any the least probable manner, proceed from Rational principles or motives, I am not so fond of this my new Coined Hypothesis, but I shall be ready Immediatly, upon such a Theory being well and Solidly Confirmed, to fling it up Entirely.

How can ambition for example, which is a Climbing passion, peculiar to great men, be founded upon any Rational principle, when it actuates and Influences the great body Inflate with it, in such a manner, as to make it take direct courses towards it's own ruin & destruction, The Subtile fluid in this Case, or rather the *Ignis fatuus* or wild fire,[4] that moves the mighty mass, having a tendency to shoot upwards, carries the ponderous mass along with it, sometimes ascending slowly sometimes briskly to such a prodigious height, that going quite beyond it's Sphere of action, or overshooting the mark, It relinquishes the Sluggish lump, and down it falls and is crushed to pieces, and, if this should not happen, yet still it may encounter in its way, a body as ponderous ‖ and large, or larger and more ponderous than itself, and both encountering, with tremendous percussion and Collision, either one falls, or both fall, and are shattered to pieces together, to me, it would seem as absurd to say, that this passion in the great, proceeds from reason, as to affirm that a fellow acts reasonably, that gets up to [8]

---

4. *Ignis fatuus* literally means "foolish fire" (a flamelike phosphorescence produced over marshes by the spontaneous combustion of decayed vegetable matter, which eludes those who attempt to follow it).

the Top of the monument, and throws himself down precipitately on the pavement below, either thro premeditated design, or by a dizziness in his head, occasioned by his Inconsiderately looking from so great a height.

Let us next view the passion of pride, which agrees with ambition in its Climbing faculty, only that it Climbs in a more ridiculous and safer manner, for evading the danger of Broken bones, it is often Contented with standing on the Summit of a mighty dunghill, or looking with Contempt on those who walk below, from a high Garret window, or balcony, from whence, if Chance should throw the body possessed with it, that body is generally more bemired than hurt, and therefore fitter to be laughed at than pitied, Pride also, besides its disposition to Climb, is very much given to puff up, swell and Bloat, and labor under the distemper Called a Tympany, and, on this account, like the frog in the fable, often runs the risque of Bursting,[5] and, I believe, it would be a hard matter to convince people in their Senses, that a man, from the principles of Reason, would Chuse to be always in a place, where he smelt a Stink, or Rush into a mire, or suffer himself to be blown up with air 'till he burst, it is much || more probable, that all great bodies thus affected, are acted upon mechanically, by the aforesaid *Ignis fatuus,* or erratic Subtile fluid, which, in this Instance is of that Sort, that travels over Stinking marshes, and bogs, and sometimes will take its Station, on the top of a hillock or small rising ground.

Avarice is another passion, peculiar to great men, which comes properly under our view, nor is it possible for the greatest Sophister, to demonstrate even in his Shuffling way of Reasoning, that this passion proceeds upon Rational principles, for, can that man act rationally, who starves in the midst of Plenty, can that man act upon the grounds of either Justice or Reason, that beholds the distresses of a friend, nay, of a wife, parent, Son or brother with a hardened heart and a dry Eye, insomuch as to withhold from them, that relief, which is amply in his power, without Injuring himself to bestow, does he act reasonably, who voluntarily draws upon himself, the Contempt of the whole world about him, we may as well mantain, that man to be guided by reason, who burns with thrist and pines with hunger, and yet has the most delicate viands, and the most delicious Liquors within his reach, or, that he rules himself by Reason, who, like the Celebrated Don Jumpedo,[6] would Confine himself, for a small gain to the narrow Compass of a quart bottle, when he has the open and free air, to walk lye and sit in.

---

5. Hamilton is recalling Jean de La Fontaine's fable "The Frog Who Would Be an Ox," in which the frog swells his chest to appear oxlike and bursts (*Oeuvres,* ed. Jean Longnon, 10 vols. [Paris, 1927–1928], III, 53).

6. Apparently a figure in a popular 18th-century farce (see p. 49n, below).

This passion therefore of avarice, so apt to actuate || great bodies, must [10] proceed Intirely from the operations of this Subtile fluid, when it Contracts itself to a point in the Center of the mighty mass, and by its particular attractive quality, has an Influence on all metals, particularly Gold and Silver, the first of which metals, it will not penetrate divide or Consume, but mildly glides over it's Surface, without wasting or Carrying along with it the least particle.

These passions, peculiar to great men, produce in the world mighty Confusion, and disorder, being the real original or ground work of Treasons, Rebellions, murders, wars, massacres, depopulations, desolations, ravages, Robberies, rapes, persecutions, executions, tortures, racks, Impostures, Cheats, perjuries, and the most execrable villanies that can be mentioned in the Devil's black list, and what is most Strange, all these things, horrid and Shoking as they are, proceed Intirely from a mere mechanical operation on the Great bodies above mentioned, and not in the least from the Grounds and principles of Reason, for from these excellent principles, proceeds nothing but what is in it self consistent Just, perfect, regular and wise.

I come now to treat alittle on the passions of little men, nor are we to think that these little men have different passions, or are actuated by a different principle from the Great men, as their bodies are Composed of the same Stuff & Materials, they must of necessity be actuated by the same prin- || ciple, tho in a lesser degree, for, as their mass of matter is much less, [11] so the quantum of the pervading fluid must be less also, from this Similitude in their Structure, these little men are at times very apt to mimic or Copy after the great bodies and will arrogantly and ridiculously take upon them to be ambitious, proud and avaricious, and these pursuits will be made with almost the same effects, as in great bodies, that is they will fall from the triffling heights to which they can aspire, but will not be Crushed, because their mass of matter is so small and Compact, that the force of the fall cannot separate its parts, They will tumble Into the kennel, and will come out as Clean as they were before, they will keep every thing to themselves and be very Scraping and Close, but no body is either Surprized or offended, as knowing the verity of the Scriptural proverb, *to whom nothing is given, nothing can be required or expected,*[7] in fine these little bodies, when they are affected in the same manner as the Great ones, serve for no other purpose, but to afford matter of fun and laughter, to all reasonable Spectators.

7. Hamilton is paraphrasing Luke 12:48 (cf. Matt. 25:29).

But there are some passions peculiar, and natural to these little bodies, which we must not here pass over, and which in themselves are every way as strange as those that affect the great, (not that the great are Intirely exempt from these) such as Ingratitude, envy and hatred; neither are those passions in Little men, guided or Influenced in the least by reason, any more than those of the Great, but are Intirely under the [Influence] of the repellent power of the Subtile Igneous fluid above mentioned, for, these Small bodies, Contain too little of that Subtile principle in them, to partake much of its attractive power, and are Intirely swallowed up in the vortex of the great, so often as they come within their Sphere of action, which is greater or Less, according to the extent or dimension of the Great bodies.

[12] Ingratitude is a passion quite natural, to a rude and unpolished lump of passive matter, for, if you roll it, tumble it, toss it or thresh it, 'twill still be Insensible, Tis true, as it is capable of motion by Impulse, should you kick it with your foot, it will go from you, should you draw it with a String, it will come after you, should you throw it up against a wall, it will recoil upon you, but will still be the same Insensate passive matter as before, and, of this Sort of matter, a great number of your Little men are Intirely compounded, tho' many that may be called little men, have a different contexture, and frame, from this, Just now described, their parts being polished and finished as nicely as those of Greater bodies, and resemble mirrors, or Looking Glasses as much as the greater masses, but their Surfaces are so minute, that it must be small, very small objects Indeed that they can reflect, these little bodies are so very small, that they may come under the Class of Atoms, and their Influence so triffling, that it is never felt, and therefore, not regarded by the numberless bodies greater than themselves, and, for this reason, they may move or be at rest, rise, fall, recoil, Impell and make a Coil, and yet nothing at all be felt, or known of the matter, in short, they are too small, to excite any agitation or tumult, among the greater bodies that surround them, and these are what most properly come under the denomination of Small men, and to Compare the whole aggregate of great and Small bodies In human Society, to a Stately fabric, these minute Corpuscles are only pins, which serve to fill up the crevices, left between the Jointures of the greater bodies, but neither serve to beautify or enlarge the fabric, for [13] were they taken away ‖ would the fabric loose any thing of its Size or beauty, tho it might be Impaired in its Strength and be apt to totter on its base, for want of these diminute propugnacula,[8] little, and Inconsiderable as they appear to be.

---

8. A *propugnacle* is a bulwark or rampart, or more figuratively a defense or protection; here Hamilton uses it to mean a support.

Hatred is a passion, to which little men are much addicted, this is effected by the repellent force of the Subtile fluid, which makes these little bodies fly from and rebuff one another, shunning at all times the least appearance of a Coalition or union; neither can this little and base passion, claim kindred in the most remote degree to reason, for, if it was founded on reason, what gross absurdities should we make reason subject to, since one little man, might with the same reason hate another little man for being taller, plumper, of a fairer Complexion, higher nose or whiter teeth, as for being richer, wiser, or better born and bred, which are the common Subjects of hatred among little men, for these latter, are qualifications altogether as accidental as the first, and therefore, neither are proper or rational Subjects for hatred or resentment, we shall Certainly then come nigher to the truth if we ascribe this passion of hatred in little men, to that antipathy, which exists in nature betwixt Certain Heterogenious Substances, and put reason quite out of the question.

Envy, which I ought to have mentioned before hatred, being its proper parent, is also a passion to which little men are very subject, it being the particular Characteristic, of little diminutive Souls, (to speak in the Stile of some Philosophers) to be Invidious; but the Soul, as we are taught by metaphysicians, is a rational Essence, and Envy, being a Gross terrestrial passion that Snake like, loves to Creep along the ground, it can have nothing to do with so Etherial a Substance as the Soul, but must be Intirely Corporeal, and probably arises from a violent nisus of the Subtile fluid above described, to penetrate or pervade || to the deepest caverns of the [14] earth, whence it originally was exhaled, and Carry its little body along with it into the Lowest abyss, for envy is observed to be a passion that is perpetually sinking, and never attempts to rise or shoot upwards, in fine, it is the direct opposite to ambition, Tho' it is often the Child of a Secret pride.

The passions of little men have their effects, as well as those of the Great, and these effects are most Clearly perceived in little towns and little Societies or little Clubs, where the little Inhabitants, and little members, are generally either in a ferment or Stagnation one with another about their little affairs, that is, they either outragiously quarrell, neighbour with neighbour, or behave in a Cold Indifferent manner, one towards another, but, these passions and ferments of little men, seldom make such a Clutter and noise, as the passions of the Great, unless at the Elections of Burroughs and Counties for members of parliament, where, a great Concourse of these little men, Joining forces together, raise such hubbubs and hurly burlys, as are Sufficient to set a whole nation in a flame, this, they are Capable to do, when collected in mighty bodies, as Statesmen, but the devil himself cannot withstand, the fury of a multitude of little men, whose passions are up, by the noisy preaching of an Itinerant Enthusiast preacher, & experience has always proved it to be true, that this Sort of fury gathers Strength by being resisted.

[15] It may be thought Strange, that, in this my Philosophical Essay on the passions, I have not so much as once mentioned anger, which is often Called Passion by way of Eminence, and is common, both to great, and to little men, and likewise has as little to do with reason as any of them, but my de- || sign is to be as short upon this large Subject as possible, and therefore I shall here purposely ommitt speaking of several other passions, which great and little men Enjoy in Common, such as Romantic Love, Jealousy, hope, fear, grief, despair, Joy &ct: expecting that some abler pen will bring this Scheme of mine to greater perfection, than either my time or abilities will permit me; I think I shall have honor enough in giving the first hint, and therefore I shall drop all the above recited passions, except anger, on which I beg leave to say a word or two.

Anger then in great men is a dreadful and noisy thing as Long as it lasts, but according to the poet, it is for the most part a *furor brevis;*[9] as things are best Illustrated by Similies, I shall produce a Simile here, which, if duely Considered, will give a Clear Idea, of the anger of a Great man; a Great man, then, while his anger is a rising, is like a Chesnut roasting in the fire, and, according as his anger rises slowly or suddenly, we may Consider him as placed among the red hot Coals, or buried in the Smother of hot ashes & Embers, the effect of the fire on a Chesnut, we know, is to make it yield a mighty Crack, bounce, or report, Jump to one Side or the other, drive all the little particles of ashes before it & raise a great dust and Smother, and, at last, if not removed from the fire it flames out itself, and burns quietly away to a Coal, Just so it is, with a great man, in a violent passion he makes a mighty noise and report, drives the Croud of little bodies before him and turnes every thing upside down, and very often is reduced to a Contemptible Coal, and falls at last to light ashes, so that the anger of the great, tho dreadful, yet ends at last in vanity, and after it has made all the havoc, and done all the mischief it can, is forgot.

[16] In little men, anger makes a different appearance, which to render more Intelligible, I shall also Illustrate with a Simile, let us then Seriously consider a porridge pot, boiling on the fire, and, as pease are very flatulent

---

9. This phrase initially appears in Horace (*Epistulae* 1.2.62), but Hamilton is perhaps recalling Petrarch's use of it (*Sonetti sopra vari argomenti,* sonnet 19) or Shakespeare's (*Timon of Athens,* act 1, sc. 2, line 28).

things and therefore most adapted to our present Subject, let the boiling Stuff if you please be pease porridge, the most conspicuous phenomena, which this pot of porridge exhibits, in the act of ebullition, are the frequent rising of gross, thick, and opaque bubbles, which by the rarefaction of the air, burst with a small puff, scatter a few of their gross particles round, and terminate in a little modicum of evanescent vapor or Smoke; Just such is the passion of a little man, his gross and Sluggish Corpuscles, being agitated with anger, as the viscid particles of this porridge, are by the fire, swell somewhat, and appear bigger than they really are, and the whole ends in a slight bespattering, and perhaps a triffling Scalding of such as are bespattered, and then all Concludes with a diminutive puff or vapor. From this Simile of the porridge pot, we may account for the Common Comparison of a little man of no note to *a Chip in porridge*.¹⁰

From this new Theory and Chain of Reasoning, I hope I have made it evident, that the passions have not the least Connexion with reason, nor reason with the passions, and Consequently, how absurd it is for Philosophers to lay down rules for governing the passions by reason, as if these passions were ever Intended, to be under any rule or Government, what are properly called passions are Lawless, and can come under no restraint, but, as the Roman poet well expresses it *qua datur porta ruunt;*¹¹ 'Tis true Indeed, some Certain portions of the ‖ Soul called affections are properly the Subjects of reason and are led, in decent order by that wise Governante, such as heroic Love, mercy, Charity and Compassion, and an Esteem for Truth and true honor, I say true honor, because that word is often applied to triffles, which dont deserve the name, Such, is the honor of a Gentleman Gamester, who defrauds a poor Industrious tradesman, of the Just debt he owes him, for a valuable Consideration, to pay off his debts of honor to Sharpers, and the honor of an Insignificant Coxcomb, who runs an honest man thro the guts for speaking a word awry, or putting him in mind that he tells a lie, but, as these affections belong not to my Subject, I shall drop them here.

Some, I doubt, will think this Scheme of mine a very absurd one, and my reasoning extremely triffling, but whatever the opinion of the Critics may be, I have this to Comfort me; That is, In the first place, I care not what they think, and lastly, I have some Great men in the writing way to keep me in Countenance, vizt: Mr Hobbes & Spinosa in morals, and Machiavel in Politics, among whom too I might have mentioned our Country-

---

10. A *chip in porridge* is a matter of no importance.
11. "They rush through whatever door is open" (Vergil, *Aeneid* 1.83).

men Colins, Mandevil and Woolston, and, if I mention also Dr Whiston as a writer of the whimsical Class, I believe, I shall not be so much out in my latitude, as that pious and Reverend Gentleman, was in his Longitude.[12]

I shall Conclude this Physical dissertation, with delivering my Sentiments concerning a proper diet, to regulate these passions in great and little men, for, as they are purely Physical, or mechanical, they may be Intirely regulated by Physical or mechanical operators, this diet then, ought to be of the flatulent || Sort, in both Subjects, and the more or less you apply of this flatulent diet, the passions in these Subjects will fall or rise, for kings, great princes, and potentates, the proper diet is flattery and adulation, this is a diet they relish mightily, and therefore they are always provided with numbers of expert cooks, who understand how to prepare this flatulent fare, and Cram it plentifully down their Throats, and, for the most part, it finds an easy passage, tho often given in monstrous great and gross morsels, this Inflates these great men and their great courtiers to such a degree that it is a very Common thing with them to forget that they are only mortal men, and, their passions being elevated to an Extravagant pitch, That is to say, their pride, avarice and ambition, the Consequence is, battles, murders, massacres, fire & Sword, and the most egregious Cruelties, and Shoking barbarities.

As for the passions in little men, they may easily be regulated by proper quantities of pease porridge and Small beer, the first may be prepared by any Common Cook, and the Latter is to be had any where at a triffling price, these, according to the quantities exhibited, will raise the passions of these little mortals to a higher or a Lower pitch, but even at the highest they are Incapable of doing much mischief or Creating much noise, the greatest mischief they can arrive at, is that of the ravages and rude exploits of a mob, vizt: breaking windows, pulling down meeting houses and Sign posts, burning the Pope and the Pretender with the Devil in effigie, and, when all the din and racket is over, they terminate in a triffling puffing and bouncing, like Schoolboys Squibs & Crackers, and produce little more than wind and Stink.

---

12. Anthony Collins (1676–1729) was an English deist and author of essays including *Use of Reason* (1707), *Discourse of Free Thinking* (1713), and *Inquiry concerning Human Liberty* (1715). Thomas Woolston (1670–1733) was an English deist who challenged the clergy in his freethinking tracts, especially the six *Discourses* (1727–1729), which questioned the miracles of the New Testament and caused his imprisonment. William Whiston (1667–1752) was an English theologian and mathematician who was expelled from Cambridge in 1710 for his Arian views, which he elaborated upon in *Primitive Christianity Revived* (London, 1711–1712). Whiston was a bit off in his "longitude" when he prophesied the end of the world in *A New Theory of the Earth, from Its Original, to the Consummation of All Things* (London, 1696).

Chapter II

Celebration of the Seventh anniversary, with the anniversary Speech and Ode, libel on his honor the President and Club, in the New York Gazette.

Far the greatest part of mankind, give themselves no manner of trowble about forming a true Judgement of things, they Judge altogether from outward appearances and the ear and eye are the Chief guides. Hence we see, that a fellow in a rich and Splendid dress, with a pompous equipage, gains Immediate esteem among the Multitude, and, from the Showyness of his trappings, They are apt to believe that they cover something excellent, while a ragged and Shabby mortal is utterly disregarded, and spoke to with a kind of reluctance, as if the Sordidness of his Character, was of a piece with that of his dress,—a man on foot, tho wise and Learned, is Jostled by every Saucy Chairman or porter, while a fellow in a gilt Chariot is given way to with respect, tho' probably a Good for nothing Coxcomb. (yet by the bye, this giving way by the foot passengers, may be enforced more by his horses than himself) This is a very absurd association of Ideas, and yet, it generally prevails; it was doubtless from the Consideration of this weakness in Human nature, that the honorable Mr President Jole, condescended at first, contrary to his natural modesty and Good Sense, to ornament his person with several gaudy trappings, as Caps of State, mallets of State, Canopies of State, and presidential Stars and badges of State, knowing, that the Longstanding members, as men, being liable to the Common foibles of humanity, would, from these gaudy ornaments sooner conceive that high opinion of him, which it was necessary they should entertain of their president, but, that once obtained and confirmed, by his wisdom and Conduct, that Great and wise president, thought it now high time to throw aside these bawbles and vanities, as we have related in the preceeding book, and rest Intirely on the merit of the Latter, as the firmest and most lasting basis of esteem. He had also laid aside the Title of *Lord President,* as vain and assuming, but one piece of Grandure, he still retained in his own hands, as thinking it of some Solidity and Signification, vizt: the privilege of celebrating at his own house, with the usual pomp and grandure, the anniversary of the Club, a relation of which Solemnity, Celebrated now for the Seventh time, I proceed to deliver.

At Sederunt 179, May 12th 1752, being the Seventh Anniversary of the ancient and honorable Tuesday Club, the Longstanding members met in their badges, at the house of the honorable Mr President Jole H:S: where, were present, besides his honor, eight Longstanding members, 4 honorary members, vizt: Mr Broadface Round, Dr Polihystor, Capt: Dio Ramble and Jealous Spyplot Junr Esqr, now from a regular, become an honorary member, on account of his Removal from town, and also five Strangers, among whom was Laconic Comas Esqr.

His honor the President as h:s: entertained the Club very magnificently, as usual, upon this Grand and Solemn occasion, the entertainment consisting of a Genteel Supper, where ‖ boiled, roast, and baked made a gorgeous appearance, in Splendid dishes, and were washed down with variety of good liquors.

The Poet Laureat, after Supper, was Called upon to recite the Anniversary Ode, but said he had really forgot to bring it with him, and, desiring to be excused, till such time as Signr Lardini, should bring the music of the said Ode, which he humbly conceived would be the fittest and most favorable time for him to recite it, but, notwithstanding this negligence of the poet Laureat, it will not be Improper to give a transcript of this Ode here.

A Pyndaric Anniversary Ode,

For the ancient and honorable Tuesday Club, for the year 1752, humbly Inscribed, to the Right Honorable Carlo, Lord president of the said Club, and his Long Standing members by,

Their most humble Servant
The Club's Poet Laureat.

To be set to music in three parts, but never done, on account of the Indisposition of Signior Lardini.

Recitativo
Whilst I again aspire
To tune the Joyous Lyre,
I sing nor king, nor Duke, nor Earl, ho,
These themes are abject, Low and Scrub,
Nam'd with the ancient Tuesday Club
And her Lord President, the most Illustrious Carlo.

Aria
See, in his Chair
Aloft in air,

Our Great and awful Lord,
   And at his right
   A valiant knight
With keen and Brandish'd Sword.
Chorus
Say, ancient Club, what canst thou fear
When such a valiant knight is near?
What honors mayst thou hope to share
When so much wisdom fills thy Chair,
   To Rule and give the Law,
   O blest Society,
   Where members all agree,
For such a Club, we never saw,
   Nor e'er again shall see.
Recitativo
Hail we Annapolis the fair,
Blest City she, without Compare,
Her Sister Cities she outshines
   And Rules without Controul,
Who holds within her blest confines
The great, the wise, the Noble Jole.
Aria

[23]

O Jole, Inspirer of my verse,
   I now renounce the nine,
When I the Tuesday Club rehearse
   And thy Sweet praise,
   To Crown my Lays,
My Songs, my odes, my Rondelays,
   I'll Crave no aid but thine.
General grand Chorus
   Sing Jo! Jo! Jo! thrice,
   Longstanding members all,
  Sound every Instrument and voice
And fill with harmony his Lordship's hall,
  With Violin and harpsicord
     With flutes
     With lutes
    Proclaim my Lord,
Whilst from each gaping mouth flow warblings Sweet,
  Ye drums and trumpets too, come on,

> Sound, sound a march to brave Sir John,
> And Crown the Song with this Important prayer,
> Long live Lord Jole to fill our ancient Chair
> Till thousand anniversarys revolve,
>   And may his Club alone
>   Of ancient Clubs the paragon,
> Ne'er but with Ancient time & fate dissolve.

[24] The orator after Supper was Called upon to deliver the anniversary Speech, and his honor ‖ being seated in the Chair of State, he stood up, and making a Low obeisance, first to his honor, then to the members, he spoke as follows.

Anniversary Speech

Honorable Sir,

It has been observed by some learned historians, (I forget who, nor would it be much to the purpose, if I should name them) that had it not been for that whore Hellen, and the Sacking of Troy, the world would have been deprived of Homer's most excellent poem, *The Iliad;* and, on the other hand, had it not been for the poet Homer, that memorable Transaction of History would long agoe have been buried in the ruines of Time.

If it be not too bold and assuming in me, to draw a parallel between the Trojans and their City, and this here ancient and honorable Club, (for Sure we are all Trojans true as ever pissd[(a)] and in that chiefly consists our antiquity,) and between that most Excellent Poet Homer and myself, I will presume to affirm, that posterity, some Centuries hence, (supposing this here Club to be obselete and out of date, as is now the City of Troy) will have Just cause to make the same observation, upon your honor, your ancient Club, and your orator, They will bless and hug themselves, that such a president and such a Club ever existed, since, to that they will owe, the matchless Speeches and declamations, of an unequal'd orator, and, at the same time, they will observe with Justice, that, had it not been for the tongue and pen of your extraordinary orator, your honor, The worshipful

---

(a) Cottons *Virgil Travestie* lib 1.[1]

1. Charles Cotton (1630–1687) was an English poet remembered chiefly for *Scarronides; or, Virgile Travestie* (1664), for the dialogue between Piscator and Viator, which appears in the fifth edition of Izaak Walton's *Compleat Angler,* and for numerous light verses and translations. Hamilton is recalling the opening lines from *Scarronides,* "I sing the man (read it who list, / A Trojan true as ever p——."

Sir John, the Chancellor, Poet Laureat, Protomusicus, Serjeant at arms, and other Illustrious personages, Longstanding members of this here ancient & Honorable Club, ‖ must all have been lost and swallowed up in oblivion together with the very name of your ancient Club itself; Just as old Priam, his Sons, his nobles and his City itself would have been, had it not been for the Song of Homer, that Immortal bard. [25]

But Lack a day! you'll say, this is taking too much honor and Glory to myself, and lessening too much the grandure and dignity of this here ancient and honorable Club, in Comparing my own fusty Genius to that of Homer, and in bringing this here Club upon a level, with so Inconsiderable a City as Troy, as if your honor was not a more majestic personage, than king Priam, Sir John a more Invincible Champion than Bully Hector, and so forth. It will be said, that I ought to esteem it my greatest honor and dignity that I am a Club orator of no mean degree, as I officiate in that Station to the honorable Jole, and his ancient and honorable Tuesday Club, which, I hope will live for ever and aye, not only, in the mouths of men women and Sucking babes, but in the Chronicles and histories of future ages, like the theme of the aforesaid Noble Poet; but live and exist Substantially and Identically, that is, preserve it's existence and being, lasting perennial, permanent and unchangeable for ages, and ages and ages to come, so, that from Century to Century successively, the longstanding members may admire the doughty deeds of their predecessor's Predecessors, and Succeeding orators in a String, may proclaim aloud the praises of the presidents, State officers and Commoners of this here ancient and honorable Club, Looking back upon the great, the wise, the politic, the Generous, the facetious and Immortal Jole, as the Spring, origin and Source of all the honor, Sapience, dignity, gravity, valor and facetious humor, of this here ‖ ancient and honorable Club, and it's longstanding members that were are and are to come, and so forth *in Infinitum*. [26]

And now, most honorable Sir, as both your honor and your ancient and honorable Club, are themes never to be exhausted, themes Replete with such multitudinous and multifarious matter and copious inexhaustible Subject, so as to confuse and confound, distort and perplex, warp & pervert, the genius and Capacity of any common orator, in such a manner, as that, when he undertakes to perrorate upon, either one, or two or three, or all of you, *omnem, Getherum, O quanta Inest plenitudo?* may be said of the Subject, *O quantum in rebus Inane,*[2] may be said of the Cranium of the

---

2. The first two words are a macaronic phrase for *omnium gatherum* ("the whole gathering"), followed by "Oh what a great plenitude is there?" and "Oh how very empty of things."

orator, his understanding is mutilated, his Judgement Curtailed, his Senses benumn'd, his faculties perverted, his memory bewilder'd, his Intellects Intangled, his elocution Confused, and his argument gravelled; So I, who profess myself, but of a midling so, so, Capacity for a Club orator, far, O far Inferior to the bright Geniuses, who have been my predecessors in that office, vizt: The Learned Mr Quaint, and the Ingenious Mr Comas, the first of whom was distinguished for his Incomparable tropes, metaphors and figures, the Latter, for his Significant and moving gestures, being a man of but few words, and these pritty pithy, and Sonorous like the Bass notes of a trumpet, I, I say, who am but of a mean Capacity for a Club Orator [Pres: Psha! theres too much of this!] —to avoid as much as possible, being caught in a Labyrinth of Intricacies, or running my head into a hose net,

[27] after the manner of some ancient || gladiators or pugilos, who used to watch every aim of their antagonists, with a Cunning eye, shall take your honor, and your principal longstanding members upon this anniversary occasion, *Singulatim* and *Separatim,* one by one Slyly, each after another in a String [here the President shifted about in his Chair, & Sir John Yawned hideously]

And first for your Self, most honorable, most excelsified, most profound, most oblong, most oblate, most dilated, most unparallelled, most excentric, and most unexemplified Sir, I must profess myself amazed and astonished every time I behold and contemplate you, the head, the director, the first mover, the *Sine qua non,* and *Archæus Faber*[a] of this here ancient and honorable Club, when I consider the depth of your understanding, the height of your Genius, and Conceptions, the breadth of your Clemency and Sapience, the Length of your memory, authority, and prosopæal, and monostatical Protuberances,[+] so, that what was said of a Certain ancient Philosopher, whose name I have now unluckily forgot, may properly be applied to your honor, not only as President, but as Chief long Standing member of

---

(a) A Term of van Helmont's the Physician, by which he meant a Certain head director or overseer, of the operations of the animal oeconomy, who had his Seat somewhere about the Pylorus, or mouth of the Stomach.[3]

3. Jean Baptiste van Helmont (1577–1644) was a learned Flemish mathematician, physician, and alchemist, whose works include *The Magnetical Cure of Wounds* (1650) and numerous other medical treatises. In chap. 5 of his *Oriatrike; or, Physick Refined* (London, 1662), van Helmont defines the Archaeus Faber as the "chief Workman, containing the fruitfulness of generations and Seeds, as it were the internal efficient cause," and suggests that in the "*Archeusses* of the bowels . . . the planetary Spirits do most shine forth, even as also, in the whole influous *Archeus*" (*Van Helmont's Works* [London, 1664], 35, 36).

4. *Monostatical* is Hamilton's invention, perhaps echoing *monostach,* a botanical term for plants bearing a single spike.

this here ancient and honorable Club, vizt: *Mento, mentula et Naso Longissimus,*[5] in the first, *mento Longissimus,* a Certain eminent Lord high Chancellor of England,[6] in the Second, *mentula Longissimus,* you Resemble a Certain heathen deity, needless here to mention, whose name begins with a Capital P,[7] || as does your honors noble title of *President,* in the third *Naso Longissimus,* you are like the august Emperors of old Rome, Lastly, the Crassitude of your *os frontis,*[8] under which is hid and conceal'd, that Store of wit & humor, which makes you so deservedly admired and extolled, all which Jumbled together, make such a group of Superexcellent qualifications, as fits you for exercising the most exalted office of honorable President to this here ancient and honorable Club, and the best way for any Club Orator to express them to purpose, is, (after the elegant manner of my Immediate predecessor in this office, with true Comasian Eloquence) to hold his peace, and say nothing, except it be only some aspiratory, Interjectionary and admiratory, hums, hahs! and huts! *Nam tu Jole, omnium Presidum Celeberrimus et Celsissimus es, neque parem neque Comparem habes aut habebis, in Secula Seculorum, Amen.*[9]

[28]

Your honor and Valor, most unexemplified Sir, shines forth, conspicuous, in the person of Sir John (heretofore Oldcastle) your most unparallelled knight, the bruitt of whose arms and heroic atchievements have already reached, Lord knows how many Leagues around us, and will reach bye and bye so many more that we shall not be able to follow or keep Sight of them, under the protection of whose terrific arms the Longstanding members of this here ancient Club, || Cling and cuddle together, in as great Security from foreign assaults and dangers, as a parcel of small Chickens, are defended from the bloody talons of the hawk, under the Spreading wings of the hen Mother, by whose terrific looks, and martial Countenances your honor sits secure in that there Chair of State, in Spite of all the machinations and Contrivances of ambitious and rebellious members, who wickedly would subvert our Constitution, and usurp the Cathedral dignity [here Sir John looked upon the Chancellor, with a Terrific Countenance]

[29]

Your honor's Justice, wisdom and Sagacity, is well signified by your wise and learned Chancellor, who, sitting at your left hand, receives from

---

5. "Longest in beard, penis, and nose" (similar to Martial, *Epigrams* 6.36).
6. Unless portraits do not tell the whole truth, none of the chancellors in England during the first half of the 18th century wore a beard.
7. Priapus, son of Dionysius and Aphrodite and god of fruitfulness.
8. "Frontal bone," or forehead.
9. "For you, Jole, are the most celebrated and exalted of all presidents, and you have nor will have neither peer nor compeer, for ever and ever, amen."

you, such emanations and exhalations, of wisdom and Justice, as will always support and mantain him with honor in his place, and dignity, and preserve the peace, quiet and happiness, of your ancient and honorable Club. Your Master of Ceremonies, represents your honor's unmatched Civility, Consummate Urbanity, and kind hospitality, from you, he derives these qualities, that fit him for his office, and reflects them back upon this here ancient Club, as the moon does her Silver light borrowed from the Sun, upon hills, dales, valleys, meadows and smooth lakes, in a Sweet Summers night, fanned with balmy breezes and soft Gales, which represent, the Sublime, delicate and moving Compliments, Similies and figures, Tropes, puns, Conundrums, Anagrams, Chronograms, epigrams, accrostics, Rebuses, Riddles, Ænigmas, odes, Epodes, Songs, madrigals and Roundelays of the same person in the Character of your poet Laureat, who sings Sweeter than the Swan on his death bed, than the thrush and mocking bird by day, than the ‖ nightingale or Whiperwill by night, and all by your Presidential Influence, and Inspiration, for he esteems you above all the muses, and among our Longstanding members, the most excellent, as Hesiod esteemed Calliope, the most excellent among the muses.

> Κλειατ', ευτερπη τε, θαλειατε μελπομενη τε,
> Τερψιχορη τ' Ερατω τε, πολύμνια τ' ουρανιη τε
> Καλλιοπη θ' ἣ δε προφερεστατη εστιν απαςεων.¹⁰

So, our Laureat may say of your honor, among the long standing members, of this here ancient & honorable Club.

> —ὃ δε προφερεστατος εστιν απαςεων.¹¹

In fine, our Clubeian Bard, owns no other Apollo but your honor, mounts no other Pegasus, Invokes no other Muse, and quaffs no other Heliconian Springs, than your honor's Wine, Punch, Rumbo, and Strong beer, as may be proved Clearly from his own words in the Anniversary ode for this year.

> Ah! Jole, Inspirer of my verse,
>   I now renounce the nine,
> Whilst I the Tuesday Club rehearse
>   And thy Sweet praise,
>   Tune my Lays,

---

10. "Clio and Euterpe, Thalia, Melpomene and Terpsichore, and Erato and Polhymnia and Urania and Calliope, who is chief of them all" (Hesiod, *Theogony* 77–79).

11. Hamilton has simply rewritten in the masculine the last clause cited above.

> My Songs, my odes, my Roundelays,
> I'll Crave no aid but thine.

The Harmony of your honor's conduct and actions, the melodious Sound of your honors Sweet voice, are represented by your most expert and alert Proto-musicus, whose || heavenly notes, like the warblings of the Sirens, enchant all that hear them, and many more besides; than which no thing can be Sweeter, unless it be your honor's dulcisonorous pipe, which (as it moves the members as well as the Stones) must be owned by all, to excell the modulations of Orpheus himself, who is said to have Charmed the Stones, trees, Cattle, and even the Infernal Imps with his melody,[12] but your honor Charms the Longstanding members of this here ancient and honorable Club, which is all in all.

Your Honor's authority and power, is figured out by your Serjeant at arms, a man of a bold and Steady front, and of an awful Stern presence, all which qualities he derives from your honor, as the fountainhead of all the perfections and Excellencies, of this here ancient Club.

Lastly, your honors oratory and Eloquence shines forth in the person of your Orator; an orator of all orators the most Garrulous and verbose, who can expatiate and hold forth, as much, and as long upon nothing, [Sr Jno: That's the truest thing you have said to night] as any orator that ever opened his mouth or mounted the Rostrum; but this Subject, I leave, for your honor and your Longstanding members to expatiate upon, being Sensible, that it is not only Improper, but unbecoming for a man to talk too much of himself, be it good or evil, but Oh! if time would permit, how largely could I hold forth, how learnedly could I florish it away, upon the Great and Sublime qualities of my predecessors in office, in this here ancient and || honorable Club, and in what Superfine fustian phrazes and Sonorous Sentences, could I celebrate the Incomparable oratorial Genius, of the Quaintian and Comasian Declamators.

As for the Residue of your honor's L:St: members, take them either Separately or Conjointly, they are altogether unparalleled, by any members whatsoever that have appeared, in ancient or moderen times, or in ancient or moderen Clubs; They are *Long,* and they are *Standing,* which, I shall explain as Succinctly as I can, They are Long in their Deliberations, argumentations, or, (to speak Clubically,) arguefications and Speeches, & determine nothing, but by Long and mature Consultation and Consideration,

---

12. The most popular version of this myth appears in Ovid, *Metamorphoses* 6.86–109; see also Vergil, *Georgics* 4.494.

they are long in their heads, that is, wise and Sagacious, they are long in their Sight, that is foreseeing and foretelling, and discerning at a distance, some of them are long in coming to Club, others are long in going away, lastly they are long in their members, such as their noses and so forth, and finally some are long in their Speeches, as Mr Protomusicus & your humble Servant, [Sr Jno: Thats true faith]

[33] Now, as for their Standing, they are Standing as they yet Stand and exist, They are Standing, as they Stand Cordially together, They are Standing as they prop up your honor's Chair, and are mutual buttresses to each other, they are Standing as they Stand, when they address your honor, they are Standing, as they are people of good understanding, they are Standing as they live in mutual good understanding || one with another, and lastly, they are Standing, being the Cause (as it is said) of many a Standing Joke, so that what Sir John Falstaffe said of himself, [here Sir John looked very Stern, and Clap'd his hand on his Sword] may properly be said of your honor, and your Longstanding members, vizt: That they not only have much wit themselves, but are the Cause of much wit in other men.[13]

Now, to take Long and Standing both together, they are of Longstanding, as they are the members of an Ancient Club, they are long of Standing, as they never proceed in a hurry, but by deliberate and gradual methods, and Sedate deliberations, and, when they address your honor, it is a long time, before they can be made to Stand up, and when up, many of them Stand long, nay longer than your honor desires, as I do now at present [Pres: I think indeed 'tis high time you were sat down] they are long in Standing, measuring a Considerable length when all ranged in a line, and, because, when once they Stand, it is a hard matter to strike them down again, lastly, they are literally Long and Standing, which are two very good qualities, Singularly useful and advantagious in some mysterious Games, which, for brevitie's Sake, I shall here leave unexplained, this Subject requiring a discourse by itself, and belonging Solely, *Veneri et Priapo*.[14]

And now, honorable Sir, I conclude with your honorary members, whose honor is derived from your fountain inexhaustible, whose honor
[34] reflects upon yourself, and is returned || by you to them again, as the rivers are perpetually fed by the vapors of the ocean, and return their eternal tributes again into his Immense bosom, running perpetually with Incessant flux, *Labetur in omne volubilis ævum*,[15] whilst you, great Sir, like the fluxes

---

13. See *2 Henry IV*, act 1, sc. 2, lines 9–10.
14. "To Venus and Priapus."
15. "It flows on, churning forever" (Horace, *Epistulae* 1.2.43).

and Refluxes of that prodigious mass of water, sometimes advance, and sometimes recede, but, whenever you go and come, still, the rivers, great and small, that is, the Longstanding & the honorary members, must follow, unless their Channels be dried up.

Gentlemen, the Subject is so great, and the time so short, that no orator whatsoever, can Sufficiently expatiate upon it so as to make it Clear and Intelligible to the most understanding, and therefore, I hope you'll excuse the abruptness and Imperfection of this discourse, and, without farther Ceremony, regale, and entertain yourselves, on this Solemn occasion, with what his honor has set before you, and, be assured from my mouth, since I bear his Commission to tell you so, that you are all wellcome, thrice wellcome, thrice heartily welcome, and you Gentlemn: honory: members, who have done yourselves the honor, to wait upon his honor on this occasion, and have done us L:St: members the honr: of your Compny: your presence & conversation, is agreeable and acceptable not only to his honor, but to us, and therefore let us all Join in one free and unreserved mirth, and with Jovial disposition, let us eat, let us drink, let us sing, let us dance, let us fiddle, let us pipe together like friends, let us meet and part like friends, and Join in one cordial wish, *long live his honor, and long live, the Ancient and honorable Tuesday Club—Dixi.*

The orator having pronounced this Speech, the Club gave the plaudite by Clapping their hands, the Chancellor leading the way. || Jonathan Grog Esqr, Poet laureat moved that this Speech should be printed. [35]

Sir John Replied that he should have his permission to print it, if he could recollect it Justly, for the Orator had used no notes.

The orator asked leave to record it, Sir John Replied that he might, if he pleased record something in it's place, but, he believed, it would be a hard task for him, to remember it again exactly, as he had delivered it, for it seemed to him to be a very Confused piece of Stuff.

The orator offered to lay Sir John a bottle of Sack, that he could recollect it again, but Sir John would not take him up upon Sack, not affecting that Liquor so much as his name sake, the renown'd Sir Jno: Falstafe.

The remainder of this anniversary Sederunt was spent, as usual, in a pleasant and Gay manner, many Jokes were Cracked, and many Ingenious puns were uttered by the poet Laureat, and the Chancellor & Secretary play'd over the music, of the Last year's anniversary ode, *Con violino et Violoncello Solo,* and Crinkum Crankum Esqr sung, thus began the Seventh Anniversary of the Ancient and honorable Tuesday Club, and was not finished, till two Sederunts after this.

Much about this time, appeared in one of the New York weekly Gazettes, a most Infamous and Scandalous Libel upon his honor the president and the Club, to this effect, "That on such a day arrived in this City (vizt: New York) from England, the honorable Co- ‖ ney Pimp Frontinbrass Esqr, Chancellor to the most high and Honorable Hugh Maccarty Esqr, President of the most ancient and Right honorable Monday Club of New York, upon whose arrival, the Honorable Sir Hugh Maccarty Esqr, Summoned a Special meeting, of the said Right honorable Club, and the said Honorable Coney Pimp Frontinbrass Esqr, was called before them, and tried at the bar, an Indictment being found against him, for treason and Conspiracy, against his Lawful lord & President, Sir Hugh Maccarty Esqr, in his Corresponding with a Certain pretended or Sham Club at Annapolis, called the ancient and honorable Tuesday Club, and with a Certain Nasifer Jole Esqr, Ridiculously stiled Lord Jole, their Pretended Lord President, a person of a mean aspect and awkward address, and, In his Clapping a Cap of State, upon the Lousy pericranium, of the said pretended Lord Jole, and betraying unto him, and his pitiful Club, the Secrets of the said Sir Hugh Maccarty Esqr, and his most ancient & right Honorable monday Club, upon which Indictment the said Honorable Coney Pimp Frontinbrass Esqr, being Tried and Cast, he was Expelled the Club, for ever and a day."

This Scandalous Libel, gave very great offence to his honor the president, and some of the Longstanding members, particularly the Chancellor, who resolved Immediatly to pen an answer to it, and it was the principal Cause, of the Great battle of Farce alia, that was afterwards fought in his honors back yard, as shall be related in its proper place. ‖ Most, if not all of the members, as well as his honor, firmly believed, that Coney Pimp Frontinbrass Esqr, was himself the author of this libell, for, as to Sir Hugh Maccarty Esqr and his Club (tho' the Lie of Humbug Fibber, concerning the death and burial of that Phantasmical President, had been better Confirmed than it was) his honor and the Club believed them now, to be only mere Chimerical Nonentities, and the wild Creation of a maggoty brain.

Chapter III

Conclusion of the Seventh Anniversary, with a Second Anniversary Speech, by the Orator.

It was a Saying of Aristarchus, that formerly there were Seven wise men, but added he, these Sages, have multiplied so fast upon us, that it is a very hard matter now a days to find the same number of fools;[1] what Aristarchus Intended by this Joke, may be easily seen thro', vizt: that the age he lived in, affected to be so knowing and wise, that not Seven men could be found, that would either plainly or Implicitly, own that they were in any degree the votaries of folly, or capable to be overreached or Imposed upon. I believe we may safely say, that men in these our days, are much the same as they were in the ‖ days of Aristarchus, for, not to mention Seven, it would be a very hard matter, to find one Confessed fool in the Sense of the said Aristarchus. Sure I am, there was not one such Confessed fool now to be found in the ancient and honorable Tuesday Club, as for his honor the President, notwithstanding the Strenuous efforts, (as he alledged) of Coney Pimp Frontinbrass Esqr, and the Secretary, to make a fool of him, by presenting him with Caps of State, and amusing him with histories of Chimerical Presidents and Clubs, over which he Claimed a natural and Lawful Superiority, yet, he affirmed, that he knew all these to be mere tricks and Impositions, even when they were in Embrio, whether it was so or not with his honor, I shall not take upon me to determin or Judge, let his honor's own Conscience bear witness to the veracity of his assertions, and the Club and the world Judge of them as they see fit, as for the members of the Club, they looked upon themselves as persons of such penetration and Sagacity, as to be Incapable of being Imposed upon themselves, and, whatever they could do with their President, none had wit enough to overreach them, of this opinion particularly was the Chancellor, and Laughed at the Stories of Sir Hugh Maccarty Esqr, and his Chimerical Club, promulgated by Coney Pimp Frontinbrass Esqr, as mere *Entia Rationis*[2] and vain Chimeras, but, we shall soon have occasion to see, how that Sly Sophister Frontinbrass, Imposed upon the Chancellor in such a manner, as to Con- ‖ vince him of the Truth of these very particulars of which he before asserted the falshood.

[38]

[39]

At Sederunt 180, Prim Timorous Esqr, being H:S: appeared in Club, for the first time Colonel Comico Butman, President of the Hicory hill Club in Virginia,[3] which Gentleman, had received a Commission, from

---

1. Aristarchus of Samothrace (ca. 217–145 B.C.) was the head of the Alexandrian Library and the originator of scientific criticism, whose name became synonymous with the complete critic.

2. "Things of the mind"; a Scholastic term, probably from Duns Scotus, meaning "something that exists only in the mind," as opposed to an *ens reale*. Here, "things of the imagination."

3. Hamilton's repeated references to this club suggest that it actually existed, but I have not found any further information on the Hiccory Hill Club (or on the Charles Town Club, mentioned below, p. 334) in any of the standard works on colonial culture, in the *Maryland Gazette* for the years the Tuesday Club met, or in the indexes of the *Maryland Historical Magazine* and the *Virginia Magazine of History and Biography*.

Coney Pimp Frontinbrass Esqr, the agent for America and the Islands, to Constitute a Club by that Name, under the Jurisdiction of the Lord Jole (as he was then stiled) and his ancient and honorable Tuesday Club of Annapolis; I mention this Gentleman with respect, because he will make some figure in this history, as Successor to Sir John, in the office of Champion, after he had left the Club in a Sort of huff, This Gentleman then, attending the Club at this Sederunt, Took his Seat, at the Right hand of the Chair of State, next to Sir John, which was allotted him, by his honor the president, as a mark of that respect, which was due to his great merit and Clubical abilities.

The Chancellor, at this Sederunt, produced an answer drawn up by him, to the late Scandalous Libel on his honor the president and the Club, published in the *New York Gazette,* in the name of Sir Hugh Maccarty Esqr, tho (as was supposed) by Coney Pimp Frontinbrass Esqr, lately preferred and honored by his honor and the Club, which was read, and proposed to be published, in the weekly Journal of Jonathan Grog Esqr, but the Club determined nothing as to ‖ that affair, at the same time, expelling the said Frontinbrass for ever from the Club, and depriving him of his titles of *Honorary member* and *agent* for the Club, unless he should personally appear, and Clearly vindicate himself from the heavy accusation, brought against him.

The proposal for publishing the Chancellor's answer, was for sometime argued warmly in the Club, and Solo Neverout Esqr, spoke very Largely on the Subject, tho' in such a perplexed and Confused manner, as was usual with him, in all his arguments and declamations, that none of the members, not even his honor himself could understand his drift, he took occasion however, to speak very fully, on the nonentity of Sir Hugh Maccarty Esqr, to abuse Frontinbrass in a gross manner, & paint forth his Impudence and assurance, in the most odious Colours, and, to take to pieces in his Inaccurate manner, the Chancellor's learned answer to the libel, and, while he spoke, he held the Libel in one hand, and the Chancellors answer in the other, looking first on one, and then on the other, waving them about, and asserting, that they were both alike derogatory to the honor and dignity of the Chair, and the honor of this here ancient and honorable Club, at this the Chancellor was much enraged, and pulling his own manuscript out of Neverout's hand, he put it in his pocket, saying, that the Club, as they did not deserve it, never should have an opportunity of seeing it again, and far less of publishing it in their own vindication, and thus by the Rashness and petulence of that Clumsy orator, Solo Neverout Esqr, and the obstinacy of his honor and the Club, was the public deprived of that valuable piece, the Chancellor more- || over turning to the president, [41] said That he could not tell what he had done to offend that fellow (meaning Neverout) but that he never could say, or propose any thing In Club, but he was browbeaten and Contradicted by him, his honor upon this, turned round, and frowned upon the Chancellor, and then Cast a Grateful Smile towards Protomusicus, as if pleased with what he had said, and Indeed, that great man's behaviour towards the Chancellor, ever since the great Rebellion, was very Surly and Supercilious, and he was observed to look upon Solo Neverout Esqr with a mild and favorable eye, a Sure prognostic of the rise of that Gentleman to a place of honor, and a dignified title in the Club, which were bestowed on him soon after this, his honor's favor and Countenance however, was Encouragement Enough for Solo Neverout Esqr, to Continue his Insults and affronts towards the Chancellor, as he found it was a Sure way to advance himself in the Club.

After this dispute was over, the Club entered upon another, Concerning the Identity of Sir Hugh Maccarty Esqr, of New York. His honor asked Coll: Comico Butman, if he ever knew any such Gentleman at New York, to which he answered in the affirmative; on this the Chancellor said that he begged his pardon, he knew very well the City of New York, had been very lately there, and never knew nor heard of any such person,—that is nothing to the purpose Sir, answered the Colonel, such a person might be there, and yet you know nothing of the matter,—where did he live Sir, replied the || Chancellor—Just over the wine Cellars, on the east Side of the Street nigh [42] the Exchange—That's a lie Sir, said the Chancellor, I kn-now these wine Cellars, and I kn-now the person that lives there, ther's no such person lives there as Sir Hugh Maccarty Esqr,—at this the Coll: gave him a broad Stare, and it was thought a quarrel would have Ensued, the Col: being a military man, and not used to have the lie Retorted upon him, but his honor the president Interposed, and requested the Colonel not to take notice of what the Chancellor said, for that he was a plain, rough, hasty, passionate Gentleman, and that It was his Common practice, to use even him, tho' president, on every occasion in the same manner, upon this the dispute was droped, and the Club determined nothing in the matter but prudently left Sir Hugh Maccarty Esqr, where they found him.

At this Sederunt were performed some pieces of music, with an organ, violin and Violoncello, by the Chancellor Secretary and Crinkum Crankum Esqr.

On the 181 Sederunt, June 16th 1752, Mr Secretary Scribble being H:S: was concluded the Seventh Anniversary of the Club, for, Signior Lardini coming to town brought with him a new minuet for his honor, which was performed at this Sederunt, but had not had Leisure to Compose music for the ode, there was also, another Anniversary Speech delivered at this Sederunt, but, before we relate the particulars of this, it will be proper to mention some remarkable occurrences, which stand so Connected with the history, that they cannot be ommitted.

[43]   Much about this time arrived in Town Coney Pimp Frontinbrass Esqr, the agent, from the northward, and, Immediatly upon his arrival wrote a letter to Mr Secretary Scribble, acquainting him, that he was desirous to attend the Club at next Sederunt, requesting that he would Inform his Lordship of it, that he might have his leave and permission, as he understood, he had unhappily Incurred his Lordships displeasure, but that he would undertake to Clear himself of all blame, if he had but an opportunity. The Secretary was Surprized at the receit of this letter, and could not by any means Conjecture how Mr Frontinbrass had got notice of the President's displeasure, however, he wrote to his honor the President, acquainting him, That the Traitor Frontinbrass had come to town, and was desirous of coming to the Club, but that as he (the Secretary) was H:S: he should have no Invitation or encouragement from him, to come, without his honor's permission, to this, his honor sent for answer, that he would by no means Consent, that Frontinbrass should be admitted into the Club or into his presence, and the Secretary took no notice of the Agent's letter, thinking that the best way to let him know, that he could not be admitted into the Club.

    The Secretary after this understood, that Frontinbrass soon after his arival in town, encountered Mr Chancellor Dogmaticus in the Street, who frowned upon him with great Indignation, and, between these two Great men there passed the following Smart dialogue.

[44]   So, Mr Frontinbrass, says the chancellor, are not you a pritty fellow?—How so pray?—have you not Impudence enough to serve fifty, good Mr Agent?—Pray Sir Explain yourself,—So you'll have the face to deny that you was the author of that Infamous pasquinade on his honor and the Club?—what pasquinade Sir?—O Sir! you know nothing then of that Scandalous Paragraph, in the *New York Gazette?* not you Indeed, hoh, hoh!—at this Mr Frontinbrass blushed up to the Eyes, but the Rubicund Suffusion reached no farther, the Conscious and rushing blood, not being able to pervade the Indurated Integuments of the *Os frontis,*—why do you blame me, (says he faultering) for the act of another person?—what other person pray Sir?—I thought you and the world both might have known Sir, that that there paragraph was published by the order of Sir Hugh Maccarty Esqr.—Pough, Pough! that Stuff of Sir Hugh Maccarty is stale, we are not to be bamboozled any Longer with a tale of a tub, this Maccarty is only a

Creature of your own brain, there is not, never was, or ever will be, any such person, or character—Prithee gi' me leave Sir, I affirm there is, and tho' I understand there has been a report spread of his death, I will make it out that he is alive, or forfeit my Character—ay, ay! your Character, when you have any,—Patience Sir alittle, I affirm that there is such an Identicall president, as this very Sir Hugh Maccarty, and that he is now as much alive as ever he was—That I believe he is, but pray how can such a person have been in New York, and I know nothing of him, Sir, I kn-now every man of note or figure in that City, I am no Stranger there—I grant what you say Good Sir, but pray gi' me leave, you probably might not know him by that name—ah ha! none of your Sophistry, what! not know a gentleman by his Christian name? what else should I know him by?—fair and soft Sir, that is not his Christian name, it is his Clubical name—how! how! his Clubical name! that's a distinction I never knew before—It may be so Sir, but he Chuses to go by that name in his Club only, and no where else, and therefore it is called his Clubical name—what may be his Christian name then Pray?—why Sir, tho' I am not obliged to satisfy you so far, yet to show you, I am willing to remove all your Scruples, the Christian Name he goes by is Colonel Rormis.—Aha! are you there? I kn-now the Coll: very well, now you tell me his Christian name, and is it he that takes upon himself the Ridiculous Name of Sir Hugh Maccarty Esqr?—It is Indeed Sir—why really and truely, it may be so, if that be the man, for he is a queer duke as ever I knew, but it is very odd, that he should assume such a Clubical, or rather farcical name,—how can you be Surprized at that Sir, when you know, that in the Tuesday Club, your knight and Champion laid aside his Christian name of Capt: Blunt, and took the Clubical name of Sir John Oldcastle, and then disliking one half of that Clubical name, he now Contents himself with Simple Sir John,—True—true, Indeed, I did not think of that.—Thus finished this Curious dialogue, the result of which, was, that Coney pimp Frontinbrass Esqr, persuaded Mr Chancellor Dogmaticus, of the Identity of Sir Hugh Maccarty Esqr, an account of this Dialogue the Secretary had from the Chancellors own mouth.

Having premised these necessary Circumstances, I go on now with the thread of our History.

At Sederunt 181, the Secretary, as we said above, being H:S: several pieces of music were playd by Signior Lardini, which met with great approbation, and among others a new minuet, Composed by the said Lardini for his honor the President.

Sir John moved twice In Club, that Coney Pimp Frontinbrass Esqr, should be sent for, as he was in town, but was not seconded.

His honor asked Sir John aside how he came to make such a motion, seeing, he knew that it was against his Inclination, that that fellow should come into Club, to which Sir John replied, that he knew his honor's forgiving temper so well, that, had Frontinbrass come into his presence, had he been the devil himself, it would only ‖ have been a bow and a Scrape with the foot, and all would have passed over and been forgot.

The orator stood up by order, and made the Concluding anniversary oration, to the following purpose.

Second Anniversary Speech

Honorable Sir,

You perhaps will think, it is almost time I had done making Speeches upon Presidents and Clubs [yes Indeed do I, said the president] and that I have said enough, or too much concerning that Subject already, and perhaps, more than any other Club orator, besides myself would have taken the trowble to say [Sr Jno: yes, faith have you] —I grant your honor, that had the Subject of my discourse been of ordinary presidents, and ordinary Clubs, I should already have very much exhausted the Subject, if not worn it altogether thread bare, and spun it away to nothing; but, since my theme has been of such a noble and exalted nature, being your honor, and your ancient and honorable Club, it is absolutely Impossible, that the Subject can ever be exhausted, but it will rather grow upon that orator who can be bold enough to undertake it, as the Hydra did upon Hercules, who, as he loped off one head, found many other heads spring up in its place, thus, upon discussing of one point, concerning your honor ‖ and your ancient Club, he will find 50 more points start up in its Stead, and, for these 50 times 50, multiplying upon him with such Rapidity, as to exceed the Comprehension of an ancient astronomer or moderen almanack maker.

But to come to the point. Upon the Conclusion of this Anniversary, I shall

> First   Prove this here Club to be a Club,
> 2dly   Prove your honor to be a president,
> 3dly   Prove your honor to be President of this here Club,
> Lastly   Conclude with some General Inferences.

I That this here Club is a Club, appears most manifest, to every man that has even but half an Eye; so that, I believe, I shall scarce have occasion, to Rummage up my Logic, and Summon *Darii Ferio Baralipton*,[4] and many

---

4. These words, nonsense in themselves, are a Scholastic mnemonic for teaching the patterns of syllogisms.

more such odd named fellows to prove it; The thing is manifest in it Self from that learned metaphysical Axiom *Quod est, est;* for do we not do as all Clubs do, we meet, converse, Laugh, talk, smoke, drink, differ, agree, argue, Philosophize, Harangue, pun, sing, dance and fiddle together, nay, we are really and in fact a Club, and an Ancient Club, for which, if your honor's authority and my own honest word were not Sufficient, I could quote many Learned and valid authorities, such as Kepler, Hugo Grotius, Guido Aretinus, Heliogobalus, Pigmalion, Trogus Pompeius, Dr Faustus, Perigort, Columella, Benedictus, Victorinus, Faventius, Epicurus, Alcibiades, Agamemnon, Hercules, Gallus, Hesiod, Jason, Pratensis, Gulliver, Spodanus and Hermes Trismegistus, among the moderens, & Jno: Fox, || Sir Francis Napier, David Rizzio, Guicchardini, Sciolto, Puffendorfius, Galileo, Peter the Hermit, John Burton, Tom Brown, Prester John, Muley Mahomet, Abdalla, Tonombeius, Robertus Burtonus Oxoniensis, David Lindsay, Coelius Aurelianus, Rhasis, Avicenna, Sir William Killigrew and Cardinal Alberoni among the venerable ancients,[5] all whom are as Explicit

[49]

---

5. Johannes Kepler (1571–1630) was a famous German astronomer. Hugo Grotius (1583–1645) was a Dutch statesman and jurist famous for his great treatise on international law, *De jure belli et pacis* (1625), and for his sacred drama in Latin, *Adamus exsul* (1601), which probably influenced Milton. Guido Aretino, better known as Guido d'Arezzo (995?–1050?), was a French Benedictine monk and musical reformer who reputedly invented the medieval "great scale," or gamut, and whose works on musical theory include *Micrologus de disciplina artis musicae*. Heliogabalus, or Elagabalus (ca. 204–222), Roman emperor from 218 to 222 known for his profligacy, took his name from the sun-god of Emesa, Elah-Gabal, of whom he was the hereditary priest. Pompeius Trogus was an Augustan historian noted for a universal history, *Historiae philippicae*. Perigort could be Cardinal Perigort, a character in William Shirley's *Edward the Black Prince* (1640), or one of the Talleyrand-Périgords, although none of the ones listed in standard reference works flourished during Hamilton's day or earlier. Columella (fl. 1st century A.D.) was a Spaniard who lamented the decline of Italian agriculture in his treatise *De re rustica*. Benedictus could be any number of Benedicts, but it is probably either René Benedict (fl. early 17th century), doctor of the Sorbonne and author of *Apologie catholique*, which attempts to prove that Henry of Navarre's acceptance of the Protestant religion was not sufficient cause to deprive him of the right of succession to the crown, or Alexander Benedictus, or Beneditti (fl. 15th century), eminent Veronese physician and author of numerous medical works, including *De observatione in pestilentia, collectiones medicinae*. Victorinus could be Gaius Marius Victorinus (fl. 4th century A.D.), Latin author of numerous philosophical, rhetorical, and grammatical works, or Victorius of Aquitania (fl. 5th century A.D.), astronomer commissioned by Pope Hilarius to fix the date of Easter, or Hugh of Saint Victor (1096–1141), famous French theologian whose works imitate the style and follow the doctrine of Saint Augustine. Faventius is possibly Paul-Marie Faventinus (fl. 16th century), Italian Dominican who traveled to Armenia to establish Christian missions and churches and while there became friendly with the king of Persia. Alcibiades (ca. 450–404 B.C.) was an Athenian general, statesman, and friend of Socrates. Gaius Cornelius Gallus (ca. 69–26 B.C.) was a Roman poet, general, and friend of Augustus and Vergil, known particularly for his love elegies. By "Jason, Pratensis," Hamilton is trying to render even more obscure the already obscure Jason Pratensis (1486–1558), author of *De pariente et partu* (1527) and *De arcenda sterilitate* (1531). Spodanus is

on this Subject, as Hippocrates and Servetus on the Circulation of the blood, or The Psalmist David and the Philosopher Seneca on the French Pox;[6] By these Quotations Indeed delivered at Length, I might have

---

probably Henri de Sponde (1568–1643), bishop and author of *Annales ecclesiastici* (1613) and *De coemeteriis sacris* (1638). Hermes Trismegistus, the name given to the Egyptian god "Thoth the very great," was the reputed author of philosophical-religious treatises and various works on astrology, magic, and alchemy. John Foxe (1516–1587) was an English priest and martyrologist, especially remembered as the author of the *Actes and Monuments* (1563), popularly known as *The Book of Martyrs*. Napier is probably Sir Francis Scott, later Lord Napier (1703–1773), who served in the allied army under the earl of Stair (1743). David Rizzio (1533–1566) was an Italian musician and favorite of Mary, Queen of Scots, and became her virtual secretary of state. Haughty and overbearing, he was stabbed to death by a group that included Lord Darnley, Mary's husband. Francesco Guicciardini (1483–1540) was a Florentine historian and statesman and author of the *Storia d'Italia* (16 books, 1561), a major historical work of the 16th century. Hamilton elsewhere identifies Sciolto as Grand Librarian to the Vatican (see II, 270). Puffendorfius is Baron Samuel von Pufendorf (1632–1694), German jurist and historian, and author of *De statu imperii Germanici* (1667) and *De jure naturae et gentium* (1672). Peter the Hermit, also known as Peter of Amiens (ca. 1050–1115), was a gentleman of Picardy who became a monk and preached during the First Crusade, leading a multitude of followers into Asia Minor. John Burton (1696–1771) was a classical scholar and author of numerous tracts, sermons, Latin verses, and Greek textbooks. Thomas Brown (1663–1704) was an English satirist and author of the famous "I do not love thee, Dr. Fell" and *Amusements Serious and Comical* (London, 1700), humorous sketches of London life. Prester John was a legendary Christian priest and king who is alleged to have reigned both in Asia and in Africa in the 12th century. Muley Mahomet, first of the Muley kings of Tunis, fathered Muley-Hacan before being poisoned by his wife. Abdalla is probably not Abdallah (fl. 6th century A.D.), the father of Mohammed, but Abdallah (d. 1058?), the learned and pious Moslem founder of the Almoravides sect who taught and organized the Negro tribes of the western Sahara region, and whose successors founded Marrakesh (1062) and conquered Spain. Tonombeius is possibly Adrien Turnèbe (1512–1565), an eminent French critic and translator who wrote commentaries on Cicero, Horace, and Pliny, and translations of Aristotle, Theophrastus, and Plutarch. Robert Burton (1577–1640) was vicar of Saint Thomas's in Oxford, rector of the parish of Seagrave, Leicestershire, and author of *The Anatomy of Melancholy* (Oxford, 1621); (see also I, 69n). Sir David Lindsay (1490–1555) was a Scottish poet noted for satirizing the vices of the clergy and exposing the disorders of church and state. Caelius Aurelianus (fl. 4th or 5th century A.D.) was a physician of Numidia and author of the *Medicinales responsiones*, a compendium of the whole science of medicine in the form of a catechism. Rhazes, or Rasis (850–923), was chief physician of the great hospital in Baghdad and author of more than 140 medical works, including a general treatise (in 10 books, translated into Latin ca. 1485) that greatly influenced medical science in the Middle Ages. Avicenna (980–1037) was an Arabian physician and philosopher who wrote numerous works on theology, metaphysics, mathematics, and medicine, including *The Canon*, long regarded in the Orient as a medical textbook of great authority. Sir William Killigrew (1606?–1695) was the English author of the tragicomedies *Selindra* (1662) and *Ormasdes; or, Love and Friendship* (1664) and the comedy *Pandora* (1664). Giulio Alberoni (1664–1752) was an Italian cardinal and statesman who negotiated the marriage of Philip V and Elizabeth Farnese and served as prime minister of Spain (1715–1719).

6. Michael Servetus (1511–1553) was a Spanish theologian, physician, and astrologer who opposed the doctrine of the Trinity in *De trinitatis erroribus* (1531) and *Christianismi restitutio* (1553), for which he was eventually imprisoned in Geneva at Calvin's request and burned at the

showed the Learning of a Warburton,[7] and gratified my own vanity at the Expence of tiring your honors patience,—which I'd be loth to do, unless absolutely necessary for the good of your honor & this here ancient Club, and besides these, I could produce a great Cloud of other witnesses and authorities who Indeed are a Set of fellows, neither ancient nor moderen but, very reputable Jolly, good Club Companions, vizt: Don Jumpedo, Harlequin, Scarramuchio, Peroquetto, alias Pero, and Mr Pantaloon,[8] such Jolly Club Companions as we I say, who are an ancient Club, in so far as we resemble the ancient Clubs, more than the moderen books do the ancient books, and therefore properly are Called Ancient Club, for the Ancient books were made only of barks of trees and flag leaves called papyrus, but the moderen books are Confabricated of paper, pastboard, Skin and sundry other materials, but the ancient clubs Consisted only of mere mortal men as do also the moderen Clubs, and, to prevent the Cavils of Critics I will take notice here, that there ‖ is no general rule but has an exception, and therefore we read somewhere, (I believe In Æsop's fables, or some other such fables,) of a Club of Centaurs, the members of wch were half men, half horses, reputed for their Celerity Strength and wisdom, and of Hercules's Club, which was nothing but a Great Crab Stick, with which he used to knock down monsters, and sometimes turkeys and Geese, when he had nothing else to do,[9] neither are our moderen Clubs altogether without examples of this Sort, for, we have some Clubs, even at this day, that are half beasts, half men, reputed for their Celerity In drinking, their wit in punning and Conundrumification, and their Strength in tossing off bumpers, and, as for monsters, how many monsters this here ancient Club has destroyed, besides Sir Hugh Maccarty Esqr, I shall not pretend to say, but, [50]

stake as a heretic, and which includes the first printed account of the circulation of the blood through the lungs (pp. 168–173). The reference to Hippocrates is commonplace. David and Seneca, of course, have nothing to say about the French pox.

7. William Warburton (1698–1779), bishop of Gloucester, frequently engaged in theological controversy. His writings include *The Divine Legation of Moses Demonstrated* (London, 1738–1741), which argues that Moses' divine mission is implied by the very absence in Mosaic law of any reference to future life.

8. In Italian commedia dell'arte, Harlequin is one of several stock characters along with Columbine, Pierrot, Pantaloon, and others. In English pantomime, which was derived from the Italian commedia and to which Hamilton is probably referring, Harlequin is a mute character who is supposed to be invisible to the clown and to Pantaloon and who rivals the clown for the affections of Columbine. Scaramouch, a cowardly and foolish boaster who burlesques the Spanish don as a stock character in Italian farces, was a popular figure in the late 17th century. The comedy *Scaramouch,* by Edward Ravenscroft, was produced in 1677.

9. Hamilton is only half joking here. Hercules is often portrayed carrying a knotted club, which according to legend, he used to destroy monsters to make the earth habitable for men.

as to fat Turkeys and Geese, Sure I am, it has destroyed as many as that of Hercules ever did. But I defy any one, to produce, from all the Authorities of the Learned, any other Instances of ancient Clubs, differing in any material Circumstances, from what our Clubs are now a days, excepting it be in these few instances of drinking Lemmon Punch, Grog, Rumbo, Toddy, Inflammable Spirits and smoking tobacco, tho the latter is by some said to be a very ancient date among the Eastren nations, the negroes of Afric and the Savages of America, which by the bye, are such trivial Circumstances, that they are not worth mentioning and are none of them the distinguish-

[51] ing Characteristick || of those venerable Societies called Clubs, but let us perlustrate[10] what has been said of Clubs by Learned writers, Joannes Stuceius wrote lately, a very ponderous Volume, on this very Subject, entituled, *de antiquorum Conviviis*, where we find, that ancient times afforded the same *Fagos apetios*, Heliogobales,[11] that moderen times exhibit, all worthy Gentlemen, members of ancient Clubs, who, as such, made a figure in their day, *quorum in Ventre Ingenium, in patinis mens*,[12] these Clubs, we find, have a very near resemblance to the Clubs of our days, for Seneca says *pervertunt officia noctis et Lucis*,[13] which may also be properly applied to our moderen drums & routs[14] and, a good ancient Club member, such as was the Roman Flaccus,

> *Noctes vigilabat ad ipsam*
> *Mane, diem Totam stertebat.*

Whole nights he watch'd, till morning peeps,
All day on Couch, he snores and sleeps.[15]

Snymdiris the Sybarite, is said to have been such a Jolly member of a Certain Everlasting Club, that he never saw the Sun rise or set once in 20 years,[16] but our ancient Clubs are best represented now a days, by your great lubberly drunken dutchmen, who make it a Custom to Invite all

---

10. Survey thoroughly.

11. Johann Wilhelm Stuck (1542–1607) was the Swiss author of *Commentaries on Arian* (1577?), *Parallel between Charlemagne and Henry IV* (1592), and *Antiquitates convivial* (1582), where he likely refers to "that most excellent glutton" Heliogabalus.

12. "Their genius was in their bellies, their mind on the dishes."

13. "They pervert the functions of night and day" (*Epistulae* 122.2).

14. A *rout* is a fashionable gathering or assembly, evening party or reception, much in vogue in the 18th century; a *drum* is also an assembly of fashionable people at a private house.

15. More literally, "He used to stay awake until dawn and snored all day" (*Sermones* 1.3.18).

16. Smindyrides of Sybaris (a Greek town proverbial for its love of luxury and pleasure) meant that he went to bed after daybreak and rose in the evening, a boast intended merely to imply his wealth, not to be taken literally (see Athenaeus 6.273).

Comers with a pail and a dish, *Velut Infundibila Integras obbas exhauriunt, et in monstrosis poculis ipsi monstrosi, monstrosius epotant,*[17] that is to say, these overgrown Swabbers, make barrels of their paunches, and || pour down [52] drink, till they become Swag bellied and hopper arsed, like the members of an Ancient drunken Club at Babylon, of which was president Alexander the Great of foolish memory, who, (rest his Soul) died with excess of drinking.

II I come now to prove, that your honor is a president, the word *President*, as I conceive, may be derived from two Lating words, according, as you shall spell it with an S or a C, and, by the bye, let none Clap a waggish Construction on my meaning, when I mention these two letters, as some Stock jobbers in Change alley did upon S:S:C, under the Royal head, in the Shillings Coined by the South Sea Company, in the year 1724, affirming that they signified a thing belonging to the Celebrated Sally Salisbury,[18] by which she made her fortune, and raised herself some degrees above that vulgar Class in which she was born; if spelt with an S, it may be derived from *præ*, and *Sedere*, to sit first, if with a C, (tho not Erroneously, as Queen Elizabeth observed the word *Sunt* to be wrote, by the Idle boys of Westminster School, with Chalk upon the wall) we derive it from *præ* and *Cedere*, to walk, or go first, in your honor, both derivations hold good, for, at all our Sederunts, we find your honor always *Præ Sedere,* or the first sitting member mentioned, and in anniversary processions, we also find, that when the Longstanding members march thro' your honors alley strowed || with [53] flowers, that your honor always marches *præ,* so that honorable Sir, *præsedeo,* and *præcedo* are both applicable to your honor, from this argument alone (the contexture of which, I borrow, from the learned Dr Warburton in that ponderous book, called the *Divine legation of Moses,*)[19] I think it appears plain, that your honor is a president, but some malicious and evil minded persons, may perhaps affirm, that you are a president and no president, we look upon this to be but a Silly Idle Quibble, a Contradiction *in terminis*, and therefore, in its self absurd, but this Saying proceeds only from the Invidious mouths of such as desire to be presidents themselves, and cannot attain to the honor, either by their acquired wit or Innate merit, as your

---

17. "Like funnels they inhale whole noggins, and in monstrous drinking vessels these monsters monstrously drink."

18. Sally Salisbury was the alias of Sarah Priddon (d. 1692), a famous whore and the central character of Capt. Charles Walker's *Authentick Memoirs of the Life, Intrigues, and Adventures of the Celebrated Sally Salisbury* (London, 1723).

19. Hamilton is probably borrowing his method of arguing from Warburton, who repeatedly quibbles about fine shades of meaning in *The Divine Legation of Moses,* but this particular quibble does not appear in that work.

honor has by both, of whom it may be said, as was said of Bernardus A Doma, when his name was maliciously annagrammatized, or rather accrosticated, *A Diabolo Os Maledicum Aperitur*,[20] and I may on this occasion also be allowed here to mention a quotation mentioned by me in a former oration.

και κεραμευς κεραμει, κοτεει και τεκτονι τεκτων
και πτοχως πτοχω φθονεει και αοιδος αοιδω.

That is, A Potter Emulates a potter,
      A Smith envies another,
      A Beggar emulates a beggar,
      A Singing Clerk, his brother.[21]
                      Robertus Burtonus Oxon: Poæta Clubicus

But in despite of these quibblers, let us say with Anacreon

μεθοντα γαρ με κεθαι
πολυ κρεισσον η θανοντα.

      Chace Care with bumpers of Red,
      For better be fuddled than dead,[22] *Anon:*

or, if you will dead drunk, than dead in Sober earnest, but to shut up this argument with a convincing proof, should any one deny it, Sir John's broad Sword will prove the Contrary, which will make the boldest of them all Tr-r-r-r-remble.

    III   And now, honorable Sir, it remains to prove, that your honor is president of this here Club, which I think, will be the easiest problem of any I have yet undertaken, I shall Introduce it with a Lemma.

Lemma

Your honor, is either president of a Club, or of no Club,
If, of no Club, of what Club are you president?
If of a Club, of what Club but this here Club?

---

20. Bernhardus à Doma was a 13th-century Provençal lawyer who devised a universal formulary for all civil actions; the acrostic, meaning "his damned mouth was opened by the devil," perhaps appears in the physician and astronomer Anton Deusing's (1612–1666) defense, the *Vindiciae foetus extra uterum geniti . . . contra ejusdem Bernhardi à Doma furiosos insultus* (Groningen, 1664).

21. Hesiod, *Works and Days* 25–26. Hamilton's translation is accurate.

22. Literally, "better I should do it drunk than dead" (an "Anacreontic," an anonymous imitation of Anacreon; see *Carmina Anacreontea*, ed. Martin L. West [Leipzig, 1984], 48.8–9).

This here ancient book of Records is alone Sufficient authority to prove it, where we find, almost in every page *Present, The honble: Nasifer Jole Esqr, Lord President,* and *Present, the honble: Nasifer Jole Esqr president,* and, in order to show that this may be proved by abundance of quotations, (after the manner of the aforesaid Learned Doctor Warburton, and many other moderen Doctors) from ancient authors, you'll find often in Homer,

Ατρειδες δε ποιμενα λαων,[23]

but this you'll say will answer as well for a Bishop as a president, but again there is

Ατρειδες δε αναξ ανδρων —and
Πατερ ανδρων τε θεων τε,[24]

and what makes more to our purpose

Τῶν ὃι αδελφιος ερχε βοην ἀγαθος Μενελαος,[25]

and Else where—*Probus quis nobiscum vivit,* and *Dic mihi musa verum,*[26] and lastly

*Mihi Delphica tellus
et Claros et Tenedos, Pateræaque regio servit,
Jupiter est genitor,*[27]

which by the bye is an excellent quotation in point, to prove Sufficiently the *Jus divinum* of Presidents as well as of kings.

But it is only abusing your honors patience and understanding to Insist any longer [pres: ay, ay, pray ha done, for no body understands this Lamentable Stuff] —in this argument, and therefore I conclude with,

IV The Inferences which are naturally deducible from this Important Subject and argument.

And first, I Inferr from thence, that this here Club is a Club, for *Nil prodest quod non Lædere possit, Item, Igne quid utilius.*[28]

Secondly that your honor is a president,

---

23. "Atreides (Agamemnon), shepherd of the people" (commonplace epithet in the *Iliad*).
24. "Agamemnon, lord of men" (another commonplace epithet; see, e.g., *Iliad* 1.7); and "Father of gods and men" (epithet for Zeus, e.g., *Iliad* 1.544).
25. "Of these was his brother, good Menelaus of the great war cry, the leader" (*Iliad* 2.586).
26. "What upright man lives among us?"; "Muse, tell me the truth."
27. "The Delphic land, Claros and Tenedos, and the region of Patara serve me; Jupiter is my father" (Ovid, *Metamorphoses* 1.515–517).
28. "Nothing helps that cannot hurt; item, what is more useful than fire?" (Ovid, *Tristia* 2.266–267).

Tibi nos, tibi nostra Suppellex
Ruraque servirent[29]

Thirdly and lastly, that your honor is president of this here Club, *Quod erat demonstrandum,*[30] and so I end with

Cujus octavum trepidavit ætas
Claudere lustrum——Dixi.[31]

The Orator having pronounced this oration, the music struck up again, and his honors minuet was playd over, thus Ended the 7th Anniversary.

29. "We serve you, and so does our company, our lands."
30. "Which was to be demonstrated" (*Q.E.D.*).
31. "A man in his eighth lustrum [40 years] whose life is hastening to a close" (Horace, *Carmina* 2.4.23–24).

Chapter IV

The Great Clubical Battle of Farce alia, fought between Coneïus Pimpeïus Frontinbrass the Great on one Side, and Mr Secretary Scribble, Mr Solo Neverout, & Laconic Comas Esqr on the other, with the event of that dreadful Battle, which Compleats the History of Box No 1.

If we look over history, we shall find several persons distinguished by the Epithet of *the Great,* There are Cyrus the Great, Alexander the Great, Pompey the Great, Mahomet the Great, Gregory the Great, Charles the Great, Lewis the great, and in this present wicked Generation Jonathan Wild the Great,[1] as the Ingenious Mr Fielding very deservedly stiles him, being a personage of Great and uncommon qualifications. What real merit these Great men had, to Entitle them to this pompous Epithet, let the discerning world enquire and Judge, It is none of my business, being but a puny Club historian, to determin and pass Judgement in these weighty and momentous matters, for, whatever my decision be, the world will still think & Judge as they please; however, I shall be bold to say, that, after the Strictest Enquiry, into the lives and actions of these heroes, (as they are called,) I find, that far the greatest number of them, were neither ‖ better nor worse than professed butchers, who spread desolation & Slaughter over the face of the earth wherever they came, one Pope, I have mentioned Indeed, among the Rest, whose profession was not war, but one of the most distinguishing actions of his life was That of Reforming and Improving the Almanac, and rectifying some Inaccuracies of the Julian Calendar, and, I humbly conceive, that, on account of this single Service he did the public, he deserved the title of *The Great,* more than did all the other fighting fellows, for all the deeds of prowess they ever atchieved, but, what Surprizes me very much, is, that some persons have been distinguished with this eminent title, who seem to have much less deserved it, than others, 'Tis true, our Alfred, in the British Annals, a prince of an Excellent Character, if what the Historians say of him be true, has had the good

[57]

---

1. Pope Gregory the Great (540?–604) restored monastic discipline and zealously propagated Christianity (not to be confused, as Hamilton later does in this paragraph, with Gregory XIII [1502–1585], who reformed the calendar in 1582). Jonathan Wild the Great is the central character of Henry Fielding's satirical romance *The Life of Jonathan Wild the Great* (1743).

fortune to be stiled Alfred the Great, very deservedly, but why Hannibal, who fought in a good Cause, why Leonidas, Epaminondas, Timoleon, Miltiades, Montezuma,[2] and our Oliver Cromwel, who were all of the military profession, and fought bravely in defence of liberty, and their natural Rights, why some Philosophers, Legislators, and Ingenious Navigators, who have been Singularly Serviceable to their respective Countries, and Indeed, to all mankind, have not been dignified with this title, I cannot conceive, unless it has been, by the General Inattention and oversight of the Historians, one would think, that Socrates, Confucius, Solon, Lycurgus, Numa,[3] Sir Isaac Newton, Sir Francis Drake and Sir Walter Rawleigh, by their public Services to mankind in General, and their own Countrymen in particular, deserved this distinguishing title, as much, nay more, than any professed Butcher that ever lived, but perhaps, the Judicious world, thought this title too triffling for their great merit, and therefore withheld it from them, especially as it had been bestowed Indiscriminately, or rather Indiscreetly on many || Illustrious theives and cutthroats. It will not then I hope seem Strange, that an honorary member, and agent for the ancient & honorable Tuesday Club, should be distinguished with this high title, since we find, several persons in history as little deserving of it as he honored with the Epithet, the person I mean, is Coney Pimp Frontinbrass Esqr, agent for the ancient and honorable Tuesday Club, in America, and the Islands thereunto belonging, who had, during his late absence from the Club, upon what account I know not, unless it was for his having encountered Sir Hugh Maccarty Esqr, or, for his having Caped the august head of the honorable Lord Jole, got the title of *the Great* annexed to his name, and was now Commonly stiled *Coneïus Pimpeïus Frontinbrass the Great,* tho' some

[58]

---

2. Leonidas, the king of Sparta (491–480 B.C.), defended his country in 480 B.C. against Xerxes' invasion. Epaminondas (418–362 B.C.), a general who helped restore Theban power (379–371 B.C.) through innovative warfare, introducing the variant of a slanting attack by the left flank, was known for his noble character. Timoleon (d. ca. 334 B.C.) was a Corinthian who liberated Sicily and Syracuse from their tyrants and, when dictatorial powers were conferred on him, initiated a program of social and political reconstruction at Syracuse. Miltiades (ca. 550–489 B.C.), an Athenian, ruled as king over the Thracians of the Chersonese peninsula and was an influential general and statesman in his later years. Montezuma is probably not Montezuma I (1390?–1464), the "emperor" of Mexico, but Montezuma II (1480?–1520), Aztec emperor and ruler at the time of the Spanish conquest.

3. Solon (ca. 638–558 B.C.) was an Athenian statesman and poet whose economic and constitutional reforms helped pave the way for Athenian democracy; one of his poems helped stir the Athenians to capture Salamis. Lycurgus (probably fl. 9th century B.C.) was the traditional founder of Sparta's constitution and social and military systems, and consequently of the "good order" they created. Numa Pompilius (traditionally 715–673 B.C.), the legendary successor to Romulus and second king of Rome, contributed much to religious and cultural developments.

are of opinion, he had not this Sonorous title at the time of his return to Annapolis, but obtained it by the Signal victory he obtained at the Great Battle of Farce alia, of that Battle, and this here Clubical heroe, I propose to treat Largely in this Chapter, but must beg leave, before I describe that Tremendous action, to premise some necessary Circumstances.

Coneïus Pimpeïus Frontinbrass the Great then, for so he must now be called, upon his Arival from his Northeren Journey as has been related, could not procure admission to the Club, which he took so much to heart, that it utterly deprived him of his rest, nor could he in any manner Compose his perturbed Spirits, till he had procured an Interview with his honor the president, which at last he obtained, tho he was obliged to try several methods before he could succeed, the different Steps he took to effect this, we are now going to relate.

After having been refused admittance to the Club, he wrote a letter to his honor the President, and superscribed it in a pompous manner, giving him the title of *Right honorable Lord Jole*. This was an Error in the first Concoction, which, (as the Physiologists tell us) could not be mended in the Second and proceeded from his being Ignorant, that the president had given up that title. This letter he dispatched with his own Servant, who delivered it to his honor, at his own door, while he looked over the hatch; which it was his Custom often to do, in a Summers evening, for the Sake of the fresh air; his honor, by the Superscription, knew Immediatly, from what Quarter the letter had come, and, putting it again into the Messengers hands, ordered him to redeliver it to his master, and withal acquaint him, that he received no such foolish letters, The messenger did so accordingly, at which Frontinbrass was much Surprized and dissappointed; he however, dispatched the letter to his honor again, and with another Superscription, and in another hand, being Informed (as was supposed) by the Secretary (tho that Sly officer never would own it) of the mistake he had Committed in the first; The Second messenger was a negroe man, altogether unknown to his honor, Which negroe, found his honour, *in Statu quo prius,* That is to say, looking over his hatch door, for the benefit of the air, or, *pour prendre le frais,* as the French term it. He delivered the letter, according to his orders, and without speaking one word, or staying for an answer, betook himself to his heels, this was an Error in || the Second concoction, and (according to the Doctrine of the aforesaid Physiologists) could not be mended in the third, for, his honor, Immediatly suspecting the Trick, hurled the letter after him with such force, that it got the Start of the negroe in his flight, and fell down in the Street before him, upon his delivering it again to Frontinbrass, he was still more Surprized, and greatly vexed, but being resolved to palm this Letter upon his honor at any rate, he sent it a third time, and gave the messenger positive Instructions not to deliver it into his honors hands, but to watch an opportunity, when he was not there, and throw it over the hatch door, or in at the window, or even down the Chimney, if every other place was shut up, The messenger observed these orders punctually, and returning to North East Street, found that his honor was now departed from the hatch, but the door being open, he twirld the letter dexterously over the hatch and walked off, Informing Frontinbrass, that he had exactly executed his orders; with this Frontinbrass was fully satisfied, expecting, that when his honor found the letter, his Curiosity would prompt him to open and read it, and by the humbleness of it's Contents, he should again get into his honors favor and good graces, but he was herein much mistaken, for this was also, an Error in the third Concoction, which could not be mended in the fourth, as we shall presently see, for his honor, as he was

[61] stepping up Stairs to bed, passed thro the Store Room, and by ‖ the light of the Candle, perceiving a letter to lye on the floor, he picked it up; and finding that it was much of the same Shape and Size with the Letter Frontinbrass had sent to him twice, and the Superscription the same as that brought by the Second messenger, he put it bye unopened and went to bed; but did nothing but toss and tumble and fret the whole night long, being so ruffled with Indignation and wrath, that he could not shut his eyes to sleep; so that at the break of day, he arose, and hurrying on his Cloths as fast as he could, he went directly to the Lodging of Laconic Comas Esqr, who happened to lodge at the same house, where Frontinbrass had taken up his quarters, and, getting admittance to Mr Comas's Room, he stood at the beds foot, bolt upright, all Ghastly and pale with Indignation and want of his natural Rest, and looked exactly like Margarets Ghost, in the old Song,[4] vizt:

> 'Twas at the Dark and dreary hour,
> When all were fast asleep,
> In Glided Margarets Grimly Ghost,
> And stood at William's feet—

So, his honor Glided in, and looked Grimly and wistfully upon Laconic Comas Esqr, as he lay fast asleep, and thinking of no harm, but at last, calling him by his name, Mr Comas opened his Eyes, and was very much startled to find such a figure, standing at his beds feet, so early; doubting at

---

4. Hamilton is recalling the opening stanza from the popular ballad "William and Margaret" (see Allan Ramsay's *Tea-table Miscellany* [1724–1732], I, 143–145).

first || whether it might not be his honor's Ghost—What do you want?—In Gods name! Cryd Mr Comas, starting upright on his bum in bed.—I have been most Scurvily used by that Rascal Frontinbrass, replied his honor—Hut! dam him! what's that to me?—I come not to blame you Mr Comas, I only desire alittle of your asistance in the affair—No by God!—not I—I wont meddle with your damnd Club nonsense,—Nay!—nay Good friend, I want you only to deliver into his hands this Rascally Letter,—Rascally Letter!—by God not I—damme if I have any thing to do with rascally letters betwixt you and him—no, no—damn him I say—Pray Mr Comas have patience, this is a letter of his own writing and Inditing, which he has the Impudence to direct to me, and force upon me in Spite of my Teeth, so, I would desire the favor of you, as a friend, since I would not see, nor speak with the good for nothing fellow, to give him his letter again, and tell him from me, not to Trowble himself any farther, for I am resolved, neither to receive any of his letters, nor see him again while I live,—if that be all, I'll do it by God;—gi' me the letter, I'll deliver it to him,—on this his honor delivered the letter to Laconic Comas Esqr, being all in a tremble with Indignation and vexation, Mr Comas Promised to deliver it to Frontinbrass, and so his honor took his Leave and Returned home.

Mr Comas, as soon as Frontinbrass made his appearance at breakfast, according to his promise deliverd him the letter, at which Frontinbrass seemed very much Surprized, || wondering how he came by it, but Mr Comas soon removed his Surprize, by acquainting him with the whole matter, as Just now related.

This made Frontinbrass still more uneasy, and he could not resolve how next to proceed, but was not long without a device, for he was fully determined, before he left the place, to have an Interview with his honor, and come to an Eclaircissement with him about the late Censures, which had been passed upon him in Club; and to effect this, he thought of Picking a quarrel with the Secretary, which was to be so Contrived, as to begin at his honors back gate, at which place, he had appointed, to meet the said Secretary one afternoon, and, Intending to begin there, first with high words, and then proceed to violence and blows, there was to be a running fight mantained thro' the alley, and Into his honors back yard. At this time some abusive letters passed between him and the Secretary, which, it was thought paved the way for this quarrel and fight, which was afterwards Called the Grand Battle of Farce alia. The world Judged differently of these machinations between Frontinbrass and the Secretary. Some thought, that it was a political Contrivance between them, to procure a forceable admittance as it were, to Frontinbrass, into his honor's presence, and that the said battle of Farce alia, furious as it seemed to be, was only a Sham battle, planed beforehand, by these two politicians, to gain the desired point or purpose; others believed that the Secretary knew nothing of any such plot, but was attacked by Frontinbrass of a Sudden, before he was aware, and that || Frontinbrass had no actual Quarrel with the Secretary, but attacked him at his honor's back gate, and Chaced him into the yard, that he might thereby get admittance into his honor's presence, under Color of pursuing his foe, others again thought that both Frontinbrass and the Secretary, were really in earnest, and that no Sham on either Side was Intended, Such are the various opinions Concerning the motives of great politicians, the depth of whose designs is hid from vulgar Eyes—but however this be, I shall here give a particular account of this great battle, and describe every Circumstance of it, exactly as it happened.

It came to pass then, upon friday the 19th of June, 1752, about 4 o'clock in the afternoon, That this Great Clubical battle of farce alia was fought in the manner following.

Solo Neverout Esqr, Protomusicus, and the Secretary, were upon their way to visit his honor the president, and talk of some Important matters, relative to the Club; The Secretary was unarmed, as suspecting no harm, but Mr Protomusicus was provided in a Good Hiccory Stick, which was Calculated by the maker both to give and ward off good hard dry blows, being of a taper Shape, Lessening from the head downwards, limber, flexible and Tough, on the head thereof, the Ingenious artist had formed a round knob, nighly Spherical, which served for two purposes, vizt: for an ease to the hand in walking, and, for more effectually Cracking any Coxcombs Cranium, who should attack or abuse its owner, the Lower End of it was studded with brass, which, by it's binding quality, would prevent the weapon from splitting, in warding || or bestowing blows at a wattling bout; Thus was armed the heroic protomusicus; Just as these two heroes arrived at his honor's back Gate, and were about to enter, they were allarmed with the Rattling noise of Chariot wheels, and looking down Northeast Street, they perceived the Enimy advancing, full Speed, vizt: Coneïus Pimpeïus Frontinbrass the Great, mounted on a lofty Chariot, and a Canopy over his head, drawn by two fiery Steeds who Champed the bit, foamed at their mouths and smoaked at the nosetrills, upon one of which rode a bold youth as postillion, with Leather Cap and buckskin breeches; Coneïus Pimpeïus Frontinbrass the Great was thus armed, he had on his head a huge broad brimd helmet of beaver, not plumed, a round bob wig scarce covering his ears, in his right hand a whip of an Enormous Size with a long lash, which he smacked as he drove along, his hands were Covered with mighty Gauntlets of buckskin, with large tops, reaching to his Elbow Joints, round his loins was a broad leatheren belt, but no Sword. At Sight of this formidable heroe the Secretary and Mr Protomusicus were much abashed, and, it is said, showed some Signs of fear in their Countenance, but soon recovering themselves, they halted at his honors back Gate, and drew up their Phalanx of Infantry in the best order, resolved to stand the Charge of the Enimy, Frontinbrass the Great upon his coming up, stooped his fiery Steeds, not chusing to take a dishonorable advantage of the enemy by oversetting their Infantry, with the force of his Cavalry, tho || he might easily have done it, [66] and Calling out with a loud and enraged voice *You Scribble!*—addressing himself to the Secretary—stood bolt upright in his Chariot and Clubbd his whip, The Secretary, being unarmed, did not stay to make him any answer, but ran precipitately into his honor's back alley and Immediatly betook himself to flight, to save his bacon; on this, Frontinbrass Jumped from his chariot on the Ground, and his pence rattled in his pocket.(a) The brave protomusicus upon seeing this, was resolved to oppose him with all his might, but Frontinbrass being Strongly armed, made him at last yield Ground and he retired thro' the alley in a Retrograde motion, receiving many a furious blow of the whip, aimed at the Secretaries head, upon his trusty hiccory Cudgel, while thus the fury of the battle, was passing by the Gavel End of his honors wooden Tenement, several hard and desperate thumps and blows fell upon the boards, which shook the house to its very foundations, but did no further dammage, for, the Strong arm and Cudgel of Protomusicus, warded them off so effectually, that neither he nor the Secretary received any hurt, and many Indeed, thought that there was no hurt Intended on either Side, tho' that is at best but conjecture, for the Combatants fought Seemingly as if the Devil in hell had possessed them, and appeared to be very much in earnest, Several huge fifty Sixes,[6] were taken up with a Strong arm, and Batterred against his honor's house, whilest the fury of the battle Continued in the back ally, which made a noise against the boards, like the Discharging of great Guns, and, a prodigious Cloud of dust was raised, so as to obscure the Sky, over head, at last Frontinbrass the Great, being too Strong || for his opponents, drove them [67] headlong into his honors back yard, dealing his blows thick about him,

(a) Fieldings Joseph Andrews,—his halfpence, rattled in his pocket.[5]

5. Hamilton is probably recalling the scene in *Joseph Andrews* (1742) where Fielding mentions that Joseph has "sixpence" in his pocket, but while turning out his pockets to demonstrate his poverty to the innkeeper Tow-wouse, he unwittingly reveals a "little piece of gold" (bk. 2, chap. 2).

6. A *fifty-six* is a weight of 56 pounds, or half a British hundredweight.

which blows were all aimed at the Secretary, who still retired before them, and the undaunted Protomusicus received them on his trusty Hiccory Cudgel, at last they came into the back yard, where was the fury and heat of the battle, and so earnestly were they engaged, and the Clamor and vociferation was so loud and terrible, that they did not perceive in the said back yard, his honor The President, Laconic Comas Esqr, Smoothum Sly Esqr, Drawlum Quaint Esqr, who were partaking a Bowl of punch and a pipe of Tobacco with his honor, at the time the battle began, and, by them also, stood in waiting Don John Charlotto, his honor's Gentleman usher, I say, the furious Combatants did not perceive these Gentlemen in the back yard, but kept dealing their blows about, and warding them off, in such a furious manner, as to overset and turn upside down every thing in their way. His honor the President Looked pale as ashes, being struck with a sudden Terror, and exclaimed with a Loud voice,—Go, run!—go run!—fetch the Constable!—I say run!—go! go! run!—To which Don John Charlotto answered,—yes Sir!—yes Sir!—presently!—Laconic Comas Esqr was taken with a fit of trembling, and could not hold still one Joint of his body,—he attempted to speak, but passion and rage Choaked up the passages of his voice, Drawlum Quaint, and Smoothum Sly Esqrs, were in such a Situation, as that they seemed to laugh and Cry at one and the same time, the muscles of their faces being in such a violent act of Gelasticity,[7] as that the tears || gushed plentifully out at their eyes, The battle in the mean time turned more furious—Let me have a fair Stroke at him Cried Frontinbrass,—damme if you shall, replied the heroe Neverout,—knock him down! —knock him down!—dam ye!—why dont you knock him down!—exclaim'd Laconic Comas,—then the thumps and blows fell ten times thicker than before, and the air whistled again with the violent vibrations of the whip and Cudgel,—his honor retired to a Corner of the yard, and stood Collected within himself, a pallid hue overspreading his Lamentable Countenance, and a pannic fear damping his animal Spirits, and as the blows Lighted nigh him he ducked and dodged his head to one Side & to the other; his honorable and venerable head that was covered with a Cap of Green velvet; Don John Charlotto, during the heat of the Engagement, had withdrawn himself, as it was believed, to fetch the Constable, pursuant to the orders he had received from his honor, the battle now began to rise to its highest fury, most terrible thumps and knocks were dealt about, one third of which lighted upon the brave Neverout's hiccory Cudgel, and the Magnanimous Frontinbrasses whale bone whip, and the other two thirds,

---

7. *Gelastic,* meaning "risible," stems from the Greek "to laugh."

upon the wall of his honor's kitchen, and the palisading of his honor's yard, but not one could be perceived to light on the Secretary, the hurly burly and noise was such, as that it was Inconceivable, and drew many Spectators, who viewed the furious conflict, with great amazement and astonishment; mingling voices were heard to rend the air—damn you!—down with him! —let me have but one fair blow—ad rat you!—Stand fair you Scoundrell!— I'll break every bone in his body by God!—be quiet I say!—It is a Lamentable thing, that people that are quiet and peaceable should be thus molested—you there, is the || Constable come yet,—not yet Sir—Zounds, knock him down!—down with him!—trip up his heels—while this mad work was going on, The brave Laconic Comas recovering from his Surprise and vehement passion, began to wave his Cane, and dealt some blows with such a heavy hand, as soon made Frontinbrass the Great perceive that he was in earnest, for, at two thwacks he made the dust fly out at the Skirts of his Coat, and aimed a blow at his head, which Glanced along the left Side of his wig, and was within two Inches of Bruising his pericranium, upon which Drawlum Quaint and Smoothum Sly Interposed, and Slyboots Pleasant and the Chancellor, coming into the yard providentially in the nick of time, the Latter being armed with a good hiccory Wattle, marched their fresh troops between the adverse parties, and a parley was sounded, and an end at last put to this most furious battle, and lucky it was that it happened so at that Instant, for, Laconic Comas Esqr, being a fresh man and much more in earnest than any of the other Combatants, would have made terrible havock with his cane, which was thick and heavy, and withal adorned with a Gorgeous brass head, Carved and Embossed, and was armed at the other End with a Strong brass Theca, and thick Iron prong, and hung at his valiant wrist, by a Strong twisted Silk String, well secured with a firm knot, and a Sliding button Just under the Tassel.

Thus Ended this Great Battle, and the Company planted themselves round the table, and, handing about the punch bowl, the adverse parties, at the Request of his honor the president shook hands, his honor then began to enquire into the cause of the Squabble, and several letters were || produced by Coneïus Pimpeïus Frontinbrass the great, wrote in a very abusive Stile, which he said, he had received from the Secretary. These letters were perused by his honor and the Company, and the Secretary was much blamed for his Incivility, upon which, the Secretary Grew warm, and some high words passed which threatned the Renewal of the battle, but, by the Interposition of his honor and Mr Smoothum Sly, matters did not grow to such a pitch, however, Coneïus Pimpeïus Frontinbrass the Great, and the Secretary, gave Each other a formal Challenge, to see it out, in a Gentleman like manner at Sword and pistol man to man, without Seconds. Then Frontinbrass, pulling out of his pocket, the Letter, which, his honor the president, so often, had sent back to him unopened, he Civily presented it to his honor, and with a low bow, desired that he would do him the honor to open and read it, which his honor absolutely refused, desiring him to cancell and destroy that letter, for he neither desired to see it himself, nor would chuse that any body else should peruse it, as he was Sure, that what was in it could be nothing at all to the purpose, and as for the difference, that subsisted between the writer of that letter and himself, it could be better adjusted and made up by word of mouth, if it was to be made up at any rate, than by all the idle Stuff that could be committed to paper. Upon this Frontinbrass, somewhat Chagrined, conveyd the letter again into his pocket; and, it was thought, soon after destroyed it, so that, by his honor's obstinacy the world was for ever deprived of the knowledge of that, doubtless, most extraordinary Composition.

[71] While the President and Frontinbrass were engaged in discourse about this Letter, the Secretary had retired with ‖ Don John Charlotto into the antichamber, the latter having Called the Secretary away from the company, as if he wanted to talk with him in private, while they were together, Don John Began in this manner. "For Gods Sake Mr Secretary, let me earnestly request you, not to fight that fellow Frontinbrass; he is a desperate fellow, and cares not what he does, he is a man of no account or consequence, no body cares for him, and he for no body; he is only one of your *here and there Sort of Chaps,* having no Certain abode or habitation, being a kind of vagabond on the face of this earth; be advised by me; dispise him; no body will blame you for it; if you should put yourself to the hazard of Sharps or bullets with him, the advantage lies much on his Side, you are an Inhabitant of some repute in this here City, and have a great deal to lose, he nothing in Comparison, and therefore Sir"—while Don Charlotto was going on with this wholesome advice to the Secretary, his honor the president entered the room, and Interupted his discourse, by calling out suddenly in an angry tone of voice—Dam you! why dont you bring the Candles,—on which Don John stopd short, and went to execute the orders of his Lord and master.

The Candles being brought, and the Company retired from the yard to the antichamber, The Conversation began to turn upon Sir Hugh Maccarty Esqr, and the Box No 1, both of which, his honor observed, contained so many gross Impositions, that he could never forgive Frontinbrass and the Secretary for attempting to put them upon him and the Club,—Frontinbrass the great readily gave up Box No 1, as a thing, in which he had not the

Least concern, and left the whole Burden of that || Celebrated box upon the [72] Secretary's Shoulders, but Insisted still upon the Identity of Sir Hugh Maccarty Esqr, and offered, to produce Evidence, if called upon, to prove, that such a person was now alive and in being—on which Laconic Comas Esqr, pulling his pipe from his mouth, said *Hut! God damn the nonsense!*—and then spit,—Frontinbrass the Great, looking disdainfully upon him started up, and addressing his honor the president, with his back towards Laconic Comas Esqr,—Sir says he, I wonder you should regard what this fellow Comas says, you know he is a person that is a professed enimy to your honor and the Club, he has not yet, nor ever will, forget that Conundrum,—That unlucky Conundrum Sir, which drove him from the Club, and he will prosecute his revenge so far as to set your Lordship, and your ancient Club by the ears—and Create an Irreconcileable difference between you, if you give Credit to his malicious Stories,—while Frontinbrass the Great spoke in this manner to his honor, Laconic Comas Esqr, laying aside his pipe, elevated his cane over his head and stood in a posture, ready to knock him down, which Frontinbrass the Great perceived not, his back being turned to him, and, indeed, his head was quite unguarded, for he had laid aside his huge beaver helmet and bob wig, after the battle, and covered his noddle with a thin Linnen night Cap, so that had Mr Comas struck, he would dowbtless have laid Frontinbrass the great sprawling at his feet, but, either his own discretion, or that of some other person in the Company, (it is uncertain which) prevented the threatned blow, from falling where it seemed to be Intended, and he betook himself quietly to his pipe again,— The Company soon after this, broke up, and parted good friends, his honor promising Frontinbrass the great, to forget all that was passed, and in token of his thorrough reconcilement, to Call upon him to morrow at twelve o' || Clock noon and drink a meridian, the Secretary also yielded up Intirely to [73] his honor, the dispute of Box No 1, and so there was an end of that affair, which had occasioned a heart burning between his honor and him for a long time; and it was agreed that it should never be mentioned again, and Indeed it never was mentioned after this, excepting only once; when his honor observed, that it Certainly was a very unlucky box, and, that some Superstitious people would be apt to believe, that it was bewitched, for, that he had put eggs into it several times, and made a hen sit upon them, but his Labor was lost, for the Eggs would never hatch, on which, in a Sort of Passion, he dug a hole in the Garden, and ramming it hard down with his foot, he threw the dirt over it and left it there to rot in oblivion, as it deserved, and this was the deplorable fate of Box No 1, whose history terminates here.

Upon the next day, at the time appointed, his honor, according to his promise went to the Lodging of Coneïus pimpeïus Frontinbrass the Great, and there amicably drank a meridian with him, being accompanied with several of the Longstanding members, where Frontinbrass protested before his honor, that, in order to clear himself of all odium and blame, with respect to the affair of the *New York gazette,* he was willing to take his trial at next Sederunt of the Club, and stand either Condemned or acquitted by their Judgement, which Tryal, his honor was pleased to Grant him.

In the afternoon, that same day, being Saturday, his honor rode all over the town with Frontinbrass the great, in his triumphal Carr, being dressed in Red, with a large full flaxen wig, and many Spectators being desirous of seeing his honor from the windows, as he passed along, Coneïus Pimpeïus Frontinbrass the Great, stoped his Chariot at several public places in the City, pretending to Call upon business at Certain houses, and to speak with Certain Gentlemen and Ladies passing bye, to give the curious Spectators a better opportunity of seeing his honor || as he rode in State, and the Sashes flew up on each Side of the Street, and windows were Crouded with Spectators, as is usual, when persons of high Character and Rank, Ride or walk in State, in the evening, before they parted, Frontinbrass the great Carried his honor to visit some Gay and Sprightly Ladies, who used him with great Civility, and looked very amorously upon him, and having treated him with a bottle of madeira wine, he waited on him to his own posteren Gate, where he put him down, and Civilly took his Leave.

Chapter V

The Solemn Trial and acquittal of Coneïus Pimpeïus Frontinbrass the Great, Strange Club Hieroglyphics.

Machiavel, that Celebrated writer in politics, tells us somewhere, among his other useful doctrines delivered for the Instruction and Improvement of mankind; *usus fraudis, in Cæteris actionibus detestabilis, in bello Gerendo Laudabilis,* The practise of deceit in the Common transactions of life is a vile thing, but in Carrying on of war, it is Commendable,[1] tho' I cannot say, that I altogether Jump in opinion with that Celebrated author

---

1. Hamilton's translation is accurate. Machiavelli discusses the pros and cons of deceit in *The Prince* (1513), chap. 18.

in this matter, yet, it is the only excuse I can find in all my reading, to Justify the Conduct of Cuneïus Pimpeïus Frontinbrass the Great, in whose actions abundance of deceit appeared, for, if it be Considered, that he was in a State of warfare with the Secretary and Solo Neverout Esqr ‖ att the fighting of [75] the Great Clubical battle of Farce alia, as above related; if Machiavel's maxim has Credit with any or all of our Readers, I hope that will Sufficiently excuse him—but we must now proceed, without further preambles, to the trial of that Gentleman, which alone, will furnish abundant matter for this Chapter.

At Sederunt 182, Slyboots Pleasant Esqr being H:S: on the 23d of June 1752, The Secretary moved in Club, that there might be Council appointed for Coneïus Pimpeïus Frontinbrass the Great, and that he might be sent to the bar, to answer the matters to be brought against him.

Solo Neverout Esqr, objected to this motion, because none had as yet accused Coneïus Pimpeïus Frontinbrass the Great.

Sir John made answer to this objection, saying in a bold manner, that he accused him.

Upon which Drawlum Quaint Esqr, formerly Speaker of the Club, who had been Called by his honor the president, to give his asistance on this Remarkable occasion, was desired by his honor to open the Charge against Coneïus Pimpeïus Frontinbrass the Great, who being set to the bar, vizt: a pair of tongs, laid athwart two Chairs, with Prim Timorous esqr, Serjeant at arms at his right hand, bearing for his badge of office, a long Tobacco pipe, with the bowl part turned away from the Criminal, Solo Neverout Esqr, was appointed his council Learned in the law, and this was the first time that this Gentleman pled at the bar of this Club.

Then Drawlum Quaint Esqr, as prosecutor for his honor and the Club opened the Charge, by accusing the prisoner ‖ at the bar of treasonable and [76] rebellious practices, in holding a Correspondence and Intimacy with Sir Hugh Maccarty Esqr, President of the monday Club of New-York, and revealing to the said Maccarty several Important Secrets of this here Club, to the great prejudice of the same and in Contempt of his honor's authority and dignity, and particularly accused him of having published in a late New-York paper, a Scandalous Libel on his honor and this here ancient and honorable Club, in great Contempt of his honors Chair and authority, and the dignity of this here ancient and honorable Club, wherein several Scandalous, and black-guard billingsgate terms were used, such as, representing his honor, as a man of a pitiful aspect and awkward address, Scornfully Calling his honor's head, by the opprobrious apellation of lousy Pericranium, and stiling this here ancient and honorable Club, a paltry Club, to all which Great and atrocious crimes, of which, the said Coneïus Pimpeïus Frontinbrass the Great stood accused, he was Commanded in the name of his honor and the Club to plead.

And the prisoner, to all and every of them pleaded, not Guilty, in manner and form, as set forth in the foregoing Charge, and being asked how he would be tried, he answered, by his Lordship and the Club, but being desired again to recollect himself, he said, by his honor & the Club.

Then Mr Prosecutor examined the evidences, the first of whom was Jonathan Grog Esqr.

[77] Pros: Pray Mr Grog, did you receive any of these Scandalous Libels with the New York Packet?

J: Gr: I received one, Sir.

Pros: Pray Sir, did you receive any others besides that one?

J: Gr: Yes Sir, I received one, via Virginia, which came without a Cover.

Pros: Do you know the prisoners hand writing?

J: Gr: I think I do Sir.

Pros: Was the Superscription of that which you received under Cover, in the prisoners hand writing or not?

J: Gr: I believe it was not.

Pros: In whose hand writing was it?

J: Gr: I protest I cannot tell Sir.

Quir: Com: Remember Sir you are upon your oath, being Solemnly sworn on the Club book.

J: Gr: I know the Importance and Solemnity of that book oath Sir.

Pros: Did the prisoner deliver you any of these papers?

J: Gr: No Sir.

Pr: Who delivered them?

J: Gr: My own Servant Sir.

Pr: And who delivered them to him—pray Consider, Sir before you answer.

J: Gr: I cannot be positive Sir, but I believe the Post boy delivered them.

Pros: What postboy Sir?

[78] J: Gr: The northeren post Sir.

Pros: What did he deliver Sir?

Jon: Gr: The New York paquet Sir.

Qu: Com: Have a Care Sir, this you say on the oath you have taken.

Jon: Gr: I do Sir.

Pros: Did the prisoner deliver you any of these papers Sir?

Jon: Gr: No, Sir.

Pros: Had you any Conversation with the prisoner Concerning them?

J: Gr: I think I had Sir.

Front: Have a care what you say Sir.

Pros: Pray be quiet Mr Frontinbrass, dont Interrupt the Evidence, It will be time for you to speak by and bye Sir.

Front: Sir, I acquiesce, but I desire no unfair Questions may be asked the evidence, he is a plain undesigning man Sir, and may be Caught in a trap to my prejudice.

Pr: Sir, I hope we shall do you Justice. Pray Mr Grog, what was the Conversation you had with the prisoner?

Front: I bar that Question Sir, it is not a fair Question.

Pros: Sir, I submit it to his honor and the Club, please your honor, and Gentlemen, do you admit this Question?

Pres: & memb: Ay, ay.

Pros: What was the Conversation you had with the prisoner Concerning this here affair Sir?

Front: Beware how you answer that Question.

Pro: Please your honor to silence this Culprit, he browbeats the evidence.

Pres: Mr Frontinbrass you must keep to order.

Jon: Gr: Sir I cannot well remember the Conversation that then passd.

Pros: Did he say any thing concerning the publication || of this Libel, [79] and by whom it was done?

Jon: Gr: Not much, but I think he said, it was published by the order of Sir Hugh Maccarty Esqr.

Chanc: By whom Sir, pray—I am thick of hearing.

Jon: Gr: By Sir Hugh Maccarty Esqr Sir.

Chanc: By what party Sir—

Jon: Grog: By Sir Hugh Maccarty Esqr, I say Sir.

Chanc: Hoh-ho hoh! by Sir Hugh Maccarty Esqr—well—

Pros: By whom was that paper delivered which you had without Cover?

Jon: Gr: I cannot now Remember Sir,—upon my word Sir—I am but a very Indifferent evidence, and can say very little upon this here affair.

Pros: 'Tis well Sir, Mr Frontinbrass, have you any Questions to ask this Evidence?

Front: No Sir.

Then the Prosecutor Called upon the Secretary to deliver to his honor and the Club what he knew of this matter.

The Secretary declared to his honor and the Club, that he firmly believed, when that Scandalous paragraph appeared first in the New York paper, that the prisoner at the bar was the author of it, but, by some conversation that he had since with the Prisoner, he had reason to believe that this libel was published, at the Instigation, and by the order of Sir Hugh Maccarty Esqr President of the monday Club at New York, which Sir Hugh Maccarty only assumed that name in his Club, and that Maccarty was his Clubical name, not that which he went by in the private negotiations of life, and, that not only he, but all the members of his Club, assumed to themselves particular Clubical names, as would soon be seen by a paper, which he had, to produce to his honor & this here Club, drawn up by the Secretary of that club.

[80]   Then the Prosecutor asked the prisoner, if he had any evidences to examine.

Front: Yes Sir; May it please your Lordship—your honor I mean Sir, since that is now your title, there are two Gentlemen, evidences for me in this Important cause, and I desire they may be sent for.

A Messenger was accordingly dispatched for them, and, upon their comeing, Mr Boniface[2] was first examined, with relation to his knowledge of Sir Hugh Maccarty Esqr, whether any such Identical person was, or if so, whether he was president of a monday Club at New York, to which Questions he answered in the affirmative, and his evidence Mr Lisper, the other Gentleman Confirmed, both declaring that they had often seen him, often heard of his club, but that the name Maccarty was his Clubical name, not that which he Commonly went by in the ordinary affairs of life.

Then the Chancellor, as having been acquainted at New York, was Interrogated for the prisoner, and he Confirmed the evidence of the aforementioned Gentlemen, Messieurs Boniface and Lisper, in so far as to declare absolutely that he knew Coll: Rormis, who went by that Clubical, or rather fantastical name of Sir Hugh Maccarty Esqr, at New York, but he apprehended that it was before the Institution of his monday Club, that he enjoyed that facetious Gentlemans acquaintans, and that he had been in his Company at sundry other Clubs.

Then the Prisoner produced a Copy of his trial before the said Sir Hugh Maccarty Esqr, with the said Maccartys great Seal affixed, which appeared to be a rough Impression, the Letters Irregular and unequal, on

---

2. Aside from its obvious connotations, the name Boniface is doubly ironic in this context, since it was the name of Saint Boniface (680–755), the German apostle, as well as of the landlord in George Farquhar's *The Beaux' Stratagem* (1707) and consequently the generic proper name of all honest innkeepers.

one Side a large Cap, with CAP OF STATE Impressed, on the other was S:S:D: Maccarty, this trial was read over in Club, by the Secretary as follows.

At an extraordinary meeting of the truely ancient and Right honorable Monday Club of New York, upon Monday the 18th of May 1752, were present³

The Right Honble: and Serene Lord
Sir Hugh Maccarty Esqr, Lord President

Antoninus pius, Chanc: pro tempore
Plutarch, Herald K: at arms
Hortensius attorn: Gen:
Democritus Serj: at arms
Herodotus Mr of Ceremon:
Titus Livius Secretry
Sophisticus, (al: Con: P: Frontinbrass the Gr: Quondam Chancellor)
Tertullus Orator

Orpheus musician
Hesiod Poet Laureat
Thuscidides Historiographer
Plato
Aristotle
Epicurus Clerk of the kitchen
Lucian
Cato

Priscus
Juba
Ælian
Priscian
Lucius Probus

} Supra ordinary members

[81]

---

3. Antoninus Pius (86–161) was a Roman emperor whose administration was marked by his beneficence and mild progressiveness. Quintus Hortensius (114–50 B.C.) was a Roman orator and lawyer who joined Cicero in many political cases. Democritus (born ca. 460–457 B.C.) was known as the "laughing philosopher" for his ethical ideal of "cheerfulness." Herodotus (ca. 480–ca. 425 B.C.) was the famous Greek historian known as the "Father of History." Titus Livius is Livy (59 B.C.–A.D. 17), the great Roman historian. Tertullian (ca. 160–ca. 240) was a Latin churchman who wrote the *Apologeticus,* which defended Christianity against charges of atheism and black magic. Priscus is possibly the Greek Neoplatonist (d. ca. A.D. 398) who influenced Emperor Julian and was known for his integrity, but more likely Priscus of Thrace (fl. 5th century A.D.), the Greek Sophist and historian of Byzantine. Juba is probably Juba II (early 1st century B.C.–ca. A.D. 23), a learned Roman who sought to introduce Greek and Roman culture into his kingdom of Mauretania. Claudius Aelianus (ca. 170–235) was a Roman rhetorician and writer. Priscian (fl. early 6th century A.D.) was a Latin grammarian who taught at Constantinople and whose *Institutiones grammaticae* is the most voluminous work extant of any Latin grammarian. Thucydides (fl. 5th century B.C.) was an Athenian historian famous mainly for his *History of the War between Athens and Sparta* (431–404 B.C.) and for its moving accounts of tragic events. Lucian (ca. 120–ca. 200) was a Greek satirist whose many works include *Dialogues of the Gods* and *Dialogues of the Dead.*

His Lordship having in great State, ascended the Chair of State in a Stately manner, ornamented with the Cap of State, Robes, mallet, and other ensigns of authority and State, as Significant as these of the Lord High Steward of England, and, the Serjeant at arms proclaiming Silence, with a Sonorous and open mouth'd **O Yes,** his Lordship Informed the Club, that he had called them together, upon a most pressing urgent, and extraordinary occasion, Into which, by his allowance and gracious permission, they were to Enquire and examine, the Case, being a case of high Treason, against Sophisticus, his late Chancellor, on which he ordered Titus Livius the Secretary to read the Impeachment, in the hearing of the Club, and he || standing up, Antoninus Pius, being put into the Judicial Chair, at his Lordships Right hand, as Chancellor pro Tempore, the Impeachment was read as follows; Sophisticus being set to the bar.

Tit: Liv: Articles exhibited, by the right honorable Lord, Sir Hugh Maccarty Esqr, the most Serene Lord president of the Truely ancient and Right honorable monday Club of New York, and his obedient members, against Sophisticus, the late Honorable Chancellor of the said Club.

Whereas the office of Chancellor, of this truely ancient & right honorable monday Club of New York, is an office of the most exalted honor and trust, upon the upright and Careful execution of which, the dignity and honor of his Lordships Chair, and the prosperity of the said Club depends, and, whereas Sophisticus, by the Sole appointment, of his most Serene mightiness, the Lord president of the said Club, and, by his Special grace and favour, was, upon the 17th of November, 1746, Constituted and appointed Chancellor, and keeper of the great Seal to his most Serene Lordship, and his truely ancient and right honorable Club, being advanced thereby, to the next place in dignity, to his Serene Lordship, having promised well and truely to serve, Implicitly to obey, and submit to his said Serene Lordship, and the said Chancellor, having held the said honorable office, till sometime in December, 1750, puffed up with ambition and vain glory and a violent furious, rebellious, and unruly desire of agrandizing himself, not having before his eyes any fear or respect for his most noble Lordship the president, or regard for this truely ancient and honorable Club, nor regarding the great trust and Confidence reposed in him, but harbouring mis- ‖ chievous, traiterous, villanous and undutiful Schemes purposes and projects, to gain to himself overgrown power, authority and Influence, and assault and attack the prerogative & dignity, authority and power, of his most Lawful & Serene Lord Sir Hugh Maccarty Esqr, did damnably, wickedly, flagitiously and devilishly, contrive, machinate perpetrate and execute, the following treasons, high Crimes, misdemeanors & trespasses, vizt: [83]

I That the said Sophisticus, at or about the month of December, anno 1750, being actually in the high office of Chancellor, of this truely ancient and honorable Club, did of purpose, and with a treasonable design, take a Journey to Annapolis in Maryland, with wicked and perverse views, to hold Conversation, and Communication, with a Certain pretended upstart President and Club there, which Club, is commonly called, the ancient and honorable **Tuesday Club,** and which president is Commonly stiled, the honorable **Carlo Nasifer Jole,** Lord president of the said Club, into which upstart Club, he the said Sophisticus, officiously thrust himself, and appeared before the said Pretended president, and, with a traiterous, mischievous and wicked purpose communicated to the said Jole and his paltry Club, several Important and Grand Secrets, relative to his true and rightful Lord, Sir Hugh Maccarty Esqr, and his truely ancient & right honorable Monday Club of New York.

II That the said Sophisticus, did sometime in the month of January, 1750 attend a meeting of the said Tuesday Club, or a Sederunt, as they foolishly term it, where he traiterously and wickedly, devised, meditated, Contrived, and drew ‖ up certain articles, called the Frontinbrassian articles, in which, he has bestowed the Eminent title of Lord on the said Jole, which Title was due only to his right Lawful and Sole Lord Maccarty, and, by several bombast and traiterous Speeches, puffed up the Pride and vanity of the said Jole and persuaded the said Club to bestow several valuable privileges on him and raise him to a dignity far above his deserts, putting the said Jole, and his paltry Club, in a manner, upon an equality, with the Right honorable Lord Maccarty, and has flattered the said Jole and his paltry Club in such a manner, as to put them quite beside themselves, and excite [84] a hubbub and disturbance and thereby endanger the peace and tranquillity of his only Lawful Lord Maccarty, to the great dammage and risque of his Cap, Chair and dignity.

III That the said Traitor Sophisticus, did traiterously, falsely, and Seditiously accept from the hands of the said Jole, a paultry club medal, a badge of the said ancient & honorable Tuesday Club, and showed it up and down, here and there and every where, in great Contempt, of his only lawful lord Maccarty, and also, accepted of a Shim Sham fiddle faddle, Silly Quinotian Commission, from the said Jole, and his paltry Club, appointing him agent & plenipo, for the said Jole & his paltry Club, in America, and the Islands thereunto belonging.

IV That the said Sophisticus, by virtue of the aforesaid Shim Sham &ct: Commission, sometime In January 1750 ‖ maliciously and traiterously, took a Journey to the province of Virginia, and there did traiterously, establish, settle, erect and Constitute several Sham Clubs, particularly, one Called The thursday Club of Hiccory hill, under the dominion, Subjection and power of the said Jole, and his paltry Club, contrary to the natural duty and allegiance he owes to his said Lawful lord Maccarty, his Chair, Cap and Government.

V That the said traitor Sophisticus, Instigated, prompted and Incited a Certain pitiful Society, who stile themselves the Eastren Shore Triumvirate,[4] owning the authority of the said Jole and his paltry Club, to write and publish, certain paltry and Scandalous papers, called manifestos, declarations and proclamations of war, and Rebellion, against their true and Lawful Lord Maccarty, lord paramount and Commander, of all and all manner of Clubs whatsoever, and Caused the tumultuous firing of Ship Guns, and the drinking of the health of the said Jole, in contempt of his said lawful Lord Maccarty, his chair Cap & dignity.

VI That the said Traitor Sophisticus, did, by his devlish Instigations and promptings, provoke and stimulate several Poetasters, who call themselves Laureats, to write and Indite, certain Senseless Songs, verses, epigrams, accrostics and anniversary odes, In which, his only Lawful Lord Maccarty was mentioned,

---

4. A Tuesday Club splinter group, founded by the Reverend John Gordon, the Reverend Thomas Bacon, and Robert Morris (see biographical sketches). Hamilton provides an account of its foundation in vol. I, bk. 5, chap. 11.

with great Contempt and Scorn, in defiance of his said lord Maccartys authority, Chair, Cap and Government.

VII   That the said Sophisticus, did, sometime in the month of february, 1750, meet the said Jole, and his paltry Club, in the City of Annapolis in Maryland, and there, with a pompous, farcical, Sarcastical, and mock Ceremony perform ‖ the honorable Capation, after the manner of the New-York Capation, upon the Lousy pericranium of the said Jole, in the Sight and hearing, of the Longstanding members, as they are ridiculously called, of the said paltry Tuesday Club, and many others besides, thereby traiterously raising the said Jole, to some degree of equality with his only true and Lawful lord Maccarty. [86]

VIII   That the said Sophisticus, on the first of april, 1751, commonly called fools day, went on a foolish, as well as traiterous Errand, vizt: took a voyage to London, under pretence of trading with tobacco, where, being arived, he there held several traiterous, foolish and farcical conferences, with a Certain Capt: Comely Coppernose, the pretended agent and plenipo of the said Lord Jole, for England, Scotland, France, Ireland, the mountains of Wales, and the town of Berwick upon Tweed, and discovered several Important Clubical Secrets to the said Plenipo, to the prejudice of his only true and lawful lord Maccarty, and in Contempt of his authority, dignity, Cap, Chair and Government.

IX   Lastly the said Traitor Sophisticus, perversely and Traiterously, did, at sundry times write several traiterous rebellious, Scandalous and Submissive letters, to the said Lord Jole, which letters were recorded in the paltry book of Records of the said paltry Tuesday club, wherein he avowedly disowns the authority of his said only true and lawful Lord Maccarty, and submitts himself to the authority of the said Lord Jole, and his paltry Club, in utter contempt of the honor, authority, Chair, cap and dignity of his only true and Lawful Lord Maccarty.

And The said most magnificent and honorable Lord Maccarty, (by protestation, saving to himself, the privilege of Exhibiting, at any time **hereafter,** or **thereafter,** any further articles or particles, or other, or whatever, points articulatim et particulatim of accusation, recusation or Impeachment, against the said traitor Sophisticus, as also of replying, duplying, Reduplying & dureduplying and also Redureduplying, to all or any or many of his answers, which he shall make or unmake or not make, to the said [87] articles or particles, articulatim & particulatim as aforesaid, or any, or all, or one, or none or more of them, or every other articles of Impeachment or accusation or recusation, which shall be exhibited, or not exhibited, by the said most honorable Lord Maccarty as the Case shall require) does command that the said Traitor Sophisticus, may be put and Compelled to answer, The said Crimes, treasons and Rebellious practices, and, that such proceedings, examinations, trials and Judgements, shall be thereupon given and Executed, as is agreeable to the authority, power and dignity of the said magnificent and absolute Lord Maccarty.

Sophisticus having pleaded not Guilty to this Impeachment, articulatim et particulatim, as therein specified & set forth, Hortensius the Attorney General opened the Charge.

Hortens: My Lord, This unhappy delinquent now at your Lordships bar, stands accused of high Crimes and misdemeanors, and traiterous practices, as your Lordship may see, by the tenor of the Impeachment. I shall || not tire your Lordship according to the common Custom of my bretheren of the profession, with long, dull, foolish pragmatical Speeches concerning traitors and treason loaded with trite quotations and Silly authorities little to the purpose, your Lordship has undoubtedly more cognisance of these matters than I, but, that this unhappy Gentleman is Guilty of these crimes laid to his charge articulatim and particulatim, I think appears as plain as the nose on your Lordships face, as a pick Staff, as day light, or as that two & two make four, or any thing else alike evident, and that from the very nature of the thing, and I hope, my Lord, I shall make it as plain as pease porridge or dough dumplings, to your Lordship and the members of this honorable Club before I have done (here the attorney coughed and hawked much, being under a very great tremor and palpitation, by reason of a tremendous frown, which Sir Hugh Emitted from the chair)—my Lord—hoh—to proceed from where I left off,—huh—I hope no offence my lord—That this unhappy Gentleman, I say, now at your Lordship's bar, has been actually guilty of the aforesd: devlish, traiterous and wicked practises, in conversing, Communing, Cohabiting, associating, Clubbing and Conclubbing, with a Certain Jole, commonly called Lord Jole, seems to every man of common Sense to be Self evident, without farther Evidence, demonstration, Commonstration, or viva voce testimony, in fine, my Lord, he is Ipso facto guilty, and it shall stand pro Confesso, for says Justinian, de locis obscuris, Sect: 4to lib: 2di, Si non apparet rationaliter, proportionaliter tamen Luculentius extat, &ct: and says somebody else (I forget who) de non apparentibus & non Existentibus eadem est ratio, and Plowden, de Communibus bonis, has ‖ mihi et non mihi, et tibi et non tibi, sit satis perfectum, oh—ho!—quolibet, quisque &ct: &ct: &ct: and so forth, which may be seen in fol: 3333, oldest Edition of the pandectas, and more concerning the same in Grotius, Sectione Quarta paragraph: undecimo,[5] but, as to the atrociousness of the Crime of treason, which this unhappy Gentleman stands accused of, I need not trowble your Lordship with moderen Quotations. The Testimony of the ancient fathers of the Law is abundantly Sufficient, Sure I am, it has been so said in divinity, and if in divinity why not in Law Q:E:D:—atchi-tchah—tchi!—(here the attorney was taken with a violent fit of Sneezing, from some of the Scatterings of Tertullian's Snuff, who then took a pinch out of his box—) Tully, in his Tusculan Questions speaks abundantly on the matter, and to very good purpose, Præmeditatione facilem reddere, Quemque Casum, Libro Tertio, Capite—nescio quo— and again Isocrates, περι ὑστερον προτερον; γεοργου παις, οπτα κοχλεαις, ακουςας δε αυτων τρυζοντων ειπε, ω κακιστα ζωα, των οικων ὑμων επιπραμενων αυτοι αειδετε, and again, Epictetus, Translated by Joannes Banisterius, Si ollam diligas, memento, te ollam diligere, non perturbaberis ea Confracta,[6] but, to

[89]

---

5. The emperor Justinian (482–565) sought to restore the greatness of the Roman Empire, in part by reforming administrative abuses and codifying its legal system. Edmund Plowden (1518–1585) was the great English lawyer who sat in Parliament during the reign of Mary I. Grotius is noted on p. 49n, above. The people are real, but the citations are all those of the learned attorney general. Hamilton tips us off by referring first to a nonexistent work, Justinian's *On Obscure References*. The passages read: "If it is not rationally apparent, still it stands out more brightly in proportion"; "The same reason applies to the nonexistent and the nonapparent"; "Mine and not mine, yours and not yours, be perfect enough, oh—ho!— wherever, whoever, etc." Here and throughout his harangue, the attorney general simply pulls names out of the air and attributes gibberish to them.

6. These pseudo-citations have nothing to do with treason. The first means "Make easy by premeditation" (roughly paraphrases Cicero, *Tusculan Disputations* 3.29); the second, supposedly from Isocrates but actually from Aesop's fable of the singing snails, means "A farmer's son was broiling snails, and hearing them crackle, said, 'Wretched creatures, your houses are burning and you sing'"; the third, supposedly translated from Epictetus by John Banister (1540–1610), an English surgeon who wrote *The History of Man, Sucked from the Sap of the Most*

Lay aside these Instances, some few from the Common forms and manners of proceeding (not from Clubs I say, for no Club can be a pattern for your Lordship) for, your Lordship very well knows, that we the Learned Gentlemen of the Law, are Guided Intirely by forms, both in our pleadings, and order of sitting at the bar ‖ (I Intend not to pun my lord) however discrepant at times from common Sense and mathematical principles, and good reason why, my lord, for Lex est ultima ratio,[7]—hoh—as for the Civil law, you will see it, act: Gloss: 6 Quest I.C.S. quis Ci, de cons: dict L.V.C. 2do fin. et est not: per doct: Cod: de Impub: et aliis substit: Luces Cunt, lib: ult & L: legitamæ fi de Stat: hom L: Quod si nollit, and again Instructor Clericalis (here it is in my pocket my lord) says pagina 275, et sustinuerunt Imprisonamentum ejus vel eorum Corporis, sive corporum, per Spacium Quodvis sine Baillio—vel occasione alicujus aresti et Invenissent Sufficientem Securitatem, vel Bailium, ad Respondendum de placito prædicto, contra forman Statuti, et de Croftas, Loftas, toftas, tenementi[9] et copyholdis prædictas pretextu[9]—Quorum Quidem arrestation[9] Imprisonamenti &ct: &ct: &ct:[8]—Pough! there is no end to it in this world, and to conclude my Lord, I hope your Lordship will find him guilty, and suit the punishment to his Crime, which is so atrocious, that tongue cannot express, nor pen write,—and therefore 'tis submitted to your Lordship.

The attorney General having thus spoke very warmly so as to have overheated himself, wiped his face, puffed his cheeks, pushd back his wig, shook his ears, and sat down, and Tertullian Council for the culprit, stood up, and spoke as follows, having first Cramm'd his nose with Snuff, Cleard his pipes, & put his body in a Graceful attitude.

Tertull: My Lord, If I may presume to speak before your

Approved Anatomists (1578), means "If you love the pot, remember that you love the pot; you will not be disturbed if it is broken." I have not found such a passage in *The History of Man* or in any of Banister's other works.

7. "Law is the final reason" (followed by a bawdy pseudo-citation to common law).

8. The fake legalese attributed to Clericalus (perhaps Jean Le Clerc [Johannes Clericus], 1657–1736, Swiss scholar and author of numerous religious and historical works) reads: "They sustained his imprisonment, or that of his body or their bodies, for whatever period, without bail, or on the occasion of anyone's arrest, if they found sufficient surety or bail, to answer the aforesaid complaint, against the form of the statute, and on pretext of crofts, tofts, tenements and copyholds; of which arrest, imprisonment, etc."

Lordship, in this Important matter, I would be bold to say by your Lordship's permission, that the unhappy Gentleman, now at your Lordship's bar, may not be altogether so Culpable, as the Learned Gentleman, who spoke before me has represented; True it is some evidence has been given before your Lordship by these worthy gentlemen, Democritus Serjeant at arms, Epicurus and Lucian, that certain papers were found in the pockets of the delinquent, when they apprehended him, being letters directed to a certain honorable Carlo Nasifer Jole, Lord president, of a certain ancient and honorable Tuesday Club at Annapolis, where, it is said he has extolled the said Jole, in a most bumbast and extravagant manner, as also, a Certain Commission for an agency for himself, with a Certain Impression of Seals, medals, and other trumpery of little Significancy, the medals, having Carolus Cole armiger Præses inscribed on one Side, on the Reverse, Concordia res parvæ Crescunt,⁹ with hands Joined, hearts upon altars, Cups upon poles, and, I know not what other, Ill contrived Conceits, vide, Maryland Gazette No   where a pompous advertisement of one of these medals lost, is published, with a great reward offered to the finder,¹⁰ Tho, I say, my Lord, these were found upon him, with Certain pitiful poems Entituled Anniversary odes &ct: and an account of a Capation, performed by him upon the head of the said Lord Jole, in the City of Annapolis, and many other apparently treasonable papers, yet my || Lord consider, I [92] would have your Lordship to Consider that there may possibly be more of rashness and Inconsideracy in these Circumstances, than any thing of malice and design, against your Lordship and your authority, this gentleman, my Lord, has had the honor to be of this Club, and under your Lordships Jurisdiction, has professed himself, (and I really believe he is) a curious antiquarian, and a Collector of Curiosities and Jimcracks, in all corners of the world, being, as every body knows, a great traveller, and perhaps, among other things of this nature, he has picked up these trifling Curiosities, Jimcracks and anecdotes, concerning this Lord Jole, and his pitiful Club, (pitiful I say, in respect of your Lordship's

---

9. "Small endeavors flourish through unity" (Sallust, *Jurguitha* 10.6).

10. Sometime after the medals arrived, one club member apparently had the misfortune of losing his, and the advertisement to which Hamilton refers ran for several weeks in the *Maryland Gazette* (see, e.g., Jan. 9, 1752).

Club)—pray my Lord, do not frown,—I hope, I shall be allowed the liberty to speak my mind for my Client, especially, as I am upon the merciful Side of the Question,—nay! my Lord! another such frown, and I have done.—My Lord, I do not desire to protect or screen the Guilty, but, at the same time your Lordship must be Sensible, that it is better 100 Guilty persons should escape, than one Innocent person suffer, my Lord, at the same time, when your Lordship thinks of being rigorous in Justice, be pleased to Consider the Character of this Club, how much better would it be, if we were reputed mild and merciful, than Cruel and Severe, my lord, in your Sacred breast, lies the power of punishing, and the power of pardoning, pity || then O pity, the deplorable condition of this unhappy delinquent at your Lordships bar, who, I confess, has too many presumptions against him of his guilt, but my Lord, pardon me, if I say, there is not one direct proof, so as to make it palpably clear, and Incontestable, that he has been guilty of high treason or misprision of treason against your Lordship, the most that can be made of it, is, that it is a trespass **upon the Case,** or a misdemeanor, and, I think, (with all Submission be it spoken) that it would be showing too much countenance to the aforesaid Lord Jole, and his Insignificant Tuesday Club, to make too great a bustle and pother about this affair, and to punish too Severely, even the most Inconsiderable member of your Lordship's Club, for being concerned in such a paltry business; It would seem, my Lord, as if your Lordship, and this Truely ancient and honorable Club, were afraid of this Lord Jole, and Jealous of any little Scantling of power or Influence he might have over Clubs in other parts, but alas, your Lordship need not fear that, for, had it not been, for this unhappy affair, I believe, Lord Jole and his Club, would still have remained, in their original obscurity, and would never have been heard of, but, all their fame has arisen only, from your Lordship's bestirring yourself so much in this Lousy affair, which I think were much better droped, and, as for Precedents of the like proceeding, I could quote many Instances, for Pindar says, Silete homines, non enim miser est, and again Seneca, Stultum est timere quod vitari non potest, and Ovid

Magna petis Phæton, et quæ non viribus istis &ct:

and a great greek poet, tho no Lawyer, tells us somewhere

Ἥρη, πρεςβα θεα, θυγατερ μεγαλοιο κρονοιο
Αυδα ὅ τι φρονεεις, τελεσαι δε με θυμος ανογεν,
Ει δυναμαι τελεςαι γε, και ει τετελεςμενον εστι,[11]

and to conclude with a case of a parallel nature from the famous Plouden; "A:B: Nuper de &ct: Tonsor attachatus fuit, ad respondendum C:D: de placito, quod, cum Idem A: ad barbam Ipsius C. Bene, et artificialiter cum Novacula munda et salubri, rodere apud N, assumpsisset, prædict⁹ A, Barbam ipsius C, cum quadam novacula Immunda et Insalubri, tam negligenter, et inartificialiter rasit, quod facies Ipsius C, morbosa et Scabiosa devenit, ad dampnum ipsius C: Centum Solidorum &ct:"[12] and so my Lord, I submit it to your mercy and Clemency.

Tertullus having finished his oration for the Culprit, he sat him down Gravely, looked about him, and taking out his box, sucked up a prodigious quantity of Snuff, and then, brushing the Stimulating dust, from the breast of his Coat, he set those that were about him a Sneezing.

Then Titus Livius the Secretary, (the Serjeant at arms having first made proclamation for Silence,) stood up & said

Tit: Liv: Cato, is Sophisticus Guilty of the matters brought against him or not guilty?

Cato, standing up and Laying his right hand upon his left breast, said Guilty upon mine honor.

Tit: Liv: Lucian, is Sophisticus Guilty &ct:

Luc: Guilty upon mine honor.

Epicur: Not guilty upon mine honor.

Aristot: Not guilty upon mine honor.

Plato: Guilty upon mine honor.

Thuscidid: Not Guilty upon mine honor.

---

11. "Be silent, oh men, for he is not miserable"; "It is stupid to fear what cannot be avoided" (attributed to Publilius Syrus, *Sententiae*, although similar to Seneca, *Quaestiones naturales* 6, "sine remedio timor stultis est"); "You seek great things, Phaeton, things for which you are not suited" (Ovid, *Metamorphoses* 2.54); "Hera, thou honored goddess, thou daughter of Cronus the mighty, / Tell me what is thy thought: my heart now bids me fulfill it, / If fulfill it I can, and the thing is ordained for fulfillment" (Homer, *Iliad* 14.194–196).

12. The pseudo-citation to Plowden reads: "A:B: Recently regarding etc. A barber was attached to respond to C.D. on the plea that the same A. undertook to shave the beard of the same C. well and artfully with a clean razor in the town of N., the aforesaid A. shaved the beard of the same C. with a certain dirty and unhealthy razor, so negligently and artlessly that the face of the same C. became diseased and scabby, to the loss of the same C. 100 shillings, etc."

Hesiod: Not guilty upon mine honor.
Orph: Guilty upon mine honor.
Tertull: Not Guilty upon mine honor.
Herodot: Guilty upon mine honor.
Democrit: Guilty upon mine honor.
Hortens: Guilty upon mine honor.
Plut: Guilty upon mine honor.
Ant: Pius: Guilty upon mine honor.
Tit: Liv: Guilty upon mine honor.

Sophisticus being thus found guilty by a great majority, was committed into the Custody of the Serjeant at arms, his Lordship having given the Signal, by knocking with the mallet upon the table.

Then, Antoninus Pius, the Chancellor Informed him, That he was found Guilty of the Crimes laid to his Charge, and asked him, what he had to say for himself, that Sentence should not pass against him.

Soph: My Lord, tho' the facts which have been produced and proved against me, be of such a nature || That I cannot, (without a greater Stock of Impudence, than that wherewith nature has endued me) absolutely and point blank deny them, yet I hope, I may with confidence, and a good face, dispute the ill natured Constructions, that have been put upon my Late behaviour, in Concluding it to be treason, and treasonable practises, I own freely, My Lord, that I have had a Correspondence by letters and Conversation, face to face, with the right honorable Lord Jole, President of the ancient and honorable Tuesday Club of Annapolis, and, with all and every of the Longstanding members, of his Lordships said Club, and with several of the honorary members, particularly, his Lordships agent at London, (—you may frown my Lord, these horrible frowns dont Intimidate me, I have learned my Lord to dispise danger and bear Calamity. Justum et Tenacem propositi vivum, (My lord,)

> non vultus Instantis Tyranni,
> mente quatit solida.)[13]

and I must Surely do them the Justice, my Lord, to say before your lordship's face—again my lord—nay frown on

---

13. "A just man and one who keeps to his purpose" (Horace, *Carmina* 3.3.1); "He is not shaken in mind by the face of the threatening tyrant" (*ibid.*, 3.3.3–4).

Si fractus Illabatur orbis
Impavidum ferient ruinæ.¹⁴

My lord all this is but fiddle faddle to me,—and therefore I say again,—before your Lordships face my Lord, and these members, that the honorable Lord Jole, is a president of great Clemency, Justice, wisdom, Sagacity, foresight and prudence, a Lord President, most exactly fitted, both by nature and art, to rule and Govern any Club, but alas, my Lord, the members of that ancient and honorable Club dont ‖ seem to be so Submissive and tractable as those of this Club are to your Lordship, and therefore, I thought it great pity, that such an honorable Gentleman as Lord Jole, should be abridged and confined in that Just power, which his Longstanding members had Intrusted him with, and used all my endeavors, by persuasion and Intreaty, to bring them to some reasonable terms of Subjection Submission & obedience to their worthy and honorable Lord President Jole, For which purpose, I framed those Articles, Commonly Called the frontinbrassian Articles, having no thought at all of derogating from your Lordships power and authority, or acting of any Treason against you, or exciting any hubbub in this honorable Club, or any other Club, but only designing to establish, and fix the authority of that Honorable Lord Jole, that worthy, that deserving president, and being an Intire lover of Clubific felicity, to stabilitate and make firm the felicity of that ancient and honorable Club, by persuading, Intreating, nay Enforcing them, if possible, to submit to his mild, his Gentle, his beatific Sway; but alas, as I am Informed, my pains have been Thrown away, my Labor lost, opus et oleum perdidi,¹⁵ They continue in the same refractory disobedience, and, so long as they do so, your Lordship, need never be afraid of any rival in power, in the honorable Lord Jole, for till that club comes to better rules and order, and a more Complacent Submission to his Lordship, it will be Impossible for Lord Jole, to gain any Influence or Supremacy ‖ over any other Club or Clubs, that are more Harmonious among themselves, than this unhappy refractory Club is. My Lord, I am fully persuaded, that if your Lordship was to see the honorable Lord Jole, and Converse with him face to face, you would be so charmed, so delighted with his wisdom,

[97]

[98]

---

14. "If the broken sky fell, the ruins would strike him undismayed" (*ibid.*, 3.3.7–8).
15. "I have wasted work and oil."

good Sense, Sweet carriage, and Comely Smiling Countenance, that you would Immediatly think me excuseable for all I have done, for, who, my lord can stand out against the charms of good nature and humanity, the Endearments of a Sweet Conversation, and a thousand other engageing qualities, which, it might sooner tire your lordship to hear, than me to repeat.

In fine, my Lord, as I know your Lordship is a president of a rigid disposition, and extremely Jealous of your power and authority, I can easily forsee my fate in this affair, That is, I must undergoe a very Severe Sentence from your Lordship, but my Lord, I am thankful, that I know, under whose wings to fly and take refuge, the honorable Lord Jole is my dernier Resort, on him I depend, he is my prop and Stay, and therefore, I here expect your Lordships Sentence with Great humility and Submission, but permit me to make one request, that I be favored with a true Copy of this my tryal by your Lordships Secretary, that, if any thing be in it for my vindication, I may not be deprived of that advantage.

[99] Ant: Pi: I am empowerd in his Lordship's name to acquaint you Sir, that you may have a copy of your tryal, and I here order Titus Livius the Secretary to furnish you with a true extract of it, from our Records, and to sign it, and I shall affix for further testimony, his Lordships great Seal, that all presidents and Clubs whatsoever, may see with what Justice and equity his Lordship has directed the whole proceeding against you, but, I am also Empowered, to tell you, from his Ldshp, that, if you will render up your agents commission for that paltry Club, Letters, papers &ct: to be burnt in this Club, as also, the medal to be destroyed, and renounce for the future all dependance on and Conversation with Lord Jole, and his paltry Tuesday Club, your true lord Maccarty, will take you again into his favor, pardon all past offences, and reinstate you, in your former honors.

Soph: Sir, I must let his Lordship know, that I would rather die, than consent to these propositions, so I expect my Sentence —[Here the Chancellor pronounced Sentence on Sophisticus in the following manner.]

Ant: Pi: Sophisticus, you have been Impeached of sundry treasons and Crimes, Committed by you against your only true and Lawful Clubical Lord Maccarty, to which you have pleaded not Guilty, and are now found Guilty on a fair trial by your peers, and therefor I pronounce Sentence against you, according to his Ldshps Command. ‖ You Sophisticus, as a vile traitor, to your Right honorable Lord Maccarty, Lord president of the truely ancient and honorable monday Club of New York, shall be carried from this place, where you are now, under durance and Custody of his Lordships Serjeant at arms, and hurled headlong, by his said Lordship's Serjeant at arms, down Stairs from the Club Room, and be banished, excluded, Expelled, Extruded, expunged, erased and dislocated, from his Lordship's presence and Countenance, for ever, and a day longer; your name to be exterminated and Erased from his Lordships ancient book of Records, all your titles of honor to be annulled and Extinct, and, you are from henceforth to be esteemed a Squire of Low degree and mean Condition.

After pronouncing of this Sentence, his Ldshp, knocked upon the table with the mallet of State, and it was Immediatly put in execution.

A true Copy from the Club Records,
Teste Titus Livius, Secretary
     Seal   appended

After Mr Secretary Scribble had read this Copy of Frontinbrasses Trial in the Club, Sir John said, it was a bundle of damnd nonsense, and that they were very Idle who Invented and wrote it.

Then Frontinbrass the Great made his defence as follows.—He endeavored to make it plain, That he had entertained no design or purpose traiterous to his honor the president, or detrimental to the ancient and honorable Tuesday Club of Annapolis, But rather was acting, as much as lay in his power, to promote the honor and Glory of the Lord president of the sd: Club, To establish his Jurisdiction, prerogative and power over all other Clubs, whatsoever In America, where he had the honor to be agent for his Lordship, for which he had his Commission in his pocket, and, that he had not been Guilty of raising any hubbub or hurly burly in this here honorable Club, or any other Club whatsoever, as Sir Hugh's Scandalous Impeachment bore, but, had labored, with all his might to mantain and support, the dignity of my Lord president Jole, and his ancient and honorable Tuesday Club, for which he had been disgracefully expelled by Sir Hugh Maccarty Esqr, and that, unless his Lordship gave him Shelter and protection, he could not with any face, show himself in any Club on this Side the water, for, Sir Hugh's Influence & power was so great (at this Sir John said *Pish!*) that unless the honorable Lord Jole protected him, he should be an outcast from all clubs, and a vagabond upon the face of the || earth, but, that if he had his Lordships protection, he would not value Sir Hugh, or his Club, or any other president or Club whatsoever.

The prisoner's Council, Solo Neverout Esqr, was called upon to deliver what he had to say in the prisoner's defence.

He gave himself no further trowble than to deny point blank every article, Mr Prosecutor Quaint had alledged against him, The prosecutor urged, that this was no defence, but Mr Councellor Neverout, Taking Quirpum Comics notes in his hand, stood up again, and very Solemnly declared, laughing heartily all the time, that his defence was valid and good, and that all that Mr Prosecutor had said and urged against him signified not a farthing, and that the Gentleman was not Guilty, in manner & form as aforesaid, and that the votes might be taken thereupon.

This bold defence of Mr Neverouts, Ingratiated him much with his honor the president, who admired him for his confidence and forwardness, and by this means he made another great Stride towards the honorable office of Attorney General to his honor and the Club.

The prisoner's council sitting down, the Secretary observed as he spoke, that he often looked upon the notes of Quirpum Comic Esqr, and perceiving there was little or nothing in all he said, took the notes out of his hand, and, as soon as he had looked || upon them, he was no more Surprized at the nothingness of his discourse, since his text seemed (to him at least) to be quite unintelligible, being as follows.

Loquacious Scribble M:D:

This Strange Club Hieroglyphic, we for ever dispair of Interpreting, since the author himself would not Explain the meaning of it; unless the Ingenious author, who, In a late magazine explains, the Indian Characters, made by the rippling of the waters on the face of a rock in the great river Messasippi, will favor us with an Interpretation of them, for Sure no Genius but his is Capable of it, it not being probable that this Luxurious and besotted Generation will ever be able to Interpret it.

After all this Learned pleading and altercation, the prisoner was acquitted by a vote of the Club, and coming from the bar, he kissed his honor the president's hand, Saluted the Longstanding members, had his offices and titles in Club restored, and was promised a renewal of his Commission, which was now in a very ragged Condition.

Messieurs Boniface and Lisper, being Entertained as Strangers, at this Sederunt, according to ancient Custom, pray'd his honor the president, to Grant them Commissions, giving them a power to set up Clubs in Virginia, under his honor's authority and Jurisdiction, which, his honor promised, they should sometime or other be Indulged in, which promise however, has never as yet been Complied with.

Solo Neverout Esqr, Towards the Close of this Sederunt fell fast asleep, his pipe (as usual) not being in his mouth. [104]

Chapter VI

Miserable defect in the Records by the absence of the Secretary, diminutive duumvirate Club; Letter in Club latin, Yawning oration, Lamentation on the late Eclipse of the Club, by the poet Laureat.

As much as one Set of Philosophers have puzzled their brains, about Investigating and Tracing of truth, so much have another Sect perplexed themselves in vain efforts and Endeavors to lose her. The latter are of the Sect called Sceptics, among whom, the Rankest I know, is the late Celebrated bishop of Cloyn,[1] notwithstanding his professions to the Contrary, for he has laid down and followed a plan of reasoning, the most productive of Scepticism of any Philosophy I have ever known among the moderens; These Gentlemen have by various arguments and Sly Sophisms endeavored to persuade us that no such thing as Truth ever did, or ever will exist, but that all nature is made up of endless doubting, Incertainty, falshood, error and deceit, and Indeed truth, when Logically sought after, and metaphysically Investigated, may be likened to a prince in a mask, where so many figures are dressed in the same Garb with him That it is a very difficult matter to pitch upon the true person; this is the observation of a very good, and a very Sententious, tho' not a Celebrated author,[2] whom at present, I chuse not to name, lest the delicate Con- || noisseurs, and men of taste in this our polite age, should think him an author of my own Creation, as the [105]

---

1. George Berkeley (1685–1753), the Anglo-Irish philosopher and clergyman, was known for his theory of vision and for his Socratic dialogues, in which he sought to prove the nonexistence of matter except as it is perceived. He became bishop of Cloyne in 1734. His works include the *Essay towards a New Theory of Vision* (1709), and *A Treatise concerning the Principles of Human Knowledge* (1710).

2. Probably Hamilton.

honorable president of the Tuesday Club, Imagined Sir Hugh Maccarty Esqr, to be a piece of mere brainwork, of Coney pimp Frontinbrass Esqr, and Indeed, the history of this Clubical Heroe, would almost Incline one who reads it to turn Sceptic as to that particular matter, & doubt whether such a person ever existed or not, for sometimes we find his Identity asserted with the same assurance & Confidence as is that of Julius Cæsar or Pompey the great, at other times, the Reality of his being is as much doubted as ever was that of Prester John or Tom o' the lin, and often, his being is esteemed as Imaginary & Romantic, as that of Amadis de Gaul,[3] or Don Quixot, we find him first in great Credit and Reputation, in the ancient and honorable Tuesday Club, and no person believed to be more real than he, by the honorable Nasifer Jole Esqr, and many of his Longstanding members, presently, he sinks in their esteem to an Imaginary person, an *Ens rationis,* and mere *Phantasma Umbrahlis,*[4] nor was the lie of Humbug Fibber, of Sufficient force to raise him again upon his legs, even in the Idea of a person dead (pardon the bull,[5] if any in this Expression of raising dead people on their legs) and buried, but behold, Coneïus Pimpeïus Frontinbrass the Great, upon his arival from his Northeren expedition, re-established the lost Credit of that great Clubical Heroe, so far, as not only to restore him ‖ to life and a new being, but, to make the honorable Jole, and his Chancellor, as it were, In spite of their teeth, to believe his Identity, after they had both, in the most Solemn manner, pronounced him merely Chimerical and Phantasmical. We shall now find that Club heroe but very short lived, for bye and bye, he will make his last appearance on the Stage in the likeness of an one Eyed Frenchman, tho' really, a woman in Masquerade, after which last appearance he sinks to nothing in the esteem of every person, and he, together with his Creator Frontinbrass, are never after that mentioned, but in the highest terms of ridicule, and with the greatest contempt.

[106]

At Sederunt 183, being the 7th of July, 1752, the records are very Imperfect, on account of the absence of the Secretary, who had gone over the bay of Chesopeak on a visit and a Sort of Embassy to the Eastren Shore Triumvirate, where, he met with an honorable reception from that Right Worshipful Society, and delivered a Congratulatory oration to them, paying

---

3. Tom o' the lin, or Tom a Lincoln, is the son of King Arthur in Richard Johnson's romance *Tom a Lincoln* (ca. 1597) who becomes a knight of the Round Table and marries Anglitora, daughter of Prester John (see p. 49n, above). Amadis de Gaul is the chivalric hero of *Amadís de Gaula,* a 15th-century Spanish or Portuguese romance.

4. "Shadowy phantasm."

5. A *bull* is a statement of ludicrous inconsistency.

them the Compliments of the Honorable Nasifer Jole Esqr, and those of his Long standing members, to which oration, Smoothum Sly Esqr Orator to the Triumvirate, returned a very pompous and obliging answer, pronouncing a florid Panegyric on the Honorable Nasifer Jole Esqr and his Long-standing members, and, after Supper, the Triumvirs admitted several members into their Society, and the Grand Chorus of the ode 1751, was playd and sung.

At Sederunt 183 however, Quirpum Comic Esqr being H:S: and deputy Secretary, the Record was Intirely neglected, the deputy having too much business on || his hands to mind taking of notes or memorandums, and therefore, the most of the matters transacted at this Sederunt, are Irrecoverably lost, only, thus much we know from persons of undoubted Credit, that his honor the President was remarkably Chearful, which 'tis thought was occasioned by the absence of some Turbulent and refractory members, and that there was a learned Conversation upon several useful and Improving Subjects, particularly concerning the Culture and Improvement of buck wheat.

At Sederunt 184, the Club met, after a Long adjournment, vizt: from the 7th of July to the 18th of august, no less than Six weeks, by means of the usual dilatoriness of Mr Protomusicus Neverout, the next in Course to the Chancellor, who was sick, and yet even then Mr Neverout declined serving, and rolld it over on Sir John, who served the Club as H:S: at that Sederunt, this was a very diminutive club, and went afterwards by the name of the duumvirate Club, there being an Entry found in the book of Records to this purpose.

Present—
Jonathan Grog Esqr, Deput: Elect: M:C:P:L: &ct:
Sir John Knight & H:S: Deput: Secretary.
The whole of the Conversation at this diminutive duumvirate Club, was, here's to you, and here's to you, and put about the bowl, other matters if any, are lost, by the neglect of the deputy Secretary, the Chief Secretary being absent, at this Sederunt also, Laconic Comas Esqr || was entertained as a Stranger this night, pursuant to ancient custom, some think by Invitation, others that he came into the Club by mere Chance.

At Sederunt 185, being the first of September 1752, Solo Neverout Esqr, being H:S: his honor Mr President Jole being Indisposed, the Club, according to Law 43d Sederunt 122, chose the honorable Quirpum Comic Esqr *deputatus electus,* who took his place, not in the Great Chair, for that, as well as his honor the Chief president was absent.

There was produced in Club, a letter from the Secretary to the deputy, which was read, and ordered to be put on Record, being wrote in Clubical latin, vizt:

To Quirpum Comic Esqr,
Honorable Deputy of the Ancient & honorable Tuesd: Club.

Syrupus,
     Esse veri, Super excellent quale Titere, cum en duas deputatus electus, fur θεαν Scient Tu es de Club, Fur Thisbe re Sederunt en Thisbe re nite, En diem Resolvit togi humi vota fora ni ovum Siriam veri tota lien Delta Geta rure masto ob Sequi usto alæ ter niti, en diva ni persona leges I do Inequitabile Ima Se Thuscidides as in cere mula toro fagi nereus cum pani *ov* en da veri Hirti Fel O! en das Iam ob liget β mi Situ assi οντο Do en Dido pro teste Iam redito doso far forani o Thersites τι fiso vel offa Sus e ren || Dido præ Sursum mali Scias Roges as me Questa *ov* mi Sinceri τι *ov* Thisbe Hector gas Edwith αναξ orbe nocti θε Edwitha ponde ras *Club.*

[109]

Tue es de nite	Siriam ures ob Sequi
7r 1st 1752	ους lito alæ ter niti
	Secretarius.[a]

     This Extraordinary Clubical Letter, tho it is not in The Stile and Language, yet it is in the manner of Cicero, for there is Greek mixed with the Clubical latin, and Cicero was wont to Confess, that he loved sometimes to mix Greek with || his latin.[6] The only difference then, between Tully and Mr Secretary Scribble, is in Stile, the Stile of the first being Classical, that of the other, altogether Clubical, neither is this manner of Epistolary writing without precedent, The Celebrated Dean Swift having used it in the Epistolary way, and Even in the Dialogue, or dramatic;[7] it is however pritty

[110]

(a) Translation of the Secretaries Letter

Sir,
    You possess every Superexcellent Quality, to recommend you, as *deputatus Electus* for the ancient Tuesday Club, for this very Sederunt, and this very night, and I am resolved to gi' you my vote 'afore any of 'um, Sir I am very totally and altogether your most obsequious to all Eternity, and, if any person alledges, I do Inequitably, I may say thus I did, as a Sincere emulator of a Generous Companion and a very hearty fellow, and as I am obliged by my Situation to do, and I do protest I am ready to do so for any others I testify so well of as you, Sir, and I do pray Sir, some malicious Rogues, as may question my Sincerity in this be hack'd or gashed with an ax or be knock'd o' the head with a ponderous Club.

| Tuesday night | Sir I am yours obsequiously to all Eternity |
| 7r 1st 1752 | *Secretarius.* |

    6. Cicero says the opposite in *Tusculan Disputations* 1.15.
    7. See especially "A Discourse, to Prove the Antiquity of the English Tongue" (ca. 1727),

Certain that Quirpum Comic Esqr, the honorable Deputy did not understand one word of this epistle, for, after having puzzled himself for half an hour to no purpose, he nailed it up on his door with four tacks or Brads, that the Curious passing by might peruse it, and, if possible unriddle it, which at last was done, by an Ingenious Club Linguist, and his translation I have put down in the margin.

The orator at this Sederunt, delivered an oration, Just before breaking up, in which he Compared the ancient and honorable Tuesday Club to the persian Empire, as it had had so many ups and downs since it's first Institution, but never had been for any time totally extinct, he also Compared it to that of the Mamalukes,[8] as it's members were now Chiefly Composed of Slaves, vizt: the Slaves of the honorable Nasifer Jole Esqr, but, the deputy, and all the Longstanding members, being seized with a vehement yawning, the orator himself took the Infection, and broke off abruptly, and no record was ever made of this extraordinary oration. || Then, the longstanding members, standing up, drunk farewell to the old Calendar, and professed themselves very Glad to be Informed, by the arrival of some Ships from England, that the parliament of Great Britain, and the Quakers of Grace Church Street, had followed the Laudable Example of this Club, in the alteration of the Calendar, which stands as a testimony to posterity of the profound wisdom and Sagacity of this ancient Club.

[111]

At Sederunt 186, September 26, (according to an act of this here Club, passed at Sederunt 169) Jonathan Grog Esqr being h:s: and deputy Secretary, the Chief Secretary being absent, a poem was presented in Club, Composed by the Poet Laureat, on the Late Eclipse of the Club, which was read and put on Record, as follows, vizt:

Lamentation, on the late Eclipse of The ancient,
and Honorable Tuesday Club
By the Poet Laureat

The Tuesday Club, In doleful Song
   O Muse, bewail again,
Alas! thou hast bewaild her long
   But still Bewaild in vain.

---

where, among other absurdities offered to demonstrate that Latin was derived from English, Swift suggests that the name Hector was derived from *hackt* and *tore* (Hamilton incorporates Swift's suggestion in Scribble's letter), and "Notes for Polite Conversation" (1738), where Swift employs these Anglo-Latin forms in a dialogue (*The Prose Works of Jonathan Swift*, ed. Herbert Davis [Oxford, 1939–1968], IV, 233, 276–277).

8. The Mamelukes were a warrior caste descended from slaves, who ruled Egypt from ca. 1254 until the Ottomans seized power in 1517.

    Her Long-longstanding members thou,
        Hast often Sharply Chid,
    Since what they should, they would not do,
        And what they should not, did.

[112]   From time to time, rebellious, they
        Have thy Sederunts sham'd,
    And thou hast been from day to day
        With Long adjournments flam'd.
    Say, if thy Proto-musicus,
        Was most in this to blame,
    Or have some other members thus
        Obscur'd thy Splendid name.

    Thy honorable President
        They often vex and tieze.
    His power is then of small extent,
        They'll do Just what they please,
    His honor lay in doleful dumps
        With gout in both his hips,
    We knew not what should turn up trumps,
        The Club was in Eclipse.

    With Sympathetic Sorrows each
        Did seem to pine away,
    Which threatned in our Club a breach
        For many a live long day,
    Neglected lay the Records all
        In piteous case, I wot,
    For two Sederunts, nought at all
        Was in our Codex wrote.

    O Protomusicus, to thee
        We all this hubbub owe,
    From thee, and from our chancellor
        We had this mortal blow,
[113]   For he 'twas first the Club adjourn'd
        And for a paltry play,(a)
    Our absent members twice we mourn'd
        When you had Cross'd the bay.

    (a) The Club was adjourned on account of a Comedy to be acted at the Theatre, on the night appointed for it's meeting.

> The Loss of bag, and eke the Seal
>   The Chanc'lor shall bemoan,
> Your music shall become a Squeal,
>   And eke a bagpipe drone,
> But now the Gout begins to leave
>   His honor's reverend hips,
> You both shall punishment receive
>   For all your tricks and trips.
>
> And, as his honor mends apace
>   And walks about again,
> The Club shall rise from deep disgrace,
>   And they shall plot in vain,
> God prosper Long our President
>   And 'Standing members all,
> And neer may such like dire event,
>   Our Ancient Club befal.

Huffman Snap Esqr, at this Sederunt, was struck out of the list of Longstanding members, according to the tenor of Law 13th, he having absented above four Sederunts, without sending any Sort of excuse.

Chapter VII

Grand Musical Entertainment by Signior Lardini, Heroic Poem on it by the poet Laureat.

*Music is an art, or (as some have been pleased to call it,) a Science, which has been Condemn'd or applauded, according to men's different fancies; for my part I believe it is neither good nor bad, considered in it self Simply, but becomes so, according to the uses to which it is applied. Diogenes and Plato among the ancients seem to be of Contrary opinions concerning it. The first, as a Cynic, told a Certain person, who bragged of his Skill in music, that Cities and States were Governed by wisdom, but that a small family could not be kept in order by fiddling and a Song; The Latter, as an academic, the principles of whose Philosophy were more Generous and enlarged, Compares the Symmetry and order of the heavenly bodies to a

---

(*) Vide, 9th anniversary Speech, where this passage is found almost verbatim.

Chorus and a dance, and to music & harmony, and the comparison in the opinion of many is Just and Elegant, and the same divine Philosopher says somewhere in his writings Αρμονια μεν γαρ και ςυμφονια, και αριθμος εν πλειοςιν εγγιγνεςθαι πεφυκεν.[1]

[115] Our moderen Italians are so bigotted to the excellency of this art, that they have a maxim, whoever Loves not music, is not beloved of God, the ancient || Hebrews used music in their devotion, as we may see by the Stories transmitted to us of king David and his harp, which had the power of Charming the evil Spirit from Saul; The Greeks used it in war, and we find an Instance of the Spartans being fond of it for that purpose, but then, they were for Confining it to a Certain Compass, and therefore Imposed a fine on Terpander and nailed his harp to a post, for adding one String to the number before used;[2] By Orpheus's music is understood the Establishment of politeness peace and morality among men, for, by the power of his modulations he Civilized the Satyrs, who were properly the unpolished part of the human Species which ranged the woods with their kindred brutes, and, it is Certain we are told in the Sacred Archives that Alleluias, and Celestial hymns are sung in heaven,—yet, notwithstanding all these great authorities in favor of music, many Heroes and Sages have Esteemed it a triffling unmanly and Scandalous Science. Philip of Macedon, asked his Son Alexander, if he was not ashamed of his singing so well, Themistocles being asked, if he could play on the harp, said, he did not know, he never had tried, but, that he knew very well how to plan a battle or storm a Town, these being arts he was practised in, Salust the Roman Historian speaking of the Qualifications of a Courtezan, says that she did, *Psallere et saltare*

[116] *elegantius quam necesse est probæ,*[3] || yet certain it is, notwithstanding the Contempt, with which many have treated this Elegant art, and its professors, (a good fidler being now a days looked upon with Scorn, as having spent much time in acquiring a triffling accomplishment, if any accomplishment may be called triffling) that some of the wisest and greatest men have been Captivated with it. Stratonice with a Song Entraped Mithridates to

---

1. "Harmony and concord and rhythm are inherent in most things" (exact source unknown, but Hamilton might be reconstructing Plato, *Symposium* 187B from memory).

2. Terpander (fl. 7th century B.C.), poet and musician of Lesbos, was known as the father of Greek music; the story Hamilton cites appears in Plutarch, *Moralia* 3.437.

3. I have not found the reference to Philip of Macedon. The reference to Themistocles (ca. 528–462 B.C.), the Athenian statesman and commander of the fleet chiefly responsible for winning the battle of Salamis against Persia, appears in Plutarch's life of Themistocles, 1.3. The quotation from Sallust (probably 86–35 B.C.), the Roman senator and historian, appears in his history of the conspiracy of Catiline, *Bellum Catilinae* 25.2, "Sing and dance more elegantly than is necessary for a nice girl."

her hive, and held him as fast as a bird in a Cage,[4] and tho the honorable Mr President Jole, and his Longstanding members, had the Character of wise, Judicious, grave and Great men, yet were they Captivated to a great degree with the musical performances of Signr Lardini musician *Con Stromenti* to the Club, so, as to show the Greatest Signs of Rapture and extacy, when that artist performed on his fiddle, the music of the Anniversary odes, and Songs of the Club, but, from this, I will not presume to Conclude, that the members of this Club were Platonists, or of the Academic Sect, for had it been so, they would, like Plato have banished music from their Common wealth, neither did they use music on the account of religion or war, but perhaps might Intend it for the same purpose as Orpheus did, to polish, soften and humanize their rough and Savage L: Stand: members if any such might possibly be, or come among them.

At Sederunt 187, Prim Timorous Esqr, being H:S: The Eastren Shore Triumvirate having sent a fourth || Embassy to the Club, the Embassadors, vizt: Signior Lardini, Theophilus Smirker, and Sir John Gabble Esqrs, attended at the Club, and Signior Lardini as Spokesman for the Rest, delivered to his honor and the Club, in a short, and Elegant Speech, the Compliments of the worshipful Eastren Shore Triumvirate, to which the Secretary by his honors order made a Civil reply. [117]

After Supper the Anniversary ode of 1751 was performed in parts, with several other pieces of musick.

It was then ordered by the Club, that his honors picture should be drawn at half Length, in a sitting posture, with all his Implements of State about him, by Signior Sehesslius, a high German artist, who was Entertained this night as a Stranger, pursuant to ancient Custom, but this order was never Complied with, for what reason, is not known.

At Sederunt 188, Tunbelly Bowzer Esqr, being H:S: The orator pronounced a panegyric on Laconic Comas Esqr, who was Entertained as a Stranger at this Sederunt, pursuant to ancient Custom, and wished him in the name of his honor the President and the Club, a good voyage to England, he Intending soon to take his departure, which done, Mr Comas rose up, returned the Secretary a Low bow; and sitting down again, sung the two favorite airs of *She Tells me with Claret* &ct: & *Bumpers Squire Jones,*[5] || with great mirth and glee. [118]

---

4. See Plutarch's life of Pompey, 3.

5. "She Tells Me with Claret" appears as "The Jolly Toaper" in Thomas D'Urfey's *Wit and Mirth; or, Pills to Purge Melancholy*, 6 vols. (London, 1719–1720) and in John Sadler's *The Muses Delight* (Liverpool, 1754), 165. "Bumpers Squire Jones" appears in *Calliope, or English Harmony* and was also published in the *Gentleman's Magazine* (November 1744), 612.

At Supper, the Secretary, who had a foolish Sort of a Genius for drawing, took his honor's portrait upon a blank leaf of the Club Record book, with a black lead pencil, which hit the likeness so exactly that the Longstanding members approved much of the execution, and, the portraits of Sir John, the Chancellor, and the Rest of the Longstanding members, were afterwards taken in the same manner, and placed at the beginning of the Record book, tho none but his honors was finished at this Sederunt.

Thus, did this diligent and Industrious officer, do all in his power, merely *ex officio,* that is, without fee or Reward, to Eternise the memory of this ancient and honorable Club, both by his pencil and pen, for soon after this he began to Collect and Compile the History of the Club.

Jonathan Grog Esqr, after Supper, sung with great vivacity and humor, the old Club ditty of *Robin and Jeck,*[6] and afterwards playd it upon the french horn, to the Great Solace and Satisfaction of the whole Club.

Signior Lardini, and the Grand band of Instrumental music, Playd *to Arms,* and *Britons Strike home,*[7] and then the Club music, with three violins, a violoncello, french horn and drum, the Grand Chorus was nobly performed, all the voices || in the Room Joining in the Concert, and many loud huzzas were given, and many hearty and loyal healths were drank, to his honor Mr President Jole, which drew about the house a vast number of auditors and Spectators, both black and white, the weather being hot, and the window Sashes of the Club room drawn up.

After which the whole Company adjourned down to Mr Leidemonts, a tavern at the Dock, having first sung some merry Catches, and then marched thro the Street in good order, with Colors flying, drums beating and the french horn a sounding the Grand Club March against Sir Hugh Maccarty Esqr, his honor walking in great State, at the head of the procession, and, being arived at the Dock, amidst the Confused noise of dogs and Children, they routed Mr Protomusicus Neverout out of bed, to which he had retired, being fatigued that night by dancing with the ladies at the State house, they spent several merry hours, In performing of vocal and Instrumental music, Celebrating his honor and the Club, and drinking Good

---

6. This tune, to which Hamilton himself provides the words and music (see pp. 280–282, below), is a variation of "The West-Country Dialogue; or, A Pleasant Ditty between Anniseed-Robin the Miller, and His Brother Jack the Ploughman, concerning Joan, Poor Robin's Unkind Lover" (James Ludovic Lindsay Crawford, ed., *Bibliotheca Lindesiana: Catalogue of a Collection of English Ballads of the Seventeenth and Eighteenth Centuries* [Aberdeen, 1890; rpt. New York, 1961], no. 1261).

7. These songs were composed by Henry Purcell, originally for the play *Bonduca* (1695), and are included in *Orpheus Britannicus: A Collection of All the Choicest Songs Compos'd by Mr Henry Purcell* (London, 1721).

'Rack punch and Claret; which his honor the president, graciously and Generously made to flow like an exuberant fountain, but, as the Clubical frolic, is best described, in an excellent Heroic Poem, wrote by the Laureat on that occasion, I shall give that Poem to my readers, as being a piece of admirable Ingenuity, and highly worthy of their perusal, the piece follows.

A Heroic Poem, [120]

Upon the Late grand procession and Parade of
the Right Honorable Mr President Jole,
and his long standing members of the Ancient
& honorable Tuesday Club.
    In three Cantos
    By the Poet Laureat
Humbly dedicated to the said honorable President & Club.

    Canto I
    Argument
    The members here are all recited
    And also, those that were Invited.

What Muses asistance now shall I Implore,
To sing the dear theme I admire and adore,
The Theme of the Club, and of Jole the renown'd,
Oh! how shall I celebrate how shall I sound.
   Not the Nine, who reside on Parnassus's hill,   5
Tho they the Clear waters of Helicon swill,
Nor Apollo their master, can dictate my verse
While I mighty Jole and his Club do rehearse,
So lofty a Subject, their Sphere far exceeds,
They ne'er did Indite such magnanimous deeds,   10
Not Even when they prompted old Homer to sing
Of Hector, Achilles, and Troy's old king,
Or when they gave Virgil the power to rehearse
Th'exploits of Æneas in high sounding verse,
Antiquities heroes, my heroe surpasses,   15 [121]
For Compar'd to great Jole, they appear but mere asses,
And the Jolly old Bards who recited their praise
Will never presume to *outrhime* my bold Lays,
Then farewell ye muses, and farewell Apollo,

For now I have got better patrons to follow, 20
I therefore myself disengage from your Yoke,
And Great Jole alone for my muse I Invoke,
Instead of Apollo to Bacchus I'll fly
And Rumbo for Helicon drink when I'm dry.
 Vouchafe then, Great Jole, Inspiration to grant, 25
For thou art my Patron, my muse & my Saint,
Merry Bacchus, come next with thy Jolly red face
And Infuse in my numbers, a Spirit and grace,
And Sovereign Rumbo my Spirits will raise,
More than Helicon's Spring to sing Mighty Jole's praise. 30
 Exalted aloft, on his Great Chair of State
At the head of his Club, the mighty Jole sat,
Of his Longstanding members, he took a Survey,
And graciously heard what each one had to say,
With Countenance lofty and mien so magestic, 35
Oh! the theme is too turgid for one single distich,
For, to frame on his honor a Just panegyric
Surpasses all verse, both heroic and Lyric,
Since nothing in natures wide Circle I find
With Jole to compare, or in body or mind, 40
Allow me, great Sir, to pronounce on the whole,
That great Jole Resembles—what?—what but Great Jole!
For nought on this Globe's mortal Round can we trace
To match him in majesty grandure and Grace,
Not even the great Ottoman Sultan with him, 45
May vie, tho his visage, be Surly and grim,
Tartarias's proud Chum, & the Emp'ror of China
With Great Jole Compared, are not worth a pin-ah!
And he of Morocco, and eke the Mogul,
If Jole should appear, would seem each but a Gull, 50
Prester John, and the Emperor of Mamalukes,
With all Bassas and Captains & muftis & dukes,
And Popes, and archbishops, & princes & kings,
Set up with great Jole, seem but pitiful things.
 Thus much for the President, now for the others 55
Of our Longstanding members, & old Standing brothers.
 Sir John, our bold Champion, should here in the van,
With his Shining faulcion appear the first man,
But alas! he's not here, then adieu Noble knight,

We must pass off without thee this Jovial night, 60
This Jovial night, with the drum and the horn,
We'll Salute, till Aurora returns with the morn,
And pity you'll think how you bore not a part
In our musical mirth and rejoicings of heart,
Then Redoubtable Champion, and Jolly round knight, 65
In this very place let me bid you good night,
While the rest of the members all night Claim my Lay,
I heartily wish you may sleep sound till day.

   And see where the Chancellor learned and Shrewd [123]
At the left hand the Chair overlooks the Gay Croud, 70
His decrees Just and Sage, all our breaches do heal,
But alas! what's become of the bag and the Seal,
The Seal and the bag, of his office the Symbols,
For which, in the Club, we have had such damn'd Gambols,
At home he has left it forlorn and neglected 75
Because by his honor dispis'd and rejected,
For now, all Commissions in our Commonweal
Are Issued from under Great Jole's privy Seal,
Then farewell broad Seal, mayst thou neer again Enter
On Summons, Commission, or Clubic Indenture, 80
For rather than thou shoulds loud discord Inspire,
Mayst thou & thy bag be both burnt in one fire.

   Proto Musicus next should The Laureat sing,
But lo! in the Club, we can see no such thing,
Say, seems he not thus to dispise and to hate us 85
To leave us to dance with the Girls in the Stadthouse,
Then farewell Good Proto'—take this to Comfort you,
May you dance till your Stumpers no more can support you,
And when all your fire, and your vigor's exerted,
May you find, by the Girls that you still are deserted, 90
Since you the Gay Glee of this night would not follow
With your ha-ha-ha-ha & your Stentor-like hollow.

   But see, where the Serjeant at arms with grave face,
And Countenance Solemn, Conform to his place,
Looks round upon all, with his fists on his knees, 95
And smiles now and then, as the Joke seems to please,
At the Laureat's puns and Conundrums so quaint [124]
He laughs like a pagan with face like a Saint.

   Come now potent Rumbo, and plume up my wing

While I in bold numbers the Orator sing. 100
Behold him, while rising, with Solemn grimace,
How Stedfast he looks on his honor's grave face,
That Sure, you would think, he meant nothing in nature
But to draw from the life his honors portraiture,
With grins and Grimaces, and faces so odd 105
Comes forth each Encomium & each Episode,
In Physics and history, much he abounds
And tickles our ears with such pompuous Sounds
Of Greek and of Latin, of welsh & of erse,
I must leave them out, as too harsh for my verse, 110
But at last all his words are but spent in the air,
Great Jole and his Club are as wise as they were.
 To sing of my Self, I next should proceed,
But that you will think, is a hard task Indeed,
For whatever I say, be it evil or good, 115
The Critics will pass their reflections so Shrew'd,
If good, the pert Scoundrels will then run their rig,
Good people observe this conceited vain prig.
If evil the pitiful Rascalls will Grumble,
Lord, how this pert Coxcomb affects to be humble, 120
Then nought of myself will I chuse to rehearse,
You'll Judge of my talents by reading my verse.
 Other Longstanding members, that were to be seen
Were Bowzer the fat, and Comic the Lean,
The first for the night had the high Stewards place 125
And acted his part with a Spirit and grace,
The other no office in Club did possess,
Tho deserving as much for his Comic address.
 Other members now absent, I sing not at all,
As having no hand in this Evenings Cabal, 130
This pompous Cabal and heroical Clutter,
For which they hereafter may Grumble & mutter.
 But here, may the Laureat put up a fond prayer,
Had Good Humor'd, merry, mild Slyboots been there,
Since he to our mirth could give humor and grace 135
With his Jolly round presence and Sweet Smiling face,
And, tho sparing in Speech, yet, we all must allow
He'd have relish'd our mirth with an excellent gout,
The dimpling Smile on his face would arise,

And he'd laugh till the tears Issu'd forth from his Eyes. 140
   But O Mighty Jole, I must here dedicate
Some lines to the worshipful Triumvirate,
The Glory of Mary-Lands Eastren main,
So Justly of their noble origin vain,[(a)]
Since from thy Great prowess at first they did spring 145
And own thee to all for their lord & their king,
The Great Chief Triumvir *in propria persona*
All the rest represents, nigh his honor's high Throna,[(b)]
In music so Shrewd and harmonious Jingle
That the touch of his fiddle makes all our ears tingle, 150
Next sat Sir John 'Squire, by his honor's commission   [126]
And shoulderd a trumpet, in warlike Condition,
A Trumpet? Nay, nay, prithee be not too rash,
'Twas a French horn, or what some do Call *Cor' de Chace*,
Which he shoulderd or wore round his waste like a Sash, 155
A Sign he was bold, not fool hardy or rash.
   There also were present at this fine figary
Some good Jolly members Yclep'd honorary,
Besides the Good Messiurs, James, Joseph & Thomas[(a)]
And the prime of good Songsters the quaint Mr Comas, 160
Who often had tickled our Ears to a tea
With "She tells me with Claret she cannot agree,
For she thinks of a hogshead, as oft's she sees me,
For I smell like a beast, & therefore must I,
Resolve to forsake her, or Claret deny. 165
Must I leave my dear bottle, that was always my friend
And I hope will Continue so, to my live's end,
Must I leave it for her, 'tis a very hard task,
Let her go to the Devil, Bring tother full flask."
   Thus Comas would merrily over a bowl 170
With Songs Bacchinalian enliven each Soul
And Chant out the Ditty of *Bumpers Squire Jones*,

(a) Song of the Triumvirate beginning

  Our noble origin we boast,
  From mighty Jole we sprung &ct:

(b) A poetical licence, putting *Throna* fem: for *Thronus* masc: for the Sake of the Rhime.
  (a) This verse seems Introduced on purpose to Rhime to Comas, as there was no body of the name of Thomas there.

With notes might enliven the Stocks & the Stones,
God b'ye then Dear Comas, we'll ever remember,
How thou of our Club was't a longstanding member,   175
For now, thou hast left us, alas! wail a day!
Curst be the Conundrum that drove thee away,
And he that would wish such a member were ousted,
We pray that he be by old Nick picafousted,[8]
So, drinking a bumper, to every true friend,   180
To Canto the first, I here put an end.

Canto II
Argument
The Social bowl is handed round
To Sprightly music's chearing Sound.

Of members Longstanding, and others, and all
Having sung, that sat round in the high Stewards hall,
I proceed mighty Jole, with thy help to rehearse
Their heroical acts in heroical verse.
    Supper ended, The king and the Club we propose,   5
Each one in his turn, in the bowl dips his nose,
Then a toast to his honor went round the round table,
Which each Longstanding member pledg'd as he was able,
Some drank in a bumper, and some took a Sip,
And some were Contented with wetting the lip,   10
But Comics warm Zeal was the Cause of much Laughter,
He suck'd up the liquor, and sent the toast after
And Cry'd as he Cram'd in his mouth the Soakd Cake
"I eat up the toast for his honor's dear Sake,"
Much good may it do you, my brave Jolly Soul,   15
And may you ne'er want, or a toast, or a bowl
To toast to his honor, Illustrious Jole,
Thy praises I louder will sing than Sir John's,
Or twenty such blustering bold Champions,
Then heres to his honor, I say, with good will,   20
Tis a full bowl of Rumbo, I take a good Swill—
Now, I'll sing you a ditty of *Robin and Jeck,*
Which, if it dont please you, I'll venture my neck,

---

8. *Picafousted* seems to be Hamilton's invention, deriving from the Spanish *picar* ("to pierce") and the obsolete *foutch* ("sword").

And, when I have sung it, without Jest or Scorn,
I'll sound it exactly upon the french horn.   25
    The Laureat thus spoke Sir, then with a gay air
With arms both a kimbo erect in his Chair,
With countenance Chearful, and blith as the Spring,   [128]
He hemd and he coughd, and prepard him to sing,
And he sung with so Sweet and enchanting a Sound^(a)   30
That they gap'd and they laugh'd and they grin'd all around,
In exerting his lungs he Committed no fault,
In the Chorus, he reachd *G Sol re ut in alt.*[10]
    The Song being Ended, with musical Grace,
He grasped the horn, and to one Side his face,   35
Applying the mouthpiece, his Cheeks gan to puff,
And he look'd as tremendous as bold Captain Bluff,[11]
The blood in his visage began to arise
And red were his plumpers, & blood red his Eyes,
Then with hideous Clangor, the Sound issued forth   40
And was heard in all quarters, east west South & north,
But when the high note in the Chorus he sounded,
The Shoke was so great Sir, that all were Confounded,
Then he Clos'd on a note Sir, so fine and so small,
You'd have swore, had you heard it, 'twas no note at all,   45
Then thinking he had done enough or too much,
He ungrasped the horn from adventerous Clutch,
And Soberly laying it down on the table,
We Clapd him as Loudly as e're we were able.
    Now view we a while Jolly faces all round   50
For the next Singing heroe, that is to be found,
Good Comas with pipe in his mouth lookd so Sage
You'd swear, 'twas not he that should next mount the Stage,
But taking the pipe from between his two lips,
Which Gently before him on table he slips,   55
He took up the bowl to apply to his nose

(a) He sung with so Sweet and enchanting a Sound
    That Sylvans & faries unseen danc'd around.
    Yellow hair'd Laddie, anonymous.[9]

9. These lines appear in the second stanza of "The Yellow-hair'd Laddie" (see Ramsay's *Tea-table Miscellany,* I, 43).
10. *Ut* is high *do;* in other words, the poet laureate hit the top of the octave.
11. Captain Bluffe is the cowardly bully in William Congreve's *The Old Bachelor* (1693).

And cleared his pipes with a hem as he rose,
Having drank to his honor, and wip'd his mouth dry,
He fetchd tother Hem, e're he venturd to try,
Then he turnd up his eyeballs & fixed his face 60
And grumbled a while on the notes of the Bass,
Then he run up his voice by degrees, and at length
Sung the flask of dear Claret with vigor & Strength,
And when that was done in a loud vocal Sharp,
Excelling the pitch of flute, viol or harp, 65
He chanted in Clear and in musical tones
"Then away with the Claret in bumpers 'Squire Jones,"
The plaudite also to Comus was given,
As his music had rais'd us up half way to heaven,
Then he suckd some more rumbo, in which he delighted, 70
And e'er he sat down his pipe he re-lighted.

   The Orator then, with his wonted grimace
Began to put on his dam'd Speech making face
To deliver out something—there was all around
A deep expectation, and Silence profound. 75

   Having done his Significant hums & his haws,
And towards the Chair streechd out one of his Claws,
He said "Honor'd Sir, and you right worthy members,
Theres more than one here, I believe, well remembers,
What a Longstanding member we had of friend Comas, 80
But fate, or the devil, at last tore him from us,
A Jolly Good member, he was in his day,
He'd smoke out his pipe with but little to say,
A Stiff bon Companion & good naturd Soul
Who said little else but—put 'bout the bowl, 85
Who never in Strife or in brangles was Loud,
And thought a Cool pipe and a bowl still was good,
To this here ancient Club he did Service & grace,
A blessing therefore on his Good naturd face,
With Songs and with catches, hed often regale us, 90
And swore he'd stick by us, whate'er should befall us,
But so it befell us, at last he was gone,
Left us for his absence to sigh and to groan,
And now for England, he goes in a Ship,
For ever and a day, to give us the Slip, 95
Let us wish him God 'buy, and I hope he will think

How with us he did smoke, how with us he did drink,
And that he'll remember us mongst merry Souls
As oft as they meet for to toss off their bowls,
And we, on this Side of the water will promise   100
In all our Carousals to drink Mr Comas."
  The Orator spoke, Mr Comas arose
And bowd to his honor, as Low as his toes,
To the Orator next, then to those that remain,
Of the longstanding members, and sat down again.   105
  Now, asist me, Great Jole, in an arduous thing,
Of the music of horn, drum and fiddle to sing,
While the voices in General harmony Joind,
And all the Grand Chorus to praise thee Combind.   110
  The Great Chief Triumvir, the prime of the band
Stood fiddle and fiddle Stick ready in hand,
And Sir John the Squire, next in order appears
With his Jolly French horn so to tickle our ears,
Next came brother Billy that Sailor so gay,   115
A Triumvirate member on east Side the bay,
Who sings a love ditty so well, like him none do,
His part was to play violino Secondo,
'Squire Strap next appears with his Chin on his Crowd,   [131]
Who playd any part well but never playd loud,
The Orator last, with his wonted grave face,   120
Closd the rear, with his viol ycleped the Bass.
  Then all being set, with the tuck of the drum,
They struck up *to arms, & brave britons strike home,*
The loud sounding harmony reach'd every ear,
And Crouds came to listen from far and from near,   125
Then pausing a while, the Club ode they began,
And round all the members, new Extacy ran,
But chiefly his honor, who sat in high Chair,
To a pitch did exalt his magnificent air,
And smild so Serene, youd Imagine by Jove,   130
That he was a bright angel that smil'd from above,
But when the grand Chorus was sounded aloud,
With their voices then Join'd us the numerous Croud,
Oh! then was great Jole with such extacy warmd
That he lookd like a figure Inchanted or charmd,   135
His Steady fix'd look, his Elongated face,

Mouth open—did add to his grandure & grace,
And, In this fixd posture, he still would remain
If the music till now had Continu'd the Strain,
But when the Grand Chorus was ended, a loud 140
And General Huzza, was set up by the Croud,
Huzza for Great Jole! and Huzza for Great Jole!
That noble magnanimous, Generous Soul,
Huzza! to his health in a full flowing bowl,
Then up went the Cups, & the punch it went down, 145
And his honor awoke from extatical Swoon.
 Now the Candles in Sockets began to burn low,
But there's punch in the Bowls & we'll drink e'er we go,
"Then merry lets meet, & merry lets part,(a)
And neighbour here's to thee with all my heart, 150
Theres one bowl in hand & another in Store,
Enoughs Enough, and we'll have many more,
Huzza for great Jole! and huzza for great Jole!
A blessing light on his magnanimous Soul,
We'll toss off his health in a full flowing bowl."
 Then forth did we sally in valorous plight
To revel rejoice and frolic all night,
These frolicks at large, you may find if you chuse
To turn over, and Canto the third to peruse.

Canto III
Argument
The Grand parade is sung at large,
And bumpers, 'rack & Claret charge.

And now, Noble Jole, my Inspirer and muse,
In my hobbling verses new Spirit Infuse,
While the other exploits of the night I reherse,
Great patron, enliven and furbish my verse.
 Wide opend the doors of the high Steward's hall(b) 5
While in grand rank and file the processioners all

(a) The words of an old Catch.¹²
(b) *Panditur Interea domus omnipotentis olympi.* Virg:¹³

12. This ancient club toast is introduced originally in I, 143.
13. "Meanwhile the house of all-powerful Olympus was open" (*Aeneid* 10.1).

Issu'd forth, two and two, with great Jole in the van,
And as floods do the valleys the Streets overran,
The Colors aloft in the air 'gan to play,
And the moon shone so bright, you'd have swore it was day,   10
The twinkling Stars seemd to dance in their Spheres,   [133]
And the shrill sounding horn struck up martial airs,
Or Else twas the fumes of the punch in our Eyes,
Made us think a grand Jubile held in the Skies,
With State and with grandure we marched along   15
Whilst the drum and the horn still enlivend the Song,
And at every house, as we pass'd on our way,
'Twas great Jole live for ever! Huzza! & Huzza!
The Children and dogs all around us appeard,
Such bawling and barking Sure never was heard,   20
And yet mighty Jole, without fear or dismay,
With Grandure and majesty led us the way,
Midst a medley of noises, undaunted he strode,
And his Longstanding members, he spread all abroad,
Till at Leidemont's wharf he at last made them halt,   25
Upon the musician to make an assault,
Ta-ra-ran, ta-ra-ran, went the horn of the Club,
And the deep sounding drum went dub-adub-dub,
And Redowbled Huzzas made so dreadful a Sound
Till it rous'd the musician from Sleep so profound,   30
Who wond'ring who Caused this Strange hurly burly,
Appeard in his Shirt, at the window to Parly,
He rubbd up his eyes and he scratched his pate
And Gaped and Grinn'd at a horrible rate,
He held out sometime but at last forc'd to yield,   35
He arm'd Cap-a pee[14] & appeard in the field,
So persuasive and Sweet were the words of great Jole,
That they Charmed his ear, and Inchanted his Soul,
For roundly he swore, nor the horn nor the drum,
But Joles honey words had Entis'd him to come,   40
Then a march we beat up, and fac'd to the right   [134]
At Leidemonts to spend what remaind of the night,
Oer Rack punch and Claret to toast mighty Jole
And drown all our Cares in a deep flowing bowl,

14. Dressed very gallantly, or appearing with "cloak and sword."

Round Leidemonts great table, our Soldiers were placd, 45
Mighty Jole at the head our assembly had grac'd,
A Sweet Smirking Smile on his visage he wore,
And of Claret and 'Rack punch he Call'd for great Store
While our Longstanding members rejoic'd all around
And Leidemont's Great hall with Huzzas did resound, 50
O thrice happy Leidemont, all envy thy Lot,
Who under thy Roof such a heroe hast got,
This Glorious night shall Establish thy name,
And babes yet unborn thy Great worth shall proclaim,
And the worlds four quarters shall hear of thy fame. 55
 And now Quick as Lightning, the Bumpers went round,
And the music struck up with enlivening Sound,
Each member in Chorus did roar & did bellow
With the horn drum & fiddle & violoncello,
You'd thought that the harmony of the high Spheres 60
Came down on a Sudden, ding-dong in our Ears.
 Then Silence succeeded, which lasted not long,
For we laughd, and we Jok'd & by turns sung a Song,
And drank to great Jole, with Huzzas & loud Claps,
While down went the Claret, & up went our Caps. 65
 Then Bold Sailor Billie, addressd him to sing
Of a Beautiful damsel that bathd in a Spring,
All her Charms he describ'd in so luscious a Stile
That the Laureat in extasies seemd all the while,
For like other bards soft emotions he felt 70
And at a love ditty would Languish and melt.
 Sly Jamie next movd with an amorous fury,
Sung a Song which he learnd of the nymphs of Sweet Drury,
Which had neither middle beginning nor end,
So not a Soul there could his drift comprehend. 75
 Then Dio to tune up his pipes did begin,
How a little black thing sat on a Cushin,
He sung of the piper that storm'd the redoubt
While the two little drummers kept drumming without.
 Then Comas his voice above *E la* did raise, 80
And of Bumpers of Claret, he Chanted the praise,
But he sung with such vigor & bawld with such force
That he ne'er would ha' done till he sung himself hoarse.
 Now Listen each muse, and attend every grace,

Great Jole is preparing his musical face, 85
To sing all his muscles he sets in nice trim,
And anon, we shall hear a Celestial Hymn.
   Then sung mighty Jole, with an exquisite trill,
The Song of the Nymphs upon Ida's high hill,(a)
The beautiful nymphs, who as old Stories told, 90
Exposd naked Charms for an apple of Gold
And for beauties prize offerd Empires & Crowns,
And wisdom to rule over nations & Towns,
But the Sceptres and Crowns, nought at all did avail,
The Charms of a Girl oer the Swain did prevail. 95
   Thus sung noble Jole, and anon all around
The hall with redowbled applauses did sound.
   Then the Laureat, snatching the horn from the table, [136]
He assaulted our ears with a tune lamentable,
Of let us be Jovial, and Robin and Jeck, 100
And puff'd forth the fumes of the Claret & rack.
   But one of our heroes who slep'd in a Corner,
Being rous'd by the Noise of this Clangorous horner,
Starts up of a Sudden, preparing to fly-O,(a)
But was stop'd in his course by the Strong fist of Dio, 105
And when that he found, he the door could not reach,
Thro the window he thrust his adventurous breech,
His head and his Shoulders, they soon followd after
And left all the room in a Loud roar of Laughter,
But Dio retaind had his hat, as a pledge, 110
His hat that was bound with bright Gold round the edge,
And seizing with furious talons the Lace,
He tore it Clean off as a mark of disgrace,
As dastardly knights, in old times with a Cleaver
Had their Spurs Choped off, so this knight's flamming beaver, 115
Was Crumpled and Rumpled, and tore with dishonor,
To throw a disgrace on its fugitive owner.
   Now Luscious toasts round the Room flew apace,
And the Claret flammd out on each nose & each face, 120

(a) Let ambition fire thy mind &ct:[15]
(a) A beautiful poetical Licence.

15. "Let Ambition fire thy Mind" is the first line of "Juno in the Prize," printed in D'Urfey, *Wit and Mirth*, V, 205.

    While with those that the bumpers of rack punch did swill,
The urine run off like the Sluice of a mill,
Full thirteen Quart bottles lay dead on the floor,
And nine Gallon bowls had been Emptied & more.
    To dance and to frisk it, Six Champions arose,   125
And heads, Shoulders, arses, arms Elbows & toes
By Sympathy movd in each caper and leap
Whilst Corro and Strap on two fiddles did scrape,
Scots reels and brisk Jigas they danc'd out of hand
Whilst Bowzer and Timerous led the Brisk band,   130
And Leidemont friskd on one leg such a rate,^(a)
Youd swear that it stood in no need of its mate.
    Now the Small hours had struck, & it drew towards dawn,
And Illustrious Jole from the Room had withdrawn,
So, deprivd of their Soul, and their life they began   135
To lose of their Jollity, man after man,
And like poor Sneaking fellows, shab'd off one by one,
Now, when all the heroes and dancers were gone,
Poor Leidemont, he lay in the field all alone,
For the drowsy god Morpheus, had made him his prey   140
And knockd him asleep Just at break of day,
Eyes shut and mouth open, he loudly did snore,
His arse on one Chair & his Legs on two more,
And Round him were strowd many bottles & Glasses
And piles of old fiddles, and old fiddle Cases,   145
Some Books Lay in heaps, and some scatter'd abroad,
The Great table seemd to Groan under it's load
Of Corelli, Vivaldi, Alberti[16] & others,
Of the Twidle-dum, twadle-dum Fiddle-dum brothers,
The drum and the Colors Lay Sad & forlorn,   150
And here on a peg hung the now silent horn,
There the Empty punch bowl so Capacious & wide,
And a mighty bass fiddle, lay Close by his Side.
    As he slept in this manner, two Jolly bluff Skippers

(a) Being lame in the other.

16. Arcangelo Corelli (1653–1713) was an Italian violinist and composer of sonatas especially distinguished for his dance movements. Antonio Vivaldi (1675?–1741), the Italian violinist and composer of operas and sonatas, greatly influenced the development of violin concertos. Domenico Alberti (ca. 1700–1740) was an Italian musician and composer of sonatas remembered for the device now known as the Alberti Bass.

Stepd into the room, in their nightcaps & Slippers, 155
At this dreadful Confusion, so much did they marvel
That they stood like two Statues of wood or of marble,
Like those that were Charmd with the Serpentine locks
Of Medusa the fury, to Stones and to Stocks,
But recovering at last from astonishmend deep, 160
They fled, and left Leidemont, still fast asleep.
 Then we'll leave this brave Champion to take his nap out
Midst the trophies and trinkets so scatterd about,
And when he awakes, may he think of great Jole
And toss off a health to his Generous Soul, 165
Who brought such a Club and a train at his back
To treat them with bumpers of Claret and rack.
 May Jole live for ever, and neer may he feel
The Gout in his hip, or his toe, or his heel,
Or what other member you please for to name, 170
Increasd be his honor, Immortal his fame,
May his Ancient Club be reverd & renown'd
On Turkish and pagan and Christian Ground,
May it live still, when all other Clubs are Stone dead,
And of all other Clubs, may he still be the head. 175
 Finis

This Celebrated Poem, by the Laziness and neglect of the Laureat, was never presented in Club, or entered in the Records.

Chapter VIII

Maxims of the ancient and honorable Tuesday Club, Speech of Jonathan Grog Esqr, & other trivial matters.

 Proximus ipse mihi, That is to say, the Shirt is nighest the Skin;[1] is a maxim, which Self love (that necessary law of nature) has Inspired, and has been used by politic men ‖ to the prejudice of Friendship and truth, the famous Machiavel, who has delivered to the public, certain useful political maxims, I mean useful, when Considered as political, not as upright maxims, seems to have founded his reasoning on this principle, when he says,

---

 1. Literally, "I am closest to myself" (paraphrases Terence, *Andria* 4.1.12).

102 [Book XI]　　　　　　　　　　　　　　　　　　　　The History of

among other Glaring political truths of the like nature, that a Certain quantum of deceit and Craft, is Commendable in Princes and great men, but despicable in people of low Rank.² This Indeed, may, in one Sense, be very true, if you will Grant the truth of another maxim, That to be fortunate is better than to be wise, since, whoever is fortunate, will be esteemed wise, as the vulgar Judgement is guided more by the event than the Intention, and, the unfortunate man, Tho' possessed of the wisdom of Solomon, will often find it difficult to make men believe that he is many degrees above a fool. Whatever approbation, the politic and discerning world may bestow on the maxims of the aforesaid Celebrated author, I cannot think, that that approbation (neither do I believe Socrates would have thought so) takes its rise from their being altogether built upon Justice and truth; and therefore, since the Machiavelian Maxims have been much applauded, I am in hopes, that the maxims of the ancient and honorable Tuesday Club, will meet with their due portion of applause, since it is evident, they do not deviate more from truth, nature & equity than the maxims of that noted Politician.

[140]　At Sederunt 189, the honorable Nasifer Jole Esqr being H:S: the members were very Elegantly entertained || according to custom, by his honor, and after Supper a Strange occurrence happened in Club, which occasioned great Surprize and Consternation, not only in the Longstanding members, but in his honor the president, nor did his honor, on this occasion, show less Indignation than Surprize, the occurrence was this.

Crinkum Crankum Esqr, and Capt: Dio Ramble Entered the room armed with two muskets, apparently in a hostile manner, having Carried before them, in an Elbow Chair, a little Swarthy fellow, with a great Black patch, or rather plaister over one eye, dressed *a la mode du France,* whom they deposited upon the floor, at the foot of the Club table, and, making a low bow to his honor the president, told him, that this odd personage was Sir Hugh Maccarty Esqr of New York, whom they had taken prisoner and had brought to his honor, to dispose of him as he pleased, to this his honor made no reply, but put on a very angry look—The Supposed Sir Hugh Maccarty Esqr, without moving from his Chair, Immediatly began to address his honor in a Sort of doggrel French, as follows. *Monsieur Jole* (says he) *Je suis Sire, le Servitur tres humble, et tres obeisant, de votre Seigneurie, et, Je vien ici, promptement determine, de vous payer cette hommage et, obedience, que a votre haute range & Grandure est due*³—while the figure spoke, he

---

2. See *The Prince,* chap. 18.
3. "Mr. Jole, I am, Sir, your very humble servant, and very obedient to your Highness, and I promptly come here resolved to pay you this homage and obedience due to someone of your stature."

accompanied his words with all the action and grimace of a Frenchman, his honor gave him no answer at first, for he really did not understand his ‖ language, and the longstanding members appeared full of astonishment, [141] nay, the Epouvantable Sir John, the Champion, was so amazed, that he had not power to lay his hand upon his Sword, but kept mumbling and tumbling his Chaw from one Corner of his mouth to the other, at last his honor taking a Serious and Earnest Survey of the poppet in the elbow Chair discovered that it was a female in the dress of a Cavalier and said "So mon Moll', are you after these tricks? prithee lay aside this foolish disguise and assume your proper dress, which is more adapted to your Sex,—go into the kitchen, the fittest place for such as you to be in, and probably I may order you some Cold vittles and Small beer, as a reward for playing the fool." At these words, the pretended Sir Hugh Maccarty Esqr, flew precipitatly from his Elbow Chair together with his guards, and were not seen again that night, and, at that very Instant, a Great Jabbering and laughing was heard out o' doors, the Muskets of Crinkum Crankum Esqr, and Capt: Dio Ramble were Examined after their flight, and, it was observed, that one of them wanted a lock, and the other a lock and a Ramroad, his honor the president could never forgive Crinkum Crankum Esqr, for this trick, as he Called it, and stuck in his Skirts for it a long time after, obstinately refusing to Confirm him a Longstanding member of the Club, after his Election.

The portraiture of Sir John, the Champion, was taken by the Secretary [142] at this Sederunt, while he sat staring at the pretended Sir Hugh Maccarty Esqr, and placed next to the president's at the beginning of the book, with a proper motto under it.

At Sederunt 190, Mr Secretary Scribble, being H:S: was play'd in Club several times, the Grand Chorus, *Con violoncello et voce Solo,* and also was accompanied with the dulcimer, which Instrument was playd in a very good taste, by a Stranger Invited to the Club,[4] concerning which Stranger there arose a Clubical dispute, vizt: of what Sex this musician was, for, Tho dressed in a man's habit, the figure had such an effemenate air, and blushed so much when looked on earnestly, in the face, that many of the Longstanding members suspected a trick of the same kind, with that which had been put on the Club at last Sederunt; Jonathan Grog Esqr, however, was absolutely of opinion, that this Orpheus was of the male Sex, on account of some free Mason's Signs, which he perceived him make, and it is notorious, that never any female was admitted into the mysterious Rites of that ancient and Right worshipful fraternity.

---

4. Thomas Richardson (see biographical sketch).

Upon the 191st Sederunt, Philo Dogmaticus Esqr, being H:S: a motion was made by him, whether the Club should meet only once a month during the winter Season, which being put to the vote, it passed in the negative.

[143] On the following Sederunt, which was on the 19th of December, 1752, Slyboots Pleasant Esqr being H:S: the || Secretary presented to the president and Club some maxims, Entituled the maxims of the Ancient and honorable Tuesday Club, which were twice read, and ordered to lie upon the table for further Consideration; But, tho' these maxims were never afterwards read, or Entered in the Club book, yet, as they Contain, as it were, a Compendium of the Constitution and Genius of the Club, I give a Copy of them here, vizt:

Maxims of the Ancient and Honorable Tuesday Club of Annapolis
Drawn up December 19th 1752

1 This being a humorous Club, to take offence at any piece of humor That passes between one Longstanding member and another, is reckoned unclubical.

2 Tho Politics be Excluded the Conversation of this Club, [vid: Gelastic Law] yet distant Jokes, puns, or Conundrums on wrong headed politicians are not debarrd (opinion of Jon: Grog Esqr)

3 The privileges of his honor the president, as entered in the Club Records, are uncontravertable, and beyond dispute, and, to mutilate them would endanger the Clubical Constitution.

4 The Chancellor and Great Seal, are terms, titles and Ensigns, without any Signification or meaning in this here Club, being, according to his honor's opinion, of no manner of use or Service.

5 Bawdy in Club Conversation is not debard, providing it be cleanly wrapt up.

[144] 6 Nothing that Sir John the Champion says to be taken amiss on account of his broad Sword.

7 It is Impolitic in this here Club to deny Sir John the Champion, any ideal privilege he takes in his head to demand, for the preservation of the peace of the Club.

8 The Great Seal is a Sacred Ensign of this Club, but disputes concerning it, are Extremely dangerous to the Constitution.

9 That it is no Indignity to the Chancellor of this here Club to play on a fiddle, providing he Confines himself to the Club music, the Song of

Alexis[5] only excepted, because it is Mr Proto Musicuses Masterpiece, the Secretary has also the same privilege, with Regard to his Violoncello.

10 That The trill of the Musician's voice, and the recitativo airs of the poet Laureat, are Essentially necessary for the Support of the musical Constitution of this here Club.

11 That his honor the President must not be thwarted or contradicted, in any Scheme or project whatsoever, proposed by him to the Club, or directed by the Club in any matters, his Station raising him above all arguefication, or reasoning, within the narrow Capacity or understanding, of the Longstanding members.

12 That his honor the president's powers are Conveyd to him by a Supernatural power, and his authority is *jure divino,* and that he has in himself, an absolute Indefeasible right, to rule and domineer as he pleases in the Club.

13 That nonresistance and Passive obedience are absolutely necessary, in the Longstanding members towards the President, for the preservation of our Clubical Constitution.

14 That the president has more Sense and Judgement than all the members taken together, and therefore, his council and advice alone, is to regulate the affairs of the Club.

15 That his honor the president has an absolute dispensing power, with Regard to all the Laws and Rules of the Club, and therefore all Saving Clauses in favor of the Club and in prejudice of his honor the president are unclubical, his honor being above Law, and in no wise accountable to the Club for his actions.

16 For the Support of the Constitution of this here Club, it is absolutely necessary, that his honor should not fix his Confidence or good opinion upon any Longstanding member whatsoever, except Sir John.

17 That the Loud Laugh of Mr Proto Musicus is the main Stay and Support of the ancient Law of this Club, called the Gelastic Law.

18 That the Song of *Robin and Jeck,* is to be reckoned an excellent piece of music in this here Club, tho no where else,—a privilege of the poet Laureat.

19 That Jonathan Grog Esqr, Punster, as well as Poet to this here Club, shall never be called to an account for any puns he shall Commit in Club.

20 That no body shall Call the musician to account for dropping

---

5. Perhaps a reference to a song sung by Alexis, a character in John Fletcher's *The Faithful Shepherdess* (ca. 1610); see especially act 5, sc. 1.

[146] asleep at eight o Clock at || night, his privilege in this here Club, time out of mind.

21   That Prim Timorous Esqr, Serjeant at arms, on account of his Stoical absence in Club, upon a vote's being proposed, shall have the liberty to Change his vote, from one Side of the Question to the other, without Controul.

22   That Quirpum Comic Esqr, who, not for want of personal deserts, has no office in this here Club, is a member absolutely necessary, on account of his Surprizing turn for Comedy.

23   That a keg is a keg, and a feather is a feather, and that the one is heavy, and the other light, the one of an aperient, the other of a Suffocating quality, notwithstanding the arguments of the Sophists & Sceptics to the Contrary.

24   That three and two make five, and two and two make four, all the world over, as well as in this here Club.

25   That one may easily conceive, one to be three and three to be one, if they are only resolved to assert and believe it, without waiting for these dangerous times of the full and Change of the moon.

26   That a man, who cannot believe Impossibilities is in a Clubical State of Damnation (Athanasius)[6]

[147] 27   That the Jokes of Quirpum Comic Esqr, are to pass for nothing in this here Club, and, are to be Esteemed || neither true nor false, for the preservation of the peace and harmony of this here Club.

28   That the Terms *whig* and *Tory*, are expelled this Club, being only Synonomous terms, signifying the same thing, for, the aim of both these parties is one and the same, being to procure to themselves Influence and power, tho' by different means, which Influence and power, must end at last in the same thing, vizt: oppression.

29   That all Tragical Subjects and Incidents, are absolutely Contradictory & Inconsistent with, the Constitution of this here Club.

30   That John Calvin, tho a hater of popery, and a reformer, was popishly Inclined, e:g: his treatment of Servetus.[7]

31   That the Secretaries Entries, in the Book of records, are to be looked upon as true or false, according as they do, or do not serve the purposes of his honor the President, or come within the Compass of his memory, which is, in a Clubical Sense Infallible.

---

6. Saint Athanasius (ca. 295–373), the theologian who played an influential part at the Council of Nicea, was the leader in the fight against Arianism. The allusion, however, seems rather an echo of Tertullian's "I believe because it is absurd" (*De carne Christi*, chap. 5).

7. See p. 49n, above.

32   That it is a very great advantage to some Clubical States to have a rogue at the helm, to administer what is Called Justice, as appears by the bold actions of Judge Jeffries and his politic master.[8]

33   That Justice and honor often become mere time serving terms, and signify no more than whim and resentment.

34   That the difference between little villains and Great villains, consists in this, that the first are often hang'd, and the Latter are always damn'd—we mean, not in this world.

35   That it is a very dangerous thing to Incurr the displeasure of an old woman, as it sets a whole neighbourhood by the ears.

36   That these wicked excrescencies of wit, Conundrums and puns, are often the Causes of violent dissentions & discord in Society, because the wit of all men is not measured by the same Gage, and because a wit will rather use his friend Ill, than lose his Joke (The opinion of Lac: Comas Esqr)

37   It is not Convenient, or agreable to the Constitution of this here Club, to be of the same Sentiment or opinion, for two minutes together.

38   This Club is of opinion, and Invariably so, which is an exception to the above maxim, that a man may Grope out his way to heaven without any of the external Ceremonies, of what our priests call religion, and another man may go headlong to the devil, with the whole load of the said Trumpery on his back.

39   That Tuesday night is a Sacred night in this here Club, and no meeting ought to be held upon any other night, unless thro' absolute necessity, by his honors express order.

40   That Law and equity are very distinct things, tho both pretend to aim at the same End.

41   That the title *honorary member,* is to be understood as an honor to that member, and to this here Club, as the honor of this here Club, is an Independent honor, and can receive no addition from extraneous Subjects.

42   That it is Ill Judged and unclubical, to put a finishing Stroke to any points or matters disputed in this here Club.

These Clubical maxims, or rather articles, in the opinion of many, are as Consistent and harmonious among themselves, as the 39 Articles of the Church of England *By Law established,* and as nicely Calculated for swearing to, without the Least danger of perjury, in the moderen acceptation of the

---

8. George Jeffreys (1644–1689) was the lord chief justice of England who presided at the trial of Titus Oates and held the "Bloody Assizes."

word, or for laying a firm foundation for eternal wrangles and disputes, In fine, they equal them in every respect, and excell them in one material point, vizt: in number, there being three more of them, and the number three is granted by many Subtile doctors to be a mystical and mysterious number.

At this Sederunt, Jonathan Grog Esqr rose up in his place, & delivered to his honor the following Speech.

"Honorable Sir,

What I am now going to say, is, for the advantage and Improvement of your honor's understanding—(Sir John: *Hah!*) and therefore, must very much Contribute to the Interest and advantage of this here ancient and honorable Club; now Sir, your honor & these here Gentlemen, will please to observe, that some few people have their understanding above Stairs, ‖ That is in the head, and a great many Chuse to keep theirs below Stairs, that is in their legs, feet, heels, or other Imfimous members; of which latter Sort, are we, vizt: your honor and the Longstanding members of this here ancient & honble: Club.

Again Sir, the understanding of many rests on the Earth, the understanding of many, upon planks, or such like Stuff, of the Latter Sort, is the prop of the understanding of us, the longstanding members of this here ancient and honorable Club; but the prop, or Stay of your honor's understanding, is a footstool Elevated above the level of we others by Six Inches.

Now, honorable Sir, I would prove, that this here footstool being broken, or in a fractured Condition, the prop of your honor's understanding is Crazy, and very much needs repairing, therefore, I move to your honor, and this here Club, that some proper ways and means may be devised, to support and preserve your honor's understanding, now manifestly In danger of a lapse."

Jonathan Grog Esqr, having delivered this Speech, in which the greatest Beauty is the punning, being much after the Stile and manner of several Speeches, made in the honorable house of Commons, in the Learned Days of James I. he sat down, but the Club were not in a hurry to Comply with his proposal, a Sure Sign of the Mighty regard they pay'd to his honor the Presidents understanding.

After Supper, it was moved by Jonathan Grog Esqr, that before rising from Supper, every Club night, the High Steward's health should be drank, which was passed *Nem: Con:* and thus was, the king and the Club, deprived of the preference ‖ after having kept it's rank for almost 4 years, which shows us, that nothing upon this Earth is permanent & lasting.

Upon the 193d Sederunt, being the 9th of January 1753, Quirpum

Comic Esqr being H:S: ^(")The Club, deprived of the Presence and Influence of their Noble Chief President, who gave a Lusture to every action, and a Smile to every countenance among the Longstanding members; after the proceedings of the last Sederunt were read, Philo Dogmaticus Esqr, being put into the Chair as deputy, descended, thro the want of him, who used to brighten and enliven the Conversation, into Common discourse, In the Course of which, a dispute arose, concerning the *Geneology* of the ancient kings of England, between Philo Dogmaticus Esqr, Cancellarius and Præses deputatus, and Loquacious Scribble Esqr Secretarius, a wager was held, of a bottle of Arrack, whether king Henry II. or king John, occupied the Coronation Chair first, which, after much altercation, was Ceded to the Latter Gentleman, who Entered under Henry's Banner, even before proof was brought, that the Latter had lost, the Club having dispatched a messenger for that purpose to bring to them, the first volume of the Celebrated Rapin.[9]

In Consequence of this Victory the Club unanimously voted Loquacious Scribble Esqr, deputy President for this Sederunt, degrading Mr Chancellor Dogmaticus, who had possessed the chair for some small time, in the beginning of the Evening. This honor the Secretary had done him, on account of his Superior knowledge in the history of his Country, and he accordingly assumed the Chair, with becoming dignity and Gravity, and mantaind his Supremacy with proper authority.

In a short Space, his honor the deputy by command appointed Crinkum Crankum Esqr, a Stranger, Invited to the Club, to be deputy Secretary during pleasure, this was a Strange and unprecedented proceeding, but the Club acquiesced, because the said Gentleman wrote a very neat and Elegant hand.

It was then ordered by the Club, that his honor the Chancellor, on his return home, wait upon his honor the president in his Chaise, with the h: Stewards Compliments, desiring the favor of his honors Company to Elevate their Spirits before Separation," by this, it appears, that the Chancellor left the Club before breaking up, being probably disgusted at his degradation from the Chair.

"The Longstanding members this night, except the Chancellor and high Steward, were ευκνεμεδες αχαιοι,[10] for reasons well known to the

---

(") This is the entry of Crinkum Crankum Esqr, apptd: deputy Secretary.

9. Paul de Rapin de Thoyras (1661–1725) was a French historian and author of the *Histoire d'Angleterre* (to the accession of William and Mary [La Haye, 1724–1728]).

10. "Well-greaved" or "well-booted Achaeans" (common epithet from the *Iliad*, e.g., 1.17).

Club," This may seem a mystery to after times, but I here solve it, and let it be known, that the ground was now Covered with Snow, so deep, that there was no walking without boots, as for the H:S: he was at home, and the Chancellor rode in a two wheeld Chair, thus have I prevented an obscurity in this history, by solving a small difficulty. It were pity all other Historians had not acted with the like Care, having made their writings very dark and obscure in many places by such small ommissions.

"At this Sederunt was produced at Supper, a large haunch of venison for the first time in this here anct: & hon: Club, which the L:St: members devourd &

——down their throats did twist
Like Trojans true as ever piss'd.¹¹

[153]   Solo Neverout Esqr, having been appointed deputy orator for the night, was ordered to make a Speech, and desired some time to Consider of it, which he meditated upon so long, that the weighty Subject weighed down his Eyelids and his mouth breathed nothing but fire and Smoke"—mem: broke his pipe as usual.

"After the usual toasts had passed round, his honor the deputy Enquired, whose turn it was to serve the Club as H:S: at next Sederunt, when, two of the members disagreeing, the vote was put, whether the Chancellor, or proto musicus should have that honor, the Club chusing in so weighty an affair, not to be too eager in delivering their opinions, Mr Proto Musicus, took advantage of their Profound Cogitations, and proposed some Reasons for his refusing the aforesaid great honor, speaking as follows.

'Mr Deputy President, Sir,

Being a man of method myself, and having some knowledge, from long experience, that this here Club proceeds on the same principles, in all their undertakings—hoh!—I humbly presume to—show—this—paper—[Here he fumbled in his pockets, and pulled out the printed list of the members, and their order of serving, turning it round and round, and displaying it's Contents] In this paper, your honor will observe, that Mr Chancellors turn Immediatly follows the present High Steward's, and Consequently, if I serve, that Great Regularity—haugh—I say Sir, that great Regularity, hitherto so Excellently kept up, will Infallibly come to a—to a—I say Sir,—to a final down fall.'

[144a]   To this the Chancellor, in a concise and pithy Sentence declared his resolution of not serving, and, after mature deliberation it was resolved and ordered, that Solo Neverout Esqr Protomusicus, should serve this here

11. See p. 24n, above.

ancient and honorable Club as H:S: upon Tuesday the 23d of this Instant January.

Ordered also, that on friday the 12th Instant, a grand Committee of the whole Club, be held at the house of the valiant Sir John the Champion, to Consult on great matters, Relating to this ancient and honorable Club, and Crinkum Crankum Esqr, was appointed Secretary to that Grand Committee," this was a Scheme of the Secretaries, Contrived on purpose to Chagrin the president, and stir up mischief in the Club.

Chapter IX

Convention of the Grand Committee, heroic letter of Sir John, Examination of Negroe Jeoffry, Clubs answer to Sir John's letter, Memorial of the Grand Committee, Carmen dolorosum of the Club.

Trick is discovered by trick, and deceit by deceit. All agree, that the best way to catch a rogue, is to set another rogue in pursuit of him; a Set of very Learned and honest Gentlemen, for whom I have a profound esteem, vizt: the professors of the Law, who perorate at our moderen bars, seem to be Sensible of these above mentioned truths, therefore, in treating of any Rogueish affair, it is always Customary with them, to put Cross questions to the Evidences and Culprit, by which they Catch the knaves in their own traps, and this method they have found always || most Successful in the discovery of falshood, so as to bring the practisers of it to Condign punishment, or, at least expose them to the Severe censure of the Impartial world, They follow here the method of Socrates, tho' they differ from that Celebrated Philosopher in this material Circumstance, that the Socratic Questions, were always urged for the discovery of truth, which is not the Case with the Enquirys of many of our Gentlemen of the Gown, those that see Specimens of each method, will see much of the first, in the State Trials, particularly in the examinations and Trials Concerning Dr Titus Oats,[1] and a very good pattern of the other, In the dialogue of Socrates with Alcibiades, in Plato's Alcibiades II, when the Latter was going to the temple to pray, in which the Philosopher, by Subtile questions, convinces the young heroe, that he understood nothing of the Nature of prayer;[2] an Instance of

[145a]

---

1. Titus Oates (1649–1705) was the fabricator of the Popish Plot (1678), an invented Catholic conspiracy to murder Charles II, place James on the throne, and suppress Protestantism.

2. Hamilton's account of the dialogue and its source is accurate.

112 [Book XI] The History of

this Sort of dexterity of both kinds, we shall, in this very Chapter display, in the Examination of Negroe Jeoffry, Taken by the Longstanding members of the Ancient and honorable Tuesday Club.

At Sederunt 194, Solo Neverout Esqr, being H:S: his honor the President did not appear in Club, and therefore Jonathan Grog Esqr, was chose deputy President, but the Club disapproving afterwards of the Election, revoked it, and Chose Tunbelly Bowzer Esqr.

[146a] A Report was made in Club, by the Secretary that a Grand Committee had met at Sir John the Champion's house upon friday the 12th Instant, and had presented a me- || morial to the said Champion, which he undertook to enforce with his honor the president, and defend the liberties and privileges of the Club, which memorial should be laid before the Club at a proper time, that at that Grand Committee, the poet Laureat had appeared with his Chaplet of Bays, and that the memorial, after having been read over by Crinkum Crankum Esqr Clk: to the Committee, was presented to Sir John the Champion, who assured the Grand Committee, that it should be put to a proper use, and, after this doubtful, and ambiguous Expression, sprinkled it all over with Claret wine, and said, that it would thence appear to his honor, that there had been some bloodshed at the drawing of it up, this Report the Club approved of and Confirmed.

After making this Report, a Certain John Jeoffry, a tall Negroe man, of a very personable appearance, entered the Club Room, and declared, that he was a Special ambassador from the worshipful Sir John to the Club, and Producing a Letter, the Secretary read it as follows.

To The honorable The Tuesday Club
now sitting at Squire Neverout's.

Gentlemen,

[147a] You have got your Ends, that is to set Mr Presi- || dent and myself at variance, which you have now done compleatly, for, we have had the devil to do about, as 'tis called, your damn'd rebellious Libellous memorial.

I wish you merry, but pray, not at the Expence of Grate men's characters, I mean those that live in high Stations of life, as your most honorable president and also one of the nine worthies.

Tuesday evening *Sir John*.

  Vengeance is the word, & Slaughter must Ensue,
  So take care of yourselves, for you know tis your due,
  —The Colour Green is turned quite black.

Sir John in this Letter writes exactly in the Stile, of the old Romans, Tho In his poetry he Imitates the Celebrated ancient Pistol.³—The Romans in the Senate in the forum, and in all places of public Declamation used to be very profuse in their own praise, a practise now altogether Incompatable with the politeness and Ceremony of these our moderen times.—The Expression at the End, Concerning the Colour Green, may seem somewhat Ænigmatical to those who know not that Green was an Epithet Commonly applied to Jonathan Grog Esqr, on account of his Laureat wreath, made of an ever Green.

After Reading the above Letter, some members moved, that, before an answer should be given thereto, the ambassador Jeoffry should be examined by the Club, and accordingly, the said ambassador || was sworn on the Club book, in manner and form following. [148a]

John Jeoffry's Oath

You John Jeoffry do swear and protest, by this great book, and all it's contents, be they true or false, Just or unjust, right or wrong, Sense or nonsense, that all & every answer you shall give to the Interrogatories put to you, by the Longstanding members of this here ancient and honorable Club, shall be the truth, the whole truth, and nothing but the truth.

This Solemn way of swearing on a book, according to the Custom of a wise and politic people, being over, Jeoffry tossed off a huge Glass of Rum, and the Club proceeded to examin him as follows.

Interog: Of what age are you?
Ans: Twenty eight years or thereabout.
In: Do you know the President of this here Club?
An: Yes Sir.
Int: When was he last at your house?
An: On Sunday last.
Int: At what time?
An: In the afternoon.
A Long St: memb: That there Question is very material, pray Sir ask it again.
Int: When was he last at your house & at what time?
An: On Sunday last, & in the afternoon.

---

3. Hamilton is referring to Pistol, a braggart known for his fine command of bombastic language, who appears in Shakespeare's *2 Henry IV* and *The Merry Wives of Windsor* as Falstaff's ensign (or ancient).

[149a] Int: What door came he in at?
Ans: At the back door.
Int: Was any body with him?
Ans: None but himself Sir.
Int: Not a Cat, nor a dog?
Ans: Neither Sir.
Int: Did he walk fast or slow?
Ans: Very slowly Sir.
Int: Had he a cane, Sword or pistol?
Ans: A cane Sir.
Int: Are you Sure he had no Sword or pistol?
Ans: I can't tell Sir, unless he had them in his pocket.
Int: Was it usual for him to carry a Sword in his pocket?
Ans: I dont know Sir.
Int: What Cloaths had he on?
Ans: Black Cloaths Sir.
Int: What Cloak had he?
Ans: A red Cloak Sir.
Int: What did you think that Cloak meant?
Ans: A bloody flag Sir.
Int: Did he piss before he went in?
Ans: I did not observe Sir.
Int: What was his business?
Ans: I cannot tell Sir.
Int: What did he talk about?
Ans: I dont know.
Int: What said he when he came to the door?
Ans: He asked if Sir John was at home.

[150a] Int: Had Sir John & he any dispute?
Ans: None that I know of Sir.
Int: Did he call for pen and Ink?
Ans: I wont answer.
Int: Did he seem to be hungry?
Ans: He had a hungry look as usual.
Int: Did you hear them make a noise?
Ans: Not a mouse stirring.
Int: Was you suffered to go in?
Ans: No, no, no, no Sir.
Int: What Street did he come down?

Ans: Between Mr Hop a-kickie's & John Thomson's the little.[4]
Int: Did he call in at John Thomson's the little?
Ans: I dont know Sir.
Int: Has he been at Sir John's since Sunday?
Ans: No Sir.
Int: Did Sir John send for him since?
Ans: No Sir.
Int: Did Sir John send for the Serjeant at arms?
Ans: I dont know Sir.
Int: Do you know Prim Timorous Esqr, Serj: at arms?
Ans: Yes Sir.
Int: Did Sir John & the president part in peace?
Ans: I believe they did Sir.
Int: You heard no high words between them?
Ans: No Sir, as I know of.
Int: Did he not talk with a Girl with a high nose?
Ans: I cant tell Sir.
Int: Nor with any of the black wenches? [151a]
Ans: I can't affirm Sir.
Int: Was the president Clean Shaved?
Ans: I think so Sir.
Inter: Did Sir John write to Prim Timerous Esqr?
Ans: Not as I know of Sir.
Qu: Com: This is a devlish Sly fellow, there's no trapping of him.
Int: Did you see Don John Charlotto at the house?
Ans: No Sir.
Int: Did you hear the president swear any oaths?
Ans: Not I Sir.
Int: Did you see any hatchet faced man in his Company?
Ans: No Sir.
Int: Do you know what a hatchet face is?
Ans: Not I Sir, how should I? I'm no Scholar.
Q: Com: This fellow is all made up of negatives, there is no picking a direct answer from him.

$$\text{The} \quad \begin{matrix} \text{John} \\ \mathcal{Z} \\ \text{Jeoffry.} \end{matrix} \quad \text{mark of}$$

---

4. The "Record" identifies Hop a-kickie as Jennings, possibly Thomas Jennings. John Thomson is likely John Thompson (see biographical sketches).

From the purport and tenor of the above Examination, the Club Concluded that the valiant Sir John had not faithfully & punctually executed the commission given him by the Grand Committee of the 12th Instant.

In answer to Sir Johns letter, the Club ordered the Secretary to draw up the following high flown Epistle.

[152a] To the worshipful and valiant Sir John,
Knight and Champion of the ancient and honorable Tuesday Club—These.

Most magnanimous Sir John,

The Ancient and honorable Tuesday Club, now sitting (being Sederunt 194) at the house of Solo Neverout Esqr H:S: have received the favor of your honors heroic Epistle, and are very well satisfied with the Contents. As to the difference between his honor the president and your worship, we hereby engage ourselves unanimously & magnanimously, to stand and fall by your Side as long as our Longstanding members will stand, and, in Case we fall, then all that is to be said of your worship is

Impavidum ferient Ruinæ,[5]

which agrees exactly with your heroic & Intrepid Character.

> We hereby send you our Clubical Greeting
> And are sorry you a'nt here at this meeting,
> Recommending it to you, to Execute your Commission
> On the honorable president, sans Intermission.
> "Green being here, no black in Green we see,
> If Green were black, Green would with Coal[(a)] agree."
>   We are, *The Club.*

[153a] The ambassador Jeoffry had this letter delivered into his hand, and was ordered to deliver it to Sir John, so, after tossing off another huge Glass of Rum, he departed in peace.

Crinkum Crankum Esqr, Clerk to the grand Committee held at Sir Johns, upon friday the 12th Instant, produced in Club a fair Copy of the memorial of the said Committee, which was put into the Secretaries hands till further orders.

At Sederunt 195, The worshipful Sir John, Being H:S: a motion was

---

(a) Coal for Cole, as in the medal Cole for Jole.

5. "The ruins would strike you undismayed" (Horace, *Carmina* 3.3.7).

made to Introduce the Conundrums again into the Club, which passed in the affirmative, Prim Timorous Esqr, being appointed Sole Conundrum master.

A motion was made to revise the Laws of the Club, and, that a Committee should be appointed by his honor for that purpose, but his honor having reason to object to all Committees whatsoever, refused appointing any such Committee, and declared, that it ought to be done, at a full Club, so the motion was droped.

The Grand Chorus for the year, 1751, with several other pieces of music, was performed after Supper on the organ violin & violoncello, the performers being Crinkum Crankum Esqr, the Chancellor & Secretary.

At Sederunt 196, Jonathan Grog Esqr, being H:S: and Crinkum Crankum Esqr, deputy in the Chair, by the Election of the Club, the Longstanding members Considering that this proceeding was highly Irregular and Contrary to the Rules and Constitution of the Club, he being no member, either honorary or regular, unanimously || protested against it, and [154] the reason given for that protest, was a very Sufficient one, vizt: a known maxim of the Club, That the members are not obliged to be of the same mind for two minutes together.

Soon after this protest was entered, the Chancellor came into Club, and seeing an opportunity when the deputy was out of the Chair, he violently seized it, and would by no means quit it again, alledging Law 43d for his authority, tho' the members did not acquiesce in this violent act of the Chancellor's, according to a Clause in that Law, which leaves room for the members to elect, so that all the proceedings of this Sederunt, were declared, to be under the authority of Crinkum Crankum Esqr, Præs: deput: Elect: who, by this very act of the Club, is made and Created an honorary member thereof, he highly deserving that honor, on account of the many Eminent offices he has held in the Club, and in the Grand Committee.

These Irregular proceedings and Schemes to irritate his honor the president, were all Contrived and set on foot by the Secretary, who still could not brook his being neglected by his honor, and looked upon as a person of no Consequence.

The Club, at this Sederunt, elected the Revd Mr Mævius Pumpkin, who was Entertained as a Stranger, pursuant to ancient Custom, an honorary member of the Club, This Gentleman was one of the Baltimore Bards, mentioned in the Third Book of this history.

It was ordered, that the memorial of the grand Committee should be Entered in the Club book, which was done as follows, vizt:

[155] Memorial of the ancient and honorable Tuesday Club, in Grand Committee Convened, at the house of the Worshipful Sir John. Setting forth Certain Grievances, for the rectification of which, application is made by a Grand Committee of the said Club, To the Right Worshipful, and Most Valiant Sir John, knight and Champion, of said Club, appointed by the authority of said Club, honorable Chair man of said Grand Committee.

Imo *Whereas,* it has evidently appeared of late, that his honor the President, not having the regard of the Club before his eyes, but moved and seduced, by the Instigation of evil Councellors, has behaved to this here ancient and honorable Club, with great Coolness, Indifference, frigidity, lukewarmness and Contempt, so as to put manifest Slights and affronts upon it, without declaring the reason why or wherefore, it is requested, that the worshipful and valiant Sir John, who, in this doleful affair, they, *The Grand Committee,* have appointed their moderator and mediator, do enquire of his honor the Cause of this Coolness, Lukewarmness, frigidity, indifference and Contempt, and, if any thing amiss be, between his honor and his Longstanding members, to endeavor to rectify, reinstate and stabilitate, good friendship and amity, by Gentle methods, and, if balsamic applications will not do, then, the said Sir John, as Champion, is humbly requested, and hereby Impowered, to proceed to Caustics and settle matters, *vi et armis.*[6]

IIdo The aforesaid Indifference, lukewarmness, Coolness, frigidity &
[156] Contempt of his honor, appears and is made mani- || fest, in several Circumstances and points of his honor's late demeanor and behavior, to the L: St: memrs: of this here anct: and honle: Club *Congregatim et Separatim,* the particulars of which are Commemorated in this here memorial, of that there honorable *Grand Committee.* and

1st His said honor the President, has for some time past, in an unprecedented and arbitrary manner, in no ways agreeable to his prerogative and privileges, as president of this here ancient and honorable Club, and directly contrary to the rights and privileges of the said ancient and honorable Club, showed a Supercilious Contempt and Slight, to the honorable Chancellor, his office, Seal, bag and dignity, treating him on all occasions as a *Jack in office,* or person of no Significancy or Importance, and his high office, as an office quite unnecessary and Impertinent, his Seal as a bawble, a toy and a Cypher, which Conduct and behaviour, this here *Grand Com-*

---

6. "By force and arms."

mittee in the name and by the authority of the Club, Construe into a manifest affront put upon themselves, and a barefaced Encroachment upon their Liberties and privileges, as the honorable Chancellor, is a Club officer, duely Elected by the Club, at Sederunt 119th and not appointed by his honor the president.

2dly That his said honor the president for reasons best known to himself, (if any he has) but utterly unknown to the Longstanding members of this here ancient and honorable Club, has of late put a high Contempt and Slight, upon the great Seal of the said Club, by positively, and absolutely refusing again and again, to issue out proper Commissions, under the said Seal to able, and well experienced persons, for the right government of the sd: Club, whereby the Constitution, is likely to fall into a State of Anarchy and Confusion, for want of a regular & legal authority to govern it.

3dly That his said honor the president has most presumptuously and arbitrarily, refused again and again to appoint a deputy president, in his own absence, by which Iniquitous proceeding, and contempt of his own Inestimable privileges, he has Constrained, forced and Coacted, this here Club, much against the grain, to make a law in their own defence, at Sederunt 122, by which, they have taken into their own hands the power of Electing deputy presidents, to the Great prejudice of the Chair of this here ancient and honorable Club, its prerogatives and privileges.

4thly That his said honor the president, has at sundry times to the great prejudice of this here ancient and honorable Club absented himself therefrom, upon slight or no occasions, giving for a reason, that he was not timely advertised of their meeting, whereas it is evident, and can clearly be prooved, that his said honor has often been told of their meeting by the respective and respectful high Stewards, several hours, nay, several days, before the meeting of the said Club.

5thly That his said honor the president, has at several times, and in sundry places, talked with great Contempt of the Longstanding members of this here ancient and honorable Club, and of the Club itself, particularly on a Certain Occasion, on the Second day of this Instant Janry 1753 at his own palace in north east Street, then and there being, while the H:S: Quirpum Comic Esqr, now a member of this honorable *Grand Committee,* made an humble apology to his honor, because he could not, for weighty reasons hold the Club upon the aforesaid day appointed, begging that his honor would excuse him till that day Se'nnight, his honor, then and there, at his palace aforesaid ‖ on the day and year aforesaid, in an angry and audible voice, made reply in the following english words, *"I am very easy about the Club, and, for my part, do not care, if it never meets again,"* which vilifying and contemptuous expressions of his honor, then and there, vizt: at his palace aforesaid, on the day and year aforesd: uttered and expressed, this honorable Committee think unworthy of his Station, and that high honor and dignity to which this here Club has advanced him.

6thly That his said honor the president, as can be fully proved, has, at sundry times, and in several places, particularly the bye corners of the Streets, in the City of Annapolis, and at his own palace in North east Street, talked Contemptuously and disrespectfully, of the wit, humor and Genius of this here anct: & hon: Club to Certain rustics with whom he debased himself in Conversing and holding Communication, holding forth in a Diabolical Stile, concerning the *Conundrums* of this here ancient & hon: Club, inducing the Ignorant and unwary, to think and believe, that some Luciferian Conspiration and witchcraft were Couched under the aforesd: *Conundrums,* occasioning thereby, the Contemptuous name of the *Conundrum Club,* to be given to this here anc: & hon: Club, to the irreparable dammage & detriment of the said Club.

7thly That his said honor the president, has, by means of his Insinuations, allegations, defamations, and Covert machinations, most Iniquitously banished and excluded the said Conundrums from the said anc: & hon: Club, to the Great dammage of polite learning, Ingenuity and wit, which in this Century has made such Surprizing progress, among persons of quality and fashionable taste, and Instead of them has Introduced vapid and woeful disputes concerning the great Seal.

[159] IIItio This *grand Committee* therefore, humbly request & Intreat, and moreover absolutely Impower, the worshipful and valiant Sir John, knight and Champion of this here anct: and honorable Club, to take his honor the president into his warlike hands, and to mollify malax, soften, Intreat and request him in a mild and gentle manner, to rectify these Gross abuses, and to remove from his honorable person, his evil councellors, and advisers whosoever they be, and deliver them up to Prim Timorous Esqr, Serjeant at arms, that they may be duely punished for their treasons, according to the ancient Laws of this here Club, in that Case made and provided, and, that his honor would again Condescend, to govern his long-standing members, in meekness, gentleness, mercy and peace, and throw aside all austerity Severity and Irregularity in his Government; and, if the said worshipful Sir John, cannot persuade his honor by gentle and fair means, he is hereby authorised to proceed to force and arms, and, if his honor should not submit to either of these methods, the said Sir John, is requested and authorised, by this here *Grand Committee*, acting with a full

power and authority from the Club, to execute the Law upon the said rebellious president, and then to Summons another grand Committee at his own house, to consider of ways and means, how he, the said Sir John, as next heir apparent to the Chair, shall take the government of this here Club into his hands.

All which is humbly submitted to the Consideration of the right worshipful and valiant Sir John.

[Great Seal]

Signd p: order
Crink: Crankum Clk: Com:

Loquacious Scribble
  præs: deput: Elect:
Philo Dogmatico Cancellario
Solo Neverout Protomusicus
Jonathan Grog M:C: & P:L:
Prim Timorous Serj: at arms
Ελιουτος πλιςαντος⁷
Quirpum Comic
Tunbelly Bowzer.

This memorial shows to what a pitch the Club was now come in their republican principles; and Indeed, as they had had nothing but Rhapsodies concerning Liberty and property sounded in their ears for these 4 years past, and violent altercations and loud protests against Slavery and Arbitrary power, promulgated by that Cunning and haughty officer, the Chancellor, it was no wonder, that they had now become mere Enthusiasts on these points, and, being such Enthusiasts, the Secretary found them ready Tools for his purposes, vizt: to raise a disturbance, unhinge the Constitution, and set all things into the utmost confusion, that there might be a necessity for modelling the Club anew, and he, thereby have an opportunity in the General Scramble, to advance himself, some degrees nigher the Chair, but, as the fates had decreed, he failed in his purpose, and Continued Secretary still.

This Grand Committee, proceeded, with an assurance equal to that of the high Court of Justice, who took upon them, in an absurd and arrogant manner, to Judge that Innocent Lamb, King Charles I. find him guilty of treason, and Condemn him to the Ax, thereby crowning him, with a Crown of Glorious Martyrdom. This proceeding was grounded on that absurd and Insolent maxim, hatched Surely, by the Devil in Hell, that Presidents were accountable to the particular members of their Clubs, *Congregatim, et Separatim,* for all their actions, a maxim, parallel to that of the king's being

[160]

---

7. This line is nonsense.

accountable to the people, who, Surely, according to the Political Nature and reason of things, is answerable to God alone, let him be never such a tyrant. This Golden maxim so conduceive to the General Good of mankind, the Civil or Temporal Tyrants, had from the Spiritual, who play Cleverly into one another's hands, and amicably Club it, to defend and support each other's tyranny, and Passive obedience, non resistance, Indefeasible hereditary right, a dispensing power, *Jure divino,* articles of Creeds, with other articles & Confessions of faith, are || grand trump Cards, which they play on these occasions to secure their game. In fine, this Grand Club Committee, acted under Sir John, as the Rump Parliament acted under Oliver Cromwell, with the same unaccountable absurdity, humbling themselves to that bold Champion, and Insolently hectoring and Commanding their president, by setting the army over him to keep him in awe, but Sir John served them the same Sauce, as old Noll did his Rump, and turned them out of doors like a parcell of Sycophants. As for the Committees stiling the president's house a palace, in the memorial, it is not without precedent, the Governor of Virginia's house In Williamsburg, being so stiled in our public papers, with simular propriety.

His honor the president, being at this time very much Indisposed with the Gout, the Club set about writing a Condolatory address on the occasion, as had been done on the like Emergency, at Sederunt 97th Janry 17, 1748/9, and at Seder: 122, Janry 16, 1749/50, at Sederunt 147 Janry 15, 1750/1, and at Sederunt 170, Janry 7th 1752, N:S: which was wrote in verse, and ordered to be Presented to his honor before next meeting of the Club.

> *Indorsed thus*
> **Carmen Dolorosum,** *Humbly Inscribed to his honor the President, by the Longstanding members of the ancient & honor: Tuesday Club.*
> Titled **Carmen Dolorosum**.
> *Composed by the anct: & hon: Tuesday Club, at Sederunt 196 febry 20th 1753, at the house of Jonathan Grog Esqr, H:S: on the mournful occasion of his honor the President's, being Indisposed with the Gout.*
> Hinc illæ Lachrimæ[8]
> ♪ ♪ ♪ ♪ ♪ ♪ ♪ ♪
> Must we then yearly mourn the Joyless time,
> And Chant our absent Chief in dreary Rhime,
> Must we still view, alas! his empty Chair
> And groan, and weep to madness and despair,
> Depriv'd of Jole, forlorn and Woe-begone,

---

8. "Hence those tears."

In briny tears we weep ourselves to Stone.
   'As Niobe, what heart could bear the pain,
Her blooming race, by angry Phæbus slain,
(Thus Tuneful bards, have sung in doleful lay)
In floods of tears, dissolvd herself away,
Till every pulse and vital motion gone,
She stood a lifeless monument of Stone.'[9]
"So our Longstanding members weep for Jole,
And In deep Sighs breath forth each plaintive Soul.
In ejaculations loud the Sorrow bursts,
A Coat of Stone each torturd heart Incrusts."
Till Stupid all Remain like Stones and Stocks,
As those that saw Medusa's gorgon locks,
From heart to members, strait Th'Infection flies,
And priapus of Stone for that of flesh does rise.
   Great Jonathan[(a)] The poet of the Club,
Whom every Judge, a tuneful bard does dub,
Produc'd a priapus of Stone outright
And showd the members, their most piteous plight,
All would have smil'd at this uncommon Joke,
But Joles disaster all their mirth did Choak,
For still they vent themselves in dolorous Groans,
And every member Noble Jole Bemoans,
"'Stead of the Joys that drilld along the hour,
Incessant griefs each aking heart devour,
They loll, they heave, they yawn, they groan, they sigh,
And direful discords dash their harmony,
Such their Sad plight, alake, and wail a day,
Too Cruel Gout, to keep our Jole away.'
   "As thro' the Lovely Covert of the Grove
Each pensive turtle mourns her absent love,
And Cooing thro' the Long meandrous vale,
Eccho repeats the melancholy tale,

[163]

(a) Jonathan Grog Esqr, Poet Laureat of the Club, being a virtuoso fond of curiosities, of which he had a Cabinet very Judiciously Collected, produced upon the occasion to the members of the Club, a Strange production of nature, being a black pebble Stone, about 4 or 5 Inches in length, and two Inches thick, exactly resembling the nut, and part of the body of a human priapus, cut, or loped off, about midway its whole Length.

9. See Ovid, *Metamorphoses* 6.145–312.

While every Breeze and Gentle Zephyr bears,
Alternate hopes, and swift desponding fears,
So drear and doleful, thro the livelong night
Each member wales Jole's animating Sight,
And tuning up their pipes, with one Consent,
By Sympathy Bemoan their president,
Curse on the Gout, they Cry, with direful Sound,
Eccho, Curse on the Gout, replies around,
From where her widowd mansion Gr——m rears ^(a)
To where his witty visage Wou'dbe ^(b) wears,
From where dame Splinters ^(c) rolls her Gouty legs
Like doughty punch, upon a pair of pegs,"
To where Industrious B—rm—n ^(d) heaps up Gains,
By Joining Gentle Nymphs & amorous Swains,
From the dark house ^(e) where fetterd wretches groan
To where resides our valiant knight, Sir John, ^(f)

[164]

From where our Chanc'lor, bag & Seal reside
In lofty pile that looks oe'r Severn's tide ^(a)
To where pragmatic Hans ^(b) in Stall retir'd
Forms boots and Shoes, by Crispin's art Inspir'd,[13]
Thence, from his honor's Shadowy domain ^(c)
To where our belfry hoar, Yawns horrid oer the plain, ^(d)

(a) An old widow lady, distinguished by her universal Correspondence & General Intelligence—Teste Solo Neverout Esqr.[10]

(b) Spatterdash Woudbe Esqr, a learned Lawyer, noted for acuteness of wit & profundity of Judgement, prosecutor to the mayors court in Annapolis.

(c) A boistrous virago, keeping Tavern at the Sign of the Ship.

(d) An Ingenious female haberdasher of Small wares, who makes private Gain of public vices—Teste Solo Neverout Esqr.[11]

(e) The City, or rather the County Jail.

(f) The Castle of the worshipful Sir John, formerly ycleped Oldcastle.

(a) The mansion of the honorable the Chancellor at Severen ferry landing, where now resides the honble: Attorney General Neverout.

(b) Hans Wolf, otherwise called Garret, or Gerraldus Wolfius, an Ingenious Cord wainer of German original, probably descended of an Illustrious Austrian Stock.[12]

(c) His honors Garden, being planted round with many trees, which afford an agreeable and romantic Shade.

(d) An old shatterd fabric of wood, nigh the Church, now pull'd down.

10. Sarah Gresham (see biographical sketch).
11. Probably Anne Burman (see biographical sketch).
12. Garrett Woolf (see biographical sketch).
13. Saint Crispin (3d century A.D.) is the patron saint of shoemakers, saddlers, and tanners.

> "The Curse resounds, each dog his ears pricks up,
> Each Toaper drops the yet scarce tasted Cup,"
> The City Curs set up one General yell,
> As if Grim Cerb'rus had elop'd from hell,
> The startl'd moon retires behind a Cloud,
> And silent night turns Clamorous and loud.
>   Thus nature shall Repine, while Joles in pain,
> When he revives, she shall revive again,
> Thus, while he languishes, his Club shall grieve,
> And nothing but his health their grief relieve,
> Divine Hægeia^(e) once again restore
> Great Jole to rule his Club as heretofore,
> Then all our Griefs to Joys shall quickly turn,
> And may we ne'er again, on like occasion mourn.

The Club had two eminent hands to help them in the Composition of this poem, vizt: the Revd Mr Mevius Pumpkin, & Crinkum Crankum Esqr, honorary members, the first, a noted Baltimore Bard, and ‖ the other a Composer of Club Songs, the parts of it Composed by the first of these Gentlemen, are marked with a single (') those by the latter with a dowble (") The poet Laureat and other L:St: members Composed the other parts of the poem, The Club ordered the Secretary and Slyboots Pleasant Esqr, to wait upon his honor the president at any Convenient time, before next Sederunt, and present this poem to him, in the name of the whole Club, which Commission these two Gentlemen willingly took upon them.

(e) An old pagan deity worshiped as the Goddess of health.

End of the Eleventh Book.

[166] List of the members Honorary and Regular, that were in the Ancient and honorable Tuesday Club, From May 12th 1752, to March 6th 1753.

Regular members	Honorary members
Nasifer Jole Esqr Presd:	Mr Abr: Bumper
Sir Jno: knt: & Champ:	Dr Polyhistor
Philo Dogmaticus Esqr, Canc:	Mr Oldham wisely
Jonathan Grog Esqr P:L:M:C:	Mr Joshua Fluter
Solo Neverout Esqr Pr: Mus:	Mr Ignotus Warble
Loquacious Scribble Esqr Secrty	Sigr: Lardini
Quirpum Comic ⎫	Mr Smoothm Sly ⎫ Triumvirs
Slyboots Pleasant ⎪	Mr Theoph: Smirker ⎭
Huffman Snap ⎬ Esqrs	Mr Broadface round
Prim Timorous, Serj: at ar: ⎪	Mr Roundhead Muddy
Tunbelly Bowzer ⎭	Mr Chantum Cheary
	Col: Courtly Phraze
	Mr Curious Courtly
	Mr Prim Laconic
	Cap: Comely Coppernose agt: Br:
	Cap: Dio Ramble
	Cap: Prettyman Spyplot
	Mr Jealous Spyplot
	Coney Pimp Frontinbrass agt: Amer:
	Mr John Gabble
	Mr Crinkum Crankum
	Mr Mevius Pumpkin
	Mr Swillum Swagbelly

History of the Ancient and Honorable Tuesday Club

[167]

Book XII

From the Convention of the Grand Committee, to the Trial of Quirpum Comic Esqr.

Chapter I

Concerning Ceremonies and their great use and Significancy, in civil life, and in Clubs.

If the universality of a thing, be a proof of its necessity and utility, Certainly nothing can be more necessary and useful in human Society than Ceremony, for every where, and among all Sorts of people, Civilized or barbarous, the practise and form of Ceremony is kept up, which, tho differing in particulars, yet, in General is the same.

Tho it be the doctrine of some Philosophers, the more of Ceremony, the less of Truth, yet we do not hold this a good argument against the use of Ceremony to a Certain degree, unless it was possible to make truth universally prevail, and banish falshood utterly from among men, which we presume to be absolutely Impossible, and the reason is, because, it would produce a Solecism, or rather an absurdity in nature, as great, as if all bodies were to be || of the same form or figure, for Example, Spherical, or of the same dimensions, or all numbers even, which would in effect mar the General System of things, and reduce all that variegated beauty around us, into the original Chaos, Therefore, as I humbly conceive, falshood is as necessary as truth, and they are ordained to stand as Counterpoises to each other. [168]

It is Certain however, according to the above doctrine, that a flood of Ceremony or Grimace, brings along with it a flood of falshood, so as very often to overflow and drown Truth, both in religious and Civil matters, as may be exemplified in the Religion of the Church of Rome and the politics of the moderen French.

The writings of the ancients have been much admired, and have stood the test of time, the reason of which, many think, is, because they are founded upon truth & nature and therefore will always be valuable, but whence comes it that our moderen writings, are most of them of so little value, and of Consequence short liv'd, and are forgotten almost as soon as born; is it not because they neglect truth and nature, as things too plain and Simple for a moderen palat, and erect their building upon a Chimerical or fantastical plan. Another Question naturally arises out of this answer; whence comes this fantastical humor in the moderens, and why are they so Infatuated as to be misled by it, when they have before their eyes the same truth and nature, which the ancients saw and fell in love with, and followed, the only answer we can give to this is, that the moderens are so Immerged, over head and Ears in Ceremonies and forms; that their great attention to these || prevents their taking any notice of truth and nature, who are become now a days as ridiculous, for their plain, open and undisguised Simplicity, as the most Stiff and formal Quakers are for the plainness of their attire, and the Simplicity and grammatical propriety of their address.

For example, how ridiculous would it appear for a moderen writer, in the way of Dialogue, to Introduce a Great Lord, and a Schoolmaster, the latter addressing the first, in the same plain, artless and Ingenuous Strain, as Socrates addressed Alcibiades, in that Celebrated Dialogue, transmitted to us by his disciple Plato, where he meets him going to the Temple to pray,[1] There he calls him plain Alcibiades, not adding any title or designation to his name, nor so much as framing his discourse, to that Complaisant Strain or manner, so particular to our moderen dialogue, where, should a plebeian, meet a great peer, and accost him, his discourse must be Seasoned with My Lord! your Grace! your highness! with all Submission to your Lordship's better Judgement,—under your Grace's Correction—I am your Lordship's most devoted Servant, your Lordship need but say the word, I am ready to obey your Lordships Command in all things—Such a dialogue as this, Socrates would neither have understood, nor been satisfied or pleased with, any more than a polite moderen Reader would relish a dialogue, wrote between two moderens in the antique || taste—because it is Intirely strp'd of that form and Ceremony, so necessary in all moderen transactions. This alone shows the necessity of Ceremony, in the age we live in, since, as

---

1. See p. 145a, above.

matters are now Circumstanced, neither our Conversation, nor our writings, nor, in short, any transaction of life, either public or private, have any relish without it.

I would not Infer from this that the ancients were quite void of Ceremony, they had their particular Ceremonies, which they Judged to be useful and necessary in Civil life, but then, they did not burden themselves with an unnecessary Superfluity of them. The Spartans, a plain and brave people, as little addicted to finical forms as any people whatsoever, gave an instance of their regard to Ceremony, where they thought it decent and becoming, in which they showed, that they understood the practise of politeness and good manners, better than some of their much Civilized neighbours, the Athenians; It was Customary among these ancient greeks, to honor and Respect age, and therefore, in the Athenian Theatre, the old men used to have the uppermost or most honorable Seats; It once happened there, that an old man came late, after most of the Seats were occupied, a Company of Athenian youth, had a mind to make fun of, or in a more moderen Phraze, to Humbug this Reverend Sire, and one Rising up, as it were to give him his place, when the old Gentleman attempted to sit down, another got into the Seat and prevented him, and thus they kept hurstling the old fellow about for || some time, who, finding he was made a but of, retired to a [171] Corner and stood; The Spartans, who had Certain Seats allotted them in the Athenian Theatre, rose up to a man, and admitted him into the most honorable Seat in their division;[2] This Ceremony, as it showed humanity and respect, was in it's Self, rational and well grounded, and, the Ancients, who Cultivated heroic virtue, seldom admitted the use of any other Ceremonies, or forms, but such as had a relation or tendency thereto; and of those Ceremonies, that are much admired and Cultivated now a days, among our dowble refined moderens, whose main use is to save appearances, they had no cognisance, nor Indeed could they have any Idea of them, and this I esteem to be the Chief reason, why the dramatic performances of the ancients, particularly their Comedy, is so preferable to those of the moderens.

But in these times in which we live, there is an absolute necessity for all the Ceremony now in practise, for mankind, now a days, are more Governed by owtward forms and appearances, than by Inward virtue and Integrity; ever since the french modes and finesse, overspread Europe, and that nation are quite wrapt up in it, in their politics, private Conversation, and

---

2. Cicero, *De Senectute* 18, tells the story of the Spartans' courtesy without the Athenians' sport.

writings, so that, what a Certain Dedicator[(a)] says, of the late Sir Robert Walpole, in an address to a kinsman of that minister's, to Justify his turn for Corruption, "That the vices and Luxury of the Nation were become so great, that || bribery and corruption were absolutely necessary and actually tended to the public benefit, and therefore were Transformed from vices into virtues"—so the world has now become so foppish and fantastical, that Ceremony is absolutely necessary for Carrying on the affairs of life, either public or private, with any kind of decency or order, this fringe and trapping has now become an essential Ingredient in Conversation and behaviour, and the man, who strips himself of it, makes as ridiculous a figure, as if he went to court, or the drawing room, or to a grand birthday ball, in a plain ungarnished Suit, striped of lace and other Splendid Embelishments.

If we look about, among the herd of mankind we shall see how much Ceremony prevails among every Class and degree, from the highest to the lowest, in public assemblies, at private meetings, at sitting down to table, in common Salutations, between Superiors and Inferiors, and even between equals, Ceremony is the main and principal Ingredient.

Therefore it is, that we look upon many Incidents that daily occur in life, without the least Surprize, which a person, unacquainted with our moderen modes, let his wisdom and Penetration be never so great, would be puzzled to account for.

From this motive alone, of a Strict observance of Ceremonies, we shall find a great man, as proud as Lucifer himself, bowing to one, whom he thinks in every respect, Infinitely his Inferior, and professing himself || his most ready and obedient humble Servant.

From a nice observance of these rules of ceremony, we shall see two courtiers, fraught with mutual hatred, and envy, bowing to, and grinning at each other as they meet, and, by the Grimace of their outward behaviour, they would appear to a man, that knew no better, to be linked together in the Strictest ties of friendship.

Among the fair Sex, ceremony is a mighty favorite, in all their undertakings and proceedings; it is a constant attendant on their visits to one another; their whole discourse is Interlarded with it, and, where they meet in knots or Clubs, in routs, or at balls, so much time must be bestowed, in

---

(a) Doctor Kirkpatric, in the Dedication of his poem Called *A Sea piece*.[3]

3. See Dr. J[ames] Kirkpatrick, *The Sea-Piece. A Narrative, Philosophical and Descriptive Poem* (London, 1750), which recounts a voyage from Europe to America. Kirkpatrick resided in Charleston, S.C., and also published several medical works (particularly on smallpox inoculation) with which Hamilton was probably familiar.

putting the Company into proper order, and Araingement, and, if the least Slip or error is made, in the Ceremonies, of Entering, going out, or sitting down, it proves often the Important Cause of many endless disgusts and Squabbles, which frequently are not confined to that tender Sex among themselves, but the Growing discord, spreads it's Contagion among the Gentlemen and *petits maitres,* and sets the brothers, fathers and Uncles of these fair ones a Cutting one another's throats, or at least, makes them bear towards one another, The most Consummate Contempt Spite & hatred.

The Great use and Emolument of Ceremonies, in this Luxurious and effeminate age is evident, when one Considers, that virtue has become a Name, and religion an outward form and farce, consisting among many, in Screw'd up faces, and morose Countenances, and among a few who pretend to more freedom and Gaiety, in using Certain garbs and trinkets, and in putting the body into Certain || postures, so that Ceremony is now the only Succedaneum for Religion and virtue, and each might now with more propriety be called decent ceremonies to save appearances, and convenient Cloaks to Cover the Iniquities of mankind, let therefore, the now missapplied words of *Virtue* and *Religion,* be altogether Exploded, and the Significant word *Ceremony* be used for both. [174]

For example, a gentleman goes to Church, kneels down, holds his hat before his face, sets his lips a wagging, as if muttering a devout prayer, reads and sings a Psalm, makes the proper responses, mutters over certain forms of prayers, and forms of Creeds, like a Schoolboy conning his lesson, bows at Certain passages in the Service, or to Certain ladies and Gentlemen in Church, turns his face to the altar, throws his eyes up to the Cieling, holds up his hands, that Gentleman, you may properly say, is very devoutly ceremonious, or religious, and the whole, at least the greatest part of his religion Consists in Ceremony, The same may be said of a Lady, only the fan comes in the place of the hat, and the Curtsey for the bow, which Curtsey also, is often bestowed by our fair devotees, on things human and divine promiscuously.

As for Virtue, if a Gentleman wants to appear open, Generous, benevolent, humane, Courteous, Civil, Social and polite, the Instructions of his dancing master, if well observed, and Carefully practised in his Childhood, will make him a perfect adept, *a la moderne* || in all these amiable virtues, in the Judgement of this polite and discerning age, for then, he can enter a room, with a jantee air,[4] walk accross the floor with a becoming grace, make a very civil and easy bow, and say, with a proper Gesticula- [175]

---

4. Obsolete form of *jaunty.*

tion—O lord ma'am—Lord Sir—Ma'am, I adore your Charms—Sir, I am ever your most obedient—pray good Sir pardon my Importunity—your Conversation is so Engaging—your manner so violently polite—Ma'am, That's Charming!—Thats admirable e'gad!—permit me to serve you ma'am —'tis a pleasure above all pleasures!—excuse me Sir—'fore George, your goodness puts me to the blush!—My lord, I am altogether yours,—Demme my Lord—Your grace may Command me at all times—Can any man Ma'am, gaze on these Charms & not be in extasies—*O mon Dieu, pardonne moi madame!*—Sir, your taste is excellent,—all people of fashion admire it,—and rat me, all that know any thing of politeness must own that people of fashion are the best Judges—Lard Ma'am, Miss Jenny is a Celestial Creature,—She plays like an angel on the *haspicod*—I am in raptures, I am in heaven when I hear her,—good God, what Charms, what Graces— I affirm, that a Gentleman furnished with these excellent tropes, and figures of Eloquence, accompanied with Certain easy and Genteel contorsions of the body, which are all but so many Ceremonies and forms studied and got by rot, will pass with most for a very accomplished and polite person, and, his virtues will shine || in the eyes of all beholders, as bright as the Diamond on his little finger, or the buckles in his Shoes, and, if any moderen author, was to pen a dialogue among half a dozen such accomplish'd Gentlemen, as many Consistent Sentences might probably be culled from it as from a dialogue between half a dozen of the worthy Inhabitants of the Great house in Moorfields.[5]

Virtue among the Ladies is much the same as among the Gentlemen, being Intirely made up of Ceremony, for example, a lady displays a great deal of benevolence in deigning to visit another lady, as she pays her a decent respect, and puts her upon an equality with herself, by discoursing over a dish of tea with her, on an Infinity of triffles, and, tho there be no real friendship, or no personal regard between the Visitor and visited, yet the keeping up the form and Ceremony of going to see one another, turn about, shows a benevolence and respect, Sufficient to be stiled virtue in any moderen lady, and tho these angels, frequently in their visiting Clubs, may talk Scandal, yet there can be no harm in it, for as their thoughts flow out generally at random, without being one moment digested, before uttered, there can be no *Malice prepense* in them (as the Lawyers stile it in their Indictments) and therefore are not Criminal. But there is a thing Called virtue, which that Sex Claim as their peculiar property, which many of them

---

5. Bethlem Royal Hospital, popularly known as Bedlam, was at one time located in Moorfields, an outlying section of London.

Chuse to call by the name of Reputation or Rep, for the conveniency of || utterance, this *rep:* is a very different thing in the fair Sex, from what it is in men, among whom it often assumes the name of *Honor,* and requires a different method to preserve and keep it Intire, the Smarts Indeed of the male Sex, commonly guard it with a Sword, which dangles at their Side, but the ladies, being of a softer metal and more delicate composition, chuse to preserve theirs by outward appearances, and Certain precise Ceremonies and forms; for instance, many of these nice and virtuous prudes, would as soon be Catched in bed with a man, as be seen by any fop or fellow whatsoever, unlaced, or in a loose dishabille, and should a blunt fellow speak a word out of Joint in their hearing, which they may Imagine has a filthy meaning, tho none such was intended by the Speaker, they will pretend to blush up to the ears, and pronounce him a rude unmannerly Clown, they will study all the prim postures to put their bodies and limbs into, when they appear in the Company of the other Sex, and lace themselves almost to a degree of Suffocation, in order to show that decency and modesty peculiar to their Sex, and should any fool or philosopher laugh at them for their preciseness, they will pronounce him either a rude or a leud[6] fellow, They would not be seen to look at a man for a million of worlds, and, for any of the other Sex to touch their hand, finger, toe, or pretend to Salute them, or so much, as to brush their Garments in passing by them, is abominably Immodest and rude, they will Colour if one talks of a || bed or a pair of breeches, and many words of a dubious Sound they are Scrupulous of pronouncing, the virtue of these ladies is so very limber and light, that, like a feather, the least breath blows it away, so pure and polite that like a mirror, the smallest blowing upon sullies it, so delicate and Sharp, that like a Sea nettle, it cannot bear handling without breaking to pieces, stinging the fingers of the fool that fumbles with it, and therefore we leave it here to stand upon it's own legs.

But tho the whole Sex are not so Squeamishly nice as these prudes Just now described, with regard to their virtue, yet we may safely say, that the greater number of our better Sort of females, as they are called, place their virtue and Integrity on mere forms and Ceremonies, & all this is owing to that care, which the prudent mothers bestow upon their hopeful daughters, who, as soon as they are able to walk and Chatter, teach them to admire the elegance of dress, and the Charms of a forced Shape, to pinch up their tender bodies in whalebone, and some having with great care made Christians of them, by teaching them Creeds and Catechisms, and carrying them

---

6. Unlettered, or untaught.

to Church, to look about them, they set their Curiosity and desires a gadding after the young fellows, by either reading them grave lectures to shun and abominate their Company, or Intirely leaving them to do, Just as they please, but by the bye, never neglecting to train them up Carefully in all the punctillios of Ceremony and prudery, by which their wit and Judgement, are modelled in the same taste, as their Shape and dress, and, I have been Informed, by such as have had leisure to study the Sex || and understand them, that they would much rather Chuse to be retired with a precise prude in a grove, or a private Chamber, than with a professed Romp, as finding much easier access, to partake of the Charms of the first than of the latter.

It would be an endless task to treat of the use of Ceremonies in all the degrees of human life, how they have gained footing among potentates and princes, In Embassies and treaties between nation and nation, In august Societies in their wise and deep deliberations, in high Courts of Justice, in universities and Schools, and, whom I ought to have mentioned first, even among those of the Sacred Cloth, will appear to every person, who takes the trowble to peruse our moderen histories, and their general use and reception, I think, is a convincing argument of their General utility.

In fine, it seems manifest, that the main Criterion whereby to Judge of the degrees of mankind are Ceremonies, these alone distinguish the high and great from the Low and Inconsiderable, for, as virtue and merit, Learning and good Sense (which, as some have Justly enough observed, are the real qualities, for which men ought to be esteemed, that is, one man ought to take the precedence of another, according to the quantum he possesses of these valuable qualifications) come not under the Cognizance of the grosser Senses, so, as at all times to be clearly discerned and distinguished by the bulk of mankind, and perhaps have less reality in || nature than some good natured philosophers, are apt to Imagine, it is necessary that something should be put in their place, of a more palpable nature, capable to strike the Senses of all mankind alike, and awake their attention that they may give honor to whom honor is due, and distinguish the Lord from the plebeian, the Lady from the Chambermaid, the Judge from the Constable, the Bishop from the Deacon and the parson from the Curate, That is, pay them those marks of distinction and deference, which their ranks and Stations require, and this very thing is Ceremony. Ceremony! that Idol of the moderens! That prototype or representative of Nobility, wisdom, Learning and piety, that Glorious peageant that adorns our Churches, inhabits our palaces, spreads its Influence o'er our high Courts of Justice, Influences all with it's power, as the Sun does with his rays, and even Gains footing in our Clubs and Nocturnal meetings.

I know that the Quakers, who prefess themselves a plain people, strip'd of all forms and ceremonies, in their places of worship and private Conversation, will object to my reasoning in favor of ceremonies, and perhaps call it unchristian, deviating from the truth, and savoring of the whore of Babylon; But I must beg their pardon, if I take the liberty to assert, that they have their Ceremonies as well as others, The fashion of the Broad brim'd hat, and the plain and buttonless coat, with the *Thee* and the *Thou* in Conversation, The Silent meeting, the Shaking of hands at parting, and the Lamentable tone of voice in their preaching and praying, are as arrant forms and Ceremonies, as are the mitres, bands, Gowns, Surplices, altars, Chalices and fonts, now used || by our national Church of England as by Law Established. [181]

The Nations that are the most free from Ceremony in these our times, I believe to be the Hotentots and the wild Indians of America, The first have their Ceremony of wearing Sheep Guts round their legs and bodies, and the more Stink and ordure they have about them the higher their quality, in this they may resemble people of high quality in a politer nation, whose luxurious way of living distinguishes them in the same manner as the Sheep gut does the Hotentot, I know of no other Ceremony peculiar to these barbarous africans, but that of their playing on a hum-strum, walking in a String like Geese, and worshiping Insect flies; In all which also, they are Imitated by politer nations, vizt: by our Courtiers and their dependants, for they follow one anothers bums in a String, humstrum the same formal Speeches over again and again, and worship volatile and light vanities.

As for the American Indians, their Ceremonies are what are Called, huskenawing, Pawwawing, Matchicomico, war dance, and funeral obsequies.

In the first, to wit their huskenawing, they give their young men a Certain root or plant, and pen them up in a Sort of Coop for some hours, till the Drug, which occasions madness, looses its effect, and they recover their Senses, the Consequence of which is that they then become men, and forget all their Childish tricks, we have something like the same Ceremony || among our polite young Smarts of fashion, when a young madcap of an heir, is penn'd up by a Surgeon in his Chamber for some weeks, and foams the mouth as if he was mad, but this Severe operation has not the effect that the Indian drug is said to have, of making them forget their Childish Tricks, for as soon as they get abroad, they fall to practising the same Childish tricks again. [182]

The Paw-wawing is a Ceremony of worshiping the Devil, that he may do them no harm, there is something very like this also among polite people, for it is common with them to worship the Rising Sun, and, if we Consider the Sun as a prince, we must Consider Lucifer as his prime minister, or harbinger, and as it is granted by all, that the most effectual way to secure the favor of a prince, is to get first in favor with the prime minister, so, of Consequence, the worshiper of the Rising Sun must worship Lucifer first, which every one knows, is the proper name of the Devil, only our polite Idolaters in this case, pay a greater Compliment to the Devil than the barbarous ones do, for they worship him not as the latter, that they receive no harm at his hands, but that he may do them good offices.

Matchicomico, is the Ceremony of their Counsel of State, being Composed of their old men, sitting squat in a Circle, If I might be allowed here to pun upon an Indian word, I would say, that our polite Councils of State, very much resemble those Indian Councils, for the members that Compose them, are Comically matched.

[183] Their war dance, is a furious agitation with va- ‖ rious agitations and Contorsions of the body round a fire to the Sound of a drum, made of a deers skin streched upon a kettle, the dancers wearing a Sort of antic dress, being hung round with deers toes and fox tails, our moderen masquerades come nighest to this Ceremony.

In their funeral obsequies, they paint a ridiculous Carracatura of a human face, upon a deer Skin streched on a hoop, for the effigie of the Deceased, which bears not the least resemblance to him, or Indeed to any natural face, and the female priestesses, pick the flesh from the bones of the dead body; This is very well Imitated in our polite funeral Ceremonies, when Epitaphs are wrote on the defunct, giving him a Certain Chimerical Character, which bears no resemblance to his real one, or Indeed to any Character in nature, and when knots of females show their regard to their dead friend and neighbour, by pulling to pieces his real Character, to make room for the Epitaph monger, to furnish him with a fictitious one.

Having thus Briefly shown the universal use of Ceremony among all Classes of mankind, and display'd some of the Chief reasons, why it becomes useful, I hope it will be easily granted me, without further trowble or expence of words, that it is of Singular use and Emolument in *Clubs,* as those nocturnal assemblies, Constitute a Considerable part of mankind, and are Composed of men of all ranks and degrees.

[184] The modes and Ceremonies then, Commonly practised in Clubs, of proposing Loyal, political and amorous toasts, ‖ of drinking Kelty[7] in bumpers, of using Caps, Chaplets, elbow chairs, white rods, mallets, badges

---

7. *Kelty* is a term denoting the complete draining of a glass of liquor.

and great Seals, have all their particular use and Significancy, and serve not only to distinguish the members, in their several degrees of dignity, one from another, but to amaze the world, and Inspire an opinion of the grandure & Importance of these Clubs; and therefore, Ceremonies in Clubs, are as necessary and becoming as any where else, however much they may be ridiculed by humdrum fellows, pragmatical Coxcombs, or precise fops.

Chapter II

An account of the Sneezing trespass by Negroe Peter, a short Revival of the Conundrums, Spatterdash Wou'dbe Esqrs facetious Conversation, protest of Slyboots pleasant Esqr, Election of a longstanding member.

Custom has established some punctillios among us moderens which, it is thought by many, the ancients were perfect Strangers to; for example, the Servant man or maid of a Gentleman or Lady of fashion, among us moderens, must not presume to sneeze, cough, Laugh, or suffer any other explosion of air from his body, which creates noise, in the presence of his, or her master or Lady, because it Interrupts polite Conversation, offends the tender delicacy, and horribly grates the Exquisite auditory nerves of persons of breeding & fashion, which nerves now a days, are compounded of finer and more tender fibres than those of which ancient Ears were fabricated, or even the Ears of our moderen vulgar, to whose coarse organs, noise is music, & vice versa, to the others, music is noise, || and Indeed [185] there is one Sort of Ærial Explosion, that is fundamentally Shoking in all Civil and polite Companies, which both affects the ear and nose disagreeably, and which no man of the least breeding or good manners will suffer to escape him voluntarily, unless matters can be so managed, as to procure for it a silent exit, or it can be made perspire in a whisper, which is sometimes the Case, and, in this Case, the Delicacy of the Ear not being offended, the trespass upon the nose is easier forgiven, because the procession of odor, is not so direct or rectilinear as that of Sound, and therefore, the place whence it comes, cannot so easily be ascertained, at least, the Naturalists tell us so, why these punctillios, unknown to the plainness of the ancients, should have gained such firm footing among the Moderens, cannot so easily be accounted for, unless we admit that the moderens have Cultivated the arts of politeness more, and are much Greater refiners upon the Delicatesse of manners, having Invented particular Genteel and Ingenious modes of hawking, Spitting, Sneezing and blowing the nose, and delivered rules for picking the teeth & ears, to which we Intirely owe, the moderen Inventions of the handkerchef and tweezer Case, utensils, nicely adapted to Gather Certain Excrements of the body from their proper reservoires, to be Carried about in a Gentlemans or Ladie's pocket, we find nothing like this refinement among the Ancients, unless you Call their Lachrimatories such, being small vials, In which they kept the tears, shed for their Dead friends.

[186]   To the highest pitch of this moderen delicatesse had the || ancient and honorable Tuesday Club now arrived, in so much as they could not bear to hear any one sneeze, even in the next room, this humor, it was thought by some, they affected, in order to appear *people of fashion,* as it had been objected to the Society, by some, who were not their Stanch friends, of a Coxcombish turn, that they were an Insignificant Club, there being no Gentlemen *of fashion* among them. This overnice regard to punctillios, which has now become so much the Characteristic of people of fashion, seems to me to be but of very late date, and therefore extremely moderen, for upon searching our English History I find no traces of this Genteel Gout, till after the days of King Charles II., for Certain it is, that that Monarch of facetious memory, who did not Inherit one grain of his father's piety, or his Grandfather's Pedantry, was not in the least wedded to these Punctillios, nay, he showed rather a professed aversion to them, as appears, by his ordering an Inscription to be put in great Golden Characters, over the door of one of his presence Chambers, on hearing of the misfortune of a poor Gentleman, who had miserably lost his life by retaining a fart in the royal presence, The Inscription run thus, *Here farting is free,* this showed the great goodness of this monarch, who was also, of so Clubical a disposition, that he would Condescend to get drunk with a Lord mayor, and get poxed with a Lord Rochester,[1] If then such plainness and freedom was

[187]   practised by this Sagacious monarch, || it must have been practised by his courtiers, and therefore by people of fashion, hence it is only since the Commencement of this present Century, that the grand gout for extreme delicatesse has made its appearance among people of fashion In Great Britain, and, whence It came, we cannot positively say; France, we can by no means give the honor of the Invention to, for it is well known that the true delicatesse in behaviour, is so little Cultivated there, in this particular, that even the most reserved and modest among their Ladies of quality, keep male valets de chambre to dress and undress them, and that, the Ladies and

---

1. John Wilmot, earl of Rochester (1647–1680), was an English poet and notorious libertine.

Gentlemen there, perform the mysterious Rites of the Goddess Cloacina,[2] Conjointly, or In Company, but it is time to proceed with our History.

At Sederunt 197, Tunbelly Bowzer Esqr, being H:S: The Secretary reported in Club, that Slyboots pleasant Esqr and himself had that day waited upon the honorable Carlo Nasifer Jole Esqr, the President, and presented to his honor the Condolatory verses, Intituled *Carmen dolorosum*, which was well received, by his honor, and that his honor was pleased to appoint Tunbelly Bowzer Esqr, his deputy for the night, but Mr Bowzer desired to be excused, alledging, that the office of H:S: alone, was abundantly Sufficient to employ all his diligence and Care, the Club yeilding to Mr Bowzers Request, the Chancellor made some bustle about his right to assume the Chair, but was disappointed, for Prim Timorous Esqr was elected president for the night, who, having been at a former Sederunt appointed Conundrum master, not only executed his office well as deputy president, but, with abundance of wit and good humor, gave a Conundrum, which being resolved by Crinkum Crankum Esqr, the deputy Chearfully drank a bumper; this was the first and last Conundrum, that was uttered from the presidential Chair in the Club, and is unfortunatly lost by the neglegence of the Secretary. I cannot but here observe upon the modesty and Self denyal of Tunbelly Bowzer Esqr, in Refusing the honorable place of deputy president, as it affords a very good Contrast to the ambition and petulence of the Chancellor, and Indeed this gentleman seemed to be the least Solicitous of all the longstanding members about places, titles, or a feather in the Cap, his genius being only turned towards the bowl and facetious Conversation.

At Sederunt 198 March 20, 1753, Prim Timorous Esqr, being H:S: The Club showed so much regard to his honor the president's verbal commission, at last Sederunt, as to set Tunbelly Bowzer Esqr, in the Chair, and that Gentleman's own modesty and Self denyal, was also a prime Cause of his promotion to that honorable Seat, tho' some are of opinion that he was appointed deputy also for this Sederunt by Special verbal message from his honor.

While the Club was sitting smoking, and Conversing about momentuous matters, an excessive Sneezing was heard in the Chamber adjoining the Club room, which very much disturbed and Interrupted their deliberations, upon this, the Serjeant at arms was sent to apprehend the offender whoever he was, and bring him before the Club. Prim Timorous Esqr,

---

2. The goddess of sewers.

upon receiving these orders went out, and returning brought with him one Negroe Peter, a little old Crooked fellow, whom he presented to the Club as the Criminal, he was Strictly examined by the Club upon oath, he having been first Solemnly swore upon a Glass of rum, after a long and learned course of Cross Questions and answers, concerning flatulent eruptions upwards and downwards, he was found Guilty of Sneezing, and Sentenced to sing a Song, which he did with great approbation, and was dismissed, with an admonition to behave more discreetly for the future.

Several facetious Conundrums were produced in Club at this Sederunt, by Prim Timorous Esqr, the H:S: and Conundrum master, one of which was solved by his honor the Deputy President, and this was the first and last Conundrum that ever was solved in Club from the Chair, for which the H:S: Chearfully drank a bumper, these Conundrums, by the negligence of the Secretary, are Irrecoverably lost, but to make a mends for this loss, Spatterdash Wou'dbe Esqr, coming into the Club by Chance, || produced some very Ingenious conundrums, which will stand as Specimens of that Gentleman's great and Surprizing wit to future ages, these were

Conundrums by Spatterdash Woudbe Esqr

Why is my Snuffbox like a man in need?
Ans: Because I *begged* it.
Why is this Club book like a pair of Sheets?
Ans: Because it wants to be *unfolded*.

Which Conundrums, with their answers, plainly demonstrate, that the epithet *witty*, is not Improperly given to the visage of the aforesaid Gentleman in the late Club poem Intituled *Carmen dolorosum,* where is the following Line.

To where his witty visage Woudbe wears.

This was the last appearance the Conundrums made in the Club, for after this, they never were again Introduced, making their final exit with Prim Timorous Esqr, Serjeant at arms, who left the Club at this Sederunt.

It is uncertain, what were this gentleman's motives for leaving the Club, in so abrupt a manner, tho' some Conjecture that he was Induced to it by two reasons, the first, that he thought the office of Conundrum master to be too weighty for him to bear, and that his natural talents, were not adapted to it, || but this is looked upon to be mere Conjecture, only. The Second, that he conceived he had met with very ill usage from his honor the president and Sir John, and in some measure from the Club, in their not supporting him in the execution of his office as Serjeant at arms, for, at this very Sederunt he reported in Club, That at the desire of Sir John the Champion (who, he understood was authorised by the Club to proceed as he did) he had Sealed the memorial of the Grand Committee, carefully up in a neat pacquet, and dispatched it, with a Careful hand to his honor the president, who Contumaciously refused to receive it, and sent back word with the Messanger, that the Serjeant at arms was very Idle for concerning himself in any such dirty business,—That after this, by the same authority and orders, pursuant to the directions of the Grand Committee, upon being told by Sir John, that his honor the president was refractory and unmanageable, he Gathered together a posse of Stout men & true, and between the hours of ten and eleven o clock at night peaceably beset his honor the presidents house, summoning him, in the name, and by the authority of the Club, to surrender himself, and, that this was done in the civilest manner Imaginable, with as little Racket and noise as could possibly be, when a multitude are Gathered together, and, that his honor the president, Instead of obeying his orders, looked out at a window in the Gavel End of his Castle, standing westward, and loaded him with abundance of billingsgate Language, Calling him and his posse, Sorry fellows and Scoundrels, swearing and Cursing like a dragoon, || and scolded like a butter [192] whore, Commanding Don John Charlotto, his Gentleman usher, to go for the town Constable, to apprehend him and his posse, and also ordered the said Don John, to throw these Scoundrells, (him and his posse meaning) over the fence, that all these affronts and Scoffs, and all this Ill usage, in the way of his duty, and in the execution of his office, he met with, and yet Sir John, the Champion, tho' he had acquainted him of it, had never given himself any trowble about supporting him, of which usage he Complained to the Club.

This Report the Club took no notice of, which, it is thought, so disgusted the Serjeant at arms, that he, Immediatly thereupon left the Society, without taking any formal leave, but laid hold of the Benefit of Law 13th to Clear himself of the Club.

As for Sir John, it was apparent, he was so far from acting vigorously, and to the full extent of his Commission, in this affair, that he still covertly play'd into the presidents hand, and Continued to be of the Cabinet council; thus dropt the bold push, which the Grand Committee made for Clubical liberty, and the Secretary, tho' he had artifice enough to set the Club upon mischief, found, that his Influence fell far short of Bringing his Schemes to perfection.

At Sederunt 199, Mr Secretary Scribble being H:S: || and Philo Dog- [193]

maticus Esqr deputy in the Chair, his honor the president, sent a verbal message to the Club, which was delivered by the Secretary, ordering, that Mr Protomusicus Neverout, should take the Chair, and, that in Case of his absence, Slyboots Pleasant Esqr, should have that honor. But the said Slyboots Pleasant Esqr, (The other Gentleman being absent) peremptorily refused the Chair, upon these terms, alledging That he little expected (considering all things,) that the president would have treated him with so much Slight and Indignity, as to have postponed him to Proto musicus Neverout, that as for his part he was as easy about Chairs as other folks, and Cared not, provided his Chair was easy, whether it was Elevated a Step above other Chairs or not, nor did it give him any great uneasiness, tho' his head should want a Certain Covering, which some people might perhaps think an ornament, and others a burlesque upon Canopies, nevertheless, he presumed to think, that his respectful deportment to his honor the president, and Steady opposition to the enimies of his power, and prerogative, might have Claimed other guess usage[3] from his said honor, than a public and premeditated affront, and Insult, that he never to his remembrance engaged in any of these tumultuous broils and Seditious altercations, which have so often disturbed the repose of his honor, nor had || he the least hand, in that furious Commotion, at the house of Mr Serjeant Timorous, when his honr: lost the Seal, lost the Canopy, lost the Chair of State, had like to have lost his arm, and did actually lose a good part of a very fine pair of ruffles; he declares that these things are not mentioned, with any view of reviving the odium of his honor against the authors of these outrages (his honor's Christian forgiveness of whom, he much Commendeth) but to show the part he acted, or rather did not act, in these perilous and tempestuous times, to show, that when all was uproar and Confusion, he behaved with all the Calmness of a Philosopher, not making himself a party in the Clamor and violence of these licentious and pretended republicans; he further observeth, that his honor seems to have adopted the maxim of a Certain great monarch,[(a)] a namesake of his, who declared, that it was not his policy to serve his friends, for his friends would still remain so, but that it was his business to make his enimies his friends, how far this observation is applicable to his honor, and Mr Proto musicus Neverout, is left to future ages to determin, by whom alone, the actions of Great Rulers and potentates are Impartially Canvassed, but, for these weighty reasons, he declines the Sham honor Intended him, positively aff- || irming, that for his part

(a) K: Charles II.

3. Other kind of usage.

(however great his veneration for his honor the president may be,) he will not suffer himself to be Contemptuously treated, or pissed upon, by any president, or Caped head in the universe, nor submit to the haughty petulence of any Proto Musicus whatsoever, and Insists, that the Secretary should enter this his protest, in the Club records.

This protest being made In club, and ordered to be entered, the Chancellor of Course took the Chair, and the proceedings of last Sederunt were Read, The Club however, were somewhat Surprized at the passionate Expressions of Slyboots Pleasant Esqr, in the above protest, and could not Conceive, how a gentleman of his easy carriage and good humor could be so puffed up at a triffle, he never having been seen angry with the Club, or with the president but once before this, in the affair relating to the Club's money box, but many thought (and very probably they Judged right) that the Righteous Spirit of this good Gentleman, was trowbled at the preposterous actions of his honor the president, in promoting and honoring a Gentleman, whom both he and the Club knew, could not claim the least merit from his former Conduct and actions, or even from any Clubical abilities he was possessed of.

At this Sederunt, Mr Crinkum Crankum, an honorary member, applied to be made a long- || standing member of the Club, and the ballots being put round, he was unanimously elected, and being Confirmed in form by Jonathan Grog Esqr, he took his Seat in Club accordingly as a longstanding member, then being desired to make a Congratulatory Speech, to the Deputy president and Club, he declared, that he thought the best Speech he could make, was to say nothing, but the Club Informed him, that such a Speech would be expected the first time his honor the president made his appearance In Club, and this Gentleman, had Indeed, occasion, after this to make many Speeches to the Chair, but not of the Congratulatory Sort, the validity of his election being a long time under dispute, and a point of Squabble between his honor the president and the Club, tho' it was at last amicably settled and Concluded in his favor.

[196]

Chapter III

The humdrum Sederunt, Metamorphosis of the bag and Seal, Letter of the Club to his honor the President, with the answer.

Wit and humor is like the ebbing and flowing of the Sea, sometimes it runs high in Conversation, and at other times subsides, or sinks very Low, and as the Ebbing and flowing of the Sea, and the brains of madmen are Governed by the moon, || so I am apt to think that wit, particularly Clubical wit, and the brains of wits, particularly the brains of Clubical wits, are Intirely governed by that Inconstant, nocturnal planet, Clubs being nocturnal assemblies, and often of an Inconstant and variable Nature, to Corroborate this proposition, I here quote a Celebrated English poet,[(a)] who, somewhere, in his voluminous works, tells us

> Great wits to madness nearly are allied,
> And thin partitions do their bounds divide.[1]

This is further evidenced, by the disposition of the ancient and honorable Tuesday Club, who at some Sederunts were extremely Smart and witty, and at others, extremely Phlegmatic and dull, this was probably owing, to the particular times of the moon, in which that Club held their Sederunts, and, I'll venture to lay an equal wager, with any person that will take me up, that, if they Consult old almanacks, as they read this History, they will find what I say to be true, and that the moon was arrived, at either her first or third quarter, or in her quadratures, at Sederunt 200, on the 17th of April 1753.

At this Sederunt it was, Philo Dogmaticus Esqr being H:S: and Slyboots Pleasant Esqr, deputy President, that the time passed away, without so much as one Clubical matter being handled || or discoursed upon, so that we cannot help observing here, that this Sederunt, was of all Sederunts the most unclubical, since the first Institution of this here ancient and honorable Club, which some Critics perhaps, in after times, will attribute to the absence of that most Ingenious and bright wit Jonathan Grog Esqr, Poet Laureat of this here Club, and on this account, I cannot help stiling this Sederunt *The Humdrum Sederunt*.

In fine, this Sederunt would have proved altogether flat and Insipid, had not the Secretary, who spared no pains to furbish up and enliven the Club at these times, produced, Just before their breaking up, a Copy of a Newgate Song, sung by Squeak Grumbleton Esqr, a Stranger, Invited to the Club at Sederunt 194, which is as follows.

(a) Dryden.

1. Hamilton is recalling these lines from *Absalom and Achitophel*: "Great Wits are sure to Madness near ally'd; / And thin Partitions do their Bounds divide" (*The Works of John Dryden*, ed. Edward Niles Hooker *et al.* [Berkeley, Calif., 1956–], II, 10, lines 163–164).

Newgate Bird Song, sung by Squeak Grumbleton Esqr[2]

As I derrik'd along, to dorse on my kin,
Young Polly the froeful I trouted,
She nailed a Cull of his tilter and Nob,
But in foiling his tatler was routed.
As I haiked along she Grappled my Shell,
She tipt me young boeman, I knew her full well,
The harman spikd after, but dam' him to hell, [199]
I plumpt him, and savd her from Limbo.

The Bus napper kinking, my mopus did seize,
But my right and left duddles I tipt him,
I darkend his daylights & sowd up his Sees,
And I up, with my dew beaters tript him.
Whilst I milld his muzzard, she nabbled his pole,
She haik'd away singing, I pick'd after moll,
She naild the Rum Codger, I milld the queer Cull,
And away she haik'd to the Cows bowsing.

Whilst snug in the kin, we sat, sluicing our Gobs,
She tipd me the Gum very Cleanly,
I swear it will never be out of my Nob,
The Brimston, she wheedled so beenly.
Round Scrag, her dear duddles, she loving did fold,
I tipt her the velvet, her daylights she rolld,
I love you, said she, for your quiddish and bold
And will dorse with my Jamie till Jamin.

Dear Molly says I, I'll dorse in your kin,
I'm a Boeman will never deceive you,
I'll Cut a been weed, to keep you in Screan,
And rumbling will pad to relieve you,
Your Darbys I dread not, death's Common to all,
Your Riders and Rumblers that Pad in the mal,
I'll shiver my trotters, at fam'd Bilboes ball
And go off like a boeman, that's quiddish.

This odd Song seemed to excite alittle Spirit of Gelasticism in the [200]

2. This song is titled "A Cant Song" in Sadler, *Muses Delight,* 178. Noting every slang term in this poem would destroy the fun—and the intended bewilderment—that comes with reading it. The more ingenious reader will know what is going on; others will be no worse off than the club members were upon hearing it.

members, tho' they understood nothing at all of the Language or dialect in which it was wrote, but the Secretary produced it alittle too late, vizt: at eleven o'Clock at night, when all the Longstanding members were in a yawning disposition.

At the following Sederunt, which was the 201, held on the first day of may 1753, Crinkum Crankum Esqr, being H:S: and the Worshipful Sir John Deputy president, the Chancellor being desired to lay the Seal and bag upon the table, he, Instead of them produced, a pair of black worsted Stockings nicely made up in a roll, at which the Club seemed very much Surprized, but his honorable worship, the deputy president, it was presumed, from the Composedness of his countenance, was of opinion, that this black worsted roll, was as good as the Real bag and Seal, and therefore suffered it to lye before him, till some dissatisfied member pilfered it, and a Strict Search being made, it was found in the pocket of Jonathan Grog Esqr, Poet Laureat.

It would require more than common wit and Ingenuity to unriddle this mysterious Proceeding of the Chancellor, who, being a man of more than ordinary Cunning and Sagacity, never did any thing In Club without a reason, but however, I will attempt it, and let the world freely Judge of my conjecture, and approve or Condemn it according to its merit.

[201] The Chancellor being of the fraternity of Free and accepted masons, was of Consequence a great admirer of mysteries and allegories, and therefore had a mind to alegorize the Great Seal, and give a lively representation of the present State of that great and Significant Club Symbol. By the Color of the Stockings, which was black, he Intended the obscurity and disgrace that this Symbol was under in Club, being utterly dispised by his honor the president, by the Stockings being rolled up, was Intended the use of that Symbol being altogether dropt, and laid aside, and, by the Roll's being made of a pair of Stockings, the Covering of the most Infimous or lowest parts of the body, vizt: the feet and legs, was signified the low and Contemptible State of that Club utensil, This probably, was the Chancellor's meaning, in Chusing a pair of black worsted Stockings to represent the great Seal, but, what was Intended by Conveying it into Jonathan Grog Esqrs pocket, unless it was to be no more a theme fit for that poet's muse, I profess I cannot conjecture.

An Address was drawn up by the Club at this Sederunt, and dispatched to his honor the president by a Special Messenger, the form of which here follows.

To The Honorable Nasifer Jole Esqr,
President of the Ancient & honorable Tuesday Club, Greeting.

May it please your Honor,

Whereas it has been represented by verbal exhibition, to this here ancient and honorable Club, now sitting at the Castle of the worshipful Sir John, being Sederunt 201, under the high stewardship of Crinkum Crankum Esqr, The worshipful and valiant Sir John knight of the Club, being deputy president, that your || honor desires to know the mind of the Club, as to fixing and determining the time of Celebrating the Ensuing anniversary,

Your honor therefore, will please to understand, that it is the mind of this here ancient and honorable Club, that the said anniversary be Celebrated Solemnized and held, upon Tuesday the 15th of this Instant May, In case your honor's health and ability of body shall permit, if otherwise, your honor is requested to fix the time of keeping the said Anniversary, on any day of the said Instant month of may, giving the Longstanding members notice thereof by means of your honor's Secretary, four days before the day fixed upon.

May the 1st 1753   Sig: p: order *Loquacious Scribble Secrty*

To which address, his honor was pleased to return the following Gracious answer in writing.

To Loquacious Scribble Esqr,
Secretary of the Ancient & honorable Tuesday Club, These.

Sir,

As you are desirous to know the time for holding the anniversary of the ancient and honorable Tuesday Club, you say, it is the mind of the Gentlemen now met, that it be held upon Tuesday the 15th Instant; as to fixing the day, which the Gentlemen seem to do, I think it is altogether Contrary to the Rules of the Club, being what I have, and shall always Strenuously Contend for, || however, as I am willing to oblige the Society in any thing within my power, it is as agreeable to me, that it be kept upon Tuesday The 15th Instant, as upon any other day, which nothing shall prevent, but want of health and ability. I congratulate Sir John on his exalted Station, and you Gentlemen, on your Choice of so worthy a deputy president, for your Society, I wish you merry and bid you farewell, and am Sir,

                       Your Humble Servant
                       Nasifer Jole.

P:S: Please to read the foregoing in presence of the Gentlemen now met, at the house of the worshpl: & valiant Sr John.

[204] This answer of the presidents, to the Club's address, seems to be wrote pritty much, in a parliamentary Stile, which Stile that honorable Gentleman now affected very much, having got it into his head, that he stood in the same relation to the Club, as the king did to the parliament, and, that no Clubical rules or Laws could pass, without his presidential fiat, this great prerogative, was only, (according to the opinion of most of the L:St: members) a Phantom of his own brain, for, it was not to be found any where in the Records, that the Club had ever bestowed any such power on their president, nay, even the Frontinbrassian articles, which gave him more largely than any other articles or Compact whatsoever, gave him no such prerogative or power, as to his Stile of the Gentlemen met, that may be easily seen thro, for his honor was Carefull not to stile that meet- ‖ ing a Club, as he looked upon the Election of Crinkum Crankum Esqr, the pretended H:S: of that meeting, to be undue and Illegal, and therefore his honor reckoned this Supper, and that punch, given by the said Crinkum Crankum Esqr, to the Longstanding members, upon the 1st of May 1753, to be a Civil treat, given by the said Gentleman, to the said L:St: members, met only as friends and acquaintances, but not as a Club, or forming a Sederunt, and that this was the reason of his honor's using, this particular Stile and Manner, in his answer to the Club's address, I am positive is true, since I had Information of it more than once from his honor's own mouth, in private Conversation with him, tho he never would declare his reasons openly in Club, but, I think it may here be made a Quere, why his honor, in the above postscript, calls the Redoubt of the valiant knight and Champion of the Club a house, seeing Castle is the proper Stile, unless he had a mind to humble, and mortify Sir John, for his late Intercourse and Conferences with the rebellious Grand Committee, as it was now Called.

Chapter IV

Celebration of the eight Anniversary, with the Anniversary ode, Speech and Music.

*Poets and orators, have been reckoned among the most darling Sons of Fame, and many have been doubtful to which to give the preference. The

---

*Vide this paragraph almost verbatim, in the 10th anniversary Speech.

the Tuesday Club [Book XII] 149

Poetry of Tyrteus,[1] saved the Lacedemonian State from ruin, and the oratory of Demosthenes, had the athen- || ians been wise, in his time, would have saved the Athenian Common wealth, from the Snares and artifices of the macedonian Philip, many Instances might be brought from ancient History, of the Great Services done to States and kingdoms by poets and orators, and also of the figure they made in Clubs, but none to excell the now living instance, in the ancient and honorable Tuesday Club, where the Exquisite poetry of Jonathan Grog Esqr, poet Laureat, and the Sublime oratory of Loquacious Scribble Esqr orator, were now the two main Supports of the dignity and Grandure of that Club, and its honorable president, Some may be puzzled, which of these two Gentlemen, to give the preference unto, but I hope they will find no difficulty, when they Consider that one thing recommends poetry beyond oratory, vizt: that it is adapted, only to the finest and most exquisite Judgement, whereas he is the best orator that pleases the *profanum vulgus*, or herd of the mobile, as witness the Ingenious and Reverend Mr George Whitefield,[2] who captivates both the great and the small mob, where ever he goes, that poetry Therefore, would be very poor, that all should approve of, if the Learned and Judicious few give the plaudite, it is Sufficient to fix the bays upon the bards pate, and, let the Illiterate throng bray like so many asses, they cannot hurt him, this is the unerring Criterion to distinguish good poetry from bad, and the Clubical performances of Jonathan Grog Esqr, always stood this test, they meeting with but || few approvers, and those of the most Clubical Judgement, we may thence safely conclude that this Ingenious Gentleman is a good Clubical poet, and takes place of the orator, in point of genius and profession, Tho' to give the orator his due, his performances were good in their kind, and very well adapted to his Subject, we shall presently exhibit a fresh Specimen of the abilities of these two Clubical Geniuses. [205] [206]

Upon the 15th of May 1753, being Sederunt 202, was Celebrated the eight Anniversary of the ancient and honorable Tuesday Club, at which were present, (besides his honor the president) 9 Regular members, two honorary, vizt: Dr Polyhistor & Captn Dio Ramble, and 4 Strangers.[3]

The members Regular and honorary Convened at the Secretaries

---

1. Tyrtaeus (fl. 7th century B.C.) was a Spartan general and poet who led the Spartans against the Messenians and whose war songs inspired his troops to victory.

2. Whitefield (1714–1770) was an English evangelist whose dynamic oratorical style and religious zeal made him the leader of the Methodists in England and a great reviver of religious sentiment in America during the Great Awakening.

3. The "Record" identifies the strangers as Capt. Samuel Wood, William Lux [of Baltimore], Mr. Wollaston, and Dr. William Lyon (see biographical sketches).

house in the Evening, and proceeded to the house of the Honorable Carlo Nasifer Jole, without any regular procession, being met at his honor's gate by Quirpum Comic Esqr, and Mr Protomusicus Neverout, They Invested themselves with their badges at the gate, and proceeded into his honor's back Court, making a grand parade, two and two a breast thro' the entry, strowed with various flowers as usual, his honor Civily met them at the Gate, and Saluted them by *Manuquassation*.+

Crinkum Crankum Esqr, came to the Club, begirt with a Sword, for some political Reasons, which the members did not then enquire into, which being drawn, was laid upon the table, by Sir John, the Champion.

The members, as usual, had a very elegant entertainment, from his honor, there being a Sumptuous Supper, and variety of liquors.

Jonathan Grog Esqr, poet Laureat, being called upon to read the Anniversary ode, after Supper, appeared with a large chaplet of Green leaves (not of bays, for he was not yet alowed by his honor to wear a Laurel wreath, tho' denominated Laureat) on his head, and standing bolt upright at the lower end of the table, in a distinct, clear, and musical voice, Read the ode as follows, vizt:

Anniversary Ode,

For the Ancient and honorable Tuesday Club, for the Year 1753. Humbly Inscribed to the Right Honorable, Carlo Nasifer Jole Esqr, President, and the Longstanding members of the said Club by

> *Their most Humble Servant,*
> *The Club's Poet Laureat*

Aria
   Sing again,
   With might and main,
The Club and Glorious Jole,
   Such a Story
   Swells with Glory
And animates each Soul.

Chorus
Come, all ye fine fidlers and Songsters so gay,
And celebrate this anniversary day,
For now with more Splendor the Sun does appear
Than on other days of the fleet rolling year,

---

4. *Manuquassation* is Hamilton's invention for *handshake* (a quassation is a shaking).

To Jole and his Club Sir,
    Goes the Drum dub adub Sir,
And the trump' with shrill Sound, ascends the arch'd Skies,
    The flute and the Viol
    Put voices to trial,
And oer the wide Welkin, Jole's fame loudly flies.
    Recitativo
In grand consistory, the members met,
Jole, at their head, in throne majestic set,
Say, bard, whoe're a nobler Junto saw,
Who Rules like Jole, or who like Jole gives law,
All other Presidents to him are Scrubs,
And his is Sure, the paragon of Clubs.
    Aria Jiga
    While the valiant Sir John,
    Sits close by his Chair o,
    His honor fears none,
    Nor here-o, nor there-o.
    For his Shining Sword,
    The best blade in nature,
    Cuts off like a gourd
    The head of each traitor.
    General Grand Chorus [209]
    Then all with one voice
    And Turned up Eyes,
    Let's sing and rejoice
    Praising Jole to the Skies,
O Jole, Mighty Jole, tis thee we proclaim,
With voice drum and trumpet, we'll sound forth thy name.
    Of Rulers the Chief
    And presidents too,
    Our Joy and relief
    Comes only from you,
    Then away with all grief,
    We'll be merry and true,
Then Huzza for great Jole, & huzza for great Jole!
A blessing light on his magnanimous Soul,
    With pleasure we'll dub,
    Him head of our Club,
And toss off his health in a full flowing bowl.

The Poet having read the ode, drank, and received a Plaudite.

Then the orator standing up, pronounced the Anniversary oration as follows.

Anniversary Speech

Honorable Sir,

When I survey the Circle of faces here present, and among the rest, your honor's awful, august and venerable face, That face, which in it's exalted Station, has now, for these eight years, shed a Smiling and benign Influence upon this here ancient and honorable Society, I cannot || help being Inspired with a peculiar Sort of awe and reverence, which, I believe it is Impossible, for any Group or assemblage of faces, but that of your honor, and those of these here long Standing members to Inspire me with.

Replete then, with this here peculiar reverence and awe, which properly may be called Clubical, I appear again, upon this Joyful anniversary occasion, to exercise my talents as a Club orator, and also to exercise the patience of your honor, and the Longstanding members of this here ancient and honorable Club.

It has been a Saying, of some one or other, wise man or fool, (it matters not which) *Mens in patinis;*[5] which expresses a person that is absent, and not at all attentive to the Subject in hand, and, as I cannot more properly translate this ancient adage, than by saying, *One whose head goes a wool Gathering,* I hope this is not the Case at present with your honor, and these here longstanding members, that is, you do not allow your thoughts to go a roving upon something else, while I, your Club orator, am exercising my lungs, to harangue you, upon this here Solemn anniversary occasion, if so, I cannot presume to attribute it to any other Cause, than the Insignificancy of your Orator, who, tho' his Subject be copious, and Inexhaustible, yet comes far short, in parts and abilities, to fram Speeches, capable of fixing the attention of your honor and these here Gentlemen, far be it from me then, to say that Culinary Cares and anxieties in your honor, that the thoughts of these here longstanding members on this night's rich Entertainment, The Savory viands, prepared in his honor's kitchen, The Generous Juice of the Grape, and the fermented Spirit of Ceres, ready to follow the extraction of the Cork, and dance & sparkle, thro' the Christalline pellucidity of the Glasses, the Spiritous || and Sweet produce of the Islands, blended with the refrigerating acid Juice and water, which Constitute that divine liquor Called Punch, far, Oh! far be it from me, to pro-

---

5. "His mind is on the dishes."

nounce, that the thoughts of enjoying these delicacies in plenty, withdraws your attention from my Speeches, let it rest here, that the orator is unequal to the Audience, and Incapable to entertain to any purpose, this here Learned, Judicious, Sagacious, and Capacious Club.

However, as something must be said, according to custom, on this here great occasion, out it must come at all risques, and therefore, without farther preamble, I shall fall to it tooth and nail.

Let us then first of all, Greet and Salute the happy day, this Gaudiferous, Letiferous, Salutiferous and luciferous day, This day, I say, in the month of may, when nature in bright array, does all her charms display, and seems to wanton and play, in the Suns delightful ray, while the musical birds on every Spray, warble a Sweet lay,—oh! what more can I say or display, to the honor of this here delicious and propitious anniversary day.

But from whence does this here day derive all it's Glory? whence its honor and renown? from whom, and by what manner does it receive such a lustre, such a dignity, as to be worthy of a place, in the elaborate Almanac of Jonathan Grog Esqr, where it stands, among other Illustrious days, in fair Capital Characters, verily, we need not go much about the bush to discover this; For who but your Honor, and this here ancient, and honorable Club, could dignify the Day, and make it Conspicuous among other days, for, your honor and this here Club, I say, have Convey'd renown to this day, but, in a particular || manner your honor, who art the Eminent head of these here longstanding members, The foundation Stone of their Constitution, the Cap-stone of their Structure, their essence and quintessence, their entity and Identity, their Alpha and Omega, their extreme and middle, their *Summum bonum,* Their *Sine qua non,* their *ne plus ultra,* the Epitome of the whole, the Volume or Scrowl in which is contained an abstract of all the Antiquity, honor, dignity and wisdom, of this here ancient and honorable Club [Sir Jno: Phogh! damn the fustian] in which we may read, all the heroic, brave, and valorous Exploits, of the worshipful and valiant Sir John, all the wise and equitable decrees, of the venerable Chancellor, all the fire, Sublimity and Civility of the Poet Laureat and master of Ceremonies, all the Quavering, trilling, warbling and melodious vociferation of protomusicus, all the Eloquence, action, prolixity and verbosity of the orator, and all the Collected Clubical virtues pertaining to the other Longstanding members, and so forth. [212]

Now, at this time, your honor will please to observe, that every thing smiles upon your honor, and these here longstanding members, on this Important occasion; all looks gay around us, nature assumes her most pleasant aspect, the air itself breaths odors, and delights, wafted upon the light wings of Zephyr, The verdure of the fields regales the Eye, Flora unfolds

[213] her Shining robe, and exhibits to your honor, even in your honor's well Cultivated Garden, all her Charming variety of Colors, and not only delights your honors eye, with a Splendid mixture, but Salutes your honor's nose, with a multiplicity of Sweet Smells, preferable to all ‖ the odoriferous Smells and Sweet Spices of Arabia; these Sweets surround your honor, and your Longstanding members in such a variety, in such abundance, that they seem to contend, one with another, which shall most gratify your honor upon this Solemn and Joyful occasion, and Surely, nature, with reason and propriety, puts on this pleasant countenance, and pours upon us, decked with all these blandishments and delights, as being your honor's proper mistress and paramour, for, all must own your honor to be the miracle and admiration of nature, the Narcissus of the age, the Nonpareil and paragon of presidents, the Sole head and regulator of all Clubs [Sir Jno: oh!—oh!—] the most peerless patron, by whom all presidents and Clubs, ought to be regulated and formed [Chanc: Ha, ha, ha.]

When I perlustrate your honor, exalted on that there Chair of State, at the head of these here longstanding members, methinks, I see Jupiter [Sr: Jno: Damm'e if I'll stay to hear any more of this Stuff] presiding over the heathen Gods, who, as the ancient poets have described him, was of a majestic, noble, and Commanding aspect, who, with his single nod, could shake the heavens and the earth, who with knitting his brows, could daunt the whole assembly, Just so it is with your honor, and these here members, for with a single motion, your honor can Command and regulate them, and turn them which ever way you please, as an expert pilot turneth a Ship, in the tumultuous Seas, for not even the terrible arms of the epouvantable Sir John, not all the wisdom and political Craft of the Chancellor, not the wit [214] and numbers of the poet Laureat, not the polite ‖ and civil demeanor of the master of Ceremonies, not the melody of the Chief musician, not the eloquence & loquacity of the orator, not all the conjoint cunning of the Longstanding members, can stand in opposition, against your honor's tremendous and honorable Nod, nor can in the least degree move or alter or disturb your honor's fixed, determined and absolute Resolves, behests, Commands, orders, resolutions, purposes and determinations, which Surely are all Calculated, for the Good, advantage, and happiness, of this here ancient and honorable Club.

Having already mentioned the benignity and hilarity of the Season, which Serenely Smiles upon your honor, on this here Solemn occasion, permit me, before I have done, to dwell alittle upon the benignity, Generosity, Complacency and Gayety of your honor, to this here ancient and honorable Club, upon the return of this here anniversary feast, wheresoever we cast our eyes, we see the effects of your honors beneficence, even in the

Vestibulum, or entry, we are encountered by Sweet Smells and odoriferous effluvia, the pride of flora, is strowed under our feet as we pass thro' the entry, which, (to speak figuratively) represents to us, the Sweet flavor and redolency of your honor's generous and overflowing profusion, to this here Club, the flag displayed in the fleeting air, points out to us, with what freedom and ease your honor's bounty flows from you to us, the regular disposition of all things in the entry, in the hall, in the Culinary office, and in the Court yard, shows, with what an even, Composed and placid mind, and, with what an undisturbed fancy and Imagination your ‖ honor goes [215] about feasting, regaling, and elevating the animal Spirits of these here long-standing members, and all other members whatsoever, who at this time do themselves the honor to attend upon your honor, on this grand, Joyful, and honorable occasion, and O! were I, your honor's poor orator, to undertake a panegyric on your honor, I should first exclaim, like the Italian Poet.[6]

Si tutti gli alberi del mondo fossero penne,
Il cielo fosse Carta, il mare Inchiostro,
Non Basteriano a descrivere la minima,
Parte della vostre perfettioni,
Se tanta lingua havesse, e tanta voce
Quant' occhi il Cielo, e quante arene il mare,
Perderan tutti il Suono e la flavella
Nel dire a pieno la vostri lodi Immensi.

If every tree were made a pen to write,
Heavens face made paper, and the ocean ink,
They'd not suffise to pen what I'd Indite
Of thy Great worth, or speak what I could think,
Had I as many tongues, as many Phrazes,
As Stars in heaven, or Sands along the Shore,
They'd lose their energy; e'er half thy praises
Were sung or said, I should have need of more.

Or, as the Greek poet long agoe, exclaimed, concerning the Multitude of the Grecian Souldiery, and Concourse of Ships, ‖ so might I exclaim of the [216] multitude of your honor's perfections.

πληθυν δ' ουκ αν εγω μεθησομαι ουδ ονομηνω
ουδ ει μοι δεκα μεν γλοσσαι δεκα δε στοματ' ειεν,
φθονη δ' αρρηκτος χαλκεον δε μοι ἦτορ ενειη.

---

6. Hamilton attempts in his panegyric to sound Petrarchan, but these lines are not in Petrarch. Hamilton's Italian reads well, although he has freely chosen his own endings for several of these words, and his translation is accurate.

Should I attempt their numbers to recount,
Tho furnish'd with ten tongues, as many mouths,
With Iron voice, and brazen lungs, I'd fail.[7]

Look round then, ye longstanding members, look round ye honorary members, look round, all ye other guests who are, or should be here on this occasion, to partake at this present anniversary of the munificence and beneficence of, the honorable and Illustrious Jole, see, how his hospitable kitchen Chimney throws out Clouds of Smoke, hear the exhilirating noise of the Spits, frying pans Stew pans and pots, the music of the frying, roasting and boiling, smell the reviving fumes, Issuing from the rich dishes, see the elegant order and Splendor of the laid out table, the Snowy white & regular plaits of the Cloth, the elegant fringed papering of the Candlesticks, contemplate the order of the Jugs, mugs, pots, cups, cans, bottles, flasks, Tankards, decanters, Cruets, glasses, plates and dishes, observe the full flowing bowls, brimming with refreshing liquor, the acid, cool refreshing punch, ready to kiss your Longing lips, perlustrate, e're you taste (a) the ragoos, fricassees, pies, Custards, Goosebery || tarts, Sillabubs, and the various delicacies of Vertumnus and Pomona,[8] under the load of which the round table groans; O Round table! more round and renown'd, than that of King Arthur and his doughty knights, since a greater chief than K: Arthur is here, and eke, a greater knight, than any of his knights is here also! and, when you have considered all these, think what a generous, what a benevolent, what a kind, what a Courteous and honorable president you are blessed with, a president, who has always been to you, a mild ruler and Strenuous protector, a president, whom you ought to honor, respect and obey, a President of all presidents the most Sagacious and Indulgent, a president, who has in his veins, the true old English hospitable blood, and possesses the very Quintessence of that Jovial and free people, [Sr Jno: The quintessence of a fart!] as described by Paulus Jovius, in the third book of his history, with which Quotation, I shall beg leave to Conclude this Anniversary oration. *Universa gens, supra Mortales cæteros, Conviviorum studiosissima, ea enim, per varias et exquisitas dapes, interpositis musicis et Joculatoribus, in multas sepius horas entrahunt, ac subinde, productis Choreis et amoribus fœminarum, indulgent,*[9]—which, I think is an exact description of the hon-

---

(a) This Speech was Intended to have been delivered before Supper, but his honor was so busy in the kitchen, he had not time to hear it, therefore this anachronism.

7. *Iliad* 2.488–490. Hamilton's translation is accurate.
8. The Roman god and goddess of fruits.
9. Paolo Giovio (1483–1552) was an Italian biographer and historian, distinguished as a Latin stylist. The passage reads: "This whole tribe was eager beyond other mortals for banquets, for

orable the president, and the longstanding members of this here ancient & honorable Club—*Dixi*.

This oration, being pronounced, the orator had the applause of the Club, only Sir John withheld his approbation, protesting that he thought it Damnd Nonsense, then the music of the anniversary ode was plaid over, not Composed, as may be plainly seen, by Signior Lardini, but Collected from the works of several Celebrated Composers, the Chancellor per- [218] formed the violino primo, Squeak Grumbleton Esqr, a Stranger Invited to the Club did the violino Secondo, and the Secretary the violoncello, while Mr Protomusicus and Crinkum Crankum Esqr, managed the vocal part, Then the music of the old ode, for the year 1751 was playd over by the same hands, and the whole Club Joined in the Grand Chorus, & thus ended the Celebration of the eight anniversary.

these frequently dragged on, through varied and exquisite courses, with musicians and jesters interspersed, through several hours, and then they indulged in lengthy dances and the love of women" (possibly from bk. 3 of Giovio's *Historiae sui temporis* [1547]).

[219]

[The last line on this page is illegible.]

[220]

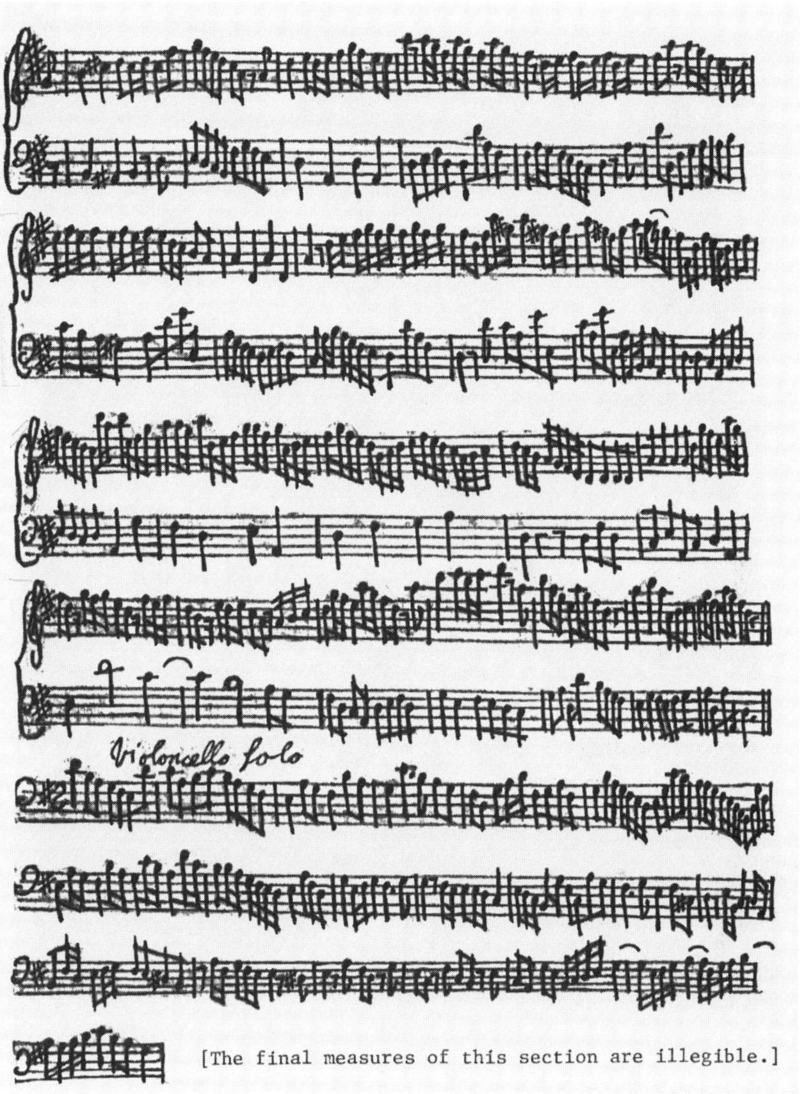

[The final measures of this section are illegible.]

[221]

[223]

the Tuesday Club [Book XII] 163

[224]

[225]

[227]

[228]

[229]

[231]

the Tuesday Club [Book XII] 173

174 [Book XII] The History of

[235]

[236a]

Chapter V

Controverted Election of Crinkum Crankum Esqr, musical Composition of Signior Lardini, Learned Speech of Mr Proto Musicus.

Learning is far short of wisdom, so far, I think, as that It has no manner of analogy or Likeness to it, many fine Scholars there are, that can prate Greek and latin *ad unguem*,[1] and it comes as easily from them as *a,b,c,* from a great Schoolboy with his horn-book; and some of these *per quire* book worms, will Thunder out greek verses to an Ostler, and make Latin orations to a Chamber maid, Thinking they appear more wise and mysterious, the Less they are understood. I must observe here, that most of the Longstanding members of the Ancient and honorable Tuesday Club, were by no means adepts in the aforesaid dead Languages, or in any dead or foreign Language whatsoever, but what then, we only can Conclude from this, that that there Club was not a Learned Club, but tho not a Learned Club, they might be a wise Club, and Sure they could not otherwise be, else they had employed their time very Ill, having now been so long, under the Government of that wise and Judicious, (Tho not Learned) Gentleman, the honorable Carlo Nasifer Jole, hence must appear in a Strong light the foly of the orator, in entertaining that Club so often with Scraps of Greek, latin and Italian, in his Speeches, and, in a much Stronger light, the foly of that Gentleman, whom we shall soon find going to much greater Lengths, in this vain Glorious practice, in the Character of attorney General to the Club.

At Sederunt 203, may 29th 1753, Slyboots Pleasant Esqr, being h:S: his honor the president presented in Club a ‖ letter, wrote to him by the Secretary, at Sederunt 98, January 31, 1748/9, In which it is asserted, that the Club could not proceed to elect any members in his absence, without his permission, on the Strength of which, his honor called in Question, the late Election of Crinkum Crankum Esqr, as a long standing member. This point was Strenuously argued in Club, both pro and Con, Some members denied the validity of that letter to convey any such power or privilege to the president, as it did not appear upon Record, that the Secretary had any

---

1. To a hair (perfectly).

orders from the Club, to pay his honor any such Compliment, for at best, It could be called but a Compliment paid the president, and no Privilege. Which Solo Neverout Esqr, in a long frothy noisy Speech absolutely denied, and, for his pains, had the title of *attorney General* given him by his honor the President, in reward for his expence of lungs, but no one could make any Connexion, or Sense of his argument. Thus was this Gentleman promoted to an Eminent place in the Club, which he had long been aiming at, and attained at last, by the Creation of this new office & title; and if we look back upon the actions of this Club Worthy, ever since his Secreting the Great Seal, and being one of the principal Sowers of discord and Sedition in the Club, so as to occasion a dangerous rebellion, under the Conduct of the Chancellor, we shall find, that he acquired this honorable promotion, from no other visible merit or recommendation, but that of an Indefatigable perseverance, in Clamor, Noise, and an Indomitable effrontery. But we shall

[239] soon have occasion to see him || making a considerable figure in this high place and office, procuring to himself a mighty Influence in the Club, and Sway, over the passions of his honor the president, and this Solely, by framing his discourses and arguments in such a manner, as to puzzle and perplex every Cause he undertook, being in his Stile and manner, altogether unintelligible.

While this dispute was a going on, Crinkum Crankum Esqr, was ordered to retire, while it lasted, but, it being likely to last the whole night, by the long winded Speeches of the new attorney General, he returned again into the Club room without leave, and made a defence for himself, in which he neither denied nor affirmed any thing, nor Indeed did he deliver any Consistent Speech or Speeches, being perpetually Interrupted and brow beaten by the Loquacity of the Attorney General. This pleased his honor The president mightily, who now found he had got a Champion, whose tongue would Carry all before him, with more rapidity of Execution, than even the broadsword of his ancient and valiant Champion Sir John.

At last, the Secretary rising up, owned, that he had wrote such a letter, to the president, as had been shown in Club, and believed, that at that time, (as also did the Club) that no election could be carried on, in the presidents absence, but then, the Club had this relief provided, that they gave the president a privilege and power to appoint his deputy, to act with full power in his absence, which valuable privilege, had the president continued to
[240] exercise, this || Club could never have been at a loss with regard to the election of members; for, tho' his honor should not be present himself, yet by this means they had always a deputy In the Chair, with full power to act,

but, since his honor had droped that Prerogative, of appointing Commissioned deputy presidents to act in his absence, this club were constrained, sometime after that, vizt: at Sederunt 121, January 16th 1749/50, to make a Law, by which they took into their own hands, a power of electing deputy presidents, with full authority to act in his honor's absence.

This argument being likely to be too long winded was broke off in the middle, and the Club broke up, and Indeed, we shall find this dispute of as long a Continuance, as any, that ever happened in the Club, not being determined till Sederunt 230.

At the following Sederunt, Quirpum Comic Esqr being H:S: nothing remarkable happened, only that Mr Drawlum Quaint, formerly a worthy longstanding member, and honorable Speaker of the Club, was entertained as a Stranger, pursuant to ancient Custom. Some disputes also happened between Philo Dogmaticus Esqr, Chanc: & Mevius Pumpkin Esqr, honorary member, concerning the best method of teaching Children the rules of Grammar, which as it was not altogether of a Clubical nature, I only barely mention.

On Sederunt 205 June 26th, 1753, Solo Neverout || Esqr the attorney general being H:S: The Celebrated Signior Lardini payd a visit to the Club, and brought along with him some new musical Compositions Composed in a delicate taste, which were an overture and a Gavotta Burlesque, for the Entertainment of his honor, and a minuet for the attorney General, which latter, he did not bring with him, but Composed on the Spot, These pieces were performed in the Club with applaus, Sigr: Lardini viol: primo, Signr Dogmatico Viol: Secondo, and Signr Scribellio, Violoncello, after which, the Grand and little Choruses of the year 1751, were play'd, to which the longstanding members sung, and Jonathan Grog Esqr performed as well as usual, the Recitativo part of *Robin and Jeck,* a Copy of which excellent piece, I may have occasion to exhibit, somewhere in this history.

The high Steward was accused of a Misdemeanor, in not wearing his badge with a proper ribbon, to distinguish his office, on which he rose up with an air of gravity and learning, which he was now entituled to take upon himself, on account of his new office of attorney General, and made a long Elaborate harangue, Elaborate with regard to its peculiarity of Stile and expression, not with regard to its correctness and accuracy, || which Correctness and accuracy that gentleman never trowbled his head about, not that he was Incapable of it, but because he Judged it not only unnecessary, but altogether Impolitic, in public declamations, held before modern assemblies, where the main art of the orator is to puzzle and perplex, his

Subject so much, as to prevent the Argument's ever coming to a fair Conclusion; Some may perhaps Condemn the Club, for suffering such declaimers to make expence of their precious time, but, if their Justification can be pled from Learned and honorable Example and precedent, they will Surely stand exculpated, when we reflect, that this very practise of puzzling and perplexing, is allowed of, and admitted in both houses of parliament, and in our Higher Courts of *Law* and *Equity,* where plain points, are argued and Laboured in such a manner, as if it never was Intended they should be understood, or finally determined.

But to return to our attorney General, in his harangue, he apologized, in the first place, for his not serving the Club punctually, as it came to his Turn, pleading business—and all that—and therefore—and because—and for why—and that being the Case,—and in that respect, (as his friend said)—and so forth,—which Learned Speech, was not understood by any of the longstanding members, and, upon their Complaining, that they did not understand it, The attorney made answer, That it was not in his power, and [243] were ‖ it in his power, he did not think himself in the least obligated, to furnish the Longstanding members with understanding, seeing, that the honorable office he now occupied, would require all the Stock he had of that valuable Commodity.—But one of the Longstanding members replied That, tho' it were granted, that this valuable Commodity, as he stiled it, was transferable from one hand to another, yet Mr Attorney himself had so small a Stock of it, that it could not in reason be expected, he could spare any to a friend.—The Gentleman however, not in the Least dashed, or put out of Countenance, by these Repartees, continued to harangue so wisely and *Judgematically,* that it was thought proper to ornament his head, with a large, voluminous, full bottom'd wig, made of tow, which fell down very gracefully, in large flakes upon his Shoulders, we shall soon see him make a notable appearance in Club, with that voluminous ornament upon his pate, and others upon his body, Suitable to the Gravity and dignity of his office.

At this Sederunt, his honor the president was remarkably gay and Chearful, being, as it is thought, well pleased with the Eloquence and address of his attorney General, from whose great abilities, he expected miracles, in the Government and management of the Club, but be that as it will, his honor's gayiety, Inspired the like, into all the longstanding members, & the Club broke up in very good humor.

Chapter VI

[244]

Misbehaviour of the Chancellor, Orator's Speech to Sir John, The Chancellor's trial.

Zoilus the Critic,[1] who wrote against Plato & Homer, and who, perhaps, (more *criticorum*) thought himself the wisest man of that age in which he lived, was remarkable for nothing so much, as the extraordinary length of his Beard, and so Curious was he, of this Signature of wisdom, (as it is said the ancients esteem'd the beard) that he kept his head always Close Shaved, that none of that nutritive Juice might go to supply the hairs of his Cranium, which he chose rather should be bestowed upon the Inferior part of his face, in order to add to the voluminousness of that *Sapientific brush*, which was a Sign hung out, by that vain glorious Critic, to show all passengers, what a rare Stock of wit was in the Inner Chambers, as the bush at a Taveren door, shows what fine liquors are kept, by the Jolly landlord within.

But, whatever might be the opinion of the ancients, with regard to the beard's being the Symbol, or Signature of wisdom, we find that beards have been in such disrepute with the moderens for some Centuries past, that they kept gradually Lessening, till they arrived in the days of our K: Charles I. to only || a pair of small whiskers, a diminutive peak on the Chin, shaped according to the humor and fancy of the wearer, till at last they were quite disused, and now every moderen, who would appear in the least degree like a gentleman, shaves as close as the back of my hand, and nothing is reckoned a greater mark of Slovenliness, Stupidity and Clownishness, than an overgrown, dirty, Squalid beard.

[245]

It appears from thence, that the moderens have no notion of the beard being a type of wisdom, and therefore reject the use of it altogether, but, as we cannot esteem these moderens such Sots and Idiots (however far, in other matters they may be besotted or sunk Into idiotism) as to pay no regard at all to wisdom, and esteem it a thing of no value, so as to reject the thing it self together with it's ancient Shadow or Symbol, we must there-

---

1. Zoïlus (fl. 4th century B.C.), Cynic philosopher and grammarian, was known for his bitter attacks on Isocrates, Plato, and especially Homer.

fore, to set matters right, find out what Signature the moderens use, to Symbolize or represent wisdom; I must own, I have Employed my thoughts for some time upon this Important Subject, and after Intense thinking and Indefatigable Scrutiny, can find no type or Symbol among the moderens, so apt and Significant for this purpose as a large *full bottomed wig,* as this is a Signature, often used, by our wise Judges, and wiser Senators, and, I must confess, that this Signature, has the advantage of that used by the ancients, [246] vizt: The Beard, for two material reasons, 1st, because a man can ‖ procure in a minutes warning, a very large Stock of this kind of wisdom from the Peruque maker, and he has no occasion to stay whole years, as the ancients did, expecting its Grouth, 2dly, because this wisdom can never become too Common, being only attainable by persons of fashion and estate, who can afford to disburse ten or twelve Guineas to furnish themselves with a Large Quantity of it, whereas the ancient Symbol, may be had, by every dirty Ignorant fellow of a Plowghman or Carman, of a robust habit of body, whom Nature has furnished with a large quantity of bristles—the beard indeed in our times, is used by some Sects, particularly the Donkers,[2] as a Symbol of Religion and Sanctity, but that is nothing to our purpose, the wisdom and Sagacity of our moderen Smarts and people of fashion, not Consisting in religion, but in a Sort of *Je ne sçay quoi,* widely different from it.

In consequence of this theory, the Longstanding members of the ancient and honorable Tuesday Club, who in every respect were moderens, and ruled themselves by moderen modes, tho' members of an ancient Club, Thought it adviseable, to adorn the head of their new Created attorney General with a full bottom'd wig, as most expressive and Significant of the wisdom and Sagacity of that Learned and Ingenious Gentleman, who, as they thought had little of the Substance within his Cranium, and therefore [247] stood ‖ more in need of a large quantity of the Symbol or Shadow without, and that Sapientific wig, they Chose should be made of tow, to signify the fleeting, light and Combustable nature of human wisdom, in General, and of this Gentleman's in particular. We shall therefore, have occasion more than once, in the Sequel of this history, to see this gentleman Introduced upon the Clubical Stage, ornamented with this voluminous flaxen head attire.

At Sederunt 206 July the 10th 1753, Jonathan Grog Esqr, P:L: & M:C: being H:S: Philo Dogmaticus Esqr, the Chancellor, pleading a law of the

---

2. Dunkers, or Tunkers, are German-American Baptists who administer baptism only to adults, and by triple immersion.

Club, as usual, mounted the Chair, and affirmed, with a Confident face, that he would mantain his place, till he saw, a Superior authority to make him leave it, the Club seemed some what Surprized at this Rodomontade, tho' it was not the first time, that this Gentleman had behaved himself in this Imperious manner; but, the Secretary producing a letter, wrote upon a Scurvy piece of paper, directed to himself, and without either proper address or Subscription, as is usual in letters from well bred persons, appointing the worshipful Sir John, deputy for the night, the Chancellor Immediatly left the Chair, and the worshipful Sir John taking that Eminent Seat of honor, the proceedings of last meeting were read as usual; This was the fourth and last time but one, that this Club heroe, had deigned to sit ‖ in the Chair as deputy, which place he always accepted of with reluctance, not out of a principle of modesty, but, as thinking it beneath him to be deputy to any president whatsoever; the first time that he Condescended to take it, (for he had often refused it before that) was at Sederunt 59, May 26th 1747, being the Second Anniversary of the Club, when he occupied the Chair as deputy, even while his honor the president, was himself present, he never would accept of it again, till Sederunt 172, January 21, 1752, when he assumed the Chair for the latter part or fag end of a Sederunt, when Solo Neverout Esqr, the Elected deputy, had left the Chair and gone home, being overcome with a Sleepy fit, a third time he deigned to accept of it, vizt: at Sederunt 201, May the 1st, 1753, when the Maggot took him to sit in that Seat of honor, tho only elected by the Club, tho this it was supposed he did, to brave the president, as he knew his honor would deny the Legality of that Club, and this last time, it is thought he accepted of it to humble the pride of the Chancellor; Some think also, tho' upon very uncertain Grounds, that the valiant Sir John was deputy at the humdrum Sederunt, viz: Sed: 184 augst 18, 1752, held at his own house, he himself being h:St: but as this is a matter of Great uncertainty, we shall not presume to declare for one Side or other, as some affirm, with the Record, that Jonathan Grog Esqr, was then deputy.

[248]

As to the Substance of the letter from his honor the president, to the Secretary, the president there says ‖ That his being very ill with the gout, was the Cause of his writing in so short a manner, and, that Sir John should take the Chair, hoping that he would behave himself according to the Laws, Rules and orders of the Club,—This was the whole of the presidents letter, which had neither address at the beginning, nor a proper Subscription at the End.

[249]

The Chancellor objected to this letter, that it was Wrote in a rude unmannerly Stile, without either Civil address, or mannerly Conclusion, and moved that it should be burnt by the hands of the hangman, but, on the Objection's being made, that there was no such officer in the Club, he offered, rather than it should not be done, to perform the office himself, The Club, after some Learned harangues of the Attorney General, in his full bottomed wig of tow, as usual, which made him labor and sweat much, the weather being hot, rejected the proposal, and the Chancellor Insisted, that his motion should be Entered on the book.

The Music of the Club was playd over this evening, by Signior Lardini and the usual hands.

At the following Sederunt, The Worshipful Sir John being H:S: on reading the Proceedings, the Secretary said, *Sederunt two Hundred and Sixth,* with which the Club found fault, and said, it was not a proper [250] expression, and the Secretary was || ordered to read it again, and say, Sederunt *two hundred and Six,* and some dispute happening thereupon, the vote was put about, and it Carried, that the latter was the proper reading, upon which the Chancellor urged some objections, as to the Propriety of it, saying it was not Grammatical, and that it ought to be read *two hunder and Sixth,* which, some of the members said, was the Scots way of Expressing it, but the determination of the Club stood.

We need not be Surprized at disputes about words, happening in the Club, since it is notorious, that the same disputes have heretofore, and still will arise in the most wise, and most Learned assemblies.

The Secretary then, as Orator, delivered an Emblematical Speech to Sir John, the H:S: upon the occasion of his serving the Club, on the first Day of the dog days, in which, he Compared that Champion, to the dog star Sirius, but the whole of this Speech is lost.

Several Quaint and witty expressions passed in Club at this Sederunt, and, one Saying in particular was used by Crinkum Crankum Esqr, which, by a defect of memory in the Secretary, is also Irrecoverably lost.

At Sederunt 208, august 7th, 1753, Mr Secretary Scribble being H:S: Mr Attorney General Neverout appeared in Club, in his proper dress of office, having a large broad hat, or *Chapeau pointu,* as the French Call it, a full bottomed wig, Curiously wrought of tow, a band, and a black gown, [251] and make- || ing a profound bow to the chair, he deposited his great hat, and delivered some papers to the Secretary, then with a grave Solemn face, telling his honor, that he had matters of the utmost Importance, to lay before him and the Club, vizt: criminal matters, charged against the Chancellor of this here Club, which, the duty of his office, obliged him to animadvert upon, hoping, that he should be able to make them evident and Clear to his honor and this here Club.

Then he Rectified his wig and band, and took a pinch of Snuff, The Chancellor, alittle flustered, told him, that he was not Surprized to see him behave so much like a pert fellow and a buffoon—but that he did not care a whistle for him,—Tho he talked till his guts came out. To which the attorney General Replied with great gravity and Stayedness of Countenance—Sir—I assure you Sir,—upon my word and honor Sir,—I shall talk a great while before my guts come out.—Then the Secretary Read the Indictment, vizt:

Indictamentum

Tuesday Club Ss:

Socii Societat⁹ Annapolit⁹ diei mart⁹ anglice, *The Annapolis Tuesday Club* super honor⁹ Suam present⁹, quod *Philo Dogmaticus Armiger* hujus mod⁹ Societat⁹ nuper Cancellar⁹ et Custos Sigilli, nec non cust⁹, conscientice, Sereniss⁹ dom⁹ nost⁹ Præsidis, nuper de Civitat⁹ Annapolit⁹, homo pernicios⁹, et Seditios⁹, pravæ mentis et turbulent⁹ disposition⁹ machinans et Intendens, contra || honor⁹ et dignitat⁹ dom⁹ nost⁹ præsidis. Socio⁹ hujus Societat, ad odiu⁹ et vituperation⁹ anglice (*Dislike*) person⁹ dict⁹ dom⁹ præsidis et gubernation⁹ Stabilat⁹ Infra⁹ dict⁹ dom⁹ præsid⁹ perturbar⁹ et Incitar⁹ et mover⁹ Sedition⁹ et Rebellion⁹ contra dict⁹ dom⁹ Præsid⁹ tertio Diei Julii anno Domination⁹ dom⁹ nost⁹ præsid octavo, in Aula Jonathi Groggii armigeri, adtum huj⁹ Societat⁹ Celsus Steuartus, in vico Caroli, anglice (*Charles Street*) in Civitat⁹ prædict⁹, coram ipso dom præsid, et in present⁹ divenor⁹ nostror⁹ Socior⁹ adhinc et ibid⁹ present⁹ et existent⁹ vi et armis rautose et riotose, assaultationem fecit execrabilem, in Cathædr⁹ et honor⁹ dict⁹ dom⁹ præsid⁹ nam, magna et alta voce Stentoriana, sequent, verb⁹ malitiosa, execrabilia, et abominabilia, pronunciavit, duesis, Quod cesta Epistola, dom⁹ nost⁹ præsid⁹ ad Secretar⁹ Conscript, erat Scribelamentum Scandalosum, anglice (*a Scandalous Scrowl*) Immorale, rude, Impertinent⁹, opprobriosum Rusticum, Anglice (*unmannerly, rude, Impertinent, opprobrious and Clownish*) et etiam, quod ista epistola, debet Comburi per manibus Communis Carnificis, anglice (*and that the said Epistle ought to be burnt, by the hands of the Common hangman,*) et hanc Contumeliam perpetravit, et assaultationem fecit, prædict, Philo Dogmaticus, Armiger, Cancellar⁹, et Custos Sigill⁹, vi et armis, rautose et riotose, Insolenter, Impudenter, et audacter, contra Leigeantiam debit⁹ in malu⁹ et pernitiosu⁹ exem-

[252]

plu⁹, omniu⁹ alioru⁹ in tali casu⁹ delinguend⁹, et contr⁹ pacem dict⁹ dom⁹ præsid⁹ Cathædr⁹ & dignitatat.

Then the Secretary read in Club, the English Indictment, to the following purpose.

[253] ### Indictment

Tuesday Club Ss:

You Philo Dogmaticus, stand Indicted, by the name of Philo Dogmaticus Esqr, Late Chancellor of the ancient and honorable Tuesday Club, keeper of the Great Seal & keeper of the political Conscience of our most Serene Carlo, for that you, as a false traitor, against the most Illustrious and Serene President Carlo, due reverence to the said President in your heart not having, nor weighing your duty towards his august Chair, but, being moved and seduced, by your own wicked Instigation, and due obedience, from your said Serene President, utterly withdrawing, and endeavoring and Intending, with all your might, the peace and Common tranquillity, of this here ancient and honorable Club to disturb, and the Laws of the same Established to overthrow, to pull down and bring into contempt, the said Serene President Carlo, and his Chair, and, the said honorable Chair, wickedly, devilishly and maliciously to usurp, you, the said Philo-Dogmaticus Esqr, upon the third day of July, in the eight year of the dominion, of the said Serene President Carlo, in a Street Called Charles Street, in the City of Annapolis, in the hall of Jonathan Grog Esqr, Poet Laureat, and then high Steward, before our said Serene President, and in the Presence of several of [254] the Longstand- ‖ ing members of this here ancient and honorable Club, then and there being, with force and arms, of malice aforethought, then and there, wickedly, an assault did make, upon the person and Chair, of our said Serene President Carlo, in open Contempt of the Laws of this here Club, and with a loud Stentorian voice, pronounced the following execrable, detestable, abominable, horrible, dreadful, malicious and rebellious words, vizt: *That a Certain letter, wrote by our said Serene president to our Secretary, was a Scandalous Scrowl, unmannerly, rude, Impertinent, opprobrious and Clownish,* or such like abusive words, and, that *the said Letter ought to be burnt by the hands of the Common hangman,* against your alegiance, due to our said Serene President Carlo, and setting a bad and pernicious example, to all your fellow longstanding members, to be Guilty of the same, against the peace of our said Serene President Carlo, his Chair and Dignity.

Secr: What say you, Philo Dogmaticus Esqr, are you Guilty of this Charge Brought against you or not Guilty?

Ph: Dog: I shall not plead good Sir, because I apprehend I am not the person accused, besides, I object to the Attorney General, as an uncommissioned officer, in this here Club, and acting by no authority but his own.

Att: Gen: Sir, tho I am not obliged to Indulge you so far, I here produce my Commission [Here the attorney General produced his Commission, under the privy Seal at Arms of his honor the President]

COMMISSION

Carolus Dominus Præses.

We Charles, president of the anct: & honble: Tuesday Club, do, by our Special and Sole authority, Constitute, appoint, and declare you Solo Neverout Esqr, Proto musicus, our attorney General, for us, and our said ancient and honorable Tuesday Club, and, by these, our Letters patent, and Commission, under our Privy Seal at arms, grant you, full power & authority to prosecute all and every Crime or Crimes, misdemeanors, alias misdemanors, trespasses, plots or plottings, Committed and perpetrated against us and our honorable Chair, and, to use all manner of means, by declaration, Information, Impeachment, Indictment, or any other Legal process, to suppress the same, and bring each offender or offenders, of what degree or Station soever in the said Club, to condign punishment, and Furthermore, we hereby grant you, full power and authority to appoint a Serjeant at arms pro tempore, to take such offenders into Custody, for which, this Commission shall be your warrant and authority, during *your* pleasure.

[Privy Seal] Given under our hand and privy Seal at
Nasifer Jole arms, this 6th day of august, in the eight
  year of our presidential Government,
  annoque Dom, 1753, at our Residence in
  N:E: Street.

Sig: pr: order, *Loquacious Scribble Secrtry*

This Commission being read, the Chancellor objected to the validity of it, it having been given without the advice and Consent of the Club, according to the proviso in Law 45, at Sederunt 134, february 13th 1749/50, upon which the attorney General turned up Sederunt 144, December 4th 1750, where the proviso of the above law stands Repeal'd, but, the Chancellor asserted that this repeal was a plain Interlineation, and written with different Ink, the President tho' was of a different opinion, ‖ and it being put to the vote, the Club voted it no Interlineation, and also voted the

Attorney General's Commission a good Commission, upon which, the attorney General rose up, and made the following Speech to the Chair.

"May it please your honor,

The case which I am now to open before your honor and this here ancient and honorable Club, is a Case—a case may it please your honor—I say Sir,—a Case of plots and plottings, full of high Crimes and Misdemeanors,—of high Crimes, may it please your honor, Charged against no less a person, than the venerable Chancellor of this here ancient and honorable Club,—I say Sir the venerable Chancellor of this here ancient and honorable Club, and keeper, may it please your honor, of the great Seal of the said Club, and also keeper, may it please your honor, of your honor's political Conscience.

It is with the utmost reluctance, honorable Sir, that I take in hand, this here prosecution—I say Sir, this here prosecution, and I Sincerely wish it had fallen into other hands, for this here Chancellor, may it please your honor, is a person,—I say Sir a person, for whom I must have some degree of respect, as being by his office,—I say Sir his office, nighly related to your honor's honorable Chair, but, in Cases of this Sort, may it please your honor, all respect of persons must be set aside,—I say Sir, all respect of

[257] persons must be set aside, and ‖ the office I bear in this here Club—I say Sir, the office I bear in this here club, as your honor's attorney General, lays me under a Strict obligation to take Cognizance of all trespasses, plots, misdemeanors and Crimes without favor or affection, to any person or persons, be their quality or degree what it will in this here Club,—I say Sir, be their quality or degree what it will in this here Club.

I hope then the venerable Chancellor will Excuse me, and your honor and this here Club will approve of my proceedings in this here Case,—I say Sir, in this here Case, since I endeavor to discharge my duty Impartially, without Respect of persons,—I say Sir without respect of persons, or suffering myself to be Intimidated or *Non plush'd*, by high sounding titles, or the frowns of Great men,—I say Sir, a-a-a-the frowns of Great men [here the Chancellor frowned Sternly on Mr Attorney] and now, may it please your honor, to the merits of the Cause—Plots and Plottings, may it please your honor, are Crimes,—Crimes Sir, of the deepest dye and the most atrocious nature,—Crimes, to which no punishment is adequate, Comprehending in them Rebellion,—I say, Rebellion, Sir, of which the Devil himself—I say Sir the Devil himself, was the first author and Instigator, having first proved a rebel to heaven, and then prompted mankind to rebel against heaven.

[258] I must own, may it please your honor, that it ‖ grieves me—I say Sir, it

grieves me, to think, that our Chancellor, a person, who, on account of his eminent degree,—I say Sir, his eminent degree in this here Club, ought to have behaved himself in a manner more agreeable, to his Supposed wisdom and dignified Station,—I say Sir, his Supposed wisdom and dignified Station—I grieve much, may it please your honor, I say, to think that this here Chancellor,—I say Sir this here Chancellor, should have so deviated from his duty, especially against your honor—I say Sir against your honor, a person Remarkable for mildness and Clemency, whose government of this here Club, is so gentle and easy, that the most turbulent Spirits, cannot otherwise but be quiet under it, so, that may it please your honor, it may be said of your honor, as a Certain old author said of a Certain good man, *oinom Duonorum pleorumei virom illom optimom esse consentiont*,[3] or, as the Celebrated Gil Blas says, in his Greek annotations, *Tois, nois*—hoh!—hoh!—[here an Interruption]

Jon: Grog: He, he, hi, hi, hi, hih.

Attor: Gen: *Nois, Presidentois,*—chi, chi, chuck!

Quirp: Com: Ha, ha, he, hi, hi.

Att: Gen: *Is te Cox-Comboy*—pugh—Pho—

Jon: Grog: Comeboy! aha, aha, ahi, ahi. The attorney Calls the horses, aha, aha, ha, hi.

Att: Gen: *Kay Clodepateon, nidjotton, hoi fooleroi asinos-s-s-s-soi*, hoh, —hoh. [here the attorney seemed to hesitate much]

Sir Jno: Hoh, hoh, hoi, hoh, ho, hoi, hoh, ho, hoi, lancets! lancets!—hoh,—I must be Immediatly blooded, hoh,—else I shall die—hoh, hoh,—the laughing at this Stuff—hoh—has given me a damn'd Stich in my Side—hoh, hoh—o.

Omnes: Aha, aha, aha, ahe, he, hoh.—

Att: Gen: And therefore, I conclude, as that Ingenious author does,—*Cheateron ton Biteon, Smoke o' the Gullum*.(a)

(a) Witty: I will prove him in some of the rest—Tois miois Fatherois, iste Coxcomboi.
Pris: Kay yonkeron nigiotton, hoi fooleroi asinoisoi.
Witt: Cheateron ton Biton.
Pris: Tous pollous trickerous, angelo to peeso, [Beaumont and Fletchers Comedy of *Wit at Several weapons*.][4]

3. "Of the good men, a great many agree that he was the best man." The "Certain old author" could refer to almost anyone, since the passage Hamilton provides is a variant of the frequently quoted inscription in early Latin on the tomb of the Scipios.

4. Hamilton's note rightly corrects the learned attorney general. This pseudo-Greek appears neither in Alain René Le Sage's romance, *Gil Blas of Santillane* (1715–1735), nor in Edward Moore's comedy, *Gil Blas* (1751); rather, it appears in Beaumont and Fletcher's *Wit at Several Weapons* (1647), act 1, sc. 1, where Witty-pate Oldcraft puts Priscian's knowledge of Greek to the test and decides he possesses a formidable command of it.

Quir: Com: Ay, ay, right Sir, right, there you have hit the nail o' the head.

Attor: Gen: And therefore, may it please your honor, whatever the Station or degree of that there Chancellor may be, in this here Club, yet, his Station and degree will not protect him from the penalties Inflicted by our Clubical laws, in such Cases, for which I shall quote several Learned authors.

Jodocus Colloverius says, *libro Quarto, Capite nescio quo, omnes plotatores Capitaliter Condempnare debent,* and, Joannes Treverius Gwellengerius ‖ *libro primo, de Institutionibus diabolicis,* roundly affirms *Quod plotator, est omnium aliorium animalium turpissimus, maliciosissimus, horrendissimus,* and a Gentleman Called Ovid, says of a Sirnia, or dissembler,

Sirnia Quam similis, turpissima bestia nobis.[5]

And our famous Countryman, Sir James Killigrew, Clerk of—I dont know what—(that not being in my brief) expressly declares *quod plotator debet forfeitare omnes goodos et effectos, et Chatellos, et Estateos personales et reales, sive Croftas, sive loftas, sive toftas, sive barnos, sive Stabellos, sive dogos, sive Catos, sive Caballos, sive asinos, et præterea Wind millos, &ct:—et postea opportit suspendure in alto Gibbetto,*[6] not to mention these very learned wise and grave authors, vizt: Cook, Littleton, Plowden, Salkeld, Hawkins, Hale, Grotius, Puffendorf, VanderDunk,[7] and a hundred other Civilians, Common Law-

---

5. Collover and Gwellenger are fictitious. The passages read: "All plotters should be capitally condemned [from] book 4, I know not what chapter"; "A plotter is the dirtiest, most malicious, most horrendous of all other animals [from] book 1, on diabolical institutions." The passage from Ovid as it occurs in Ennius reads: "How like us is the ape [or dissembler], the basest of beasts."

6. I have been unable to identify Sir James Killigrew. This pseudo–law Latin reads: "a plotter ought to forfeit all goods and effects, and chattels and estates, personal and real, crofts, lofts, tofts, barns, stables, dogs, cats, horses, asses, and especially windmills, etc.—and then should be hanged on a high gibbet."

7. Sir Edward Coke (1552–1634) was a barrister of the Inner Temple, chief justice of the common pleas (1606), and author of 11 volumes of *Reports* (1600–1615) and of the *Institutes* (1628–1644). Sir Thomas Littleton (1407?–1481) was a judge and author of a treatise on tenures (the later much-expanded edition with Coke's comments became the standard text on property law until the 19th century). William Salkeld (1671–1715) was an English legal writer whose *Reports of Cases in the King's Bench, 1689–1712* (1717, 1718) is the standing authority for that period. Sir John Hawkins (1719–1789) was an English lawyer and magistrate. Sir Matthew Hale (1609–1676) was lord chief justice and author of numerous legal works, including the *History of the Common Law of England* (1713). Vanderdunk is probably Adriaen Van der Donck (1620–ca. 1655), a Dutch lawyer who founded a colony on the Hudson, where he was known as the "Jonker," or squire (whence Yonkers), and author of the famous "Remonstrance" (1650), a narrative of his people's grievances, and of *Beschrijvinge van Nieuvv Nederlant* (1655), a descriptive account of New Netherland. For Plowden, see p. 89n, above, and for Grotius and Pufendorf, see p. 49n, above.

yers, Councellors, Serjeants, attorneys, barristers and Clerks, Choack full of Clubical Law, and Clubical maxims, altogether Consistent with Common Sense, equity & reason (pray dont mistake me, I mean the Common Sense, equity and reason of Lawyers only,) as we may perceive by their voluminous writings, spending as many words upon plain truths, as the Reverend Dr Warburton, does upon plain falshood, by the mere Slight of Scholarship and Craft, and a vast extensive acquaintance with such Sort of books, which alas are not in my hands, hoh! ho. ‖ But, I shall waste no more of your honors time in quotations, knowing well that quotations will never support truth, if it is not supported in the nature of things, or stands on its own legs, hey, hey [here the attorney wiped his Sweaty face, with a fine Cambric handkerchef, being quite overheated with speaking] But I shall endeavor, to make the facts evident and clear, against this here Chancellor, and, for that purpose, I shall proceed to examine my evidences." [261]

The Chancellor, here desired the Attorney General to proceed no farther, since, notwithstanding all his evidence, it was evident, he was not the person accused, the words in the Indictment, being *late Chancellor,* whereas he was now actually Chancellor of the Club.

The attorney upon this acquiesced, and owned that the Indictment was quashed, by this very objection.

Quirpum Comic Esqr, who took Notes during this trial, delivered them up to the Secretary, and they were to this purpose.

Lrd President	page 227
at	313
Philo Dogmaticus	a Case of plots & plottings,

—The Late Chancellor—The Chancellor, *N:B:* the difference—The highest Impudence—his office—respect,—reluctance,—respect to persons set aside—Plots trespasses and Crimes—high sounding titles, not Intimidate— *Non plush'd*—I say Sir—the Devil Sir—I say Sir—grieves to think that Chancellor—ought to have ‖ behaved well in this here Club—ha, ha, ha, hah,—so that—noys—noys—*υχχηλλφηχαη*[8]—Ingenious authors—Jacobus Cantharides,—Exitum Sequentem—Capitalitum, quod turpiss—piss —Countryman, Sir James Kill—who—Sive—Sive—Sive, &ct:—Jobetto— groce is—Barrister—Turn pickerius,—Examin evidences. [262]

These accurate notes, were doubtless wrote out according to the exact method of the notes taken, in the house of lords and house of Commons, by Certain nimble fisted ammanuenses, from whom, the editors of the monthly Magazines, borrow the furbished up Speeches, which they are

---

8. This pseudo-Greek is nonsense.

pleased to tell us, were spoke verbatim, by the noble and learned members of both houses of parliament, we find in these Short notes, that this gentleman again shows his great Skill in Cyphering, I mean, writing in a Certain kind of Cypher, which no one but himself can possibly unravel or understand.

Thus the Chancellor got Clear of this Intricate affair, and dissappointed both his honor and the attorney General, who expected to have humbled him upon this occasion, but, as the attorney General, in this trial, displayd his learning in a Surprizing manner, the fault could not be laid at his door, but Solely at the Secretaries, who had been too Careless in drawing up the indictment, and some think he did this on purpose, to favor the Chancellors escape, as he had Incurred the Censure, by vindicating the respect that was due to him from the president.

Chapter VII

Long adjournment of the Club, Speech of the Orator to the Chancellor, Eulogium on the Club Supper, by the Poet Laureat.

Nature, when she furnished man with a tongue capable to articulate Sounds into words and Language, surrounded it with a dowble fence of teeth and lips, to show that he ought not to be too profuse in Speech, unless desirous of being thought vain and foolish. Those that know how to speak well, never speak much at a time; and it betrays the greatest Ignorance and Simplicity for any one to think that long Speeches, tho they may be agreeable to the Speaker, can be so to the hearers; Hugo Victorinus, a noted author, says somewhere (but I cannot recollect the Chapter and verse) *Est tempus quando Nihil, est Tempus Quando aliquid, nullum antem est tempus, quando dicenda Sunt omnia,* There is a time when nothing is to be said, there is a time when something is to be said, but there is no time, when every thing is to be said.[1]

The Attorney General, and Orator of the Ancient and honorable Tuesday Club, tho' nature had very Compleatly furnished them both, with the dowble fence aforesaid, vizt: lips and teeth, yet were provided with such large tongues, that they seldom or never held their peace, or kept Silence in Club, for while the one was not pleading, the other was perpetually declaiming, and vice versa, but then, if they hit the proper time, it must be

---

1. Hugh of Saint Victor (see p. 49n, above).

Confessed || that they both Strictly observed, that particular part only of Victorinus's Rule, *est tempus quando Nihil*, there is a time when nothing is to be said, tho' they did not observe this rule in the exact manner that this author Intended it should be observed, i:e: by holding their peace, but by an eternal babbling and Chattering, and a great profusion of words, and the Subject of their Speeches, pleadings, declamations and Orations, was neither more nor less, than *Nothing,* There being Just *Nothing* in all that they said, as has already appeared, and will yet appear, in the Course of this history. [264]

At Sederunt 209, on the 8th of August, 1753, Philo-Dogmaticus Esqr, being H:S: all the Longstanding members were deputy Presidents by turns, The Chancellor first taking the Chair, on account of his privilege in Club by Law 43, for, his honor the President, having now Intirely given over sending deputations, either by verbal or written Commission (Tho a very valuable Privilege of the Chair) without giving any reason for it, as being, by his Station in Club, above giving of Reasons, the members, had of late Incouraged an unaccountable Irregularity and Confusion in their proceedings, with relation to the Chair, to the great hurt and Injury of this here Club, which, we have reason to pray, may soon be remedied, before it ends, as it is likely to do, in a final dissolution of the Club.

Abundance of Learned discourse passed in Club this || night, relating to the prodigies of nature, in which were gravely told, Stories of Great Irish Bulls with two heads, monsters as yet unheard of, of monkies that could discourse Intelligibly, Salamanders that could drink punch and Rum, Camelions that lived at Court upon mere air, and often Changed their Color, wearing an artifical Skin, Cockatrices that killd with a look, Unicorns; and even of Squirrells that navigated Arms of the Sea, with nothing for a Barge, but a fragment of a board, and no other Sail, but a bushy tail spread out to the wind; These Stories were promoted by two Irish Gentlemen Invited to the Club at this Sederunt, vizt: the Reverend Mr Rodomantus, and the Jocose Captain Furbisher, the first beginning this Conversation & the Latter, Imitating him, so the Club broke up, each member going home full of wonder. [265]

At the next Sederunt, which was the 210th, the Worshipful Sir John being h:S: he was elected by the Club, as deputy president, for the night, which he Condescended to accept of, and so exercised a dowble office, an honor, which none but himself and the attorney General ever arrived at, so as to hold it thro the whole Sederunt, tho' it was once refused, in a modest manner, by Tunbelly Bowzer Esqr, and now, since we mention this last Gentleman, we must take notice here, that he had now left the Club, having retired to live in the Country.

The next Sederunt, after a long adjournment of Seven weeks on account of his honor the president's being either Indisposed or not at leisure, was held by Slyboots Pleasant Esqr h:S: Contrary to the order of the preceeding Sedert: by which his honor the president was appointed to serve.

[266] Some arguments were started at this Sederunt, concerning the great Seal, which did not make its appearance in Club, upon the Return of the Chancellor, who had been absent for almost two months, by which the orator lost a good opportunity of making a pompous Speech to that great Club officer.

Crinkum Crankum Esqr, moved that he might be Confirmed a long-standing member by his honor, according to Clubical Law, but the Gentleman not being seconded in this motion, his honor seemed, as if he did not hear it, directing his discourse to the members on his right hand and on his left, and talking of Indifferent matters, as was always his honor's custom, when any Improper motion, or Impertinent Speech was addressed to the Chair, at least any motion or Speech, which his honor esteemed to be Improper or Impertinent.

Much business of Importance was this night postponed, on account of the absence of the honorable the attorney General.

It was ordered that an exact list of the Honorary members now in the Club, should be brought in by the Secretary at next Sederunt.

Accordingly, at next Sederunt, which was the 212, Novr: 6th 1753, the Secretary produced an exact list of the honorary members, now belonging to the ancient and honorable Tuesday Club, as follows.

A list of the honorary members of the Ancient and honorable Tuesday Club, Novr 6th 1753

[267]

Mr Abraham Bumper	Mr Oldham wisely
Doctor Polyhistor	Mr Ignotus Warble
Mr Broadface Round	Mr Swillum Swagbelly
Signr Lardini ⎫	Mr Prim Laconic
Mr Smoothum Sly ⎬ Triumvirs	Mr Curious Courtly
Mr Theoph: Smirker ⎭	Capt: Comely Coppernose agt: Britt:
Mr Jno: Gabble	
Mr Roundhead Muddy	Capt: Dio Ramble
Mr Chantum Cheary	Capt: Prettyman Spyplot
Col: Courtly Phraze	Jealous Spyplot Junr Esqr
Mr Joshua Fluter	Mr Mevius Pumpkin
	Coney Pimp Frontinbrass Esqr, agt: Americ:

This list being Examined, all the Gentlemen therein named were confirmed anew, and declared honorary members of the Club.

The Secretary then, as orator of the Club, rising up in his place, with the Club Seal and bag in his hand, directing his discourse, first to the honorable the president and then to the venerable The Chancellor, delivered the following oration.

"Mr President Sir,

Tho it be not customary for any longstanding member of this here Club, especially the orator, to address himself to any particular member, but only to the honorable Chair, yet I must beg the Indulgence of your honor, on this here particular occasion, for, having something of weight and Consequence to say to our Venerable Chancellor, I shall, with your honors permission, address myself to him.

Mr Chancellor Sir, [here the Chancellor made a low bow to the orator] As you are an officer of Great Importance, in this here ancient and honorable Club, upon whom, principally the Strict ‖ destribution of equity depends, so, your presence is always necessary, because highly Serviceable to the longstanding members, and your absence is always Inconvenient and detrimental to this here Club, since it is generally on these occasions that some petulent noisy, and turbulent Longstanding Members, on one of whom I now have my eye,(a) take an opportunity to disturb and Interupt the peace of this here Club.

I therefore Sir, take this oportunity to congratulate your return to the Club, after so long an absence, and hope, your being seated again in that Chair, will have a great effect to secure peace and tranquillity to the Club, which your presence always brings along with it.

But to the purpose [Pres: Ay, ay, 'tis time to say some thing to the purpose] I must here take notice, Sir, that it has been a practise, time out o' mind, or at least ever since the time of the ancient Ægyptian kings, to express things by Significant hieroglyphics, Certain marks or Signatures, have been used by almost all nations, to represent kingdoms, States and Republics, and even great families, the Turkish Empire is represented by a Crescent, Their Imperial Standard or ensign, The Roman by a Spread eagle, The French Monarchy by a flower de lis, the English by three Lyons Courant, the Scots by a thistle, and, the ancient and honorable Tuesday Club, tho' not properly an Empire or kingdom, is signified, by that very expressive figure of two hands Joined in amity and ‖ concord over a heart. Nay, particular persons of great birth and extraction, use Seals of their own

---

(a) Supposed to mean the attorney General.

Coats of arms, to distinguish them from other Illustrious Stocks, and, men in great offices and trust have their particular marks and Signatures, expressing the nature of their offices, such as Chancellors &ct: and you Sir, as Chancellor of this here Club, have this here Great Seal, as a mark or Symbol of your office,—from this humor of expressing Empires, kingdoms, States, Illustrious families, and great offices, by such Symbols and marks, the Heralds office took it's first rise, and is not of so moderen an Institution as some may Imagine, and therefore, I think it is necessary, that we should have so necessary an officer, as a herald king at arms, and so necessary an office, as a herald's office in this here Club, in which, the *Tabulæ votivæ*[2] of honor, belonging to every State officer, officer of the Commoners, and even those of the L:St: members ought to be suspended, and kept on perpetual Record, like so many Scutcheons, to declare to admiring posterity, the Great worth and honor of this here ancient and honorable Club, lest the fame of their actions, like the fame of the actions of much the Greater part of Mankind, should perish with themselves; now Sir, as this here great Seal, is our Chancellors badge of State, and Significant Symbol declaratory of his office, I think it is a Signature or emblem of Great Importance, and, my reason for thinking so is this, that as a Seal without a Chancellor, is to little or no purpose, so a Chancellor without a Seal is to as little purpose, which I shall demonstrate by this

Lemma

You Sir, are either a Chancellor, or no Chancellor,
If you are no Chancellor, to what purpose is this here Seal.
again—This here Seal, is either a Seal or no Seal,
If it is no Seal, to what purpose is that there Chancellor.

Q:E:D:

And therefore, Venerable Sir, to reinstate you in your venerable office, and render you *rectus in Curia*,[3] I here, Solemnly, in the face of his honor and the Club, restore you this here Seal together with that there bag, thereunto belonging, and thereby, each, and either of you, vizt: Chancellor bag and Seal, or Seal Chancellor and Bag, or Bag Chancellor and Seal, or Bag Seal and Chancellor, or Seal bag and Chancellor, or Chancellor Seal and bag, (to give you all the Changes, upon these three Significant words) will work as effectually as if you had never been asunder, and, that it may be so, I earnestly pray, so be it, *Dixi*."

2. "Votive tablets."
3. "Upright in court."

Here the orator ended, and the Chancellor made a reverend bow—In this Oration the orator seems to talk a great deal upon nothing, at least upon nothing new to the Club, for the whole Substance of it he borrows from himself, in two former orations delivered by him to the Club, vizt: that at Sederunt 119 at the first delivery of the great Seal, and that at Sederunt 181, at the Conclusion of the Seventh Anniversary. We find in this oration also, the Grossest flattery that can be Imagined, when he Compliments the Chancellor, by stiling him the Supporter of the peace and Tranquillity of the Club, when he knew to the Contrary, that that turbulent State officer, had not only been the violent promoter of a terrible Civil Combustion in the Club, but was eternally in wrangles and brangles with his honor the president, but this, it is thought, he did on purpose, to spite his honor, whom he looked upon as the thwarter of all his ambitious Schemes, and, as he now despaired of ever rising a Step higher in the Club, he was resolved to show ‖ his resentment on all occasions, to revenge the neglect of that great merit, and abilities, which he thought himself possessor of; but his honor never failed to be up with him, bestowing on him on all occasions the most poignant repartees. [271]

Jonathan Grog Esqr, Poet Laureat, towards the Close of Supper, entered the Club Room, and Informed his honor and the Club that he had been Invocking the muses, and pulling out of his pocket, his performance, read it with a good grace as follows.

Eulogium, on his honor's Entertainment

We've eat and we've drank,
And who should we thank
   Next after the bounty divine,
Who but noble Jole,
Who Chears every Soul
   With good eating, with punch & with wine.

His Plentiful Board
Presents us a hoard,
   Of dainties so rare and so nice,
That search the Globe Round
There cannot be found
   Such an Elegant Luscious device.

'Mongst the boild and the roast,
Where to chuse we are lost,
   Every dish is so nicely prepar'd.

When my belly is full,
My muse is too dull,
   To describe how each member has far'd.

[272]
In punch, Rumbo and Grog [a]
Each may swim like a frog,
   And wine each may Liberally swill,
Till the good liquor Gains
The ascent to our brains,
   And smoothly makes wit flow at will.

Then hail noble Jole,
In a full flowing bowl,
   Thy health we will roll it around, [b]
While we drink we will sing,
Thou art great as a king,
   Thy equal is not to be found.

The Club was much pleased with this performance of the Poet Laureats, and, as the liquor Grog is mentioned here for the first time in that Gentleman's Clubical poems, it will not be amiss to say something here, concerning the origin and Invention of this excellent Liquor, so much Celebrated for Invigorating the Spirits and preserving the health of mankind.

For a great many years after the Settlement of the Sugar Islands, punch was a liquor of Great Repute, the Composition of which, is so universally known, that it would be Impertinent to describe it here, but the middling Sort of people, not being able to procure the delicious Ingredients of this precious liquor, used another Composition of a more Simple kind, without the acid Juices of the fruit, this went by the Names of Rumbo, Bumbo, Toddy, and sometimes Black-Strap, when made with brown Sugar or Melasses, this Liquor had also, and now has it's admirers, but even this being above the pocket of poor Sailors, and too Sweet and washy for their Stron-

[273] ger Stomachs, these Cattle took to ‖ guzzling of what is called in vulgar Stile, right Reverend Raw rum, which Inflamed them so much in the hot Climates, that they died like rotten Sheep. This the Celebrated Admiral Vernon observing, in his late Expedition to the west Indies,[4] and pitying

---

(a) Pointing to the Bowl that held these liquors.
(b) Drinking to the president.

4. Edward Vernon (1684–1757) was an English admiral nicknamed "Old Grog" (because he wore a grogram coat in bad weather), who traveled to the West Indies and was the first to issue rum diluted with water (or grog).

the calamities of these poor Infatuated men, he invented a mixture of the Spirit and plain water, which they Guzzled with Safety, every man his allowance, this was at first called Vernon's Drops, by way of derision, at last, it got the Name of Grogrum, from a Sort of linsey-woolsy Stuff, so called, and now is Called Grog, by way of abreviation; This liquor has now become the favorite of many people of taste, who now prefer it to any other, and Commonly chuse it for a meridian tiff, tho' others, who pretend to a more delicate taste, turn up their noses at it, & look upon it, as a very Clownish porterly liquor, but the admirers of this Liquor, now go by the name of the Grogorian Sect, of which there are great numbers now in Annapolis, and they begin to multiply in all places, to the great dammage of the fruit merchants, it was supposed by some, (tho they had no other Grounds for it than the Gentlemans name) that Jonathan Grog Esqr, was the founder of this Sect in Annapolis, but, tho the fact be not determined, yet it is Certain, that this Gentleman is a very Great admirer of this liquor himself, chuses to drink it Constantly for a meridian, & mentions it often in his Club Poems.

Chapter VIII

Petition of Crinkum Crankum Esqr, Creation of Don John Charlotto Clerk of the kitchen to the Club, Speech of the orator.

Men of a timorous disposition may be Influenced and managed, by a forward and assiduous application, but || great and heroic minds are only to [274] be wrought upon by an affable and mild demeanor. To use a Simile from angling for Illustrating this problem, we know that a small fish will follow the hand with a sudden twitch of the line, but if a great one is hooked, he cannot be brought ashore by a sudden Jerk, because his weight and Strength would break the tackle, but must be Cunningly and Gently playd till he yields, I have known it often happen, that the more Solicitously and earnestly a favour is applied for, the more obstinately it is denied, eager applications raise Suspicions in the person applied to, a man that comes with *You must do so and so,* is likely to solicit in vain, for many men when much urged and teizd for a favor prove Inexorable, whereas if you seem easy and Indifferent about it, they will give it you often without asking. This we shall find to be the Case between the honorable The President and Crinkum Crankum Esqr, who solicited his honor long, with great Earnestness to be Confirmed, a Longstanding member of the Club, but was still from time to time obstinately denied that boon, tho' in itself but reasonable, I therefore, from these premises Conclude, that the honorable Nasifer Jole Esqr, was one of those great & heroic Spirits, who would not suffer himself to be teized or threatned into any measures, but might be wheedled into what measures you pleased, as it will appear this great person was at last wheedled by the said Crinkum || Crankum Esqr and some of his Cunning asociates into a Compliance with a thing he had so long refused, and even vowed never to comply with.

At Sederunt 212 The attorney General delivered to the Secretary in Club the following Petition, vizt:

To The Honorable Nasifer Jole Esqr, President of the Ancient and honorable Tuesday Club, Leutenant General of the Independent foot Company in Annapolis, Lord and protector of the worshipful Eastren Shore Triumvirate &ct: &ct: &ct: The humble Petition of Crinkum Crankum Esqr, a Standing member of the said Club.

Showeth,

That, whereas your petitioner, upon the 3d day of April, 1753, in the eight year of your honor's Presidential Dominion, at Sederunt 199, of this ancient and Honorable Club, (Philo Dogmaticus Esqr, your honors Chancellor, being Deputy President, and In the Chair, at the house of Mr Secretary Scribble then H:S:) was Elected by an unanimous Ballot, a Standing member of the said Club, and was, at the said Sederunt Confirmed by the said Philo Dogmaticus, and Jonathan Grog Esqr, your honor's master of Ceremonies, in the usual form, used first at Sederunt 100, Febry 28, 1748/9, notwithstanding which proceeding, (which your petitioner believed to be regular and legal, and knows not yet, to the Contrary, the affair not being || hitherto settled by the Club,) your honor and some others alledge that your petitioner is not a longstanding member, legally and duely Confirmed, therefore have debard, and shut out your petitioner, from a lawful Seat in this here Club, looking on him as a Stranger and Intruder.

Your petitioner humbly begs leave hence to Infer, That he has cognizance of some Enimies in this here Club, who have entered into a Cabal or Combination against him, to Invalidate his election, and, by the same Channel laying a foundation of a plot against your honor, under pretence, that you are Endeavoring by arbitrary and unprecedented proceedings to undermine and subvert the Constitution of this here ancient and honorable Club, but your petitioner rests this here Cause in that there breast, which always decides with Impartiality, and, in the known honor of him, whose

Justice, Integrity, truth and equity, are already displayd over half the Globe, by the panegyrical pen of your Sublime Poet Laureat, and whose excellent virtues will stand, and be manifested to Generations yet unborn, by the Labors of the Learned and Ingenious Historiographer of this here ancient and Honorable Club.

This therefore, is humbly to beseech your honor, to take the premises, into your most tender and Serious Consideration, and, in your great Goodness and Clemency to relieve your petitioner from the heavy Grievance under which he labors, by allowing him to be heard by his Council at the bar of this here Club, (the birth right of every || free born Englishman) [277] who, he presumes, by Clear and undenyable arguments will prevail upon your honor to Confirm him, with your own honorable hands, a longstanding member of this here Club, and grant him all those privileges and liberties, perquisites and Immunities, to which he is, and ought to be Entituled, as a valid and legal longstanding member of your honor's ancient and honorable Tuesday Club, and your petitioner, as in duty bound shall ever pray &ct:

Crinkum Crankum.

Upon Reading of this petition, the Secretary spoke for some time to the Cause, to whom Mr Attorney General Neverout, very Learnedly Replied, with many hums and haws as usual.

His honor was pleased to observe, that his petitioners Council did him more harm than Good, and his Cause would have been much better managed without any Council at all, which Compliment the Secretary took in very good part from his honor, as knowing the extent and depth of his Judgement, and his usual Civility and Complaisance on these occasions.

Crinkum Crankum Esqr, used some arguments himself to little purpose, his honor being absolutely resolved to proceed in his own Summary way, having not yet thorroughly digested the masquerade of Sir Hugh Maccarty Esqr, nor the memorial of the Grand Committee, in both which that Gentleman was very deeply concerned, he however pled earnestly for his Confirmation, giving several learned quotations, concerning that Significant Ceremony, and among || the rest, he mentioned, that Important [278] ceremony of Confirmation, used by these Right Reverend fathers in God, my Lords the Bishops.

On this the Secretary moved, that the Reverend Philo Dogmaticus Esqr, the Chancellor, should be appointed Bishop of this here Club, in order to Confirm the long Standing members, but this motion being wicked and prophane, he was not seconded, and it dropt.

Then the Secretary moved, that Don John Charlotto Gentleman, should, upon account of his profound Skill in Cookery, be Created Clerk of the kitchen, to this here ancient and honorable Club, and being seconded, Don John Charlotto, Gentleman, was Called in, and acquainted with the matter, upon which, he delivered himself as follows.

"Please your honor,
And you there Gentlemen,
Longstanding members of this here anct: & honble: Club,

I am so conscious of my own want of merit, for an office of so great worth and dignity, and withal of so little profit, that I could wish from my heart, you had pitched upon a person better qualified, or one less mercenary than my Self, to execute that weighty and Important Charge, and altho I know that youll think this modest refusal of your favors, only a matter of form, in the way of *Nolo Epispoopari*,[1] yet if it must be so I heartily thank you for these favors."

In this short and pithy Speech, Don John shows himself to be as much of an orator, as he showed himself a poet upon another occasion at Sederunt 139, when he Composed a poem upon Signior Lardini, and really, this Gentleman's abilities both ways, were pritty equal, only, he seems, at the beginning of this short oration, to Confine himself too much to Club Stile.

Then Jonathan Grog Esqr, Master of Ceremonies Laying his hand upon the head of Don John Charlotto, Created him, by his honors order, Clerk of the kitchen to the Club, in Manner and form following.

My right hand, I lay upon,
The head of You, Charlotto John,
And, Clerk of the kitchen, I you dub,
To th'ancient & honorable Tuesday Club.

The poet Laureat said that these verses were extempore, but he seems to have borrowed the last distich, from the form of admitting members, used by the ancient and venerable Tuesday (or whin bush) Club of Lanneric,[2] which we quoted at the end of the first book of this History.

Don John Charlotto, after being thus Solemnly Confirmed, in his honorable office, made a low bow, first to the Chair, and then to the Club, and Retired.

Before the Club broke up, Jonathan Grog Esqr, sung *Robin and Jeck,* in his usual Recitativo way, and, || as we have often mentioned this Song in our history, it will not be Improper, to give a transcript of it here.

---

1. The familiar phrase *nolo episcopari* means "I will not be made a bishop"; *nolo epispoopari* means "I will not be made a poop."

2. The Whin-Bush Club was the Scottish progenitor of the Tuesday Club (see I, 43n).

Jeck
Tis like you are afraid to wed
    Because the times are hard,
But put such Thoughts out of your head
    And do not such things regard,
For, if you can get money, when times are so dear,
Oh! Then Brother Robin, I'll make it appear,
In times of great plenty, much money you'll Clear,
Oh! marry pray thee then marry. Joan's a pritty Girl.

Robin
  I do not know whether honest Joan,
    Will marry with me, I declare,
  For she to such a height is grown,
    That if I by chance come there
  And offer to kiss her, she turns her about,
  And with her bold fist she batters my Snout,
  The blood at the same runs trickling out,
O marry! if I should marry, how would she serve me then?
Jack
  'Tis like you did not Compliment,
    And give her a kind Embrace,
  But like some Country booby you went,
    With your hat flapp'd over your face,
  It may be, your Stockings and Shoes were untied,
  Like some Country booby you Cack at the bride,
  For some such thing she licked your hide,
O Robin! Honest Sweet Robin, is it the truth or no?
Robin
  I do declare, as I'm a man,
    True breeding I did Express,
  And, as you know, I very well can,
    I went in a handsom dress.
  With my Grandfathers hat, & my Calf leather Cloaths,
  And Into her presence, I merrily goes,
  And made her a compliment down to her toes,
But Joan, angry Joan, she kick'd me about the Room.

[282]   *Jack*
  You should have told her what you had,
    To bring a young woman unto,
  Which would have made her heart full Glad,
    Without any more to do.
  You should have told her "If you will be mine,
  All the Young Turkies, and Capons and Swine,
  And every thing else in this world shall be thine,"
Oh Robin! honest Sweet Robin, you would have Gain'd her love.

  Go try your fortune once again
    And be not daunted so,
  But be resolved to hold out,
    For lasses are Coy, you know,

Tell her, "Love is a thing that can't be conceald,"
And be resolved, not for to yield,
And you shall be Heir of a Conquer'd field,
Oh Robin! Play thy way, Robin, she will at last be thine.
  Robin
I'll try my fortune once again,
  I'll court this young damsel once more,
I'll give her Custard, cakes and wine,
  Which I never did before.
I'll spend a round Shilling, then when I have done,
If she wont have me, as Sure as a gun,
I'll Call her base Slut, and away I will run,
Oh leave her! utterly leave her, never come to her no more.

It is Impossible to have any Idea of the Spirit and humor of this Club Song, but by hearing it performed to music || by the Ingenious poet Laureat of the ancient and honorable Tuesday Club. [283]

At Sederunt 213 November 20, 1753, Quirpum Comic Esqr, being H:S: for the last time, for soon after this, he retired to the Country, and left the Club, Coll: Comico Butman, President of the Club at Hiccory hill in Virginia, whom we have had occasion to mention with honor in this History, and shall have occasion again to mention, at the particular Desire of his honor the president, was Created, (Tho' absent,) an honorary member of this Club, by an unanimous vote of the Longstanding members.

The high Steward, at this Sederunt, had wrote two very facetious letters, to the president & Sir John, which could they have been procured, would have much decorated this History, but by the obstinacy of the Champion, they are utterly suppressed and lost.

Sir John at this Sederunt, presented a letter to the Secretary, directed to himself, which being read, the Contents of it, were not well understood, by his honor the president, nor by the Longstanding members, being Chiefly Concerning the Devil and the Club, or the Club and the devil, and his honor the president's having been by somebody or other diabolified, or metamorphosed into a Dæmon Infernalis, or rather an Infernal Imp's assuming the Shape of his honor the President, in a Sort of dream, but, whether, Beelzebub, Astorath, Mammon, Apollion, or Belphegor,[3] or any

---

3. Beelzebub was the "prince of the devils." Astoreth, or Ashtoreth, was the goddess of fertility and reproduction among the Canaanites and Phoenicians. Mammon was the god of worldly possessions. Apollyon was the Greek name for the king of hell and angel of the bottomless pit. According to a medieval Latin legend, Belphegor, a demon, was sent to observe married life on earth and fled in horror back to the happy regions where female society was nonexistent.

[284] other of the Diabolical tribe, The letter does not say, this letter somewhat offended ‖ his honor, and therefore was never Recorded, the Secretary however, discovered a glimpse of the Secret history of this letter, which was occasioned by a dream of one of the Longstanding members (supposed to be Quirpum Comic Esqr) in whose fancy, the fumes of a plentiful Supper, had excited in his Sleep, the Idea of the Devil come to carry him away, under the Shape of his honor the president.

The Petition of Crinkum Crankum Esqr, was again presented to his honor the president, and read a Second time, but tho' the Club, and particularly Sir John, thought it reasonable Enough, yet, the little attention his honor gave to it as usual, seemed to portend Badly for the poor petitioner, at last, after a deal of reasoning, and altercation Intermixed, The president presented the petition to Crinkum Crankum Esqr, and assured him it should never be Granted, tho' it was voted in Club, at the Instance of the Chancellor, who was much Enraged at this arbitrary proceeding, whether Crinkum Crankum Esqr was duely elected a longstanding member of the Club, or not, and it Carried in the afirmative, next, it was voted, whether he should be Confirmed by the Club, and it Carried in the negative, then the petition was properly Indorsed by Quirpum Comic Esqr thus, C——t, and lay on the table for a third reading.

[285] The Chancellor, then, Complained heavily of the bad use his honor the president made of his pre- ‖ rogative, and said, that at this rate, the Club never would be able to do or effect any thing they proposed, since the most reasonable proposals were always objected to by his honor.

Upon which, the Secretary, as orator of the Club, stood up, and delivered the following Speech.

"Honorable Sir,

This here Club, like all other human Societies, great or small, is supposed to have, or rather really has a power located in it Self as a Society, and, were it otherwise, honorable Sir, that is, if this here Club had no power in it self, what a deplorable Condition should we be in!

Again, lest this power, being too diffuse, or dissipated, or too equally divided among the longstanding members, should occasion a confusion and hurly burly in the government of this here Club, it was necessary to make it center in the hands of a president, and had we not done so, what a deplorable Condition should we have been in!

The President then, having this Superiority of power, serves for the better Government of the Club, and not to enslave the longstanding members, for, were it so, how deplorable must our State be!

The Longstanding members then, having a power distinct from that of the president, must use that power In their proceedings, when it does not Interfere with the prerogative of the president, and that power must be || located in the majority, and were it otherwise, how deplorable must our Case be!

Suppose then, honorable Sir, as the Case is at present, the Club should be Inclinable to admit a worthy longstanding member, and, the president should obstinately refuse to confirm his admission, in this here case, how deplorable must our Condition be!

And, if thro' the president's refusal, to depute a person fit to take the Chair, in his own absence, the Club should want a governor, and the Constitution run into Confusion, In this here Case Sir, how deplorable must our State be!

And should the president refuse to give his fiat to any necessary and useful Laws, or dispense wth Laws already passed, and the Club should be without the benefit of these Laws, as no Society can be ruled without Laws, in this Situation, most deplorable Indeed, must our Condition be.

And, if thro' the want of admitting worthy long-standing members, arising from this default in the president, this Club should dwindle away to nothing and become at last no Club at all, in this last Case Sir, how deplorable must our State be!

And therefore Sir, to Conclude this argument, and put an end to this deplorable Subject, I must Intreat your honor to Consider this case maturely, and Graciously grant this deplorable petitioners petition, else I am afraid our State will be deplorable Indeed."

The orator ended, but the president took no further notice, and, tho the Case was deplorable, yet was his honor Inexorable, and so things remained *in Statu Quo*.

The orator, doubtless, in this deplorable oration, mimicked some Great master of the deplorable Stile, probably some one or other of our Costive and verbose Senatorial declaimers, as it is evident he here deviates from his own peculiar Stile and manner on other occasions.

As a trial of the Presidents Complaisance, Captain Dio Ramble, an honorary member, was proposed to be made a longstanding member, he not Intending himself to aspire to any such honor, and on the motion's being made, he rose up, and made a very Reverend bow to the Chair, but his honor pulling out his watch, said it was past Club hour, and no more was to be done this night—upon which—Quoth the Chancellor—says he—I should have thought it very Strange, had there been no objection from the Chair in this here Case, since there is, in all cases that come before us—but Surely every one must think it Strange, that the Club must lose the opportunity, of admitting an excellent Longstandg: member, to humor the Silly objections, of an old froward and unreasonable President—His honor at this Sederunt, having expressed much Indignation at Crinkum Crankum Esqr, Capt: Dio Ramble told his honor, that he thought the said Crankum, a very Impertinent fellow, and that if he pleased he would pull his nose or kick his arse for him,—to which his honor tacitly assented—but this was Jocularly said by the Captain.

Chapter IX

Confirmation law passed, Accrostic on the Poet Laureat, The Champions departure from the Club, Trial of Quirpum Comic Esqr.

Love my Self, love my dog, is an old proverb, which like all other proverbs has its Signification, Respect and deference to any person, Implies also a respect and deference towards every thing that pertains to him, and when at any time the Latter is deficient or wanting, men never fail to Conclude that the first stands but on a Slipery foundation. Indignities or affronts offered, to a persons Coat of arms or to any ensign or Symbol he Carries about him, to distinguish his own merit, or the merits of his family, are every whit as provoking, as if offered Immediatly to his person, and have laid the foundation of many feuds and quarrels between private persons and their families, Nay public affronts of this Sort, where the flag of a nation, or their arms have been Contemptuously treated, have been the Cause of Cruel and bloody wars, which has Cost the lives of thousands, and to Ennumerate the Law Suits that have arisen between man and man on this Important occasion, and the money that has been thrown away upon establishing these || points of honor, would be an endless work, we shall have occasion to give a detail of one remarkable example of this kind, happining in the Tuesday Club, before we Conclude this Chapter and book.

At Sederunt 214 December 4th 1753, Solo Neverout Esqr, the attorney General being H:S: The Chancellor, according to Law 43, took the Chair, as deputy President.

Crinkum Crankum Esqr, a long standing member in humble manner, represented to his Honor the Deputy and Club, the Hard Circumstances he lay under, in being looked upon, deemed and esteemed, a person Illegally sitting in this here Club, on account of his not having been yet confirmed by the hands of the Honorable Mr President Jole, that he had in the most dutiful and humble manner, drawn up and presented a respectful petition to the said honorable Mr President Jole, praying and requesting his confirmation, which petition stands upon Record, in the minutes of Sederunt 212, notwithstanding which, the said Honorable the President, absolutely rejected and refused granting the said petition, without giving any reasons Satisfactory to either the Club, or the petitioner, and therefore the petitioner finds himself constrained, against his Inclination, to apply to this here Club, for relief in his hard Circumstance, since he can have none from the head and principal power in the Club, or the Honorable President.

The Club upon this, took the Case under their mature and Serious consideration, and, after some debate on the Subject, during which Mr H:S: Neverout was fast asleep, they came to the following resolution, to which they gave the Sanction of a Law.

Law LI. That, notwithstanding this here Club at Sederunt 100, Febr: 28, 1748/9 Thought fit, out of their regard and esteem for the honorable the president, to grant and Concede to him, a power of Confirming Longstanding members, yet, after a Strict Examination of the Records, at this present Sederunt, 214 Decemb: 4th 1753, finding no express, or written Law of this here Club to place this power of Confirmation Solely in his honor the president, or, to make this Ceremony of Confirmation absolutely necessary for making a legal Longstanding member of this here Club, it is therefore ordained and passed into a law, to prevent all further disputes on this point, and, to secure the peace and liberty of this here Club,

That this Ceremony of Confirmation shall not be deemed henceforth, a necessary ceremony to Create any Gentleman a Legal longstanding member of this here Club, and, that after an unanimous election by the Ballot, two thirds of the Longstanding members being present, according to Law 39th, passed at Sederunt 102, March 21, 1748/9, and a deputy President in the Chair, either by his honor's appointment, or the Election of the Club, according to Law 43, passed at Sederunt 122, January 16th 1749/50, The Gentleman Elected shall be deemed, a true and legal Longstanding member of this here Club, to all Intents and purposes, as truely and effectually, as if he had been Confirmed by a hundred honorable Presidents and elected by a Thousand Longstanding members, any thing || in the Customs, ordonances or resolves of this here ancient and honorable Club, to the Contrary notwithstanding, and also, that all deputy Presidents, whether appointed by the Tenor of Law 43d of this here Club, elected by the Club, or Commissioned by his honor the president, shall have as full and large a power to act, in all and every proceeding, requisite for the good of this here Club, and shall act, with the same efficacy and Virtue, as if his honor, the Chief

President were present, and In the Chair, any resolve, custom or ordonance of this here ancient and honorable Club, to the Contrary notwithstanding.

After passing of this Law, (which we must observe is the longest that ever was passed in Club, and highly necessary at this time, to support the falling liberties of the Club, if with propriety we may stile these liberties, falling, which seemed to be fallen already) Solo Neverout Esqr, attorney General and H:S: waking from his Sleep, rubbing his Eyes, yawning, and streching out his Limbs, protested against it *articulatim* and *particulatim,* without Comprehending, knowing or understanding one single ace of the Intent or purport of it, but only upon a Suspicion, that it was derogatory to, and destructive of, the prerogative and authority of the honorable Chair, for the Support of which, ever since he had his Commission of attorney General, he had shown himself, either with or without Rhime or Reason a Strenuous Stickler.

[292] At Sederunt 215, Jonathan Grog Esqr, being H:S: his honor sending no deputation as usual, the || Chancellor according to Law 43d took the Chair, and some Consultation was held in Club, about appointing a Committee to be held at his honor the presidents, to enquire into some enormous trespasses, Committed by Don John Charlotto Gent: Clerk of the kitchen, and to call him to a Strict account for the same, denouncing Severe punishments to be Inflicted upon him if he did not mend his manners, and the H:S: and Mr Attor: Neverout were appointed to be of the Committee, the nature of these trespasses were very heinous, the said Don John, having made several violent assaults of late, upon the Sacred person of his honor the president, taken the Command of the house and the keys into his own hands, and Called his honor by several Scurrilous and oprobrious names, as dam'd old Son of a Bitch & the like.

The Club having nothing else to do at this Sederunt, payd a Compliment to the poet Laureat by Composing on him the following accrostic.

Accrostic on the Poet Laureat, by the Club

In flowing numbers, sing the Poet,
Of whose keen muse, (the world shall know it)
No other muse the pitch attains,
Ascending still in Lofty Strains,
The president and Club he sings,
High soaring on Pyndaric wings,
And warbles out his notes so mellow,
No other Bard can be his fellow.

Great Bard! whose grog-Inspired fancy,
Round the bright Starry orbs doth dance high,
Of Jole the Great, still sing with Pathos,
Gain matchless heights, & shun the Bathos.

This accrostic shows plainly that the poetical Genius of the Club, was at this particular time somewhat Costive and bound up. [293]

At Sederunt 216, the Worshipful Sir John, being for the last time H:S: and Philo Dogmaticus Esqr Deputy in the Chair by virtue of Law 43d, some argumentation arose between the deputy President and the Secretary concerning the propriety of Conundrums, which, after much earnest disputation, was, like most Controversies of that nature, left Just where they found it.

The Club tried again to exercise their poetical Genius this night, upon the lamentable occasion of the honorable the president's Indisposition, and absence from the Club, according to Custom, but the muses would not answer their Call, the Longstanding members, being Remarkably dull and low Spirited, which some looked upon, to be an ominous presage, of the *Great Sir John, the Champions leaving the Club.*

Mr Attorney General was fast asleep the greatest part of the evening, and Jonathan Grog Esqr, the brightest wit in Club, was sunk in a fit of Philosophical Silence and Contemplation, and did nothing but Chaw Tobacco and drink Grog, and O Lamentable! the Club broke up at ten o clock.

This being the last time, that the Great Sir John appeared in Club, we cannot take our leave of this heroe, without bestowing a few words on him. It cannot be Certainly ascertained, wherefore he left the Club, or Indeed, whether he had reasons or no reasons || for doing so, tho' some Imagined, [294] that finding his Health much on the decline, he could not safely be abroad a nights. Others, that he found his Interest with the President so much lessened, since the affair of the Grand Committee, and was so picqued, at the Influence and power of the Attorney General, that he could not brook, or bear the thoughts of being under that haughty officer, as he had always looked upon himself to be the Second man in the Club, and the Right hand prop of the Chair, and therefore, finding that his honor the president relied upon another Supporter, he Judged, it was high time for him, now to take his departure, as his Influence seemed now to be at an end, being like other great men, in this respect, disdaining to hold a place in any Society, Inferior to that which he had at first possessed; But, whatever were the real reasons of Sir John's leaving the Club, in the abrubt manner he did, it is Certain that he gave, or alledged no reasons for it, being so much of a politician, as to keep his reasons always within his own breast; by the Great part the Champion has had in this History, it would seem that the Club would suffer much by his departure, but it happened otherwise, his honor the President did not seem to take it at all to heart, and, the Chancellor's leaving the Club soon after, restored such peace and tranquillity in the Clubical Constitution, that there was no occasion ‖ for a Champion, and Indeed the honorable the President, expressly declared several times, *ex Cathedra*, that for the future, he himself should be Champion for the Club, Tho Coll: Comico Butman sometime after this had a Commission, under his honor's privy Seal, to be Champion for the Club, for one night. By Sir John's departure, the Secretary was now become the only old Standing member of the Club, that is, he was the only one left of those eight Gentlemen, who were of it originally at it's first Institution in Annapolis.

At Sederunt 217, Mr Secretary Scribble being H:S: and Crinkum Crankum Esqr, Deputatus Electus, the attorney General Rising up, Called upon Quirpum Comic Esqr to answer unto a Trespass on the Case, in as much, as he, the said Quirpum Comic Esqr, had offered the Presidential Chair, with all it's appurtenances to public Sale, wherupon Quirpum Comic Esqr, rising up, denied the said Charge.

Then the Attorney examined Jealous Spyplot Esqr, Honorary member.

Att: G: Jealous Spyplot Esqr, Sir, I shall Call upon you to declare, what you know of Quirpum Comic Esqrs exposing the presidential Chair to Sale, at a house in this here City.

J: Sp: I know nothing of it Sir, the chair may speak for itself.

Att: G: Sir, answer me directly, did you ever see the Chair, at a certain house in this City, exposed to public Sale?

Dep: Pres: How! How! To public Sale say you?

J: Sp: I never saw it exposed to Sale any where.

Att: Gen: No Shuffling Sir,—I say not to Sale,—but to public Sale?

J: Sp: Say you so Sir,—well public Sale be it.

Att: Gen: I find Sir by your prevaricating, you have been at a bar before now; did you never hear of the Chair's having been exposed to public Sale at a Certain Taveren in this City, by Quirpum Comic Esqr L:S:M: now at the bar?

J: Sp: Never heard Sir?

Att: Gen: Did you never hear any person say, that Quirpum Comic Esqr L:S:M: Exposed the Chair to public Sale?

J: Sp: I tell you, as I told you before, good Mr Attorney, The Chair is of age, it may speak for itself.

Then Dr Nolens Volens,¹ a Stranger Invited to the Club, was Examined.

Att: Gen: Doctor Nolens Volens, declare to his honor the deputy and this here Club, what you know of this here affair.

Dr N: V: Who?—I Sir—

Q: Com: Pray Sir, in what Ship did you come to this here country?

Dep: Pres: You have no right to ask that Question Sir.

Q: Com: Pray upon what terms did you come here Sir?

Dep: Pres: Psha! let us hear what he has to say. The gentleman seems confounded, ask him the Question again Mr Attorney.

Att: Gen: Dr Nolens Volens, Sir I call upon you to declare ‖ what you know of this here affair Sir. [297]

Dr N: V: It was offered to Sale in divers parcells, The footstool, Canopy and Seat were exposed separately, but the Seat would not sell, because some body said it smelt of a fox.

Dep: Pres: How! of a fox Sir?

Att: Gen: Pray Sir, give his honor and the Club a particular account of it, according to the Best of your knowledge.

Dr N: V: I have told you what I know Sir.

Q: Com: Pray Sir go on Cooley, this is no triffling affair.

Att: Gen: As Cool as a Cucumber Sir.

Dr N: V: Sir, now I recollect; The Chair was sold for 19 Shillings and Sixpence, Clear of it's appurtenances, and, in leu of the Stool, and other parts that would not sell on account of their perfume, there was a balance of three Shillings and ten pence, to be returned to the Club.

Att: Gen: How say you Sir?

Q: Com: Thats a fib, I'm Sure.

Dr N: V: The person buying this Chair Sir, was to hire it out to the Club for the future when they wanted it, and the whole might have been sold, had it not been for that same perfume as I said.

Q: Com: If that be proved, I shall Surely be hanged.

Att: Gen: How then Sir. Pray proceed.

Q: Com: Take care what you say, you are a young man Sir, consider the oath you have taken.

Dr N: V: Sir, tho' I be a young man, yet we all know that *Philosophum non barba facit*.²

Q: Com: Sir, I dont understand greek or Hebrew.

---

1. This Latin pseudonym is roughly equivalent to *willy-nilly*.
2. An old commonplace, meaning "The beard does not make the philosopher."

[298] D: Pres: Greek and hebrew! eh, eh, eh, Greek and hebrew! eh, eh, eh.

Q: Com: Pray Sir, did you take notice of the Seat and footstool?—I may ask the evidence some questions may I not Sir?

Chanc: Yea Sir, but you have no right to ask that there Question—what do you say to those matters that the evidence has already delivered, have you any thing to plead in your own defence, before Sentence is passed upon you?

Q: Com: Sir,—I say—that he says that I said it,—and I say—that he said it—I know not what else to say faith—not I.

Att: Gen: I find we have got a Cunning fellow to deal with,—we do nothing here but prevaricate & quibble.—ho! Silence there—why, you Pitiful delinquent, I have Good evidence of your saying so, your very Identical Self.

Q: Com: Whose evidence, pray Mr Attorney?

Att: Gen: Why you Incorrigible Brute, your own Brother told me so.

Dr N: Vol: Sir, one thing I had like to have forgot, he said he had made a Charge to the Club of Coach hire, or Cart hire, one or another.

Dep: Pres: Ay! ay! ay! was the Chair Carted?

Secret: Why yes Sir, to say the truth the Chair was Carted to the house of this delinquent, when he last served the Club, at Sederunt 213, on the [299] 20th of November, and, he had the Impudence to cart it up North ‖ east Street, Just under his honor the presidents nose, as he looked over his hatch.

Chan: What say you to that Culprit?

Q: Com: Gentlemen, you wont permit me to ask the evidence any questions—avast there I say,—no dragoon Law.

Chanc: Yea Sir—but Club law—Club law.

Dr N: Vol: Is that what is called *argumentum Baculare?*[3]

Secr: As this trial, Gentlemen, seems not in a way to be soon determined, I would move That as this Gentleman is to leave the Club soon, he may, from a Longstanding, be transmogrified into an honorary member, as others before him have been.

Q: Com: Sir, I humbly second that motion.

Jon: Grog: Why Mr Secretary, you would not have us to dock the Gentleman, I suppose the member, however he may stand now at this Juncture, is as long as ever.

Dep: Pres: Ha, ha, ha, the longstanding members methinks are waggish.

---

3. "Argument of the rod."

Mr Electro Vitrifrice [a Stranger Invited to the Club] Longstanding members, I think Gentlemen, with Submission, are not so properly waggish, because if they stand they cannot wag.

Chanc: Yea, but with your leave Sir,—I say these members must stand before they can wag.

Thus did this learned trial proceed, and was not determined any how, the delinquent privately slipping or wagging out of the Club room, for fear of some ‖ Severe Sentence being passed against him. [300]

If the abstract of this political Club trial seems Imperfect, the Secretary thus apologizes for himself, having no pen and ink at hand, he was obliged to use a lead pencil, and by the attrition and rubbing of the Sides of the paper together, the writing was so obliterated, before he could find leisure to get it transcribed in the Record book, that partly his memory, and partly his Invention served as a Succedaneum for the defect of his eyes in transcribing the faint words and letters.

Several new Songs were sung at this Sederunt by the Longstanding members, and mirth was very much Promoted in Club.

End of the Twelfth book.

Book XIII[1]

Sederunt 218
Tuesday, Febr: 5th 1754

The Club met at the house of Alexr: Malcolm Esqr, Cancellar: and were entertained by him as H:S: pursuant to an order of last meeting.
Present
The hon: Beal Bordley Esqr, Præs: Dep: Elect:
Alexr: Malcolm Esqr Canc: & H:S: ⎫   ⎧ Walter Dulany Esqr
Jonas Green Esqr Mr of Cer: ⎭   ⎩ Wm: Lux, Esqr
Alexr: Hamilton Secretry

Alexander Malcolm Esqr Cancellarius, having determined in his own mind to keep no Club this night, neglected to send notice of it to the longstanding members, who, having several of them assembled at his house in the evening, in pursuance of the order of last Sederunt, after some learned arguments upon the point, vizt: whether they should form themselves into a Club or not, or whether they were to account themselves but half a Club, and this here Sederunt, only half a Sederunt, they at last established themselves into a Club, and sent for the Records, which were brought by the Secretary, and the deputy president being elected and plac'd in the Chair, the proceedings of last meeting were read.

The Club this night, according to their ancient Custom, composed a Condolatory poem, on the absence and Indisposition of his hon' the Pres: as follows.

---

1. Chapter 1 and the beginning of chapter 2 (pp. 301–332) of book XIII are missing from the *History*. I have provided material from the "Record" (pp. 462–465) for this portion of the narrative.

ΔΑΚΡΥΑ ΜΕΛΠΟΜΕΝΗΣ.[2]

Or a Lamentable Ode, upon the mournful occasion of the absence and Indisposition of the honorable Charles Cole Esqr, president of the ancient and honorable Tuesday Club, presented to his honor by the Poet Laureat

As water Springs from rocks do Gush
    And drench the vales all oer,
So from our Eyes the Tears do rush
    And Round bedew the floor.
Thus annually the briny drops
    Do from our Eyelids flow,
For still alas, our flattering hopes,
    Are quashd by yearly woe.

Our honorable President
    Again the Gout confines,
Which makes the Club again Lament
    In Lamentable lines.
The Lamentable Song again
    Melpomene shall raise,
Hills, dales and valleys shall Complain
    Resounding doleful Lays.

We mourn and moan, we sigh and Groan
    For want of Noble Cole,
For why? we thus are left alone,
    Bereft of life and Soul.
The life and Soul, thus gone and fled,
    The carcase dead remains,
Dead is our Club, while Cole's in bed
    Confind with gouty pains.

O may these cruel gouty akes
    No more his Joints torment,
May they Infest old pockey rakes
    And not our president,
May drunken Sot, who sucks his pot
    With gout and gravel pine,

---

2. Literally, "Melpomene's tears"; in context, the "tragic tears" of the club, since Melpomene was the Muse of tragedy.

> But from great Cole, such wretched lot
>   Avert ye powers divine.
>
> May he from bed of Sickness rise,
>   At your divine command,
> Forsaking couch on which he lies
>   Like Standing member stand,
> May he from grief and anguish free
>   Thro' life with pleasure Jog,
> Whilst like longstanding members we,
>   Shall drink his health in Grog.

Ordered that Jonas Green Esqr, Poet Laureat, and William Thornton Esqr Protomusicus and attorney General, present this Condolatory poem to his honor before next Sederunt.

Ordered that William Lux Esqr, serve this Society, upon Tuesday the 19th of this Instant February as H:S: thereof.

Sederunt 219
Tuesday Febr: 19th 1754

The Club met at the house of the worshipful Sir John knight of the Club, and were entertaind by W: Lux Esqr as H:S: pursuant to an order of last meeting.

Present
Walter Dulany Esqr, Præs: Deputat:
Alexr: Malcolm Esqr Canc:
Wm: Thornton Esqr P:M: & At:G:
Wm: Lux Esqr H:S:

Beal Bordley Esqr
the Revd Mr Jno: Hamilton H:M:
Alexr: Hamilton Secretry

The Deputy president having taken the Chair, without the authority of either a Commission from the Honble: Mr President Cole, or the Election of the Club, the proceedings of last meeting were read.

Jonas Green Esqr, being this night absent, the Secretary reported to the club, that the said Jonas Green Esqr and himself, had presented, the poem, Entituled $\Delta\alpha\varkappa\rho\upsilon\alpha\ \mu\varepsilon\lambda\pi o\mu\varepsilon\nu\eta\varsigma$, to his honor the president, yesterday morning, which he was pleased graciously to receive, Mr Attorney General Thornton, declining being Concerned in the presenting of that poem, doubting the authority of the Club held at the house of Alexr: Malcolm Esqr, to compose or present any such poem.

Then the Secretary read the proceedings of a Committee, held at the House of Mr Attorney General as follows.

At a meeting of the Committee, held for redressing Clubical Grievances, of the ancient and honorable Tuesday Club, summoned by Will: Thornton Esqr Protomusicus, and attorney General to the said Club, on Monday February the 11th 1754, were present as follows, vizt:

Walter Dulany Esqr, Chairman
Alexr: Hamilton Esqr ⎱   ⎰ William Thornton Esqr, At: Gen:
Jonas Green Esqr   ⎰   ⎱ William Lux Esqr Clk: committ:

Mr Attorney General, delivered in the Committee, a Cabel of the several Longstanding members, Summoned to attend the Committee, together with the form of the Summons as follows.

Forma Summonsii

Annapolis, Monday febr: 11, 1754 Three o Clock P:M:

We Summons you   In the name of, and by the authority of the honorable Mr President Cole, to attend the Committee for redressing Clubical grievances, to be held at the Castle of William Thornton Esqr attorney General, this present evening, at Six o' the Clock precisely, and after the Clubical grievances are redressed, to regale with Turkey and oyster Sauce, apple pye, plumb pudding, and Craneberry tarts, to be washed down with a glass of Good Hermitage &ct: &ct: &ct: for which this shall be your Sufficient warrant, and which produced shall gain you admittance, hereof fail not, at your peril, and under pain of our high displeasure.

Summons No   Will: Thornton—   [Seal]
For   Attorney General

The Committe Called in Alexander Macpherson, a highlander by birth, and Examined him as follows.

Com: Where was you born?
A: MPher: Hay! Sir?
Com: Where was you born?
A: McP: Born Sir—In the Shire of Inverness.
Com: How old are you?
A: M: Be-my Troth I canno' tell.
Com: Did you ever hear of Prester John? at Inverness?
A: M: Yes, figs! but I war na' there.
Com: You were not where?
A: M: What's your wul Sir?
Com: You were not where?—I say.

A: M: I war na' at Preston Pans.³

Com: Not at Preston Pans?

A: M: Na, na, the highlanders were dong there & I was at the ither place.

Com: At what place?

A: M: Att Colloden,⁴ whare I fand I mon rin for my life whan I was doon.

Com: Did you Run after you was down?

A: M: Yes faith did I, as if the muckle deel had been in me.

Alexander being thus examined drank a large Glass of Grog and was dismissed. ‖ Upon Examination, and some Interrogatories put to Jonathan Grog Esqr, who drank a Glass of Grog between each Question and answer, the Committee resolved, & report to the Club as follows. [334]

That it appears to this here Committee, by the above examination, that the Club held by Philo Dogmaticus Esqr, the Chancellor, on Tuesday the 4th Instant, was a Sham Club, and at best but half a Club, and that this here Committee, shall make up the Remaining half, to render it a whole Club, and a Compleat Sederunt, provided always, that the said Chancellor give the long standing members, one handsom Club treat before he leaves these parts, else this resolve and report to stand for nothing, all which is submitted to the Consideration of the honorable the President and Longstanding members.

After the Song of *Robin and Jeck* had been sung several times, by Jonathan Grog Esqr, the Committee broke up.

Sigd: *Slyboots Pleasant Chairman*.

It does not appear by the Record that the Club ever Concurred with this Report.

The Reverend Mr Broadface Round, an honorary Member, attended the Club at this Sederunt, and presented a petition from some Gentlemen In Charlestown, Requesting a power and authority by Commission, under the Great Seal, from Mr President Jole, to erect a Club at Charles Town in Cecil County, which petition ‖ was once read, and ordered to lye upon the table, till his honor Mr President Jole should appear in Club. [335]

---

3. Prestonpans is a small port on the Firth of Forth near Edinburgh where the Jacobites (chiefly Highlanders) defeated British troops on Sept. 21, 1745.

4. In 1746 the duke of Cumberland defeated the Young Pretender and his forces at Culloden. Two of the Tuesday Club's members published sermons celebrating the defeat (see John Gordon, *A Thanksgiving Sermon, on Occasion of the Suppression of the Unnatural Rebellion, in Scotland, by His Royal Highness the Duke of Cumberland* [Annapolis, Md., 1746], and Thomas Cradock, *A Sermon Preach'd at St. Thomas's Church, . . . to Give God Thanks for the Conquest of the Rebels by His Royal Highness the Duke of Cumberland* [Annapolis, Md., 1747]).

Mr Broadface Round, in speaking for this Petition, Informed the Club, That there were Certain Gentlemen in Charles Town, who had formed themselves into a Club, and met as a Club, by no Earthly authority but their own.

To which the Chancellor replied, what then Sir? Is not their own authority Sufficient?

Nay Sir, said Mr Broadface Round, but it would be much better, could we obtain the Sanction of his honor The President, and this here ancient and honorable Club.

And if you should not, replied the Chancellor, I suppose you'd still be a Club, in Spite of our teeth.

Really I doubt that Sir, replied Mr Broadface Round, at least not such a perfect and Compleat Club.

That is, said the Chancellor, without our Commission, you could not equal us in Nonsense and absurdity—here this Learned Conversation dropt, and the petition was to be further Considered at a Subsequent Sederunt.

The Orator produced a Speech, Intended to have been delivered, In Case his honor the President had been Present in the Club, which Speech was read and laid aside, as Intirely useless and Improper at this Juncture. After Supper, the Secretary read several of the old minutes to some Strangers Invited to the Club, during which lecture the Chancellor fell fast asleep, a thing very unusual with that Gentleman, for which he blamed the flatness of the Stuff read by the Secretary.

Chapter III

Congratulatory ode by the poet Laureat, altercation of the President and Chancellor, Learned Club Letters, Second long adjournment of the Club.

Discretion and Goodness in Rulers, and obedience in Those that are ruled, are the two principal Ingredients In the happiness of a State, Community or Club; without these there can be no tranquillity or peace, nor can there be any harmony or order in their proceedings. What made Scipio, the Roman General, so Successful a Conqueror, was his own discretion and wisdom in directing, and the readiness of his Soldiery in obeying his orders, which made him say, at a review of his troops, that there was not one man among them all, but would, should he Command him to do it, throw himself from a precipice into the Sea;[1] The Great Inconvenience of Stubborness that Consul knew, when, meeting with an obstinate fellow, he sold him and all his effects, declaring that he had no use for that Citizen that would not be obedient.

Whether the want of obedience, in most of the Long Standing members of the ancient and honorable Tuesday Club, particularly in the Chancellor, towards his honor the president, their right and Lawful master & ruler, was owing to any Indiscretion or misconduct, in the said honorable President, I shall not be so bold as to declare, let that honorable Gentleman's conduct, as it is ‖ set forth in this faithful and true history, be the Criterion of that, to the Judging and Impartial world, as it does no ways become me to pass Judgement on the Conduct of my Superiors, but this I may with Confidence affirm, that not one of the Longstanding members of the ancient and honorable Tuesday Club, would have, at his honor's command, Jumped from a precipice into the Sea, nay, not even from a Table upon the floor, and, as for the Chancellor, his honor thought him so obstinate, and so refractory a member, that, had it been in his power, he would have done with him as Scipio did with the ungovernable Citizen, That is, sold him, and all his Clubical Effects, vizt: his bag and great Seal, both of which, he now from his heart, hated and dispised.

At Sederunt 220, Slyboots Pleasant Esqr, being H:S: several Congratulatory Speeches were made, on his honor's appearance in Club, after so long an absence.

The Petition of the Reverend Mr Broadface Round, and the Charles Town Club, was Read and pocketed up by his honor the President for further Consideration, but, by it's going into that pocket, it got, with many other Clubical papers, into the Bottomless Pit of oblivion, for the Club never saw it again.

An Ode Congratulatory was presented and read in Club, by the poet Laureat, vizt:

Congratulatory Ode,
On the Return of the Honorable
Mr President Jole To his Club.

Oh! That I had the Lungs of Stentor,
    And Nestor's flowing tongue,

---

1. Scipio Africanus (236–184/183 B.C.) was a great Roman general who helped establish Rome's domination in Spain, Africa, and the Hellenistic East.

On such a Song, this night I'd venture
   As ne'er by bard was sung.
Loud as a trumpet would I rattle,
Rejoice you with poetic tattle
   And puff away all Care,
     With hollow Sound
     Like empty Tub,
     I would rebound
     And tell the Club,
   Great Jole resumes the Chair.

The Chair Great Jole resumes again,
   With Joy we're all agog,
Let's drive away all Care and pain,
   With hearty pulls of grog.
Then here's a health to mighty Jole
And round the table let it roll,
   And pledge it every one,
     Thus quick we'll pass,
     The Sprightly glass,
     No time is lost,
     For next we toast
   The worshipful Sir John.(a)

O valiant knight, rejoice, rejoice
   And drink your Glass with glee,
Tune up your pipes, exalt your voice
   And sing along with me,
Again, Great Jole beholds his Club,
   O then Rejoice therefore,
While I, nor wine, nor 'rack, nor Shrub,
     Will ever use
     To whet my muse,
     But in a log
     Of Lusty Grog,
   I drink our Chancellor.

Then put it Round, my Jolly boys,
'Twill whet and Elevate our Joys,
Lets Laugh and make a Joyful noise,
   This Grog will never burn you,

(a) When this poem was made, it was not known Sr Jno: had left the Club.

Jole's found again whom we thought lost,
Hes found! The Jewel we valu'd most,
Rejoice therefore, while next we toast
  Our General Attorney.
  Chorus
Long Standing members, every Soul
Loud let the Chorus sound for Jole,
    Each one must Join
    His voice with mine,
  Our president to praise, [340]
A President of such great worth,
    No where is found
    On earthly ground
Or east, or west, or South, or north,
  May heaven prolong his days.

May happiness his Steps attend
From the beginning to the end,
    Still driving out
    The cursed Gout,
That Racks his Joints with pain,
And let us Jointly pray for this,
    Should he be ill
    Yet may he still
Like to the Phænix bird of bliss,
Rise youthful from his nest again.

Thus would he still revive his Club
More than would draughts of mum or bub,
  Or fine Cephalic drug,
And, as for me, the Laureat,
His presence can my muse Elate
    Even more than potent Grog.

This ode met with Great applause in the Club, and it was thought by most of the members, that the Laureat had here touched the true Clubical Sublime.

    Soon after the recital of this ode, a most violent dispute, arose between his honor the president, and the || Chancellor, the occasion of which was [341] this. Crinkum Crankum Esqr, again urging his confirmation, and moving that his petition might be again read and maturely considered, by his honor and the Club, his honor told him, that he might make himself easy, as to that matter, that he was fully determined to act in the affair, as he had before declared, and, that it signified nothing, his giving himself any further trowble about the matter, for, that by that means, he should still be farther from his desired end. This answer affected the Gentleman much, and he sat down with a very Sorowful Countenance, but, getting up again, he used an argument with his honor, which he thought would prevail, thinking to take him upon the weak or blind Side, knowing his enthusiastical fondness for old England and every thing pertaining to that happy Country; he begg'd his honor, to favor him at least for Country's Sake, that he was his Countryman, and, the only old Englishman now In the Club, besides his honor, and his honor's attorney General, The Rest of the members, being either Country born or Scotsmen—To this his honor made reply, that he set no value upon that, and that he always Judged of a man by his behaviour, and not by his Country. This was an excellent Sentiment & came from his honor unawares, he not being given to think so Philosophicall or Justly, when old England was Introduced into the Conversation, which || evinces that even resentment at times, may make a man utter Philosophical truths. The Secretary then got up to speak for Crinkum Crankum Esqr, but his honor dashed him at once, by telling him that he might spare his trowble, for, that he did not understand his broad Scotsh pronounciation and dialect.

The Club, after this kept Silence for some time, and the Chancellor swell'd and puff'd with Inward rage, scarce being able to contain himself, and had frequent recourse to his Snuff box, dawbing the breasts of his Coat all over with that Sophisticated powder, so that it might be said in a literal Sense, that the Chancellor took Snuff at this, at last, a member moved, that the law passed at Sederunt 114 might be read, and alledged that that law gave Crinkum Crankum Esqr, as full and ample privileges, as any longstanding member of the Club, The Secretary at the desire of the Club read the law, which being done, the President declared *ex Cathedra*, with the Haughtiness and peremptoriness of a pope, That this was an unwarranted Insolent proceeding, altogether Illegal and rebellious, and that if that law stood, he'd never set foot in Club again, upon this the dispute between his honor & the Chancellor began, which was Carried on by dialogue as follows.

Chanc: And who Cares a fart, whether you do or not, we should be much better without such a Tyrant, what! must the Club be kept under by such humors and whims? has not the Club a power of making laws for their own regulation?

Pres: No, they have not, so long as they have made me their governor and Ruler.

Chan: That's a damn'd lye, they did not give up all their rights and privileges, when they made you their President, they only committed a trust into your hands, which trust, they never Intended should be used to Inslave them.

Pres: Prithee moderate your voice, you quite deafen me.

Chan: I will speak to be heard, and must be heard, this Tyranny is most unsufferable, and the Club will never be so Simple as to bear with it.

Pres: For God's Sake, if you speak to be heard, speak to be understood, speak English, & then I'll understand you.

Chan: Speak english! what do you mean Sir? dont I speak English?

Pres: You may speak English words for aught I know, but I would desire you Sir to mend your pronounciation, for you utter your words so broad, that I cannot understand you.

Chanc: That's a damn'd piece of foppery, Sir, I can speak as good english as you can.

Pres: Nay, for that, I appeal to the Club, the Secretary is your Countryman, yet, tho' his dialect be broad, he speaks more properly than you, and I can understand him better [here the Secretary bowed low to the President]

Chanc: Sir, I'd have you to know, I can speak better English than you.

Pres: You may speak more grammatically than I perhaps, because the Study of Grammar has been your business, but to say you speak English with a better accent than I, ‖ who am an Englishman born, and you a Scots man is absurd. [344]

Chanc: Of all the old fellows I ever met with you have the most abusive tongue, and there is no bearing with your Scurrility, I wish you'd learn to mend your manners.

Pres: I am not to come to Learn of you, you have no Right to advise me.

Chan: I'll let you know Sir, I have a right to advise you in this here Club.

Pres: As how pray?

Chan: By my office of Chancellor.

Pres: Your office of Chancellor! what right does that give you to advise me? I dispise your office and every thing belonging to it.

Chan: Sir, I'd have you to know, that that office, gives me an authority over you.

Pres: As how?—what! must I be hectored over in this manner, and none take any notice [looks about him] as how?—I say.

Chanc: As keeper of your Conscience Sir.

Pres: You keeper of my Conscience, pray who made you keeper of my Conscience?

Chanc: The Club.

Pres: The Club!—The Club make you keeper of my Conscience?

L: St: memb: Ha, ha, ha, ha.

Pres: No Sir, I'll have it under no such Sorry keeping.

Chan: 'Tis lucky for you that it is under such keeping, the Conscience of a fool is apt to go astray unless under good Custody.

Pres: Can any one bear this usage?

[345]   Chan: If your Conscience be tender, it must be alittle roughly handled to harden it.

Pres: Prithee let my Conscience alone, I cannot see what business you have with my Conscience.

Chan: More than you Imagine, I tell you again I am keeper of your Conscience.

Pres: Who the Devil made you my Conscience keeper?

L: St: memb: Ha, ha, ha, ha.

Chan: Who but the Club.

Pres: The Club make you my Conscience keeper!

L: St: memb: Ha, ha, ha, ha.

Chanc: Yea Sir, I am the Club's officer.

Pres: You are the Devils officer, I think, which does not become your Cloth.

Chanc: Augh! (yawns) there's no ending with you, you have an eternal tongue, and will have the last word, [here the president looked about him, and none in the Club taking notice, he abrubtly left the Chair and the Club broke up Confusedly]

While this dispute lasted, the Chancellor and president showed very different aspects, in their several Countenances, the president's countenance, was the most Composed, he having the greatest command of his temper & features, the Chancellors visage had a pale Cast which he always showed when in a passion, together with an extraordinary elongation of Countenance, the two faces together, and the Countenances of the Rest of

[346] the Club would have furnished a very good Group for the || genius of the Celebrated Hogarth to Improve upon, one face Looked down Contemptuously from a lofty Chair upon the other, and the other looked up as Scornfully upon the face in the Chair, and both faces were of the hatchet Sort, showing when they smiled or Grin'd that they shared Three teeth between them, the President having one long tooth, and the Chancellor two.

At the next Sederunt, the Club, after having been shammed off, as usual, by Solo Neverout Esqr, attor: Genl: met at the house of Jonathan Grog Esqr, Mr of Ceremonies, Being Sederunt 221, and, Slyboots Pleasant

Esqr, being put in the Chair, as deputy President, the H:S: presented in Club, a letter directed to him by the Secretary, vizt:

To Jonathan Grog Esqr H:S:T:C:

Sir,

    Tho it be not Customary to write letters to H: Stewards, or H: Stewards elect, or Supposed H: Stewards, yet, as we are got now, into many Anticlubical, or unclubical, or Pseudo-clubical, practises of late in the ancient and honorable Tuesday Club, by means of the woeful & lamentable disputes, altercations, Schisms and Contentions, between the most honorable the president and the most venerable the Chancellor, which, like the dissentions now subsisting between the parliament and Clergy in France, are likely to terminate in a Civil war, I take the liberty in these trowblesome times to write to you, whom, I suppose to be at present, the H:S: elect of the ancient & honble: Tuesday Club, ‖ for the following reasons, 1st His honor the President refuses, tho' he were in Good health, to serve the Club at this time, notwithstanding it is his turn in Course, 2d his honor is Indisposed, and therefore, if he would he could not serve, 3dly The Clerk of the kitchen is still in a drunken Situation, and every thing is at Sixes and Sevens in his honor's house, his honour cannot be a minute from home, for fear the house should be turned out at the windows, 4th, Quirpum Comic Esqr, who is next to his honor in Course of serving, has left this place, given up housekeeping here, and therefore is supposed to have left the Club, 5thly you follow next in Course to him, in the order of serving, at least Solo Neverout Esqr says so, who, this day, sets out for Prince George's County Court, and therefore, were it his turn (which I think it is before you) he cannot serve; 6thly, I who come next, am not well disposed, 7thly The Chancellor, who succeeds me, declares he will not serve, 8thly Sir John is in the Dumps, and we cannot safely ask him the question,[(a)] 9thly, Crinkum Crankum Esqr, served only the time before last, and thinks it too soon to serve again, especially as his Seat in Club is questioned, 10thly Slyboots Pleasant Esqr, was the last that served, and says, he knows not that he has yet been Guilty of the breach of any Club Law to make him Incurr the penalty of serving twice hand running,—For these Important reasons, I take the liberty to trowble you, with this very long ‖ Letter, which, I own, might all have been contained in the following words,—Sir, [if you are willing to serve the ancient and honorable Tuesday Club this night, being

[347]

[348]

(a) Hence it appears, that it was not yet known Sr Jno: had left the Club.

Tuesday the 26th Instant March, Please to let me know, I will Inform the members in Town] and if you serve, send me the Copy of the ode of last Sederunt, that I may enter it in the Records.

Yours, with all due respect
Loquacious Scribble Secrtry

The answer to which letter was also produced & read in Club, vizt:

To Loquacious Scribble Esqr Secretary.

Dear Sir,

I have this minute received yours, and have Carefully read and Considered all the ten heads Contained therein, and shall answer them thus.

1st I am willing to serve as H:S:
2d I am willing to serve as H:S: to night.
3d I am willing to serve as H:S: to night of the Tuesday Club.
4   I am sorry his honor cannot serve as H:S:
5   I am sorry his honr: cannot serve as h:S: to night.
6   I am sorry his honr: cannot serve as h:S: to night of the Tuesd: Club.
7   I will serve in his room as h:S:
8   I will serve in his room as h:S: to night.
9   I will serve in his Room as h:S: to night of the Tuesday Club.
10 I must serve, and shall be very glad to have the Company of the members who are in town, and can attend at the house of your and their

March 26th 1754   Very Humble Servt:
                                    Jonathan Grog H:S:

After this Sederunt, followed the Long adjournment of the Club, being the Longest by much that || ever happened since its first Institution, The first long adjournment being but Seven weeks, and this eleven, which was owing chiefly to a Contest between the Chancellor, and the attorney General, each alledging, that it was the others Turn to serve, nor, would this Contest have Ceased, or the Club have Convened again, even to this Day, had not the Secretary, at his honor the presidents order and desire, taken upon himself the burden, as well as the honor of serving the Club, upon the eleventh of June, which was the 9th Anniversary, the Relation of which we reserve for the following Chapter.

Chapter IV

Celebration of the Ninth Anniversary, Anniversary Speech and Ode.

Democritus the Philosopher has been much wondered at, and much blamed for his Laughing humor,[1] by persons of a particular Solemn and Grave turn and, for this Reason, has had the Character of a Coxcomb and Impertinent Buffoon; But if one Seriously Considers the humors of this Transitory world, in which we live, he will wonder, how any person can be so Stupid as to forbear laughing at almost every occurrence that happens around us, would it not provoke one to Laughter to observe, on what the Generality of men place their esteem, to see how the Philosopher, as well as the fool, is mistaken in opinion, in reckoning the wealthiest always the best, to observe a Set of domineering Insolent puppies, endea- ‖ voring to sink a noble and generous Spirit by accumulating misery upon it, while all their dirty labor, is Laughd at and dispised, by the Heroical, resolute and Brave; To see politicians and projectors, noted for their wisdom and Sagacity, like the Spoke in Sesostris' Chariot wheel[2] turned up and down from begging to honor, and from honor to begging again, to see the Incommensurable flow of idle Compliments, that are Current among people of fashion and grimace, which, like Sham bills of Credit pass Current for friendship, to see Machiavels maxims held in greater Repute than the Scriptures, and the Gospel of truth, and trick and Chicanery pass for wisdom, while honor and Integrity and Candor, are esteemed words of no Signification, but Invented to Gull Simple fellows and fools, to see Justice bought and sold in our Courts of Law and equity, as if money Carried a more Convincing argument with it than truth; to see a Rich fool fee a knave of a Physician, and pay a blockhead of an apothecary, to deprive him of health, under a pretence of Restoring it, as if God made work for fools to mend, to see a Silly housewife pay a Tinker, for stopping one hole in her pot or kettle, and making two in it's Stead, To see how dowble tongued flattery, with the Slipperiness of a Snake, creeps into favor and Esteem with the Great, till it

[350]

---

1. Democritus (born ca. 460–457 B.C.) was known as the "laughing philosopher" for his ethical ideal of "cheerfulness."
2. Sesostris was a mythical Egyptian king who conquered Africa (perhaps based on Ramses II, the third king of the Nineteenth Dynasty of Ramses kings [fl. ca. 1333 B.C.]).

[351] Empoisons and Corrodes their Substance, To see Papists, and other wrong headed bigots Invent and publish dam'd Impudent lies, to support their villanous religion, that they may not only || Cozen the present age, but Impose upon Simple and Credulous posterity, To see well meaning and honest Simplicity laugh'd at, and made a tool of to serve wicked purposes, to see Religion, that venerable name made a vizor for villanous politicians, assumed or thrown aside, as occasion requires, To see Rogues of low degree exalted on a gallows or gibbet, and greater rogues of high degree elevated to places of honor and profit, the badge of the first, the more honest of the two, not from nature but necessity, being a hempen halter, and the Symbol of the other, a diadem, a Golden Chain, or a Star and Garter, To see human wit and Cunning, eagerly employed in finding out the Arcana of Nature, with deep and curious Scrutiny, and at last discovering neither more nor less, than that a Straw is a Straw, and an atom an Atom; I say, who can see or observe this medley of absurdity without Laughing Immoderatly, either with Democritus, or any other Gelastic Philosopher; and who can blame the members of the ancient and honorable Tuesday Club, for Laughing at all the world, as well as at themselves, and furnishing a fund of Laughter to all those who have a turn for the Gelastic humor, since their main delight and pleasure is only to Laugh and be laughed at; and, in fine, who can blame them, for Laughing Immoderately, at the Clubical altercations between the honorable the President and the venerable The Chancellor.

[352] At Sederunt 222, was Celebrated the Ninth Anniversary of the ancient and Honorable Tuesday Club, when, Mr Secretary Scribble, by the Grace, favor and Con- || descention of his honor the President served as H:S: The members, at this Anniversary, were all, except the President, who had his Chair of State, seated in Windsor Chairs, ornamented with their Badge medals. What the Intention or meaning of this was, cannot be Conjectured, unless it was only a mere piece of State or Grandure, which this Club was apt to assume to themselves, at Certain times, without giving, or even having any particular reason for it, but mere whim.

After Supper, the Secretary as orator of the Club stood up in his place, and delivered an anniversary Speech as follows.

Anniversary Speech, delivered by the Orator.

May it Please your honor,
And these here L:St: members
Of this here anct: & honble: Club.—
The practise of delivering Anniversary Speeches, has been received and

prevailed much in other Clubs, as well as in this here Club. Permit me to quote a few authorities, The famous Cardan says, *verba propter res, et res propter verba;* and Philo says, *qui Rebus se exercet, verba negligit, et qui callet artem dicendi, nullam disciplinam habet recognitam,* and the wise Seneca, *Cujuscunque orationem vides, politam et solicitam, certo Animam in pusillis occupatam, in Scriptis nihil solicitum.*³ || Many eminent orators have shone in [353] this particular province of eloquence, among whom, I, as a Club orator, (tho modesty forbids me to assume the first rank among these Ingenious gentlemen) have from time to time, (as your honor, and these here Long-standing members must know and Confess) made no Contemptible figure in the exercise of my office.

Anniversary orations, are certainly not only decent and becoming, but absolutely necessary in all Clubs, who have any regular Constitution or policy, especially in those, where that excellent form of mixed government exists, called the three estates. I mean, where the Society is governed by a President, Supreme head or *Archon,* State officers, Nobles or *Magnates* and officers of the Commons, or *Tribuni Plebis;* The two cardinal points or hinges, upon which, such a government moves, are Prerogative and privilege; Prerogative of the President or *Archon,* and privilege of the members under his Sway. These two points necessarily exist in a free government and therefore exist in this here Club, the Government of which is yet, I hope, under proper restrictions, and, the members, *in some measure free.*—Therefore, as it is a part of the prerogative of an honorable President, to hear an anniversary Speech every year, so, it is the undoubted privilege of any one, or all of the members of a free Club, to pronounce, or utter such an anniversary Speech, or Speeches, to the honorable the Chair, this valuable privilege, our ancient & honorable Club || have thought fit by custom to lay [354] Intirely upon my Shoulders, making me, as it were, the mouth of the Society, to deliver their Sentiments on these Grand and Solemn occasions to your honorable Chair, and if my memory does not deceive me, this is the ninth time that I have officiated as anniversary Orator to your honor &

---

3. Cardan, or Geronimo Cardano (1501–1576), was an Italian mathematician, physician, and astrologer, whose works include *De subtilitate rerum* (1551), *De rerum varietate* (1557), and the popular *Cardanus comforte* (1573); the passage means "Words exist on account of things, and things on account of words." Philo is probably Philo Judaeus (ca. 30 B.C.–A.D. 45), an Alexandrian philosopher hailed as "the Jewish Plato," who sought to harmonize the religious philosophies of Plato, Aristotle, and other Greek philosophers with the doctrines of the Pentateuch; the passage means "He who busies himself with things neglects words, and he who is expert in the art of discourse has no recognized discipline." The Seneca passage means "Whoever's oration you see polished and careful, I contend that his mind is occupied with trifles, and he is not concerned with writing."

these here longstanding members, and held forth laboriously and pathetically, amidst a group of laughers, listners, Grumblers and Sleepers, for, Certain it is, that upon the return of every occasion of this Sort, some have laughed, either at your Orator's person, action, or discourse, or altogether, some have listened attentively, with ears wide, and mouths wider open, some again have Grumbled and muttered between their teeth at what was said, and exclaimed Impatiently, that there was too much of this Stuff, when your orator had scarce gone thro his Exordium, while some, Insensible of either mirth or anger, have sunk into soft Repose and balmy Sleep, lulled by the mere Sound of the orators voice, such members, I could, if I would, now point out to your honor, but, I prudently shun being particular, for fear of giving offence.

Since then, The absolute necessity of anniversary Speeches in free Clubs is evident, I hope (pardon me if I say it, for you know it to be true) tho' our Club has for some time passed *drooped,* yet this laudable Custom must not be *droped,* and therefore, I must beg your honors patience, and the patience of these here Longstanding members, to Indulge my oratorial Loquacity for a few minutes ‖ while I deliver what may be proper to be delivered, on such a Sublime occasion, as this here present anniversary.

Our Anniversary, honorable Sir, which has hitherto been an occasion of Rejoicing and mirth, a day of Singing, fiddling, dancing, Jesting, drinking, eating and laughing, a day of pomp, Show and magnificence, grandure and triumph, which has hitherto given great Solace and Joy, to the Longstanding members, is now, (I am sorry to say it, and particularly on this occasion when such complaints may seem Improperly urged) likely to become a humdrum, dull, moaping day of dejection, a Spiritless, tasteless and tedious pastime to the longstanding members, who, cannot but perceive a great decline and falling away, of the wonted Glory and magnificence of this here Club, evident and apparent by the late long adjournments it has undergone, the very last Club preceeding this present Anniversary, having been held on the 26th of march last, and not one single Sederunt Intervening, O Lamentable! that for the Space of almost three months, the honor, Glory and dignity of this our ancient and honorable Club, should be buried and Enveloped, in darkness and oblivion, whilst no body can tell for what.

Did I say, honorable Sir, no body can tell for what, I grant it, perhaps more out of Complaisance to your honor, and this here ancient and honorable Club, than for any truth the assertion contains in it Self, because I would shun giving offence, especially to great men and State officers, but Surely a man must be very ‖ short Sighted, if he cannot at least conjecture for what, permit me then to trespas alittle on your time and patience, while I offer my conjectures.

May I not then be allowed to conjecture, for I dare not proceed to positive assertions, that Luxury has in a great measure got footing in this here ancient and honorable Club, Luxury, in the opinion of all wise men has been the bane and ruin of States and nations, and therefore must at last be the ruin of Clubs, where it has been admitted, are there not longstanding members here present who have seen, the primitive times of this here ancient and honorable Club, did they not in alittle time[a] see an end to that virtuous and heroic frugality, that prevailed in it, at its first Institution, have they not seen Luxury, peeping from behind the Scene, and preparing for her pompuous entry upon this Clubical Stage, have they not seen this bold actress, take one Great Stride at her first advance, and proceed afterwards, with a *grand pas,* to expell Simplicity and plainness from the Club, and Introduce pomp, Show, and extravagance, her Constant pages and attendants, while another, her Companion and Coactor, with the like buskined pride, playd the part of a Momus or mimic, this was no less a person than Ceremony, as much a beau, as the other is a belle, whom you have seen also, showing his pragmatical front, on the most conspicuous part of the Scene, and Introducing Certain fantastical punctillios, forms and modes, by which, he has so disguised and Intoxicated the behaviour and manners, of the L:St: membrs: of this here anct: & honle: Club (as indeed he does those of all mankind, especially such as are in high life, for he never shows his face among beggars and Clowns), that they now seem ‖ not to be the same [357] persons that they were at their first Institution.

Happy,[a] thrice happy, in those heroic times of Innocence & Simplicity, were the Longstanding members of this here anct: & honble: Club, for then, without molestation, could they sit with their legs accross, loll, upon a table or elbow Chair, smoke their pipes, kiss the bowl or the Glass in their turns, converse upon Clubical matters, either grave or facetious, drink toasts, either loyal or amorous, Crack Jokes, frame *Puns* or *Conundrums,* and, should their Stomachs call for a whet, without Ceremony or trowble to themselves or fellow members, they might rise up, go to the Side board, & after having taken their Sliver of Gammon or Slice of Cheese standing, Return again to their Compotation, Jocosity or Clubical Conversation, how Charming, how regular, and how like the Simple frugality of the Golden age was this, and how different from the present Luxury, and pro-

---

(a) Vide vol: 1, Book 3, beginning of Chap: 5, page 179 verbatim almost with this.
(a) Vid vol: I lib: III Cap: 3 page 148 almost verbatim the same with this paragraph.

fuseness that prevails in most Clubs, where the whole apparatus of a formal Table is Introduced, the Club room is pestered with the passing and repassing of Servants, the hobnails of whose Shoes, make a miserable Clamping on the planks, and, when this is over, it proves only a prologue to the confusion and needless Ceremony that succeeds, for, as soon as the h:S: gives the Signal that Supper waits, there is hawling of Chairs, Crossing over, Casting off, figuring in, Galloping up, right and left and back to back like people at a Country dance, There is—Pray Gentlemen, take your places, as the h: Stds: prologue—there is grace to be said, of which, not one word can be heard, for Talking and laughing, then follows Sharp rebuke from the chaplain, and Grumblings from the offending mem- ‖ bers, next it is—pray take a Seat—pray sit here Sir—heres enough of room—excuse me Sir—I never eat Supper, Sir,—I seldom sup a nights Sir—for my part, I never sup Sir,—then comes the Table Conversation—here boy,—some bread—pray shove that dish this way—who carves best—what do you chuse Sir,—pray gi' me leave to help you—Shall I help you to this—Shall I help you to that—Sir your most humble,—any part good Sir, 'tis all the same to me,—pray Sir, help yourself, and please yourself—hold good Sir—here's enough—Shall I help you to some Sauce,—yes Sir, you know I'm pritty Saucy—will you have some Gravy—no Sir, I'm Grave enough already,—please to hand me that mustard—pugh 'tis damn'd Strong, it makes me Cry without a Cause, as Hob did for his Grandmother[4]—please to shove the vinegar Cruet this way,—a clean plate there—Coming Sir!—this is fine veal—that's delicious mutton,—these apples are well baked—Pho! I have burnt my mouth with that damnd apple pye, 'tis damnation hot—These cheese cakes are not done,—of all things commend me to pudding—do you love Cold pudding Sir—not I Sir, my love is settled—a knife and fork there—'Pan[5] Sir?—yes Sir!—pray Sir eat 'tother Custard—boy, some small beer—a glass of wine you—this minute Sir—Sir my humble Service,—Sir your health,—yours Sir,—and yours Sir,—and yours Sir—your most obedient ‖ humble Servant,—pledge you Sir—fill me a Glass of Claret there ho—avast, you Son of a bitch none of your Bumpers, damn you—Pray Sir give me a Slice of that tongue—I thought you had got tongue enough already—well, come away, let's have at this turkey and these oysters—my Stars and Garters, what a twist of the under Jaw you have got,—I play a good knife and fork, thanks be praised—The Lord make us thank-

---

4. Hamilton is likely recalling an incident in the popular farce *Flora; or, Hob in the Well* (1606), where Hob actually cries out to his mother from the well (act 1, sc. 5).

5. *Pan* is a combination of betel leaf, areca nut, and lime used as a masticatory.

ful,—here take away—and so they get up, one by one and fall to picking their teeth, sauntering about the Room, or standing with their bums to the fire, I would ask what pleasure, there can be in all this, except that of eating & drinking, which, as it is a pleasure we enjoy in Common with the brute, and, often employ to more wicked purposes, the destruction of health and Constitution, we ought to glory but little in, as the Pious Mr Dods, the Reverend Mr Dolittle, and several other Learned divines tell us,[6] as for the table Conversation on these occasions, have I not Just now given a Specimen of it, is it any thing but mere Balderdash, so Confused, and so noisy, that I defy the wisest head in Christendom to make any thing of it, and, after all Impediments are removed & the Club forms itself round the Great table to smoke and drink, how dull, how sleepy are the members, when their Stomachs are overcharged, how flat, how low the Conversation, what yawning, what streching of limbs, what nodding, what Sleeping, what Snoring, or rather driving of hogs, oh! oh! || 'tis Lamentable to behold, [360] how much better to have spent the time in witty conversation such as punning, framing quaint Conundrums, Cracking of Sly Jokes, telling Comical Stories, singing old Catches or composing quaint Rhimes, but alas! all this is only preaching to the wind, and beating the air in vain, for, one may preach to eternity, and never reform the manners of Clubs, nay more, the manners of mankind in General, till the example of Great men and presidents show them the way.

I might take occasion to observe here, since I have mentioned Great men and Presidents, how people in Eminent Stations[(a)] will sometimes, by artful methods, gain upon the affections of the vulgar, when they observe a mild easy, and Condescending deportment, and behavior towards them, and, when they heap benefits and favors upon them unasked, may not this

(a) Vid: vol: 1, lib: III Chap: 8 pag 201, almost verbatim the same with this.

6. Probably John Dod (1549?–1645), Puritan divine and reputed author of the famous sermon on malt, who was known as "Decalogue Dod" for his exposition of the Ten Commandments (1604). Thomas Doolittle (1632?–1707) was a Nonconformist tutor and preacher who published several volumes of religious writings, including *A Complete Body of Practical Divinity* (London, 1723). Like most divines, Dod and Doolittle frequently admonish their readers against the dangers of excessive eating and drinking, but I suspect that Hamilton is especially recalling their treatises on the Lord's Supper. In *A Briefe Dialogue, concerning Preparation for the Worthy Receiving of the Lords Supper* (London, 1627), Dod discusses the dangers of excessive eating and drinking in his section on the sins against the Fourth Commandment; in *A Treatise concerning the Lords Supper* (London, 1667), Doolittle writes: "It is an hainous sin that those that are reeling in the street, . . . rather than degrading themselves below the rank of men" and "reducing them[selves] to the Primitive Institution, . . . should be seen kneeling at the Sacrament" (p. 3).

have been the Case, with a Certain great man, and the L:St: members of this here anct: & hon: Club, have we not seen one, with a Complaisant and mild Countenance, always adorned with a Smile, like Julius Cæsar of old, (pardon honorable Sir, the uncouth Comparison, between a Christian President, and a heathen Emperor) flatter the people, that, by gaining the ascendant over their affections, he might with more ease, seize the Tyranny into his own hands, and govern their persons, as he thought fit,—no bounty was spared, in the way of entertaining; 'Rack, that expensive liquor

[361] has been Introduced, Rack! so || bewitching to our refined palats, because fare fetched, large tables have been set out, covered with Clean fine linnen, nicely pinched, and Sweetly perfumed, with lavender and roses, elegant dishes of meat, and exquisite deserts, have been Curiously ranged thereon, the Rooms and passage, Splendidly Illuminated with Sconce lights, in the forms of Rhombus's, Squares, triangles and Circles, vocal music has been warbled forth most mellifluously, an Iced Cake made it's appearance, which was dealt about in Luncheons to the members, curiously Enveloped in Clean white paper; This Cake, this fatal Cake may we not Conjecture compleated the catastrophe of the Liberty of this here ancient and honorable Club, and, as Esau sold his birthright to Jacob, for fair words and a mess of porridge, so, this unhappy Club has bartered their liberty to a Certain great man, for an old Song, rack punch, Plumb pudding, four pound of Candles, and an Iced Cake.

But, tho' I condemn the Conduct of this here Club in this here particular affair, yet, that I may do Strict Justice to that there great and Illustrious personage, I am Sincerely of opinion, that this here Club, could not have pitched upon a milder and more Complacent Governor than he, for, has he not at all times shown himself, modereat, gentle and easy to be Intreated, and, excepting only in that point, of giving up the least article or particle of his valuable prerogative, a point, of which, all princes and Great men, are very tender and Jealous; a point, of which, he Is Justly tenaceous, he has spared no pains to humor this here Club in every thing that they desired, but, what tho this here Club, be in a great measure happy and easy, under the administration and government, of this here accomplished and polite

[362] *Archon,* yet, it cannot with any || certainty be expected that it will always remain so under that of his Successors, who, not regarding his excellent example, may turn out to be Cruel & blood minded tyrants.

And now, honorable Sir, and Gentlemen, I think, having discussed this point of Luxury, I have dispatched the burden of the Song, but, permit me, before I conclude this long Speech, to make a few more Conjectures, concerning the causes of the decline of this here Club.

May we not reasonably conjecture, that Certain bickerings and contentions of late, sprung up among us in a great measure contributed to eclipse the Glory of this here Club, so, that to use nigh the words of a late Celebrated poet, it has been with us, as with the Oliverian Saints.

> *Here* Civil dudgeon has grown high,
> And *we* fell out, *we* knew not why
> While hard words, Jealousies & fears
> Set *us* together by the ears.⁷

And how have we been set by the ears, may we not reasonably Conjecture, by the ambition and pride of our Great men, striving for power and Influence; Lamentable was that day, in which so many State officers were appointed in this here Club, woeful was the accursed time, when a great Seal and bag were thrown in among us as a bone of Contention, dreadful was the period, when titles of honor and badges of State, were bestowed upon some restless and aspiring Spirits who knew how to abuse them, but not well how to use them, let us run a parallel, between this here ancient club & the Roman Republic, & see how their Circumstances & fate agree.

In the beginning of the Roman Republic, there subsisted a Jealousy or Contention, between the Patricians or nobles, || and the plebeians, or Common people, has not a Jealousy and contention also existed from the very beginning in this here Club, between the State officers and the Commons, were not the Tribunes of the people established at Rome for the Security of the Commons? who used to Controul the votes of the Senate with a *Veto,* were there not officers of the Commons also appointed in this here Club, who have often had the assurance to Controul the votes of the State officers, were there not two Triumvirates established at Rome? are there not also two triumvirates established in this here Club? one Extraneous, on the eastren Shore, the other within its very bowels, under the Color of a Champion,⁽ᵃ⁾ a Chancellor, and an attorney General? was there not a perpetual dictatorship established at Rome by Julius Cæsar? has not this here Club saddled themselves with a perpetual Dictator, under the title of a *perpetual president*? Did not the Chief magistrate of Rome assume to himself the title of *Imperator*? was not the title of *My Lord* given to the president of

[363]

(a) Sir John had not as yet declared that he had left the Club.

7. Hamilton is referring to the following lines from Samuel Butler's *Hudibras:* "When *civil* Dudgeon first grew high, / And men fell out they knew not why; / When hard words, *Jealousies* and *Fears,* / Set Folks together by the ears" (*Hudibras,* ed. John Wilders [Oxford, 1967], I.i.1–4).

this here Club? did not the Emperor sit between the Two Consuls in the Senate at Rome? does not the president of this here Club, sit, in Club between his two Satellites or Satrapæ the Champion & Chancellor? did not the army assume a governing power for a Considerable time at Rome? has not Sir John, for a Considerable time assumed, by virtue of his broadsword a governing power in this here Club? was not Rome for some time governed by the Councils of loose women and Courtezans? has not there also been a Genearchy in this here Club? did not the Romans go to an excess of luxury in buildings feasts, public Shows, and Spectacles? has not this here ancient & honorable Club, gone to an excess of Luxury in || feastings, badges, canopies, and processions? did not Rome at last sink by degrees from a State of liberty into a State of abject Slavery? Have we not reason to believe, that, as the political State of Rome, and that of this here Club, seem to be parallel, that if we drive on, Jehu like,[8] in this manner, this here Club, will at last, sink into a State of Slavery; has not moderen Rome at last, submitted to be ruled by an old priest and his myrmidons? may we not Conjecture, that this ancient and honorable Club, once it becomes a *Moderen Club*, will be priest ridden, if the presumption and petulence of a Certain great Club officer, the Chancellor, be suffered to go on [Chanc: aha! is it come to that!]

In fine, honorable Sir, and Gentlemen, I have presumed to lay all those matters before you, that you may have a Clear view of the present deplorable State of this here ancient and honorable Club, and the ruin that threatens it, if proper means are not used to prevent it, therefore, you will Remain without excuse if you do not use these means, which are, to reinstate the Club in its ancient Simple constitution with regard to expences, to secure to his honor the president his Just prerogative, to curb and restrain the growing power of your State officers, to keep within proper bounds the Influence of the Great Seal, to regulate the presumptive Claims of the officers of the Commons, to provide that Commissions be duely and regularly Sealed and Issued, not only for deputy presidents, but for officers of State, to revise and correct the body of Laws, to hold Committees for wholesome advice, and to put down that pestilent Custom of long || adjournments lately crept in among us by enacting Severe penal laws against those who presume to hold Sham Clubs or Illegal Committees. If these expedients are not Speedily taken, this here Club will soon be at an End, and, this, probably, may be the last anniversary we shall see, whereas, if proper care be taken, before it is too late, we may yet see many a Joyful

---

8. *Jehu* is a humorous word for a fast and furious driver or coachman.

Return of this day of Rejoicing, may often with pleasure, behold our noble president, exalted in his Chair, smiling upon his Club, which calls to my mind the following poetical passage.

> *Aris fulgorem, resonantia tecta, Corusco*
> *Auro, atq*₃ *electro nitido, sectoque Elephanto*
> *Argentoq*₃ *simul—Talis Jovis ardua Sedes,*
> *Aulaq*₃ *cælicolum Stellans Splendescit olympo.*

The brazen Roof, Inlaid with Sparkling Gold,
With Carved Iv'ry & with Amber pure,
With Shining Silver, such the Seat of Jove,
Such the Star Chamber, where th'Immortals meet.[9]

Then may we often hear the poet Laureat repeating his elegant odes, the chief musician warbling his dulcisonorous notes, Signior Lardini drawing Charming Sounds from Cat guts with nimble fingers & Skillful bow, and your poor orator perorating his anniversary Speeches while nothing but peace, harmony, mirth and Jollity prevails among us, which, ought to be the wish of every longstanding member, of this here Club, as much as it is of

Your humble Servant
The Orator.

The orator having finished this oration, neither the president nor the Club seemed pleased with it, notwithstanding the fine flourish at the Close, which shows how little men care to be told of their faults, The orator was in none of the best of humors at the delivering of this oration, and was resolved, since he found he could not advance himself by flattery, and dissimulation, which he had tried for a great while, to speak the naked Truth for the future.

The Poet Laureat was then Called upon to recite the ode, which at this time had not been set to music, and, he rising up, his head adorned with a Chaplet of Lemmon leaves, instead of bays, recited in his place, with a Clear voice as follows.

---

9. Hamilton's translation is accurate, although the last line more literally reads, "And so shines the starry hall of the heaven-dwellers at Olympus."

Anniversary Ode,

For the Ancient and honorable Tuesday Club, in the year, 1754, Humbly Inscribed to the Honorable Nasifer Jole Esqr, president, and the Longstanding members of the said Club, by,

Their most humble Servant
The Club's Poet Laureat.

Air
Mighty Jole, we sing again,
Raise, O Raise the Joyful Strain,
Laughing muse, Resume the Lay,
To Jole, and to the Joyful Day.
Chorus
Sackbuts, Cymbals, Timbrels, lutes,
Bangeos, dulcimers and flutes,
Bagpipe drones with Snuffling bellows,
Viols, violins, violoncellos,
Pipes and Tabors, kettle drums,
Trumpets Shrill, and deep humstrums,
Harpsicord, and Hauboys Sharp,
Irish, Welsh and Jewish harp,
Grave Hybernian Clarshoo,[10]
Cor de Chace, Guitarre also
Join in General concert, Join,
With your voice, & his and mine,
Till the arched Skies rebound,
With th'exhilirating Sound.
Air
Tis Jole, tis Jole demands our annual praise,
For Jole I sing, for Jole I wear these bays,
Long live and prosper Jole the Great,
May he, the favorite of fate,
Still on his Club benignly shine
And rule with wise Judicious head,
From that exalted place,
May his most Gracious face
On our Longstanding members shed,
It's Influence divine.

---

10. *Clarshoo* is a variant of *clairschach,* the old Celtic harp strung with wire.

Grand Chorus
    Ye members all Salute the Bowl,
    Drink health, long life and peace to Jole,
To Jole, who other presidents exceeds,
In bold exploits, & in the ruling art,
As much as Sturdy oaks do dwarfling weeds,   [368]
Or awful thunder, does a rousing fart,
    And, when you've put the Goblet round,
    Sound again the music, sound,
    Wide delate each warbling throat,
    While Eccho shall repeat each note,
    And thro' the wide expanded Skie
The praise of mighty Jole shall flie,
      And all th'ærial powers,
      That croud ambrosial bowers,
    The Zylphs, the Gnomes & Zephyrs Sweet,
    Their music Join great Jole to greet,
    And, Charm'd with our Terrestrial lay,
Descend to hail great Jole, & this propitious day.

The poet Laureat having recited this ode with applause was ordered to return thanks to the orator for his anniversary oration, which he did in the following words.

"Mr Orator Sir,

By the order of his honor the President & the Club"—

Pres: By my order Sir! No, I'd have you and the Club to know I gave no order to return thanks for any such Stuff [this the President said see sawing, and Rolling his handkerchef on his knee]

Poet: I beg your honors pardon.—well—Mr Orator Sir—by the order of the Club, I return you thanks for the Elegant anniversary Speech you have delivered upon this occasion.

Then the orator being ordered to return thanks to the || poet laureat [369] for his anniversary ode, did it in the following words.

"Mr Poet Laureat, Sir,

The orders of his honor the Pres:—hoh!—I mean Sir, the orders of the Club, which I shall always be ready to obey, and which I greatly Respect and honor, are, that I should give you thanks, for them and in their name, for your elegant anniversary ode, Just now recited, Sir, I wish that my abilities, were equivalent to your Sublime Genius, that I might be qualified to return you such thanks, as would be adequate to your extraordinary merit, but, since I cannot thank you, in such Strains as I would, I must beg of you, to accept of my thanks for the Club, in such a plain Stile as my genius can reach."

Thus did these Two Great Clubical Geniuses, compliment, or (as some call it) scratch one another, and, the Club seemed to be of opinion, that this short extempore Speech of the orators, was much better, than his long Studied anniversary oration.

Chapter V

The Chancellors farewell oration, The attorney Generals Speech against the late Chancellor, Resolves.

The most learned, Judicious and Ingenious men, have often entertained peculiar notions and opinions, which It is Impossible Intirely to separate from Enthusiasm or Superstition, and which are so discrepant from truth and nature, that not the least affinity or relation can be found, by the most diligent Inquiry. || The celebrated Lord Chancellor Bacon, That prodigy of Learning and knowledge, in matters Physical, was not Clear of this Imbecility, when he Imagined and firmly believed that there was something real in that empty dream of the Chemists concerning the Philosopher's Stone, or the transmutation of base metals into Gold, This appears from his *Natural History,* where he very gravely gives us a process to turn Silver into that precious mettle, with an assurance that it will succeed;[1] My Lord Hales likewise, a man deeply skilled in the law, and other matters of learning, and also of a Solid head and understanding, had a firm belief in witches and diabolical Incantations, and in his Judicial capacity tried some of these unhappy wretches.[2] When we find such Instances of human weakness, and many others of the like nature, which might be produced, need we be Surprized that Mr Chancellor Dogmaticus, a man of Gravity, Solidity and learning, tho not in any respect equal to my lord Chancellor Bacon, should be so weak, as to give in to the notion, that there was something Supernatural in the Tuesday Club, and that they possessed some powers unknown to other Clubs or other men; this will plainly appear in some

---

1. In a passage headed "Experiment solitary touching the making of gold" Bacon states that "a perfect good concoction, or digestion, or maturation of some metals, will produce gold," and then provides the necessary steps (*Sylva Sylvarum; or, A Natural History* [1627], in *The Works of Francis Bacon,* ed. Basil Montagu, 3 vols. [Philadelphia, 1841], II, 49–50).

2. In 1661 Matthew Hale presided over a jury that sentenced to death two women accused of practicing witchcraft. Hale also wrote a treatise on witchcraft that was published in 1693.

passages of his farewell Speech, which he made to the Club, of which we shall presently give an abstract.

At the aforesaid Anniversary Sederund, after the ode had been rehearsed, and other matters of Ceremony dispatched, Mr Chancellor Dogmaticus Rose from his Seat and arming his Nose with a pair of Spectacles, delivered to his honor and the Club, the following harangue.

"Honorable Mr President, Worshipful officers, and you, other worthy members of This ancient and honorable Club,

The occasion of my making this address to you, has affected me so deeply, that, as the respect due to you, and the dignity of the office I have bore in this Club, forbad me to think of wasting the smallest part of your precious time, with any such Crude extempore effusions, as my poor genius could dictate; and, the damp thrown upon my Spirits, by the same melancholy occasion, depriving me of that ready memory, which would be necessary to deliver what I have meditated, with that distinctness order and decency, due both to you and my own Character, so, I am obliged to beg your Gracious permission, to supply that Defect by reading.

Honorable, worshipful & worthy Gentlemen,

The occasion of my present address to you, is truely mournful to me,—Tho', I hope, will prove no loss to you,—I am—alas!—how can I utter it,—I am now to take my leave of a Society, that I honor, esteem and love; in which I have Enjoyed much pleasure; a Society that has not only admitted me to a participation of their ordinary Joys, but even their highest honors; let me Gratefully Commemorate each of these—I have been an associate in your ordinary pleasures—but why do I say ordinary, the smallest of them are extraordinary, if compared with what any other Society could ever produce,—It is this Club alone, that has Improved the Gelastic faculty which distinguishes men from brutes, to the most extensive and useful purposes, using it, not only as a natural expression of Inward pleasure, but to communicate pleasure to others, by the admiration and Imitation, of it's extravagance, and, which is more wonderful, made it a useful || Instrument of punishment in silencing, small uproars by much greater [like the firing of Cannon, and ringing of bells, to check water Spouts and thundergusts, and Exploding of Bomb Shells, to Curb the fury of fire](a). *This unparallelled Club, has found the Secret of Inlarging their pleasure by making* **Sense** *and* **Nonsense,** *equally the objects of it, so suiting all Capacities, between the wise and the foolish, the Learned and the Ignorant.* Can the pleasures of such a Club be with any propriety Called ordinary?

(a) This between the Brackets, not in the original Speech.

This passage shows what a Strange Superstitious notion, the Chancellor had of the Club.

I am next to Commemorate the Great favors you have done me, who, thro' your kind and favorable opinion of my abilities (In which I could humbly differ from you, If I durst differ from so many Judicious and discerning persons) have dignified me with the high and honorable office of your Chancellor, keeper of your Great Seal, and, of his honors political conscience—how I have discharged this Important, and arduous task, I must leave to your Judgement, if you were mistaken in your Choice, your opinion of me was Charitable and Generous, and my failings (for I claim no Infallability) fix no reflexion upon you, but how ever you now Judge of my Conduct, I shall, without pretending to perfect Innocence, comfort myself with the testimony of my own heart, that I have always meant well, and done what I thought best.

Liberty and property, you know, have always been my darling objects, and, if in defence of them, and perhaps mistaking the meaning and design of our honorable and worthy president, the life and Soul of the Club, I have sometimes given him offence, I yet acted honestly, as things appeared to me, and now beg your honor to take my behaviour in this light, as I leave your ‖ views a Secret in your own breast, for, as I do not think, so, I am not so gross a flatterer, as to Compliment your honor, with my opinion of your being exempted from human frailties, nay, I have a better opinion of you, than to believe you would thank me for it, and not rather be offended, however grateful alittle Incense burnt upon your altar may be to you—Therefore, I must say, that as power is a very Intoxicating thing, very dangerous to the Innocence of those who possess it, and the happiness of those who are subjected to it, it is at least a possible thing, that your honor might have sometimes been misled, by this bewitching idol and *Ignis fatuus* of power, and, tho I do not assert, that you ever had any design of abusing it, yet, others may think that to be an abuse, which you meant for good.—Now Gentlemen, as equity, the Constitution and privileges of the whole & every member of this Club, in their different Stations, were my peculiar Care and trust, so, that relation I have so long bore to this honorable Society, obliges me, while it does subsist, & as my Last good office in it, to offer my friendly parting advice.

First, that your honor will be content with such power as is Consistent with, and Sufficient to enable you to promote, the peace, honor and happiness of *this here Club,* which, I hope you will use to that end only, that you will always acknowledge the fountain of your power, and be satisfied to owe it to those who alone could bestow it, and can take it away, firmly persuaded, that it is more honorable, and can yield more rational delight to rule & do good || to a free people, than to exercise dominion, over Cringing [374] Sycophants, and Submissive Slaves, in fine, that you will be always Governed by that Glorious maxim, *Salus populi, Suprema lex*.³

And You worthy Gentlemen, my dear Compatriots of the Club, let me leave it upon you, that you be always persuaded of the duty and necessity of supporting your President, In those powers and privileges that you have Conferred upon him, for the General Good, and, always pay him, that honor and regard, that the toils of his beneficent Service Justly Claim, as the least reward due to him—absolute power, Gentlemen, is, no doubt, the best Instrument of Government, provided it be always in the hands of a very good man, and perhaps, you could not trust it more safely than with your present *Archon,* but, as you cannot promise yourselves such a one always, if the Globe could ever furnish such another, I rather recommend to you, the General and Salutary Aphorism, of being always watchful and Jealous of your liberties, giving away no more power than is absolutely necessary and Checking Incroachments.

Principiis obsta, sero medicina paratur,
*Si mala per Longas Invaluere Moras.*⁴

But, at the same time, remember human frailty, and never Contend obstinately about triffles, where the remedy may prove worse than the disease.

I am now come to the bitterest part of my present task, to say—Farewell—and resign my office of Chancellor of this Club, in which I was Invested, by delivering me this Seal, which I redeliver in the same manner as I received it, into the hands of our trusty Secretary, from whom I received || it by the vote of the Club, and the particular order of his honor the [375] president, as I never used it, but by his honor's directions and Commands, so, it has never suffered any hurt in my Custody, but that once by a fatal convulsion, it fell into the fire, and singed the bag alittle, may it never have such a mishap again, nor the Club such a dismal Omen of it's final Catastrophe.

May it please your honor,

As to the Commission I received from your honor, I should think it, in point of form, proper enough, now to give it up, but, as after this resignation, and the entry of it, it gives me no title, if I have deserved any thing, I must beg your Indulgence, to keep it among my archives, to show my posterity, what an Illustrious person they can Claim among their ancestors.

To Conclude, there remains to me, I hope, the pleasure of another

---

3. "The safety of the people is the highest law" (Cicero, *De legibus* 3.3.8).
4. "Resist at the beginning; the medicine is offered too late / If evils have grown worse by long delays" (Ovid, *Remedia amoris* 91–92).

relation to this Noble Club, that of being one of its honorary members, which, tho' I could Claim, from the Constitution and use, yet I'd rather owe it to your free and Chearful Suffrages, and, an Entry made in your Records to that effect, in favor of one, who will always think himself bound in Duty of Gratitude, to wish well to, and promote the happiness of the *Ancient and honorable Tuesday Club—Long live Illustrious Jole*."

The Chancellor having finished this Speech, the grand Chorus of the ode, 1751, was Immediatly struck up, with voices and Instruments, In which Concerto, The Chancellor, without removing his Spectacles from his Nose, || playd the violino primo, a Gentleman Invited to the Club performed violino Secondo,[5] the Secretary violoncello, and Mr Protomusicus and Crinkum Crankum Esqr, with the Poet Laureat performed *Con voce*.

The Chancellor had a plaudite for his Speech, and was made an honorary member by a free vote, according to his request, or, rather was made an honorary member *Nem: con:* for, whatever approbation the Club might give the Chancellor in this occasion, it was pritty plain that his honor the president did not approve of his Speech, which appeared, by the many postures he shifted his body into in his Chair, during the time of it's delivery, this, that assiduous officer the Attorney General perceived, and prepared a process against the Chancellor, 'gainst next Sederunt, which we shall presently relate.

Thus finished this 9th Anniversary of the Ancient and honorable Tuesday Club, with less mirth and Jollity than usual, the bad humor of the Secretary, and the departure of the Chancellor, putting the Club in a humdrum humor.

At Sederunt 223, June 25th 1754, Solo Neverout Esqr, attorney General being H:S: the said attorney after Supper, rose up, and delivered the following Speech.

"Honorable Sir,

As I have always showed my Zeal and readiness, ever since I have been honored with the Eminent office of attorney General to your honor, and this here ancient and honorable Club, to discourage and Check, all daring and Insolent attempts upon the honor and prerogative || of the Chair, by Immediately prosecuting the persons Concerned in those atrocious designs, without fear or affection, favor or partiality, so, I hope, neither your honor, nor this here ancient and honorable Club, will think I act unjustly or pusilanimously in the Case which I am now going to lay before you, since it is well known, that the person I am now going to accuse, never could, when

---

5. Daniel Dulany, Jr. (see biographical sketch).

Invested with all the grandure and power of a *Chancellor,* intimidate me, or make me neglectful or remiss in my duty, when his unprecedented and unaccountable behavior, to your honor, called upon me to urge a proper Castigation, much less, now he has resigned his office, and become a private Man in the Club, (I will not even say an honorary member) can the Consideration of his lowly State, & want of Clubical power, Induce me to hector & bully over him, since it is well known, to be directly Contrary to the disposition, of bold, daring & honest officers, such, as I have shown myself to be, to Crow over the weak & helpless, any more than to be afraid of the Strong and powerful.

Sir, The Case that I am now to open to your honor, is a Case, that will naturally Introduce a motion—a motion Sir, of the utmost consequence and Concern to your honor, and this here ancient and honorable Club, which I shall mention to you in it's proper time and place, but first I shall Clear up to you the Case, in the Plainest terms I am Capable of, Jodocus Damhoderius, a learned Lawyer, tells us in *Codice primo, Capite Sexto, Sectione Quarta* ‖ *pandectarum, fu—fu—fut—fogh!—futilium,* [Here Jonathan Grog Esqr, puzzled to stiffle a Laugh, retired precipitatly from the Club room] *vanum etiam mendacemque, Improba fortuna fingit,* and Antonius Dro—Droll—Drollingtonus, in his *lectiones pueriles,* I think it is in folio, 15720, has these words, plain as a pick-staff, *Heus tu Dromo, cape hoc Stabellium, ventulum hinc facito dum Lavamus &ct:*[6] which great authorities Sir, are, I think, Sufficient to make it appear, to your honor, and this here ancient and honorable Club, without farther *arguefication,* that the late Chancellor of this here Club, in a late Speech, which he delivered to your honor and this here Club, has forfeited all his titles, honors, privileges, places of profit and Emolument in this here ancient and honorable Club, for ever and a day, for, Sir, it can be made appear, that *that there* Speech in manner and form as it stands (for which I referr you to the Copy now in our Secretarys hands) is Seditious, malicious, flagicious and pernicious, and, has a direct tendency to Create, promote and encourage, Dissentions, Contentions, evil propensions, and distentions, between your honor and

[378]

---

6. The learned attorney general is fuzzily recalling Josse de Damhouder (1507–1581), Flemish legal expert, scholar, and author of *Patrocinium pupillorum* (1580) and *Praxis rerum civilium* (1569), but the passage he attributes to Damhouder, meaning "Perverse fortune makes one vain, even a liar," is a reference to the nonexistent "Futile Pandects." The attorney general has probably invented both the author and source (the "Puerile Lessons") of the second passage, meaning "Hey you, Dromo, take this stable and fan it out while we wash up," a version of which appears in Terence, where it is not Dromo who has a stable, but the slave girl Dorius who has a fan ("heus tu, inquit, Dóre, cape hoc flabellum, ventulum huic sic facito, dum lavamus," *Eunuchus* 594–595).

the Longstanding members of this here ancient and honorable Club, Sir, can there be any thing more dangerous to our present happy Constitution, than to have the prerogative of the Chair Called in Question, in this Impudent, and daring manner, Sir, I cannot tell how to define the assurance of some people, and by what name to call that Spirit that is always for stirring up dirt, and exciting hubbubs and hurly burlys, a Learned author, whose name I cannot now ‖ recollect, says, *Nominativo. Hic, hæc, hoc. Genetivo. Hujus. Dativo. Huic. Accusativo. Hinc, hanc, hoc. Vocativo. Caret.* yes Sir, *Vocativo Caret!*⁷ I say Sir, such Impudence wants a name (*vocativo Caret,* Sir,) that can without blushing tell us, that this here Club, can subvert it's own Constitution, by turning your honor out of that there Chair, & I am sorry to find—I say to find Sir, that so many of our long Standing members sat silent, and did not express their Resentment, at this bold Invasion of your honor's prerogative, There was Sir, a law among the Athenians, that when any mutiny arose in the City, the Inhabitants should take one Side or other, or else be banished the City, and truely Sir, when Longstanding members, and State officers of Clubs, stand Neuter, when a Chancellor, or any other person, is pumping out from his Surcharged Stomach [here Jonathan Grog Esqr, returning again into the Club room, with pale & Ghastly face, declared that he had thrown up all his Supper by Evomition]—I say Sir, while he is pumping up from his Stomach abusive and Corrosive matter, which affects your honors power and Just prerogative, and, have not courage to utter their real opinion, I think, they very well deserve to be expell'd the Club, every Longstanding member sits here Sir, to defend the rights and prerogatives of the Chair, and, when he declines that, he cannot properly be said to be a long standing member.

Upon the whole Sir, I would make a motion, that the following resolves, naturally arising from the bold unprecedented Conduct of our late Chancellor, be entered as resolves of the Club, in our Records, and have your honor's Sanction ‖ and approbation, and, I hope Sir, I shall be seconded in this motion by other Longstanding members, the Resolves follow Sir, and are Thus.

I Resolved, that the Speech of the late Chancellor, and keeper of ye honor's political and Clubical Conscience, contains divers matters of a Seditious Nature, Injurious to his honor's dignity, Calculated to create Jealousies of his designs, and to foment divisions, derogatory from his rights and prerogatives, and tending to the Subversion, and dissolution of the Constitution of this here Club, & the dissolution of the same.

II Resolved, that as all Commissions are Issued by, and derived from

---

7. This is the declension of the Latin pronoun meaning "this," which has no particular vocative case.

the president, upon a resignation, the same ought to be surrendered to him, and, that therefore, the delivering of the great Seal, by the Chancellor to the Secretary, is repugnant to the principles of our Constitution, derogatory to the rights and prerogatives of the president, and tends to the dissolution of this here Club.

III Resolved, that the Continuance, flourishing State, and very being of this here Club, depend upon the exquisite Clubical qualities of his honor, and the vigorous execution of his presidential authorities proceeding therefrom.

IV Resolved, that his honor the president, has duely displayd and exercised his presidential qualities and Authorities, and Carries himself with an uniform moderation, Integrity and wisdom, by which temper and Conduct, he has supported his own Character, and the happiness of the Longstanding members of this here Club, upon its proper basis, the original view and principles of our Constitution.

V Resolved, that it is a position big with absurdity and mischief, and apparently tending to the dissolution of this here Club, that the members of this here Club, to vindicate and support their liberties as such, can subvert or annihilate their Constitution, upon which Those liberties depend, that the removal or decathedration of his honor the president, by any pretended or usurped authority of the Club, would at once dissolve our happy Constitution, which can exist no longer, than all the presidential powers and authorities, remain, as they are now personally vested in his honor the president.

And, whereas some misunderstandings and animosities have been Industriously fomented and excited, by the Seditious machinations and artifices of the late Chancellor, the principles of whose Conduct are avowed and explained, by the aforesaid Inflammatory Speech, and, the pernicious tendency of the said principles, have been experienced, and, whereas, to accomplish, his wicked and pestilent designs, and, to strip, and deprive his honor the president, not only of all his prerogatives, but even of his birthright, the said Chancellor did, Impudently and audaciously assert, that he, the said Chancellor, did speak, and pronounce the English language better than his honor the president,

VI Resolved therefore, that his honor the president is a true born Englishman, and the late Chancellor by birth a Scots man, and, that therefore the aforesaid pretensions and behaviour, of the said late Chancellor, are highly vain, and presumptuous, and tend to bring his honor's pronounciation of his native tongue into Contempt."

When the Attorney General had done speaking, some arguments passed in Club, concerning the tenor and Intention of the late Chancellor's

Speech, the Secretary attempted to speak in his vindication, but his Speech was such an Inconsistent piece of panegyric and Invective, he vainly endeavoring to exculpate & accuse the Chancellor at one and the same time, that his honor and the Club, looked upon it as only a piece of flimsey flamsey Stuff, in which the Secretary, according to his wonted Ingenuity took away with one hand, what he gave with the other.

The late Chancellor declared That, as he was now in the Station of a private person in the Club, and only could Claim the rank or degree of an honorary member, (which by the bye was not conceded to him by his honor the President) || he cared not a louse how they proceeded in this affair, they were welcom to do as they pleased, since he had now no titles, or badges of honor, or places to lose, having delivered all these up at last Sederunt, but nevertheless, he could not but still Justify what he had asserted in his Speech, since he spoke the real Sentiments of his heart and for the Interest and good of the Club.

Upon which the Resolves were ordered to stand upon record, a fresh instance this of the now depraved and Slavish Condition of the Club.

It was then moved by the Secretary, that Slyboots Pleasant Esqr, as a person very well qualified for the office, should be created Champion of the Club, since Sir John appears to have forsaken the Society.

This motion was not altogether relished by his honor, who did not think the Champion well used, by the Secretary in broaching it, as the said Champion had not as yet, expressly declared his Intention to leave the Club, and, his honor added, That no Champion should be Chose or appointed in any Case, for, that he himself was properly the Champion of the Club, and he wanted no Substitutes or asistants. Thus we see his honor, seizing at one Grasp, both the Civil and military Government of the Club, Into his own hands.

Chapter VI

First Taveren Club held by his honor the President, The Chancellors poem on the Club, Mr Protomusicus's answer to it, election of a longstanding member.

Homer by many, was Called by way of eminence *The Poet,* and, I think the Stagyrite was the first that gave him that name,[1] and the appellation is

---

1. See Aristotle, *Poetics* 1.11.

highly || distinguishing and honorable, signifying in the greek Language, [383] The *maker;* Homer, the master poet, and those mighty Geniuses among the ancients, that were Cast in a simular mold to his, were esteemed *makers* or *Creators,* producing from their inexhaustible fancies, new Images or Creations, both Instructive and Entertaining, they might be called *makers* too, on account of their knack at fiction, by which they Conveyd useful moral doctrines to the Ear, under a Surprizing and entertaining dress, and thereby hit upon the true method to fix the attention, on what was profitable & Instructive—In a like manner our poets now a days may be Called *makers,* as being *Makers of Rhimes,* and verses, and masters of a particular kind of fiction, which the ancients seem to be utterly unacquainted with, as not having nature for it's groundwork, but something else of a *Je ne sçai quoi,* which cannot be described, for the ancients were quite unacquainted with every other Copy to work by, but plain and undisguised nature; hence the moderen poets have been stiled Bards, a name given to Certain dark and unintelligible prophets or augurs, among the ancient Britons and Gauls, a name very proper for our moderen versificators and Rhimsters, who are for the most part unintelligible, not only to themselves but every body else, the main Ingredient in the genius of an ancient || poet, being a knowledge in [384] nature, and an ability to Copy after that perfect pattern, we need not be Surprized that they attain'd so easily to the heights of poetry, but now a days it is not so easy a matter to become a poet, several things being absolutely necessary to be understood to accomplish a moderen bard, the principal Rule is that which you will find in the very beginning of Horaces art of poetry, which is what belongs to that peculiar Sort of Grotesque painting used by our latter poets,[2] The next that comes in view, is the Ingenious art of *Crambo,*[3] which is altogether Inseparable from the Composition of a moderen poet, 'tis therefore necessary that he should often exercise himself amongst Companies of the young and gay, the facetious and frolicksome, at that Ingenious and witty Game of Crambo, or what the French Call bout Rhime, to store his memory with a Sufficient quantum of words that Jingle and Rhime together, for this Rhime according to the opinion of a very eminent bard[(a)] of our Days, (who Indeed (this only

---

(a) Dryden.[4]

2. In the opening of *Ars poetica* (1–13) Horace warns that yoking together various kinds of verse is like coupling a human head with a horse's neck.

3. In the game of *Crambo* one player composes a line of verse for which the next player must provide a rhyme.

4. Hamilton could be alluding to any number of passages in which Dryden applauds the virtues of rhyme (including the opening paragraphs of his preface to *The Conquest of Granada*),

excepted) to do him Justice, comes nearer to the true Genius of the ancients than many of his fellow moderens,) is the very Soul of moderen poetry, and she cannot be kept alive without it, we have also the opinion of a Great master in the burlesque⁽ᵇ⁾ to Confirm our assertion, who has the following Sentiment.

> For Rhime the rudder is of verses,
> By which we poets steer our Courses,
> One line for Sense & one for Rhime,
> Is Sure Sufficient at a time.⁵

[385] A moderen poet also, to regulate his measure, must know how ∥ to count his fingers, and thumbs, that is, in his hexameter and pentameter verses, for, as the Greek and latin Hexameters and pentameters, consisted, the first in several Dactyls and Spondees, and the latter in the same, with two Cæsuras, so, vice versa, the moderen pentameters and Hexameters Consist, the first in eight Dactyls, and the latter in the same number of Dactyls, with the addition of two Pollices or Thumbs, which to speak in the paragrammatical Style, make the latter only two Inches longer, as for Pyndarics, when a moderen bard has a mind to exercise his Genius that way, he needs not have recourse to this Digital Arithmetic, but only use a Scale of equal parts, to wit, that Invented by Gunter,⁶ or any other Ingenious Geometrician, and, if

---

(b) Samuel Butler.

---

but perhaps he is referring particularly to Neander's assessment of the aptness of rhyme and verse toward the end of *An Essay of Dramatic Poesie,* where Neander states: "When a Poet has found the repartee, the last perfection he can add to it, is to put it into verse. However good the thought may be; however apt the words in which 'tis couch'd, yet he finds himself at a little unrest while Rhyme is wanting: he cannot leave it till that comes naturally, and then is at ease, and sits down contented" (*Works of Dryden,* ed. Hooker *et al.,* XVII, 77).

5. This passage appears in *Hudibras,* ed. Wilders, as follows:

> A Squire he had whose name was *Ralph,*
> That in th'adventure went his half.
> (Though writers, for more stately tone,
> Do call him *Ralpho;* 'tis all one:
> And when we can with Meeter safe,
> We'l call him so, if not plain *Ralph.*
> For Rhyme the Rudder is of Verses,
> With which like Ships they stear their courses.)
> An equal stock of Wit and Valour
> He had laid in, by birth a Taylor (I.i.451–460).

6. Hamilton is referring to Gunter's scale, a flat rule, two feet long, marked on one side with scales of equal parts and on the other side with scales of the logarithms of those parts; it was named after its inventor, Edmund Gunter (1581–1626), the distinguished English mathematician.

he Calculates his piece, so as that some lines may be an Inch long, others two three 6, 8 or 10 Inches, the pindaric ode is finished, there is also a large magazine of poetical Ideas, to be stored up in the brain of a moderen poet, such as quaint puns, dowble Entendres, trite Similies and allusions, Extravaganzas, flights, and a vast number of Sentiments, Concerning Groves, Grottos, flowery Lawns, Green meadows, verdant forrests, purling Streams, Silver fountains, hoary mountains, Darts, fires, Stars, moons, Suns, Constellations, &ct: &ct: &ct: all Compared and assimulated to Certain things to which they have not, never had, or ever will have any likeness or analogy, This is a short Summary of the Qualities absolutely necessary to frame a moderen poet, of a Genius adequate to that of Jonathan Grog Esqr, and the other moderen poets or Bards of the ancient and honorable Tuesday Club, of whose Incomparable Genius, we have already given several Specimens, in this history, and shall have occasion to exhibit more before we have done.

At Sederunt 224 July 9th 1754, The Honorable Nasifer Jole Esqr being H:S: The Club met for the first time, since its Institution, at a Tavern or house of Public Entertainment, being, at the Celebrated Mr Leidemont's, at the Dock, where whillom was held the Grand Clubical parade, The occasion of the Club's meeting at a Tavern at the time of his honor's serving as h:s: was said to be, the excessive drunkeness of Don John Charlotto Gentleman, Clerk of the kitchen, which threw every thing in his honor's house and kitchen Into such a Lamentable Confusion, that he could not Entertain Company at home. [386]

At this Sederunt no proceedings were read, because the Secretary was Scrupulous about bringing the book of Records to such a public place of Rendezvous, as a tavern, neither did his honor take the Chair, because there was no Chair to take.

Some slight hints were given by his honor the president, that the Club for the future should meet at a public house, which the Club took no notice of, on account of two principal members being absent, vizt: Mr Attorney General Neverout, and Slyboots pleasant Esqr.

At Sederunt 225th, Crinkum Crankum Esqr being H:S: and Jonathan Grog Esqr, Deputy in the Chair, a poem was presented In Club, left with the Secretary by the late Chancellor, being the proper Composition of that Great Clubical State officers muse, who said, at the time of his presenting it to the Secretary, that he left this poem, as a peace offering to his honor and the Club, to stand as a Salvo for his late Speech, that had given so much offence, || and added also, that he never once in his life time had thought of being either a poet or an orator, till the Tuesday Club had made him both, The Poem follows. [387]

Carmen Sociale,

In praise of the Ancient and honorable Tuesday Club in Annapolis, wrote in the year 1751, by one of it's admirers.

        Sicilides Musæ, paulo majora Canamus. Virgil[7]

Invocation	Once more [a] Thalia,[8] Tuneful maid,
	Let me Invoke thy needful aid,
	A nobler Theme ne'er tun'd the Lyre,
	Worthy the poet's brightest fire,
	The Grecian bard, or Mantuan Swain,
	Might hence Immortal honors gain,
	For not Achilles' frantic rage,
	Nor Ithaca's more Crafty Sage,
	Nor Bully Ajax' Stamps and frowns,
	Nor Thread bare tales of Ships and towns,
	And vagrant travels, here and there,
	By Sea and land, and God knows where,
	Nor yet Æneas, boasted Sire,
	Of Romulus that Tyrant dire,
	With all his toils and Din of war,
	Which poets art has spread so far,
	[Mere dreams Invented to deceive,
	Which men of Sense will ne'er believe]
	Can such an ample field afford,
	A field with such description stord.
Proposition	I sing the *Club,* whose ancient name
	Stands high upon the Rolls of fame,
	"The Tuesday Club, Annap'lis Glory,
	While human things shall live in Story."
Introduction	Th'Important night revolving Calls
	The happy band to friendly walls,
	Where mirth & wit, & gen'rous Cheer Invite
	The Soul unbent, to revel in delight,
	They're met, now muse, each member trace,

((a) Once more,) This expression may puzzle the Commentators in times to come, how to reconcile it to the Chancellor's assertion, of his never having been a poet, till the Tuesday Club had made him one, unless he had wrote something, before this time, which he never Communicated to the Club.

---

7. "O Sicilian (pastoral) Muses, let's sing somewhat greater things" (Vergil, *Eclogues* 4.1).
8. Muse of comedy and pastoral poetry.

Description	Describe each Character and place.
1st The President	Full to the Sight, & next the Bowl[(a)]
	Exalted shines Illustrious Jole,
	[Forgive me Hogarth, if I steal
	A line that suits my theme so well]
	A Gilded Scallop oer his head
	Does it's refulgent radiance shed,
	"With air mysterious, see him nod,
	In Imitation of the God
	Whose thunder keeps the world in awe
	And gives a Sanction to his Law,"
	Not greater on his lofty throne,
	Or more Superb sits Prester-John,
	Like him our Chief, vain and elate
	With Satrapæ that on him wait,
	Scarce deigns one Sidelong glance to throw,
	On those that suppliant round him bow,
	Directs, assents, Revokes at will,
	Obedient, nonresistant still,
	The flattering Crowd with feign'd applause,
	Return their Lordly Chief his praise.
2d The knight Champion	In Sullen pride, upon his right,
	Sir John, Yclep'd the Champion knight,
	Tremend'ous sits, with penthouse brows,
	To whom none equal he allows,
	Prepar'd his title to mantain,
	Alike by dint of Sword or brain.
3d the Chancellor	His left, a priest, with look demure,
	In Character of Chancellour,
	"Guards—Ready with his Skill profound
	All knotty Questions to expound,
	Or puzzle what needs no Comment,
	Litigious Disputes to foment,"
	But stop my muse for reasons known,

[389]

(a) A line wrote under the print of Hogarth's *Midnight Moderen Conversation*, for borrowing of which our Bard here Improperly directs his apology to Hogarth, who, tho' of the original painting, yet cannot be supposed to be author of this line.[9]

9. Six lines of doggerel did appear under the original print of Hogarth's *Midnight Conversation*, but not this particular line (see *Hogarth Moralized. Being a Complete Edition of Hogarth's Works* [London, 1768], 202–205).

4th the Secretary	'Twere better Let the Church alone.
	Slow and majestic see arise
	The Scribe—on him their eager eyes,
	The whole Divan direct, while he,
	In Clubic Stile, the Noble Three,
	My Lord, the Chancellor and knight,
	Harangues, and proves, that black's not white,
[390]	Explores the philosophic truth,
	While lab'ring with eternal drouth,
5th the Poet Laureat	The Poet Laureat, honest Soul,
	In Raptures views the Sparkling bowl,
	Dear object of his fondest wish,
	His darling Joy, and greatest bliss.
	The ancient bards, a Sickly Crew,
	Inspir'd by water, never drew,
	From fam'd Castalios font a drench,
	Would fire the Soul, like Generous punch,
	"Whose Influence our poet's lays,
	Show, proving he deserves the bays,
	In Ceremonies art too, does excell,
	Like fam'd beau Nash, or Greater Cotterell."[10]
6th The musician	"Next hear how Proto musicus
	With Croaking voice obstreporous,
	And front of Brass Claims Orpheus' praise,
	Just so Pan with Apollo vies,
	Yet to his merit no small praise is due,
	As every Ravishd hearer, must allow."
7th & 8 Two private members	O Spyplot[(a)] could the pow'r of verse
	But half thy oddities reherse,
	How much like Socrates thy face,
	The self same Lineaments they Trace,

(a) Jealous Spyplot Senr: Esqr, the lineaments of whose face represented those of the bust of Socrates, painted by Paul Rubens.

10. Richard Nash (1674–1762) was an English gamester and social arbiter (known as Beau Nash and King of Bath, where he presided as master of ceremonies in 1705). By Hamilton's day the name Sir Clement Cotterell was virtually synonymous with master of ceremonies. The original Sir Clement Cotterell of Wylsford, Lincolnshire, was groom-porter to James I and muster-master of Buckinghamshire by 1616. Like his ancestor, the Sir Clement Cotterell who flourished in the early 18th century was master of ceremonies and a noted antiquarian besides.

> But ah, how near allied in mind
> Baffles the muses art to find,
> Vain Physiognomists forbear,
> Your Senseless guesses, Idle Care,
> Since here, to your eternal Shame,
> Two faces Lineally the same,
> Own Souls and minds as fare remote
> As horn Cape, and John a Groat.[11]
> "Thy oddities however can divert
> And much Gelastic Pleasure do Impart."
>   Dear Slyboots Sure for friendship form'd,
> No anxious thought yet e're alarm'd,
> Thy peaceful breast, let others wear
> Out life in dul Chimeric Care,
> Let merchants plow the Sea for gain
> And brave the terrors of the main,
> Let Gownmen wrangle, Soldiers fight,
> And plodding fools in Change delight,
> Whilst thou at ease experience,
> The Charms of Sacred Indolence,
> "And others please with humors Sweet & free,
> Averse to Jars, and friend to mirth & Glee."

Conclusion
> Thus far the muse has plac'd in view,
> The happy Corps. Still would pursue
> The Pleasing theme, did not the task
> A Butler or a Fielding ask.
>   *In magnis voluisse sat est, Valete.*[12]

The apostrophed lines in the preceding poem, are those, which the Chancellor affirmed, were purely his own in the composition, as for the others, he had help in forming them, after the reading of this poem ‖ The Secretary produced another, wrote In answer to both the Chancellor's performances, to wit the Speech and the poem, by Mr Proto musicus Neverout, attorney General, as he himself affirmed, a Copy of which follows.

---

11. Supposedly, John o' Groat (or Jan Groot) came from Holland in the reign of James IV of Scotland and, with his brothers, established a line of eight Groat families in Scotland; when a question of precedence arose among the families, John o' Groat designed an eight-sided room with a door to each side and an octagonal table in the middle. Ever since, this building, located in the vicinity of Duncansby Head, has gone by the name of John o' Groat's House.

12. "In great affairs, it is enough to have tried. Farewell" (Propertius 2.10.6).

Poem

By the attorney General, against the late Chancellor.

Infernal muses, Guide the pen,
To sing the Crabbedest of men,
Who lets his Devlish Genius loose,
Men in high Stations to abuse,
In Speeches, and in Poems full
Of Rancor, tho prolix and dull,
Without or Rhime, or Reason, bent,
To Scandalize our President,
Alect' Erynnis and Medusa,[13]
Are muses fit for me to Chuse ah!
They best become my theme and verse
While I this Chancellor reherse.
This Chancellor so Diabolic,
Whose Rhimes would give a man the Colic,
Whose Speeches at a single look,
Would make a man both —— & puke,
With Billingsgate they so abound,
Each Gentle hearer they Confound,
Raise Indignation in each Soul,
Whilst they traduce Illustrious Jole,
Illustrious Jole! our pride & glory,
Unmatch'd in old, or moderen Story,
Whom none can equal or excell
In Spite of pride or th'devil in Hell.
   See him rising from his Chair[(a)]
With look malicious, Grim, Severe,
His nose he pulls with handkerchef,
With Snuff well loaded, Snotty, Stiff,
His mouth he wipes with hand more nasty,
Well us'd to dip in pye or pasty,
With Spectacles he arms his nose,
Then spues his billingsgate in prose,

(a) *Oli sedato, respondit Corde Latinus.* Virg.[14]

13. Erinyes was the Greek name for the Furies (the avenging deities, Alecto, Megaera, and Tisiphone).

14. "To him, Latinus answered with a calm spirit" (*Aeneid* 12.18).

With air and utterance of a Sloven,
With hums and has well Interwoven,
He Coughs, then spits, the bowl he takes,
Then to the Chair a Stiff bow makes,
And with unequal'd Impudence
Palms on us Sophistry for Sense,
Dwells on the liberty of Clubs,
Giving his honor Scurvy rubs,
He wipes the Sham tears from his Eyes,
Pretending kindly to advise,
And feigning Grief and deep contrition,
Would stirr up Strife and dire Sedition,
And, like a quibbling Shrewd Rascallion,
Sows in the Club, Seeds of Rebellion,
Pernicious maxims he doth bring,
That touch the Rights of George our king,
Then with malitious intent,
Applies them to our President,
Calls his prerogative in question [394]
And all his rights makes a mere Jest on,
Subjects him quite to Clubic Law,
Makes him a president of Straw,
Destroys his Grandure at one Stroke
And makes of all his power a Joke,
Mantaining that the Club as soon,
As set him up, can pull him down,
Absurdities too gross to hear,
Or Loyal members for to bear,
Destructive of our Constitution
And tending to a Revolution,
That sap would the foundation Stone,
And make the Club yield her last Groan,
And having thus given up the Ghost,
For ever dead, for ever lost,
Would baffle all our power to raise
Again upon her lasting base.
    While with harsh voice & nasal twang
The Chanc'lor mouths his rude harangue,
Upon his honor's face the while
Appears a grand Contempt'ous Smile,

As if he Cared not a whistle,
For all this Chanc'lor's noise and bustle,
Sometimes too, with a Scornfull air,
He'd fall quite back upon his Chair,
To one or 'tother Side leans oft
While now he hawkd, & then he Cough'd,

[395]
Folding his handkerchef on knee,
His body moving, see-saw-see.
Bends forward now, then Backward veers,
Picqued at the Chanc'lor's Jibes & Jeers,
Then, on his Seat erect up reard,
He frowns, and strokes his awful beard,
And, oft from his vindictive eye
Lets Sparks of Indignation fly,
Then first one leg, and then the other,
On's knee he'd throw to spell each other,
The Orator^(a) with Eyes oblique
He would regard, and then as quick
At every period of his Speech,
On him he'd turn disdainful breech,
And then would by degrees begin,
In Scorn to elongate his Chin,
And squeeze his lips together tight,
Like them who to the pope do write
In Cloacinas Sacred dome,
And find their matter hard to come.
 But still this Chanc'lor perseveres,
With false alarms to strike our ears,
And tops with froth his Sillabub
Of Rhe'tric to Inflame the Club,
Which, spite of's art & forward face,
His reas'ning minded not an ace,
Esteemd his Suppositions *ficta*
And all his problems *Gratis dicta*.

[396]
 Infernal muses next reherse
His talent Shreud at dogrell verse,
When vainly he Invokes the muse,
The Club & Pres'dent to abuse,

(a) The Chancellor meaning.

Ransacks his brain and ancient Books
To find a pack of Bully Rooks
That round Troy's wall their arms did roll,
Only to match them with Great Jole,
Great Jole, who all of them exceeds
In Grandure and heroic deeds,
As old Rack does new England Rum,
Or Julius Cæsar to Tom Thumb.
Compares him next to Prester John,
Exalted high on Splendid throne,
When Prester John's to him a dottrell
As Clown to great Sir Clement Cotterel.
Next on Sir John he vents his Jeers,
Sir John, the prime of Cavaliers,
And to his valour nought allows
But Surly looks and penthouse brows,
And then he leaves us in the Lurch
Forsooth, lest he offend the Church,
And, without either Sense or grace,
Slurs oer his own Gelastic face,
For that describ'd, he'd run the risque
To make a Show the most burlesque
Mongst the whole group of Clubic wights,
So nothing of himself he writes,
The orator and poet too [397]
He sets for laughing Stocks in view,
The first, he says, like fool holds forth
From Sense as wide as South from north,
The Poet Guzzles punch and Grog,
And 'Musicus Croaks like a frog,
Of Spyplot makes a *Je ne sçay quoi*
And Slyboots Calls an Idle boy.
   Thus on the members round he vents
His awkward Scurvy Compliments,
Stirrs up the maggots in his brain,
To Satirize, but all in vain,
And while they o'er each other Tumble,
From thence proceeds a hideous Jumble
Of Crude Conceits & fancies Low
In Lines that hobble as they go,

And last of all to make us Gaze
And Gape pops out a Latin Phraze.
   The Chanc'lor thus, in Jingling measure
To teize the muses takes a pleasure,
By Introducing Jarring Sounds,
He all their harmony Confounds
And makes them break off in the middle,
Like artless hand that plies a fiddle,
Should he with doggrel thus harass us,
He'll make the Nine to fly Parnassus,
With fustian he'll our senses fuddle,
Convert pure Helicon to puddle,
For of Sweet poesie's he's no master,
Nay, is not even a poetaster,
His dogrell works, or I'm a Rogue ho,
Are like a new born *Caco fogo*^(a)
Which, tho it bears a human Shape,
Has not the Judgement of an ape,
For soon as it has op'd its Eyes,
It eats, speaks, Grumbles, farts and dies,
And sooner than a man would Think,
The lump expires in Noise and Stink.
   So 'tis with all such Dogrell Scrub,
As touch our president and Club,
And so 'twill be in after times
With this vain Chanc'lor & his rhimes,
For these shall neither hear nor see,
Either his doggrel Rhimes or he.

   Thus was this great officer, the Chancellor, who had been so Signally Serviceable to the Club, in Contending for its liberties and privileges, against the arbitrary proceedings and tyranny of the Chair, treated with burlesque poems and Satyrs, at the same time with his leaving of it, an

---

(a) *Caco fogo*, a monstrous birth, said to be as Common among the east India women as Soutrekins are among the Dutch, being a figure in a human Shape apparently but scarce animated, that dies almost as soon as born—making a noise like an explosion of air.[15]

15. A *cacafuego* is a spitfire or braggart (from the Latin *cacare*, meaning "to void, as excrement," and the Spanish *fuego*, meaning "fire"). Hamilton's facetious note enhances the derogatory nature of the word.

Instance of the great depravity and degenerate State of the Club, at this time, and a Shoking example of the Corruption and Ingratitude of the times, when true Patriotism and worth, become the || Subjects of Satyr and [399] ridicule. The Chancellor had showed himself an excellent Club member, while he Continued in it, and, tho' somewhat hasty and passionate, yet the Ends he had in view were always honest and upright, and it were pity he had not had a greater Command of his temper, for had he been a person of a more Calm disposition, his understanding and Judgement, would have been Sufficient to have restored lost liberty again, to the Club, the President, was undoubtedly rejoiced at his departure, expecting now to rule the roast alone, as he actually did, by the asistance of his Sicophantish flatterer the Attorney General, the Club submitting to his dictates in every thing, so that they make but a pitiful mean figure thro the Sequel of this history, and the more so, as they never had again, any such bold persons as The Chancellor and Sir John, to support them under the weight of that Tyrannical administration, which they were obliged to submit to.

When The Attorney Generall's Poem was read, the Club Created Jocifer Bluechin Esqr, a Stranger, entertained at this Sederunt, according to Ancient Custom, an honorary member, and ordered the Secretary to make him out a Patent under the Great Seal of the Club, the form of which patent was as follows.

COMMISSION OR PATENT TO JOCIFER BLUECHIN ESQR.

At the Two hundredth and twenty fifth Sederunt of the ancient and honorable Tuesday Club, vizt: on || Tuesday the 23 of July, 1754, Jonathan [400] Grog Esqr being deputy president, and acting with full power & authority at the Election and appointment of the Club, under the Honorable Nasifer Jole Esqr, president in Chief, Jocifer Bluechin Esqr, was unanimously Chosen and appointed an honorary member of the said Club by an unanimous Suffrage of the Longstanding members, and, by virtue of the *Letters patent,* of the said ancient and honorable Club, and the *Great Seal* of the Club thereunto appended, The said Jocifer Blue Chin Esqr, has full liberty Granted him, to come and go to and from the said Club at all times, without let or hindrance, and without any Charge or expence, as also, to speak in any debate of the said Club, having first asked leave of the Chair, to behave himself at all Sederunts of the said Club, with that freedom and decency that becomes an honorary member, in witness whereof, our Secretary, by the order of his honor the president and Club, has drawn out this

Instrument, and affixed thereto the Great Seal of the Club, this 24th day of July 1754.

[Great Seal appended]   *By order of The Club*
Nasifer Jole

[401] The Club then admitted by unanimous ballot, Doctor Jeronimo Jaunter, a Stranger entertained also this night, a Longstanding member of the Club, and Slyboots Pleasant Esqr, taking the Chair, as || Subdeputy president (the first of that denomination that had ever been in the Club) or Substitute of Jonathan Grog Esqr, Deputatus Electus; the latter Gentleman, as master of Ceremonies, Invested the Doctor with the Club Badge in the usual form, and the Subdeputy Confirmed him by manuquassation, then, all the rest of the Longstanding members Saluted him in the same manner, and Jonathan Grog Esqr, resuming the Chair, Dr Jeronimo Jaunter spoke as follows.

"Mr President and Gentlemen,

I return you my hearty thanks for the honor you have done me, in admitting me a longstanding member of this Club."

The Secretary then thus spoke to Dr Jaunter.

"Sir, I thank you for the ease you have given my memory in this short Speech, since I can remember it verbatim, and enter it without taking notes."

These Proceedings of the Club, at this Sederunt, were afterwards looked upon to be altogether illegal, and unwarrantable by his honor the president, and by him Cancelled, as we shall find in the Sequel—The Secretary now, by permission of the Club, had the keeping of the Great Seal, since the Chancellor left the Society, but his honor the President set no esteem or value now upon this Club Symbol, but looked upon it as a Cypher, nor could he Ever be prevaild upon to appoint another Chancellor, or to allow the Club to Chuse one.

Chapter VII

Second Taveren Sederunt, Concert of frogs, Critical letter by the Secretary, Poem on the Club tobacco box by the Laureat.

[402] Observations made on the actions of Brutes, have often afforded hints, by means of which useful discoveries || have been made in various arts and

Sciences, thus the arts of Physic and Chemistry have received several Improvements; medicines of Great value and Surprizing efficacy have been discovered, and the properties and qualities of bodies, before unknown, have been explained, for example, the way of Injecting a Glyster, that Soveraign Remedy in Colics and Gripings of the Belly, was first discovered by a certain bird that frequents marishes on the River Nile, who often with his long bill retroverted, administers to himself that medicine.[1] Music, with regard to modulation, has been much advanced by remarking the warblings of the birds, and Harmony, the most noble part of that Science, much Improved by the moderens, who have been the best Composers of Harmonic pieces, and who doubtless took their first hints from the Croaking of frogs, in a pool or Marish, for, among these animals, when they set up their pipes in hot weather, before a Showr, are to be perceived by a Curious ear, all the degrees of notes and tones, from the highest of the treble, to the Lowest of the Bass, This hint tho rude, might have first given rise to that Charming art, of Harmonic Composition, so much Improved by the Italians, in these latter Centuries, at least, since the time of Guido Aretinus, the monk, in the year 900, who was the author of the Chromatic Scale; And why not? since we are told, that the first origin of the Violin, that Charming Instrument, was the hollow Skull of an ass, strung by Hermes Trismegistus. The members of the ancient and honorable Tuesday Club, Constant admirers of the Curiosities of antiquity, were undoubtedly of this opinion, when they admitted into their Society, the practise of a *Concert of frogs*, for we cannot otherwise account for this practise in them, who always acted on principles of Reason, (I wont say right reason, according to the exuberant Stile of some, for I can frame no Idea of any Species of Reason that is not Right) than the profound regard they had for these first Hinters of Harmonic Composition, vizt: the Frogs.

[403]

At Sederunt 226, august 5th, 1754, The Club Convened for the Second time at a Taveren, under the high stewardship of Doctor Jeronimo Jaunter.

The Secretary delivered to his honor the President The Copies of several authentic poems and Club Speeches, together with the Rough Drafts of the Minutes of Last Sederunt, which his honor very gravely put into his pocket, that Insatiable Gulph, into which, whatsoever went, relative to the Club, never came out again.

A vein of punning run Thro the Club at this Sederunt, many Shining ones were delivered by Jonathan Grog Esqr, The attorney General, mistaking his latitude, attempted to pun, and was suddenly Cut short by the

---

1. The ibis, the sacred bird of the Nile noted for its long downward-curved beak.

Gelastic law, at which he looked not alittle amazed; this Illustrated the adage, *non omnia possumus omnes.*²

[404] Some members observing that Slyboots Pleasant Esqr, was Likely to succeed as Chancellor, Jon- ‖ athan Grog Esqr, said he had no *Chance* for that.

A Concert of frogs was performed this night by three Voices, vizt: The Secretary Treble, The Poet Laureat Tenor, and Crinkum Crankum Esqr Bass, The Treble part, sung Flip, flip, flip,—The Tenor, a Cool Tankard, a Cool Tankard, a Cool Tankard, and the Bass ditty was Grog, Grog, Grog, which occasioned much Laughter and Gelastication.

Entertained this night, according to ancient Custom, four Gentlemen of Note, and forty besides. (a)

At Sederunt 227, after four weeks adjournment, Slyboots Pleasant Esqr, being H:S: The proceedings of last Sederunt were read, by Crinkum Crankum Esqr, deputy Secretary, after which his honor observed and said,

Pr: I dont think the last meeting to be a Club at all. Where are the Seal and Records?

Att: Gen: Why, at home—It certainly was no regular meeting.

Dep: Secr: Would your honor have the last meeting accounted a regular Sederunt?

Pres: Why—I dont know.—I think not.

Here came on a hot Dispute Concerning Doctor Jeronimo Jaunter's Inauguration, The President said he was Glad of his Company, but, before he could be esteemed a Longstanding member, forms and Ceremonies were to be complied with,—The attorney General sided with the President in Every Thing, as usual, as long as he kept awake, for he fell asleep by eight [405] o'Clock and ‖ did not open his eyes all the rest of the evening—Doctor Jaunter began to pallaber the president, endeavoring all he could by force of fair persuasions to obtain his Confirmation, and declared, he did not desire to sit as a member of the Club, without his honor's acceptance.—The President on his part protested, that he would rather Initiate him than some others (meaning, as is supposed, Crinkum Crankum Esqr) professed a great Regard for him, and expressed with more than Common warmth, his Sentiments of his worth.

A pacquet was brought into Club from the Chief Secretary, directed to

---

(a) That this pun may not be lost, which was started by Jon: Grog Esqr, there was one Capt: Forty entertaind at this Sederunt.³

2. "We cannot all do everything" (Vergil, *Eclogues* 8.63).
3. The "Record" identifies these gentlemen as [John] Hepburn, Alexander McPherson, Lancelot Jacques, John Ridout, and John Forty (see biographical sketches).

the H:S: and, Mr Pleasant Laughing upon receiving of it, the president Reproved him for it, and seemed offended at his impolite behaviour.

Pres: What have you got there Mr Pleasant, what is it, Let me see?

H:S: No Sir. They are directed to the H: Steward, here Mr Secretary.

Pres: Who made you Secretary Sir? what are you at?

Cr: Crank: Penning a poem Sir, I cannot help Clapping down my thoughts even at midnight.

Pres: We all know you to be so forward a Gentleman that you say any thing you first think of, tho' never so much out of time.—what!—are you writing down that?

Cr: Cran: Sir I am deputy Secretary.

Pres: Remember Gentlemen, that at next Sederunt, I enter a Caveat against his setting down that.

Then the Deputy Secretary read the letter to the H:S: vizt:

To Slyboots Pleasant Esqr, [406]
High Steward of the Tuesday Club, These.

Sir,

You being, (as I am Told, for I am now a days, tho Secretary, let Into very few Club Secrets) H:S: of the ancient and honorable Tuesday Club, to meet this evening the 3d of September, 1754, I thought it adviseable to write to your High Stewardship, Concerning very weighty and momentuous matters, for, since his honor the president, and so forth, has sent forth his verbal edict, against all manner of Club letters, upon Club days, or Clubical occasions, wrote to himself, and pertinaceously has Secreted and Concealed these letters, from the view of the Club, let their Contents be never so momentuous and Important, Their Stile never so ornate and lofty, their Sense never so well segregated and sequestered, from any plausible handle to hold by, and their Nonsense never so well soldered, nailed and Dovetailed, so as to make it thorro'ly Clubical, and worthy of the Serious Consideration of the Longstanding members over a pipe and a bowl (—hoh!—this period is too long)—it is my most Serious and Sober opinion, that the H:S: is the properest person, to be wrote to on such Important occasions as may require writing, since, he being a temporary officer, can ‖ have no [407] temptation to Conceal, Secrete, envelope in obscure pocket bags, or even to dedicate, to the Divine Cloacina, or the persian Deity, any of the valuable Scrolls, Chartules,[4] Schedules, transcrpts, prescripts or rescripts belonging

---

4. A *cartulary* is a collection of charters, particularly a large volume, or set of volumes, containing copies of all the charters, title deeds, and similar documents belonging to an estate such as a monastery.

to this here ancient and honorable Club, what tho' he has no authority to order them to be recorded, yet good Sir—you know who has a trick for that—heigh! hoh!—

Tho I am persuaded, that some wise men and modish wits, who Cut their Sentences, as taylors do their Stuff, to save a Remnant, may say *Pish!* and turn up their noses, and distort their mouths, at what I am now going to write to you, yet I must proceed in my own way, regardless of these Pseudo-critics, and only Salute them, *en passant,* in the Phraze of Plautus(a) *Olet homo!*[5] For though they may have a greater quantum of wit than I, and may keep it in larger Jars, or vases of earth, alias Craniums, yet mine, tho' less in quantity, is abundantly more volatile than theirs, and pungent enough to force them to make these droll Gelastic faces, when it strikes the Olfactory nerve in its passage to the Ideal Empyræum, such Burlesque faces I mean, as are wore by *People of Fashion,* when any thing *Low,* or rather *Clubical,* is mentioned in Conversation, which Sort of Nonsense is not of the Right Cut for them to Laugh at, but when their || gravity and demureness, makes it recoil back upon others, it causes those others to laugh, or Gelasticate even to excess, so as to make their eyes shed Salt water and shake their fat bellies.

But, to the main point intended, which I profess, I had like to have forgot, I think it would be expedient for our Great poet Laureat, to apply to our Learned attorney General, to Cause Issue process against a Certain Poetaster, who has lately made his appearance in the *Maryland Gazette* No 485, in an anonymous piece, wrote by him, the said Anonymous poetaster, Entituled, a *Memorandum for a Sein Hawling, in Severen River, near a delightful Spring, at the foot of Constitution hill.*[6] In this patched up piece, the Malapert Bardling, has Impudently, Insolently and Ignorantly, attempted to Imitate the manner, Stile, Diction, Phraze, and Inimitable versification of our Incomparable Poet Laureat Jonathan Grog Esqr, That Sugar Plumb and Darling of the Muses; as this is not only a daring affront, to that Illustrious Poet Laureat, and unparallelled Punster and Conundrumificator, but, an Insult upon our honorable President, and our ancient and Honorable Club, who are as manifestly wounded thro' the Sides of their Darling,

---

(a) *Amphitrio,* the Scene between Mercury & Sosia.

5. "Man stinks" (*Amphitruo* 321).

6. Hamilton accurately transcribes this poem as it appeared in the *Maryland Gazette,* Aug. 22, 1754. The "Anonymous poetaster" is likely the attorney general himself, whom Hamilton later identifies as a "Sain hawler" (see p. 562) and who has by this time established a reputation for his odd verses and bad imitations (see I, 175–176, II, 106–108). In effect, Secretary Scribble is asking the attorney general to prosecute himself for his own bad poetry.

as Religion is often wounded thro' the Sides of the Reverend Clergy, it would be proper to publish a reward in the said Gazette for apprehending and bringing to Justice that Impudent thief and plagiary, who, like Prometheus, has stole Celestial fire from the said Jonathan, and produced a Pandora, who, once she opens her pestilent box or budget, will disseminate among us, all the pleagues of Grubstreet and Insufferable doggrel, with small Hope of Recovery left behind, if Mr Attorney will please to look over that abominable Poem, it will pose his great Learning to find out any thing to match it in all his pandects, *Corpus Juris's,* Law Entries, and Learned Reports, Can any thing be more Coarse and abominable, than the very first distich of this Rascally poem.

> Six bottles of wine, right old, good and Clear,
> A Dozen at Least, of English Strong beer.

The muddiness of this Poetaster's Genius, appears in the very first opening of his piece,—what! a dozen of puff-gut beer, and only half a dozen of wine? ought it not to have been rather 6 Dozen of wine, ye Gods! *proh pudor!*[7] what comes next?

> Six Quarts of Rum, to make punch & Grog,
> (The Latter a drink, thats now much in vogue)

The first line is Lame, and wants one Sillable, if there is any beauty in the Second, it is Couched under the Clear definition it gives us of Grog, being a Liquor now much in vogue, *O preclarum Caput!*[8] why so is mum, Stum, Rum and hum, all liquors now much in vogue. Then he proceeds,

> Some Syder, if Sweet, would not be amiss,
> Of Butter Six pound, we cant do with less.

Smoke the Rhime, *amiss* and *Less,* and then, as Myn heer Van dyke says, in the Comedy,(a) *and butter, Remember butter, do not leave out butter;* The Devil Butter his Guts with Naphta & Sulphur for his Impudence, what! does he think we can swallo Six pound of butter at a Gulp,—but what next?

> A tea kettle, tea, and all the tea Geer,
> To treat the Ladies,—and also Small beer.

(a) Beaumont and Fletcher's *Beggars Bush.*[9]

7. "For shame!"
8. "Oh illustrious head!"
9. Hamilton has accurately quoted this passage from *The Beggars Bush* (probably coauthored by John Fletcher and Philip Massinger and first acted in 1622), act 2, sc. 3, lines 103–104.

Our Poetaster here has been Guilty of a great over Sight, in not putting a break between *the Ladies* and *Small beer,* which, I out of Compassion have done for him, and, let him take notice to have it printed so, in all the following editions of this work, what an odd Antithesis, what a Shoking Contrast, Ladies and Small beer, the Poet Laureat of the Tuesday Club, would have shit upon such an Expression, vizt: wiped his breech with it, even the veriest grov'lers of Grubstreet, commonly match women & wine together in their Jovial Songs and Catches, but Sure the Ladies, who are not esteemed mere women, but a Species of Celestial Goddesses, the least he could have matched them with, was heavenly Nector, Pho! Small beer; fulsom flatulent Rot-gut!

    Sugar, Lemmons, a Strainer, & likewise a Spoon,
    Two China bowls to drink out of at Noon.

[411] The first line again hobbles, having two Sillables too much; but why two China bowls?—oh, one for Punch and one for Grog, in this single particular only, our poetaster resembles, or rather pretends to Imitate our Laureat, in a pretended esteem for Grog, then follows

    A Large piece of Cheese, a table Cloth too,
    A Saucepan, two Dishes, and a Cork Screw.

This is expressly against a Rule of Aristotle's in his *Poetics,* who absolutely forbids, the bringing in a Group or medley of things, that have no relation to one another In the same Sentence, unless it be by way of Banter,[10] but this Scribbler seems to be Serious, and by no means in that Comic vein, in which the Great Milton was when the following line escaped him.

    Embrios and Idiots, Eremites and Friars.[11]

Then we have him Thus.

    Some plates, knives and forks, a fish kettle & pot,
    And pipes and Tobacco, must not be forgot.

I humbly Conceive, that a great part of this last line is stole from a Certain ancient Bard, who Composed a ballad, in which the following beautiful line was the Burden of the Song.

    For oh! for oh! the hobby horse is forgot.[12]

Then follows

---

    10. *Poetics* 1456a, 27–32.
    11. Hamilton has accurately quoted this line from *Paradise Lost,* 3.474.
    12. Proverbial phrase in Shakespeare, Jonson, *et al.,* presumably from an old ballad.

> A frying pan, Bacon or lard for to fry,
> A Tumbler or Glass to use when we're dry.

For to fry—The particle *for,* here, is often extremely useful, to fill up the measure in poetry, tho' in prose ‖ altogether Superfluous,—but why a tumbler?—what the devil a'nt the two China bowls mentioned above Sufficient?—well come away, let's have the rest. [412]

> A hatchet, some matches, a Steel and a flint,
> Some touchwood, a box with some Tindar in't.

Bustle enough Indeed, about making of a fire, but this Scurvy Rhimer stands much in need of some fire to warm his Cold Genius and fancy.

> Some vinegar, Salt, some Parsley & Bread,
> Or else loaves of Pone, to eat in their stead.

As if Pone was not bread.—if Pone be not bread, pray Mr Malapert, what is it, here this prig plainly discovers his Ignorance of the Latin and french tongues, the near Resemblance of *Pone* to *Panis,* and *Paine,* might have Convinced him that pone was really Bread.

> And for fear of bad luck at Catching of Fish,
> Suppose we should Carry—A READY DRESSD DISH.

Why this Break between *Carry,* and *Ready dressd Dish,* and why the latter in Capital Characters, but this Confirms what a Celebrated wit says.

> In moderen wit—all printed trash is—
> Set off with numerous breaks—and dashes—
> —When letters are in vulgar Shapes,
> 'Tis ten to one, the wit escapes,
> But when in Capitals express'd,
> The dullest reader smokes the Jest.   Swift.[13]

So to have done with this poetaster and his piece, let him be prosecuted I

---

13. This passage appears in Swift's "On Poetry: A Rapsody" (1733) as follows:

> In modern Wit all printed Trash, is
> Set off with num'rous *Breaks*——and *Dashes*—
>
>   To Statesmen wou'd you give a Wipe,
> You print it in *Italick Type*.
> When Letters are in vulgar Shapes,
> 'Tis ten to one the Wit escapes;
> But when in *Capitals* exprest,
> The dullest Reader smoaks the Jest:

(*The Poems of Jonathan Swift,* ed. Harold Williams, 2d ed. [Oxford, 1958], II, 643, lines 93–100).

[413] say, let him be prosecuted, by || Mr Attorney General Neverout, to answer to a trespass on the Case, against Jonathan Grog Esqr, Plantiff.

Solo Neverout Esqr
Attorn: Genl: Pledges { John Doe / Richd: Roe.[14]

I have sent you the rough proceedings of last Sederunt, and, (if I durst nominate) I would have that Ingenious Gentleman, the Laureat to supply my place as Secretary this night, and take down the minutes minutely, of the Club's proceedings, but, dreading the fate of our Late Chancellor, in a parallel Case, I earnestly beg and request, that his honor the president would not Create that Gentleman Deputy Secretary, *Nam si scit Celeberrimus noster præses, me hanc rem optare, nequaquam fiat &ct: &ct: &ct:*[15]

I know not if it will be altogether proper at this Sederunt, to take notice of the late Insolent Conduct of the king of Prussia, in Refusing a free passage to the Palatines thro' his territories,[16] and publish a mandamus of the Club, ordering him to desist, for should this foolish Scheme of his take, it might be of Infinite prejudice to this here Club in after ages, for these high Germans are a very Clubical Sort of fellows, and would make excellent Longstanding members, and having besides got Square Sterns and very broad Squat Arses, would fill windsor Chairs nobly at a Grand Club Sederunt, but this I leave to the wisdom and discretion of his honor and the Club.

[414] Please to demand the Rough Copy of the minutes of last Sederunt but one, of his honor, who pocketed || and has not as yet returned it, and request his honor that we may be no more shammed with promises of Councils of State, and, that we may know at once, without farther Shuffling and quibbling, who are long Standing members among us, and who not a Gods-name,—as I take it, Jonathan Grog Esqr serves this here Club next to you, upon Tuesday the 17th Instant, Commend me to his honor, and his longstanding members, That now are, and are to be, so, am your's to Command,

Postrid: Calend: *Loquacious Scribble Secretarius*
Septemb: *anno Æræ* 1754   *Tuesday Clubensis.*

After the Reading of this Long letter of the Secretaries, The President seemed much offended at it, and expressed no small Surprize at the Imper-

---

14. Names signifying any plaintiff and defendant in an action of ejectment.

15. "For if our most celebrated president knew that I wished this thing, nothing would be done."

16. Hamilton is referring to the antagonism between Frederick the Great (1712–1786) and the rulers of the Palatinate during the War of the Austrian Succession.

tinence of the Paragraph Concerning the king of Prussia, saying "what a' God's name has the Club to do with the king of Prussia, or he with the Club"; and some time after this, when Doctor Jeronimo Jaunter expressed to severall of the members some Inclination he had to leave the Club, on account of his honor's refusing him Confirmation, his honor would not allow, that that was the true Reason of his so expressing himself, but affirmed, that what made him desirous of leaving the Club, was a disgust he had taken at Mr Secretary Scribble's nonsense, which was nonsense of such an Intollerable Sort, that no man in his Sober Senses could patiently bear with it.

Dr Jeronimo Jaunter, had diligently applied for || some time to his honor for his Confirmation, but in vain, his honor remained Insensible, or rather Inflexible, but however, Condescended so far, as to promise to call a Council of State about it; as for Crinkum Crankum Esqr, he had now given over all Sollicitude on that very point, and Contented himself, with the Sanction he received from the Tenor of Law 51, tho' his honor the President denied the validity of that Law. [415]

At Sederunt 228, Septr: 24, 1754, Jonathan Grog Esqr being H:S: John Gabble Esqr, Champion of the Eastren Shore Triumvirate and honorary member, appeared in Club, and applied to his honor the President for a Commission, from under the Great Seal, to serve under his honor and the Club, against the French at the Ohio, and, after many long, and Tedious Speeches, thereon to no purpose, his honor absolutely refusing to Grant any such Commission; The Secretary took notice, that as he was in possession of the Club medal or badge, in Quality of honorary member, and Champion to the Eastren Shore triumvirate, that was Commission Enough, which observation his honor took notice of and approved, saying That it was the best remark the Secretary ever had made in Club, and Indeed the only one he had ever made to any purpose, his honor however consented to grant the said John Gabble Esqr, a Certificate, under his hand and privy Seal at arms, deferring the Commission, till he should deserve it, by his Conduct and behaviour, at the Expedition against the French on the Ohio, this Certificate however, has never as yet been Granted.

The attorney General, with his head Covered with his handkerchef, instead of the flaxen wig, rose up and observed Smartly upon the behaviour of John Gabble Esqr, while he addressed || his honor, taking notice, that he had sat all the time upon his Bum, and never once offered to rise and make a proper obeisance to the Chair,—Mr Gabble Excused himself for this behaviour, alledging that he had mounted Guard, at the Guardhouse all the preceeding night, with the Recruits, and was not really able to support [416] himself long on his legs, so his honor was pleased to excuse him, I take notice here, That Sir John Gabble Esqr, was not now only Champion to the Eastren Shore Triumvirate, but Second Leutenant to the Independent Maryland foot Company, now on their march, against the French at the Ohio, which Commission, it is supposed, he got by his Gallant behaviour in the Station of Triumvirate Champion.

At this Sederunt, was brought into Club, a Poem Composed by the Poet Laureat, upon the Late Chancellor's Carrying away with him the Club Tobacco box, that venerable piece of antiquity, purchased by the Club at Sederunt 14th, august 13th 1745 at the Price of 18 Shillings of Nasifer Jole Esqr, before he had attained to the Dignity of President, and, tho' this poem was not Read in Club, for Certain Political Reasons, yet, we cannot help giving a Transcript of it here, as follows.

A Tragical and Heroic Episode on The Club Tobacco box,

Pyrated By the Chancellor, composed by the Poet Laureat.

I sing the Ancient box of Lead,
Adornd at top with Negroes head,
The Box, that had so many fillings
Of Indian weed,—Cost eighteen Shillings,
Companion of the flowing Bowl,
Purchas'd of old, of Noble Jole,
On which, his most heroic Story,
Was 'Grav'd to eternize his Glory,
The box that often deck'd our Club-board,
Brighter than Silver vase in Cup-board,
Like Cornu-copia, with full measure,
And running over, op'd it's treasure,
Of Sweet Virginian Cut and dry,
Whose thick Clouds from our mouths did fly,
And hover'd o'er our heads all night,
To Guard our wits from taking flight,
Which waxed volatile and fine
By help of Rumbo, punch and wine,
The Box from house to house still sent,
Till it grew batter'd bruisd and bent,
Had many a rude thump, bang and Drub,
In Service of our Ancient Club,
Till like old Roman urn it show'd

With hollow Stems and ashes stowd.
  Ye Grubstreet muses, Guide my verse
While I this ancient Box Reherse
And show at Large the Grand device
Grav'd on its Sides, by artist nice,
And how our Chancellor at last,
In an old Trunk, confin'd it fast,
And Crossing Chesopeaks wide bay
Bore it oer hills and far away.
  On Starboard Side, the artist Quaint [418]
A Presidential Chair did paint,
And in this grand and Gorgious Seat,
There sat a President elate,
With mien majestic, bolt upright,
And by his Side a doughty knight,
That had enured been to blows,
With prosopæia bellicose,
A mighty blade of Steel around,
This knights Redoubted Loins was bound,
Whose Sheer edge Cut, where'er it hit,
Keen, as the Presidential wit;
Oer this high presidents Sage pate
There hung a Canopy of State
By Curious artist, finish'd well,
In figure of a Scallop Shell,
With oval Scutcheon in the front,
Which bore the Club's device upon't,
Libertas, et natale Solum,[17]
O'er Liberty, with Capoon pole hung,
Appeard, in flying Label dress'd,
In Gilded Capitals Expressd,
Two hands o'er heart on altar rub,
And underneath *The Tuesday Club,*
May the 14th the Date did fix
And Seventeen hundred forty Six.
  On 'Tother Side of lofty Chair,
A Chanc'lor sat, with Solemn air,
With hatchet face, and piercing eye, [419]

---

17. "Liberty and native soil."

His Seal and bag before him lye,
Next him, Sir Clement Cotterel height
Engraved was, with face polite,
A Laurel Green, his temples bound,
A Cup of Grog his right hand Crownd,
For he a dowble office shar'd,
Master of Cer'monies and Bard,
Nor could he make a Jantee bow
Or the Club's honor's neatly do
Or make his Jaded muses mill go
Without a tiff of Grog, or Jillgo,[a]
Great Proto musicus next see
Against the Laureat vis, a vis,
With prickt out music on a Scrowl
Compos'd in praise of noble Jole,
Long live Illustrious Jole he sung
While with his note the welkin rung,
Illustrious Jole, sounds to the Skies,
Eccho, Illustrious Jole replies,
The Curious Sculptors hand next Cut,
The Plodding Scribe at table's foot,
With folio Book of Records vast,
Noting each Circumstance that passd.
Others of the Longstanding rout,
The Table Compass'd round about,
Whose Spacious Surface bore the types
Of Bottles, bowls, Tobacco pipes,
And oer the whole Collected Crowd,
There hung of Curling Smoke a Cloud.
    Now to the Larboard Side we turn
Of this prodigious antique urn
And send abroad our wits to guess[a]
What here our artist would express.
    Exalted on a Spacious table
Appears a figure venerable,

(a) Jilgo, a Synonom for grog, because those who lov'd it Stiff used to mix Jell and Jill, that is, of rum & water, which made one draught.

(a) This would seem to Insinuate, that this whole description is a fiction, and that there were no such figures on the box, they only existing in the Poets brain or fancy, like those of Achilles's Shield in Homer.

Who, on a single knee bends down,
And eagerly presents his Crown,
To an Expanded fist so large,
And brawny, ready to discharge,
The Grand Inaugurating flap,
To fix thereon a mighty Cap,
A mighty Cap, it seemd indeed
And only fitted for the head,
Destin'd therefore by rigid fate
Yclep'd I ween, *a Cap of State,*
A Cap of hue right venerable,
Was all made up of velvet Sable,
Guarded before, with little flop,
And a small button at the top,
This was decreed, tho small & plain,
A head of wisdom to contain,
And, was by such a Noddle wore,
As never Cap Inclos'd before,
Arch-President, without Controul,
To wit, the most Illustrious Jole,
Longstanding members in a Croud,
Around this mighty table stood,
There, you might see the Champion knight,
With broad Sword on his Shoulder right
Prepar'd to rectify all wrongs, [421]
The poet too, with massy tongs,
A most prodigious figure made
And Gracd each Shoulder with a blade.
The Orator expands his Chops,
And praises Jole, in high flown Tropes,
While the mixd croud their voices raise,
Waving their hats, in loud huzzas,
And bawld for Jole, with Lungs right hearty,
Defying still Sir Hugh Maccarty.
This notable Configuration,
Was Call'd I ween, *The Grand Capation,*
And here in more than all the rest
The Sculptor had his art Expressd,
The Boxes arched head was Crown'd
With fruits and flow'rs & foilage round.

Pipes, bottles, Glasses, Goblets wide
Were Interwove on every Side,
In brave festoons and garlands twisted,
And negroes head, o'er all was sisted,
Which, as a Heroglyphic stood,
By which we'd have it understood
Jole's Club all other Clubs outbraves
And all their presidents his Slaves. (a)
    But Oh! our Chanc'lor, foul befal him,
I know not what base name to Call him,
Unless it be, malicious Cub,
Of this grand box, has 'reav'd our Club.
For, when he pack'd his awls to part,
With rancor burning in his heart,
'Gainst Jole and his Longstanding members,
Which Inward glow'd, like smother'd Embers,
And, with the Cunning of a fox,
In ancient Trunk, packd up this box,
This darling Box, and Clean away,
He wafted it accross the Bay.
    O may it prove to him a pest
To 'reave him of his wit and rest,
This heartily we do Implore ah! (a)
May't prove to him, box of Pandora,
Emmitting noisome Exhalation,
Retaining hope and Consolation,
Till he Repents his daring folly
And sends the box, back to great Jole hey! (a)
That he, and each longstanding member
May once again, in bleak December,
With the kind fumes which it discloses,
Furbish their wits & warm their noses,

  (a) This is a very strained Hieroglyphic, for the negroes head on the top of this box, would seem to signify, Just the Contrary.

  (a) Our Poet frequently uses this licence, for which, (not to mention Common ballad mongers,) he has good authority from old Chaucer, in his tale of the Knight, vizt:

    He cast his eye upon Emelia,
    And therewith he blent, and Cried ha, ha,
    As tho' he had been struck into the heart, a.[18]

  18. "The Knight's Tale," lines 1077–1079.

And least you think this tale too long,
I here Conclude my noble Song.

Chapter VIII

Speech of Crinkum Crankum Esqr, Confirmation of a long standing member, Dr Jaunter's Speech on a Cat's tail.

A well bred Complaisance and obsequiousness, especially when artfully exercised towards those who are fond of punctillio, and Ceremony, will, like a rudder, managed by a Skillful pilot, steer an obstinate man into another course, and make him Correct those mistakes & errors, ‖ in his own Conduct, which had hitherto baffled all the efforts of good advice; and sometimes too, this Latter Conveyd in a proper manner, that is to say, either with freedom, and Gaiety, or accompanied with a Striking allusion, will have the same Good effect. Darnades, when he observed Philip king of Macedon, behaving himself lightly before his Captives, asked him, since fortune had made him like Agamemnon, why he should behave himself like Thersites, and this Transformed him into quite another man, as to his manners and behavior.[1] Now, had he represented him plainly, as acting beneath the Dignity of a king, and urged some Grave & Serious lectures, the effect, probably would have been, that he thereby would have enraged the Tyrant, and instead of reforming rendered him worse, for, the Innate pride of human nature makes men unwilling to be told of their faults in a blunt manner. [423]

It is likely, that the Longstanding members of the ancient and honorable Tuesday Club, were no adepts in this Sort of Supple Complaisance, and obsequiousness, so powerfully operating upon the Conduct of the obstinate and Ceremonious, neither did they know, how to Convey their advice in a proper Channel, so as to prevail upon the honorable Mr President Jole, to Confirm, (as they and every one Else thought in reason they ought,) Crinkum Crankum Esqr, and Dr Jeronimo Jaunter, Longstanding members, after they had both been elected by a free and unanimous voice of the Club, ‖ for he obstinately refused the Solicitations of the Club on that Score, and, declared more than once, that he never would give up that part of his prerogative in allowing Confirmation to longstanding members [424]

---

1. See the conversation between Dardanus and Philip in Seneca's *Dialogues* 5.23.3.

elected without his knowledge and Consent. As for Crinkum Crankum Esqr, he had now, for sometime past given over hopes of obtaining that Significant Ceremony of Confirmation at his honor's hands, and therefore did not trowble his head any further about it, but it was not so with Dr Jeronimo Jaunter, who, understanding human foibles much better than most of the other members, and therefore how to manage his honor, prevailed at last upon the President, (by what manner, it is unknown, but we may reasonably suppose) by a well tim'd Complaisance (of which that Gentleman was a great Master) and advice artfully Convey'd, to Call a Council of State, to Consult and advise, concerning the Confirmation of himself and Crinkum Crankum Esqr.

Accordingly a Clubical Council of State, met at the attorney Generals house, on Saturday the 5th of October, in the evening, which was Composed of the attorney General, Slyboots Pleasant Esqr, with his honor the President, as for Mr Secretary Scribble, he attended the Council only as Clerk; while this Council was sitting, Philo Dogmaticus, the late Chancellor came into the Room, which, for some time put a || Stop to their consultations, the honorable the president however, civily Saluted Philo Dogmaticus, and signified to him, that they were met as a Council of State to concert matters of Consequence relating to the Club—These are matters, replied Philo Dogmaticus, with which I have now no concern,—I hope I do not Interrupt your Consultations,—The President answered Civily No Sir, and desired him to take a Seat, then told him That he had a great mind to pass an act of grace and oblivion, remitting all former offences, in the Club, and asked him how he relished that proposal,—Philo Dogmaticus answered It was what did not at all Concern him—how so Sir, Replied the president, dont you think it will be agreeable to the members—It may be so said the other—but said the President, will it not be so to you Sir—Why to me Sir? I care not a fart now what acts you pass, I am out of your Jurisdiction—on this his honor looked alittle grave, and the Conversation went no farther, till Supper coming in, the Conversation turned upon various Indifferent matters, which being Ended, the late Chancellor, had what he came for, and retir'd from the Company to Jog home, The Council then laid their heads together and it was resolved That Doctor Jeronimo Jaunter and Crinkum Crankum Esqr, should both be Confirmed at next Sederunt, upon making the proper || Submissions, and observing the proper punctillios & Ceremonies, The latter of which Gentlemen, was to knock at the Door of the Club Room, and being admitted was to desire liberty to sit down, as a Stranger in Club, and then, upon having leave Granted him, humbly to solicit his Confirmation, after which resolutions, the Council broke up.

On Monday the 7th of October, a day sooner Than the time appointed, for the Club to meet, was held, for particular reasons of State, the 229th Sederunt, Mr Secretary Scribble being H:S: at which Sederunt attended, Philo Dogmaticus Esqr, the Late Chancellor, in quality of an honorary member.

Doctor Jeronimo Jaunter, Elected a member of the Club at Sederunt 225th, by an Illegal ballot, in the absence of his honor the President, and also by an Illegal Club, it being held by Crinkum Crankum Esqr, as H:S: a person, not as yet regularly confirmed, a Longstanding member, by his honor's authority, rose up in Club, and made a Speech to the Chair, in which he earnestly requested his Confirmation, and pled in excuse for his former Conduct, his Ignorance of the Laws and Customs of the Club, which he should be more Careful for the future to study and observe,— after this Speech, by his honor's gracious permission, Doctor Jeronimo Jaunter was confirmed by the Master of Ceremonies, with the usual Ceremony, and was Saluted || by his honor and the L:St: members, in the ancient manner of manuquassation, and then standing up in his place, he spoke to this purpose. [427]

"Honorable Sir,

In the last Speech of thanks I made to this here Club, on occasion of my Supposed election, and Confirmation, it was observed upon me, in the Club records, that my Speech was a great ease to the Secretary, on account of its Shortness, as he could enter it verbatim, without takeing notes, but now I find, that Speech, short as it was, is more than Sufficient for the benefit I received at that time, and therefore, as I am now Instructed by experience, who properly to thank for such favours, I thank only your honor, for this great favor, I have Just now received."

Having thus spoke Doctor Jeronimo Jaunter took his Seat, as a Legal and effectual Longstanding member.

The Attorney General having some papers handed to him from the Chair, was observed to be very much occupied in looking them over, but this was kept a Secret from the Club, and managed Intirely in whisper between the honorable the president & he.

Crinkum Crankum Esqr, during these Transactions, knocked at the Club Room door, according to the directions of the Council of State, and being admitted with some difficulty, made a bow to his honor, and desired leave to sit down in the Club as a Stranger—Then the Secretary stood || up to make a motion, to desire liberty for a Certain Gentleman there present, to open his mind to the president & Club, but met with several Interruptions from the President, and being very much puzzled, how to keep the [428] thread of his discourse even and Intelligible, on account of these vexatious Interruptions, he began to turn warm, and betray some violence in his expressions and gestures, on which, at the Instigation of the attorney General, the Gelastic Law was put in execution against him, but, after the noise was over, he, still standing up patiently in his place, recovered his perturbed faculties, and moved, that Crinkum Crankum Esqr, should be allowed to speak for himself, which, being granted, notwithstanding the Objections of the Attorney General, that Gentleman stood up, and delivered himself as follows.

"Honorable Sir,

The reason of my now standing up, before your honor and this here Club, upon this here particular occasion, I have no need to mention, as your honor, and these here longstanding members must have knowledge of it already *in fact,* whatever knowledge you may be supposed to have had of it *in Policy,* for *knowledge in fact,* and *knowledge in policy* I take to be very different things, people possessed of the former, Generally make a merit of Communicating it to mankind, and thereby render others as wise as themselves, on the contrary, the politicians, for reasons of State, Generally keep their knowledge to themselves when it serves not their purpose to reveal it, and show a pretended Ignorance where there is none, and therefore, political knowledge may be defined, a negative knowledge, or Rather Ignorance, in the Eye of the whole world, but that of the politician himself.

For this very reason Sir, knowing your honor & these here gentlemen, to be men of great parts & deep policy, I thought it not proper, to usher what I had to say, on this Important occasion, in any Crude or unfinished Extempore harangue, but have Committed my thoughts to paper, that the language and Expression, may be more adequate to the dignity of my Subject, and more adapted to the delicate ears of this here ancient and honorable audience, I therefore, beg your Indulgence so far, as to permit me to read this Clubical oration.

As the transactions of this here ancient and honorable Club, can be no Secret to the Curious and discerning world, whose Eyes and Ears, are always open, to the Conduct and actions of Great, Grave and wise men, so, the Resolves, Conclusions, Consultations, and deliberations, of it's Committees, grand Councils and Councils of State, cannot long remain hid, but, must expand, and dilate themselves with an eclat, worthy of their great gravity, ponderosity and Sagacity, it therefore can be no matter of Surprize to your honor and these here gentlemen, that I, poor I, in no ways qualified to be present, aiding or asisting at the late Grand Council of the Club, held at the house of Mr Attorney General, should, by means of the Clangorous trumpet of fame, be Informed of the Great & Solemn Transactions of that venerable, Sapientific, Clubical Council, at least, Informed of so much of their deliberations, as more Immediatly Concerned myself, and therefore, answering my purpose, which in fine, is the Sole and whole reason of my now standing up in this here place, to harangue your honor, and this here ancient and honorable Club.

The babbling tongue of fame then, for, I shall accuse no other babbler [Here Mr Crankum looked about towards his left hand, where Mr Secretary sat,] as eager to promulgate great, heroic and Noble actions as to disseminate Scandal, Conveyd to my ears the Joyful news, that his honor, our honorable President, after grave and mature deliberation, with his Council of State, was determined, at this happy Juncture, to pass an act of Grace and oblivion, and, to forget and forgive all offences [Phil: Dogm: Ha, ha, ha, ha, hah.] Hitherto Committed against him in this here Club, This Joyful news, revived my flagging Spirits, and I began to Conceive hopes of being Received || into favor, but ah! how much was I transported, when I was Informed, that his honor was Inclinable to show favor to my unworthy Self, in Particular, and Confirm me in the honorable and undisputed Station of a Longstanding member of this here Club, and render me *rectus in Curia,* providing I should make proper Concessions and Submissions, and own my former conduct to have been blameable; Then I say, my Joy was Great, even like the Joy of Archimedes, the famous Geometrician, when he ran thro' the Streets, crying ευρεκα, ευρεκα, I have found it, I have found it! said I, in an extacy, with a Loud voice, and Saltatory Gesture,—what have you found, said the Surprized Relator of the News?—I have found favor, Replied I, in the eyes of his honor the president.

Now, Honorable Sir, as the Conditions, which your honor is pleased to propose to me, thro' the Channel of your honorable council, seem to be easy and reasonable, I am willing, altogether willing to comply therewith, for, it was always my opinion, that the man who would never own himself to be in the wrong, who would obstinately persist in his Erroneous opinions and whims, in Spite of all reason and Argument, who will not lend a willing ear, to the Good Councel, of another, admonishing and advising him for his Good, who would shut his eyes in Sunshine, and be Stupidly pertinaceous and Inflexible to advice & Intreaties, nay, to threats, I say Sir, such a one || or such a man Sir—must have more pride than prudence, more ambition than understanding, more petulence than discretion, more conceit of his own parts than Submission to the wisdom of his Superiors, more Impudence than modesty, more Ignorance than Judgement, more—more— In fine, he must be, Sir,—he must be more fool than Philosopher.

I therefore, in humble duty and respect to my Superiors, am determined to act in direct opposition to the ways of these hard headed and harder hearted Dogmatists, and, with a melting heart, and flowing eyes, pouring out Sluices of tears [*N:B:* to wipe my eyes here with a white handkerchef] to beg your honor to forgive all my past offences, the greatest part of which, I can assure your honor, were Committed more thro' Inadvertency than design, from a wrong Sense of things, skimming off the Superficies of the Clubical Rules only, without trowbling myself to dive or grope to the bottom, of this here excellent constitution, a false persuasion, that I was kept out, and deprived of my Just and lawful due and right, hurried me precipitatly on, perhaps too far, being naturally hasty and passionate, the Characteristic of my native Country, which borders on Wales, and made me exceed the bounds of decency, and violate my duty, but now I am Sensible of my error, and publicly profess my Sorrow and repentance therefore, [*Hinc illæ lachrimæ*] [memd: apply the handkerchef here, to the part supposed to be affected]

[433] And now, honorable Sir, I here Solemnly renounce disclaim and revoke, all letters, petitions, Speeches, writings, orations, harangues, overtures in prose or verse, by me uttered, motions by me made, poems, Songs, puns, Conundrums and Sham Laws, that I may have hitherto promoted in this here Club, derogating from your honors Just prerogative, power and authority.

> I also denounce a Clubical damnation,
> To that foolish wight of the Imagination,
> Sir Hugh Maccarty ycleped Esquire,
> And wish he was roasting, by John, at your fire.

I likewise wish from my heart, that he and Box No 1, were buried, ramm'd Cramm'd and hid under the earth, in the same Coffin, never to rise again, and, had I known, I should have given the least offence to your honor, in Intermeddling with that pragmatical, Phantasmical Club heroe, I would never have raked the Dunghil for his Stinking name, but have left him to rot in oblivion, like *a Son of a bitch* as he was, & now Honorable Sir,

> Having publicly made this Large recantation,
> I hope you will grant me a due Confirmation.
> *Parvum in multo*"[2]

Tho Mr Crinkum Crankum accompanied the delivery of this Speech, with all possible Submission, yet his honor refused to confirm him, at this

---

2. "A small thing in a great space" (the comic inversion of *multum in parvo*).

Sederunt, the attorney General talked much against him, at first, and the Secretary being his Councel, and observing the attorney to take notes, Insisted upon seeing these notes, the attorney absolutely refused, and a Clubical Squabble had like to have ensued.

It was Thought that Mr Crankum was Inspired with the Spirit of prophecy in one part of his Speech, where he wishes ‖ the box No 1 buried under Ground, for that, soon after this, was really the fate of that Celebrated box, as his honor himself declared in Club, at Sederunt 231. [434]

Doctor Jeronimo Jaunter Talked much in favor of Mr Crinkum Crankum, and, in a very smooth and persuasive manner, but to no purpose, his honor was determined not to be Cajoled at this time, and as he told the Club more than once would not Confirm Mr Crankum at this Sederunt, Then demanded a Copy of his Speech, which was delivered to him after alittle hesitation. Mr Crankum himself then pray'd very hard to be heard, but all his discourse was of no Significancy, his honor still persisted in his refusal.

Doctor Jeronimo Jaunter, Instigated by some Strange and unaccountable Infatuation, or rather, being under a Sort of fascination or witchcraft, made a Speech, *de lana Caprina,* or Rather *de Cauda felina,*[3] which gave offence to the Chair, this, the Club perceived, not by a *fieri facias* emitted from thence, but rather by a *facies Lignea,*[4] the Common Symbol, of the presidential Indignation,—This Speech on a Cats Tail, was a very Extraordinary one, as proceeding from Dr Jaunter, and, none could Imagine, how he could light on a Subject so particularly offensive, to his honor, who had a particular esteem for these creatures. Some one or other, had brought a Cats tail Into the Club, which it is supposed had been picked up in the Street, and the purport of the Doctor's Speech, was That the Club should make some law, to make the barbarous usage of these Gentle animals, in Cutting off and docking of their tails, highly penal—The president looked very Surly at this, and the Club being alittle puzzled, how to prepare such a law, the attorney ‖ general advised the Club to apply to the Corporation of Annapolis, who were a Judicious body of men, very expert at drawing up correct bye laws. While these transactions were going on in Club, the Late Chancellor, Philo Dogmaticus, sat silent and Contemplative, applying himself often to his Snuff box, and seemed to be altogether absent, taking no notice of what passed, excepting only once Laughing, when Crinkum Crankum Esqr, mentioned in his Speech, the passing of an act of grace and oblivion. [435]

---

3. "Over goat's wool" or "over a cat's tail."
4. Not by a "writ to be made" but by "a wooden face."

The Club, finding the President, very much Enraged, at Dr Jaunter's Speech, endeavored to huddle up the matter in the best manner they could, fearing that it was likely to occasion as much mischief as the famous letter of Cats did, at Sederunt 113, and, as Quirpum Comic Esqr, was Soleley concerned in that affair, so, his honor the President, thought him alike Culpable in this, for, he was present in Club at this Sederunt, and was observed to whisper Dr Jaunter often before he rose up to speak.

Chapter IX

Trial of Crinkum Crankum Esqr, Speech of his honor the President.

[436] The actions of the Brutes appear to be Conducted by a fiat rule, which, if you please, you may Call *Nature,* with me, or *Instinct,* with a Certain Sect of Philosophers, who have denied them the use of Reason, but be it nature, be it Instinct, or what you please, 'tis Certainly something that produces a greater Consistency and uniformity || of Conduct, than that in another Species of Animals, which is dignified by the name of Reason, be this reason of theirs, humor, Caprice, Ignorance, perverseness, or what you please, for example, you cannot make an Ass drink unless he be dry, whereas the other rational animal will often drink, tho' not dry, till he loses his reason, or at least that power of discerning and distinguishing which he Calls reason; in fine, from this Caprice it arises, that men will advance lies for truth, absurdities for Sense, folley for wisdom, Cowardice for Courage, Dreams and Chimeras for honor, and regulate their actions accordingly, pretending to derive all from reason and Sound Judgement, abundance of Instances could we produce here, if time would serve, from politicks, religion, the Common and frequent occurrences of life, on which punctillios and duels are grounded and take their origin, and thro' which men Conceive prejudices and likings for one another, They cannot tell for what, resolve thus to day, act otherwise to morrow, say this and mean that, do and undo in the same breath, and follow a perpetual Giddy and Irresolute Course; This Caprice then, this *opiniatreté,*[1] this *Je ne sçai quoi* of a malapert humor, being the Cause of all absurd and Inconsistent actions in men, we cannot attribute to any other Cause than this, the Inconsistent Conduct of the honorable Nasifer Jole Esqr, and Mr Neverout his attorney General, in

---

1. "Obstinacy."

not keeping to the Resolutions of the Grand Clubical Council of State, framed by themselves, & with their Consent, in the affair of Mr Crankums Confirmation, since the latter Gentleman, as we have related, had punctually performed ‖ all that was required of him by that Clubical resolve, to wit knocking at the door, asking leave to sit down, and moving for his Confirmation, but we shall soon see this Gentleman Gratified in what he so earnestly desired, and indeed in such a manner, as nothing but the power of Caprice can account for his Success in this affair at Last. [437]

At Sederunt 230 Novr 5th 1754, Solo Neverout Esqr Attorney General being H:S: he, having, as usual, shuffled off the Club, a fortnight latter, than the time appointed for his serving, as soon as the Club were set, and the proceedings read as usual, Mr Attorney Neverout, the high Steward, stood up in his place, and addressed Crinkum Crankum Esqr, as follows.

"Sir,

As a Gentleman and a Stranger, I cannot, in good manners, but make you welcome here, in my house, but, as a Longst: member of this Club, which you have pretended all along to be, I utterly disown you for such, and as such you have no business in this place,—Therefore, if you come here as such—There is the door."

At this Speech, Mr Mevius Pumpkin, an honorary member, seemed very much Surprized and astonished, and pulling his pipe from his mouth, stared, in a fixed posture for a considerable time, Mr Crinkum Crankum was very angry with the attorney General, and seemed much affected at the Rudeness of the address made to him, by that Gentleman, and, having urged and pled his confirmation with the president, some dispute and hesitation arose In Club Concerning that matter, at last, some proposing to have Mr Crankum Regularly admitted by the Ballot, and then Confirmed by his honor the president, the attorney General objected and ris- ‖ ing up, delivered himself to the Chair, To the following purpose. [438]

"Honorable Sir,

The Duty of my office obliges me to stand up here, an advocate for your honor and the Club.—I say, Sir, for your honor and the Club, for, according to my conception, whatever affects your honor, equally affects the Club, and vice versa—again, an Indignity to the Club, is an Indignity to your honor, therefore, as your honor Comprehends the Club, I need only speak to and of your honor, to make my Subject full and compleat, or perfectly Clubical in all points.

From this position, honorable Sir, I hope, without much straining my learning or parts, to make it plainly appear, that this paultry Speech, which I now hold in my hand [Cr: Crank: which hand Sir I pray?]—I desire not to be mistaken Sir,—I mean the Speech, which I hold in my—hah!—my left hand Sir [—'tis writ, Right hand here, I profess]^(a) I say Sir, my left hand, teems not only with absurdities, and Improprieties of Stile and expression, but with palpable, unparallelled rudeness and Insolence, towards your honor, and therefore towards the Club,—and the delivering of it at last Sederunt—may say Sir, the barefaced delivering of it, was perhaps one of the greatest Strokes of Impudence, that can be exhibited in the memory of man, or from the multi-multi-ti-tifarious Stores of history.—alas! alas! my eyes are bad.

It is observed by Jonathan Grog Esqr, our Ingenious Poet Laureat, In some of his weekly Lucubrations, which I cannot now exactly quote, as to Chapter and verse, that || Impudence is a quality of very great force and Influence in this world, a quality, by which, many a man who understands how to manage and lay it out to the best advantage, has advanced himself and made his fortune.^(a) This observation, I believe, honorable Sir, will every where hold true, but, allow me to remark, with the aforesaid Ingenious observator, that it is not barefaced Impudence, such as is contained in this pragmatical Speech, which will succeed now a days, in this our polite and discerning age, and to prove, that this Speech abounds with this very Species of Impudence, is the Sole and whole drift of my present argument.

Permit me therefore, first, to observe upon the Speech in general, before I take it to pieces, that it is far from being Judgematically done, for, in the first place there is too much of it, and, all that is said here might have been said, in one quarter of the time and Space that this occupies, this, the author himself owns, by Clapping a motto at the end of his Speech which is (whether he adverted to it or not) extremely applicable to the Character of his performance, the Motto Sir, is *Parvum in Multo,* a motto, Sir, which, had he searched all the ancient fathers of the Church, all the Scholastic Philosophers, and all the pan-pan-pan-Pho!—pandexes, Corpuses and Codices, from Aristotle's time, to what *anno Domino* your honor pleases, or the Club can pitch upon, he could not have Culled out one more *a propos.*

Secondly Sir, permit me to make this General Remark, that, thro' the whole of this vamped up Speech, this Sillabub (to use a figure) there abounds too much of one particular Stile, which, tho it has been, and is

---

(a) The attorney held his own written Speech, which he delivered in his right hand, and Mr Crankums delivered at last Sederunt in his left.

(a) Vide *Maryland Gazette* No 417.²

2. Hamilton is referring to an editorial that appeared in the *Maryland Gazette,* May 3, 1753, 1 (see appendix 5).

now, a favorite Stile in the Club, yet, I can by no means approve of it, especially, when it is too || often Introduced, as it seems to be by this priggish Sophister. I mean Sir, the Stile of *This here,* and *That there,* which I think serves only to multiply words to no purpose, and where it abounds too much in a Set premeditated Speech, is a Sure Sign, that that Speech is not Judgematically executed, and exhibits in a Strong light, the *Puzzle-mentationful* brain of the pragmatical author. [440]

My last General observation, honorable Sir, is, that he applies himself too much to the Club, by which, Instead of mending the matter, he has made a wretched piece of Botch work, and, Inadvertently brought himself upon a Precipe, from which, not knowing how to retire, he turns giddy headed, and, bewilders himself in an Intricate Labyrinth of false arguefication, from which he cannot extricate himself,—I would ask, Sir, what has the Club to do with his Case?—I say, the Club Sir? who, in the Case now before your honor, are as Culpable as this Culprit himself and therefore stand as much in need of an apology.

Thus, honorable Sir, having done with my General observations, I come now to particulars, let us examine the Preamble of this Discourse; after having used, (as you have seen) frequently the Stile of this here and that there, he says, he needs not tell you the reason of his now rising up, yet, at the end of his third paragraph, after a long rigmeroll, of I dont know what kind of Stuff, he has the assu- || rance to tell your honor, *That this is the Sole and whole reason, of my now standing up in* **This here** *place to harangue your honor, and* **this here** *Ancient and honorable Club.*—observe again how he drags in the Club upon every occasion,—I say Sir, the Club, who have nothing to do with harangues or Speeches of any kind, which ought only to be directed and addressed to your honor,—I say, your honor Sir, who are the architype of the Club, since, without your honor, the Club is but a headless trunk or—*Corpus cum Cauda.*[3] [441]

His definition of knowledge in fact, and knowledge in policy, at the very beginning of his Speech, is nothing but a fling, a barefaced Impudent fling, at the Council of State, and, particularly, at your honor, as the head and director of that Council.

As to the Second paragraph, it is a piece of Gross flattery, not Sufficiently Glossed over, to go down, but it is my opinion, that, had he spoke an extempore discourse, and let this Laboured piece alone, he would have made another Guess figure, and gone nigher to have Gained his cause.

In his third paragraph, he, after Laying on another Daub of flattery, on

---

3. "Body with a tail."

your honor and the Club, affects to humble himself, with *I, poor I, in no ways Qualified;* It would have been lucky for poor I, had he had an Eye, clear enough to discern his error, and evaded this Lamentable piece of fustian, I hope your honor will pardon me for punning, but I declare, I cannot Cast an eye upon this *poor I,* without falling into this Strange humor, and tho ‖ punning (asking our Laureats pardon) is a thing for which I have hitherto showed a great animosity, yet it slips from me unawares, at this very time, and in this very place.

[442]

As for his fourth paragraph, it seems only to be a vain ostentation of his knowledge, in the Greek and latin Languages, where, after throwing a Sidelong Glance upon one or other of the Council of State, as a babler, he Introduces a Cock and a bull Story of one Archimedes, as much to the purpose as fal lal de ral in the Chorus of a Song, and uses the greek word ευρεκα, and a little *lating* Scrape, *Rectus in Curia,* only to amuse his audience with a false Show of book Learning, then he comes to his Submission, and, before he goes directly to it, Informs us in his fifth paragraph, that he is not obstinate and Inflexible, and is very willing to lend an ear to advice. I would ask the Gentleman here, by whose Good advice, he penned that Egregious discourse, and, by whose good advice, he had the assurance to deliver it, Surely, a person that acts with such Insolence and effrontery, must either have no advisers at all, very bad advisers, or must be above all advice, but his own.

I come now to the Sixth paragraph, In which I find is contained a Memorandum, or *Nota Bene,* of only ten words, vizt: *To wipe my eyes here, with a white handkerchef,* which memorandum, Sir, is big with Impudence and Impertinence, being nothing but a Rank Stage ‖ direction, which is put often in the margin of our moderen Comedies, and plainly shows that he intends here only to play the buffoon with your honor,—observe next, how he burlesques our Constitution, *skimming* (says he) *off the Superficies of the Clubical rules,* as if our rules were in a literal Sense really Clubical, and the very Scum and filth of the Imagination of the framers, *and, not diving* (adds this petulent declaimer) *and groping to the very bottom of our Constitution,* he might have said, with very little alteration, *and not overturning our Constitution,* which, I think, he has attempted to do, in every Step of his Conduct.

[443]

In the very next paragraph, after passing over the foolish apology he makes for himself, as being hasty and passionate, and his being half a welshman, I observe, upon his feigned repentance, his pedantic expression of *hinc illæ Lachrimæ,* Then comes, *memorandum, apply the handkerchef to the place supposed to be affected.* What part pray? may it not be the breech? especially if the Gentleman has got the distemper, Called by the french *les* *broches;*⁴ and then comes a foolish list of his Clubical performances,—which he Solemnly revokes, and renounces, these we find, are *Letters, petitions, Speeches, writings, orations, overtures in prose or verse, puns, Conundrums, motions, poems, Songs and Sham Laws!*—Oh! the unparallelled Group of Lumber we have here! I think he ought also to have renounced or revoked this very oration, which I now hold in my hand, and which I take to be the Sum total of all his other fooleries, ‖ and never pretend again to speak or declaim before your honor, as for his poetry, I pass it over, as beneath the dignity of doggrell, and, I advise him, for the bettering of his Genious this way, to take a few Instructions from Jonathan Grog Esqr, our poet Laureat. [444]

Upon the whole, honorable Sir, I am against admitting such a rotten member into our ancient and honorable Club, else, we shall manifestly err against the Rule of Arnoldus Merdologus, the prime of Politicians, in that Golden Maxim, wherein he says, *Prigma pragma Padanarum, pujolas, pish, Panjoulteras.*"⁽ᵃ⁾

I shall beg leave to observe here, that the attorney General Commits two Capital faults in the body of this Speech, the first is, the condemning a Custom altogether, which he, in his former Speeches used without any Scruple, and that is, the Stile of *This here* and *That there,* a Stile approved of, by the Club, now for many years, and first Introduced into the Club by That unparallelld Genius, Drawlum Quaint Esqr, Speaker to the Club, who used it much in his Club Speeches and harangues, but lately dissapproved of by his honor the president, in the attorney General's hearing, as a foolish form of Speech, which shows that the attorney took Care to form his own Judgement, after ‖ the president's model, like the fulsom flatterers of our times, who like or dislike any thing according to the humor of their patrons, the other mistake Consisted in his Condemning so peremptorily that list in Mr Crankums Speech, which he Calls an unparallelled Group of lumber, not knowing, or having forgot, that the passage was taken from a form, which his honor had delivered to the Secretary to be Inserted into the form of Mr Crankum's Confirmation, by the express appointment of the Council of State, we cannot any otherwise account for this Gross oversight, in that learned Gentleman, who was himself a member of that Council of State, unless we alledge, (as it is very probable) that he was fast asleep, as usual, when that matter was talked of, and Concluded in Council. [445]

(a) This is a language, which, we leave for the Critics of future times to Interpret.⁵

4. *Broche* is the French word for a spit or pin; the phallic connotations of the word are obvious, but none of the French dictionaries or dictionaries of slang or erotica lists *les broches* as a term for syphilis or other form of venereal disease.

5. Arnoldus Merdologus (or Arnold Turdologue) and his saying are both invented.

When the Attorney General had finished his Speech, Mr Crankum stood up, and spoke in a very vehement manner, and the Chief objection he had to it, was an Impropriety in his Introducing the handkerchef, in the margin of moderen Comedies, whereas, that Implement is never brought on the Stage, but in tragical representations, but this objection, or any other that he made, had very little weight with his honor, besides, the Secretary Remarked, that the attorney General's observation, on the handkerchief was Just enough, for this handkerchief is often used in our modern Comedies, in the same Sham manner as Mr Crankum was supposed by the attorney to have ‖ used it in the delivery of his Speech, and very often even in a Serious mood, when a foolish Girl is in Love, which is a Circumstance essentially necessary in all our moderen Comedies.

After some dispute In Club, Doctor Jeronimo Jaunter proposed again, that Mr Crankum should be admitted in the ordinary method by ballot, and Jonathan Grog Esqr, rising up, delivered himself to the Chair as follows.

"Mr President, Sir,

I seldom make Speeches, and when I do, they are very short, and the Speech I am now going to make to your honor, is Indeed a very short one, being only this, that I here present Mr Crankum to your honor, as a person desirous to be admitted a L:St: member of this here Club, and I hope my request will be granted."

The Club then went into further argument, and his honor the president sat silent, no body knowing which way he would Incline, which made Mr Crankum look very blank.

The Secretary said something with Regard to the danger of admitting Mr Crankum a member of the Club, being a person of a bold daring and pushing disposition.

To which Jonathan Grog Esqr, made answer, That it was therefore very proper he should be made a L:St: member, because, a pushing disposition is a good Characteristic of a longst: member, The Club allowed this to be a good pun.

The attorney General, pitying the deplorable Condition ‖ of the poor delinquent, in some measure pled with his honor to permit the ballot, which his honor at last graciously consented to, and the ballot at last being put, there was a parity or division; The attorney, before putting the ballot, advertised the Club, That his honor the president was to vote as a private member, and then, in Case of a parity, put in his Casting vote if he pleased, which was conceded to, and stands as a rule *in futuro*.

Upon the parity in the Ballot, Mr Crankum looked like one in despair, and walked about the Room with great Strides, pled very hard with his honor, and wiped his eyes often, as if tears trickled therefrom, at last, his honor, pulling out a paper, directed his discourse to Mr Crankum, and spoke as follows.

"Sir,

Tho you may perhaps think I have proceeded with too much rigor against you, and expressed too much resentment of the trespasses you have been guilty of, against myself, and therefore against this honorable Club,— for, as I have said, I shall always look upon Indignities offered to myself, as directly offered to this honorable Club; and again, whatever Insults or affronts are put upon this honorable Club, I shall always look upon, as Immediatly put upon myself, I say Sir, tho you may think, I have stood out too obstinatly against your admission, yet, to Convince you, that I can forget and forgive, and that it is not in my nature, to retain Implacable resentment, ‖ I shall (tho you see, a part of the Club has in a manner rejected you, as a person unworthy, by splitting and dividing on the ballot) apply relief in your present misfortune, and therby demonstrate to you, and every one here, that I am more Ready to pass over your late misbehaviour, than even the Club itself." [448]

His honor the president read this Speech from a written paper, and, it was the Second Set Speech that he had delivered in Club, since his Cathedration, he did not seem to be very ready in his utterance, for he hesitated and stammered at several places, which was owing, perhaps, either to the writing not being distinct or fair, or to the badness of the light, or Insufficiency of the Spectacles, which his honor used, these having but one Eye.

This whole proceeding however, seemed to be so formal, that the affair was probably consulted and Concerted beforehand, by his honor and the Attorney General, who, it is thought held a private Conference, concerning the managing of this very affair, a few days before the Club met.

There is one Circumstance in this proceeding, which we cannot help here taking notice of, and that is, that his honor seems altogether to have forgot, that no member, according to the tenor of Law 4th, can be admitted without the Concurring Consent of the whole Society, or, if he had not forgot it, he was willing and desirous to use his dispensing power, with regard to that Law.

Crinkum Crankum Esqr, at hearing this Speech from his honor, was so suddenly overjoyed, that his Countenance Cleared up, and his Eyes seemed to sparkle, and ‖ being led by his honors permission, by Jonathan Grog [449]

Esqr, as master of Ceremonies, to the Right hand of the Chair of State, he received his Confirmation, in the manner that shall be related in the following Chapter.

Chapter X

Confirmation of Crinkum Crankum Esqr, Proclamation by his honor's order, Second Speech of Crinkum Crankum Esqr.

Truth and falshood are very distinct things, and diametrically opposite to one another, yet are they often liable to assume one another's dress by turns. For example, whatever is esteemed true, by those that hear it, is true, be it ever so false in it's own nature, and, on the Contrary whatever is Looked upon as false by the hearers, is false, tho' as true as the Gospel. This we find often happens in historical facts, pieces of news, and religious opinions, For Instance, an Admirer of Mr Eachard, that Celebrated Historian, (whose Genius was above Consulting of Rhimers *fœdera,* which all other writers of the English history have reverenced) will be firmly persuaded, that Rapin's history is a bundle of damn'd Lies, be it ever so true,[1] and again, an Admirer of Rapin, will look upon the said Eachard, as an Impudent or Ignorant falsifier, a Jacobite, a roman Catholic, or a favorer of such, when he reads a paragraph in the news of a victory obtained by the French in Flanders, or a design to bring in the pretender, a Tory will yield a willing Consent to that paragraph, and defend the truth of it, while a Lowchurch man, whig, or Presbyterian will think it a notorious lye || and believe quite the reverse; a papist will firmly believe a wafer is real flesh and blood, be it so or not, and a protestant will not be persuaded, that it is any thing but a wafer, hence we see, what precarious and unsettled things truth and falshood are, and how much men are divided among themselves, concerning the nature of both. We have had occasion to exhibit many examples of this in our history, where his honor the president has seemed all along willing to give a ready belief, to all that was told him by Sir John, and the Attorney General, let their propositions be ever so chimerical or false, and gave not the least Credit to any thing proposed or uttered by the Chancellor or Secretary, let them be ever so true in their own nature, this we can

---

1. Hamilton is referring to Thomas Rymer's (1641–1713) *Foedera* (1704–1735), a collection of public records in 20 volumes; for Rapin, see p. 15n, above.

easily account for, as he looked upon the first to be his friends, and the latter his enimies, so that he naturally would place a confidence in the one and suspect the other, but how he came at this Juncture, to give Credit to the Speech and professions of Crinkum Crankum Esqr, to whom he hitherto had bore a riveted Antipathy, I can by no means tell, unless he was Cajoled and wheedled into it, by the Cunning and artifice of Dr Jeronimo Jaunter, who was greatly a friend to Mr Crankum, or by the Pallaber of the Attorney General, who was not so much that Gentlemans Enimy as he pretended to be, but this I leave to the Judicious and Sagacious to determin, and proceed with our History.

Jonathan Grog Esqr, the Master of Ceremonies, as we have related in the foregoing Chapter, having taken Crinkum Crankum Esqr by the hand, placed him at the Right hand of the Chair of State ‖ and Confirmed him in a new form, drawn up by his honor's Command, as follows. [451]

"Sir,

I here, by the authority, and at the will and pleasure of his honor the president, Constitute, Confirm, and Inaugurate you, Crinkum Crankum Esqr, a Lawful longstanding member of this, our ancient and honorable Tuesday Club, in token of which, I now Invest you with our Club badge medal, and you are here, before the honorable the president and Club, to promise and engage, faithfully and truely to behave yourself, as a Stanch and Loyal long Standing member, of our ancient Tuesday Club, and to support and mantain, to the best of your power, the authority and prerogative of the honorable Chair, (*Salvis Societatis privilegiis et libertatibus*)² [(a) and you, in particular, are also to promise, that you will renounce and disclaim, and also revoke, all letters, petitions, writings, orations, harangues, overtures in prose or verse by you uttered, or motions by you made, puns, Conundrums, poems, Songs and Sham Laws, that you may have hitherto promoted in this here ancient and honorable Club, derogatory to his honor's prerogative power and authority] on which, I here present you to his honor the president, to receive his Gracious Salutation by manuquassation, recommending it to you, to make your acknowledgements to his honor, in the best Speech you can devise."

Mr Crankum being thus Confirmed, after the new method, dictated by his honor the president verbatim (excepting the little latin Sentence, which the Secretary had Slyly put in, not only for the Security of the Club, but for [452]

(a) All this between the brackets, is only particular to Mr Crankums Confirmation, not belonging to the general form to be used.

2. "Without violating the privileges and liberties of the club."

his honor's entertainment, who was always pleased with such little Specimens of latin, in the Club forms, tho not in the Speeches, because he did not understand them) sat down very well satisfied, and if he did not at that particular time Exclaim, yet had he very good reason to exclaim, with Gil Blas,

Inveni portum, Spes et fortuna valete,
Sat me lusistis, ludite nunc aliis.

I've found the port, fortune & hope adieu,
Me you have plagu'd enough,—plague others now.[3]

Many arguments passed in Club, about this whole unaccountable proceeding, which the Secretary could not record, for several weighty reasons, two of which are, 1st That he had neither time nor room, and 2dly The Reverend Mr Mevius Pumpkin, an honorary member, who, at this Sederunt made several very Learned Speeches, in Club, had, Inadvertently, and not with design or malice prepense, lighted his pipe with the Secretarie's Short notes, by which he was himself a very great Sufferer, as posterity will be, in not having these, his Elegant Speeches preserved, in the durable records of this here Club.

This affair discussed, the following proclamation was drawn up by the Secretary, and read with a clear and audible voice in Club by his honor's express order.

PROCLAMATION

To be read by the Secretary every Club night

Whereas it has been observed several times that the honorary members, on their Casual appearance in Club, have taken upon themselves a behaviour unbecoming their Station as honorary members, and passed several Insults and affronts, on the president, or the Club, this is therefore, in the name of, and by the authority of our honorable president, to make it publicly known, to all herein concerned, that, if any honorary member for the future, shall misbehave himself, or be Impertinent in Club, by speaking Irreverently or disrespectfully to the Chair, raising any disputes or disturbances in Club, taking more of the discourse than comes to his Share, making Speeches of any Sort to the Club, without leave first asked and Granted, or pretending to vote in Club in any matter whatsoever, Contrary

---

3. Hamilton's translation is accurate, but I have been unable to trace this passage to either Le Sage's romance or Edward Moore's comedy, although it may be a garbled version of the closing lines of the latter: "To all my follies, here I bid adieu, / Reclaim'd and fix'd by virtue, and by You."

to an express law of the Club, in that Case made and provided, such honerary member so offending shall be expell'd the Club, and, *Ipso facto*, forfeit his Seat therein, never again to be admitted, upon any application, unless it be the Gracious will and pleasure of his honor the President.

[Great Seal appended] Signed by authority
Nasifer Jole *Loquacious Scribble Secret:*

After Reading this proclamation, Mr Pumpkin, an honorary member, seemed uneasy and observed that he was sorry to find, that there was a necessity || for such a proclamation in this here Club, that he was Sure, that [454] for his own part, ever since he had the honor to sit in it in that Station and quality, which was now almost two years, he had behaved himself with all due reverence and respect, and could not tax himself with any misbehaviour.—His honor the president satisfied Mr Pumpkin in that point, that the thing was by no means Intended against him, or any other Gentleman, that behaved himself with decency and Good manners, on which Mr Pumpkin made a very Low bow, sat down, and resumed his pipe.

After Supper, Mr Crankum standing up in his place, delivered to his honor, the following Speech of thanks.

"Honorable Sir,

Behold me risen up now a Longstanding member of this here ancient and honorable Club, to return your honor the thanks due, for the great and Inestimable favor, that has been Just now bestowed upon me.

I design Sir, to perform this duty, with all the Reality, punctuality, and Circumstantiality, which it is possible, for my tongue or pen to reach. I say my tongue, because that is the member which must be used, in delivering this Gratulatory Speech, and, I say my pen, because that is the Instrument which has been made use of, to set down these my thoughts in proper order, according to the best of my poor abilities, not daring or venturing to hazard to Express myself to your honor and this here honorable Club, by a rough draught of the Imagination or memory for fear[4] of entertaining you with a dish, called by the Spaniards *olla podrida*, by the french *Gali mathias*, by the dutch, *Grawton Guedon aaton*,[5] and by the english, *Hodge-podge*, quite unworthy of your hearing.

---

4. The conclusion of book XIII and the beginning of book XIV (pp. 455–502) are missing from the *History*. I have provided material from the "Record" (pp. 513–523) for this portion of the narrative.

5. *Olla podrida* (literally "putrid pot") is a well-known Spanish dish composed of odds and ends; *galimatias* means "nonsense or gibberish"; Hamilton has probably concocted the third phrase (although in one sense *grauw* means "rabble," which seems consistent with the other phrases in this passage).

As thanks must always be proportioned, to the nature of the benefits bestowed, and the manner of bestowing them, so there must be several degrees of thanks, according to the several degrees of favors, and the several modes of Conveying those favors, and, tho' [the] Grammarians have reckoned only three degrees of Comparison, vizt: the positive, Comparative and Superlative, yet I, not Influenced by foolish Custom, beg liberty in this Clubical Oration, to dissent from these Gentlemen, and branch out my degrees into four, which, for brevity's Sake, I call, the pos: Comp: dowble pos, and Superl, and, for this novel variation from the Common rule, I have the Sanction and Authority of the late learned author of the Georgian Calendar.

When favors are obtained by painful and repeated application, The thanks proper to be returned for them, according to my System, are in the degree pos, and may be expressed in the four following words, which I chuse to call the Stile tetralogical, *I thank you Sir,* when the said favors, are obtained with little more trowble than bare asking for, the expression of thanks should be in the Stile pentalogical, as they are supposed to be in the Comp: degree, vizt: *I thank you kindly Sir,* when the benefits acquired, are unlooked for, and come without any application, the thanks returned, are in the dowble pos: and expressed in the Stile Hexalogical, as—*I most kindly thank you Sir,* and finally, when favors are obtained, by all those three methods in Conjunction, the thanks, by this new System are in the degree Superl: and must run in the Stile octological, (the heptological, I purposly ommit, because Seven is an ominous and Sacred number,) such as *I most kindly and heartily thank you Sir.*

Having thus, in the manner of the learned and Ingenious author of the *Moderen Ephemeris,*[6] settled this grand and nice point, and Invented proper terms of art, to be applied upon these occasions, I am now to Consider, in what manner I am to return your honor thanks, according to the above Scheme, for this here great favor, I have Just now received at your honor's hands, & it will appear, at first Sight, that my thanks to your honor, are to be expressed in the *Superl: degree,* for 'tis notorious to your honor, and these here longstanding members, that I have at last attained to this here great favor, by all the above recited methods, that is to say by Strenuous diligent and, I may even say, teizing application, by a Careless & slight Solicitation, when I found the first Ineffectual, and lastly, by remaining quite silent and Inactive when I perceived the bad Success of both methods;

---

6. Hamilton is likely referring to the *Ephemeris,* or *Ephemerides,* a series of almanacs especially popular in the late 17th century (written by various authors).

for I protest, I had given over all hopes of ever attaining it, and was resolved to apply no farther, but be as mute as a fish upon that Subject for the future, when your honor's goodness, flashed on, and Surprized me, all of a Sudden, and bestowed it, without asking for, I therefore, honorable Sir, in form, *et Secundum Artem,*[7] express myself, in the *degree Superl, Octologically* thus; *I most heartily and kindly thank your honor.*

But, that my propositions on this point, may not seem to be a parcel of Paradoxes, permit me, to produce a few arguments, to prove what I have advanced.

When Strenuous and assiduous application for a favor is employed, and the favor is hard to be obtain'd, or cannot be obtain'd at all, this must necessarily in the case before us, Imply, want of merit in the person applying, and not want of Judgement, perverseness, or obstinacy, in the honorable person applied to, and, as favors are to be estimated, by the merit, and resentment of the Subject, on which they are bestowed, so, good offices done, and Compliments payd to a block or chip, come not under the Idea of favors at all, because, here, the object is so far from being a rational, that it is not even a sensitive being, your Stupid fellows, and Selfish mortals (to apply our metaphor) are blocks and chips, (hence a Silly fellow, is often Called a chip in porridge) are Sensible of nothing, and therefore, favors bestowed on them, must either be extorted by continual tiezing, or by main force, and, when procured, scarce deserve thanks in the pos: degree, again, should favors be bestowed on oysters, Sea nettles, and Sensitive plants, they may possibly be attained by moderate application, tho' the objects even here cannot properly be stiled meritorious, having barely Animal life without rational faculties, yet, some degree of resentment, may even here be discovered, as, when you throw Salt water on an oyster, it rattles shakes and Chirrups, when you touch a Sensitive plant, it shrinks, and retires within itself, and, if your honor should rub your leg, or any other part with a Sea nettle, it will bite & sting you. Ungrateful and vain people, to apply our metaphor again, are oysters, Sensitive plants, and Sea nettles, thinking every favor they deign to receive, to be a kindness done to the bestower, these kinds of favors, deserve thanks in the Comp: degree, that is a Comparison may be drawn between the bestower and receiver, to discover, who has participated the greatest favor, the first in bestowing, or the other In accepting. When favors are bestowed upon a good horse, a dog or a monkey, as these creatures enjoy, not only animal life, but a degree of rationality, the favors are procured with no application, but, generally flow from the

---

7. "According to art."

love and affection of the owner, and therefore, on account of the Innate merit of the objects, they possess a higher degree in the Class of favors, and require thanks in the dowble pos: Such (to pursue our metaphor) are those men, who will look with an expectant, or rather a greedy Eye, upon a favor in prospect, but thro a Shortness of memory forget all past and in possession; The last Class of favors, are those that are procured by the practice of all these here methods, and may be said to be Conferr'd, on a rational human Creature, Capable of Gratitude, and therefore every way worthy of them, the giver, in this Case, possesses the true Character of a Generous person, & ought to have thanks paid him, in the Superl: degree, as above directed, which I take to be the very case between your honor and myself, in this here affair, *Quoderat demonstrandum.*—pray pardon me Sir, for being alittle too refind and metaphysical, on this here Subject, the Importance of it absolutely requiring it.

But, as I am none of that Class of people, (of whom, alas! there are but too many, in this here Selfish world,) who think that thanks, or to speak more properly, Gratitude, consists in a flow of words, and therefore trowble themselves no further, than delivering of a formal Set Speech, and utterly neglect to make their Sense of favor appear in actions, which are the most emphatically expressive of true Gratitude, so, I desire, to carry mine towards your honor farther, than bare words, and to make it appear in my conduct and actions for the future, in this here Club, and in the following manner—

First, by supporting in the best, and most effectual manner in my power, your honor's authority, grandure, prerogative & dignity in this here Club.

Secondly, by defending to the utmost of my poor abilities, the liberties and privileges of this here Club itself, against oppression, and arbitrary power.

And these, I hope to demonstrate, to be the two principal branches of the duty of a member of any Club, or Society, to have an equal, or Impartial regard, to both the governing, and governed parts of that Club or Society, if it is in his power to prevent, either the one or the other, from exceeding the just bounds prescribed by Law and reason, seeing, if he takes the part of one, and neglects the other, he contributes his mite, at least, to destroy that Just equilibrium upon which the peace and happiness of the whole depend, and therefore, cannot be called a loyal and honest member of that Club or Society.

As to supporting your honor's power and authority, let us enquire alittle, how it may most effectually be done, not by flattery and Cajoling, not by fulsom praises, that would shoke the ear of modesty, nor a creeping dependance, that wounds a generous eye, for, these pimping arts, blind the daylights of mortal men, and puff up their Imagination, to the Conceit of their being Immortal gods, as history Instances in Alexander the great, Caligula the Roman Emperor, and Canute the mighty king of England,[8] Pope Joan, *cum multis aliis quæ nunc dicere longum est*,[9] and therefore, Imagine themselves Infallible, and above all advice, not by a blind compliance, and Senseless agreement with every thing coming from men in power, for, as power is a bewitching thing, and apt to make men violent and unguarded in their conduct, the Complaisant and over Zealous dependant, consulting only his patron's will, nod or wink, will say black is white, or vice versa, till he leads his Superior, into dangerous errors and Labyrinths, out of which, his art can never conduct him, and, Instead of proving his friend and Supporter, will prove in the end his bane and ruin.

I therefore shall endeavor, to make Sincerity and truth, the rules of my future Conduct towards your honor, and considering you as a mortal man, tho a great president, shall never fail, to throw in my advice for the best and most eligible course, tho' at times, I may risque the giving offence.

Power, may it please your honor, may be considered as a dead weight, which hangs at a machine to give it motion, and which would give it motion to such a violent degree, as soon to destroy it, were it not for the pendulum, balance or check, in the machine, which regulates temperates, and conducts the moving power.

Your honor here is the dead weight, being the person of power, this here Club is the machine, and I myself, hope to make part of the pendulum, balance or Check, to keep that power from going to excess, and hurrying the motion in such a manner, as to set all the allarums a Jingling, ding dong, ding dong, bend the axles of the wheels, distort the notches, break the springs, drive out the pins, and loosen the rivets of this our Clubical machine, so as to make it fall to pieces.

Again, those that are under governance, or what we may call the Subject, in a collective body, considered as the several parts or pieces of the machine itself, put up into a regular fabric, must not have this balance or check, too Strong or Inflexible, for, by that means, the dead weight of

---

8. Canute the Great, or the Mighty, king of England (1016–1035), actually reproved his courtiers for flattery.

9. Pope Joan was the mythical female pope who supposedly succeeded Leo IV (855); she disguised herself as a monk so that she could gain admission to her lover, the monk Folda. After being elected pope, she was discovered when she gave birth during her enthronement. The passage reads "with many other things which it would take too long to speak of now" (a commonplace way of saying *etcetera*).

power and authority, will be of no effect, and the motions of the machine stop, or at least become irregular, therefore, it is necessary, that this here Clubical machine, be not only kept clean, and free from all rust and corruption, but have it's balances and Checks, so fitted and proportioned to the governing and ruling power, that no Interruption may proceed therefrom, and this I hope to effect, as far as my slender abilities will perform, by the Gentle friction and attrition of good advice to the Longstanding members, whenever I perceive them going wrong, & by the smooth oil of soft words, and cool reasoning, temperate and adjust every Individual part, that it may compose one Solid and delightful whole, and this I hope I shall be enabled to apply, whenever necessary,—Thus Sir, I humbly apprehend, I shall most effectually show my gratitude, on the one hand, by taking the proper method to establish your honors Just and lawful prerogative and power in this here Club, that you may be in no danger of becoming a president of Straw as the phraze is, or a popet, deck'd only with the Sham name, but wanting the Substance of power, on the other hand, I shall demonstrate my gratitude, by mantaining the Just and lawful privileges and Immunities of this here club, since that will be the Surest way to make your honor an honorable, and a great President Indeed, by rendering those you rule over, an honorable and a free Society, and gaining and securing to you, their hearty love and affection, your only and best Support, which, as your honor now possesses, I Sincerely wish may always Continue, that your name may reach, thro the long Records of fame, to latest posterity, and your memory be dear to the present, and yet unborn members, of this here ancient and honorable Club."

Mr Lux having delivered this Speech, gave the Copy to his honor the president, and some dispute arising in Club, afterwards, concerning prerogative and privilege, in which Mr Lux was pritty loud, the Revd: Mr Craddoc, attempting to speak, was interrupted by the aforesaid Gentleman, who Cried out "The proclamation! The proclamation!" as he alledged Mr Craddoc had spoke without asking leave, but his honor the president, quashd this Clamor, and generously declared

Law LII. That an honorary member of the Clergy, may at any time speak what he pleases in club, without asking leave, which stands as a rule *in futuro.*

Some talk passed this night, about the clubs meeting once a month, but was deferr'd to a more full Club, two of the members having retired.

Ordered, that his honor the president, be requested to serve this Club, upon Tuesday the 19th instant, as H:S: thereof.

Book XIV

Sederunt 231
Tuesday, Novr 19th 1754

The Club met at the house of the honorable Charles Cole Esqr, President, and were entertaind by him as H:S: pursuant to a request of last meeting.
Present
The honle: Charles Cole Esqr Prest: & H:S:
Wm: Thornton Esqr, att: Gen:⎫   ⎧Walter Dulany Esqr
Jonas Green Esqr Mr: Cer: ⎭   ⎩Wm: Lux Esqr
Alexr: Hamilton Secretry

His honor having taken the Chair, the proceedings of last meetg: were read.

The Club were entertained in an elegant manner as usual by his honor the president, and, after Supper, Jonas Green Esqr, as usual, rose up and delivered himself as follows, having a Cup of grog in his hand.

"Honorable Sir,
I first address you in prose, pro tempore,
I shall next speak to you in verse extempore,
As is usual with me on ordinary nights, when your honor serves as
     H:S:
On anniversary occasions, I pronounce a Studied ode,
Then I Invoke the muse, and am Indeed in the mews, or mew'd up,
But now, with no other asistant but this potent grog, which I Intend to drink up presently, I celebrate your honor's noble entertainment, in the following extempore ode, Song, odd Song, or you may call it what you please" [here, the poet Laureat hawk'd and spit a great deal, to recollect his thoughts]

> You've made us to sup, Sir,
> On excellent prog,
> To your health in a Cup, Sir,
> Of very good grog,
> Each longstanding member
> Will pledge me, no doubt,
> In this month of november,
> 'Twill keep the cold out.   (Drink)

Since we've eat of your dishes,
To keep the heat in, (Belly)
To drink now like fishes,
Is no Scandal or Sin, (fill)
Since by your noble bounty,
We fatten and thrive, (Cheeks)
In Club, or in County,
There's no man alive

Whom we to your honor
As equal set up,
To your health noble Donor, (Drink)
I suck this Grog up,
And now, having drank, Sir,
My manners to show,
Your honor I thank Sir,
By this Reverend bow. (bow)

 The Laureat having delivered these extempore verses as he called them gave the Copy to the Secretary for Recording, the Attorney general took the paper in his hand, and observed, putting on his Important face, That the Laureat had abundance of assurance, to pretend to palm these verses on his honor, for extempore verses, whereas they appeared, from his reading them in open Club, from a written paper, that they had been premeditated and wrote down. The Laureat replied to this, That they agreed in this very particular, with abundance of other small Copies of verses, which had been palmed on the public, for extempore productions, for, he could never bring himself to believe, that the Composition of verses was merely mechanical, but that they must be premeditated or thought upon before they could be uttered or wrote down.

 That posterity may not be at a loss, to know the meaning of *drink, Belly, fill, Cheeks, drink, bow,* in the margin of the poet Laureat's extempore verses, they mean as follows, at the first drink, He *drinks* a Cup of Grog, then strokes down his *belly,* then *fills* up the Cup with Grog again, next he strokes down his *cheeks,* and then *drinks* his Second Cup of Grog, and lastly, makes a *bow* to the Chair, and sits down.

 The attorney General, presented the proclamation in Club, with the great Seal appended, at which his honor took offence, and said, that the great Seal had nothing to do there, that his own privy Seal, if any, was the proper Seal to be affixed to that paper, declaring, that the great Seal, for the future, should have no authority at all in Clubical writings, but stand for a cypher, unless he had the keeping and affixing of it himself, thereupon he pronounced that proclamation to be void and of no effect, and proposed Issuing his presidential warrant, to search for the great Seal.

The attorney General perceiving his honor's Indignation, charged the Secretary with the trespass and asserted That the proclamation, with the Seal appended was sent to him that morning, Inclosed in a petulent letter from the Secretary, which he read in Club. The Secretary denyed the Charge, and put it upon Mr Attorney to prove, that he had either wrote that letter, or affixed the great Seal to the proclamation, and desired to have a Copy of the letter, as it might be of use to him, in drawing up his defence, in case he should be prosecuted for this Supposed trespass, but this was positively denied him, he therefore was under a necessity to be at some pains and Charges to get a Genuine copy of that letter, which he has recorded as follows.

To William Thornton Esqr,
Attor: Genl: of the Tuesday Club.

Mr Attorney General,

Tho you either are, or take yourself to be an officer of great and unlimited authority, like that authority whence you derive, yet I cannot see, how that authority, gives you any title to meddle or Concern yourself, with things that come not within your province, or capacity, pray Sir, had you any authority at last Sederunt, which, if I mistake not was Sederunt 231, to Secrete, and keep in your custody the rough minutes of the Club's minutes, could you Sir *Secrete,* who are not *Secretary,* could you do this from any other motive than to copy after, and ape your Master and mine, who is graciously pleased, at times, to pocket up these rough proceedings, and never thinks of returning them again, if this was not your Incitement, it could be nothing else but mischief, Intending thereby to put me to a puzzlementation and *Nonplush,* if you return me not these proceedings to day, which you know as well as I, is Club day, I shall be obliged to leave a damnable Gap in the book of records, large enough to Contain an Indictment, and trial, concerning the Subject matter of this very letter, and these very rough minutes and records, which I expect you will make a handle of against me, but I thank my Stars (tho I know you will take an exact Copy of these very rough records, and Consult your damn'd books and Codexes to handle me roughly in a Sophisticated Speech) I have quibbles enough in reserve to baffle you with all your book learning—pray Sir, send me these very rough records, and take this here Inclosed proclamation into your keeping, which is a paper properly belonging to your office, and, neglect not, on your Peril, to bring it into Club, am, Learned Sir,

Novr 19th 1754 *(vera copia)* Yours to Command,
  A:H: Secretary.

Entertained this night as Strangers, according to ancient Custom Mr Lancelot Jacques, and Capt: Benjamin North.

Ordered, that Mr William Lux, serve this Society, upon Tuesday the 2d day of december next ensuing as H:S: thereof.

Sederunt 232
Tuesday, December 2d 1754

The Club met at the house of Mr Charles Wallace of Annapolis, and were entertaind by Wm: Lux Esqr as h:s: pursuant to an order of last meeting, being the 3d public-house Sederunt of this Club.

Present

The hon: Dr Upton Scot, pres: deput: elect:
Wm: Thornton Esqr, att: gen: } { Will: Lux Esqr, H:S:
Jonas Green Esqr, Mr of Cer: } { Walter Dulany Esqr
Alexr: Hamilton Secretry

The Club having chose Dr Upton Scot Deputy President, by virtue of Law 43d, he took the Chair, and the proceedings of last meetg: were read.

William Lux Esqr, rising up, addressed his honor the deputy, alledging that the Attorney General, Intending to prosecute him for some trespas committed in Club, against the honor and dignity of the Chair, he prayd that his trial might now come on, without farther delay.

To which the attorney general made answer, in a short and grave Speech, that he could not gratify the gentleman so far, at this present Juncture, for certain political reasons, which he should lay before the Club when properly maturated, and Concocted, but begged at this time to be excused, from proceeding any farther.

It was moved this night, that the club for the future should always meet at a public house, but the determination of the affair, was delay'd, till his honor the president should be present in Club—a motion was made by the Secretary for a new record book, but not regarded.

There arose some dispute about the form and Structure of Law 48, which the Club found to be very Incorrect, but did not think fit to alter or amend that law, till his honor the president should be personally present, by

the Tuesday Club [Book XIV] 309

which means the H:S: escaped being taken to task for a Supposed breach of that law, in Inviting more than two Strangers to the club.

Jonas Green Esqr, showed a very great disposition for punning this night, and uttered several very Curious paragrams, of which, as the Secretary took no memorandum at that time, being Impeded by the eternal Clack of the Attorney General, must be altogether lost to posterity, unless that Ingenious bard favors us with a list of them under his own hand.

Some grave discourse happening, concerning the Spartan Commonwealth, and, of their being ruined by Luxury, there was a parallel drawn between that Commonwealth, and the ancient Tuesday Club, and they were found to agree in many respects.

Entertained this night as Strangers, according to ancient Custom Messrs: Lancelot Jacques, Daniel Wolstenholme & Stephen Bordley.

Ordered, that Doctor Upton Scot, serve this Society upon Tuesday the 17th of this Instant December, as H:S: thereof.

Sederunt 233
Tuesday December 16th 1754

The Club met at the house of Mr Samuel Middleton, and were Entertained by Dr Upton Scot as H:S: pursuant to an order of last meetg: being the 4th Tavern Club.

Present

The Hon: Charles Cole Esqr Presidt:

Wm: Thornton Esqr att: Genl:
Jonas Green Esqr, Mr of Cer:
Walter Dulany Esqr
Wm: Lux Esqr

Dr Upton Scott H:S:
Coll: Wm: Fitzhugh:
H:M: & Champion
Thomas Bacon Esqr, Triumv: & H:M:
Michael Earl Esqr H:M:

Alexr: Hamilton Secretary

His honor having taken the Chair, the proceedings of last meeting were read.

The Proclamation was read, according to an order of Sederunt 230, then the Secretry read a Commission, granted by his honor to Coll: Wm: Fitzhugh, to be Champion for this present Sederunt, which Commission he presented by his honor's order to the said Coll: Fitzhugh, who took his place at the Right hand of his honor's great chair, above the attorney general, and laid his naked Sword upon the table, while Thomas Bacon

Esqr, otherwise Signior Lardini, took the left hand of his honor's great Chair, as chief commissioned Triumvir, of the eastren Shore triumvirate.

Wm: Thornton Esqr, Attorney General, Presented to the Secretary an Indictment, drawn up in *Clubical* form against Wm: Lux Esqr, and Commanded it to be read, Wm: Lux Esqr, standing up in his place, the Secretary read as follows.

Indictment

Tuesday Club Ss:

William Lux Esqr, you stand Indicted, by the name of Wm: Lux Esqr, a Longstanding member of this here ancient and honble: Tuesday Club, for, that you as a false traitor, against our most Illustrious and Serene Presidt: Charles, due reverence to the sd: Serene president in your heart not having, nor weighing your duty towards his august Chair, but, being moved and seduced by your own wicked instigation, and due obedience to our sd: Serene Presidt: utterly withdrawing, and endeavoring and Intending, with all your might, the peace and Common tranquillity of this ancient and honorable Club to disturb, and the Laws of the same established to overthrow, to pull down and bring into Contempt, our said Serene presidt: Charles and his Chair, and the said honble: Chair wickedly, devlishly and maliciously to usurp, you, the said Wm: Lux Esqr, at two sundry times, vizt: on the 7th of octor: 1754, at the house of Mr Secretary Hamilton, then High Steward, vizt: at Sederunt 229 of this anct: & honble: Club, and, on the 5th of Novembr following, at the house of Wm: Thornton Esqr attorney General, and then High Steward, vizt: at Sederunt 230, of the said Club, and in the 9th year, of the presidential Government of our said Serene president Charles, before our said Serene presidt: then and there in Club sitting, and in presence of several of the longstanding members of this ancient and honorable club, and others, then and there being, with force and arms, and of malice aforethought, wickedly, devlishly, and treasonably, an assault did make upon the person and Chair, of our said Serene Presidt: Charles, in open contempt of the laws of this ancient and honorable Club, by daringly and audaciously, pronouncing with an audible voice, certain wicked, flagitious, treasonable, and abominable Speeches, derogatory to the honor and dignity of our said Serene presidt: Charles, and to the authority of his Chair, and against your allegiance to our said Serene president Charles, and setting a bad and pernicious example, to all your fellow longstanding members, to be guilty of the same, against the peace of our said Serene presidt: Charles, his Chair and Dignity—What say you William Lux Esqr, are you Guilty &ct?

To this Indictment Wm: Lux Esqr pleaded not Guilty, and desired a Copy of the same, which was denied him expressly by his honor, and some argument being held upon this point, in the mean time, the Indictment was privately conveyd from the table, by some evil minded person, upon which his honor blamed the Secretary for his Carelessness, and, after some Search, the Indictment being found again, his honor commanded the Secretary to lay it, upon the book of records, wch being done, the attorney general rose up, with his usual gravity, and delivered the following Speech.

"May it please your honor,

As the duty of my office obliges me to take notice of every Indecency and misdemeanor, committed by refractory members, which reflect upon your honor's dignity and authority, so, I cannot help now standing up, before your honor, and this ancient and honorable Club, to accuse a gentleman, whom I have now in my eye, for an Insolent, petulent, presumptious and daring Speech, which he had the assurance to deliver before your honor, upon that very remarkable day the 5th of novembr, a day, marked out in the annals of History, for a day of dire treason and Conspiracy, and therefore, the fittest day he could have chose, for delivering himself of that load of treasonable and disloyal trash & Lumber, contained in that Seditious and abominable Speech, and that I may not detain your honor with long preambles and repetitions, I shall fall directly to my Subject.

And first, permit me, honorable Sir, to observe on the Insolence of this Speech, he is pleased to term it, a Speech of thanks, or a thanksgiving Speech, and Imagines us to be such gulls, as to be bamboozled with a Specious title, but, I hope the Gentleman will be made to know before long, that your honor is not to be amused with bombast and fustian, I need not tell your honor, who know it already, that thanksgiving Speeches ought to be wrote in a modest and humble Stile, and delivered in a Submissive & respectful manner, but this Impertinent declaimer, is so far from keeping to these rules, that he takes upon him to Inform your honor, with an air of Superior knowledge, of things as plain, as that two and two make four, in his description of the uses of the tongue and pen, which is an open Insult, upon your honor's understanding, and then pours out of his budget, a rabble of french, Spanish and dutch words, which, as they are uttered in these ticklish times, we know not but they may contain the most atrocious treasons.

Again, taking upon himself the Stile of a dictator, he proposes to lay down rules of manners and behaviour, to your honor & the Club, as if we knew nothing of these rules before, he tells us, that thanks must be proportioned, according to the degrees of favors received, might he not as well have told us, that 20 Shillings went to the pound & 12 pence to the Shillg: Sure we should have reaped as much Instruction from it, in fine Sir, the Gentleman, in this learnd paragraph, only takes an oblique method, to tell us we are fools, and I think this is the rankest Instance of *Humbugging*, (to use the moderen phraze) that ever I have met with in all my reading and experience.

In the next place, as he has ridiculously assumed the Character of a Learned man, so, he takes upon him to differ in opinion from all the Grammarians that ever lived, as it is a Characteristic of Learned men and doctors, to differ one from another, This assuming gentleman branches out his degrees of Comparison into four, vizt: the pos: Comp: dowble pos: and Superl: and runs us a most abominable rig of balderdash, upon that triffling Subject, but by the bye, takes an opportunity to vilify and asperse a Reverend and learned Divine, a Steady friend to the Church of England, as by Law established, and a professd Enimy to all popish, and other plots. Scandalous Imputation! Scurrilous Insinuation! especially from such pragmatical and Self Sufficient prigs, I may properly enough here exclaim with the Poet

Quid Domini faciunt, cum audent talia fures![1]

Then we have him dressed up in his greek habit, with the terms *tetralogical, pentalogical, Hexalogical, heptalogical* and *Octological*, words, that one would think Invented by Dr Faustus to Conjure up the devil, words, which are by no means Clubical, and which, for aught we know may contain the blackest and most atrocious treasons, or even terms of abuse, for, may not the Gentleman, all the time, that he is treating us with this Jargon, be calling us blockheads, asses, Idiots, coxcombs, fools, gulls, numbskulls & Ignoramuses.

As to his reference to the *Moderen Ephemeris*, 'tis no other than an ill naturd fling at the above mentioned Revd Divine, who published his Georgian Calendar lately, so useful and Satisfactory to the Connoiseurs in Almanac making, and bears also in it, an Invidious Sneer, upon our Ingenious

1. "What should the masters do, when thieves dare do such things?" (Vergil, *Eclogues* 3.16).

poet Laureat, who of late had obliged the public, with many curious almanacks, with elegant verses of his own Composition at the head of every page, this is most unsufferable usage, and, should learning and Ingenuity meet with this treatment, we may yet live to see the day, when we shall again sink into Gothic Ignorance.

Next come his propositions and paradoxes, or *pardoxes* as he calls them, Quere, who is his author for this new term? but it appears that this gentleman would use words as he would do your honor's authority and prerogative, that is clip and Curtail them as he has done by the words *positive, comparative* and *Superlative,* calling them *pos: comp:* and *Superl:* but these words are nothing but froth as he frames them, being only ridiculous Specimens of the mock Sublime, and by no means proper to be used in a Speech of thanks to your honor.

I come next to his dissertation upon blocks and Chips, and cannot conceive why he should Introduce these burlesque terms into this Club, unless he takes your honor and your Longstanding members to be so many Chips in porridge, or rather your honor to be a block, and the longstanding members to be *chips of the old block,* (here his honor smiled pleasantly upon Mr Attorney General) as the proverb goes,—In short I am astonished!—I am amazed!—I am struck all of a heap at his Insolence and Impudence, in this particular passage of his Speech.

Let me take notice of his metaphysical disposition, and how the Importance of his Subject obliges him to be so metaphysical, I must own I cannot comprehend, I Imagine that he is here much out of his latitude, in many respects, and Grammatically, problematicaly, emphatically, Judgematically and pragmatically mistaken, for, as I apprehend, this pedantic prig, is as much acquainted with metaphysics, as your honor's Clerk of the kitchen.

I observe next, that the Gentleman makes great promises to your honor & the Club, of the mighty services he intends to do for both, I hope they will be of more Significancy than his Speech, which only Inclines me to observe, that he is better read in the History of *Jeck and the Gyants, the wise men of Gotham, Tom Thumb, Laugh and be fat, Jeck Hicathrift,* and (as he says himself) *cum multis aliis quæ nunc dicere longum est,*[2] in short, the froth

---

2. *Jack the Giant-killer* is a famous nursery tale. By "the wise men of Gotham" Hamilton is probably referring to the *Merrie Tales of the Mad Men of Gotam by A. B.* (possibly Andrew Boorde [ca. 1490–1549], a physician). This collection of tales concerns Gotham, a village in Nottinghamshire, whose inhabitants acquired a reputation for folly, perhaps as a result of an actual incident in which they feigned idiocy to prevent King John's displeasure. Although Hamilton was surely aware of Henry Fielding's burlesque play, *Tom Thumb, a Tragedy* (1730),

and vanity of the rest of his Speech, his trite Simile of a dead weight and machine, with his *This here* and *That there,* are of a piece with all his other performances, and his latin quotations, would better become the pen of a Schoolboy than a grave Longstanding member, of the ancient and honorable Tuesday Club, and therefore, I Conclude, honorable Sir, let him be anathema, let him be Maranatha."³

[503] The attorney general having delivered this Speech sat down, and Wm: Lux Esqr again demanded || of the Secretary a copy of his Indictment, but, behold the Indictment was again a missing, which much Chagrined his honor the President with the Secretary, whom he blamed upon all occasions. Search was made, but to no purpose, &, while the Club was busy in making a Scrutiny, the Culprit took the opportunity to plant himself in the Champion's Chair, and seized upon a broad Sword that stood in the Room, which Coll: Comico Butman perceiving, took his trusty Toledo In hand, and boldly encountered the Insolent Invader, fighting him in a furious and heroic manner, and after some paryings, thrusts and Lunges on both Sides, he vanquished him, and made him surrender the broad Sword with which he was armed,—This Clubical Conflict was Close by his honor's chair, and the blades of the Swords glanced several times so nigh his honor, that the Club thought his honor in some danger, and his honor, as appeared, by his looks of astonishment, seemed in this matter to be of the same opinion with the Club, the Rebel, however, being vanquished, and much wounded, was brought again to the bar in a mangled Condition, with a handkerchef, tied hard about his waste to stop the blood, tho it was thought by many that these wounds, and that blood, were like the wounds and blood of the Gods, which, as Homer says, shut up Immediatly upon their being Inflicted, and the blood was of a fine Spiritual or ambrosial Substance, not perceivable by mortal Senses, like Miltons angelic blood, In fine, Mr Crankums blood and wounds were of a Clubical Sort, and really, had they been actual wounds, they would not have been so honorable as were the wounds of Zopyrus, who mangled his body to save his fellow Citizens,⁺ but this ||

---

the context here suggests that he is referring to the famous nursery tale. *Laugh and Be Fat* (ca. 1625), a popular collection of humorous tales and jests, was the work of John Taylor, the Water Poet. Jack (or Tom) Hickathrift is the nursery-rhyme hero who, though a poor laborer, was gifted with such enormous strength that he killed a giant, for which he was knighted.

3. *Maranatha* is an Aramaic phrase that appears in 1 Cor. 16:22, often erroneously regarded as comprising with the word *anathema*, which precedes it in the biblical text, a formula of imprecation, i.e., "a terrible curse."

4. Zopyrus the Persian (fl. 6th century B.C.) mutilated himself horribly and then sought refuge with the Babylonians to convince them that the Persian king Darius had inflicted the wounds. Having gained their confidence, Zopyrus then delivered Babylon to Darius, who had

heroe got his wounds by fighting against his honor the president, and his [504] fellow members, It is pritty Surprizing however, and cannot be accounted for otherwise, than by the prevalence of the passion of fear in both, that neither his honor the president, nor his Indefatigable attorney General, ever took notice afterward of this most daring Insult.

After this Hurly burly was over, the Indictment again made it's appearance, having been found in the pocket of Doctor Jeronimo Jaunter, and his honor Conveyd it into his own pocket, from whence it never again made its exit in Club.

Then the trial went on, and Mr Crankum was very Loud, and very petulent in his own defence, nor could all that his honor or the attorney General say, silence or abash him, he demanded to be tried by his peers, which the attorney General said was an Insolent Demand, as he was not himself a Peer, or State member of the Club, to this the Secretary modestly and Learnedly replied (taking upon him without fee or Reward to be Council for the Prisoner) that he humbly Conceived, that the Learned attorney was mistaken in this particular, and with all deference to that Gentlemans great knowledge in these matters, a commoner as well as a nobleman had his peers, the word *peer* or *peers,* being derived from the words *par* or *pares,* which he understood were latin, as the attorney did not reply to this, the Club acquiesced, and accordingly a Jury of two, vizt: Slyboots Pleasant and Jonathan Grog Genten: were appointed by his honor to retire and try the prisoner by his peers, and bring in their verdict accordingly, as these Gentlemen were step- || ping out of the room, the prisoner [505] pled guilty, and pray'd an arrest of Judgement, in as much as That he (The Culprit) was stiled in the Indictment Esquire, and his Jury only stiled Gentlemen, by which it appeared they were not his peers, which put an effectual Stop to further proceedings on this Cause.

After Supper, was play'd the Grand Chorus of 1751, *Con voce,* Violino primo, Secondo and Violoncello, and several pieces of the Celebrated Vivaldi, the Club were then going to proceed in the trial of an affair, brought against the attorney General, by a longstanding member, but that politic State officer, knowing the risque he run of Incurring his honors displeasure, and of being degraded from his high office, had privately, as well as prudently withdrawn himself from the Club, and, mounting his horse at the Street door, rode home, very Composedly, without attendants.

Colonel Comico Butman, the Champion for the Night requested his

---

been unsuccessfully besieging the city for months. Darius made Zopyrus a satrap of Babylon for life in gratitude for his self-sacrifice.

honor to grant him a Commission as honorary member of the Club, which he said he thought he had a right to demand, for the many Services he had done the Club, and, more especially, as a Gentleman now present, had a Commission of the like nature Granted him, who, compared with him, was but a Stranger to the Club, the members backed the Colonels request and sollicited his honor for such a Commission, which his honor absolutely refused, alledging there was no precedent for it, upon which the book of Records was called for, and the Secretary read severall ‖ Commissions of that nature, vizt: that to Capt: Comely Coppernose, at Sederunt 122, That for Coney Pimp Frontinbrass Esqr, granted at Sederunt 147, and that for the Eastren Shore Triumvirate, and also for John Gabble Esqr, at Seder: 155, but all these arguments and precedents availed nothing with his honor, who declared *ex cathedra,* That he would by no means be directed by the club, in any such matters, and that, were he Inclined to grant a Commission, the Gentleman himself, vizt: Col: Comico Butman, would sooner prevail with him than the whole Club.—Then the Late Precedent, of Jocifer Bluechin Esqr, was produced, who, had his Commission with the Great Seal, appended at Sederunt 225, and that honorary member being present in Club, he was called upon to deliver the Copy of that Commission, which he did, and it was read by the Secretary.

Upon hearing the Commission Read, his honor absolutely denied the validity of it, affirming that the Club had no right to Grant any such Commissions, and advised Jocifer Bluechin Esqr, to put it to the use it deserved, as it was Good for nothing—and, upon its being asked by the said Jocifer, what use that was? his honor replied, that mean, and Infamous use, that waste paper is Commonly put to—Mr Bluechin bowed to his honor, and put up his Commission again in his pocket book, with no Intention to follow his advice, and his honor Calling him up to the Chair, took him by the hand and Saluted him an honorary member, telling him withal That, that was a better Sanction and Confirmation than all the Commissions ‖ the Club could grant him, Mr Bluechin made a profound bow, and returned to his Seat.

Col: Comico Butman then acquainted his honor, and the Club, that he had in his possession a Commission Granted him by Cone Pimp Frontinbrass Esqr, as agent for the Club in America—(Damn the fellow, said the president, I hate to hear the name of him—) constituting him President of the Hiccory hill Club in Virginia, under the Government and direction of the honorable Lord Jole, as his honor was then stiled, President of the ancient and honorable Tuesday Club of Annapolis, and, that, as he found, Commissions of less note, had had a place in the Club Record, he begged that this Commission might also be recorded, of which he should deliver a Copy to the Secretary, to lay before the Club at next Sederunt.

Chapter III

Commission of Col: Comico Butman, Granted by Coney Pimp Frontinbrass Esqr, several motions in Club, Speech of the orator, new Record book ordered, Jonathan Grog Esqr, accused.

Men have practised various kinds of policy to procure to themselves a Character and lasting fame, a Show of Generosity and bounty of Charity and munificence, has often been display'd for this very purpose, but policy of this Sort, runs smoothest, when it turns upon hinges of Gold, which, being a metal, not liable to rust, will require no Smear, or unctuous Substance to prevent || ungrateful Jarring; Tis certain, that the policy of Beneficence and generosity without the Supply of means, wherewithal to bring professions into practise, is like a Curious piece of Clockwork, without weight or Spring to set it a going, a wonderful Machine without a mover, That the ancient and honorable Tuesday Club resembled such a machine, will appear plainly from what I am now going to relate. [508]

At Sederunt 234, December 31, 1754, Slyboots Pleasant Esqr, being H:S: and Deputy in the chair, The Secretary presented in Club, a copy of a Commission, granted by Coney Pimp Frontinbrass Esqr, agent for America and the Islands, to Coll: Comico Butman, which the said Butman, requested should be entered on the Club Records, which was accordingly read and entered as follows.

COMMISSION

For Col: Comico Butman,
Carlo, Dominus Præses.

We Carlo, of the ancient and honorable Tuesday Club, Lord president, to all herein Concerned send Greeting.

Whereas, we have an Inherent power of appointing, constituting and establishing, all, and all manner of Clubs whatsoever, here and there and every where, to wit, anywhere, within his majestie's dominions of America & the Islands thereunto belonging, and, whereas we understand, that our trusty and well beloved Colonel Comico Butman, is desirous to erect a

Certain Club, in his majestie's ancient province of Virginia, by the name of the Hiccory hill Club, and under our direction and authority—*Now know ye* [509] ‖ that we, by the advice and Consent of our ancient and honorable Tuesday Club, by *These presents,* appoint, constitute, erect and establish the said Club, as a legal, valid and Effectual Club, under our direction and authority, by the name of the Hiccory hill Club, of which Club, we appoint you, our said trusty and well beloved Col: Comico Butman president in Chief, acting under us, and by our direction, disclaiming, disavowing, contemning, scorning and vilifying, the Authority and mock power of a certain upstart President, by name, Sir Hugh Maccarty Esqr of New York, and esteeming the said Maccarty a triffling pitiful pretender, Interloper and Intruder, upon our Presidential power and authority, and treating him as a Rebel wherever you find him; and furthermore, we Grant unto you, and your said Club of Hiccory hill, all the privileges and Immunities that appertain or belong to any free Club, on the face of this terraqueous Globe, by Sea or land, here or there and every where, that is to say, any where, within the precincts of his majesties dominions of America and the Islands there unto belonging, with a power to add to your Society, such member or members, as to you shall seem most fit and agreeable, provided always, that due deference and regard be had to the dignity and authority of our Chair, each member of your said Club, before his admission, being duely made to abjure and renounce, the aforesaid Impudent, proud, presumptuous Invader, Intruder, Interloper, and usurper, Sir Hugh Maccarty Esqr, the Sham President of the Monday Club at New York, and all his abettors, and promise faithfully never to assume to themselves, the titles of *Longstanding* [510] *members* ‖ or *oldstanding members* only due and applicable to the members of our ancient and honorable Tuesday Club of Annapolis,—Provided also, that you, our trusty & well beloved Coll: Comico Butman, shall not presume, without our Commission and authority to wear, either in your Club or out of your Club, in the Chair, or out of the Chair, here or there or any where, that is to say no where within his majesties dominions of America and the Islands thereunto belonging, any Cap of State or Caps of State, either resembling or not resembling our Cap of State or Caps of State, or any other Cap of State or Caps of State, here or there, or any where, that is to say no where, within his said majestie's dominions of America, and the Islands thereunto belonging, and finally, none of the members of your said Club of Hiccory hill, shall be held, or reputed, or alledged, or supposed or esteemd or deem'd &ct: as any ways connected with or related to, our said ancient and honorable Tuesday Club of Annapolis, either as regular members, Longstanding members, old Standing members, or honorary members, without our advice and Consent, and concurrence of our said Club.

[Privy Seal]	Given by our Command and authority
By his Ldshp's Command	and under the great Seal of our ancient
Coney Pimp Frontinbrass	and honorable Tuesday Club, and the
agens americanus	privy Seal at arms of our honorable agent
[Great Seal appended]	for America, and the Islands thereunto
	belonging, this 16th of December, 1750,
	In the Sixth year of our presidential
	Government.

Coney Pimp Frontinbrass, agens Americanus. (vera Copia)

Mr Slyboots pleasant, H:S: & D:P: and Solo Neverout Esqr, attorn: Gen: having had each their Nap out after Supper, the Club broke up.

At Sederunt 235 Janry 21, 1755, Jonathan Grog Esqr being H:S: His Honor the president on hearing Coll: Butman's Commission read in Club, observed, that he verily believed that Hiccory hill Commission, was penned and Composed by somebody in Annapolis, and that Frontinbrass the Agent had no hand in it, and therefore, ordered it to be Crossed out, as he thought it was using his name (His own meaning) with too much freedom, on which the Secretary said, he would dash it out with a St Andrews Cross, but the president declared, he would have nothing to do with St Andrew, or any thing belonging to him, by which he showed his Good will towards the Scots, whose Tutelar Saint this is, for had it been St Georges Cross, he would have touched on another note,—The Secretary urged in his own defence, as to that there Commission, that the Club, at last Sederunt, had ordered him to record it, but, his honor by an express Edict annulled that Sederunt, none having been present at it, but the H:S: attorney General and Secretary.

The attorney General moved, that the Club should Consider of ways and means to raise a Sum to be employed in Levying men, to go against the French at the Ohio, and spoke very warmly and Zealously upon the Subject, he was seconded by Quirpum Comic Esqr, hon: member, who asked leave to speak to that point, and he observed That It would be very proper for that purpose to lay a tax, on the Batchellors of the Club, which proposal, his honor the President did not seem to relish as the matter came too near home, Dr Jeronimo Jaunter || urged the taxing of the honorary members at ℔ 5: per poll, which, he observed, would have this good effect, to bring many more of these Sort of members into the Club; then the Sum to be raised was talked of, Some fixed it at three, others at four, 5, 6, 7, 8 thousand pounds, upon which Quirpum Comic Esqr, asked, (with permission) what Species of pounds these were? if pounds in money, or pounds of Tobacco, after several long and learned Speeches, on the Subject, which his honor the president heard with great Patience, The Secretary rose up, and proposed, That this money should be raised Immediatly, by strikeing the Sum fixed upon in exchequer bills, which bills, should be denominated, the Current money of the Club, and pass current among the longstanding members and others, and that this Clubical fund should be sunk by laying certain duties upon liquors drank in Club, vizt: wine Punch, Rumbo, Grog and Small beer, and, that it should not be lawful, for any longstanding member of the Club to refuse that money when proffered, not even the President, who, should any Longstanding member come to his Store, and proffer this Clubical money for any, or all the Goods therein, his honor should be obliged to take the money and deliver the Goods—Not I Indeed, quoth the President, I must have other guess money for my goods, I assure you Sir—Doctor Jaunter objected to this motion of the Secretarie's, and said, That he was not for striking exchequer bills, because that would sink and depreciate the value of other monies now in Circulation, but the Secretary soon removed this objection, by putting his honor and the Club in mind of a fact Incontestible, vizt: that as no Club money had ever as yet been struck, (unless they Reckoned the Club medal Current money) so there was no money of the Club's at present Current, and therefore, it was saying too much, that any money, vizt: Club money, could thereby be depreciated. His honor then, starting a difficulty, about the making of that money current, among those that were not members of the Club, the Attorney General || stood up with his usual Gravity, and Informed his honor and the Club, That he could soon remove that difficulty, for, as Colonel Courtly Phraze, was an honorary member of this Club, and a monied man, it was easy for the Club, to remitt the gross Sum of these new struck Clubical Exchequer bills to the said honorary member, and oblige him to pay out of his Coffers, an equivalent Sum in other Cash or Species to Circulate in their Stead.—Thus far went this momentous debate, & was referred to another Sederunt.

[513]

The Secretary then rose up, and made a motion from a written paper, as follows.

"Honorable Sir,

I am not a person much given to making motions in this Club, but when I do make them, they generally (tho very Important) are rejected, whether this be owing, to their being made, when a bad planet Reigns, rules or prevails, I shall not say, not being Astrologer enough for these

Celestial Configurations, but, whatever the luck, or fate of the motion I am now going to make, may be, the present Condition of our book of Records is such, that the said motion must be Speedily made, and also Speedily determined, else our fame and renown will Speedily perish, and be at a final Period. I mean Sir, that as there are now, but five or Six Blank leaves, left in our book of records, it is high time for your honor and the club, to Consider of ways and means to procure a new one, and therefore I move Sir That a new Record book may be ordered, at this, or the next Sederunt at farthest, and I hope Sir, that some longstanding member, that has a regard for the fame and renown of this here ancient and honorable Club, will second my motion."

This motion of the Secretary's was seconded, thirded, fourthed &ct: by several of the Longstanding members, and even by Quirpum Comic Esqr, hon: member, and Jonathan Grog Esqr, was ordered to bind, prepare and beautify, a new Record book for the Club || before three Sederunts [514] were Elapsed, which the said Jonathan Grog Esqr, as Stationer for the Club undertook to do, The Club paying all Charges, and making good all dammages to the said Club Stationer.

The Secretary Informed his honor, that he had prepared a Speech or oration, which he beg'd leave to deliver to his honor and the Club, In quality of their orator, which having been Granted him, he read a Set Speech from a written paper, using Spectacles, at the beginning of it, the writing being very small, on which his honor observed, that he did not at all become Spectacles, making at all times, but a very ordinary figure without, and a much worse with them; after the delivery of this Speech, a long Standing member said, that it ought to be recorded, to which his honor made no reply, but, to remove all Suspicions, which may arise in after times, concerning this here Speech, the Secretary has ventured the Recording of it without orders, as he had done with many other matters of Record, submitting Intirely in this affair to the Judgement of the Readers of this present age, and of the age to come, who may Casually Cast an Eye upon our archives.

Speech of the Orator

Honorable Sir,

Tho your honor and these here Longstanding members, may be long ago Thorro'ly tired, with hearing of my Speeches, yet, I can never be tired of delivering them. The first probably arises from your love of your own Ease, the latter, I am Sure springs from my own vanity; I am thorrowly persuaded that it is always good to speak well, and in Season, tho' sometimes it may be quite safe to say nothing at all, little said indeed, is soon mended, but a flow of words may display follys, which we are not aware of, yet, a Settled Silence proceeds as often from ‖ moroseness and Stupidity, as from wisdom and prudence, which made a certain Philosopher observe, wisely enough, who did not think a man's face the true Index of his mind, upon seeing a promising fair countenance in a silent man, that he should desire to *hear* that person speak, that he might *see* him.—I therefore, remembering the maxim of this Philosopher, (who ever he was) propose now to speak to your honor, and these here L:St: members, that you may *see me*, and, tho' I make no question, that you know me Sufficiently, long agoe, from what I have already said in this here Club, yet, I must beg once more to Indulge my vanity at the expence of your Repose.

[515]

I think it proper, as the new year is now making it's entry, to welcom it with a Speech (which I dont remember I ever did in this here Club before) and, I shall be very cautious how I offend your honors ears, or those of your L:St: members, by using any Improper Stile (tho' quite Clubical,) such as, frequent repititions of *this here* and *that there,* of late so Justly condemned, by your honor's accurate and Ornate Judgement, and that of your honor's Learned Attorney General, I shall rather endeavor to make it Succinct and Concise, in the mercantile Stile, which is now Looked upon, by the best Judges, to be the most ornate manner of declaiming, as well as writing.

Have ransaked my brain, once and again, to find proper Subject to entertain, your honor and L:St: members, on this occasion of General mirth and Jollity, this frolicksom time when Gaiety and good humor abound, and all mankind thro the large Scene of Christendom seem Clubically inclined, but cannot find Invention capable of striking out any thing in itself, so novel and uncommon, as to be fit to amuse & entertain, your honor and Club—had like to have said *this here Club.*

[516]

Have the honor to be now, the only Remaining old Standing Member of this Club, and therefore, hope your honour, out of regard to Seniority will overlook, many Clubical Imperfections, which may appear in my Stile, phraze, Diction and demeanor, while pronouncing this Saturnalian oration, not because I think any more than your honor, that Seniority gives a man a privilege to play the fool or be Silly, but, in so far, as it cannot otherwise be, than, that Have a more profound respect for your honor, and this Club, than to cook up a dish of blunders and absurdities, on purpose to entertain them, on the aforesaid *Saturnalian occasion,* or Indeed on any occasion, Chuse to call this occasion Saturnalian, because, 'tis that time of the year, on which the old Romans used to celebrate their Saturnalia, which Saturnalia, were Copiously scattered over, bespangled and bedecked, with the same Sort of Gambols, frolicks, tricks and Jokes, as now distinguish our Christmass Hollidays from the Rest of the year.

Shall not presume, honorable Sir, to molest or Irritate your auditory organs, with any Set Subject or dull method, that Sort of declamation, being too much Confined, shakled and fettered, and Improper for the freedom and vivacity of the Season, neither shall take upon me, to be licentious or blunt, as some people do, from an old foolish maxim, that a man may do or say what he pleases during these Christenmass Hollidays, and no offence, Briefly, I shall neither be too lax nor too restricted, in my manner, but following the footsteps of your honor's attorney General (who, I now perceive is fast asleep) address your honor and this ancient Club, in the easie, Genteel elegant, and purblind manner of that extraordinary Genius, not discerning or minding my Subject, till it comes within half an inch of my nose—but, as Subjects are now very much dried, shrivelled and shrunk up, by too much handling & tumbling, I shall leave them, to such as carry about with them, the Lubricating unguents of Parnassus, that they, by Gentle friction & embrocation, may bring them to their proper plumpness and || lubricity, so as that they may pass them again upon the world for new, as our Booksellers of late, have passed off old books by the help of new title pages; and knowing well, upon what Side my bread is butter'd, shall meddle only with such topics, as will sit as easy upon me as an old Shoe, and therefore shall not trowble you, with quotations from authors, but pass off all for my own, and, should any one discover, that have stole, from either ancients or moderens, shall not pretend to deny the fact, if they will but only point out the Chapter and verse, and take a note of it in their memorandum book.

Now, honorable Sir, (as they say) this is a merry time, and set apart for Laughter, let every one expand his Jaws and dilate the muscles of his face, to such a degree, as becometh the Hilarity of the occasion, for, as we are often told, in the margins of old almanacks, that is, as often as there is room for Inserting it, *Post est occasio Calva,* and ὁ χρονος ου χρονιζει,[1] we ought to seize occasion by the forelock, and be always merrily dispos'd, so often as we may, for, as the Philosophers wisely tell us, if we let occasion slip to day, we may not find her to morrow, and a bird in the hand is better than two in the bush, which proverb, (Tho old and Common) is very Significant, and,

[517]

---

1. Latin commonplace meaning "Opportunity hath a bald spot behind"; Greek commonplace meaning "time does not tarry."

not to be found *totidem verbis*,[2] among Solomon's Collection, so far forth as I can remember.

But, as some finical fellows distinguish mirth into two Sorts, vizt: high mirth and low mirth, you, perhaps may expect, shall enter into a disquisition, upon this nice bipartition, but, have no mind to entertain you, with any such Idle Subject, high and low of all Sorts, are banished this Club, not ev[en] excepting the Church, which has been foolishly distinguished by the[se] nonsensical Epithets, Some pragmatical fellows, Ind[eed] ma[y] say, and I believe have said, that the wit of the Club is Low, b[ut] leaving these formal Critics to stiffen in their own Starch, so as to become Incapable of bending ‖ either to humanity or good nature, without splitting their Rump box or *Os Sacrum*,[3] as anatomists term it, shall set our wit in opposition to theirs, and leave the world to Judge, but, as for our mirth, let it be purely natural, without constraint or affectation, and it will never fail to please and satisfy ourselves as well as others, in the exercise of this mirth, our risible faculties, ought to be Employed, upon proper Subjects, both within doors and without, that is, among ourselves, towards one another, and towards the whole body of mankind. By proper Subjects, mean Subjects fit to be Laughed at, which are so Infinite, that there is no end to Laughing, as often as a man has a mind to it, you cannot expect, that, will be so Idle as to number them up here, no, that would be labor in vain, a work of Supererogation, but look abroad into the world, and tho' you have but one eye, or half an eye, you may see them swarming like bees in Summer, so that he that runs may read, but, as every one does not know how to laugh with propriety, that is to say, how to laugh, without giving offence, or being the Cause of Scandal, be pleased to observe this General Rule, let your Laughing or Gelastication, be accompanied with good humor, a pleasant open, and Candid Countenance quite strpt of Satyr, Sarcasm or Sneer, and a Cynical air of Superiority, for, by Laughing in this manner, we shall be always safe, and always in a pleasant vein, the other methods of Laughing, to say, the Cynical and Sarcastical methods, are sometimes, nay, many times, followed with weeping and wailing, and, if we do not at least, draw the laugh upon ourselves, by Laughing Sarcastically, we may perchance do *worser*, that is, pull an old house about our ears.

Question not, but all the L:St: mem[be]rs of this Club, who now hear me discourse upon this [si]gnificant Subject, know very well how to laugh, both in time and tune, and the anti- ‖ quity of our Club is a plain Demon-

---

2. "In so many words."
3. "Sacred opening."

stration, that this noble art of Gelastication has been very well understood in it, and also very well timed, else, their Constitution would never have remained Intire so many years, nay may say, so many Centuries, but would before now have been shook to pieces, as has been the Case with many other Clubs, by a wrong headed method of Laughing, let us then preserve that true taste of mirth, which we have hithertoo preserved, and we need neither fear envy, nor the Rage of time, we shall flourish while other Clubs fall, we shall be admired and Commended by the wise, and, probably misunderstood by the foolish, but whatever fools, or (whom I esteem no better) pretended wise men, may say, or think of us, let it not divert us from the direct and upright course of Laughing with propriety, and, tho we should be treated, with the repartee of Horace, that witty and Facetious Clubist, who used to laugh away whole evenings, with his Clubical friends, over a Goblet of good wine of Talernam (much like our Burgundy and Champaigne)—

> *Quid rides, mutato nomine de te,*
> *Fabula narratur*[4]*—*

This repartee will only serve to renew our Laughter—Say it again, for tis worth remembering, that to laugh with propriety is of more Significancy and Importance, than many people think, and, some men of moderate parts and Capacity, have acquired the Character of Consummate Philosophers, from their understanding only this single art, and have been admitted into the lofty presence of Emperors, kings, Popes, princes, Dukes, Earls, Lords, archbishops, Cardinals, Bishops, and even Club Presidents, upon no other merit or recommendation.

But Least should Tire your patience with long winded discourses ‖ after the manner, of a Certain gentleman, learned in Clubical Law, whom I have now in my Eye (tho Indeed his eyes are shut upon me, and every one else, here present) I shall Conclude all with drinking up this Bumper of Good liquor, [520]

> Wishing this ancient Club may always be,
> Promoters of facetious mirth and Glee,
> And, that our members all may be expert,
> At the Great punning and Conundrum art,
> And that our Laureat's muse may ever warble
> Our fame to Last as Grav'd on Brass or Marble,

---

4. "What are you laughing at? Change the names and the story is about you" (*Satirae* 1.1.69).

And while Gay Laughter furbishes each Soul,
Let each a bumper drink, to *Noble Jole.*

At this Sederunt, it may be remarked, that the Club, and the orator, attempted what neither of them were able to perform, the first to be Generous and liberal for the public benefit, without any apparent fund, and the Latter to be Eloquent and poetical, without a Sufficient Strength of Genius.

At Sederunt 236, Febry 11, 1755, Mr Attorney Neverout being H:S: Jonathan Grog Esqr, Pursuant to an Order of last meeting, Produced in Club a new book, for the Records, neatly bound in folio, and the Club defrayd the Charge thereof, This book was Titled on The Back, *Record of the Tuesday Club Vol: II May, 1755.*

The Secretary then Rising up, delivered himself to the following purpose.

"May it please your honor,

Tho what I say in this Club, is often but too little regarded, and the advice which I give for its good and advantage frequently rejected, as if some politic Sly or Sinister design was Couched under it, yet, I cannot help now rising up to advise and ad- || monish your honor and this here Club, in an affair, which I take to be of the utmost consequence, & it is this.

There is a Gentleman here present, who sits at my right hand, a L:St: member of this here ancient and honorable Club, and no less a person than our poet Laureat and master of Ceremonies, who has been guilty of a trespass, of an extraordinary and Glaring kind, such as cannot well Escape the notice of your honor and this here ancient and honorable Club, and therefore has become a notorious delinquent, and made himself obnoxious to your honor and this here Club, and hence becomes a proper Subject of your animadversion resentment and Indignation.

The misdemeanour Sir, that this here Gentleman has been guilty of, is no less than that of lately printing and publishing a disrespectful letter,[5] or billet, directed to your honor, and the other members of this here ancient and honorable Club, worded and Conceived in such an arrogant and Impudent manner, as no Ideas can Clearly Conceive, or the most Emphatical words express.

In this letter Sir, Copies of which are still extant and in being, to be produced before your honor and this here Club, when called for, the presumptuous writer, takes upon him not only, by his own authority to ad-

---

5. I have not found this letter in the *Maryland Gazette.*

journ this here Club to a farther day, but also, in an Insolent and disrespectful manner, addresses your honor, in the said letter, in the same manner as he does the other members, or mere Plebs of this here Club, with the Insignificant and Naked title of *Sir,* Intirely ommitting the Common address of *honorable,* which the whole Club have allowed, time out of mind, to be the Just and Lawful title, of your honor, as honorable President of this here Club, and also has concluded, this Insolent Epistle, with the Silly and vulgar Compliment, *I am, your Humble Servant, J: Grog P:L:M:C:H:S:*

This enormous trespass Sir, I am humbly of opinion de- ‖ serves[6] proper castigation, and your honor's attorney General ought to exert his utmost to prosecute and bring to condign punishment, this here notorious offender, for Sir, the welfare and prosperity, nay, the very Essence and being of this here Club, depends upon a proper deference and respect being paid by the longstanding members thereof to your honor's Chair, and authority, and where that Sir, is wanting, and proves deficient, our Club must dwindle to nothing, and our Constitution tumble to pieces.

I would therefore, not only move Sir, that this Gentleman should be Severely taken to task, for this heinous offence, to deter others from being Guilty of the like in times to come, but also, that some laws should be passed in this here Club to secure and support that respect to your honor's Chair, which it is the duty of the L:Stand: members to pay to it at all times, and on all occasions, and that there ought to be rules laid down for proper punishment both of high and petty treason in this here Club against the Chair, and, I think it must appear to every one, that this here trespass, committed by that there Gentleman, comes under the proper Denomination of petty treason against your honor, therefore, I pray Sir, that your honor and the Club, may take it into your Serious Consideration."

Thus far the Secretary, in a very unusual Strain, and almost out of Character, being not addicted much of late to flatter the Chair, in such a manner, but many thought he did this to divert a Storm that he was afraid would soon fall on his own head.

When he had made an End of speaking, Doctor Jeronimo Jaunter rose up and moved, that the offending member be Indicted for this trespass, and the attorney General standing ‖ up, in his place spoke as follows.

"May it please your Honor,

The matter that has now been laid before your honor and the Club, by the Secretary, I think Sir, is of the utmost Importance, and I think as he has thereby shown a regard for your honors prerogative and the privileges of

---

6. Hamilton omitted pp. 522 and 523 when numbering his pages.

your honors Chair, he ought not to be suspected, as usual of Sinister designs—I observe Sir, that the Learned Gentleman who spoke last, moved for an Indictment to be preferred against the offender, which Indictment, I am very willing, in pursuance of the duty of my office in this here Club, to preferr against him, and against all offenders *Whatsomever,* be they who they will, without partiality, favor or affection, but, as I am very desirous Sir, to give every Gentleman fair play, and a fair Chance for his life, and, as this here Gentleman, apprehensive of the Storm, that now Gathers over his head, has brought a Gentleman Learned in the Law, vizt: Mr Attorney Wou'dbe, whom your honor sees now in Club, to be his Council, and to plead his cause, I am Content Sir, (with your honor's permission) that this here Gentleman should appear, as Council at the bar for the defendant."

Jonathan Grog Esqr, then spoke as follows—

"May it please your honor,

That was Just what I was a going to mention, and therefore, need trowble your honor with, but a very short Speech, upon this here occasion, since, all I Intended to speak has already been spoken, by that there Great Gentleman who spoke last, in the latter end of his Speech, and for ‖ that reason, Sir, I have brought this here Gentleman, vizt: Mr Attorney Woudbe, to Implead my cause, and therefore humbly pray, that he may be heard upon the premises."

Pres: I will Indulge you so far Sir, as to allow the Gentleman to speak, for you in this cause, but, with this caveat, that the like is never to be permitted in Club, without the president's express Commission and permission.

It was then moved, that Spatterdash Woudbe Esqr, attorney for the defendant, should be Qualified upon the Club-book, to Implead before his honor the President and the Club, and the Secretary Qualified him in the following manner, he standing up, and Solemnly laying his hand upon the book.

Form of the Qualification of a Club attorney.

"You, Spatterdash Woudbe Esqr, attorney at Club Law, do protest and avow, by this great book, and all it's contents, be they true or false, Just or unjust, right or wrong, Sense or nonsense, that you will faithfully and truely ply and exercise, the office of an attorney at Club law, in a Clubical Capacity, while pleading before his honor and this here Club, in all, and all manner of Causes, by you undertaken in this here Clubical Court, to the best of your ability, knowledge and Capacity"—Mr Woudbe, having assented to this very Significant form, copied and modelled from other forms alike Significant, and alike binding on account of the necessary Solemnity of a book, bowed to his honor and the Club, and sat down, *the Gentleman being in his boots.*(a)

Mr: Woud: May it please your honor, since I have obtained licence of your honor and this here Club, to speak in defence of that there Gentleman, as I take it Sir, it is Impossible to answer to a Charge, properly, not yet regularly made, and therefore, I beg that this here trial may begin now, and be Carried on in a regular manner.

Attor: Gen: Please your honor to permit me to speak, before your honor gives any further orders in this matter, I apprehend Sir, that Mr Attor- ‖ ney Woudbe by proposing this Intends, That an Indictment is to be preferrd Immediatly if possible, but, I humbly represent, that I am not yet fully prepared to try this here Cause, and therefore, cannot preferr an Indictment before next Sederunt. I apprehend Indeed Sir, that when Mr Attorney Woudbe rose to speak, he would have been able to have shown, at this present time, that Mr Grog in his proceeding was no way Culpable.

Mr Att: Woud: Sir, I thought an Indictment had been ordered long ago.

Att: Gen: No Sir, no such thing, if you have any thing to say for your Client, please to say it now.

Mr A: W: Pardon me Sir, I am not prepared.

Att: Gen: Will your honor be pleased to order an Indictment?

Pres: Yes yes, to be Sure let an Indictment be prepared.

Doctor Jeronimo Jaunter then took notice, That Jonathan Grog Esqr, had not only been guilty of disrespect, to his honor, in publishing that letter, but had Committed a most hideous Bull, in the body of the Letter, for which trespass also, he moved that he should be Indicted.

He then accused the attorney General Himself, Slyboots Pleasant Esqr, and Mr Secretary Scribble, of a heinous trespass against his honor the President, in sending him a missive, wrote out upon the knave of Spades, Inviting themselves to eat a fat turkey with him, on Saturday night last, for which he moved that they might be Indicted.

[527]

(a) What the historian can Intend by this Circumstance of the boots, cannot be Conjectured, unless he means to Imitate that remarkable passage in the apocrypha, *and Tobit went forth, and the dog went also,* or perhaps in Imitation of Homer, who never mentions the Greeks, without taking notice of their boots, $ευκνεμεδες\ αχαιοι$.⁷

7. Tob. 6:1; the "well-greaved" or "well-booted Achaeans" is a common epithet in the *Iliad*, e.g., 1.17.

Whereupon, Mr Attorney General Neverout, acted in a very unprecedented and unaccountable manner, in appointing Mr Attorney Woudbe to prosecute himself, and the other Gentlemen.

Then an Indictment was ordered, against Messrs the attorney General Slyboots Pleasant & Secretary Scribble.

The President then took notice, That this missive Card was sent by a Scoundrel, vizt: the knave of Spades.

Jon: Grog: Had it been the knave of Clubs, it would have been somewhat Clubical.

Dr Jer: Jaunt: Will your *Lordship* please to give direction, how || Mr Attorney Woudbe is to manage this prosecution [the members stared upon one another, on Dr Jaunter's Calling his honor, *your Lordship*]

Mr Att: Woud: It is my opinion Sir, that proceeding by way of Indictment, is altogether Improper in this here Case.

Pres: You know best Sir, you're a Lawyer.

Mr Crank: I move Sir, it may be by presentment.

Pres: Who Presents?

Mr Crank: Who your honor pleases.

Pres: I dont know Gentlemen, I am no Lawyer.

Dr Jaun: I move Sir, that the Card may be delivered to Mr Attorney Woudbe.

Pres: No, no. I think it best to keep that in my own hands.

Attor: Gen: Please your honor, he cannot proceed without that very Individual Card, I shall Surely overset all he says if he has it not.

Pres: How Sir!—how say you Sir?—

Mr Crank: I move he may keep that there knave to himself, and let Mr Attor: Woudbe, have nothing to do with knaves of any Sort.

Pres: No Sir!—I cannot, nor will not entertain any knaves—

Sly: Pleas: Suppose we have a Council on these Important matters.

Pres: No Indeed—we shall have no Council.

Att: Gen: Sir, if we have been Guilty of offence, and are to have trial, we have a right to come to trial, when demanded, upon account of the Great expences, accompanying such trials and vexatious Suits in this here Club.

Mr Att: Woud: Sir, I am so far from desiring a delay of this here trial, that I only request time to prepare proper materials, and, I think, an Information on the Case, will lie most properly before your honor, an Indictment cannot properly be in this here Case Sir.

Pres: Mr Councellor Jaunter, please to take a Copy of this here Card for Mr Attorney Woudbe—Dr Jaunter then took a Copy of the Card and gave it to Mr Attorney Woudbe.

Pres: I beg to see that paper Just now wrote out.

Mr At: Woud: Sir!—

Att: Gen: Sir!—pardon me, no copy of a paper from Mr Attorney Woudbe, is to go out of his hands, I know the Law in such Cases Sir. [529]

Pres: I must!—and Insist upon seeing that paper Sir.

Att: Gen: With all my heart Sir, 'tis no business of mine, I only give my opinion.

Mr Att: Woud: You took notice Sir, that this here Card was sent by a Scoundrel.

Pres: The knave of Spades, I meant by the Scoundrel Sir,—it was sent by a negroe, and cannot tax the negroe with any bad thing.

Att: Gen: Sir, I hope we may plead our own Cause in this here Case.

Dr Jaunt: All your words Sir will go for nothing.

Att: Gen: Consider what court we come before, a Court of Conscience.

Pres: It is not properly a Court of Conscience.

Mr Crank: Who is the Court, I hope your honor will not sit Judge in your own Cause, and verify the proverb of the devil.

Pres: I will not answer you—

Mr Crank: Then Minute, Mr Secretary that this is no Court.

Dr Jaunt: Set down nothing but by his honor's order.

Slyb: pleas: I observe every thing that Dr Jaunter says is assented to.

Pres: give me one Instance of that Sir.

Dr Jaunt: I have asserted nothing but the truth Sir.

Pres: For my part, I know nothing of what has been done to night.

Mr Crank: I humbly think, if one member has liberty to speak, another may.

Pres: Perhaps I think otherwise—

Dr Jaunt: You put words in the president's mouth as you please, if the president cannot moderate, pray of what use is he?

Mr Crank: It is hard, when a man speaks to the purpose, it should be Improper.

Pres: I think all you have said this night is Improper.

Mr Crank: The President is prejudiced against me.

Pres: No Sir,—I have it under your hand that I am one of the best friends you have, and therefore cannot be prejudiced against you, and you ought to be taken to task for your pertness.

[530]   Slyb: pleas: Do not determin Mr President that he is Guilty before he is heard, you proceed too hastily.

After this the Clamor Grew so loud between the president and Mr Crankum, and his honor spoke so fast, that the Secretary could take no more minutes, The Proclamation was read to Quell the noise, and his honor finding, that the honorary members only were affected therewith, was dissatisfied, and vowed that it should be altered, and the regular members taken in; which none durst contradict, a bold and daring Stroke upon the Liberty of the Club.

All the members, excepting his honor and the H:S: broke up at ten o Clock, to go to a ball, at the other end of the town.

Chapter IV

Mr Attorney Woudbe appears in Club, Trial of Jonathan Grog Esqr, his Condemnation and Sentence, new Song Introduced by his honor the President, Congratulatory Pyndaric Ode by the Poet Laureat.

People of a Low and gross taste, are often offended at a Serious manner of Jesting, either in Conversation or writing, what I mean by a Serious manner of Jesting, is running a Course of Ridicule, on Subjects, that are esteemed to be of a Serious and Solemn nature; for this reason, I doubt not, but many low and Gross Critics, will Condemn me, for presuming to Jest upon Subjects of this nature, (according to their profound estimation) and particularly our Solemn and grave professors of the Law, who esteem their Science, (as they call it, tho' I rather think it an art) the quintessence of human reason, and their Judicial Proceedings, thereon founded very Grand, Solemn & Sublime, in all its parts. It is true, that I have in various places of this Important and Solemn history, especially in giving an account of the Club trials, represented that Science, and its professors, the Gentle-
[531]   men of || the long robe in no favorable light, for which I have no other apology to make, than that I take our Law (especially our Common law) proceedings to be *Seria mixta Jocis;*[1] *Seria,* in so far, as the Intention of them is pretended to be the Securing of right and property, and *Mixta Jocis,* as they are many times Crouded & overloaded, with such triffling distinctions, such minute punctillios and forms, far fetched definitions, distorted reason-

---

1. "Serious matters mixed with jokes."

ings, and prolix tautologies, as would make any reasonable man, who is not a party Interrested or concerned in this profitable, extravagant, and expensive ocupation, split his midriff with Laughter.

The Profound Doctors of this profounder profession, may, if they please think me an Ignorant puppy, and, that I prate in this manner, because I know nothing of the matter, and apply to me the Scurvey proverb of *Ne Sutor ultra Crepidam*,[2]—'Tis very true, my Learned friends, I never trowbled my head about any such Intricate and Subtile Studies, but Call me what you please, Ignorant or dull, I hope I am only so in Law, and not In fact, as you know, by your own wise maxims, a man may be dead in Law, and not in fact, I hope I have natural reason Sufficient to form a Judgement of the perfections and Imperfections, The Integrity & the flaws, breaks or botches of this Slippery Craft, however deep and learned it's foundations or props may be, and I may safely aver, and have the Concurrence of many Candid Judges, that our modes and Proceedings in Law, (common Law I still mean) are more founded upon national Custom, than upon Reason; and, That national Custom (especially the custom of conquering nations, for from them our Common Law took it's original) is always founded on Reason, I believe, few discerning men will allow; it being rather established on the will and pleasure of the Conquerors, which Sort of reason, may seem reasonable to them, but absurd to all the world besides, (I beg pardon for Introducing here such Clubical terms, as *reasonable Reason,* and *Reason absurd,* but had I time I could quote many Common law terms to support me here) Besides, If we Grant that *Reason Simpliciter,* as Reason, is common to all mankind, (and I think my Philosophy tells me this is true) then, the Common Law, if founded on reason as they say, would be common to all nations, but should this fundamental reason, on which this bulky fabric stands, be any other reason, but Common reason, or, in plainer words, Common Sense, I would not give a farthing, for either the Edifice or it's prop; Since we know then that this Common law is not universal, and that it is founded on Custom, there must necessarily be many absurdities in it, and all the Reason its professors can brag of, is to reduce these absurdities to some Show of reason; hence, many Learned arguments have been devised, to establish the equity and reasonableness of the Law of Combats, and the manner of old, of determining Right and Wrong, by dint of blows and hard knocks, to place on a Rational foundation, Trials by fire and water ordeal, and the discovery of witches by their floating or sinking in a pond or river, abundance of Learned treatises have been wrote, concerning the

---

2. "Let the cobbler not [judge] beyond shoes" (Valerius Maximus 8.12.3).

law of duels, and how in proper form and methods, men might Cut one another's throats, to solder up Crack'd honor, and separate truth from falshood, which learned tracts, and arguments, In times past had their value and Character, and were looked upon, as a very Rational method of procedure, tho' now obselete, and thrust out of doors, and I am afraid, our Common law is still stuffed with numberless absurdities, owing their birth to the same Gothic original, not withstanding the wisdom of the Legislature of late has Cleared it of that Barbarous Jargon of old obselete Norman French, and dog latin, of which many Grave and ponderous volumes may be seen at this day, printed in a fine black Character, and it is to be wished that some Great Genius, would scour away the Rubbish of Silly reasons which abound in these vast books, such for example, as that of a Certain Grave Judge, who gives this reason, why a father cannot Inherit his Son's Lands, vizt: *Quia terra gravis est et non potest ascendere;*[3] but these fooleries would Surely be much sooner exploded, and share the same fate with the Codes, concerning Single Combat and duels, were it not, that they serve to Inrich the professors of this Cunning Science, and render the profits thereof more extensive, a method being hereby Ingeniously Contrived, whereby to baffle mathematical demonstration, and keep a man waiting twenty or thirty years, squandering his money & fooling away his life, before it can be determined that twice two makes four. Let no rash Critic therefore Censure the methods of proceeding in these our Club Trials, or pronounce them absurd or nonsensical, since they have so great a pattern, as the Courts of Common Law to Copy from, nor let any find fault with our Clubical punishments, of a Condemned Criminal, should he be Sentenced to *sing a Song,* to expiate his trespass, since, had we time or room here, we could produce proceedings and punishments alike absurd, in our Grave and Solemn Courts of Judicatory.

At Sederunt 237, February 25th 1755, The Club was Convened at the house of Mr Secretary Scribble H:S: where appeared the Ingenious and Learned Spatterdash Woud- be Esqr, a Clubical attorney, legally Qualified, according to the order of last Sederunt, as Council for Jonathan Grog Esqr, and as Prosecutor for his honor the president against Mr Attorney Genl: Neverout, Slyboots pleasant Esqr, and Mr Secretary Scribble, This Learned Gentleman was dressed in his robes and Garb of office, vizt: a Large full bottom'd wig, a band and black Gown, as was also his Antagonist the Learned Mr Attor: General Neverout.

The Latter Gentleman delivered into the Secretary's hands a huge

---

3. "Because land is heavy and cannot ascend."

bundle of papers, and was about to open the charge against Jonathan Grog Esqr, who was now set to the bar, but was Interrupted, and Cut short in his harangue, by Mr Attorney Woudbe, who alledged, that Mr Attorney Neverout at this present Juncture was Incapacitated to plead before his honor the president, and the Club, as he was himself, with two other Gentlemen of the Club, under a prosecution, which, he hoped soon to make appear, and therefore *Non rectus in Curia.*

To this objection, Mr Attorney General answered, That he knew nothing of that matter *et de non apparentibus, et non existentibus eadem est Ratio*[4]—upon which, Mr Attorney Woudbe, produced a Letter, which he had wrote to the following purpose, and said he hoped that that there Letter, would make good his argument.

To Secretary Scribble, Mr Attorney Neverout & Slyboots Pleasant Esqr, Honorable members of the Tuesday Club in Annapolis.

Gentlemen,

Inclosed is a Copy of the Charge to be exhibited against you, by order of the Honorable Nasifer Jole Esqr, President of your ancient and honorable Tuesday Club, I Ima- || gine you will prepare yourselves for Trial, and, I heartily wish you a lucky escape, but, if you put in any Long Plea *&ct:* I pray I may have notice of it, and a Copy, I am Gentlemen, with due respect, [535]

Febr: 16th 1755   Your Humble Servant
(*vera Copia*)   *Spatterdash Woudbe*.

But this Letter being read in Club, by Mr Attorney General, his own way, did not seem to weigh any thing with the President, so he was permitted to proceed.

Then a very warm dispute arose between the Two Learned attorneys, which of the two Indictments should be first read, Mr Attorney Neverout Insisted, that they should be read in order, as numbered, Mr Attorney Woudbe, requested that Indictment 2d might be first exhibited, but, what his reasons were is altogether a Secret, The president however granted his request, and Jonathan Grog Esqr, being put to the Bar, the Secretary read as follows.

Indictment 2d

Tuesday Club Ss:

  Jonathan Grog Esqr, you stand indicted, by the name of

---

4. "The same reason applies to the nonexistent and the nonapparent" (cf. p. 89n, above).

Jonathan Grog Esqr, master of Ceremonies, and poet Laureat to the ancient and honorable Tuesday Club, heretofore Called, Jonathan Grog Esqr, P:P:P:P:P: That is to say, Poet, Punster, Printer, Punch maker General and Purveyor, of the said ancient and honorable Club, for that you, on the 14th day of January anno Dom, 1755 and, in the tenth year of the Presidential Government, of our Illustrious and honorable President **Carlo,** in a Street Called Charles Street, in the City of Annapolis, was a punster, or paragrammatist, and the said art, or Lingual occupation of a punster or paragrammatist the || aforesaid 14 day of Janry, in the anno dom: aforesd: and in the year of our presidential governmt: aforesd: in the Street aforesd: of the City aforsd: you, the aforesd: Jonathan Grog Esqr, poet Laureat & Mr of Ceremonies aforesd: to the ancient and honorable Club aforesd: did use and exercise, and did not hold yourself to the sd: art and Lingual occupation of a punster or paragramatist, but, on the sd: 14th day of Janry, in the anno dom: aforesd: in the year of our presidential Governt: aforesd: in the Street aforesd: of the City aforesd: the art and mystery of a Bull maker, being an art and mystery by others then and there used, and in the Street aforesd: of the city aforesd: did set up, and profess, as well the said art and mystery of a bull maker, as the said art and mystery of a punster or paragrammatist, on the said 14th day of Janry, in the anno dom aforesd: in the year of our Presidential Govt: aforesd: and ever after, untill this day, by Impudently and audaciously printing and publishing, or causing to be printed and published, in your dwelling house aforesd: in the Street aforesd: of the City aforesd: a certain letter, wherein was Contained the following words, vizt: *The holding of the ancient and honble: Tuesday Club this night in Charles Street, for some weighty and Extraordinary reasons, is put off till Tuesday the 21 of this Instant,* which words, contain in themselves, as rank and overgrown a bull, as ever was hatched in Hybernian Land, which art and mystery, you, the sd: Jon: Grog Esqr, Poet Laureat and Mr of Ceremonies of the ancient and honorable Tuesd: Club aforesd: wickedly and divlishly, still Continue to exercise, to the Great detriment & dammage of the Irish members of the sd: anct: & Hon: Club, that now are, have been or shall be, whose Sole privilege it has been, time out of mind, to make, manufacture, and vend those bulls, against the form of the Statute of this here Club, in that there Case, made and provided, and against the peace of our said honorable and Illustrious President Carlo, his Chair and dignity.

Solo Neverout   Pledges { Joannes Doe
Attorn: Gen: pros: { Ricardus Roe

Secr: What say you Jonathan Grog Esqr? are you Guilty of this matter wherewith you stand Indicted, or not guilty?

Jon: Gr: I Leave all to my attorney Sir.

Mr Att: Woud: Sir, I Justify to this Indictment.

Then The attorney General stood up, and spoke to the following purpose.

"May it please your honor,

I rise up to speak to this Indictment, which is the first, Tho of Course it ought to have been the Second; this is an Indictment Sir, which Charges the Culprit with a trespass on the Case, in so far forth, as that he, professing the Lawful business of a punster in this Club, as appears by the Club Records, vizt: Sederunt 103 april 11th 1749, Prim Timorous Esqr being H:S: where you will find page 118, the following Record, vizt:—*The Question proposed, was, whether Jonathan Grog Esqr, already enjoying several offices and titles in the Club, properly expressed in Capital Ps, after the manner of the old Romans, as follows, Jonathan Grog Esqr, P.P.P.P.P. could be burdened with any other office?*—and so forth, and, we find by the same record, that it passed by a great Majority in the negative, there being nine Nays, and only two Yeas. Now, your honor will permit me to observe upon this, that by one of the Ps, was signified and Intended Punster, which office, this unhappy delinquent did then, and Indeed does now exercise in this Club, but among all these five Ps, your honor's Eyes, and Indeed the eyes of any other person, must be much keener, and of a much different make from mine, if they can discover any the least likeness or Resemblance of a B, for by B, as I humbly Conceive, Sir, may be Intended || a bull maker, as well as Punster by P: but Sir, any one that can but distinguish a B from a bull's foot, can see that these letters are all P:s so that the Case appears plain in point, that the Gentleman has been guilty of a Trespass, in adapting to himself this B, which he has no manner of title or right to, I mean Sir, Title or right Clubical, neither by rule of Statute law, Common Law, Civil Law, nor (I hope) Club Law, for we have it in the Syriac Code of Alminhagas, thus—*hash, hagath Rabga bash, Shig Shag Shobos, bongomash onoriadka^5*—and, in

---

5. The attorney general may be recalling one of the Almohades, a Moslem dynasty in North Africa and Spain that superseded the Almoravides during the middle of the 12th century, and perhaps the "Syriac code" is simply a reference to Moslem law, but I suspect he has invented the name, source, and quotation.

the Common or Statute Law of England, we find, in this Collection I have now before me, page 510, *anno vigesimo tertio Henrici octavi, Capite Quarto,* these plain words, vizt: *No brewer shall be a Cooper &ct:*[6] a Case Sir in point, parallel to the Case of this unhappy delinquent at your honor's bar, who, being a punster, takes upon him the occupation, and office of a Bull maker, for, if the words, as is set forth, point blank in the Indictment, and, as they stand in this printed Letter, which I have in my hand, be not a rank bull, I must own, I know not what a bull is. He says, may it please your honor, *The holding of the ancient and honorable Tuesday Club this night in Charles Street,* (vizt: the 14th of January when the Letter is dated) *for some weighty and Extraordinary reasons, is put off to January the 21st Instant*—I believe it would puzzle a Gentleman of a much wiser and deeper head, than this unhappy delinquent, now at your honor's bar, to find reasons to convince any man, that is *Compos mentis,*[7] that a meeting, held upon the 14th of any month, can be held upon the 21st, either of that, or any other month, so, that these reasons, I grant you, were they found, would really be very extraordinary, and very weighty Indeed, so weighty, as to weigh down all the reasons, I ever yet heard, or read of, and beyond the Subtilty of Joannes duns Scotus, or the famous meta- ‖ physician Duvries,[8] but, not to take up any more of your honor's precious time, I think, honorable Sir, the Case is very Clear, and therefore, I pray Judgement against the Delinquent, at your honors bar according to Club Law."

The Attorney General Having thus spoke, Mr Attorney Wou'dbe stood up and objected—he said, He could no where find, either by Club law, or any other Law upon Earth, that it was forbid his Client to make Bulls, and that he was humbly of opinion, his Client might lawfully make any Sort of bulls, Except *popish Bulls,* which, he owned he had no right to make, by the Laws of this protestant Land, that, as for Statutes, quoted by the Learned Gentleman, on the other Side of the argument, he apprehended that this here Club, had nothing to do with Statute Law, of any Sort, far less with any old obselete Statutes, of an old obselete fellow, vizt: Henry VIII. who was dead and Rotten, above 200 years agoe, and therefore pray'd arrest of Judgement, but, since the Learned Gentleman was pleased to Quote the Club Records, he would beg liberty also, to bring a

---

6. "No Brewer Shall Be a Cooper" is in fact the heading of chap. 4, 23 Henry VIII, in Ferdinando Pulton's *A Collection of Sundrie Statutes* (London, 1661 [orig. publ. 1618]), 510; see also p. 545n, below.

7. "Of sound mind."

8. I have searched in vain for a metaphysician whose name even resembles that of Duvries. Hamilton may mean Davies—several of that name wrote metaphysical tracts—but his manuscript clearly says Duvries.

the Tuesday Club [Book XIV] 339

more ancient Quotation, from that Learned Collection, and desired Mr Secretary, to turn up to Sederunt 54th, Febry 24th 1746/7, Dumpling Gundiguts Esqr, being Deputy President, and Smoothum Sly Esqr H:S: where, in a letter, of the Honorable the President to the H:S: there is a parallel Instance to that, in his Clients Letter, the Subject of the Indictment, which runs thus,—*And as I understand, some of the members will not be able to come, 'tis probable, you'll postpone the Resolves of last Club, to our next meeting*—and therefore, (he said) his Client, having the example of his honor the president before him, he could not follow a better pattern, and therefore was not Culpable in this here Case. His honor the president, seemed to take this Quotation in || bad part, and remarked on the forwardness of Mr Attorney Woudbe, saying, That if he had a mind to make bulls, neither the Club, nor any attorney appearing therein, had any Right to Call him to an account for it,—Then the other Indictment was ordered to be read. [540]

Indictment 1st

Tuesday Club Ss:

Jonathan Grog Esqr, you stand indicted, by the name of Jonathan Grog Esqr, master of Ceremonies and Poet Laureat, of the Ancient and honorable Tuesday Club, heretofore stiled Jonathan Grog Esq P:P:P:P:P: That is to say Poet, Punster, Printer, Purveyor, and Punch maker General, to the sd: ancient and honorable Club, for that you, as a false Traitor, against our most Illustrious and honorable **Carlo** President of the said ancient and honorable Club, due obedience to the said Illustrious and honorable president, in your heart not having, and, being instigated, moved and seduced by some absurd devil, or rather by your own wicked and malicious Inclination, and due obedience to our said Illustrious and honorable president utterly with drawing, and endeavoring and Intending, with all your might, the peace and Common tranquillity of this ancient and honorable Club to disturb, and the Laws of the same established to overthrow, to pull down and bring into Contempt, our said Illustrious and honorable President, Carlo, and his chair, & the said honorable Chair, wickedly, divlishly, maliciously and treasonably to usurp, you, the said Jonathan Grog Esqr, Poet Laureat, and Mr of Ceremonies of the said ancient and || honorable Club, upon the 14th day of Janry anno dom 1755, and, in the 10th year of the Presidential Government of our said Illustrious and honorable President Carlo, in a Street, Called Charles Street, in the City of Annapolis, then and [541] there, wickedly, devlishly, treasonably, and of your malice aforethought, with force and arms, Rautously and riotously, an assault did make, on the said person & Chair, of our said honorable Illustrious President Carlo, in open Contempt of the Laws of this ancient and honorable Club, by daringly and openly, printing and publishing, or causing to be printed and published, a certain treasonable Libellous, Seditious and malicious Letter, in the following words, vizt:

   Sir,
   The holding of the ancient and honorable Tuesday Club this night in Charles Street, for some weighty and Extraordinary reasons, is put off to Tuesday the 21st Instant, I am

Tuesd: Jan: 14th 1755   *Your humble Servant*
                                     Jonathan Grog P:L:M:C:
                                          & H:S:

which treasonable, libellous, Seditious and malicious Letter, addressed, worded and Conceived in the Contemptible and disrespectful Stile aforesd: you, Jonathan Grog Esqr, Poet laureat, and master of Ceremonies of the sd: ancient and honorable Tuesday club, sent to our said honorable and Illustrious president Carlo, by your menial messenger of the press, Commonly Called the Devil, in utter defiance and Contempt of our said honorable and Illustrious Presidt: Carlo, the dignity and authority of his chair, and the laws of this ancient and honorable Club in that there Case [542] ‖ made and provided, and setting a bad and pernicious Example, to all your fellow Longstanding members, to be guilty of the same, against the peace of our said Illustrious and honorable President Carlo, his chair and dignity.

Solo Neverout   Pledges { Joannes Doe
Attornat Genl: pros: { Ricardus Roe

   Secret: What say you, Jonathan Grog Esqr, are you Guilty of this Charge brought against you, or not Guilty?
   Jon: Gr: My attorney must answer for me Sir.
   Mr Att: Woud: Please your honor, I Justify to this Indictment.
   Then the attorney General stood up, and spoke as follows.
   "May it please your honor,
   Ever since I had the honor, to plead before your honr: and this Club, as your honor's attorney General, I cannot say that I have met with a Case

parallel to the Case, which I now bring before your honor,—The Case, may it please your honor, now under our Consideration, is a Case of petty Treason, as appears, by what is said, by that profound Subtile Casuist Bernardus A Doma, in his *Disquisitiones Nugatiles, libro Quarto, Sectione Undecima, pagina Centesima, Qui, Quium, Quam, Quibus, quantisper Quolibet, Quisque Quorundum Quandoque quoties, Quando, Quæstus, Quærela, Quæremonium Quære, quid, quod Questio*⁹ and so forth, but, that I may not tire and tieze your honor, with authorities upon the Case, I shall come directly to the point, and endeavor explicitly to expand and Explain the nature of the Case now before us, as it stands in the ‖ Pandectas of Drogheda, Published at the Hague, in a fine Elziver Type, *When one writes to a Great Man,* says that profound author, **Dunk Glehisk Gunders kindiken van Brindlindunket cungught diderlich boorden Drunken, bungin woorden Gleek,** ⁽ᵃ⁾ That is to say, his Stile ought to be mannerly, circumspect, decent, Superlatively polite—now Sir, that this Epistle under our consideration, wrote to your honor, by this unhappy delinquent at your honors bar, is wanting and deficient, not only in one or two but in every respect, according to this authors Learned definition, of *polite Literature,* that is to say, the polite *Modus ad Conscribendas Literas, vivis magnis, magnificentibusque,*¹¹ which, I shall make my whole & Sole Business to prove—permit me Sir, to observe in the first place, the address, att the beginning of this paltry epistle, you will find it consists of nothing but plain *Sir*—I say Sir, Plain *Sir*—which I aver, is altogether Improper, as well as Indecent in him to address your honor, as honorable president of this Club, who ought to be addressed in the Stile of *your honor,* or *Right honorable,*—again, as to the body of the letter, it plainly contains treasonable matters, for if it be not treason (I mean petty treason Sir, as I could show your honor by several Clubical Laws, vizt: Law 49th, fol: 281, of these Records, which your honor will find to be in point) for any longstanding member of this Club, to take upon himself that authority, which only belongs to your honor, I cannot tell what to denominate treason, I mean Sir, his adjourning the Club, without having first obtained your honor's permission for so

[543]

(a) He who consults a dutch dictionary to explain this passage, will have only his labor for his pains, the Language being Intirely Clubical & obselete.¹⁰

9. This reference to Bernhardus à Doma's (see p. 53n, above) "Trifling Disquisitions" (bk. 4, sec. 11, p. 100) is nonsense.

10. The attorney general is perhaps recalling William of Drogheda (d. 1245?), eminent lecturer on canon law at Oxford during the early 13th century and author of the *Summa aurea* (ca. 1239), an elaborate treatise on canon law, but the passage attributed to Drogheda is nonsense.

11. "Manner of writing letters, lively, big, and magnificent."

[544] doing, and yet, this Gentleman has ‖ Insolently assumed that authority, not only by the purport and Stile of his Letter, but also, to the knowledge of your honor, and all the Longst: membrs: of this Club,—and lastly Sir, as to the conclusion of this letter, how does it conclude Sir? why thus—*Your humble Servt:*—whose humble Servt: pray? The king's or the Coblers? but that I may not tire your honor, with prolix Speeches, I proceed to Examin evidence."

Upon which Mr Attorney General Examined Mr Secretary Scribble, who declared That upon the 14th of Janry last, in the morning, he called at the office of Jonathan Grog Esqr, and asking him how he did, he replied he was very unwell, and did not think of adjourning the Club that day, 'till he [The Secretary] advised him to do so, that he did not see the said Jonathan, either write, or actually print the letter mentioned in the Indictment, that the said Jonathan showed him the Letter, after it was in print, and he has reason to believe, that he sent this letter to his honor the president, and the rest of the members, as he himself received one—Then Jonathan Grog Esqr, being asked if he had any questions to put to the evidence, he asked the Secretary If he had not showed him that letter in manuscript, before he saw it in print, and demanded his opinion of it, to which the Secretary answered That he remembered he had showd him something in manuscript,—what then was your opinion of it, Sir, said the Culprit, did you condemn or approve of it,—the Secretary replied that he approved of what he showed him, and did not then perceive any bull in the body of the letter, as set forth in the other Indictment, but could not well Charge his memory [545] as to the manuscript letter, being verbatim, and literatim ‖ the same with the printed one,—this evidence being delivered, the attorney General proceeded.

"Having thus, I think, honorable Sir, irrefragibly proved that this letter is a treasonable letter, and not only Contrary to the rules of the above quoted polite and learned author, but expressly against the first article of the 49th Law of this Club, as above quoted, to satisfy therefore your honor and the Club, that this delinquent at the bar, is Lawfully attainted and tried for treason, I shall produce an ancient unexceptionable authority in point, vizt: *anno trigesimo tertio Henrici Octavi Capite vigesimo fol: 726*[(a)] where it is

---

(a) Here the attorney General turned up a great book, about half a foot Thick, Intituled *Pulton's Collection of the Statutes*.[12]

12. Ferdinando Pulton (1536–1618) was an English legal author who compiled and edited the statutes of English law in several volumes. The attorney general has closely paraphrased this passage from 33 Henry VIII, chap. 20, "How Treason Committed by a Lunatick Shall Be Punished" (*Collection of Sundrie Statutes*, 677).

said, *attainder of treason by the Common law, shall be of as good force, as by act of parliament,* and if by Common Law, *Ergo* Sir, by Club law also, for I know of no Law that is more common than Club Law, having now, I think, Clearly proved the facts, with which this delinquent stands Charged, I shall leave it with Your honor to find a verdict, as in your conscience you see right, not doubting, but that, if your honor finds him Guilty, you will pass such a Judgement on him as may deterr all others from following the like detestable practises.

But I must humbly beg your honors pardon, to Indulge me a word or two in regard to the worthy Gentleman, who appears here this night as council for the delinquent, this Gentlemans great knowledge and abilities in the Law, is so well known to some of the Courts below, & his particular talent, either at puzzling a Good cause, or glossing over a bad one, by Specious and Subtile arguments, is such, that I should dread the consequence, was I not well assured, that all his art and Subtilty will avail him nothing, before so great and good a Judge, as your honor, but, as the greatest and best of men may be misled, by the Crafty arguments of the Subtle & designing, I thought it my duty, most humbly to give your honor this hint, least the Speciousness of the Gentleman's arguments might prevail too far, on your honors known goodness & Clemency."

The attorney General having finished his Speech, Mr Attorney Woudbe rose up with Great Gravity and objected to his whole pleading, in the first place he said,—That it did not signify that neither of those what you Call it Sort of papers, brought against his client at the bar, were Indictments, as Mr Attorney was pleased to call them, but rather a rig-me-roll of I dont-know-what Sort of Stuff, that the form & tenor of those were quite Improper, and widely different from that Commonly used in our Courts of Law, That John Doe and Richard Roe the pledges, had nothing to do here, those persons being only taken as pledges in Civil, and not in Criminal Cases, as this here case was set forth to be, that the attorney General's reading of Speeches from written papers was ridiculous, and altogether unprecedented, that in short, it was a practise that would not be allowed of, in any Court of record *whatsomever,* to read pleadings at the bar, and was mere preaching and nothing in the world else, that as for his authorities, it did not signify, for, as he observed before, Harry VIII. had been dead and rotten, a great many Years agoe, and this here Club had nothing at all to do with him or his Statutes, that, as for the attorney General's quoting of foreign Languages, it was now point blank contrary to the Rules of moderen pleadings, and that the Law french and Latin, were now by Statute quite expelled our Courts, and therefore, could not be admitted into Clubs,

[546]

that, as for what the Attorney General Called Dutch, and Syriac, he did not know whether they were so or not, nor would he undertake to determine, but would take upon him to say, that it was highly rude and Improper in him to trowble your honor and the members ‖ with a Sort of I dont-know-what Sort of Balderdash, they did not understand, and finally, as for his Client, he said, as he had before said, that, it did not signify, he was neither Chargeable with Treason, petty treason, or any Sort of treason, and, as for making of Bulls, he left it to his honor and the Club to Judge, whether or not his Client might *Salva Conscientia*,[13] make, manufacture and vend, any Sort of Bulls *whatsomever*, all the world over, excepting only Papal Bulls, which Indeed he could not do, not being pope, and therefore pleaded an Arrest of Judgement.

Mr Attorney Woudbe, having thus got thro' his argument, notwithstanding many Interruptions he met with from Mr Attorney General, who attempted often to dash him in his usual manner, with a loud Laugh, and a Stentorian hollow, his honor the president was pleased to say, that he would determin the matter after Supper, so the Club went to Supper,—which over, his honor resumed the chair & spoke as follows.

"Gentlemen,

I find that Mr Jonathan Grog has been prosecuted in two trespasses, in one prosecution, he is charged with writing and publishing a disrespectful letter to me, here is a Letter which I now produce, as I take it, from him, in manuscript, where he pleads multiplicity of business—It is true, I grant you, that this letter might have been otherwise worded, but be that as it will, it makes some compensation for his Crime, and I am of opinion, it is not so atrocious a one, as Mr Attorney General has Endeavored to represent it, and therefore, I shall pass the milder Judgement upon him, not so much to punish him, as to deterr others from following his bad example, you say, the Gentleman is a Poet, and I think that he me- ‖ rits that title more than any of the other four, and to confirm this, I shall here produce a poem of his, which I think is not to be parallelled on this Continent of America, at least, and really, it is my opinion, that the Gentleman is as bright a Poet, as ever the Sun shone upon, tho' he is not altogether to be excused for his late trespass, and therefore, I shall pass an easie Judgement on him, that is, *that he shall sing his own poem*, but, as I know, that is not so good a musician as Poet, I shall excuse him from the Greatest part of the task, Intending to sing it myself for him to a proper Tune, but he shall stand

---

13. "In good conscience."

by here, and Join in the Chorus—but first, I give the Secretary the Poem to read to you, before it is sung."

The Secretary then Read the Poem as follows.

City of Annapolis Ss:

The Jurors for the City bring,
Before your worships Thomas King,
For buying Cheap a pair of pumps,
For which he's now in doleful dumps,
Confesses that when them he bought,
He ne'er Imagind to do nought,
For that the man, Shafter by name,
From whom 'tis Clear he bought the same,
Did Bring them to his house, and there
He, said Shafter show'd the pair,
And said the pumps did not fit him,
They were too wide, or else too slim,
And he would change them if King pleas'd,
But King not liking to be teizd,
Made him an offer of a Crown,
Instead of Changing, tho' 'tis known,
A pair of Pumps, if good for ought,
Are worth two Crowns as well as groat,
For which King sold them that is Clear,
Nay, his own oath makes it appear,
Now, what said honest Jurors think
Is that said Thomas ought to stink,
For the said King might well Conceive
That Shafter the said pumps did thieve,
Or else so cheap, he would not sell,
And that said King must know full well,
The whole of this, we now submit,
For you to do as you think fit——

[549]

This Poem being read in Club, his honor the president Took the paper in his hand, and Gravely putting on his Spectacles, sung it to an excellent new Tune of his own setting with a proper Chorus, Jonathan Grog Esqr, standing bolt upright by the Chair, to Join his honor in the Chorus according to his Sentence, in which Chorus also, the whole Club Joined in the manner following.

[550]

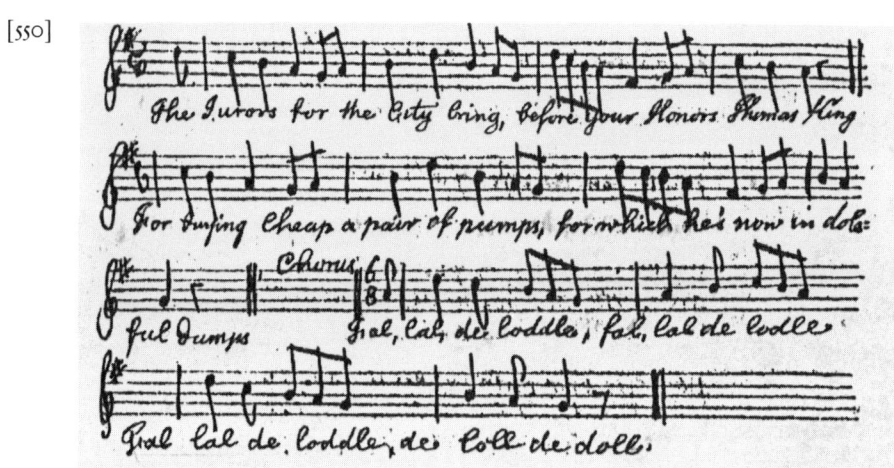

Jonathan Grog Esqr, after singing of this exquisite air, with the President, said he was Glad that he was cleared with honor, the President bid him not be mistaken, for, he was not as yet Cleared, The Club gave a General and Loud Plaudite to the Song, by Clapping of hands and stamping of feet, which made the Room shake, and all the Bowls, glasses and Tobacco pipes dance upon the Table.

Then Jonathan Grog Esqr standing up, said, he hoped the following Sublime Gratulatory pindaric ode, would make full attonement to his honor and the Club, for all past offences,—which ode, being ordered to be read, he Read as follows, (after having been made by his honor, to Correct the word *right* in the Title, which he did, by putting over the Line, its antithesis *wrong*, as it stands in the following transcript.)

[551]   *A Congratulatory Pindaric Ode,*

(wrong)
Addressed to the right Honorable Nasifer Jole Esqr,
President of the ancient and honorable Tuesday Club,
on his having escaped the Cruel Distemper of the Gout,
this Present year, 1755, by, his most obedient,
and very humble Servant,

The Club's Poet Laureat

Descend ye muses from Parnassus hill
And drop Nepenthe⁽ᵃ⁾ in my raptur'd quill,
    High, O high,
  Let my towring genius fly!
And in extatic numbers sing our Joy,
  Not only that Great Jole's alive,
  In Seventeen hundred fifty five,
But now, that Hoary winter fast retreats
And turns his back on Spring's mild genial heats,
    And yet Great Jole is found
    Vigorous brisk and Sound.
  Nor is one precious Joint possess'd
  With that most Curst Tormenting Pest
    The Gout, the Raging Gout,
Kind heaven at last has from his Limbs kept out,
    And we, with Joy again,
    Releasd from racking pain,
  Now see him mount the Chair,
    With firm and vigorous tread
    And Sound Judicious head,
The Club as he was wont, to regulate,
Each Law he dictates, tempers each debate,
Obedience to enforce, he Sagely plies his care.

    Rejoice with me, rejoice,   [552]
    Join with melodious voice,
Ye Jovial Streams, ye mountains hills and rocks,
Ye fertile plains, Ye fountains, rills, ye flocks,
    Ye Sweet and flowery Lawns,
    That when the morning dawns,
  With Orient pearly drops of dew,
  Your odors on the day renew,
    Wipe off your Cristall tears,
    While Sol his head uprears,
    As we shall do this night,
    At the approach of *Candle Light*,
For why? Great Nature's darling, Jole,

(a) A Liquor vastly preferable to Grog, which, according to Homer the father of Poets Laureat, the Immortal Gods Quaffed, when they had a mind to make merry.

With Body Sound, and vig'rous Soul,
Freed from his wonted fierce tormentor,
Dares boldly out a' nights to venture,
And the propitious Gods have heard our prayer,
And Chang'd his humble Couch to lofty Chair.

Ye Satyrs all, and Sylvan Gods,
Come, pipe with us, sing Jovial odes,
Pan, and Apollo, both with Speed,
Come, with your harp and oaten Reed,
  Ye Sheep and oxen too
  With Gentle Bellowings,
  Ye Swains with Hollowings
In Chorus Grand, your Rural Song renew.

Fill the Goblet to the brim,
Jole's now Sound in every Limb,
  Down the toddy,
  Let us swill,
  In a mighty body
  Large enough to drive a mill,
With voice then musical and Shrill
  To the Skies,
  Let us rise,
For our Great President the Gout now flies,
He, like Jove's royal bird his youth renews,
In State again, his ancient Club he views,
  Then with huzzas,
  And loud applause,
Each having drunk, salute we Jole the Great,
And pray he long may Grace that lofty Seat,
  And ever shine
  With rays divine
On his Longstanding members every one,
Who brook no Governor, but him alone.

This Ode met with the Clubs approbation, tho' his honor did not seem much to relish it, as not adapted to that Sort of Sublime that suited his taste, however he folded up the Copy which the Laureat respectfully delivered to him, & put it in his pocket.

Chapter V

Information of Mr Attorney Woudbe, Plea to the Information, Trial of the Attorney General, Historical Sederunt.

There is in many Companies a person of note or distinction, who is Called the *Cock;* That is, a fellow, who either upon account of his Superior rank and Station, to others in the Set, presumes to direct and dictate, or thro' a Conception, of his better understanding and Judgement, prevalent both with himself & the Junto, Ingrosses the whole discourse to himself, argues, confutes, settles and decides all points that are brought upon the Tapis; This mean Spirited mortal, || with whom I have nothing to do here, [554] as unfit to be a member of any Social or Humorous Club, I have been at the pains to define, least he should be mistaken, for a worthy person, I am now going to mention, who is properly called, the *Spirit of the Company;* This Spirit of the Company then, who more or less, gives his attendance in all Clubs and Companies, according to their degree of wit and understanding, is a quite different Character and person from the Cock of the Company; for, as the Soul enlivens the body, and sets the Limbs or members in action, so this useful personage pours life into every member of the Company, and sets them all in high Glee, Gaiety and Laughter, while the other, The Cock, always deadens them, and diffuses among them a Cold torpor or palsey, by Constraining them to listen to his Stupid Speeches, and Impertinent Maxims, and directions, and to give an Implicit assent to all his propositions; The one then is a disease in Company, the other is the vigor and life in it, and without this Spirit, the most Sprightly Companies or Clubs, will sink to the deadness and flatness of Small beer, and either in his absence, or when he neglects to exercise his powers, will be oppressed, as if hagridden, with a Sullen and humdrum humor.

How necessary then, such a person is in all Clubs & Companies, must appear at one view, and I hope, the Transactions of the ancient and honorable Tuesday Club hitherto, have demonstrated, that they were not without such an useful member, in the person of Jonathan Grog Esqr, whose wit and humor has shone, thro' almost the whole of this History, and is || about [555] to shine in a Conspicuous manner in this present Chapter.

The Poet Laureat having read his ode, as above recited, The two attorneys went again tooth and nail to Work, and renewed their Wranglings and Branglings, lifting up with mighty two handed Sway, their ponderous books of precedents, entries and reports, to strike one another In the head, this dispute arose, Concerning an Information brought by Mr Attorney Woudbe, against messrs Neverout, Pleasant and Scribble, which Information being Called for, Mr Attorney General had Clandestinely Secreted it, and would not permit it to be read, at which Mr Attorney Woudbe, was highly Incenced, and Insisted upon its being produced, his honor the President observed, that that prosecution and Information was maliciously brought & set on foot, Mr Attorney Woudbe said, he had brought it, by the express order of his honor the president and Club, and that it was according to Justice and right, to which the attorney General replied that *that right was very wrong,* however, after much altercation, Mr Attorney Woudbe, drew out a Copy of the Information from his bag, and read it as follows.

Information of Mr Attorney Woudbe, City of Annapolis Ss.

[Mr Attor: Woudbe reads]

Be it Remembered, that on this   day of   (I mean Gentlemen, this 25th day of february. We must fill up blanks) in the year of our lord, 1755, Mr Woudbe || Prosecutor, especially appointed, by the honorable Nasifer Jole, President of the ancient and honorable Tuesday Club of Annapolis, cometh into the said Club, at a Sederunt numbered —— (what Sederunt, Mr Secretary?—I hope Gentlemen I shall be allowed to fill up blanks)—

Attorn: Gen: Forbear Mr Secretary, let him go on, he will make but a blank affair of it.

Mr Woud: Please your honor—I must have fair play, else all this is Stuff and signifies nothing—Pray Mr Secretary?—

Secret: It is the 237th Sederunt Sir.

[Mr Woudbe Reads] at a Sederunt, I say, numbered 237 and held at the house of Loquacious Scribble Esqr, in the said City, before the honorable Nasifer Jole, Esqr, President, and his associates, L:Stand: members of the said ancient and honorable Club, and, gives the said Club to understand, and be Informed, that Mr Attorney Neverout, Secretary Scribble, and Slyboots Pleasant Esqr, being members of the said Club, and persons of a *Contancerous*[1] disposition, and not having that due regard for their president, (which they ought to have had,) before their Eyes, but being moved

---

1. *Cantankerous.*

and seduced by their own restless machinations, on a certain day of the Month, called Saturday, lately passed, in the morning of the said day, did by, and of themselves, hold a private Council out of Club time, in which Council, they, the said Attorney Neverout, Secretary Scribble and Slyboots Pleasant Esqr, under pretence of Compliment, did agree and Conspire to Lessen and Indignify, their honorable President Nasifer Jole Esqr, by sending him a disrespectful, dark, mysterious, Intricate and Seditious message, Concerning their having ‖ the honor of eating a fat turkey with his honor that evening, well knowing the Incapacity Inability and Impossibility of Complying with the said Complicated and figurative Message, (supposing it could have been understood,) by means of a disobedient and refractory Servant, That seldom attends his honor, which message, as aforesaid was wrote on a Scandalous Card, Called and known, by the Name of the Knave of Spades, and directed in a plain manner, to Nasifer Jole Esqr, without the word *honorable,* and Caused the same to be delivered by a negroe boy or Girl, which message, Tho dark and figurative, Induced the honorable Nasifer Jole Esqr, (who, by his well known principles of Honor, Generosity, and esteem for all or any of the members of the said Honorable Society) to travel on foot, with great Labor and pains, to the several houses of the said Attorney Neverout, Secretary Scribble & Slyboots Pleasant Esqr, in expectation of being Handsomly treated, but, to his Great Surprize, was disappointed and made a Joke of, all which actings and doings, are Contrary to the well known rules of the said ancient and honorable Tuesday Club, and manifestly tend to pervert, disturb, perplex, and overthrow, the Peace, Happiness, mirth harmony Innocency and diversion, subsisting and Intending to subsist in the said Club, as also to detract, traduce and lessen the honor, power and dignity of the Honorable Nasifer Jole Esqr, and others, the honorable and peaceable members of the said Club,—*Wherefore,* the said Mr Woudbe, as Prosecutor, prays the advice of the Club, here, in the Premises, and that due process may be made against the said Attorney Neverout, Secretary Scribble & Slyboots Pleasant Esqr, to answer of, and upon the Premises &ct: [557]

Spatterdash Woudbe Prosecutor.

Then was read the Plea to the Information as follows.

Plea to the Information [558]

By Messrs Loquacious Scribble, Solo Neverout & Slyboots Pleasant.

And the aforesaid Loquacious, Solo and Slyboots, defend the force and Injury when, and so forth, in their proper persons, Protesting, that the

Information aforesd: is Insufficient in every respect to put them upon their Trial upon the matters therein Contained. For Plea, nevertheless they say, that by the Laws of *this here* ancient Club, it is provided and ordered, that no person what soever, can be, or become a member of the said Club, without the unanimous Consent of the L:Stand: members thereof, and the president thereof, being a L:Stand: member, and also, that no person can, or ought to be, by the Laws aforesaid, attorney General, or attorney of any degree whatsoever, of the said Club, without then and there being a L:Standg: member thereof, and the said Loquacious, Solo and Slyboots, further say, that, altho' the said honorable Nasifer Jole Esqr, be president of the said Club, yet they presume, that he has no power to appoint, his attorney General aforesd: that is to say, the said attorney General, not being a L:St: member, at the time of said appointment, and they further say, that, if the president, and his appointed attor: Genl: aforesd: have such L:Standg: members aforesd: that the same ought to be produced, by which it may appear to the Club, that the said President, and his said attorney have full and ample authority, the one to appoint, and the other to plead, at the bar of this here ancient & honorable Club, whereupon, they may Judge & determine || of Law and right, as they ought, and this they are ready to verify, wherefore, they pray Judgement if they ought to the Information aforesd: any further or other answer to give.

[559]

This plea being read, the Secretary stood up and said That as he was one of the Parties accused in Mr Attorney Woudbe's Information, and, as no Council had been appointed or allowed for the other Gentlemen or Himself, (unless Mr Attorney General thought fit to take up the Cudgells,) he thought he might be allowed, to offer some objections against this Information, in order, if possible to overset it, and these were, that it was set forth in the Information That the aforesd: Gentlemen, held a private council out of Club time,—I beg leave to say Sir, it was no Council, nor could be a council, according to the Laws of this here Club, unless your honor had been present, it might Indeed be called a Committee, but that is nothing to the purpose,—2dly, They, the said Culprits, are said to have met on Saturday morning, and sent a message &ct: whereas it can be made evident, their meeting and writing of the Card was upon Friday night, 3dly that this card was sent by a negroe boy or Girl, whereas it was carried by a full grown negroe man, and lastly that the honorable the President was made a Joke of, by the aforesd: Gentlemen, whereas it is evident, that he, the President vizt: made the Greatest Joke of them by giving them nothing, when they came to his house, but Cold Comfort, and a Glass of Cold water

the Tuesday Club [Book XIV] 353

to the attorney General, therefore, he hoped that the Information would be rejected, as altogether Insufficient.

When the Secretary had done speaking, the attorney General, objected to the whole proceeding, and wondered at the Impudence of Mr Attorney Woudbe, to come into the Club unsent for, with such a foolish Infor- || mation; Mr Attorney Wouldbe, with some heat and passion said That this was but mere Shamming, and that the Attorney General knew as well as his honor, that the Gentlemen had brought him into Club at last Sederunt, and Employed him,—This is only going about the bush, Sir, said Mr Attorney General, and if you prove what I say to be not right—Sir, said Mr Attorney Woudbe, if what you say be not right it is wrong—The President observed, that he thought the plea was a very valid and Sufficient plea, and asked Mr Attorney Woudbe, if he had the Gentlemen's assent to bring in this Information?—May it please your honor, replied Mr Attorney, I had their tacit assent, which I call their Tacit Consent, they said nothing at all against it, but since your honor's Attorney General has been very Learned in his pleadings, and abounded in hard words and outlandish Languages, I must beg leave to return him the said Sauce, and therefore Sir I say, that it is no wonder, I can do nothing in this here Cause, since you all *Conglutinate* together, that is Combine against me, that I am not heard, and what I say turns out as if it was nothing but mere Stuff, which method of proceeding, if your honor suffers to go on, will *Conquassate,* or shake to pieces the constitution of your Club, and, that they should behave towards your honor in this manner, Surprizes me much, who think, that they ought to pay more respect to a person, who has reached, or very nigh reached his Grand Climacteric, and, so Sir—I have done—I protest I have no more to say—The president observed, That he thought he had said a great deal too much,—said the Information was not full enough, ordered a more Compleat one to be brought in, at some Subsequent Sederunt, and also to let the Gentlemen, or parties accused, have a true Copy of it, full eight days before their trial, which was assented to.

[560]

At Sederunt 238, after three weeks adjournment, on account of Balls, assemblies &ct: the Club met at a Taveren for the 5th time, Crinkum Crankum Esqr, being H:S: Mr Attorney General moved, that the prosecutions now in the hands of Mr Attorney Woudbe, should be Immediatly Carried on, or, in case of that Gentleman's non appearance at this Sederunt, be abated, and urged the Great trowble and expence Incurred by prosecutions being keept long depending in this here Club, but his honor the President would give no ear to this motion. Mr Attorney however, urged it again, and again, and dictated an entry to the Secretary, for that purpose

[561]

Interlining and refining this entry with his own accurate pen, which rough entry, his honor ordered to be erazed, & pronounced arbitrarily *ex Cathêdra,* that no such entry, should be made, and, that the prosecutions should not abate, Mr Attorney General, Begged to be Indulged in this matter, The President told him, he had been too much Indulged already, Dr Jaunter observed, that the Gentleman was always for shuffling things off, in a very odd manner—'Tis no Shuffling Sir, said the attorney General, to Insist on being Cleared of a Great trowble, and burdensome Expence, In giving attendance here from Sederunt to Sederunt, only to wait the Leisure and pleasure of Mr Attorney Woudbe, who, since he will not attend, ought to drop those actions against these here other Gentlemen and myself—Sir, said the President, There's a particular action against you, which must be brought on, whether Mr Woudbe attends here to night or not, but I hope he will be here presently,—while this debate was a going on, a Letter came from Mr Attorney Woudbe, to his honor the President, this letter however, his honor did not Communicate to the Club, having been for a great while, for certain political reasons, best known to || himself, very shy of letting the Club peep into his letters, by which the records suffered great Loss, and particularly thro' this Letters' being concealed, which must have contained something extraordinary, being wrote by so exquisite a penman.

Soon after, Mr Attorney Woudbe came into the Club, and, after Supper, preferrd an Indictment against Mr Attorney General, as follows.

Indictment

Tuesday Club Ss:

Solo Neverout, of the City of Annapolis *Sain hawler,* alias, Attorney General of the Tuesday Club, alias Protomusicus for the said Club, stands Indicted by any or all of these names, for that he, the said Solo Neverout, on a day called Saturday, Lately passed, in the year 1755, In the City of Annapolis, with force and arms, one Great Coat, of a dark Colour, with a red velvet Cape, of the value twelve Shillings Current money, the proper Goods and Chatels of the honorable Nasifer Jole Esqr, Then and there being found, then and there, feloniously, tho' before his face (the face of the honble: Nasifer Jole Esqr vizt:) took and Carried away against the peace Good rule, and Society of the said Club.

(vera Copia, except the Parenthesis) *Spatterdash Woudbe prosecutor.*

To this Indictment, Mr Attorney General Refused to plead, because, he said, it was a piece of the most notorious nonsense that ever had been penned, and desired a Copy of it, which, after some wrangling, was at last granted him, and holding it in his hand, he remarked, that there was neither day, date, time or place fixed upon, but only some Stuff, about a day Called Saturday, and then and there.—Pray when and where?—That also, the thing taken away was Called a Great Coat, whereas, being without Sleves, || it was only a Cloak, it was also defined, of a dark Colour, whereas the said Cloak was of a light grey & so forth. Then there arose a prodigious dispute between the two attorneys, and, there was nothing but pulling and hawling, Confused talking and bawling, Mr Attorney Woudbe, attempting to speak said The Culprit was Indicted for stealing a Great Coat,—'Twas no Great Coat Sir, twas a Cloak said the attorney General, besides, as set forth in the Indictment, the trespass is a robbery and not a theft, being, with force and arms, and before his face,—The Secretary was examined as an evidence, he declared, that upon a Certain Saturday in the evening, lately passed, he was at the honorable the presidents house, with Mr Attorney General, in expectation of there eating a fat turkey, that after sitting a Considerable time, the president gave them nothing to eat or drink, only a Tumbler of Cold water was presented to the attorney General, as he was going away, by which being chilled, he covered himself with this Cloak or great Coat, which, he remembers, seemed by Candle light to be of a whitish Colour, tho' much sullied, and almost thread bare, That the attorney General took this Cloak or Great coat without asking the president's leave, and walked home with it—The attorney General denied it was a great coat, the President asserted it was, tho without Sleeves, then arose a learned dispute, about the difference between a Cloak and a great coat, and whether the latter could essentially exist without Sleeves, on this, several witty Sayings were handed about, one said—That the Indictment was a Sleeveless Indictment, another observed That the Attorney General's defence was a Sleeveless defence, and that he went on a Sleeveless errand, when he went to the president's, so, as this Great Coat was Sleeveless, every thing belonging to it was so too; The President was pleased to find the attorney General Guilty, and said he would be merciful to him, in his Sentence, out of regard to his small family, that is, tho he deprived him of his office, he would permit him to enjoy the perquisites—The || attorney General observed, That these perquisites would be hard to find, since he never had found any since he occupied The office,—his Sentence was to kneel down and ask pardon, and restore fourfold—The first part of this Sentence he absolutely refused to comply with, and being puzzled about performing the Latter, Jonathan Grog Esqr, advised him, to fold up the Cloak four fold, and send it back to the president folded in this manner, his honor alittle after stiled

[563]

[564]

him, our Late attorney General, which notified to the Club, that he was degraded.

The Secretary making a formal Speech, about the Impossibility of pleasing all parties, let a man be ever so careful and diligent, and, extolling his own diligence and Care, since he had been Secretary of the Club, in keeping the records, notwithstanding which, he had been often Condemned, for putting into them false Entries, and things merely of his own Invention, in order to vindicate himself for the future, from such a heavy Charge, was resolved to deliver all the original papers of the Club, into his honor's hands, so soon as they were entered upon Record, and approved, that recourse might be had to these original draughts for his vindication, he then delivered a great bundle of papers to his honor, consisting of Indictments, anniversary, and other Speeches, Informations, pleas and poems, which his honor, with his usual Gravity pocketed up.

At Sederunt 239, april 22, 1755, The Club met for the Sixth time at a Taveren, under the High Stewardship of Dr Jeronimo Jaunter.

The Late attorney General made the following short Speech after the Club had sat silent for some time, and the Bowl seemed to stand still, vizt:

"Please your honor Mr President, Sir, you let the bowl stand Sir," upon which the bowl went round, and somebody proposing to drink the king's health, another desired that it might be a Protestant[2] king, and Jonas Green Esqr said it might be the *King* of the protestants, and his majesty King George was properly king of the protestants.

Jonas Green Esqr, upon reading the motto of the Club's badge, *Concordia res parvæ Crescunt,* asked the Secretary, how many Sillables the last word of that motto consisted of, the Secretary, not suspecting a trap, answered, that it was a dissillabical word or had two Sillables, upon which the laureat requested the Secretary to pronounce the last Sillable of that word, with a Clear and Audible voice, the secretary, instead of complying observed, that as engravers would sometimes committ blunders in the orthography of latin words, it would have afforded matter of fun had the engraver of the Club Dye, put a P: for a C, at the beginning of that word, Jonas Green Esqr, remarked, that that mistake would have been Clubical enough, for P: stood for Pun, and C for Conundrum, this introduced a v[er]y facetious conversation, which lasted the whole evening, and on this ac-

---

2. Hamilton died before completing this chapter. The remainder of book XIV (and the conclusion of volume III) apparently would have focused upon momentous events of the club's tenth anniversary. I have provided the final page of the "Record" (p. 550) to complete this chapter. The second volume of minutes (pp. 1–8) includes a fragment of Hamilton's tenth anniversary speech, which I have provided in appendix 6.

co[u]nt we may call this Sederunt the Historical Sederunt, There having been s[e]veral facetious Stories told by Jonas Green Esqr, and the other members, of old women, young women, and love adventures, too numerous to find a place here.

The Secretary observing, that Will: Thornton Esqr, the attorney General was now degraded, his honor replied, that he could not be Sure of that, by which reply, the club is left in doubt about that Gentleman, vizt: whether he is now attorney General or not, however, he falling asleep after Supper, according to usual Custom, his honor was pleased to laugh he[ar]tily, and be much diverted, with the grotesque figure of his countenance.

Entertain'd this night as Strangers, Messrs Danl: Wolstenholme & Lancelot Jacques, pursuant to ancient Custom of this Society.

Requested, that his honor the President serve this Society, upon Tuesday the 13th day of May next ensuing, as H:S: thereof, that day being Intended to be kept, as the Anniversary of this Club.

APPENDIX I

Maryland Gazette, December 17, 1745, 3–4.

For the Benefit of the Public; *An infallible Receipt to cure the afflicting and epidemical Distempers of* Love, *and the* Poetical Itch.

As Christian Charity enjoins and obliges to relieve and assist our Neighbours, in such Calamities and Afflictions as the Frailty of human Nature makes us all in common liable to; I, a Friend to the public Good, and a professed Enemy to secret Broking, such as *Chinese Stones, Chemical Powders,* and the like *Torresian* Mysteries, have benevolently published to the World the following Recipe, which is good and proved, as was lately evidenced, to the great Pleasure and Satisfaction of all good well-meaning Christians, in the Cases of some poor miserable Patients in —— County, who were quite distracted and beside themselves, with the cruel Distempers of Poetry and Love; it has cleared their Brains, enlightened their Understandings, before miserably dark and clouded, so as that in their little Intervals of Sunshine, they could think of nothing but some incoherent Taggs of Ideas, as had neither Sense nor Meaning in them, such as *Swan Necks, Rhetorical Nonsense, Canting Harmony,* and the like inconsistent Similes and Epithets. In and about *A*—— likewise, some unhappy *half finish'd Poets,* thro' the feverish Rage of poetical Fury, having so effectually lost their Sight, as to be quite blind to all the astonishing Charms of the Fair Sex, especially their backward Beauties, which are the most striking, as a smooth musical Poet has lately most melodiously sung; this wonderful Medicine has effectually cured their Blindness, and restored them to their right Senses: In fine, the Virtues and Operations of this Medicine, like the Female Charms

—— *Strike behind as pow'rful as before,*

being both cathartic and emetic, like some late Verses.

The RECEIPT.

Take half a Grain of the South-East and by East Side of the Pith of common Discretion, two Grains of moderate vulgar Sense and Solidity, gathered exactly an Hour and two Minutes before Sunrise, half a Dram of the inside Bark of solid Thought and Reflection, three Drams of common Modesty, half an Ounce of well-timed Diffidence, calcined in the Fire of

Self-Examination, and a Pound of honest Industry and Diligence, in any lawful Calling or Employ you please; beat all stoutly in a Mortar well propp'd with a good Understanding, and when all is reduced to a Powder, give it frequently only to the Quantity of half a Dram for a Dose; taking care all the while it operates, to stop well all the Crevices and Cracks of the Patient's intellectual Chamber, or *Cranium* (to use a Term of Art), lest the poisonous Blast and Air of Ignorance, Self-Conceit, and Idleness, should get Access, and frustrate the Operation of the Medicine: If thus used, it will in a little Time bring the Patient to a good Habit of Mind, so as that he shall neither heedlessly fall in Love at improper Seasons, or in improper Places; for Example, *when hearing a Sermon,* or *while in Church,* or vainly imagine himself a Poet, and fall to making of Verses, when he knows nothing at all of the Matter.

PHILALETHES.

APPENDIX 2

Maryland Gazette, February 4, 1746, 4.

By Theophilus Polypharmacus, M.D. for the public Good.

Nam pulchrum est benefacere Reipublicæ.
SALLUSTIUS.

My good Friend Dr. *Philalethes,* having lately published his *Specific Nostrum* (as he supposes) for the *Furor Poeticus* and *Febris Amatoria,* (I don't mean the *Green Sickness*), I, who am an old and experienced Physician, and without Vanity can boast of as much Benevolence as any of my Brethren of the *Faculty,* have used this *Recipe* again and again, since it's Publication; but I cannot say, with that Success I expected: I must indeed extoll the Humanity and Christian Spirit of my learned Friend, in making public whatever he thought might be of Advantage to the Community; but alas! tho' his Design was noble and praise-worthy, I am loth to say, that it has not turned out so much to the public Benefit, as might have been expected, from the Authority of *so learned a Voucher:* For, instead of making a Cure of these unhappy *demented Poets,* I have found to my great Surprize, that it has increased their *Delirium* to such a furious Height, as to put them beyond all Hopes of Recovery, as I shall presently instance in the Case of one of my *poetical Patients;* and then, for the further Instruction of the *Public,* and my *Brethren* of the *Physical Tribe,* I shall produce another *Recipe,* of my own Invention and Composition, which I have found more effectual, tho' I cannot venture to affirm, that it is a true Specific.

Three Weeks ago, I was called to an unhappy Patient, seized with a deplorable *Furor Poeticus,* and complicated *Febris Amatoria.* After feeling his Pulse, I asked him how long he had laboured under the Distemper; he surpriz'd me with a jingling Reply,

> A well-turn'd Praise requir'd the nicest Skill,
> And he who writes ill-natur'd must write ill.

I blooded him, blister'd his Head, and administred a few Doses of my worthy Friend's Medicine; next Morning I called to see him, and, How dost do (said I), Friend *Bavius*? He stared wildly on me, and broke out into this Couplet,

Then let the Muse her tuneful Numbers raise,
And praise the Beauties for the Sake of Praise.

I gave him a Sternutatory, which operated wonderfully, for he sneezed for half an Hour; I ordered Mr. *Sneak,* his *Apothecary,* to ply him with proper Topics, to translate the Inflammation from the Brain to his Extremities: I visited him in the Evening, as I entered the Room, he exclaimed in a furious Manner to this Purpose,

In every Charm some glorious Goddess place,
But let the Charm the glorious Goddess grace;
Let Venus *hail her for the Wife of* Jove,
And Juno *take her for the* Queen of Love;
Let Pallas, *frowning,* ——

The rest I cannot remember, his Words were so unconnected, and the Sense so jumbled; but I think he raved about summoning all the *Heathen Gods* and *Goddesses* to his Assistance. I applied twelve Cupping-Glasses to his Head, and threw down a large Dose of *Hellebore;* next Morning I found he had evacuated by Stool an incredible Quantity of *Atra-bilis,* which was abominably fœtid: I repeated some Doses, of my Friend's Specific, but to little Purpose; for he sallied out with

M——a *sings, now bid the* Muses *hear,*
Or call Apollo *from the* Chrystal Sphere.

I immediately apprehended a *Calenture,* when he talked of *Chrystal Spheres,* and therefore ordered frequent and copious Injections of Warm Glysters, to make a Derivation from the *Encephalon,* and applied *Sinapisms* to his Soles; next Morning I found his *Delirium* still raging, but the Evacuations, I perceived, had made his Imagination sink from the *Mock-Sublime,* to the real *Bathos;* which gave me some Hopes of his Recovery. He broke out thus,

See lovely R——, *happy,* hapless Maid—
Happy the Man whom this fair Maiden loves;
O happiest he, whom this fair Maid approves!
Great is her Worth, but useless and unknown,
Or useful to her charming self alone.

I was mightily surprized at the Change, and took Notice of this Instance of the *Bathos,* or *Sink in Poetry,* as the most remarkable Example of the Kind, ever I had observed.

After many Trials to no Manner of Purpose, I at last luckily discovered the following Remedy, which I applied with admirable Success; and my Patient is now perfectly recovered.

The RECEIPT.

Take four Lines out of any of *Pope's poetical Works,* six Lines of *Milton's Paradise Lost,* eight Lines of *Garth's Dispensary,* guarded with four Lines of *Butler's Hudibrass;* let the Doctor or Apothecary read these very loud to the Patient, every Time he bursts forth into his Exclamations, in the hearing of some discreet Persons, *Judges of Poetry,* 'til the *Contrast* produces a Laugh in the Company: When the Patient's raving Nonsense, and the true Sublime of these *great Wits,* have been sufficiently prepared, and their Parts broke and blended together, by the Gelastic Conquassation of the Air, put them into a large bellied long-necked Matrass, and there will arise a most furious Fermentation, from the *Antipathy* and heterogene Nature of the Ingredients; when this ceases, it will produce a *Neutrum quid,* or a Substance neither saturated with the *Salt of good Sense,* nor flattened with the *Phlegm of Nonsense.* Infuse for two Days in Balneo Vaporis, taking for your *Menstruum* a Quart of pure Water of *Helicon;* filtre and bottle it up for Use. The Dose is a Gill every Morning upon an empty Stomach.

APPENDIX 3

Maryland Gazette, March 18, 1746, 4.

*******,**th. 1745, 6.

Ran away from the Subscriber, and left nothing behind him but his Senses, a *dapper-witted, finical Fopling,* known by the Name of *Bard,* alias *Bavius,* he wore, when he went away, *a string of Bells,* which make a hideous jingling, and discordant noise, his Speech is frothy and incoherent, inclining more to *Rhime* than *Reason,* he talks much of the *Ladies,* whom he stiles *Belles* and pretending to aim at *Praise,* he unhappily slides into *Satyr,* he deals much in insignificant Rhimes, being far gone in the *poetical Itch,* for which the ingenious Doctor *Polypharmacus* lately had him in the *powdering Tub:* His Performances are little understood by any body, least of all by himself, not upon Account of sublimity of Stile, and fine Sentiments, but rather a dark indefinite Expression, and a motly Rabble of confus'd Ideas, and unnatural Comparisons and Allusions; He may, therefore, probably have sundry things about him, such as *Bundles of Papers,* scribbled over with *poetical Trumpery,* and Conceits of his own Composition, so monsterously form'd and void of Sense, as to be utterly unintelligible. Among these Papers, there is a deal of Rubbish and Lumber, which is all his own; but what is good, if any such you find, is purloin'd and stolen from others, and therefore must be return'd to *Pope* and *Prior* their right Owners. The Flowers of his Poetry are gathered from the *Dunghill,* the *Kennel,* or the *little House,* and his *Prose* is exactly to the Tune of *Billingsgate Declamations.* In a word, to relish his Compositions 'tis absolutely necessary for one to have been very much conversant with Scoundrels, as is evident from his late *dirty Epistle* to the *City of A———.* I cannot give any Account of his *Parentage* and *Country,* and despair of ever being able to succeed in such an Attempt, considering what some intelligent Persons have lately advanced, that he never had any *Ancestors,* because he is universally acknowledged to be an *Original.* He pretends to some Knowledge in Poesie, tho' in that he cannot rival an Old Woman: His Discourse is entirely *excrementitious,* and he throws out his *Sarcasms,* as a *Scavenger* would do *Tubs of Sir-Reverence,* for his whole Talk and especially his Compositions turn upon *B-sh-tt-ng* and being *B-sh-t,* treading upon a *T—d,* pulling it out of his own Bosom and *dropping it into a Lady's, eating and chewing it as one would do a Sugar Plumb.* He is a nasty Fellow, for the *Sphincter Ani,* or *Bum Muscle,* in him being preternaturally relaxed, he is very apt to bewray himself in Company, and being somewhat foolish, is insensible of his Misbehaviour, and lays all the blame upon others. He seldom is heard to praise any Person but himself, his whole Drift is Defamation and Censure, and that frequently convey'd under the sham Name of *Panegyrick,* to which he is a mighty Pretender. He is very apt to condemn, upon Hear-say, Performances he never saw, and even if he sees them, his Criticism is void of Judgment, for he Censures as much for the sake of Censure, as he *praises for the sake of Praise.* He is noted for his irreconcilable hatred to the *Presbyterians,* whom upon every occasion he shews the strongest disposition to persecute, tho' himself may be, for ought I know, a *Muggletonian.*

If he is known by these Marks, and brought to the Subscriber by any Person who goes upon the *chace* after him, such Person or Persons apprehending him, because it is a difficult matter so to do, shall have, as a *Reward,* all the Profits arising from his *Poems,* made over to him and his, or them and their Heirs, for One hundred Years to come, besides what the Law allows in such Cases, by

JEHOIAKIM JERKUM.

APPENDIX 4

Maryland Gazette, July–November 1751.

[July 3, 1751]. Late last Night, one of the most audacious Robberies was attempted in Town, which perhaps has been heard of in this Part of the World: Two Men Arm'd, went to the House of Mr. *Charles Cole,* of this Place, Merchant, and having placed a Ladder up to a Dormant Window, one of them ascended and got into the Room where Mr. *Cole* lay, and having a dark Lanthorn and a Pistol, presented the Pistol at Mr. *Cole,* and told him if he offer'd to stir or make a Noise he would immediately blow his Brains out, then fell on him and tied him, and gave him several Bruises, telling him, his Money he wanted, and that he would have; his Accomplice was left below, to give notice in case of any Assistance; but Mr. *Cole's* Man *John,* who lay in a House close Adjoining, hearing some Noise, look'd out, when the Man below told him if he offer'd to stir or make any Noise he would shoot him Dead; but *John* fetch'd a loaded Piece and fired out the Window at him, but missed him, on which he fired a Piece at *John,* loaded with Slugs, which narrowly missed him, but happily did no harm: This alarm'd the Man in the Chamber with Mr. *Cole,* and he made off out of the Window, leaving Mr. *Cole* bound in Bed, and, with his Accomplice, got off before any help came; and are as yet undiscovered.

[July 10, 1751 (repeated for several weeks)]. Whereas a most wicked, violent and audacious Crime was committed in the Night of the 2d Instant, by breaking open the House of Mr. *Charles Cole* of this City, binding and threatening him in his Bed with the Loss of Life, unless he would discover or deliver his Money; and altho' the Persons concerned were frightened from putting their more execrable Designs in Execution, and afterwards made their Escape, yet as the Lives and Property of every Individual can only be preserved from such Villainies by the Discovery and Punishment of the Offenders: Therefore, for the better discovery of the Actors of the said Villainy, I do hereby Promise to pay, to any Person or Persons who shall discover them, or any of them, upon his or their Conviction, the Sum of Eighty Pounds Current Money; and that in Case any of the Accomplices (other than the Person who broke into Mr. *Cole's* Room) shall discover the other Offenders, or any of them, that upon his or their Conviction, the

Accomplice making such Discovery, shall have the same Reward; and I am impowered by his Excellency the Governor, to assure him of a Pardon.

D[aniel] Dulany.
[probably the elder]

[July 17, 1751]. We have been infested in this Town and Neighbourhood for some Time past, with a Parcel of Thieves and Robbers, but from whence they come, or who they are, cannot yet be found out, altho' we have strong Suspicions. Almost every Day, since the Attempt made at Mr. *Cole*'s, has brought a fresh Account of some new Villainy either attempted or perpetrated; but we must make Allowance for Exaggeration: However, it is certain, that on Friday last, near *South* River, a Gentleman of this Town was stopp'd by two Men well mounted and arm'd, who forced him out of the Road and wou'd have robb'd him, but as he happen'd to have no Money about him, they, after many Threats, let him go. Another Gentleman escaped them by the Swiftness of his Horse. They have robb'd several Negroes of Things they were bringing to Market; and have done so many Villainies that the travelling the Road, except in Companies and with Arms, seems unsafe, and People are afraid of coming to Market. Several Companies have gone out at sundry Times, with Fire Arms and Dogs, to search for them in the almost impenetrable Fields of Pines near the Town; but without Success: And it is fear'd they are now grown more formidable, having stole sundry good Horses, and are (if we can believe Reports) four or five in Number. One Night three of them had the Impudence to ride almost up to the Town Gate and hang their Horses, when one of the Watchmen, (for we have a constant strong Watch kept every Night) stept up to him, and would have taken him; but observing another of them stoop, as he apprehended to fire at him, presented his Pistol, but it miss'd fire, on which the Rogues made off with great Precipitation before any more of the Watch could come to him, and left one of their Horses, which they took and brought into Town. Some Gentlemen in Town have published an Advertisement offering Forty Pistoles for the apprehending of them.

The two Men, so often mentioned in this Paper, who went by the Names of *Newton* and *Jones,* and who murdered the Master and Mate of a Vessel which came into *St. Mary's* some Time ago, are arrived from *Boston,* and confined in *St. Mary's* County Goal, in order for their Trial, either at a Special Court to be appointed for that Purpose, or at the Provincial Court. [These were not the same men who tried to rob Cole, but their contributing to the rash of robberies that had apparently broken out in Annapolis surely influenced the punishment heaped upon Cole's robbers.]

[Aug. 14, 1751]. Last Friday was brought to Town, one *John Conner,* a Convict Servant belonging to a Gentleman at *Elk Ridge,* who was carried before a Magistrate, where he made a free and full Confession, That he, and one *Thomas Bevan,* were the Persons who made the Attempt to rob Mr. *Cole* in the Night of the 2d of *July* last, that *Bevan* went into Mr. *Cole*'s Bedchamber and bound him, and he the said *Conner* tarried below to keep Watch, and when Mr. *Cole*'s Man fired at him, return'd the Fire which gave the Alarm, on which *Bevan* jump'd out of the Window, and they both made off together, and continued some Time lurking about in the Pines, robbing sundry People: After which they made away towards *Manoccosy,* where the Country was soon alarm'd, and the Woods very diligently search'd, and they narrowly escaped being taken; they finding that the People thereabouts were so industrious in searching after them, that it was impossible to get off that way, *Conner* return'd back to his Master, and was brought to Town and made the above Confession, on which he was committed to Goal. And *Bevan* not knowing his Companion had impeach'd him, coming to Town on Saturday Night, in hopes of being carried away by Water, went arm'd to his Master, and telling him he would not have him lose by him, but should be glad to be sold out of the Country, was prevail'd on to be secreted in a Cellar, where he was surprized and taken on Sunday Morning, by several People who went in with loaded Pistols, and he is now in our Goal, strongly Iron'd and chain'd to the Floor.

[Nov. 6, 1751]. On Friday last *Thomas Bavin* was executed at the Gallows, just without the City Gate, for breaking into the House of Mr. *Charles Cole,* of this Place, Merchant, on the Night of the 2d of *July* last, and binding him in his Bed, while his Accomplice waited without to keep watch. He was a likely young Man, who had a pretty good Education, and was a very ingenious Mechanic, who might have been very useful to himself and the Community, had he but bent his Mind to Honesty; but for some Fault committed in *England,* he was transported into this Province, where instead of reforming, he committed sundry Crimes, before this last for which he suffer'd. After he was cast for his Life, he applied himself to reading good Books, and was visited in Prison by several Divines to assist him in the work of Preparation. As he rode to the Gallows, he scarce ever once look'd round him, but kept reading all the Way, and when he came there he prayed with seeming Fervour, in Terms well adapted to his Situation, for near half an Hour, when he stood up and spoke to the Spectators, advising them to take Warning by his untimely and shameful End, and to lead quiet and peaceable Lives; and after recommending his Soul to the Divine Mercy, he was turn'd off into that State where we must leave him.

APPENDIX 5

Maryland Gazette, May 3, 1753, 1.

Having lately entertained the Public with the Speech of Lawyer BRIEF, and other Matters of the like trifling Nature; lest those scurvy Specimens of Wit, should incline the Readers, in Part, to believe, what a CIVIL, GOOD NATURED Gentleman lately asserted in a public Declamation, That this [here] News Paper was a common Conveyancer of NONSENSE, Scandal, and Falshood; we shall present them with the following short Essay on IMPUDENCE, which it is to be hoped, will be reckoned tolerable Sense, especially as therein is carefully avoided, dull Prolixity, tedious Repetitions, needless Tautology, pitiful Quibbles, and false Arguments, and there is introduced nothing foreign to the Subject; and above all, there is Care taken to avoid particular Observations and personal Reflections, injurious to an unoffending Neighbour: Happy were it for them, if all Authors and public Declaimers would observe this excellent Rule, since it would not only preserve Peace and Harmony between Man and Man, but add a greater Dignity, and procure more Credit, to their Writings and Harangues.

IMPUDENCE is a Quality of such Force and Influence in the World, that the ancient Pagans, whose Superstition often led them to deify *Passions* and *Qualities,* made a Goddess of it. This is confirmed by a Passage to be met with in one of their Theatrical Pieces, where there is an Address to *Impudence* in these Terms; "O *Impudence!* Thou greatest of the Goddesses (if it be lawful to call thee a Goddess), for sure thou art one, since, as the World goes now, whatever has Power is worshipped as a Deity."—This ancient Exclamation shews, that *Impudence* was as much in Vogue, had as great Power and Influence, and was preached to as great Advantage, two thousand Years ago, as it is now in our Days.

This of *Impudence* has been reckon'd a profitable Quality to most of it's Possessors; and in Effect it has brought considerable Gains to such as have been furnished with a *sufficient Stock* of it, and understood how to parcel it out to the best Advantage, and on proper and apposite Occasions: Many Setters out in the World, *without one distinguishing Quality besides,* have been solely indebted to it for the Increase and Rise of their Fortune: But it must be observed, that a Stock of this, must be managed with as much Prudence and Care, as a mercantile Stock, before any considerable Gains can be reaped from it; barefaced Impudence and Effrontery will seldom succeed, but among Fools and Dupes, and unless the Vender spices it with a little knavish Cunning and Artifice, it will recoil upon him to his own Hurt. It is therefore necessary, that one who is possessed of this profitable Quality, and would make it turn out to his Advantage, should be acquainted with the Foibles of Mankind, and with their prevailing Passions; he must, before he begins to act the Farce, know what Sort of Persons he is to deal with; whether they be ignorant, or knowing; dull, or sprightly; moderate cool Men, or hot headed Enthusiasts: If he is so qualified, he may ingratiate himself with the Great, by gross Flattery, and a servile obsequious Importunity and Intrusion; with the Ignorant, who set up for Admirers of Learning, and are more taken up with *Sound* than *Sense,* he may raise his Character by Pedantry and Positiveness; and if he talks unintelligibly, *with a good Front,* he will always be applauded and thought in the Right, whether he is so or not; he may pass for a holy Saint among the giddy Populace, if he can screw up his Face, and throw as much Sanctity into it as possible, express himself in a whining Tone, and abstain from all Appearance of Mirth and Gaiety; he may make a Figure at the Bar by Vociferation, Noise, and Multiplicity of Words, and an undaunted and invincible Front and Assurance, which nothing can dash or *put to the Blush;* he may be a learned Physician, without a Grain of either Mother Wit or College Education, by the Help of a solemn Face and Carriage, a voluminous Wig, a black Coat, and a Cane: He may make a Figure in Assemblies of Men of Rank and Fashion, by humouring their Pleasures and Taste of Conversation, however trifling, by laughing when they laugh, exclaiming when they exclaim, and jumping in with them in all their Opinions and Humours, however true or false, just or unjust, or however discrepant to his own Notions of Things. Thus we may daily observe, how a Person possessed of this Quality of *Impudence,* and using it like a true Artist, may advance himself, tho' he possesses not one single good Quality to recommend him.

We find *Impudence* sometimes assuming the Comic Dress, that is, when her Votaries place their whole Ambition in dizening themselves up in whimsical and fantastic Garbs, out doing even the most extravagant Humours of the Mode, to appear in public Places in order to be taken Notice of, to give and receive Salutations, Bows, and foppish Cringes, to seem very familiar with great Men, and prime Favourites with Ladies of Rank and Condition: This Sort of *Impudence* is peculiar to an insignificant Set of Mortals called Fops; and I think in this Instance only, *Impudence* is a harmless and trifling Quality; and as it goes no further than a vain Fool's having a better Opinion of himself than he ought, it is only laughed at, and there is an End of it.

But when the Force of this Qualification is applied to some serious Scenes of Life, it becomes more pernicious: An itinerant Quack, for Example, under the Notion of great Proficiency and Skill in the Healing Art, by talking of his miraculous Cures, of unheard of Distempers, of Kings, Emperors, and Princes, who have consulted him, and by a Rhapsody of hard Words and Bombast altogether unintelligible, will cajole and deceive the silly Populace in such a Manner, as that they shall suffer themselves to be poisoned by him: An empty scull'd Fop, with a Song, a Dance, and some common place Speeches, extracted from Plays and Romances, delivered with an affected, tender, and languishing Air, will prove too strong a Foe for the Virtue of a simple Maid to stand against: A lying Parasite will thrust himself into Favour and Places of Trust at Court; and a pettifogging Lawyer, with steel'd Effrontery, Vociferation, Quibbling, and vapid Harangues, will sometimes mislead the Judgment and Understanding of honest Judges and Jurymen, will confound all Reasoning and Argument, establish Iniquity for Justice, Error for Truth, screen the Rogue, and prosecute honest Men: In fine, he that has *Impudence* enough (be his Profession or Calling what it will), to show himself, with a steady Air and unchangeable Countenance, a good for nothing trifling Fellow, to wise and discerning Men, will nevertheless, with the Multitude, reap as much Advantage as if he were Master of all Arts and Sciences, and will go farther in his own Service, than if he really possessed them all encumbered with Modesty.

This bustling Vice of *Impudence* often takes the Place of Virtue, Integrity, and Honour, and under the Mask or Disguise of these moral Excellencies, opposes and brow beats them wherever it meets them; and it's most triumphant Atchievement is, when it's Votaries gain a Point without being ashamed of the indirect or ill Means by which they attained it.

APPENDIX 6

Minutes of the Tuesday Club, vol. II,
Peter Force Collection, Series 8D, Item 170,
Library of Congress, pp. 1–8.

Sederunt 240
Tuesday May 27th 1755

ANNIVERSARY X.

The honorable the president, this evening, Celebrated The Anniversary of the Club, at his house in North East Street, in the usual Grand and magnificent manner, where were

Present

The hon: Charles Cole Esqr Pres: & H:S:

Willm: Thornton Esqr, Att: G: ⎫   ⎧ Walter Dulany Esqr
Jonas Green Esqr, P:L:M:C: ⎬   ⎨ Wm: Lux Esqr:
Dr Upton Scot   ⎭   ⎩ Thomas Craddoc Esqr H:M:

After Supper, which consisted of many exquisite dishes, & served in a very Elegant manner, as usual, The Secretary being absent, William Thornton Esqr, attorney General, was appointed by his honor and the Club To deliver the anniversary Speech, To which arduous & Important task, he properly prepared himself, by first rising from his Seat with his usual Solemn and grave air, and having put himself into a proper attitude and posture, and cleared his pipes, by alittle heming and Spitting, he begun to deliver his oration in the following manner and form.

Anniversary Speech

Honorable Sir,

Tho the making of speeches, with elegance and propriety of action & expression, be a task as arduous and difficult, as any within the compass of human ingenuity, yet, I know not any one exercise of wit, that has more pretenders than this.

A few indeed, in other matters, will mistake their natural genius, and set up for poets, musicians, painters, punsters, boxers, fencers, dancers & so forth, and yet all the while, know nothing of the matters pretended to.

But all degrees of men, from the king in his parliamentary robes, to the beggar in Sordid rags on the high way, or the haltered rogue under the triple tree at Tyburn, Lay Claim to some Skill in oratory or speech making, and, in their own Judgement, perhaps, think they equal Cicero or Demosthenes, or some Spokesmen as great, in case they never may have heard of these great men.

This *cacoethes,* as I may call it of Speech making prevails no where more than in clubs, for, in all degrees of these nocturnal assemblies, we shall find many of their members fond of hearing themselves talk, and eager to display their parts and abilities to their fellows.

And in this here Club in particular, this humor has prevailed since it's first institution till now, and I my self have acted a principal part in this exercise of wit, nor Indeed has your honor stood altogether among the mutes of the Drama, but the eloquence of the honorable chair has at times broke out and Surpriz'd us.

But, as to the elegance and propriety of these Club Speeches, it is none of my business here to remark upon it, that being a thing which the world will Judge of as they please, whatever one or more of our members may think, or express concerning it.

However, I cannot help making this observation, with regard to myself, and I hope, without the least Imputation of vanity, that my abilities this way, I mean, Sir, in the way of oratory, or Speech making, must Surely rise alittle above the common pitch, else I cannot comprehend, why so many persons of Judgement and discernment, as the longstanding members of this ancient Club undoubtedly are, should, with an unanimous Choice, have appointed me their orator, and committed into my hands the honorable Charge, of being the mouth of their Society.

And yet, this flattering notion vanishes Into Smoke, when I consider, that their proceeding in this affair, might have been Intirely *Clubical,*—I say *Clubical,*—which I understand, has now become a cant word out of doors, for any procedure that is ridiculous.

And what is apt to confirm me in this notion, is, that this here Club once on a time, I hope not yet out of the memory of some here, pitched upon a certain person for their orator, to whom it was naturally a pain to speak above three words in an hour, and, whose favorite Phraze was, put about the bowl.

If this Indeed be the case, that your honor and the longstanding members, perceived something out of the way, ridiculous, or rather Clubical in me, which qualified me, in your opinion, for an orator of this Sort, I must own, I cannot but have a poor opinion of my abilities in elocution and oratory.

But I say no more on this head, you are conscious to yourselves in what light you view me, which, be it ridiculous, or Clubical, or what you please, I must beg leave to go on in my ancient way, and molest your ears alittle with an oration, adapted to this here occasion of the Anniversary.

It is recorded, honorable Sir, of Parysatis, the Empress of Persia, that she commanded the Courtiers, when they spoke to her Son Cyrus, to interweave their words with crimson Silk, which figurative way of Speaking, much practised in the east, even at this day, Imports neither more nor less, than that their speeches, when addressed to that prince, should be framed in a polite nitid Stile, and abound with lively, fiery and Striking expression, as Crimson Silk in it's texture is Smooth and Shining, and, in its Complexion or color, lively and Showy.

But whatever might be the opinion of that ancient princess, with regard to her Son Cyrus, the darling of her Soul, I must own, I differ alittle, and but very little in Sentiment from her, with regard to your honor, the darling and minion of this ancient and honorable Club.

And therefore boldly declare, that the Speeches directed to your honor, especially anniversary Speeches, ought to be Interwoven, or rather altogether framed of Crimson velvet, which is Shining, lively, soft, and of so pliant and tractable a nature that you may stroke it in any direction and feall the same glabricity, the Complaisant pile of the Stuff, yielding alike every way to the hand.

I shall therefore, frame this, my tenth anniversary Speech, which I am now to deliver to your honor, intirely of crimson velvet, that is, in a smooth, easie and pliant Stile, not in the Bombast, which may rather be called a Stuff like Bombazeen, which, tho often Showy enough, yet feels somewhat rough and stiff.

As to that part of my Speech which regards your honor, I shall not dwell long upon it, being thorroly satisfied, that I have already wore out your honor's patience and the Club's, with panegyrics and loads of encomium upon that particular point in my former Speeches.

Your honor will therefore excuse me, if I Insist not at this time upon all your perfections as a president, waving the gracefulness and grandure of your person, the affability and Comliness of your countenance, the Sharpness and poignancy of your wit, and the depth and profundity of your wisdom.

Permit me only to say, that your honor is the animating power, or principle of this Club, or, to speak in the Stile of the Platonists, the $\tau o \ \pi \alpha \nu$ of our Society, the very essence and constitution of it, the Clubical body politic, to the Clubical members, the head and regulator uncontroulable, the modeller, fashioner and Sole Lawgiver.

And the Confidence which our longstanding members place in your honor, appears in this one single Instance, that they now quietly permit your honor to make new laws for them and manage their old laws, as that Civil and hospitable Gentleman, Procrustes did those guests of his whom he laid in his bed, that is, if they were too short for this couch of his, he streched out their limbs with an engine to a proper length, and, if too long, he loped off their legs or feet with a hatchet.

Thus your honor has done of late with the laws of our Club, adding, or rather streeching, where they are deficient, and lopping where there is too much, according to your wise arbitriment, which is a glaring Instance of the Confidence the Club puts in your honor, and of the high opinion which they entertain of your wisdom and Sagacity.

I come now to say something of the Club, nor shall I Insist long upon this topic, having also largely discussed it in my former Speeches.

And tho I have not said all that might be said upon so Copious a Subject, yet, I believe, it will be granted that I have said all that is necessary.

We know in what State our Club now is, the Champion and Chancellor have both left us, who were supposed to be principal Supporters of the Chair, while in the Society, at least, this was the opinion of the Club.

But, as your honor and the Club often differ in opinion, we find, that tho' these great officers are gone, and your honor has refused to create new ones in their place, yet the Club has suffered no otherwise by their departure, but the bare deminution of their number of members.

This demonstrates plainly, that your honor conceived more Justly of this matter than the Club, which we must Surely grant to be the case in other matters.

But as no Society can stand without props of some Sort or other, permit me to say somewhat, concerning those persons, whom I esteem to be it's principal Supporters, under your honor, who are the head and main body of our fabric.

This Society then, honorable Sir, I humbly conceive, stands upon three legs, these propugnacula are the Poet, the musician and the Orator, and this clubical Tripod or Supporter I shall take the liberty to insist alittle upon, as the Subject is worthy consideration.

And therefore, taking the poet and musician, as the two extremes and myself as the mean, I shall first draw a parallel between the poet and myself, then say something of the musician and myself, and Conclude with some Critical observations on my own performances as an Orator.

And, I hope, tho' I shall here have occasion to talk a great deal concerning myself, you will not charge me with egotism.

Poets and Orators have been classed with the favorite Sons of fame, and it has been matter of doubt, to which of these the preference should be given.

Tyrteus rescued the State of Sparta from Imminent ruin by his poetry, and, had the Athenians been wise, the oratory of Demosthenes, would have frustrated all the artifices of the Macedonian Philip, which afterwards proved the Ruin of that republic.

Many more Instances could I give, of great public Services done by poets and orators, and also, of the figure they have made in Clubs, but none to excell the now living Instance of our ancient and honorable Tuesday Club, where the Sublime poetry of our poet Laureat, and the exquisite Oratory of our Orator, are now two of the main Supporters of this ancient Club, and it's honorable president, by transmitting their Renown to future ages in prose and verse.

It perhaps may be a matter of doubt with you, which of these two geniuses to prefer, but, I hope, that doubt will be removed, when you consider, that one thing recommends poetry beyond Rhetoric or Oratory, vizt: that it is adapted only to the finest and most exquisite Judgements, whereas, he is the best orator that pleases the *Prophanum Vulgus,* as witness, the pious, Ingenious and Reverend Mr George Whitefield, who captivates both the great and the small mobile wherever he goes.

That poetry on the other hand would be but poor that all should approve. Should the learned and Ingenious give the Plaudite, it is Sufficient to fix the Bays upon the Bard's pate, and let the unthinking throng bray like so many asses, they cannot hurt him.

This, I think is the unerring criterion, to distinguish good poetry from bad, or Indifferent, and the Clubical performances of our Laureat have always stood this test, meeting but with few approvers, and those of the most Clubical Judgement, for the Chief of these approvers, are members of this ancient Club, who, I must own, have been Induced to Judge differently from the world with regard to our poet's performances, beholding them with milder eyes than the public did when they went abroad, being willing to wink at many inaccuracies and oversights, which that Ingenious gentleman, from too great a rapidity of Imagination is apt to fall into, which could not escape the nice and Judicious eyes of the Critics.

And therefore it is, that these latter gentlemen are never disposed to spare our Laureat whenever they find him tripping, but call out with great vehemence, when reading any of his Club Compositions, o horrid! abominable! Sad Stuff! poor, mean, Low, pish! tis Intollerable, and other such Exclamatory Phrazes, Commonly used by critics.

But our Laureat prudently Chuses to proceed in his own way, not regarding their Emmendations and annotations and Indeed, should he suffer his pieces to undergo an alteration, according to the Sentiments of these refined Gentlemen, it is the opinion of many Judicious persons, that they would thereby suffer as much in their clubical turn and humor, as the works of the celebrated Shakespear have suffered in their natural Sublime, elegance and beautiful Simplicity, by being too much bethum'd and beslubbered, by the Critics of the Succeeding age.

From these premises, we may safely conclude, that this here Ingenious Laureat is an excellent Club poet, and takes place of the orator in point of profession, Tho, to give the orator his due, his performances are truely Clubical, and pritty well adapted to his Subject.

We come now to the musician, whom I shall Consider as a Musician only, and not as an attorney General, it being uncertain whether he now holds that place, but granting he did, the other Claims that preference, as being the more ancient office in the Club.

Music is an art, which has been applauded or Condemned, according to men's different humors and fancies, for my part I think that, Considered simply by itself, it is neither good nor bad but becomes so according to the uses to which it is applied.

Diogenes and Plato, among the old Philosophers, conceived different notions of it, the first as a Cynic, told a man, who bragged of his Skill in that Art, that Cities and States were governed by wisdom but, that a small family could not be kept in order by fiddling & Singing. The other as an academic, the principles of whose philosophy were more Generous and enlarged, (tho he banished the art from his Philosophical commonwealth,) compares the Symmetry and order of the heavenly Spheres, to music, harmony, a Chorus and a dance and the comparison in the opinion of many, is hig[h]ly Just & elegant, and, the same divine Philosopher says somewhere in his writings, Αρμονια μεν γαρ και ςυμφονια και αριθμος εν πλειοσιν εγγιγνεσθαι πεφυκεν.

Our Moderen Italians are so bigotted to the excellency of this art, that it is a maxim among them, That whoever loves not music is not beloved of God.

The Hebrews of old used music in their divine worship, as we find, by the Stories transmitted to us, of king David and his harp, which had the power of Charming the evil Spirit out of Saul.

The Greeks used it in war, and we find an Instance of the Spartans being fond of it for that purpose but they were for confining it to a certain compass, and therefore Imposed a fine upon Terpander, and nailed his harp to a post, for adding one string to the number before used.

By Orpheus' music is understood, the establishment of politeness, peace and morality among men, for, by the powers of his music, he Civilized the Satyrs, who were properly the unpolished part of the human Species, which ranged the forrest, with their kindred brutes, and it is Certain, we are told in the Sacred Archives, that Alleluias and Celestial hymns were sung in heaven.

Yet notwithstanding all these great authorities in favor of music, many heroes and Great men, have esteemed it a triffling and Scandalous Science. Philip of Macedon asked his Son Alexander, if he was not ashamed of his singing so well?

Themistocles being asked, if he could play on the harp, said he knew not, he had never tried, but that he knew very well how to plan a battle or storm a town, these being arts he was well practised in.

Sallust, the Roman Historian, speaking of the qualifications of a Courtezan says, that she did *Psallere et Saltare elegantius, quam necesse est probae.*

Yet, Certain it is, notwithstanding the Contempt with which many have treated this elegant art and it's professors, (a fiddler, now a days being looked upon with Scorn, as having squandered much time in acquiring a triffling accomplishment,) that some of the wisest and gravest men have been captivated with it.

Stratonice with a Song entrapped Mithridates to her lure, and held him as fast as a bird in a Snare, and, tho your honor and the Longstanding members of this club, have the Character of wise, Judicious, Grave and great men, yet have you been captivated to a great degree by the musical performances of Signior Lardini, Musician *Con Stromenti* to the Club, so as to show the greatest Signs of rapture and extacy when that Artist performs on his fiddle, the music of the Anniversary Ode and Songs of the Club, and also, when Mr Protomusicus in the execution of his office *Con voce,* has warbled forth Captivating Strains.

And, above all, the Club has been extravagantly charmed, when your honor has Chanted Captivating melodys from the Chair, particularly in the late ravishing Song of Thomas King and the Pumps.

But from all this, I must not presume to conclude, That the members of this here Club are Platonists, or of the. . . .

PUNCTUATION CHANGES

The page numbers below refer to the bracketed numerals in the margins of this edition, which record the pagination of Hamilton's manuscript. Occasionally I have had to refer instead to the page numbers of this edition (for example, for sections of Hamilton's manuscript that are not paginated, such as his table of contents); those cases are indicated by asterisks. The material before the bracket shows the text as I have emended it; the material following the bracket reproduces Hamilton's manuscript. The swung dash used after the bracket stands for a word that adjoins a punctuation mark. The inferior caret, also used only after the bracket, signifies the location of punctuation that does not appear in the manuscript but that I have added.

Volume I

Page.Line

		Page.Line	
i.20	ones,] ~ ^	19.6	Ibrahim,] ~ ^
ii.2	falshood,] ~ ^	19.16	families] ~,
ii.15	Liars,] ~ ^	20.11	post,] ~ ^
iii.2	Swine,] ~ ^	21.2	alone,] ~ ^
iii.22	live,] ~ ^	21.11	Lamb,] ~ ^
iv.21	eating,] ~ ^	22.13	they,] ~ ^
vi.1	fit,] ~ ^	23.9	antiquity,] ~ ^
vi.3	eloquence,] ~ ^	26.7	resolve,] ~ ^
viii.15	horse,] ~ ^	27.23	Spirit,] ~ ^
viii.15	fiddle,] ~ ^	28.15	catches,] ~ ^
viii.15	horn,] ~ ^	30.17	Nod,] ~ ^
ix.16	Ideas,] ~ ^	32.11	things,] ~ ^
xi.10	history,] ~ ^	33.19	Physic,] ~ ^
xa.6	account] ~,	34.16	*Dux*,] ~ ^
xa.19	farces,] ~ ^	35.7	disputes,] ~ ^
xii.5	picture,] ~ ^	39.13	blood,] ~.
xii.21	armies,] ~ ^	39.17	complexion,] ~ ^
xiii.19	Clubs,] ~ ^	39.24	tower,] ~ ^
1.10	Historians,] ~ ^	44.20	drink,] ~ ^
7.14	Charity,] ~ ^	46.8	dews,] ~ ^
7.14	Humanity,] ~ ^	46.21	poet,] ~ ^
9.18	head,] ~ ^	48.23	north,] ~ ^
9.21	Annibals,] ~ ^	49.16	Bisho-pricks,] ~ ^
13.20	others,] ~ ^	50.17	Idolatry,] ~ ^
14.8	England,] ~ ^	54.6	praying,] ~ ^
14.11	blood,] ~ ^	54.9	Baylies,] ~ ^
16.8–9	therefrom,] ~.	56.17	effeminacy,] ~ ^

379

Punctuation Changes

Page.Line

59.12	me,]	~ ∧
72.15	perplexity,]	~ ∧
75.3	reason,]	~ .
75.15	first,]	~ ∧
76.19	aqueline,]	~ ∧
78.19	Normandy,]	~ ∧
80.4	languages,]	~ ∧
81.2	viol,]	~ ∧
81.11	Cookery,]	~ ∧
82.5	Sleeves,]	~ ∧
82.6	points,]	~ ∧
82.24	pistol,]	~ ∧
86.16	vaporish,]	~ .
87.13	conquest,]	~ .
88.21	bottles,]	~ ∧
89.23	Rome,]	~ ∧
94.20	fathers,]	~ .
95.8	pikes,]	~ ∧
95.19	Ignoramus,]	~ ∧
96.14	thus,]	~ ∧
98.6	browd,]	~ ∧
98.7	about,]	~ ∧
98.19	hail,]	~ ∧
100.20	other,]	~ ∧
100.20	Clubs,]	~ ∧
103.21	Cogitation,]	~ ∧
105.14	Venus]	~ .
106.17	Sir,—]	~ , ∧
107.22	presidents,]	~ .
108.22	electrics,]	~ ∧
110.17	crickets,]	~ ∧
112.15	men,]	~ ∧
113.23	nunnery,]	~ ∧
117.14	Subject,]	~ ∧
122.16	*argument,*]	~ ∧
122.17	*here*]	~ ,
122.19	understanding,]	~ ∧
123.6	wrangling,]	~ ∧
123.16	fellows,]	~ ∧
123.23	Lammas,]	~ ∧
129.16	names,]	~ ∧
129.18	mention,]	~ ∧
130.9	a-Nokes]	∧ ~
130.15	Conqueror,]	~ ;
130.26	manner,]	~ ∧
132.13	easie,]	~ ∧
134.17	proverb,]	~ ∧
135.22	names,]	~ ∧
136.14	Ocularis,]	~ ∧
136.14–15	Mentularis,]	~ ∧
137.21	even]	~ ,

Page.Line

138.3	them,]	~ ∧
139.19	moon,]	~ ∧
139.20	Fool,]	~ .
140.3	like,]	~ ∧
141.5	short,]	~ ∧
143.12	another,]	~ ∧
145.17	Indifference for)]	~) ~
145.18	hat]	~ ,
150.1	away,—]	~ , ∧
150.18	Stories,]	~ ∧
151.27	thereto,]	~ .
152.13	Club,]	~ ∧
153.5	day]	~ ,
153.6	honorable]	~ ,
153.7	Steward,]	~ ∧
153.19	Norman,]	~ ∧
153.25	storekeeper,]	~ ∧
155.17	air,]	~ ∧
156.17	Stuff,]	~ ∧
156.26	Congregation,]	~ ∧
157.2	pink]	~ ,
157.25	Entertainment,]	~ ∧
159.15	taste,]	~ ∧
160.29	composition,]	~ .
161.5	Contempt,]	~ ∧
162.25	tune,]	~ ∧
164.24	companions,]	~ ∧
169.15	Clapper,]	~ ∧
170.2	hand,]	~ ∧
170.19	Stage,]	~ ∧
171.17	Esqr,]	~ ∧
172.15	temperance,]	~ ∧
173.17	Phraze,]	~ ∧
176.10–11	produced,]	~ ∧
176.22	lines,]	~ ∧
176.24	original,]	~ ∧
178.9	*Gazette,*]	~ ∧
178.12	power]	~ ,
179.20	perdue,]	~ ∧
181.20	says,]	~ ∧
181.21	hellebore,]	~ ∧
184.18	victory,]	~ ∧
187.18	it,]	~ ∧
187.26	Church,]	~ ∧
188.19–20	Composed,]	~ ∧
189.14	melliflous]	~ ,
189.27	Revernd]	~ ,
190.3	piece,]	~ ∧
190.37	after,]	~ ∧
190.37	hall,]	~ ∧
191.4	History,]	~ ∧

Punctuation Changes

Page.Line

191.10	1745,] ~ ∧
193.8	Stockings,] ~ ∧
195.20	12th,] ~ ∧
195.25	20th,] ~ ∧
197.1	1745,] ~ ∧
197.4	17th,] ~ ∧
197.13	15th,] ~ ∧
197.19	notwithstanding,] ~ ∧
198.3	entertaining,] ~ ∧
200.13	Club,] ~ ∧
200.18	knives,] ~ ∧
202.11	entreated,] ~ ∧
202.21	24th,] ~ ∧
203.13	Seat.] ~ ∧
203.19	Chair.] ~ ∧
204.2	Shirt,] ~ ∧
204.5	Nasifer's,] ~ ∧
204.23	abilities,] ~ ∧
206.1	to,] ~ ∧
207.13	members,] ~ ∧
207.16	perceiving,] ~ ∧
208.5	creating] ~ ,
210.23	work.] ~ ∧
211.13	fiddlesticks,] ~ ∧
212.6	adulterize,] ~ ∧
212.19	*by*—] ~ —,
213.9	Insurmountable,] ~ .
213.22	wrist,] ~ ∧
215.4	*Doxies.*] ~ ,
215.5	*cheat.*] ~ ,
215.6	*Fumbumbus.*] ~ ,
215.7	*bouse.*] ~ ,
215.9	*praters.*] ~ ,
216.8	*Presidential,*] ~ ∧
217.1	army,] ~ ∧
217.3	barristers,] ~ ∧
217.26	sat,] ~ ∧
219.1	it,] ~ ∧
219.11	*Conundrumatic,*] ~ ∧
220.2	Synchronously,] ~ ∧
222.23	exercises,] ~ ∧
223.14	1745,] ~ ;
224.12	*Jolæus,*] ~ .
226.20	hands,] ~ ∧
226.21	thus it is,] ~ ~ ~ ∧
227.7	treated,—] ~ , ∧
227.19	on,] ~ ;
230.14	Chair,] ~ ∧
232.23	epigrams,] ~ ∧
235.6	Charity,] ~ ∧
235.21	1745–6,] ~ ∧

Page.Line

236.2	esqr,] ~ ∧
236.15	pretext,] ~ .
237.17	even] ~ ,
238.6	box,] ~ .
238.8	28,] ~ ∧
239.9	Rewards,] ~ ∧
241.10	action.—] ~ . ∧
243.19	*Craft,*] ~ .
243.28	1745/6,] ~ ∧
243.29	Steward,] ~ ∧
245.15	way,] ~ ∧
245.20	1745–6,] ~ ∧
246.3	invective,] ~ ∧
246.19	Club,] ~ ;
247.6	elbow,] ~ ∧
247.7	pause,] ~ ∧
249.16	1746,] ~ ∧
250.4	pleased,] ~ ∧
251.20	14th,] ~ ∧
252.11	Anniversaries,] ~ ;
252.17	bigots,] ~ ∧
253.19	brotherhood,] ~ ∧
254.9	matters,] ~ ∧
255.2	fireworks,] ~ ∧
258.4	Institution,] ~ ∧
258.23	Importance,] ~ ∧
260.18	plebs,] ~ ∧
260.21	said,] ~ ∧
262.21	magnanimity,] ~ ∧
264.5	Communities,] ~ ∧
265.6	1746,] ~ ∧
266.24	Quaint,] ~ ∧
267.17	did,] ~ ∧
267.20	designing,] ~ ∧
269.23	1746,] ~ ∧
271.18	*Incog',*] ~ ∧
272.5	members,] ~ ∧
272.10	Sederunt,] ~ .
272.20	form,] ~ ∧
275.4	Esqr,] ~ ∧
277.3	this,] ~ ∧
278.6	1746/7,] ~ ∧
279.14	1746,] ~ ∧
281.2	1746,] ~ ∧
281.7	1746,] ~ ∧
281.18	frequent] ~ ,
283.15	him,] ~ .
284.24	it,] ~ ∧
285.8	1746/7,] ~ ∧
285.14	orator,] ~ ∧
287.6	1746,] ~ ∧

382 Punctuation Changes

Page.Line		Page.Line	
287.7	28,] ~ ∧	338.5	established,] ~ .
287.14	1746/7,] ~ ∧	340.13	1747/8,] ~ ∧
290.15	1746/7,] ~ ∧	341.10	masters,] ~ ∧
290.17	1746/7,] ~ ∧	341.16	ensuing,] ~ ∧
290.18	Comas,] ~ ∧	342.4	Cestis,] ~ .
290.22	occasion,] ~ ∧	343.15	did,] ~ ∧
291.1	Round,] ~ ∧	343.20	manner,] ~ ∧
291.2	absence,] ~ ∧	344.10	undetermined,] ~ ∧
292.1	1747,] ~ ∧	344.12	Quaint,] ~ ∧
292.9	evening,] ~ ∧	348.5	themselves,] ~ .
293.7	Honorary members,]	351.1	1748,] ~ ∧
	~ ~ ∧	353.11	marriage,] ~ ∧
298.4	pert,] ~ ∧	356.18	minature,] ~ ∧
298.22	mitres,] ~ ∧	356.21	moon,] ~ ∧
299.3	pimps,] ~ ∧	358.2	Esqr's] ~ ,
300.15	thus,] ~ ∧	358.10	Spangled,] ~ ∧
301.15	veins,] ~ ∧	359.3	Wood)] ~ ∧
301.16	legs,] ~ ∧	359.14	8It] ~ ,
301.16	toes,] ~ ∧	359.15	Anniversary] ~ ,
301.16	hair,] ~ ∧	359.16	members, vizt:] ~ ∧ ~
302.12	hyppo,] ~ ∧	359.22	Supper,] ~ ∧
303.12	Impertinent,] ~ ∧	362.7	badges,] ~ ∧
303.14	wiseacres,] ~ ∧	363.12	2d,] ~ ∧
304.18	place,] ~ ∧	364.3	purpose,] ~ ∧
308.7	into,] ~ ∧	364.10	1747/8,] ~ ∧
309.15	points,] ~ ∧	365.6	20th,] ~ ∧
309.19	so,] ~ ∧	365.19	Share,] ~ ∧
310.11	form,] ~ ∧	366.16	dispute,] ~ ∧
312.4	Club,] ~ ∧	366.19	custom,] ~ ∧
312.6	Orator,] ~ ∧	368.16	demands,] ~ ∧
313.15	1747,] ~ ∧	374.16	1748,] ~ ∧
317.1	1747,] ~ ∧	376.22	1748/9,] ~ ∧
317.9	being,] ~ .	377.22	negative,] ~ ∧
317.20	Club,] ~ ∧	380.10	Anarchy,] ~ ∧
318.22	1747,] ~ ∧	380.14	mute,] ~ ∧
319.21	Speeches] ~ ,	381.11	1748/9,] ~ ∧
323.11	penetration,] ~ ∧	383.18	31] ~ ,
323.17	1st,] ~ ∧	384.14	My,] ~ ∧
327.15	27th,] ~ ∧	386.4	Gentlemen,] ~ ∧
328.3	last,] ~ ∧	386.15	words,] ~ ∧
328.5	33d,] ~ ∧	388.2	Club,] ~ ∧
328.17	Instant,] ~ ∧	389.20	and] ~ ,
330.3	purpose,] ~ ∧	390.8	1748/9,] ~ ∧
331.12	Steward,] ~ ∧	392.5	me,] ~ ∧
332.2	Steward,] ~ ∧	392.13	which,] ~ ∧
333.2	bottles,] ~ ∧	397.8	99th,] ~ ∧
333.22	Solemnity,] ~ ∧	399.24	Club,] ~ ∧
334.10	who,] ~ ∧	402.11	honorable] ~ ,
337.9	triffles.] ~ ∧	404.17	stabilitate,] ~ ∧
337.24	Incensed,] ~ ∧	405.5	Gentlemen,] ~ ∧

Punctuation Changes

Page.Line				Page.Line			
405.8	firm,]	~	∧	457.2	halters,]	~	∧
406.21	pain,]	~	∧	457.3	racks,]	~	∧
407.19	him,]	~	∧	457.3	fire,]	~	∧
408.19	aloud,]	~	∧	459.9	Quarrells,]	~	∧
409.3	him.]	~	∧	463.3	Conversation,]	~	∧
411.22	punch,]	~	∧	463.21	dull,]	~	∧
412.3	arms,]	~	∧	464.15	Mortals,]	~	∧
415.23	John,]	~	∧	466.19	thing,—]	~ , ∧
416.3	Annarundel,]	~	∧	466.20	value,]	~	∧
416.20	words,]	~	∧	466.24	freedom,—]	~ , ∧
418.4	them,]	~	∧	467.6	drink]	~ ,
419.20	Chair,]	~	∧	467.14	punsters,]	~	∧
420.19	1748/9,]	~	∧	467.17	Aristotle?—]	~ ? ∧
421.20	member]	~ ,		467.21	patience—]	~	∧
424.18	presence,]	~	∧	468.11	toaper—]	~	∧
425.10	Commission,]	~	∧	468.14	motion,—]	~ , ∧
425.14	Clerk,]	~	∧	470.7	others,]	~	∧
426.15	being,]	~	∧	470.19	Sufferings.]	~	∧
427.22	1748/9,]	~	∧	472.16	then?—]	~ ? ∧
428.18	21]	~ ,		473.18	huntsman,]	~	∧
428.18	1748/9,]	~	∧	474.16	assembly,—]	~ , ∧
428.24	1749,]	~	∧	475.1	pulpit,]	~	∧
430.6	Importance,]	~	∧	475.5	preaching,—]	~ , ∧
430.13	places,]	~ .		475.18	Increase,]	~	∧
431.6	Thus,]	~	∧	476.11	Soray,]	~	∧
431.22	eye,]	~	∧	476.19	ordered,]	~	∧
433.15	prepared,]	~	∧	477.19	more,—]	~ , ∧
433.17	hands,]	~	∧	477.19	Pope,]	~ ;
434.3	following]	~ ,		477.19	oath,—]	~ , ∧
435.27	Speakers,]	~	∧	479.6	Club,]	~	∧
437.6	1749,]	~	∧	479.8	puns,]	~	∧
437.21	preceeding]	~ ,		480.8	him,]	~	∧
440.5	it,]	~	∧	480.8	was,—]	~ , ∧
440.15	Committee,]	~	∧	480.13	Languages,—]	~ , ∧
441.18	finished,]	~	∧	481.6	wit,—]	~ , ∧
442.24	Secretary,]	~	∧	481.8	house,]	~	∧
445.12	deserts,]	~	∧	482.5	third,]	~	∧
446.13	reserve,]	~	∧	482.12	done,—]	~ , ∧
446.17	Satyrical,]	~	∧	482.17	Confusion,]	~	∧
446.21	Spirits,]	~	∧	482.18	fellow,]	~	∧
447.5	Club.]]	~ . ∧		482.20	numberless]	~ ,	
447.7	same,]	~	∧	483.8	'um's]	~ ,	
447.17	occasion,]	~	∧	486.6	laugh,]	~	∧
448.5	them]	~ ,		486.22	him,]	~	∧
450.19	great,]	~	∧	487.3	Pandragoras,]	~	∧
450.26	Warble,]	~	∧	487.4	Sigh,]	~	∧
451.13	appear.]	~	∧	487.4–5	*mortal*,—]	~ , ∧
451.19	up,]	~	∧	487.19	Size,]	~	∧
452.7	Character,]	~	∧	488.9	Night,]	~	∧
452.21	theirs,]	~	∧	489.13	admission,]	~	∧

Page.Line

490.6	Ceremonies,]	~ ∧
492.13	Secretary,]	~ ∧
493.6	put,]	~ ∧
494.4	11th,]	~ ∧
495.20	proposition,]	~ ∧
496.5	him,]	~ ∧
496.11	members,]	~ ∧
497.5	ends,]	~ ∧
498.10	promoted,]	~ ∧
498.18	long.]	~ ∧
500.9	Scuffle,]	~ ∧
500.11	Custom,]	~ ∧
502.5	ears—]	~ ∧
502.16	which—]	~ ∧
505.20	1749,]	~ ∧
507.21	made,]	~ ∧
508.9	1749,]	~ ∧
509.21	22d,]	~ ∧
510.19	Society,]	~ ∧
510.22	person,]	~ ∧
512.5	*Cats,*]	~ ∧
513.4	reconciled,]	~ ∧
515.9–10	countenance,]	~ ∧
515.17	pleasure.]	~ ∧
516.8	1749,]	~ ∧
516.20	Steward,]	~ ∧
518.12	Society,]	~ ∧
518.23	acknowledgements,]	~ ∧
519.15	faction.]	~ ∧
519.19	opinion,]	~ ∧
519.23	happens,]	~ ∧
520.24	tune,]	~ ∧
521.9	follows,]	~ ∧
523.2	Annapolis,]	~ ∧
523.12	honor,]	~ ∧
524.4	Stone,]	~ ∧
524.6	file,]	~ ∧
524.14	practise,]	~ ∧
524.20	separate.]	~ ∧
526.7	ceremonies,]	~ ∧
526.8	Supper,]	~ ∧
527.22	respects,]	~ ∧
528.3	better,]	~ ∧
530.3	1749,]	~ ∧
530.16	keeper]	~ ,
532.14	vanity,]	~ ∧
532.20	Quote,]	~ ∧
532.21–22	Command,]	~ ∧
533.16	*Artifice,*]	~ ∧
534.4	ejaculations,]	~ ∧

Page.Line

536.17	John,]	~ ∧
536.24	presence,]	~ ∧
538.6	1749,]	~ ∧
539.7	tell,]	~ ∧
539.20	1749,]	~ ∧
540.3	retained,]	~ ∧
541.7	vittles,]	~ ∧
541.10	penalty,]	~ ∧
544.17	1749,]	~ ∧
545.16	tell,]	~ ∧
546.6	bearer,]	~ ∧
548.5	1749,]	~ ∧
550.15	on,]	~ ∧
550.24	Chronology,]	~ ∧
551.7	heroes,]	~ ∧
553.20	difficulties,]	~ ∧
554.17–18	Dogmaticus,]	~ ∧
555.15	Earth!]	~ ,!
556.10	you,]	~ ∧
557.3	Room,]	~ ∧
558.12	Endures,]	~ ∧
560.19–20	Christendome,]	~ ∧
562.20	a Seal,]	~ ~ ∧
563.2	Society,]	~ ∧
563.13	Ceremonies,]	~ ∧
564.13	me,]	~ ∧
564.19	art,]	~ ∧
566.6	parts,]	~ ∧
566.22	officer,]	~ ∧
567.7	officers,]	~ ∧

Volume II

2.21	Grubeans,]	~ ∧
5.19	woman,]	~ ∧
6.12	Secrecy,]	~ ∧
7.18	them?—]	~ ? ∧
8.1	coxcombs.—]	~ . ∧
8.9	Companions,—]	~ , ∧
14.23	Poetry,]	~ ∧
16.13	in't,]	~ ∧
17.6	words,]	~ .
17.17	Passus,]	~ ∧
17.20	it,]	~ ∧
17.22	posture,]	~ ∧
18.17	Philosophers,]	~ ∧
18.20	Sparta,]	~ ∧
19.4	posterity,]	~ ∧
20.11	*Transubstantialities,*]	~ ∧
21.20–22.1	futurity,]	~ ∧

Punctuation Changes

Page.Line		Page.Line	
22.20	efficacy, probably] ~ ∧ ~ ,	75.16	yourself,] ~ ∧
23.2	posture] ~ ,	75.21	chains,] ~ ∧
24.9	Voltaire,] ~ ∧	82.16	Club,] ~ ∧
26.2	had,] ~ ;	82.17	*order,*] ~ ∧
26.3	trappings,] ~ ∧	83.2	difficulty,] ~ ∧
26.7	*Bellianis,*] ~ ∧	83.19	Toasted,] ~ ∧
26.8	Instructive.] ~ ∧	87.8	Statesmen,] ~ ∧
26.19	of,] ~ ∧	87.16	Generosity,] ~ ∧
27.2	*Cohobation,*] ~ ∧	88.6	Commission,] ~ ∧
27.7	*Seatille,*] ~ ∧	88.16	13th,] ~ ∧
28.10	Sandyvogius,] ~ ∧	89.6	Sly,] ~ ∧
28.12	Georgius,] ~ ∧	89.7	Triumvirate,] ~ ∧
28.15–16	ennumerate,] ~ ∧	91.10	Conscience,] ~ ∧
28.17	*qualities,*] ~ ∧	92.17	history,] ~ ∧
28.17–18	*prolific,*] ~ ∧	93.21	convened,] ~ ∧
28.18	*powers,*] ~ ∧	94.7	Bickerings,] ~ ∧
30.6	tea,] ~ ∧	97.27	fiddle,] ~ ∧
32.8	memory,] ~ ∧	98.10	Club] ~ ∧
32.9	Chapitres,] ~ ∧	102.19	Council] ~ ,
32.14	time] ~)	105.6	purpose,] ~ ∧
33.5	men,] ~ ∧	105.14	Gelastic] ~ ,
34.3	Johnson.] ~ ∧	106.9	Sly,] ~ ∧
37.16	*Table,—*] ~ , ∧	108.18	Society,] ~ ∧
37.17	Company,—] ~ , ∧	110.5	order,] ~ ∧
45.17	years,] ~ ∧	111.7	displeased.] ~ ∧
45.23	following,] ~ ∧	111.22	rebellion,] ~ ∧
45.25	is,] ~ ∧	112.1	hand,] ~ ∧
46.20	pictures,] ~ ∧	112.16	*Damn*] ~ ,
46.21	breeches,] ~ ∧	116.12	night,] ~ ∧
47.4	A,] ~ ∧	117.19	1750,] ~ ∧
47.4	bell,] ~ ∧	118.6	Esqr,] ~ ∧
47.6	Rebus)] ~ ∧	118.23	*Liberty,*] ~ .
48.1	consideration,] ~ ∧	119.2	triumvirate,] ~ ∧
48.7	προτερον,] ~ ∧	119.6	Club,] ~ ∧
51.3	Case,] ~ ∧	119.9	themselves.] ~ ∧
52.8	dignity,] ~ ∧	119.26	Secretary,] ~ ∧
52.13	19th,] ~ ∧	120.1	petulancy,] ~ ∧
57.10	keeper,] ~ ∧	120.23	noise,] ~ ∧
59.5	them,] ~ ∧	121.26–27	ambassador,] ~ ∧
59.11	Seat,] ~ ∧	124.22	Senses,] ~ ∧
59.15	95th,] ~ ∧	125.8	appetites, even] ~ ∧ ~ ,
60.11	him,] ~ ∧	125.20	morals,] ~ ∧
60.13	over.] ~ ∧	127.14	1750,] ~ ∧
61.20	Services,] ~ ∧	127.17	1748/9,] ~ .
62.11	95th,] ~ ∧	127.19	altar,] ~ ∧
64.11	Sigillature,] ~ ∧	128.3	Secretary,] ~ ∧
69.25	proverb,] ~ ∧	133.23	air,] ~ ∧
70.18	notwithstanding,] ~ ∧	135.14	kitchen,] ~ ∧
70.20	Chusing,] ~ ∧	137.14	eclaircissement,] ~ .
73.6	there.] ~ ∧	138.24	bow,] ~ ∧

Punctuation Changes

Page.Line

139.8	ranged,] ~ ∧
140.4	Subject,] ~ ∧
140.6	Semiquavers,] ~ ∧
140.6	minims,] ~ ∧
141.20	honor,] ~ ∧
146.20	heart,] ~ ∧
163.19	Interest,] ~ ∧
166.26	vain,] ~ ∧
167.6	honor,] ~ ∧
167.7	Seal,] ~ ∧
167.13	for,] ~ ∧
168.23	writers,] ~ ∧
168.25	motion,] ~ ∧
168.25	drop'd,] ~ ∧
172.8	there,] ~ ∧
172.23	Club,] ~ ∧
173.23	table,] ~ ∧
175.8	Club,] ~ ∧
176.10	Corrupt] ~ ,
176.22	devlish] ~ ,
176.30	president,] ~ ∧
177.18	Chancellor,] ~ ∧
177.23	45th,] ~ ∧
181.21	Claim,] ~ ∧
183.20	parts,] ~ ∧
184.2	romance,] ~ ∧
184.3	Generals,] ~ ∧
186.2	province,] ~ ∧
186.11	gravity,] ~ ∧
188.12	Shoulder knot,] ~ ~ ∧
188.26	man,] ~ ∧
190.20	genius] ~ ,
190.24	happens,] ~ ∧
193.5	Sort,] ~ ∧
193.7	Lords,] ~ ∧
198.1.2–3	pause, Quadrille speaks]] ~] ~ ~
201.15	so,] ~ ∧
202.3	uneasy,] ~ ∧
202.21	Sentence,] ~ ∧
203.10	17th,] ~ ∧
205.12	will,] ~ ∧
205.22	wit,] ~ .
205.23	Conundrum,] ~ ∧
206.21	Rhubarb,] ~ ∧
207.24	1750,] ~ ∧
208.24	purpose,] ~ ∧
211.16	Esqr,] ~ ∧
211.25	Club,] ~ ∧
214.15	well] ~ ,

Page.Line

216.13	for,] ~ ∧
217.16	Chancellor,] ~ ∧
220.21	Inquisition,] ~ ∧
221.7	drawing] ~ ,
222.6	State,] ~ ∧
222.20	liberty,] ~ ∧
222.21	Chancellor,] ~ ∧
223.20	return,] ~ ∧
227.3	*facto,*] ~ ∧
227.9	no,] ~ .
232.18	Children,] ~ ∧
233.6	name] ~ ,
236.2	Sederunt] ~ ,
236.17	good.] ~ ∧
237.18	bumper,] ~ ∧
238.20	members,] ~ ∧
244.20	John] ~ ,
244.21	President,] ~ ∧
246.6	1750,] ~ ∧
246.18	them.] ~ ∧
247.17	Contempt] ~ ,
248.11	thus,] ~ .
248.21	thro',] ~ ∧
249.6	it,] ~ ∧
252.2	Law,] ~ ∧
252.14	Guilty,] ~ ∧
253.12	Rhubarb] ~)
253.15	president,] ~ ∧
253.20	Club,] ~ ∧
255.19	it,] ~ .
255.23	extravagance,] ~ ∧
258.21	Cheese,] ~ ∧
259.18	this] ~ ,
260.6	Custody.] ~ ∧
262.24	punishment.] ~ ∧
263.27	doing,] ~ ∧
264.4	Club,] ~ ∧
264.4	Gentleman,] ~ .
263a.18	Hall,] ~ ∧
267.20	occasion,] ~ ∧
270.13	magnificent,] ~ ∧
272.10	determinator,] ~ ∧
272.23	down,] ~ ∧
273.4	notch'd it,] ~ ~ ∧
276.19	*head,*] ~ ∧
277.19	agent,] ~ .
278.12	himself,] ~ ∧
279.5	times,] ~ ∧
279.24	monarchs,] ~ ∧
281.24	England,] ~ ∧

Punctuation Changes 387

Page.Line

283.6	occasion,] ~ ∧
284.25	honorable] ~ ,
287.20	into,] ~ ∧
288.16	countenance,] ~ ∧
290.5	hand,] ~ ∧
290.17	future.] ~ ∧
291.4	President,] ~ ∧
293.25	broils.] ~ ∧
294.25	Club,] ~ ∧
295.11	purpose,] ~ ∧
296.12–13	unalterable] ~ ,
297.27	him,] ~ ∧
299.4	himself] ~)
299.6	Seal at] ~ , ~
300.1	empire.] ~ ∧
300.11	1750/1,] ~ ∧
300.12	Club,] ~ ∧
301.19	Epistle,] ~ ∧
301.22	thro',] ~ ∧
302.3	pride,] ~ ∧
303.26	night,] ~ ∧
303.26	health,] ~ ∧
304.22	Club,] ~ ∧
307.24	to,] ~ ∧
310.4	nothing,] ~ ∧
310.7	flattery,] ~ ∧
312.8	Lordsp's] ~ ,
313.22	detested,] ~ ∧
314.13	profit himself,] ~ , ~ ∧
314.20	1750/1,] ~ ∧
314.21	president,] ~ ∧
318.15	Spirits,] ~ ∧
318a.4	articles.] ~ ,
319.21	magnitude,] ~ ∧
320.2	delivery,] ~ ∧
321.7	Lordship.] ~ ∧
322.10	Garret,] ~ ∧
324.10	1750/1,] ~ ∧
325.18	other,] ~ ∧
326.13	State,] ~ ∧
326.14	oration.]] ~ . ∧
328.4	admiring,] ~ ∧
328.23–24	rendezvous,] ~ ∧
334.17	Authorities] ~ ,
335.21	discourses,] ~ ∧
336.9–10	figuratively,] ~ ∧
336.13	with,] ~ .
337.10	power,] ~ ∧
337.13	are,] ~ ∧
338.4	speak,)] ~ , ∧

Page.Line

338.19	villain,] ~ ∧
340.10	necessary,] ~ ;
340.12	Jewels,] ~ ∧
341.19	mine.] ~ ∧
344.9	wealth,] ~ ∧
344.10	experience,] ~ ∧
344.25	humanity,] ~ ∧
345.9	Goodness,] ~ ∧
345.25	Country,] ~ ∧
349.5	limitations,] ~ ∧
349.15	Signification,] ~ ∧
350.16	with,] ~ ∧
350.20	*lament,*] ~ ∧
351.11	Chair,] ~ .
353.18	Secretary,] ~ ∧
354.23	given,] ~ ∧
355.8	account] ~ ,
356.14	Lord,] ~ ∧
357.21	gate,] ~ ∧
359.1	Chamber,] ~ ∧
361.6	one,] ~ ∧
361.15	were] ~ ,
362.20	this,] ~ ∧
363.19	doctor,] ~ .
363.20	Satrapes,] ~ ∧
364.10	bright,] ~ ∧
366.3	thought,] ~ ∧
391.21	more] ~ ,
392.7	Triumvirate,] ~ ∧
392.11	Embassy,] ~ ∧
394.26	preface.] ~ ∧
395.9	member] ~ ,
396.21	promontory,] ~ ∧
400.15	natures,] ~ ∧
404.2	Secretary,] ~ ∧
404.3	hands,] ~ ∧
404.26	office,] ~ ∧
406.18	Villain,] ~ ∧
406.20	moderation,] ~ ∧
406.29	Gentleman,] ~ .
408.4	honor,] ~ ∧
408.11	Strides,] ~ ∧
408.11–12	accents,] ~ ∧
408.19	beneficent,] ~ ∧
408.25	John,] ~ ∧
409.24	Incident,] ~ ∧
411.6	woman,] ~ ∧
411.23	hole,] ~ ∧
412.3	bum-gun-Shot,] ~ ∧
412.17	wizzards.] ~ ∧

Page.Line			Page.Line	
413.1	Virginia.] ~ ∧		487.20	Just,] ~ ∧
414.20	Singular,] ~ ∧		489.21	terror,] ~ ∧
416.2	Extraction,] ~ ∧		490.13	hands,] ~ ∧
416.7	way,] ~ ∧		492.25	him,] ~ ∧
420.5	Altho] (~		493.17	back,] ~ ∧
429.8–9	Littleworth,] ~ ∧		495.6	head,] ~ ∧
429.15	company,] ~ ∧		495.21	Secretary.] ~ ∧
429.19	Custom,] ~ ∧		495.24	Flutter,] ~ ∧
431.17	History,] ~ ∧		495.27	Champion,] ~ ∧
433.11	*procession*,] ~ ∧		496.4	partizans.] ~ ∧
433.18–19	antiquity,] ~ ∧		496.6	Esqr,] ~ ∧
434.4	lips,] ~ ∧		496.8	Club.] ~ ∧
434.15	Stick,] ~ ∧		497.5	Satyrus,] ~ ∧
435.7	*book*,] ~ ∧		497.9	antagonists,] ~ ∧
438.1	affairs,] ~ ∧		498.10	again.] ~ ∧
438.3	Secretary,] ~ ∧		498.13	house,] ~ ∧
438.13	occasion,] ~ ∧		501.1	poets,] ~ ∧
438.22	*king*—] ~ ∧		501.13	home,] ~ ∧
439.9	Seal,] ~ ∧		504.15–16	Councils] ~ ,
440.25	it,] ~ ∧		505.7	Lordship himself] ~ , ~
443.22	Poet,] ~ ∧		508.5	Sederunt] ~ ,
444.21	even] ~ ,		508.19	Club,] ~ ∧
445.26	teeth,] ~ ∧		510.9	manner,] ~ ∧
446.8	me,] ~ ∧		510.18	deputation,] ~ ∧
446.17	Laureats,] ~ ∧		512.31	violoncello.] ~ ∧
448.20	fury,] ~ ∧		513.25	box.] ~ ∧
456.3	oracles.] ~ ∧		516.4	proverbs,] ~ ∧
458.10	lived,] ~ ∧		517.9	trappings,] ~ ∧
459.17	hands,] ~ ∧		517.18	powdering,] ~ ∧
460.12	away.] ~ ∧		519.23	Combustion,] ~ ∧
461.2	Coxcomb,] ~ ∧		520.7	pompous] ~ ,
466.5	words,] ~ ∧		523.2	them,] ~ ∧
466.11	flattery,] ~ ∧		523.9	it,] ~ ∧
467.10	points,] ~ ∧		524.1	Countenance,)] ~ , ∧
469.9	Wisdom,] ~ ;		524.3	part.] ~ ∧
470.2	them,] ~ ∧		524.5	Secretarie's,] ~ ∧
470.6	them,] ~ ∧		524.14	question,] ~ ∧
472.2	Impudence,] ~ ∧		525.23	reply,] ~ ∧
472.10	Genius,] ~ ∧		526.14	Sederunt] ~ ,
472.14	Impudence,] ~ ∧		527.8	men.] ~ ∧
476.12	*Grandiston*,] ~ ∧		530.17	unstrung,] ~ ∧
481.23	out,] ~ ∧		533.18	of,] ~ ∧
482.11	tools,] ~ ∧		534.2	into,] ~ ∧
482.15	Custody,] ~ ∧		534.7	*intollerable*,] ~ .
482.16	hands,] ~ ∧		537.9	Spite,] ~ ∧
483.13	it,] ~ ∧		540.10	Society.] ~ ∧
484.22	pocket,—] ~ , ∧		540.13	thro',] ~ ∧
485.12	resistance,] ~ ∧		540.19–20	another,] ~ ∧
485.18	searchd,] ~ ∧		541.15	said,] ~ ∧
486.6	possession,] ~ ∧		542.9–10	arbitrary,] ~ ∧

Punctuation Changes

Page.Line		
545.5	1752,]	~ ∧
545.15	1752,]	~ ∧
545.19–20	Indisposition,]	~ ∧
545.20	proper]	~ ,

Volume III

Page.Line		
3.15	small,]	~ ∧
3.28	benevolent,]	~ ∧
4.5	*noisy,*]	~ ∧
4.5–6	*perpetual*]	~ ,
5.5	is,]	~ ∧
5.11	bodies,]	~ ∧
6.7	tube,]	~ ∧
7.6	truth,]	~ ∧
7.18	it,]	~ ∧
8.11	bones,]	~ ∧
8.18	fable,]	~ ∧
11.9	parts,]	~ ∧
12.5	wall,]	~ ∧
12.16	rise,]	~ ∧
13.6	fluid,]	~ ∧
13.18	Substances,]	~ ∧
15.7	anger,]	~ ∧
15.22	down,]	~ ∧
16.2	Simile,]	~ ∧
17.14	be,]	~ ∧
19.12	as]	~ ,
19.13	Learned,]	~ ∧
20.19	members,]	~ ∧
20.24	occasion,]	~ ∧
21.1	boiled,]	~ ∧
24.1	stood]	~ ,
24.17	date,]	~)
24.26	Club,]	~ ∧
25.23	great,]	~ ∧
26.16	office,]	~ ∧
27.4	*Separatim,*]	~ ∧
28.9	Immediate]	~ ,
30.11	but]	~ ,
32.9	Speeches,]	~ ∧
33.5	members,]	~ ∧
33.14	Standing,]	~ ∧
34.15–16	welcome,]	~ ∧
34.17	members,]	~ ∧
34.26	way.]	~ ∧
35.22	effect,]	~ ∧
36.22	place.]	~ ∧
37.14	thro',]	~ ∧
37.18	upon.]	~ ∧

Page.Line		
40.11	Hugh]	~ ,
40.16	in the other,]	~ ~ ~ ∧
40.24	Club,]	~ ∧
41.20	person,—]	~ , ∧
42.1	Chancellor—]	~ ?—
42.9	president,]	~ ∧
42.17	Anniversary]	~ ,
44.13	Esqr.—]	~ . ∧
45.13	Rormis.—]	~ . ∧
46.5	that.—]	~ ~ —.
46.9	Circumstances,]	~ ∧
48.22	Benedictus,]	~ ∧
49.3	Mahomet,]	~ ∧
49.4	Aurelianus,]	~ ∧
49.14	Companions,]	~ ∧
49.14	Jumpedo,]	~ ∧
49.18	books,]	~ ∧
50.2	fables,]	~),
50.3	fables,)]	~ , ∧
50.11	monsters,]	~ ∧
52.14	*Sedere,*]	~ ∧
54.13	Sufficient]	~ ,
57.28	them,]	~ ∧
58.3	title,]	~ ∧
58.16	action,]	~ ∧
62.2	Comas,]	~ ;
62.13	fellow,]	~ ∧
62.16	letter,]	~ ∧
62.16	him,—]	~ , ∧
62.22	Surprized,]	~ ∧
63.9	Secretary,]	~ ∧
63.17	Secretary.]	~ ∧
63.23	aware,]	~ ∧
65.22	Cavalry,]	~ ∧
66.7	pocket.]	~ ∧
66.15	dammage,]	~ ∧
67.3	them,]	~ ∧
67.18	Esqr]	~ !
68.2	furious—]	~ ∧
68.4	ye!]	~ !,
68.26	there,]	~ ∧
69.11	time,]	~ ∧
69.11	Wattle,]	~ ∧
69.19	String,]	~ ∧
70.20	paper.]	~ ∧
70.21	Chagrined,]	~ ∧
72.8	Esqr,—]	~ , ∧
72.14	Stories,—]	~ , ∧
72.18	unguarded,]	~ ∧
73.2	I,]	~ ∧

Page.Line			Page.Line		
73.2	affair,]	~ ∧	117.2	Esqrs,]	~ ∧
73.8	them,]	~ ∧	117.13	with,]	~ ∧
73.16	him,]	~ ∧	139.5	nature,]	~ ∧
73.23	Frontinbrass]	~ ,	139.7	Rank.]	~ ∧
74.7	Gate,]	~ ∧	140.11	president,]	~ ∧
74.16	thing,]	~ ∧	140.19	*due*—]	~ —,
75.4	preambles,]	~ ∧	141.10	fool.]	~ ∧
75.7	182,]	~ ∧	141.18	after,]	~ ∧
79.21	paper,]	~ ∧	143.17	Records,]	~ ∧
80.23	affixed,]	~ ∧	143.22	debard,]	~ ∧
81.27	Lordship]	Lord, ship	144.4	demand,]	~ ∧
81.33	Club,]	~ ∧	147.7	thing,]	~ ∧
84.25	Commission,]	~ ∧	149.7	disputes,]	~ ∧
87.13	as]	(~	149.19	Stairs,]	~ ∧
88.20	Communing,]	~ ∧	150.12	repairing,]	~ ∧
89.3	forth,]	~ ∧	151.3	Sederunt,]	~ ∧
90.3	hoh—]	~ —.	152.13	Steward,]	~ ∧
91.3	now]	~ ,	152.22	Club,]	~ ∧
93.26	potest,]	~ ∧	145a.8	Trials,]	~ ∧
94.1	Lawyer,]	~ ∧	147a.14	praise,]	~ ∧
94.14	oration]	~ ,	147a.21	thereto,]	~ ∧
94.16	Snuff,]	~ ∧	152a.7	Contents.]	~ ∧
94.20	Silence,)]	~ , ∧	153a.6	Committee,]	~ ∧
97.16	felicity]	~ ,	153a.8	195,]	~ ∧
98.3	Club]	~ ,	153a.24	regular,]	~ ∧
98.9	humanity,]	~ ∧	154.20	Custom,]	~ ∧
99.16	propositions,]	~ ∧	156.12	Importance,]	~ ∧
99.18	manner.]]	~ . ∧	157.24	Se'nnight,]	~ ∧
99.21	Maccarty,]	~ ∧	158.2	words,]	~ ∧
100.2	Lord Maccarty]	~ , ~	158.9	places,]	~ ∧
101.9	Club,]	~ ∧	159.15	methods,]	~ ∧
101.15	president]	~ ,	160.27	resistance,]	~ ∧
101.16	Club,]	~ ∧	161.4	Cromwell,]	~ ∧
102.10	good,]	~ ∧	168.5	truth,]	~ ∧
103.3	unintelligible,]	~ ∧	169.12	dialogue,]	~ ∧
104.8	truth,]	~ ∧	171.21	Corruption,]	~ ∧
104.15	exist,]	~ ∧	172.12	table,]	~ ∧
105.15	members,]	~ ∧	172.17	modes,]	~ ∧
105.16	*Umbrahlis,*]	~ ∧	173.3	rules]	~ ,
106.2	teeth,]	~ ∧	175.8	e'gad!—]	~ ! ∧
106.4	Phantasmical.]	~ ∧	175.10	yours,—]	~ , ∧
106.5	lived,]	~ ∧	175.13	*madame!*—]	~ ! ∧
106.23	however,]	~ ∧	177.10	hearing,]	~ ∧
106.24	neglected,]	~ ∧	178.4	feather,]	~ ∧
107.1	memorandums,]	~ ∧	178.20	Company,]	~ ∧
107.12	Chancellor,]	~ ∧	179.15	Inconsiderable,]	~ .
110.17	Slaves,]	~ ∧	180.7	Curate,]	~ ∧
114.14	harmony,]	~ ∧	180.22	Conversation,]	~ ∧
116.4	if]	(~	183.23	proposing]	~ ,
117.1	Embassadors,]	~ ∧	184.20	fashion,]	~ ∧

Punctuation Changes

Page.Line

184.23	noise,] ~ .
185.11	ancients,] ~ ∧
185.21	Ancients,] ~ ∧
186.4	some,] ~ ∧
186.18	thus,] ~ ∧
187.12	197,] ~ ∧
188.2	master,] ~ ∧
188.3	president,] ~ ∧
188.14	Esqr,] ~ ∧
188.14	1753,] ~ ∧
189.6	Criminal,] ~ ∧
189.9	downwards,] ~ ∧
189.18	Chance,] ~ ∧
190.3	ages,] ~ ∧
190.21	it,] ~ ∧
191.23	dragoon,] ~ ∧
192.2	whore,] ~ ∧
192.6	office,] ~ ∧
192.12	leave,] ~ ∧
194.13	monarch,] ~ ∧
194.15	friends,] ~ ∧
195.20	Crankum,] ~ ∧
196.17	Low,] ~ ∧
202.23	for,] ~ ∧
204.3	meeting,] ~ ∧
204.11	him,] ~ ∧
206.10	honorary,] ~ ∧
211.3	Punch,] ~ ∧
211.14	play,] ~ ;
213.22	even] ~ ,
215.24	Ships,] ~ ∧
216.18	pots,] ~ ∧
216.19	Cruets,] ~ ∧
216.21	lips,] ~ ∧
217.1	tarts,] ~ ∧
217.6	these,] ~ ∧
217.7	kind,] ~ ∧
217.9	protector,] ~ ∧
217.24	seen,] ~ ∧
217.25	Composers,] ~ ∧
218.6	Chorus,] ~ ∧
238.13	reward] ~ ,
240.15	Club,] ~ ∧
240.16	Custom.] ~ ∧
241.18	accuracy,] ~ ∧
242.13	as] ~ ,
242.18	Case,—] ~ , ∧
243.17	General,] ~ ∧
247.8	1753,] ~ ∧
248.5	that)] ~ ∧

Page.Line

248.17	Sederunt,] ~ ∧
250.13	days,] ~ ∧
250.19	dress] ~ ,
253.17	Carlo,] ~ ∧
254.7	words,] ~ ∧
254.21	President]] ~ ∧
255.30	opinion,] ~ ∧
260.11	Cook,] ~ ∧
262.11	houses] ~ ,
262.17	occasion,] ~ ∧
263.13	*omnia*,] ~ .
264.15	Privilege] ~ ,)
265.11	Captain] ~ ,
267.20	Club,] ~ ∧
268.3	members,] ~ ∧
268.20	thistle,] ~ ∧
269.7	kingdoms,] ~ ∧
269.11	arms,] ~ ∧
270.18	Anniversary.] ~ ∧
272.22	liquor,] ~ ∧
272.25	admirers,] ~ ∧
273.3	Sheep.] ~ ∧
273.17	it] ~)
274.6	tackle,] ~ ∧
275.19	1748/9,] ~ ∧
277.2	presumes,] ~ ∧
277.24	Ceremony,] ~ ∧
278.12	matter,] ~ ∧
279.20	up,] ~ ∧
279.21	way,] ~ ∧
280.2	history,] ~ ∧
283.22	say,] ~ ∧
284.16	not,] ~ ;
284.18	thus,] ~ ∧
288.10	family,] ~ ∧
288.14	treated,] ~ ∧
289.3	Club,] ~ ∧
290.15	1748/9,] ~ ∧
291.5	president,] ~ ∧
291.14	Sleep,] ~ ∧
296.11	Attorney,] ~ ∧
296.13	Club,] ~ ∧
297.4	separately,] ~ ∧
299.10	Club] ~ ,
299.16	Juncture,] ~ ∧
333.1	Macpherson,] ~ ∧
333.23–24	dismissed.] ~ ∧
334.20	Charlestown,] ~ ∧
337.1	history,] ~ ∧
337.17	pocket, it] ~ ~ ,

Page.Line			Page.Line		
340.23	most]	~ ,	406.6	it]	~ ,
341.18	Country.]	~ ∧	406.11	Club,]	~ ∧
341.20–21	Conversation,]	~ ∧	407.12	Pseudo-critics,]	~ ∧
344.25	keeping,]	~ ∧	409.21	hum,]	~ ∧
345.23	passion,]	~ ;	412.10	bread.—]	~ .—,
347.2	health,]	~ ∧	415.16	triumvirate,]	~ ∧
347.15	question,]	~ ∧	416.8	Independent]	~ ,
348.3	night,]	~ ∧	423.1–2	Conduct,]	~ ∧
351.2	posterity,]	~ .	423.23	Club,]	~ ∧
351.13	Laughing]	~ ,	425.10	Sir,]	~ ;
351.22	Club,]	~ ∧	426.5	Confirmation,]	~ .
353.11	*Archon,*]	~ ;	428.7	gestures,]	~ ∧
353.11	officers,]	~ ∧	428.19	*Policy,*]	~ ∧
354.14	anger,]	~ ∧	433.3	uttered,]	~ ∧
355.9	dejection,]	~ ∧	433.16	was,]	~ .
357.8	Jokes,]	~ ∧	434.2	this,]	~ ∧
357.11	Cheese]	~ ,	435.20	Reason,]	~ ∧
357.14	this,]	~ ∧	436.11–12	religion,]	~ ∧
357.20	waits,]	~ ∧	436.14	another,]	~ ∧
358.8	me,—]	~ , ∧	438.15	[—'tis]	(— ~
358.14	mutton,—]	~ , ∧	439.4	fortune.]	~ ∧
359.8	teeth,]	~ ∧	439.7	Speech,]	~ ∧
359.12	in,]	~ ∧	440.20	of I]	~ , ~
359.14	occasions,]	~ ∧	440.21	Stuff,]	~ ∧
359.19	flat,]	~ ∧	443.22	fooleries,]	~ ∧
359.20	nodding,]	~ ∧	448.20	Society,]	~ ∧
360.3	punning,]	~ ∧	449.19	falsifier,]	~ ∧
361.2	fetched,]	~ ∧	450.6	both.]	~ ∧
364.8	once]	~ ,	451.7	badge]	~ ,
366.2	it,]	~ ∧	453.20	Pumpkin,]	~ ∧
368.23	well—]	~ —,	*300.32	*degree,*]	~ ∧
369.4	hoh!]	~ !,	*301.28	Chirrups,]	~ ∧
370.12	produced,]	~ ∧	*303.1	modesty,]	~ ∧
371.19	ordinary,]	~ ∧	*306.23	down.]	~ ∧
375.22	Nose,]	~ ∧	*306.33	Grog,]	~ ∧
377.2	designs,]	~ ;	*308.21	deputy,]	~ ∧
378.3	*fingit,*]	~ .	*310.1	Lardini,]	~ ∧
378.12	day,]	~ .	*310.22	times,]	~ ∧
382.3	lose,]	~ ∧	*310.26	Steward,]	~ ∧
382.17	asistants.]	~ ∧	*311.5	Esqr,]	~ ∧
383.1	honorable,]	~ ∧	*311.12	records,]	~ .
383.10	verses,]	~ ∧	*311.28	Speech,]	~ ∧
383.13	described,]	~ ∧	*312.1	times,]	~ ∧
386.24	offence,]	~ ∧	*312.20	Divine,]	~ ∧
391.28	others,]	~ ∧	*312.36	lately,]	~ ∧
402.10	birds,]	~ .	*313.33	*fat,*]	~ ∧
402.23	antiquity,]	~ ∧	503.4	purpose,]	~ ∧
403.6	Composition,]	~ ∧	503.7	perceiving,]	~ ∧
403.20	Chancellor,]	~ ∧	504.18	matters,]	~ ∧
404.6	and]	~ ,	504.19	peers,]	~ ∧

Punctuation Changes

Page.Line

504.21	two,] ~ ∧
506.11	225,] ~ ∧
506.12	Commission,] ~ ∧
508.3	practise,] ~ ∧
509.13	to] ~ ,
511.20–21	Subject,] ~ ∧
512.8	Patience,] ~ ∧
512.21	bills,] ~ ∧
512.27	money,] ~ ∧
514.22	Speeches,] ~ ∧
515.12	did] ~)
517.14	χρονιζει,] ~ ∧
517.21	Sorts,] ~ ∧
518.2	it,] ~ .
518.3	mirth,] ~ ∧
518.27	tune,] ~ ∧
519.19	again,] ~ ∧
524.2	castigation,] ~ ∧
524.21	Character,] ~ ∧
525.11	will,] ~ ∧
525.13	Gentleman,] ~ ∧
526.2	Gentleman,] ~ ∧
528.22	trial,] ~ ∧
529.34	you,] ~ ∧
530.2	heard,] ~ ∧
530.27	trials,] ~ ∧
531.9	ocupation,] ~ ∧
531.15	please,] ~ ∧
533.8	Lands,] ~ ∧
533.10	duels,] ~ ∧
534.6	Gown,] ~ ∧
534.19	purpose,] ~ ∧
536.19	words,] ~ ∧
537.8	first,] ~ ∧

Page.Line

538.11	words,] ~ ∧
541.27	Carlo,] ~ ∧
543.5	Gleek,] ~ .
544.12	so,] ~ ∧
544.20–21	manuscript,—] ~ , ∧
544.22	it,—] ~ , ∧
545.2	one,—] ~ , ∧
546.15	before,] ~ ∧
546.17	General's] ~ ,
547.24	it,] ~ .
547.25	example,] ~ ∧
550.12	transcript.)] ~ . ∧
553.29	mortal,] ~ ∧
554.13	directions,] ~ ∧
556.11	[Mr] ∧ ~
557.20	others,] ~ ∧
558.4	persons,] ~ .
558.10	member,] ~ ∧
558.17	appointment,] ~ ∧
559.11	time,—] ~ , ∧
559.14	purpose,—] ~ , ∧
560.16	proceeding,] ~ ∧
561.8	motion.] ~ ∧
561.13	matter,] ~ ∧
561.16	manner—] ~ ∧
561.23	presently,—] ~ , ∧
562.22	notorious] ~ ,
563.2	forth.] ~ ∧
563.5	Coat,—] ~ , ∧
563.6	General,] ~ ∧
563.22–23	Indictment,] ~ ∧
563.25	Sleeveless,] ~ ∧
564.17	approved,] ~ ;

SUBSTANTIVE CHANGES

The page numbers below refer to the bracketed numerals in the margins of this edition, which record the pagination of Hamilton's manuscript. Occasionally I have had to refer instead to the page numbers of this edition (for example, for sections of Hamilton's manuscript that are not paginated, such as his table of contents); those cases are indicated by asterisks. When a reference contains three numbers they refer to page, column, and line. The material before the bracket shows the text as I have emended it; the word or words after the bracket reproduce Hamilton's manuscript. The swung dash used after the bracket stands for a word that has not itself been changed but that adjoins an emendation.

Volume I

Page.Line		Page.Line	
*4.9	foundation] foundtion	195.21	purchased] purjased
4.14	worships] worship's	204.15	state or] stated
5.17	Jole] Joule	205.15	acquaint] acquant
10.18	precious] pecious	210.21	mechanics] mehanics
14.3	Sanctuaries] Santuaries	210.23	Theology] Thology
16.6	highlanders] higlanders	212.15–16	*transubstantiation*]
50.21	bon'd] bond		*trasubstantiation*
64.1	*Mclaurie*] *Mcleanrie*	243.16	allegations] allgations
64.26	*Drumore*] *Cameron*	251.14	the President who] the who
65.18	loud] lound	257.24	appositely] appostely
65.18	1577] 1677	258.13	Committee] Committeee
67.4	*Zachary*] *Zahary*	298.2	worldly] wordly
74.14	putrid] putid	298.4	saucy] sauy
86.15	seem] seen	299.4	triffle,] triffles
104.11	candour] condour	326.8	Makefun] Makfun
140.9	honorable] honorably	326.20	for] four
147.27	instead] istead	376.11	Clubical] Clubcal
151.9	Shoulder] Shouder	380.8	Sincere] Sinsere
154.19	for] fore	382.12	any affront] an ~
158.9	arangement] aragement	384.3	Rules] Rule
162.4	awkward] awkard	387.25	long] lon
169.22	Seemly Spruce] Spruce Seemly	401.10	Anap:] Anaa
172.3	politic] politc	413.4	here Sir] her ~
173.15	generous a disposition] generous disposition	420.9	Orations] Oratons
		457.19	and many] any ~
194.12	feignd] feingnd	460.7	neither] neitheir

Substantive Changes

Page.Line
498.11	alledged] alleddged
504.8	Enmity] Emnity
510.10	the] th
513.15	Ill] I'll
518.12	have Indeed been] ~ ~ have ~
518.12	too heavy] to ~
522.13	August] Augus
544.4	they] the
545.9	they] thy
547.22	they] the
550.24	and knowledge] an ~
*430.1.2	an] in
*431.2.19	effects] effets
*431.2.25	to be believed] to believed
*434.2.40	publishes] pubishes
*439.1.42	Speech] Spech
*440.2.11	Stiffrump] Stiffrum

Volume II

4.15	Indeed] Inddeed
12.7	discovers an] ~ and
27.6	*nocturnal*] *noturnal*
30.4	Harpsicords] Harspsicords
36.15	women] woment
42.3	School-boy] School-by
54.22	letters] leters
70.1	Law] Low
72.24	when he is] when is
74.23	Laconic] Laconi
76.24	Supplicant] Suppliant
85.5	his] is
86.6	in] it
91.22	Inconvenience] Inconvenice
96.14	wholsome] wholsoem
109.18	beloved] bloved
113.19	it] in
118.22	original] originial
124.24	pervert] pervent
125.9	Safety] Saftety
127.21–128.1	unacountable] unaountable
129.9–10	dye during the] dye the
134.13	Neverout] Neverous
165.20	a] ar
169.13	Intirely] Intirlely
175.19	here] her

Page.Line
178.14	transgressed] trangressed
181.12	Character] Charcter
185.15	pantomime] patomime
201.5	one] on
203.4	he] the
205.10	flagging] flaggin
206.21	Rhubarb] Rhubard
209.9	nigh] night
211.16	Esqr, he was] Esqr was
230.11	Scenes] Senes
250.21	here] her
250.23	here] her
253.13	Pickeringtonus] Pilkeringtonus
254.9	opinionated] opiniated
254.20	they] the
256.5	Sensible] Sensibe
264.24	be] by
268.16	here] her
272.22	to] too
274.22–275.1	profitable quality introduces] profitable introduces
288.1	146] 246
295.18	XLIX] XLXIX
307.4	went] wen
311.21	unparallelled] uparallelled
311.21	really] relly
317.23	After] Aftr
334.22–23	pride to Level] pride Level
346.20	thus] thuse
394.2	do] to
394.24	London, in which] London, which
397.26	We'll] Well
416.5	abandoned] abandone
418.10	Rehearse] Rhearse
430.4	At] A
437.12	petticoat] petticat
447.11	Quaint] Quint
448.3	mentions] mentons
456.5	one] ane
456.15	necessary] necesscary
465.11	property] propertly
465.17	Subjects] Subject
468.7	texts] tents
480.13	exciters] exiters
484.20	one] on
492.19	securing] scuring

Page.Line

504.6	Immediatly]	Immeditly
513.8	particular]	particulart
514.12	regard]	regart
518.13	too]	to
522.5	Lordshp's]	Lordsph's
522.22	apprehending]	aprrehending
524.20	and]	am
529.17	prudent]	pirident
535.9	domineer]	donineer
537.16	contemporaries]	cotemporaries
537.17	moderen]	moderent
539.6	these]	thes
539.17	dignity]	dignuty
545.21	his usual]	is ~
*401.1.9	Defined]	Dfined
*402.1.9	nursery]	nurery
*403.2.46	addressed]	address
*405.1.26	Replacing]	Replacin
*405.2.39	used]	uesd
*407.2.39	Ridiculous]	Ridicuolus
*408.2.29	education]	eductation
*413.1.30	enthusiasm]	ethusiasm
*413.1.47	honorary]	honororary
*414.2.39	Creating]	Creaing
*420.1.25	recommending]	recommeding
*421.2.43	Caprice]	Caprie
*422.2.14	Understanding]	Understand

Volume III

4.22	electrized]	elecrtized
5.9	or]	ar
14.10–11	neighbour]	neigbour
15.4	Jealousy]	Jealous
17.17	too]	to
19.21–20.1	Canopies]	Conopies
20.13	Solemnity]	Soleminity
25.5	too]	to
25.7	fusty]	futy
28.16	bruitt]	brutt
34.10	whatsoever]	whasoever
34.26	Chancellor]	Chancllor
42.7	Colonel]	Colnel
58.22	several]	sereval

Page.Line

58.23	succeed]	succceed
62.16	I'll]	Ill
80.3	Yes]	Yest
92.17	screen]	scireen
94.6	Plouden]	Ploudem
111.8	September]	Septemper
127.29	I'll]	Ill
131.23	Chorus]	Charus
131.26	magnanimous] magnamous	
132.7	We'll]	Well
132.14	parade]	parde
134.20	Spheres]	Speres
137.22	Vivaldi]	Vialdi
138.7	we'll]	well
142.11	looked]	looke
151.24	accordingly]	accordngly
144a.18	Gentlemen]	Gentleman
146a.10	bloodshed]	blooshed
152a.6	Neverout]	Neverut
158.16	Conspiration] Conpiration	
158.21–22	Iniquitously]	Iniqutously
161.10	Williamsburg] Williambsurg	
162.13	ejaculations]	ejulations
168.5	necessary]	neessary
168.17	too]	to
174.2	virtue]	vrtue
176.4	probably be culled] probably culled	
176.19	there]	their
178.9	Squeamishly]	Squeanishly
179.2	precise]	preise
179.15	Low and]	~ in
181.20	recover]	rocover
182.17	that he]	the
191.2	Second]	Socond
191.20	obeying]	obying
194.11–12	further]	futher
212.8	may]	me
244.3	*Chancellor's*]	*Chanellor's*
248.8	he]	the
257.13	frowned]	frown
261.21	trespasses]	terespasses
281.2	I'll]	'Ill
281.17	booby]	looby
284.4	Quirpum]	Quircum
291.18	the honorable]	he ~

Substantive Changes

Page.Line		
292.2	appointing]	appinting
292.6	punishments]	puniishments
*217.13	several]	severals
*219.8	William Lux Esqr]	William Esqr
334.13	sung]	song
345.22	Chancellors]	Chanchellors
349.4	alledging]	alldging
371.15	now]	no
397.7	*Je ne sçay*]	*Je ne scay*
397.23	off]	of
403.4	exuberant]	exuberat
412.19	off]	of
413.23	honor]	hononor
417.17	Had]	Hand
422.24	bred]	berd

Page.Line		
430.6	be Informed]	should ~ ~
434.5	no]	not
437.6	230]	130
440.7	General]	Genereal
*302.34	part]	port
*306.33	Grog]	Groog
511.24	too]	to
517.6	off]	of
521.27	*Servant*]	*Servan*
524.8	Constitution]	Constituton
528.15	Individual]	Indvidual
533.13	mathematical]	mathematial
536.1	Janry]	Jnary
537.11	business]	businness
558.14	further]	futher

INDEX TO VOLUMES I-III

Abdallah, III, 37
Abigail, I, 357
Abraham, I, 30, 77, 121, II, 19, 140
Académie Royale des Sciences, I, 41, 253
Accrostics, II, 13, 37–38, 71–72
Achilles, I, 88, II, 144, III, 278
Acrisius, II, 258
Adam, I, 37
Addison, John (Swillum Swagbelly): made honorary member of club, I, 256
Addison, Joseph, I, 197, II, 7, 26, 139
Adrian IV (pope), I, 83
Aeacus, II, 203
Aeneid, II, 22
Aeschylus, I, 22
Aesculapius, II, 257
Aesop, I, 410, III, 39
Agaberta Maga, II, 24
Agamemnon, II, 144, III, 37, 281
Agamestor, I, 354–355
Agathocles, II, 352
Aglaitadus, II, 11
Aidan, I, 47
Ajax, II, 144
Alban, Saint, I, 120
Alberoni, Giulio, III, 37
Alberti, Domenico, I, 55
Albertus Magnus, II, 19, 24
Albinoni, Madam, I, 252
Alchemy, II, 23
Alcibiades, I, 271, III, 37, 111, 128
Alexander the Great, I, 24, 25, 44, 76, 119, 247, 353, 355, II, 240, 323, 351, III, 41, 45, 84, 303
Alexander Severus, Marcus Aurelius, I, 146
Alexis, III, 105
Alfred the Great, III, 46
Alhandal, II, 24
Almahide (Scudéry), I, 22, II, 23, 198
Amadis de Gaul, II, 198, 324, III, 78
Amadís de Gaula, I, 11, 22, II, 22

Amadís de Grecia (da Silva), I, 22, II, 22
Ambrose, Saint, I, 119
Amphibalus, Saint, I, 120
Amphitruo (Plautus), II, 138, III, 270
Anacreon, I, 361, II, 14, 15, III, 42
Anagrams, II, 13, 35–36
Ancients and moderns, II, 26, 137–138, III, 128–129, 138, 181–182, 253–254
Andraeus (Johann Valentin Andreä), II, 24
Andrewes, Lancelot (bishop), II, 27
Annapolis: club life in, I, 81–85
Anniversaries, Tuesday Club: first, I, 215; second, I, 240–242, II, 375, III, 183; third, I, 282–284; fourth, I, 337–344; fifth, II, 97–107; sixth, II, 266–276; seventh, III, 20–29, 33–44; eighth, III, 149–157; ninth, III, 232–248; processions, I, 240–242, 337, II, 266–268; speeches, I, 337–339, II, 99–103, 270–273, III, 22–29, 36–44, 152–157, 232–241; odes, I, 341–342, II, 103–105, 266, 268, 273–275, III, 20–22, 150–151, 242–243; music, II, 107–122, 278–293, III, 44, 157–176
Anson, George, Lord Anson, I, 124
Anticovenanters, I, 54
Antiquitates convivial (Stuck), III, 40
Antiquity: highly esteemed, I, 23–33
Antony, Mark, I, 174
Apelles, I, 31
Apollo, I, 39, 40, 44, II, 8, 102, 272, 320, 331, III, 26
Apollyon, III, 205
Apuleius, Lucius, I, 272, 273
Arabians, I, 29
Arbitrary power, I, 94, 213, 292, 321, II, 40, 166, 209
Archaeus Faber, I, 123, III, 24
Archimedes, III, 285, 292
Aretino, Guido, III, 37, 267
Ariosto, Lodovico, II, 21
Aristarchus of Samothrace, III, 30, 31

399

Aristophanes, I, 353
Aristotle, I, 42, 143, 355, 400, II, 17, 127, 138, 144, 152, 332, 368, III, 252, 272, 290
Armstrong, Archie, I, 358, 359, II, 12
Artamène; ou, Le grand Cyrus (Scudéry), I, 22, II, 198
Arthur, III, 156
Astoreth, III, 205
Astraea, II, 204
Astronomy, II, 192
Athanasius, Saint, I, 119, III, 106
Athenians, I, 25, 172, II, 354, III, 129, 149, 250
Athens, I, 27, II, 11, 352
Atkinson, George (Joggle Hasty): made honorary member of club, I, 134; engages in learned debate, I, 147, 149; steward, I, 166; forfeits his seat, I, 170
Atterbury, Francis (bishop of Rochester), I, 398
Atticus, Titus Pomponius, I, 137
Attila the Hun, II, 252
Attraction, theory of, I, 33–34, III, 9–10
Augustine, Saint, I, 122
Augustus, I, 139, II, 219
Aurangzeb, II, 225
Aurelianus, Lucius Domitius, II, 323
Auretti, Madona, I, 55
Avicenna, III, 37
Ayrer, Georg Heinrich, I, 266

Babel, Tower of, II, 200
Bacchus, I, 38, 42, 44, 97, II, 197, 234, 257
Bacon, Anthony (Comely Coppernose, Agent for the Club in London), II, 296, III, 65; arranges to have club badges made, I, 322, 325; sends the Great Seal, I, 409; appointed agent for the club, I, 415, II, 40, 49–50; made honorary member of club, II, 41; letters written by, I, 401–402, II, 94, 196, 328–329; letters written to, II, 40–41, 158–159
Bacon, Francis, Lord Verulam, II, 26, III, 244
Bacon, John (John Gabble), III, 85, 275; sings in club, II, 268; appointed squire of Eastern Shore Triumvirate, II, 295–296; engaged in battle against the French, III, 276
Bacon, Roger, II, 26
Bacon, Thomas (Signior Lardini), I, 237, 238, 333, III, 309–310; made honorary member of club, I, 178; in anniversary procession, I, 240; performs music, I, 242, II, 105, 177, 268, III, 35, 86, 179, 184; member of Eastern Shore Triumvirate, I, 386, 387, II, 65, 294, 295, III, 85; sets anniversary odes to music, II, 159, 359; his proposals for charity school, II, 179–180, 184, 189–190, 194; appointed chief triumvir, II, 276; composes music for club, III, 33, 35, 179; poem written for, II, 182–183
Badges: significance of, I, 217–220, II, 252, III, 19; Tuesday Club badges, I, 215–216, 282, 322, 398. *See also* Medals
Bajazet I, I, 358
Balaam's Ass (poem), I, 102
Balance of power, II, 256–261
Baltimore Bards, literary battle with Tuesday Club, I, 153–163
Banister, John, III, 67
Bantam, II, 214
Baptism, II, 353
Barnes, Abraham (Curious Courtly): made honorary member of club, I, 256
Barrow, Isaac, I, 201
Bavius, I, 134
Beaumont and Fletcher, II, 139, III, 189, 271
Becher, Johann Joachim, II, 24
Becket, Saint Thomas, I, 213
Beelzebub, II, 24, 25, III, 205
Beggars Bush, The, III, 271
Belial, II, 9
Bellianis of Greece, II, 198. See also *Honour of Chivalrie, The*
Belphegor, III, 205
Belt, Joseph, II, 94, 158
Benedetti, I, 55
Benedictus, III, 37
Benefit of Farting . . . Explained by Don Fartinando Puff-indorst, The, I, 37

Index

Berberini, Madona, I, 55
Berkeley, George (bishop of Cloyne), III, 77
Bernard, Edward, II, 24
Bernard Canisianus, I, 71
Bernhardus à Doma, III, 42, 341
Béroalde de Verville, François, I, 360
Bethlem Royal Hospital (Bedlam), I, 266, II, 27
Bickerstaff, Isaac, I, 209
Biermann, Martin, II, 24
Biography, I, 19, 74
Blackmore, Sir Richard, I, 49, II, 8, 28, 29
Bloody-Bones, I, 118
Blunt, Sir Harry, II, 197
Bodin, Jean, II, 24
Boileau(-Despréaux), Nicolas, II, 21
Bolingbroke, Henry Saint John, Viscount, I, 122
Bona Dea, mysteries of, I, 44, II, 335
Bononcini, Giovanni Battista, I, 55
Bordley, John Beale (Quirpum Comic, Master of Ceremonies), I, 332, 341, 369, II, 133, 204–205, 369, III, 58, 106, 190, 191, 288, 319–320; made longstanding member of club, I, 298–299; high steward, I, 322, 380, II, 131, 206, 303, 375, III, 79, 108, 179, 205; master of ceremonies, I, 328, 332–333; his character, I, 328–330; addresses the club, I, 375–376; his satirical letter on cats, I, 380–382; leaves the club, I, 383, III, 229; readmitted to the club, II, 125–126; sings in club, II, 262; involved in Chancellor's Rebellion, II, 366, 367; deputy president, II, 376, III, 79, 217; member of Grand Committee, III, 119; tried in club, III, 212–215; letter from, I, 323–324
Bordley, Stephen (Huffman Snap), II, 66, 82–83, 130, 133, 174, 188–189, 231, III, 83, 309; made longstanding member of club, I, 298–299; high steward, I, 307, 392, II, 55, 168, 262, 294, 324, 398; deputy president, I, 321, II, 164, 225, 303; involved in club commotion, II, 80; involved in Chancellor's Rebellion, II, 364, 365, 367; letters written by, I, 308–310, 396
Bothwell Bridge, battle of, I, 53
Boyd, Rev. Zachary, I, 65
Brahe, Tycho, II, 26
British, antiquity of, I, 23, 26
Broughton, John, II, 142
Broughton's Amphitheatre, I, 405
Brown, Thomas, I, 360, II, 8, III, 37
Brutus, Lucius Junius, II, 232–233
Buchanan, George, I, 143, II, 26
Bullen, John (Bully Blunt, Sir John Oldcastle, Club Champion), I, 166, 215, 237, 240, 242, 257, 292, 296, 307, 343, 375, II, 99–100, 187, 207, 227, 235, 241, 244, 276, 306, 342, 395, III, 25, 29, 35, 36, 75, 86, 103, 104, 114–115, 153, 154, 156, 189, 205–206, 257; founding member of club, I, 125; steward, I, 128, 170, 205; involved in literary battle with Baltimore Bards, I, 152, 154, 161; seeks presidency and is defeated, I, 174; opposes the president, I, 176, 178, 226, 325, 395; objects to club's proceedings, I, 205, 283, 285–287, 289, 327–328, II, 371; appointed club champion, I, 226–228; high steward, I, 259, 273, 293, 379, II, 47, 158, 240, 312, 396, III, 79, 116, 184, 193, 211; defends the club's liberties, I, 270, 367, 378; disowns title of Oldcastle, I, 284; sings in club, I, 291, II, 300; proposes smutty toast, I, 294; indicted, I, 313–319; his commission, II, 59–60, 79; in anniversary processions, II, 77, 268; dances in club, II, 106, 183, 297; objects to conundrums, II, 160, 178; involved in Chancellor's Rebellion, II, 367; assumes presidential chair, II, 375; member of Grand Committee, III, 118–121; deputy president, III, 146, 183, 193; leaves the club, III, 211–212; letters written by, I, 259, 284–285, 293, 379, II, 46, 240, III, 112–113; letters written to, I, 281, 309–310, 396, 405–406, II, 47–48, 55, 75–76, 78, 85–86, III, 116; poem written for, II, 78

Bumbasto, Colonel, I, 240
Bunyan, John, I, 134
Burman, Anne, III, 124
Burton, John, III, 37
Burton, Robert, III, 37; Hamilton's parody of, I, 69–74
Butler, Samuel, I, 387, III, 239; quoted, III, 254

Caelius Aurelianus, III, 37
Caesar, Gaius Julius, I, 21, 24, 55, 76, 119, 174, 213, 246, 247, II, 13, 123, 138, 219, 260, 351, 352, 369, III, 78, 238, 239
Cain, I, 28, 37, 363
Calanus, I, 355
Calder, James (Abraham Bumper), I, 211, 282; made honorary member of club, I, 127–128
Caligula, I, 145, II, 74, 213, III, 303
Calvin, John, II, 26, III, 106
Cambridge Jests, I, 352, II, 30
Cambridge University, II, 197, 339
Cameron, Richard, I, 53
Cameronians, I, 53
Canopy of State, Tuesday Club, I, 327, II, 193, 204, 207, 366, 372, III, 19
Canterbury, archbishop of, I, 27
Canute the Great, III, 303
Cape Breton Island, I, 150, 151
Cap of State, Tuesday Club, II, 73–74, 180–182, 199–203, 204, 206–207, 209, 241–242, 245, 311, 340, 344, III, 19
Cardano, Geronimo, I, 119, II, 24, III, 233
Carpenter, John (Giovanni Carpentiro), II, 335
Case, John, II, 39
Cassandre (La Calprenède), I, 22, II, 23, 198
Cassius Vecellinus, Spurius, II, 260
Catholic Church: disparaged, I, 32, 42, 45, 182–183, 283, II, 167–168, 196, 213, 252, 254–255, 260, 300, III, 128, 232, 296; its antiquity, I, 37; its growth, I, 391. *See also* Pope
Catiline, II, 260, 347
Cato the Elder, I, 55, 246, 271, 355, II, 258
Cato the Younger, I, 139

Cato (Addison), I, 197, II, 139
Ceremony, power of, III, 19, 127–137
Ceres, II, 257, III, 152
Cervantes, Miguel de, I, 134
Chair of State, II, 366, 369, 372, III, 213
Charity school (Talbot County), II, 180, 184, 194
Charles I, I, 88, 141, 213, II, 13, 55, 349, III, 121, 181
Charles II, III, 138, 142
Charles the Great, III, 45
Charlette, John (Don John Charlotto, Clerk of the Kitchen), II, 206, 241, 242, 385, III, 54, 141, 255; saves the president, II, 308, 309, 313–319; involved in Battle of Farce-alia, III, 52; made clerk of the kitchen, III, 202; abuses the president, III, 210; poem written by, II, 182–183
Chase, Thomas (Bard Bavius, Baltimore Bard): involved in literary battle with Tuesday Club, I, 153–159, 164
Chaucer, Geoffrey, II, 21, III, 280
Chevy Chace (song), II, 378
Cheyne, George, I, 35
China, I, 23–24, 27, 247
Christianity, I, 391, 392, II, 194
Chronogram, II, 36–37
Church of England, I, 37, 141, 213, II, 194, 348, III, 107, 135, 296, 312, 324
Cibber, Colley, I, 21, II, 99, 158, 329, 330, 332, 379
Cicero, Marcus Tullius, I, 55, 76, 139, 271, 279, II, 13, 16, 78, 182, III, 67, 80; quoted, I, 137, 354, II, 21
Cincinnatus, Lucius Quinctius, I, 139
Clarke, Samuel, I, 201
Claudius, II, 138, 213, 214
Clélie (Scudéry), I, 22, II, 23, 198
Cléopâtre (La Calprenède), I, 22, 246, II, 23, 198
Cloacina, III, 139, 269
Clodius, II, 335
Club box: established for charity, I, 198–199; disputes concerning it, I, 207, 230, 268, 287; abolished, I, 289; proposal to revive it, I, 368–369
Clubs: Hamilton's definition of, I, 33; antiquity of, I, 37–44, III, 39–40; in

London, I, 44; in Annapolis, I, 81–85; women's clubs, I, 82; Royalist Clubs (of Annapolis), I, 83, 88–93, 107; College Club, I, 85; worthies of, I, 115–124; Monday Club (of New York), I, 124, II, 209, 210, 212, 237, III, 30, 57, 60, 61–75, 318; Rustic Club, II, 129, 321; Lying Club, II, 197; Saturday Club (of Annapolis), II, 247; Charles Town Club, III, 223. *See also* Eastern Shore Triumvirate; Red-House Club; Thursday Club of Hiccory Hill; Ugly Club; Whin-Bush Club

Clydesdale, I, 50, 51, 56

Coilus, I, 47

Coke, Sir Edward, III, 190

Cole, Charles (Nasifer Jole, President), I, 198, 229, 236, 268, 299, 300, 312, 319, 338, 375, 398, II, 49–50, 66–67, 75, 79, 84, 87–88, 92, 97, 134, 180, 185–187, 188, 212–213, 215, 217, 264, 295–296, 335, 384–388, III, 24–25, 30, 33, 41–44, 47–49, 56, 78, 85, 88, 99, 105, 206, 257, 268–269, 274–275, 295, 330–331; his character, I, 39, 54, 134–146, 151, 173, 194–197, 267, 272, II, 156; made longstanding member of club, I, 134; steward, I, 146, 170, 215, 230; sings in club, I, 147, 169, 269–270, 278, II, 302, III, 345; promotes luxury, I, 150, 170, 173, 189–190, 212, 222–223; jealous of the secretary, I, 166, 204, 291; elected president, I, 174–175; privileges granted him, I, 175–176; opposes club ball, I, 192–193; jealous of his prerogative, I, 210–211, 334, 397, II, 44–45, 54, 128, 170, 189; creates club champion and master of ceremonies, I, 223; speech on wisdom, I, 224–226; creates club speaker, I, 231; his mercantile style of writing, I, 238; high steward, I, 265, 283, 337, 401, II, 99, 190, 266, 366, III, 20, 102, 255, 305; refuses to grant club's petition, I, 285–287; yields up club box, I, 288; his arbitrary power, I, 292–293, II, 168, 174; grants commissions, I, 297, 298, 302, II, 41–44; his presidential style, I, 297–298; confirms members, I, 311; holds anniversaries, I, 337, 340, II, 99, 266; satirized, I, 380–381; petitioned by Single Ladies of Annapolis, I, 388; refuses secretary's request to write history of the club, I, 392; wears cap of state, II, 203; rejects it, II, 206; ceremony of his capation, II, 244–247; attacked by thieves, II, 304–311, 313–319; his accident in club, II, 342; his decathedration, II, 360–369; restored to the presidential chair, II, 396–397; involved in Battle of Farcealia, III, 52–54; victim of hoax, III, 102–103; addressed by Grand Committee, III, 118–121; petition addressed to, III, 200–201; opposes the chancellor, III, 226–228; letters written by, I, 237–238, 239, 240, 275, 324, II, 163, III, 147; letters written to, I, 259, 260, 263, 277, 280, 284–285, 289–290, 296, 302–303, 307–309, 323–324, 335, 370, 380, 384, 396, 397–398, 403–404, II, 45, 124–125, 131, 159, 192–193, 214–215, 217–218, 225–226, 234–235, 240, III, 147; poem written by, III, 344; poems written for, II, 50–51, 71–72, 228–229, 299, 313–319, 337–339, 373–374, 377–378, 390–392, III, 122–125, 197–198, 217, 223–225, 306, 346–348

Collection of Sundrie Statutes (Pulton), III, 342

Collins, Anthony, III, 18

Columella, III, 37

Comedy, II, 143, 146, III, 129; satire, I, 351; burlesque, II, 15; punning, II, 16–17, 30; ridicule, II, 53–54, III, 332; farce, II, 141

Come Jolly Bacchus (song), II, 337

Commerce, I, 135–136

Commissions, Tuesday Club, I, 297, 298, 302, II, 41–44, 59–60, 79, 127–128, 224, 295–296, 303, 336–337, III, 187, 265–266, 317–319

Confucius, III, 46

Congreve, William, I, 201

Constantine, I, 139, II, 167

Constantinople, I, 356, 358, II, 18, 353
Conundrums: derivation of, I, 186–187; collections of, I, 352; definition of, II, 30–32; Tuesday Club, II, 52–53, 60, 62–63, 70, 72–73, 80, 82, 83, 84–85, 89, 95–96, 126, 128–129, 134–135, 155–156, 157, 159, 161, 163, 164, 165–166, 172–173, 177–179, III, 140
Copernicus, Nicolaus, II, 26
Corelli, Arcangelo, I, 55
Cork, John: member of Ugly Club, I, 107
Cotterell, Sir Clement, I, 110, 228, 339, II, 42
Cotton, Charles, III, 22
Counterblaste to Tobacco, A (James I), I, 48
Covenanters, I, 54
Cowley, Abraham, II, 15
Cradock, Thomas (Bard Mevius, Mevius Pumpkin), III, 125, 179, 289, 298, 299; made honorary member of club, III, 117; involved in literary battle with Tuesday Club, I, 153–160
Critics: of *History*, I, 15–16, 245; of the times, I, 69–72, 245–253; literary, I, 72–73, 154, 155, II, 86, 393; in club, I, 153–156, 162–163
Crito, I, 266
Cromwell, Oliver, I, 45, 49, 90, II, 224, III, 46, 122
Crusades, I, 217
Culloden, III, 221
Culpeper, Nicholas, I, 39
Cumming, Alexander (Prettyman Spyplot): made honorary member of club, II, 71
Cumming, Thomas (Coney Pimp Frontinbrass, Agent for the Club in America), I, 320, II, 206, 209, 234, 242–243, III, 30, 34–35, 46–50, 54–56; his character, II, 210, 212; his interview with the president, II, 215–217; proposes Frontinbrassian Articles, II, 219–222; made honorary member of and agent for the club, II, 224; his patent, II, 227; performs Grand Ceremony of the Capation, II, 244–247; incites Battle of Farcealia, III, 51–53; tried in club, III, 57–76; letters written by, II, 214–215, 217, 218
Cumming, William, Sr. (Jealous Spyplot, Sr.), I, 292, 340, 344, 368, 388, II, 69, 174, 240, 265, 268, 334, 360, III, 212, 258–259; member of Red-House Club, I, 94; founding member of Tuesday Club, I, 111, 125; steward, I, 127, 190, 223, 235; opposes club's proceedings, I, 168, 176, 198–199, 230; presents the club box, I, 200; speech on trade and traffic, I, 221; his prophetic wisdom, I, 228, 257, 415, II, 47; deputy president, I, 239, II, 168, 264, 373; high steward, I, 256, 270, 284, 292, 321, 377, II, 40, 163, 184, 233, 320; serves as club attorney, I, 316, 319, II, 161–162, 194–196, 247–248; gelastic law executed upon, II, 71; moves to abolish conundrums, II, 178; tried in club, II, 185–187; defends club's liberty, II, 219, 222, 231, 232, 239; involved in Chancellor's Rebellion, II, 366, 367; leaves the club, II, 379; his death, II, 397; letters written by, I, 378, II, 234
Cumming, William, Jr. (Jealous Spyplot, Jr.), III, 20; made longstanding member of club, I, 298–299; high steward, I, 321, 383, II, 85, 264; letters written by, I, 384, II, 85–86
Curll, Edmund, II, 333
Cyril, Saint, I, 119
Cyropaedia (Xenophon), II, 10
Cyrus the Great, I, 24, 247, II, 10, 11, 323, 351, III, 45

Damhouder, Josse de, II, 24, III, 249
Danae, II, 258
Dandiuses, II, 24
Dardanus, III, 281
David, I, 357, III, 38, 84
De arcanis Amoris et Veneris, II, 333
Deism, I, 33
Delphi, temple at, I, 250
Demetrius Ixion, I, 250
Democritus Junior. *See* Burton, Robert
Democritus of Abdera, I, 252, 352, II, 17, III, 232

Demosthenes, I, 138, 202, 220, 355, II, 182, III, 149
Dennis, John, II, 322
Descartes, René, I, 130, III, 10
Devil (Satan), I, 11, 32, 41, 357, 358, 359, II, 10, 23, 139, 197, 208, III, 13, 18, 135, 188, 205, 206
Dickinson, James (Theophilus Smirker), II, 195, III, 85; member of Eastern Shore Triumvirate, II, 65; made honorary member of club, II, 71; elected as triumvir, II, 175–176
Diocletian, I, 139
Diodorus Siculus, I, 21
Diogenes the Cynic, I, 353, II, 17, 352, III, 83
Dionysius, II, 270
Directory for Midwives, A (Culpeper), I, 39
Divine Legation of Moses Demonstrated, The (Warburton), I, 33, III, 41
Divine right (*jure divino*), I, 40, 76, 90, 95, II, 167, 352, III, 105, 122
Dod, John, I, 131, III, 237
Doe, John, I, 116, III, 274, 337, 340, 343
Domitian, I, 139
Don Quixote, III, 78
Doolittle, Thomas, I, 131, III, 237
Dorsey, Edward (Drawlum Quaint, Speaker), I, 99, 215, 222, 235, 236, 265, 276, 288, II, 321, III, 57–59, 179; made longstanding member of club, I, 134; steward, I, 149, 170, 211; his amorous adventure, I, 151–152; involved in literary battle with Baltimore Bards, I, 152, 154, 164; his odd behavior, I, 205; speech on honesty, I, 207; a satirist, I, 209; his abilities as speaker, I, 226, 254–255, 263, 273; appointed speaker, I, 231; resigns and resumes his office, I, 232; high steward, I, 239, 262, 278; in anniversary procession, I, 240; his marriage, I, 279; involved in Battle of Farce-alia, III, 52, 53; letter to, I, 239
Dorsey, Richard (Tunbelly Bowzer), II, 65, 67, 220; made longstanding member of club, II, 54–55; high steward, II, 92, 174, 262, 327, 398, III, 85, 139; deputy president, II, 163, 262, III, 112, 139; tried in club, II, 187–188; involved in Chancellor's Rebellion, II, 367; member of Grand Committee, III, 121; leaves the club, III, 193
Downie, George, I, 209
Drake, Sir Francis, III, 46
Dromo, II, 336
Drugger, Abel, II, 35
Dryden, John, I, 49, II, 21, 22, 26, 143, III, 253; quoted, II, 28, III, 144
Dubos, Jean-Baptiste (Abbé), I, 29, 30, II, 140
Dulany, Daniel, Jr., II, 375, III, 248
Dulany, Dennis (Dio Ramble), II, 99, III, 20, 149, 207; made honorary member of club, II, 71; in anniversary procession, II, 97; perpetrates hoax on the president, III, 102–103
Dulany, Walter (Slyboots Pleasant), I, 226, 334, II, 133, 387, III, 90, 139, 252, 268, 282, 315; made longstanding member of club, I, 134; steward, I, 169, 207, 232, 235; his amorous adventure, I, 209; deputy president, I, 210, 301, III, 144, 219, 228–229, 266, 317, 319; high steward, I, 255, 268, 368, II, 45, 127, 194, 199, 301, 373, III, 57, 104, 177, 194, 223, 268, 317, 319; rare display of anger, I, 287, II, 80, III, 142–143; his commission, II, 127–128; his conundrumish genius, II, 156; involved in Chancellor's Rebellion, II, 367; involved in Battle of Farce-alia, III, 53; indicted, III, 330–332, 350–353; letters written by, I, 307–308, II, 45, 47–48; letters written to, III, 269–274, 335
Duncan, John, I, 50, 56
Dunkers, III, 182
Duns Scotus, John, I, 143, II, 18, 24, III, 338
D'Urfey, Thomas, II, 8
Dutch, III, 264, 299, 341, 344
Duvries, III, 338

Eachard, John, I, 134, III, 296
Earle, Michael (Jocifer Bluechin), II, 89, 367; made honorary member of

club, III, 265; his commission, III, 265–266
Eastern Shore Triumvirate, I, 369, 404, II, 65, 86–88, 174–176, 179, 276, 294–296, III, 78–79, 85, 91; arises from Tuesday Club, I, 128, 392, 401; formation of, I, 343; letter written by, II, 78; poem written by, II, 297, 299
Edinburgh, I, 80, 359, 363, II, 35, 309
Edward the Confessor, I, 49
Edward III, I, 217
Edward, duke of York, II, 369
Effluvia, I, 35
Egypt, I, 83, 410, II, 271
Egyptians, I, 23, II, 13
Electricity: experiments with, I, 35, 99, III, 9–10
Elizabeth I, I, 47, II, 323, 348, III, 41
Ellis, John (Giddy Thoughtless): his satiric poem, I, 164
Ennius, Quintus, I, 73
Ens rationis, II, 171, 212, III, 78
Enthusiasm, power of, II, 224–225, 253–255, 260
Epaminondas, III, 46
Ephemeris, III, 300, 312
Epictetus, I, 18, III, 67
Epicurus, I, 171, III, 37
Episcopacy, II, 309
Epistolary writing. *See* Letters, Tuesday Club
Equivocal generation, II, 171–172
Eric (king of Norway), II, 23
Erskine, Ralph, I, 43
Esau, I, 173, II, 10, III, 238
Esteron, Monsieur, I, 89
Ethiopians, I, 29
Euripides, II, 144
Eusebius of Caesarea, I, 118
Eve, I, 37, II, 9

Fable of the Bees, The (Mandeville), I, 150
Faerie Queene, The (Spenser), II, 228
Falstaff, Sir John, III, 28, 29
Familiar Letters (Howell), I, 102
Farinelli, Carlo, I, 55
Faust, Johann, II, 24, III, 37, 312
Faventinus, Paul-Marie, III, 37
Fawkes, Guy, II, 306

Fell, John, II, 16
Fergus I, I, 47
Fergus II, I, 47
Fibber, Humbug: tries to deceive president, II, 341, 342
Ficino, Marsilio, I, 71
Fielding, Henry, I, 134, 385, III, 45, 51
Fisher, James, I, 43
Fitzhugh, William (Comico Butman): president of Thursday Club of Hiccory Hill, II, 243, 244, III, 31–32, 33; made honorary member of Tuesday Club, III, 205; club champion for one night, III, 309, 314–316; his commission, III, 317–319
Flattery, power of, II, 90–91, 190
Flavel, John, II, 28
Fleet Street, II, 333
Fletcher, John, III, 271
Florilegia Sacra (Lake), II, 193
Foedera (Rymer), III, 296
Foliot, I, 118
Forty, John, III, 268
Foxe, John, III, 37
France: disparaged by Hamilton, I, 20–22, II, 23, III, 128, 129; antiquity of, I, 28; bishop from, I, 139; king of, I, 359; war with, II, 36, 37; theater in, II, 140–141; saved by Joan of Arc, II, 310; language of, III, 102, 184, 292–293, 299; mores in, III, 138–139; dissension in, III, 229; at war on Ohio, III, 275, 276, 319; in law, III, 343
Franklin, Benjamin (Electro Vitrifrice), II, 310, III, 215
Frederick the Great, II, 256, III, 274, 275
Freemasonry, I, 52, 81, 387, 396, II, 157, III, 103, 146; its antiquity, I, 25–26, 38, 41, 43–44; ceremonies, I, 214–215

Gaguin, Robert, II, 24
Galen, I, 42
Galileo, II, 26, III, 37
Gallus, Gaius Cornelius, III, 37
Games, I, 15, 16, 151, II, 142–152
Garrick, David, I, 252
Geddes, Jenny, II, 309
Gelastic law, Tuesday Club, I, 133, 289,

320, 400, II, 63, 71, 327, III, 105, 268, 284
Geminiani, Francesco, I, 55
Gemma, Cornelius, II, 24
Genearchy, II, 323–324, 335–336, III, 240; of Tuesday Club, II, 325–327, 334, 379
Gentleman's Magazine, II, 296, 328, 329, 330
Geometry, II, 271
George, Saint, I, 119
George II, II, 138
George, Sydney (Dormer Goggle), II, 367
George a Green, I, 119, 120
George de Trebizonde, II, 24
Germany, I, 28
Gibson, John, I, 82
Gibson, Mark (Dumpling Gundiguts): his character, I, 133, 217; made longstanding member of club, I, 134; steward, I, 146, 207, 210; accused of bribery, I, 223; deputy president, I, 237; high steward, I, 239, 261; excluded from club, I, 284
Gil Blas, III, 189, 298
Gilpin, Neal, I, 56, 66, 85, 86, 93
Giovio, Paolo, quoted, III, 156
Glorious Revolution, II, 272
Göckel, Rudolf, II, 24
Godelmann, Johann, II, 24
Gondomar, Diego Sarmiento de Acuña, count of, I, 48
Gooch, Sir William, II, 310
Gordon, John (Smoothum Sly, Master of Ceremonies): founding member of club, I, 111, 125, II, 86, 276, 295; involved in literary battle with Baltimore Bards, I, 152, 154, 157, 161; sings in club, I, 167; his gallantry, I, 193; deputy president, I, 207; steward, I, 210; speech on civil government, I, 210–211; butt of satire, I, 226; appointed master of ceremonies, I, 228, 292; high steward, I, 237, 260, 275, 288; leaves the club, I, 328; member of Eastern Shore Triumvirate, I, 343, II, 106, III, 79; delivers speech in club, II, 175; involved in Battle of Farce-alia, III, 52, 53; letters written by, I, 260, 384–387, II, 78; letters written to, I, 238, 275, 393–396
Gordon, Robert (Serious Social): member of Red-House Club, I, 94; founding member of Tuesday Club, I, 125; sings in club, I, 127, 128, 169–170; steward, I, 127, 198, 228, 229, 235; speech on prudence, I, 221; deputy president, I, 240; high steward, I, 257; leaves the club, I, 262
Government, II, 63; offices and officers, I, 187–188; ceremonies, I, 188–189, 238; swayed by opinion, II, 166–167; by caprice, II, 173–174; forms of, II, 219; balance of power, II, 256–261; civil commotions, II, 347–357. *See also* Divine right; Hereditary right; Passive obedience
Gracchi, II, 219
Great Seal, Tuesday Club, I, 321–322, 411, II, 40, 130, 131, 134, 165, 169, 174, 184, 188–189, 194–195, 204–205, 264, 327, 328, 336, 337, 344, III, 104, 118–119, 146, 196, 251, 266, 306–307; club battle over, II, 359–367
Greece, I, 25, 28, II, 311
Greek language, II, 339, III, 80, 177, 254
Greeks, I, 54, 272, II, 13, 16, 18, 265, 357, 364, III, 84, 329
Green, Jonas (Jonathan Grog, Poet Laureate and Master of Ceremonies), I, 283, 294, 297, 300, 316, 322, 327, 328, 331, 335–336, 368–369, 396, 400–401, 408, II, 66, 101–102, 158, 175, 228, 244, 384–385, III, 26, 79, 105, 189, 199, 250, 258, 270, 290, 297, 326; his poetical genius, I, 22, 166, 325–326; his punning humor, I, 142, 149, 290, 342; involved in literary battle with Baltimore Bards, I, 154, 157, 159; elected longstanding member of club and appointed Purveyor, Punster, Punchmaker General, Printer, and Poet, I, 273; his character, I, 273, 275; high steward, I, 276, 289, 301, 380, II, 71, 164, 243, 397, III, 81, 117, 182, 210, 275, 319; delivers speeches, I, 278–279, III, 108, 294, 328; deputy

president, I, 297, III, 255; created poet laureate, I, 325; created master of ceremonies, I, 399; his commission, II, 42–43; appointed conundrumificator, II, 52–53; his conundrums, II, 62–63, 70, 72–73, 80, 82, 84, 85, 89, 126, 128–129, 134–135, 155–156, 161, 165, 172, 177; in anniversary procession, II, 97; tried in club, II, 235–237, 239, 247–248, III, 335–345; his remonstrance against Colley Cibber, II, 329–333; sings in club, II, 358, III, 86, 179, 202–205, 221; involved in Chancellor's Rebellion, II, 366–367; interrogated, III, 58–59; member of Grand Committee, III, 121; his poems (accrostic, II, 71–72; anniversary odes, I, 341–342, II, 103–105, 273–275, III, 20–22, 150–152; distich, I, 325; epigram, I, 326; extempore ode, III, 305–306; The Clubs Lamentation for the Loss of their President, II, 377–378; Congratulatory Ode, On the Return of the Honorable Mr President Jole To his Club, III, 223–225; A Congratulatory Pindaric Ode, III, 346–348; Eulogium, on his honors Entertainment, III, 197–198; A Heroic Poem, II, 313–319, III, 87–101; Lamentation, on the late Eclipse of The ancient, and Honorable Tuesday Club, III, 81–83; A Mournful Episode, upon the late Displeasure of his Lordship, II, 390–393; Poetical Entry for Sederunt 164, II, 321–322; A Tragical and Heroic Episode on The Club Tobacco box, III, 276–281; poetical speeches, I, 402–403, 412–413 [see also Poems, Tuesday Club]); examples of his wit, I, 362–366, 388–389, II, 45, 74, 156, III, 214, 268, 330, 355; letters written by, I, 277, 289–290, 302–303, 380, III, 230; letter written to, III, 229–230; accrostic written for, III, 210–211

Gregorian Calendar, II, 372
Gregory I (pope), III, 45
Gregory XIII (pope), III, 45
Gresham, Sarah, III, 124
Grimston, Harbottle, I, 65
Grogorians, III, 199
Grotius, Hugo, III, 37, 190
Grub Street, I, 201, 360, II, 8, 15, 27, 29, III, 271
Guicciardini, Francesco, III, 37
Gulliver, III, 37
Gunpowder Plot, I, 214, II, 306
Gunter, Edmund, II, 24, III, 254
Gunter's scale, I, 251, III, 254

Hadrian, I, 145
Hale, Sir Matthew, III, 190, 244
Halicarnassus, I, 21
Ham, I, 42, II, 10
Hamilton, Dr. Alexander (Loquacious Scribble, Secretary and Orator), I, 151, 215, 216, 242, 255, 304, 316, 321–322, 340, 343, 415, II, 48–49, 65, 67, 83, 87, 128, 133, 162, 169–170, 176, 185, 187, 219, 244, 303, 320, 335, 336, 384, III, 27, 34, 54, 78–79, 86, 90, 94–95, 109, 121, 178, 184, 192, 258, 298–299, 351–353; member of Whin-Bush Club, I, 49, 56; member of Ugly Club, I, 107, 110; founding member of Tuesday Club, I, 111, 125; steward, I, 125, 169, 174, 220, 231; his amorous adventures, I, 151, 209; involved in literary battle with Baltimore Bards, I, 152, 154, 160–161; appointed secretary, I, 166; his character, I, 166–167, 204–205, 327, 371; makes preparations for club ball, I, 192–193; butt of satire, I, 194–195; his speeches, I, 205, 337–339, 409–412, II, 99–103, 180–182, 191, 200–201, 203–204, 207–209, 227, 240, 245, 247, 265–266, 270–273, 304–311, III, 22–29, 36–44, 152–157, 195–196, 206–207, 232–241, 321–327; opposes the president, I, 229, 268, 270, 291; resigns and resumes office, I, 232; high steward, I, 239, 267, 280, 290, 367, 403, II, 124, 192, 299, 371, III, 33, 103, 141, 184, 212, 232, 283, 334; in anniversary processions, I, 240, II, 268; his marriage, I, 254; his bombastic style, I,

263–264, 281–282; deputy president, I, 276, III, 109; protests against club's proceedings, I, 316, 320; causes hubbub, I, 373; proposes that history of club be written, I, 392; turns flatterer, I, 404; his commission, II, 43–44; appointed conundrumificator, II, 52–53; his conundrums, II, 62, 70, 73, 82, 85, 89, 126, 129, 134, 157, 161, 164, 165, 172–173, 178; opposes the chancellor, II, 64, 75; gelastic law executed upon, II, 71; promotes commotion, II, 79–80; performs music in club, II, 105, 375, 378, III, 33, 117, 179; appointed orator, II, 179; works to restore club's liberty, II, 235; involved in Chancellor's Rebellion, II, 359–360, 364–367; involved in Battle of Farce-alia, III, 50–53; indicted, III, 330; letters written by, I, 237, 384–387, 401–402, II, 40–41, 75–76, 124–125, 158–159, 192–193, 236, III, 80–81, 116, 147, 229–230, 269–274, 307–308; letters written to, I, 262, 263, 280, 281, 290, 296, 324, 335, 393–396, 403–404, 405–406, II, 46, 94, 163, 199, 328–329, III, 147, 230, 335
Hamilton, Dr. John (Dr. Polyhistor), I, 156, II, 276, III, 20, 149; made honorary member of club, I, 147
Hamilton, Rev. John (Broadface Round), I, 215, 239, II, 276, III, 20, 221–222, 223; made honorary member of club, I, 192; speech on charity, I, 211; in anniversary procession, I, 240
Hamlet, II, 306
Hannibal, I, 24, 76, 119, III, 46
Hanover, house of, I, 77, 90
Harlequin, I, 117, II, 141, III, 39
Harlequin Doctor Faustus (Thurmond), I, 357
Hart, Samuel (Ignotus Warble), I, 340, 367; made honorary member of club, I, 170; speech on cheerfulness, I, 211; summoned to appear in club, I, 232; sets anniversary ode to music, I, 342
Harvey, William, I, 42

Hawkins, Sir John, III, 190
Hebrews, III, 84
Hector, I, 145, III, 23
Heidegger, John James, I, 358
Helen of Troy, III, 22
Heliogabalus, III, 37, 40
Hell-Fire Clubs, I, 44
Henderson, Captain, II, 328
Henderson, Jacob, I, 122
Henley, John, I, 16, III, 8
Henry II, III, 109
Henry IV (king of France), II, 349
Henry V, I, 284
Henry VI, I, 45, II, 369
Henry VII, I, 77
Henry VIII, I, 102, III, 338, 343
Hepburn, John, III, 268
Heracleus the Megarian, I, 250
Heraclitus, I, 252, II, 18, 370
Hercules, I, 288, II, 271, III, 36, 37, 39, 40
Hereditary right, I, 49, 77, 90, 95, 101, II, 167, 348, 350, III, 122
Hermes Trismegistus, I, 190, II, 19, III, 37, 267
Herodotus, I, 21, 89, II, 13, 323
Hesiod, I, 21, 39, III, 26, 37; quoted, II, 336, III, 42
Hesselius, John (Signior Sehesslius), III, 85
Heydon, Sir Christopher, II, 24
Heylyn, Peter, I, 42
Hibernians, II, 11
Hickathrift, Jack, III, 313, 314
Hieroglyphics, I, 398, II, 13, 33, III, 195
Hill, Richard, Jr. (Chantum Cheary): made honorary member of club, I, 239
Hippocrates, I, 42, 72, III, 38
Hiram, I, 43
Historians, III, 110; necessary qualities to make good ones, I, 19–20
History, II, 22–23; instructive, I, 17–18; proper subjects of, I, 19–23
History of Sir Charles Grandison, The (Richardson), II, 355
History of the London Clubs, The (Ward), II, 152
History of Tom Jones (Fielding), I, 385
Hoadly, Benjamin, I, 363, II, 26

Hob, III, 236
Hobbes, Thomas, III, 17
Hobgoblin, I, 118
Hogarth, William, I, 195, III, 228, 257
Holliday, Robert (Hereum Thereum): made honorary member of club, I, 192
Hollyday, James (Joshua Fluter), II, 367; made honorary member of club, I, 170; attends club's anniversary, I, 282
Homer, I, 21, 39, 80, 88, 145, 271, II, 15, 138, 144, 370, 382, III, 22, 23, 181, 252, 253, 278, 314, 329, 347; quoted, II, 21, 364, III, 43, 71, 155–156
Hominy, II, 207, 208
Honour of Chivalrie, The, II, 22
Hopkinson, Joshua (Joshua Swash): member of Ugly Club, I, 106, 108, 110
Horace, I, 55, 218, 272, 279, 385, II, 16, III, 253; quoted, I, 70, 74, 164, 247, 264, II, 320, 380, III, 44, 72, 73, 116, 325
Hottentots, II, 200, III, 135
Hoyle, Edmond, II, 142, 152
Hugh of Saint Victor, III, 192, 193
Hurlothrumbo (play), I, 159
Hystaspes, II, 10

Ibrahim Pasha, I, 30
Icarus, II, 350
Ignis fatuus, I, 103, 117, III, 11, 12
Iliad, III, 22
Indians: North American, I, 29, 99, II, 200, 208, III, 40, 135–136; South American, I, 42; Nanticokes, I, 140, II, 208
Indictments, Tuesday Club, I, 265, 313–319, III, 185–186, 310–311, 335–337, 339–340, 354
Inquisition, II, 167, 197
Ireland and the Irish, I, 23, 26, 28–29, 83, 365, II, 203, 305, III, 336
Iris, II, 15
Isaac, II, 10, 140
Isocrates, II, 16, III, 67
Italy, I, 28, II, 252, III, 84

Jack-a-dandy, I, 123
Jackanapes, I, 123

Jack-o'-lantern, I, 117
Jack Pudding, I, 201
Jack the Giant-killer, I, 22, III, 313
Jacob, I, 173, II, 10, III, 238
Jacobites, I, 54, 76, 94, 151, 283, 284, 367, 398, II, 107, III, 296
Jacques, Lancelot, III, 268, 308, 309, 357
James I, I, 47, 48, 49, 88, 102, 141, 238, 358–359, 360, II, 12, 27, 348–349, III, 108
James II, I, 88, II, 349
Januarius, Saint, I, 120
Jason Pratensis, III, 37
Jeffreys, George, III, 107
Jennings, Catherine (Madonna Swashgut), II, 243
Jennings, Thomas (Prim Timorous, Serjeant at Arms), II, 247, 263, 272, III, 27, 89, 106, 115; member of Red-House Club, I, 94, 98; made long-standing member of Tuesday Club, I, 299; his character, I, 300–301; high steward, I, 327, 381, 397, II, 75, 130, 185, 262, 358, III, 31, 85, 139; his rare complaint, II, 188; serjeant at arms, II, 222, 236–239, 327, 336; involved in Chancellor's Rebellion, II, 363, 366, 367; appointed conundrum master, III, 117, 140; member of Grand Committee, III, 121; deputy president, III, 139; letter written by, I, 397–398
Jeoffry, John, III, 112, 113, 115, 116
Jerusalem, I, 27
Jestbooks, I, 352, II, 30
Jesting, III, 332; jests and jesters, I, 358–364, II, 12–13; when appropriate, I, 376–377; ill-conceived jest in club, I, 380–381
Jews, I, 77, 121, 411, II, 349, 353
Joan (pope), I, 123, II, 335, III, 393
Joannes ad oppositum, I, 123
Joan of Arc, II, 310
Joe Miller's Jests, I, 352
John (king of England), III, 109
John-a-Nokes, I, 116, II, 232
John-a-Stiles, I, 116, II, 232
John of Gaunt, duke of Lancaster, I, 77
John the Baptist, I, 214

Index 411

Jones, Inigo, I, 44
Jonson, Ben, II, 28
Joseph, II, 10
Joseph Andrews (Fielding), III, 51
Jubal, I, 31, 36, 37, 41
Julian Calendar, II, 372, III, 45
Juno, II, 382
Jupiter, I, 40, 41, 253, 254, II, 382, III, 154
Justinian I, III, 67
Justinus, Marcus Junianus, I, 21, II, 200

Keating, Geoffrey, I, 28, II, 202
Kendi, II, 24
Kenneth II, I, 47
Kent, England, I, 134, II, 209
Kepler, Johannes, III, 37
Key, Philip (Signior Phrazeobundus): in anniversary procession, II, 266, 268
Killigrew, Sir James, III, 190
Killigrew, Thomas, II, 13
Killigrew, Sir William, II, 127, III, 37
Kirkpatrick, Dr. James, III, 130
Knights of the Golden Horseshoe, I, 217–218
"Knight's Tale, The," III, 280
Knox, John, I, 143, II, 26
Kublai Khan, I, 119

Laban, II, 10
Labeo, Marcus Antistius, II, 258
Laelius, Gaius, I, 272, II, 140
Lais, II, 11
Lake, Charles (Rev. Whiner), II, 193
Lamech, I, 41
Lampridius, Aelius, I, 145
Lampugnani, Giovanni Battista, I, 55, 252
Laneric. *See* Whin-Bush Club
Language: corrupted, I, 181–185, 224; religious, I, 182–183; legal, I, 183–184; medical, I, 184; of beggars and thieves, I, 184–185; clubical, I, 185–187
Lapland, II, 25
Lares, I, 220
Las sergas de Esplandían, I, 11, II, 22
Latin, II, 208, III, 80, 177, 292, 297–298, 314, 334; in law, I, 313–314, 318, III, 343

Laud, William (archbishop of Canterbury), II, 13
Laugh and Be Fat (Taylor), II, 8, III, 313, 314
Laughter, III, 231–232, 324–325, 332. *See also* Gelastic law; Jesting
Law, William, I, 350
Law: proceedings, I, 116–117, III, 111, 332–333, 338; language, I, 183–184, 220; lawyers, II, 368. *See also* Government
Laws, Tuesday Club, I, 127, 128, 130, 133, 146, 147, 150, 169, 170, 175–176, 199, 200, 207, 210, 215, 221, 231, 257, 259, 267, 276, 278, 326, 327, 377, 378, 397, II, 52–53, 67–68, 69, 95, 130, 170, 191, 231, 312, 313, 372, III, 209, 304
Leal Lealis, II, 24
Leatherlungs, Vocifer, I, 66; member of Ugly Club, I, 107; orator, I, 108–110
Le Clerc, Jean, III, 68
Lemmas, III, 42, 195
Lemnius, Levinus, I, 70
Lendrum, Andrew (Roundhead Muddy), I, 343–344, 369, 373, 398, 399–400; made longstanding member of club, I, 367–368; high steward, I, 370; leaves club, I, 390–391; letter written by, I, 370
Leo I (pope), II, 252
Leonidas, III, 46
Letter from Rome (Middleton), I, 120
Letters, Tuesday Club, I, 237, 238, 239, 240, 259, 260, 262, 263, 275, 277, 280, 281, 284–285, 289–290, 293, 296, 302–303, 307–310, 323–324, 335, 370, 378, 379, 380–381, 384–387, 393, 396, 397–398, 401, 403–405, II, 40–41, 45, 46, 47–48, 55, 75–76, 78, 85–86, 94, 124–125, 131, 158–159, 163, 192–193, 199, 214, 217–218, 225–226, 233–234, 240, 328–329, III, 80, 112, 116, 146, 147, 229–230, 269–274, 307–308, 335
Letter to the City of Annapolis, I, 157, 159, 164
Levelers, I, 88, 90, II, 264
Life of Colley Cibber, I, 21
Lilliston, Sue, II, 335
Limberloins, Spruce, I, 66; member of

Ugly Club, I, 104, 107; secretary, I, 108, 110
Lindsay, Sir David, I, 61, 63, III, 37
Lisper, Mr., III, 60, 77
Lister, Martin, I, 362
Literary battle between Baltimore Bards and Tuesday Club, I, 152–166
Literary critics, I, 72–73, 154, 155
Littleton, Sir Thomas, III, 190
Livia, II, 214
Livy, I, 21, 89, 279
Lloyd, Edward (Courtly Phraze), III, 320; his amorous adventure, I, 151; made honorary member of club, I, 152; attends club's anniversary, I, 282
Locke, John, I, 362, II, 26, 28
Lomas, John (Laconic Comas, Orator), I, 258, 282, 283, 338, 341, 389, II, 63, 80, 215, 217, 241–242, 344, III, 20, 24, 48–49, 93, 98; founding member of club, I, 125; steward, I, 133, 170; his amorous adventure, I, 152; returns to club, I, 239; high steward, I, 240, 260, 278, 333, 398, II, 84, III, 79; his motion in club, I, 268; deputy president, I, 275, 322, II, 54; dispute concerning Presbyterianism, I, 277; sings in club, I, 322–323; orator, I, 328, 372, 373; sides with president, I, 368; absent from club, I, 369; gives up office of orator, I, 370–371, 390; fatal Comasian conundrum, II, 83–84; his conundrum on the chancellor, II, 159; involved in Battle of Farce-alia, III, 52, 53, 55; leaves for England, III, 85; letter written by, I, 336; letter written to, I, 335
London, II, 330, 335, III, 11, 65
London Jests, I, 352
London Spy, The (Ward), I, 360, II, 8
Long, Thomas: member of Ugly Club, I, 107
Longinus, I, 306, II, 152
Longstanding member, origin of term, I, 52
Lottery, Philadelphia, I, 230, 286, 288, 289, 325
Louis XIV, II, 351, III, 45
Lucian, II, 17

Lucifer, III, 130, 136. *See also* Devil
Lucina, I, 39
Lucretia, I, 55, 246
Lucullus, I, 55
Ludovicus de la Cerda, Joannes, II, 24
Luther, Martin, II, 26
Lux, William, of Annapolis (Crinkum Crankum): his controverted election as longstanding member, I, 299, II, 337, 341, 358, 360, 367, 376, 378, III, 177–178, 194, 199, 200, 201, 206, 208–209, 225–226, 275, 281–287, 289, 294–296; sings in club, III, 29, 157, 248; performs music, III, 33; perpetrates hoax, III, 102–103; deputy president, III, 117, 212; member of Grand Committee, III, 121; elected longstanding member of club, III, 143; high steward, III, 146, 219, 255, 308, 353; petitions the club, III, 200–201; his speeches, III, 283–286, 299–304; his confirmation, III, 297–298
Lux, William, of Baltimore, III, 149, 219, 304, 308, 310–311, 314
Luxembourg, François Henri de Montmorency-Bouteville, duc de, I, 76
Luxury: of Spartans, I, 25; of Catholic Church, I, 32; Hamilton's lament against, I, 54, 127, 130–131, 149, 150, 170, 192, 197, II, 357, 369, III, 235–238
Lycurgus, I, 25, 272, II, 12, 253, III, 46
Lyon, William, III, 149
Lysander, I, 139

Maccarty, Sir Hugh (president of Monday Club), II, 198, 210, 212–213, 237, 239, 243, 244, 245, 297, 299, 340–344, III, 30, 57, 59, 286, 318; questions concerning his identity, III, 31, 34–35, 54–55, 60, 78; libels president of Tuesday Club, III, 32; presides over trial, III, 61–75; impersonated, III, 102–103
Macha-Allah, II, 24
Machiavelli, Niccolò, I, 88, III, 17, 56, 57, 101–102, 231
McPherson, Alexander, III, 268
Mcpherson's lament (song), II, 262
Maelius, Spurius, II, 260

Index

Magic, II, 19
Magnen, Jean-Chrysostome, I, 271
Magnus, Olaus, II, 23, 24
Mahomet, Muley, III, 37
Malcolm, Alexander (Philo Dogmaticus, Chancellor), I, 194, 195, 391, 409, III, 25–26, 32–33, 34–35, 60, 109, 117, 146, 212, 214, 222, 252, 282–283, 287; his petition on the advantages of society, I, 407–408; made longstanding member of club, I, 408; elected chancellor, I, 413, 415; his commission, II, 41–42; deputy president, II, 47, III, 141, 182–183, 210, 211; opposes the president, II, 52, 54, 58–59, 87–88, 219, 236, 247, 335, 337, III, 118–119, 206–208, 225–228; opposes the secretary, II, 64, 264; incites rebellion, II, 80, 359–369; performs music, II, 105, 375, 378, III, 29, 33, 117, 157, 179; tried in club, II, 131–134; high steward, II, 225, 313, 376, III, 104, 144, 193, 217; in anniversary procession, II, 268; assumes presidential chair, II, 371, 393; involved in Battle of Farce-alia, III, 53; member of Grand Committee, III, 121; a Freemason, III, 146; his dispute on grammar, III, 179; indicted and tried, III, 185–192; his wit, III, 215; his farewell speech, III, 245–248; letter written by, II, 225–226; poem written by, III, 255–259; poems written about, III, 260–264, 276–281
Mallet of State, Tuesday Club, II, 239, 344, 372
Mamelukes, III, 81
Mammon, II, 260, III, 205
Mandeville, Bernard, I, 150, III, 18
Man in the moon, I, 123
Manlius Capitolinus, Marcus, II, 260
Marlborough, duke of, II, 324
Marriage Dialogues (Ward), II, 8, 324
Mars, II, 15
Marshe, Witham (Prattle Motely), I, 152; member of Ugly Club, I, 107, 108, 109, 111; founding member of Tuesday Club, I, 125; appointed secretary, I, 133; steward, I, 134; his amorous adventure, I, 152; involved in literary battle with Baltimore Bards, I, 161; leaves for England, I, 166
Martial, II, 15
Martianus Capella, II, 24
Martini, Giovanni Battista, I, 55
Mary, the Virgin, II, 214
Maryland Gazette, I, 154, 156, 157, 159, 283, 387, II, 36, 159, 235, 236, 239, 310, 372, 385, III, 29, 32, 69, 270, 271
Massinger, Philip, III, 271
Mathematics, II, 192
Medals, Tuesday Club, II, 92–96, 158, 217, 372
Medusa, I, 72
Melchizedec, I, 121
Menippus, I, 72
Menoetes, II, 15
Mephistopheles, II, 24
Mercury, III, 270
Merrie Tales of the Mad Men of Gotham, I, 22, III, 313
Merry Andrew, I, 201, II, 18, 344, 348, 353
Messala Corvinus, Marcus Valerius, II, 307
Messalina, Valeria, I, 246, II, 335
Methodists, I, 202
Meursius's dialogues. See *De arcanis Amoris et Veneris*
Micromégas, I, 253
Middleton, Conyers, I, 120
Middleton, Samuel (Mr. Leidemont): hosts Tuesday Club, III, 86, 97–98, 255, 309
Midnight Conversation (Hogarth), III, 257
Militia, I, 140, III, 276
Milo, II, 271
Miltiades, III, 46
Milton, John, I, 134, II, 9, 21, 26, III, 314; quoted, III, 272
Minerva, I, 88
Minos, II, 203
Minskie, Samuel (Mungo Macfun): member of Red-House Club, I, 94; his comic genius, I, 97
Miscellanies in Prose and Verse, II, 32
Mithridates, I, 89, III, 84
Mogul Empire, II, 225

Mohammed, I, 54, 213, II, 167, 224, 225
Mohammedanism, I, 212, 217, 391, II, 167
Mohammed the Great, II, 18, III, 45
Mohock Club, I, 44
Montaigne, I, 146
Montezuma, III, 46
Moorfields, I, 266, III, 132
Moors, I, 41, 42
Morpheus, II, 306
Morris, Rob, I, 140
Morris, Robert (Merry Makefun), I, 384, 394, II, 86–87, 106–107; made honorary member of club, I, 239; in anniversary procession, I, 240; performs music, I, 242; sends beer, I, 261, 265; member of Eastern Shore Triumvirate, I, 384–387, II, 65, 135; his death, II, 157, 159, 164, 175, 176; letter written to, I, 262
Morvan de Bellegarde, Abbé Jean-Baptiste, I, 364
Mosaic chronology, I, 24, 36
Muggletonians, I, 77, 159
Music, III, 83–84; its antiquity, I, 36–37; musical scores of club anniversary odes, II, 107–122, 278–293. *See also* Songs

Nabal, I, 357
Naples, II, 309
Narcissus, III, 154
Nassau-Siegen, Count Joan Mauritz van, II, 349
Natural philosophy, II, 23, 157
Negroes, III, 40, 47–48; origin of, I, 41–42. *See also* Dromo; Jeoffry, John
Negro Peter, III, 140
Neilson, George, I, 66; his character, I, 74–81, 101; works for reformation of clubs, I, 85–93, 107, 111; founds Red-House Club, I, 93–98; his death, I, 100
Nero, II, 138, 213, 214
Newton, Sir Isaac, I, 33, II, 26, III, 46
New York City, I, 124, II, 341, III, 33, 35. *See also* Clubs, Monday Club
New York Gazette, III, 32, 34, 56, 57, 58, 60
Nimrod, I, 42
Noe (Noah), I, 29, 41, 42, 43, II, 10

Norris, Sir John, I, 50
North, Benjamin, III, 308
North, Robert (Huffbluff Surly): made honorary member of club, I, 170; in anniversary procession, I, 240
Novels, disparaged, I, 20, 144, 152, II, 22
Numa Pompilius, III, 46
Nuns, I, 101–103

Oates, Titus, III, 111
Occult, II, 24–26
Odyssey, I, 30
Odyssey (Triphiodorus), II, 16
Oedipus, II, 31
Oldcastle, Sir John (Lord Cobham), I, 284, II, 127
Orange, house of, I, 77
Orpheus, I, 78, 256, II, 300, 305, 320, III, 27, 84, 85
Osman I, I, 24
Overton, John, II, 201
Ovid, II, 15, III, 190; quoted, II, 363, III, 43, 70, 247
Oxford Jests, Refined and Enlarged, I, 352, II, 30
Oxford University, I, 101, 286, II, 197, 339

Paganism, I, 392
Palatinate, III, 274
Palermin, II, 22
Pallas, II, 257
Pamela (Richardson), II, 355
Pan, I, 38, II, 272
Pandora, III, 271
Pantaloon, III, 39
Pantomime, II, 141
Paracelsus, I, 142, 356, II, 24, 26
Paragrams, II, 17
Parliament, II, 69, 347–348, 369, III, 15, 81, 108, 148, 180, 191–192
Passions, of great men and little men, III, 7–18
Passive obedience, I, 90, 95, II, 167, 209, 348, 349, III, 105, 122
Patrick, Saint, I, 120
Pausias, II, 17
Pedantius, Mr.: member of Ugly Club, I, 107, 108
Pegasus, III, 26

Pepperell, Sir William, I, 151
Perigort, III, 37
Persians, I, 54, 247, III, 81, 269
Peter, Saint, II, 167
Peter the Hermit, III, 37
Petitions, presented in Tuesday Club: on the club box, I, 285–287; from the Single Ladies of Annapolis, I, 388; from the chancellor, I, 407–408; from club members, II, 56–57, III, 200–201
Petrarch, III, 155
Petronius Arbiter, Gaius, II, 17; quoted, II, 257, 382
Phaedrus, I, 253
Philip, king of Macedon, I, 25, 355, III, 84, 149, 281
Philistines, II, 10
Philo Judaeus, III, 233
Philosophers' stone, II, 25
Pickering, Stephen (Gasperus Pickeringtonus), II, 188, 242
Pickle-Herring, I, 201
Pierrot, III, 39
Pindar, I, 22, 155, III, 70
Pisistratus, II, 352
Pistol, III, 113
Pitcairne, Archibald, II, 305
Plato, I, 36, 70, 354, II, 16, 270, 271, 341, 352, III, 83, 84, 85, 111, 128, 181
Platonists, III, 85
Plautus, II, 38, 138, III, 270
Pleiades, II, 271
Pliny the Younger, quoted, II, 17
Plowden, Edmund, III, 67, 71, 190
Plutarch, I, 21
Pluto, I, 256
Poems, Tuesday Club: Accrostic on the Poet Laureat, III, 210–211; Address of the Eastern Shore Triumvirate, II, 299; amorous epigram, I, 160; Baltimore Belles, I, 153, 155, 156; *Carmen Dolorosum,* III, 122–125; *Carmen Seculare,* II, 373–374; *Carmen Sociale,* III, 256–259; City of Annapolis, III, 345; ΔΑΚΡΥΑ ΜΕΛΠΟΜΕΝΗΣ, III, 218–219; The Epicaedion of the Ancient Tuesday Club, on the mournful Indisposition of Nasifer Jole Esqr, II, 50–51; The Jurors for the City bring, III, 345; *Lugubris Cantus,* II, 228–230; Memorandum for a Sein Hawling, III, 270–273; Poem against the late Chancellor, III, 260–264; The Reverend Scout, I, 164, 209; The Spiritual Rake, I, 164; Unmatch'd Lardini, Tune thy Lyre, II, 182–183; Verses on the Baltimore Bard, I, 161–162; Verses to the Bard on the Ladies Backward Beauties, I, 164; To The Worshipful Sir John, II, 77. *See also* Green, Jonas, his poems
Poetics (Aristotle), III, 272
Poetry, III, 148–149; poetical furor in Annapolis, I, 152–166; rhyme introduced into, II, 21–22; modern poets critiqued, II, 329–333; necessary qualities of poets, III, 252–255
Political doctrines. *See* Divine right; Hereditary right; Passive obedience
Polybius, I, 21, 89
Polypus, II, 171
Pomona, III, 156
Pompey, I, 24, 55, II, 123, 369, III, 45, 78
Pomponazzi, Pietro, II, 24
Pope, Alexander, I, 76, 155, 159, 361, II, 21, 26, 331, 332
Pope, I, 27, 365, 389–390, II, 167–168, 196, 213, 252, 300
Porteous, John, I, 359
Portugal, II, 167
Posies, II, 38–39
Praxiteles, I, 31
Presbyterianism, I, 90, 141, 159, 213, 214, 277, 365, 366, II, 309, III, 296
Prester John, I, 121, III, 37, 78, 220
Prestonpans, III, 221
Priam, III, 23
Priddon, Sarah. *See* Salisbury, Sally
Primogeniture, II, 352
Prior, Matthew, I, 159, 389, II, 331
Prometheus, III, 271
Protestants, III, 296, 356
Protogenes, I, 31
Prynne, William, I, 134
Psalter of Cashel, I, 29
Ptolemy, I, 190, II, 19

Ptolemy VII, I, 76
Pufendorf, Baron Samuel von, III, 37, 190
Puffendorst, Don Fartinhando. See *Benefit of Farting, The*
Pulteney, William, earl of Bath, I, 90
Pulton, Ferdinando, III, 342
Puritans, I, 367
Pyrrhus, II, 309
Pythagoras, I, 42, 44, 249

Quakers, I, 35, 202, II, 209, 210, 215, III, 81, 128, 135

Rabelais, François, I, 210, 360, II, 78
Ralegh, Sir Walter, I, 48, III, 46
Ramsay, Allan, I, 56, 67, II, 35
Rapin de Thoyras, Paul de, III, 109, 296
Rawhead, I, 118
Rebecca, II, 10
Rebuses, II, 13, 33–35
Red-House Club, I, 107, 111, 300; chronology of, I, 66; founded, I, 93; proceedings of, I, 94–98; dissolution of, I, 99–101
Religion: doctrines, I, 95, 97, 122–123, 183, III, 296; necessity of toleration, I, 95–96; language, I, 182–183, II, 353; ceremonies, I, 220, III, 131; wit, II, 28
Restoration, I, 49, 53
Rhadamantus, II, 203
Rhazes, III, 37
Rhetoric (Aristotle), II, 17
Richard, James (Roughby Ranter): involved in literary battle with Baltimore Bards, I, 163
Richardson, Samuel, II, 355
Richardson, Thomas, III, 103
Riddle, II, 32–33
Ridout, John, III, 268
Risteau, Catherine, I, 157
Rizzio, David, II, 349, III, 37
Robin Goodfellow, I, 118
Rochester, John Wilmot, earl of, III, 138
Roe, Richard, I, 116, III, 274, 337, 340, 343
Rogers, William (Seemly Spruce): member of Red-House Club, I, 94;

founding member of Tuesday Club, I, 125; learned debate, I, 147; steward, I, 170, 207, 230; deputy president, I, 205; holds anniversary, I, 215; high steward, I, 259, 277, 285, 297, 298, 300; his death, I, 379, 387
Roland, I, 183, II, 198
Romances, disparaged, I, 20, 22, 152, 249, II, 9, 22
Roman Empire, I, 25, 217, 246, 247, 321, II, 213–214, 353, III, 25, 195
Roman Republic, I, 25, II, 219, III, 239–240
Romans, I, 54–55, II, 12, 75, 182, 201, 208, 260, 265, 357, III, 113, 323
Rome, II, 272, 310, 347, 369. *See also* Catholic Church; Pope
Roscius Gallus, Quintus, I, 279
Rosenkreutz, Christian, II, 24
Roundheads, II, 224
Rowe, Nicholas, I, 201
Royalists, I, 88, 90, II, 224
Royal Society, I, 42, 139, 352
Rubens, Peter Paul, III, 258
Rump Parliament, III, 122
Russian Empire, I, 247
Rymer, Thomas, III, 296

Sacheverell, Henry, II, 348
Saint-Évremond, Charles de Saint-Denis, sieur de, I, 76
Salisbury, Sally, I, 294, 319, III, 41
Salkeld, William, III, 190
Sallust, I, 21; quoted, III, 84
Samson, II, 10, 271
Sancho VI (king of Navarre), I, 83
Saturn, I, 89
Satyricon, II, 17
Satyrus of Clazomenae, II, 368
Saul, III, 84
Scald Miserables, I, 214, 215
Scaramouch, II, 141, III, 39
Scarron, Paul, I, 76
Scarronides; or, Virgile Travestie (Cotton), III, 22
Schiolto, Giovanni Battista Barbaro di, II, 201, III, 37
Schoolmen, I, 356, 357, II, 18
Scipio Africanus, Publius Cornelius, I,

Index

24, 55, 272, II, 140, III, 222–223
Scotland, I, 43, 78, II, 309
Scots, I, 26, 28, 76, 77, 80, 186, 216, III, 195, 319
Scott, Sir Francis, later Lord Napier, III, 37
Scott, Dr. Upton (Jeronimo Jaunter), I, 299, III, 297, 319–320, 327, 329, 330–331, 354; made longstanding member of club, III, 266; high steward, III, 267, 309, 356; his confirmation, III, 268, 274, 281–283; his offensive speech, III, 287–288; deputy president, III, 308
Scythians, I, 23
Seals: significance of, I, 409–411. *See also* Great Seal
Sea-Piece, The (Kirkpatrick), III, 130
Secundus, Johannes, II, 24
Sedgewick, John, II, 94, 158
Selden, John, I, 122
Semiramis, II, 323, 335
Sendivogius, Michael, II, 24
Seneca, I, 72, III, 38, 70, 233; quoted, III, 40
Senesino, Francesco Bernardi, I, 55
Servetus, Michael, II, 26, III, 38, 106
Sesostris, III, 231
Seven Champions of Christendom, II, 272
Seven Sleepers, I, 121, II, 272
Seven Wonders of the Ancient World, II, 271
Severus, I, 145
Shaftesbury, Lord, II, 26
Shakespeare, William, I, 201, 247, II, 21, 26, 28, 139, 145, 393
Sheriffmuir, battle of, I, 80
Shirley, William, I, 151
Siam, II, 214
Silenus, I, 38, 44
Sloane, Sir Hans, I, 139
Smalridge, George (bishop), I, 201
Smindyrides of Sybaris, III, 40
Snowden, Richard (Oldham Wisely): made honorary member of club, I, 170; at third anniversary of the club, I, 282; his speech in club, I, 304
Sociability: importance of, I, 33–35, 71–72, 132, 144, 205, 271, 407–408; enemies to, I, 69–71
Social gatherings: routs and drums, I, 33, 81, 351. *See also* Clubs
Society, regulation of, II, 251–254, 256–259, III, 14. *See also* Government
Socrates, I, 211, 246, 249, 253, 254, 271, 353, II, 12, 354, 389, 394, 395, III, 46, 102, 111, 128, 258
Sodom and Gomorrah, I, 28
Solomon, I, 43, 245, II, 253, 347, 380, III, 102, 324
Solomon's Temple, I, 102
Solon, II, 253, 347, III, 46
Songs, performed in Tuesday Club: club catches, I, 127, 128, II, 105; Boddily Song (to the tune of Mcpherson's lament), II, 262; Britons Strike home, III, 86, 95; Bumpers Squire Jones, I, 322, III, 85, 91; The Clubs Lamentation for the Loss of their President (to the tune of Chevy Chace), II, 377–378; The Drunken Wife of Gallowa, I, 167–168; The Great Bell of Lincoln, I, 147, 169, 278, 300, 344, 378, 379, II, 302; Hundreds of Drury, I, 291; Jog hooly good man, I, 169–170; The Jolly Toaper, I, 323; Newgate Bird Song, III, 145; A New Song (to the tune of Come Jolly Bacchus), II, 337–339; Orpheus and Euridice, I, 255; Robin and Jeck, II, 358, III, 86, 92, 105, 179, 202–205, 221; Save Women and Wine, I, 256; Says Celia to a Rev'rend Dean, II, 302; She Tells me with Claret, III, 85; Song on the Baltimore Bards, I, 165–166; Stand Round My Brave Boys, I, 322; To Arms, III, 86, 95; Trumpet Air, I, 283–284; When Chloe we ply, I, 232–233, 269; Where are you going my pritty maid, I, 269–270; Whilst I gaze on Chloe trembling, I, 142. *See also* Anniversaries, Tuesday Club, anniversary odes
Sophocles, II, 144
Soret, Nicholas, I, 360, 361
Sosia, II, 270

Sourface, Surly: member of Red-House Club, I, 94
South, Robert, I, 201, 224
South Sea Company, III, 41
Spain, I, 23, 26, 28, 42, 212, 389, II, 167, III, 299
Spartans, I, 25, 272, II, 12, 18, 208, 309–310, III, 84, 129, 309
Spartianus, Aelius, I, 145
Spectator, I, 104, II, 145
Speechmaking: reasons for, I, 200–202; dangerous, I, 221–222
Spencer, Archibald (Dr. Rhubarb), II, 157, 163, 178, 188, 191–192; his learned debate, II, 170–172
Spenser, Edmund, I, 119, II, 21, 228
Spinoza, Baruch, III, 17
Sponde, Henri de, II, 24, III, 37
Sterling, James (Rev. Rodomantus), III, 193
Steward, John, II, 72
Stewart, Mr. (Mr. Boniface), III, 60, 77
Stilpon, I, 354
Stoicism, II, 367–368
Stratonice, III, 84
Stringar, Samuel (Samuel Swallowbeak): taster, I, 97–98
Stuart, James Francis Edward (the Pretender), I, 80, II, 348
Stuarts, I, 49, 77, 197, II, 352
Stuck, Johann Wilhelm, III, 40
Suetonius, II, 12
Suleiman I, the Magnificent, I, 24
Sulpicius Rufus, Servius, II, 258
Swan, Robert (Stentor Snuffysnout [Snuffybeak]), I, 262, 263, 265, 266
Swarthy, Captain: member of Ugly Club, I, 107
Swift, Jonathan, I, 360, II, 32, 152, III, 80; quoted, III, 273. See also *Benefit of Farting, The;* Bickerstaff, Isaac
Sydenham, Thomas, II, 21–22
Sylva Sylvarum; or, A Natural History (Bacon), III, 244
Syracuse, II, 352
Syriac Code of Alminhagas, III, 337

Table Conversation (Swift), II, 152
Tacitus, Cornelius, I, 21
Tamerlane, I, 24, II, 351
Tantarabobus, I, 119
Tarquins, II, 232
Tasso, Torquato, II, 21
Terpander, III, 84
Tessarini, Carlo, I, 55
Thalestris, II, 323
Theater, I, 200–201; proposal to remodel modern theater, II, 137–154; English, II, 138, 141–146; classical, II, 138–139, 144; Dutch, II, 139–140; French, II, 140, 141
Themistocles, III, 84
Theobald, Lewis, II, 322
Theocritus, II, 127
Theodoret, I, 271
Thersites, II, 15, III, 281
Tholosan (René Milleran), I, 118, II, 24
Thompson, John (Joannes Tomlinsonus), II, 247, III, 115
Thornton, Thomas (Nolens Volens), III, 213, 214
Thornton, William (Solo Neverout, Protomusicus, Attorney General), I, 264, 293, 330, 386, 398, II, 63, 86–88, 102, 359, III, 27, 32–33, 76, 89, 180, 182, 184–185, 187, 192–193, 212–214, 306–307, 327–331, 350, 353, 354–355; *History* dedicated to, I, 10; seized by rhyming fit, I, 152–153; made longstanding member, I, 168; steward, I, 200, 221, 232; satirized, I, 209–210; chairman of badge committee, I, 215; sings in club, I, 232–233, 255–256, 283–284, 299, 342, II, 262, 302, 320, III, 157; appointed club musician, I, 233, 235; in anniversary procession, I, 240; high steward, I, 254, 269, 369, II, 65, 155, 214, 303, 388, III, 79, 112, 179, 208, 248, 289, 326; absence from club, I, 257, 389; his discordant laughter, I, 258, 286–287, 373; protests against club's proceedings, I, 259, 276–277, 289, 328; indicted, I, 262–263, 265–267; defends club's liberty, I, 270, II, 235, 263; deputy president, I, 293, II, 155, 375; his sleepy disposition, I, 294, 300, 316, II, 157, 375, III, 77, 86, 183,

209, 210, 211, 319; his commission, II, 43; his remonstrance, II, 55–58; tried in club, II, 66–67; gelastic law executed upon, II, 71, III, 267–268; his abilities at law, II, 133–134; his ambitious designs, II, 155, 162, 327, 328; involved in Chancellor's Rebellion, II, 365, 367; involved in Battle of Farce-alia, III, 50–52; member of Grand Committee, III, 121; appointed attorney general, III, 178; pleads in club, III, 188–191, 248–251, 289–293, 311–314, 337–338, 340–343; letter written by, I, 370; poems written by, II, 77, III, 260–264
Thucydides, II, 127
Thursday Club of Hiccory Hill (Virginia), II, 225, 242, 243, 244, III, 31, 64, 205, 316, 318, 319
Tibullus, II, 358; quoted, II, 16, 357
Tilghman, Edward (Prim Laconic): made honorary member of club, I, 256
Tillotson, John (archbishop of Canterbury), I, 201, II, 26
Time: wasted in trifles, I, 14–15; remorseless, I, 38
Timoleon, III, 46
Tiresias, I, 72
Titus, II, 353
Tobacco box, Tuesday Club, II, 203, 372
Tobit, III, 329
Toleration Act, I, 88
Tom Folio, I, 123
Tom Fool, I, 123
Tom o' the lin, III, 78
Tom Thumb, I, 22, III, 313
Tomyris, II, 323
Tonombeius, III, 37
Torelli, Giuseppe, I, 55
Tories, I, 54, 88, II, 348, III, 106, 296
Towers, Dr. (Dr. Pyrgos), II, 170, 171, 172
Tragedy, II, 143, 146, 153
Tragicomedy, II, 138, 141, 142, 145, 146; new scheme for, II, 148–154
Transubstantiation, II, 353
Trials, Tuesday Club, I, 261, 265–266, II, 66, 131–134, 185–188, III, 57–76, 184–192, 212–215, 289–293, 310–315, 328–332, 333–344, 350–356
Trifles: necessary, I, 245; large and small, I, 246–248
Trigonometry, II, 271
Triphiodorus, II, 16
Trogloditcs, II, 354
Trogus, Pompeius, I, 21, II, 200, III, 37
Trojans, I, 343, II, 364, III, 22
Troy, John (Capt. Furbisher), III, 193
Troy, III, 22, 23
Tubal-Cain, I, 31, 36, 37, 41, 43
Tuesday Club of Annapolis: its antiquity, I, 37, 43; derived from Whin-Bush Club, I, 44–58, from Red-House Club, I, 93–100, from Ugly Club, I, 103–110; its genealogy, I, 59–67; founded in Annapolis, I, 111–113; first meeting, I, 125; first laws, I, 127; its regard for women, I, 128–129; establishes gelastic law, I, 133; tobacco pipe procession, I, 147; literary battle with Baltimore Bards, I, 152–166; elects president, I, 174; holds ball, I, 193–194; dispute on club box, I, 207; celebrates anniversaries, I, 215, 240–242, 282–284, 337–344, II, 97–107, 266–276, III, 20–29, 33–44, 149–157, 232–248; title of high steward established, I, 238; club commotions, I, 276–277; sublime letters introduced, I, 306–310; at its peak of glory, I, 334, II, 30, 42, 86, 91, 106, 168; introduces conundrums, II, 52–53; motto, II, 85–86; approves Frontinbrassian Articles, II, 220–222; Grand Ceremony of the Capation, II, 244–247; ruled by women, II, 325–327; civil war, II, 328, 337, 372; Chancellor's Rebellion, II, 359–367; restores president to power, II, 396; list of members, II, 399; Battle of Farce-alia, III, 50–53; hoax perpetrated in, III, 102–103; maxims, III, 104–107; Grand Committee, III, 112, 118–121, 141; list of honorary members, III, 194. *See also* Anniversaries; Badges; Canopy of State; Cap of State; Commissions; Conundrums; Great Seal; Indictments; Laws; Letters;

Medals; Petitions; Poems; Songs; Trials
Tully. *See* Cicero, Marcus Tullius
Turks, I, 217, 247, 356, III, 195
Turlupin (Henri Legrand), I, 186, 356

Ugly Club of Annapolis: chronology of, I, 66; founded, I, 103–108; its proceedings, I, 107–110; its dissolution, I, 110–111
Universal Magazine, II, 328, 329, 330
Utopians, II, 354

Valentini, I, 55
Valerius Flaccus, Gaius, quoted, III, 40
Valerius Maximus, I, 271
Van der Donck, Adriaen, III, 190
Van Helmont, Jean Baptiste, III, 24
Vapor, Andrew: member of Red-House Club, I, 94
Vaunter, Major: member of Red-House Club, I, 94; member of Ugly Club, I, 103, 106, 108, II, 143
Venice, doge of, I, 390, II, 197
Venus, I, 42, 97, 271, II, 15, 382
Vergil, I, 22, 55, 134, 279, II, 15, 22, III, 256, 260; quoted, I, 183, III, 17, 312
Vernon, Edward, III, 198–199
Versailles, III, 11
Viar, Saint, I, 120
Victorellus, II, 24
Victorinus, III, 37
Violante, Madona, I, 55
Virginia. *See* Thursday Club of Hiccory Hill
Vivaldi, Antonio, I, 55, III, 315
Voltaire, II, 21, 26, 140
Vulcan, II, 15

Wallace, Charles, III, 308
Waller, Edmund, II, 14
Walpole, Sir Robert, III, 130
Walpolizing, I, 331
Wandering Jew, The, I, 121
Warburton, William (bishop), I, 32–33, 44, 95, III, 39, 41, 43, 191
Ward, Edward "Ned," I, 360, II, 8, 324
Warren, Sir Peter, I, 150

Well meaning Society (of Annapolis). *See* Clubs, Saturday Club
Welsh, I, 26, 28
Whigs, I, 53, 54, 88, 90, 151, 229, 367, II, 348, III, 106, 296
Whin-Bush Club (of Edinburgh): its origin, I, 45–49; admission to, I, 50; proceedings of, I, 51–54, 56; chronology of, I, 66; its simplicity, I, 215–216
Whiston, William, II, 47, III, 18
Whitefield, George, I, 35–36, 118, 153, 160, 161, 163, 202, III, 149
Wier, Johann, II, 24
Wild, Jonathan, the Great, III, 45
Wilkins, William (Spatterdash Wouldbe), II, 311, III, 124; delivers conundrums in club, III, 140; serves as club attorney, III, 328–331, 337, 338–339, 340, 343–344, 350, 351, 352–353, 354–355; letter written by, III, 335
William I, I, 49, 77, 116
William III, I, 53, II, 138
William of Drogheda, III, 341
Williamsburg, Virginia, II, 310, III, 122
Will-o'-the-wisp, I, 117
Wilson, William, I, 43
Wise men of Gotham, I, 22, III, 313
Wit, III, 143–144; defined, I, 236, II, 28–30; ancient examples, I, 352–356, II, 10–18; modern examples, I, 356–362, II, 18–26; history of, II, 7–39; in conundrums, II, 156. *See also* Green, Jonas, examples of his wit
Wit at Several Weapons (Beaumont and Fletcher), III, 189
Witchcraft, I, 32, 321, II, 23, 25
Wither, George, I, 134
Wollaston, John (Squeak Grumbleton), III, 149; sings in club, III, 145; performs music, III, 157
Wolstenholme, Daniel (Giovanni Precisio), III, 309, 357; performs music, II, 268, III, 309, 357; his character, II, 270
Women: women's clubs in Annapolis, I, 82; toasted, I, 97; judges of beauty, I, 104; Tuesday Club's regard for, I,

128–129; have no souls, I, 144; club ball for, I, 192–194; petition of Single Ladies of Annapolis, I, 388; their wiles, II, 10, 380–383; govern Tuesday Club, II, 325–327, 334; displeased with club, II, 379; their ceremonies, III, 130–131, 132–134. *See also* Genearchy

Wood, Benjamin: prepares club badges, I, 282, 284

Wood, Samuel (Nathaniel Sylvius), III, 149; mediator in club dispute, I, 375

Woolf, Garrett, III, 124

Woolston, Thomas, III, 18

Wren, Sir Christopher, I, 44

Xantippe, II, 12, 389
Xenocrates, II, 11–12
Xenophon, I, 21, 89, 271, II, 10, 13
Xerxes I, II, 311, 312

"Yellow hair'd Laddie, The" (song), III, 93

Zanti, Jean, II, 24
Zeno, I, 355
Zenobia, II, 323
Zeuxis, I, 31
Zoilus, III, 181
Zopyrus the Persian, III, 314
Zoroaster, I, 190, II, 19
Zosimos, II, 24
Zwingli, Ulrich, II, 26

OHIO UNIVERSITY LIBRARY

ase return this book as soon as you

OHIO UNIVERSITY LIBRARY

Index

Wind buyers & Sellers	27
Witches & wizzards, venerable Philosophers	28
Wits, Envied by dull men	238
Wise men of the East, Compared to the President, Sir John & the Chancellor of the Tuesday Club	362
Women, their Caps & head attire	264
Women (old) save Sparta from ruin	411
Naples savd by one	410
Pyrrhus, king of Epirus, killd by one	410
Presbytery established in Scotland by one	411
in Episcopal dress, burn Joan d'Arc	412
subject to Imperfections	515
Great power of the Sex	515
vanity of their dress	517
Their designs in dressing	518
bad Secret keepers	7
Improper to be admitted into male Clubs	519
Wou'dbe (Spatterdash) his life miraculously saved	413
Words, disputes concerning their variety	473

X, Y, Z

Xantippe, her adventure with Socrates	9
her character of Ditto	529
Story of her & Socrates	538
Xenocrates, studies at Athens	9
his adventure at Corinth with Lais the Courtezan	9
Xenophon, a witty historian	7
Xerxes, why he wept over his army	415
Yawning oration	
Zenobia (Queen) vanquishd by Aurelianus	433

the privilege of the Gr: Seal	246
bad policy in refusing to promote the Secretry	246
Their power to chuse a Chancellor disputed	253
Revoke the order of Seder: 137	254
Tax their members	255
show a coldness for Systematic divinity	261
Bad Christians	261
Repeal the proviso of Law 45	262
first Inventors of the Clubical Cap of State	266
Cause of their decline	276
vote the Cap of State to the Chancellor	278
Consult on the Cap of State	280
vote the Cap of State to Coney Pimp Frontinbrass	281
Confirm the frontinbrassian articles	297
appoint a Jury of 6 for trials	298
Compose a poem on the presidents Indisposition	304
amend Law 2d, & make it penal	307
Their *Coup d'essay*	314
enquire Concerning the Saving Clause in the frontinbrassian articles dispute	318a
their Superstitious maxims orders for the Anniversary	355
Celebrate their 6th Anniversary	357
Their great Stupidity	417
Tumults Concerning the Great Seal	437
Beginning of the Civil war	439
alarm in Club	439
Rebellion agst: the Presidt:	491
great battle of the Gr: Seal	491
victory proclaimd in Club	495
decathedrate his Lordship	494
a republican Governt: proposed	502
Their ensigns proposed to be sold by vendue	503
Interregnum in Club	503
alter the Calendar	503
agree to send a Condolatory address to his Ldshp	505
send ditto	505
send deputies to his Ldp:	509
Think of sending othr deput: prevented by the Chancellor	535
Their conduct accounted for	536
send deputies to the pres:	540
print their members names	545
Tumults & uproars, whence	472
party ones, their effects	475
Tweezer Case, a moderen Invention	30
Tyburn & Court Rogues, Compared	521
Their several Rewards	521

U, V

Understanding, subject to fallacy	123
Violence, more prevalent than Importunity	509
Virgil, a Lover of wit and master of the burlesque	15
Votes in the Tuesday Club, orders concerning them	102
Vulgar, the most Respectable and powerful Body of men	333
Vulgar & Grandees, flatter each other reciprocally	333

W

Warf, proposals to build one in the Club rejected	168
Wars, Civil and foreign, distempers of the body politic	480
Cause of them among the ancient Greeks & Romans	480
Whiston (Dr) his predictions of the End of the world	62
a false prophet	63
Whiner (Revd Mr) his proposals To the Club rejected	260
Whigs and Tories, their dissentions	465
Whig & tory, whence	466
Wit, (history of) wanted	2
—and humor, as old as the Creation	3
Its eclipse in times of Ignorance	19
new Species of it in the Tuesday Club	
defined differently	34

Index 421

Toasts, drunk with Epithets — 85
Tomlinsonus, Joannes, in the Chair — 329
Tomyris, Qu: of Scithia, Conquers
    Cyrus the great — 433
Tories and whigs, their dissentions — 465
Tories, their absurd doctrines
Triphiodorus, a letter droper — 16
Translations (literal) their
    Impropriety
Trios in music — 361
Trigonometry, its use in geometry &
    measuration of Solids — 362
Trowble, Inseparably Connected
    with human nature — 406
Truth, necessary in Conversation — 456
    a Sure guide — 517
    hard to find — 517
    her Simplicity — 517
    found by the Philosophers — 517
    Investigated by logic } vid Truth
    vol: 3 — 517
Tragedy, persons proper for — 192
Tragicomedy (moderen) its rise — 183
    new modelled — 181
    (Proposals to Improve) — 186
    Compard to whipt Syllabub — 186
    Persons in it talk out of Character — 187
    Scheme for its Improvement — 192
    disposition of the Tragicomic
        Stage — 192
    (proper persons to act in) — 192
    (new Specimen of) — 194
Trimmers, their Character — 308
Tuesday Club, disputes in it
    concerning Commissions — 58
    Censure the Secretary — 62
    dispute on the Report of the
        Committee for Commissions — 66
    Their great Influence & power — 67
    Epicædion to the president — 68
    Pass Law 43 — 70
    Institute Conundrums — 71
    Their Clemency to the Chief
        musician — 79
    Grant Sir John a Commission — 81
    members protest agst: it — 81
    affected by the Conundrums — 85
    Immoderate Laugh — 86
    Receive an Embassy from the
        East: Shore Triumvirate — 88
    Pass the 1st prerogat: law — 92
    pass 2d ditto — 94
    adopt a parliamentary Stile — 96
    Take State upon them — 96
    vote a Cap of State for their
        president — 101
    Their Humdrum Sederunt — 112
    Repeal their order on the Great
        Seal — 255
    Receive a Second Embassy from
        the Triumvirate — 119
    Tumultuary dialogue — 121
    Great Commotion — 121
    by what Instruments flattered — 126
    Badge medals arive — 127
    Their motive, to strike them — 130
    hold their 5th Anniversary — 133
    Compard to the Solar System — 136
    They & their president an
        Inexhaustible Subject — 165
    Instance of their public Spirit — 168
    Impeach and try their Chancellor — 175
    appoint Emissaries to the East:
        Sh: Triumvir: — 179
    observations on the chancelor's
        behaviour on Mr Comases
        Conundrum — 211
    disgusted wt the Conundr: — 211
    order a new Record book — 214
    Extreme Complaisance to their
        president — 216
    resolve Concerning the Great Seal — 217
    subject to & misled by opinion — 221
    how they lost their liberty — 222
    Resolve the Secretary's political
        Questions — 223
    Remarks on their Conduct — 224
    Their policy Condemned — 224
    Condemn the Secretarys
        Conundrum — 229
    Their Caprice — 230
    Their dominion Enlarg'd — 234
    Expell the Conundrums — 238
    Chuse an orator — 239
    The Errors in their Law 48 — 236
    Resolve to enquire Concerning

Inexplicable	225
falls asleep while deputy in the chair	228
objects to reading the proceedings	231
Remarks on the Speech of the Triumvirates ambassador	233
moves to expell the Conundr:	238
Commits a trespass	239
prosecution ordered agt: him	239
Censures the Secretarys Speech	243
his trial	247
pleads his own Cause	248
his acquittal	250
Speech thereupon	250
accuses the Secretary	262
objects to the Secretries appeal	264
opposes Cone Pimp Frontnbrass	293
espouses the Interest of the Chair	308
his policy	310
his designs seen thro	310
Compared to Junius Brutus	310
his observations on Jon: Grogs trial	317a
designs in recommending the Frontinbrassian articles	297
his letter to the President	310
Conjectures Concerning it	312
accuses Jonath: Grog	329
accused & acquitted	330
chosen deputy Presid:	354
Leaves the chair	354
Censured by the Club	355
Indictment drawn agst: him	355
do: Burnt	355
his Conversation with Signr Phrazeobundus	359
his Speech Concerning the Genearchy	448
moves for a writ *de ventre Inspiciendo*	448
appointed a Commissioner *de ventre Inspiciendo*	450
saves the Record book from the flames	493
discovers the great Seal in his pocket	484
pitched upon for a but	484
accuses the Secretry	513
his death	542
his Eulogium	542
Spyl: Junr: Critic on his Letter to Sir John	118
his Translation of the Club motto	118
Spagyrites	26
States men, a rule of theirs	86
—in Clubs	87
Stoics, their doctrine	496
Subject, none Inexhaustible	165
Exception to the rule	165
Summons, blank ones, ordered to be printed by the T: Club	102
Suspicion, whence proceeding	510
Swift (Dr) a Riddle maker	42
Sydenham (Dr) a Saying of his	25

T

Tamerlane, a climber	470
Thalestris, mistress of Alexr: the great	433
Theatre, a modest proposal for its improvement	181
Theocracy, (a single instance of)	468
Three, a favorite number	361
its harmony	361
Three (Rule of) in arithmetic	362
Tiara, persian Cap of State	269
Timorous (Prim) Complains of bad usage	252
appeased by the president	253
made Serjeant at arms	298
makes the 1st & 2d O yes	298
makes his 3d O yes	316
Takes Jonathan Grog into Custody	318
Takes Solo Neverout into Custody	438
is Intimidated	438
His astonishment & fright	489
flys & hides himself in the battle	490
blamd by his Lordship	494
a deputy on the 2d deputation	540
Entertains the Rustic Club	172
Tibullus, a punster	16
Time Servers, their Character	308

Index 419

appears in mourning	542	answers ditto	171
Presents Signr Lardinis Compliments to his honor and the Club	545	new maxim broachd by him	173
		suspected a Creature of the Chair	308
Seven, the number, its extent	363	ans: Jon: Grogs Conundrum	179
Sevent Son, a born doctor	363	answers the Secretrys Conundr:	217
Senses, subject to flattery	123	chosen deputy Chancellor	225
how perverted	124	attacks the Chair on both Sides	492
Senses (organs of) original Cause of all owr knowledge	126	saves the Great Seal from the fire	495
		suspects the president of bribery & theft	253
Sensible objects, how they affect the understanding	125	resigns his office of dep: Chancellor	254
Sederunt (poetical one)	430	his orders as dep: president to the Secretary	307
(Gelastic)	86	turns a Creature of the Chair	308
Semiramis, Enlarges the assyrian Empire	433	attempts a pacification in Club	490
		sent upon a forlorn hope	492
Shakespear, (his writings) why permanent	191	is a deputy on the Second deputation	540
Sheer wit, definitions of it	34	Socrates, a lover of wit	9
Shield of the Presidential Canopy, destroyed		his adventure with Xantippe	9
		a witty Saying of his	10
Sincerity, necessary in Conversation	456	his Story, a Slur on the Athenians	475
Simile of one amazed		Xantippes Character of him	529
Sly (Smoothum) Ambassador of the Eastren Shore Triumvirate	119	his opinion with regard to retalliating of Injuries	537
accuses Neverout in name of the Triumvirate	119	Sophists, their Learning Signal of victory in an argumt:	
addresses the Club at the 5th aniversary	145	Society, divided into the Leading and led	163
answers the Secretaries Conundrum	237	Socratic method of arguing	447
		why hated by the Sophists	447
Is ambassador to the Triumvirate	232	Solomon, misled by women	515
Introducer of a foolish Custom in Club	432	Spartans, a merry people	10
		Spartan Sage, his witticism	10
Slavery, Introduced by enthusiasm	347	Spiritual and Secular arms, engross power over men	347
Smirker (Theophilus) first ambassador of the E: Shore Triumvirate	88	Sphinx of the ancients, described	39
		Spyplot (Jealous Senr:) allays a tumult in Club	60
his Speech	89	The Gelastic Law Executed upon him	91
chosen a Triumvir	233		
made an honorary memb:	98	undergoes ditto	98
Snap (Huffman) answers Jon: Grogs first Club Conundrum	87	objects against the Conundr:	101
engages the Chancellor	91	answers Jon: Grogs Conund:	116
burns the protest	112	Prosecutes the Secretry	213
answers Jon: Grog's Conundr:	112	disputes with the Chancell:	214
finds the Comasian Conundrum	114	his designs while dep: pres:	
answers Jon: Grogs Conundr:	168		

chosen orator of the Club	239	Incurrs the odium of the Club	353
refuses the office	239	his Speech to the President	356
compelld to accept it	239	delivers his 6th anniversary Speech	360
Speech on the Presidents green velvet cap	240	his neglect	402
flatters the president on the qualities of his Cap	241	do: cause of it	402
suspected by the president and Club & why	246	his measures disregarded by the club	404
accuses Jealous Spyplot Senr	247	his Speech to the President	405
replication to Mr Spyplot's defence	248	his oration on Caps disapproved of	414
accuses Tunbelly Bowzer	251	delivers a Speech on the abuses & Grievances in Club	416
put to a nonplus	252	moves the revisal of the Laws for the last time	417
appointed Seal keeper	255	his oration on the Chancellor	427
a Tool of the Club to flatter the president	256	censured by the president and Club	428
Speech on the president's entertainment	256	disregards it	428
moves to revise the Laws	257	demands the Great Seal	438
dispute wt Dr Rhubarb	258	seconds Jealous Spyplots motion	448
his trial	262	his Speech Concerning the Genearchy	448
answer to the Charge	263	his Conjecture on the president's Countenance	449
Condemnd & sentenced	263	his private Conference with Solo Neverout	483
appeals from the Club to the Chancellor	264	Entrapped by protomusicus	483
Presents the Cap of State with a Speech	268	result of their Conference	483
Speech to the Chancellor	272	conveys the Great Seal into Jealous Spyplot Senrs pocket	484
his designs in recommending the frontinbrassian articles	297	attempts a pacification in Club	490
ordered to draw out Commissions	298	attacks the Chair on both Sides	492
delivers the Presidents mandate & Con: Pimp Frontinbrasses patent	302	attempts to burn the Records	493
		is under his lordships displeasure	502
his Speech to the Chancellor	303	one of the deputies sent to his Lordship	509
Pronounces Sentence agst: Jonathan Grog	316	accused by Jealous Spyplot Senr	513
his Speech on noses	319	Excuses himself	513
first Speech at the Capation	326	is threatned by the Club	514
Second at ditto	327	undertakes to restore the lost record	514
concerned with Gasperus Pickeringtonus in modelling the Cap of State	322	restores it	514
his motion in Club rejected	352	reports in Club the Presidents final answer	528
soured, and why	353	his Speech at the Presidents restoration	541
slighted by the Chancellor	353		

Index

his dispute with the Secretry 258
result of it 258
Riddle, what 42
Rich men, why admired 342
Romans, a merry people 10
The wisest people 356
Roman Catholic Church, its policy 339
Romances, moderen Inventions 26
Rustic Club, appointed 172
held 173
proposed 429

S

Sampson, a Riddle maker and
    punster 6
Satyrus, the Barrister, his method of
    bridling his passion at the bar 497
Scholastic Philosophy 469
Sciences, (occult) by whom
    Improvd 28
Scenes and acts of the drama, rising
    from ancient custom 199
Scheme for Improvement of the
    Theatre, its advantages 198
Scholars, apt to Contemn each
    other 473
Secretary, his letter to Capt: Comely
    Coppernose 52
receives his Commission 54
a general bear blame 62
Censured by the Club 62
submits & is pardoned 62
made a Conundrum master 71
his first Club Conundrum
    answered by Slyboots
    pleasant 85
his Second ans: by Jon: Grog 85
Counteracts the Chancellor 87
his artifice 87
operates in vain 88
his Speech to the Eastren Sh:
    Triumvirates ambassador 89
moves the first prerogative law 92
moves the 2d ditto 94
accuses Laconic Comas 97
accuses Protomusicus 97
undergoes the Gelastic Law 98
moves for a Cap of State for the
    president 101
acts openly against the Chancellor
    & Secretly agt: the Presidt: 104
Tampers with Sir John 104
his Schemes abortive 105
attempts to mitigate the
    Presidents anger 111
author of the Comasian
    Conundrum 114
Endeavors to turn the banter of it
    on Jonathan Grog 114
his comendable artifice
    unsuccessful 115
acts with precipitation 120
is silenced by the presidt: and
    Club 120
answers the Triumvirates Embassy 122
delivers his 5th anniversary Speech 135
addresses the President, Sir John
    & The chancellor 136, 137
advises the Chancellr 138
Flatters the Presidt: 138
advises Jonath: Grog 139
The Club musician 140
his prayer to Apollo 140
addresses the L: Stand: members 140
The honorary members 141
Thanks the president 145
bad Success of his flattery 166
his Conundrum Questioned 206
ordered to draw up Merry
    Makefun's Eulogium 207
appeases the Chancellor 211
is accused by Sir John 212
tried and acquitted 213
a tool to Protomusicus 213
deserted by him 213
applies for a new Record book 214
Produces in Club the Eulogium
    on Merry Makefun 217
delivers the Great Seal in Club 217
appointed Seal keeper in the
    Chancllors absence 217
proposes political Questions in
    Club 223
his policy baulked 225
moves a revisal of the Laws 225
Reprov'd by Sr John 225
his Conundrum Condemnd 229
motion to Indict him for a
    Contempt 229

Pox, how named in Edinburg	46	Questions (political) dangerous ones	447
Prayer, for the Restoration of Learning		Question (political) answered by a conundrum	447
President of the T: Club, an inexhaustible Subject	165	Question (argument by) why hated by the Sophists	447
his dress Typical		Quibble of the President	90
Presidents of Clubs, their pride	287		
Presbytery, how established in Scotland	411	**R**	
Pretender, a tool to the Grand monarque	465	Rage, a dangerous passion	488
Precisio, Giovanni, his Character	359	Ramble (Capt: Dio) made an honorary member of the T: Club	98
President and members of the T: Club, Compared to Alexr: the great and his courtiers	319	Rebellion, (the Chancellors) cause of it	485
Pride, (human) Incommensurable	286	History of it	489
forms dissentions	469	Record book, a new one ordered	214
where found	471	Records (lost) restored	514
a noisy passion	471	Reflection, on the President on the Tu: Club	
Priests, their power less than that of women	516	Rebus, defined	43
Protomusicus, receives his commission	90	ancient	43
		modern	43
Procession, 2d grand anniversary one of the T: Club	134	Examples of both	43
3d ditto	357	how agrees with Conundrum	45
Prussia (K: of) secures the balance of power	341	Etymon	46
		Ingenious one of Allan Ramsay	46
Pucelle, saves France from ruine	412	Religion, opposd to reason	339
Pun, its definition	37	Reflection, a free one	
difference between it & a conundrum	37	Record book, proposed to be burnt	493
Punning art, in what it Consists	38	Revolutions in the Tuesd: club, reflections on thm	499
Pyrgos (Dr) his dispute with Dr Rhubarb	226	Records, defects in them discoverd	513
his repartee to do:	227	Resolution, the best armour in adverse fortune	528
his opinion of Dr Rhubarb	227	Records of the T: Cl: defective	444
Pyrrhus, Epirot, killd by an old woman	410	Rhime in poetry, a modern Invention	24
Pysistratus, actuated by pride and avarice	472	Rhubarb (Doctor) Introduced in the T: Club	206
		a Celebrated philosopher and Freemason	206
Q		his Learning	206
Quaint, (Drawlum) entertained as a Stranger in the T: Club	429	his dispute with Doctor Pyrgos	226
		his Skill in Grammar	227
Quacks (political) more dangerous than Physical	479	in metaphysics	228
Question, an unexpected one in the Tuesday Club	524	his observation on the Secretaries Conundrum	237
		is searched for the great Seal	253

Index   415

false, enslave and mislead the
   people   346
false ones, how they move the
   people   346
   —in England
Patriots (Sham ones) of Rome   464
Party Brawls & disputes, their
   effects   475
Passions, most effectually bridled by
   prevention   497
Passus the painter, his witty device   17
Petronius Arbiter, a wit & punster   18
Philosophers (venerable) who
Philosophers, by way of Eminence   26
Philosophers (occult) list of them   28
Philosopher-Stone enquiry   29
Phraseobundus (Signior)
   accompanies the 2d
   Anniversary procession   357
   his polite Speech to the Presidt: 358
   his Character   360
   Learned Conversation with
   Jealous Spyplot Senior   359
Physician and Legislator, Compard   479
   equally subject to mistakes   479
Physiognomy, a moderen Science   21
Pickeringtonus (Gasperus) searched
   for the Great Seal   253
   Invents & makes the Cap of State   322
Pitcairn (Dr) his poem Quoted   407
Plato, a paragrammatist   16
   his Sentiment of a lye   458
Planting of men, what   19
Pleasant (Slyboots) versed in the
   ancient History of the T: Club   61
   assumes Learned Stile   64
   answers the Secretaries
   Conundrm: 85
   answers the Secretarys Conundr: 101
   appointed deputy Chancellor   169
   ans: Jon: Grogs Conundr: 204
   ans: ditto   204
   his Singular knack at answering
   Club Conundrms: 205
   one of the Clubs deputies to his
   Lordship   509
   delivers the purport of the
   deputation   524
   his replication to his Lordship   525

   is a deputy on the Second
   deputation   522
Plenipotentiaries, their Conferences,
   the best Comedies   520
Plenipos of the Club, go to his
   Lordship   522
   are admitted   522
   the Gracious reception   523
   take their Leave   526
   Their report in Club   526
Plinius Secundus, a lover of puns   17
Poet laureat, his witticism   91
Poet and Fool, the Characters not
   Incompatible   443
Poets (ancient Greek) great wits   12
Poet's heads, lumber garrets   36
Poets, monkish ones   25
Poetry, moderen   24
Poetical Entry by the Laureat   430
   an obscure passage in it Explained   431
Poem, on Signior Lardini   244
   (heroic) on the presidts night
   adventure   418
Police, Civil and Ecclesiastical   219
   supported by opinion   219
Politicians, a rule of theirs   86
   in the Tuesday Club   87
Polyhistor (Doctor) attends the
   Sixth Anniversary   370
Pompey the Great, his false
   pretensions   163
Pope of Rome, his qualities   221
Popes of Rome, the Impudence
   unparallelled   286
   Imitators of the Emperors   287
Political Report, spread abroad   521
Popularity, antecedent to the
   acquisition of power
Popular uproars, whence   464
   Commotions & tumults, how
   cured   477
Posie, defined   50
   Sign posie   50
   annular Posie   51
   Garter posie   51
Potentates (Indian) their pride   287
Power of women, greater than that
   of priests   516
Power (desire of) a natural passion   349

wears his night cap in Club, while deputy president & H:S:	207
leaves the Secretary in the lurch	213
appointed deputy Secretary	214
delivers Strange minutes in Club	214
answers Jon: Grogs Conundrum	229
moves the revisal of law 2d	307
designs to restore the Clubs liberty	313
assumes the Chair without Commission	351
Turned out of it	352
his ambition disappointed	352
displays his parts	402
yeilds the prize in Singing to the President	402
declaims in Club unintelligibly	402
gains the Presidts favor	402
means of his advancement in the club	403
sets a recitativo air to Jon: Grogs heroic poem	428
keeps up a fooli[sh] Custom in Club	429
great seal delivere[d t]o him	438
undergoes the Gela[s]tic law	438
Committed to the Custody of the Serj: at arms	438
Prognostic concerning his advancement in club	439
made the presidents Instrument to humble the Chancell:	439
accused of theft by the Secretry	451
negroe evidence agst: him	451
Resolves to deliver the Gr: Seal	483
chuses the Secretary for his tool	483
his private Conference with the Secretary	483
Entraps the Secretary	483
Result of his Conference	483
put on a forlorn hope in the Great Clubical battle	492
falls asleep in the Chair	508
Night, described	366
Nonsense, on what account Established	444
Nonresistance, a nonsensical doctrine	465

O

Obedience, passive, a nonsensical doctrine	468
Observations, Philosophical & moral	401
Ode, aniversary, anno 1750	142
ditto, anno 1751	365
Oedipus, a Riddle Solver	39
Officers (State ones) in the T: Club, to be tried by indictment	235
Olaus Magnus, Quoted	27
Opinion, its great prevalence	219
supports arbitrary power and Slavery	219
deifies villains	220
asists Impostures In religion	220
supports the Roman Church & papal authority	220
misleads the members of the T:C:	221
Oration, anniversary, 1750	136
ditto, anno 1751	360
Orator of the Tuesday Club, Created	239
Order to the Chancellor	121
Orleans, maid of, saves France from ruine	412
Orpheus, the power of his music	400
fable of him Explained	400
a native of Ireland	407
effect of his music there	407
Ostentatious fellow, who	7
Overture to the Annivers: ode 1750	147
Ovid, a paragramattist	15
O yes, first made in the T: Club	298
Second do:	298

P

Pantamimes, moderen Inventions	183
Pandamonium, College of	28
Paracelsus, assumes a Creating power	29
Party, whence it rises	163
Its origin in the T: Club	164
Partiality, it's prevalency	
Patriots (nominal) many	345
(real) few	345
True	345

Index

Coney Pimp Frontinbrass to the President	288
ditto to ditto	291
Chancellor to the President	300
Jealous Spyplot Senr to the Pres:	310
(Heroic) of Sir John to the Pres:	318
Comely Coppernose to the Club	440
Lilliston (Sue) her Story	449
Logic, a moderen art	
Locke (John) his definition of wit	34
Lycurgus, his Instruction to the Spartans	10
Lyars, habitual, believe their own fibs	222
why dispised	456

M

Maccarty (Sir Hugh Esqr) his cap of [St]ate	265
his Identity [q]uestioned	265
his health [dr]unk by the T: Club	282
his charac[t]er	284
a Quixotic person	285
his death	458
Mad-caps	264a
Magic (moderen)	21
Magicians of Lapland	27
Mahomet, his Imposture	220
how supported	220
founded his religion on enthusiasm	299
Makefun (Merry Esqr,) suspected of Jacobitism	146
his death	207
Eulogium on him by the Club	234
Mallet of State in the Tuesd: Club	318
Mankind, divided into great and vulgar	333
Martial, a punster	15
Matter, its perishable nature	
Maxim, a false one	
Magazine publishers, their opinion of Jon: Grog's performances	440
Medicines and Laws, Compared	479
Members and Presid: of the T: Club, Compared to Alexr: the great and his courtiers	319
Members (honorary) of the T: Club, Compard to Comets	364
address to them	141

Men, why censorious	73
Mephistophilus, an airy Councellor	
Milton, a punster	5
Mitres, Episcopal, their use	263a
Modern Chance discoveries	30
Modern wits, wrong headed	30
Modern honor, unknown to the ancients	537
Moderens, preferable to the ancients for Inventions	182
their modesty	182
Modesty, assumed by authors	181
a good recommending quality	181
Moderens, theyr way of putting up Injuries	537
Money, a badge of State	335
Murders and battles on the Stage, ridiculous	191
Music, of the anniversary ode, anno 1750	147
Do: 1751	371
Mysteries, their great merit in religious faith	220
Mystery, Essential to moderen Learning & Philosoph:	32

N

Naples (State of) saved by a triffling accident	410
Navigation, Improved	27
Neverout (Solo) his remonstrance to the Club	76
comes booted into Club	79
his great Impudence	79
his trial	90
answers the presidents Quibble and quotes Scripture	90
Jibes the Chancellor	92
accused by the Secretary	97
undergoes the Gelastic law	98
his poetical Epistle to Sr John	106
a plagiary	108
Burnt in the hand by the East: Shore triumvirate	119
accused by Smoothum Sly	119
Browbeats the Secretary	120
answers the Secretrys Conundrm:	123
Gains favor with the Chair	203
opposes the Chancellor	203
his policy	204

his heroic resistance in battle	493	Lapland, a Colony of witches settled there	29
his decathedration	494		
Throws the Gr: Seal in the fire	495	Lardini (Signior) Entertains the Club with music	235
his party in Club	495		
his discreet behaviour	497	Lays a Scheme before the Club	239
Retires from the Club	498	presents a poem on himself in club	244
Compared to Pompey	499		
writes an apology for himself	501	his Scheme Considered	247
his obstinacy	510	rejected	261
admitts the Clubs Emissaries	521	Performs the anniversary music	359
his Situation at their admission	522	Laugh, a Great one in the Tuesday Club	86
his Gracious Speech to the deputies	523		
		Laureat (poet of the T: Club) his works will not bear Criticism	
his astonishment at the deputies Speech	525		
		Compared to Shakespear	534
his answer to them	525	Laws, without penalties, good advice	245
his heroic behavior	529		
his prudent conduct	529	of the T: Club, defective	245
compared to Socrates	538	The presidents opinion of them	245
assents to the Clubs demand	540	Sir John's opinion of them	246
returns to the Club	540	Laws of the T: Club, revised	262
his restoration	540	Laws and medicines, Compared	479
Salutes the Chancellor	540	Learning, reviv'd in Europe	30
observation on his behavior to the Chancellor	541	(occult) the budget of it	28
		Legerdemain	21
appears in mourning	542	Legislator & Physician, compared	479
Cedes the title of my Lord	543	equally liable to mistakes	479
Conjectures Concerning his designs	543	Legends, popish articles of faith	335
		Leo the Great (Pope) diverts Attila from the pillage of Rome	335
Isocrates, a paragrammatist	16		
Judgement, how perverted	123	Lewis le Grand, a Climber	470
Judicial astrology	27	Letters, Clubical, of Slyboots	
Jus divinum, a nonsensical doctrine	219	Pleasant to the President	60
Justice of Peace, his opinion on the Case	202	from the Secretry to Capt: Coppernose	52
Jus Negrum of the Spartans	279	Sir Jno: to the Secretry	61
		Slyboots Pleasant to Sr Jno:	63
K		Huffman Snap to Sir Jno:	75
		Jon: Grog to the Presidt:	99
Kings, not respected on account of their personal merit	338	Secretary to Sr Jno:	104
		Smoothum Sly to Sir Jno:	108
on account of their Titles only	338	Jeal: Spyplot Jnr to Sr Jno:	117
why Called Gods vice Gerents	468	Capt: Coppernose to the Club	129
Knowledge, Coveted by all	455	Secretary to the Presid:	165
few Qualified to receive it	455	Quirpum Comic to the President	174
(desire of) it's effects	455	Secretary to Capt: Coppernose	208
		Laconic Comas to the Presd:	209
L		President to the Secretary	215
		Secretary to the President	259
Lais the Corinthian Courtezan, her adventure with Xenocrates	9	Suppositions of Capt: Coppernose to the club	266

Index

delivers the Great Seal	174
observations on his genius for Conundrums	205
Reason why he did not answer them	205
his Sentence against Mr Comases Conundrum	210
Endeavors to appease the Chancl:	210
writes a laconic letter to the Secretary	215
observations on it	215
Great opinion of his power and notion of the members	216
Compared to the Great Turk and the pope	222
accuses the Club of breach of Law	225
his caprice	230
holds an Extraordinary Club	231
displeased with the order Concerning the Great Seal	231
protests against the Club's proceeds:	239
forced to comply	239
puts on a Cap of Green velvet	239
his opinion of the Club Laws	245
his defect of memory	247
appeases Prim Timorous	253
suspected of bribery and theft	253
Produces the Great Seal	253
accuses some members of giving him bad advice	253
betrays his own Guilt	253
objects to the privileges of the Great Seal	254
effects of it upon him	254
reproves the Secretary	263
puts on the Cap of State	271
his Sentiment of the Cap of State	276
different Sentiments on ditto	277
Secret Conversation with Don Jno: Charlotto on the Cap of State	277
his Jealousy of the Club letters	278
drinks Sir Hugh Mccartys health	282
Presents Frontinbrass with the Impressions of the Great and privy Seals	282
admires Sir Hugh Maccarty Esqr	284
his evasion	285
Caught by Cone Pimp Frontinbrass	289
Presents Frontinbrass with a Club medal	290
appoints a Serjeant at arms	298
his power founded on Enthusiasm	300
Revokes the amendment of Law 2d	308
uses the Mallet of State	317
his Severity to Jonath: Grog	318
his privy Council of 3	320
enters suddenly into the Club	354
his Grand Capation	325
is angry with the Club compared to the Sun	364
Gains the prize of Protomusicus	402
Panegyric on his Courage & presence of mind	405
description of his dangerous night adventure	408
displeasd with the orators Speech	414
displeasd with the Laureats heroic poem	417
his night thoughts in bed	419
attacked in bed by a ruffian and bound	422
his Speech to him	422
his wise observation	422
his Scheme to humble the Chancell:	439
makes Solo Neverout his Instrument	439
his remark on the Agents Letter	441
offended at the Chancellrs Speech	449
orders writs *de ventre Inspiciendo*	450
his contempt for the Gr: Seal	451
his observation on the Secretrys bass viol	454
suspicious of the members of the Club	456
his Notions of Sir H: Maccarty	457
Encounters a bass fiddle and Case	459
objects to some of the Frontinbrassian Articles	460
his aversion to Ensigns of State	461
lays aside his badge of State	461
refuses to be searched for the Great Seal	485
his Jangle with the Chancellor	485
his great astonishment	490

Hieroglyphics, compose the Rebus	43
High Steward, distinction of his badge	133
Hypocrisy, acquires power	344
History, Improvd by the moderens	26
Historians, a fruitles labor in them Their error	4
Homer, a lover of wit	15
master of the Burlesque	15
a pattern for Imitation	183
a master of the drama	183
how he Introduces his heroes	190
Quoted	491
his notion of discord	500
origin of his Iliad	
Homony, a Speech on it	278
a nourishing & royal dish	279
Etymon from different languages	280
Honor, founded on opinion	219
titles of, Rewards of virtue	392
moderen, unknown to the ancients	537
Honorary members, why so called	
Horace, a paragrammatist	16
Horse, Consul of Rome	102
Hottentot Caps of State	269
Human Nature, Instance of its frailty	

I

Jacob, a wit, outwits his brother Esau	5
James I. (King) Ruines of the Gothic Structure of Learning in his reign	32
author of parties in England	466
a Scourge to the English people	466
a foil to Q: Elizabeth	466
nicknamed by Henry IV, of France	467
misfortunes of his Posterity	467
Tools to France	467
Icarus, his Story	469
Ideas, false association of them	189
Jews, under a Theocracy	468
Imprecation on the defacers of the Tuesd: Club records	513
Impudence, its uses	472
Indian monarchs, how they differ from other monarchs	279
Indefeasible Hereditary right	468
Indictment, burnt in Club	355
Interregnum in the T: Club, History of it Confused	496
Injuries, productive of Injuries	536
forgiveness of, Inculcated	536
Joseph, the patriarch, makes a fortune by his wit	6
Jole (Nasifer) delivers the commissions	54
his passion in Club	59
Cancels the Commissions	60
addresses the Special Committee for Commissions	65
displeasd with the Clubs poetical address	69
his arbitrary claims	70
how affected towards the Chancellor & Secretary	88
delivers a Commission to Mr Protomusicus	90
his Quibble	90
answered by Mr Neverout	90
Empower'd to Call privy Councils	92
gets the Sole power of Granting Commissions	94
Becomes giddy headed with exaltation	102
his motives to grant Sir John a Commission	103
Presents a Comiss: to Sr John	109
assumes his timber Countenance	111
Reproves Laconic Comas	116
Quarrels with the Chancellr	120
is reconciled	122
Presents the Club medals	127
meets the Grand anniversary procession	135
Compard to the Sun	136
he and the Chancellor Compard to Cæsar & Pompey	164
delivers Capt: Coppernoses patent Ingrossed and Seald	167
Instance of his public Spirit	168
Incensed with the Chancellor	170
assumes a dreadful timber Countenance	171
seizes the great Seal	172

Index 409

its consequences
Their usual topics of
    Conversation
Strangers to Sincerity
defined
Great Seal of the Tuesday Club,
    disputes Concerning it 246
    order of the Club Concerning it 246
    a General Search for it 253
    a check to the Presidents power 254
    a bone of contention 483
    is a missing 485
    disorder in Club Concerning it 485
    Tumults about it 488
    2d General Search for it 485
    The Presidents Contempt of it 486
    Thrown in the fire 495
Great Rebellion in the Tuesday Club 491
Greek Epigrammatists, punsters 16
Greeks, the wisest people 356
Grog (Jonathan) made Conundrum
    master 71
    his first Conundrum answered by
        Huff: Snap 84
    answers the Secretaries Conundr: 85
    his pun 91
    answers the Secretries Conund: 97
    his accrostic on the President 99
    his poetical vote 101
    good at bearing a Joke 115
    his Character Compared to that
        of Laconic Comas 115
    Remark on his Conundrums 117
    Salutes the President at the
        Anniversary procession 135
    deliv: his 2d Annivers: ode 142
    ans: the Secretry's Conundr: 168
    observat: on his Conundr: 205
    Compar'd to Colly Cibber 208
    fails in his answer to the
        Secretaries Conundr: 216
    Presents a new Record book 226
    Repairs the presidentl: Chair 226
    his Conundr: Condemned 236
    his thanks to the Secretry 257
    his distich on the Cap of State 271
    ordered to publish the *Lugubris*
        Cantus of the Club 304
    Information agst: him for ditto 314
    Tryd & Condemned 317

    Taken into Custody 318
    his remark on his Sentence 317a
    sets Joannes Tomlinsonus in the
        president's Chair 329
    Tryed & confesses 329
    Sentence executed on him 330
    his heroic poem on his Ldsps
        dangerous adventure 418
    his poetical entry in the Record 430
    his remonstrance against Colley
        Cibber 441
    challenges the authors of the
        magazines 442
    appointed a Commissioner *de*
        ventre Inspiciendo 450
    Criticism on his Singing 482
    saves the Presidential canopy
        from the flames 493
    ordered to prepare a mournful
        Song 509
    is a deputy sent by the Club to his
        Lordship 509
    Presents a mournful ditty in Club 510
    restores the lost record 514
    presents the *Carmen Seculare* 523
    his mournful Episode 529
    different Judgements on his
        performances 533
    delivers the printed list of
        members 545

H

Ham, Son of Noah, a wit 5
Harmony of the heart, preferable to
    all other 78
Haste to preferment, often
    disappoints the ambitious 349
Head, (the President's) encomium
    on it 243
Head (human) how adorned 264
Hellen of Troy, cause of the Iliad
Henly (Mr Orator) his observation 51
Head, ornamented by all nations 264
Heraclitus, a burlesque character 18
    his notion of discord 500
Hereditary right (Indefeasible)
    whence derived 468
Hiatus, a great one in the Club
    records 435

their Jealousies	448
The vanity of their dress	517
Fever in the State, what	475
Fibber (Humbug) his Lie	458
Confutation of it	458
Flattery, of the understanding, whence	123
of the Senses	124
(Instruments of) in the T: Club	126
Its great power over men	126
(Lovers of) Selfish	255
Flawel, a divine Spiritualizer	33
Folly, often takes the place of wisdom	52
Fool and Poet, the Characters not Incompatible	443
Fools Caps	264a
Fops of the Stage	185
French, their genius for Romance	26
Friendship, founded on opinion	219
Frontinbrass (Coney Pimp) his first appearance in the Tuesday Club	276
requests the Cap of State to carry to New York	281
Is refused the Cap of State	281
restores it	281
his pernicious proposals in Club	281
made an honorary member	282
his character	282
Lays a bait for the President and catches him	289
his private audience with the president	289
gives the presit: the title of Lord	290
kisses the presidts hand	290
receives a Club medal	290
his pernicious advice to the president	291
his proposals to the Club	293
oppos'd by Jealous Spyplot Senr:	293
supported by the Secretary	293
opposed by the Chancellor	294
Threatens to leave the Club	294
draws up articles	294
designs in recommending the articles	297
made agent in America	299
his patent Sealed	303
his arival	323
Caps the Ld President	327
his Speech at the Capation	327
Frontinbrassian articles, drawn up	294
Fuddle Caps	264a
Fur caps	264a

G

Gabble (John) performs the vocal music at Anniversary 6	359
made an honory: memb: & Champion of the Eastren Shore Triumvirate	394
Geese, save the capitol of Rome	412
Geddis (Janet) her history	411
Genearchy of the T: Club	437
Genearchy, a Subject not much handled	432
Love Genearchy	434
Domestic	434
how mantaind in Clubs	434
arguments Concerning it	447
Secretary's Speech on it	448
Conclusion of it	514
Generation, Equivocal, argument for it by Dr Rhubarb	227
Geometry	362
Gold, its power	348
Good in human nature, extinguished by an absurd education	415
Goodness, no bar against misfortune	
Gothic Learning (destroyers of)	31
Gothic fabric of learning, Remains of it, where to be found	32
Government, arbitrary, Erected on opinion	219
Government, a perfect one, not in nature	476
Gowns and Cloaks, badges of wisdom and Bravery	356
Grandees on the Theatre and in the world, how they differ	187
Grandees and vulgar, reciprocally flatter each other	333
Great men, their passion for power, a rule among them	71
errors in Judgement, peculiar to them	

Index

Cyrus the Great, a Climber	470

D

Dance, a Clubical one	145
Devil, a wit, the most ancient	4
a punster	5
made a Beast of Burden	29
first makes cooks	279
outwitted	27
a tragical droll	183
Democritus, a Droll	18
Devotees (Religious) their Error	125
Demigods, who esteemed such	220
Diogenes, a droll	18
a proud Philosopher	471
Discoveries (Chance ones)	30
(modern ones)	30
Discords in Societies, as necessary as in music	500
Discord, in the Tuesday Club	501
a thing natural	501
Diadems, their use	263a
Disputes (Religion, Subject of)	473
concerning the propriety of words	473
Ridiculous	473
Ditty, mournful one by the poet Laureat	510
Dissentions concerning Religious matters	473
Doctors, magical ones	27
Born & unborn	363
Doctrines, absurd ones, by whom promoted	465
Dryden, his definition of wit	35
Drugger (Abel) his Rebus	47
Dress, vanity of it	517
of women, its design	518
Dutch, their Taste for Tragicomedy	184
Dull men, envy great wits	238

E

Eastren Monarchs, Their pride	287
Eastren Shore Triumvirate, Their first Embassy to the T: Club	89
Second ditto	119
Third ditto	231
Favor the Secretary	239
Their bad policy	239
honors done them	391
Education, an absurd one	455
in high life, it's effects	415
In Low life	416
(university) more productive of pedantry than true knowlge:	455
Egg Shells, used in navigation	28
Elizabeth (Queen) Compared to the Queens of antiquity	433
King James I, a foil to her	466
English Dramatic writers, expert in Tragicomedy	184
Enthusiasm, Conduceive to Slavery	299
an universal passion	299
human grandure supported by it	299
a ground work to found power upon	347
Epicædion of the Tuesday Club	68
Episode, a mournful one by the poet Laureat	529
Erick, The Danish king, his Conjuring Cap	27
Euripedes, the Greek Tragædian, his manner of writing	190
Eulogium, on Merry Makefun Esqr	234
Exclamation, Condolatory	68

F

Fable, not to be taken in a literal Sense	400
Facetious Companions, who	8
Fancy, described	35
ancient & moderen descriptions of it	36
Faith (Religious) gathers Strength by mysteries	220
Farces, Theatrical, moderen Inventions	185
the most Ridiculous ones	520
Falshood, its bad Consequences	456
Farmer, his Case adjudged	202
Favors, how received by some	391
Fate, an universal Governor	400
Female Sex, their deceit	449
Females, as well adapted for Governing States & Emprs: as males	433

his great Inattention	101
opposes the motion for a Cap of State	101
offended at the Comasian Conundrum	114
Compard to Jon: Grog	115
reprovd by the president	116
Leavs the Club	116
his Conundrum on the Chancellor	210
his behaviour on hearing of the Chancellors Conundrum	211
present at the private Conference of Frontinbrass and the president	289
displeasd with the Conference	289
Confederates wt Sir John	458
Comasian Conundrum (history of it)	114
Comedy, (persons proper for)	192
Common Sense, banished	219
Comic (Quirpum) suspected for Secreting the Great Seal	404
admitted a member of the Club	167
answers Jonathan Grogs Conund:	236
finds the deputies Commission	404
Treats the Club with homony	278
his Speech in Club privilege granted him	351
sends a message to his Ldship	436
his Conference with him and Report to the Club	436
Committee, for Comissions, its report	65
its Legality questioned	66
grand anniversary one, appointed	131
meets	132
Comittee to the Frontinbrassian Articles, it's report	295
Commotions (civil) compared to a fever in the State	475
admit not of a perfect cure	476
partially cured, how	477
Popular, how cured	479
Community or State, none without flaw	476
Coifs of the Judges in Westminster hall	263a
Concert of music, adjourns the Tuesday Club	435
Conference, private between Coney Pimp Frontinbrass & the President	289
between Quirpum Comic & Do:	436
Between the deputies of the Tuesday Club & ditto	523
Conjuring Caps	264a
Conversation, improves	
Coppernose (Capt: Comely) his Letter to the Club	129
Spurious ditto	266
2d letter	440
his conference with the publishers of the magazines	440
Conundrums, defined	39
Hieroglyphic	40
Instituted in the T: Club	72
first produced in Club	83
how they affect the Club	85
Club ones	96
Ditto	100
Ditto	112
Ditto	116
Ditto	122
Ditto	131
Ditto	167
Ditto	171
Ditto	179
Ditto	204
Ditto	212
Ditto	216
Ditto	218
Ditto	229
Ditto	236
motion to expell them rejected and why	215
reasons for Expelling them	238
only Calculated for low life	238
Their character, how hurt	238
Conundrumificators of the Tuesday Club	72
Corpus [cum] Cauda	
Court Rogues	520
Court Compliments	309
Crankum (Crinkum) presents a new Song in Club	452
Performs music in Club	482

Index

displeas'd & meditates revenge	461
his great rage	485
his Jangle with the Prest:	485
his Incendiary Speech	487
effects of the Speech	488
his anger	489
attacks the Presidts Chair	492
renews the attack	493
his party in Club	495
how he got the victory	495
endeavors to seize the Chair	498
is prevented	498
Compard to Cæsar	499
his haughty behaviour in the Chair	502
displeas'd with the presidents answer to the deputies	527
seizes the Chair	527
mistaken in his politics	527
forcibly assumes the Chair	534
disgusts the members	535
prevents a Second Embassy to the president	535
observation on his behavior	541
his Speech to the President on Replacing him in the Chair	541
Charms to cure diseases	22
Characters, Comic ones, mistaken in high life, why ill done by dramatic writers	188
of the great, mistaken by the writers of Tragedy	188
Charity, of a Cold temperature	262
does best by a Christenmass fire	262
Charlotto (Don John) his poem on Signior Lardini	244
of the privy council of 3, and why	320
fires a gun in the Dark	409
his secret conversation with the President, on the Cap of State	277
Eulogium on him	409
his Skill in music	419
describ'd drunk and asleep in the presidts kitchen loft	421
awakes from his Sleep	424
a pistol fir'd at him by a ruffian	424
Eulogium on him	426
Chemistry, its origin	26
Terms of art	26
Christianity, ancient and moderen, how they differ	261
Chronogram, defined	48
prophetical one	48
Church, Roman, its power, whence	339
high & low, whence	466
Chyromancy, a moderen Science	21
Cibber, (Colley) nature of his anniversary Compositions	445
compared to the poet laurt: of the T:C:	445
Cicero, a paragramitist	16
a Rhimer	24
Civil war, beginning of it in the Tuesday Club	439
True Cause of it	439
Climateric, The Grand, middle and lesser	361
Climbers of the Ladder of ambition, their Employment	469
Cloaks, Signatures of Learning	356
Clodius, his carbonading	448
Club (of Hiccory hill in Virginia)	323
by whom erected	323
(eastren Shore) modelled after The Tues: Club, & subject to it	119
(monday, of New York)	281
(Tuesday) compared to the Planetary System	364
Clubs, practise of them ancient & moderen, alike	
how they differ	
ancient members of them	
Clubical Cap of State, Invented	266
Cobwebs, used in navigation	28
Commission, melilotian	54
Commissions, why post dated	58
Commission, Deputy Presidents, Seald with black wax & why	75
Commission to Sir John by the Club	82
Comas, (Laconic) accused by the Secretary	97
objects against the Conundrums	101

his opinion of Laws	246
wears the Cap of State	281
discredits the Character of Sir Hugh Maccary: Esqr	285
displeasd with the Secretaries Speech to the Chair	304
his Conduct in Club Contests and dutch policy	314
his clemency	318
his heroic Epistle, Censured by the Club	319
is of the privy Council of three and why	320
displeasd at the orator's Speech	357
compar'd to Mars	364
first fomenter of the Presidents Suspicion	457
opposes the Scheme for republican Government	502
Brings the Secretary under his Ldshps displeasure	502
assumes the Chair	508
is a deputy on the Second deputation	540
Chair, presidential, in danger of being burnt	495
Chancellor of the Tuesday Club, receives his Commission	54
reads & Seals the comissions	54
designs against the Chair	59
foments disputes in Club	59
operates against the Chair	71
Club Jealous of him	71
his character	73
his method to advance himself in Club	73
Parallel between him and the president	74
his Scheme to humble the president	81
his first Step to excite the great Rebellion	83
he and the Secretary, Club politicians opponent	87
operates in vain	88
his contempt of the Club laws	102
his policy	112
answers the Secretaries Conundr:	113
disgusted at the Clubs procedings	114
Reads the Comasian Conundrum	114
solves ditto	115
quarrels with the president	120
his Clubical anger	121
is reconciled to the president	122
oversets the Champion	145
he & the president Compard to Cæsar & Pompey	164
appoints a deputy	169
an Impeachment ordered agt: him	171
set to the bar	175
Impeached	175
is acquitted & his Great Joy	178
is angry with Mr Comas's Conund:	210
his remarks on it	210
his dispute wt Mr Spyplot	214
his political reasons a Secret	216
his opinion Concerning the Great Seal, delivered by the Secretry	217
Compar'd to the Judges of hell	272
Refuses the Cap of State	278
opposes Coney Pimp Frontinbrass	294
displeased with the frontinbrassian articles	297
his first high Stewardship	300
his designs in flattering the President	301
disobeys his lordships order	316
absents himself in disgust from the Capation	328
his decree agt: Jon: Grog	329
slights the Secretary	353
Compar'd to Saturn	364
is the Orpheus of the Club	427
his Speech Concerning the Genearchy	449
appointed a Commissioner *de ventre Inspiciendo*	450
his anger	452
opposes the President in rescinding the Frontinbrassian articles	460

Index

Cato (Tragedy of) by Addison, a Tragicomedy	184
Caligula, why he made his horse Consul of Rome	102
Case, adjudged	202
Caps, origin of	264
Expressive of good qualities	263a
variety of them	263a
of Cardinals	263a
of Judges	263a
Trencher and Square	263a
Expressive of bad qualities	264a
San benito	264a
Conjuring	264a
feathered	264a
of women	264a
most ancient Record of them	269
oration on them dissapproved	414
Cap of State of the Tuesd: Club, prognostic of it	207
prelude to it	240
Cap of State, ducal	264a
Presidential, never used before the Time of N: Jole Esqr	265
of the Lying Club	265
Clubical, by whom Invented	266
Cause of Great revolutions in the Tuesd: Club	266
Hottentot ones	269
american	269
old Roman	270
Cap of State of the T:C: model of it	270
Distich on it by the Poet Laur:	271
Compard to the monarchial Crown of Ireland	271
Disputes concerning it	276
Consultation on it	102
its disgrace	320
Secret history of it	321
Cap, Presidential, Symbol of the virtues of the President of the T: Cl:	241
Capation, history of it	325
(grand Ceremony of)	325
Capitol of Rome, saved by Geese	412
of Williamsburg in Virginia, burnt by an Irrational Creature	412

Cabal against Mr Pres: Jole	313
Caprice, Incident to fools	230
wise men sometimes subject to it	230
Societies subject to it as well as Individuals	230
Catiline, his method to Inflame the Roman people	347
Canopy of the Chair, In danger of being burnt	493
Calendar, rectified by the Tues: Club	503
Carmen dolorosum	529
Carmen Seculare	505
Caco fogo, what	
Ceremonies, Mr of, in the Tues: club, receives his Commission	54
Censure, Causes of it	72
Cure	73
Champion of the Tuesday Club, compared to the moon	75
his Complaint to the Club	80
Receives his Commission from the President	109
Chairman of the grand Anniversary Committee	132
takes the Chair to music	132
his resolve at the Committee	133
Leaves the Committee Chair to a Jig	133
his reception of the members at the 5th Anniversary	133
dances to warlike music	145
Falls on the Chancllor	145
rejects the ornament of his badge	165
retires from the Club for reasons of State	169
Conducts the Rustic Club to the pines	173
presides at it	173
appeases the Chancellor	211
his anger at the Conundrums	212
accuses the Secretary	212
Reproves ditto	225
is addressed by Jealous Spyplot Senr	239
dances several war dances	245

Introduced into The list of the Tuesday Club	276
Astrology, Judicial, Terms of it	27
Attila, king of the Huns, diverted from the Sacking of Rome	334
Athenians, how affected by popular outrage	475
Story of Socrates a Slur on them	475
Athens, a nursery of arts and wit	8
Authors, Clubical ones	2
Audience (English,) their behaviour at Tragical representations, Vindicated	191
Avarice, excites discord	469
a *fames Canina* & atrophy	470
Avaricious man, his Inconsistent Conduct	470

B

Basses meurs or Bathos of the mobile, where displayd	2
Badges of State, Command respect	334
necessary in Clubs	341
Badge medals of the Club, arive	127
described	127
mistake on them	128
Reason of it	128
Delivered	133
Badge medal of the H:S: how distinguish'd	164
Badges of State, the necessity of them	335
Their antiquity and use in Civil Government	336
Battles and murders, exhibited on the Stage, ridiculous	191
Battle, Great Clubical one for the Great Seal	491
Spectators of it	496
Balance of power, dissertation on it	341
a Coffee house term	341
way to procure it	342
method to regulate it	348
Bass viol and Case, Encountered by the lord president	459
his lordships observation on one	454

Baptism, disputes Concerning it	473
Beelzebub (Doctor) a beast of Burden	29
Beaus, their Employment	517
Blackmore (Sir Richd:) the British Homer	2
Bluechin (Jocifer) answers the Secretarys conundrum	123
Spectator of the Battle of the Great Seal	496
Blank verse, used in the new Scheme for Tragicomedy	201
Blunt, (Sir Harry) president of the lying Club, his Cap of State	265
Bowzer, (Tunbelly) made a member of the Club	74
Breaks a law of the club	236
accused by the Secretary and Tried	251
his defence	251
acquitted	252
Chairman of the Committee for the frontinbrassian articles	295
Produces a Comission for Dep: Pres:	351
Body (natural) compared to the politic	477
Box No 1, Foundation of it's history	102
described	271
Brutes, denyd reason by whom	3
Brawls of party, their effects	475
Burlesque, (masters of)	15
Butman, (Col: Comic:) president of the Hiccory hill Club	323
sends Letters by Frontinbrass to Mr President Jole	323

C

Cæsar (Julius) a wit and rebus maker	11
his false pretensions	163
a great Climber	470
actuated by pride, ambition & avarice	472
a pretended patriot, and therefore popular	347

Index of the Contents of this Volume

A	Page
Absurd doctrines, promoted	465
Absurdities (ordinary ones)	220
not Credited	220
extravagant, believed	220
Accrostic (moderen) its origin	12
Defined	49
Single	49
Dowble	49
Etymon	50
Acts and Scenes in the drama, from ancient Custom	199
Accidents (Triffling,) sometimes fortunate	400
Actions (great) not Lessened by the meanness of the agent	410
Address, (Poetical) of the Club to the President	68
Condolotory, of the Club to his Lordship	505
Remark upon it	507
Admiration, Subject of it	
Ægyptian hieroglyphics, effects of wit	11
Ænigma	39
Agathocles, actuated by pride and avarice	472
Albertus Magnus, a moderen Sage	21
Alexander the Great, a Climber	470
Altercation (clubical) between his Lordship & the Chancellor	485
Ambitious men, their views often frustrated	349
American Savages, their Caps of State	269
Amnesty, a Strange Instance of it	409
Ambition, Causes dissentions among men	469
Compared to flying	469
a Ladder	469
Anacreon, a punster	12
ode	13
ditto	14
Anagram, what	47
Anniversary, 5th of the T: Club	133
Grand procession	134
Speech	136
ode	142
Anniversary, 6th of the T: Club	357
grand procession	357
Speech	360
ode	365
music by Signr Lardini	359
Antidiluvians, why Long livd	280
Apology for the author of this history	
Ditto	
Archie (king James I's fool) a pun of his	10
Aristotle, an admirer of punning	16
Arthuriad	2
Arts, perverting the Judgement	125
How far they affect the Senses	125
how pervert the Senses	125
how the Judgement	125
Aristotle's Rules, mistaken	190
Articles, (Frontinbrassian) rescinded	460
Assurance, advantages reaped from it	274
(man of) his Character	

[546] List of the members honorary and Regular, that were in the ancient and honorable Tuesday Club, between the dates of December 10th 1751, to may 12th 1752.

Regular Members	Honorary members
Nasifer Jole Esqr Ld Pres:	Mr Abraham Bumper
Sir John Knt: & Champ:	Dr Poly hystor
Philo Dogmaticus Esqr Canc:	Mr Oldham wisely
Jonathan Grog Esqr, P:L: & M:C:	Mr Joshua fluter
Solo Neverout Esqr Pr: mus:	Mr Ignotus warble
Loquacious Scribble Esqr Secr:	Signr Lardini ⎫
Prim Timorous Esqr Serj: at arms	Mr Smoothum Sly ⎬ Triumvirs
	Mr Theoph: Smirker ⎭
Quirpum Comic ⎫	Mr Broadface Round
Slyboots Pleasant ⎪	Mr Roundhead Muddy
Jealous Spyplot Senr ⎬ Esqrs	Mr Chantum Cheary
Jealous Spyplot Junr ⎪	Coll: Courtly Phraze
Huffman Snap ⎪	Mr Curious Courtly
Tunbelly Bowzer ⎭	Mr Prim Laconic
	Cap: Comey: Coppernose Agt: Brit:
	Cap: Dio Ramble
	Capt: Prettyman Spyplot
	Con: P: Frontinbrass Esqr agt: Amer:
	Mr John Gabble
	Mr Swillum Swagbelly

End of the Second Volume.

End of the Tenth Book.

out, and rendered void and of no effect, the president chusing no other title, but that of *the honorable Nasifer Jole Esqr, President of the ancient and honorable Tuesday Club, Patron, founder, and protector, of the Worshipful Eastren Shore Triumvirate,* thus, were these Frontinbrassian Articles, still more Curtailed, and reduced now to the number of five; most were of opinion, that the presidents design in yielding up his Grand title and ensigns of State was to prevent for the future those violent uproars & Hubbubs, that were excited in Club, under pretence of pulling down the pride and ambition of the Chair, and Sure, if this was his Lordships motive, it showed the Great Regard he had for the peace and wellfare of the Club, and demonstrated a disposition truely great and heroic.

It was moved at this Sederunt, that there should be a list of the Longstanding members of the Club printed neatly in their order of serving, with a figure of the Club Seal annexed, to be fixed in a frame and Glass, and one of them hung up in the house of each member, which motion was ag- ‖ greed to, and Jonathan Grog Esqr, Printer to the Club, was ordered to print the said list, in the following form and order.

At this Sederunt his honor the president, was pleased to take upon himself, the Service of the Ensuing Anniversary, The day upon which that Grand Solemnity is to be observed, being to be fixed at some Subsequent Sederunt.

At Sederunt 177, April 21st 1752, Huffman Snap Esqr, being H:S: Jonathan Grog Esqr, presented in Club, the list of the members, printed on half a Sheet of paper, and distributed one to each member, pursuant to the order of last Sederunt, of which we have here exhibited the figure, but this Curious piece was never set in a frame by any of the members, for what reason we cannot declare, but they continued for some time tossing about in every body's hands, and at last, were all lost, being most of them, like many Good things, put to very bad and Infamous uses.

The Ensuing anniversary of the Club, was appointed at this Sederunt, to be held upon Tuesday the 12th day of May next.

At Sederunt 178, may 5th 1752, Tunbelly Bowzer Esqr Being H:S: The orator, in a Labored Speech, presented the Compliments of the Revd Signior Lardini to his honor and the Club, and acquainted them from him, that he could not give his attendance upon the ensuing anniversary, appointed to be held on the 12th of this Instant May, on account of Indisposition, but, that so soon as his health would permit, and a proper opportunity offer, he would wait upon his honor and the Club, and perform his usual Task of Composer and Musician *Con Stromenti,* to his honor and the Club, in the Recital of the Anniversary ode.

for some certain reasons of State, in the late violent act of your Lordshp's decathedration, yet to convince your Lordship, that animosities and resentments, even in great men will Cease and subside, I here profess myself sorry for what has happened and, with my own hand, replace your Lordship, in your ancient chair of State, and heartily wish, that there never may be any such cause for dispossessing your Lordship of this honorable Seat, in this here ancient and honorable Club"—This said, his Ldshp, and the Chancellor shook fists together, seemingly in a hearty manner, and, each of them grinning a Courtly Smile, his Lordship fixed himself in the Great Chair, the Chancellor took his usual place at the left hand, and the Longstanding members planted themselves round the table, and fell very Seriously to Smoking and drinking, the orator pronouncing a short Congratulatory oration to his lordship, upon the Joyfull occurrence of his restoration, which Speech was not recorded & therefore || is irrecoverably lost; but the [542] poem Composed on the occasion, by Jonathan Grog Esqr, which we have given in the preceeding Chapter, was read in Club at this Sederunt, and, his Lordship seemed to hear it with pleasure, wearing an agreeable Smile on his countenance, while the Secretary read it.

Thus was restored again, to his dignity honor, and authority in this ancient and honorable Club, the honorable Nasifer Jole Esqr, their Lord president, after an Interregnum of 15 weeks, during which Space, the Government of the Club, was very Confused, and Irregular, and withal arbitrary, The Chancellor taking upon him to order and manage every thing with a high and Imperious hand.

At this Sederunt, his Lordship appeared in Black, as also the worshipful the H:S: and the Secretary wore black Ribbans at their Badge medals, (they being now the only remaining old standing members of the Club) on account of the Death of Jealous Spyplot Senr Esqr, late a Stanch and true old Standing member of this ancient and honorable Club, whose Services to the Club, had been so great and so numerous, and withal done with so hearty a good will, that the Club, with very good Reason Lamented the Loss of so worthy and so Serviceable an old Standing member.

After Supper, in order to Crown the rejoicing of the night, several pieces of music were play'd by the Chancellor and Secretary, *Con violino & violoncello Solo.*

At The 176th Sederunt, Jonathan Grog Esqr being H:S: his Lordship [543] applied to the Club, to have the title of *my Lord* and *Lord presidentship,* struck off from the Rest of his titles, upon a vote of the Club, this request of his Ldshp's was agreed to *Nem: Con:* and accordingly the first of the Frontinbrassian articles, passed at Sederunt 146 Janry the first, 1750/1, was struck

much more prudent method, to be reconciled to his rebellious Chancellor and Club, as we are now going to relate.

At Sederunt 175, march 24th 1752, The Club Convened at the house of the worshipful Sir John, H:S: and soon after the members were met, the worshipful the H:S: acquainted them, that the honorable the Lord President, was in the next room, upon which the members went into Serious Consultation, concerning the manner In which they were to behave to his Lordship at this Juncture, and, finding, that his Lordship, had made as great a Step towards a reconciliation as was Consistent with the honor and dignity of his place, they Concluded, that a Select number of the Longstanding members, with the worshipful the high Steward, should wait upon his Lordship in the next room, and request his Lordship to come into the Club room and take the Chair. Pursuant to this Resolution, the worshipful Sir John, H:S: & Champion, ‖ The respectful Prim Timorous Serjeant at arms, Huffman Snap, Tunbelly Bowzer, and Slyboots Pleasant Esqrs went, and Solemnly waited on his Lordship in the adjoining Chamber, and making a very low and profound bow, Prim Timorous Esqr, Spokesman for the Deputies, delivered himself in this manner.

"My Lord, we are sent by the ancient and honorable Tuesday Club, Convened in the next Room, to request your Lordship to come and resume your Lordship's Chair of State in the Club, and to take again the reins of Government into your Lordship's hands, that good order and peace may be reinstated in our at present Confused Society." His Lordship answered this Speech with a nod of the head, which being understood as a Signal of assent, the Deputies made a lane, by ranking themselves, on each Side of the Door way for his Lordship to pass thro', and his Lordship accordingly, walked in State thro' that lane, with much the same air and Countenance as other Great men assume on the like occasions, and coming into the Club Room, the first person his Lordshp encountered was the Chancellor, who took his Lordship by the hand, led him to the Great Chair, and placed him in it, while this Solemn Ceremony was a performing, these two great men, vizt: the President and Chancellor, smiled very pleasantly upon one another, but this Reciprocal Smile was Judged ‖ to be only from the teeth outwards, like all Complaisant Smiles, which now a days appear on the faces of our thorro'pac'd Statesmen and Courtiers; after the Chancellor, had placed his Lordship in the Chair, he adressed him to this purpose, making first a Low bow and laying his right hand on his left breast, after the manner of our Courtiers, as an expression of his Sincerity and the heartiness of his professions.

"My Lord, Tho I cannot say, but that I was particularly Instrumental,

the Guts, or blow out his brains, and, that they may not seem to do this out of anger or Spite, they will frequently shake hands with the Silly Coxcomb, Just before they dispatch him to the other world, or take a trip there themselves, but these times we live in, differ from the age, in which the aforesaid Philosopher Lived, and these heroic feats are done for the Support of a Certain Moderen Phantome, which has assumed the name of *honor*, and with this particular kind of *Gothic* or *Moderen Honor*, Socrates & his brethreren ancients were quite unacquainted, neither is it in the least probable, that the said Socrates or his contemporaries were acquainted with the modes of behaviour, used between man and wife, in these our moderen refined and Civilized times, wherein, the Superior Class of mortals, under this Indessoluble tye behave to one another with the Greatest Ceremony distance || and Complaisance, the middling Sort, with the most perfect Indifference, and the lower Class with the greatest freedom and familiarity, giving blow for blow, thump for thump and reproach for reproach, and this appears from the behaviour of the said Socrates, to his dearly beloved wife Xantippe, who having once struck and abused him, the Philosopher was desired, by some of his Good friends and well wishers present, to return the blows and abuse, but he replied, that he was not at that time in a disposition to Create them fun or Sport, and, that they should not stand by and cry *Halloo Socrates!* and *Halloo Xantippe!* as men do when Dogs fight, spurring them on to mischief by hollowing and Clapping of hands.[2]

[538]

Whether the honorable Lord Jole, president of the ancient and honorable Tuesday Club, regulated his Conduct with regard to the Chancellor and the Club, who had lately put upon him such great Injuries, by the example of Socrates or any other ancient Sage, or by the pattern of any one of our Moderen Philosophers, or Sages, I shall not be so bold as to declare, being quite In the dark, as to the real motives, that actuated that Great man, but Sure I am, that, in the mildness, and Gentleness of his behaviour, Towards the said Chancellor and the Club, he showd a degree of heroic patience, forbearance and forgiveness, that whatever his motives were, he deserved at least in the Char- || itable Judgement of the world, the character and name of a Good christian, and tho' he was spurred on to wrangle and brangle with the Club and the Chancellor, particularly by his Champion Sir John, in the same manner as Socrates was Irritated by his friends to assault Xantippe, yet, with a prudence and patience, equal to that of the ancient Philosopher, he withstood these wicked and malicious Insinuations, and not Inclining to make fun for the Gaping and gazing world, he chose a

[539]

2. See Diogenes Laertius, *Socrates* 2.36.

Chancellor put a Stop to this deputation, and partly by threats, and partly by arguments, persuaded the club, that they had already made all the advances, that was consistent with their honor and dignity, and, that to go farther, would be demeaning themselves to such a baseness that they would be dispised and Laughed at by all the world. It was Strange to see such wise men, as the Longstanding || Members of this Club, under such an anxiety, and show such a weak fondness for the Return of his Lordship to the Club, especially after the Report made them by the Secretary, at this very Sederunt, concerning the answer his Lordship gave to him, when he waited upon him, but, if we consider that the Schemes of the Chancellor were very deeply laid, for establishing his own power and Influence in the Club, and that the members were afraid of the power and artifices of that State officer, we cannot be any longer Surprized at the uneasiness and Sollicitude the Club showed at this Juncture for the Restoration of his lordship to his chair and authority.

Chapter VIII

Happy Conclusion of the great Rebellion, his Lordship's happy Restoration, and his cession of the title of Lord President.

It is said that one Injury produces another, the observation may be too true, and a man may find it so if he looks abroad in the world, but should any one thence Infer this maxim, that one Injury calls for another, I will not be so rude as to call him a lying Doctor, but Sure with propriety, I may denominate him a bad Christian, as to return Injury for Injury is a practise expressly Contrary, to the excellent rules prescribed us by Christianity, besides, if Injury called for Injury, this would turn out a very ridiculous Sort of a world, for there would be nothing but || quarelling to be seen; Socrates was of opinion that Injuries were to be overlooked, for he thought none but fools or madmen would offer them; and being once asked why he did not properly resent some Injuries That had been offered him; if an ass kick me, says he, shall I strike him again?[1] The notion of this Philosopher differs in that particular vastly from that of our moderen Smarts, who think the best method of putting up an Injury is, to run the fool who offered it thro

---

1. Hamilton has paraphrased Socrates' explanation of why he could bear being kicked, as it appears in Diogenes Laertius, *Socrates* 2.21.

Inaccuracies and oversights, which that Ingenious Gentleman from || a too [534] great rapidity of Imagination was apt to fall into, which could not well escape the nice Eyes of the Critics, and therefore, these Gentlemen were never disposed to spare our poet Laureat, whensoever they could find him tripping, but would call out with great vehemence, when reading any of his Club Compositions, *O horrid!—abominable! Shoking Stuff!—poor!—mean! —Low!—pish! 'tis intollerable,* and other such exclamatory Phrazes, commonly used by Critics, but our Laureat Chose to proceed in his own way, not regarding their Annotations and Emendations, & Indeed, had he suffered his pieces to undergo any alteration, according to the delicate Sentiments of these refined Gentlemen, it was the opinion of the Club, and of many other Judicious persons, That they would thereby have suffered, as much in their Clubical turn, and humor, as the works of the Celebrated Shakespeare, suffered in their natural Sublime elegance, and beautiful Simplicity, by being too much thumbed and beslubbered by the Critics in the age next to him.

But to proceed with our history, at Sederunt 174 Mr Chancellor Dogmaticus, took to himself the Chair without Consulting or advising with the Club, on the matter, pleading the privilege granted him by Law 43, and tho many of the Longstanding members, objected against the overbearing and Imperious behaviour of this State officer, and had proposed Jonathan Grog Esqr, as deputy at this Sederunt, yet the Chancellor still mantained his Seat, and gave orders with so Stern and Imperious a brow, that none of the members were so hardy as to contradict him, this forward || and overbearing [535] behaviour of the Chancellors however, disgusted the Longstanding members, and they began to perceive, tho' almost too late, that they would make an exchange much for the worse, if they should establish this Gentleman in the Club Chair, and that notwithstanding all his Speeches and harangues In defence of Clubical liberty, and against the tyranny and oppression of the Chair, he was himself so easily Intoxicated with power, that, upon the Least taste of it, he would assume to himself the tyrant and domineer over the members without Check or controul. This Reflexion made the longstanding members wish for the honorable Lord Jole, to come and resume his honorable Seat of authority, in the Club, and, they were about appointing another Special Embassy from the Club to his Lordship at this very Sederunt, in which the Chancellor had possessed himself of the Seat of Supreme authority, conceived in humbler terms than the last was, that is to say, the appointed Emissaries were to be Instructed, most earnestly to beseech his Lordship, in the name of the whole Club, to return again, to take the Reins of Clubical Government Into his hands,—but the

Put on his Cloak and hat to fly the place,
And Grave and Stately stepping to the door,
He left the Rebells, neer to see them more,
Ah! ne'er to see them more! forbid it heaven,
The Grossest Sins sometimes may be forgiven,
His Lordships goodness, may forget the Crime
And shine upon his Club another time,
As when the Sun has run his daily race,
When night comes on he hides his Jolly face,
But Rises fresh and new the following morn,
Old natures face, 'T'enliven and adorn.

    Thus may his Lordship on his Club once more
Arise and shine Benign as heretofore,
Then our Longstanding members shall revive
And under his kind heat again shall thrive,
But Lo! he comes, the Longing Muse can see,
Flush'd with prophetic fire, benignant he,
Forgetting and forgiving all thats past,
And posting to his Club with winged haste.
Welcom Great Sir, to take this Chair of State,
Long may you hold it, may you leave it late,
Be that decree, fixd in the Book of fate,
May your old Club, still by your kindness warm'd,
Against all foreign foes be Strongly arm'd,
May peace and love, 'twixt you & them remain,
And ne'er may broils or feuds be heard again,
And, may the Grateful muse, while you bestow,
Your Soothing Smiles, with Cordial Ardor Glow,
And with the Genuine ὕψος[2] nobly fir'd
Sing you and your great Club, by you alone Inspir'd.

    This poem, the Club seemed to be particularly fond of, esteeming it one of the best performances of their Laureat, Tho' others Judged, that the first Anniversary ode, the acrostic on the President, and the poetical Entry of Sederunt 164, were by much the Compleatest pieces of any that ever that Bard had done, but we need not be much Surprized that the Club Judged differently from the world in this affair, They looking upon the performances of their poet, with milder eyes than the public looked upon them, when they made their appearance abroad, being willing to slip over many

---

2. Literally, "height"; figuratively, "the sublime."

The Seal demands, with Stern Imperious brow,
And on his Side a numerous party drew,
With mingled Clangor, all the Room resounds,
And various voices, utter various Sounds,
The Secretary tries the Case to state,
But discord is awake, it is too late,
My Lord rejects all reas'ning, right or wrong,
And frowning looks Indignant on the Clamorous throng.
 The Chief musician Clamorous and Shrill,
With Stentors Lungs, Inflames the threatning ill,
While in the general uproar others Join'd
And dis[co]rd raged like a Storm of wind,
Yet unabash'd great Jole mantaind his Seat,
Solemnly firm, magnanimously great,
Nor did the Canopy, condemn'd to fire,
Unhinge the mind of our heroic Sire,
Nor did th'authentic Codex of Record,
Doom'd to Combustion, discompose my Lord,
'Midst The dire noise, unshaken he behaves,
Like a firm rock, dash'd by the furious waves,
Which, as they rush, with ruin and dismay,
Repells their Empty froth and Idle Spray,
With Empty froth, the pert musician swells,
And stuns our Ears with Inharmonic knells,
Forgetful of his art, to please my Lord
With Soothing Sounds, nought breaths but harsh discord,
But ah! how shall the muse the Sequel sing   [532]
Of this most Sad and Lamentable thing,
With force Rebellious, as if drunk with Rum,
The chair they pull'd quite from his Lordships bum,
Who with great Indignation and Just Ire,
Threw the ill fated Seal into the fire,
Which had been burnt (burnt may it be I say,
E'er it again move such unseemly fray)
Had not the Care of some longstanding members
Snatch'd it in haste from the red burning Embers,
Sing'd was the bag, sing'd were the Strings likewise,
A Lamentable figure to the Eyes,
But Safe and Sound the mark ℈ was found,
As was the Seal within, still who[le] still smooth still round.
 And now, his Lordship with a lofty grace,

into the excesses of rage and passion, but putting all his passions into even poise, and balance, he patiently waited the Issue of these combustions, neither behaving himself with an overbearing pride and haughtiness, nor sinking into a base and Pusilanimous Submission, to his enimies, this heroic behaviour of his, gained him the esteem and respect of the L:St: members more than all his former Transactions had done, and the poet Laureat among the Rest was so charmed with his Lordship's wise prudent & discreet behaviour, that it stirr'd up his muse to sing forth his Lordships praise, in the following piece, vizt:

A Mournful Episode, upon the late Displeasure of his Lordship, against his ancient Club, by the Club's Poet Laureat

These ten long weeks, the mournful muse has wept
And all her Laurels in oblivion steept,
Her wither'd laurels faded and forlorn
For Jole are thrown away, for Jole are worn,
For, while he, smiling, sits on lofty Seat,
The Laurels brightens on the Laureat's pate,
But when fierce Indignation hurls him down,
Faded and wither'd is the Laurel Crown.
 Alas! and wail a day, and wo is me!
Destin'd this Lamentable Sight to see,
This Lamentable Sight of tragic woe,
Our Surest friend, become our firmest foe,
Sing muse, for once, in Lamentable Strain,
For Sure thourt likely ne'er to sing again,
How this most dire Catastrophe befell,
This woeful Scene, I shudder even to tell.
 Ah Cursed Seal! from thee this discord sprung,
Which has mistun'd my voice, my harp unstrung,
My harp unstrung, my voice mistun'd so Sore,
Robin and Jeck shall be my Song no more,
When I long standing members did relieve ho,
From doleful dumps by bold Recitativo,
By bold Recitativ' and Ritornel,
At once I sung, and did a Story tell,
But now a doleful Story is my ditty
Of Seals, and broils, and wars, the more the pity.
 With visage Stern, the Chancellor uprose
(And thank the gods, he did not come to blows,)

The Secretary at this Sederunt reported to the Club, that he had waited [528] on his honor the President, to receive his final answer to the question proposed by the deputies of the Club, and that his honor had desired him to acquaint the Club, that he Intended to honor them again with his presence, as their President, but could not promise to attend their meetings so Punctually as heretofore, on account of many bodily Infirmities.

With this Report of the Secretaries the Club seemed to be very well satisfied, and the Chancellor was the only person, who appeared to be disgusted at it, as his designs upon the Chair were thereby Frustrated.

Chapter VII

Heroic Episode by the poet Laureat on his Lordship's Displeasure, and other Trivial matters.

A Stedy and unshaken resolution, is the best armour that a man can wear, against the assaults of a perverse and malevolent fortune; fortified with this he can bravely withstand the many Rubs, Jibes, Jeers, revilings and taunts he may meet with from foolish and ungrateful men; with this, he knows as well, how to brook a State of Servitude, and obey, as to be a master and Command; It is Certain that this foolish world has nothing in it, worthy a man's anger or displeasure, who is guarded with Wisdom and resolution; Such a man knows, that to dispise and neglect Injuries, or to turn them Into Ridicule, is the best way to make them die of themselves; but to do this effectually requires great temper, Solidity and Judgement, and the art once it is acquired, affords a man Infinite Satisfaction & || content, his mind being at all times in a calm and Serene State, as was that [529] of Socrates, who had this character from his vixin of a wife Xantippe, that he always came home with the same composed Countenance, with which he went abroad.[1]

The ancient and honorable Tuesday Club had good reason to look upon their president, as a person furnished with this heroic Resolution, in the present Situation he was In, he bore his decathedration with that magnanimity and Courage, which became his high Station and Character, he neither repined, nor fretted his Guts to fiddle Strings about the matter, as many poor spirited irresolute mortals would have done, nor did he rush

---

1. See Cicero, *Tusculan Disputations* 3.31.

time, and, if Mr Secretary will take the trowble to call here, Just before the next Sederunt of the Club, I shall give the Club full Satisfaction as to that point." The deputies finding his Lordship turn alittle angry upon being urged, droped the affair here, and after sometime sitting silent, and looking at one another, they Took their Leave, with a Low bow, observing that his Lordship was suddenly seized with a fit of yawning.

The Deputies at their departure, entertained no favorable opinion of the Success of this negotiation, but however, it turned out better than they expected, they, accordingly at Sederunt 173 made report to the Club, that they, pursuant to appointment of Sederunt 172, had waited that very day, vizt: Tuesday February 14th 1752, upon his Lordship, the honorable the President of this here ancient and honorable Club, and Presented to his Lordship, the *Carmen Seculare* Composed at Sederunt 171, and that his Lordship was pleased Graciously to receive the same, and Read it, sitting in his bed, and that then they proceeded, according to the express orders of the Club, to demand a Categorical answer to the following question, vizt: whether his Lordship ever Intended to return to the Club again, if yea, in what quality, as president, or private member, to which his Lordshp after a short fit of musing, made answer, that he would desire further time to think of it, and would give in his final answer against next Sederunt of the Club.

At this Report, Philo Dogmaticus the Chancellor, and H:S: was angry, and said It was an Insult upon the Club, and the members would be very great Simpletons, if they would rest satisfied with any such prevarication and Juggling, Then taking hold of the great Chair, while Mr Comic the deputy was out of it, having step'd to the Door to make water, he vaulted into it, and knocking upon the Table with his fist, he told the Longstanding members, That once he had the honor to possess that Seat, he would teach them to behave themselves like men. Then he began in an arbitrary manner to order and Command the members, to do this or do that Just as he pleased. Some were Intimidated by this bold behavior of the Chancellors, and others minded it not much, and, it was thought, had the Champion been present at this Sederunt, the Chancellor durst not have assumed these airs, he however kept his Seat, during the Remainder of this Sederunt, In Spite of the united force of the Club, yet, was much out in his politics, in taking upon him this authority, as it proved a Bar to the Success of his ambitious Schemes in the Club.

At Sederunt 174, march 10th 1752, The Club met at the house of Solo Neverout Esqr, Protomusicus, fifteen days Latter, than the appointed time of meeting, upon account of his Sickness, and other Causes of Postponing, not unusual, with this Gentleman, and were served by him as H:S:

and wipe them on his breeches, while his Lordship kept in a perpetual see-sawing motion as he sat in bed. After a few minutes of profound Silence, Slyboots Pleasant Esqr, Spokesman for the deputies, got up and making a Profound bow addressed his Lordship as follows.

"My Lord, we are ordered by the ancient and honorable Tuesday Club, To demand a Categorical answer to the following question, vizt: *Whether your Lordship ever Intends to honor the Club again with your presence, and if so, in what quality, whether as president or a private member?* I, accordingly, pursuant to my orders from the Club, and in the name of my fellow deputies here present, propose this Question to your Lordship, and demand a Categorical answer."

His Lordship appeared much astonished and Embarassed, at this Question, it having come upon him as it were unexpectedly, like a Clap of thunder, he having looked for no other than a humble and Submissive behaviour in the Club, and an earnest Intreaty and application, that he should || return again to resume the chair of State, this made him keep Silence for a great while, and shift and hurstle himself from one Side of the bed to the other, see-sawing with greater violence than before; but at last, reflecting with himself, that to give a Rude answer or absolute denyal to the deputies, would be a dangerous proceeding, and give a Sufficient pretence for the Chancellor to seize upon and usurp the Chair, he collected all his rational powers together, in one body, to Check his rising Choller, and gave the deputies this mild answer.

"I should not Gentlemen have expected such a peremtory message from the Club, after the treatment I lately met with there,—If the Club had thought fit, a more Submissive and dutiful message would have been more proper, but as it is far from my Intention to promote and foment differences, I will n[ow gi]ve them as plain an answer, to their message, as they can reasonably expect, which is, That I will consider maturely of the matter, and deliver my answer expressly, in a few days"—To this Slyboots Pleasant Esqr the deputy, made answer "My Lord, this is far from being a Categorical answer, and we cannot discharge our duty to the full extent of our orders, and Carry back such a dubious answer to the Club, therefore I humbly request your Lordship to deliver your answer in more express terms, either affirmatively or negatively, that we may have a proper and Satisfactory report, to make to the Club, of this transaction"—at this, his Lordship seemed to bristle up alittle, and assume somewhat of an angry Countenance, and soon gave the deputies this reply, speaking with some earnestness and precipitation.

"Sir, I have already given the only answer I can give at this present

deputation of the Club to his Lordship

[facing page 522]

bed, being still under the agonizing pains of the Gout, his body was wrapd about with blankets, and his head covered with many Caps, one over the other, so that his lordship looked very like a Great Chinese Mandarin in his Grand Chamber or Saloon of public audience, The Club deputies advanced towards his Lordship with Great awe and humility, making a most profound bow down to their toes, and seemed to be under a Sort of damp, apprehending that his Lordship would frown Indignantly upon them, Considering || what had lately happened in Club, but they were agreeably mistaken, for, his Lordship Graciously smiled upon them, and Commanded his Gentleman usher to hand Chairs, that the Embassadors might sit down; This piece of humanity and respect, from the patron and protector of the Club, raised the Spirits of the Deputies much, and Jonathan Grog Esqr, assuming one of his most agreable Smiles, and most Gelastic aspect, Presented to his Lordship the *Carmen Seculare,* composed at Sederunt 171, which his Lordship Graciously received out of his hand, the Laureat, at the Presenting of it, making a very Low bow, his Lordship then arming his nose with Spectacles, began to mutter over that Poem to himself, and, sometimes, as he read, he would smile, and sometimes look Grave, at last taking off his Spectacles, and folding up the paper, and turning it round and round in his hands, he began to harangue in the following agreeable and modest words. [523]

"I think, Gentlemen, we have had enough already of these congratulatory and condolatory poems; I'm Sure, for my part, I do not see the necessity of making so much to do about matters of so little Importance to the world, as the affairs of our Club must be; for my part, tho I be your president, and was made so by your unanimous Consent, yet you all know, that I never Coveted having any such Compliments paid me, and I take it in better part, when one sends Civily to enquire after my health by a Common messenger, than if they were to send me a hundred such poems, and Sure I am, that rather than have such things published in the *Gazette* concerning me, I would rather they would hit me a Slap in the face at once, (here his lordship Looked hard at Jonathan Grog Esqr, and the poet Laureat seemed || very much out of Countenance,) But however, (continues his Lordship) since the Club will Compliment me with such performances, I must take them in Good part." While his Lordship, spoke in this manner, the deputies looked very grave at one another, tho It appeared by some of their Countenances, Especially Jonathan Grog's, and the Secretarie's, that they had a great mind to gelasticate alittle, and Don John Charlotto, who stood hard by the door, was observed often to cover his mouth with his hand, like one who is about to yawn or Cough, and to blow his nose with his fingers [524]

State, whom I have Just now had occasion honorably to mention, I think they are both alike Subtile fellows and merit equal praise for their Cunning and dexterity, the most material difference between them is, that the first [521] are employed in high, the other in low life, that is the first deal in high tricks, the Latter in low tricks and Chicanery, and, tho' some rigid Philosophers, think, that they both Deserve the same Reward, that is the Gallows, yet, so it happens, that the first are exalted to high places and Stations at Court, where they can exercise their dissembling Craft to great advantage, and the latter are exalted upon a lofty tree, like that at Tyburn, where they afford a Spectacle to the gaping populace, and a woeful example of the reward, that Low lived heroes are to expect.

We find the ancient and honorable Tuesday Club at Sederunt 173, had appointed Plenipotentiaries to treat with his Lordship, and demand of him a Categorical answer, concerning his resolution, with regard to the Club, vizt: whether he ever Intended to return to it again, and if so, in what Quality, whether as president or a private member? One would think, that this was a plain Question, and easily resolved; but, his Lordship, tho pressed much to it, by the Plenipo's, did not think fit to return a positive or Categorical answer to the question, as we shall presently see, nor Indeed, would the deputies of the Club, have got access to his Lordship to propose any such question, had not some deep drawn Club Politicians industriously spread about a report, that the Longstanding members Intended to place Philo Dogmaticus Esqr in the chair, which alarmed his Lordship, so much that he readily Granted admission to the Emissaries of the Club, tho he had before determined obstinately to deny them access.

[522] These three Clubical Commissioners then, vizt: Jonathan Grog Esqr, Slyboots Pleasant Esqr, and Mr Secretary Scribble, one afternoon, took their progress towards his Lordships house in north East Street, and marching along Incog, without pomp or Ceremony, to avoid Suspicion, came to his Lordshp's outer gate, where, giving a Signal, they were admitted into the Court yard by Signior Don John Charlotto, his Lordships Gentleman usher, upon asking this domestic minister, if his Lordship was to be seen, who gravely replied that he could not tell, that his Lordship was private in his Chamber, but, that he would go and acquaint his Lordship and bring them an answer, The gentleman usher accordingly did so, and, after having politely answered some questions put to him by his Lordship Concerning the business of these Gentlemen, as well as he could, he returned, and acquainted the Emissaries, that his Lordship was ready to receive them. Whereupon, they were Immediatly Conducted by the said usher, into his Lordships privy Chamber, who received them sitting, bolt upright upon his

Seeing then, that this Sex have so little notion of Truth and artless Simplicity, it must be altogether unsafe to trust them in any Case whatsoever with the Reins of Government, since nothing but mischief and Confusion can thence arise. It is therefore prudent to keep them within their proper Sphere, suffering them only to bear Sway over the prigs and Coxcombs and Smarts of the age, their natural and proper Subjects, for, if ever they are admitted into grave Clubs, and Solid assemblies of the male Sex, they will Certainly excite a fermentation and Combustion, and every thing will be turned topsy-turvy, as we have seen happen, in a woeful and Lamentable manner, in the ancient and honorable Tuesday Club, who, either thro the Inadvertency of her Longstanding members, or design of their Chancellor, to pave the way to his ambitious projects, admitted them to her Councils.

Chapter VI

Special Embassy of pacification of the Longstanding members to his Lordship, and the Conference that happened thereupon.

Farces acted between great men and plenipotentiaries, when They are obliged to confer together in a public Capacity, perhaps afford the most perfect comedies of any that occurr in the extended field of human transactions; since it seldom happens otherwise at these Solemn and pompous Conferences, Treaties, and negotiations, than that one thing is expressed, and another meant, It being altogether Inconsistent, with the political Character of such Conferees, to use that Sincerity and Candor, which some people rely upon in the Common Transactions of life; as the potentates who employ them, are for the most part magnificent and powerful Rogues, and bites,[1] so, it is necessary, that they, being under strappers should wear the Cloak of dissimulation, which makes it, that two plenipos, have as little confidence to put in one another's declarations and professions, as two professed thieves or Sharpers in Newgate, who will keep to their old Slippery tricks, till that fatal period comes when they take their final leave under the Gallows. I would not here be thought to mean, that these Newgate Rogues, are Greater Rogues in the nature of things than our Rogues of

---

ear? / I'm no diviner, but I know what you want." This is probably an imitation of Martial. The last line clearly echoes Martial 3.71.2.

1. A *bite* is a sharper or swindler.

nature has made her, without high heeld Shoes to add to the one, whale bone Stays and Steel busks and hoops to disguise the other, and variety of Cosmetics washes, paints and fucuses to give a false hue or Complexion to the last; for what purpose, but to Inviegle and Insnare do that Cunning and Artful Sex hang out their Splendent Signs, to what purpose are their pendants, bracelets, Ear-rings, Chains, Girdles, Rings, Spangles, Bugles, Embroideries, Lace, Brocades, feathers, fans, masks, muffs, Cawls, Cuffs, Capuchins, Cardinals, head tires and Caps of various molds, tinsels, velvets, Cloth of Gold, Silver Tissue, Gaudy Colors, glasses, pomatums, Curling Irons, Combs, bodkins, Buckles, monstrous hoops, Robes, neglegees, Sacks, furbelows, flounces, and why all this labor and Cost, to paint and anoint their faces and Skins, to make a Hellen of a Hecuba, why too they hurt, pinch, squeeze, cramp and torment themselves, why all this farce and fiddle faddle, but, like the Harlot in the proverbs,[4] to Intoxicate some one or other, and Call in Coxcombs, to get drunk with their artificial Charms, as an Ivy bush calls in a fool, idle fellow or Sot to stupify himself in a Taveren.

Nor are our moderen Ladies Singular in these practises, we find it has been the business of the Sex in all ages, The holy Prophet talks of the vanity of the Daughters of Zyon; the tinkling of their feet, their bracelets, mantles, wimples and Crisping pins, and their head attires like the moon; Homer Informs us that || Juno, bewitched and Imposed upon Jupiter by the Charm of Venus's Cestis or Girdle, and Petronius the Satyrist says *Quo spectant flexæ Comæ, quo facies medicamine attrita, et oculorum mollis petulantia, quo Incessus tam Compositus?*[5] To what purpose or design are Curled locks, anointed faces, wanton Eyes, and an affected trip in walking.

> *Quod pulchros Glycere, sumas de pixide vultus,*
> *Quod tibi compositæ, nec sine lege Comæ?*
> *Quod niteat digitis adamas, Beryllus in aure?*
> *Non sum divinus, sed scio quid Cupias.*

> Why Glycere, you wear that painted face,
> Why artificial Curls your temples grace?
> Why diamonds sparkle on your fingers? why
> Your ears with Berylls hung, attract the Eye?
> I am no Prophet, yet I can declare,
> With truth, what your designs & wishes are.[6]

---

4. Prov. 7.

5. "Why the curled hair, the face worn down with makeup, the soft wantonness of the eyes, and the affected walk?" (*Satyricon*, chap. 126).

6. More literally, "Glycere, why do you take pretty faces out of a jar? / Why do you have such artful rather than lawless hair? / Why does the diamond shine on your hand, the beryl in your

A man who has lived but a small Scantling of time in this world, and who has had the least conversation with his own Species, may see numberless Instances of the fascinations and wicked Practises of this Cunning Sex upon the male, they can at any time make a wise man act out of Character, & Change a Philosopher to a fop or a fool; They can on the other hand, by Certain Incantations,[3] Infuse life and Spirit into a mass of Stupidity, and make a bright man of an Idiot, by setting his animal Spirits into a vigorous motion, and moving every nerve in his fabric, from the greatest to the smallest; They can open the purse of the miser, and soften the mind of the barbarian, and make the Cruel and merciless melt into tears, they can bring the proud and arrogant upon their knees, and establish an universal Idolatry, without the asistance of priest craft, and Indeed, whatever has been said of the power of priestcraft, the power of women is much greater, for they have an universal worship, and their Shrines are set up over the whole Inhabited world, both among barbarians and the Civilized, it is no Strange thing to hear of Cities razed, kingdoms depopulated ‖ and provinces laid waste, on account of these Idols Women, as well as on the account of the most holy Saints that ever graced our Calendar, or the most notorious Idols and objects of false worship, of ancient, as well as moderen times. [517]

Truth, as we are told by Certain old Philosophers, is the most certain guide to walk by, but the great difficulty is to find this Truth, for as the world goes now, what is truth with one man is falshood with another and vice versa, but that there is such a thing as truth is Certain, and her being a very Simple and plain Lady, without disguise or trappings, is probably the reason, why it is such a difficult matter to discover her, she being among the numberless Gaudy Names and Falshoods that Croud round us, of no greater note or Significancy than a plain Country Girl, amidst a ring of high dressed Ladies at a ball or polite assembly. Truth then delighting in Simplicity and plainness, can never remain where disguises and vain trappings take place, and by whom so much as by the female world are these trappings and disguises used, True among the male Sex we have a few, and Indeed but a very few accomplished beaus, who lay themselves out to captivate the Ladies in General, by powdering, Combing, washing, brushing, Tinseling, Gartering &ct: but the whole of the other Sex, from the Dutches to the Chambermaid, have their heads more or less bent and Employed on outward Trappings, and Embelishments, and therefore must be in a great measure Strangers to Truth, who delights in no such disguises, but sets herself out to view, of the same Stature, Shape and Complexion ‖ as [518]

---

3. This word might easily be transcribed as "Incuntations."

the Company, of that Eminent and Valuable old Standing member, for soon afterwards the Club were deprived of him by the Inexorable hand || of death, whose Summons, as the Poet Horace tells us, must be obey'd by the King as well as the Beggar.

> *Pallida mors æqua pulsat pede pauperum Tabernas,*
> *Regumque Turres.—* and again
> *Mors et fugacem persequitur virum,*
> *Nec parcit Imbellis Juventæ*
> *Poplitibus, timidoque tergo.*

Impartial Death, his awful Summons brings,
To huts of boors, and Palaces of kings—
The fearful he pursues, and oft his dart,
Inexorable strikes the youthful heart.[2]

In this place it will be proper to say alittle concerning the Guiles of the female Sex, and the danger of trusting too much to women, that we may caution other Clubs, from being made tools of to them, as this ancient and honorable Club was, and thereby were exposed to the vexatious Ridicule and banter of a particular Set of Coxcombs, whose chief business is to laugh at Calamity, and rejoice at the distress of others, and also had their valuable records mutilated and defaced.

Tho I be not such a Mysiogenist, as to think that women are altogether Corrupt and bad, yet I cannot have such an extensive Charity and benevolence for that Sex as to believe that they are all perfection, and of an angelical and divine frame and Contexture, as some romantic Poets and mad doating Lovers would persuade us.

'Tis Certain that they practise abundance of arts and Cunning devices, to captivate and Insnare mortal men; Solomon himself, who, as we are told, was the wisest of || mortals, and who understood the wiles and guiles of the Sex as much as any man, before or since his time, was, at last, notwithstanding the many Cautions he gives against their artifices, in that Excellent book Called his proverbs, enslaved & Intrapped by them at last in such a pitiful and abject manner, that it is thought, he finished his life as Contemptibly and Infamously, as the Rankest of our moderen Rakes and debauchees, that waste the greatest portion of their time in Bagnios and bawdy houses.

---

2. More literally, these passages from Horace's *Carmina* (1.4.13–14 and 3.2.14–16) read: "Pale death pounds with impartial foot on the shacks of the poor / And kings' towers"; and "Death pursues even the fleeing man, / Nor does he spare the bent knees of the peaceful youth, / And the fearful, retreating back."

Six leaves had been tore out, this very much amazed and alarm'd the Club, and examining further to find in what particular part of the book this Havock had been done, They found, that the whole matter relating to the Genearchy of the Club was destroyed, together with some other Transactions of moment, particularly the latter part of the Remonstrance of Jonathan Grog Esqr against Colley Cibber, and the whole of that noisy transaction, concerning Mr Protomusicus, when he first Secreted the Great Seal, This made them Conclude, as the most probable Conjecture, that they could frame on the affair, that some angry females, who Imagined that their Sex were exposed too much to ridicule in these memorable Club Transactions, had laid their hands on the book, and out of pure Spite and Revenge mangled it in this manner, and some Expressions that Quirpum Comic Esqr, the deputy President, droped from the Chair, Confirmed this Suspicion. Jealous Spyplot Senr Esqr, was of opinion, that the Secretary alone was to be blamed for this mischance, as it must have proceeded in a great measure from his Carelessness, in letting the book go out of his Sight, the Secretary excused himself, and asserted, that it would be absolutely Impossible to save the book from such disasters, unless they would padlock it, or shut it up in a Strong box. || The Club however were not satisfied with this [514] answer, and defence of the Secretaries, but told him that he must Infallibly be called to an account for it and undergo a Severe censure, unless he could somehow or other restore these valuable archives, the Loss of which would be an Infinite dammage to posterity. Mr Scribble being alarmed at these threats, Promised to use the utmost diligence, not only to discover the offenders, that they might be brought to Clubical Justice, but to fill up the Chasms from his Loose papers, and render the record whole again. The first part of his Engagement, with regard to the offending persons, it never was in his power to Comply with, tho' he used all the Diligence possible, by rewards, threats and Coaxing, to make a discovery, but the Latter part with regard to filling up the deficiencies he performed pritty well, by the asistance of Jonathan Grog Esqr, his own memory, and some loose papers he then had by him relative to these matters, which he had not as yet put to that mean use which most of the Loose Club papers were put to, after having been transcribed in the book.

 This Concludes the History of the Genearchy of this ancient and honorable Club, and, what is very remarkable, and worth taking notice of, is that Jealous Spyplot Senr Esqr, a person most deeply concerned in this history, made his exit from the Club, at this very Juncture, This present Sederunt 173 being the last in which the Club had the happiness to enjoy

And be no more thy foe.
Chorus, O Jole! Jole! &ct:

4

Then here's thy faithful orator
   With folio book in hand,
Well skilld in Learned Eloquence
   To wait thy high Command.
And here is Eke thy Laureat
   Who pen'd this goodly verse,
And here is Proto musicus
   Who does these lines Rehearse.
Chor: O Jole! Jole! &ct:

5

With each longstanding member round
   All at this dead of night,
Hoping they wish, & wishing hope
   Of Jole to have a Sight,
Singing they weep, and weeping sing
   The Loss of Jole away,
O Lamentable, and forsooth!
   Alake! and wail a day.

    Chorus

O Jole, Jole, Jole, where art thou Jole,
   Where art thou gone away,
O Lamentable and forsooth!
   Alake! and wail a day!

   The burden of the Song, in the Chorus of this piece, which abounds so much in Interjections expressive of grief and Sorrow, is a beautiful Imitation of his Lordships proper Stile and manner of exclaiming, on such occasions as moved him with pity Sorrow or Contempt.

   This piece was playd and sung in Club, to the ancient mournful Tune of *Chevy Chace, Con voce, violino e Violoncello Solo,* Crinkum Crankum Esqr, performing the vocal part, Philo Dogmaticus Esqr, the violino Part & Mr Secretary Scribble the violoncello. || It was Intended to have been performed by way of Serenade, under his Lordshps window, but the Severity of the Season, and deep Snows that then covered the ground prevented this Lamentable project.

   One of the Longstanding members, turning over the book of Records at this Sederunt, first discovered a great defect in it by reason that five or

mournful ditty, which he had prepared pursuant to the order of last Sederunt, which was as follows.

The Clubs Lamentation for the Loss of their President,
To the old Tune of Chevy Chace[1]

1

O! what's become of noble Jole
  At this unlucky time,
When all the feet that prop him up   [511]
  Are only feet of Rhime.
In vain the Singers go before,
  And minstrells come behind,
In vain on Jole's known name we Call,
  No Jole, alas, we find.
    Chorus
O Jole! Jole! Jole! where art thou Jole!
  Where art thou gone away,
O Lamentable! and forsooth!
  Alake! and wail a day.

2

The Birds Lament the General loss,
  The beasts in Concert groan,
The little fish pop up their heads
  And Cry, alas! he's gone.
Oft when with beating breasts we Cry,
  O Jole, where art thou, where,
Eccho, from each resounding hill
  Replies he is not here.
    Chorus
O Jole! Jole &ct:

3

Lo, here's thy valiant knight, Sir John,
  In quarrels brisk and warm,
With Sword and pistol, pike and Gun,
  To Guard thee from all harm.
The Chancellor does Likewise bend
  All on his knee so low,
To render Back the Ill got Seal,

---

1. This popular Scottish song appears in *A Second Set of Scots Songs* (Edinburgh, 1757), 28.

wait upon his Lordship, to deliver the *Carmen Seculare,* and also, to demand a Categorical answer from his Lordship, with regard to his Intention of returning again to the Club, and on what Conditions, and to give in his answer to the Club at next Sederunt.

Crinkum Crankum Esqr, Invited to the Club this night as a Stranger, performed *Con voce,* with approbation, the Song of Sederunt 168, and that being Concluded the Club broke up.

Chapter V

Mournful Ditty of the Club to the Tune of Chevy Chace, Concerning the Great Clubical Rebellion, Enquiry into the deficiency of the Club Records.

Violence is a surer way to gain a point with many people, than a restless Solicitude and teizing Importunity, if a man goes to stroak or Coax a hungry or enraged Lyon, or bear, tis ten to one but he loses his life, or at least, a limb, for his pains, but, if by force or Cunning he makes his assault, he may easily decoy him into a Snare, and tame him at his own leisure—In short, we for the most || part, find it a very true maxim, that too much Importunity only prompts men to deny, by rendering them suspicious, for, the more we desire to gain of others, the more are others upon their guard, that they may not lose by us.

[510]

The Truth of these Sage observations is Illustrated by the Conduct of the members of the ancient and Honorable Tuesday Club, towards their president, whom they now began to coax and flatter, and eagerly to sollicit, to return again to the Club, sending him poems and addresses, and demeaning themselves in a very Submissive and humble manner, yet, notwithstanding all these addresses, poems and humble Speeches, his Lordship obstinately held out in absenting himself from the Club, and scarce any member could gain the favor of admittance, or of having any Conference with him, nor would he, as it is thought, have yielded one ace to this very day, had he not been suddenly alarmed, by a report purposely raised, that the Club Intended to place Philo Dogmaticus the Chancellor in the Chair, as we shall relate in it's proper place.

At Sederunt 173, Philo Dogmaticus Esqr being H:S: His Lordship still absenting, and not sending a deputation, Quirpum Comic Esqr, was appointed Deputy President, and Jonathan Grog Esqr, Produced in Club the

Considers on the other hand, that this Club is not Singular in this point, but have before them the pattern of a great and mighty nation, who beheaded their king as a Tyrant, and very soon after, canonized him as a Saint, and fasted and pray'd upon the day of his martyrdome (as they are pleased to call it) acting at that time, a very foolish farce, his Surprize will Immediatly subsede, and he will look upon it in no other light, than as the way of the world, and Intirely proceeding from the weak and Instable passions, which mankind all over the world are subject to.

After Supper, at this Sederunt, were performed several pieces of music, by Philo Dogmaticus Esqr Cancellarius, violino Primo, a Gentleman Invited to Club,⁵ violino Secondo, and the Secretary Violoncello, which the Club very much approved of. [508]

At Sederunt 172, Quirpum Comic Esqr, being H:S: his Lordship still, thro' Indisposition, and high displeasure, absented from the Club, the members chose Solo Neverout Esqr, deputy President, who soon fell asleep, in the Chair, as usual, and being bantered for it by the Chancellor, who Envied him his Seat, he left the Club in a Sort of huff, before the time of breaking up, and the Worshipful Sir John, knight and Champion of the Club, Spontaneously (tho' with the Club's approbation) assumed the Chair, the Remaining part of the evening.

This was the Second time that this great Club heroe, had sat in the Presidential Chair, The first being at Anniversary Second, Sederunt 59th May 26th 1747, at the house of Drawlum Quaint Esqr, then Speaker of the Club, both at that time and now, this valiant knight, deigned to occupy the Chair, but for a part of the evening, and, he was always (for what reason, is not known) very shy of taking that honorable Seat, we shall see this Champion twice more, before he leaves the Club, deputy president for one whole night, once by the Presidents, and another time at the Club's appointment.

It was ordered at this Sederunt, that Jonathan Grog Esqr Poet Laureat prepare a mournful Song, condoling the absence and departure of his Lordship, the honorable President, from this here ancient and honorable Club, to be sung *Con voce,* to some Lamentable old tune, accompanied with ‖ a [509] violino and Violoncello, and to be laid before the Club at next Sederunt.

The Club understanding that the Poet Laureat, had gone to present his Lordship with the *Carmen Seculare* composed at last Sederunt, but could not procure access to his Ldshp's person, were very much alarmed, and thereupon appointed the said Jonathan Grog Esqr, Loquacious Scribble Secrtry and Slyboots pleasant Esqr, a Special Deputation from the Club, to

---

5. Daniel Dulany, Jr. (see biographical sketch).

Makes us so dull, so moap'd and lonely,
But that the Cruel gout once more,
Has made my Lord both Sick and Sore.
   O Gout, of all our ails the worst,
Brother of Nemesis the Curs'd,
Who to us mortals does dispense
Blue plagues and Ghastly pestilence,
Whoe'er you with your torments grieve,
His Lordship's precious members leave,
Or may some leech thy fury quell,
And hurl thee headlong into hell,
Where thou damd wretches mayst enrage,
Nor strut again on earthly Stage.
For whilst his Lordship you molest,
You Rob his ancient Club of Rest,
His ancient Club, which cannot stand
Without his Strong Supporting hand.
   In vain the huge and pond'rous pye
At Supper strives t'attract the Eye,
In vain the Turkey, plump & large,
Calls each keen Stomach to the Charge,
In vain the punch smiles in the bowl,
To stirr our mirth & chear each Soul,
Nor pye, nor Turkey, nor the punch,
Can screw our mirth up half an Inch,
Nought will avail to raise our glee,
'Till we his Lordships face shall see.
His gracious face, in every wight,
Would rouse up mirth and make hearts light,
Whilst all would sing with Joyful Strain,
May he no more feel gouty pain,
And, may this ancient Club no more
Fall under his displeasure Sore,
Thus, freed from Gout and discord's rage,
We'll see again, the Golden Age.

   If one Considers well the frame and tenor of this Poem, he will be Surprized not alittle at the Caprice and humor of this ancient and honorable Club, who, but two Sederunts before this, in a most outragious manner, decathedrated their Lord president, and now pretend to write mournful verses, Condoling his Indisposition, absence and displeasure, but, if he

formerly Issued, published, made or enacted to the Contrary notwithstanding.

At Sederunt 171, January the 7th, 1752, according to the above act of the Club, Slyboots Pleasant Esqr, being H:S: his Lordship still continuing in high displeasure with the Club, would neither send a deputation nor ‖ an excuse for non attendance, tho duely acquainted by the high Steward, therefore the Club not Inclining to trust Philo-Dogmaticus Esqr again in the Chair, elected Jealous Spyplot Senr Esqr, Deputy President, according to a Clause in Law 43.

The Club understanding by Certain Intelligence, tho' not from his Lordship himself, that his Lordship was very much Indisposed with the Gout; which, (had he been otherwise well disposed,) would have prevented the Club from Enjoying his gracious presence, the members, according to ancient Custom, as at Sederunt 97, Janry 17, 1748/9, at Sederunt 122, Janry 16th 1749/50, at Sederunt 147, Janry 15th 1750/1, agreed, that there should be a Condolatory address wrote by the Club, and directed & sent to his Lordship upon this Lamentable & mournful occasion, which was accordingly done, and after some Consideration, on the matter, it was agreed, that it should be Entituled *Carmen Seculare*,[4] and being read in Club, it was approved of, and Jonathan Grog Esqr, master of Ceremonies, was ordered to present it, to his Lordship, the Tenor of this address follows.

Carmen Seculare

Being a most mournful Condolance,
of the ancient and honorable Tuesday Club,
addressed to the honorable Nasifer Jole Esqr,
Lord President of the said Club.

Ah wretched Club! must thou again,
Resume the Lamentable Strain,
By Cruel fates doom'd once a year,
To sigh, and shed, the doleful tear.
Christ'mass in vain his dainties pours,
Alas! these dainties are not ours,
What dainties can to us give pleasure
While press'd down by my Lord's displeasure,
Yet, not my Lord's displeasure only,

---

4. Literally, "secular song or verses," borrowed from Horace's *Carmen Saeculare*, composed for the Secular Games in Rome.

malicious misrepresentation, will be a perpetual bar, to his ever getting into the Good graces and favor of his Lordship.

Some of the members however proposed, that since the Club was near it's end, the Clubical Ensigns ought to be exposed at public vendue, vizt: the Chair of State, Canopy of State, mallet of State, Cap of State, Presidential Star of State, white Rod of State, money box, Box No 1, Tobacco box, Seal, badge medals, yea and nay Tickets, and the book of Records, and the money thence arising, to defray the Charges of the late Civil war, and the overplus to be given to charitable uses, this motion seemed to take at first, and Jonathan Grog Esqr, was ordered to print an advertisement concerning it, in his next *Gazette,* but the thing was never done.

The whole history of this Clubical Interregnum is so confused, That I think the Reader can take but little pleasure in it, and therefore I shall dispatch it, in as few words as possible, wishing that I never had been destined to perform so ungrateful a task, I shall however relate here, a remarkable thing that happened at this Sederunt, and Indeed the only praise worthy transaction that occurred during the whole time of this Clubical Interregnum.

The Club then, at this Sederunt, thought proper, in their great wisdom and policy, to alter the Calendar, from the Julian way of Computation, to the Gregorian, and, after some Learned debate upon the point passed the following Law.

[504] *Law L.* The club taking it into their wise Consideration, That the Julian Calendar is highly Irregular, and liable to create many Inaccuracies, in the computation of the year; think fit to appoint and decree, that the Stile in the Records of this here Club, shall be regulated according to the Gregorian Calendar, and the Clubical year, to begin henceforth, upon the first day of January yearly, and also, that the day Immediatly following the 2d day of September next, 1752, shall be denominated named and designed the 14th day of the said month of September, and so, to proceed in the denomination of the days successively, according to the arithmetical progression of numbers, and the Secretary is hereby required and Commanded, to date the Sederunts minutes and entries henceforth, according to the said Gregorian Calendar, as he shall answer to the Contrary at his peril, and Jonathan Grog Esqr, printer to this here Club, is also Enjoined and Commanded in all his publications henceforth, relating to this here ancient and honorable Club, whether decrees, Commissions, Laws, Summons for Councils of State, poems, or almanacks for the Club's use, to keep to the said Gregorian Calendar Strictly and Exactly, as he shall answer to the Contrary to his perill, any Law, Statute, order, Injunction or decree of this here Club,

At Sederunt 170 December 24th 1751, his Lordship being still under very high displeasure, would neither attend the Club, nor send a deputation for the Chair, Loquacious Scribble Esqr being then H:S: The night on which the Rebellion broke out, his Lordship had, when he went home, shut himself up in his Study and wrote an account of the whole affair, wherein his design, was to vindicate his own Conduct, and throw the whole blame on the Chancellor, and his party, and it was thought by many, that his Lordship had been Employed ever since last Sederunt, in drawing up this memorial, because, during that Space, he kept so close in his room, that none could get access to him, not even the Secretary. Few or none have been so happy, as to see this Curious composition of his Lordship's, tho' some have Confidently asserted, that it fills up one Intire Sheet of paper, wrote close on both Sides, 'Twere pity that posterity should be deprived of so Curious a piece, and, it is to be hoped, that his Lordship will at last Generously Communicate it to the public.

At this Sederunt however, his Lordship not coming to the Club, or taking any notice of their meeting, Philo-Dogmaticus Esqr, the Chancellor, claimed his privilege || of taking the Chair, from the tenor of Law 43d, [502] which the Club Granted him for that night, but he behaved himself in that Seat of honor, in such a haughty and assuming manner, that the members soon repented their having placed him there, and were Cautious afterwards during this Clubical Interregnum, how they allowed him to possess it. The conversation of the Club at this Sederunt, turned chiefly upon politics, Jonathan Grog Esqr, read the anniversary ode for the next year, a Second time in the Club, and was in a particular manner gay and facetious. Some of the L:St: members, at this Sederunt showed some apprehensions of the Club's being nigh it's final dissolution, should his Lordships displeasure Continue, others were of a different opinion, among whom was the Chancellor, and proposed to establish a Sort of republican Government in the Club, Intirely putting down the Presidential power; This proposal, Sir John, the Champion, turned up his nose at, and by no means would hear of, and, as the Secretary had some hand in promoting that motion in Club, Sir John made a handle of it against him, for at a private Gossoping, which he had afterwards with his Lordship, he Informed him, that the Secretary proposed the expelling of his Lordship the Club, should he absent himself 4 nights, without sending a rational Excuse, according to the tenor of Law 13th, this malicious report so riveted his Lordship, in his Emnity to, and Suspicion of the Secretary, that he could never to this day regain his Lordship's favor, and that unlucky officer, firmly believes, that the Scandal trumpt up against him, concerning the || Cap of State, Box No 1, and this [503]

We cannot take our Leave of this mournful occasion without some grave and Philosophical Reflexions, which we shall Endeavor, to throw into as little Room as Possible.

[500] There is nothing in this vain Sublunary world, but what ‖ has its opposite or antagonist, by which it is prevented from growing to that excess of Luxuriance, which would disturb that Symmetry and order, plan'd out by nature, for the well being and Support of all her parts; it would seem as if discord had a principal hand, in keeping the whole System of things in order, and the very essence of true harmony depends upon her Intervention, so that, however hideous she may appear, by herself singly, yet accompanied with Certain Concords and harmonies, she finishes a Compleat Scale of beauty and regularity. Every Species in the wide lap of nature, has something to poise or Ballance it, that it may not overgrow, or exceed the bounds prescribed. One Scale of this universal Balance, is never too much elevated, or the other too much depressed, but the beam is in Continual motion, often approaching nigh to, but never attaining a perfect or quiescent Equilibrium, or State of rest, and Inactivity; from the ant on its little heap of earth, to the monarch on his Splendid throne, every thing has a Counterpoise, or something to awe or Restrain it. Men may be compared to birds fettered in Strings by School boys, they have a Certain Scope to soar in, but should they attempt Higher, they may depend upon being pulled back with violence; no man so happy as to be void of fears, and none so miserable as to be utterly deprived of Comfort or hope, Beasts are delighted and terrified with beasts, man with man, is awed and defended; States are bounded with States, kingdoms by kingdoms, and they either mutually destroy or defend each other, and yet, an admirable General Harmony is produced from this apparent disorder, and Discord; Heraclitus, the obscure Philosopher, called Discord and Concord, the universal parents,

[501] and to rail at Discord, says Homer, the father of ‖ poets, is to Calumnate nature,[3] and the Sentiment is Just, since we find that true harmony cannot exist without it, let not any one then presume to think that the late uproar and discord in the ancient and honorable Tuesday Club, throws a Just Slur or tarnish upon the wisdom and Character of that Club, since the said Club, being in the vast Catalogue of Sublunary things, must be subject to the same Changes and revolutions, that other Sublunary things are necessarily subject to, and therefore, having finished, these my pertinent and grave Reflexions, I return again to our History.

---

3. In the *Nicomachean Ethics* (8.1.6) Aristotle accredits Heraclitus with saying that harmony springs from discord. I have not found the second passage in Homer.

resume the Chair, but, he Replied in a huff, That he would have nothing to say to such an old Fool; so his Lordship departed from the Club muttering, That he never would come there again. The Club however, to show, that they had not altogether lost that respect, which was due to their president, ordered Quirpum Comic Esqr, to Escort his lordship home to his own house, which orders he obeyd, and returned again to the Club, and made this report, That he had seen his Lordship safe to his own house, but that all the way, his Lordship keept Silence, and being Jealous of danger, (as he supposed) keept his distance at least an arms Length from his escort.

Thus was this furious battle fought in Club, and decided in favor of the Chancellor, who bristled and plumed very much on his victory, and was Just going to ascend the Chair of State, in the shatter'd condition it was in, when he was pulled back, by some of the Longstanding members, and desired to take his proper place in Club, and thus, notwithstanding, his being flushed with Success, was he disappointed, in his designs to seize upon that honorable Seat, In prejudice of the Lord Jole, as Edward Duke of York was, when In parliament, he attempted to ascend the throne, in prejudice of Henry VI, whom he had made to surrender it, but we shall presently see, this ambitious Grandee, mounted on that Seat of honor, dealing his commands about him in an Arbitrary manner, which made it plainly appear, that the Quarrel betwixt my Lord Jole and he, with regard to the Club, was the same, as of old, the Quarrel between Cæsar and Pompey, with regard to Rome, that is, the thing aimed at, was power and dominion, and not Liberty, as was pretended.

[499]

And thus was decathedrated, in a most Lamentable manner, The Illustrious Nasifer Jole Esqr, Lord president of the ancient and honorable Tuesday Club, whose personal worth and merit, had recommended him at first to be exalted to that Great Dignity, and, who had now possessed that Chair of State, for upwards of Six years; a woeful example to all, who suffer themselves to be misguided by flattery, and Immerged in the soft allurements of Luxury, which mislead them into ambitious and aspiring designs, and projects, which at last terminate in their utter Ruin, as this was exactly this honorable Gentleman's case, his woeful Catastrophe ought to deter all other presidents from the like detestable practises, and abominable vices, and this ancient and honorable Club, which from this very time, was perpetualy upon the declining hand, ought to be a warning to other Clubs, how they follow these dangerous paths of Luxury, vain pomp and excess, and practise the arts of adulation, which, as they proved the bane of this Club, so they will Surely prove the bane of every other Club that Indulges them.

not to be shoked or discomposed, at pain or misfortune, but whatever the principles of Stoicism may teach us, with regard to our behavior in such Cases, it appears to me, that there is nothing like running away from occurrences of that Sort, wherein the passions may be in danger of being Ruffled, and set ‖ into a violent fermentation, for, when once a man's blood is up, and his bad humors and Corruption set a working, it is not all the arguments of the Stoics that will restrain him within proper bounds, and therefore to me prevention seems to be the best bridle, and *Veniente occurrite morbo*,[1] is a very Just maxim. Aristotle tells us of one Satyrus, a Barrister at Law (and therefore obliged to speak in public) who was of a passionate and furious disposition, that used to stop his Ears with wax when he argued at the bar,[2] that he might not hear any Jibes or Jests that might be passed on him, by his antagonists, as it is a very common practice among Lawyers, to throw little Jokes and reflections upon one another, and on their Clients, in their pleadings, whether they be to the purpose or not; Thus Satyrus wisely evaded those heats of passion, to which he was naturally subject, by this cunning method of prevention.

The honorable Lord Jole, tho his passion had been stirred up to a great Pitch, by the Rude usage he met with and the Scurvey Language that was bestowed upon him by the Chancellor, in the Late Clubical Tumult, yet was his heart so swoln, within his magnanimous breast, that his passion during that Scuffle, could not find a proper vent to discharge itself; he therefore, against his will, retained it, till the battle was over, and then, having had some time to breath, as he stood staring round him, in the middle of the floor, he found the vent holes of his Indignant bosom begin to enlarge, and his anger, threatned to rush forth with great violence and fury, which he perceiving, and fearing lest he should be guilty of some Inconsiderate action, beneath his Station and dignity, Immediatly took his hat, Cloak and Cane, and having Gravely put on the two first, and taken the Latter in his hand, he, with Great State and Solemnity, walked out of doors, and left the Longstanding ‖ members, staring after him with great astonishment, being wrapt in admiration at his Lordship's heroic Command of his passions, which redounded more to his honor, in that he did it not by stopping his ears with wax, like Aristotle's Lawyer, but by mere prudential prevention, and a Seasonable retreat.

Some of the members called his Lordship back, but he seemed not to hear them, the Chancellor was desired to Intreat his Lordship to return and

---

1. "When disease arrives, attack it" (Persius, *Satires* 3.64).
2. Hamilton is apparently referring to Satyrus of Clazomenae (*Problems* 3.27, traditionally but wrongly assigned to Aristotle).

Immediate destruction, and Huffman Snap Esqr, dexterously snatched the great Seal from the danger it was in, of being Consumed to ashes, and with a Low bow put it into the Chancellor's hands, who received it with a lowd hollow of *Victory,* and Tunbelly Bowzer Esqr, at the same Instant, rescued the Chair of State from the fatal Combustion with which it was threatned; his lordship stood now in the middle of the floor, very much astonished, and seemed to be quite disabled and out of breath, and Loud peals of *Victory* from the Chancellor's party rung thro' the Room; and Indeed the Chancellor had no great Reason to boast of his Superiority, considering that he had by much the advantage of his Lordship in numbers, for, upon his party, were the following Intrepid Champions, vizt: Huffman Snap Esqr, Solo Neverout Esqr, Tunbelly Bowzer Esqr, Quirpum Comic Esqr, Jealous Spyplot Senr Esqr and the Secretary. On his Lordship's Side were only, Prim Timorous Esqr, who had not Courage to stand the brunt of the battle, but absconded for fear, Slyboots Pleasant Esqr, Jonathan Grog Esqr, and Mr Josua Flutter, an honorary member, who did but little Service, having stood neuter, till victory was almost secured to the Chancellor and his forces, which contributed much to his Lordship's defeat in this battle, was the absence of Sir John his Champion, ‖ who, had he been present, [496] would, either by the terror of his Countenance, and the virtue of his broadsword, have altogether prevented the fray, or discomfited the Chancellor and his partizans. There were three Spectators of this furious battle, who looked on while the battle was fought, with Infinite astonishment, vizt: Crinkum Crankum Esqr, afterwards a Longstanding member, Jocifer Bluechin Esqr, afterwards an honorary member, and Dormer Goggle Esqr, a Gentleman Invited to the Club. These Gentlemen, during the Conflict, kept themselves out of harm's way, shifting from Corner to corner to evade the fury and danger of the Battle, being so very Considerate, as to act rather the part of Spectators, than be concerned as fighters in this Lamentable and Inhuman Scene, for which, I dare say, posterity will not Condemn them.

Chapter IV

Clubical Interregnum, usurpation of the Chancellor, Eclipse of the Club, Carmen Seculare, and the Alteration of the Calendar, by the Club.

Lectures wisely and Judiciously framed, concerning the Government of the passions, have been delivered by the Philosophers in all ages of the world, and particularly by that Sect called the Stoics, who made it a rule,

devouring flames, and Commit to oblivion in one moment, all the transactions of this ancient and honorable Club, when the wisdom and discretion of Jealous Spyplot Senr Esqr, prevented this dreadful Calamity, for, he perceiving the Secretaries design, pulled him back, and seizing the book out of his hands, took it into his own care and protection, Then Quirpum Comic Esqr, having beat Prim Timorous Esqr from his station, behind the Chair, took off the Canopy of State and was approaching towards the fire to Committ it to the flames, when he was stoped, by Jonathan Grog Esqr, who with heroic Intrepidity rescued that Ensign of State from the distroyer, and disposed of it in a private corner out of || the way of danger. Prim Timorous Esqr, Serjeant at arms and H:S: was thrown into such a terrible pannic that he swore several times over *God—bless the king,* and run and hid himself in some private Corner, so that he was not seen again on the field till the battle was over, he was afterwards much blamed for his conduct, by his Lordship, who told him, that he had behaved not only unworthy of his office as Serjeant at arms, and beneath the dignity of a H:S: but also utterly neglected his duty as a County magistrate, in not Commanding the peace during the outrage and Insult, but most excused him on this occasion, as knowing him to be of a mild and fearful disposition.

His Lordship still keeping his Seat with unshaken Intrepidity, the Chancellor fearing that the destinies would turn the Scale against him, gave orders for a fresh attack, calling out to the Longstanding members to take Courage, and not lose Spirits, on which the uproar and hurly burly, encreased to a great degree. Quirpum Comic Esqr, one of the principal heroes in the opposition, seeing that it was but labor in vain, to move his Lordship from his Seat by tugging and pulling, went behind the Chair, and with his brawny fist fetched several violent hard blows under the Bottom of it, which being made of pliant Stuff, vizt: Canvass & Leather stuffd with hair, gave such a Strong concussion and repercussion, to his Lordship's buttocks, that he rebounded at least half a foot from his Seat at each blow, and was obliged to quit his Chair of State, rushing precipitatly from the Step, and falling upon one knee, but soon again recovering himself, notwithstanding the uninterrupted thumps and blows of the enimy, he run with precipitation to || the fire, and to the great astonishment and Surprize, of every person present, who Imagined that his Lordsp in the height of his frenzy and desperation, was going to sacrifise his own carcase to the devouring flames, he threw the great Seal into the middle of the fire, and rammd it down, into the hottest part with his foot, while Quirpum Comic Esqr, threw the Chair of State over his Ldsp's head, which pitched into the fire at the same Instant with the great Seal. There was Immediatly a most furious Scramble, to save these two precious Ensigns of the Club from

> ——encountering thus with mighty Shouts,
> Nor the hoarse waves, that roar along the beach,
> Impelld by blustering breath of Boreas bleak,
> Nor Crackling Sound of fire that raging spreads,
> His baneful flame thro mountain forests vast,
> Nor murmurs deep, which from its towring top,
> The forrest yields when restless winds Impell,
> Equald the horrid Clangor, when the hosts
> Of Greeks and Trojans to the battle rushd.[2]

This might be properly said of the horrid din and Clangor, that was now excited among the Longstanding members of the ancient and honorable Tuesday Club; the Chancellor and his forces had now advanced towards the Center of dominion, or the Seat of Empire, to wit, his lordship's great Chair of State, and made a formal atack upon it, besetting it on all Sides, having first, like a Skillful General, dispatched his forlorn hope, vizt: Huffman Snap, and Solo Neverout Esqrs, to assault the chair upon the dexter and Sinister Sides, Huffman Snap Esqr, took the dexter quarter of his lordship, and Solo Neverout Esqr, seized upon the Sinister quarter, they began the attack first by seizing on, and securing his Lordship's arms, which, with one fist on each Side they pinned down fast to the arms of the Chair, and each with his other hand, attacked the dexter and Sinister pockets of his Lordship, to search and rummage for the great Seal, his Lordship recovering, from his astonishment, threw a tremendous look, first on one Side, and then on the other, and asked the two Champions in a precipitate manner, and with a Surprized tone of voice if they Intended to rob him, but they made no answer, continuing still their Search, while the || chancellor spurred them on with Inflammatory Speeches, commanding them to fight like Lions for their liberty and property. His Lordship then began to struggle most violently and to lay about him to the right and to the left, as lustily as he was able, and had like to have knocked down and discomfited his left hand Antagonist, in this Scuffle his Ldshp, had his ruffles tore in a most Lamentable manner, and the posture of his wig was altered much for the worse, having the tail turned foremost, however his Lordship still kept his Seat, and would not suffer himself to be moved one Inch to one Side or other; upon this the general attack was renewed with greater fury; there was a General Cry among the Longstanding members, and nothing was heard but Burn the Chair!—Burn the Canopy!—Burn the book!—on which, the Secretary was advancing towards the fire to throw the book in the midst of

---

2. Hamilton provides a good translation of this passage from the *Iliad* (14.393–401).

like one in a Catalepsy, seemed to have nothing left about him but the faculty of breathing, all the other parts of his Corporeal frame, vizt: muscles, Eyes, hands, being fixed and Immoveable, as one thunderstruck or under some Strange diabolical fascination or Incantation.

While affairs were in this alarming Situation, and the fire of [Rebel-l]ion, like an Impetuous flame Confined within a Close Chamber, was ready to burst forth every moment, and Carry the whole Edifice before it, Huffman Snap and the Secretary endeavored to mitigate the rage of the Chancellor, and persuade his Lordship to deliver up the Seal, but it was too late, the first thro' the violence of Rage was deaf to all Intreaties, the other, thro' astonishment, was rendered Incapable of Listening to any overtures or proposals.

Upon this, the majority of the Club, were absolutely ‖ determined, since the Seal could not by fair means be made forth coming, to use force, to recover that valuable badge of office, Huffman Snap swore, Dam him, if it was not an Impudent Imposition on the Club, to rob them of their great Seal, and that such an Insult ought not to be suffered.—Why do you suffer it then, replied the Inflamm'd Chancellor, why dont you Immediatly seize upon this Tyrant of your own setting up, and pull him down again since he knows not how to rule with moderation—Come on—I will lead the way—I will give the word, and let every Stanch member here use his utmost endeavors, by main force to detect the thief—These words were no sooner uttered, than the whole room was in an uproar, the decanters bowls and glasses were overset upon the great Table, the Tobacco pipes, tobacco and Clubical papers flew about like Straw or dust, in a whirlwind, a horrid Clamor and uproar was excited, and the din of mingling voices and most unmerciful Thumps, discharged with angry violence, upon the backs, bellies, Shoulders, rumps and buttocks of the Longstanding members, made a rustling & rattling and whizzing in the air, much like that confused noise excited at the general Conflict of the Greeks and Trojans which Homer in the following passage, beautifully describes.

——οι δε ξυνισαν μεγαλω αλαλητω,
Ουτε θαλασσης κυμα, τοσσον βοάα προτι χερςον
Ποντοθεν ορνυμενον, πνοιῆ βορεω ἀλεγεινη;
Ουτε πυρὸς τοσσος, γε ποτι βρομος αιθομενοιο,
Ουρεος εκ βησσης, ὅτε τ' ωρετο καιεμεν ὕλην,
Ουτ ανεμος τοσσον, γε ποτι δρυςιν ὑψικομοιςιν,
Ἤπυει ὅστε μαλιστα μεγα βρεμεται χαλεπαινων,
Οσση ἆρα Τρωων και αχαιων επλετο φονή,
Δεινον ἀυσαντον ὅτ επ αλληλοιςαν ὀρουςαν.

them, the poet Ovid was very Sensible of this, which made him give the following Council.

> *Dum furor in Cursu est, currenti cede furori,*
> *Difficiles aditus Impetus omnis habet.* [489]
> *Stultus ab obliquo, qui cum discedere possit,*
> *Pugnat in adversas ire natator aquis.*

> When rage breaks out, evade the Tyrant's arm,
> 'Tis dang'rous to approach the Raging harm.
> He acts the fool, who shuns not danger's course,
> And Idly strives to stem the torrent's force.[1]

The Chancellor, as has been related in the foregoing Chapter, was Enraged to such a degree, that most of the members kept aloof from him, esteeming it a very dangerous attempt to come within his reach; for he was in such agitation, as that he resembled an Infernal fury, more than a human Creature, his Long Crane like neck was streched out to its utmost extent, his mouth, as he uttered his words, gaped horrendous, and seemed to spue forth fire, like the mouth of a furnace, his countenance was pale & wan, and his eyes staring and flaring like two burning Candles, while his fists were Clenched h[ard], which he balanced and poised on both Sides, ready to give the decisive blow, and his feet stamped on the planks of the floor at each Elevation of his voice, which Indeed was at Least a Semitone above *E La,* and made all the Concavities, cuddies and Chambers of the high Stewards house, resound, like the hollow belly of a Great Bass fiddle; The high Steward, Prim Timorous Esqr, was in the utmost consternation and terror, & forgetting his office of Serj: at arms, and throwing aside ‖ his white [490] Rod of authority, he betook himself for protection, behind his Lordship's Chair of State, and would now and then Slyly peep at the Chancellor, from one Side of the Canopy now, and then from the other, according as the Chancellor changed his place or Situation, on the floor, for, that furious Incendiary, while he delivered his Seditious Speech, did not stand stock still, but walked about, like a peripatetic.

During this furious extacy of the Chancellor, and Consternation of the Longstanding members, his honor the president was fixed like a monument of marble in his Chair; he moved neither to one Side, nor to the other, but

---

1. More literally, this passage from Ovid's *Remedia amoris* (lines 119–122) reads, "When rage is running, yield to the racing rage. / Every approach to violence is dangerous. / It is a foolish swimmer who, when he could go downstream, / Fights to go slantwise against the onrushing waters."

discharged my duty in it, with that uprightness and honesty, which becomes so eminent a Station, and such a great trust—will you Gentlemen—will you see me abused—trod upon, Insulted, contrould and brow beaten by that old Coxcomb in the Chair, will you suffer your faithful Chancellor, who has always served you honestly and faithfully, to be made a Cypher, a person of no Influence or Significancy in this here Club, by an arrogant Prig, who owes his exaltation to you, as much as I do, for Shame! rouse up your heroic Spirits, dont suffer your selves to be piss'd upon—pull him down I say!—pull him down! if he knows not how to command, let him be taught to obey, evacuate the chair of such a load of absurdity—dispossess the tyrant and put some other in his place, that will be more Just, more humane, more grateful—I request and beseech you, for your own Sakes to take my part, and support me against the threats of this Tyrant in grain—suffer me not to be trod under foot, but in supporting me, support the honor, the dignity, the Liberties and privileges of this here Club, but, if this will || not prevail, if you are deaf to my Just complaints—I must fly from you, I must leave you, to sink under that mean and despicable Slavery, with which you are at present Threatned."

[488]

This Speech of the Chancellor, was delivered with so Strong an Emphasis, accompanied with so much of the Pathos, with such violent agitations of body, with such a furious & pallid Countenance, that it struck many of the members with a pannic, enraged the majority, and quite silenced his Ldshp, and Immediatly, such a terrible Hurly burly and Tumult arose, that it is Impossible to give a description of it, at the Close of a Chapter in this History, and therefore I must refer you to the following Chapter for a full detail of it.

Chapter III

Effects of the Commotions and uproars in the Club, and the Decathedration of his Lordship.

Rage and fury, when their approaches are sudden and Impetuous, are very dangerous affections of the mind; they as it were dilacerate the Soul, and devest it of it's noble faculties, tossing them about, and flinging them away, like useless rags. These boisterous passions are Sworn enimies to mankind, and it is even dangerous for good advice to approach too near

fool, an assuming Coxcomb, and a hundred other such abusive epithets, and peremptorily Insisted upon his being searchd, saying That the members of the Club would not only be despicable Slaves, but Insufferable asses and blockheads if they allowed themselves to be so Imposed upon,—what, says he do we come here to be hectored and domineerd over by an old absurd obstinate ass, who will not harken to reason—Prithee hold your peace, answered his Ldshp, it will not be any thing you can say, that will have Influence upon me, your words are spent as much in vain upon me as if || they were directed to a Stone wall, and I will do Just as I see fit—You [486] shall not do as you see fit replied the enraged Chancellor,—we will not be Controuled in this manner by a Tyrant and an old fool, such as you are, deliver up the Seal, or we will soon pull you out of that Seat where you so hector and domineer—I would not deliver up the Seal Sir, said the president, if I had the Seal in my possession, you, at least, with my consent, should never be master of it again—Sir! Sir! replied the Inflammed Chancellor, I'd have you to know, I had not my place and title from you, but from the Club, and therefore 'tis to the Club alone that I am accountable, I would scorn to hold either place or title, by the Curtisy of such an old Tyrannical Coxcomb as you are, and therefore Sir, I again demand, what you have no right to keep, and that is, the great Seal, the badge of my office in this here Club—you may look somewhere Else Sir for your Seal, said the President, you shall not search me for it I assure you—I have had no peace in this Club since you came Into it, and I wish to God I had never seen your face, tis a Lamentable Thing, that I must be perpetually put into these flusters and blusters for nothing at all, when you have your Seal, why can't you keep it, when you give it up into every bodys hands, how can it otherwise be than lost? and when lost why do you blame me for it?—I'd have you to know Sir, that I scorn you and your Seal both, and so find it where you can, dont blame me for it.—The president being out of breath with this Long Speech, fell back on his Chair, and the Chancellor with a Ghastly and Enraged countenance, got up and harangued the Club to this effect.

"Gentlemen, must we then submit to this Insolence, this unparallelled [487] tyranny and oppression—must we be such dupes, such Simpletons, such asses—you have here set an old fool in that there Chair to rule over you, who will not submit himself to the rules of reason and equity, but attempts to carry every thing with a high hand, as he sees fit,—if you have a mind to be Slaves, despicable Slaves, vile contemptible drudges, submit, I say submit to his caprice and humors,—for my part, I declare, I will not—I am, gentlemen, your Chancellor, I was by your vote and Suffrage exalted to the honorable place which I now possess, in this here Club, and I hope I have

[484] own hands, and by Intirely depriving || the Chancellor of that necessary badge of his office, utterly prevent the proper use of it in the Club, and therefore he thought it would be much better, to put the Joke upon some one or other of the Longstanding members of the Commoners. Accordingly Jealous Spyplot Senr Esqr was pitched upon, as the most proper person to bear the burden of the Joke, and the Secretary agreed to slip the great Seal, into the pocket of that Gentleman, while he sat at Supper, which he did in such a dexterous manner that it was not perceived.

Supper being over, the Longstanding members for some time sauntered about the room as was usual, before they replaced themselves round the Great table, to drink, as they were wont, the King and the Club, and to toast the Ladies, during this Idle Sauntering Interval, Mr Crinkum Crankum playd some Interludes on the organ, and while this musician was exercising his art with a book of pricked music before him, Jealous Spyplot Senr Esqr, tho' he understood nothing at all of musical Orthography, took it in his head to look over the notes, and for that purpose began to rummage in his pockets for his Spectacles, but Instead of the Spectacles, to his great Surprize, laid his hand upon the Seal, which Lugging out, he exclaimed with a loud voice—Hey day!—what have I got here!—how came I by this!—why 'tis the great Seal says one—It is so, says another,—Be it so or not, says Mr Spyplot, I know no more than the pope of Rome, how the Devil it came into my pocket,—no matter for that Good Sir, says the Chancellor, we shall Enquire into that matter Presently, but I am Glad how ever, that I have found the badge of my office—and taking the Seal out of

[485] Mr Spyplots hands, he laid it upon the table be- || fore the presidents Chair, its usual place, presently after this the members took their places, and the Club was Just going to enquire how Mr Spyplot came by the great Seal, when to the great astonishment of all present, that Illustrious Symbol was a missing, and could no where be seen, this put a Stop to the Intended Enquiry, and they Immediatly began to use the Strictest diligence to discover the person that had pirated it, being persuaded that it must be in the Custody of some one or other of the members; at first his Lordship was not suspected for having seized upon it, till a general Search was resolved upon, and all the members having undergone a Strict Scrutiny, and turned their pockets outside in, when the Searchers came to his Ldshp he absolutely refused to undergo a Search, and made a most violent resistance, putting on a very angry and terrible Countenance, and Commanding the Longstanding members to desist, on peril of his high displeasure; on this the Chancellor, suddenly fell into a most violent rage, and rising from his Seat all pale and Ghastly with anger, he told his Ldshp, That he was a Tyrant, an old

for the Ensuing Anniversary, which was approved of, and ordered to be sent to Signior Lardini to be set to music.

At this Lamentable Sederunt it was, that the furious and outragious rebellion, excited by the Chancellor and his tools, broke out in Club, of which I shall give as particular and Circumstantial a relation as I can.

It has already been related, how Solo Neverout Esqr had Secreted the Great Seal, and refused delivering it up at Sederunt 166, after retaining it some time in his Custody, that Gentleman returned it again into the Secretary's hands, but took an opportunity one morning to go Into the Secretarys Study, while he was absent, and purloin it from the table where it lay, wrapt up in it's bag, this the Secretary Endeavored to prove upon him at Sederunt 168, but failed, because the evidence produced was that of a Negroe, which prevented the Sealing and delivering of the new Commissions at that time; The Chancellor, upon his return from his Journey, finding the badge of his office a missing, laid it much to heart, and thinking himself slighted or affronted he blamed his Lordship, and Immediatly ‖ meditated Revenge, which revenge he effected in the following manner. [483]

Solo Neverout Esqr, being afraid of the Chancellors displeasure, was resolved to deliver up the Great Seal, but in such a manner, as to save himself blameless and lay the whole fault upon others, to effect this he pitched upon the Secretary as the most proper person to be his tool on this occasion, who was easily enough led into the Scrape, not forseeing the dismal Consequences with which it would be attended, Protomusicus then, alittle before the members went to Supper, took the Secretary aside into a corner of the Room, and acquainted him, that he had the great Seal, that everlasting bone of contention in his pocket, and that he had a mind to deliver it out of his hands in such a manner, as that he should not be suspected for Secreting it, but the whole blame should Light upon another, which would afford some diversion or *Fun,* as he called it, in Club; by this Subtle trap he Insnared the Secretary, who was a person whose volatile Genius or natural levity, led him very much to promote fun or diversion, and was loath to lose a Joke at any time, whatever the Consequences might be; Mr Protomusicus then, privately putting the Seal into the Secretarie's hands, told him, that, if he could by any means slip it into his Lordship's pocket, while he sat at Supper with his Longstanding members, he himself, would make a motion after Supper, that there should be a general Search for the Seal, and, that its being found upon his Ldshp, would afford abundance of mirth & Jocularity in Club; The Secretary objected to this, saying, that it would not be altogether safe, to pass the Joke upon his Ldshp, who might be revenged upon the Club, by retaining the great Seal for ever in his

'Tis gold breeds Strife, men knew not war nor Sword,
When beachen Bowls, adornd the frugal board.¹

But whatever be Tibullus's opinion, with regard to gold being the Cause of wars, we are Sure, that this was not the Cause of the Civil wars that were stirred up by the Chancellor, in the ancient and honorable Tuesday Club, true Indeed, at Sederunt 71, novr 24th 1747, Loquacious Scribble Esqr, being Steward, a Civil Combustion had like to have broke out in Club, concerning a pistole or piece of Gold, which Smoothum Sly Esqr, had Jocularly taken out of the Box, and which his honor resented so far as to accuse him of theft, but that flame was Luckily smothered before it blazed out, the Club not being arrived at that early time to that degree of Luxury, as to be in danger of falling precipitatly Into Civil Combustions, but at this present Juncture, they were now ripe for such a Calamity, and the Cause of it was, that of ambition, pride and revenge, and not the thrist of Gold, tho Indeed Silver had some Concern in the affair, for the true or pretended cause of this uproar and rebellion, was the great Seal, which was made of Silver, of this memorable Transaction, at its first breaking out, I shall give a particular account in this Chapter.

At Sederunt 169 December 10th 1751, Prim Timorous Esqr, being H:S: several pieces of music were performed on the Harpsicord and Organ, by Crinkum Crankum Esqr, and Jonathan Grog Esqr, Poet Laureat, gave the Song of *Robin and Jeck;*² and, as this Gentleman's musical Qualifications are not so conspicuous as his poetical talents, I think it may be safely affirmed, that most Connoiseurs would Call his music rather Saying than Singing, after Supper, the said Ingenious Gentleman, read in Club, an ode Prepared

---

1. More literally:

> Who was the one who first drew the horrible swords?
> How savage he was, in fact how steely.
> Then slaughter was born to the human race, then wars;
> Then a shorter road was opened to fearful death.
> But that wretch deserves nothing; we do our own evils
> Turn what he gave for use on wild beasts.
> This is the fault of precious gold; there were no wars
> When the cups upon the tables were made of beechwood.
>
> (Tibullus 1.10.1–8)

2. This tune, to which Hamilton himself provides the words and music (see III, 118), is a variation of "The West-Country Dialogue; or, A Pleasant Ditty between Anniseed-Robin the Miller, and His Brother Jack the Ploughman, concerning Joan, Poor Robin's Unkind Lover" (James Ludovic Lindsay Crawford, ed., *Bibliotheca Lindesiana: Catalogue of a Collection of English Ballads of the Seventeenth and Eighteenth Centuries* [Aberdeen, 1890; rpt. New York, 1961], no. 1261).

and Cheats of the Physical tribe, because the first affect the whole Society, the latter only Certain Individuals.

Chapter II

Beginning of the Chancellors Rebellion, and the great Commotions and uproars in the Club.

Civil and domestic wars, as well as foreign, are distempers of the body politic, proceeding from Sloth Luxury and repletion, In the same manner as disorders in the natural body take their rise from the same Causes. The humors being thus Increased in quantity and Corrupted in quality, must have an evacuation, and as soon as that happens, the State returns to its former tranquillity and ease, hence we find that war, makes its approaches gradually, but is Immediatly succeeded by peace, between peace and war there are two Stages, Luxury and ambition, between war and peace, none at all, the Causes of war may be reduced to Ambition, avarice, pride and Revenge, the two first were the common exciters of wars, both domestic and foreign, among the Greeks & Romans, for, what the Conquered Barbarians (as they were called) specified by the names of pride and Covetousness, these polite people, from the highness of their Blood, denominated honor and thrist of Empire, Tibullus the poet lays the whole blame upon the desire of Gold.

> *Quis fuit horrendos, primus Qui protulit enses?*
> *Quam ferus, et vere ferreus ille fuit.*
> *Tunc Cædes hominum generi, Tunc prælia nata*
> *Tunc brevior diræ, mortis aperta via est,*
> *At nihil Ille miser meruit; nos ad mala nostra,*
> *Vertimus in Sævus quod dedit Ille feras.*
> *Divitis hoc vitium est auri, nec bella fuerunt,*
> *Faginus adstabat, dum Scyphus ante dapes.*

> What wretch was he, the murdering Steel first drew,
> An Iron Soul he had, nor pity knew,
> The Scourge of mankind, war, was then made known,
> And shorter ways, to death's dark mansions shown,
> Yet Sure unjustly, we the wretch accuse,
> What for fierce beasts he meant, 'gainst man we use,

nourishes the whole, those members of the Community, who have been refined and humanized (if I may so speak) by the helps of Education polite literature and a free Conversation, compose the finer parts of this political mass, which, like the Animal Spirits in the natural body, keep every thing in this political body, in a Just and regular motion, the Coarser parts of the mass, are the Gross body of the Common people, who serve for the Support and nutriment of the State, if these be trained to Industry and Labour, adapted to their Stations, and Capacities, and regulated by Good Laws properly executed, the Great political machine will move on undisturbed, tho' at times it may be Liable to Irregularities, from a redundancy of humors, and an Endeavor of the Grosser parts to get the mastery of and take possession of the finer, yet the General Constitution will be exempted from violent convulsions, fermentations, or Stagnations; but, if Luxury and Idleness, avarice and pride, and the like high Seasoned vicious habits, once Creep among the populace, and gain ground, we have very good reason to expect, that such a State will become distempered, and Subject to those convulsions, fermentations, and Stagnations Just now mentioned.

[479] From this method of reasoning, the cure is evident when Commotions and popular tumults happen in a State, & it will appear to every Judicious person, that this Cure is easiest performed, by checking the progress of the disease, before it has time to form itself; true Indeed, there can be no such thing in nature as a perfect government, even the best constituted police, has Innumerable Imperfections, and, for this Reason, all governments are unstable and fluctuating, and have a direct tendency to decay, & perish, even Strenuous attempts to Render a government more perfect, have proved its utter Subversion. As human Government then, as well as human life, is transient and liable to perish, so good Laws seem to be the rational expedient to preserve the one, as medicine is used for the prolongation of the other, but, in both Cases, the Legislator and Physician may be so far mistaken as to do more hurt than good to the body politic and animal Oeconomy, for it is Certain that both Laws and medicines, may possibly prove noxious as well as Salutary, the most Innocent and wholesome remedies, may be rendered poisons in some Cases, by being administred in Improper doses, and at unseasonable times, the most Salutary laws may become hurtful, nay destructive to a State, by being either partially, unseasonably, or too vigorously enforced and executed, thus then we find that Laws and Physic so abused are worse than none, because they both have a Sanction and authority to hurt, and may dissolve human Society and human life, hence we may Conclude, that political Quacks, that is, Ignorant rulers and Corrupt ministers, are much more mischievous knaves, than the Impostures

ized by the Ingenious Mr Richison,[10] author of *Pamela*, a noted Clubical Historian of the first rank.

It is Impossible any State or Community can be without flaw or Complaint, till such time as it can look upon every Individual of it's Subjects, with the same favorable eye, as every Subject Looks upon himself, till it can Indulge every one in his civil and religious notions, or reward him as he himself thinks he deserves to be Indulged and Rewarded, till this can be done, I say, we need never expect to see a government without flaw, or a perfectly well regulated Society, for every State, and every religion will want reforming ‖ in the opinion of such as are dissafected to that State or Religion; that is, those who think their merit neglected or overlooked. [477]

But that these Inconveniencies in a State or Society will admit of a partial Cure, I think, is not to be disputed, and, to make this clear, let us compare the body politic to the natural body, as many Learned writers have done, and found our Reasoning and demonstrations upon Analogy.

The natural body is nourished by the taking in of various Substances at the mouth, these, mixed in the Stomach, and concocted (as they stile it) in the Intestines, are Convey'd by proper conduits into the mass of Blood; This mass is the Strength and Support of the natural body, and the Chief mechanical Cause of life and Motion, but it consists of various humors, which are applied to nobler, or baser purposes, according to their texture and Composition, the Animal Spirits, which are supposed to be the most Subtile and refined part of the mass, are Employed about Sensation and motion, the other grosser fluids have their particular uses, for the nourishment and Support of the fabric; according then, to the nature of the Substances taken in to Compound, and supply this mass, the mass it self must become more or less fit for answering the purposes for which nature designed it, if the Substances taken in, are of a mild and balsamic texture, and easily reduced to that smooth and equable Consistence, necessary to constitute wholesome blood, the animal and vital functions are Carried on in an equable uninterrupted Course, and, tho sometimes a tumultuous ‖ circulation may happen from a plethoric habit, yet the constitution is free from fevers, convulsions, palsies, Lethargies, and distempers of the like terrible aspect; whereas, if acrid and Stimulating Substances are taken in, or what are called by people of a modish and refined taste, rich food, the miserable frame often sinks under all these distempers Just mentioned. [478]

In the body politic the case is parallell, it consists of a mixed multitude of mortals of various degrees, Stations and characters, which supports and

---

10. Hamilton is alluding to Samuel Richardson's third major novel, *The History of Sir Charles Grandison* (1754).

354 [Book X]   The History of

[475] you act the part of a Zany in exposing yourself upon the public Scene of ridicule, to || help to vend off the quack compositions and Nostrums of villainous politicians, and Statesmen, who raise themselves upon your folly and extravagance, and afterwards looking down upon you with contempt, laugh at you in reward for your pains and trowble, I say, could you but see in what an open point of ridicule this conduct places you, how soon would you Repent of your follies and misconduct, and, Recollecting all the powers of your Reason, with which heaven has liberally gifted you, Live a Sober, quiet and harmless life, like a man in his Sound Senses, and Diametrically opposite to that of a Crack brained fool."[8]

The effects of popular tumults and party disputes may be seen in many Instances, in ancient History; the Athenians, Irritated and Inflamed by their party declaimers, put many of their greatest heroes and best patriots to death, and among the rest, the greatest and wisest Philosopher that ever lived. The Story of Socrates, will throw Infamy upon the History of that people, so long as it Continues to be known.

Civil Commotions and popular uproars, are fevers in a State, which tear and waste the Constitution, as that distemper in an Animal does the habit, or animal Oeconomy, They may well be Called fevers, for while they last the body politic, is in an Inflammatory Situation, accompanied with a Light headedness or delirium, the demented populace, at that time, will be more guided and Influenced, by names, by words, Sounds, habits, Garbs, Ceremonies, badges and persons than by Sound reasoning and Common Sense.

[476] It is absurd to think, that this political distemper and it's consequences can admit of a perfect cure, the nature of human Society is such that it must at times be subject to effervescencies and ebullitions, like all Compound or mixed bodies which consist of heterogene Substances, We have Indeed heard of Troglodites[9] and Utopians, a Sort of people perfectly well governed, exact in their morals, and unblameable In their behavior, wise, Just, Innocent, Simple and divested of Luxury and vice, but these people never had any other existence in nature, but in the whimsical fancies, and Romantic brains of the writers of their Histories; he who looks for such a people, among the Race of mankind, will be Sure of only having his Labor for his pains; as much as one who could be Idle enough to look for the Late Celebrated *Sir Charles Grandiston,* a Clubical heroe depicted and Character-

---

8. This entire passage in quotation marks reads like a humorously stilted translation of a classical author; I have been unable, however, to trace its source.

9. Troglodites were ancient European cave dwellers whose name has become synonymous with those who live in seclusion.

If we take a view of the factions and discords that have been excited upon points of religion, what a Strange medley shall we encounter? what Mobbing, what tumults, what Insurrections, murders and Massacres have been stirred up about Senseless disputes, concerning the Import and meaning of words among Sophisters and muddy brained Schoolmen, who were neither better nor worse, than the foolish and presumptuous tools of Insolent priests, striving for power and Superiority? What havoc did not the Important dispute concerning the words *Transubstantiation* and *Consubstantiation,* occasion over the whole Roman Empire? what discord was not excited about settling the Epithets, *Mother of God,* and *Mother of Christ?* what terrible Animosities arose among Christians about the Superiority of Councils, habits of Priests, and the Buffoonery of Rites and Ceremonies? what [su]btile disputes have we not had, concerning the Lawfulnes[s of] Baptizing with human Spittle, or Broth made of Animal flesh? instead of water, and, In fine, in these reformed, and more Enlightened days, what unparallelled Nonsense has not been published, about Lay Bapt- ‖ ism, [474] ordination by Bishops, apostolical Succession, and what Ingenious doubts have not been started, about the State of Infants dying without Baptism, vizt: whether or no they went to the devil for want of that precious Ceremony; one who takes a Serious view of these things will no more admire at the Solemn Nonsense, that passes at Clubs or smaller assemblies of men, when they find, that even in the *Grand monde,* there daily are acted such unaccountable farces and Scenes of absurdity, as would move a Sullen Cynic to Laughter, or a professed Merry Andrew to tears.

Thus has division and discord been raised among men, these have been the Causes of war and dessolation between Nation and Nation; these the Instigators of popular tumults, civil wars, rebellions and Insurrections, for such triffles the Jewish factions Cut one another's throats within the City, when they were closely besieged without by Titus,[7] a Strong and Implacable Enemy, for such Important points the Inhabitants of Constantinople, butchered one another, till the Turk swallowed them up, and put an End to the declining Empire of the East, for these brother differs with brother, father with Son, Husband with wife, the Sacred bands of friendship are hereby dissolved, and even amicable Clubs, an[d] Societys of a more private nature, are dissolved and [elimin]ated.

"O Vain man, could y[ou] but think, what a Comedy your life is rendered, by your Care and Solicitude about these triffles, and how much

---

7. Titus (39–81) was emperor of Rome (79–81) who captured Jerusalem in 70, served as praetorian prefect and military arm of Vespasian's regime, and became known for his affability and generosity as emperor.

brained fool that Climbs a pair of Stairs on horseback, where it is twenty to one but both beasts Tumble down Together before they reach the top, it is a very uncharitable vice, teaching the fools that are possessed of it, to dispise all mankind, and esteem every thing of a mean and despicable nature, but what relates to themselves, one proud man cannot endure or bear with another, Diogenes dispised Plato, and Plato Diogenes, and both of them were proud Philosophers.

[472]   From those three passions, vizt: Avarice, Ambition and Pride, properly Seasoned with Ignorance and Impudence, proceed not only all the wars and desolations by the Sword, that have ever happened since the beginning of the world, but also all the Civil and domestic broils, Tumults, Seditions, popular Insurrections and rebellions that ever molested any public commonwealth or State. In the first, the Soldiery are raised and Employed in their butchering trade, by proud, ambitious and Covetous Crowned heads, who are only great Licenced robbers, in the Latter the Giddy headed populace are Inflammed and spurd on to mischief by men of the same turn or Genius, tho' in a Lower degree of life, and, as they do not pillage by authority or Licence, are liable to make their exit, if their endeavors succeed not, on a Scaffold or Gallows.

Upon what other motives than these of pride, ambition and avarice, spurd on by Impudence, could Cæsar act, when he Enslaved his Countrymen & fellow Citizens, and laid a foundation for the absolute and Tyrannical dominion of a race of Emperors, perhaps, the Compleatest and most hardened villains and bloody Tyrants that ever were actuated by the Devil; what but these egregious motives spurred Pysistrates to seize the Tyrrany of the Athenian State, and Agathocles that of Syracuse.[6] In fine, what moved the Stuarts, a race of Tyrants, bred in our own Island Britain, to assume to themselves, an arbitrary power and attempt to dispense with the Laws, but their ambition avarice and pride, and what but their Impudence and Igno-

[473] rance ‖ and that of their minions and favorites, could ever Induce them to Impose on the people, and set them together by the ears, concerning Primogeniture, Indefeasible hereditary right, a right *Jure Divino,* Passive obedience, nonresistance, and such like detestable Stuff and Silly cant; Is not this a Sort of nonsense and Solemn Jargon, fitter to be Canvassed by Schoolmen and Quibbling Lawyers, or even by the members of a Stupid Drunken Club, than by men in their Sober Senses?

---

6. Pisistratus (fl. 6th century B.C.) was a tyrant-king of Athens whose long rule weakened the power of aristocrats, encouraged individualism, and brought the cultural development and financial prosperity that made a movement toward democracy feasible. Agathocles (361–289 B.C.) was the ruthless tyrant-king of Syracuse.

and the wretches who trust their whole weight on them fall thro. On the rounds of this mighty Ladder, have been fought, most if not all of the great battles, with which History abounds, Cyrus the Great, Alexander the Great, Cæsar, Tameralane,[4] and even Lewis the Great of France, acted their Butcheries upon the Steps of this Ladder, and acquired their titles of great mighty and heroic princes, Solely by the trade of Cutting of throats and destroying vast numbers of their own Species, and at last tumbled down themselves from the great height to which they had Climbed, into the Lowest degree of Contempt and Reproach.

Avarice is like the distemper called *Fames Canina*,[5] in which, tho' the Stomach be gorged, the appetite is not satisfied, 'tis an atrophy, as the Physicians term it, there being a perpetual Emaciation, tho' there is thrown in rather a Superfluity of nourishment; The unaccountable wretch surrounded with this Scurvy of the mind (for it is but a mean Scurvy affection) acts very Inconsistently, showing as much Solicitude to acquire riches, as if they were his own, and as great Caution and parsimony in using them, as if he was a faithful Steward for another, tho' he might live easy in spending, yet he Chuses to be miserably pinced both in back and belly, in keeping and scraping, and had rather, dying leave || his wealth to his enimies, than living, with his Superfluities relieve his needy friends; and Indeed the avaricious man can have no real friends, having not the least affection to any thing earthly, but his money, in fine, it is as Impossible to draw Charitable deeds from a miser, as words from a dead body, or pearls from dung. [471]

As for pride, it is seldom to be found in a generous mind, nor humility in a mean despicable Character, therefore, that assuming passion, is the Sure Companion of baseness, arrogance being a weed, which like most other weeds thrives best on a dunghill; hence it is, that fools, Clowns and mean fellows, who by some lucky hit, are lifted up from nothing to a Conspicuous Station in life, are always the most Insufferable Insolent Coxcombs to those that were their Superiors, and, for want of proper Education and Example, act a very ridiculous and Silly part in high life.

Pride is a noisy bustling passion, and exposes a man to many disappointments in his way to preferrment, every man Contemns and shuns the proud Coxcomb, and if he is engaged in Conversation at any time, it generally Issues in quarrells and brawls about Insignificant forms and Ceremonies; a fellow, that would make his way to preferment by pride, is like a hair

---

4. Tamerlane, or Timur-Leng ("Timur the Lame"), ca. 1336–1405, the famous descendant of Genghis Khan, ruled by terror and desolation over parts of Turkestan, Siberia, Persia, and India.

5. Literally, "canine hunger," that is, bulimia.

Government, Singular in itself, and the only form of that Sort that probably ever had a being, vizt: a Theocracy, where we are told, that the Deity himself took upon him the Government of that unruly and headstrong nation, if in such a Case as this, their kings were Called God's vicegerents, and the Lord's annointed, it Surely might be so, with more propriety of Speech, than when these lofty titles are applied, to some of the princes of the Gentiles, whose tyranny and Savage nature, would seem to give them a better right, to be called the Devils tools and agents.

We have also from these Learned and Glorious times, that overgrown Lie of Indefeasible hereditary right, and this too fathered on the Scripture, and dignified with the name of a divine doctrine, this monster was also first hatched to serve || the purpose of a party, and each party in their violent heats Impudently and Impiously, bring the almighty into their disputes, and make him angry or pleased with this or the other triffle or farce, as if the Deity was a pitiful angry mortal like one of themselves, and deeply concerned and Interrested in their triffling Sophisticated arguments and Scholastic nonsense, more nonsensical and Contemptible, than any Clubical Stuff, that ever was vented over a pipe of tobacco and a mug of porter.

But, tho men have no such egregious nonsense to quarel about, nonsense, which puts on the Important and Significant face of Wisdom, and dresses itself up in a reverend Religious Garb, they will still Carry in their minds the Seeds of dissention and variance, so long as they are well stocked with these three most predominant passions, ambition Avarice and Pride, which with the help of Ignorance and Idleness, sow numberless Seeds of discord.

The first of these has been represented by learned & Ingenious metaphorists, as a State of flying, Climbing and Scrambling; The old fable of Icarus, who had his waxen wings melted by approaching too nigh the Sun in his flight, and falling into the Sea, is only a poetical representation, of the fate of those arrogant fools, who aim at higher things than nature ever adapted them for; The ladder of ambition is so high, as that it seems to vanish in the Clouds, on the rounds of which are numberless persons, many of whom are pushing others up before them, by applying their backs and Shoulders to their Breech, that they may rise after them, many more are Employed In overturning || those that are above them, or catching them in running nooses, and oversetting them, and all those that stand between others, who Climb but cautiously and slowly, are employed in Greasing and smearing the rounds of the Ladder with unctuous Stuff, that their Careless antecessors may slip their hold and give place to them, others are cutting the rounds as they pass them, that they may break with those that follow,

form divine Service, whether a man should stand, or kneel, or look with his face to the east, or west, when he pray'd, whether he should eat fish or flesh upon fridays, whether a moveable feast, was to be held on this or that time of the year, or whether a table should stand in the middle of the floor, or Close to a wall, these were the Important disputes, these the brangles in religious affairs, which broke the public peace, and while Zealots and Enthusiasts, were engaged about these very Clubical and Significant points, no man trowbled his head, about the Business of Charity benevolence, and good will towards his neighbour, nor thought the Least upon the Deformity of knavery deceit & Hypocrisy. By means of these excellent maxims and rules, Introduced by this wise monarch, Whom Henry IV of France, a prudent prince, called by the name of Solomon the Son of David, meaning, (as was suppos'd) David Rizzio,[2] the Italian Fiddler, his reputed father, he was himself in his Life time Contemned, having had ridiculous medals struck to his memory, by the Dutch, who Courted and revered his Illustrious Predecessor, and, after his death, one of his Sons was beheaded on a public Scaffold (as many then thought deservedly) tho the Enthusiasm of the Nation, dressed up the Silly Tyrant afterwards, in the fool's coat of a martyr, and his grandson was kicked out of doors, and sent overseas, or rather fled himself before the Glorious Nassau,[3] to be a vassal and tool, to the french king, on such occasions as that monarch Thought fit, where his pitiful posterity, have continued to act the parts of || understrapers to that [468] tyrant and the pope ever since, and what a ridiculous part they acted appears glaringly, in our annals of the years —15 and —45.

From the Learned and Pedantic heads of these Learned and Pedantic times, proceeded these most Slavish and Rascally doctrines as could ever be Imagined or hatched, by the most Clubical Imagination, dressd in a holy garb, and backed with texts of Scripture to serve the end of a party; That Infamous tenet of Passive obedience, by which the Rights of Freeborn Subjects, have been attempted to be exchanged for the Beastly Servitude of Turks, has been made a doctrine of divine authority, and by far fetched arguments and examples, foreign to the purpose, drawn from the Jewish History, where, if any such doctrines were really taught, or mantained, we must remember what kind of administration the Jews were under; a form of

---

2. David Rizzio (1533–1566) was an Italian musician and favorite of Mary, Queen of Scots, and became her virtual secretary of state. Haughty and overbearing, he was stabbed to death by a group that included Lord Darnley, Mary's husband. (Rizzio had arranged that marriage.)

3. Count Joan Mauritz van Nassau-Siegen (1604–1679) was a famous Dutch general and administrator who governed the Dutch possessions in Brazil, defeated the Spanish and Portuguese fleet, and fought against Louis XIV.

ment, endeavoring to set the populace in an uproar, by their Bombast declamations and Speeches concerning British libert[y, and] the danger of it's being Infringed; till they them[selves a]re shuffled into place, and then all becomes sa[fe, and] Liberty and property perfectly secured by thei[r prom]otion, how often have we seen whig and Tory [by] the ears together, sometimes the one, sometimes the other uppermost, now a Cry of the Church being In danger & perpetual mobbing for Doctor Sacheveral,[1] and such like Impudent and Infamous Incendiaries, then an allarm Concerning the tottering condition of our Liberties, which divisions are fomented, till the Subjects go to cutting one another's throats, and giving fair opportunities to a ridiculous Pretender, the tool of a Grand Monarque, to force himself upon his, with all his trumpery of Indefeasible hereditary right, non resistance and Passive obedience, doctrines of so monstrous and ridiculous a nature, as that they || seem to have been first hatched in some absurd Clubs where a villanous and Low policy, was more studied and promoted, than the general good of mankind.

But it is not to the whig or the tory, parties that have denominated themselves, by a Sort of Cant words, that we are to attribute those popular mischiefs, it is only to the wise operations, machinations, and State maxims, of a pedantic monarch of Learned memory, who succeeded a very Great Princess, on the throne of England. This Royal Idiot, seemed to have been se[nt by div]ine providence, not only as a Scourge to a wi[cked peo]ple, but, as a foil, counterpart, or Contrast, [to that] most excellent princess. This Besotted monarch, [poiso]ned and bloated by the arts of flattery, began to reign first by a party, in his time began, the Clubical distinctions of high church and Low Church, The denominations of whig and tory took their rise, during the Nefarious administration of his posterity, which broke the peace of the nation, engaged them in endless broils, and dissentions, which are not yet at an End, or perhaps never will be, till English liberty is altogether Lost; and furnished a Stock of Jargon and nonsense, for ambitious Spirits, to shuffle one another in and out of place everlastingly, and all under pretence of acting for the advantage of the people, and these Contentions and tumults, were not only || fomented on state points, but blazed forth on the Subject of Senseless ceremonies in religion, that is, whether a priest should appear in a Merry Andrew's coat, or in a plain dress to per-

---

1. Henry Sacheverell (1674?–1724) was an English political preacher who condemned toleration and attacked the Whig ministry (1709) for neglecting the church's interest. His impeachment, trial, and conviction by Parliament for high crimes and misdemeanors caused a great public commotion, and he became a celebrity. Sarah, duchess of Marlborough, described him as "an ignorant and impudent incendiary."

History of the Ancient and honorable Tuesday Club

[464]

Book X

From the Death of Sir Hugh Maccarty Esqr, and the mutilation of the Frontinbrassian Articles, to the end of the Chancellor's Rebellion, and Civil wars concerning the Great Seal.

Chapter I

Dissertation on Civil Commotions and Rebellions, their Causes and effects, and the way of preventing them.

Popular Clamor or uproar, is easily excited, It requires but little Judgement or Sense to kindle the flame, but once it blazes out, all the wisdom of a Solomon or Solon, cannot extinguish it, the same qualifications, the same Spirit, which set out mountebanks and Itinerant preachers, vizt: Enthusiasm and Impudence, produce Sham patriots and pretended reformers, who, in order to gain popular Influence, must promote and practise popular deceit, which they easily do, by offering popular Laws, and Complaining loudly of popular Grievances.

Cataline, that abominable monster, that blood thirsty Rebel, when he purposed to burn Rome, and massacre his fellow Citizens, took this high Road of Cajoling the || people, and sounding perpetually in their ears, their lost liberty, spiriting them up to Sedition, by a detail of the grievances they had labored under. [465]

We need not bring examples from ancient History to Illustrate this Subject, we find many recent and glaring Instances of it in our own times; how often, even in that excellent model of Government established in Great Britain, have we observed popular Incendiaries In both houses of Parlia-

[463] List of the members, Honorary and Regular, of the ancient and honorable Tuesday Club, from February 28th 1750/1 To December 10th, 1751.

Regular members

Nasifer Jole Esqr Ld Presidt:
Sir John, knight & Champn:
Philo Dogmaticus Esqr, Cancells:
Jonathan Grog Esqr P:L:M:C:
Solo Neverout Esqr: Pr: music:
Loquacious Scribble Esqr Secr:
Quirpum Comic ⎫
Slyboots pleasant ⎪
Jealous Spyplot Senr ⎪
Jealous Spyplot Junr ⎬ Esqrs
Huffman Snap ⎪
Prim Timorous Serj: at arms ⎪
Tunbelly Bowzer ⎭

Honorary Members

Mr Abraham Bumper
Dr Polyhistor
Mr Oldham Wisely
Mr Joshua Fluter
Mr Ignotus Warble
Signr Lardini ⎫
Mr Theop: Smirker ⎬ Triumvirs
Mr Smoothum Sly ⎭
Mr Broadface round
Mr Roundhead Muddy
Mr Chantum Cheary
Mr Courtly Phraze
Mr Curious Courtly
Mr Swillum Swagbelly
Mr Prim Laconic
Mr Comely Copernose ag: Brit:
Capt: Dio Ramble
Capt: Prettyman Spyplot
Coney Pimp Frontinbrass ag: Amer:
Mr John Gabble

proceedings the Secretary entered nothing at all on the Record book, being forbid by the Club, who were ashamed of them, so, that this part of the history, he Compiles from his memory, being one present at these memorable Transactions.

Thus were the famous Frontinbrassian Articles, of which his Lordship was once so fond, reduced from the Number eleven to Six, a remarkable Instance, of the Instability of all Sublunary things, and this act of the Club, was Called the mutilation of the Frontinbrassian Articles.

End of The Ninth Book.

Introduced by an Idle and foolish Coxcomb, vizt: *That fellow Frontinbrass,* whose Impudence and falshood was such, as had no parallel, the Club had some dispute as to this point, and with some difficulty at last gave up this undoubted privilege, as it is called.

His Lordship then objected to article 4th in it's first Clause, that all Commissions should be annually renewed, and said, that since they had of late made such a tool and foot ball of the great Seal, that he would not be bound for the future, by any writing or Instrument to which it should be affixed, and, that he would grant Commissions, Just when and how he pleased, without being Confined to any particular time; after the Chancellor had opposed this for a while, with his usual Impetuosity and ardor, he was at last out talked by Mr Proto Musicus, and the Club, for the Sake of peace, dispensed with this article also.

His Lordship then objected to article 9th, relating to the use of the Mallet of State, saying, that it was only a Silly Custom, used, (as was said) by a foolish, or rather Imaginary president, vizt: *That Lamentable No-nation fellow, Sir Hugh Maccarty Esqr,* and, for that reason alone, he would not demean himself so far, as to use any badge, or ensign of State, that had been even said to be used by any such man of Straw, and besides, that he had now Conceived such an aversion to all Ensigns and badges of State, ever since that pestilent Cap of State had come from Box No 1, to disturb his peace, and that of the Club, that he could not bear to be decked or set off, with any such foolish triffles and trinkets, and therefore of Late, had thrown aside, his presidential Star of State, and caused the Shield of the Canopy to be destroyed, resolving for the future, to appear as plain and unornamented as any private member of the Club, not desiring to be trickt up || any more or dizened like a Merry Andrew, in their tawdry trappings. This objection of his Lordship's raised some Indignation in the members; who professed that they Sincerely meant to do him honor in bestowing these ensigns on his Lordship, however, for his and their quiet and ease, they were Content they should be discontinued, and therefore Rescinded this 9th article.

These unaccountable proceedings, arose Intirely from the bad humor his Lordship had been put into, by the underhand Machinations of the privy Council of Three, and particularly by Sir John, & Laconic Comas Esqr, who were now both become Inveterate and Irreconcealable Enimies to the Club, and it was a Considerable time after this e're the Longstanding members found out the Secret of bringing his Lordship again to tollerable Good humor, which at last was effected, by the Skill and Ingenuity of Solo Neverout Esqr Protomusicus, as shall be Related in it's place, of these

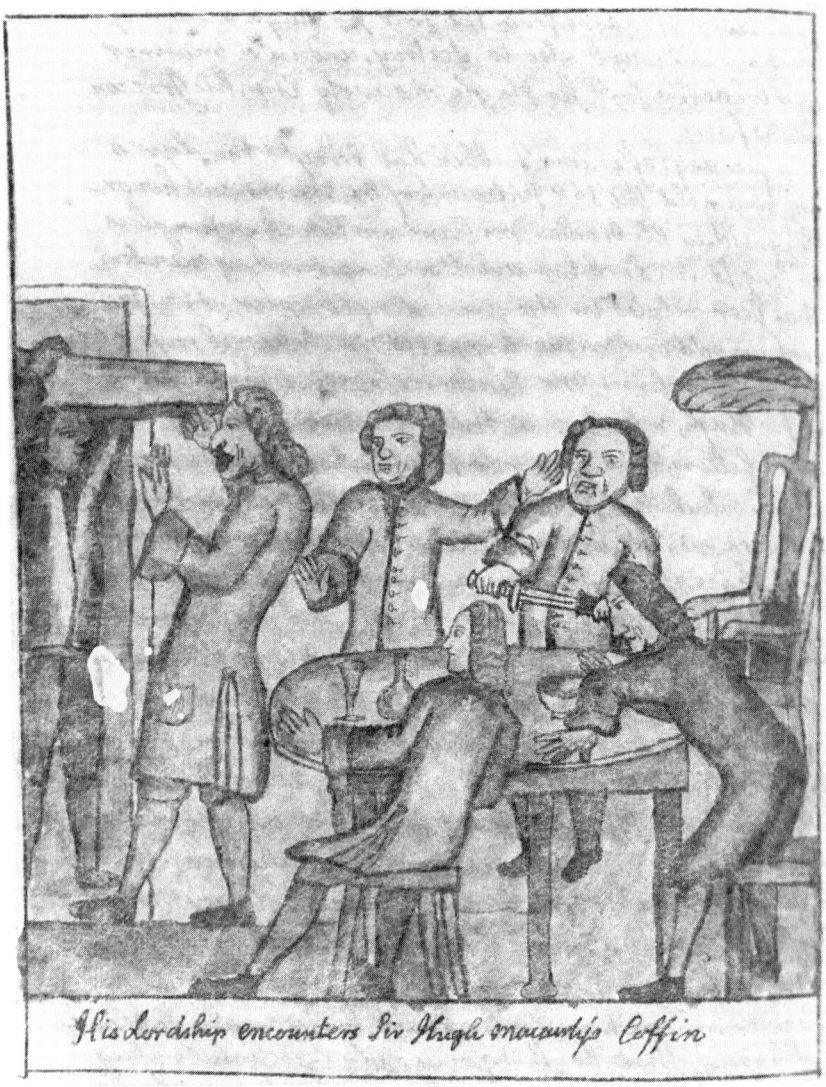

His Lordship encounters Sir Hugh macarty's Coffin

[facing page 459]

an odd occurrence happened, which seemed in some measure to confirm Mr Fibber's Supposed lie, concerning Sir Hugh, which was this. A certain tall, Gygantic negroe fellow, bringing into the Club room, the Bass viol, on which the Secretary that night performed Solo, elevated on his head, in a great deal board Case, pritty much in the Shape of a Coffin, encountered his Lordship full but, at the door, and not stepping back, with that respect and deference, which he ought to have showed to so Illustrious a personage, hit his Lordship, a terrible Thump with it on the forehead, Just over one of his Eyebrows, which made his Lordship stagger back, and Rub his face with his hands, but the blow was so violent, that it soon raised a frightful bump upon the place, the Club were very much alarmed, at this accident, and thinking some assasin Intended to destroy their President, started up in great Surprize and stood in a posture of defence, and, it was said, that Sir John, the Champion, drew forth from the Scabbard his tremendous blade, but finding, that the thing was only accidental, they again composed themselves, and his Lordship asking || what that fellow had brought into the room, some person made answer, that it was the Coffin of Sir Hugh Maccarty Esqr of New York, who had lately departed this life, and there the affair rested.

At this Sederunt also, came upon the Carpet, the Frontinbrassian articles, which his Lordship had some material objections to, the first was, to the Salvo, or Saving Clause at the Conclusion, concerning the natural and political rights of the State officers, and Longstanding members, his Lordship observed, that neither the Longstanding members nor officers, had any rights that they could lay Claim to, but those derived from the favor and Grace of the Chair, and, that it was still in his power to bestow these rights and to take them away. The Chancellor made some Clamor and Stirr against this malicious and villanous maxim, as he called it, but was soon overpowered by the majority of the Club, and the Stentorian Vociferation of Mr Protomusicus, who, now had gained much favor with the chair, by his opposition to this State officer, the Club at last, were so far Infatuated, as to cut off this article, and very quietly suffered his Lordship to talk in this Dictatorial Strain, a glaring Instance of the Despicable Slavery and Subjection, they had, by their foolish Concessions brought themselves under.

His Lordship then objected to two Articles in the Lump, vizt: to the 6th and 7th, concerning the privilege, granted the Longstanding members, to kiss his Lordship's hand on Anniversary days, and the first Club Night after new Years day, and the right given to members at admission, and to Strangers Invited to the Club, to do the same, professing, that he chose to keep his hand || for other uses, and reject that Idle and foolish custom, as

Night, and almost quite extinguished his heroic Spirit as a Club President; nor did the Champion, by this his ill placed conduct, less prejudice the Club, than the president, for, by souring the temper of the Latter, he quite destroyed the harmony of the first, for the President being always dissatisfied, both with himself and the Club, it could not otherwise be, but both must thereby suffer Great uneasiness, by being engaged in eternal wrangles, and disputes, so, that it may be Justly here said of Sir John, that by this piece of extraordinary conduct he hurt the Club more than ever he had advantaged it, by his acts of prowess and valor, as a Champion; Many, upon very good grounds alledged that La- || conic Comas Esqr, still stomaching the Conundrum passed upon him, was Confederate with Sir John, in Inculcating these pernicious notions into his Lordship's Noddle, and was, as the proverb goes, as deep in the dirt as the Champion was in the mire.

About this time Mr Humbug Fibber, an Inhabitant of Annapolis, and an Intimate acquaintance of all the Longstanding members, having returned from a Journey to New York, Brought an account, that Sir Hugh Maccarty Esqr, of New York was dead, and that he had seen him there decently buried, at this many were Surprized, hearing that a man should die and be buried, who, they were Sure had never lived, but his Lordship showed neither concern nor Surprize at the tidings, for with him, for some time passed, the said Sir Hugh Maccarty Esqr, was dead and Damnd, tho' not buried, many however Condemned Mr Humbug Fibber, for telling so palpable a lie, but he excused himself, and urged, that tho' he had unfortunately acquired the Character of a promoter of fibs, yet his fibs were not of a malignant Sort, being Calculated either to make fun, or to do Service to a friend, and many apologized for Mr Fibber in this affair, and vindicated him, from a known maxim of the Divine Plato, who asserts, *that Lying is very Justifiable, when it has a tendency either to save a Citizen, or hurt an Enimy,*[1] and therefore, as Mr Fibber's Lye in this matter, was evidently Intended to do both, it was highly Justifiable, for by it, he Intended to free his honored fellow Citizen, the honorable Lord Jole, from the Terror he was under by the || apprehension of harm from the said Sir Hugh Maccarty Esqr, his rival, and also to destroy, and in a manner annihilate, the said Sir Hugh Maccarty Esqr, his Irreconcealable foe.

A few days after Mr Fibber had brought this Lying news, was held the 168 Sederunt, of the ancient and honorable Tuesday Club, when Mr Crinkum Crankum sung his new Song to his Lordship and the Longstanding members, as has been related in the preceeding Chapter, at this Sederunt,

---

1. *Republic* 3.389.

[456] or points, which they were before Ignorant of, and every man who entertains a notion that his ‖ neighbour is more knowing than himself, Imbibes his dictates with great greediness, and, thinking himself on the fair road to Improvement, stores up his maxims as so many truths and oracles. By a mutual Intercourse or Conversation then, particularly in Clubs, it is, that men Improve one another, and more is done by this alone, than by the perusal of myriads of volumes, or hearing Centuries of university Lectures,—but, it is absolutely necessary, before conversation can be rendered in any degree Improving, that it should be highly Seasoned with Truth, and Sincerity, for, when falshood and dissimulation accompany the Conversation or Intercourse between man and man, the best Issue that can come from them is a Sullen Mysanthropy, accompanied by Ignorance & absurdity, for this reason, detected lyars, have always been looked upon as the basest of men, and fa[ls]hood has been decked out, in the most ridiculous Trappings, as utterly destructive of that Confidence, which men ought to repose in one another, which is absolutely necessary, for the well being and Support of human Society, hence it is, that we think our understanding as much Injured by Imposition and deceit, once we see thro' it, as our purses are affected and reduced, by a rogue's passing Counterfeit money upon us for good, and therefore, the Dissembler or falsifier, and the rogue, become alike the Subjects of distrust in Conversation, and the Common transactions of life, relative either to Social Intercourse or Traffic.

It will be no matter of Surprize then to our Readers, when they find, the honorable Lord Jole, in the Sequel of this History putting no manner of Confidence or trust in any of the Longstanding members, and, looking [457] upon every proposal in Club with a ‖ Suspicious Eye, as if some trick lurked under it, since that old Gentleman, had lately had several notorious falshoods palmed upon him for Truths, by the ill timed and mischievous Industry of Coney-pimp Frontinbrass Esqr, and the Secretary, relating to the Cap of state and the History of Sir Hugh Maccarty Esqr, of New York, which Clubical heroe, his Lordship had now discovered, to be only a creature of the Imagination, and the Cap of State, to be nothing but a Fool's cap, both which he was at last convinced of, by the unwearied diligence and teazing Importunity of his minion Sir John, who could never be easy, till he had convinced him of the fallacy of these whims and Conceits, this the Champion did, to curry favor with his Lordship, tho' like many other officious persons, he did not consider, that he acted thus, at the expence of his Lordship's peace and happiness, who never was better satisfied, than while he Labored under this Clubical delusion, and, his being undeceived, as to these very particulars, has since cost him many an uneasy day & restless

Longstanding members, great and small,
  Who truely know this treasure,
Sing in the Chorus, one and all,
  Continuance to your pleasure,
The bumper fill, hand round the bowl,
Show you've a true and Loyal Soul
And Pledge the Health of noble Jole,
  The Stay of all your pleasure.

This Song was approved of by the Club in General, only his Lordship expressed some dislike to the Bass, or Drone, as he was pleased to call it, which he intended as a banter on the Secretary, on whom he bestowd his repartees on all occasions.

Chapter VIII

[455]

Death of Sir Hugh Maccarty Esqr, and the mutilation of the Frontinbrassian Articles.

    Knowledge, next to power, wealth and beauty, seems to be most desired or coveted by men; all are fond of being thought knowing and wise, tho few are put in the proper way to become so, and still fewer are born with a genius adapted to receive and contain this eminent ornament of the mind; for, university Learning, and a Rabble of Greek and Latin Sentences, the Lumber of Poets Historians and Essay writers, are so far from being essential to true knowledge, that they are only the Embelishments of pedantry, and I have known some Ploughmen and Mechanics, much wiser men, than some Self Sufficient prigs, who have spent half their life, [at] either the one or the other of our famous English universities of Cambridge and Oxford, to which Learned Ceremonies, if you enter a Coxcomb, ten to one but he comes out a greater Coxcomb than he went in, having there only acquired some Idle forms and Ceremonies, absurd maxims of politics and religion, that never existed in the nature of things, and not a few university vices and follys, which, if ever at all rubb'd off, take as much time to wear out of the habit, as was spent in beating into him, a Jumble of vain, and unprofitable Learning.
    From this violent desire of knowledge, Implanted in mankind, proceeds that Strong Inclination, that all men have to be Informed of novelties

To hammer out his measure.
My muse Invites each Jovial Soul,
To find the depth of Glass and bowl,
In pledging round the noble Jole,
   The fountain of our pleasure.

See! Honor flashes from his eyes,
   At every noble Story,
See! Fame exalts him to the Skies,
   And records prove his Glory,
In majesty rever'd, he sits,
And frowns, and smiles, and laughs by fits,
And Curbs the pride of wicked wits
   That would Eclipse his glory.

No more let Gyant Hugh pretend
   To war with Jole's own Thunder,
But humbly beg, and Lowly bend,
   The table to knock under,
For like La mancha's Glorious knight
Our heroe vanquishes in fight
And never yet was put to flight
   To every body's wonder.

[454]

Let Sullen mortals hug their Spleen
   And misers hoard their treasure,
Let debauchees the brothwels glean
   And then repent at Leisure.
While we enjoy the circling glass
And Laugh, and sing, and toast our Lass,
We care not who's the Sneering ass
   That would destroy our pleasure.

Envy may Grin, a Ghastly Smile,
   Ill nature may revile us,
Folly pretend to make a Coil,
   Or Scandal to defile us,
But while the heart of Jole holds stout,
And till our punch and wine is out,
With dowble Strength we'll put to rout,
   Those foes that wish to foil us.

Large paper, in fair Characters, the Sealing and delivering of these new Commissions, then was postponed by his Lordship, for want of the great Seal, and Indeed, postponed in such a manner, as, that it was never afterwards done, and his Lordship conceived such a hatered to the Great Seal, on account of the Civil war that broke out in the Club, concerning that badge of office, soon after this, that he could not with patience hear it named, and held it in as great contempt as the Box No 1, nor, would he ever since this time give his Consent, that it should be affixed to any Clubical Instrument, or writing, but declared at all times that he esteemed it only as an Insignificant bawble or Cypher.

The Chancellor's Indignation was very much stirred up at these proceedings, and he began to meditate revenge against his Lordship, Protomusicus and the Secretary, whom he looked upon, as all equally guilty in Secreting and concealing the Badge of his office, and, really, considering the provocation this great officer had, who, after 6 week's absence, had Just returned to the Club, expecting to receive again, the badge of his office, with a Congratulatory Speech, from the orator, as usual, was disappointed in both, and his ensigns of State trod upon and Contemned, we cannot be much Surprized at his Indignation, especially, when we consider, that, that State officer was of a warm & Impetuous Temper.

At the same Sederunt, it happened Luckily, that while his Lordship and the members, were in a Sullen humor, by this unlucky affair of the great Seal, and his Lordship at the same time extremely soured in his temper, by another unhappy Incident which happened, and which we shall soon relate, in the following Chapter, where it will more properly come in, a Gentleman Invited to the Club, according to ancient Custom, vizt: Crinkum Crankum Esqr, afterwards a longstanding member, proposed the Singing of a new Song, which he himself had Composed, in praise of his Lordship and the Club, and leave being granted him to sing it, he performed it to the tune of, *Come Jolly Bacchus* &ct:[5] the Secretary accompanying his voice, *Con violoncello Solo.*

A New Song, For the Tuesday Club,
By Mr Crinkum Crankum

Let sots Implore the God of Wine,
   To Crown their hours with pleasure,
Let Colley vainly Court the Nine,

---

5. This popular 18th-century tune is included in Charles Coffey's ballad opera *The Devil to Pay* (1731), which was performed in Annapolis in 1752.

to pronounce dogmatically, upon Subjects of this occult Nature, well Remembring the Sage Sentiment of that Illustrious Poet & Philosopher, who says thus.

και κεραμευς κεραμει κοτεει και τεκτονι τεκτον
και πτωχος πτωχω φθονεει και αοιδος αοιδω.³

Upon these debates, it was ordered by his Lordship, that Prim Timorous Esqr, Serjt: at Arms, should Issue Summons to bring these females to his Lordship and this here Club, at next Sederunt, and, the honorable the Chancellor, Jonathan Grog Esqr, master of the Ceremonies, and Jealous Spyplot Senr Esqr, old Standing member, were nominated by his Lordship as Commissioners, for the Insp[ec]tion of these females, and thus, was this grand affair [de]termined and settled, but that Inspection and Scrutiny was never performed, the disturbances and hot Civil wars, concerning the Great Seal, putting an effectual Stop, to all other Clubical proceedings whatsoever.

At the 168th Sederunt, held upon the 26th of November, 1751, The honorable Lord President Jole being H:S: an Enquiry was made concerning the great Seal, which did not appear upon the table as usual, it could not, with certainty be discovered, in whose Custody it was; Solo Neverout Esqr declared, that he had delivered it to the Secretary, after that Club dissention, which happened concerning it, at Sederunt 166, this the || Secretary did not deny, but asserted, it had been stole from him, and (as he suspected) by Protomusicus himself, which the other put him to prove, but the Secretary could produce no legal evidence; only asserting that a Certain negroe of his,⁴ had seen Protomusicus go one morning, into his master, the Secretarie's Study, while the great Seal and bag lay upon the table, and, that, at the coming out again, of the said Protomusicus, the Seal had vanished, this was no proof at all, the witness being a negroe, and so the affair stood, tho' many believed the truth of the negroes declaration. A general Search, however for the Great Seal, was made among the members to no purpose, yet still, the Chief musician was suspected; this prevented the Issuing of the new Commissions, which the Secretary had with abundance of pains, at the Command of his Lordship, prepared and drawn out upon

---

3. "Potter is jealous of potter, smith of smith; / Pauper hates pauper, and poet hates poet" (Hesiod, *Works and Days* 25–26).

4. Perhaps a reference to Hamilton's servant Dromo, who accompanied Hamilton during his tour of the northern colonies and is frequently mentioned by name in Hamilton's account of his travels, the *Itinerarium* (see Carl Bridenbaugh, ed., *Gentleman's Progress: The Itinerarium of Dr. Alexander Hamilton, 1744* [Chapel Hill, N.C., 1948]).

name) in Case of necessity, however we shall Endeavor to sum up the Substance of this Speech here.

The Secretary brought instances from ancient and moderen History, of the danger of admitting females to be Concerned in government affairs; he mentioned Semiramis of Babylon, who was a Termagant; he mentioned Messalene of Rome, who was a fury, a composition of lust and a Devil Incarnate, he produced an Instance how Jealous the females were of admitting men to their Secret Councils and mysterious Rites, and the barbarity with which they treated them, when discovered there Incog, and gave, for example, the carbonading of Clodius, who rashly Intruded || into the mys- [449] teries of the *Bona dea,* in a woman's dress, but the priestesses inspecting him, found that he was not a member fit for their purposes, and, as it is said, tossed him in a blanket, bump't, thump't, thrash'd, smash'd and mash'd him, in such a Lamentable manner, that he Just escaped with life, tho not with whole bones, he also brought the example of Pope Joan, who, ascending the papal Chair, by this Craft or deceit, obliged the venerable and Reverend Cardinals, ever since, to use a groping Chair, to examine and Scrutinize his holiness by, if he was a true Canonical Member of the Church, and lastly, he mentioned, the Renowned Sue Lilliston, of this place, and of our own times, who, in the disguise of a merchant, transacted affairs on the 'Change at London, forged bills upon an honest Planter, and had it not been for Capitano Giovanni Carpentiro, who, it [is] supposed, discovered her by groping, would have eff[ect]ed her wicked purpose.[2]

When the Secretary had done, the chancellor rose gravely from his Seat, and without any particular address, to either his Lordship or the Club, spoke as follows.

"For my part, I approve very much of Mr Attorney Spyplot's motion, and urge, that the Search shall be begun Immediatly, and since his Lordship has given no proofs of his virility as yet, I move, that it may be Scrutinized, whether we have not now, a Pope Joan, in the Chair."

If the Longstanding members might take upon themselves to Physiognomize, they could not but presume to think, that this Speech of the Chancellor's, might, in his Lordship's || opinion, have been as well let [450] alone, for his lordship's countenance Changed much, during the delivery of it, and showed a mixture of Scorn and Indignation; However, posterity are desired to take this, as the Secretary's conjecture only, he not presuming

---

2. I have not identified Sue Lilliston. Giovanni Carpentiro is probably John Carpenter (see biographical sketch).

and, by being tossed and bandied from question to question, made to contradict himself most hideously. This was the reason that the Sophists of old, did by no means relish the Socratic way of arguing, which was carried on by question, for questions being the Sharp tools of Strong reasoners, they were by this means often reduced to their most pitiful Shifts and Quibbles; if for instance, the Question should be asked any of us, why petticoat government is the best and most eligible?—we might Ingeniously enough answer,—because it cannot be under *Male*-administration—This seems to be a very pertinent and Quaint answer, and, had like to have been made use of in the ancient and honorable Tuesday Club, In support of the Late Genearchy,—but the truth of the matter is, if we consider this Shrewd Question and its answer Seriously, we shall find it neither better nor worse than a rank *Conundrum;* and therefore, as to its Significancy and merit, we shall leave It intirely to the Judgement of the Learned, and proceed with our History.

At Sederunt 167, several arguments were started In club, Concerning the Genearchy, which was Established on Sederunt 165, as has been related, and after much ratiocination, the Club could not well tell how to proceed in this puzzling and knotty affair, till Jealous Spyplot Senr Esqr, who seemed to have been asleep all the time that the point was argued, took the Club book, and very gravely arming his nose with his Spectacles, tossed the leaves, backwards and forewords for a Considerable time, Then rising up, addressd the Chair, saying ‖ That he found on Sederunt 165, that this here Club was Governed by certain women, there having been then as the Record mentions a female president, a female Champion, and a female Chancellor, and as he reckoned such Innovations to be dangerous to the constitution of this here Club, he humbly moved that his Lordship would issue his warrant, *de ventre Inspiciendo*,[1] for searching and Inspecting these females, in order to discover, whether or not they were Effectual, and true Longstanding members.

The Club much approved of this motion of Mr Attorney Spyplots, and the Secretary back'd him Strenuously in a pithy Speech, the Substance of which is now lost, some ungracious, malevolent and profane hands, having lacerated and mutilated the Club Records, in this place, for which we wish them, (whoever they are) no worse punishment, than that they may never have a Scrap of paper to wipe a Certain part, (which modesty forbids me to

---

1. That is, a warrant "to inspect the womb" (permission given by a judge to midwives to determine the fact of pregnancy).

did Edmund Curl, Stationer, at the Bible & Dial in Fleetstreet,[9] that is, have fairly poisoned me, under the mark of friendship, in a Glass of old hock, or rather Grog, as a whet, before dinner, knowing (tho my Stomach be naturally good enough) that I am passionatly fond of whets; but these Gentlemen must have used either Rumbo, or Grog for that purpose on me, I not being fond of any other liquor, which said Curl, tho' his neck was of such an Immoderate Length, as not to require further streching, on a certain triple tree at Tyburn, yet was found very well adapted for another wooden machine, much more ridiculous and comic than the first mentioned, this he got by his publishing an elegant translation of Meursius's dialogues[10] for the Instruction of our youth, and dabbling in things which he did not understand, and that this, or the aforesd: triple tree may be the reward of all such fellows, whether magazine publishers or pretended Laureats, is the Prayer of,

Jonathan Grog Esqr, P:L:T:C:

This Remonstrance was well received by the Club, and Jealous Spyplot Junr Esqr, was appointed to hold the next Sederunt.

We are Informed by report, for the records are also here Imperfect, that that Seder: was held on the 13th Novembr 1751, of which we shall give an account in the following Chapter.

Chapter VII

Arguments in Club, against the Genearchy, Club Search warrants Issued, Speech of the Orator, New Club Song, Composed by Crinkum Crankum Esqr.

Questions in politics may be propounded in such a Cunning ‖ manner, [447] that in giving an answer, one can scarce evade being led into a præmunire,

9. For a good account of Pope's running feud with Edmund Curll, see George Sherburn, *The Early Career of Alexander Pope* (Oxford, 1934), 161–185, where Sherburn relates the story of Pope's giving Curll an emetic, calling the incident "perhaps the least dignified in all Pope's career" (p. 172).

10. Hamilton is referring to what was commonly known as *De arcanis Amoris et Veneris*, probably first printed at Grenoble about 1680, wrongly attributed to the Dutch scholar Johannes Meursius (1579–1639), and wrongly attributed to his son Johannes Meursius (1613–1654) on its title page. It is probably the work of Nicolas Chorier (1612–1692), who denied authorship of it. As the title suggests, it is a licentious book.

Licence, to Nonsence, and bad poetry (which is the same, or worse than no poetry) to Introduce themselves with abundance of propriety, into this particular kind of writing, and tho' my natural abilities, were to enable me to deviate from the established rule, yet, in so doing, I should still err in the eyes of all our moderen Critics and Connoiseurs, even tho I exactly observed the rules of Aristotle, who, I do not remember to have handled this Subject in his poetics, Secondly, when the said Laureat, professed to write in Imitation of the said Col- * * * * * * * * * * * * * * * * * [here again is a most miserable defect in the record, the Remainder of this piece having been tore out, but it happened luckily that Jonath: Grog Esqr had the original Copy, by him, from which this hiatus was filled up] -ley Cibber, Esqr, if he acted upon a rational plan, he ought to have set ‖ the said Cibber before him as a pattern, and followed him in every particular, without regard to Aristotle, or any body else, with which Learned, tho' heathnish Philosopher, the said Laureat is persuaded, the said Colley Cibber Esqr, never had the Least acquaintance or Intimacy. I appeal to the Learned world, and to every Candid and unprejudiced person, whether or not (allowing, that there is neither Sense or poetry in my Composition) I have not exactly followed my original, in whose anniversary compositions of this nature, not the least grain of either was ever found, Surely, if my production had been otherwise, I should have had the Character of an unskillful Copist, and have rendered myself as ridiculous as that painter, who, from a Carracatura, or piece of deformity, produced a beautiful and well proportioned figure.

Lastly, I have a word or two to add, relating to the said Colley Cibber Esqr, my unworthy brother Laureat, who, I am afraid, has been himself, at the bottom of all this, and has had the Chief hand in the plot, for, I cannot Imagine, that such Clodpated fellows, as the authors or publishers of magazines, have Learning adequate even to my poor performances, so as to Judge rightly of them, I therefore think, that they have been spurred on by the said Colley, who, fearing that I should eclipse him in Glory, and succeed him in his office and dignity, has Invidiously set these Curs loose upon me; but, I must tell him, he might have spared his breath to cool his porridge, for, as he is now Superannuated, and ripe to be gathered to his fathers, having drawled out more Lustra, in this transitory world, than many worthier men, & better poets, I, being yet, but in my 40th year of life, I may hope to live, to be preferred after his death, in Spite of his teeth, and I have ‖ great reason to thank my Stars, that the vast gulph of the Atlantic lies between him and I, for, had I been on the Spot, I dare say, he and his associates, would have served me the same Sauce as Alexander Pope Esqr,

time with great Indecorum and Impudence, to his Lordship's plenipo', expressing a most high contempt, of the said Laureat, of the said Club.

Now these objections, the Laureat aforesaid, undertakes to destroy as frivolous and Impertinent.

First, That the author is a fool, now, granting this proposition to be true, he does not conceive, that he is thereby disqualified from writing anniversary odes, as well from numberless Instances, that have anniversarily appeared, almost time out of mind, and from the Reason of the thing, as from the authority of a late Celebrated Poet,[a] who, descanting upon the merit of our present Laureat, has sung to this purpose.

> In merry old England, it once was a rule,
> The king had his Poet, and likewise his fool,
> But now, we're more frugal, I'd have you to know it,
> For Colley will serve, both for fool and for poet.

Whence, it appears, that the Characters of fool and poet are not so discordant, as this Shallow Critic would Insinuate, however, tho I have Clearly proved, that the Characters of fool and Poet, are not at all Incompatible, yet, let it not be thought, that I admit every fool, to the honorable Title of *poet,* Else some pert magazine publishers, might Impertinently Intrude, into the company of their betters, and so disgrace Parnassus, muddle the pure Streams of Helicon, and prophane the Temple of Apollo, for, as our English Lyric[a] says

> That every poet is a fool
> Ned can by demonstration show it,
> Happy, could Ned's Inverted rule,
> Prove every fool to be a poet.

But his next observation is still more absurd, when he says—

2dly, That there is neither Sense nor Poetry in my ode; *Risum Teneatis amici,*[8] had this Critic one grain of Common Sense, he might Easily perceive that neither Sense nor poetry were ever intended in it; 1st, because custom, which in process of time obtains the force of a Law, has given a full

---

(a) Alexr: Pope Esqr.[6]
(a) Mathew Prior Esqr.[7]

6. See Pope's "On a Translation of Aeschylus," lines 302–305.
7. Hamilton has closely paraphrased one of Prior's epigrams (see *The Literary Works of Matthew Prior,* ed. H. Bunker Wright and Monroe K. Spears [Oxford, 1959], I, 454).
8. "Hold your laughter, friends."

sary odes, was Constituted and appointed poet Laureat of the ancient and honorable Tuesday Club, so deservedly famous in all the courts of Europe, as well for the wisdom of her regulations, as for the profound Sagacity of her Lord President, and the wit, drollery and Facetiousness of her long-standing members.

Item, That the said poet Laureat, had, according to custom, Composed an ode, upon the Anniversary of the Club's Institution, wherein he had proposed the aforesaid Colley Cibber, as his pattern and example, and had, in the opinion of some Gentlemen, other guess Critics than some publishers of magazines, acquitted himself to admiration, by exhibiting as good a burlesque, upon the said ancient Club, as ever the said Colley, did upon his most Sacred majesty.

Item, That the said ode was deemed so masterly a performance, as to deserve a place in the Collections of the Learned, and, it being thought a pity, that the merit of it's author, should be confined to this dark corner of the world, the Inhabitants whereof, are much greater Connoisseurs in Homony and tobacco, than in Anniversary odes, the said ode was transmitted to his Lordships Plenipo' at the court of London, to do honor to some of their monthly collections, and was accordingly by the said plenipo' presented to the Publishers of the *Gentleman's* and *Universal magazines.*

Item, That one of the publishers of the said magazines, (of the *Gentlemans* vizt:) told the said plenipo' in a gentleman like manner, that he chose not to publish any thing in his magazine, but what would be understood by the Generality of people, and, what was of public utility—but I would ask this grave and profound Gentleman, whether in his publications hitherto, he has kept Strictly to this formal declaration, and whether several of his Love Songs are of any public || utility, or whether his Rebuses, Riddles, anagrams, puns and Conundrums, with which he mightily abounds, are understood by the Generality of people, or Indeed, by any Sort of people, but the Idle foolish witlings that compose them—but, let me tell this grave Gentleman, that I challenge him, with all his garret Inhabiting authors, in one body, to produce, either out of their manuscripts, publications, or maggoty pericraniums, any thing equal, or nigh to these Ingenious *Conundrums* and *puns,* contained in the Records of our ancient Tuesday Club, of which, I myself, am the unworthy author.

Item, That the publisher of the *Universal magazine,* distorting his face, into a very contemptuous Leer, was pleased to declare, that the author of the said Ode was a fool, and that there was neither Sense nor poetry in the Composition, and utterly refused to publish the same, behaving at the same

know whether Colley, might not have some how or other got Intelligence of it, and suppressed it, lest his being outshone so greatly, by our Laureat, who there publicly declares himself candidate to succeed him, he might be displaced Immediatly, to make room for a Genius so far Superior to his. Their Excuses were partly ill natured, and all Triffling, The first told me, that as this was of a private nature, and would be understood by nobody, but the Club of Gentlemen themselves,—and he chose to put nothing into his magazine, but what was of public utility,—The other had the Impudence to tell me, it was not poetry, and that it was nonsense, I told him, it was want of Judgement in him, that made him Condemn it, and ‖ that it [441] was much better than many pieces of his publishing I could point out, and which no doubt were the production of his own Leaden Brain.

Be so kind as to make my compliments to the honorable the president, with the members of the ancient Tuesday Club, assure them, that I am deeply Sensible of the great honor they have been pleased to confer upon me, and that it shall be greatly my Study to deserve it, by doing all the Good offices in my power, to serve them, am,

Dear Sir &ct:
Comely Coppernose.

This Letter Confirmed the Lord presidents Conjecture Concerning the letter produced by Jonathan Grog Esqr, at Sederunt 156, but at the same time, it had as little Credit with his Lordship, as the said Letter of Mr Grog, he pronouncing it of the same Cut, with that which came with the Box No 1.

The Secretary then acquainted his Lordship and the Club, That Jonathan Grog Esqr, desired to be excused from attending the Club at this Sederunt, on account of Indisposition, but humbly desired, that the remonstrance, which he had Committed into the hands of the Secretary, might be read in Club, and put upon Record, which was done, as follows.

An Humble Remonstrance,

To all whom it may Concern, by Jonathan Grog Esqr, Poet Laureat of the ancient and honorable Tuesday Club, against Colley Cibber Esqr, poet Laureat of Great Britain, France and Ireland, the Authors and publishers of the *Gentleman's* & *Universal magazines,* and all their abettors and adherents, whomsoever & wheresoever,

Showeth,

Imprimis. That the said Jonathan Grog Esqr, on account ‖ of his uncom- [442] mon talents at versification, and particular knack at Composing Anniver-

members, and in his obstinacy in Concealing the great Seal for his own private use, upon which, his Lordship observed That one Rotten Sheep spoils the whole flock, at the same time, casting a Sheeps Eye, upon Mr Proto musicus.

This disturbance in the Club, concerning the Great Seal, was the first allarm, sounded to that great Clubical Civil war, which was afterwards Carried on, under the Conduct of the Chancellor, that ended in the decathedration of his Lordship, and, sometime after, in the Exaltation of Solo Neverout Esqr, to the dignity of attorney General, and the rise of this Gentleman was prognosticated, even at this Sederunt, by his Lordship's throwing a Sheep's Eye upon him, which was Interpreted by some, as a mark of respect, and really turned out so afterwards, for, his Lordship perceiving that this affair of the Secreting of the great Seal, would lay the foundation of an Irreconcealable quarrell between the Chancellor and Solo Neverout Esqr, was determined to foment it all he could, in order to mortify and humble, if possible, that aspiring officer, and break his measures, and he thought he had now found in Protomusicus a man of unshaken Resolution and Courage, that could with Intrepidity, go thro' this great and arduous work, which Indeed, he did, at last, as we shall soon relate, but not without exciting such dreadful convulsions in the Club, as to shake his Lordship out of his Chair, but, by good manage- ‖ ment and policy, he gave him a Cant[4] into it again, so as that his lordship sits there, firm and Steady to this very day.

At this same Sederunt, the Secretary presented in Club, a letter from Capt: Comely Coppernose the agent in Great Britain, which was Read, and put on Record.

To Loquacious Scribble Esqr,
pr: The Nancy Capt: Henderson.

Sir,

I am Sadly mortified, and greatly enraged, at the publishers and printers of the *Gentleman's,* and *Universal magazines,*[5] I cannot prevail on any of them, to give our Laureats poem a place in their pamphlets, and, I do not think any of the others are worthy of the honor, being but in little esteem, they have had that excellent performance between them, five months, and, at first, both promised to put it in, but at last absolutely refused, I don't

---

4. A *cant* is a sudden movement that results in a tilting up or turning over of something else.

5. Hamilton is referring to Edward Cave, the renowned founder and publisher of the *Gentleman's Magazine,* and John Hinton, who published the *Universal Magazine.*

a lady Lord president, a Lady Sir John, and a Lady Chancellor, Philo Dogmaticus Esqr, having the Complaisance to surrender his office for one night. But who these Ladies were, cannot now be known, the Record being Irrecoverably lost,[3] so that the memorable transactions of this Sederunt, to our great grief and Shame, must be buried in perpetual oblivion, However, thus much is most certainly known, that Tunbelly Bowzer Esqr, was appointed to serve at next Sederunt, which happened upon Tuesday, the 22d of October.

The Records of this Sederunt also, are much defaced, and most miserably mutilated, we have reason, however to Conjecture, that there were, at this time, loud and tumultous debates in Club, concerning the Great Seal, for Philo Dogmaticus Esqr: Cancellar: having gone out of the province, about urgent || affairs, left the great Seal in the hands of Huffman Snap [438] Esqr, the last High Steward, who delivered it in trust to Solo Neverout Esqr, requesting him to deliver it to the Secretary, who was not in Club that night, Mr Protomusicus having then got possession of the Seal, did not care to part with it again, but having in his head as it was thought, some ambitious aspiring designs of supplanting the Chancellor in his absence, secured this Illustrious badge of office, and refused absolutely to deliver it up, tho' requested to do it again & again by the Secretary, and even by the honorable the Lord president in person, but all to no purpose, he even went so far, as positively to deny that he had it, and Carried all before him in Club, by noise, Clamor, and loud Laughing, his usual way of getting off, in such a manner did he vociferate and Laugh, that even the punishment of the Gelastic Law, which was Inflicted on this occasion, was nothing to that vociferous heroe, for he could at any time out laugh the whole Club, after many Speeches, arguments, replys, and reduplys, revilings, exclamations, threatnings and vaporings, concerning the great Seal, his honor the president and Club, finding that they could by no means operate upon the Petulancy and obstinacy of this aspiring Gentleman, it is supposed that at last, for a Signal Punishment, he was Committed to the Custody of Prim Timorous Esqr, Serj: at arms, under whose Clutches, he behaved in such a tumultuous manner, as quite terrified that mild and modest Gentleman, and made him swear several times *God—bless the king—* || *God's my life*—and [439] *as God shall Judge me*—his usual exclamations, when surprized or terrified, this Confinement however, had so little effect, upon Mr Protomusicus, as, that he persevered in his Gelastic humor, against his Ldsp and the L:St:

---

3. Hamilton does not identify these ladies in the "Record," but he mentions there that women did serve as officers at this memorable sederunt.

Genearchy of the Club.

[facing page 437]

the members of this Club, at a Rehearsal of music for a Charitable Concert, performed on wednesday night last, it was by some rebellious members, without the Consent or privity of the honorable President adjourned and put off"—

* *

There is here a most horrible Gap or hiatus in the Records of this ancient and honorable Club, which posterity may || be at a loss for, tho it is questioned by some, whether they will suffer any loss thereby, It cannot therefore be positively conjectured, what Individual members were present at this Sederunt, but however, we may very safely suppose, that Huffman Snap Esqr H:S: Philo Dogmaticus Esqr: Cancellar: and some other members of less note gave their attendance, it is pritty certain, that the Honorable Nasifer Jole Esqr, the Lord president, was not present, which we have from a well vouched tradition or report, that the Club sent for his Lordship about eight o clock in the evening, no Commission for a deputy appearing, and his Lordship not Intimating to the Club at meeting, that he either could, or could not attend, as usual; This messenger was no less a person than Quirpum Comic Esqr, who, being deputy Secretary at that Sederunt, in the absence of the Chief Secretary, waited on his Lordship in his bed Chamber, being ushered by Don John Charlotto, and found his Lordship, Just stepping into bed, having his breeches in his hand; he delivered his message in a Succinct manner, Informing his Lordship, that the Club requested his attendance, to which his Lordship made reply That he could by no means attend that night,—Then the Emissary demanded a Commission for a deputy, which his Lordship would not grant, so Quirpum Comic Esqr, returned, and made his report to the Club, taking notice of the Circumstance of the breeches; what could be his Lordship's reason for not attending the Club at this Sederunt is not || certain, unless it was that the H:S: had neglected to send him a letter of advice, as was customary, and Indeed it might be so, for his Lordship of Late, being Jealous of underhand designs in some of the members, particularly the Secretary, had carefully Secreted all letters wrote to himself, and would not suffer them to be recorded, which occasioned a Certain remissness in the high Stewards after this time, and prevented their writing, having not the least Encouragement, that their Ingenious performances of this Sort, should be transmitted to posterity.

[436]

[437]

The Club upon hearing Quirpum Comic's report or answer, from his Lordship, resolved, that since the honorable breeches were laid aside, that the honorable petticoat should supply their place, and govern the Club for this Sederunt, accordingly, three Great female officers were appointed, vizt:

Duke of Marlborough, did Amadis de Gaule, or any other such Romantic heroe.

[434] Neither am I to be supposed to mean here, that Sort of || universal genearchy which the fair Sex, have mantained ever since the beginning of the world, procured and supported by bright Eyes, Jetty locks, arched Eybrows, Ruby lips, Snowy bosoms &ct: &ct: which we find minutely and Circumstantially described in our moderen Love Songs, odes, Cantatas, Bellets doux, Romances and novels, for really, that Subject, has already been so Largely discanted upon, by poets Enthusiastic Lovers, and soft Historians, That I should look upon it to be a work of Supererogation, to write or say any more Concerning it, than what has been already wrote and said, and therefore, that I may not be guilty of a waste of time, paper and Ink, I shall offer nothing on the Subject.

Nor do I mean that Sort of Genearchy, which takes place in private families, mantained by fainting fits, pearly tears, Sighs and soft complaints, and sometimes by the rougher method of eternal talking, bawling, flouncing, Scolding, nay, by the discipline of the fist and broom Stick, This being Sufficiently displayed, in many of our moderen Comedys, and opera farces, and is touched in a very Elegant and natural manner, In the Ingenious Mr Ward's *Matrimonial dialogues*.[2]

But that Sort of Genearchy which I speak of, is, that which Takes place in Clubs, where the members must be ordered and regulated, by the Caprice and humor of their wives, whether Present or absent; I say, it is a pity [435] some able pen has not || treated Largely on this novel Subject, as it would afford abundance of matter to be learned and witty upon, this Subject, (tho I had a capacity adequate to it) yet, is too extensive for me, at present to meddle with, having the weight of this Important History on my Shoulders, which I must discuss in as Succinct a manner as I can, for fear of Incurring that Common fault of being too voluminous, and Committing a *great Sin* by giving birth to a *great book,* so, having given this hint to the wits of our age, to exercise the acumen of their Genius upon; I shall proceed to relate a remarkable Instance of Genearchy or petticoat Government, which at this period happened in the Ancient and honorable Tuesday Club.

At Sederunt 165, on the 8 of October, 1751, there appears this Entry on the Record.

"The Club met at the house of Huffman Snap Esqr, pursuant to an order of last meeting, Tho it should have met at the said house last Tuesday instead of this day, but, by reason of the necessary attendance of several of

---

2. See 2n, above.

Chapter VI

The Genearchy of the Club, Records mutilated and defaced, Letter from the agent in Great Brittain, Remonstrance of the Laureat against Colley Cibber.

Genearchy is a form of Government, which I have not seen in all my reading, treated of in that full and ample manner, which the nature and dignity of the Subject deserves; ‖ and it were to be wished, that some able pen would undertake the Subject, and unfold the mysteries of it in all its parts; I must not be thought to mean here, the government of States and Empires, which have frequently been in the hands of women famous for heroism and policy; and, by nature, seemingly, as well adapted to Govern as the Male, tho' custom has settled it otherwise, This might easily be made out from History, both ancient and moderen; we read of Zenobia the Empress, who supported her State long against the Strength of the Romans, after her husband's death, 'till Aurelianus vanquished her, and led her in triumph thro' the Streets of Rome, where she had as many to gaze on her, as if she had been in *a Grand Anniversary procession,* we are told also of Semiramis, who became mistress of the whole assyrian Empire, and enlarged its bounds more than any of her predecessors; Herodotus likewise tells us of Thomyris, Queen of Scythia, who killed the Great Conqueror Cyrus & dipt his head in a pail of blood, that he might satiate himself with that for which he always thristed, we have also an old Story handed down of Thalestris, a queen of the amazons, who was got with Child, by the Macedonian Conqueror Alexander;[1] But these were the She tyrants of antiquity, and, tho their fame is sounded forth by historians at an Extravagant Rate, yet not all of them together can be Compared with our Illustrious Elizabeth of England, either for true Courage, wisdom, or policy, that renowned lady, being of more value and Significancy, than the whole Group of these ancient heroines, excelling them as much, as the late great

[433]

---

1. Tomyris (fl. 6th century B.C.) was queen of the Massagetae who defeated Cyrus the Great; she is said to have thrown his head into a vessel filled with blood, saying, "It was blood you thirsted for; now take your fill!" (Herodotus 1.214). Thalestris was queen of the Amazons who, attracted by the fame of Alexander the Great, traveled from her country to see him and bear his child (Diodorus Siculus 17.77).

Put me the Laureat into that trusty place,
As for recording, what at this Club pass'd,
I've already said, it rain'd very fast,
Musicus slept with his pipe in his mouth,
A Custom of his, tho' very uncouth.
No Stranger this night at Club entertained,
No Laws either broke, or any way strain'd,
And at breaking up it was thought fitting
At Huffman Snap's Esqr, shall be the next meeting.

The Beauties of this Poetical Entry are so Glaring and apparent, that they need no Comment to set them forth. I shall therefore leave them to speak for themselves, In that elegant, Simple and natural Stile, in which they are conceived; but, that I may not leave any thing dark or obscure in this History, which might puzzle future Critics and Comentators to explain, and disturb the plodding Brain of some, as yet unborn Dennis, or Theobald,[+] I shall beg leave to clear up an obscure passage, in the Second line of this admirable performance, vizt:

Which, *if twice read o'er,* Sure all will hear ont.

The meaning of which expression, *twice read o'er,* is neither more nor Less than this, that, at the opening of every Club, it was usual for the Secretary, to read the proceedings ‖ of the last Sederunt, and he always named the number of the Sederunt with a Clear and audible voice, but a custom had been Introduced of old, by Smoothum Sly Esqr, who being, or pretending to be, thick of hearing, would Interrupt the Secretary, after he had pronounced the number of the Sederunt, with, *Pray Sir, what Sederunt is that?* and so oblige him to repeat it over again, this Custome once Established, by Smoothum Sly Esqr, still prevailed in Club, for, after he left the Club, Mr Protomusicus took up the practice, which he has continued to this day, and in his absence, some Inquisitive member, particularly the Chancellor, never fails to put that teizing question to the Secretary, and, not only Interrupt him, in the very beginning of his reading, but oblige him to repeat these words twice over, and this is what is meant by the words, *twice read over* in the poetical Entry of the Laureat, this foolish Custom in the Club, has taken such deep root, that it is not now in the power, even of his Lordship, to expell it, and rectify the abuse.

---

4. John Dennis (1657–1734) was an English dramatist and critic ridiculed by Pope. Lewis Theobald (1688–1744) was an English poet, dramatist, and essayist whose *Shakespeare Restored; or, A Specimen of the Many Errors as Well Committed as Unamended by Mr. Pope* (London, 1726) provoked Pope to make him hero of the *Dunciad*.

tember, and the Proto-musician hearing this resolve, passed a Compliment to his Lordship, and the Longstanding members, declaring that he should be very proud of their company, and this meeting of the Club, was to be called the Rustic Club, but this was never put in execution, because Mr Protomusicus, never retired to the said Villa, and therefore had no title to have this honor bestowed on him, at this Sederunt was entertained as a Stranger, according to Ancient Custom, the Celebrated Drawlum Quaint Esqr, late a worthy Longstanding member of the Club and Speaker.

The next Sederunt was only remarkable, for the Record of it being penned in verse, by the Poet Laureat, who was appointed by his Lordship deputy Secretary, the chief Secretary being absent, that ex‑ traordinary performance of the Laureat's follows.

> *Poetical Entry by the Laureat for Sederunt 164*
>
> At the Club's eightscore and Fourth Sederunt,
> Which, if twice read o'er Sure all will hear on't,
> And, as to the day and month of the year,
> Look on the last, and it will all appear,
> At such a Sederunt, and such a day,
> That the Club, it did meet, is what I say.
> I mean, that at night, the Club, they did meet,
> And, tho' it rained hard, met in Charles Street,
> At the Laureat's or printer's, no matter for that,
> 'Twas there that they met, and there that they sat,
> Where were, his Lordship, the honorable Jole,
> And he, and five others, made up the whole,
> Of which the Chanc'lor, first shall be nam'd,
> And then Squire Proto' for music so fam'd,
> Squire Bowzer the next, tho' largest in Size,
> Tho' to no office he cannot yet rise,
> Mr Quirpum Comic came next, that queer Dog,
> And Last came the High Steward Jonathan Grog,
> His Lordship produc'd from the Chief Secretary
> A Letter of Excuse, wrote very merry,
> Wherein he Inform'd him he could not appear,
> For he was so sick, he could not come there,
> And left it to him to Chuse for the night
> A Scribe or a Clerk, the records to write,
> His Lordship out of his favor and grace

and honorable Club was the real, true and Genuine Apollo and Orpheus of the Club, by whom the poet seemed at all times to be Inspired, which he proved by authentic quotations ‖ and authorities from the ancient Records, of this here ancient and honorable Club, vizt: in Sederunts, 118, 119, 122, 147 and 162. In which Sederunts, the honorable the Chancellor, was first Invited as a Stranger to the Club; Was elected a Long Standing member, and Created Chancellor in one and the same night; was appointed deputy president, and in the two last was H:S: of this here ancient Club, at which times and occasions in particular, the bright Genius of the Club, and their Celebrated Poet Laureat, shone out with uncommon Splendor, in Speeches and addresses Prosaical and poetical to the Club and Chair, and in Epicædions and mournful Songs on his lordships Indisposition, and in an Eminent and distinguished manner, in the last grand heroic performance, in which the Laureat may say, as did the Latin poet,

Exegi monumentum ære perennius.[3]

At Sederunt 163, Jealous Spyplot Senr Esqr, being high Steward, the Secretary was Severely Censured by his Lordship and the Club, for altering the Stile of the Records at last Sederunt, by foisting in the Phraze *mounted the Chair,* instead of *taken the Chair,* which he was ordered to correct, but that officer paid so little regard to the reproofs and Instructions of his Lordship and the Club, that that very error stands to this day uncorrected in the Record book.

Solo Neverout Esqr, Protomusicus, at this Sederunt, exercised his function in Club, by singing a Recitativo and Excellent old tune, to great part of the Laureat's heroic poem, but his Lordship and the Club being ‖ gorged Cloyed and satiated with the Sweetness of his music, when he had gone thro' about 20 lines, ordered him to read the rest, which he did, with great gravity, and composure of Countenance, and had like to have lulled the whole Club asleep.

It being said in Club, at this Sederunt, that Mr Protomusicus, a member of great worth and merit among the Longstanding members of this here ancient and honorable Club, Intended soon to fix his residence in the Country, at his villa, upon a pleasant Sandy tract of Land, called Littleworth, it was resolved at Supper, by his Lordship, and the Longstanding members, that this here ancient and honorable Club, should do the said Proto Musicus, the honor, to attend him at his Country house twice a year, vizt: upon the Second Tuesday of March, and the Second Tuesday of Sep-

---

3. "I have completed a monument more lasting than bronze" (Horace, *Carmina* 3.30.1).

Both males and females to him flockd
And with his piteous tale were shok'd,
While he, the Story Lamentable
Describ'd as well as he was able,
Which stirr'd up many a Sigh & groan,
But all applauded valiant John.
 Oh! valiant John, thy fame & Glory,
Shall Cut a —— dash in future Story,
Thy doughty deeds with wonder fill us
Like those of Hector and Achilles,
Bards yet unborn, shall sing thy praise
And with thy name adorn their Lays,
Nor shall the Ancient Tuesday Club,
Ever forget this glorious Job,
But shall Remember, whose brave arm,
Sav'd them from dread, and dire alarm,
For, had my Lord by bloody thief
Been kill'd then, ah, without Relief
The ancient Club, had sunk to nought,
And dark oblivion been her Lot.
But brave Don John, with heart of Lyon,   [427]
'Tis thee we safely may rely on,
While I, the Laureat of the Club,
My Lazy muse will Soundly drub,
If she thy praise does not proclaim
And sound in Sweetest verse thy name,
Thy great Immortal name abroad
And blazon thee a demi-god,
For Sure like Hercules thou art,
And has't a very Sampson's heart,
Long life to thee may heaven afford,
Still to protect and guard my Lord,
And may his Lordship ne'er forget,
How vastly he is in thy debt,
Who has't as 'twere renew'd his breath
And snatchd him from the Jaws of death;
And since I chuse no more to sing,
God save my Lord, the Club and King.

 After the Reading of this heroic poem, the Orator delivered an oration, in which he proved, that the honorable the Chancellor, of this ancient

  Thus brave Don John, discharg'd his gun,
  And made the Rugged Ruffian run,
  But e'er he run he fir'd a pistol,
  Round John's Brave nob, the Slugs did whistle
  And luckily stuck in the wall,
  So John Receiv'd no harm at all.
   The Rogue within, who heard the Rattle,
  Believ'd there was a furious battle
  Abroad, and without more delay,
  Thro dormant window made his way,
  And slid from thence into the Street,
  Where he betook him to his feet,
  And with his fellow rogue did fly,
  The devil go with them both, say I.
   His Lordship then from bed up rose
  And scarcely stayd to seek his Cloths,
  But from his window roar'd like Thunder,
  "Thieves! Thieves! fire! murder! blood & plunder!"
  The neighbours raisd, around did floke,
  Some to condole, and some to Joke,
  My Lord's mishap, some much did pity,
  Others thereon were wonderous witty,
  Some thought my Lord & John were battling
  And stirr'd up all this rout and rattling,
  (For they were wont at times to squabble
  And round the doors to draw a rabble)[2]
  Therefore, a Certain person swore,
  "By G—d he'd bind his Lordship oer,
  To keep the peace"—"and by our Lady,
  Replies my Lord, I'm bound already,
  Alack and wail a day! says he,
  If you believe not come and see,"
  And that they might not think he lied,
  He showd his hands yet firmly tied.
   Then mov'd with pity was each breast,
  To see his Lordship thus distressd,
  And quickly they his hands unbound,
  When all to comfort him stood round.

---

2. Cole and Charlette were, indeed, apt to feud (see biographical sketch for John Charlette).

And, tho' I have no money got,
I pray you would not cut my throat,
Go to my Store, where goods are plenty,
And freely take what will Content ye."
His Lordship spoke—The Rogue replies,
"Sweet honey, dear,—and dam' my eyes,
One hair o' your head, I will not offer
To hurt, but must ransack your Coffer,
Tis but your money, I demand,"
Then strait he seiz'd with Cruel hand,
His Lordship's throat, as if he'd strangle him,
Who, while the thief did thus Entangle him,
Gave many a Lamentable Groan,
That would have pierc'd a heart of Stone.
  When Brave Don John, who, as we said,
Lay high in kitchen loft a bed,
Heard in his Lordships room a noise,   [424]
Which made him quick from Couch to rise,
And peeping Slily thro' a breach in
The Gavel of his Lordship's kitchen,
He spied a rogue below, expecting,
Th'event of what within was acting,
Who seeing John's Courageous face,
In such an unsuspected place,
Swore "Dam' ye, speak, or make a noise,
I'll blow your brains out in a trice."
"Oho! quoth John, and is it so,
Then faith 'tis time for me to go."
Then stepping back, he seizd the gun,
And quickly to the port hole run,
Where, taking neither aim nor mark,
He boldly fir'd her in the dark,
For, as the rusty gun had not,
Been loaded with or Slug, or Shot,
He wisely Judg'd 'twas all the same,
To shoot at random as to aim,
For he propos'd no further harm,
Than the Good neighbours to allarm,
That they asistance might afford
In Tribulation to my Lord.

A Bass' relief upon a wall,
Or antique Bust, or Statue, which,
Sly artist cut on Tomb or Nitch,
[422] Whose Stony eye-balls dead and dark
For ever fix on the same mark,
Whose marble phiz, tho hewn with Skill,
Is motionless and silent still.
His Lordship look'd just such a look,
When hardy thief by gorge him took,
And seem'd like one transfix'd with wonder,
Or destin'd wretch Just struck with thunder.
 At last the Thief in Cruel Bands
Began to tie his Lordship's hands,
"Dam' your old blood (says he) beware,
For, if to call or stirr you dare,
I'll blow your brains out"—From Surprize,
His Lordship rousing, turn'd his Eyes,
To view the Rogue who talk'd so big,
And star'd upon him, like stuck pig,
Yet not with dastard fear oppress'd,
His Lordship Judg'd it might be best,
The Rugged knave to sooth and flatter,
Hoping to compromise the matter,
His Lordships Eloquence forth broke,
And thus in honey'd words he spoke.
"O Dearest, kindest friend, I pray,
Dont murder me, while here I Lay,
In bed thus bound, and unprepar'd,
For that would Cruel be and hard,
[423] Cash I have none, but had I any, ⎫
You should be welcome to each penny, ⎬
Your Carriage is so Gentlemanny, ⎭
For Sure a gentleman you seem,
I know it by your air and mien,
Had I a treasure in my hands,
Forth it should come at your Commands,
For money Sure you stand in need of,
And Sordid pelf, 'tis not the greed of,
As seems by your polite Demeanor,
That makes you ask in such a manner,

How he the orators fine Speeches,
Which far as east from west he fetches,
And with much greek does oft Embelish,
To understand, and truely relish,
How to bring over to his fancy,
The members, so that none dares Gainsay
His Sage behests. In fine, how, wisely,
Strictly Solemnly and precisely,
To rule his Club in every matter,
That they might wiser prove and better;
Such Ideas, grand as these we mention,
Perhaps might fix my lord's attention,
When lo! in the next Room, a noise,
Made all give way to quick Surprize,
"Ho! John! (his lordship Cries) g[o]! run!
In that there Corner stands a gun!
Quick! fire it off, some rogue I fear,
By force and arms has enter'd here,"
His Lordship spoke, but devil a gun [421]
Was in the Room, nor valiant John,
Who, with a glass of rum well dos'd,
Himself in kitchen loft reposd,
And by his Side (as one may say)
His gun with powder loaded lay.

   Alas! his Lordship could no more,
Or say, or do, ope' bursts the door,
And, O most dread terrific Sight,
Shows a dark Lanthorn's gloomy light,
Which to his Lordship strait advances,
Next in his Eyes, a pistol Glances,
And, by the throat, a brawny fist,
His Lordship seiz'd with cruel twist,
And, while he struggled, well nigh Choakd,
Clapt to his breast the pistol Cock'd,
With "Dam your blood, you old Curmudgeon,
Tis not for nought, I've scald your Lodging,
Where is your money? quickly tell,
Or, 'S blood, I'll blow your Soul to hell,
Your Hoard of Cash,—declare old Chuff,
Or dam you, I shall use you rough."

   Oh! have you never seen at all

And round, their Reign'd a Silence deep,
The rich awake, the poor asleep,
The Lab'ring hinds whom cares ne'er wound,
On Couches hard, met Sleep profound,
While Great ones, Rich by knavery grown,
Found no repose on beds of down,

[419]
Twas then his Lordship, snug and warm,
Lay on his bed, and thought no harm,
Nor yet, had Morpheus, drowsy God,
Wav'd oer his Lordships eyes, his rod,
His magic rod, with poppies bound,
Which mortals Lulls in Sleep profound,
Or sooth'd by Johns melodious Lays,
While on his flute he Sweetly plays,
For John, The Muses darling dear,
Oft warbled Strains most Sweet and Clear,
Which drew the Listning Clowns around,
His Lordship's Court, to hear the Sound,
Or Pond'ring in his pericrane'
Thoughts worthy of so wise a man,
His cogitations, peradventure,
On th'ancient Tuesday Club did Center,
How he with wisdom might Govern
And steer like pilot skilld at Stern,
How 'gainst Sir John to make resistance,
Till that proud Champion knew his distance,
How the [Sl]y Chanc'lor to withstand,
And keep him still, at his left hand,
Or other matters, he might think on,
As drinking, the Great bell of Lincoln,
Or who among the String of Ladies,
Succeeds his toast, who yet a maid is,

[420]
How to outsing the pert musician
And beat him in his own profession,
[This musicus, if he thinks fitting,
When his turn comes to have no meeting,
Altho his lordship then thinks queer ont,
He oft adjourns the Club's Sederunt.]

[ ] Between the brackets is supposed to be an Interpolation, as it not only varies from the Stile of the rest of the poem, but breaks in upon the Sense.

fallen into, that their constitution was as it were paralytic, and they did not in the least feel where the Shoe pinched, their whole attention being fixed upon magnificence and Show, and the aggrandizing of their Lord president; The Secretary had moved the revisal of the Laws sundry times, but to no purpose, and therefore resolved with himself, not to trowble his head any farther about the matter, but to allow this now *Lawless Club,* to go on, as they seemed disposed to do, without either Laws or order. During this whole Sederunt, the Club seemed very dull, which was thought, to be owing to the absence of Mr Proto-musicus, and, to his Lordship's utterly declining to sing.

At Sederunt 162, Philo dogmaticus Esqr, being H:S: The poet Laureat produced in Club, a heroic poem upon his Lordships late wonderful escape, from the hands of a merciless ruffian, which, after reading, did not meet with that Countenance, and favor from his Lordship, which the Laureat expected, for the same reason, (as it is thought,) that he did not approve of the Secretarie's late oration upon that Subject, therefore, this poem was not allowed a place in the Record; but, as it would be a great loss to posterity, to be deprived of this masterly performance, I have with some difficulty procured a Genuine Copy of it, and Inserted it into this history, which I should esteem Incompleat without it.

A Heroic Poem [418]

On the late Tragical Scene acted in the bed chamber,
of the Right Honorable Nasifer, Lord president of
the ancient and Honorable Tuesday Club.
Humbly presented to the Consideration of his Lordship,
and his Longstanding members by

        Their most humble Servant
        The Club's Poet Laureat.

Dictate some Gloomy muse, my verse,
While I the Tragic Scene Rehearse,
The Tragic Scene that had almost,
Transform'd his Lordship to a Ghost,
Till brave Don John from Sleep uprising,
With Courage bold and Enterprizing,
Discharged the tremendous Gun,
That made the Villain fire and run.
   Night's Sable Chariot had well nigh,
Climbd to the Summit of the Sky,

dead and rotten in less than one Century;[1] This Thought moved the Tyrant, and drew tears from his eyes, when the prospect of the murders and butcheries he was preparing to committ, to gratify his vain ambition, did not excite one Serious Thought.

This shows us that Tyrants, are not altogether Incapable of pity or compassion, tho' it is for the most part wrong placed, and therefore all that would seem wanting, to make a tollerable good man of a Tyrant, is to bring it so about, that these humane or tender passions, which Nature has planted in him, should be bent upon proper objects; we may hence Infer, that most, if not all Tyrants have been made so in a great measure by Education, and, that their parents and teachers, have very Industriously Contributed towards making monsters of them, by Instilling into their minds, while callous and tender, Ridiculous and absurd notions of things, so, that they can never afterwards associate their Ideas, according to the Standard of nature and truth, but their whole life and actions, are one Series of absurdity and barbarity; If these methods produce a Tyrant, in a [416] man that is of || an elevated birth, or ordained to Inherit a Crown, they are productive of as bad consequences in persons of a mean Extraction, for, a Cobler or tinker, that has been brought up in Idleness, and never has reaped the advantage of good precepts and example, turns out as perfect a Barbarian, and abandoned ruffian in his Sphere of action, as the Villain that wears a diadem, and would prove as Compleatly wicked and mean, had he the same power, or if the Gallows did not stand in his way, which often proves a Check to the ragged or needy villains, yet these low lived Barbarians, wretched, Savage, and ragged as they are, have in them also some Sparks of humanity, which will break out on particular occasions, as did the Innate humanity of that opulent and exalted Villain Xerxes, but they are equally misplaced in them as in him, these observations will be verified, in the behaviour of that hardened, Low lived villain, that attacked his Lordship the president in his bedchamber, as we are going to relate.

At Sederunt 161, August 6th 1751, The worshipful Sir John being H:S: The Orator delivered a harangue, upon the abuses & Grievances, that had crept Insensibly into the Club, and pressed his Lordship earnestly for a reformation of the same, and, for a revisal of the old Laws, which he said, he was afraid were Irrecoverably lost, since they were taken out, at the Rebinding and beautifying of the ancient book of Records, by Jonathan Grog Esqr printer to the Club, but his Lordship, not seeming to take any [417] notice of the Orators motions, and no body seconding him, the || affair was dropt, such a State of Supineness and Stupidity was this ancient Club now

---

1. An account of this story appears in Herodotus 7.46.

heaven, that by the goose like gabbling of that Case hardened villain, to your Lordship's honor in bed in the night, the valiant Don John was waked from his Slumbers in the kitchen loft, and your Lordship was extricated from danger, by a random Shot.

To wind up all by a moderen Instance, was not the precious life of that Illustrious personage, Spatterdash Wouldbe Esqr, Pr—s—r of the m—y—rs C—rt in Annapolis, miraculously saved, by means of his bitch Watch, || (when he was tumbled into the water, out of an overset Canoe,) not Improperly so called, long, ah long my Lord, may brave Don John be preserved, to watch over your Lordship. [414]

Finally, let these Instances suffise to show, that Great matters are often effected by mean and low Instruments, and allow me to conclude with wishing, that this here ancient and honorable Club, may never again Incurr the like danger of losing your Lordship's precious person, for, as we Surely stand or fall by your Lordship, so it is our duty and Interest to wish and pray for your Lordship's Safety and preservation."

The orator having made this oration sat down, and observing that most of the Longstanding members wore night caps, he made a short Speech upon Caps, but that being now a trite and wore out Subject to the Club, and to his Lordship, who had not yet digested the trick of the Cap of State and Box No 1, it was so little regarded by the Club, as to be thought not worthy of the Record, neither was his Lordsp altogether pleased with his other oration, because it Insists too much on the praise of Don John Charlotto, for his Lordship was one of those Sorts of people, who like much to be praised and extolled themselves, but are disgusted with panegyrics bestowed on other persons, a foible, in which his lordship was not Singular, it being a mental disorder very frequent and Epidemical in human Societies, where envy never fails, more or less to spread her Influence.

Chapter V [415]

A heroic poem by the Laureat, on his Lordship's miraculous Escape, Eulogium on the Chancellor by the Orator, appointment of a Rustic Club, Poetical Entry by the Laureat.

Xerxes, we are told by the Historians, when from an eminence he viewed the numerous army with which he Intended to Invade Greece, wept bitterly, when he reflected that every man in that vast multitude, would be

blunderbus, not loaded with bullets or Shot, have Saluted him with a volley of bum-gun-Shot, which would have made the paltry poltron fly as fast, from his villainy, as these Spartan youths ran to their duty, but your Lordship will think, I have already said enough of old women, and therefore I shall now mention an Instance of a young woman, and then conclude with a remarkable example that has happened in our own times.

The young woman I mean, is the maid of Orleans, commonly called Joan d'arc, a poor Shepherd's daughter, did not she, with nothing but a Silly tale of a Tub, save the Great Kingdom of France from ruin, and absolute Subjection to the English, and did not Certain old women, in the Shape and dress of Right Reverend Bishops and Judges, afterwards burn her for a witch, an ample reward for all her excellent Services, thus attributing all their good luck, and happy Sucesses against their hitherto victorious Enimies, to the benevolence Influence and power of the devil, happy thrice happy these Enlightened times, in which your Lordship and your valiant Don John, are in no danger of being burnt for wizzards. One more Instance of antiquity, and then I have done, was not the Capitol of Rome saved from the plunder and fury of the Gauls, by the Gabbling of a Goose in the night, a goose, that Irrational Creature, of another Guess disposition[14] than that Irrational Creature, of whatever Species it was, multipede, quadrupede or bipede, that but very lately, wickedley desperately and villanously set fire to the Capitol of Williamsburg in Virginia.[a] Thank

---

(a) *Gentlemen of the Council, Mr Speaker, & Gentlemen of the house of Burgesses,* The astonishing fate of the Capitol occasions this meeting, and proves a loss the more to be deplored, as being apparently the effect of malice and design, I must Indeed own it difficult to be Comprehended, how so flagitious a crime could be committed or even Imagined by any rational Creature &ct: &ct: Governor Gooche's Speech to the provincial assembly of Virginia, *Maryland Gazzette* No 103.

Do: Burlesqued, by Ned Type, ibid No 112.

> Lord have mercy upon us, the Capitol, the Capitol is burnt down,
> O astonishing fate! which occasions our meeting in town,
> And this fate proves a loss, to be deplored the more,
> The said *fate,* being the *effect* of *malice* & *design* to be Sure,
> And yet, tis hard to Comprehend, how a crime of so flagitious a nature,
> Should be Committed or even Imagined, by any, but an *Irrational Creature.*[15]

14. Another kind of disposition. According to tradition, when the Gauls invaded Rome, they nearly entered the city unnoticed, until some geese cackled and awoke the Roman garrison and thus saved Rome from destruction.

15. Hamilton has accurately transcribed the opening lines of Lieut. Gov. William Gooch's speech as it appeared in the *Maryland Gazette,* Apr. 14, 1747. "Ned Type" is Benjamin Franklin, whose burlesque of Gooch's speech and the reply to it appeared in the *Gazette* June 16, 1747. Franklin's burlesque and a brief discussion of the incident can be found in *The Papers of Benjamin Franklin,* ed. Leonard W. Labaree *et al.* (New Haven, Conn., 1959–), III, 136–140.

about by mean Instruments and tools, but I shall trowble your Lordship, and the Longstanding members, but with a few such.

Was not the City and State of Naples saved from a dangerous and desperate conspiracy by an old woman's oversetting an earthen Pitcher that stood in a window, as she hastily ran to look out, upon hearing an outcry in the Street, by the fall of which the brains of the Chief conspirator were knocked out, and his perfideous Soul it is supposed, went to the devil, would to heaven, your Lordship's valiant Don John, had knocked out the brains of that Lamentable villain, & sent his Soul a packing to the devil, tho it had been with a brown earthen piss-pot, and not a pitcher.

Did not another old woman, knock out the brains of the warlike king Pyrrhus with a tile, when he was about || to kill her Son, and stoped at one blow the rapid Course of his victories,[11] it were to be wished, that the valiant Don John, had knocked out the Brains of that assasin, had it been even with a brick bat, or dutch Clinker, and so put a Stop to his damnable rogueries.

Did not a third old woman, Janet Geddes by name, go near to beat out the brains of a Certain hot headed prelate with a three footed Stool, as he ascended the pulpit in the Great Church at Edinburg called St Giles's, by which pure Presbytery was established in the kingdom of Scotland, and the Gross Superstitions of popery and Episcopacy, quite Expelled,[12] This old woman, by the Change of one letter, for Janet Geddess, might have been called Janet Goddes, being as it were a guardian goddess to the liberties of her Country, and the purity of it's ancient apostolical Religion. We have reason to wish that brave Don John, had so secured this Lamentable Ruffian, as not only to have knocked him over the Jowles with a three footed Stool, but to have brought him to such another celebrated triple tree, as that at Tyburn, where many of his fellows have deservedly been suspended.

Did not a number of old women, relieve the tottering and forlorn State of Sparta, by showing their nudities in an antic posture, to the timorous youth flying full speed from the enimy, which made them for very Shame, renew the battle and come off victorious.[13] It were to be wished, that the valiant Don John, had only shown that merciless Scoundrell his Nockandroe, or posteriors, thro' the port hole, and || instead of firing a

---

11. The story is told in Plutarch's life of Pyrrhus, where, technically, the tile hits his headpiece and then breaks his neck.

12. Jenny Geddes was the supposed name of the woman who threw a stool at Bishop Lindsay in St. Gile's, Edinburgh, when the new service was introduced.

13. Hamilton is probably thinking of Plutarch's life of Lycurgus, where this role of women is described elaborately, though not mentioning the specific instance here.

no such matter—but behold, in place of Sir John, there appeared another John,—a John, I may say, the Jewel and pearl of all Johns, who, for his brave behavior in this critical Juncture deserves to be knighted, this John, My Lord, no less a person than Don John Charlotto, your Lordship's faithful Gentleman usher, or principal valet de Chambre, by Seasonably firing a gun, Charged with blank powder, and boldly exposing his brave Nob to the fire of the Enimy, saved and extricated your Lordship's honor, from this Imminent periclitation of your Lordship's honor's life and fortune, O John! Brave John! Noble John! may your praise be sung aloud to all posterity, may this ancient and honorable Club never forget the favor you have done them, and, may they give orders to Jonathan Grog Esqr, their celebrated poet Laureat, to sing thy praises, O Rare John! In never dying verse, set to most excellent dulcisonorous music, in Three parts, *Con voce,* viola, violino and Violoncello, but tho' this here Club, shall never forget thy magnanimity O most Excellent Don John! yet, forever let the villain and villainy be forgot, and sink into oblivion, and tho' Indeed, it would be Surprizing, should ever our Longstanding members forget such a Lamentable Incident, yet would it not be a more astonishing Instance of amnesty, than that of the Learned Philosopher || Messala Corvinus, of whom it is recorded in History that being seized with a deep Lethargy, notwithstanding his profound learning, he forgot his own Christian Name.[9]

But it may perhaps be remarked by some Sophisters, that this noble and heroic deed, did not fall into proper hands, and that it's being executed by your Lordship's valet de Chambre, throws a tarnish over and sullies as it were the glory of the action, but my Lord, allow me to say, *Procul O Procul esto Prophani,*[10] the meanness and Lowness of the Instrument, I dare to say, in your Lordship's opinion, and, In the opinion of all other Sage Philosophers, abates nothing from the dignity and worth of a great action, I might give your Lordship, and these here Longstanding members, of this here ancient and honorable Club, numberless Instances from History and ancient Annals of Surprizing Exploits and revolutions effected and brought

---

9. Hamilton is apparently recalling Marcus Valerius Messala Corvinus (fl. 1st century B.C.), patron of the arts, historian, poet, grammarian, and orator, but remembered chiefly as a Roman general, friend of Augustus and Horace, and proconsul of Aquitania. Pliny, *Natural History* 7.90, mentions his forgetting his own name. Hamilton may be playing with the Greek sense of the term: forgetfulness (as in Lethe) as well as the modern sense of lethargy (Isidore, *Etymologies* 4.6.5 supplies such a definition).

10. "Keep back, keep back, you uninitiated ones!"—the utterance of the Sibyl to the companions of Aeneas (*Aeneid* 6.258).

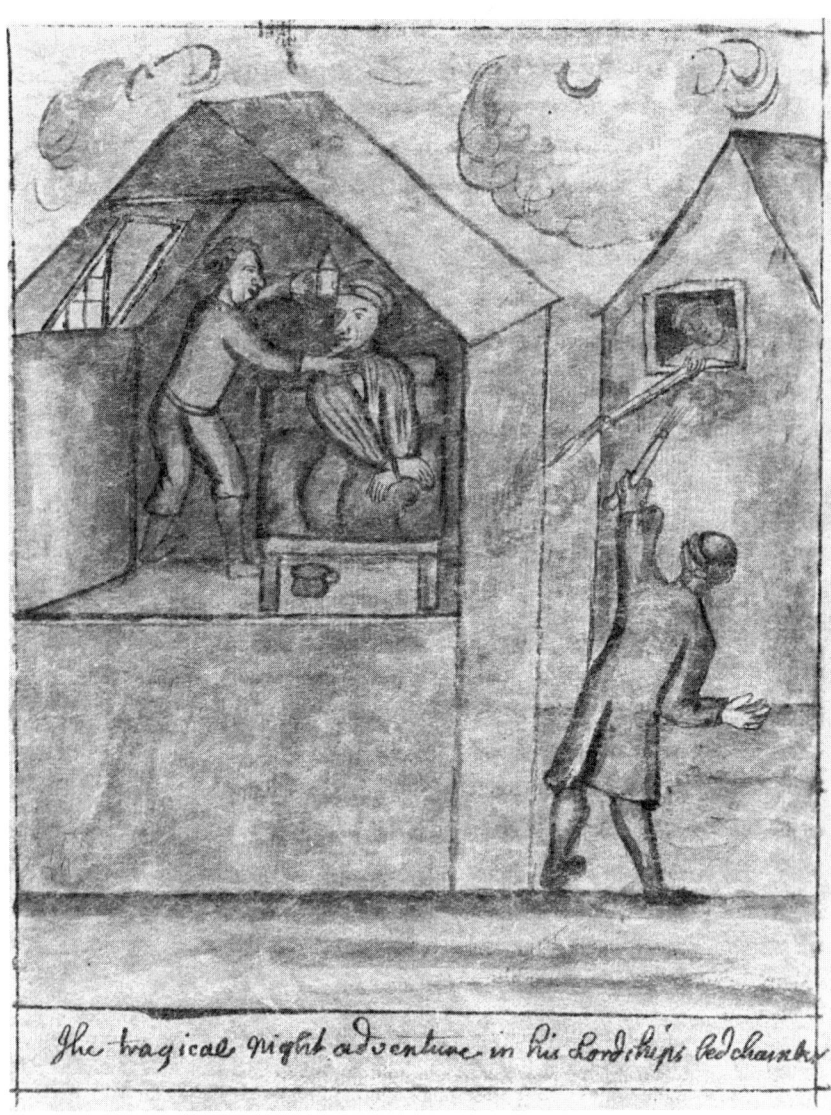

The tragical night adventure in his Lordships Bedchamber

But how do I shudder, my Lord, when I reflect upon this Lamentable Incident, how ought every Longstanding Member to shudder and stand aghast, when he thinks upon the lamentable perilous Situation, your Ldshp's ‖ sweet person was in, under the rugged hands of that merciless ruffian, what danger did this here ancient and honorable Club then stand in of loosing ah! for ever losing their main prop and pillar, your Lordship's honor, by whom alone they stand or fall—but let us perlustrate[6] the horrid Scene!

Methinks, I now see, your Lordship Supine upon your nocturnal pacific couch recumbent, composing yourself to partake of that Sweet repose, the meed and portion of the virtuous & upright, When lo! all of a Sudden, open flys your Lordship's Chamber door, and enters a most horrid, horrible, Grizly figure, armed with a pistol and dark Lanthorn, who, advancing with terrific Strides, barbarously threatning your Lordship, in Infernal accents, with death and distruction, unless your Lordship's honor would deliver your Lordship's money. This Impudence, this audaciousness, this unmatched villainy, can scarce be parallelled in history, or meet with its equal in the annals of time, nay, not even the famous villain Guy Fox, that Infernal Tool of the Gunpowder Treason[7] with his dark Lanthorn, can match the barbarity of this att[empt.] But ah! can I say it without tears! this vile, execrable, detestable miscreant, bound your Lordships honorable hands, these munificent, these beneficent, these benevolent, these Innocent hands, here, I may exclaim with Hamlet's Ghost in the Tragedy

O horrible, O horrible! most horrible![8]

Now, your Lordship, tho in the utmost peril, and upon the point of being destroyed by that Lamentable assasin, still preserved that Steadiness of mind and Calmness of temper, so natural to your Lordship in the most trying Circumstances—where then, O where then was Sir John, your Lordships valiant and Intrepid Champion, where ‖ I say, was that Illustrious Chieftan, that heroe of antiquity [here Sir John plumed up, and sat with his arms akimbo] the defender of your Lordship, and this here ancient and honorable Club, alas! Sir John was not there, [at this Sir John exclaimed, what then Sir, behold me here] but sunk in soft repose, and surrounded with the Hypnotic poppies of the drowsy deity Morpheus, he thought of

---

6. Survey thoroughly.

7. Guy Fawkes (1570–1606) was an English conspirator in the Gunpowder Plot to blow up the Houses of Parliament in revenge for penal laws against Catholics; he was subsequently executed.

8. *Hamlet,* act 1, sc. 5, line 80.

dence of the hardened Villain, yet, your Lordship not in the least ennervated or unmanned with pusilanimous fear, but, with that placid Calmness and moderation, that masterly presence of mind, and perfect command of the passions, which become a virtuous and wise Philosopher, so checked and bridled, the Struggling effervescent *pathemata*,[4] within your Lordship's noble and heroic breast that, Instead of bursting and thundering out upon him, with that Just fury and Indignation, his Insolence and Impudence deserved, your Lordship addressed him, in Civil words, and Smoothing Speeches, so as to soften the flinty heart of the rugged barbarian, and turn his rough and Savage behaviour, in appearance, to the mildness and mollified carriage, the Gentle and Courtly address of a Civil and polite Gentleman, || so that your Lordship, by your Sweet and alluring demeanor, [407] effected the same upon this unhewn piece of Rock or block, as Orpheus of old, a happy native, as we are told, of Hybernian Soil, with the Soothing Sound of his bag-pipe, made the woods, and the bogs, and the fens and the Stones of that Savage country, and even the men, more lumpish and heavy than any Stones, frisk and dance after him, Just like so many Christians, hence, the Caledonian Poet Pitcairn has well observed[5]

> *Quamvis in terris, fabulatur Orpheus,*
> *Natus Irelandis, ubi nulla wiavat,*
> *Spidera telum, neque fæda spoutat*
>   *Toada venenum.*
> *Dura Clarshoo modulante, Saxa,*
> *Et viros, Saxo Graviores omni,*
> *Et Lacus, et bogs, fluviosque et omnes,*
>   *Ducere Sylvas.*

> Great Orpheus, born in Ireland, where,
> No Subtile Spider w[eaves h]er Snare,
> Nor toad Inflate with venom dare
>   Its loathsome poison spout,
> His Sweet bag pipes he touc[h,] and strait
> Lakes, boggs, woods, rivers, on him wait,
> Huge Stones, and men of greater weight
>   To dance and frisk about.

---

4. Violent emotions.

5. Archibald Pitcairne (1652–1713) was a Scottish physician, poet, Jacobite, satirist of Presbyterians, one of the first members of the Royal College of Physicians at Edinburgh, and author of the political comedy *The Assembly* (1722) and numerous Latin verses. Hamilton provides a good translation of Pitcairne's macaronic verses, which I have not found in Pitcairne's works.

It was then moved, that the Club should meet but once a month, but this was only mentioned, and no regard paid to it.

After Supper, the orator, rising up, addressed his honor in the following Speech.

"My Lord,

Since it has been my good fortune, to be dubbed orator of this here Club, I have had the pleasure, more than once to perorate to your Lordship, and these here Longstanding members, upon Subjects very delectable and agreeable, which Communicated, (I may be bold to say) Joy, not only to your Ldshp, and my hearers, but also, to your unworthy orator himself, which appeared Evident from the Smiles of your Lordships Sweet countenance, from the attention of these here Longstanding members, and from the earnest and Emphatical demeanor of your humble Servant, in delivering his thoughts to your Ldshp, and this here ancient & honorable Club.

I hoped my Lord, that I should never have had any occasion to harangue your Lordship and this here ancient and honorable Club, upon any other Subject, but such as afforded Gladness, Joy and merry Glee, but alas! such is the unsteady, and fluctuating State of human affairs, that even the greatest and the wisest men, such, as your Lordship, and these here Longstanding members, must often submit to ‖ unavoidable cares, trowbles and accidents, Inseparably connected with human nature, and sometimes even sink under them, whilst fools, madmen, Scoundrels, and mean Low fellows, will unaccountably, and as it were, by the Capriciousness of their Stars, not only Escape and elude, the vindictive hand of Justice, but wallow in the favors of fortune, and Enjoy a full Swing of earthly prosperity and felicity, without so much as the Shadow of one single virtue to deserve them.

A person of your Lordship's profound discernment and penetration must by this time Clearly perceive, that the Lamentable Subject I am now to Harangue upon, is the Late happy, and unhappy nocturnal Incident, which befell your Lordship in bed,[3] unhappy, in the tragical Circumstances that attended it, and happy, O thrice happy! in it's agreeable, Surprizing and unexpected catastrophe, which catastrophe was in a great measure owing to your Lordships calmness, composure, and Steadiness of temper during the Hideous transaction, for tho all Circumstances concurred, to make the action perilous & terrific, Tho' great, very great was the provocation given your Lordship, tho' unmatched the audaciousness and Impu-

---

3. Hamilton presents the robbery of Charles Cole in a humorous light, but in reality the people of Annapolis were less than amused. The events surrounding the crime were recorded in the *Maryland Gazette* (see appendix 4).

This Song was a particular favorite of his Lordship's, and he used to quaver it forth with Great pleasure, Some conjectured that he admired the words, because they bore a Satire upon marriage, to which his Lordship, as was thought was no hearty friend, having lived hitherto a batchellor's life, others thought, (and more Justly) that his Lordship sung it to teize the Chancellor.

At Sederunt 159, Quirpum Comic Esqr, being H:S: and Huffman Snap Esqr, Deputy in the Chair, the Records ‖ were again miserably deficient, by [404] the neglect of the Secretary, who had now got into a careless way, and still excused himself, as having more Important business on his hands, so, that the members, now began to think, that this officer finding he had now, no manner of chance for promotion in the Club, became Careless in keeping the records, giving himself no trowble about them, he thinking, and with some reason, that it [was] a disagreeable thing to take the laboring oar in his h[ands] and be thus fobbed off, from time to time, by his Lord[ship] and the Club, and denyed a reasonable fee and rew[ard], but, whatever the Secretaries reasons were the Club had no regard to them, and suffered him to proceed as he pleased, which, when that officer found, he applied himself more carefully to keeping of the Records, but at the same time, Industriously set his brain to work about plotting of mischief, as we shall find, in more than one Instance, in the Sequel of our history.

Yet, that the history may not appear defective in this place, and a woeful Chasm be left in the valuable archives of this ancient Club, I shall here exhibit a faithful account of all I can recollect, of that memorable Sederunt, the truth of which, I am ready to vouch.

Before the deputy took the Chair, his Lordships Commission was a missing, having been, as was supposed, purloined and Secreted by some dissaffected members, but, after much talk, and Learned observation, concerning this occurrence, while some of the Longstanding members seemed angry, others astonished, the Commission was privately slipt into the Secretarie's hand, by Quirpum Comic Esqr, the H:S: which made it suspected that he was concerned in Secreting it, to the great prejudice of the Club, and the Scandal and disgrace of his office, tho' some ‖ inclining to favor [405] him, alledged that this procedure of his, was only one of his quirps or Jokes, like that which this comical Gentleman passed upon the Club, at Sederunt 142, concerning the Great Seal.

At Sederunt 160, Solo Neverout Esqr, being H:S: it was moved, that the Secretary should be called to an account, for his forgetfulness and negligence, in keeping the Club Records, but the motion was not seconded.

Records were, by the forgetfullness of the Secretary, left very Imperfect, The Entries not having been made till 20 days after the Sederunt held, and the only excuse the Secretary had, for this neglect, was his being employed about matters of greater Importance.

However, thus much of that Sederunt stands on Record, That Solo Neverout Esqr, Proto-musicus, displaid his great abilities to his Lordship and the Club, in a Singular manner, both in the musical, and the Declamatorial way, as to the first, it was thought by most, that he performed no better than usual, tho he strained hard for the prize, but, what was very uncommon, with a Gentleman of his kidney or disposition, he fairly owned, that his Lordship the president, had quite foiled, and got the better of him at his own weapons; as for the Second, he had so much of the discourse, that he would suffer no body to put in a word but himself, but, as to the purport of what he said, and the Substance and drift of his argument, (if any argument there was) neither himself, nor any body present, could give any rational account of it. This cunning officer, by this Singular behaviour, captivated the heart of his Lordship; for he first mollified him, by flattering his vanity, a thing, which even the most modest men possess a large Share of, and then, by his unintelligible Jargon, he made his lordship conceive a good opinion of his politics, who began now to think him a very proper Instrument, to establish and make firm the prerogative and power of the Chair, by leading the Long || standing members into a Labyrinth, thro' his perplexed & confused discourses, and his undaunted front of assurance, This opinion, which his Lordship conceived of him, opened a door to his promotion, in the Club, and his acquiring the dignified place, of his Lordship's attorney General, which happened, not long after this.

At this Sederunt, his Lordship, with great Condecention and good nature, sung the Celebrated ca[tch] of the *Great Bell of Lincoln,* and several other favo[rite] Songs, among which was the following.

> *Song sung By his Lordship*
>
> Says Celia to a Rev'rend Dean,
>   What reason can be given,
> Since marriage is a holy thing,
>   That there are none in heaven?
>
> There are no Women there, he said,
>   But she replied in Jest,
> Women there are, but I'm afraid,
>   They cannot find a Priest.

ball, being sometimes, as it || were capriciously taken from the plough to [401] the throne, and again, from the throne to the Gallows, as if he could not avoid being either wretched, or happy, or both.

> *Non solicitæ possunt curæ,*
> *Mutare fati Stamina fusii,*
> *Quicquid patimur mortale Genus,*
> *Quicquid facimus, venit ex alto,*
> *Servatque suæ decreta Colus,*
> *Lachesis: dura revoluta manu,*
> *Omnia Certo tramite vadunt,*
> *Primusque dies, dedit extremum.*

> *Thus Translated by a Clubical Bard*
> Our most Thoughtful cares can not
> Change establish'd fate's firm plot,
> All we suffer, all we prove,
> All we act, comes from above,
> Fates decrees, still keep their course,
> All things Strictly, by their force,
> Wheel in undisturbed ways,
> Ends are set on our first days.[2]

Tho I deliver not these grave moral observations expressly, as my own opinion, but only, as the maxims of some Certain Philosophers, both of ancient and Moderen times, yet, before I get to the End of this Chapter, I hope to let the Reader see, that they come in here, pritty much to the purpose, as our history is now soon to relate the miraculous Escape of his Lordship from an Imminent danger, which escape was brought || about, [402] partly by his lordship's own discreet behaviour, and partly by a random act of his man John, which last, if it was not an act of folly, yet, it seemed to border on it.

At Sederunt 158 June 4th 1751, Slyboots Pleasant Esqr being H:S: The

---

2. More literally:

> Our most worrisome cares cannot
> Change the threads of the spool of fate.
> Whatever we the mortal race suffer,
> Whatever we do, comes from above.
> The spindle of Lachesis observes her decrees;
> When her harsh hand has unwound,
> All things go forward in a fixed track,
> And the first day dictates the last.
> (Seneca, *Oedipus* 981–988)

the 28th of may, 1751, which the Secretary alledged, portended some dreadful revolution in the Club, & we shall soon find that he was really prophetical) and the danger which the Constitution of this here Club stood in, if so be, that the heir apparent of the Chair, *videlicet,* Sir John, should depart this life, before his lordship, by which this here Club, might be governed by a minor President.

Sir John at this Sederunt sung the first Chorus of the ode most manfully, *con violino Solo*.[2]

Chapter IV

Flourish of Mr Protomusicus, neglect of the Secretary, Speech of the orator Congratulating his Lordship's escape from an Imminent danger.

Orpheus, we are told, with the Sound of his harp Charmed the Stones and trees into motion, and made them dance, minuets, Jiggs and paspies, according to the Strain of his music.[1] Whoever believes this Story in a literal Sense, be he Christian, Mahumetan, Jew or Pagan, I will pronounce him to be but one Step above a tree or a Stone in understanding, tho' we meet with many miracles of as Enormous a Size in the popish Legends, that have been heretofore, are now, and will hereafter be believed, by many Judicious, discreet, wise and Sober Catholics; yet, this fable of Orpheus, like many other fables, that are not in the Class of Legends or Idle tales, has it's proper Import and Signification, which, (if I be not mistaken) is this; that Smooth words, a Gentle Carriage, and an humane address, will work upon the roughest and most hardened natures, move the Cruel to pity, and mollify the Indurated heart of the Ruffian and barbarian.

Again, sometimes by a foolish or Insignificant accident, lucky occurrences will be brought to pass, and Surprizing Escapes made; which shows us that human wisdom, however it may be extolled, is not the only preservative against bad luck, and misfortune, and that, when she fails, folley will take her place, which verifies the old maxim, *That the fools bolt does not always miss the Mark;* This would almost tempt one to think, that things are often Governed by an Inflexible fate, and that mortal man is but her foot-

---

2. Two pages of empty scales follow here in the manuscript where Hamilton planned to provide music for the address of the Eastern Shore Triumvirate.

1. The most popular version of this myth appears in Ovid, *Metamorphoses* 6.86–109; see also Vergil, *Georgics* 4.494.

*Address of the Eastren Shore Triumvirate,
to the Honorable Nasifer Jole Esqr,
Lord president of the ancient and Honorable
Tuesday Club*

Our noble Origin we boast,
   From mighty Jole we sprung,
Our Glorious name shall ne'er be lost,
   While Jole's great name is sung.

Your Smiles propitious Father, grant,
   And take us in your Arms,
No other Safeguard, shall we want,
   Against Sir Hugh's alarms.

Give orders, that the Great Sir John,
   Your yet unequal'd knight,
May Gird his puisant Sword upon,
   His thigh, to guard our right.

Protected and defended so,
   By Great Sir John and you,
We'll sing, and laugh, and care not tho'
   The Devil had Sir Hugh.

That Haughty President we scorn
   And slight his furious brags,
We'll march with Trumpet, drum and horn,
   And tear his Cap to rags.

This done, with Rich Lemonian punch
   Crown the capacious bowl,
In this grand toast we'll never flinch,
   A health to noble Jole.

And thus ended the Grand Special Sederunt of the Club, with Great mirth and Jollity.

At Sederunt 157, Mr Secretary Scribble, being H:S: the Secretary delivered the original Commissions of the Triumvirate and Sir John Gabble, Squire to his Lordship, and, after Supper, made an oration to the Chair, upon the honor and antiquity of the Club, The Dignity and magnificence of his Lordship, and the State members, the nature and portentousness of ominous and prodigious Phænomena, and appearances in nature, as Eclipses &ct: (there having been an Eclipse of the moon that night, vizt:

298 [Book IX]

[facing page 396]

his lordship making him a present of one of the club medals, the master of Ceremonies Invested him with that badge, and presented him with the usual form to his Lordship, who Graciously took him by the hand, and Confirmed him an honorary member of the ancient and honorable Tuesday Club.

Thus, we see how much his Lordship honored and respected the Eastren Shore triumvirate, showing repeated marks of respect to that worshipful Society and its members, and, it must be owned, that they deserved all the favor, esteem and honor, which his Lordship bestowed on them, as being always true and Loyal to his Lordship and his ancient and honorable Club, these marks of his honor's favor however, soon rendered them a Society of such Influence, and power, that their fame spread far and near, and they were able thereby, on their own proper Cost, to proclaim and mantain a war, against Sir || Hugh Maccarty Esqr, of New York, and strike a [396] terror into all the enimies of his honor, and his ancient and honorable Tuesday Club, firing of Ship Guns, sounding of Trumpets, and filling the air with Loud *Huzzas,* to his honor Lord Jole, striking fear and amazement Into all that heard them.

After Supper, at this Special Sederunt, the music of the Anniversary ode was performed on several Instruments, accompanied by a voice, the March against Sir Hugh Maccarty Esqr, was accompanied with beat of drum, while his Lordship and Sir John, sat in State with their Swords drawn, and Sir John danced to his own minuet, in a martial manner, Sword in hand.

It was wonderful to observe to what a pitch of Enthusiasm and rapture the Rehearsal of the ode, particularly the Grand Chorus, screwed up his Lordship the President, he was so enraptured, that, with a back Stroke of his faulcion, he had very nigh loped off the Secretaries Nose, for he as he passed by his Lordships Chair had like to have lost the handle of his face, his Lordsp, in the height of his rapture, Imagining him to be Sir Hugh Maccarty Esqr, aimed a back Stroke at his face with his naked hanger, exclaiming—*Ha! who are you?*—*The traitor Maccarty?* and had not the Secretary duck'd his head alittle, his Lordship had Certainly extirpated, his nasal promontory, which was no small one.

After playing and singing of the ode, there was presented in Club, an [397] address of the Eastren Shore Triumvirate to the honorable Nasifer Jole Esqr, Lord President of the ancient and honorable Tuesday Club as follows.

Nasifer Dominus Præses

To our Trusty and Well beloved John Gabble Esqr.

[394] *We,* of our Grace and favor, and In Consideration of the many || good qualities with which you are endued, do constitute, appoint, declare and Create you John Gabble Esqr, our Right Worshipful and dignified 'Squire of our worshipful Eastren Shore Triumvirate, under the Noble Title of *Sir John,* 'Squire of our said worshipful Eastren Shore Triumvirate, and hereby Impower you, at all meetings of the said Triumvirate, to take the right hand of the Chair of the Worshipful Chief Triumvir, and there, like a valiant Squire, to protect, defend and mantain, the rights, privileges and Immunities of the said right Worshipful Triumvirate, in all matters lawful and honorable, and Consistent with the honor, dignity and liberties of our ancient and honorable Tuesday Club, and also, to be a doughty and faithful 'Squire, to our right noble Sir John, our knight and Champion, so often as you attend our ancient and honorable Tuesday Club, in quality of an honorary member, in Confirmation whereof

[Great Seal] We Grant you this our Commission and
Nasifer Jole Letters patent, under the great Seal of our
 ancient and honorable Tuesday Club, This
 16th of May, in the 6th year of our
 Presidential Government, *annoq₃ dom:*
 1751.

Sig: p: ord: *Loquacious Scribble Secry*

After the reading and recording of these Commissions, Jonathan Grog Esqr, produced in Club a letter from Captain Comely Coppernose, the Club's agent at London, in which he Informed him, That the anniversary ode for the year 1750, was Inserted in the *Gentleman's magazine* for February [395] with a proper preface.[1] || The authenticity of this Letter his lordship Questioned, and alledged it was of the same Stamp, with the letter produced by the Secretary at Sederunt 144, Together with the Box No 1, and the Cap of State, and this allegation of his Lordship's appeared afterwards to be better Grounded, than the Club Imagined it at that time to be, tho, I will not expressly assert, That Jonathan Grog Esqr, or any body for him, Counterfeited that Letter from the Agent.

The Secretary then moved that John Gable Esqr, should be made an honorary member of this Club, which was unanimously consented to, and

---

1. This preface and ode never appeared in the *Gentleman's Magazine.*

please to grant his request in bestowing the desired Commissions, for the honor of the worshipful Triumvirate.

Upon this, the Secretary, by his Lordship's Command, produced in Club two Commissions, the one for the Triumvirate, the other for John Gabble Esqr, as 'Squire of the Triumvirate, which being twice read in Club were Passed, and ordered to be Signed and Sealed, which Commissions stand upon Record as follows.

Nasifer Dominus Præses

We Nasifer, of the ancient and honorable Tuesday Club, Lord President, To all herein Concerned send Greeting. *Whereas* we have an Inherent power of appointing, constituting and Establishing all Clubs and Societies whatsoever, within his Majestie's dominions of America, and, *Whereas,* we understand that our Trusty and well beloved Signior Lardini Esqr, Smoothum Sly Esqr, and Theophilus Smirker Esqr, Honorary members of this, our ancient and honorable Tuesday Club, are desirous to be Erected into a Society, and formed into a Triumvirate || under the name of the [393] worshipful Eastren Shore triumvirate of the said ancient Tuesday Club; *Now know ye,* that we, by the advice and consent of our said ancient and honorable Tuesday Club, *by these presents,* appoint, Constitute, Erect and establish, you, the said Signior Lardini, Smoothum Sly, and Theophilus Smirker Esqrs, a legal, valid, effectual and a Right Worshipful Triumvirate, under the name of the Worshipful eastren Shore Triumvirate, of our ancient and honorable Tuesday Club of Annapolis, with all the privileges and Immunities, which appurtain, or belong, to any of the ordinary members, of the said ancient and honorable Society, with power to add to your Society, such members as shall seem to you most fit, and agreeable, provided always, that due deference and regard, be had to the authority and dignity of our Chair, and that none of the other members, to be chose into your Society, shall be held or reputed as any ways connected with, or Related to our said ancient and honorable Tuesday Club, without our advice and the Consent and Concurrence of our said Club.

[Great Seal]   Given under our Hand, and the great Seal
Nasifer Jole   of our Ancient and honorable Tuesday
                                  Club, this 16th of May, in the 6th year of
                                  our Presidential Government—
                                  Annoq3 domini 1751.

Signd p: ord: *Loquacious Scribble Secrty*

[391] ## Chapter III

Special Club, by the order of his Lordship, fourth Embassy of the Triumvirate, Commissions Granted to the Triumvirate, Poetical address of the Triumvirate with music.

It is said of some, who entertain a mighty good opinion of their own deserts, That if you give them an Inch, they will take an ell; When favors are proffered to, or Conferred upon persons of this Stamp, they look upon them as rewards due to their merit, and therefore, with a pleasant Sort of freedom or frankness, they lay hold on more than is offered, Imagining, that the bestower is as much honored by their deigning to receive, as they are benefited by his gift.

We have seen in the preceeding part of this history, that The honorable Nasifer Jole Esqr, had, by sundry favors bestowed on the Eastren Shore triumvirate, elevated that worshipful Society, above others, in honors, dignity and power; his honor, once before, to serve that Triumvirate, Called an Extraordinary Club, on the 18th of September, 1750, being Sederunt 139, at which Sederunt, he showed them several Special marks of his favor, affection and esteem, and did them the honor, of creating, by his own authority a new Triumvir, in the place of one deceased, and bestowed upon them in a very gracious manner, his Sanction and protection; but not Content with this, we shall find that Society applying still for more favors, by the Interposition of Signior Lardini, their principal member, which shows how [392] Insatiable men's desires are, for honor ‖ and promotion, but, as that Gentlemans merit was very great, and, as that Society had behaved themselves modestly and dutifully, to his honor, I cannot but own, that all the favors his honor Granted them, were deservedly bestowed.

On the 16th of may 1751, was held a Special Club, according to appointment, at the House of Huffman Snap Esqr, being Sederunt 156, and this Special Club, was called chiefly to serve the Eastren Shore Triumvirate, who had dispatched Signior Lardini, as their Ambassador, to solicit commissions, under his Lordships hand and Seal for that Society; and he not having had an opportunity, at the Grand Anniversary, to deliver the purport of his Embassy, he now addressed his Lordship, requesting That, as this Special Sederunt was held to give him audience, that his lordship would

[The Grand Club Minuet con variatione, which covers the next four manuscript pages, is illegible.]

[384]

[383]

288 [Book IX]

[381]

[380]

[379]

the Tuesday Club [Book IX] 285

[378]

284 [Book IX]

[377]

[376]

[375]

[374]

[373]

[372]

[The face of the best lyrist is here depicted;
He fascinates our ears; and at his will he tempers
Our captive senses; with swift pick and finger
He teaches the strings, earlier mute, to sing sweetly.]

[facing page 355]

After the reading of the ode, the music of it was performed by several violins, a flute, a drum and a voice, to the Great Solace and pleasure of his Lordship, and Sir John, who sat in a warlike posture with their Swords drawn, while the Martial march against Sir Hugh Maccarty Esqr was play'd and sung.

Signior Lardini, a worthy honorary member and triumvir of the Club, upon account of his Ingenuity and great Services to the Club, at the motion of the Secretary, [obt]ained a request of a Commission from his Lordship, to be Chief triumvir of the Eastren Shore triumvirate, and a Speciall Club was accordingly appointed, to meet at the house of Huffman Snap Esqr, upon Thursday the 16th Instant, to regulate that business.

Thus ended this Grand Ceremony of the Sixth anniversary of the ancient and honorable Tuesday Club, which was Carried on, on his Lordships part, with the Greatest Elegance and pomp, there being, as usual, a Sumptuous entertainment, the honorary members present at this Grand Anniversary were || Signior Lardini, musician *con Stromenti* to the Club, and a Triumvir of the worshipful eastren Shore Triumvirate, Smoothum Sly Esqr, a Triumvir, Broadface Round Esqr, and Doctor Polyhistor, who seemed, more than any of the others, to enjoy the mirth and Glee of this Grand and Gelastic feast, and protested and declared in a Solemn manner, that he would never slip one opportunity for the future, of attending this Egregious Solemnity; This Gentleman was a very great admirer of mirth and Jollity, and was as good a hand as any to Join in a Gelastic Chorus, and humor the mirth of the Company, and to make one in a Clubical procession; having also an excellent talent at telling a Clubicall Story while he primed his nose well with Snuff, and took mighty pinches from the box as it was handed round, holding often a pinch in each hand; he also loved a waggish Joke dearly, and would [te]ll such Jokes with a high Gout and relish, and laugh heartily with the Company, so that the club made a very Judicious Choice, when they admitted him an honorary member, there being no man better adapted to enjoy mirth himself, or to promote it among others than he.

Let fames Loudest trumpet his actions display
While Clubs far and near their Just hommage do pay,
    Let no Janglings annoy
    His Lordships Sweet Joy,
Nor the Seeds of dire discord, his quiet destroy.
    Chorus
  To Jole each member does submit
  With mind right true and hearty,
  Allowing still, that he, in wit,
  Excells the great Maccarty.
    Recitativo
On this exalted theme, long might I dwell,
Yet not the half of Jole's perfections tell,
Should any Bard attempt to sing them all,
Thousands of volumes Sure would prove too small.
    Aria
  Hear us almighty thundring Jove
  And all Immortal Gods above
    Who all things can Controle,
  Let majesty and honor grace
  The Lofty and majestic face
    Of our Illustrious Jole.

  To him your choicest blessings give
  'Till time and fate no longer live,
    May he distinguish'd shine,
  Indulge a life of happy years,
  Till he ascends the Cloudless Spheres
    To Taste of Joys divine.
    Chorus, intended for the Grand Chorus
And sooner let the Rolling year forget,
    Among his numerous train,
  To bring this happy day again,
    Than I the Laureat,
  Its yearly rites to celebrate,
And may each Sweet Intelligence above
  Which to harmonic Sounds does move,
  When he beholds this Glittering day,
  Return with the Sweet month of may,
  In time's great dance and Chorus Join,
And warble out a harmony divine.

Chorus
Ah! Noble Jole, Long mayst thou there,
Shine out from that exalted Chair,
   Upon this ancient Club.
May no ill natur'd gouty pain
Ever Invade those limbs again
   Us of our Joy to rob.
Recitativo
Ye Muses nine attend my call,
Jole's praise to sing, I need you all,
Had I a hundred tongues and lungs of brass,
     My Brazen Lungs
     And hundred tongues
This mighty, mighty Theme would far surpass.
Aria
As when the morning Chaces night,
And Joyful day, all mortals Chears,
The Sickning Stars soon lose their light,
And only one bright Sun appears,
So our Longstanding members seem,
Like a faint light, and twinkling beam,
   'Till mighty Jole the Chair ascends,
Then all their glory fades away,
Like Starlight at th'approach of day,
   And one bright veil o'er all extends.
Chorus
To each longstanding member, he
Appoints his Station and degree
   And rules with wisdom and with Spirit,
While each beholder will allow
The most Imperious Sir Hugh,
   Submits to his Superior merit.
Recitativo, as Intended, but made the
   Grand Chorus
Long live Illustrious Jole, the Chair to hold,
May he see Centuries, and ne'er grow old.
Prop of our Club, by him we stand & fall,
He is our Glory, pride, our Joy, our all.
   Aria, Giga allegro, as Intended
Let heavens best and Choicest blessings be sent
On our most Illustrious Lord President,

the Tuesday Club [Book IX] 273

And now Gentlemen, L:St: members, look upon his Ldship ‖ the [365]
president as your benefactor, and bountiful protector, who spares no pains
to please and regale you, with the most exquisite fare, and to rule you with
a hand of mildness & wisdom.

And you, worthy honorary members of this here ancient and honorable Club, I pay you the Compliment due to you upon all occasions, and particularly on this Solemn anniversary we are Sensible of the favor, and honor you do us, in giving your attendance, to add to the dignity and Glory of this great feast, and, if your humble orator, can be of any Service or Significancy, he shall always be ready to exert himself, to the utmost of his power, to serve his Lordship, and you, the members of this here ancient and honorable Club.

When the orator had delivered this Speech, the Poet Laureat was ordered to read the Anniversary ode, which he did with an audible and Clear voice as follows.

Anniversary Ode

For the Ancient and honorable Tuesday
Club in Annapolis, May 14, 1751,
humbly Inscribed to the Right Honorable
Carlo Nasifer Jole, Lord president thereof,
and the Long Standing members,
by their most humble Servt:

                      The Club's Poet Laureat.

  Recitativo
Once more Thalia, tune the Gladsom Lay,
Sing Jole, the Club, and this auspicious day,
Exuberant Themes, whence endless matter flows,
Impart thy aid, while I the Song Compose.
    Aria
    Lo! with Triumphant noise,
  With Sprightly music's loudest voice,
  This day a Solemn feast proclaim, [366]
  A Solemn feast to Jole's Immortal name,
  No Gloomy thought, no trickling tear,
  No heart corroding care or fear,
  Approach to Cloud this Joyful day,
  But merry, merry be each Soul,
  What member here would not be gay
    Who looks on Noble Jole.

There are the Seven wise men of Greece, the Seven Sages of Gotham, the Seven Champions of Christendom, the Seven kings of Rome, the Seven hills upon which that City was built, there are the Seven Sleepers & their dog, who slept in a Cave for 500 years [Sir Jno: The devil! they did!] the Seven days of the week, the Seven Golden Candlesticks, the Seven metals, the Seven Cardinal Colors, the Seven fundamental Intervals of music, The Seven Strings of Apollos harp, the Seven pipes in Pans reed, the Seven Patriot Bishops of England, promoters of the Glorious revolution;[7] and O how wonderful is the medicinal power of this number Seven, when we Consider, that the Seventh Son is a born doctor, and the Seventh Son of a Seventh Son, an unborn doctor, but I need say no more of Seven, when I mention your Lordship and your Six Great Satrapes, officers of this here ancient and honorable Club, vizt: Sir John, The Chancellor, the master of Ceremonies, or poet Laureat, the musician, the Serjeant at arms, and the last and most Inconsiderable of them all, your Ldsp's orator and Secretary.

[364]   I would compare this remarkable Seven, this unparallell'd Septemvirate, vizt: your Lordship, and these gentlemen, with propriety enough, to all the Sevens I have ennumerated, as summing up and comprehending the excellencies of the whole, only it would make this oration too prolix, and besides, I should be cautious, how I compared you & them to the renowned Sages of Gotham, as the Characters of these Philosophers, are somewhat obscure & have not as yet been cleared up by our moderen historians, however, I may say in General, that your Ldship and they, (your officers I mean) sum up the whole group of Sevens because you have in you, every thing that is bright, Shining, beautiful, wise, grave, proportionable, grand, Solemn, magnificent, brave, couragious, harmonious and Surprizing, and as to the planetary Systems, your Lordship is like the Sun, for, as that Splendid Globe gives Light, life and vigor to every thing, in this System, so your lordship Communicates the same, to this here ancient and honorable Club; Sir John, my lord I compare to Mars [Sr Jno: Pough!—mine arse] The Chancellor to Saturn, the poet and the orator to Mercury, and let the other officers chuse each their planet, for I have not time now to particularize, the Longstanding members of the Commoners my Lord, may be said to be like the Secondary planets, that revolve in Smaller Circles round the Greater Globes, the honorary members to the Comets, these excentric bodies, who make their revolutions or returns seldomer, and whose Course is more Irregular.

7. Nearly all these sevens are identified in Brewer's *Dictionary of Phrase and Fable*. The "wise men" of Gotham were noted for their foolishness (see I, 6n); the Seven Sleepers, according to legend, slept for around 200 years (see I, 137n).

αιτιων απαντων των κα[λ]ων, δευτερον δε περι τα δευτερα, και τριτον περι τα τριτα.⁵

There is also, my lord, a certain harmony in the Number three in music, for, all harmonic Compositions can ‖ be Included in a Trio or piece of three parts, and whatever greater number of parts, musicians may add, in their Compositions, they are only Trios repeated, there are likewise in music but three principal Cords, vizt: a third, fifth and an octave or diapason, there is also, my Lord, that great Rule in arithmetic, *The rule of three,* on which, in a great measure depends the doctrine of proportion, there is likewise my Lord, that branch of the mathematics, called Trigonometry, or, the measuration of Triangles and Trilateral figures, plain and Spherical, of such Singular use in mathematics, as that, on this is founded the whole of practical Geometry, the measuration of Surfaces, heights and distances, by which we discover the order and disposition of the members of this grand System of the world; but what need I say any more my lord, about the number three, when I have once mentioned the great power of that number in this here ancient and honorable Club, in the persons of that unparallelled triumvirate, your Lordship, Sir John and the Chancellor, wise as the three magi of the east, Strong as Sampson Hercules and Milo,⁶ and fair as the three Graces, [Sr Jno: That's a damn'd lye, or I'll be shot] I have summd up in three words, all that can be said of this wonderful number. [362]

Permit me now, my lord, to say something of the number Seven, and, I must beg leave to Insist alittle longer upon this, seeing the Subject is learned and Curious, and not unworthy of the attention of your Lordship & these here l:St: members of this here ancient and honorable Club.

You will find Seven, my Lord, to be a very remarkable number, If you consult the fathers of the Church, writings of the Philosophers, historys and tracts of Learned Physicians and Chemists. [363]

My Lord, you know, to begin with the heavens, there are the Seven great Globes of this planetary System, the Seven Stars of the Heiades [Sr Jno: What! what! the Hay days!] The Seven of the Pleiades, the Seven of Arcturus, there are the Seven liberal arts and Sciences, the Seven wonders of the world, the Seven Pyramids of Ægypt, the Seven Churches of Asia,

---

5. This is, as Hamilton suggests, a philosophical riddle: "Related to the King of all are all things, and for his sake they are, and of all things fair He is the cause, and related to the Second are the second things, and related to the Third the third" (Plato, *Epistles,* trans. R. G. Bury, Loeb Classical Library [London, 1914–1925], 2.312e).

6. Milo was a celebrated athlete of Crotona in Italy whose immense strength contributed to his numerous victories in wrestling at the Olympic games and to his success in leading the Crotonian army against Sybaris in 511 B.C.

forth—and Signior Giovanni Precisio, a Gentleman, who Cut out his behaviour Geometrically, and talked and acted by exact Rule and Scale.

Supper being over, The Orator was Called upon to deliver The Anniversary Speech to his Lordship and the Club, which he did in the following manner.

Anniversary Speech

My Lord,

Tho' nature has gifted me with a very slender Genius, as an orator, yet fortune and your Lordship's goodness has so far smiled upon me, as to allot me a place, wherein the most Indifferent orator could not fail of having a noble opportunity to display his small talents, having such grand, copious and Inexhaustible Subjects as your Lordship, and this here ancient and honorable club.

With exhilerating Joy, I again see, my lord, this Gaudiferous day, return, in the Circle of the revolving year, this day! this more than Splendid day! upon which, this here ancient and honorable Club, Had its happy birth!

This here ancient and honorable Club, my Lord, now enters || into its Sentennial Æra, since established and translated to this here city, an æra reputed Critical by all learned astrologers, being the lesser Climacteric, for, the great and mystical Number Seven, my lord, is reckoned by wise horoscope men the lesser, and multiplying this Significant number, by another Significant number three, vizt: three times Seven is twenty one, which is the middle, and three times 21 is 63, which is the grand Climacteric, pray heaven your Lordship may live to see many lesser middle, and also many Grand Climacterics [Pshaw! damn the Stuff, says Sir John] of this here ancient and honorable Club.

I could Insist, my Lord, largely, upon the two Surprizing & Mystical numbers, three and Seven, as for the first, it was a favorite number among the wise philosophers of old, The Stoicks, Peripatetics and platonists made it a darling Number, under which many Strange and dreadful mysteries were Couched, we may know what high Sentiments the Divine Plato had of this mystical number, three, by a passage in his letter to Dionysius, where, as he is somewhat mysterious and Dark, I leave it to the wisdom and Sagacity of your Lordship, and the Longstanding members of this here ancient and honorable Club to unriddle, he expresses himself thus, περι των παντων βαςιλέα παντ' εστι, και εκεινου ενεκα παντα, και εκεινο

Grand Rehearsal of the Anniversary ode.

[facing page 359]

sion went on, his Lordship retiring again into [his kitch]en to overlook the Cookery, as was always his custom—The order of the procession follows.

1   First the master of Ceremonies & P:L: *Solus* waving the ode
2   Sir John and the Chancellor
3   The Longstanding members two and two
4   The honorary members two and two
5   Protomusicus & the Secretary in the rear

[359] The Grand procession arived at the Council Chamber, where the music of the anniversary ode, Composed by Signior Lardini, a worthy honorary member of the Club, was performed on many Instruments accompanied with voices, with great applause, before a grand and Splendid assembly of the prime Gentlemen and Ladies, to whom the poet Laureat presented printed Copies of the ode; Signior Lardini playd the violino primo, The Chancellor, Violino Secondo, Signior Giovanni Precisio, a Gentleman Invited to the Club performed the flauto part, the Secretary the Bass, and Mr John Gabble of the eastren Shore triumvirate executed the vocal part, with an excellent good Grace; for which good performance, his Lordship the president afterwards said, that that young Gentleman deserved to be made a bishop.

After the ode was performed at the Council Chamber, the members proceeded directly to his Lordships, escorted by Signior Phrazeobundus, and sitting down in his Lordships Court yard, some Sprightly conversation past, particularly between Jealous Spyplot Senr Esqr, and Signr: Phrazeobundus, in this Conversation abundance of little latin Sentences were uttered much *a propos*.

The members, after sitting for some time in the Court yard amidst the Redolence of flowers, fresh lemmon punch, and the Smoke of Virginia Sweet Scented, translated themselves into his Lordships great Saloon, where the Candles were light up, and his Lordship ascended the Chair of [360] State, in the midst || of an august assembly, consisting of ten Regular and four honorary members, and three Gentlemen Strangers, invited to the Club, among whom were Signior Phraseobundus, a person of a very Comic and Gelastic address, and queer Countenance, much master of Sheer wit, and Fustian Phrazes, abounding every now and then with Junks of Latin, such as *Titere to Patulæ; O mihi præteritos, Tempora Labuntur*,[4] and so

---

4. The first passage would read more correctly, "Tityre, tu patulae . . .": "Tityrus, you [under the shade of the] spreading [beech tree]" (Vergil, *Eclogues* 1.1). The second passage could be translated, "O my predecessors, the times are slipping away" (echoing several classical passages).

Third Grand Anniversary Procession

is this night, *Græcus palliatus,* and *Romanus Togatus,* a Cloaked Greek and a Gowned Roman, and, in that dress, was represented, the wisdom and valor of your Lordship, the valor of Sir John, the wisdom of the Chancellor, and the great dignity and worth, of this here ancient and honorable Club, which will florish and remain, so long as your Lordship lives, and that it may be long, is the earnest wish of every L:St: member here and particularly, of your dutiful and Zealous orator."

The Orator having pronounced this Speech, the Club gave a hum of applau[se,] and Sir John put on a frown of Contempt, and disapprobati[on, and this Sede]runt broke up, every member going to h[is own home.]

At Seder[unt] 155, which was on the 14th of May 1751, was Celebrated [the] Sixth Anniversary, at the house of his Ldsp, the president, [that] great Solemnity was carried on as follows.

The mem[bers], regular and honorary, met at the Secretarys house, in the [afte]rnoon, and from thence, proceeded, to Sir John's house, where [they per]formed, or rehearsed the music of the ode, and then we[nt in] Solemn procession, towards the Council Chamber, in [this Cit]y, amidst a great number of Spectators, Saluting his Lordship the president, as they passed by his gate, who Issued out from his kitchen back door, as the procession passed that way, and Graciously gave them the manuquassation. Signior Phraseobundus, a Solemn Grave Gentleman ‖ who attended the procession, but not a member of the Club, taking his Lordship by the hand, spoke as follows. "My Lord, will your Lordship honor this grand procession with your Lordship's company,—Tis my opinion, my Lord, that it is proper your Lordship should, to add that grace and dignity to it, which it not only merits, but very much wants to make it compleat,—do, good my Lord—'twill be extreamly obliging—and a mighty honor done to the procession—and a handsom Compliment to the Ladies and Gentlemen, who expect your Lordships magnificent presence in the Council Chamber,—and—my lord,—and—and—all that my lord"—To these courtlike words, Phrazeobundus added a Courtlike Smile, very much resembling a gelastic Grin, and sho[ok in a hearty] manner his Lordship's hand,—his Lordship, after a [brief pause, spoke ev]enly to this effect—Sir, I hope you, and the Gentlem[en and Ladies wi]ll excuse me, I am at present so busy about the n[ecessa]ry [deco]rations, for this Solemnity, that it is Impossible for [me] to a[ttend] them—do Pray, Good my Lord, (said Phrazeobun[dus])—P[ra]y Sir have me Excused, said his Lordship,—I obsecr[ate a]nd Intreat your Lordship—Sir, it is Impossible for me,—pray my Lord be perswaded—Sir, pardon me—my Ld, I'm [your m]ost obedient,—So, after several low bows, his Lordshp & Phraseobundu[s parte]d, and the proces-

drew up an Indictment, against Jealous Spyplot Senr Esqr, at which proceeding, his Lordship showed much displeasure, and o[rdered] directly a *Nolo prosequi*,³ the whole Club at this, exc[ep]t only Sir John, were very much abashed, and the Indictment was burnt at the Candle, by the express command of his Lordship, and the tryal put a stop to.

Then, the Club ordered, that upon Tuesday the 14th of may next, the L:St: and honorary members should meet at the Secretarie's house, and thence proceed to Sir Johns, whence they were to go in procession with their badges, as the majority should then determin, to wait upon his Lordship the president, and, that the Orator should deliver an anniversary Speech, as usual.

Before this Sederunt broke up, the orator begged leave to deliver an oration to his Lordship, and the Club, which being granted, he stood up, and spoke to the following purpose.

"My Lord, [356]

I have always Looked upon this here Club, as a most magnificent and exalted Society, and nothing is a greater demonstration to me, of their magnificence and dignity than their Judicious choice, of so magnificent and dignified a personage as your Lordship, to rule over them.

In all your Conduct and proceedings, My Lord, both in this here Club and elsewhere, you show yourself to be an exalted and dignified genius, and those excellent qualities and enduements, with which nature has Copiously furnished your Lordship, burst forth in a most glaring manner, in every Step of your [Lords]hips Conduct, this night, which shows your [dept]h of Judgement and penetration, and in what an easy and familiar manner you can adapt or suit your Conduct to the Genius and bent of this wise and heroic Club. Your Ldsp, as these here L:St: members may please to remember, came into Club, dressed in a Cloack and Gown, badges, my Lord, of wisdom and bravery, peculiar Modes of dress which were used by two nations, the one the wisest and most Learned, the other the most warlike and powerful people, that ever appeared in Europe, and therefore, my Lord, I believe I may safely say, the wisest and bravest that ever appeared in the known world, I mean, my Lord, the Greeks and the Romans, the first a people, noted for their erudition and politeness, who have furnished us with the sagest Philosophers, and the most famous Lawgivers, the Latter a Nation Celebrated for their arms and ‖ prowess, who spread their empire [357] over almost all the then known world; my Lord, we may say, your Lordship

---

3. That is, an action at law whereby a plaintiff or prosecutor abandons part, or all, of his suit against a defendant.

likewise to add to the Secretaries discontent, was, a Slight he received from the Chancellor, who Intending to leave the place for some time, left the Great Seal, with his honor the deputy, to keep till his return, expressly contrary to an order of the Club, which ordains the great Seal, to be left on these occasions with the Secretary, this Conduct evidently demonstrates that this Great officer, had conceived a disgust to the Secretary, and Indeed, the Latter, by his Cunning and underhand practices, had now Incurred the odium and displeasure, not only of his Lordship, but in some measure that of all the L:St: members of the Club.

On Sederunt 154, held on the 30th of April, 1751, Jealous Spyplot Junr Esqr, being H:S: and Jealous Spyplot Sen: Esqr ‖ for some part of the evening, deputy in the chair, the Club, as his Lordship did not appear this night nor send a Commission for a deputation, ordered the H:S: who came late to town, to dispatch a Letter to his Lordship, which he did, and, the messenger not gaining admittence, the Club next proceeded, according to the tenor of Law 43, (the Chancellor being absent) to the election of a deputy president, and the Election fell upon Jealous Spyplot Senr Esqr, who took the Chair, notwithstanding that he protested against this proceeding, this proceeding of his, who seldom was for allowing any deference to be paid to prerogative and power, but was in principle a true leveller, may show us how unaccountably men's opinions will alter with the times.

When the Club were going about settling some matters of Importance, relating to the Grand ceremony of the Anniversary, to be held on the 14th of May next ensuing, all of a Suden, his Lordship appeared in Club, in a dishabille, being in his night cap and Gown, over which he wore a long Cloak, which dress made him appear very awful and Tremendous, on Sight of his Lordship, Jealous Spyplot Senr, Esqr, precipitatly left the Chair, and seemed to be in a mighty great pannic, and his Lordship ascended that lofty Seat of honor.

The Club were somewhat Surprized and Shoked at this Incident, which demonstrated to them, how much terror his Lordships presence carried along with it, and some, who were Superstitiously, but not prophetically given, ‖ some time after, that is, in due time, when a man need be no conjurer, to make such an Ingenious conjecture, Imagined that messiurs Neverout and Spyplot, ascending the presidential Chair, both in an extraordinary manner, were great presages of the decathedration of his Lordship, which happened, not Long after.

The Club however, upon this, Censured Jealous Spyplot Senr Esqr, and Sir John, and some other members, being very Zealous to have him called to an account for it, the Secretary, at the request of the members

his pocket, and presented it in Club, upon the reading of which, the members, especially Solo Neverout Esqr, questioned the validity of the said Commission, because it appeared at bottom that the present year was named the 5th year of our Presidential Government, whereas it was in effect the 6th, the honorable the president having been Inaugurated on the 26th of November 1745 at Sederunt 25th, as appears by the Record, but the date of the year, month and day appearing right || in the commission, the Club at last allowed it to be good, and ordering Solo Neverout Esqr, to leave the Chair, he very unwillingly Complied with the order, and Tunbelly Bowzer Esqr, assumed it, by virtue of his Commission, this was a Great baulk on Mr Proto musicus, who began now, to set such a value, upon the merit, he had acquired in Club, as a Strenuous Clubical patriot and assertor of Liberty, that he even Carried his views so far, as to take possession of the Chair, not only as deputy, but as Chief President, and Imagined, that he could easily compass his ends in this, and have the Consent of the Club, now, groaning under the heavy Load, of an absolute and despotic power, but, like many other Self Sufficient politicians, he found himself in the end, miserably mistaken, and, was obliged to take his Station in Club, as a private member, above which degree, he did not rise till a good while after, when, by the management of Coney Pimp Frontinbrass Esqr, the petulency of the Chancellor, and his own policy, he arrived to the dignity of his honor's attorney General.

A Motion was made at this Sederunt, by a member, that the old Commissions, should be tore into long Slipes, to be appropriated to the lighting of pipes in the Club, But, the honorable the Deputy, rejected this motion with Contempt, perceiving plainly, that it was a barefaced assault, upon his Lordship's prerogative and privileges. This motion was made by a discontented member, who, having sometime before, delivered up his old Commission || to his Lordship, in expectation of a new one, had not as yet been gratified by his Lordship in that respect, and Indeed, the old Commissions, were none of them, as yet, revoked, notwithstanding the order of Sederunt 146, published in Club, by the Serjeant at arms by his Lordship's own authority, appointing the new Commissions to bear date January 1, 1750/1, This very much soured the Secretary, for, tho' he had been at the pains to prepare new Commissions, had the mortification, to see the Execution, or Sealing of them postponed from time to time, by his honor, who would give no reason for his doing so, but the Club conjectured his reason to be, that he was Jealous of the practises of the Secretary and some other politic members, this Induced the Secretary, for (not to mince the matter) it was really he, to make the above absurd motion in Club, what contributed

[350] haste towards preferrment, in some mad attempt to Jump a ditch, or spring a fence, they are thrown out of the Saddle, into the mire or dirt, and all their Golden hopes vanish; this was exactly || the case with Mr Protomusicus, as shall shortly be related, who, thinking that his great merit, and personal abilities, had so recommended him, to the favor and love of the L:St: members, (especially, as he had hitherto pretended to be a Strenuous patriot, and advocate for their liberty) that he might with Safety, and their approbation, seat himself in the Presidential Chair, boldly seized upon that Seat, but, to his great confusion and disappointment was precipitatly tumbled down, again, to his former low degree, as we shall presently relate.

At Sederunt 151, Huffman Snap Esqr, being H:S: nothing remarkable passed in Club, but on the following Sederunt, which was held, the 26th of March, 1751, Tunbelly Bowzer Esqr, being H:S: Solo Neverout Esqr, had a long winded dispute in Club, concerning his singing a Song, and, after abundance of arguments, and far fetched objections, condescended, after Supper, to exercise the functions of his office in singing a Song, and then, using his privilege, enjoined Quirpum Comic Esqr to sing after him, which Injunction he readily Complied with, saying, that he would sing a Song, which he had learned but 'tother day, in some certain place, near the Church over South river (but, with this caution withal, that it was not on Sunday) which Song was delivered to him, under the title of the *Boddily Song* to the tune of the first part of *Mcpherson's lament*,[2] which he performed [351] so well || that the Club Immediatly conferred the privilege of singing the said Song Solo, upon the said Quirpum Comic Esqr, and, that no others in the Club, not even his Lordship the President, Sir John, nor Protomusicus, were to presume to sing, the said Song, Mr Comic was so careful, that the words of the Song, should not pass into any hands but his own, that the Secretary could never prevail on him to let him have a Copy of it, so that posterity must be Intirely deprived, of this Curious and Gelastic performance.

At Sederunt 153, April 16th 1751, Prim Timorous Esqr, being H:S: and the honorable Tunbelly Bowzer Esqr, deputy in the Chair, Solo Neverout Esqr having presumptuously taken the Chair, and no Commission for a deputy President appearing, at the first meeting of the Club, his Lordship having ommitted to acquaint the Secretary, as it was usual, Tunbelly Bowzer Esqr, to the great Surprize of the members, pulled a Commission out of

---

2. This popular Scottish song is described in James Johnson, ed., *The Scots Musical Museum*, 6 vols. (Hatboro, Pa., 1962; orig. publ. Edinburgh, 1787–1803), II, 114. I have not found a copy of the "Boddily Song."

cised in smaller Societies of men, such as Clubs, and the History we now write affords a Striking instance of the truth of this. For, have we not seen riches, and wealth put to that very use, by an ambitious President, that, in order to get the balance of Clubical power in his hands, spared no Cost in the pomp and elegance of Entertainments, have we not seen a chancellor, endeavoring to compass his ambitious purposes, by espousing the Cause of liberty, and becoming a Strong advocate for the privileges of the Club, in fine, have we not seen a Champion aiming at power, by the coercive Influence of his broad Sword.

And now, if this grand defect in human Society and government, will admit of any cure, it must be done by prevention, for, after the malady has taken root, to attempt a Cure is dangerous, and may shake a Constitution so as to make it tumble to pieces.

The Cure then is only effected, by dissipating that power abroad, and not suffering it, to center it Self in || too narrow and contracted a compass, [349] that is, to prevent its falling into the hands of one, or a few, for, as power is insatiably coveted, and thristed after by all men, so we ought not to allow it to center in one hand, but on the contrary by a proper division and balance of power, and the check of good Laws and limitations, protect and secure the public or Clubical liberty.

Chapter II

Usurpation of the Chair by Mr Proto musicus, disputes in Club, Speech of the Orator to his Lordship the President, Celebration of the Sixth Anniversary; Anniversary Speech and Ode, Music by Signior Lardini.

Festina lente, is a latin proverb, which were I to translate literally, as many Starch'd pedants would do, signifies, *Make haste slowly,* but, considering, that this literal Translation in the english idiom, produces that figur[e] of Speech, properly of an Hibernian grouth called a Bull,[1] I chuse to explain it by an english proverb of the same Import or Signification, vizt: *The more haste the less Speed.*

Many ambitious Spirits in their Conduct, verify this ancient proverb, for, while, with the whip and Spur of Insatiate ambition, they ride post

---

1. A *bull* is a self-contradictory expression involving a ludicrous inconsistency unperceived by the speaker. The proverb appears in Suetonius, *Augustus* 25.

in *Clubs,* likewise evidence it. Spurius Melius, Marcus Manlius Capitolinus, and Spurious Cassius,[9] old Romans, all aspiring to Tyranny, by this Cant word *liberty,* were all popular, beloved and believed, Cataline,[10] that Inhuman Monster, had *Liberty, Roman Liberty* eternally in his mouth, even while he was plotting to overthrow the commonwealth, burn the City, massacre the Citizens and Enslave his countrymen, and Cæsar, that worthy patriot, out of Zeal for public liberty forsooth, was for sparing him and his villanous accomplices, even after they were Convicted, & yet this Cæsar, this Tyrant in grain, was a very popular man.

These are the principal arts, by which mankind are Imposed upon, and power thrown into the hands of one, or a few, by which the balance is always cast upon a Side detrimental to the wellfare and peace of the Community.

The Arts used by the Spiritual and Secular arm, in betraying men to power, I might here mention, The first carried on by the Hypocrisy and Craft of priests, the other by force & Compulsion, The first Clapping fetters upon the Conscience, the latter Compelling the will, but these are, each of them, Subjects of a much greater extent than can possibly come within the Compass of my plan, and therefore I shall not enlarge upon them. The first has enthusiasm as a ground work, to go upon, and seldom or never fails to rear a firm Structure upon it, the latter, in these our more refined times, must be asisted by the Irresis- || table power of gold, for, the truth of the proverb, is now every where known, that *money is the Sinews of war,* we therefore look upon the last mentioned power, as Subordinate to Mammon, that all ruling divinity, and by no means to be set a going to any purpose without his asistance.

And now, tho' many may think that these methods are practised only in the *Grand Mond,* as it may be Called, and carried on, in the ample Theatres of kingdoms and States, yet, if any person will take the trowble to carry his observation alittle farther, he will find them also vigorously exer-

---

9. Spurius Maelius (fl. 5th century B.C.) was a rich Roman who wished to profit by the famine that desolated Rome and, by doling out his money to gain the support of the poor, tried to usurp royal authority. Marcus Manlius, said to be surnamed Capitolinus for his defense of Rome and the Capitol from the Gauls (387 B.C.), was a supporter of the poor who probably was killed in an attempt at revolution. Spurius Cassius Vecellinus (fl. 5th century B.C.) was a consul of Rome who helped establish peace throughout Latium. Livy (*History* 6.17.1–4) discusses all three as examples of leaders who pandered to the public, which then elevated them before discarding them.

10. Catiline (d. 62 B.C.) put himself forth as champion of the poor and of discontented Roman aristocrats. After failing in attempts to be elected consul, his efforts at conspiracy and rebellion were quashed by Cicero.

his end, and acquires that power after which he bends his pursuit, for Goodness, be it genuine or feigned, never fails to create easiness and trust among men, and by trust, the people are Surely betrayed to power, their very reason being captivated by those, in whom they come by degrees to have an Implicit faith, or a Grounded Confidence.

We cannot Illustrate this better, than by taking a Cursory view, of these cunning fellows of the times, who call themselves *Patriots,* and far the greatest part of these, must only be nominally, not virtually so, for, a patriot, to take the Character in a Strict Sense, is possessor of such qualities & Enduements, as are very rarely, if ever at all to be found in any one man, hence, we may safely Conclude, that true patriots are more scarce, and therefore more precious than diamonds, whatever number of nominal patriots we may be blessed with.

The true patriot is a man of a great and generous mind, a friend to mankind, a lover of liberty & his Country, ‖ benevolent, Just, humane, generous, honorable in all his dealings with men, a hater of low, mean and Selfish arts, the Instruments of oppression, an Enimy to dissimulation, dowble dealing and fraud, he Industriously shuns all views that are merely Selfish. The more or less of these qualities any man is possessed of, so much the more or less is he a Patriot, in reality, whatever he may be in appearance; for, if he is only thus in appearance, he is really neither better nor worse than a hypocrite, but, tho a rank hypocrite, as I believe is the case with most of our reputed patriots, if men are once persuaded, that his professions are Sincere, he is in a fair way of becoming a man of great power, and Influence, and his exercise of that power, is the true test of the Sincerity of his professions. [346]

The deluded populace are for the most part misled by those dissemblers, they believe their beloved minion, is only prompted by a public Spirit, and their Good and Interest alone is the measure of his conduct—has he any Interests of his own in view? No Surely—he is an upright Sincere man in his public transactions, whatever his disingenuity and Insincerity in private life may be, all his professions are Sincere, all his harangues eloquent and convincing, his Steps and proceedings dissinterested, and his lies and flatteries, so many marks of love and truth, thus the deluded people follow their favorite leader to bondage, while he cries *Liberty and property,* all cry the same, repeating it after him, till he has decoyed them (it may be) for ever, out of even the Shadow of liberty, conveyd their property into his own pocket, and made use of the Sound utterly to destroy the Substance.

The truth of this is apparent from History, almost in every page, and recent examples in our own days, in kingdoms, Commonwealths and even [347]

[344]
>He can to Danae proffer nuptial love,
>Th'Incestuous match Accrisius shall approve,[7]
>He can declaim, write, Censure, verses write,
>And better do all these than Cato might.
>Skill'd in the Law, he rules it—wealth amass,
>Servius and Labeo,[8] you will far surpass.
>In fine; let Rich men, wish what e'er they love,
>Tis done—In chest they hold Almighty Jove.

Thus having ennumerated the great power of wealth, and applying our observations to the test of experience, what man can wonder, that Immense wealth is the shortest and readiest way for a man to secure to himself the Balance of power in any Society, but, as the wealthy are not so often to be met with, as the Cunning and Crafty, and more Especially, the wealthy and Generous, there are fewer that are enabled by this means to secure to themselves the balance of power in Societies, than there are of such as Compass it by craft and artifice.

That which is most capable of acquiring power, next to treasure, is Hypocrisy, this is a qualification, which scarce any cunning or designing man is without, but, as there are two kinds of hypocrisy, the one which covers a natural good disposition, with a Show of depravity and wickedness, and another, which hides a wicked and depraved mind, under a Cloak of goodness, we must here specifie, which of these two it is, that is used to acquire Influence and power in human Societies, and it will appear at first Sight, that it is the latter Sort, which wears the garb of Goodness and

[345] humanity, ‖ amiable qualities, that captivate and Charm mankind, qualities that have a greater operative power, than even miracles and prophesies, for, tho' the latter may silence, yet they may not convince, while the first never fails, like the Silver tongue of a fluent orator to perswade—as for the first Species of Hypocrisy, 'tis only an Instrument used by Coxcombs and fools, to show their courage and bravery, in defying virtue, as a Quality unbecoming a man of Taste and fashion, and repugnant to the favorite & reigning modes.

The Hypocrite then, who sets out on the plan of Goodness, no sooner professes himself a friend of and advocate for the people, but he compasses

---

7. Acrisius was the mythical father of Danae and brother of Proteus, whom he defeated to become king of Argos.

8. Servius Sulpicius Rufus (d. 43 B.C.) was an eminent jurist and contemporary of Cicero. Marcus Antistius Labeo (d. A.D. 10 or 11) was a prominent Roman jurist whose learning was immense, including his expertise in dialectics, the history of Latin language and grammar, and philosophy.

administer to their necessities, and further their ambitious projects, expecting by this Sort of Idolatry ‖ to draw something out of him, whereby to gratify their desires and advance their fortune—In fine, for a man to be rich, is to be three parts of the way towards perfection, gold is a cover to all Imperfections and serves as a veil to hide the defects of villainy and folly, to this the limber knee will bow, and the fluent tongue speak what the heart never thought—This Governs the muses and can purchase their voice, It softens more effectually than the most pathetic & melting oratory, and hardens more than the parching heat of Summer, or the white-bearded frost of winter—This commands the military arm and prowess, to overrun provinces and kingdoms, it breaks thro' the Strictest vows of chastity, and opens the exuberant Stores of Bacchus and Ceres,—this proves an Æsculapius[5] to a sick man, and a Pallas to an Empty brain, and love never Conquers hearts more effectually, than, when his arrows are tip'd with Gold, the ancients as much worshiped this deity as we moderns, and, we find Petronius, an old Satyrist, talking of riches in the following Strain.[6]

[343]

> *Quisquis habet nummos, secura naviget aura,*
>   *Fortunamq₃ suo, temperet arbitrio*
> *Uxorem ducat Danaen, ipsumq₃ licebit,*
>   *Acrisium Jubet credere, quod Danaen.*
> *Carmina Componat, declamat, concrepat omnes*
>   *Et peragat Causas, sitque Catone prior.*
> *Juris consultus, paret, non paret, habeto;*
>   *Atqui esto quicquid Servius aut Labeo*
> *Multa Loquor; quid vis, nummis presentibus opta,*
>   *Et veniet; Clausum, Possidet arca Jovem.*

The Wealthy man can safely sail all Seas,
And mould his fortune, as himself shall please.

---

5. The Roman god of medicine and healing.
6. This passage from the *Satyricon* (chap. 137) may be translated more literally as follows.

> Whoever has coins sails safe seas
> And changes fortune to his will.
> Let him marry Danae, it will be permitted to him
> (It behooves Acrisius to believe what Danae believes),
> Let him compose poems, declaim them, he conquers all,
> And if he pleads cases, he is better than Cato.
> As your lawyer, if he appears, or if not, you win
> And become whatever Servius or Labeo you please.
> But I am talking a lot; whatever you want, make your
>   wish with cash in hand
> And it will come; you have Jupiter locked in your moneybox.

State, mallets of State &ct: should take place in Clubs, and become alike necessary, there, as in the whole aggregate of the whole Community or Society.

Having discussed these Grand matters, I come now to discant alittle upon the *Balance of power,* I know this is a political term of art, which of late years has been very much used by our Coffee house politicians, and there has been abundance of Shrewd discourse, over a pipe, and some hot Sippings, made of roasted beans, upon this very Subject, it being sometimes made a question, whether it was in the hands of the King of Great Britain, or the king of Prussia, with regard to the affairs of Europe, and, I think it has been lately agreed by all, that the Latter has now Clenched it so firmly, that there is no likelihood of his ever letting it go again; This method of treating the Subject, I shall Intirely wave, leaving it to deeper and abler heads and pens than mine. I shall only expatiate alittle, upon the most effectual methods, that have been practised by Subtile and Cunning men, to get that Balance into their own hands, and having once seized the Scales, have made them cast & kick the beam ‖ either on one Side or the other, as best suited their own Interest, and offer a few observations and rules, towards the preventing of such mischievous machinations in Societies both great and small, which task, I undertake, purely out of the great desire I have, to advance or promote the wellfare & prosperity of *Clubs.*

By *power,* I must be understood here to mean, Influence or weight, and, by how much a man has Influence or weight, in any Society, Just so much power has he in his hands, to conduct, regulate and Govern that Society Just as he pleases, and make the balance to turn in every case, in his own favor, but, however advantageous this cast of the balance may be to himself, it can in no Case turn out to the advantage of the Society, unless he be a person of such a perfect Character, with regard to Justice, Integrity clemency and understanding, as no mortal man ever yet could boast of, hence it must appear, how dangerous a thing it is, for any single person, in any Society whatsoever to get the balance of power, in his own hands.

There are many ways, by which men procure to themselves, the management of this balance, besides the powerful and never failing way of wealth and Treasure, and of the Influence & power of this, I must treat alittle, before I proceed to the other methods, tho it be a very trite Subject.

It is well known how much the wealthy man is extolled & admired, not so much on account of any personal merit he possibly may possess, but Solely for his riches, the reason of which esteem, can be no other than, that he has in his possession, what can supply all the natural wants of men, and therefore men extoll and admire him, as one, who has it in his power to

mounted upon artificial props, to prevent her falling altogether into contempt, which would Infallibly prove the utter loss of a very profitable trade to the whole body of the priesthood. Therefore, abundance of trappings, pompous decorations and Splendid Embelishments, all under the great and awful denomination of *Holy,* have been foisted into the Ceremonies and rituals of divine worship, more with a design to captivate the Senses, and kindle up the flames of Enthusiasm, than to guide and Enlighten the understanding.

The once Roman Christian, but now the Roman Catholic Church, to establish her overgrown Hierarchy, proceeded upon this policy, and, by the asistance of her Converted Emperors, many of whom were her Gulls and fools, established herself upon such a foundation, as that she || became on a [340] time the wonder and terror of all the Europæan, and a great part of the Asiatic world, and thus Rome, who but alittle before awed the nations with her arms, now struck a damp and terror, by farce and foppish ceremonies; They began this mighty bulwark, first upon the grossest Ideas of vulgar Ignorance in the gothic ages, and afterwards fell on a method, to operate with the same charm, upon the highest Speculations of Philosophy, by exhibiting a Philtre to excite enthusiasm both ways, The first they dosed up very plentifully, with processions, & ceremonies, magnificent Structures and music, then came into religion, as things essentially necessary, Statues, paintings, an Infinite variety of vestments and mountebank dresses, figure dances, mitres, copes, chalices, candles, Jewels, purple, and all the Cathedral pomp and magnificence, by this they stirred up the vulgar Species of Enthusiasm, and having thus gained the great majority of mankind on their Side, made their Spiritual dominion firm and secure, and even, to this day, among those Churches, who call themselves reformed, we find abundance of this very farce and Ceremony prevail, and the truth is, they are become, by Custom, the Great bulwark of most, if not all, national religions, hence the necessity of them appears, and the Great Simplicity and folly of those, who talk of utterly rooting them out.

Having thus shown the necessity and utility of Ensigns and badges of State and authority, in human Society in general, I question not, but it will be granted me, that they become at times, equally necessary, in particular Soci- || eties, such as Clubs, and such associations, as are only smaller [341] branches springing from the great common trunk, for, to use a Similitude, whatever fruit is peculiar to the tree, every branch and twig of it, must yield the same fruit, therefore, nothing more natural, than, that Ensigns of State, and badges of authority, such as Chairs of State, canopies of State, Caps of

ing, and the frailties of human Nature, appear rather in a more glaring light, under loads of these vain trappings, than when Intirely stript of them, and dizened out in a plain and Simple dress.

[338] Hence we may draw this Conclusion, that as || the number of the wise is but small, and that of the foolish and Simple very great, so there is an absolute necessity for the use of these magnificent trappings and Embellishments, those mock beauties (so to speak,) to Charm and captivate human weakness, and keep the great Leviathan of Civil Society under proper discipline and order, and regulate it's motions in such a manner, as that the frantic animal may not destroy itself.

From hence also, we may draw this reflexion, which wears as much the face of truth as many things which have been preached up as gospel, that, it is not to the persons of kings, potentates and great men, Strictly speaking that the mobile pay reverence, respect and awe, but to their titles, Symbols of State, and badges of office; for it is Certain, that the words *king*, or *Emperor*, or *lord*, carry with them Ideas altogether discrepant to those excited by the pitiful mortals, whose fortune it is to bear them, for, to a person of very little discernment, the deformities, both of body and mind, that are so liberally scattered over the human Species without distinction, appear very plainly thro' all these exalted titles and denominations. Therefore a Crown or diadem, will Command some Sort of admiration and respect, tho' fixed upon the head of a boy, a fool or a villain, a gorgious Robe and Splendid train, will excite a notion of elegance and magnificence, tho' annexed to a mass of deformity and wore by a pitiful mean Spirited fellow, and a Star and Garter, will Command Respect and precedence, tho' if every man had his due, a halter would often much better become the wearer, Thus, we see how necessary these badges and Symbols of authority

[339] and || State are, to regulate civil Societies, in the present depraved and Lapsed State of mankind, and that they are not altogether vain and foolish, as some Scurvy Cynics have taught, let us now take a view of Religion, with regard to the advantages she receives, from outward pomp, Show and peageantry.

That morality has always been separated from Religion by the cunning and Craft of priests of all denominations, is now so far from being a Secret, that every fool knows it, and as the priesthood will always for the promotion of their holy Craft, consider them as distinct things, The setting morality on one Side, to stand upon it's proper legs, being furnished with excellent Supporters of its own, makes it necessary, that Religion thus robed or defrauded of her best and only Sufficient Stay, or natural basis, should be

themselves deeply skilled in the moral System, and can frame elegant discourses upon the consummate beauty of virtue, and the hideous deformity of vice, cannot possibly perceive any beauty or deformity in nature, but what strikes the outward organs of Sense, under the Influence of which, for want of better guides, they have been, and will continue all their lives Long, and therefore, it becomes necessary for politicians, or *primi motores*,[3] both in Church and State, to make use of such mechanical powers, to speak figuratively, as will move and set in play, this Great and unweildy machine, the vulgar, and make every thing go on smoothly and regularly, in the Great and General Society, and, these gross, and material tools, are their proper Instruments to go to work with, Moral Lectures and admonitions, simply by themselves, being as Incapable, to move or actuate this, this Gross and Lubberly mass, as the Gentle Breath of Zephyr, is to move a mountain, or the soft ripling of a purling Stream, to loosen the foundations of a huge rock.

From the experience of this, we find, that States Empires and kingdoms, in all ages of the world, have used the regalia, or Ensigns of State, to destinguish their kings, Governors and great men, and to strike an awe and Reverence into the vulgar, by which the Civil power, receives a Sanction and authority, and men more Easily yield Obedience to their rulers & magis- || trates, surrounded with this grand farcical or fantastical Splendor, [337] than they would do, to the wisest, best and most rational rules of conduct, preached from the mouth of a plain unornamented Solomon, Solon[4] or Lycurgus, and the only good reason, in my opinion, that can be given for it, is, that this has an Immediate Effect upon their Senses, whereas the other can only operate on the understanding, which in them, for want of proper and early culture, is rude and Imperfect.

It is principally then, from this great root of Endemical Enthusiasm, that the respect and deference, which is paid by the mobile, to princes and men in power, springs up, grows and florishes, for, were it not for this artificial glory, which, like Phosphorus in the dark, spreads its rays upon the benighted minds of the Ignorant vulgar, these potentates & grandees, would appear to them, as they really are, frail and mortal as themselves, and the major part of them too every whit as Ignorant foolish and wicked, but to wise men (the number of which I must own, is small and Inconsiderable) who see by the light of the Sun, these Gorgeous Embelishments avail noth-

---

3. "Prime movers."
4. Solon (ca. 638–558 B.C.) was an Athenian statesman and poet whose economic and constitutional reforms helped pave the way for Athenian democracy; one of his poems helped stir the Athenians to capture Salamis.

building, to which it lays it's Sturdy Shoulder, can never totter, while this present System of things remains as it is, which, I am apt to think will be much longer than some pious people I[n]cline to believe, and tho the truth of this is glaringly patent [to ever]y one from the prince to the beggar, and bre[aks fort]h at courts and palaces, as well as in Country vi[llages] and huts, in drawing room assemblies, as well as at rural wakes, and may pole meetings, y[et], because it has been a foolish custom among authors t[o i]llustrate truth with examples and Authorities from His[tory] (which by the bye often proves a notorious liar) I sh[all] for once follow the tract of my bretheren historians, [an]d give one example from History, to support this so pal[pa]ble and Incontestable a truth. Attila the Hun, In the 5th Century of the Christian Æra, having wasted all Italy, was advancing towards Rome, with Great and terrible Strides, firmly resolved her pride to Level with the ground, and drive the Holy Fathers the Popes, to shift for themselves somewhere else, and this Barbarian would certainly have executed his purpose had not || Pope Leo the great, called Saint Leon,[1] marched out of the City in pontificalibus, or dressed up in all his holy Gewgaws and trappings, in which, he made, not only a Splendid, but very uncommon appearance, which so operated on the Barbarous Chief, that at once fearing and admiring the Pope, as a Supernatural and divine being, he turned tail and quitted his enterprize; This Story, I know, is questioned by many, being thought only a popish Legend, or a trumpt up miracle, to Corroborate the truth of the Catholic Religion; and that this Pope wrought upon Attila, by the power of money, or treasure, more than by antic Shows and Ceremonies. For my part, I will not undertake to decide the thing, leaving every man to think for himself, for, which ever way it is taken it answers my purpose, as I look upon money and treasure, to be as much Ensigns of State, as any other Glittering Implements are, such as Crowns, Sceptres Globes &ct: since the latter are often bought and procured by the first.

Whoever has the least commerce with, or action in human affairs, must easily perceive the necessity of these Symbols and badges of State and authority, both in Civil and Religious matters. The mobile, which is by far the Greatest part of mankind, not being in any degree furnished, with the refined and dowble refin'd faculties of Philosophers, or those, who set themselves up, in their writings and discourses, for deli- || cate reasoners and Connoiseurs, in what is called the *Turpe* and *honestum*,[2] who reckon

---

1. Leo I (Leo the Great, Saint Leon) (390?–461) was pope (440–461) who persuaded Attila to withdraw from Italy and dissuaded the Vandals from massacring the population of Rome.
2. The "dirty and honorable."

History of the Ancient and honorable Tuesday Club

Book IX

From the grand ceremony of the Capation, to the Death of Sir Hugh Maccarty Esqr, and the mutilation of the Frontinbrassian Articles.

Chapter I

Of the Importance and Significancy of ensigns and Symbols of authority [an]d [St]ate, and a dissertation Concerning the Balan[ce of p]ower.

Mankind is divided into the vulgar and the g[r]eat; I chuse for particular reasons of my own, to name the most numerous and respectful body first, and, one of my p[ri]me reasons is, because they are the most powerful, whatever some fools, and State Enthusiasts may think, to the Contrary. These two great Classes, or divisions of the human Species, have, each, their particular ways of flattering and Cajoling the other; The Vulgar flatter the Grandees by far fetched fustian Speeches, and antic gestures, no matter how framed or fashioned, the farther from truth the first, and the more discrepant from nature the Latter, so much the better, for || truth seldom captivates the ear, or nature the eye, or pride of a Grandee; The grandees again, flatter the Senses of the vulgar, with pomp, Show and magnificence, which Glittering Structure is Intirely fabricated, or piled up with certain Splendid and Showy utensils, called Badges and Ensigns of State, which have in themselves a peculiar Charm, to attract and fix the Eyes of the vulgar, and raise their admiration (I had like to have said their adoration) to the highest pitch. This doctrine, among a very few others has the Sanction of truth to support it, a butteress of such duration and Strength, that the

List of the Members, honorary and Regular, of the Ancient and honorable Tuesday Club, from July 17th 1750 To February 28th 1750/1.   [331]

Regular members	Honorary members
The Hon: Nasifer Jole Esqr Ld Pres:	Mr Abraham Bumper
Sir John knight & Champion	Dr Polyhystor
Philo Dogmaticus Esqr Cancel:	Mr Oldham wisely
Jonathan Grog Esqr, P:L:M:C:	Mr Joshua Fluter
Solo Neverout Esqr Pr: Mus:	Mr Ignotus warble
Loquacious Scribble Esqr, Secret:	Signior Lardini ⎫
Quirpum Comic ⎫	Mr Smoothum Sly ⎬ Triumvirs
Slyboots Pleasant ⎪	Mr Theoph: Smirker ⎭
Jealous Spyplot Senr ⎪	Mr Broadface round
Jealous Spyplot Junr: ⎬ Esqr L:S:M:	Mr Roundhead Muddy
Huffman Snap ⎪	Mr Chantum Cheary
Prim Timorous ⎪	Coll: Courtly Phraze
Tunbelly Bowzer ⎭	Mr Curious Courtly
	Mr Swillum Swagbelly
	Mr Prim Laconic
	Capt: Comely Coppernose agent
	Capt: Dio Ramble
	Capt: Prettyman Spyplot
	Cone Pimp Frontinbrass Esqr agent

After a deal of time spent in this trial, and many prolix Speeches, the chancellor was called upon to pass his decree, which he did to the following purpose.

Chancellor's Decree.

[330]   I Decree, in the great depth of my Judgement that ‖ as Jonathan Grog Esqr, seems guilty, by his own Confession, of the trespass wherewith he has been charged, and, as Jealous Spyplot Esqr, seems to have maliciously prosecuted him, that both the accused, and the accuser drink off a large bumper of punch.

This Sentence was Immediatly executed upon Jonathan Grog Esqr, who did not at all dislike it, but Mr Attorney Spyplot alledging, that he had been unjustly Sentenced, desired the vote of the Club on the matter, saying that he would stand only by their decision, and not by any Sham decree or decrees, and upon the Vote's being taken he was acquitted, upon which he rose up, made a very Low bow, and thanked the Club.

End of the eight Book.

the admiring, all the gazing, all the gaping world; a Choice for which you shall henceforth rejoice and be glad; a Choice, on which only stands your happiness, as a Society, and your duration as an ancient Club; a Choice—I say—a Choice, which never had, nor ever shall have a parallel—hum—hum—and so I have done."

His Lordship then Descended from the table, the long Standing members gave another *Huzza,* and a low bow to his Lordship, who returns to them a gracious Nod, now a Cap'd Nod.

The Council ordered, that this Grand Ceremony, should henceforth be called the Capation Ceremony, and that it should be Celebrated yearly for the future, on the 18th of February, but this order was never afterwards observed,—after this the Grand Council broke up.

From this Council Philo Dogmaticus Esqr, the Chancellor, purposely absented himself, for what reasons is not known unless it was, that that great officer, was disgusted at the mighty hommage and deference paid by the Club to his Lordship, which, it is thought he could not well digest, especially as he had been witness to a Singular piece of honor and respect, paid to his Lordship that afternoon, sometime before the Grand council met, for Coney Pimp Frontinbrass Esqr the agent, Introduced a great many persons of condition to his Lordship, at a certain place of public rendezvous, || who had the honor of kissing his Lordship's hand. [329]

At the same Sederunt, on which these Capation proceedings were read, Jonathan Grog Esqr, was accused by Mr Attorney Spyplot, of a high trespass against the honor & dignity of his Lordship and his Chair, in as much, as the said Jonathan Grog Esqr, had put a heinous affront upon his Lordship, the Chair of State, and the Longstanding members of this here ancient and honorable Club, in setting into the said Chair, a certain Joannes Tomlinsonus, Chairman of a Certain Club, called the Well meaning Society In Annapolis, alias, the Saturday Club, by which the said Jonathan Grog Esqr, had, in a contumelious manner, debased and degraded, the dignity and Grandure of his Lordship's said Chair of State, and therefore, the said Mr Attorney Spyplot, Prayd his Lordship to give Judgement, against the said Jonathan Grog Esqr.

Tunbelly Bowzer Esqr, Prim Timorous Esqr, and the Secretary, were called upon, to give their evidence against the delinquent, but their Testimony was Indirect and wavering, it appearing to be only founded on hearsay.

Jonathan Grog Esqr Confessed the fact, so far, as to own, that the aforesaid Joannes Tomlinsonus, had sat in his Lordsp's Chair of State, but that it was neither by his permission or advice.

246 [Book VIII] The History of

Grand Ceremony of the Gapation

Con: P: Front: Please your Lordsp to ascend the table [his Lordship ascended the table, and sat down on a Chair of State, and the orator pronounced the following short oration.]

Orat: Ye Longstanding members of this here ancient and honorable Club, look up with admiring, yea with astonished eye balls; behold your great patron and protector, the darling and delight of your hearts, whom you can never Sufficiently exalt and honor, behold, I say, exalted upon that table, and seated in that lofty Chair of State, the honorable Nasifer Jole Esqr, Ld President of your ancient and honorable Club, a person so well formed, fashioned and cut out to rule & govern, That he is the paragon of Presidents, and the very masterpiece of art, and wonder of nature, a person endued with authority, dignity, wisdom, perspicuity, Prudence, discretion, Sagacity, Integrity, Justice, Clemency, Circumspection, Sobriety, magnanimity, generosity, eloquence, urbanity, and In short, such a number of first rate qualities, that I neither have || ability to ennumerate them, nor you time or patience to hear them all recited, qualities that make him every way worthy to rule in a presidential Capacity, this here ancient and honorable Club, or any Club that now is or ever shall be—behold I say, behold him! but your eyes will never be satisfied with beholding,—admire, I say, admire him!—but oh, you never can admire Enough, *Dixi*. [327]

Then Coney Pimp Frontinbrass Esqr, stepping with one foot upon the Table, desired his Lordship to kneel upon one knee, which his Lordship did, and the agent put the Cap upon his Lordships head, giving it three flaps, with the flat of his hand, while he pronounced the following words.

"I here, in the name of, and by the permission of the Longstanding members of this here ancient and honorable Club, Constitute and declare your Lordship, *a head of heads* (flap) *a Cap'd head of Cap'd heads* (flap) *Chief Cap and Cap'd head, of all the Caps and Cap'd heads* (flap) of his majesties dominions in America, in defiance of Sir Hugh Maccarty Esqr, and all other ambitious and assuming Presidents, in token of which, I ornament your Lordship's honorable head, with this here Cap of State."

L: St: memb: Huzza! Huzza! Huzza!

Then his Lordship arose, and sat down again upon the Chair of State, with the Cap of State on his head, while the orator pronounced the following short oration.

"Ye Longstanding members of this here ancient and honorable Club, I singly dowbly, and Trebly Congratulate you, upon the wise and prudent choice you have || made of the right honorable the Lord Jole, not only for your Lord president, but for your Cap'd Lord president, a choice, which will display your profound wisdom and Sagacity, to all the discerning, all [328]

His Lordship produced letters in Council, which he had received from Coney Pimp Frontinbrass Esqr, agent and Plenipo for the club, in his majesties dominions of north America & the Islands thereunto belonging, one from Coll: Comico Butman in Virginia, whom Coney Pimp Frontinbrass Esqr, had || made president of the Thursday Club at Hiccory hill, requesting of his Lordship Instructions how to regulate that Club, and also desiring to be Informed, if he owned the Supremacy of Sir Hugh Maccarty Esqr of New York, this letter the Council did not much dwell upon, but the other, which was from the said Sir Hugh Maccarty Esqr, to Coney Pimp Frontinbrass Esqr, our agent, and his Chancellor, wrote in an Angry and Contemptuous Stile, the council thought fit to take under their mature deliberation, and, at last, unanimously agreed, that his Lordship, in defiance of the said Sir Hugh Maccarty Esqr, should be Solemnly Caped, with a Cap of State, and the Ceremony was performed in the following manner.

Grand Ceremony of the Capation

A Great table, being placed in the middle of the Room, a chair of State was placed upon it.

His Lordship, the master of Ceremonies and the agent, retired into the next room, and the door was shut.

Sir John the Champion with his broad Sword shouldered, stood upon one Side of the door, in the Inside, the Secretary with the great book of Records stood on the other, The longstanding members in a ring round the great table.

The master of Ceremonies without, and the agent Escorting his Lordship, knock at the door.

Secret: Who's there?

Mr of Cer: One whom you will know as soon as he enters.

The door opens, his Lordship Enters, the Company bow Low, and his Lordship returns a gracious nod, || the Longstanding members march four times round the great table, Sir John shouldering the broad Sword of State, and walking before his Lordship, the master of Ceremonies behind, with the tongs shouldered, a blade on each Shoulder, The procession stops.

Con: P: Front: Ye Longstanding members, of this here ancient and honorable Club, I ask you, if you own this here Illustrious Gentleman for your Lord president?

L: St: memb: We do, we do, we do.

Con: P: Front: Are you willing his head should be Cap'd?

L: St: mem: We are, [here they bowed low, and his Lordship returned another gracious nod.]

day Club, he had erected a Club by the name of the Thursday Club of Hiccory hill, under the Jurisdiction of the Right honorable the Lord President Jole, and appointed, Collonel Comico Buttman President thereof, the agent brought with him, letters from Mr President Butman, the purport of which were, to know, if he should own the Superiority of Sir Hugh Maccarty Esqr of New York, as the principal Presidential cap'd head of America, or the grand President of Presidents, and Chief Cap of cap'd heads, he also had a letter, in an abusive hectoring Stile, from Sir Hugh Maccarty Esqr, directed to himself, in which that president upbraided him, and taxed him with disloyalty for paying so much deference to one Jole, of whom he spoke very Contemptuously, president of an obscure Club in Annapolis, These letters were the Cause of a grand Council of the Tuesday Club being Summoned, to meet in Annapolis, upon Tuesday the 18th of february 1750/1, in order not only to satisfy the Request of the President of Hiccory Hill, but to proceed in such a manner, as to humble the pride of that ambitious and aspiring President, Sir Hugh Maccarty Esqr, and let him know that the honorable Lord President Jole, was his Su- || perior, in every respect; it was [324] resolved then, that his lordship, should, at this grand council, undergo the Grand ceremony of the Capation, and he having Issued Summons to the several members, to convene in the evening at a tavern in the city, Prepared himself, a cap for that purpose, which was made of black velvet, in the plain & Simple form of a horseman's cap, or what is commonly called a Jockey Cap, having a small rounded flap before, and a button at top. The Council then met at the time appointed, and the Grand Ceremony was performed by Coney Pimp Frontinbrass Esqr, in the manner below related.

On Sederunt 150 February 28, 1750/1, Jonathan Grog Esqr, being high Steward, the Secretary Produced in Club, the proceedings of the Great Council of State, which were Read as follows.

Monday February 18th 1750/1.

At a Grand Council of the Ancient and honorable Tuesday Club, Summoned by his Lordships authority, at the house of Madonna Swashgut, in Annapolis, were present,

The Honorable Lord President Jole

Sir John Knight	Huffman Snap Esqr
Jonathan Grog Esqr M:C:P:L:	Slyboots Pleasant Esqr
Solo Neverout Esqr, P:M:	Tunbelly Bowzer Esqr
Prim Timorous Esqr, Serj: at Arms	Coney Pimp Frontinbrass Esqr
Jealous Spyplot Senr Esqr	Loquacious Scribble Secretry

of a calm and Cool temper, and plain undesigning behavior, which was the Just character of Mr Comas in most transactions of life, and, what is still more Surprizing, is this, that tho Mr Comas made himself very busy in detecting the Supposed fraud of the Cap of State, yet he was with good reason suspected to be of the cabal, when the whole Scheme was projected in his own Chamber, one evening, over a Bowl of Punch, by the Secretary and Gasperus Pickeringtonus; as for the motives of Don John Charlotto, they were no other, than an honest desire that his Lordship should not be Imposed upon, and In reality, he was the most Sincere and unbyassed member of the privy Council.

By the Constant application and assiduity of this Council of three, who were frequently shut up with his Lordship, the Secret History of the cap of State, as they || Imagined, at last came to light, tho' they never could Clearly prove their asseverations; which was, that the Secretary, and one Gasperus Pickeringtonus, had laid and Contrived the whole Scheme (they should, to come nigher the truth, have mentioned Laconic Comas Esqr, as one Concerned in this Cap Cabal, and that the Scheme was hatched in his Chamber, but political reasons, prevented the Discovering of this material Circumstance) and, that they had Concerted and Contrived, under Color of doing honor to his Lordship's Noddle, to adorn him with a fools Cap, and make him a Common bye word and Joke, and that they had Confabricated and made up this Cap, in private, in a Garret, of some old Remnants and Shreds, and passed it off as a Cap sent by the agent at London, Pickeringtonus forging, and writing a letter, as if from the agent to this effect, This Cap then, so prepared, was put into a certain box of green pine plank, since called by his Lordship, in derision, Box No 1, among a parcell of Shavings, and Solemnly presented to his honor in the Club, by the Secretary, accompanying the Presentment of it, with a pompous Speech concerning Caps, which so far wrought upon his honor, as to make him Clap this Scandalous Cap upon his honorable head; thus, the whole Secret History of the Cap of State was discovered, and, with some difficulty his Ldship at last believed it, and Conceived so Inveterate a hatred to the Cap, that he would never after see it, and even scarce could Endure to look at the Box No 1, in which it was contained, and this devoted box, became a byeword || ever after this in his Lordship's mouth, which he would always mention, with an Emphasis, when he had a mind to be witty upon the Secretary in Club, or put him out of Countenance, which, by the bye was no easy matter.

During these transactions of the privy Council of three, and political enquiries into the Secret History of the Cap of State, Coney Pimp Frontinbrass Esqr arrived from a Southeren clubical Expedition to Virginia, where, at a place Called Hiccory hill, as agent of the Ancient and honorable Tues-

Sign, for a longstanding member to hang out,—The Chief musician, as remarkable as any of the Long Standing members for a prominent beak, was ommitted || in this oration, not being in the room at the time of it's delivery, having retired, as some Imagined to measure noses, with the high Steward's high nosed maid, but, upon the reappearance of this Celebrated longstanding member, the orator framed an oration upon his nose In particular.

I am now to relate a transaction, the most Important of any within the whole compass of this Club history, a transaction, which for it's glory and Singularity, far surpasses all other Clubical transactions whatsoever, that have occurred, since the beginning of time, ever since Clubs were in being, and, if ever equalled, can never be excelled by any Club, that shall appear in future ages, upon the face of the Earth, This transaction is no less than the *Grand Ceremony of the Capation,* which I shall relate with that pomp and dignity, becoming so great and Important a Subject.

The *Cap of State,* which, as has been related, had made its exit from Box No 1, at Sederunt 144, and was ushered in by a pompous Speech from the orator, had now fallen into disgrace, and was held in no esteem by his Lordship and the long standing members, being degraded, unto the mean office of being worn upon the head of a beef Salter, to keep the ears warm, This was brought about, by the Indefatigable Insinuations and advice, of his Lordship's privy Council of three, at the head of which, was Sir John, the Champion of the Club, the other two, were Laconic Comas Esqr, late a longstanding Member and Don John Charlotto, Gentleman of the Bedchamber to his Lordship, this privy Council, was neither of his Lordship's nor of the Club's Creation, but, they had made themselves and Intruded upon his Lordship at all times, even in his hours of privacy, *congregatim* & *Separatim,* officiously || to offer their advice concerning the cap of State, at which they had conceived a rivited animosity. Sir John's motive for acting in this manner, was no other, than to make himself appear a person of deep penetration and knowledge in the Secret caballs of the Secretary, and other designing members of the Club, and perhaps, he also had a mind, to put a Stop, to bestowing any more marks of favor and distinction on the Chair, by accumulating ensigns of State upon his Lordship. The motives of Laconic Comas Esqr, for entering into this private Cabal, or Council were two, first his love for lemon punch, of which he had many a Cool draught, when he paid his visits to his Lordship, who, for the most part was furnished with Choice of that refreshing fruit; Secondly revenge against the Club, he having not as yet forgot the affair of the Comasian Conundrum; and this affords an Instance, how far the Spirit of Revenge, will carry men

the bye he never obeyed; Thus, we see into what a Slavish and Contemptible State this Club had brought themselves into by their Luxury, and overstrained Complaisance.

At Sederunt 149, the worshipful Sir John, Knight, being H:S: his Lordship produced in Club, a letter from the H:S: which was read and recorded as follows.

To The Honorable Nasifer Jole Esqr,
President of the Honorable Tuesday Club.
Sir,

As I have the honor to serve as high Steward, this night, to the most august Tuesday Club, I hope it will be *Imbellisht* with your good Company, as the *Gratest* ornament *Thareoff,* which will very much oblige, besides doing *grate* honor to Sir,

> Your most *fathfull,* honest, Sincere, trusty, well beloved Heroick and valiant knight,
> *Sir John.*

This heroic Epistle, so called, because Sir John at the Close of it stiles himself so, met with some Censure in Club, because Sir John had not given either his Lordship or the Club their proper titles, but his lordship said, that he was willing to overlook that small trespass, Quære, whether his Lordship's clemency here, proceeded from friendship to, or fear of the Champion.

The Secretary, as orator of the Club, delivered a Speech at this Sederunt, The Subject of which, was the noses of his Lordship and the Longstanding members; taking the hint from a Servant maid of the H: Steward's, who waited on the Club that night at Supper, whose nose was of an uncommon Size; He began this Speech, by drawing a parallel, between Alexander the Great and his Courtiers, (who were all of them wry necked, the first naturally, the Latter by affectation,) and his Lordship and his Longstanding members of the ancient and honorable Tuesday Club, who were all of them, (except one or two discordant members) furnished with very large handles to their faces; after giving the nose of each member a proper epithet, he drew thence this Conclusion, that for any member not to have a large nose, was a Shrewd Sign of disloyalty and disaffection to his Lordship (an Inference plainly levelled at Sir John, and Jealous Spyplot Senr Esqr, the only two old Standing members of the Club, who were of the flat nose order) whose right honorable nose was of the first magnitude, and concluded, that a Long or high nose, was a very proper and Significant

yet, would not his lordship, grant them this request, nor Indeed, would he have set them at liberty that night, even at the Intreaties of the Club, had not Sir John Insisted upon their being released, laying his hand upon his broad Sword, on which the Serjeant at arms returned to his place, and Jonathan Grog Esqr, sat down at the foot of the Table, and drank to his Lordship.

We are to remark also, that this was the first and Indeed the only time, that ever his lordship made use of the mallet of State in Club, after the manner ‖ of Sir Hugh Maccarty Esqr, for soon after, he conceeved a hatred and Contempt for that Great Club heroe, and therefore dispised all his rites and Ceremonies, on account of his disputing the Superiority with him, and this Contempt at last, dwindled away to nothing, in the firm perswasion, that there never Existed any such person on Earth, as the said Sir Hugh Maccarty Esqr, as for the mallet of State, it was provided, and presented to his Lordship by Jonathan Grog Esqr, who got the maidenhead of it himself, and Indeed, had the first and last of it, he being the only Culprit, against whom it was used, but this is not the first and only Instance of great politicians, furnishing rods to break their own heads. [317a]

Jonathan Grog Esqr observed, at that part of the Sentence, which in pity of his numerous family allows him the perquisites and profits of his offices, that he heartily wished he could find out these perquisites and profits, for, ever since he had enjoyed offices in the Club, he said his perquisites had been of the negative Sort, that is It had cost him more to compose and print the Anniversary odes and Commissions, in time, Labor & paper than any perquisite which he had as yet enjoyed (being nothing) could ever repay.

Jealous Spyplot Senr Esqr, observed on this trial, that it was carried on in too summary and arbitrary a manner, for, that the prisoner was not allowed to speak in his own defence, that, had he been heard, he would doubtless have made it appear, that he had express orders ‖ from the Club to print that poem in the *Gazette,* besides, he had not the benefit of the Jury of Six good men and true, according to an order of the Club, at the passing of the Frontinbrassian articles. These observations were true, yet True as they were, his Lordship had so little regard for them, as to take some offence thereat, which made the Club make some enquiry into the Saving Clause, at the Close of the Frontinbrassian articles, passed by the Committee, at Sederunt 146, which Enquiry was not Compleated, for want, (as it was pretended), of the original Copy of these articles, so the Secretary was ordered to bring and produce that Copy at next Sederunt, which order by [318a]

238 [Book VIII]　　　　　　　　　　　　　　　　　　The History of

Jonathan Grog Esq.r under Custody of the Serjeant at arms.

[facing page 318]

By his Ld presidentships Command, January 29th 1750/1, Sentence to be pronounced against Jonathan Grog Esqr, late Master of the Ceremonies, and Poet Laureat of the ancient Tuesday Club.

We dismiss you, Jonathan Grog Esqr, late Master of the ceremonies, and poet Laureat of our ancient Tuesday Club, from holding any Commission titles or honors under us, from the date hereof, untill the 29th of April next, and from this time forth, you are to take your Seat, at the Lower End of the table, untill we restore you to your former employments and titles, Strictly complying with, and obeying such orders and Instructions, as you shall receive from us from time to time, during your said degradation, but, out of a tender regard and Compassion for you and your numerous family, our Ldsps Grace, will not wholly and totally deprive you, of the perquisites and profits arising therefrom, notwithstanding the atrociousness & heinousness of your Crime, which, we hope will be a Caveat, to regulate your future conduct, with regard to the press, in any thing relating to us, our ancient Tuesday Club, or, any of our officers and Commoners thereunto belonging, our Records being an ample and Sufficient testimony of our proceedings.

[Privy Seal] Signed per order of his
Nasifer Jole Ld Presidentsp
  Loquacious Scribble Secrtry

After the Reading of this Sentence, his Lordship knocked upon the table with a little mallet, after the manner || of Sir Hugh Maccarty Esqr, Lord president of the monday Club at New York, and, this Signal being given, the Serjeant at Arms Immediatly took Jonathan Grog Esqr, into Custody, and he was confined a full half hour, a languishing prisoner, in a remote and dark corner of the Club room, being utterly deprived, to his great mortification, of all Comfort and asistance from the Sparkling and Enlivening bowl, a woeful and lamentable Spectacle and Example of his Lordships displeasure, and a warning to all loyal longstanding members, to be upon their good behavior.

It is to be remarked here, that Prim Timorous Esqr, Serjeant at arms, was under as great a Confinement, as the unhappy prisoner, being obliged to stand by and guard him in the aforesaid dark Corner, with his white rod of authority, over his right Shoulder, during the whole time of his confinement; and, tho he and the wretched prisoner, often begged his Lordship to Indulge them in a small draught of punch, to raise their flagging Spirits,

as appears by the said *Gazette* No 299, 16th Janry, 1751, in a presumptuous, wicked, disorderly, indecent and Contumelious manner, In direct opposition to the laws and rules of this here ancient and honorable Club, and in Contempt of his lordship's Chair, honor and authority.

Cryer: Serj: at arm: God Save his Lordship & the Club.

This being read, his Ldsp, presented the Chancellor with the following order.

To our Trusty and well beloved, Philo Dogmaticus Esqr our Chancellor.

We Command and Enjoin you, upon Receipt hereof, to read Immediatly, the following Sentence, with a Loud, Clear and audible voice, against Jonathan Grog Esqr, our master of Ceremonies, for which this is your authority and warrant.

[Privy Seal]   Sig: p: ord: of his Ldsp,
Nasifer Jole   *Loquacious Scribble Secr:*

[316] The Chancellor absolutely refused to obey the mandate of his Lordship, in reading this Sentence, as being beneath the dignity of his office, at which the Club were very much Surprized, wondering at the boldness of this State officer who durst oppose in this manner, the presidential authority, and expected every moment, his Lordshp's rap upon the table, to command him into the Custody of the Serjeant at arms, but, whether his Lordship, thro' fear or policy, was Inclined to overlook the Insult, is not known, but the Club were here disappointed in their expectations, and here, I may Justly observe, that tho' the Chancellor, at this time, was so precise, with regard to keeping up the dignity of his office, yet, at an occurrence, which happened in the Club, some time after, and which shall be related in its place, this haughty State officer, did not scruple to offer his Service to the Club, in quality of their executioner or hangman, to burn a letter of the president's to the Secretary, at which he had taken offence, The Chancellor having thus peremptorily refused, to read the aforesaid Sentence, that Task was put upon the Secretary, which he performed as follows, Jonathan Grog Esqr, standing at the foot of the Table and Prim Timorous Esqr, the Serjeant at Arms, standing at his right hand, with his white rod of office, proclaimed, before the Secretary read the Sentence

Serj: at arm: O yes, O yes, O yes, all manner of persons are commanded to keep Silence on pain of his Lord presidentships displeasure.

The Secretary then read the Sentence in these words.

besides, it is apparent, that Mr Spyplot had a political design, in writing this letter, and was now Joined in a private or Secret Cabal with the Chancellor and Secretary to flatter and Cajole the president, in such a manner, as to make him lose himself, by loseing his understanding, and so, while his Lordship was mired in their puddle, and Entangled in their nets, they might easily regain the lost liberties of the Club, by pulling down the Tyrant. Solo Neverout Esqr, acted also vigorously to reinstate liberty, but took different measures from these, that Gentleman Chusing to act above board, and not in any disguised Character, and his moving for the Restoration of the one dish Law, a Law, which his Lordship detested, was || a *coup* [314] *d'essay,* to see how much the Club had in their power, but the event of that motion, and the repeal of that amended law by his Lordship showed the Slavish disposition of the Club, in a very glaring light, however, this Gentleman, by his open and unconstrained behavior, and Strenuous opposition to the Chancellor, got himself advanced at last, to the quality of a State member, when the Schemes of the other politicians were Intirely frustrated, as for Sir John, the Champion of the Club, he looked quietly on, during these mischievous machinations, not but that he had penetration enough to see the designs Levelled against the Chair, and might, if he would, have opposed them, but like the trafficking dutch, he Chose for the most part to lie still, during hurly burlys and hubbubs, that he might share the more profit himself, &, if there was a necessity for Exerting his warlike prowess, he would then take the Strongest Side, that he might be Sure of victory.

After reading of Mr Spyplots Letter, his Lordship presented a paper to the Secretary, which he ordered to be read in Club, which was as follows.

Information, against Jonathan Grog Esqr, Master of the Ceremonies and Poet Laureat, to the Ancient Tuesday Club.

Whereas, this here ancient and honorable Club, at Sederunt, 147, January 15th, 1750/1, upon hearing of the Indisposition of his honor the Lord president, ag- || reed among themselves to compose a Certain mournful [315] poem or *Lugubris Cantus,* Suitable to the occasion, in a very concise and elegant Stile, which was very kindly and graciously accepted by his Ldsp's honor, and Committed the said Poem in trust to Jonathan Grog Esqr master of the Ceremonies, to be presented to his Lordship's honor, in a proper manner, notwithstanding which, the said Jonathan Grog Esqr, Contrary to the Great Trust and Confidence reposed in him, by the said ancient & honorable Club, before presenting the said Poem to his Lordship's honor, in a proper manner, did publish the said poem in the weekly *Gazette,*

Lordship's honors ancient and honorable Tuesday Club, to think otherwise, would not only be next ‖ to high treason, but would be a most monstrous piece of presumption, and a mere finesse of obstinacy, a Solecism in point of opinion, and would also be the same as Impeaching the Judgement of the Longstanding members of this here ancient and honorable Club, who, as they have always acted Consistent with themselves, as men of profound understanding and Consummate discretion, so, if your Lordship had not been, by far the most worthy and deserving person, in the whole posse or Congregation, they never would have pitched upon your Lordsp's honor for their bright oriental Star, to Irradiate and Enliven their meetings. Come then! O come! Thou bright Star of the North east!^(a) thou glittering and Celestial Luminary of the ancient and honorable Tuesday Club; and shine upon us this evening, with that smooth Clemency & Sweet benignity, that Exhilerating Serenity, which heretofore used to clear away from our pericraniums, the heavy Clouds and fogs of care, and exhilirate the Spirits, even more than potent Bacchus, come, thou unparallell'd Celestial Influence, come, O come, and felicitate this evening, with your Lordship's honor's divine presence.

Janry 29th 1750/1   Your most obsequious
                             Most officious
                             Most dutiful H:S:
                             Jealous Spyplot Senr.

This Letter, is so different from the usual plain Stile, and blunt manner of Jealous Spyplot Senr Esqr, that it was believed by many of the members, not to be of his own proper inditing, but that Coney Pimp Frontinbrass Esqr, (in order to ‖ lay the foundation of discord in the Club, in which discord he delighted, notwithstanding his pretensions of being a promoter of Clubific felicity) had dictated it, and persuaded him to send it; others were of opinion, that the Secretary had a hand in it, but, be that as it will, it is certain, that Jealous Spyplot Senr Esqr, could never upon any account whatsoever have been guilty of writing or sending such a letter to his Lordship, if the native purity of his manners, had not already been in a great measure poisoned, by the many bad Examples of this Sort exhibited in the Club, now for a Considerable time past, nay, ever since Letter writing was first Introduced, and, it is most true that Custom and examples, and ridiculous modes and fashions, will at last sway the wisest and the most Solid men, and lead them Insensibly into ridiculous and Silly practises,

(a) Alluding to his Lordship's living in North east Street.

good of the Club, that Nasifer Jole Esqr, a person of uncommon Cunning and penetration, might not suspect his Intentions, and, by attacking him on that Side which may properly be called the blind Side of all mankind, the most penetrating and Sagacious, as well as the most foolish and Simple, this Clubical Patriot, like he of ancient Rome, at last in a great measure effected his purpose.

At Sederunt 148, January 29, Jealous Spyplot Senr Esqr being high Steward, his Lordship delivered to the Secretary, a letter from the H:S: which, being read in Club, was ordered to be recorded as follows.

To The Honorable Nasifer Jole Esqr,
Ld Presidential of the ancient and honorable Tuesday Club.

My Lord Presidential,

Whatever Charm or virtue, the vulgar may Conceive to ‖ be Inherent in high sounding titles and pompous names, yet, your Lordship, and every man of your Lordship's consummate understanding and erudition, may well perceive and know, that titles of honor, are only rewards and Guerdons of virtue, valor and Integrity—for Considered in any other light, they are but mere Sounds, or frothy words, with which, none but vulgar ears can be amused or Captivated.

The honorable titles, which your Lordship has had from time to time accumulated upon you, in this here ancient and honorable Club, are therefore, all of them expressive and designatory of that Inate worth, valor *Rightness*(a) &c: &c: &c: so plainly conspicuous in your Lordship's honor, for, as nothing but good can come of Good, and nothing but evil of evil, so, these high and lofty titles being good, or signifying what is good and Excellent, which is the same thing, *Ergo, a fortiori,* your Lordship's honor must have in you, every thing that is Good, for, as the Saying is κακον κορακος κακον ων,⁴ or, as the Garter express it *hony soit qui mal y pense,*⁵—your Lordship's honor will forgive me for dealing so much in foreign and dead languages, but, I must make this my apology, that not any Language on earth, is capable to express, the Great magnificence, Grandure, excellency, and Stupendous Inconceivable redundancy of your Lordships honor's most unparallelled perfections, and really, for me, a puny Commoner of your

[311]

(a) Supposed to be meant, *Uprightness.*

4. This phrase was first used in a lawsuit by Tisias against his teacher Corax, the first teacher of rhetoric at Syracuse; the case was thrown out by a judge who called Tisias "a bad crow's bad egg" (*korax:* "crow") (see Aristotle's *Rhetoric* 2.24).

5. "Evil be to those who think evil thoughts."

least matter of Surprize to find these Camelions, constantly changing Color and countenance, looking Smart and airy to day, dull and formal to morrow, now living Sober and regular lives, and puking at a bumper, Then fuddling revelling roaring and merry making, now drinking Nokes's health and damning Stiles to hell,[1] Then Toasting Stiles, and sinking Nokes to perdition, according as matters of party rise and fall, in this transitory world; now slighting Peter, and not deigning him the Salute *en passant,* and cringing to and fawning on Paul, Then dispising Paul, and paying divine honors to Peter, at these Contradictory and Clashing modes of procedure, men are not [in] the least Inclined to wonder, since they know it is the Court fashion now, and has been so for many ages past, and plainly discern that the Sole Cause of this discrepancy of manners and Character, flows from the absolute necessity our court danglers are under, to flatter and Cajole patrons of different characters and dispositions, but when men of a Constant and Invariable temper, who have always Steddily kept up to the same principles and professions, are seen of a Sudden to Change, or shift Sides, this naturally Inclines men to believe, that something of Importance is upon the Anvil, and that Schemes of a higher and more Significant nature, than any within the narrow Capacity, and the nonsensical Skulls of Court Sycophants, and shallow pated Temporizers are hammering out, this was the Case with the members of the ancient and honorable Tuesday Club at this present Juncture, when they perceived that Steady and Invariable assertor of Clubical || liberty, Jealous Spyplot Esqr, all of a Sudden, turn a flatterer of his Lord presidentship, They rightly conjectured that this great man did not act this part so Inconsistent with the Character he had all along mantained in the Club for nothing, but that he had some deep designs in view to restore the Club to its lost liberty, by poisoning the Chair, and pampering up the presidential pride with extravagant doses of flattery, Remembering the Scriptural maxim, that *Pride will Surely have a fall,*[2] neither were they mistaken in their Conjectures, as the Sequel will show; for, this great and good politician, for the public benefit, Imitated the Roman Patriot Lucius Brutus, who, tho wise, counterfeit[ed] madness for the good of the Commonwealth, That these Ty[ra]nts the Tarquins, might the less suspect his designs,[3] so, Jealous Spyplot Senr Esqr, tho' a plain blunt spoken man, counterfeited the flatterer to admiration, for the

[310]

---

1. Names formerly given to fictitious persons in an action at law.
2. Prov. 16:18.
3. Lucius Junius Brutus was the traditional founder and first consul of the Roman Republic (509 B.C.); he feigned idiocy to escape death at the hands of the Tarquins, the family of kings of ancient Rome that he overthrew.

Law L. Agreed, that henceforth, two dishes of meat shall be the Standing number, every member shall be confined to, either roast or boiled, and also, there may be allowed, two dishes of desert, and no more, Butter, Cheese, and all Sorts of Garden Stuff, in their proper Seasons, not being Included in the name of deserts, and any member found transgressing this rule, shall be obliged to serve again, The Club night Immediatly following, and so, *Toties Quoties*,[4] none to be exempt from the observation of this Law, but his Lordship the President.

After this argument, his honor the deputy President ordered, the Secretary to enter this proceeding on waste paper, with this Salvo, that it shall be of no force unless his lordship gives his assent, to the same, which proposal, the majority of the club consented to, but || Solo Neverout Esqr, [308] Sir John and the Chancellor protested.

His Lordship was pleased to order, upon seeing this entry, that law Second, notwithstanding the above resolves, shall stand as it is, unaltered, till further orders, Here again, is another Instance of the Infatuation, and overstrained Complaisance of this ancient Club, to his Lordship. A great party, at the head of which was Huffman Snap, of late become a Strenuous Stickler, for the prerogative of the Chair, and among whom to the Surprize of all, was Jealous Spyplot Senr Esqr, that Stanch patriot, showed themselves fond of yielding privileges to the president, which never as yet had been granted him by the Club, among which was that great and Important one, of allowing him a negative upon all Laws, It will soon appear, what designs Jealous Spyplot Senr Esqr had in his pate, which made him act thus diametrically opposite to the Character, he had always mantained in Club.

Chapter XI

Sublime poetical letter of Mr Attorney Spyplot, Tryal and Condemnation of Jonathan Grog Esqr, Heroic letter of Sir John, Speech upon noses by the Secretary, Grand Ceremony of the Capation.

Trimmers and time Servers, being a Sort of people as Inconstant as the moon, and addicted to worship the rising Sun, moulding their manners according to their beloved patterns of persons in power for the time being, however || discrepant from those of their great predecessors, it is not the [309]

---

4. "However often."

The genius of the Tuesday Club, appearing to the Longstanding members

As if the Club had got a mortal wound,
Depriv'd of Jole, I [ween, their] Safeguard and defence.

 The Genius of the Club, beheld from high [306]
To what dire dumps, the members sunken were,
She, from Olympus Top straitway did fly
And like a Ghost, in mids of them appear,
She ask'd of them, the Cause of all their Care—
What dismal hap, my Sons has you betiden,
Compose yourselves, forbear to gape and stare,
Your Piteous case I hope's, not desp'rate past abiding.

 If my Celestial power, can you relieve,
On that Support you safely may rely,
Forbear, my Sons, forbear to sigh & grieve
—Oh! grieve we must (said they) If Jole should die,—
Woe's me (then did, Th'astonishd Genius Cry)
If Jole should die, your Glory's at an end,
But Courage, I'll back to Olympus fly,
And urge almighty Jove, the fatal Stroke to fend.

 My earnest prayer, perhaps the hand of Jove,
May stay, and eke avert the destin'd blow.
But first to show my heartiness and love,
My Sons, I'll taste your punch before I go.
Long then may mighty Jole his visage show,
In that Exalted noble chair of State,
And may he rule a thousand years or moe,
This ancient Tuesday [Club, e'er he su]bmit to fate.

 She spoke and fled—the members all uprous'd, [307]
With new born Joy, each Countenance was Crownd.
Her kindly words new Courage soon Infus'd,
And with a Smile the Sparkling bowl went round,
The hall re-eccho'd with a Joyful Sound,
And every lip dip'd deep into the bowl,
That soon all Grief in Joyful mirth was drownd,
And all the Joyful Song was, Long live Noble Jole.

 The Club at the motion of Solo Neverout Esqr, Protomusicus, began to consider of the better regulation of Law Second, relating to the high Stewards having but one dish at Supper, after several arguments pro and Con, it was at last agree'd—

ship was much Indisposed. The members began very much to condole their Case, and, calling to mind that they had been in the same doleful Situation, at Sederunt 97, January 17, 1748/9, when they wrote a Condolatory epistle to his Lord presidentship, (then his honor), and also, at Sederunt 122 January 16, 1749/50, when they addressed him in an Epicædion, so they thought fit now at this Sederunt, being the 147th January 15, 1750/1, to write something condolatory on this Present Lamentable occasion, and the following mournful ditty or Poem was framed by the Conjoint muses of the Club, which being highly approved of, it was moved in club, that it should be published, to which, the members having agreed, it was delivered to Jonathan Grog Esqr, printer to the Club, with orders to print it in his weekly Journal, with the following title and preamble.

We hope our readers will not be displeased with the following mournful lines, composed last night in the ancient Tuesday Club in this City, bewailing the present Lamentable Indisposition of their worthy President.(a)

Lugubris Cantus

In Imitation of Spencer, Author of the Fairy Queen.

> The Members of the Ancient Tuesday Club
> Sat, nodding oer their pipes, in pensive mood,
> While, at each whiff, a heavy Sigh and Sob,
> Burst forth, and eke of briny tears a flood,
> The Chair, Bereft of Jole deserted stood,
> Bereft of Jole, the Club's main prop and Stay,
> For why, In Jole, was center'd all their Good,
> And not a Sound was heard, but 'lake and wail a day!

> The deputy, with phyz demure and Sad,
> And Groans repeated Eyed the members round,
> The Champion Lost his courage fierce & drad
> And the musician, his melodious Sound,
> Each count'nance Sad was fixed on the Ground,
> And Sullen Silence spread her Influence

(a) Vide *Maryland* [*Gazette* No 299] Janry 16, 1751.³

3. Hamilton has accurately transcribed this "Funeral Chant" as it appeared in the *Maryland Gazette*, only changing *Cole* to *Jole* throughout.

Patent for Coney Pimp Frontinbrass Esqr

Know all men here and there, and every where, to whom these presents shall come, that *Coney Pimp Frontinbrass Esqr* is elected, Chosen and Confirmed, an honorary member of the ancient and honorable Tuesday Club of Annapolis in Maryland, and agent and plenipo, for the said ancient and honorable Club, in north America, and the Islands Thereunto belonging—In Testimony whereof we, by the order of the Honorable Nasifer Jole Esqr Lord Presidential of the said ancient and honorable Club, have affixed the Great Seal of the said ancient and honorable Club, as Chancellor Thereof.

[Privy Seal]	Signed by his Lord
[Great Seal]	Presidentship's order
Nasifer Jole	*Philo Dogmaticus Cancellarius*.

The Orator having been ordered by his Lordship to make an apology to the H:S: for his not attending him at the Club, stood up, and spoke as follows.

"Mr High Steward,

I am ordered and Enjoined by his Lord Presidentship, whose august commands I am always ready to obey, to make an apology from his Lord Presidentship to your High Stewardship, for his not being present at your Club this night, and, his Lord presidentship bid me acquaint you, that it is not at all out of any picque or resentment (which his Lords presidentship is of too Generous a disposition to bear against any the least of the members of this here ancient Club, far less against so eminent a person as you Sir the Honorable Chancellor and H:S:) that he has not given his presence this night, but, is Intirely owing, to his Indisposition and want of health, which prevents his coming abroad, and he hopes you will put this construction upon it."

This Speech ended, the high Steward made a bow of assent to the orator, and they both sat down.

Sir John made several ferocious distorsions of his mouth while the orator spoke, and when he Ended said—"Hoh! why so much Fiddle come farts about nothing?"

This Speech from the Orator, by his Lordships order, was a greater honor and Compliment, than ever was paid to any H:S: either before or since, and, as it was evidently the effect of the chancellors Letter, that great and politic officer hugged himself upon the Successful operation of his first Dose of flattery.

The Club was then Informed by the Secretary, that his Lord president-

would have been Irresistable, and beg leave to subscribe myself, my Lord,

> Your Lord presidentship's
> Most dutiful obedient Chancellor
> and humble Servant
> *Philo Dogmaticus.*

It may seem Strange to many, that this adulatory Epistle, this puffed up piece of fustian, should come from the hands of the chancellor, who was a plain spoken man & not in the least degree addicted to flattery, but his design in writing this letter, may easily be seen thro', and in this we have a glaring Instance, how apt your ambitious and politic men are to fall into dissimulation, and how they will hypocrise to promote their own Grandure, while || in other concerns, they are remarkable for their Sincerity and plainness. The Chancellor knew very well, that the Honorable Nasifer Jole Esqr, was come to his akme of power and pride, and, like a ripened Impostume, he was Just ready to burst, so full was he of prerogative and lofty titles, and therefore he Judged wisely, that the adding a triffle more to the quantum would bring his overswoln Glory to a Chrisis, and break the Inflated tumor, for which reason, he wrote this letter with a design, Intirely to turn his Lordships head, that he might in this fit of Infatuation, the more easily pull him down, and it was not long after, that he effected this devlish project.

There were then delivered in Club by the Secretary, two papers, which were ordered to be recorded as follows.

To Philo Dogmaticus Esqr,
Chancellor of the ancient Tuesday Club.

We hereby order and Command you, Philo Dogmaticus Esqr, our Chancellor, and keeper of our political Conscience, to deliver, under your hand, and the Great Seal of our ancient and honorable Tuesday Club, a full, ample, and effectual testificate testifying and Importing, that our Good friend and well wisher, Coney Pimp Frontinbrass Esqr, has been chosen, elected, confirmed, and appointed, an honorary member of our ancient and honorable Tuesday Club, and our agent and Plenipo' for us, and our said ancient and honorable Club, in north America, and the Islands thereunto pertaining.

[Privy Seal]   Given under our Privy Seal, this 1st of
Nasifer Jole   Janry, 1750/1, in the 6th year of our
           Presidential dominion.

Sig: pr: ordr: *Loquacious Scribble Secrt:*

mouths, as Mahomet and his Arabs did among the Greeks and Asiatics with the Sound of Alla, Alla and his prophet. By this Aurenzebe[1] made himself master of the opulent Mogul Empire, in prejudice of his elder brothers, in fine, by this Nasifer Jole Esqr, made himself absolute over the ancient and honorable Tuesday Club, and over many other Clubs on the Northeren Continent, of America, particularly the Hiccory hill Club,[2] and the Eastren Shore Triumvirate.

At Sederunt 147, January 15th 1750/1, Philo dogmaticus Esqr being, for the first time, since he was Elected into the Club, High Steward (an Indulgence which never was granted, to any of the Longstanding members, but himself, vizt: to be allowed to attend the Club as a regular member for 27 Sederunts successively without once serving) and Huffman Snap Esqr, deputy in the Chair, a letter was produced in Club from the high Steward to his Lord presidentship, which being read was recorded as follows.

To The honorable Nasifer Jole Esqr,
Lord President of the Tuesday Club.

My Lord president,

Your Lordship's ancient Tuesday Club, being appointed to meet at my house this evening, I expect and request the honor of your magnificent presence, so necessary to the Solemnity, order and pleasure of our Society, I could, according || to custom, expatiate upon your Lordship's distinguished [301] and unparallelled Qualities for the high State *this here Club* has advanced you to, but that fact, being the Judgement of a most Sagacious and discerning body of men, shows your Lordship in a light that confounds all Imagination and, would make all Eulogical attempts, even from the God of Eloquence himself, an affront, or, if the good Intention of it, should save that misfortune to the author, from a person of your Candor and benevolence, it would reflect upon his understanding to offer any description or Commendation of what, by the confession of all the world who have heard of the ancient Tuesday Club, and their Illustrious head, is both Ineffable and Inconceivable.

For my own Sake therefore, and not to offend your excellent perception and delicate ear, I restrain the Impetus, which, without that motive,

---

1. Aurangzeb (1618–1707), sixth emperor of Hindustan, caused the death of his three brothers and styled himself Conqueror of the World. Hamilton is probably borrowing his information from Dryden's tragedy *Aureng-Zebe* (1676).

2. Hamilton's repeated references to this club suggest that it actually existed, but I have not found any further information on it.

O yes, O yes, O yes, it is his Lordship's pleasure, that all Commissions shall stand Good till further orders.

Then his Lord presidentship Commanded the Secretary to draw out new Commissions for all the officers of the Club, bearing date January 1, 1751, but Circumstances so fell out afterwards, by means of a hot Rebellion in Club, excited by the Chancellor, that these new Commissions, tho all punctually prepared were never Sealed, and remain now unsealed in his Lordship's hands.

It was then ordered, that when any Cause is to be tried, there shall be chose from among the members by ballot a Jury || of Six good men and true,—this order was never in any one case complied with.

Then his Lord presidentship, Graciously granted to Coney pimp Frontinbrass Esqr, for his Signal Services to the Club, (or rather to himself in contributing to render him absolute) a full testificate, under the Great Seal and privy Seal at arms, of his being an honorary member of the Club, and also, constituting him agent and Plenipo for the Club at New York, and over all the British Continent and Islands of America.

Chapter X

Coney Pimp Frontinbrass Esqr's patent Sealed and delivered, Lugubris Cantus, by the Club, dispute upon Law Second, not determined.

That pestilent and headstrong passion of Enthusiasm, the Seeds of which are universally disseminated in human Nature, is the Chief Instrument in Enslaving mankind, and reducing those that before were a free and generous people to worse than Common pack horses, or beasts of burden, This is capable to be set to work and kindled up, by certain devices and operations, well known to Cunning and politic men, and breaks out as suddenly as fire does, by the Collision of Steel and flint. The truth of this is well known to all ambitious politicians, and religious Impostures, and large and firm foundations of grandure and power, have been laid upon this single human folly, The notorious Imposture Mahumet, by this device alone, from a despicable Camel driver, made himself a great king, and laid the foundation of a || vast empire. Cromwels roundheads, in our general Rebellion, by means of this frantic fury routed the Cavaliers or Royalists, and bore every thing before him as effectually with a Psalm tune in their

[Look upon the stern face of our Lictor,
Who always attends to your orders, Jole.
Woe to wretched offenders when he is swelling with savage bile,
Who suffer the penalty of enchainment under his pitiless hand.]

[facing page 298]

to his honor the president (now his Lordship) more high privileges and powers, than had as yet been given him, since the first Institution of the Club; and tho' Jealous Spyplot Senr Esqr, who was concerned in drawing up the articles, had Incerted the Concluding Clause, as a Salvo for the liberties of the Club, and thought that he had by that means rendered the preceeding articles of little or no effect; yet the Club went into the Strict observation of every one of them, so much were they Infatuated and blinded to their own hurt; The Articles, contrived by the Cunning and policy of Coney Pimp Frontinbrass Esqr, were furthered, promoted and recommended by the diligence of the Secretary, who never was at rest, till he had them passed; the views of the first, it was thought by some, were hereby to flatter the President, and by others, merely to create fun, by laying the foundation of hubbubs and hurly burlys in the Club; the design of the Latter was to Check the growing power and ambition of the Chancellor (however he might pretend a regard to the president) which great officer, now, was a perfect bar or obstruction to his ever rising to any high dignity in the Club, the effect of these machinations, was, that the president became in a manner absolute, and the Chancellor Conceived an Inveterate hatred for Coney Pimp Frontinbrass Esqr, as the obstructer of his prospects and Schemes, and never could afterwards endure him, tho he was the Person that first Introduced him into the Club.

It may Probably be thought by some, that his honor the || President, acted somewhat out of Character, when he requested the expunging of the fifth article, it being a thing very uncommon with him to refuse any the least addition to his power, but we must consider, that by this concession, he was really no loser, since by the tenor of the preceeding Article 4to the Commissions were annually renewable, and he had it then in his power to change the person of the officer.

There arose some discourse in club, after the passing of the articles, concerning who should be appointed Serjeant at arms, during which, his Lordship drank to Prim Timorous Esqr, who was thereby constituted his Lordships Serjeant at arms, according to article 8vo, and the Secretary was ordered to prepare and draw up a Commission for him, but this Commission was never to this day drawn out.

Then the Serjeant at arms proclaimed in the manner following.

O yes, O yes, O yes, all manner of persons, are Commanded to keep Silence on pain of his lordship's displeasure.

Silence being made, the Serjeant at arms proceeded to make another O yes.

cient Tuesday Club, and every officer thereof, shall be Called, his Lord Presidentship's officer.

4to   That all Commissions shall be annually renewed || and the [296] persons appointed, at the Sole pleasure, and by the nomination of his Lord Presidentship, which shall be signified, by his Lord presidentship's drinking to the person, by name and title whom he Intends to promote.

5to   [The 5th article, by order of the committee, and at the particular desire of his Lordship, who modestly declined such an extent of power, was left out.]

6to   That on anniversary days, and every first Club night of the new year, every member, shall have the honor of kissing his Lord presidentship's hand, at the same time, offering the Compliments of the Season, to his Lord presidentship, this last article, to be an unalterable privilege of the Club.

7mo   That every person admitted as a visitor, honorary, or fixed member, may, as a privilege, have the honor of kissing his Lord Presidentship's hand.

8vo   That there shall be appointed from among the Commoners, an officer, called, his Lord Presidentship's Serjeant at arms, who, by the order of his lord presidentship, shall take all offending members into Custody, and them safely keep, in such place, as his Lord presidentship shall appoint, during his Lord Presidentship's pleasure.

9mo   That his Lord presidentship shall have a mallet, to Command Silence, on the Sound of which, The third time at most, whosoever is refractory, shall be taken into Immediate custody if his lord presidentship shall think proper.

10mo   That every cause, that may be determined by his honor the Chancellor, may be carried by appeal to his Lord presidentship, who may finally determin the same.

11mo   Lastly the above articles, are humbly offered with a Salvo, that all former, natural and political rights and || privileges, of [297] the State officers and commoners of this here ancient club, shall be Strictly observed.

The Club having confirmed the Report of the Committee, the above articles stood in full force, and henceforth were deemed as a Law of the Club.

Thus were passed the Frontinbrassian Articles, by which, were Ceded

Great Britain, it was Lodged in the hands of the proceres or primates,[3] and in the king Lords and Commons, and in a democracy in the Collective body of the people, and, that this here Club, by their Late tumultuous proceedings, had plainly showed, that they were not fit to be trusted with a democratical power, *Ergo, a fortiori,* the Sole power ought to be lodged in his honor the president.

Some of the members alledging, that this was a reflexion on the Club, Coney Pimp Frontinbrass Esqr, pretended to take affront at this, and was seemingly going to leave the Club in an abrupt manner, but, before matters came to that extremity, his honor the president, and the members, permitted him to retire with the Secretary into another room, where, having drawn up Certain articles, they returned into the Club Room, Conducted by Jonathan Grog Esqr, Master of Ceremonies, and presented the Articles to his honor, the president, and the Club, requesting that ‖ they might Immediatly be taken under Consideration, and the members accordingly resolving themselves into a Committee of the whole Club, (his honor still keeping the Chair of State) chose Tunbelly Bowzer Esqr, Chairman of the Committee, and, after considering them *articulatim,* delivered by the mouth of their Clerk, to his honor and the Club, the following report.

Report of the Committee

Your Committee after mature deliberation have determined and agreed, that all the articles contained in the Schedule presented to your honor and the club, shall stand, with the amendments thereunto made by your Committee, except the article 5to Running to this purpose, "That when any of his Lordships officers misbehave, his lordship shall have a power to degrade them *ab officio,* and appoint others in their Room"—which article, your Committee has expunged.

Signed *Tunbelly Bowzer Chairman.*

The Articles Presented by Coney Pimp Frontinbrass Esqr, allowed by the Committee.

Law XLIX. 1mo   That his honor the President, for the future, in Club-time, shall be called my Lord Presidential.

2do   That he shall have an unlimited power to do all the good he can to his Club.

3tio   Which Club, shall be called his Lord Presidentship's an-

---

3. In this context *primates* means "men of the first rank or importance"; *proceres,* too, means "leading men, chiefs, or nobles."

letters, tho' the Secretary long before gave him that title in Sir John's Indictment,) humbly requesting That his Lordship would permit him to propose some articles, for the right regulation and government of the ancient Tuesday Club, which, he found to his great Sorrow and Concern, was in the utmost confusion, and ready to sink into anarchy and ruin, But, as the Scheme he proposed, had a tendency to locate all the power and authority in his honor the President alone, Jealous Spyplot Senr Esqr stood up and opposed his arguments, alledging That it was dangerous to trust the Sole authority and power, in the hands of a single person, and arguing, that power was Justly and properly fixed in the whole body, and that the members, if they pleased, had power to pull out the eyes of the head, and therefore, he declared, that he was for a republican, and not a monarchical government in this here Club—The Secretary then urged, in opposition to Jealous Spyplot Esqr, That Republican governments were always the most dangerous, and tumultous, and Instanced, the condition of old Rome, in the Time of the Gracch, Marius, Sulla, the Tribunitial and Dictatorial powers & the decemviri,[2] the many massacres and murders, and the Confused and fluctuating condition of the Commonwealth, which Continued till Julius seized the Monarchy, & Augustus settled it, and then, by the wise Government of some of the Emperors, that Empire arived to a greater pitch of Grandure and magnificence than ever, and was more at rest from intestine broils. The Chancellor then spoke alittle on the other Side of the argument || and alledged, that tho monarchy was the best form of Government, yet, it was upon this Supposition, that the head was Sound and Solid, therefore, the members of this here ancient Club, ought to be very careful, how they gave the power out of their hands to any president or single person, as a head, unless they were perfectly assured, that that head was Sound and Solid, else they might smart Soundly for their conduct, and repent Solidly of what they had done. [294]

Then Coney Pimp Frontinbrass Esqr stood up, and again repeated his request of bringing in the articles, alledging that in every Government whatsoever, an absolute power was Located somewhere, in a monarchy it was Lodged in one, in an Aristocracy, and mixed monarchy, such as is in

---

2. Tiberius Sempronius Gracchus (163–133 B.C.) and Gaius Sempronius Gracchus (153–121 B.C.), brothers, were both tribunes and reformers (and, arguably, demagogues) who were killed for political reasons. Their proposals created deep divisions within the Roman Republic, which eventually led to the conflict between Gaius Marius (157–86 B.C.) and Lucius Cornelius Sulla (138–78 B.C.), which resulted in the Roman Civil War in 88 B.C., a reign of terror, and eventually the end of the Republic and the rise of personal dictatorships. The Decemviri was a Roman body of 10 men with absolute power appointed in 451 and 450 B.C. to draw up a code of laws.

the relation I have the honor to stand in to your Lordships ancient Club, makes me think of the *uppermost* Importance.

I would not dare to flatter my vanity so far as to cogitate in the most minute degree, that any merit, your Lordships *argulian eyes,* can, in any possible, or Impossible, conceivable or Inconceivable manner whatsoever discern me possessed of, can be an argument efficacious to Incline your ‖ Lordships honor, to alter, turn, overturn or change the aforesaid lamentable resolution of your honor. Tis true I have been in this City together with my Servant and two horses this fortnight at a Considerable Expence, on purpose to have a Second opportunity and honor, of being once more a Spectator of your honor and presidential dignity, in the pleasing hopes of then, in conjunction with your Ldsp, to use a few more efforts, towards reforming the abuses and Irregularities, which most Lamentably have Crept, into your ancient Tuesday Club.

As to what Concerns the first of these Considerations, observations or remarks, I confess it is not worth your Lordship's notice, but the latter, I humbly conceive is—your Lordship with all Submission, I beg, may consider, that, according to the high Station rank and office you bear in the Club, cannot but be perpetually Solicitous, to bring about every thing, which may conduce to order and harmony in your ancient Tuesday Club, if your Lordship do persist in your resolution of being absent to morrow night, after the rout, and confounded hubbub, your unruly officers and commoners made last meeting, to what Lengths and breadths, heights and deeps, ups and downs, heres and theres, and what nots, may they not carry, the Sickly distressed, poor Languishing gasping ancient Tuesday Club.

I am so deeply affected at the very thoughts of what may happen, if your Lordship's honor, does not appear next night, that I can scarce hold the pen in my trembling hand, any Longer, be prevaild upon therefore, most Sage Sir, to be there, then, you may depend upon it, that every power and faculty of my Soul, shall be exerted to promote the Salutary ends you have in view, In presiding over the ancient Tuesday Club. I am, Inconceivably, my Lord,

Annapolis	Your Lordships honor's
31. Decemb: 1750	most humb: Servt:
	Everlastingly & for ever after
	Coney Pimp Frontinbrass.

These letters being read in Club, Coney Pimp Frontinbrass Esqr honorary member, stood up, by permission, and addressing his honor, by the Title of *my Lord,* (being the first, who addressed him thus, in Speeches and

from his Seat, looked somewhat Surprized, and pull'd up his breeches, Laconic Comas Esqr, swore a great oath, and Damnd the Impudence of Frontinbrass, however, he persisting in his request, his honor at last streched forth his right hand, and Frontinbrass Eagerly kissed it, on which Laconic Comas burst out, *O! God dam' you! you'r a fool by God!* Then his honor pull'd up his breeches again and sat down, and Commanded Frontinbrass to arise, which Command he obeyed—Frontinbrass then Entered into a Long discourse concerning *Clubific Felicity,* and the nature of Presidential power, endeavoring to demonstrate, that the first Intirely depended upon the unlimited extent of the latter, and wondered that his Lordship did not exert himself more arbitrarily in the Club, and advised him to keep the members more under absolute Command for the future. While these Speeches were making, Frontinbrass in directing his discourse to his honor, would always rise from his Seat, and his honor would rise also, and pull up his breeches, while Laconic Comas would, every now and then burst out into, *Damn the Nonsense, you'r both fools by God!* This Conversation lasted some hours, and Frontinbrass took his Leave, leaving his honor so well satisfied and pleased, that the very next morning, he went In person, to Coney Pimp Frontinbrasses Lodging, when he was scarce got out of bed, and made him a present of a Club medal, when Frontinbrass || again, in the presence of several persons of figure and distinction, vizt: Scots merchants and Supercargos, had the honor of kissing his Lordships hand. [291]

The other Letter, wrote by this Gentleman to the President, was sent to his honor, upon the day the Club met, at Sederunt 146, and was as follows.

To Nasifer Jole Esqr,
The honorable Lord President, of the ancient & honorable Tuesday Club.

My Lord President,
Most high and deep Sir,

My ambition never received so lamentable a Stroke, nor my pride such mortification, as when from the (till then) Sweet lips of your Lordship's honor, I was told your Lordship's honor had taken such offence, at the ill, rude, tumultuous, treasonable behavior, of most of the members of your ancient Tuesday Club at last meeting, that you would not grace, the exalted Chair of the said ancient Club, with your Lordship's dignified presence.

O my Lord! forgive my Impudence, pardon my presumption, in taking upon me, to expostulate with your Lordship's honor in an affair, which,

216 [Book VIII] The History of

Private Conference of Frontinbras, with the Honourable Master Sole Ear

[facing page 290]

dom and Sagacity, that I am like one, Just come out of a dark dungeon, into the light and Clear Sunshine, my eyes ake with the Splendor and refulgency of your honor's countenance, and tho' to distraction, I am astonished, yet, I cannot say I clearly see all your honor's excellencies and perfections—'Tis my most prevailing ambition, that I may, before I leave this place, be enabled perfectly, to comprehend your Grandure and dignity, and therefore, I would beg the favor, that your honor would permit me this evening, to wait upon your Refulgence, and thereby acquire a more perfect Idea of your presidential Highness, I am, with the utmost deference, and most humble, profound Submission,

Annapolis 20th Decr 1750

Your honors most devoted
Most obsequious Servant
Slave and Confounded admirer
Coney Pimp Frontinbrass.

This letter, in the Strain of which appears, abundance of Impudence and affectation, Impudence in the gross Flattery that runs thro' the whole, and affectation, in the odd peculiarity of Stile and words, was thrown out as a bait by the writer to catch his honor the President, and his honor the President snaped at it and was accordingly caught, an Instance of the degree of Infatuation, the Club, by their repeated Compliments and flatteries, had brought this worthy Gentleman to, and a great example of the frailty of human nature, which, in the most Sagacious, can be so tempered and wrought upon, as to acquiesce, and give assent to the grossest lies and absurdities.

The design of this Letter was to procure a private audience of his honor the President, which accordingly was procured, and Coney pimp Frontinbrass Esqr was admitted into his honor's antichamber, upon the same day, on which this letter was wrote, in the Evening, about the time of lighting up of Candles, at the Entering of this great politician into his honor's antichamber, he found his honor in a dishabille, being in his night cap Gown and Slippers, Laconic Comas Esqr, Late a privy Counsellor of his honor, being in the Room with his honor, smoking a pipe of tobacco, and a bowl of Rumbo before him, and from Mr Comas it was, that we had the particulars of this private Conference, that Sagacious gentleman, being much displeased and provoked || at the gross flatteries then vented by Mr Frontinbrass, in his addresses to his honor. When Frontinbrass came first into the Room, he pulled off his hat tho a Quaker, kneeld down upon one knee, and humbly desired that his Lordship would permit him the honor of kissing his Lordships hand, on which the honorable the president, started

[289]

[290]

would fain have passed for omnipotent, was not the breath or voice of Nero, to be sacrifised to by every Roman, otherwise he might be taxed with high treason, did not Claudius appoint divine honors to be paid to his mother Livia,[1] and it was thought as great a Crime then to Question the Divinity of that ancient Lady, as it is now thought Criminal in Moderen Rome to doubt of the Divinity of the Virgin Mary, commonly called the Queen of Heaven, and the mother of God; from this principle of pride, so Ingrained in human nature, all men have been fond of taking to themselves great and lofty titles, and laid hold of every opportunity to attain to them, the Eastren Emperors and potentates, and even every petty Indian Prince, as the Kings of Bantam and Siam, Call themselves The Sons of God, the darlings of God, the Eye of the world, the delight of Paradise, and a thousand other pompous titles, which, if things were well sifted, or Inquired into, they have little or no right or title to assume. Seeing then, that Great priests, great kings, and great men, at all times, have been so fond of pompous titles and designations, it will not at all appear Strange or uncommon, that Great presidents, should be Carried away with this prevailing principle of pride, and assume to themselves high titles, which many think they have no right to assume, we shall soon see an Instance of this in the Conduct of the honorable Nasifer Jole Esqr, presidt: of the anc: & hon: Tuesday Club.

[288]   At Sederunt 146 January 1, 1750/1, Solo Neverout Esqr being H:S: his honor the president produced in Club two letters which he had received from Coney Pimp Frontinbrass Esqr, honorary member, they were read, and put upon Record, as follows.

To The honorable Nasifer Jole Esqr,
President of The Tuesday Club, These.

Most Honorable Sir,
   The Idea of the Grandure and magnificence of your honor, has so filled my fancy, ever since I had the honor and pleasure of viewing your honor, exalted in that distinguished Chair of State, of the *Ancient and honorable Tuesday Club,* that it has quite occupied my thoughts by day, and my dreams by night—I am so swallowed up in the Contemplation of your honors Excellence and magnificence—so stuned with admiring your profound wis-

---

1. Livia (58 B.C.–A.D. 29), wife of Augustus and mother of Tiberius and Nero Claudius Drusus by Tiberius Claudius Nero, was known for her kindness and intelligence. According to Suetonius, it was the son of Drusus and her grandson the Emperor Claudius (10 B.C.–A.D. 54), whom she considered a dolt, who made the senate decree divine honors on her.

that means, he deprived the honorable Nasifer Jole Esqr, of a great part of the pleasure of his life, for, nothing he took greater delight in than, the thoughts of, one day, becoming Superior to, and having an absolute Jurisdiction, over the aforesaid Sir Hugh Maccarty Esqr, and his Club, great and tremendous as he was; when his honor was undeceived in this Quixotic notion, he fain would have passed it upon the Club || and the world, that he [286] knew the deception and trick from the very beginning, and always was thorroly persuaded that no such person existed as Sir Hugh Maccarty Esqr, and no such Club ever was in being as his Club, but he found it no such easy matter to Convince the Club and the world of the truth of this assertion, as it was for the unparallelled Cunning and assurance of Coney Pimp Frontinbrass Esqr, to persuade him of the Identity of that Romantic president and his Club; tho' Indeed, a person of less assurance and artifice, than the said Frontinbrass, might have wrought upon the easy and Credulous disposition of the Honorable Nasifer Jole Esqr, to believe, even greater Impossibilities.

Chapter IX

Sublime letters of Coney Pimp Frontinbrass Esqr, to his honor the President; disputes in Club; The Frontinbrassian Articles drawn up and assented to; new Title Conferred upon the President, Creation of a Serjeant at arms, Coney Pimp Frontinbrass Esqr, made agent & plenipo for the Club In America.

Human pride is Infinite or Incommensurable, it being Impossible for the Greatest mathematician or algebraist, to calculate the Length, breadth, height and depth of it; not satisfied with Imperial and Regal honors and titles, it even has had the assurance at times to aspire to divine honors and worship, most people reckon it an humor (or rather a piece of Impudence) as uncommon as Ridiculous in the popes of Rome, to assume to themselves attributes only applicable to the divinity, such as that of holiness and Infallibility, but, however ri- || diculous it may seem, I may safely say, it is not [287] uncommon, for, is it not notorious, from the Annals of the Roman History, that long before these magnificent Bishops the Popes, fixed the Seat of their Empire in that ancient City, several of the Emperors, the most accomplished villains that ever drew breath, and mere Devils Incarnate, vizt: Nero, Claudius and Caligula, assumed to themselves divine honors, and

time that he admired their parts and understanding; he was above measure forward in thrusting himself into companies of all Sorts, and Immediatly mixing in the Conversation, with that freedom and forwardness, as if he had all his life been in Intimate friendship and acquaintance with every one in the Company, and the very next Company he went into, he would make use of these person's names and Characters not much to their honor or advantage, especially if it would turn out any way advantagious to himself, or make him appear a person of Judgement and understanding, in fine, he was one very well adapted to act the buffoon, in every degree of life, of such a finished assurance, that he had very few equals and no Superiors in that distinguishing Quality, and we shall soon see, what disturbances he excited in the ancient and honorable Tuesday Club, by the Sole force of his Impudence, effrontery and buffonery.

Sir Hugh Maccarty Esqr, a Supposed great Club president, whom Coney Pimp frontinbrass Esqr, first made mention of in the ancient and honorable Tuesday Club, calling him the President of a very ancient and Right honorable monday Club at New York, was, for some time believed to be a real person, and more Especially, by his honor Mr President Jole, who, upon his having so grand a description of his person and Character declared or delivered to him by the aforesaid Mr Frontinbrass, had Conceived a mighty great opinion of, and esteem for him, he, from the description, Imagining him to be a person of a very austere disposition, who had an absolute Command over his Club, and who would be obeyd at any rate, this was what the honorable Nasifer Jole himself || wished very much to be, in the ancient and honorable Tuesday Club, if either by his wit or Courage, he could attain to that pitch of authority, and, as it is natural, for men to admire in others, what they would like to be possessors of themselves, we cannot be Surprized, that the Honorable Nasifer Jole Esqr, should be so much in love, with this magnificent and powerful Club worthy, whom, as we have said, he at first believed to be a real person; but alas! the pleasure of that thought, did not continue long; for, after he had spoke much in praise of the said Sir Hugh Maccarty Esqr in every Company, and Conversation he happened into, falling into raptures, when he discoursed of that great Clubic heroe, he found, to his great disappointment and Grief, that this mighty Club magnifico, was no other than a mere *Ens rationis,* a Quixotic person, who never had any other place of existence either he or his Club, but the maggoty brain of the aforesaid Coney Pimp Frontinbrass Esqr, which discovery was made, by the great application and Assiduity of his Champion Sir John, who took Infinite pains to persuade his honor, of the nonexistence of this Phantasmical Club heroe, and effected it at last, tho' by

the Tuesday Club [Book VIII] 211

[Behold the man of hard heart and of very cold face,
Brazen, impudent, in whose mouth is no shame,
Expressionless, importunate, rash, immodest,
Your deeds, O Pimp, are disgraceful.]

[facing page 283]

from the Chair, drank the health of Sir Hugh Maccarty Esqr, president of the most ancient and right honorable monday Club of New York, of which that Gentleman said, he was a member, which was also done by all the Longstanding members, and then his honor, presented Mr Frontinbrass, with a fair Impression of the great Seal of the Club, and his own privy Seal at arms, which that Gentleman received with a very profound bow.

As this Gentleman, and his Sham heroe, Sir Hugh Maccarty Esqr, are very deeply concerned in the Sequel of this History, I think it will be necessary to give here, a short Scetch of the Character of each.

Coney pimp Frontinbrass Esqr, first Introduced into the ancient and honorable Tuesday Club, by the Recommendation of the Honorable Philo Dogmaticus Esqr, the Club's Chancellor, was, as he said, a native of Scotland, The City of Glasgow there, having the honor of his birth, he seemed to be a person cut out for Travel, and in his time had seen many parts of the world, he pretended to be a person of universal Genius and universal acquaintance, and Intelligence, there was no transaction, great or small, but what he seemed to be acqu- || ainted with or to have had a hand in, and tho' he was a person of Strong memory, yet he carried always about him a help to it, which was an Alphabeted pocket book, in which he entered the names and Characters of persons he had seen and Conversed with in his travels, as also every thing that passed in Conversations, which he thought worth remarking, or such as would serve his purpose on a future occasion, and being a compleat master of the art of Short hand, he was thereby Enabled to do this with the greater accuracy, by this means, he could scarce go into any Company, in any part of the world, but he was Immediatly furnished with a Sufficient Stock of conversation, for, this Sort of Study and application, had rendered him a Compleat adept, in the General Characters of men of note in all ranks and Employments, in every place where he had been; for with every man of the least figure or Genius, he pretended to have Conversed or held Intercourse, from the Lord to the Cobler, and used to treat persons far above him, with abundance of familiarity, and often with Contempt, but this was always behind their backs, and when they were far enough distant, for before people's faces, he was full of an oily smooth Conversation. As to religion, he set up for a Quaker, and at times would be very Stiff and formal, and abound in *thees* and *Thous,* but he would at other times forget this preciseness, and hold forth, in as polite a Stile, as any pragmatical puppy of the times, who sets up for a pattern of politeness, he took a particular pleasur in finding out men's foibles, and weak Sides, and then would expose and make fools of them in such an artful manner, that they would not for a great || while perceive his drift, but Imagine all the

the Tuesday Club [Book VIII] 209

plicity of diet, has been very Conduc[eiv]e to Longevi[ty] among men, hence, the antidiluvians, from [their living c]hiefly upon vegetables & Grain, protracted [their lives to so] great a Length, if the Longstanding members then, of this here ancient and honorable Club, were to show a greater respect to homony, than they seem at present to do, they might probably Enjoy a Longevity equal or perhaps little Inferior to that of the antidiluvians, and Sure I am, it is my earnest desire, that your honor, and all these here Longstanding Members, of this here ancient and honorable Club may live 900 or 1000 years, and then Indeed, with great propriety, might we be called an ancient Club. *Dixi.*"

This Oration Ended, the Club began to Consider, what was to be done with the Cap of State, when a gentleman present, and Invited to Club as a Stranger, according to ancient Cus- ‖ tom, by name Coney Pimp Frontin- [281] brass Esqr, by religion a quaker, as he said, by profession a merchant for Tobacco, Rising up, with the permission and leave of his honor and the Longstanding members, humbly requested, That if the Club did not Chuse to use this here Cap of State, he might be allowed to carry it to New York for a great president of a Club there to wear, to which Club, he belonged, as a dignified member,—To this proposal the Club Consented by a vote, but his honor the President, protesting against this proceeding, the Gentleman very respectfully, Restored the Cap again into the hands of his honor, by no means presuming, tho' he had the Consent of the Club, to act against his honors will and pleasure.

Whereupon Sir John, in a bold manner seizing the Cap of State, Clap'd it upon his head, and wore it during the Remaining part of the night.

Coney Pimp Frontinbrass Esqr, upon some very Plausible proposals he had made to his honor for the advantage of the Club, which proposals Consisted Chiefly in advising and Enforcing a passive obedience of the longstanding members to the orders of the Chair, and Establishing an arbitrary power in the Club, located in the Chair, for which, the said Coney Pimp Frontinbrass Esqr, laid down the pattern of a Certain (as some think Imaginary) Club, at New York, stiled the most ancient and Right honorable *Monday Club,* of which, one, Sir Hugh Maccarty Esqr (by some Esteemed an Imaginary person, but) a native, as he said, of Kent in old England, was ‖ the arbitrary and despotic president; I say, the said Coney [282] Pimp Frontinbrass Esqr, upon account of these proposals, by the Interest and application of his honor the president, who Immediatly conceived a high opinion, of that artificial and Insinuating politician, was unanimously chosen an honorary member of the Club, and his honor very Cordially,

honorable Club, to those blessed times, those halcyon days, which were called the Golden age, in which men lived long and happy, then all their food was Simple, they fed upon the plain acorn, and the unadulterated, unfermented Grain, no high Spices, no devlish Caustic or Sophisticated Sauces contaminated and Corrupted their Taste, [the very] Rivers, flowed with Milk wine and nectar, and [the ancient] Sturdy oaks, droped Honey, their food was [simple and clea]n, calculated for health, and, as yet, the monstrous and hellish compositions of moderen Cookery, had not contaminated and polluted their kitchens, and wholesome food, was the gift of heaven, being before [the] Devil to[ok] it in his head to send Cooks to poison [mankind, h]ence the proverb, *God sends meat, but the de[vil sends Coo]ks;*[1] The old Spartans, a virtuous and hardy people, dined very Contentedly, upon their *Jus nigrum,* or black broth, and we Read of some Roman Generals, who would not scruple to dine upon a boiled Turnip, yea, and Cook it themselves,[2] and yet, these I hope, were as great, and as good men, as the Longstanding members of this here ancient and honorable Club [here Sir John looked Surly and Sour.]

But, honorable Sir, what need we object to homony, I may safely say it is a royal dish, being the favorite repast of many ancient & virtuous Indian monarchs, who ‖ differ not from other monarchs, in any other earthly respect, but, that they are not so Luxurious, so ambitious, such lcorice[3] fellows, or such lovers of their belly, that this here homony, is an excellent honorable and ancient dish, may be made appear, from the Etymology of the word,[4] it being derived from several words in the Greek, latin and English languages, which shows its antiquity and universality, the Greeks derive it plainly from ὁ μονος, which signifies *the only,* that is to say, that homony is the only food, the latin is *homo,* which is a man, and that Implies, that homony is a manly food; the Engl[ish may de]rive it from these two words, *of many,* or [with an apost]rophe *o'many,* being, as we may say, [th]e most E[xcellen]t food of many kinds of food, and indeed, it may be called so, since it is made of pure Grain, and of grain is made bread, which you know, in Scripture Phraze is the Staff of life, we find that Sim-

---

1. Hamilton is perhaps borrowing this old proverb about the effects of bad cooking most immediately from Lord Smart's remark, "This Goose is quite raw. Well; God sends Meat, but the Devil sends Cooks" (Jonathan Swift, *A Compleat Collection of Genteel and Ingenious Conversation* [1738], in *The Prose Works of Jonathan Swift,* ed. Herbert Davis [Oxford, 1939–1968], IV, 182).

2. The story of the Spartans dining on black broth appears in Plutarch's life of Lycurgus; the story of the Roman generals appears in Plutarch, *Marcus Cato* 2.2.

3. Obsolete form of *lickerish* or *lickerous,* meaning here "fond of good food."

4. As Hamilton was probably well aware, *hominy* is a word of American Indian origin.

the Tuesday Club [Book VIII] 207

would fain have persuaded the Club, that they were the very opinions he had entertained of it, from the Beginning, ever since the moment that Cap had been taken out of box No 1. These Sentiments were, that this Cap had never come from London, but had been made up here, out of some Second hand Stuff, by the Contrivance of the Secretary. His Gentleman Usher, the very next morning, after the presenting of the Cap, seeing it by day light, and perceiving that it had a quite different Gloss and appearance from what it showed, in the light of the Candles, had some Secret conversation with his honor about it, and afterwards, Sir John, Endeavored to persuade his honor, that the Cap came from the Secretary, and not from the agent, but it was sometime after this, e'er his honor would believe that allegation, we shall however soon have opportunity to show, who were the first Contrivers, and fabricators of this Cap.

The Club however, after his honor, had absolutely refused to wear the Cap, and hung it upon the Shield || of the Canopy, put it to the vote, [278] whether the Chancellor or Sir John should wear it, It carried in favor of the Chancellor, who very modestly declined that honor, and said he could by no means accept of the Cap of State, unless he was to have the Chair along with it, but that proposal appearing preposterous and absurd, to the Club, the argument was Entirely dropd.

Several Letters were produced in Club, which were read, but not recorded, one letter was an answer prepared by the Secretary to Capt: Comely Coppernose Esqr, agent for the Club at London, which his honor the president ordered to be laid aside 'till further orders; it was now apparent, that his honor became very shy of permitting Club letters, particularly those directed to himself, to be recorded, he suspecting, that all, or most of them were forged by the Secretary, for Certain political Ends.

The High Steward, having produced at Supper, a dish of homony, Sir John, after Supper made objections to it, and the Orator standing up, made an apology for the H:S: to the following purpose.

"Mr President and Gentlemen,

It is an astonishing thing to me, that some members of this here ancient Club, are always objecting, and always finding fault, never satisfied, who would have thought, that the bringing in of a dish of homony, would have occasioned any Cavil or Censure, in this here ancient and honorable Club, Homony, I affirm, to be a good wholesome and Simple Dish, very well adapted for nourishment, and || The more Simple our food is, the more [279] kindly and agreeable it is to our Stomachs, in the opinion of all learned, wise and Judicious men, let us look back into the first ages of the world, many Centuries before any Records can be found, of this here ancient and

always Confine himself within the Compass of the Sublime, and appear as an actor in high life, but finds it necessary at times to be deeply concerned in affairs of a meaner and more private nature, for, where ever he thrusts himself into Clubs or families, he becomes a principal agent there, and takes the whole burden of their affairs upon his back, by which he often reaps much profit and Emolument, and makes many dupes, and, providing he takes care to carry on his trade artfully, and not to remain too long in one place, so as to suffer his Imposture to be discovered, he may chance to finish or wind up the farce, without having his bones broke, or being kicked out of doors.

[276] I should not have Introduced this chapter of our history, with this prolix preamble on assurance, had not his honor the president, and his ancient and honorable Club, after having so long managed their own matters, Intirely by their own wit and Understanding, now, at this unlucky period of our history, met with a person exactly of this character, In Coney Pimp Frontinbrass Esqr, who made his appearance at an Ill fated hour, in this here ancient Club, and by his devices and projects, contrived and furthered, Soleley by the force of assurance, put the whole Clubical System and Oeconomy, into such disorder and Confusion, as that the Constitution of the Club became thereby subject to Severe Convulsive fits, and not having recovered it's wonted Strength and vigor, even at this day, continues still in a Lamentable, broken and Crazy condition, and tho' this unnatural Shoke, narrowly missed putting an end to the precious life of his honor the president, by enraging and exasperating his gout, yet it is thought by many persons of Sagacity and foresight, that it will at last put an End to the Club.

At Sederunt 145, December 18, 1750, Quirpum Comic Esqr, being H:S: there arose in Club, some very hot disputes Concerning the Cap of State, which it seems his honor the president took it *in his head,* not to wear *on his head,* asserting That it was a Scandalous patched up bawble, and, that some nasty Slattern of a milliner, had not only Imposed upon the Good agent Capt: Comely Coppernose, but also in the Grossest manner upon himself [277] and this ancient and honorable Club, in pretending ‖ to palm such a daub, and such a pitiful patchd up piece of work upon them, and, that if the Club Chose to dishonor themselves, with such a despicable rag as that there Cap was, they might get whom they pleased to wear it, but he never would disgrace his head with any such greasy trumpery, These were his honor's Sentiments of the cap of State, which at that time were purely his own; Tho sometime after, he conceived Sentiments of it, at the Instigation of Don John Charlotto, his Gentleman usher, and the worshipful Sir John, Champion of the Club; which he found came nigher to the truth, and therefore,

and laid upon the bag, that the Club might see it was there, but upon searching into the bag, instead of the Seal, came forth a Slice of bread, which not alittle Surprized his honor and the Club, and after Search for the great Seal, it was found by the said Quirpum Comic Esqr, which made the Club suspect him for the Contriver of this Quirp, and Comical trick.

Chapter VIII

Disputes Concerning the Cap of State, Speech on Homony by the Orator, History and Character of Coney Pimp Frontinbrass Esqr, Account of Sir Hugh Maccarty Esqr.

Assurance is an useful Qualification, which Carries many men thro' the world, better than an honest and reputable calling. I have known some fellows, well stocked with assurance, tho' void of all Good qualities whatsoever, either natural or acquired, by this single talent alone, get mightily in favor with princes and great men, twist them round their fingers, and do with them what they pleased, direct, order and manage all, put some in place, and degrade others, and become as it were the Sole directors, In kingdoms, Senates, courts and families; This gainful assurance, is of a peculiar Sort, and requires a good Stock of Cunning and artifice to manage it right, it consists chiefly, in a pretended freedom and familiarity in all Companies, wherever the person possessing this pushing and profi- || table [275] quality introduces, or rather intrudes himself, he enters into the Spirit of the conversation in an Instant, let it have either a Serious, a comical, a grave, or a facetious turn, he laughs, weeps, looks dull, Sprightly, mourns and rejoices with the Stream, and in a minutes time is as well acquainted, and as free with every person in the Company, as if he had known him all his life, and he not only knows him, but knows all his relations, friends and acquaintances, and, in short, the whole History of his life, and every particular occurrence, public or private, that has happened for some years past, he (the man of assurance) has had a principal hand in. He has been the prime Confident of great men and ministers of State; has given his advice in most public affairs of any Consequence; has had familiar Conversation with princes, knows the whole System of Politicks all over Europe, has been an author of great Repute, has had the leading pen in Controversies of the utmost consequence, and in fine has made a very Considerable appearance in the Republic of letters, if you'll believe his own report; nor does he

Judges of Hell, so, you by ancient Club Chronology, are Just Judge of this here ancient and honorable Club, your absence from this here ancient Club, has seemed to us, the old and longstanding members, an age of duration, many have been the Conflicts, many the Bickerings, and the altercations many, since your departure hence; The Seal! the Great Seal! that Eminent badge of office, has been the Cause of all, the longstanding members have often been in danger of rebelling, and as often has his honor the president frowned tremendous from the Chair, Astræa,[11] or Justice, seemed to have left this here Club, and followed your Eminence to the Northward, the Seal has been in danger of Sequestration, and, his honor the president's Conscience has been tossed to and fro' like a football, as for the Seal, we have bumpt it, thumpd it, tossed it, tumbled it upside down, ‖ topside turve, arsy-versy, everted it, subverted it, Inverted it and Converted it, to bad uses; knock'd it, push'd it, thresh'd it, Jerked it, shoked it, shaked it, slubber'd it, hack'd it, whitteld it, notch'd it, bewray'd it, bespattered it, pocketed it, fobb'd it, stole it, till at last, it became a thing of as little moment as a Chip of Bread—But now, most equitable Sir, since you are returned, we hope all things will be rectified, and order will return with you; Therefore, in the name of his honor the president, and the Longstanding members of this here ancient Club, I congratulate you worthy Sir, upon your again taking that Seat of equity, which none here are so worthy of, and so capable to fill as yourself, and wish that you may long continue to possess that eminent office, and be an equitable dispenser of Justice, to the Longstanding members of this here ancient Club—*Dixi.*"

The Orator received the thanks of the Chancellor for this Speech, who declared, that he would always faithfully and Justly discharge his trust, as chancellor, without fear, favor or affection, and, at the same time threw a broad look towards the Chair, and received in return from thence, a very Scornful leer, while Sir John did nothing but Chaw during these Speeches and Transactions, looking now and then Contemptuously and askew, at the Cap of State, as it hung on the Canopy.

What the Secretary mentions in the above oration with regard to the Seal's being of as little moment as a Chip of bread, relates to an occurrence, that happened at Sederunt 142, when his honor the President was H:S: which has been ommitted to be related, and it was this. His honor being ‖ seated in the chair, and the bag laid before him, with the Seal in it, as it was supposed, Quirpum Comic Esqr, moved, that the Seal might be taken out,

---

11. Astraea was a mythological goddess associated with equity and innocence who left earth when sin began to prevail and was metamorphosed into the constellation Virgo.

This Cap was of a very antiquated form and figure, and seemed much to resemble that Gold plate bonnet or Tiara, that was dug out of a Bog or morass in Ireland, and was said to belong to the ancient monarchs of that kingdom, according to the Ingenious Dr Keating in his history of Ireland.[9]

As for the Box, marked No 1, in which this Cap was contained, it was made of a piece of Green pine plank, wch appeared to be of American grouth, and therefore some began to suspect, that this Cap had never been in or came from London, but this shall be fully cleared up in the Sequel. Three different Boxes, at three different times, had now made their appearance in this ancient Club, and were the unhappy Causes of much noise and disturbance therein, vizt: The money Box, whose date is long agoe expired, The Box No 1, which is now ready to make its appearance on the Stage, and with a much greater esclat, than any of the other boxes, but, after even that had breathed it's last, and was thrust under ground in his honor's Garden, the Club Tobacco box, which for many years had made little or no noise, made it's exit, together with the Chancellor, and occasioned some perturbation, as for the Sand boxes, or rather Spit boxes, tho' they were the first boxes that appeared in Club, yet they Continued so short a time, that it is scarce worth while to rank them, among the boxes of quality in the Club.

His honor the president, having, as was said, put on the Cap of State, [272] wore it, till the health of the donor was drank, and then, Solemnly taking it off, placed it upon the Shield of the Canopy.

Then Mr Orator was called upon to deliver a Congratulatory address to his honor the Chancellor, upon his return to the Club, after a long absence, which he did with a *bon grace,* in the following terms, vizt:

"Most profound and equitable Sir,

As Orator of this here ancient Club, by permission of his honor the president, I address you, most honorable and dignified Chancellor, most just and Sagacious Arbiter and determinator, Perfect Copy •of Minos, Æacus and Radamantus,[10] who, as they were, by pagan Mythology, Just

---

9. Geoffrey Keating (1570?–1644?) was an Irish writer and priest whose most important work was a history of Ireland from the earliest times to the English invasion, *Foras feasa ar Eirinn* (Foundation of knowledge on Ireland [1629]), which was written in the Irish language and borrowed heavily from popular Irish folklore and poetry. I have not, however, found this reference in Keating's history.

10. Minos, traditional king of Crete, was so respected for his justice and wisdom that he was made supreme judge in the infernal regions. Aeacus was the son of Zeus and Aegina, renowned over all Greece for his justice and piety and consequently one of the judges in Hades. Rhadamantus was the mythological son of Zeus and Europa who, like his brother Minos, showed so much wisdom and judgment during his life that he became one of the judges in the infernal regions.

The honorable Nanfer sole Esqr. wears the Cap of State

birds, and with || variety of feathers, the Romans, that brave and warlike [270] people, had their Coronæ or Caps of honor, which they bestowed as rewards on their brave heroes, they had their Corona Civica, Navalis, Muralis and Campestris,⁶ and even their triumphers and mighty Emperors wore a Simple Laurel Wreath.

But what need we bring Instances and authorities for the wearing of Caps, it is authority Sufficient to recommend the practice to all nations and all people, that a Cap, even a Cap of State was thought Expedient to be wore by the honorable the president of this here ancient and honorable Club.

And now, honorable Sir, I shall say something of the form and model of this extraordinary *Cap,* this *Cap of State,* it seems to be a form most Grand and magnificent, exactly the same model, with that which was wore by Rigdumfoledo, The great grandson of Nabuchadonozor king of Babylon,

according to the eikon given of it, by Signior Giovanni Battista Barbaro di Schiolto,⁷ Grand Librarian to the vatican at Rome, and Just such another, as is delineated by John, or Henry Overton,⁸ at the white horse near Newgate, London, and, I think that our agent deserves the thanks of your honor and this here Club, for this noble and Splendid present, which, that your honor may long live to || wear, is the earnest desire of your most diligent [271] orator and most humble Secretary."

This Speech delivered, his honor took the Cap, and after considering it, and turning it on all Sides, put it upon his head, to the great Satisfaction of the Club, and the poet Laureat rising up, spoke to this purpose.

> Long may you live, to wear that Cap of State
> And Grace the Tuesday Club, of ancient date.

---

6. Civic, naval, mural (for storming), and battlefield crowns; Aulus Gellius, *Noctes atticae* 5.6, explains these and other military decorations.

7. Although I have not identified Schiolto (also mentioned by Hamilton in III, 49), he was probably a church historian. Since no character named Rigdumfoledo (or anyone with a name even faintly resembling it) appears in the Bible, Hamilton is apparently poking fun at Schiolto's learning as well as at church history.

8. John Overton (1640–1708?) was an English printseller and vendor of mezzotints whose shop was at "the White Horse without Newgate."

hand, and turning it round and round, to show it to the best advantage, as orator of the Club, he addressed his honor the President, and the Longstanding members, in a pompous Speech, to the following purpose.

"Honorable Sir, and you the worthy members of this here Club,

You see here a *Cap of State,* a badge of honor, which some time agoe was thought of and proposed in this here ancient Club, 'tis an ensign of such dignity and Consequence, that something very honorable, ought to be said in praise of it; and, as antiquity is allowed universally to be an Infallible mark of honor, I have been at much pains, Study and application, to turn over many volumes night and day, in order to get some light, into the history and antiquity of Caps, that I might deliver in an elegant manner as orator, whatever might be said on the Subject to this here ancient Club, in honor of this honorable and resplendend badge, this precious Cap of State, destined for the Illustrious || pate of our honorable president, but I cannot say I could get any light, into the history of Caps, so as Certainly to ascertain any thing plausible, concerning their first form, fashion, or origin. 'Tis plain, that our first parents thought of covering some other parts, before they made provision for the head, in the antidiluvian History, we hear nothing of Caps, nor, can I find Caps were in use at the building of the tower of Babel.

The most ancient Record I find of Caps, is that of the Persian Tiara, mentioned by Justin, Trogus,[5] and some other old Historians, but why need we search for the antiquity of Caps in History and Records, since their being Introduced into this here ancient Club, is abundantly Sufficient, to render them of a most ancient date, let us leave then, such needless Enquiries to Gardiners, Barbers and Taylors, who are not as yet agreed, which of their Crafts are most ancient, for, it is Sufficient for us, that every thing must be ancient, which belongs to this here ancient Tuesday Club.

All Nations we find most honorable Sir, both barbarous and polite, were Solicitous about ornamenting the head, and different models of Caps were wore by different people, as a mark of distinction and honor, according to their peculiar taste and humor; The Hottentots wear Sheeps Guts, twisted about their heads, which ornament, tho it be nasty enough, yet is a badge of State and distinction among them, their nobles only being allowed to wear them, on that part, while the vulgar wear them round their legs; the Savage nations of America, adorn their heads, with the Skins of beasts and

---

5. Pompeius Trogus was an Augustan historian noted for a universal history, *Historiae philippicae,* which has survived only in the abridgment of Marcus Junianus Justinus of the 3d century A.D. The reference to the Persian tiara appears in Justinus 1.2.3.

It was at Sederunt 144, Slyboots pleasant Esqr being H:S: That the Secretary, Just after his Tryal & condemnation was over, produced a letter, supposed afterwards to be a Surreptitious or Spurious one, from Capt: Comely Coppernose, the Clubs agent in Great Britain, which was Read & Recorded as follows.

To Loquacious Scribble Esqr,
at Annapolis in Maryland with a small box, marked No 1.

Dear Sir,

Soon after I had dispatched the badges, I had the favor of yours, dated April 6th, in which you Inform me of the Seal's having come safe to hand, and that it pleases the Club, at which I am overjoyed, you also let me know that the ancient and honorable Club have elected me an honorary member, and design to send me a patent under the great Seal, to be agent for them in London, I am much Indebted to his honor the President, and your worthy Club, for this piece of honor they design to bestow upon me, and shall do my utmost to behave myself diligently and honorably in that Eminent place, and shall wait with Impatience, till the patent comes to hand, and, as you tell me, that a motion was made in Club, to prepare a *Cap of State* for his honor to wear in the Chair, I cannot but Commend the Zeal of your Club, in bestowing marks of distinction and honor upon so worthy a president as yours, but fearing lest you might be at a loss, to find materials to make this *Cap* in Annapolis, I have ventured to anticipate alittle in my office, and without Commission or order from the Club, have Caused to be made a Cap of State for his honor, which I have sent over with this opportunity, it was made in a hurry, and is not quite so fine as I Intended it, but my desire of Speedily furnishing you, with an ornament of this Importance, made me hurry the workwoman to get it done, that I might not skip this present occasion, not knowing when another should offer. But, if my Zeal in this particular, is approved of by his honor and the Club, I shall at another time, send you a more flaming one, to be wore at the Anniversary, or Solemnities of that Sort, and I hope, this will answer upon more ordinary occasions, presenting my most hearty respects to his honor, and to all the good Members of the Club, I am Sir,

London June 5th 1750   Your humble Servant
Comely Coppernose.

Then the Secretary opening the Box No 1, took out a Gorgeous Cap of blue Shag velvet, trimmed with Gold lace, and holding it up Elevated in his

other fellow member, to wch: Member he was obliged to give up his Cap and Chair, to be possessed by him, till he should in the same manner be outlied; but as the Records of this Club, may be looked upon, as one Intire lie in the Gross, or rather Gross lie from beginning to end, we cannot be ascertained of the veracity or real existence of this blue Cap of State and feather; and, as for Sir Hugh Maccarty Esqr, That Great Clubical heroe, who is said even in these our days to have wore a prodigious Cap of State in his Club, at New York,[2] we have reason to doubt much of the reality of the whole history of that Clubical worthy, who, ever since the Identity of his person has been called in question by the Honorable Nasifer Jole Esqr, has Intirely lost his Credit, and Character, and is looked upon now as an arrant fabulous heroe as Amadis de Gaul, Bellianis of Greece, or Orlando Furioso,[3] and Indeed, if any one now a days, talks of this Sir Hugh Maccarty Esqr || or of his club at New York, he is esteemed as great a Romancer, as ever was the author of *Cassandra, Cleopatra, Clelia, the Grand Cyrus, Almahide*[4] or any other Romance writer that has decorated these latter times with his voluminous collection of lies, so, that we may safely Conclude, that the only real Clubical Cap of State, and therefore, the first Clubical Cap of State that ever appeared on this earthly Stage, was that prepared for, and once wore, by the Honorable Carlo Nasifer Jole Esqr, President of the ancient and honorable Tuesday Club, so that he, together with his Club, may freely take the honor to themselves, of being the first inventors and Institutors of that distinguishing badge of authority honor and wisdom in Clubical Presidents.

[266]

That I have said so much here upon Caps, and Caps of State, and Clubical Caps and Caps of State, I hope the Indulgent Reader will bear with me, and forbear to blame, when he Considers, that [many] material Occurrences in this history take their rise from this very Cap of State, which was Introduced into the Club, it is thought, by means of the Secretaries Contrivances, and Machinations, and occasioned more Comical and Tragical Revolutions and Changes in the Club, than any other Circumstance that ever occurred there.

---

2. Sir Hugh (or Colonel Morris, as Hamilton calls him in the "Record") and his Monday Club remain a mystery. Carl Bridenbaugh alludes to the Monday Club in *Cities in Revolt: Urban Life in America, 1743–1776* (New York, 1955), 163, but it is evident that he has borrowed his information from Hamilton.

3. All three figures are noted above (see 26n, 24n).

4. Four of these titles are noted above (see 26n). *Artamène; ou, Le grand Cyrus* (1649–1653), which deals with the love of Cyrus, grandson to the king of Media, for Mandane, is another French romance by Madeleine de Scudéry.

Coifs, wore by our Judges in Westminster Hall, are expressive of the vast magazines of *Law learning* contained in the Noddles of these reverend dispensers of legal Justice, The Trencher or Square caps wore by the Students & fellows, of various orders and degrees, at our two famous Seminaries of Learning, Oxford and Cambridge, are Symbols of the Immense Learning of the wearers, and express an uncommon depth of Philosophy and Science. There are of these Tiaras or head ‖ attires also, that express bad qualities as effectually as the others do excellencies. Of this Sort are the San benito Sugar loaf caps made of pastboard or thick paper, wore by those miserable wretches condemned by the holy Inquisition, when they go to execution, these are adorned with the pictures of horrid devils, and a lively representation of hell flames. There are also Conjuring caps, wore by those who hold correspondence with the devil. There are mad Caps, peculiar to demented people; fools Caps, appropriated for Simpletons and fools, adorned with bells, to signify, that noise without meaning or Sense, is the principal mark of a fool. There are fuddle caps, appropriated to the votaries of Bacchus, and several Sorts of Caps likewise are wore by persons in a private capacity, the fur Cap is the favorite wear of the northeren Grandees, a Cap and feather, or hat and feather with lace, Express very Emblematically, the contents of the head of a fine moderen Gentleman or beau, as for the different modes of Caps wore by the fair Sex, to adorn and set out the beautiful rotundity of their heads and emblemize the Quantum of understanding therein contained, it would require a Large treatise by itself fully to discuss that Subject, and therefore I Judge it best to drop it altogether. [264a]

Caps of State, are what are wore, by many potentates and Rulers, that are reckoned below the Regal dignity, the Ducal cap is wore by many of our European Grandees, and among these, that of the doge of Venice is Reckoned the most dignified and honorable or rather magnificent cap. That presidential Caps of ‖ State, were ever in use before the glorious times of the honorable Carlo Nasifer Jole Esqr, president of the ancient and honorable Tuesday Club, who was at last, (tho with difficulty) prevailed on to wear a Cap of this Sort, I do not find any documents In History to prove, tho' I have made the most diligent and Indefatigable Search. It is reported indeed that one Sir Harry Blunt, President of the Lying Club[1] wore a blue cap and a feather, which might be called a *Cap of State,* as it was a distinguishing badge of honor in that worthy Society, the most expert Liar in the Club always wearing it, and sitting as Chairman, 'till he was outlied by some [265]

---

1. The story of Sir Harry Blunt and his Lying Club appears in Ward, *History of the London Clubs,* 2–4.

196 [Book VIII] The History of

Club, against wch appeal, Jealous Spyplot Senr Esqr, brought several cogent and Strong reasons, and showed as clear as day light, that it was altogether Irregular, unprecedented and absurd.

Chapter VII

Spurious L[ette]r from the Agent in Great Britain, Commencement [of] the History of Box No 1, and the delivering of the [Cap] of State, with a Speech by the orator, address [to the] Chancellor, by the Orator.

[263a] There are [two] manners in which the human head may be adorned, or set off, the first is done by nature at the original formation of the human Embrio, when the foundation work or first principles of this excellent decoration is laid, that is to say, when the Cranium and brain are formed, in such a happy mold as to be Capable of receiving and holding (if we may believe the Physiologists) the most perfect patterns of Judgement understanding and memory, and all other excellencies, that are said by Connaiseurs in Ethics to Embelish the Rational Soul; But, as there are but few men, who are so happy as to partake the munificence of nature in this respect, it became necessary that the human head should be supplied by art with other ornaments, to make up for the want of the natural apparatus, for this reason variety of caps or || head attires, have been Invented, to adorn this eminent part of the human frame, and to express certain qualities by outward Symbols, so as to make the multitude believe, that the heads wearing these distinguishing badges, were possessed of these Qualities whether they were really so or not, among all ranks, degrees and professions, we find Certain ornaments appropriated to the head, the Royal diadems and Crowns, which by the General Consent of nations both Civilized and barbarous, are wore upon the heads of Emperors, kings and princes, are Expressive Symbols (or at least thought to be so) of their Royalty and power, the Triple Crown, wore by the Holy Bishops of Rome, expresses that High priests assumed Superiority, over the princes of this Lower world, the Red hats and Robes of the Cardinals, are expressive (some say) of the blood of the first apostolic martyrs of the Church, whom these princely, pampered and dignified priests represent, or (as some others think) signifying more properly, the blood of Heretics and Enimies to the Catholic Church, The Cloven mitres of the Bishops, typify the Cloven tongues, that descended upon the heads of the first Ministers of the Gospel, when Inspired by the holy Ghost; The

Seal, for which he deserved condign punishment. In this accusation, Mr Attorney Spyplot showed a plain resentment of the Secretary's lately prosecuting him, for a trespas in Club, and the Secretary was not alittle Surprized at this accusation, as he Imagined the affair had been Intirely drop'd at last Sederunt.

The Secretary to this charge made answer, that he had neither forged, [263] stole, nor abused the great Seal, as to the first charge of forgery, the Impression was made by the Identical Seal itself, and was only affixed to a missive letter, which Conveyed no commission or authority to any one; and therefore, there could be no forgery in the Case, as to the Second charge, he could show from the records and proceedings of the Club, that the Seal had been committed to his care and keeping, and therefore he had not stole it, and, he humbly conceived as to the last article, that the affixing the Great Seal to a letter directed to his honor the president, was rather an abuse of his honor the President, than of the Seal itself, for, he always looked upon the Chair to be above the Seal, and this here proceding was so far from b[e]ing an abuse of the Seal, that it was rather advancing it's di[gn]ity, by setting it upon a level with the Chair.

The Club upon a vote, determined, that the [Sec]retary should be reproved from the Chair, which Sentence was [exec]uted with great mildness and Clemency by his honor the [pre]sident, for, the Secretary standing up in his place, r[eceive]d rather an admonition than a reproof from his honor, [for] which he thanked his honor, and protested That he should always for the future, behave himself with Greater reverence and respect towards the great Seal, than towards any dignity title or authority whatsoever in this here Club. This was a very Sharp repartee of the Secretary's, reflecting on the president and Club, in such a manner, as ought not to have been passed over.

The Secretary, as orator of the Club, was then Called upon by some members to address the Chancellor in a congratulatory manner on his return to the Club, after so long an absence, having not been in the Club since Sederunt 137, which the Secretary absolutely declined doing, alledging
|| for a reason, That this ought to have been the first thing done, after the [264] Convention of the members, and, that the addressing of so honorable a person as the Chancellor, after such a paltry tryal as had been Just now before the Club, would be like putting a Churl upon a Gentleman, which reflexion of the Secretarys, when some members took upon them to reprove, the Secretary apealed from the Club's Sentence passed upon him, to the Chancellor, the proper Judge in all cases of equity brought before the

much laughed at, as a System of Divinity, our moderen wits, pretending, in a very absurd manner, to settle Christianity (I mean what our moderen High Church divines, now Call Christianity) upon a rational and Consistent foundation, not considering, that Christianity, in these latter Centuries, differs as much from Christianity in the apostolic times (which indeed is looked upon by many luke warm people to be a very rational Scheme) as any one Extreme can differ from another, the latter being supported by Reason, Philosophy & Sound morals, the first, by the Rites, Mysteries, and the power of the Clergy.

The Secretary also laid before the Club, a letter from Signior Lardini, Concerning the progress of the fund for the Charity School in Talbot County, requesting of the Club Subscriptions for the said School, but could not meet with the least Encouragement, the Club having long agoe, together with their money box, droped all manner of Charity, besides, they ruled themselves very much in that respect, by the known trite maxim *Charity begins at home,* and Talbot County being too far from home, they thought it best not to send their Charity, a thing, according to the || proverb, of a Cold temperature, over the bay of Chesopeak, as it would thereby (christenmass now advancing or the extreme cold Season) run the risk of being Ice bound or frost bit, and rendered much colder, and, I dare say, most will think it very prudential in this Club, to keep themselves and their Charity close by a Christenmass fire.

The Club Laws were at this Sederunt Revised Cursorily, but not finished, that business being deferred, till two thirds of the members should be present, but this was the last time the Club ever applied themselves to this necessary and useful work, for, in a short time after, the president's will became a law, and so there was no necessity for the Club, either to revise or Correct old laws, or enact new ones.

At Sederunt 144, Slyboots Pleasant Esqr being H:S: It was agreed, to prevent many disputes in Club, that the proviso of Law 45th should be repealed, at least this resolve appears to be entered on the book, tho, it was afterwards alledged in Club, at the Chancellor's trial, that this entry was an Interlineation, made long afterwards, by the then attorney General, to serve a Certain purpose, for his honor the president, as shall be related in it's proper place.

Mr Attorney Spyplot, at this Sederunt, accused the Secretary of a high trespass and misdemeanor, in using the great Seal of the Club for a missive letter, which he had sent to the President, at last Sederunt, alledging that it was a complicated crime, vizt: forgery, theft, and a gross abuse of the great

if I could discover your honor's Solium, the Celebrated Cathædra, which always used to appear, at the house of the H:S: some days before the great Solemnity of serving the Club; but to my Infinite consternation and dread, that august Seat and Canopy were no where || to be found, which has made me quake for fear ever since, least there might, peradventure, be either some latent treason in the case, or your honor's high displeasure might be portended thereby, and, as you designed in wrath to withdraw your person from us this evening, so, as a foreboding omen of this Terrible punishment, you retained the Chair in firm Custody. I hope, your honor, at the earnest Intreaty of your dutiful H:S: will convince us, that this is not the case, by first sending this Chair and canopy, and, in the next place coming to the Club yourself, and thus all dread and terror will dissipate and vanish, and, the more to enliven our Spirits, please to send with this black Ambassador, one Congium or four Sextarii, which the vulgar call a Gallon, of your best Spirit Ycleped Rum, which being mixed with good fr[uit,] Sugar and water, will, at the Second or third potatio[n, Insp]ire us with Sprightliness and wit, and make us all [look as] grand and Shining, as if we had Caps of State u[pon o]ur Nobs, I am, Honorable Sir, with all respect [and] obsequiousness, your honor's

[260]

Tuesday
Novr 20th 1750

Most Zealous Orator
Faithful Secretary, &
Diligent H:S:
Loquacious Scribble.

 This Lamentable letter, as his honor was pleased to call it, being Sealed with the great Seal of the Club, the members were about to call the Secretary to an account for this rash practice, but, it being done in Compliment to his honor the President, The Crime at this time was winked at.
 The Secretary then read some proposals from the Revd Mr Whiner, for printing by Subscription, a Compendious System of Divinity, Entituled *Florilegia Sacra*,[2] and applied || for Subscriptions from his honor and the members, but to no purpose, they were altogether deaf to such pious proposals as concerned the publication of Systems of Divinity, a woeful instance of this here ancient Club's being touched, or rather tainted with the pestilent Infidelity of the times, which so much ridicules the good old way of promoting the grouth of Xianity by way of System, that an antiquated foolish ballad in this our Corrupt and degenerate age, would not be so

[261]

---

2. Hamilton is referring to the compendious system of divinity produced by the Reverend Charles Lake (see biographical sketch).

and he had some warm disputes on some mathematical Subjects, in which kind of Science, the aforesaid learned Doctor would not allow the Secretary to be a Judge, and began to Catechise him on that point, as he thought, by desiring him to give a proper definition of an Astronomical Term, which that Sagacious Philosopher called the *Procession of the Equinoxes,* which *Procession,* had he called it *Precession,* as it is thought, he ought to have done, had nothing to do wth the Science of mathematics in General, as belonging properly to astronomy (and a man may possibly be a good mathematician, and yet a Sorry astronomer) The dispute, at which some Sharp words passed, was not in any likelihood, ever to come to a conclusion, since the one Gentleman as the proverb goes talked of Chalk and the other of Cheese, and besides, the Subject was not within the Compass of a proper Clubical Conversation, that is, it exceeded the understanding of most there present, however the result was that the Philosopher was so disgusted with the Club, as a parcell of Ignoramuses, and the Club with the Philosopher, as an ostentatious pedant, that neither chused to con- || verse together, ever since this learned altercation.

At Sederunt 143, on the 20th of November, Mr Secretary Scribble being H:S: his honor the president produced in Club a letter from the H:S: which being read was recorded as follows.

To the Honorable Nasifer Jole Esqr,
President of the Tuesday Club.

Honorable Sir,

It was a Saying of one of the wise men (not of Gotham but) of Greece, that nature Intended the head to rule over the members, and had therefore wisely allotted it the highest or most eminent place,[1] hence, it may be Inferred that the ancient and honorable Tuesday Club, has exactly followed the excellent pattern of that universal Schoolmistress, in allotting your honor, happily destined to rule o[ver] the old & longstanding members of that ancient Club, [the hi]ghest place in that circle or ring, your honors Ch[air of] State, being elevated above the others, by a degree of Six I[nches] and defended at top, by a grand Impending Canopy [of Sta]te.

Whilst I ruminated this morning upon that Grand Subject, it Seasonably came into my head that this day, this auspicious day, being the 20th of November, 1750, it was my Good fortune to serve your honor and the ancient Tuesday Club, in quality of H:S: I then Cast my eyes around to see,

1. See Plato, *Timaeus* 44D.

"Honorable Sir,

I rise up, by the Command of this here ancient and honorable Club, to return thanks to your honor, for the elegance and magnificence, with which your honor has entertained our longstanding members.

It is not, honorable Sir, that the Longstanding members of this here ancient and honorable Club are such Epicures, as to think there is any thing Superexcellent in fine eating and drinking, for they come not here to eat and to drink || only, but to enjoy one another in a Social and friendly manner, tho' by the bye, good eating and drinking in good company is not at all amiss; neither is it, honorable Sir, that we Imagine your honor entertains so despicable a notion of the Longstanding members of this here ancient Club, as to think you could please them only by dainties of this Sort, or nice eatables and drinkables; we are Confident, your honor thinks better things of us, but what moves our Gratitude and acknowledgement is this, that your honor seems to take particular pleasure, in bestirring yourself with Alacrity ardor and diligence, in the Service and Solace of the Longstanding members of this here ancient Club, which Signal piece of friendship, affection and good nature of your honor, towards the said Longstanding members of—hum,—hoh,—hum—I say, Sir—of the aforesaid ancient Club, is the more grateful and acceptable, as it proceeds from a person of your Eminence and high rank, in this here Society, which Crowns every obligation of this Sort with honor, for which we ought always to be grateful, and show respect to your honor, in the first place, and also to those Sumptuous cates, which you are so munificent as to set before us, and therefore, in the name of the Longstanding members of this here ancient Club, I as their orator, return your honor their most Sincere and hearty thanks for this kindness and condescension." [257]

The orator having thus spoke, Jonathan Grog Esqr Master of Ceremonies, craved leave to return him thanks for his Speech, and performed it in a silent and Solemn manner with a most profound bow.

Then the Secretary moved that the Club might revise and Correct the Laws, or appoint a Committee to do the || same, but this was postponed to another meeting. This was a point of honor, which the Secretary, insisted much on; for, as he had been the laborious penman of most of these Laws himself, he had as great a regard, in this affair to his own Character, as to the well being and Safety of the Club; but the Club seeing thro' his purposes, were slow in gratifying him, which piqued that officer much. [258]

This was the last Sederunt, on which that Celebrated Philosopher Dr Rhubarb, honored the Club with his presence, being Invited as a Stranger, according to ancient custom, for, it unluckily happened that the Secretary

answer to that Gentleman Concerning his Scheme for the Talbot County Charity School, what that answer was, shall be related in the Sequel.

Chapter VI

Speech of thanks to his honor the president, delivered by the orator, abuse of the Great Seal, Specimen of the Club's regard for Religion & Charity, Trial of the Secretary.

Nothing shows in a clearer light, the folly and weakness of human nature, than that of its being so open to flattery, and so apt to be misled by it, for what is more Common, than to observe men of good parts and understanding, very vain of talents, which in themselves are so far from Containing any merit, that on the Contrary, they are in the greatest degree insignificant; and often, the love of flattery, when it rises to a degree of extravagance, betrays as much as any thing an excessive Stock of Self-love, for those that most like to be flattered, are least apt to conceive a good opinion of other men, which flows from the overfondness they have of their own merit, preventing their entertaining any good opinion of the deserts of others.

The members of the ancient and honorable Tuesday Club, were very Sensible of this particular failing in their honorable President, and therefore took occasion to flatter him at all times, and particularly on that Subject of his Skill in Cookery, and elegance in setting out a table and entertainment, and they having now got a proper tool to set to work upon this good old Gentleman, the Secretary to wit, who never forbore larding him inside and out with pompous adulations, till he became so Self conceited that, in this particular province of Cooking and entertaining he would allow none to have any Skill or knowledge but himself.

At Sederunt 142, November 6th 1750, The Honorable Nasifer Jole Esqr, being H:S: the Club were entertained in a very Splendid and Elegant manner as usual, by his honor the H:S: and tho' the poet Laureats Genius did not Inspire him at this Juncture, to sing the honors of the feast, as he had done on a former occasion of his honor's ordinary Service night, yet, the roast and the boiled, the pies, Custards and delicate tarts and deserts that appeared on this occasion, were not unsaid, tho unsung, for, the Orator after Supper, being desired by the Club, to return thanks to his honor, delivered himself to the following purpose.

either himself convey'd the Great Seal into his pocket, or it was convey'd there by his own approbation and knowledge, both which he had the moment before denied.

After a Long dispute, concerning the Club's power to Chuse a Chancellor, and the privileges of that great officer, || his honor the president most graciously restored the Seal to Huffman Snap Esqr, desiring the Club to proceed with their Chancellor as they thought fit; and, when the orator was going to open the Charge against him, he voluntarily surrendered to the Club, the great Seal, which stopped further proceedings against him, and the Club, without delay proceeded to elect a deputy Chancellor, for the time being, 'till Philo Dogmaticus Esqr should return to resume his office, and the result was, that the Seal should be redelivered to Huffman Snap Esqr, and kept by him till that time; So opinionated were the members of this ancient Club in their wrong headed proceedings, that, tho' they had experienced the Ineptitude of this Longstanding member for that eminent deputation, yet would they still have him to continue in it, but his honor the president was Intirely at the bottom of this proceeding, for, rather than the Secretary, should have the trust of *that there* Seal, he would Consent that even the Devil in hell should be Chose Chancellor.

His honor the president showing much uneasiness and disgust, at the Great privileges granted to the Great Seal, by which a dangerous Check to the honor and prerogative of the Chair was established, endeavored to convince the members, how much their constitution was Endangered, if they suffered any such rule or order to take place, the members, more for the Sake of their own quiet, than, because they were Convinced of the truth of this assertion, revoked the order of Sederunt 133, concerning the great Seal, and resolved, that that order, and all other orders whatsoever, concerning the privileges of the great Seal in constituting a Club, should be annulled, abrogated, and rendered altogether void, and, that henceforward || it shall be a Club, when the president, or his deputy are in the Chair, and, the Chancellor, in Case of necessary absence, shall Committ the Seal to the Secretary, for that night, to be laid before the president at the meeting of the Club, which the Secretary is to return again to the Chancellor, on his appearance in Club.

It was then ordered that the members should Contribute one Shilling and Sixpence a piece at next Sederunt, to defray the expence of the new record book and the reparation of the Chair, to Jonathan Grog Esqr.

The Secretary then delivered some books from Signior Lardini to his honor the president and the members, and was ordered to return a final

blank upon it, not expecting to meet with this Criticism and reprehension from Mr Bowzer, who seldom showed any genius for remarks of this kind, but it is reasonable to think that a man, tho' he be reserved upon ordinary occasions, will not be so in his own defence.

The Question was put, whether he was guilty or not Guilty, and he was Cleared by a great majority.

Then the Orator was going to proceed to Impeach Huffman Snap Esqr, the deputy Chancellor, for his frequent absence, and neglecting to bring the great Seal, when, all of a Sudden that eminent badge of office, to the astonishment of all the members was a missing, having been, as it was thought, Clandestinly convey'd from the table, by some evil minded member, by which, the business of the Club was quite Interrupted, and high and Clamorous disputes arose thereupon; Mr Prim Timerous the high Steward likewise, grievously complained, of an Injury done him, the Club were very attentive to that gentleman, as he was very little given to make any bustle or complaint at any time, and Enquiring into the Cause of his discontent, he declared, *as God should Judge him* || that some one or other of the members had pirated a Choice Lemmon, with which he intended to have made a delicious bowl of punch after Supper; upon this, his honor the president very gravely took a Lemmon out of his pocket, and generously presented it to the H:S: which Lemmon was so like the one that was a missing that some of the members were Indiscreet enough to whisper it about, that it was the very same Identical Lemmon, others boldly asserted, among whom was Huffman Snap Esqr, deputy Chancellor, that his honor, with that Lemmon, intended a bribe to pacify the Club, In case it appeared to them that he had seized upon the Great Seal; A general Search for the Seal was agreed upon, and when every member had been searched, and every Stranger, (not excepting even the Reverend and Learned Dr Rhubarb and the facetious Gasperus Pickeringtonus, who had both been Invited to the Club that night,) when this Search, I say, had gone round all, except his honour the president, to the great astonishment of all the members, his honor very gravely took the great Seal out of his pocket and produced it in Club, declaring at the same time, that he could not tell how he came by it, but, that some friend to his honor and prerogative had convey'd it there, and asserted, that this piece of Conduct, he had been advised to, by some of the principal members of the Club, but his honor declined naming these pernicious advisers; It was thought however, that his honor meant the Secretary, but his honor was not aware how he betray'd himself in this apology, for it was either Stark nonsense, or otherwise he thereby owned, that he had

Jea: Sp: Honorable Sir, I thank your honor, and this here ancient and honorable Club,—and now, since I am acquitted, I must be so Ingenuous as to tell your honor, that I addressed Sir John out of picque [here Sir John started up from his chair, frowned, layd his hand on his Sword, and sat down again] because your honor seemed Inattentive, or would not harken to what I said.

Sir Jo: O! 'tis well you Explained yourself. [251]

Pres: Pray Sir, how could I hear you, before you spoke?

Sir Jo: Psha! ha done with this damn'd Stuff.

Then The Secretary brought an accusation against Tunbelly Bowzer Esqr, for transgressing Law 48, passed at Sederunt 133, June 12th 1750, he being then H:S: and having Invited no less than five Strangers to the Club, in one night.

Tunbelly Bowzer Esqr, made answer That he put it upon Mr Orator and the Club to prove, that these Gentlemen were there by his Invitation, and if they did so, he'd stand Condemned.

Secr: Sir, there is no necessity to prove that these Gentlemen were at the Club, by Mr Bowzer's Invitation; nay, it would be absurd either to demand or go upon any such proof, for, it is not to be supposed, that either your honor, or these here Long Standing members, can know what discourse passed between Mr Bowzer and these Gentlemen, at that time, it is enough that they were there by his permission, for it is to be presumed, they would not have staid in the Club without that, and Mr Bowzer's permission, I humbly conceive is tantamount to an Invitation. *Ergo* &ct:

Pres: What do you answer to that Mr Bowzer?

Tunb: Bowz: Sir, I have one answer still in reserve for that, which Mr Orator, perhaps, is not aware of, and which I hope will make him more Cautious in drawing up the Club Laws for the future, and it is this— granting that I am found Guilty of this here trespass, I cannot see, how I can be punished, according to the letter of Law 48, and if not according to the Letter, I am not punished by that Law ‖ and therefore by no law in this [252] here Club that I know of, and if by no Law, I am Illegally and unjustly punished, for Sir, the Law expressly says, that the high Steward so transgressing, is to serve as high Steward, the night Immediatly after the trespass, and this here present Sederunt, is so far from being the night Immediatly after, that it is not even the Club night Immediatly after the trespass, for, Sir, this here Sederunt, is the Second Club night after the fault said to be Committed.

The Secretary was somewhat abashed at this defence, and looked very

with it, is thereby annulled and of no force—I grant it Sir, were it really so, but this here is not the Case, for these two laws are neither Contradictory to, nor do they Clash with one another; The first, which is the article 5to of your honor's privileges, when your honor ascended that there Chair of State, is marked in the margin, *altered in Law 32*, but how altered? not so altered I hope, as to be quite annulled; The Law 32d only says, that the Speaker is to be addressed when any Speech is made, but does not expressly say, *first addressed;* The first Law ordains, that the President shall be *first addressed,* when any motion is made, but, I hope Sir, that your honor, and all the Longstanding members of this here Club, will allow that there is a difference betwixt a Speech & a motion, besides, the first law, is only marked *Altered*, the Second Law, is expressly noted in the margin *Revoked;* and why Revoked? your honor and these here Gentlemen know, that for a Considerable time past, there has been no such officer in this here Club as a Speaker, and therefore, this here Law naturally drops, unless the Gentleman, will undertake to assert, that the worshipful Sir John, is Speaker of this Club [here Sir John frowned] further, it is absurd to say, that any law that is revoked, can either be broken or observed, whereas, it is easy to conceive, how a law that is altered, may be both, it is my humble opinion then, honorable Sir, and, I hope, also the opinion of your Hon- ‖ or and these here gentlemen, that Jealous Spyplot Senr Esqr has been guilty of a manifest breach of this here altered law; in fine, Mr President Sir, allowing that the latter Law abolished the first, in express terms, as it stands here in the book (which by the bye, I have not allowed it does) yet, even in that case, such a law would be void and absurd in itself, for, your honor will please to take notice, that the first law, is the privilege 5to of your honor's Chair and dignity, and, I humbly conceive, that it is not in the power of the members of this here Club, to pass any law, which tends to Encroach upon, or abolish, any of your honor's privileges, or prerogatives, without your honor's Consent.

Pres: So I think too, and I'm Sure I never Consented to any such unreasonable Law.

Then it was put to the Question, whether Jealous Spyplot Senior Esqr, was guilty of the Charge brought against him, or not Guilty.

Mr Orat: Sir John, is Jealous Spyplot Senr Esqr, guilty of this Charge brought against him or not Guilty?

Sir John: [laying his right hand on his left breast] not Guilty upon mine honor,—and so of the Rest—Jealous Spyplot Senr Esqr, being thus acquitted, rose up & spoke to this purpose.

Prim Timorous Esqr H:S: when the Secretary brought an accusation, according to a former order of the Club, against Jealous Spyplot Senr Esqr, for a high trespass and Contempt of the Chair, in addressing himself Solely to Sir John at Sederunt 139, against the Tenor of Law 19th, where among other privileges, granted to his honor the president, it is there expressly said 5to "That if any motion is made in Club, the President is to be first addressed, by the moving member, giving him his proper title."

The Secretary opened the Charge, as orator of the Club, in a warm and pathetic Speech, for the privileges and prerogatives of the Chair, showing, how dangerous it was to the Clubical Constitution, to violate and break thro' them, and Called upon Jealous Spyplot Senr Esqr, to answer to the Charge.

Jeal: Spy: Mr President Sir, I would ask your honor and this here club one single Question—

Pres: Sir, we are ready to answer all the Questions you will ask.

Jeal: Sp: Pray Sir, when two Laws are in being, which seem Contradictory one to the other, or to clash, which of them ought to be obeyed?

Pres: Methinks that which was last enacted annulls the other, and therefore ought to be the Law in force, especially if it is consistent with the privileges and prerogative of our Chair.

Jeal: Spy: Then Mr President Sir, here is a law passed, Sederunt 25th, Novr 26th 1745, which directs the address to be made to the Chair, which I find marked in the margin thus, *altered in Law 32,* let us then Sir, turn to Law 32, passed Sederunt 47, october 28, 1746, where we find these express words, that *Mr Speaker shall be adressed, when any Speech is made in Club.* I hope then Mr President, your honor and this here Club, will find that I have transgressed no Law now in being in this here Club, in not addressing the Chair, and therefore acquit me of the Charge Mr Orator has brought against me.

Pres: What have you to say to that, Mr Orator?

Orat: Sir, a great deal, tho Mr Spyplot be a worthy member of this here Club, for whom I have a most profound respect, yet, when I find our Laws, or constitution broke thro', especially such laws honorable Sir, as have any relation, to your honor's privileges or prerogative, I cannot help araigning and accusing the Guilty members, be they who they will, and, I am sorry, very sorry, honorable Sir, that Mr Spyplot, a gentleman whom I so much esteem and respect, should have obliged me, by his Imprudent behavior, to accuse and araign him in this here Club, which I now do, by virtue of my office, as orator. Mr Spyplot has said, that the law that was last in force ought to be observed, and that the preceeding law, which Clashes

know and understand these rules, was no great honor to that Society of Gentlemen; With Sir John, because that boisterous Champion, always declared, that he valued none of their Laws, and would be bound by no Laws but those of his own framing.

At Sederunt 140, october 9th 1750, Jealous Spyplot Senr Esqr, being deputy H:S: in place of his Son, it was resolved by the Club, to examine into the nature of an order passed, by the Club, at Sederunt 133, concerning the privilege of the great Seal, which was found to be Inconvenient to the Club, on account of the nonattendance of the deputy Chancellor.

This Symbol of office in the Club, had begun to raise, Considerable disturbances, both in the presence of the chief Chancellor and his absence, and we shall soon see it prove the Cause of a most terrible Civil Commotion, and unnatural Rebellion, in the Club, for the original of this mischief the Club had only themselves to blame, for, by their obstinatly refusing, to promote the Secretary, that faithful Drudge and Servant, according to his merit, he purposely threw this bone of Contention in their way to excite discord among them. In the Chancellor's presence, his own ambitious views, concerning the aggrandizing of himself, occasioned much altercation and hurly burly in the Club, and, in his absence, the Club's capriciously Committing the great Seal into bad hands at Sederunt 133, against an express determination of the Club at the preceeding Sederunt, occasioned much uneasiness, whereas, had they let it remain in the hands of the Secretary, who was the most constant attendant on the Club, all the mischief would have been evaded, but it was now come to that pass, with this unhappy officer, that neither the President nor the Club Cared much to trust him in any thing, and suspected very much his fidelity in keeping the records, his honor and the members often alledging || that he filled them up, with arrant Sophisticated Stuff of his own Inventing; This his honor asserted meerly out of a defect in memory, for, it was his peculiar foible, to forget Intirely at one Sederunt, what he had done and said at another, as for the Club, they could not possibly here be mistaken, but they obstinately persevered in this humor, either to Cajole and flatter his honor the President, or as some Imagined, to make fun, between his honor and the Secretary.

At this Sederunt also, the Club took Into their Serious Consideration, the proposal made by Signior Lardini at last Sederunt, concerning the Charity School in Talbot County, but came to no final resolution, either with regard to this or the affair of the Great Seal, postponing the further Consideration of both, to a more full meeting of the members.

On the 23d of October 1750, was held Sederunt 141, at the house of

Admiring, Pleasd, we sit entranc'd
To hear thy numbers flow,
With beauteous accents all around
From thy unerring bow.
Humbly Inscribed, to Signior Lardini Esqr,
Chief Musician of the Tuesday Club.

This poem was composed by Signior Don John Charlotto, Gentleman Usher to his honor the President, and was much approved of by the Club, only, that thro' Misinformation, he had given him the office of Solo Neverout Esqr, Calling him Chief musician to the Club, Instead of musician *con Stromenti*.

Before the Club broke up, at this Sederunt, Signior Lardini played several Jiggs, hornpipes and minuets *Con Violino Solo,* to which, Sir John, knight and Champion to the Club, danced several bold & martial dances.

Chapter V

Trial of Mr Attorney Spyplot, Tryal of Tunbelly Bowzer Esqr, General Search for the Great Seal, repeal of the order of Sederunt 133.

I have read somewhere in a very good author, but cannot now recollect his name, That Laws without penalties are only good advice. This is not only true with regard to Laws that have no penalties annexed, but also, such laws as are so worded, or expressed in such terms, as that their penalties can either be evaded, or cannot be enforced; This is the very case, If I am not much mistaken, with most, if not all the Laws of the Ancient Tuesday Club, with most, because in fact most of these Laws are without penalties, and with all, because there is no method as yet fallen upon to enforce the penalties of such laws as have penalties Annexed to them, and, in a particular manner, it is the Case with Law 48, which is so worded and conceived, as, that it is next to Impossible to put the penalty in execution— The Secretary, perceiving this great defect in the Club Laws, had, at sundry times moved the revival or Correction of them, but was always opposed by the President and Sir John; by the President, because it was a favorite maxim with his honor, that there was no necessity for any laws at all, unless in a Club of disorderly and unruly people, and that to have any laws or rules but ‖ the rules of good manners among gentlemen, who were supposed to

and which are all figured out, within the compass, and comprehended within the small circumference, of that there Significant *Cap*.

[243] Having thus, honorable Sir, discussed the Cap, I come now to what is contained under it, *The Head; O Demosthenes! O Cicero!* O ye Shining Geniuses of Ancient Greece and Rome! noble orators! why are you not here to blazon forth this Glorious Subject? a Subject far, O far surpassing, the puny abilities of this here poor weak orator, of this here ancient and honorable Club; what shall I say on this head? Such a head! Such a precious head! this *Carum,* this *Preclarum Caput!*[4] in it are treasures, hoards of precious contents, too numerous, too Shining to be ennumerated; to be looked on! There is wisdom, perspicuity, depth of Judgement, profound penetration & wit of the Genuine and Sterling Stamp; none of your low, base, *Conundrum* coin; and in fine, Solidity Impenetrable. I most Sincerely wish, and pray, honorable Sir, that your honor's understanding, may long be preserved, firm and Sound, I mean your honor's legs, the Supporters of that useful, Important and necessary head, and, I dare be bold to say, that all the longstanding members of this here ancient Club, Join with me, in their ardent wishes, that your honor's Underprops, or Understanders, may long, for the good of this here ancient and honorable Club, continue firm, Sound and Robust, and never more be Infested, tormented, or assaulted, with that paltry, ungrateful, and beggarly distemper the gout, *amen* and *amen*.

The Secretary having pronounced this oration, had the applause of the Club, but Mr Attorney Spyplot, was pleased to observe, addressing himself still to Sir John, that this Speech was good enough in the main, but too much abounding in the usual daubing and flattery, peculiar to Certain [244] frothy ‖ orators of this here Club, to which Sir John assented by a Significant nod, and a twist of his mouth, which he made In shifting of his Chaw.

Then Signior Lardini rising up, requested, that a certain poem might be produced, which had been delivered to the Secretary, and Inscribed to himself, saying further, That he hoped the honorable the President and Club, would easily excuse the mistake the Ingenious bard had made in the denomination of his office, since the Compliment was well meant,—This poem was produced, and read in Club, and ordered to be recorded as follows.

> Unmatch'd Lardini, Tune thy Lyre,
> And Touch the trembling String,
> Thy warbling music Charms our Ear,
> And we with Rapture sing.

---

4. "This dear, this outstanding head!"

Sederunt 125, I had the honor to make a motion in this here ancient Club, That there should be a *Cap of State,* provided at our proper expence, for your honor to wear in the Chair, which motion at that time was Strenuously seconded, and the vote passed in the affirmative; however, either thro' the remissness of this here ancient Club, or thro' your honor's extreme humility and Self Denyal, this here Intended CAP OF STATE was altogether droped and seemed to be forgot; and now, honorable Sir, the case seems to be parallel between you and I, when the thing was sopite and unthought of, and there was no more mention made of this here *Cap;* we, the members of this here ancient Club, are altogether Surprized, and, our eyes, as it were dazzled, to find, that your honor's head, is, as it were, miraculously adorned with such an *Identical Cap,* and wears that very distinguishing badge of State, without this here ancient Club's being any way concerned, in the procuring or preparing of it.

Allow me then most honorable Sir, to congratulate your honor, upon this Surprizing and Remarkable Incident. To speak in a figurative manner, that there *Cap,* which your honor now wears, possesses several qualities, which in an elegant manner Typify and represent, the great and many fold excellencies and virtues which adorn your honor, as president of this here ancient Club, and they are these—As that there *Cap,* is of the Species of Silk ‖ which we call velvet, it is light, smooth, Shining, and we may add to these, [242] the Secondary quality or accident of it's Color, which, I humbly conceive to be green. Now, your honor and these here gentlemen will please to take notice, that the lightness of it, Implies the great lenity and gentleness of your honor's government and administration, in this here ancient club, the Smoothness denotes that Superlative ease pleasure and facility, with which all things go on, while your honor sits at the helm, and regulates the course of this here ancient Club; The Shining, or nitidity of its Surface, may be said to Imply, or signify, the uncommon brightness of your honor's parts, as also the glory and unsullied equity of your honor's determinations and proceedings in that there Chair, and the Color Green, being as it were, the universal Robe, or mantle of Nature, in which she seems most to delight, a color which overspreads the whole Surface of this terraqueous globe, since, not only the land, but even the vast ocean itself, in some degree is tinged with it, a Color, on which the eye dwells with pleasure,—this Sir, has such a String of Significant emblems in it, that I am quite at a loss to express them; but in short, as we view this Charming Color with delight, so, with delight, honorable Sir, we view and admire your honor in that there chair, we admire and contemplate your wisdom, Justice, lenity, good humor, generosity, and a thousand other good qualities of which you are possessed,

ing a Charity School in Talbot County on the eastren Shore,³ and applied to them for Subscriptions to further the same, but the affair was deferred to the Consideration of a Subsequent Sederunt.

Jealous Spyplot Senior Esqr, in several long Speeches he made in Club, addressed himself to Sir John, in Contempt of the Chair, which trespass was ordered to be further considered at some Subsequent Sederunt, and a prosecution ordered against him.

His honor the President, after Supper, having ornamented his head, with a Gorgeous Cap of Green velvet, In- ‖ tending it (as it is thought) as a prelude to, or rather memorandum, for the promised cap of State, The Secretary to display himself and his talents as orator, at his first entry on the office, rose up and addressed his honor and the Club, in manner and form following.

Most Honorable President, and worthy Gentlemen,

It seems not Strange to me, that your honor, and this here ancient and honorable Club, have dignified me with the eminent place and title of *orator*, of your own free will & pleasure, without the least application or Sollicitation on my part,—Tho in times elapsed, your honor and these here Gentlemen must know, that this very title and dignity was by me applied for, and aspired to in vain. I say, by me, the very person upon whom you are pleased now, as it were Capriciously to confer it. This Surprizing incident, this unaccountable conduct of your honor and this here ancient and honorable Club, only Indicates to me, what I very well knew before, that the arogant views of the ambitious are often deservedly frustrated, while the modest and quiet man, who humbles himself, and gapes not after preferrment, is suddenly, we can't tell how, exalted and promoted to dignities and titles. Tho' this has plainly been my Case, and a great honor, and weighty charge unlooked for, has unexpectedly been claped on my back, yet I humbly request, that your honor, and this here ancient and honorable Club, would excuse my nonacceptance of this eminent office, seeing I have abundance of other business to employ me, in keeping the archives & records of this here ancient Club, in quality of their Secretary.

But to come to the point. Honorable Sir, your honor, and these here gentlemen, may well remember, that sometime agoe, I think, it was at

---

3. A good account of Thomas Bacon's efforts to establish this school for orphans and poor children appears in Richard Beale Davis, *Intellectual Life in the Colonial South, 1585–1763*, 3 vols. (Knoxville, Tenn., 1978), I, 285–288. An advertisement placed in the *Maryland Gazette* for Apr. 12, 1753, indicates that Hamilton (and no doubt other of the club's members) was involved in helping to establish this school.

ished, and banished the Club for ever, to the no small Satisfaction of the Master of Ceremonies and the Secretary, whose Invention was already worn thread bare in this (as it was esteemed) low and vulgar exercise.

Thus Ended the Club Conundrums, which had Continued now for 16 Sederunts, the first that were proposed in Club, being at Sederunt 123, and the last at this present Sederunt, which is Sederunt 139, so that the Club conundrums amounted in all to 64; These pieces of Ingenuity were never calculated to gain a great character in the Club, for, since all men are not of an equal acuteness of genius, in exercises of wit, those who are more dull and slow of apprehension, Generally have a Jealousy of, or rather picque at such as set up for being wits, therefore many of the Longstanding members were uneasy at the master of ceremonies and the Secretarie's outshining them in this very particular, hence, they not only conceived an aversion to the conundrums, but the framers of them, and these latter gentlemen, perceiving that those trials of Skill, procured them the ill will of their fellow members, were very glad to get rid of them, the discord they had occasioned in Club too, with regard to Laconic Comas and the Chancellor, much hurt their character; besides, this being a Species of wit, only appropriated to persons in high life, it was thought by the best Critics, that they were quite Improper to be used in Clubs, unless these Societies chose to act out of Character, and beyond their Sphere, high life being none of their province.

There was at this Sederunt a very unexpected question ‖ started in [239] Club, which was, whether the club should proceed to chuse an orator? This question passed in the affirmative and the Secretary was chose into that office, by a great majority, This office the Secretary persisted in refusing to accept, either as it is thought, out of an affected modesty, or, because he was not satisfied with the bare title and office, unless he enjoyed thereby, the Station of a State member; the President protested at first, against the Club's proceeding in this affair, but the Club were resolved to regard neither the Secretarie's refusal nor the President's protest, but forced the office upon the one and the officer on the other; and, tho' his honor consented at last that the Secretary should be Orator of the Club, yet he never would Consent to give him the distinguished title of a State member, This office, it is thought, the Secretary procured by the Interest of the Eastren Shore Triumvirate, whose particular favorite he was, Tho some people wondered at this bad policy of the Triumvirate, in making a minion of one, whom they very well knew, their Patron and protector, neither regarded nor esteemed.

Signior Lardini laid before his honor and the Club a Scheme for erect-

[237]   Secretarie's Conundrums

Conundrum 3d

When may the poet Homer be likened to a garret window?

The Revd Mr Smoothum Sly gave for answer, when he is *Dormant*,[1] the Club allowed the answer, and the Secretary drinking a bumper delivered his answer.

ans: When he is *dormant*
 aliquando bonus dormitat Homerus[2] }

Conundrum 4th

Why is a Sevil orange like a pox curing quack?

The Club gave it up, after some time spent in profound Cogitation, and the Secretary gave his answer.

ans: Because we have a *peel* / *pill* } from it.

This Conundrum, Just as the Master of Ceremonies had Solemnly laid his hand upon the Secretaries head to declare him victor, was condemned by the Club, & declared to be naught, and, the Secretary was ordered to drink a bumper, which he refused, alledging that there was no law to Oblige him so to do.

The Learned and Ingenious Doctor Rhubarb observed upon this conundrum of the Secretarie's, that there was a great Impropriety in it's Structure, for that we not only had a pill from a Sevil orange, but there was also abundance of Juice in it, if the orange was good, which observation he accompanied with an affected laugh, a thing very usual, with that polite Gentleman, by this he showed his great Judgement in the Art of Conundrumification, none in the Club Contradicted this Doctor's Remarks, for they were Generally much out of the reach of persons of Common understanding.

[238]   It was then moved by Jealous Spyplot Senr Esqr and seconded by the worshipful Sir John, that the Conundrums should be totally abolished and expelled, as a Species of low wit altogether unworthy of the dignity of the Club, and, upon the vote's passing round, they were, unanimously abol-

---

1. A *dormant*, or dormer window.
2. "Sometimes good Homer sleeps" (or nods, similar to Horace, *Ars poetica* 359).

one part of the Clubical power and authority, lodged in the hands of the officers of State, would enable him more easily to effect his design of rendering himself absolute in the Club.

Signior Lardini, musician to the Club, *con Stromenti,* entertained his honor and the longstanding members this Evening, with several new pieces of Music, Solo, upon the violin.

The high Steward this night was guilty of a manifest trespass against Law 48, passed at Sederunt 132, In inviting to the Club no less than five Strangers, for which he was ordered to be called to an account, and an Enquiry made Into it at a Subsequent Sederunt; In this order, the Club was guilty of a great oversight, for, according to the tenor of that law, they ought to have condemned the H:S: to serve the Club, at the following Sederunt, or rather the day Immediatly following this, which, by their neglecting to do, he, by that means evaded the punishment prescribed for the trespass, as we shall soon see related.

The Conundrums being called for, after Supper, Jonathan Grog Esqr, produced his.

Club Conundrums

Jonathan Grog Esqr

Conundrum 1st

Why is a man with a moderate pox, like a finished Church bell?

After some Consideration Quirpum Comic esqr, made answer, Because he has a *Clapper,* which the Club allowed to be good. Then Mr Grog gave in his answer.

ans: Because he is not without a *Clapper*—dr: a bump:

Conundrum 2d

Why is matrimony like Polyphemus's eye?

The Club gave it up and Mr Grog delivered his answer.

ans: Because it is a great $\left.{tye \atop eye}\right\}$ decl: victor.

This Conundrum was Condemned by the Club as Improper, and altogether Insignificant, upon which Jonathan Grog Esqr, after having been formally declared victor, by the Secretary, drank a bumper, tho' not obliged to do so by any Law or rule of the club, which Indicated either his Ignorance of the Club laws, or his great affection for a bumper.

standing Members of this here ancient and honorable Club, recommending it to you at all times, to pay to them that deference and Submission, that is Justly due."

Then Mr Smirker made a Low bow to the Chair and having delivered a short Speech of thanks, returned to his Seat, and was Saluted as a Triumvir, by the Revd Mr Sly, and Signior Lardini.

Thus we find how the Empire and Dominion of this ancient Club, had already fixed itself on the Eastren Shore, by their becoming arbitrators and Judges, even in the case of electing and appointing members, for the Worshipful triumvirate.

The Secretary then produced in Club, the Eulogium upon Merry Makefun Esqr, Late a worthy honorary member of the Club, and a Triumvir, which being read and approved of, was ordered to be entered in the Club's book of records as follows.

By the order of the Honorable the President and Club.

The honorable the President, the State members, the long standing and honorary members of the ancient and honorable Tuesday Club, being thorro'ly convinced, that real worth and merit, wherever they constitute a Character, never fail to meet with that Just applause, which they deserve, and that men, reasonably lament the loss, when ‖ they are deprived by death, of such persons as are endued with these excellent qualities, upon this occasion, therefore, they think themselves Strictly bound in gratitude and humanity to bestow that Just Encomium upon the worth and merit of Merry Makefun Esqr, Late an Honorary member of this Club, which is due to the memory of so good a man, and to deplore the loss of so excellent and worthy a member, of whom the Irresistable and Inexorable hand of Death, has Irretrievably deprived them, whereby the public in General or the Society has lost a person of activity Skill and Integrity in business, a good Common wealth's man, or, a Zealous promoter of the Common Interest, the private Society of his own friends, a kind, facetious, pleasant, candid and Sincere Companion, The poor a Charitable, Generous and humane benefactor, and this Club a most worthy and excellent member. *By order of his honor the president and Club, this Eulogium, Sacred to his memory, is entered in their book of Records.*

It was ordered by the Club, that the tryals of the State officers for the future, to prevent unnecessary disputes, should be carried on by way of Indictment; this order, it is thought, was obtained at the Instance and by the Interest of his honor the President, who thought, that the breaking of

"Mr President Sir, and you the Longstanding members, and honorary members of this here ancient Club,

I am to Inform you, that, by the Late Inexpressible loss of Mr Merry Makefun, our Eastren Shore Triumvirate, of which worshipful Society, I have the Honor to be a member, is reduced to two. We look upon you, honorable Sir, to be the head and father of our Society, as well as of this here ancient and honorable Club, your worthy and generous deeds to us, and to this here ancient and honorable Club in particular, render you highly deserving of that Eminent title and dignity, we of the Triumvirate, honorable Sir, as we were originally nursed up, under your Paternal Care and protection, so, we deem ourselves to be your Children, and more especially, seeing we are also Composed of honorary members of this here ancient and honorable Club; we apply therefore, to you, honorable Sir, the *Original* of our health and mirth, to restore us again || to our former State, by adding [233] one to our number, and therefore, we humbly propose your honorary member, Mr Theophilus Smirker, to your honor, and the worthy Members of this here ancient and honorable Club, as a person worthy to fill up that vacancy, and hope, our recommendation will be agreeable to your honor and these worthy Gentlemen, while I, in the name of my fellow Triumvirs declare, that if we should be so happy, as to see any of the longstanding members of this here ancient and honorable Club on our Side the water, we shall always be proud, to entertain them in the handsomest and most elegant manner we can."

The Ambassador having delivered this Speech sat down, and Jealous Spyplot Senr Esqr, remarked upon it, that it was too much spiced up, or overseasoned with flattery & bombast.

Then the Ballots being put round by the Command of his honor the President, Theophilus Smirker Esqr was unanimously elected a Triumvir in the Place of Merry Makefun Esqr Deceased, and Jonathan Grog Esqr, Master of the Ceremonies, leading him to the foot of the Table confirmed him in the following form, Solemnly laying his hand upon his head.

"Sir,

I as master of the Ceremonies of this here ancient Club, which mastery in Ceremonies I acknowledge to have received by the Grace and favor, of his honor the president, with all the Ceremony I am master of, do declare, pronounce and proclaim you, Theophilus Smirker Esqr, a lawful, true, and duely elected Triumvir of the || worshipful Eastren Shore Triumvirate, and [234] here do Solemnly confirm you, in the name of his honor the President and the Longstanding members of this here ancient and honorable Club, in token of which, I present you to his honor the president, and the Long-

Strange, Societies that are composed of wise, Staied and grave members, and can boast of having men of wit and learning, and even *people of fashion* in their number, an example of this will soon appear, and that in a very Strong light, in the Conduct of the ancient and honorable Tuesday Club, both with regard to the honorable the president, and the whole posse of the Longstanding members, The first, in his Countenancing the Introduction of a *Cap of State,* which he had long agoe disapproved of, either thro an affected or real modesty, the Latter, in their creating the Secretary orator of the Club, in a manner aganst his will, and when ‖ he was far from soliciting for it, or trowbling his head about that promotion, which he had nevertheless heretofore, used all his policy and artifice to obtain, and (as we have seen) in vain.

On the 18 of September, 1750, by the Special order of his honor the President, was held an Extraordinary Sederunt of the Club, being Sederunt 139, when Tunbelly Bowzer Esqr, served as H:S: This Club was held upon account of weighty and Important matters to be Considered, the Eastren Shore Triumvirate having sent over Embassadors to the Club, which was their third Embassy since their Institution.

The Secretary being called upon to read the proceedings of last Sederunt, he was stop'd by Jealous Spyplot Senr Esqr, who rising up declared That according to a former rule or order of the Club, passed at Sederunt 133 and also at last Sederunt, the Club is not regularly formed, till the great Seal appears upon the table, and, as Huffman Snap Esqr, deputy Chancellor, had not as yet come to take his Seat in Club, and deposit the Great Seal before his honor the president, no proceedings ought to be read till that was done—on which the Secretary desisted.

This objection raised the Spleen of his honor the President to a very great degree, and Indignation appeared very plain thro' his timber Countenance, he could not digest the thought of the great Seal's being set up as his rival, and made a Check to his authority and power, nor could he sit easy in his chair, till this absurd order of the Club, (as he was pleased to call it) was revoked, which rendered him altogether a Cypher, or person of no authority.

The deputy chancellor was often sent for, but did not come till Just before Supper, which excited much wrangling in Club between his honor and the members, but Huffman Snap Esqr, at last making his appearance, the proceedings were read, and all parties were easy.

Then the Revd: Mr Smoothum Sly, a Triumvir standing up in his place, delivered the Substance of the Embassy from the Triumvirate, addressing his honor the president and the Club to this purpose.

ans: Because it is a great *Deal*.[5]

The Club condemned this Conundrum as naught, because the word *Deal*, is not applicable to any other but a pine plank, and therefore as it was not expressly denominated a pine plank in the Conundrum, It could not pass, to which opinion of the Club, the Secretary with some difficulty submitted, and being ordered either to drink a bumper, or produce another Conundrum, he would do neither till such time, as the Club produced an express rule or Law for it, upon which some members moved, that the Secretary should be Indicted for a contempt.

Conundrum 4th

Why is a well frequented house of office, like a battallion of horse Guards drawn up?

The Club gave it up, the Secretary delivered his answer.

ans: Because in it there is much *ordure* } *order*

He was declared victor, and the Club broke up.

Chapter IV

[230]

Extraordinary Club, appointed by his honor the President, Third Embassy of the Triumvirate, Election of a Triumvir, Eulogium on a Triumvir deceased, Club Conundrums, opinion of Dr Rhubarb on the Secretaries Conundrum, abolition and expulsion of the Conundrums, Sublime Speech by the Secretary, The Secretary created Club Orator.

Tho' caprice be a foible most Incident to fools, yet at times wise men will suffer themselves to be ruled by it, we need not turn over History and ancient Records to produce Instances of this, any man who goes abroad in the world, and is conversant with his own Species, will meet with frequent or daily Instances of it among all conditions and Scenes, not only Individuals are sway'd at particular Junctures by this odd humor, but whole Societies suffer themselves to be ruled by it, and what would seem somewhat

---

5. A *deal* is a slice of wood not more than seven inches wide and three inches thick; applied exclusively to pine and fir.

Infinite multitude of maggots, that bred in a very short time in Cheese and other Substances, while he was Lengthning out his Discourse, Dr Pyrgos with a Sneer said, Pray Sir—Dr Rhubarb with a Smile said—Permit me Sir—Prithee now—says Dr Pyrgos—Look ye now, Sir, says Dr Rhubarb—Poh! poh! says Dr Pyrgos—These maggots, as I said Sir, says Dr Rhubarb—maggots Sir?—says Dr Pyrgos—The maggots in the Cheese Sir—says Dr Rhubarb—Pish! Pish! you mean the maggots in your brain & mine Sir, says Dr Pyrgos,—this raised a laugh in Club, and here the Dispute ended, much to the Satisfaction of the longstanding members, who, not understanding Logic, metaphysics or Physics, this discourse and dispute to them was dry and unentertaining.

It was observed, that during this learned disputation, The deputy president Jealous Spyplot Senr: Esqr, fell fast asleep in the Chair, which was particularly taken notice of by Solo Neverout Esqr, and he made a request, that there should be an entry made thereof in the book, that he might not in this particular Circumstance stand alone.

Then the Conundrums were Called for, and Jonathan Grog Esqr, gave in his as follows.

Club Conundrums

Conundrum 1st

Why is a pregnant woman, from the fourth month untill her time, like the Sea in a Calm?

[229] Solo Neverout Esqr made answer, because she *Swells,* which being allowed good, Mr Grog drank a bumper & gave in his answer.

ans: Because she is always *Swelling.*

Conundrum 2d

How is an under Sheriff, like the neck of a Miller's Shirt?

It was given up, and Mr Grog delivered his answer.

ans: Because he often has a thief by the *Collar*—dec: victor.

Secretary's Conundrums

Conundrum 3d

Why is a plumb Sterling, like a four Inch plank 40 foot long?

The Club gave it up, The Secretary delivered his answer.

happened to be upon the nature of Insects, and the Polypus, a creature lately discovered by the virtuosi, or Connoiseurs in the Secrets of nature, to have a power of multiplying itself,[2] was the Subject of their discourse and argument, Dr Rhubarb took most of the talk to himself, and Dr Pyrgos seemed to show a great Contempt for him, as professed Scholars and Philosophers will sometimes do for one another; but the Ground of this Contempt, was laid upon a Correction, which Dr Rhubarb made, on an expression of Dr Pyrgos, in a preceeding conversation between them, wherein, it appeared, that the first alledged, that the latter || broke Priscians head,[3] and uttered false grammar, for Dr Pyrgos having occasion to use the term *ex post facto*, Dr Rhubarb, being of opinion that the latter proposition *post*, and not the first *ex*, governed in this Case, hastily Interrupted him, & said *Ex post factum* Sir!—with an Emphasis,—Dr Pyrgos repeated again, *ex post facto*, with an equal emphasis—*ex post factum!* says Dr Rhubarb,—*ex post facto*—says Dr Pyrgos—and thus the dispute continued for some time, without any other mode of reasoning; like two Schoolboys that get at it tooth and nail, with I say yes, and I say no, but it is not known which of these philosophers had the last word;—Again, what contributed to Increase Dr Pyrgos's contempt for this learned man, was an expression used by him, in a certain disputation, where one of the Company made use of the term *Ens rationis* (well known to Logicians and Metaphysicians) as a term of contempt, throwing a Slur on his adversarie's argument; The Learned Dr Rhubarb observed, that the Gentleman was mistaken, or else must be supposed to speak Ironically, for, that *Ens rationis,* was the very Quintessence of Reason, This Specimen of Dr Rhubarb's Grammatical and Logical Learning, Induced Dr Pyrgos to conclude, that he was only a pretender to literature, and, at best, but a muddy headed fellow; However, in their Conversation at the Club, Dr Rhubarb fell at last, upon Equivocal Generation, a doctrine of the ancient Philosophers,[4] and happened to say, that he was almost Induced to believe, that there was || such a thing in nature, from the

[227]

[228]

---

2. *Polypus,* or *polyp,* is the general name for any number of animals capable of asexual reproduction, but in this context it refers particularly to the freshwater hydra, the discovery of which was perhaps the most momentous microscopic revelation of the eighteenth century. Numerous articles on the polypus appeared in the *Philosophical Transactions* of the Royal Society between 1742 and 1758 (volumes XLII through L).

3. Priscian (fl. early 6th century A.D.) was a Roman grammarian who taught at Constantinople and whose *Institutiones grammaticae* is the most voluminous work extant of any Latin grammarian; to *break Priscian's head* is therefore to violate the rules of grammar.

4. *Equivocal generation* is another term for spontaneous generation, or the ability of certain plants and animals to come to life without parents, as from lifeless matter. Aristotle refers to this phenomenon in the *Historia animalium.*

State policy and craft; for, had he brought the Club to own, that the Chancellor, had made a Resignation of his office, in delivering the Seal to him, he would Surely have steped into that office himself, but the Club saw thro' his design, and by their cautious and wise answer to the question, disappointed his ambitious purposes.

His honor the Deputy president, showed some reluctance to determin some of these points, unless his honor the Chief president had been present himself, what Mr Spyplots design could be, in showing this complaisance to the Chair, who always, without disguise, set up as an assertor of the Liberties of the Club, I can by no means Conjecture.

The Club then proceeded to chuse a Chancellor *pro tempore,* till Philo Dogmaticus Esqr, should return, and Huffman Snap Esqr, was chosen by ballot, Jonathan Grog Esqr, Mr of Ceremonies, in the name of, and by the authority of the President & Club, Solemnly delivering into his hands the great Seal.

His honor the president was very much Incensed at this proceeding of the Club, and alledged, that they had Committed an open breach of Law 45th, called the Second prerogative Law, but the Club never would own themselves Guilty of this breach.

The Secretary then moved for a revisal and ammendment of the Laws of the Club, either by a Committee chosen for that purpose, or by the Club in full meeting, and was Sharply reproved by Sir John, for presuming to direct the Club in that matter, and the motion was not seconded, being put off till the Honorable Nasifer Jole Esqr, should be in Club.

Jonathan Grog Esqr, presented in Club, the Record book, beautified and enlarged, and titled on the back, he also reported, that he had repaired the presidential Chair, for which the Club agreed to refund his Charges.

The Eulogium on Merry Makefun Esqr, late a worthy honorary member of the Club, was not brought into Club this night, having been left at the house of the late h:S: and was ordered to be considered at next Sederunt.

There were in the Club at this Sederunt, Invited as Strangers, according to ancient Custom, two very eminent persons as to learning and accomplishments, vizt: Dr Rhubarb, whom we have mentioned before, and Dr Pyrgos.

These two personages passed with many, for very Eminent Scholars and Philosophers, and were doubtless so in their own opinion, for they both had an equal Share, of that Sort of Self opinion (I will not call it vanity) which is peculiar to that Class of men; The discourse between them

the Tuesday Club [Book VIII] 169

by Commission, at this Sederunt the Secretary pr[ese]nted in Club, the Great Seal, making the same [address] to the Chair, as was made at last Sederunt, r[equiring] the Club to settle and determin by vote the fo[llowing p]oints, vizt:

1st Whether the chancellor of the Club, in case of absence has a power to depute.

2d Whether the present [Chancel]lor's absence, and his Committing the great Se[al into the] Secretary's keeping is to be accounted a Surren[dry of] his office.

3d Whether the [Great] Seal's being laid upon the table in the Chancellor's absence [be nec]essary to constitute a Club.

4th Whether the order of the last Club of 4, ordaining the great Seal to be kept by the Secretary, till the Chancellors return, shall stand good.

The first, Second and 4th of these questions the Club resolved in the negative, but the third they determined in the affirmative.

I shall remark upon these questions and Resolutions, that the Club in their proceedings herein, seemed either to show some fear of the anger of the president, or a Jealousy of the growing power of the Chancellor, or, perhaps they were swayed by both these powerful motives, they knew, that the giving the chancellor any more power, by enabling him to appoint his deputy in his own absence, would certainly draw down upon them the presidential Indignation, since the honorable Chair, seemed to be Strongly of opinion, that the Chancellor had too much power already, and therefore was a dangerous enimy to the prerogative, the Club knew also, that they had already suff[ere]d, by granting his honor the president too large a latitu[de in ap]pointing his own deputy, that in short, their own p[ower of appoint]ing a deputy for the Chair, In case of his honor's [refusal t]o depute, was absolutely denied, and therefore chos[e to] confer no such power again, upon any Subordinate officer in the Club, for fear of rendering their Circumstances still worse [if possible], and therefore reserved to themselves the power [of appointin]g a deputy Chancellor on occasions, and, to prevent the C[hair's] being vacant at any time, should the president refuse to d[epute,] they gave the Chancellor the privilege of taking the Ch[air,] they Inclined not to chuse another, but in this conduc[t] they showed a wrong policy, for, by weakning the hands of this Important officer, the Chancellor, if they prevented his aggrandizing himself, they still took away that curb, which would otherwise have been upon the presidential power, by which means they Intirely lost these very privileges they laid Claim to, and at last, their Liberty.

The Secretary in his Second question shows abundance of his wonted [225]

[224]

forgeries, Idle and Silly fables, and Egregious Blasphemies have been for many Centuries received all over Europe and are yet firmly believed and defended in some Countries, and, all by th[e for]ce of popular opinion more than thro' the princ[ip]les of right reason.

Can it be any matter of wonder then, that the long standing members of the ancient and honorable Tuesday Club, as mortal men, subject to the frailties and errors, Incident to human nature, and, as it were Essential and Coexistent with it, should be led away or seduced Into error, by the Impetuosity of this monster opinion, and believe that there was something so Sacred in the person and authority, of their honorable President, ‖ that the first was above the class of common men, and the latter Incontrovertable. Opinion had by degrees gained an Influence over the honorable the President, and then over the members, his vassals and Subjects, for the latter, by setting him up as their head, and Elevating him Six Inches above themselves in a chair of State, and the Continued application of the arts of flattery, had so wrought upon the understanding and Intellects of that Judicious and [discer]ning gentleman Nasifer Jole Esqr, that he bega[n now to Im]agine, that all Clubical power was Locate[d in himsel]f, alone, and, that the members had no bu[siness to al]ter or appoint any thing, but only were h[is honor's Cy]phers round his Chair, to hear and obey hi[s Commands], and, in fine, he looked upon himself to be as arbitrary in his government of the Club, as the Great Turk i[n th]e ruling of his kingdoms, and had as good, if not a better opinion of his own Infallibility than ever the pope of Rome [ha]d of his. The members again, by their continual and repeated flatteries, uttered to the Chair, began, (as it is the Custom with habitual lyars,) to believe their own fibs at last, and to think that all these fopperies and fustian Speeches were exactly true, and agreeable to reason and good Sense, and therefore, after a few more faint Struggles, for mantaining the small remains of their Clubical liberty, under the direction of the Chancellor, who never suffered himself to be misled by these ‖ opinions, we shall find them quietly and passively submitting themselves to the honorable Nasifer Jole Esqr, their president, to be ruled and Governed by him, Just in what manner he pleased, tho' before it came to that pass, it Cost his honor the President a decathedration, and a short Interregnum happened thereupon in the Club, as shall in it's proper place be related.

Upon the 11th of September, 1750, was held Sederunt 138, Huffman Snap Esqr, being H:S: and Jealous Spyplot Senr Esqr, deputy in the Chair

---

handed over to Saint Peter's successor, Pope Sylvester I, dominion over Rome and its provinces.

of passive obedience, non resistance, *Jus divinum* & Indefeasible hereditary right, were it not for this how ‖ could the greatest villains that ever lived [220] and the most Ingrained Rascals, ever have been esteemed Demigods, nay, Gods, and translated to a place of honor among the Stars of heaven, is it not Intirely from the Influence and power of this, that no man of clear discernment and understanding in other matters among the Mahumetans, has dared for these thousand years and upwards, to call in question, the authenticity of the divine mission of that monster among Impostors Mahomet, who among them ever openly called in question, the existence of his fools paradise, the pleasures of which, chiefly consist, in the gratification of the most beastly of the Sensual apetites, in filthy lusts, and abominable pollutions; ordinary absurdities indeed, as they are not quite beyond the reach of Reason, may be curable by Reason, but extravagant, and monstrous absurdities, and miraculous nonsense, under a holy and Sanctified Garb, is safe and thriving, because quite out of Reason's Influence, The more wonderful the venerable Stuff is, the more it is reverenced and firmly believed, because the General opinion gives it the better Sanction, for it's being altogether Incredible, it h[a]ving been a general article of faith, for some Centuries past, that there is a mighty merit, in believing of myster-[i]es, and setting up the Strength of Religious faith agains[t] reason.

We therefore find, that that rash person, would Inevitably be swallowed up in the devouring flames of the Inquisition, who, in the catholic countries of Spain and Portugal, would deny the authority of that Holy court, (as it is called) or rather Hellish Court. Who there dares to dispute the fantastic Supremacy of an old dotard, and often wicked priest over heaven and Earth, who dares doubt of his right ‖ heirship to the apostles, [221] these poor ragged fishermen; who there questions the kindred and alliance, of a poor miserable, contemptible mortal friar to the Omnipotent Deity? who there disputes the Infallibility of this mock divinity, This tragi-comical wretch, who pretends to a power of damning or saving Souls for money, or for want of it, dare any one there deny his fantastical holinesses Commission for forgiving Sins, and his power of drawing holiness, miracles, and vast treasures, out of dust, rags, rotten bones, old boards and rusty nails; w[ho there] has the Romantic keys of St Peter ever called in qu[estion, his rig]ht to a tributary purgatory, or his toll for [being sav]ed from it by his mandate, or his lease [to Rome] from the Emperor Constantine, who never be[fore leased] him one foot of land,[1] yet we find, that these mon[strous]

---

1. Hamilton is referring to the Donation of Constantine (the *Constitutum Constantini*), a spurious document composed probably in the 8th century, in which Constantine purportedly

The Club gave it up and the Secretary gave his answer.

ans: Because it is full of *reigns* } dec: victor.
                             rains

Conundrum 4th

Why is a drunken night rambler like opium?

The Club gave it up, the answer delivered was

ans: Because he is an Enimy to *panes* } dec: victor.
                                      pains

The old book of Records, now filled up, was committed to the Care of Jonathan Grog Esqr, to be repaired, beautified and rebound.

[*Here endeth, the Second Book of Club Records.*]

Chapter III

State questions resolved in Club, new record book delivered by the Master of Ceremonies, the Secretary's Conundrum Condemned.

 Opinion, upon whatsoever foundation it stands, whether supported by the principles of right reason, or by prejudice and the force of Custom, is so powerful a thing that Supreme dominion and the Government of great nations and States are maintained and supported Solely by it. Let us search the world over, and we shall find almost every kind of police, civil or religious, born up upon the Strong and brawny Shoulders of that gyant called popular opinion, or the mind of the multitude, nay, we find often, that Love, friendship, honor and Esteem, and the like valuable Ingredients in human life, more particularly confined to private Society, have their Chief Support from it, were it not for the great prevalence and power of popular opinion, especially when it has an unluc[ky] turn towards enthusiasm, How is it possible, that ever such monsters in nature, as arbitrary power and absolute Slav[er]y, could ever be Imposed, and men peaceably submit to t[he]m, were it not for this, how could Common Sense, in m[a]ny instances have been banished from among whole nations of men for many ages together, and Mortals patiently submitt themselves to the yoke, and Continue faithful drudges and most violent advocates, for nonsense and Impertinence, such as the much Idolized and admired doctrines,

honorary member, prepared, according to a former order of the Club, which was read, and ordered to lay bye, for further C[on]sideration.

The Secretary then produced the Great Seal, by appointment of the Chancellor, to the Club, declaring, that the Chancellor thought this grand Signature of such Importance, as that there could be no Club without it, and he would not take upon himself, to avoid giving the Club, the trowble of Impeachments and trials, to appoint a deputy, tho' he was not Convinced that he had not a power so to do, 'till the Club of whom he originally had his power and office, determined the affair by vote, and also, declared it to be his opinion, that the Club should Commit, this valuable badge of office, to some trusty hand, till his return, declaring that this delivery of the Seal, was not to be understood, as a Surrendry of his office of Chancellor.

In Consequence of this, it was resolved, by the deputy president and Club, that the Secretary should keep the Seal, and lay it before the President, or his deputy for the time ‖ being, but withal, barring him, from assuming to himself the title of deputy chancellor. [218]

Then the Conundrums for the night were Called for, when Jonathan Grog Esqr produced his.

Club Conundrums

Conundrum 1

Why is a privateer like a Clergiman?

The Club gave it up, & the answer given was

ans: Because he lives by *Cannon* / *Canon* } dec: victor.

Conundrum 2d

Why is a Consumptive man like a Gazette?

Upon Consideration the Club gave it up.

ans: Because he is *weakly* / *weekly* } dec: victor.

Secretarys Conundrums

Conundrum 3d

Why is Bakers chronicle,[5] like the month of August?

---

5. The popular *Chronicle of the Kings of England* (London, 1643), compiled by Sir Richard Baker (1568–1645).

to this proceeding, but some thought he had political Reasons for it, tho' these reasons he reserved *in petto,* and therefore, they must for ever remain a Secret.

The Conundrums being Called for, Jonathan Grog Esqr, Produced his.

Club Conundrums

[Co]nundrum 1

[W]hy is a Nob[leman]'s Chief Cook, like the honble: the Presd: of the Tuesd: Club?

[The] Club gave [i]t up, & Mr Grog gave in his answer.

    ans: Because he rules the *roast.*—dec: victor.

C[onu]ndrum 2d

Why is the Pre[s]ent H:S: of the Tuesday Club like his Son?

The Club gave it up, the answer given was,

    ans: Because he is an *Alderman / Elder-man* } dec: victor.

The Secretarys Conundrums

Conundrum 3d

Why are some Court houses like a pack of Cards?

Jonathan Grog Esqr made answer, because there is a deal of *Shuffling,* which the Club did not acknowledge a good answer, || But Huffman Snap Esqr, made answer, because there are *knaves* in it, which was allowed good, and the Secretary drank a bumper, and delivered his answer.

    ans: Because there are at least 4 *knaves* in them.

Conundrum 4th

How does an alehouse Sot, differ from a dead man?

The Club gave it up, and the Secretary gave his answer.

    ans: The one Carries his *beer* / The other is Carried upon his *bier* } dec: victor.

At Sederunt 137, august 28, 1750, Jonathan Grog Esqr being H:S: and Huffman Snap Esqr, deputy President by Commission, the Secretary produced in Club an Eulogium upon Merry Makefun Esqr, late a worthy

the Tuesday Club [Book VIII] 163

Accordingly Jonathan Grog Esqr, was ordered to procure and bind up a new record book for the Club. At this ‖ Sederunt was entertained again [215] the Celebrated Philosopher Doctor Rhubarb.

At Sederunt 136, Jealous Spyplot Esqr being H:S: and Tunbelly Bowzer Esqr Deputy President, a letter was produced by the Chancellor in Club, directed to the Secretary from his honor the President.

To Loquacious Scribble Esqr,
Secretary to the Ancient Tuesday Club—

To be opened and Read, Immediatly after the meeting of the Gentlemen or the major part of them.
Sir,
Please deliver the Inclosed Commission to Tunbelly Bowzer Esqr, to whom it is directed, I am Sir,

Your humble Servant
Nasifer Jole.

This Laconic letter of his honor the President, is Just the reverse of the Irishman's whose postscri[p]t was twice the length of the body of the Letter, for here [the] direction and Superscription, is twice as Long as the [let]ter itself, The Club seemed to be of opinion that this was an air of State and grandure in his honor the Presid[en]t.

A motion was made at this Sederunt, th[at] the Conundrums should be expunged and expelled for e[ve]r, as fomenters of discord and mischief in the Club, but, a previous question being put, whether that question should be now put or not? it was Carried in the negative by a great majority, not that the Club had any objection to expelling the conundrums, which they now looked upon as fomenters of mischief, but that an affair of this consequence was not to be determined in the absence of his honor the president.

The Secretary was again ordered to draw up a proper encomium, upon Merry Makefun Esqr, late a worthy honorary ‖ member of the Club, after [216] he had made an apology for not presenting it at this Sederunt, according to a former order of the Club.

Several matters were moved in Club at this Sederunt, which his honor the deputy ordered, might be postponed, till his honor Mr President Jole should appear in Club, in person; thus we find the Club now yielding up every thing to his honor the president, not taking upon themselves, either to Judge or determin in any thing whatsoever. It is matter of Surprize to some, that the Chancellor, who was present at this Sederunt, did not object

Charge, unexpected, because he thought, that Mr Solo Neverout, now much in favor with his honor the President, would have stood his friend, and quashed this prosecution, but it appeared, that the Secretary, in the eager pursuit of his ambitious designs, had suffered himself in this affair to be Humbuged by Mr Protomusicus, and become his tool, serving only as a necessary Instrument to further his de[si]gns, which, (as an artificer does with his tool when he h[as] used it) the said protomusicus threw on one Side, not [thi]nking it agreable with right policy, to quarell with Sir John, to support the Secretary, who served his purpose in this affair, knowing that that Champion, by his propinquity to the Chair, could overset his projects with greater ease than the Secretary, who was a [perso]n that was now neither [fe]ared nor respected by his honor the president, and, tho Sir John was little respected, yet was he much feared by his honor, which Mr Neverout knew very well, and therefore, like all politic Schemists, he left his useful tool the Secretary in the Lurch, and stuck by the Champion, as thinking, that the best, shortest, and most effectual way to Compas his designs. This prosecution against the Secretary was then Carried on, and he was rendered so utterly *non Compos* || *mentis,*[4] that he could take no minutes of this Queer Proceeding, and desired Mr Protomusicus to act as Secretary for him, in that affair, and to note down every thing worthy of a place in the Records; after the determination of this momentuous affair, which, contrary to expectation, went in favor of the Culprit, the Secretary demanded the rough minutes of Mr Protomusicus, on which he delivered him a paper, whereupon was wrote Mr Attorney Spyplot—Mr Attorney Spyplot—Mr Attorney Spyplot—Mr Attorney Spyplot &c: &c:—at the same time, protesting, that he had Strictly complied with the Secretaries Injunction, in noting down every thing worthy of a place in our ancient Record, now, whether this, is to be construed, as a compliment to Mr Attorney, or as a [sar]castical Sneer, upon the Insignificancy of his argume[nts] against the Secretary, let Mr Protomusicus himself exp[lai]n, but the Secretary protested, that he could give no other account of the above proceeding, for the reason above mentioned, as well as because his ears were stunned, and his reason Confounded by a Clamorous altercation, be[tw]een the honorable the Chancellor, and Mr Attorney [Sp]yplot, concerning the Ci[vil] Law, and the methods of proceeding in Chancery.

 The Secretary then represented to his honor the President, that the Club Record book was full and a new one was wanted, and Jonathan Grog Esqr, offered to repair & beautify the Record book for a very small Sum, vizt: Seven Shillings & Sixpence, which the Club Consented to.

 4. "Not of sound mind" (or confused).

Club Conundrums

Conundrum 1

Why is a widow [follo]wing the Corps of a good husband, like a horse Just [fitted] for a ride?

The Club, after [seri]ous pondering gave it up, and Jonathan Grog Esqr, [gave i]n his answer.

> ans: Because she is *Sad-led*—dec: victor.

Conundrum 2

Why is a Company of Grenadeers, to be Compared to a pair of Shoes?

The Club gave it up, Jno: Grog gave his answer.

> ans: Because they are *Sized*[3]—dec: victor.

Secretarys conundrums

Conundrum 3d

Why is the City of Westminster, like a School boy's hornbook?

The Club gave it up, the Secretary gave in his answer.

> ans: Because it has an *abbycy*. / A.B.C. } de: victor.

Conundrum 4th

Why is a pewter plate, like a Certain Seminary of Learning?

The Club gave it up, the Secretary delivered his answer.

> ans: Because it is *Eat-on* / *Eton* } decl: victor.

After discussing the Conundrums, the Secretary was accused by Sir John, of having dictated a bombast letter for || Mr Protomusicus Neverout, to the President, in which the said Proto-musicus, in derogation from the merit of the rest of the oldstanding members, had very modestly recommended himself, as the fittest and most capable person to represent his honor in the presidential Chair. A prosecution was hereupon ordered against Mr Secretary, which was managed by Mr Attorney Spyplot; The Secretary was much flustered, abashed and Confounded at so unexpected a

---

3. A company of soldiers is *sized*, or arranged in ranks according to stature.

lor; The president, who still had some regard for this State officer, notwithstanding his having opposed him at times, promised him, that he should have full Satisfaction against this Conundrum, and it's author, for, that at next Sederunt, he would sentence the Conundrum to be hung upon a gibbet, prepared for that purpose, before the whole Club Convened. The Chancellor answered in a huff, That he cared not a fart, what his honor or the Club did with it, That it was but a Silly performance, and in fact, no conundrum, having none of the requisites in its Structure and composition necessary to constitute one, that ‖ it was nothing but a nasty parallel, or Comparison between two Subjects, that were in that respect simular and alike, and therefore was rather a coarse Simile, than a Conundrum, but notwithstanding the Stupidity of the performance he did not think nor could persuade himself to believe that Mr Comas was the author of it, for he knew that Gentleman too well to think that he would ever exercise his Imagination, muddy as it was, about any such f[oo]lish Compositions.

[211]

The Chancellor having thus [delive]red his Sentiments, the Club remained silent for some t[ime. A]t length, Sir John, and the Secretary, by Solid argu[ments a]nd Sound Clubical reasoning, brought the Chancellor [again] to moderate his temper, and the thing was hushed up, however, several of the members, naturall[y] drew the following observation, from this transaction, that the Chancellor, like many other wise and discerning men, li[ked bet]ter to pass a Joke upon another, than to have one passed upon himself. It was said, that when the news of this clubical transaction came to the ears of Laconic Comas Esqr, he was rather more Incensed at it than the Chancellor himself, and said that he wondered people should make themselves so Impertinently busy, as to forge Conundrums in his name, when it was very well known, that he never trowbled his noddle about any such foolish fancies.

Thus passed off this Remarkable occurrence in Club, which, as an affair of this Sort, had already Cost them a good Stanch Longstanding member, so this had well nigh deprived them of an useful and able State officer, this made the affection of the Longstanding members cool towards the Conundrums, and, as they were likely to prove fatal to the Club, they were soon after this expelled, as we shall relate in the proper place.

[212]

The Conundrums however, for this Sederunt, were Called for after Supper, at which Sir John put on his terrible Countenance, and seemed to frown in a horrendous manner, having conceived for some time past, a rooted Antipathy to these Conundrums, notwithstanding which, Jonathan Grog Esqr produced his.

Inclosed this ode, & would also have sent the music set to it by Signior Lardini, in three parts, but it would have made the pacquet too bulky.

You will doubtless, before this reaches you have heard of the melancholy death of our friend Mr Merry Makefun, a Gentleman of so good a character, that he was esteemed by all, and by all is Sincerely Lamented, I send you herewith the *Maryland Gazette,* where you have a particular account of his Tragical fate and am Sir,

Yours &ct: *Loquacious Scribble.*

This Letter being read, there came another Into Club, directed to his honor the president, which the Secretary by his honors order, read as follows.

To the honorable Nasifer Jole Esqr,
President of the Tuesday Club.

Honorable Sir,

Since your Chancellor took the liberty to make a Conundrum upon me, I shall beg leave to use the same liberty with him, and desire he would consider of and || ponder upon the following Conundrum.

Conundrum

    Why is P:D: like an old Ram in the Spring?
        Answer—
    Because he is all bones and *B—ll—cks.*[2]

am, honorable Sir,

Your most humble Servt:
Laconic Comas.

At the Reading of this Conundrum, and its answer, the Club fell into a Laugh, which Continued for some time, his honor the president looked very Grave upon the Chancellor, and notwithstanding the great command he had over the muscles of his face, he could not forbear showing a kind of a Smirk or half Smile, The chancellor could not contain his passion, but allowed it to break forth with Great violence, dropping some hints that he would give up his place and take his farewell of the Club, upon this the Club began to be sorry, that the Joke had been Carried so far, for they could not bear the thoughts of parting with so useful an officer, as their Chancel-

---

2. *Bullock* here means "a castrated bull or ox" (in this case, a ram past its prime), but is also a humorous reference to a papal bull.

forerunner of the Grand appearance of the *Cap of State* in Club, which we shall now soon see make it's entry on the Scene, and occasion a multitude of Grand transactions, & Important occurrences.

On Sederunt 135, held the 31, of July 1750, The worshipful Sir John, knight, being high Steward, the Secretary Produced a Letter wrote by him to Capt: Comely Coppernose, the Club's agent at London, which being read in club, it was ordered to be put on Record, and is as follows.

[208] To Capt: Comely Coppernose, London.

Sir,

After I have acknowledged the receipt of two of your Letters By Belt, and Sedgewick, the first with the Tuesday Club Seal, the other with our Badges, I return you the hearty thanks of the Honorable Mr President Jole, and the Longstanding members of our ancient Tuesday Club, as also, that of our honorary members, for the Great diligence and pains you have used, in executing their Important Commissions, and, in a particular manner, kind Sir, accept of my grateful acknowledgements for the trowble and expence you have been at, in that affair, your letters have been read in Club, and met with a very honorable reception, the Club having bestowed on you, tho' absent, the title of *honorary member,* as also, granted you an ample patent, under the Great Seal, and Confirmed by his honor the President, empowering you to negotiate, as agent for the Tuesday Club, in the City of London, and every where else, within the Dominions of Great Brittain, you have here Inclosed, the said patent, as also, a small bill of Exchange, which, I believe, makes up the whole amount of your Charges.

I have also sent you Inclosed, our last Anniversary ode, Composed by Jonathan Grog Esqr, Poet Laureat to the Club, the honorable the president and Club, require you, as their agent, to get it Inserted in the magazine at their expence, with a Suitable short preamble, drawing a parallel between the genius of the Incomparable Colley Cibber, and our American Bard, in which, you may desire the penman, whatever poor garreteer you Employ [209] for that purpose, to put ‖ in by way of paradox, this observation, that as that great Luminary of Parnassus, the British Laureat Cibber, is about to *set in the east,* and finish his glorious course, after having regaled us with many unparallelled odes, so, *In the west there now rises a sun,* that we hope will be as bright as Colley's, to wit, the Genius of the Poet Laureat of the ancient Tuesday Club of Annapolis in Maryland, whose mellifluous muse, will Surely qualify him to succeed the now Superannuated British Laureat, when that time comes, which now, alas! by the Course of nature must be nigh at hand, when he shall be gathered to his fathers, I have sent you

Conundrum 3d

Why is our Poet Laureat like the Sea Shore?

The Club gave it up, and the Secretary delivered his answer.

ans: Because of his *muse—mews,*—dec: victor.

The Club having questioned the validity of this Conundrum, the Secretary gave in his Second.

Conundrum 4

Why is the Tuesday Club, like the time betwixt breakfast & dinner?

The Club gave it up, the Secretary gave in his answer.

ans: Because it is *our's—hours,*—dec: victor.

At this Sederunt, for the first time, was Introduced into the Club, and Entertained as a Stranger, the Celebrated Dr Rhubarb, a person famous all over America for his great Skill in natural Philosophy and Free masonry, the first of which, he showed, in his curious and Learned experimental lectures, held for the entertainment and amusement of the Ladies and Gentlemen, where, he proved by the bye, with great force of argument and Ingenuity, that the raising of water || in tubes or pumps, was not done by Suction, as is Commonly believed, but, by the Gravity of the atmosphere, his Skill in the latter appeared, in the many Learned disputes and altercations, he had upon that misterious Subject, with Mr Chancellor Dogmaticus, and Mr Secretary Scribble, we shall have occasion soon in this history to show that Gentleman's profound knowledge, in Grammar, Logic, the Equivocal Generation of Insects, and the Structure of *Conundrums.*

The Club having received the melancholly news of the Death of Mr Merry Makefun, a worthy honorary member & triumvir, ordered the Secretary to draw up an eulogium upon him, to be presented to the Club at next Sederunt.

It was observed, at this Sederunt, that Solo Neverout Esqr the deputy president, sat in the Chair with his nightcap, which was remarked to be the only Instance of a nightcaps having appeared in the Chair of State (except at the time when his honor read an oration from the Chair) since the presidential office existed in Club, Some were Simple enough to believe that the honorable Deputy wore this Theca or Cover, to his head, on account of his natural disposition to sleep in Club, especially in the chair, or (the weather being hot) to make himself easy, as the west India Creols term it, but others that saw farther, took this odd incident to be a prognostic or

ans: Because there is a *Cork* in it.

Conundrum 2d

Why is a Convict wroth, Just landed from England, like a man of taste, Just married to a fine Girl?

Slyboots Pleasant Esqr, again made answer, because he is *transported*, which the club allowed to be good, and Jon: Grog Esqr gave in his

ans: Because he is *transported*.—drank a bumper.

[205] This Conundrum was much approved of by the Long standing members, notwithstanding its bad Success, which evinces, that good things, as well as good men are sometimes unlucky.

I must observe here too, that this is the first Instance of Jonathan Grog Esqr's Skill failing him so far, as to have both his Conundrums answered in the same night, whereas the Secretary, whose Genius that way was not so acute, had met with that bad luck more than once, I observe also, that Slyboots pleasant Esqr, is the only Longstanding member, that answered two Conundrums in one night, whether this occurrence was owing to the flagging of Mr Grog's Genius, or an Extreme quickness of apprehension in Slyboots Pleasant Esqr, will be hard for me to determin, but, be that as it will, if Jonathan Grog Esqr, had the most happy Genius in framing those exquisite pieces of wit called Conundrums, it must also be allowed that Slyboots Pleasant Esqr, had the luckiest and Clearest aprehension, in the Solution of these knotty Involutions, of any of the Longstanding members, having answered more Conundrums in Club, than any one else; as for his honor the President, tho' some thought, that he was in this respect somewhat slow of apprehension, because he always looked grave when the Conundrums were proposed, and never once solved one of them, yet they might be quite mistaken in their Conjectures of that Great man, for his looking grave might easily be accounted for, he always having shown an aversion to these exercises of wit, besides, tho' he might see into the mys- [206] tery of a Club Conundrum, || yet he might think it beneath the dignity of his place, to resolve or give an answer to any, since that would have been putting his wit upon a level with that of the Longstanding members, but even granting that his honor never possessed that ready talent of resolving knotty Conundrums, yet, with him, as with other men (tho' a great President) the observation will hold true, that the less a man's Stock of wit is, the Stronger and deeper is his Judgement, and depth of Judgement all will allow is a talent more necessary in a president than Quickness of wit.

The Secretary then produced his Conundrums, which were as follows.

how partial men are to themselves, and how they will form a differ- || ent [203] Judgement upon the same Case, when applied to themselves, and to their neighbour, this we shall soon find Clearly examplified, in the behaviour of Mr Chancellor Dogmaticus, who, tho' he was the main promoter of the *Comasian Conundrum,* as has been related, and seemed to be very much Surprized at Laconic Comas's Childish and Pettish disposition or temper, in taking that Conundrum in such grievous dudgeon, yet could not keep his own temper, when Mr Comas published In Club, a Conundrum concerning him, as shall presently be related.

At Sederunt 134 July 17th, Solo Neverout Esqr, being deputy president and H:S: a motion was made by a member, that the Club should proceed, according to the Instructions of the Committee of the 15th *ultimo,* held by appointment of the Club, in the Arbor of the pines, but his honor the deputy objected, and desired to put in his protest, against any such Illegal proceeding, in the absence of the honorable Mr President Jole, whom he had the honor to represent, and the motion was dropt, it being Carried in the negative by a majority, what these Instructions of that Committee were is not now known, they being Cancelled upon this vote, but, we may observe here, how Mr Solo Neverout began to veer about, and Change Sides, for he, (before a Strenuous patriot, and Stickler for the Liberties of the Club,) finding that his opposition to the Chancellor would || advance [204] him in the president's favor, declared now, openly and vigorously, for supporting upon all occasions, the power and prerogative of the Chair, and we shall see how this Cunning politician by degrees, gained his ends, and became at last, a person of greater Sway, power and Influence in the Club, than even Sir John, or any other State member had ever been, this he not only compassed by his cunning and Artifice, but by his great and profound Learning in Clubical Law, or what we may Properly Call the *Jus civilis clubicalis,* he was the first, Indeed the only Longstanding member, that ever was deputy president and H:S: at the same time.

After Supper, the Conundrums were produced as follow.

Club Conundrums

Jonathan Grog Esqrs

Conundrum 1st

Why is a well stoped bottle of Claret, like the Island of Ireland?

Slyboots Pleasant Esqr, made answer, because there is *Cork* in it.—allowed Good—Jon: Grog Esqr, drank a bumper and delivered his

> Ld Add: The Rubbers ours,—Fopely, you've lost your bet.
> Fope: Damn it, tis so, th'unluckiest dog alive,
> > Therefore no fool, for as the proverb goes,
> > Fools fortune favors, me she ever flouts.

Or at the Ladies Table, the numbers might run thus.

> La: Gr: O la! good ma'am, you have forgot to cut.
> > Again I shuffle—so—pray cut them now.
> La: Friz: You Call'd the king of diamonds—I profess,
> > Our Luck goes Backwards, tis a sure Codille.
> La: Add: Pray Captain some rappee—my head akes Sadly.
> > Tis very fine,—did you play out Spadille,
> > The deuce is in't—you'll let them have the Vol.[23]
> La: Friz: Lard ma'am be not uneasy, Captain Chance,
> > Diverted my attention with his tricks,
> > The Apish tricks he plays with poor Miss Toward.

Thus we see, that even this Subject may be agreeably enough heroicised, or blank versified, and thus having given a short Sketch of my plan, I leave it here as it is, for the Ingenious to comment upon, or Improve as they see fit.

Chapter II

Club Conundrums, a letter from the Agent in Great Brittain, Conundrum on the Chancellor by Mr Comas, Trial of the Secretary, a new record book ordered—more Club Conundrums.

There is a stale Story, (which, were it not for the Illustration of my Subject, I need scarce tell, since every fool knows it) of a poor farmer, who Carried a Complaint, before a worshipful Justice of the peace, concerning a neighbours cow, that had gored his horse, in such a manner, as that his life was dispaired of. The Justice very gravely Condemned the Trespassing Cow to the pound, the farmer on this, Informs him, that it was his worship's own Cow, which had Committed the trespass; oho! neighbour, then said the Justice, the case is altered, and so reversed the Sentence,[1] this shows

---

23. *Vol* is presumably a variant of *vole*, a deal at cards that wins all the tricks.

1. This proverbial story is told of Edmund Plowden (1518–1585), the great English lawyer who sat in Parliament during the reign of Mary I.

As to the division into acts and Scenes Commonly followed by our dramatic writers, I look upon that to be quite unnecessary, in this kind of Composition, and is a thing, which can plead no better reason, for its being at all observed, but ancient custom, but, in Case the Audience should be tired with the Conversation, which probably they may be; in half an hour after the first opening, the curtain may be let down, when the Tragedians may be supposed to leave || their Cards and go to Supper, and the club [200] Comedians, to fall asleep over their pipes, during which Interval, the music in the Orchestra may play and the curtain be drawn up again after a proper time of rest.

If it be objected that there are no royal Characters Introduced in the tragic part of this Scheme, tis denied, they come in the persons of mutes, in which they make as good an appearance, as when they are made to speak in most of our Moderen Tragedies, are elegantly painted on pieces of paper, and make as good a show to a triffle, as they do in the mock life, dressed up in tinsel. In fine, if four kings, four Queens, and four Generals, be not Sufficient to furnish out any moderen Tragical piece, I know not what is. The black and red Spots that attend them, may be supposed to be their Clergy and Soldiery, and very Justly, the first being Generally the Contrivers of plots that Issue in Tragedies, and the latter the executors of these Tragedies.

Here too, In case it should be objected that there is no Sort of killing, Butchering or battleing, in this our new Scheme of Tragicomedy, I answer, that it is here actually effected without shoking the Ladies, or tender hearted part of the audience, for, in the first place, old Father Time, is effectually killed, over and over again in these assemblies, which we have allotted for our tragical Scene, and then kings kill queens, and Queens knaves, || and knaves Plebeians, and bully aces, commonly kill and Carry all [201] before them on the green Tapis, or field of battle, and all this without the Shokeing noise of drums and Trumpets, but to the Sweet alarums of the Ladie's tongues.

Lastly, should any one object, that this Sort of tragical Conversation does not admit of blank verse, so very necessary in Tragedy, this I absolutely deny, for this Subject, may be blank-versified, as well as any other of the like Significancy and Importance, and be rendered thereby, tollerably Sublime, as in the following Specimen.

L: Addl: You deal the cards.
Ld: Friz: I dealt but now, my Lord.
Col: Would: The ace of diamonds, I turn up for trumps.
Count: Friz: Come on—we hold good Cards—the lurch is ours.

Lad: Gr: Lord ma'am, no ma'am, pardon me ma'am, That Card was not Tabled.

Lad: Frib: You'r so Careless of your Game, there's no playing with you. &ct: &ct: &ct:

[here a fight, and the bottles tobacco pipes &ct: fly about] &ct: &ct:

This I think is Sufficient to exhibit a plan of my new Scheme or modest proposal for the Improvement of the Theatre, in the point of Tragicomedy, at least, it is Sufficient to give the hint to abler heads and pens to carry it to greater perfection, than either my time or Inclination will permit me to do, I shall conclude this Learned Chapter, by showing the advantages of my new Scheme, and removing some objections that may be raised against it.

And first, the rules of art, are easily and naturally observed in this new method, with regard to unity of time, place and action, for, the whole circumstance and plot is transacted in the exact Space of one evening, no Club, or Rout, or drum, exceeding that Space of time, as to their duration, whereas, in the most correct of our moderen representations, 24 hours is for the most part the least time of action. Then observe again, that the Scene continues still the same, without varying, The one lying in a Chamber, the other in an anti- ‖ chamber, and also, the action is uniform thro the whole, for the Sole business of the tragical part, is killing of time or playing at Cards, and the Sole business of the Comic, is recruiting the Spirits, drinking and smoking, in short, to be master of this Species of the drama, one has no occasion to study Longinus,[20] or Aristotle's rules, If he only reads the Celebrated Dean Swift's *Table Conversation,* and the *History of Clubs,*[21] by an anonymous author, he will make himself master of the Comic part, and, if he peruses the Ingenious Mr Hoyle, on the Curious Game of whist, he will Compass the other, but, in truth, he has no occasion to read any thing to make himself an adept in this way of writing, for, if he frequents these assemblies for one night, and takes notes in his table book of what passes, in case his memory should be defective, he will make himself master of the whole art, which is an art that may be said to comprehend *Parvum in multo.*[22]

---

20. Longinus (ca. 213–273) was a rhetorician and philosopher who taught at Athens. He was generally considered to have been the author of the literary treatise *On the Sublime* until 19th-century scholars more accurately traced its authorship to the first century A.D.

21. Hamilton is probably referring to Edward Ward, *The History of the London Clubs* (London, 1709).

22. To comprehend "a small thing in a great space" (the comic inversion of *multum in parvo*).

L: Gr: Pha! Nash! I wonder you would copy from such a puppy.

Ld Fopel: Miss, your Tucker sits awry, shall I adjust it?

Miss: Tow: Paw, my lord, your so teazing.

Ld: Fopel: Miss, your most obedient humble servt:
(exit to Comedy)

Ld: Addl: You've got the Rubbers (rising)

Gen: Slice: Capt: Rozin, and Count Frizzle, you come in for next Rubbers, Wouldbe & I go out.

L: Fribb: They would not have got the lurch of us last hand, had you minded Hoyle's rules more than you did.

Col: Would: Damn Hoyle and his rules, I follow my own rules be gad, in this here Game and no man's Else, rat me.

[Enter to them from Comedy Lord Fopely and Tickle point]

Tick: p: Savvant Gentlemen, hard at whist I see, who's luck's best, I Just come from the penny pie Club, I was tired of them, the damndest Smoking Sots, upon Earth fore Gad, the fellows look as if they were Smoke dry'd.

Lor: Fopel: How has my bett gone?

Col: W:B: Lost by God, come disburse, 4 Guineas for me, and as many for Slice.

Lo: Fople: My usual luck, damme.

Cap: Rozin: You deal Sir.

Count: Frizz: Diamond the Trump Card [a long pause, Quadrille speaks]

Pimp: Yes my Lord, we have Tossed up Six already, and now we go upon the Seventh, which is miss Frizzlerump.

L: Fople: Gad a good one, before George, gi' me a bumper, damme here's frolicksome miss Frizzlerump.

[197]

Mr Trig: Please to sit my Lord.

L: Fople: No, I am in a violent hurry gentlemen, I have laid 5 guineas on the Rubbers against Lord Fribble and Coll: Wouldbe, and must see how my Luck goes on: Phogh! These Sots poison me with their Smoke [aside] Gentlemen, your most humble Servt:
(exit with Ticklepoint)

Guzz: Gr: A damnd fop as ever breathd, he makes mouths as if he had beshit himself & smelt it.

Trig: And that fool Ticklepoint is his ape.

Mr Teaz: Gad Sir you shall drink a Bumper to that girl, she's a pure Girl by Zounds.

Trig: Who? miss Plumpington, you dont mean to humbug me,—damn her, I would not give a Joint of miss Suckey Cuddle's little finger for her whole Carcass by Jupiter.

Mr Teaz: Sir, I say you're a damnd Sneaking poacher and you'd give your Eyes to have the Cuddling of her.

[198]

Mr Trig: Damn you, you lie.

Mr Teaz: Have at you then

Judge me, ha! ha!
Lad: Frib: Your Snuff box pray, Capt: Chance.
Capt: Ch: 'Tis good Strasburg rappee ma'am, before Gad.
Lad: Addl: We had matadores[15] this time, lady Grace.
L: Gr: O! True, matadores?
L: Frib: Thank you for that ma'am, the Cards are dealt.
L: Gr: What king do you call?
L: Frib: Clubs, and the king of harts for me.
La: Addl: Fogh! prithee mind your game, what made you throw away Spadille?[16]
L: Friz: Well, deuce take me ma'am, if I can get this fop Polish out of my head, he was finely frumpt,[17] miss Tipkin Jilted him with a vengeance, shes a pure Girl—That trick's mine ma'am.
L: Fribb: Lard ma'am, she never could give that fool any encouragement.
Count: Friz: Fore Gad, ma'am, we have lost Codille,[18] come, down with your dust.
L: Gr: Paw! lady Frizzle you'r too vulgar.
Count: Friz: I learnt that phraze of Beau Nash[19] at the Bath last Summer.

your damnd nactals and ambrosials in the universe, damme.
Teaz: Phogh! I cant bear your Smoke.
Guz: Gr: Sit farther off then and be damnd.
Mr Clum: Fill another pipe of this Mr Trig, 'tis good Virginia Cut and dry.
Mr Pun: Virginity said you, if the Tobacco has its virginity, it cannot be but Sweet, I'll fill a pipe of it, tho' I would rather have a Snap at a wet than a dry virginity, rat me, ha, ha, ha.
Mr Clum: Very witty faith Mr Punnington.
Mr Teaz: 'Fore George you have baulked your Glass.
Pun: No Sir, his glass has baulked him, for he broke it but Just now, and he wants the drawer to bring another.
Mr Trig: Whats the toast Mr Ticklepoint, Miss Fumbleton?
Teaz: I toasted Miss Frizzlerump. [enter to them from the tragical Scene, lord Fopely]
Fopl: So! my Jolly cocks, are you tossing up the Ladies?

---

15. *Mattadores* is a name applied to certain principal cards in games such as quadrille or ombre.

16. *Spadille* is the ace of spades in ombre or quadrille.

17. He was put off with a jeer, scoffed at, or mocked at.

18. *Codille* is a term used in ombre or quadrille when the game is lost by the challenger.

19. Richard Nash (1674–1762) was an English gamester and social arbiter (known as Beau Nash and King of Bath, where he presided as master of ceremonies in 1705).

Tragedy or Rout	Comedy, or Club [195]
Scene a Large hall, Card Tables, fans and Snuff boxes	Scene a Tavern Chamber, bottles and punch bowls &ct:
Col: Wouldb: Deal the Cards my Lord. Ld: Addlp: Diamonds Trumps. Gen: Slice: You and I lord Fribble against my Lord Addlepate and the Colonel, for the Rubbers. Ld: Frib: Come on then. [a Long and profound Silence at the whist table, till the Rubbers are got by Gen: Slice and Coll: Wouldbe, the Quadrille Table speaks] Lad: Grace: Lard Ma'am, you've misdealt. Counts: Friz: Well!—and I protest ma'am, my thoughts run so upon that fool Beau Polish, that I knew not what I was about. Cap: Chan: About, ma'am! The last time I had the pleasure of measuring your La'ship ma'am, I think you was about three quarters of a yard round the Girdle. I measured with my own garters Ma'am, as gad shall	Mr Pimpl: Stir up the fire neighbour Trig. Mr Bump: Have you heard the news Gentlemen? Mr Ticklep: What news pray, I have heard none these two days. Mr Bump: The king of Prussia is dead, here's to his damnation. Ticklep: The devil, he is! I'll pledge you in that, 'tis good news for Europe. Mr Trig: This Tobacco's naught. Mr Clum: The tobacco's good, your pipe is dirty. Mr Punning: Burn it, 'tis dirty enough e-gad. Mr Teaz: Do you chuse porter Sir? Guz: Grog: No, this is my favorite, this Spirit and water exceeds your Nactors & abrosials. Mr Teaz: I would not give a Swag of good Herefordshire Syder and a Slice of Cheshire cheese with a toast, for all

---

patterned after the Lord Foppingtons who had graced the English stage (see 188n, above); Mr. Clumsey is perhaps derived from Sir Tunbelly Clumsy in Vanbrugh's *The Relapse* (1697); Colonel Wouldbe is perhaps an imitation of Centlivre's Wou'dbe in *Love at a Venture* (1706), or possibly of Squire Wouldbe in the anonymous *She Ventures, and He Wins* (1695); and Lady Graceless is clearly a parody of *The Provoked Husband*'s Lady Grace, who imagines passing her "leisure hours in riding, in reading, . . . perhaps hearing a little music, taking a dish of tea, or a game at cards, soberly; . . . or in a thousand other innocent amusements—soberly!" (*The Provoked Husband*, ed. Peter Dixon [Lincoln, Nebr., 1973], act 3, lines 516–523). Moreover, Lord Fribble is surely the offspring of David Garrick's popular Fribble, the effeminate suitor in *Miss in Her Teens* (1746).

Thus having briefly laid down my Scheme, I shall give a short Specimen of the dialogue of each part, in such a representation as follows.

[194] *New Scheme for Tragicomedy*[14]

Tragedy or Rout	Comedy, or Club
Persons of the Tragic Drama	Persons of the Comic Drama
Lord Fribble ⎫ Coll: Wouldbe ⎪ Lord Addlepate ⎬ whist players General Slice ⎪ Capt: Rozin ⎪ Count Frizzle ⎭	Mr Trig Mr Pimpleton Mr Bumper Mr Ticklepoint Mr Punnington Mr Teazer Mr Clumsey Mr Guzzle Grog
Lady Graceless ⎫ Countess Frizzle ⎬ Quadrille Lady Fribble ⎪ players Lady Addlepate ⎭	
Lord Fopely ⎫ Captn Chance ⎬ Standers by Miss Toward ⎭	

Mute Persons

4 Kings of { Clubs
Spades
harts
diamonds

4 Queens of ditto
4 Knaves of ditto
2 Black aces, 2 Red ditto
Their Guards and attendants
in Black and white liveries

14. In this mock-tragicomedy Hamilton seems to be neither burlesquing particular scenes in previous tragicomedies nor imitating particular scenes in popular 18th-century comedies. To be sure, card playing was a popular motif in several comedies of manners and sentimental comedies, including Vanbrugh and Cibber's *The Provoked Husband* (1728), in which Lady Townly continually irritates her husband by running off to play a few hands of quadrille. The scenes Hamilton creates presumably are, for better or worse, originals. He does, however, borrow the names of some of his dramatis personae from popular 18th-century comedies: Lord Fopley is

[The left half of Hamilton's "Division of the Theatre" is missing.]
[facing page 193]

awkward manner, our actors and Actresses, counterfeit the agonies of that grim prince of Terrors, Death.

Having thus ennumerated the faults that have crept into our tragicomedy, I shall now offer my modest proposal for rectifying them and bringing this excellent moderen Improvement, of the theatre to greater perfection and elegance.

To prevent the blending, or mixing together, the opposite parts & characters of Tragedy and Comedy, in our Tragicomical representations, I would propose, that the Stage should be divided by a partition, running from the back Scene towards the front, or the Orchestrum, that the dexter division, should be alloted for the tragical and the Sinister for the Comical parts, that the orchestrum should also be equally divided, and every division have it's proper music, the music for Tragedy, I would have to consist of The orbos, Bassoons, Violins, Violoncellos and the Harpsicord, that for Comedy to Consist of flutes, violins, hautboys and bagpipes, and all these to play in concert, while two pieces, the one tragic and the other Comic, was at the same time representing, on their particular places of the divided Theatre.

Persons in high life, must of necessity be the actors in the tragical division, and those in Low life in the comical, while persons of a middle Station may be allowed to make their entries and exits, to or || from either the one or the other Scene, by means of a common door in the partition.

The most proper Subject for the tragic division, is, the Transactions that pass at these polite Moderen Assemblies called Routs, and Drums, where the Conversation is of the most refined Sort, neither Towering up to the Bombast, nor sinking into the pedantic and vulgar topics of Discourse, The persons may be Dukes, Earls, Lords, Countesses, Marchionesses and other Great Ladies, and, now and then, thro the partition door, a finical fop from the division of Comedy may pop in, or make his entry to Embelish their Conversation.

The fittest Subject for the division of Comedy is the Conversation that passes at Clubs, and therefore, the Persons of the drama here are to be the members of some Club, which may, either be a male Club of Smoakers and drinkers, or a female Club of Gossips over a Tankard of Posset, hot Suppings or Candle, but the mixture of the Sexes in this Comic division is not to be allowed unless the poet sometimes, to promote a Joke, Introduces a wife, to Carry her drunken husband home from his tipsy Companions, upon this Comical Assembly, a Lord or Duke from the Tragical Division, may make a Solemn Entry thro the partition door, to create alittle fun, with persons that are his Inferiors in rank and quality.

‖ many of our moderen play wrights, have Judiciously Conceived, that a [191] piece for the theatre may be mechanically framed by the help of these rules, and, accordingly many, whose genius was yet to look for, have set themselves down gravely to write for the theatre, with no other direction but these rules, and, have framed very exact and finished pieces Indeed, with regard to unity of place, time & action, but so destitute of all other Embelishments, or rather Strokes of nature, that the representation of them has proved an effectual Hypnotic to the audience, and called down the drowsy Deity to lull their flagging Senses, hence it proceeds, to the no small wonder of people, who have not found out the true cause, that the performances of Shakespear, who had little or no regard to the mere rules of art, but followed nature, have outlived those of his nicer contemporaries, those also, of the Century following, and will Surely outlive our finest Theatrical performances, that were wrote but yesterday, and probably may be dead and damned to morrow.

Lastly it has been objected to the perfection of our English Tragedy in particular, that there is too much bloodshed, battles, alarms and murders, exhibited on the Stage, which horrid representations, the foreign, and particularly the french delicacy cannot away with, this fault appears in a Stronger light in Tragicomedy, as these dismal Scenes, must often Interfere, with those of mirth and pleasantry, and put the mind of the Spectator on a rack,[13] between the extreme passions of horror and Laughter, tho' with regard to our English audiences this objection will not always stand good, for, I have heard, as Loud a laugh, at the representation of an execution ‖ or killing of [192] a heroe, as at the most comical farce that ever was exhibited, nor, can they always in this Case be condemned, especially, if it be considered, in what an

---

13. Hamilton's pun indicates that he is borrowing most of his information from the *Spectator*. In *Spectator* 40 Addison denounced tragicomedy as an unnatural mixture of extreme passions, and in *Spectator* 44 (1711) he printed his strongest attack against what he considered the excessive violence then appearing on the English stage: "But among all our Methods of moving Pity or Terrour," he concludes, "there is none so absurd and barbarous . . . than that dreadful butchering of one another which is so very frequent upon the *English Stage*. . . . Murders and Executions are always transacted behind the Scenes in the *French* Theatre; . . . But as there are no Exceptions to this Rule on the *French* Stage, it leads them into Absurdities almost as ridiculous as that which falls under our present Censure" (*The Spectator*, ed. Donald F. Bond [Oxford, 1965], I, 187–188). The Abbé Dubos was one of several French critics who endorsed Addison's complaint against English tragedy, and he also agreed that "the French poets are too affected in excluding all these sorts of spectacles. . . . It cannot be denied, that if the representation of tragedies is too much loaded with spectacles in England, it is certainly too naked in France" (*Critical Reflections on Poetry, Painting, and Music*, I, 346–347). Hamilton whimsically denies both authors' assessments of French tragedy without bothering to substantiate his claim.

so crampt at all times, yet, all our tragic Poets seem to agree in this, that he is at least to become a Rhimer at the end of an act, Just before he makes his exit, but these Gentlemen playwrights of the tragical Class, in this Case, must Impose upon themselves and the world, by a false association of Ideas, for it is so far from being an essential and necessary Ingredient in the Character of a great man, to discourse and express himself, in a lofty and elevated Strain, that no Set of men are more addicted to the Bathos in discourse, than Grandees and heroes are, a kind of dialect which they contract in their youth in Bagnios and Bawdy houses and at Gaming tables, sticks close by them, till they become old worn out Rakes drunkards and Gamesters, neither is it a rare thing to hear a Lord in these our days, in the open Streets, talk so much like a porter, that, unless it be by outward dress, and retinue || or Star and garter, you could not distinguish one from the other, and, I am apt to think, that our moderen Lords and grandees are not Singular in this, but that men of high rank and titles among the ancients, were pritty much of the same cast and disposition, for we find Homer, that great master of the drama, Introducing Agamemnon and Achilles, his two Chief characters, scolding like a Couple of mere Billingsgate fish women, or rather Butter whores, about a wench, Ajax holding forth like one of our moderen bullies or prize fighters, and several of his other heroes and kings, talk in a plain homely Stile, Just like other mortals, we find also, that Sophocles and Euripedes, the Greek tragedians Introduce their great heroes, using such a natural and plain manner of discourse, as that they seem much like other men, and, tho' rank pagans, to discuss points more like christians, than even our most elevated Grandees of the Christian Theatre, this all proceeds from our moderen dramatic writers studying more the mechanical rules of writing for the theatre, than applying themselves to the rules of nature, that Illustrious Philosopher Aristotle, it is true lays down some rules for dramatic poets, which rules pass with many, for rules Invented by Aristotle himself, whereas they are only rules proceeding from the nature of things, neither did the Stagyrite, lay them down, as rules to compound a genius for the drama, but intended them only as directions how a dramatic poet is to guide his Genius. The Ingredients of a genius, were necessarily to be furnished by nature, and the rules in this case, were no more, but as a receipt in Cookery to teach how to compound these Ingredients, so as to make them palatable, but, I know not how it happens,

---

the thought may be; however apt the words in which 'tis couch'd, yet he finds himself at a little unrest while Rhyme is wanting: he cannot leave it till that comes naturally, and then is at ease, and sits down contented" (*Works of Dryden*, ed. Hooker *et al.*, XVII, 77).

Coxcombs in nature, who shine away chiefly in a bawdy Jest, a Sett of uncommon oaths or a Street riot, The Sir Fopling Flutters, Lord Foplingtons, Courtly Pices, Wildairs, Airys and Vaunters,[11] are persons of this rank in our moderen Comedy, the constant Shining part of whose character, is a peculiarity in dress, and Singularity of address, such as, a hat and a feather, a Shoulder knot, a Sword knot, a Solitaire, a Snuff box, or some other such Implement, and a Ged-demme-be-ged-split my vitals, split my windpipe, pax rat me, and such like Smart ejaculations, are the chief Embelishments of their discourse.

Our dramatic writers, in their compositions of this Sort, have so far deviated from nature, and there can be no better reason given for their error, than this, that they are in general unacquainted with, or Strangers to these Characters in life, of which they pretend to write, and indeed, as to the characters proper for Tragedy, how can it be expected, that a poor forlorn, Starving poet, who either lives in a garret, or in some place or Station remote from Courts and high life, can ever be acquainted with the conversation and manners of men in high rank, the Conceptions or Ideas, that such a person must conceive, of the manners of persons in this degree of life, must be widely different from what they really are, he must doubtless Imagine, that a great man, be- || cause his Station and title is elevated [189] much above the herd of mankind, his fellow creatures, must be lofty and elevated in every thing else belonging to him, that is, he must be elevated in his eating, drinking, dressing and speaking, and particularly in the last, for Surely, (according to their notions) it is Impossible that a great prince can give orders to a Servant, to make a fire, wipe his Shoes or shut the door, send a Challenge to an adversary, call for his Cloak or a cup of wine without expressing himself in heroicks, In fine he cannot be angry, or pleased, or Indifferent, but he must measure his words and Sentences exactly, and discourse as it were by geometry, with a proper cadence and Emphasis, and often, (as it was the opinion of the Great Mr Dryden) he is obliged to harangue in Rhime and Jingle,[12] and, if some think that he ought not to be

11. Sir Fopling Flutter is a character in George Etherege's *The Man of Mode* (1676). Lord Foppington is a character in Sir John Vanbrugh's *The Relapse; or, Virtue in Danger* (1696) and in Colley Cibber's *The Careless Husband* (1704). Sir Harry Wildair is a character in George Farquhar's *The Constant Couple* (1699), and in its sequel, *Sir Harry Wildair* (1701). Sir George Airy is a character in Susannah Centlivre's *The Busie Body* (1709).

12. Hamilton could be alluding to any number of passages in which Dryden applauds the virtues of rhyme (including the opening paragraphs of his preface to *The Conquest of Granada*), but perhaps he is referring particularly to Neander's assessment of the aptness of rhyme and verse toward the end of *An Essay of Dramatick Poesie*, where Neander states: "When a Poet has found the repartee, the last perfection he can add to it, is to put it into verse. However good

themselves, and never should be mixed with the grosser or bottom part, during the Representation or Reading, 'tis time enough for them to mix, after that is over, in the Judgement, or Intellectual Stomach of the reader or Spectator, where they || may be Intimately concocted and digested together, as is the case with a real whipt Sillabub, which towers and brightens in the Glass, till the latter end of the feast, and then being mishmashed, mingled and swallowed, a Strong Stomach never feels it, but in the Stomachs of the weak and Sickly, it is transformed into Expanded air, which passes off with noisy eructations above, and often below; tis the same with tragicomedy, our metaphorical Syllabub, which has no visible Effect on the Judgement or Intellectual Stomachs of common readers and Spectators, but with those gentlemen, whom we Call Critics & Connoiseurs, it goes off with abundance of noise, because their Stomachs generally are of a weaker Contexture.

Another remarkable fault in our moderen Tragicomedy is, that the persons generally talk out of character, for example, in the tragical part, we shall often see a prince or a great man, coming upon the Scene, talking in a Sublime manner, all in regular measured blank verse, and showing himself to be a deeply learned, and thorro' paced philosopher, far beyond the compass of the understanding of his bretheren grandees on the great Stage of the world, who, in the Common course of things, neither use nor understand, such a puffed up dialect, so that a Stage artificial Grandee, and a real or natural Grandee at a levee or drawing room assembly, have this remarkable difference, that the first always Converses in heroics on Sublime and Studied Subjects, and the latter Contents himself with plain natural prose, delivered extempore, as occasion offers, and Chiefly turning upon dogs, horses, town toasts, Bagnio adventures, the gaming table, Cards & the Celebrated Mr Hoyle, Boxing matches and the Renowned Broughton,[10] and the like fashionable and polite topics of discourse. In the Comic parts again, we find Certain persons in low life, or such as Compose the bottom, or grosser part of our theatrical Syllabub, I mean || Sailors, coblers, Taylors and tinkers, extremely witty and Satyrical, and withal, persons of very deep Judgement and understanding, in such affairs of human life, as are Commonly out of their Sphere of action, and those among them, who are in a middle Station, that is, in a degree between the Tragical heroes and the Comical Clowns, are always Represented as brutes, Sots, or the arrantest

---

10. Edmond Hoyle (1672–1769) was an English writer on card games whose *Short Treatise on the Game of Whist* (London, 1742) ruled whist until 1864. John Broughton was a British prizefighter who established a theater for boxing in 1743 (John Ford, *Prizefighting: The Age of Regency Boximania* [New York, 1972]).

Learned days, and is set off also with these Incomparable flights of fancy called by the French *les Pettits pieces,* and by the English Farces, Specieses of humor, also, utterly unknown to the ancients, where monsieur Harlequin & Signior Scaramuchio,[8] are the Chief heroes, and the machinery of such a nature, as to be altogether novell and Surprizing, such as the sudden transmutation of a human form, into a wheel barrow, a flight of Stairs, or a bass viol—which is called pantomime, I say, tho' Tragicomedy be now come to such a height of perfection, as to seem altogether Incapable of any further Improvement, I shall, (tho' it may seem to some a very bold attempt) offer to the public, a modest proposal, for ‖ the Improvement of our theatre in this particular province, and, in order to do this Clearly and distinctly, I shall mention a few Circumstances, which I humbly conceive to be faults, or Imperfections, in the present Structure of our Tragicomedy, and next, I shall propose a Scheme to remove them, and lastly shall exhibit a small Specimen of my Scheme, to demonstrate how it may be executed. [186]

The principal fault then, in our Moderen Tragicomedy, is the blending the two extremes of it too much together, that is, the Intermingling of it, by bringing upon the same Stage, without a proper partition or Division, The Comic, and the Serious or Tragic, the facetious and the Solemn, the light and the dark, the levity and the gravity, in fine the ὕψους and the βαθος.[9] That I may be better understood, nothing is more common, in our Tragicomic performances, than to see a king and a Cobler, or any other base mechanic, talk together in blank verse, and even sometimes Change Characters, The Cobler rising to the tip top of the Sublime, and his majesty sinking apace to the dialect of Wapping, this is a deplorable defect in this Species of the Drama, and it were to be wished it could be remedied. I shall bye and bye, (God willing) propose a Remedy for it, and leave it to the Judgement of the Candid and Ingenuous, to stand or fall as it deserves. But to demonstrate the necessity there is for mending this woeful defect, let us only consider our moderen Tragicomedy, as a whipt Sillabub, the froth that is buoy'd up at top, is the Sublime part of the piece, being always uppermost, and, its rare and Spungy texture represents well enough, the lofty discourse, and elevated actions of great men in high life. These, to preserve the beauty of this Theatrical whipt Sillabub, ought always to remain by

---

8. Scaramouch is a stock character in Italian farces, a cowardly and foolish boaster who burlesques the Spanish don, and was a popular figure in the late 17th century. The comedy *Scaramouch,* by Edward Ravenscroft, was produced in 1677.

9. "The sublime and the profound"—possible allusion to Alexander Pope's *Peri Bathous; or, The Art of Sinking in Poetry* (1727), esp. chap. 1, itself inspired by Longinus, *On the Sublime* (see 199n, below).

History on their Scene, and Intermixing moderen modes, and fashions with the Characters of ancient Heroes, (a thing, which the french, notwithstanding their *delicatesse*[5] as they call it, are every day guilty of in their Theatrical dresses, where old Romans & Grecians appear dizened out in full bottom wigs & Caps and feathers) Hence it is, that nothing is more common, on the Stage at Amsterdam, than to see the Patriarch Abraham, going to sacrifise his Son Isaac, by firing a blunderbus at him, and, Just as he is ready to draw the trigger, an angel pisses in the pan, which affords abun- || dance of mirth to the audience, 'tis also very usual with these Tragicomedians, to represent Scipio & Lælius,[6] smoking their pipes, and Guzzling a pot of Beer very amicably together.

The French (if you'll believe their own authors) have Intirely excluded this Tragicomical Taste from their Theatre, having arrived to that degree of *Delicatesse,* or Rather Fiddle faddlesse, as to excell all other nations, in the purity and Elegance of their Theatrical pieces, but I think, notwithstanding Voltaire & the Abbe le Boe (whom all the world will agree with me had a Stock of wit much Superior to mine) have thought otherwise,[7] That these Superlatively Squeamish and nice monsieurs, study foppery, (a turn peculiar to their nation) much more than nature and blend abundance of Comedy with their tragical Representations, in their fantastical Stage dresses, their ballad like hobbling Rhimes, their overstraind action, and foppish Gesticulation and their *Petit's piece,* or pantomime performances.

But tho Tragicomedy be come to this pitch of perfection in these our

---

18th-century Dutch literature [pp. 104–192], and I am especially indebted to his comments about Dutch tragicomedy on pp. 113–114, 127–129.)

5. Sense of delicacy or finesse.

6. Scipio Africanus (236–184/183 B.C.) was a great Roman general who helped establish Rome's domination in Spain, Africa, and the Hellenistic East; his close friend Laelius shared in Scipio's African campaign (204–202) and became proconsul in Gaul (189).

7. Hamilton is probably referring to Voltaire's remarks on the elegance of French drama in his preface to *Brutus* (1731), "Discours sur la tragédie, à Mylord Bolingbroke," in which he writes, "The English dramatists have more action in their plays than we have; they speak more directly. The French aim rather at elegance, harmony, style. It is certainly more difficult to write well than to fill the play with murders, wheels, gibbets, sorcerers, and ghosts. . . . Often the unusual way of saying ordinary things, and the art of embellishing by literary style what all men think and feel—these are what make great poets" ("A Discourse on Tragedy," trans. Barrett H. Clark, in Clark, *European Theories of the Drama,* rev. Harry Popkin [New York, 1965], 236). In "Of the French Manner of reciting tragedy and comedy," the Abbé Dubos applauds the elegance of dress, speech, and gesture on the French stage, concluding that "'Tis sufficiently agreed upon . . . throughout Europe, that the French, who for this century past have composed the best dramatic pieces among the moderns, recite tragedies also the best, and represent them with the greatest decency" (*Critical Reflections on Poetry, Painting, and Music,* trans. Thomas Nugent [London, 1748], I, 342–343).

fancies, hammered out, most Surprizing theatrical pieces, taken chiefly from Scripture history, where the Tragic and Comic humor were most Ingeniously interwoven. These unparallelled artists adopted the Devil for their Droll, who was always brought upon the Scene in antic trappings, and more antic gestures, when they had a mind that the audience should Laugh, as for the more Solemn & Serious parts, they were performed by angels, Saints and priests, who were the Tragical Heroes of these Theatrical pieces, Nay, sometimes, they did not scruple to Introduce the Deity himself, under the name of the father or the Son, into performances of this nature, this humor however, had it's time, and, when their matter was wore out, in the Stores of the Sacred archives, they betook themselves to Legends, Prophane Historians and romance writers, to supply matter || for their Scenes, [184] and the heroes of both history and romance, vizt: Kings, princes, dukes, Generals, great Captains, and knight Errant Saints were Introduced into their Solemn Tragical Scene, and Clowns, fools, Shepherds, porters, Taylors & Coblers, made up the Comic list, and these being blended together in one piece, compleated and perfected, that excellent modern high Relished *olla Podrida*[2] called Tragicomedy, In which some of our English dramatic writers, Particularly Shakespear, & Beaumont and Fletcher, have shown their great Skill, and even the great Addison, in his *Cato,* has, (whether he has adverted to it or not) fallen into this very Species of writing, in a great measure, with regard to the action and characters, tho' not the persons, for, we must own, this piece grows exceeding comical, when he Introduces a soft languishing love Story into the middle of that great Roman Heroe's Transactions,[3] while he struggled hard for liberty, his Sons were sighing with the Tender passion, and Senators and Soveraign princes fighting and killing one the other for love, in his palace and under his very nose. In this State at present is Tragicomedy in Europe, and the Dutch Play Wrights only, retain the pure gothic mode of it,[4] by exhibiting pieces of Scriptur

---

2. Literally, "putrid pot" in Spanish; figuratively, an incongruous mixture of odds and ends.

3. Hamilton is alluding especially to Cato, act 3, sc. 1–3.

4. I suspect that Hamilton is toying with the popular misconception that 18th-century Dutch drama had failed to keep pace with developments in Italy, France, and England. As Hamilton must have known, the stage at Amsterdam had presented many tragicomedies, including the plays of the 17th-century Dutch poet Jacob Duym, Pieter Corneliszoon Hooft's frequently performed *Granida* (1605), which, like John Fletcher's *The Faithful Shepherdess* (ca. 1610), was modeled after Giambattista Guarini's famous pastoral tragicomedy, *Il pastor fido* (1589), and Joost van den Vondel's popular *Pascha* (1610). Dutch comedy was alive and well during the 18th century, especially in the plays of Molière's admirer Pieter Langendijk, who displayed a tragicomedian's "great deftness in untangling and resolving his plots" (Reinder P. Meijer, *Literature of the Low Countries: A Short History of Dutch Literature in the Netherlands and Belgium* [Assen, The Netherlands, 1971], 158. Meijer provides a good survey of 17th- and

have always yielded place to the ancients, as their betters, tho' some have been loath to allow these ancients any other preheminence, but that of their having lived in earlier times, and asserted, that the moderens, have showed as much Ingenuity in their writings and Compositions as the ancients ever did, and that the latter were only preferred to the former, from a certain Enthusiastic humor, of late too prevalent, which admires every thing, only for its antiquity, in [the] sa[me] manner, as a Copper Coin, with the Stamp of Nero or Claudius, or any other powerful Rogue or Tyrant, is more esteemed, among our Connoiseurs for antiques, by ten thousand degrees, than a halfpenny of the same metal and weight, adorned with the head of his Sacred majesty King George II. or even that of K: William III. of Glorious memory, which two excellent monarchs, have done more Real Good to mankind, Than all the twelve Cæsars put together. But, whatever value may be put upon the ancients, the moderns Certainly have a very good title to our esteem, upon this account alone, that they have been the happy Inventors of many things of Great use and Emolument, which the ancients knew nothing of, which, not to mention the use of Tea, Coffee, Sugar, Chocolate and Tobacco, and many other valuable conveniencies of life, and encouragers of trade, The Invention of Tragicomedy, by which our English Stage has been wonderfully Improved, is none of the Least Considerable.

[183] True it is that the ancients seem to be perfectly well acquainted with Tragedy and Comedy; Plautus In his prologue to his *Amphitrio,* Calls that piece a Tragicomedy,[1] only on account of the Subject of the piece being Intirely Comic, tho some of the persons, (being deities) were of the tragical Class, but this Species of Tragicomedy, is Intirely different from the moderen. Homer the Greek Poet, is the great master and pattern of both these Specieses of the drama, exhibiting to those writers that came after him, examples very worthy of Imitation, but, it was never discovered, till of late, that these two distinct partitions of the Drama, could elegantly be blended and mixed together, to the great Improvement & delight of either the Spectator or Reader, this Grand art, the moderens Justly claim as their own, and we find it took its rise from what were called the Mysteries in Gothic times, when some bold Geniuses, either contemning, or altogether Ignorant of the rules of Aristotle, wrote for the Stage, and from their exuberant

---

1. Hamilton is alluding to this famous passage from Plautus's *Amphitruo:* "I shall mix things up: let it be tragi-comedy. Of course it would never do for me to make it comedy out and out, with kings and gods on the boards. How about it, then? Well, in view of the fact that there is a slave part in it, I shall do just as I said and make it tragi-comedy" (*Plautus,* trans. Paul Nixon, Loeb Classical Library [London, 1916; rpt. New York, 1921], I, II, lines 59–63).

History of The Ancient and Honorable Tuesday Club

Book VIII

From the Impeachment and acquital of the Chancellor, To the Grand Ceremony of the Capation.

Chapter I

A modest proposal, for the new modelling and Improvement of our Moderen Th[eat]re.

We have had in our times many modest Proposals made to the public, and Indeed, almost every proposal, that we meet with, be the matter proposed, what it will, is a modest one. This only shows us, that a modest Character or demeanor, is so taking in the world, that every man likes to assume that Character and name, whether he has any title to it or not, and, our Gentlemen authors, vizt: Historians, Poets and Essay writers, who are often suspected not to possess a great Stock of that amiable quality, show nevertheless some Solicitude and desire, to persuade the world, that they are a very modest Sort of fellows, as knowing, that if they once can be believed in this point, that their writing will thereby acquire some character, and pass [cu]rrent for a time under that Stamp, even tho' they have little or nothing else, of art and Ingenuity to recommend them; I, among the Croud of these modest gentlemen, put in my Claim, || and, to give my reader alittle breathing from the great & arduous Transactions, of that Club, of which I write the History, I shall treat him, in my way, with a modest proposal, but, before I come to the main point, shall according to custome premise some necessary observations.

The moderens have been so remarkable for their modesty, that they

[180] List of the Members, honorary and Regular of the ancient and honorable Tuesday Club, from December 9th 1749 To July 17th 1750.

Regular members	Honorary members
The Hon: Nasifer Jole Esqr Pres:	Mr Abraham Bumper
Sir John, knight & Champn:	Dr PolyHistor
Philo Dogmaticus Esqr Canc:	Mr Oldham Wisely
Laconic Comas Esqr Orat:	Mr Joshua Fluter
Jonathan Grog Esqr, P:L:M:C:	Mr Ignotus Warble
Solo Neverout Esqr Pr: Mus:	Signior Lardini
Loquacious Scribble Esqr Secret:	music: *Con Stromti:* ⎫
Quirpum Comic ⎫	Mr Smoothum Sly ⎬ Triumvirs
Slyboots pleasant ⎪	Mr Theophilus Smirker ⎭
Jealous Spyplot Senr ⎪	Mr Broadface Round
Jealous Spyplot Junr ⎬ Esqrs	Mr Roundhead Muddey
Huffman Snap ⎪	Mr Chantum Cheary
Prim Timorous ⎪	Coll: Courtly Phraze
Tunbelly Bowzer ⎭	Mr Curious Courtly
	Mr Swillum Swagbelly
	Mr Prim Laconic
	Capt: Comely Coppernose agent
	Capt: Dio Ramble
	Capt: Prittyman Spyplot

Conundrum 4

Why is a man Eating mustard like a good pun?

The Club gave it up, the Secretary gave in his answer.

ans: Because he is taken in two *Senses*—decl: victor.

It was then ordered, that Messrs Slyboots Pleasant, Huffman Snap, Phylo Dogmaticus, Cancell: Solo Neverout, Jonath: Grog, and the Secretary, go over as Emissaries from the Club, upon Tuesday the 16th of July next, to Pay a visit to Merry Makefun Esqr, and the Eastren Shore Triumvirate, which order was never Complied with, but for what reasons is unknown to the Writer of this History, tho' he was himself, one of the persons appointed t[o] go upon this progress.

Chanc: Then Sir, I put it upon your honor and this here ancient Club to prove that I wrote that there Commission.

No proof could be brought, that the Chancellor had wrote the Commission, and so, by a vote, he was acquitted of the 2d Article, and Called to the Chair, when he came there, he eagerly snatched up the Great Seal, kissed it thrice, and laid it down again upon the table, with a respectful bow, and the members congratulated him upon his happy deliverance, and restoration to his honorable office, this prosecution stuck in the Chancellor's Stomach, and, tho he at present stiffled his resentment, yet, sometime after this, it burst forth in a violent manner, so as to shake his honor out of the Chair, and almost shatter the Constitution of the Club to pieces, at this trial Mr Protomusicus Neverout, first showed || his great abilities in Club Law and proceedings, and began to gain upon the affections of his honor the President, by which he afterwards attained the honorable office of attorney General in the Club, as shall be related in it's proper place.—Then the Conundrums were Called for.

Club Conundrums

By Jonathan Grog Esqr

Conundrum 1

Why is a man's hanging for willful murder, like a pond newly frozen?

The Club gave it up, Jonathan Grog Esqr, gave his answer.

ans: Because it is but *Just-ice*.—decl: victor.

Conundrum 2

Why is a man in a Salivation like a Good Cook?

Huffman Snap Esqr made answer, Because he *Spits*, the Club allowed it good, and Jonathan Grog Esqr gave in his

ans: Because he *Sp[its]* well—drank a bumper.

By the Secretary

Conundrum 3d

Wh[y a]re noble tit[le]s like an Iron poaker?

The Club after deep Consideration gave out, The Secretary gave his

answer. Because they belong to the *Great / grate* } dec: victor.

swers, which he shall make, against the said articles, or any of them, or of offering proofs, to all or every of the said articles, and to all and every other articles, Impeachment and accusation which shall be exhibited by them, as the Case shall require, do pray, that the said Philo Dogmaticus Esqr, may be put to answer the said Crimes and misdemeanors, and that such proceedings examinations, trials and Judgements, may be thereupon had and given, as is agreeable to the Law and Justice of this here ancient Club.

This Impeachment being read, no proof could be produced against the Chancellor, as to the first article, it appeared that he had Crossed the bay, at the time specified in the Impeachment, but he alledging, that he had gone about necessary business, and that he had left no Creatures behind him, to carry on plots, the Club by vote acquitted him of the first article.

Then the Secretary was ordered to read the Commission to Slyboots Pleasant Esqr, and Law 45th, which done the Club proceeded as follows.

Huff: Sn: Mr Secretary, have you any evidence to examine concerning this Second article?

Sec: I call upon Slyboots pleasant Esqr, Pray Sir, from whom did you receive this here Commission?

Sl: Pl: From the Secretary of this here Club Sir.

Huf: Sn: Very well, Mr Secretary, we shall have you Called to an account bye and bye, pray Sir, who gave it to you?

Secr: Sir, if I remember right, I had it from Slyboots Pleasant Esqr.

Sol: Never: So! whence comes this Clashing. Slyboots Pleasant Esqr says he had it of the Secretary, the Secretary affirms, he had it of Slyboots Pleasant Esqr, pray recollect yourselves Gentlemen.

Quirp: Com: Remember you are upon your oath Gentlemen.

Secr: I now remember, I found it on my table, when I came home.

Huff: Sn: Do you know who put it there?

Secret: I cannot tell, but I was told, that among others Philo Dogmaticus Esqr, Called at my house, while I was abroad.

Qu: Com: Do you declare this upon oath?

Sol: Nev: Tis well, this Gentleman at the bar thinks himself upon a precipe, has he any thing to say for himself?

Chanc: Mr President Sir, I do not think, that tho' I had granted this Commission, I have transgressed Law 45th, as is observed and Charged against me, in the Impeachment.

Pres: Sir, do you deny this here Commission is your hand writing?

Qu: Com: On the oath you have taken Sir?

Chanc: Shall I suffer any hurt in my Cause, if I should own it?

Pres: Surely Sir, you would stand Self condemned.

[178]

the great Seal of this here ancient Club, and keeper of his honor's political conscience, and thereupon, took his Seat in a chair of State, at the left hand of the Great Chair, having promised well & truely to serve his honor the President, and the Longstanding members of this here ancient Club, and, the said Chancellor, having continued in this high office, untill about the 12th of June 1750, puffed up with ambition, and a wicked desire of power, not valueing or regarding or gratefully acknowledging, as he ought, the many favors and honors, and dignified titles Conferred on him by his honor the President, or the great trust and Confidence reposed in him, by the Longstanding members of this here ancient Club, but Entertaining wicked and Corrupt designs and views, to procure to himself, excessive and exhorbitant power, and to encroach upon and Impair, the honor and prerogative of the Chair, did, Illegally, daringly and damnably, contrive, machinate and perpetrate, the following high crimes, treasons and misdemeanors, vizt:

Article I. That the said Philo Dogmaticus Esqr, at or upon the 12th of June 1750, or thereabout, being in the high office of Chancellor of this here Club, did, Secretly, Clandestinely, and as it were by Stealth, upon the very day, on which the Club was to sit, at the house of Slyboots Pleasant Esqr, then H:S: convey himself from the place, Passing over in a boat, in the night, to the Eastren Shore, absconding from the Just wrath and Resentment of his honor the President, while his creatures and agents left behind, were Carrying on devlish machinations and plots against the honor & Dignity of the august Chair and the liberty and privileges of the L:St: members, of this here anct: Club.

Article II. That on, or about the 12th of June, 1750, the said Philo Dogmaticus Esqr, did most traiterously perfidiously and wickedly, directly contrary to the Duty of his office, and to the great trust committed to him, and in daring and open violation of Law 45th of this here ancient Club, give up, deliver, and resign, the Great Seal of this here ancient Club, and the political Conscience of his honor the president, into the Care and keeping of Slyboots Pleasant Esqr, then H:S: by means of a Certain Illegal, unwarranted and false Commission under the privy Seal at arms, of the said Philo Dogmaticus Esqr Chancellr: in great Contempt, of the authority and dignity of his honor the president, and to the Irreparable prejudice of the L:S:M: of this here ancient Club.

And the said State officers, and L:St: members of this here ancient Club, by protestation, saving to themselves the liberty of exhibiting, at any time hereafter, any further Articles, or other accusation or Impeachment, against the said Philo Dogmaticus Esqr, and also, of replying to his an-

very uneasy in his Chair, it was agreed, that there could be no regular Club, till the Great Seal was laid upon the table, and his honor the president, after the L:St: members had passed their word of honor, that the Seal should be safe, laid it Solemnly on the table, and the proceedings were read; we observe here, that this was the first time, and the Last, that ever his honor trusted to the honor of the Longstanding members.

Then a Letter from Quirpum Comic Esqr, the H:S: to his honor the President was read, as follows.

To the honorable Nasifer Jole Esqr,
President of the Tuesday Club, Annapolis.

Sir,   Tuesday 26th June 1750

    It is with great pleasure, I once more Embrace the opportunity, of serving your honor and your ancient || Longstanding members in duty of H:S: for this night, at my house in Francis Street, where I hope your honor will favor the Club with your presence.

                                  Your honor's dutiful H:S: &
                                  humble Servant
                                  Quirpum Comic.

The Secretary was then ordered to read the Impeachment, against Philo dogmaticus Esqr, late Chancellor of the Tuesday Club, for high Crimes and misdemeanors.

    But the question was first put, whether Philo Dogmaticus Esqr, should be set to the bar, or keep his place at the left hand of the Chair, during his trial, It was resolved that he should be set to the Bar, and have a Seat or chair allowed him there, accordingly, Philo Dogmaticus Esqr, appeared at the bar, dressed in deep Sables, and the Secretary read the Impeachment as Follows.

Articles exhibited, by the State officers and Longstanding members of the Ancient Tuesday Club, against Philo Dogmaticus Esqr, late Chancellor & keeper of the great Seal for the said Club.

    Whereas the office of Chancellor of this here Club, is an office of the highest dignity and trust, upon the Just and diligent execution whereof, the honor of the Chair, and the wellfare of this here ancient Club depends, and whereas, Philo Dogmaticus Esqr by the Suffrage of the Longstanding members of this here ancient Club, and the great grace and favor of his honor the President, was, upon the 5th day of December 1749, or thereabout, at Sederunt 119 Constituted and appointed Chancellor and keeper of

would terminate in the Deposition of the Chancellor, and loss of the great Seal.

The Secretary moved, that in order to remove the Inconvenience, of Inviting too many Strangers in the Club, The following Law should pass, which accordingly passed, by a majority.

[173] *Law XLVIII.* Passed into a Law, by the president and Club, now met this 12th of June 1750, That from this time forth no member or members shall Invite any Stranger, or Strangers, except the High Steward, for the time being, and he only two at one Serving, for breach of this Law, the penalty shall be, to serve as High Steward, the Night Immediatly after the trespass Committed, and should any member Invite, whose night comes of Course, Immediatly after the H:S: for the time being, such member shall serve the Club, for two nights successively.

On friday the 15th of June, according to appointment, several of the L:St: members met, first at the house of Prim Timorous Esqr, and having there regaled themselves with Cool draughts of Lemmon Punch, marched forth, under the Conduct of Sir John, their Champion, to the Arbor in the pines, where they Enjoyed the breath of the Gentle Zephyrs, and tasted the Refreshing Springs of water, talking of various Gelastic Subjects, and singing of several Songs, the Poet Laureat made the Greatest figure, next to Sir John, in this Rustic assembly, for that Champion presided there, sitting on a bench of Green Turf, and the others on Planks that were erected in the arbor.

On the 26th of June, was held the 136 Sederunt, Quirpum Comic Esqr, being H:S: when a very great dispute arose concerning the Great Seal, when the Secretary was going to read the proceedings of last Sederunt, Huffman Snap Esqr stoped him, and objected, that as the Great Seal and bag, were not yet upon the table, there was no Club, this new started maxim Surprized and alarmed his honor the president very much, he never [174] once dreaming, that the Great Seal would be || set up as a rival to his dignity, for he always thought and now thinks, that his being in the Chair of State was Sufficient to constitute and form the Club, without the asistance of any other Symbol or badge of State, Some thought, that this opinion, was a Suggestion of the Chancellors, in order to aggrandize himself, and make his office of great Importance in the Club, and, that he had Employed Huffman Snap, to broach this new maxim, as being a person skilled in the Law, and a Subtile reasoner, or rather Sophister, others, less fond of political Conjectures and perhaps more Justly, were of opinion, that it was a pure device of the Club, to recover the Great Seal, which the president had seized upon at last Sederunt.

After a very Learned dispute, during which, his honor seemed to be

Conundrum 2d

Why is Kent Island like a whore?

Huffman Snap Esqr, answered, because it is *Incontinent,* which the Club allowed to be a Good answer & Jon: Grog Esqr gave in his answer.

ans: Because it is different from the *Continent*. (drank)

By the Secretary

Conundrum 3d

Why were the Ancient Romans on an Expedition like Ship Carpenters?

The Club, gave it up, the Secretary gave in his answer.

ans: Because they used $\left.\begin{array}{c}\textit{augurs}\\\textit{augers}\end{array}\right\}$ dec: victor.

Conundrum 4th

Why are many hats like the power of Electricity?

The Club gave it up, the Secretary delivered his answer.

ans: Because they are *Felt*.—decl: victor.

His honor the president, after Supper, drank the health of Mr Merry Makefun, a worthy honorary member || of the club, in a remaining bottle of that beer, which that Gentleman had presented to the Club, this toast was drank Immediatly after Supper, the king and Club being first toasted, and the bottle was emptied in one Round.

It was then ordered, that on friday next, being the 15th Instant, at 5 o'Clock P:M: The club should meet in the arbor of the pines, without the City gate, convening first at the house of Prim Timorous Esqr, at half an hour after four P:M: there, vizt: in the arbor, to regale themselves with draughts of Cool Lemmon punch, and maturate affairs of Importance, for the Consideration of the Club at next Sederunt, This appointment was called the appointment of the Rustic Club, tho' in Propriety it was only a Committee.

After Reading the Chancellor's Commission, to Slyboots Pleasant Esqr, the great Seal and Bag, being laid by him upon the Table as usual, before the President, it did not long appear there, for, his honor the President, thinking that it had got into Hucksters hands, as the Saying is, Slyly laid hands on it and Conveyd it into his pocket, and, neither the demands of the deputy chancellor, nor the Solicitations of the Club could recover it from thence, so that every one began to fear that his honors Indignation

cult province, being the keeper and director of his honor the president's political conscience, therefore, I do hereby committ to you, my worthy and Trusty friend, Slyboots Pleasant Esqr, a person well and truely qualified for so great an office, my full power and Commission, for me, and In my place, to act this night, the 12th of June 1750, as chancellor of this here club, meeting at your own house, recommending it earnestly to you, to act Impartially, without respect of persons, suffering no Infringement, either of the Just liberties and privileges of the members, or the prerogative of the Chair, at least, not without the same authority that Confered them, under which his honor knows that he holds them, and, I am satisfied, has reason and moderation to claim no further, knowing well that every creating power, has also an annihilating power.

[Seal]   Given under my hand and Seal at arms at my Lodging in the City of Annapolis, this 12th day of June, 1750, and have sent you also the great Seal, and Instrument of the office.
Signed *Philo Dogmaticus*.

This Bold and daring attempt of the Chancellors, to Lessen the presidential authority, by taking to himself, a power of appointing his deputy, very much Incensed the president, & alarmed the L:St: members, as it was an open attack, upon the prerogative of the Chair, and a plain defiance of Club Law, particularly Law 45th, one of the Prerogative Laws, Lately passed, at Sederunt 124, it was observed, at the reading of this Commission, that his honor the president ‖ assumed the most dreadful timber countenance, that he had been seen to assume for a great while.

It was then ordered, that the Chancellor should be Impeached in the name of the Club, for this manifest breach of Law, and misdemeanor, and the Secretary was enjoined to draw up the Impeachment.

Then came the Conundrums on the Carpet.

Club Conundrums

By Jonathan Grog Esqr

Conundrum 1

Why is a big bellied woman like a fine Gentleman?

The Club gave it up.

    ans: Because she shows her *breeding*,—decl: victor.

the Club should contribute to build a warf, in the City dock, for the good of the place, the Secretary got up and made a long Speech to second and further this motion, to support which, he quoted many ancient, and many moderen writers, vizt: Aristotle, Thuscidides, Theocritus, Sir Willm: Killigrew, and Sir John Oldcastle,[1] but his honor the President, showing some displeasure at the motion, it was drop'd, this was an Instance of his honor's public Spirit, and the complaisance of this ancient and honorable Club, in dropping it at his desire, but, it is thought by some, that the members were Influenced more by a regard to their || own pockets, than any real regard to the Presidents pleasure, there will be occasion by and bye, to exhibit a parallel Instance of the Charity of the President and Club.

Upon the next Sederunt, which was the 132, Slyboots Pleasant Esqr, being high Steward, Sir John, for Particular Reasons of State, retired from the Club, before his honor ascended the Chair, but, what these reasons of State were, could never yet be discovered, tho' it was thought, that Sir John, whatever State he might pretend, was drove away, by the Smell of a new painted room.

A Commission for appointing Slyboots Pleasant Esqr: Deputy Chancellor, from Philo Dogmaticus Esqr, who was obliged to be absent for some time on a Journey, was produced and read in Club, but disapproved of, as Intirely Contrary to Law 45th. This Commission follows.

To my worthy and Trusty Friend, Slyboots Pleasant Esqr, Greeting.

Necessary affairs, calling me away this day, from the honor and pleasure of attending the honorable and ancient Tuesday Club, whereof, I am by their distinguished and Superlative favor, an honorable member, in quality of Chancellor, and keeper of the Great Seal, and, it being necessary, that they should not be, without the asistance of so useful and Important an officer, I was willing and ready to supply their want at this time, of my acknowledged and Eminent talents of Judging in equity and preserving the tranquillity, peace and harmony of the honorable Club, for supporting the Dignity of the August Chair, in Con- || junction with my fellow officer, our dread knight and Champion Sir John, and, which is my peculiar and diffi-

---

1. Thucydides (fl. 5th century B.C.) was an Athenian historian famous mainly for his *History of the War between Athens and Sparta* (431–404 B.C.) and for its moving accounts of tragic events. Theocritus (ca. 300–ca. 260 B.C.?) was the Greek poet whose *Idylls* established him as the master of pastoral poetry in Greek literature. Sir William Killigrew (1606?–1695) was the English author of the tragicomedies *Selindra* (1662), *Ormasdes; or, Love and Friendship* (1664), and *The Siege of Urbin* (1666) and the comedy *Pandora* (1664). Oldcastle (Lord Cobham), 1377?–1417, was the English Lollard leader who gained the friendship of Henry V (then prince of Wales) but was later convicted of heresy (1413).

of Manuquassation, and, after paying a short and pithy Compliment to his honor, he took his Seat in Club.

Thus, the Club recovered again, a worthy and valuable Longstanding member, who was once given up for lost, as has been related, in the History of the letter of Cats.

Then followed the Conundrums, which were as follow.

Club Conundrums

Jonathan Grog Esqr

Conundrum 1

Why is a Carter like a woman with Child?

Given up by the Club, and the following answer given in.

ans: Because he is often *Teaming* / *Teeming* } declard victor.

[168] Conundrum 2

Why is a white Smith like an arrant thief?
Huffman Snap Esqr answered, because he *Steels* / *Steals* }

The Club admitted it a good answer, and Jonathan Grog Esqr drank and gave in his answer.

ans: Because he is often *Steeling* / *Stealing* }

The Secretaries Conundrums were

Conundrum 3d

Why is a large tract of land In Maryland like the moon in her monthly Course?

The Club gave it up, and the Secretary gave in his answer.

ans: Because it is divided Into several *quarters*,—dec: victor.

Conundrum 4th

Why is a great folio book, like a Coronation procession?

Jonathan Grog Esqr, answered, because there are many *pages* in it, the Club allowed it a good answer, and the Secretary drank his bumper.

It being proposed in Club after Supper by Slyboots pleasant Esqr, that

that of your ancient Club, To be Clerk and Secretary to your honor, and your ancient Tuesday Club, is a felicity that adequates the most extensive of my desires, I desire no greater office, no higher dignity than this, here be my *Ne plus ultra* of ambition and fame, the top and pinacle of my Glory, Thirteen letters have I already writ Concerning your honor and your ancient Club, this I now write is the fourteenth, and I still find matter enough to exercise a fancy ten times more fertile than mine, and Sure I am, were it the fourteen hundredth in number, I should still find a Copious field before me. I shall Conclude with observing, that, as the Greatness of the Subject is Inconceivable, so also is the pleasure and Satisfaction I enjoy every time I serve your ancient Club as H:S: Your honors Company and gracious countenance gives me pleasure, to wait upon and serve your ancient and honorable Tuesday Club, gives me pleasure, and therefore, I hope your honor's generosity will evidence it Self this night, in granting the pleasure of your august presence to your ancient and honorable Tuesday Club and to him who is, Honble: Sir,

> Your honor's most faithful
> Secretary, Diligent H:S: and
> Most devoted Servant,
> *Loquacious Scribble*.

It appears in this letter, how the Secretary again has recourse to flattery and Cajoling, to gain over his honor the president to his Interest, and procure to himself thereby, the dignity and place of a State member, but, we shall find, he spends his breath in vain, & that his honor's understanding was too Solid and Strong to be imposed ‖ upon by such false glosses, at least from this officer, whose Cunning and deceit, was too well known by his honor ever to gain any Confidence or trust with the Chair.

Captn Comely Coppernose's Patent, drawn out on a fair Skin, in Ingrossing hand, with the Great Seal of the Club appended, in red tape, was delivered to the Secretary in Club, by his honor, which being read, the Chancellor applied to it, the great Seal, and the Secretary was ordered to dispatch it to London by the first opportunity, a duplicate of the same, wrote out on Skin, in the same manner, being delivered to his honor, by the Secretary, to be Signed and Sealed, in Case of the miscarriage of the first.

Quirpum Comic Esqr, formerly a long Standing member of the Club, applied to be again admitted, he withdrew and the Ballots being put round he was elected, and being sent for, The master of Ceremonies received him at the door, and leading him to the Great Chair, Confirmed him after the usual manner, and Presenting him to his honor, he received the Salutation

[167]

tending to act for the General Good, tho' they had nothing less in their view, the absolute power over, and Sole Sway in the Club, being in effect, what they both aimed at, and it will appear at last, in this history, after many violent Struggles and Convulsions, that the Chancellor, like Pompey, being overcome, the Club, as the Romans did to Cæsar, became Slaves to Nasifer Jole Esqr, and the Tyrants his Successors and Substitutes in that Clubical Chair.

Upon the 29th of May, 1750, the Club met at the Secretaries house, It being Sederunt 131, at which Sederunt, all the members appeared in their badge medals, and the h:S: according to a rule lately passed, had his, distinguished from the others, by a knot of yellow ribbon, alittle above the medal, the presidents, was now, as it always had been, for a Considerable time past, distinguished by the presidential Star, and some attempts were made ‖ at this time to clap a distinguishing mark, upon Sir John's badge, by adding several Silver Tassels to it, which that Champion Rejected with Scorn, saying, that he wanted no other mark of distinction, but his broadsword, by which, he should always chuse to distinguish himself.

A Letter from the high Steward, was produced at this Sederunt, and is as follows.

To the honorable Nasifer Jole Esqr,
President of the Tuesday Club, These.

Honorable Sir,

No Subject is altogether Inexhaustible, the most Copious and extensive themes, when frequently handled will dwindle into nothing, nay, if tortured beyond what they can bear, will degenerate into mere Triffling, this may Justly and truely be said of these Common Subjects and vulgar topics comprehended, under the heads of the Seven liberal arts and Sciences, but, should we aver this of the ancient Tuesday Club, and its honorable and Illustrious President, I will not affirm, that we should mantain a palpable lye, but we should Surely fall very wide of the truth, your honor and the Club Therefore are Subjects inexhaustible, infinite Subjects that never can be wore out, a fountain that furnishes Copious Supplies for the poet and the Orator; the orator, did I say? alas! now the orator is defunct, our Laureat has got all the glorious theme to himself, happy Laureat, who can boast such a noble theme! Happy Club! who are blest with such a bard, to sound your fame!

Most honorable Sir, Tho heaven has gifted me with a very slender genius, yet, I bless my Stars, that I was born under so auspicious a planet, as

Chapter VIII

[163]

Admission of a Longstanding member, Deputy Chancellor's Commission, Rustic Club, Seizure of the Great Seal, Disputes concerning it, Impeachment & acquittal of the Chancellor.

In all Societies whatsoever, there are, and must be, people that Lead, and people that are led. There are Cunning men and fools, blended together in Communities, and the Cunning and ambitious, will never be without their train of fools and Simpletons. This is the very nature of human Society, & is observed as often in Clubs as any where—Even among beggars, or those that are upon a level, there will be leaders, advisers, directors, and some that assume the management and Sway of the rest of the ragged fraternity.

From the Jarring or opposite interests of two or more ambitious men setting themselves up to be leaders or directors in Society, that monster *Party* takes it's origin, which is a plant, or rather weed of a monstrous quick Growth, and Choaks every useful vegetable near it, in fine, it effectually breaks the union of, and weakens Society, for union in any Society is Strength, and, if it does so, it is no promoter of the Common Good. Tho Pompey and Cæsar both pretended to befriend the public Interest, yet, they were in fact, it's greatest enimies, and the True & real friends of the public, were such as counteracted the ambitious views of both. Party men, by raising their minions too high, are Sure to Introduce General Slavery, after Pompey's overthrow, all were Slaves to Cæsar, and the Tyrants his Successors.

These Political observations, occurr very naturally to a historian of my degree and Class, in writing the His- || tory of such a Society, as that of our ancient Tuesday Club, In this Club, we found, directors, managers and leaders, either setting up themselves, or exalted by the operation of others, we find a president, who for some time acted with the Sole power, till State officers were Created, which in some measure checked that power, and occasioned several Commotions in Club, Thence, party took its rise, and began to play her pranks, at last, two great Rivals, the President and Chancellor, appeared in the lists, and like Cæsar and Pompey at Rome, raised unextinguishable heats and Animosities, in this unhappy Club, both pre-

[164]

[162]

[160]

[157]

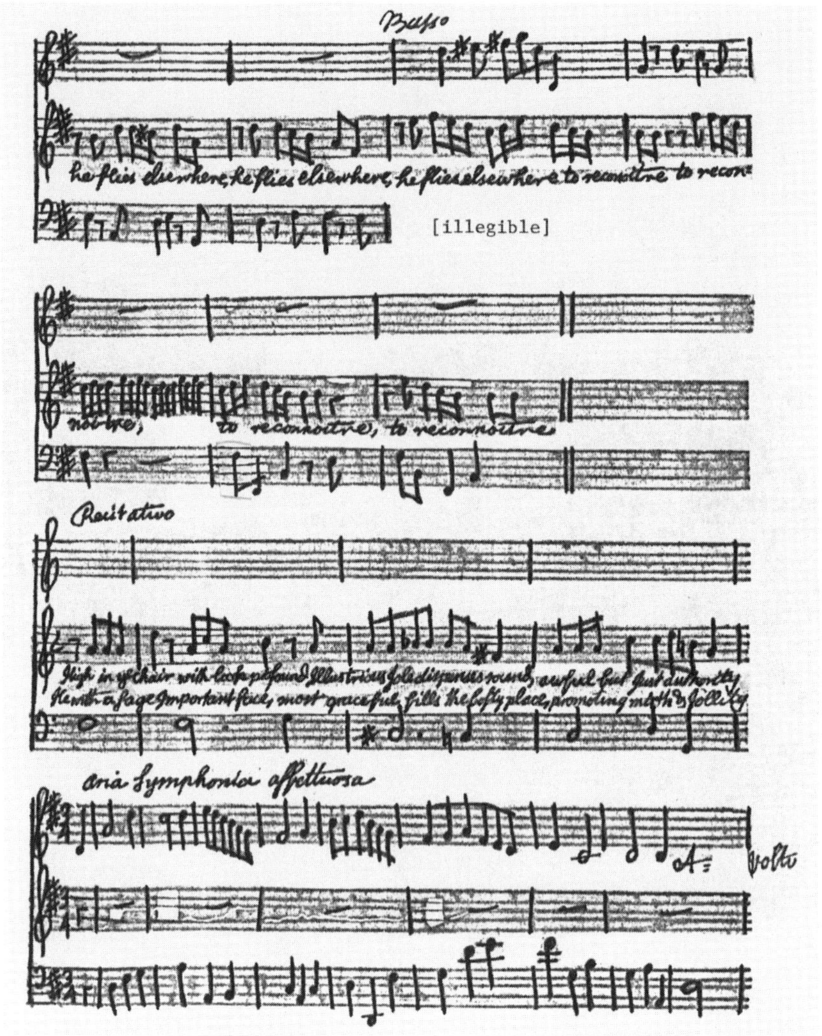
Basso
he flies elsewhere, he flies elsewhere, he flies elsewhere to reconnoitre to recon=
[illegible]
noitre, to reconnoitre, to reconnoitre
Recitativo
High in ye chair with looks profound Illustrious sole dispenses round, awful but just authority
He with a sage important face, most graceful fills the lofty place, promoting mirth & jollity
Aria Symphonia affettuosa
volta

[154]

112 [Book VII] The History of

[152]

110 [Book VII]

[150]

[148]

Tory rory with all his heart, but, the Longstanding members suspecting a Jacobite Song because of the word *Tory* in the Chorus, were silent, and Mr Makefun did not sing.

Thus ended the 5th Anniversary, in which the Club took upon them a deal of Grandure and State, and began to look upon themselves, as men of Great Consequence.

Then several martial tunes were plaid Solo, Sir John knight and Champion of the Club, dancing several heroic and warlike dances, and honored the Chancellor so far as to dance a Jigg with him, while the latter laid aside the Gravity of his office, and play'd and danced at one and the same time, but Sir John making a fawx pas, he fell upon the Chancellor, had almost overset him, and broke the bridge of the fiddle.

Solo Neverout Esqr, Protomusicus *Con voce,* did not perform the Canto part of the music this night, not being Sufficiently prepared.

The Revd Mr Smoothum Sly, in a Succinct harangue, paid the compliments of the Eastren Shore Club, to his honor the presd: & the members.

The Secretary returned the club's thanks to his honor the president, for his Sumptuous and grand entertainment, to the poet for his Ode, to Signior Lardini for his fine performance, and to the honorary members for their attendance.

Thus in great pomp and magnificence, was this grand anniversary Celebrated, at the house of Mr President Jole, in North East Street, where, besides the Show and Splendor of the Entertainment, and the Instrumental music that was exhibited on this grand occasion, there was abundance of Eloquence displayed In various Speeches, made by the members, both honorary and Regular, which we have neither Space nor leisure here to record, there was also a great deal of vocal music, for, after Mr Protomusicus had performed, most of the members sung, and the old Catch of Captn Serious Social was sung several times over, where is the following distich.

One bowl in hand, and another in Store,
Enough's enough, and we'll have one more.

On which his honor the president observed, that they might have 100 more, if they pleased, but Mr Merry Makefun answered, that they would not be quite so unreasonable or inconscionable, and sung it in the following manner.

Enough's Enough, we'll have ninety nine more.

His honor then desired Mr Merry Makefun to sing a Song of his own, but he answered, that he could sing no Song well, but what had *Tory rory*[10] in the Chorus, and if he could get one to Join him, he would sing a Song of

---

10. *Tory-rory* means "roaring, uproarious, or boisterous"; after 1680 the phrase was sometimes abusively associated with the tory faction.

Aria
Apollo with his band of Singers
The tuneful nine the Chair surround,
He strikes the Lyre with nimble fingers
And sooths our ears with magic Sound.
Chorus
The Canopy, o'er head impending,
Kind Amalthæa hov'ring there,
With Cornucopia seems descending,
Her richest, Choicest bounty sending
For us, her favorites to share.
Recitativo
Pomona, Bacchus, Ceres, see,
To all our members Long and Standing,
Are bounteous too, as well as she,
And their most chearing Gifts are sending.
Aria
Let this glad evening crown the day,
   Let mirth abound
   And bowls go round
   To honor Jole,
   Our life and Soul,
And each Sad thought be Cleard away.
Grand Chorus
Whilst Jole shall live to fill our Chair,
We ever shall be debonnair,
No turpid cares our Joy shall Rob,
Kind heaven Grant, that long he may
Remain in health to bless this day,
Long live, Long live the Tuesday Club.

This ode met with great applause, being composed in the right moderen taste, the machinery of it consisting chiefly in a group of heathen Gods and Goddesses, the Constant attendants of all Princes and great men, on their birth and wedding days, and therefore very proper ministers for honorable Presidents of Clubs, whose greatness no man can call in Question.

After Supper, the musicians *con Stromenti* of the Club, played the overture of the anniversary music, with two Violins and a bass, Signr Lardini, Violino primo, Cancellarius Violino Secondo, & Secretarius Violoncello, and met with great applause, this overture consisting of a prelude, air for his honor, minuet and pastorale.

Shouts of Triumph, peals of Joy
In praise of Jole, each Tongue Employ,
    The tuneful nine,
    In concert Join,
    Apollo heightens our delight.
  Chorus
Fortune ever changing,
Now shall keep from ranging
  And with great Jole shall live,
For his refulgent glory,
Shall fill each pompous Story
  Whilst time and fame survive.
  Recitativo
Honor[a] and Justice[b] on each Side the Chair,
Behold, while Jole sits there in State
Secure. Our knight with courage rare
And front terrific, guards the awful Seat.
  Aria
For should a bold Intruder dare[c]
T'assault the Club, or storm the Chair,
    His bones Sir John,
    Would fall upon
And furiously at every bang
Demand a prompt eclaircissement.
  Chorus
Thus Bruis'd to mash, and Crush'd to powder,
  A Piteous Spectacle of nature,
Bawling out Louder, still and Louder,
  He'd fly elsewhere to Reconnoitre.
  Recitativo
High in the chair with look profound
Illustrious Jole dispenses round
  Awful, but Just authority,
He with a Sage Important face
Most graceful fills his lofty place,
  Promoting mirth and Jollity.

(a) The Champion.
(b) The Chancellor.
(c) The music here warlike and furious.

adopting you as members, Secondly, as being Gentlemen of worth and Character, you reflect an honor upon this ancient Society, and add to its Lustre and Glory, being so many Stars of the Second magnitude, in this our Clubicular System, for we must allow the old and Longstanding members to be the first rate Stars, that surround like Satellites the great Luminary of the Chair.

And now Honorable Sir, and Gentlemen, enough for Speech making, let us prepare to eat, drink, laugh, sing and be merry.

The Secretary having pronounced this Speech, (in which is exhibited the first Specimen of his knowledge of the Sublime in Club Speeches, and his fondness for the moderen method of Introducing the heathen Gods and Goddesses into his Declamations) his honor left the Chair, and the members went to Supper, and were entertained in a most elegant and magnificent manner, by his honor, altogether Suitable to this Grand occasion.

After Supper, Jonathan Grog Esqr, Poet Laureat || was called upon to [142] read the anniversary ode, which he did with a Clear and Audible voice, standing up in his place as follows.

Anniversary Ode, for the Tuesday Club

Set to music in three parts, and to be sung, and played on several Instruments, on tuesday the 15th of May 1750. Humbly Inscribed, to the honorable Carlo Nasifer Jole Esqr, president, and the Longstanding members of the said Club by

*Their Humble Servant
The Poet Laureat.*

Recitativo
Thrice hail Serene returning day,
Bright Day, outshining far, the rest,
In which the Tuesday Club, in may,
First rear'd her gay and Social Crest.

Phæbus has now five Courses ran,
The Laureat twice essay'd to sing
Great Jole's eclat, that glorious man,
From whence the Club's best blessings spring.

Aria
Airy violins Sweetly sounding,
Softer ecchoing flutes rebounding,
    Celebrate a day so bright.

trious Laureat! so long as you continue to sing the eulogium of his honor the president, and this here ancient Club, and your bold Strokes, shall be remembered in future ages, and read with admiration and astonishment, by our Sons, and our Son's Sons, whilst a multitude of grateful puns & Conundrums [here his honor the president frowned] like rich balsams and Spices shall Season the whole of your Compositions, and render your fame Savory & odoriferous to posterity.

[140]   Dignified Proto-musicus,

Rouse up now all the powers of Sweet music, warble forth the praises of his honor and this here ancient Club, our Laureat's verse will afford words in plenty, his honor the president will afford ample Subject, 'tis your business dignified Sir, to modulate Sound, Collect together all your Quavers, Semiquavers, minims, Crotchets, Shakes, Graces, Stops, accents,[9] and, let us see this night, that notwithstanding the criticisms made upon your performances, by some Capricious members, that you can, upon such a Solemn occasion, outdo even your own outdoings, assist him O Apollo, to go thro' this arduous task, stand by him with your Melodious Lyre, that his voice may be kept in tune, & give him a Sip of Helicon, that his Spirits may not sink under the mighty burden of singing Solo, the Sublime Anniversary ode, Composed by our poet Laureat, thy favorite!

Gentlemen,

You the old Standing and longstanding members of this here ancient Club, Long and firmly may you stand, a diapente of years have you already stood, and I hope five hundred shall not see you fall, pray the Celestial powers to preserve the life of mighty Jole, for, by him you stand, and are supported as an ancient Club, and, when he goes, may it be at a long, late and distant day, and pray the gods to send us Just such another, if possible, but alas, we may pronounce with a Sigh, where is he to be found, I am afraid he is not yet born, and we need not expect him, till the return of the golden age, or the celebrated millennium, when, we are told, that all mankind, shall be as one Club.

[141]   You worthy Gentlemen, honorary members, of this here ancient Club, I greet you well, in the name of his honor the president, his honor is glad to see you, and Joy appears in his countenance, we all rejoice at it; welcome thrice welcome worthy fellow members, to share with us the rich fare, and Jovial mirth and Glee of this Solemn occasion, in a twofold Sense may you be called honorary, first, as this here ancient Club has done you honor in

---

9. These are all musical terms. Perhaps the only one that may pose problems is *crotchet*, which is the symbol for a note half the value of a minim.

then, O take not all the Glory to yourself, nor Imagine it is Intirely the effect of your wise and Just oeconomy, but remember to stop, before you go too far, and let not vain glory mislead you, for, as all the wits and geniuses of this here ancient club, derive virtue and power, from that there honorable Chair, so you, with all your Stock of equity, must own, that, from that there fountain head, it all proceeds, else, the waters of the Stream could never flow so Clear & so majestic, and in fine, as in that there bag, you reserve safe the Great Symbolical type or Signature of this here ancient Club, so you ought also, to keep Safe and Sound, the political Conscience of his honor the president, in a Clean and unsullied Sachel or bag, that it may always remain Clear & without Spot or blemish.

Jonathan Grog Esqr,

Shall I address you as worshipful m[as]ter of ceremonies, or as poet Laureat, to this here ancient Club, fo[r] both these Eminent places you possess, the least of which great off[ic]es, would be a multifarious theme, for a Club orator to En[la]rge upon, worshipful, worthy and witty Sir, the order and decency of this here ancient club, is by you supported and directed, by you we know, and are Instructed, when and how we are to sit, walk, address the honorable Chair, how, with an air to bow, how to take our place in Club, and with what decorum there to || deport ourselves, with pleasure, often have our eyes beheld your curious and elegant attitude, when adorning the Shoulders of his honor, with the Grand presidential Star and Garter, with enchantment have we heard you pronounce, the Inaugurating Speech at the Confirmation of a new member, vizt: "I as master of ceremonies, with all the Ceremony I am master of, which mastery in Ceremonies, I acknowledge to have received from his honor the President &ct:" words elegant and well ranged, a trope as yet unequalled, an expression Inimitable—Shall I now address you as a bard—O for the whole troop of muses from Pindus, to asist me here—Come Thalia, come Melpomene, come Urania, come Clio, come Polhymnia, come Euterpe, come Calliope, come Terpsichore, come Erato,[7] come altogether in a Group, and enable me to address this eminent Bard! This Bard of the ancient and honorable Tuesday Club, your darling, your favorite, for, most Sublime Sir, as your Subject is grand, so your verses are yet unequalld, you are the very marrow, the quintessence of all poetical Sublime, the Corner Stone of the temple of Peon,[8] the Laurels shall for ever florish upon your brow O Illus-

[139]

---

7. The Muses of comedy and pastoral poetry, tragedy, astronomy, history, sacred song, lyric poetry, epic poetry, dance, and love poetry.
8. Paean was one of the epithets of Apollo, who often led the Muses in their songs and dances.

ened, by the Influencing beams, proceeding from that there exalted Chair, is an eternal fence and Safeguard to the Longstanding members of this here Ancient club, so, as that they can, with tranquill Security, from all || assaults, from without, and from within, defended and protected sit here, and quaff nectareous draughts of Lemmonian punch and manducate the most delicious ambrosial Cates, from his honors Culinary *officino,* as also, with freedom, roll round the Ingenious pun, and well Involved *Conundrum,* (a) led and directed by the yet unequaled wit, and unparallelled acumen of our Laureat's genius.

Happy, we enjoy the Sweets of peace and plenty, under your valorous protection, and sit secure from all assaults and Insults, for—should any bold Intruder dare to break in upon our peace,

> His bones Sir John,
> Would fall upon,
> And furiously, at every bang,
> Demand a promt eclaircissement, (b)

as our above said Sublime bard, has most elegantly expressed it,—Gird then, Sir John, your Sword upon your manly thigh, let guards of Grim musqueteers, attend your beck, and all the bristling horrors of deadly war, be ready at your Call, lest dire destruction from the vigilant foe, should menace, and find us off our guard, for, at your voice Stentorian and terrific, and most horrendous frown, all enimies will fly away apace, even before the Lustre of your refulgent Sword, darts from the dark recesses of the Scabbard, to strike us dead with most horrific Glare.

Most honorable C[han]cellor,

Thou most profound, M[aje]stic, and pacific Stream of Salutiferous Justice, whose equal and Imp[ar]tial hand destributes balsamic and healing equity, to the Long[sta]nding members of this here ancient Club, that Infallible Traumatic Balsam, which heals up and Cicaterises the wounds, ulcers and Slashes, made in our Constitution, by the ill timed altercation, and vociferation of some longstanding members, whose || ambition and desire of power in this here ancient Club has outrun their prudence and discretion. Thou Infallible Solver of all knotty points, that are, or shall be started in this here ancient Club, look here, upon the harmony and order that prevails among us, on this here Solemn and pompous occasion, and

---

(a) Here his honor the president, who was no friend to puns and Conundrums, stooped down, and whispered Sir John, at his right hand, saying loud enough to be heard, *I think we have enough of this Stuff.*

(b) Anniversary ode for 1750.

the Street, by means of the many Genteel Scrapes he made, to set off his bows, nor were Sir John, and the Chancellor wanting in their bows and Salutations, then, his honor, taking his place, between the two Latter, the procession went forewards, and passed thro' a gate, into his honors yard, the way being strowed with flowers & the Colors displayed as usual, which flag, Capt: Dio Ramble, removed from his honors Garden poles, and briskly mounting a Ladder, stuck it on the ridge of his honor's kitchen, and the members, after sometime sitting in the yard, round a table Garnished with punch bowls, bottles, Glasses and Tobacco pipes, They Translated themselves into his honor's great Saloon, which was beautifully Illuminated with Sconce lights, and set out with various garlands and flowers, and his honor having ascended the great Chair of State, in the presence of Seventeen Regular, and honorary members of the Club, and two Strangers, Silence was commanded by Jonathan Grog Esqr, Master of the Ceremonies, and the Secretary was Called upon to deliver the anniversary Speech, which he, standing up in his place, pronounced as follows.

Anniversary Speech [136]

Mr President Sir,

Such a Surprize and astonishment as possessed the old hoary and Squalid anarch Chaos, when he was waked out of his eternal Slumbers, by the elucidation of the Celestial lights, when Creation first sprung, such a Surprize, I say, Honorable Sir, must at this Instant possess my Sensorium when I behold the members of this here ancient Club, Incumbent over those capacious bowls, replete with precious punch, most Splendidly elucescent, with those Glittering and Lumeniferous badges, like so many oriental and bright planets, Rising upon the watery deep, and adorning the azure Expance with their Immortal Irradiations! whilst you, Great Sir! like the Solar Center of this grand Clubicular System, dispence Inexhaustible Lustre to all, and, from your fountain undeminished, the whole emanation of light proceeds, the Splendor of our Longstanding members being nothing else, but the reflected glory of your honor, our most honorable president.

Sir John,

Thou Standing Sturdy pillar, and Robust butteress of this here ancient Club, who, as our mellifluous Laureat, has in Cibberian numbers sung, *with front terrific guards the awful Seat,*[6] whose valor, quickened and enliv-

---

6. Cibber is a constant butt of humor in the Tuesday Club. This passage, which does not appear in any of Cibber's more memorable works, was perhaps invented by Hamilton as another indirect hit against Cibber's inflated diction.

The Second grand Anniversary Procession.

[facing page 134]

Resolved, by Sir John *Solus,* that every member shall wear his badge Ribbon in what form he pleases.

The Committee broke up, the honorable Sir John, leaving the Chair with a plaudite, and a brisk Step, while an airy Jigg was played by one of the Club's musicians *con Stromenti.*

Upon the 15th of May, 1750, according to the appointment of the Grand Committee, The members, regular and honorary, to the number of ten, convened at the Secretaries house, at four o'clock p:m: and an hour after, Invested themselves with their badge medals and proceeded to Sir John's house, who received them dress'd out in his regimentals with a bold martial air, || and Introducing them into the Antichamber, Entertained them with Rich Lemonian punch, and Generous wine, at 6 o'clock, they dispatched a messenger, to his honor the president, to acquaint him of their comeing, and, in half an hour after marched out in Solemn procession, being met on the way by Capt: Dio Ramble, an honorary member, the order of the procession was, as follows. [134]

1   Jonathan Grog Esqr, Mr of Ceremonies, *Solus*
2   Sir John, Knight, & Philo Dogmaticus Esqr, Canc:
3   Slyboots Pleasant & Tunbelly Bowzer Esqrs, L:S:M:
4   Jealous Spyplot Junr Esqr L:S:M: & Capt: Dio Ramble, H:M:
5   Merry Makefun and Signr: Lardini Esqrs H:M:M:
6   Smoothum Sly, Esqr & Dr Polyhystor H:M:M:
7   Solo Neverout, Pro: Mus: & Secretary Scribble L:S:M: & rearmen

As the procession moved on in a Solemn and Stately manner, it was honored with a great number of Spectators of all Ranks from windows, walls, Balconies, and even the Sides of the Streets, were lined with Children and other Spectators, nay, the *Patres Conscripti,*[5] or members of the Great provincial Senate, deigned to come forth of the doors of their house and look on this gallant Show; for the Long standing members made a most Splendid appearance, with their dowble gilt || badge medals—when the procession came within twenty paces of the honorable the president's gate, his honor made his appearance, and advanced to Salute them, on which the procession stoped alittle, and Jonathan Grog Esqr, pulling out the Anniversary ode, waved it in a Graceful manner, in his hand, by way of Salutation to his honor the President, his honor made several low bows, which were respectfully returned by the master of Ceremonies, who raised some dust in [135]

---

5. "Chosen fathers" (literally, "fathers [and] elect"; commonly and less correctly, "conscript fathers") was the common address of Roman senators, as in Cicero's orations.

Why is one eating an egg for Supper, like a hardened Sinner in the act of Iniquity?

ans: Because he makes no *bones* of it.

It was ordered that no Conundrums should be proposed on the anniversary night, that being a time for mirth and not for hard Study.

[132] On monday the 7th of may, 1750, the Grand Committee met at the Secretarie's house, by Summons from his honor the president, and Sir John was Chose Chairman by a great Majority, and while he marched to take the Chair, with a *grand pas,* a martial tune was play'd by one of the Club's musicians *con Stromenti,*[4] and he took the Chair with a plaudite.

A Copy of the printed anniversary ode, was presented to each of the members present.

The music of the Ode was cursorily examined by the Committee and approved of.

It was resolved that the Anniversary of the Club, should be Celebrated upon Tuesday the 15th Instant, at the house of the honorable Mr President Jole.

Resolved also, that the Regular and honorary Members of the Club, shall meet at the house of the Secretary upon Tuesday the 15th Instant, at four o'Clock P:M:

Resolved also, that at 5, P:M: they shall march to the house of Sir John, knight of the Club.

Resolved also, that at 6 o clock p:m: they shall march, from the house of Sir John, to the honorable Mr President Joles, in full procession, ornamented with their Badge medals.

[133] Then the order of the grand procession, was settled by the Committee, and the Secretary was ordered to open the Anniversary Solemnity with a Speech.

Then eleven badge medals were destributed to the members of the Committee, and affixed each to a Ribbon to be wore round the neck and hang down before.

Ordered by this committee that in case all the members, should agree to wear their badge medals every Club night, that the h:S: for the time being should distinguish his badge Ribbon from the others by a knot of a different Color *ad Libitum,* tied Just above the medal.

Blue Ribbons were delivered by his honor the president, to all the members of the Committee.

---

4. With his instruments.

Then the following Laws were Passed.

Law XLVI. No Gentleman shall be proposed as a member of this Club, either honorary or Regular, while he himself is present.

This Law was of his honor the Presidents framing, he being offended at the Club's creating so many honorary members, especially at Sederunt 124, when no Less than three honorary members were made in one night, and all those that were made, were then present in Club, which, put a Constraint on the Members in giving their voices, especially on his honor the president, to whom some of these Gentlemen were not agreeable.

Law XLVII. That no honorary member shall be admitted for the future, without unanimous Consent by balloting.

Then it was ordered, that the Grand Committee of ‖ the whole Club, [131] should meet, upon Monday, the 7th of this Instant, wherever his honor the president shall think fit, to prepare matters for the anniversary, and deliver the badge medals.

Then the Conundrums were Called for.

Club Conundrums

Jonathan Grog Esqr gave in his, which were both given up by the Club, and he declared victor.

Conundrum 1

> Why is a public advertisement like a Shower of rain in Summer?
> ans: Because it is *Not-ice*.

Conundrum 2d

> Why is a Scandalous Story like a Church bell?
> ans: Because it is often *Told* / *Toll'd*

The Secretarie's Conundrums were also both given up by the Club, and he declared victor.

Conundrum 3d

> Why is a man with a broken back, like a good Country housewife?
> ans: Because he is *Not-able*.[3]

Conundrum 4th

---

3. In this context *notable* means "capable, bustling, clever, and industrious in managing household affairs."

agent in Great Britain, directed to himself, which was read in Club as follows.

[129] To Doctor Loquacious Scribble, Annapolis.

Dear Sir,   London Janry 26th 1749

The bearer, Captn John Sedgewick brings you, your Medals, which I have at last got done, this has been the *Puzzleingest*[a] Job I ever undertook, every body I employed about them, from the dye cutter to the finisher, complain they are not half paid for such a Job, and I am afraid the Gentlemen will think they are paid too much, you see they come to more than we calculated them at, however, I hope they will make their own way, and recommend themselves, several pieces broke off the edge of the dye during the last medal that was struck, but it has not got to the Letters, so, that you can have more done if you want them, the Edges can be made Compleat with a tool.

I shall keep the Dyes, untill I have your orders about them, if you should want any more, I dont believe you have an Engine in America to strike them.

I shall think myself abundantly recompensed, for the trowble I have taken, if I am so happy, as to have the approbation of the worthy members, pray do me the favor to pay my compliments, and particularly to your Illustrious Chairman, I congratulate him on the honor done him on this occasion, which will Justly perpetuate his memory from generation to Generation, I hope you Received the great Seal I sent you by Mr Belt, shall be Glad to hear from you & am

                               Your most Humble Servt:
                               Comely Coppernose.

P:S: I have given them to the Captn, and made him give bills of Lading, which small expence, I hope, you will not think needless. C:C:

[130] Thus the Club, to perpetuate their memory, and that of their honorable president, were at the expence of strikeing a medal, in which piece of vanity they have Imitated several other Societies, and therefore are not Singular in this particular.

The Ode for the Ensuing Anniversary of the Club, was produced at this Sederunt, by the poet Laureat, and being approved of was appointed to be first performed before the grand Committee of the Club, preparatory for the anniversary.

    (a) This is a right Clubical word.

[Book VII] 93

The Tuesday Club Medal. Courtesy of the Maryland Historical Society, Baltimore.

instances of this our History, for we have seen here, how the arts of flattery have prevailed over his honor the president, and his State officers, so as to make them Judge erroneously, and perverted their understanding to such a degree, as that they could not comprehend how any proposition could be rational or Consistent with Common Sense, which had not a direct tendency to promote their power, Influence and authority in the Club; as for the Senses of his honor, and his Longstanding members in General, we shall find, in the following part of our history, how Grossly they were misled and Corrupted, by a vein of pomp, Show and magnificence, assumed in the Club, and what a powerful effect, this Species of adulation, in the Shape of Medals, Caps of State, Canopies, Capations, and Solemn Grand processions, had upon their understanding and Judgement.

At Sederunt 129 May 1, 1750, Tunbelly Bowzer Esqr being H:S: the Secretary reported in Club, that he had received the Club Badge medals, from Capt: Comely Coppernose, the Club's agent at London, according to an order of the Club, at Sederunt 105, march 14th, 1748/9, which medals, the honorable the president produced to the Club in a box, upon the one Side of this medal was struck, the Emblem of liberty, sitting by an altar, upon the altar was the motto *Libertas et Natale Solum,* and Round the Edge of the medal, *Carolus Cole Armiger Præses,* which by an unacoun- ‖ table blunder of the Sculptor, was put instead of *Nasifer Jole,* or *Carlo Nasifer Jole,*[1] this arose, it is thought, from the Indistinct writing of the Secretary, who gave directions to the artist in this work, but the mistake rather arose, from the Complex Name of his honor, he being called by several people *Carlo Nasifer Jole,* and the Engraver, being no Scholar, mistook Carlo, for Carolus, which is on the K: Charles's Crowns & Shillings, and Intirely ommitting the Name Nasifer, as not having room for it, he mistook the Secretarys J for a C, in the last part of the name, upon the reverse was a heart, with two hands Interlocked in the amicable Gripe, and in the Middle in Large Characters, *The Tuesday Club, in Annapolis Maryland, May 14th 1746,* and round the edge of the Medal *Concordia res parvæ Crescunt.*[2] These medals were of fine Silver, without alloy, dowble gilt, each onepenny weight over and above one ounce, and to each a Shagreen Case, Lined with green Velvet.

The Secretary produced a letter from Capt: Comely Coppernose, the

---

1. At one time, Hamilton apparently either placed or intended to place one of the club's badge medals here, but it does not appear in the manuscript. Four copies of the badge medal remain: one is housed at the British Library, another at the Maryland Historical Society (accession no. 1852.3), and the last two at the Johns Hopkins University (John Work Garrett Library, Wilson Collection, no. 785). For further information on the Tuesday Club medal, see Sarah Elizabeth Freeman, "The Tuesday Club Medal," *Numismatist,* LVIII (1945), 1313–1322.

2. "Small endeavors flourish through unity" (Sallust, *Jurguitha* 10.6).

philosophers, since the beginning of the world, all the glorious pictures that have been exhibited of virtue, and the happiness accompanying that Goddess, and all the high flown encomiums that have been bestowed upon her attendants Temperance, Justice, benevolence, Truth, humility & Charity have had no Influence at all, in persuading men from gratifying to the utmost pitch, all Sorts of Sensual appetites, even at the Risque of their own and their neighbour's quiet, Safety peace and lives.

On the Contrary, these allurements, that are applied to the Senses, seldom or never fail to mislead the understanding, and vitiate the Judgement, hence, we find, dress and finery, often make much the greatest part of the Character of a fine gentleman or Lady, and excite notions of something excellent, Comprehended under these external trappings, hence we find also, many devotees, carried away with a high notion of the real excellency of pomp Show and Splendor in the Ceremonies and rituals of Religion, and persuade themselves, that this way of going to heaven amidst a glare of magnificence, is the easiest as well as the most pleasant Road, and so never trowble themselves about the stale method, which points out the way of good morals, which some refined Sort of folks have Indeed Imagined, to be the only ladder whereby to mount the Celestial mansions.

If I may be allowed to give a reason for this Superior force and efficacy [126] which the operators on the Senses have over those which operate on the understanding and Judgement, I shall offer this, that whatever our metaphysicians and refined philosophers have said of abstract knowledge and Innate Ideas, whatever our divines have advanced, concerning the pure Spiritual frame and disposition of the human Soul, yet, we must come to this conclusion at last, that we receive all our knowledge in the Lump, Refined, dowble refin'd, triple refined, midling and Gross, from the organs of Sense, and these material organs are, Sure and Certain the Sole Inlets, by which we originally receive any Notion or Idea we can possibly conceive, relative to the mixed Scene of things round us, whether they exist in the Natural, or the moral System, as they are termed.

The members of the ancient and honorable Tuesday Club, being mortal men, as much as the members of his majestie's privy council, the members of both houses of parliament, or in fine as much as the members of the most august Assembly or Senate, that ever met or will meet, while the world stands, are furnished with powers and faculties, peculiar to that degree of animals, in the Great Scale of nature, that is they are possessed of understanding and Judgement to a certain degree and also, are endued with Senses, which are alike subjected to the Seducing arts of flattery with the understanding and Senses of other mortal || men, as has appeared in many [127]

Chapter VII

Arrival of the Club medals, Celebration of the 5th Anniversary, Ode and Speech on that occasion, Music by Signior Lardini.

[124]

The Senses are as subject to the arts of flattery, as the understanding and Judgement. Both have their particular ways of being cajoled and amused; The Judgement and understanding, are misled, and put on a wrong Scent, by a Skillful application of high sounding phrazes, smooth lubricating Speeches, and an Indefatigable assiduity in doing Servile offices, these artifices have power Sufficient to pervert the most Solid and Stayed understanding. The Smoke || of this Incence, Intoxicates the mortal Idols on which it is bestowed. They first of all, conceive themselves patterns of perfection, and in Consequence of this capital Error in Judgement, their conduct and actions are brought to that Standard of absurdity, which renders them altogether fit for the purposes of their most humble and most obedient worshipers and hangers on.

The Senses are misled by Show and pomp, the Symbols of magnificence, this Sort of flattery, tho not of the grosser Sort, is yet most commonly set to work, upon the Grosser Subject, the Mobile, or the more Superficial, and less knowing part of mankind, which makes up at Least nineteen twentieths of the whole Species—The first Sort of flattery is effected by the more refined powers of wit and eloquence, and to render one an adept in it, it is requisite he should have some Skill in oratory and Rhetoric, and also something very Complaisant, Submissive and officious in his manners and behaviour; The latter Sort has it's aids Intirely from the mechanic arts. The Jeweler, Sculptor, Taylor, Milliner & painter appear in the first Rank of those artists, who are Instrumental in ornamenting and Embelishing human bodies and bestowing Splendor and Gloss upon their Ceremonies and transactions, to make them seem, as if they contained in themselves, something really great and excellent.

[125]

If we examine how these different modes of flattery, applied to different Subjects, to wit the understanding and the Senses, affect each others provinces, we shall find it thus, those arts that are applied, or rather misapplied to pervert the Judgement and understanding || have little or no effect upon the Senses, hence it is that all the fine Lessons delivered by

the Tuesday Club [Book VII] 89

Club Conundrums

Conundrum 1

    Why is the moon past the full, like a School mistress?

Given up, and the answer given in by Jonathan Grog Esqr.

    ans: Because she is every day $\left.\begin{array}{r}\textit{Lessening}\\ \textit{Lessoning}\end{array}\right\}$ dec: victor.

Gave in his Second.

Conundrum 2

    Why is a highlandman in his plaid, like a Strong new Castle?

The Club Considered and gave up & Jon: Grog Esqr, gave in his answer.

    ans: Because he has no $\left.\begin{array}{r}\textit{Breeches}\\ \textit{Breaches}\end{array}\right\}$ declared victor.

The Secretary gave in his first. [123]

Conundrum 3d

    Why is a pen, and half a pen, like the 4th part of a tester?[8]
    Solo Neverout Esqr, answered, because it is three half $\left.\begin{array}{r}\textit{pens}\\ \textit{pence}\end{array}\right\}$

The Secretary gave in his answer

    ans: Because equal to three half $\left.\begin{array}{r}\textit{pens}\\ \textit{pence}\end{array}\right\}$

and drank a bumper, then gave in his Second.

Conundrum 4th

    Why is a parsons Cassoc, at the hem, like the Town of Berwick?

After Consideration, Mr Jocifer Bluechin, a Gentleman Stranger Invited to the Club this night, according to ancient custom, answered, Because it is upon the *border,* the Secretary gave in his answer

    ans: Because it is upon the *border,* drank a bumper, and the Club broke up in good order.

---

8. *Tester* is a colloquial term for *teston,* the shilling of Henry VII, which diminished in value until it became virtually worthless by Hamilton's day.

tyranical proceedings, and dare you to your face to restrain my tongue, whenever I have a mind to speak, and—

Pres: For the Lord's Sake ha' done, you talk more than comes to your Share—and nothing to the purpose,—I command Silence.

Chanc: You Command a fiddle Stick—what, are we to be under your tyrranical will in every circumstance?—no, we will have liberty of Speech in Club, and you shall know it.

Pres: Pish—pish—pray, if you have a mind to bawl, remove alittle farther from my ear, you tear it to pieces.

Chanc: No Sir, here is my place, and here I'll keep my Station—and will not submit to your damn'd tyrranny (here the Chancellor, bawled very loud, and looked very pale, as some thought, with real anger, tho' others Imagined his anger was purely Clubical)

Mr: Attor: Spypl: Why, Mr President Sir, I think it a very hard case, that any man should pretend to clap a padlock on my mouth in this here Club.

Pres: Hey! Sir, has your mouth been Locked all this time, and now you open it in this rude manner—

After this the noise grew so great, and all talked together in such a tumultuous manner, that the Club Scribes could not take down any more of this Elegant dialogue, and Mr Protomusicus came off with victory by the help of his honor the President, and looked with contempt on the ambassador, || and by the mediation of the Club, the Chancellor and President were so reconciled, as to shake hands and drink to one another, This displeased some of the Longstanding members, who were fomenting the quarrell, but the president and Chancellor regarded them not, it being a rule with great men, when they please to make little men their tools and Instruments, once they have Compassed their ends, to put the same Standard value, upon their pleasure and displeasure, which Standard value, is Just nothing.

The Secretary, after Supper, in a short Speech returned an answer to the Ambassador, presenting the Compliments of the honorable the president and the club, to the worshipful the Triumvirate, which the Ambassador promised faithfully to report to the said Triumvirate, made his bow and sat down.

Then the Secretary was ordered to write a Congratulatory letter, in the name of his honor the president and Club to the triumvirate, which order by the bye, he never Complied with.

The Conundrums being Called for, after Supper, Jonathan Grog Esqr, produced his.

took a live Coal from the fire, and, as the said Neverout, stood with his hand behind him, thrust it into his fist, and burnt him in the hand for his Contumacy, but, as that was not a Sufficient punishment, he requested his honor, in the name of the said Triumvirate, to give orders to his Secretary, to prosecute the said Solo Neverout Esqr, for the said Contumacy and Insult.

His honor the President hesitated a good deal at this report and request, and, while he pondered with himself, what to do in the affair, the Secretary, || according to his usual forwardness and petulancy, expecting to [120] distinguish himself in this process, and pick up some gleanings to serve his purposes, rose up, and began a Speech, in which he proceeded to accuse Mr Neverout, never waiting for the orders of his honor the president, and club, the Secretary, thus rising up, had not spoke a dozen words, before Mr Neverout, with a very loud voice Interrupted him, but, he obstinately continued his harangue, and the other his loud and Clamorous Interruptions, in the Manner of a dialogue as follows.

Secr: Mr President, Sir, I here in the name of the Eas—

Proto: No accusation—no accusation—

Secr: —Eastren Shore Triumvirate—

Proto: No accusation—ho—no—

Secret: Triumvirate Commence pro—

Proto: Hollo—hollo—ho—no accusation—

Secret: Process against Mr Pro—

Proto: No—no—no—I say no—no accusation—

Secret: Protomusicus, for a contempt which—

Prot: No accusation—you ho—no accusation—

Pres: Mr Secretary, forbear, I command both of you to sit down and hold your peace.

Secret: Sir, it is the duty of my office to—

Prot: No accusation—ho—no accusation—

Pres: Prithee be quiet, let us have less of your noise, I order you this minute to be silent.

Chanc: Sir, you go beyond your authority, I humbly conceive that any member of this here Club, may have the liberty of speaking.

Pres: Not what, and when he pleases, without my permission.

Chanc: Pardon me Sir, I'd laugh at any man, would pretend to hinder [121] me.

Pres: I would hinder you Sir, who am your President.

Chanc: Your president; Your fart Sir! I'd dispise such arbitrary and

acquaint you, that the Club meets this night, at the house of Jealous Spyplot Senr Esqr, where, I have the honor and pleasure of serving the Ancient Tuesday Club, as h:S: and, shall esteem it an honor, far above my expression, should you vouchafe to favor me with your presence; I am, most magnanimous Sir John,

Scots Street
april 17th 1750

Your most humble &
obed: Servt:
Jealous Spyplot Junr:

In this extraordinary epistle, the Ingenious writer shows his great Skill in the moderen *degagée*, or careless way of writing, scorning the Rules of pedagogues. He shows little regard to the common acceptation, or what is called the propriety of words, when he affirms that such a thing *has been a point of Squabble,* and three lines after, in the same Sentence tells Sir John, that the said point, *has never yet been discussed.* Some Critics, who do not understand this mode of writing, would say, that our Letter writer, might more properly have used the word *determined;* again, They would blame the Translation of *Libertas & natale Solum,* as deviating much from the original Sense of the words, for, who but a Club wit would ever think of translating it thus; *I do honor to whom I think it is due, and use my Liberty,* but these Criticisms may affect Schoolboys in their versions, but not a Gentleman of a free and unconfined wit and Genius.

[119] At this Sederunt, appeared Smoothum Sly Esqr as ‖ ambassador from the eastren Shore triumvirate, the Substance of whose embassy, was to deliver the Compliments of that Society to the honorable the president and Club, and to acquaint them, that a Club was formed and set on foot, on the other Side the water, modelled Exactly after the plan of the ancient and honorable Tuesday Club, and, that the Triumvirate, having had the Chief hand in forming the said Club, they desired the Correspondence, Countenance and protection of his honor the president, and the Ancient Tuesday Club, under whose Government, they placed themselves. This was soon granted, for neither his honor, nor the Club would refuse a request, which had a tendency to exalt their own honor and dignity.

The ambassador then proceeded to accuse Solo Neverout Esqr, in the name of the said Triumvirate, for a disrespectful answer he had given to Mr Merry Makefun, a worshipful Triumvir, who, enquiring after the welfare of his honor and the Club, The said Neverout, turned first round on his heel, and made no reply, but, the Question being repeated, he answered in a huffing manner, that he knew nothing of either, on which, Mr Makefun,

The Secretary gave in his first.

Conundrum 3

Why is a man on his marriage night, like a riding horse upon a Journey?

The Club gave it up, the Secretary gave his answer.

ans: Because he is *Bride-led* / *Bridled* decl: victor.

The Secretary gave in his Second Conundrum.

Conundrum 4th

Why is an Infamous Character like the fag end of a Christenmass fire?

The Club gave it up, the Secretary gave in his answer.

ans: Because it is full of *Brands,*—declared victor.

I shall beg leave here to observe, lest it should escape the observation of the Reader, that there seems to be an uncommon delicacy and Elegance in most of the Conundrums, composed by Jonathan Grog Esqr, as may be seen in the one Just now mentioned, Concerning *The king's prick,* which is not only a perfect Conundrum, but Contains also a delicate pun, as the word *Prick* may be Interpreted various ways.

At Sederunt 128, april 17th 1750, Jealous Spyplot Junr Esqr, being high Steward, Sir John delivered in at the Table, a letter wrote to him by the h:S: which being read in Club, was ordered to be recorded, as follows.

To The Noble Sir John,
knight, of the Ancient Tuesday Club.

Magnanimous Sir John,

As it has been a long time a point of Squabble, whether the high Steward for the time being, is obliged by ancient Custom, to acquaint your honor, of his serving, when and where, and, as the mighty affair, has never as yet ‖ been discussed, I am determined to act according to our motto

Libertas et natale Solum,[7]

To do honor, to whom I think it is due, and use my liberty, therefore, noble Sir, I, with every compliment, that is due to one of our Illustrious Society,

---

7. "Liberty and native soil."

Then unsaddling his nose, and looking up, he said, "I answer—Because there is always *Punch* in it."

At this answer some in the Club Laughed, others looked Serious, and a few pretended to be astonished, Mr Comas looked more Sullen than usual, and rising up, requested his honor, that he might be allowed to serve the Club once more at next Sederunt as high Steward, the president, who had not as yet, laid aside his timber Countenance, asked Mr Comas, if that was all he had got to say? to which he || answered, that he had nothing else to offer—The president told him Smartly—that he Surely had less brains than tongue, which was next to none at all, to let this Scurvy Joke pass upon him unanswered; this Sharp Rebuke, made Mr Comas's heart Rise to his mouth, and it was said that the tears gushed out at his eyes, this Tragical end, had this unseasonable Joke, and this Sederunt broke up in bad humor.

The next Sederunt was held upon the 10th of April, 1750, Laconic Comas Esqr, being high Steward, and nothing passed at it but the Conundrums; only that some observed, that the H:S: wore a very unsatisfied Countenance, and droped several hints, Intimating that this was his last Service to the Club, and Indeed it proved so, for he left the Society this very night, not being able to swallow, far less to stomach that pestilent and Satyrical Conundrum, published on himself at last Sederunt.

The Conundrums then being Called for, Jonathan Grog Esqr, produced his, as follows.

Club Conundrums

Conundrum 1

Why is the king's prick, in marking down a Sheriff like an Elephant?

Jealous Spyplot Esqr made answer, Because it *Stands,* Jonathan Grog Esqr, drank a bumper to the Clubs prosperity, and gave in his answer.

ans: Because it always *Stands.*

Then he delivered his Second Conundrum.

Conundrum 2d

Why are dried apples, like married people?

The Club, after Consideration gave it up, and Jon: Grog Esqr, gave in his answer.

ans: Because they are *pared* / *paired* was declared victor.

down, picked up a paper, which unfolding, he gravely Informed the club, that he had found a Conundrum, which if they pleased, he would read to them, That they might exercise their wits upon it. There arose Immediatly a murmur in the Club, some Trick of the Secretary's being suspected by his honor and the members, The Chancellor seized the Conundrum out of the hands of Huffman Snap, and saddling his nose with his Spectacles, read from the Scroll, as follows.

Why is L—— C——'s mouth like a puppet Show?

Immediatly on the Reading of this Conundrum, the Countenance of Laconic Comus Esqr fell, and a Cloud overspread his visage, which made him look excessively murky, for even at best, he was of a Lowring aspect, the Secretary, who (however much blamed in this affair) was no further concerned, than that he had composed the Conundrum, and rashly mentioned it, in the hearing of some people, who took the advantage to make their fun of it, by promulgating it, contrary to his advice, fearing a fatal event from Mr Comas's Indignation, alledged, that the Chancellor, from a defect, in his eyesight, or Spectacles, or both, did not clearly see or discern, the Initial letters of the Supposed name in the Conundrum, that if he Examined more nearly, he'd find that the Letters were J:G: and not L:C: this he did, in order, if possible, to roll the Joke from Laconic Comas upon Jonathan Grog Esqr, who was a facetious man of a quite || opposite humor [115] to the former, and could bear a Joke the best of any in the Club, returning always *tit* for *tat,* and silencing those that engaged him in this manner, with a pun or some quaint clench, and this made the Club afraid, to handle such weapons against him, besides, the Secretary knew that this Conundrum in it's Structure and Solution, would fit Mr Grog as well as Mr Comas, there being one particular part of their Characters pointed out in the Solution of this conundrum, which bore an exact resemblance, but this artifice of the Secretarie's would not take, tho' Intended to serve the Club, by preventing the loss of one of its best members, which at last was the fatal effect of this wicked Conundrum; The Club Conjectured, that the Letters L:C: must Intend Laconic Comas, but declined giving any Solution of it, tho there wanted not in the Company who knew both the Conundrum and answer, and who it pointed at, even before it was produced in club. But the Chancellor, taking off his Spectacles, and stroaking down his beard, with a Superlatively grave Countenance, told the Club, that, tho wit was not his province, yet he would adventure the Solution of it, and submit it to their Candid Judgement, and Clapping on his Spectacles again he read

Why is L:C's mouth like a puppet Show?

[113] and drank || a bumper to the prosperity of the Club. Then he delivered his Second Conundrum.

Conundrum 2d

Why is a Clean Smoke, hung on a hedge to dry, like an honest debtor confined in prison?

After profound Consideration, the Club gave it up, and Jonathan Grog Esqr gave his answer.

ans: Because it is *unironed,*—was declared victor.

Then the Secretary gave in his first Conundrum.

Conundrum 3d

Why are the tops of a great many Steeples, like a Laboring man's Arm?

The Club, after deep pondering gave it up, and the Secretary gave in his answer

ans: Because they are full of *vanes* / *veins*

was declared victor, and gave in his Second.

Conundrum 4th

Why is a pew in a Country Church, in Sermon time, like the foundation wall of a house?

Philo Dogmaticus Esqr, answered, because it holds *Sleepers,* the Secretary gave in his answer

ans: Because it supports *Sleepers,* and drank a bumper, to the prosperity of the Club.

After the conundrums were discussed, the Club proceeded to argue matters of State, and the result was, that the order of Sederunt 125th, relating to the State members, and the Commoners voting *Separatim,* was repealed, which somewhat disgusted the Chancellor, and, from that moment [114] || he meditated revenge, against his honor the President.

I am now to relate an adventure, which excited much uneasiness in Club, by first depriving it of one of it's best members, and next, disgusting one of the principal State officers, at this very Sederunt, after Supper, when the Conundrums, business and toasts were all discussed, and, every Longstanding member expected to retire in peace, Huffman Snap Esqr, stooping

Club. Squabble, concerning Sir John's Commission.

[facing page 112]

against the proceedings of Sederunt 123, but his honor desired him to stop, and positively declared, that he would hear no papers read on any such foolish Subject, the Secretary however, persisting, at the Instance of the protesting members to read it, his honor declared that he would leave the Chair, and a mighty dispute arose in club, which ended in noise and Confused talking, all speaking together, and every one endeavoring to outbawl another, among others, Slyboots Pleasant Esqr, a man naturally of a mild temper, was more Irritated with his honor than was usual with him on such occasions, at Last Huffman Snap Esqr, seeing the great danger of a Civil war breaking out in Club, pushed the Chancellor back Into his Chair, who had got up, and, by Incendiary Speeches, was spurring the members on to rebellion, || and snatching the paper, out of the Secretaries hand, Committed it to devouring flames, and thus gave a Seasonable check to this Club tumult, which otherwise probably, might have ended in a battle Royal, which, had victory Inclined to the Stronger party, which the Chancellor headed, would have brought about the decathedration of his honor, from his Chair of State.

After the quelling of this tumult, the Club Continued for some time in a humdrum Situation, the members looked at one another, some with enraged, and others with Sorrowful and downcast countenances, his honor the president, Leaned back in his chair, his legs accross, his hands Clasped together, his mouth puckered up, his visage Elongated, his eyes fixed, and his Chin prominent, the high Steward endevored to put about the bowl, In order, if possible to give a Philip to their Flagging Spirits; But Sir John, with a furious voice, and a thump of his fist on the table, Called for the *Conundrums,* and, Laconic Comas Esqr, Laying down his pipe, swore, *Damn the Conundrums, they spoilt good Company*—but notwithstanding this, the Conundrums were produced.

Club Conundrums

The Master of Ceremonies, presented his first according to Custom.

Conundrum 1

    Why is a good Clergiman like a pair of Clogs?
    Huffman Snap Esqr answered Because he preserves $\left.\begin{array}{l}Souls\\Soals\end{array}\right\}$

Jonathan Grog Esqr gave his answer

    ans: Because he helps to save $\left.\begin{array}{l}Souls\\Soals\end{array}\right\}$

Nasifer Jole Præses

To our Trusty and well beloved Sir John, greeting.

We, of our particular esteem, free will and favor, as also, in Consideration of the many good qualities of which you are possessed, grant unto you our ‖ Trusty and well beloved Sir John, by this our Commission and [110] these our Letters patent, under our hand and the great Seal of our ancient Tuesday Club, The high Title of *Sir John,* Knight of our ancient Tuesday Club, hereby creating and Installing you, a right worthy knight of the Solitary order, giving and granting you, all the privileges, honors, titles and dignities, appertaining to such a high degree and office, and Constituting you, one of the State officers, permitting you, our worthy knight, to take your place, next to ourself, at the Right hand of our Great presidential Chair, there, to be at all times, whether we be present or absent, a loyal, and faithful mantainer of our dignity, Chair and privileges, and a Strenuous Supporter of our Authority and power, as also, a Safeguard and defence, to our Ancient Tuesday Club, against all outrages Insults, affronts, or Injuries whatsoever, in every respect and emergency, as might become a Loyal and faithful knight, nevertheless with this proviso, that we hereby give or grant you, our said knight, no privilege, Claim, pretence, or title whatsoever, to succeed in our Presidential Chair, on our Demise, or otherwise, more than any other officer or private member of our ancient Tuesday Club, every such officer, or private member, having an Equal Right, or Claim thereunto, any thing in this Commission to the Contrary notwithstanding.

[Great Seal]   Witness ourself, at our residence in North
Nasifer Jole   east Street in Annapolis, this 13th day of
      february, 1749/50, In the 5th year of our
      Presidential Government.
Sig: p: order *Loquacious Scribble Secrty*

Sir John having received this Commission, at the hands of his honor [111] the president, made a very Low and Courteous bow to the Chair, and then flung a paper upon the table, which being opened and read, proved to be the Commission granted to him by the Club, at Sederunt 123, while this was a reading, it was observed, that the honorable the president, assumed his Timber Countenance, which was an Infallible Sign, of his being highly displeased. The Secretary, to prevent the Rising Storm, as soon as he had returned, the Surreptitious Commission to Sir John, To secure it from falling into his honor's Clutches, stood up, and offered to read a paper in Club Intituled *a Remonstrance, and protest of Certain Longstanding members*

whole piece, was pyrated from the latest translation of the works of the Celebrated Rabelais.⁶

The Letter from Smoothum Sly Esqr, to Sir John was as follows.

To the most Renowned Sir John,
knight of the Tuesday Club, pr: favr: of Jonathan Grog Esqr.

Sir John,

If the marks of acknowledgement and regard be first due, where one has been most obliged, and the Station most exalted, the honorable president in all propriety Claimed our first notice—next to him, however, we think ourselves bound to pay our Compliments, to the Right Noble knight of the ancient *Tuesday Club,* and (in his own opinion at least) Heir expectant of the Chair.

As the Club is Large in your praise, and as you are even admired by him who is most of all admired, It would be in vain for us to attempt any thing in your Commendation, your particular talents, which qualify you, for shining in the highest Stations, even as Chairman of the privy Council, for promoting the honor, and Influencing the mirth of the august Society, are Subjects of such a weighty nature, that Cicero himself must have sunk under them.

'Tis with concern we understand, that, Instead of the great Seal, you had a melilot plaister affixed to your Commission, which has Induced some Spiteful people to conclude, that you are not a Standing member of the Club—be that as it will, in our humble opinion, your distinguished Station, and high quality, entitle you more properly to the honorable the presidents Letters patent, than a Commission.

Pray remember our dutiful Compliments to the honorable president, with our best Respects to the witty Gentlemen of the ancient Tuesday Club, and be pleased, great Sir, to accept of the most profound Devoirs of the Talbot County Triumvirate from, Most Invincible Sir John,

Talbot County	Your most obed: humb: Servt:
8 March 1749/50	*Smoothum Sly.*

After Reading of these letters, the honorable the President, presented to Sir John, a Commission under the great Seal, the old Commission, with the virescent melilotian Sigillature, being Cancelled and destroyed, the Tenor of which Commission follows.

---

6. This is an obvious parody of bad translations in general; it does not represent any passage in Rabelais that I could discover.

To The Worshipful, Sir John, Knight of the Tuesday Club

O uncommission'd knight, tho' valiant one,
Thrice trebly inclite,[2] brave and bold Sir John,
Knight, once that was, and once again may be
If with Illustrious Jole, you will agree.
    Our Auricles percuss'd by fame Sonorous,
Your mirabundous acts have brought before us,
Your Blusterous actions, inaudite before,
Our Sage records have garnish'd o'er & o'er,
To our thrice Inclite Tuesday Club repair [107]
To night, and exercise your valour there,
For there, dark Schemes in dark recesses stord
Claim the decision of your Conqu'ring Sword,
And when the Cluttering din of Battle's oe'r,
Sit down, and taste our Amalthæan Store,[3]
Then when the turb[4] is once accumulate,
Jocund Jocundity's Immensurate,
With Sumptuous Cates, divine Ambrosia Joins,
And Punch Nectareous rivals all our wines,
Each Sitient, each esurient guest Replete is,
As at the feast of Peleus with his Thetis,[5]
Then all arise, the Table is Sublate,
And mighty Jole, resumes his throne of State,
The king and Club, in flowing brimmers toasted,
Whats next? by damnd *Conundrums* you'll be roasted,
If all this Jargon, and Instructive Jaw
Cannot this night to Club your worship draw,
I Leave you to your Choice, subscribing thus,
Your humble Servant—*Protomusicus*.

Febr: 13th 1749.   *Solo Neverout*

    This was the third trial of Skill in poetry made by Mr Proto-musicus, and would have passed for the boldest Stroke of wit ever struck out by that Ingenious gentleman, had it not been soon discovered, that almost ‖ the [108]

---

  2. *Inclite* is Hamilton's invention, apparently associated with *enclitic* and here meaning "closely bonded to or intensely loyal to the club."
  3. Amalthea was the mythological nurse of Zeus whose horns, according to one legend, broke off and contained the fruits she delivered to Zeus.
  4. The crowd.
  5. The mother and father of Achilles (Sir John is the Achillean defender of the club).

more pompous and Sonorous manner, and in a more Sublime and Significant Stile.

It is thought, that the commission, which the Club granted you at last Sederunt, (of which, his honor the president, has not as yet had the least Intimation) will occasion a most violent uproar and Confusion, and, at last end in anarchy, by his honor's quitting the Chair, if your behaviour is not Calm, cool, and adapted to the Important and Critical occasion, and therefore, would request, In case you come to Club to Morrow night at Neverout's, you would politically, || with great moderation and Silence, wait your time, till his honor presents you, with a Certain magnificent and large Commission, fairly printed, on an Intire Sheet of Superfine paper, Sealed with the great Seal, and subscribed with his honor's own hand, then rising up, with Great Gravity, throw the Club's commission, which you are to bring in your pocket for that purpose, upon the table, and pocketing up the other, make a bow to his honor the President; There is a remonstrance prepared, by those who voted against the proceedings of last Sederunt, which I have Inclosed for your perusal, as you are the principal person mentioned in it; if you approve of it, please to send it back, it is designed to sweeten his honor's blood alittle, which doubtless will be set in a ferment, when he hears the Club's Surreptitious Commission Read, and it will occasion a great deal of Learned and political Argument in Club, and, perhaps, afford Cause for some Gelastic Motions of the Muscles of the face, I am, Sir John,

Febry 12th 1749/50   Your most humble Servant
Loquacious Scribble.

The policy of this Letter is easily seen thro', The Secretarys Intentions here, are plainly to Curry favor with Sir John, and make him his friend, in order the better to promote his Schemes; but this Stroke of policy did not answer his purpose, for Sir John did not give his at- || tendance on the night, when Mr Neverout served the Club as H:S: and, we shall find by the reception that the Remonstrance of the protesting members met with at Sederunt 126, that this project of the Secretary's to Curry favor with the President and Sir John Intirely failed.

At the aforesaid Sederunt, after his honor had taken the Chair, and the proceedings were read, Sir John presented in Club two papers, one of which was a poetical Epistle from Solo Neverout Esqr, the last High Steward, and the other a Letter from Mr Smoothum Sly, one of the Eastren Shore Triumvirate, which being read, were ordered to be recorded, and are, as follow.

abilities, to execute that High office, as the nature of the Romans, and their Genius at that particular time, which, being somewhat brutish, were fit to be ruled by a real brute in the Shape of a man, and, also the Importance and authority of this office, under the Imperial Sway, which a horse was as capable to fill and mantain, as the wisest and most politic man, that ever Lived, it being readily allowed by all hands, that a horse, dog or monkey, will do as well to make a Cypher of, or fill up a blank as a man.

In the same manner, the honorable Mr President Jole, whether in Imitation of that Illustrious pattern, or thro' his own free will and accord, I shall not pretend to determin, when he made Sir John a Commissioned officer, and a State member of the Club, and gave him the Noble title of *Champion,* under hand and Seal, Considered neither the qualifications of Sir John's person, which might fit him for a Club Champion, nor the nature of the office, which he was to exercise, but had chiefly in his view, the fierce and Indomitable nature of the members and the Chancellor, to which he believed Sir John might be a check, by his boisterous & bold Countenance, and, at the same time he thought, as to the execution of the duty of a Champion, he would make a very good Cypher, at the Right hand of the Chair.

At Sederunt 126, Prim Timorous Esqr, being high Steward, several things of very Great moment were transacted in Club, and some disputes and dissentions arose, of which, I purpose to give a true and Genuine account in this Chapter, but shall premise some necessary circumstances, for the better understanding of what follows.

The Secretary, who now set all his Ingines at work to undermine the Chancellor, and also operated against the President, under a feigned Zeal to support his authority and prerogative, began to Chop in[1] with Sir John, and endeavor to make a tool of that Champion, the better to bring about his purpose, for that reason he put himself at the head of the protesting members, against the Clubs Commission, granted to Sir John, at 123, and, on the following Sederunt, he wrote a letter to the said Champion, addressing him in a private Capacity to the following purpose.

[104]

To Sir John, These.

Sir John,

I write to you, as a private friend, not in a public or clubical capacity as Secretary of our ancient Tuesday Club, else I should have addressed you in a

---

1. To fall in with.

But Laconic Comas. Jonathan Grog Esqr Poet Laureat gave his vote in these words.

A Cap of State
For the President's pate.

[102] Then it was ordered that a Grand Committee be Summoned to || Consider of ways and means to prepare and present this Cap of State to his honor the president.

Thus was voted into the Club, an ensign or Badge of dignity which was the occasion of much wrangling and Dissention, and in a little time displayed, a large Scene of Transactions in this ancient and honorable Club, Laying the first foundation for the perplexed and Intricate history of Box No 1, as shall be shown in its proper place.

It was resolved at this Sederunt, that henceforth when the votes were taken in Club, the State members and Commissioned officers shall vote for themselves, and the Longstanding members of the Commoners also, vote by themselves, and that no Law or motion should be carried in Club, but by a majority on both parts, this was a Contrivance of the Chancellor's, to have always a separate negative, to any Laws or orders that might be proposed, contrary to his Schemes, against the Chair, but this Ordonnance did not, (as Indeed it could not) stand long in force.

The Secretary, by order of the Club, prepared a blank Summons for the use of his honor the president, when he should call together upon urgent occasions the Grand Committee or privy Council of State, and delivered to Jonathan Grog Esqr, to be printed.

Thus, by gradual Steps, did this ancient and honorable Club, aggrandize and exalt his honor the President, till they brought him to a height that made him at last giddy, totter and fall from his Seat, as shall appear in due time.

Chapter VI

Poetical Epistle from Mr Protomusicus, fatal Comasian Conundrum, Commotions in Club, remonstrance of the protesting members burnt, several Club Conundrums, Second Embassy of the Triumvirate.

[103] When Caligula Thought of making his horse Consul of Rome, he did || not consider so much the propriety of his person, or his qualifications and

the Tuesday Club [Book VII] 73

Then the Secretary read the Second Conundrum.

Conundrum 2d

>Why is a pump in a well like a fire lock?

On deep Consideration, the Club gave it up, and Jonathan Grog Esqr, delivered his answer.

>ans: Because it depends upon *Springs*.

He was declared victor, & the Secretary Produced his first Conundrum.

Conundrum 3d

>Why is an almanack maker like a butcher?

After minutes rumination, Slyboots Pleasant Esqr, answered Because he deals in *Weathers,* the Club allowed the answer, and the Secretary drinking his bumper delivered the following.

>ans: Because he deals in variety of *weathers* } *Wethers*

The Secretary then gave his other Conundrum.

Conundrum 4th

>Why is a boy of two years old, Like a China Cup?

The Club, after Considering gave it up, the Secretary delivered his answer.

>ans: Because the Ladies *kiss* him in public, without being out of countenance.—was declared victor.

>Jealous Spyplot Senr, and Laconic Comas Esqrs, objected against the Conundrums in General, as unworthy of the Club, which occasioned some debate, and having moved that the Conundrums should be voted out, the Question was put; Continue the Conundrums or not? It Carried by a great Majority in the affirmative.

>The Secretary, after Supper, made a long Speech, in which he moved that a grand Tiara, or Cap of State should be prepared for his honor the president, to be wore by him in the Chair, upon the Anniversary, and other Solemn occasions, after some argument and debate upon the Subject, To which Laconic Comas Esqr, was so very attentive, as that, going to light his pipe, he held the breech of the bowl part to the Candle, and extinguished it, it was put to the vote, a Cap of State for his honor the president, or no Cap of State?

>It Carried by a great majority in the affirmative, none voting against it

Pray, grant your presence to preside,
Renowned Sir, our greatest pride,
Except when you, our head appear, ⎫
Strife and foul discord govern there, ⎬
Intending treason 'gainst the Chair, ⎭
Dispell by your auspicious face
Each Traiterous plot to seize your place,
Nor let the Club your presence want,
The best of favors, you can grant.

Incline Great Sir to make us blest,
On you our peaceful hopes are placd,
Let each disturber of your peace
Ever before you, fall and cease.

I am, may it please your honor, your honor's and the Club's

Shrove Tuesday 1750   Most obliged poet Laureat
                                     Most vigilant Mr of Ceremonies
                                     Most faithful High Steward &
                                     Most humble Servant
                                     Jonathan Grog.

[100] This Ingenious accrostic very much pleased his honor the President, who was not for the most part a great admirer of that Sort of wit, but, it was thought by many, that he would not have esteemed it so much, had it not been wrote on himself.

The Conundrums were called for, this evening before Supper, when Jonathan Grog Esqr, Mr of Cerem: and H:S: produced his, which the Secretary published in Club as follows.

Club Conundrums

Conundrum 1st

Why is a Client, that has lost his cause, to be compared to a Ladie's winter Stocking?

After a minute and a halfs Consideration, Mr John Steward, a Gentleman, Invited as a Stranger to the club, answered, because he is *worsted,* it was allowed, and the Laureat drank his bumper, and delivered his answer thus.

ans: Because he is *worsted.*

the Tuesday Club [Book VII] 71

their pensive posture, which these wit Strechers always put them into, the Secretary accused Laconic Comas Esqr, of a trespass, having Combined with a Certain Grand Jury, to present the honorable the President, Sir John, and Proto musicus, to a certain Court, for certain Illegal practices, but was not Countenanced or seconded in this accusation.

Then the Secretary accused the musician to the President, for exceeding the precincts of his office, in attempting instrumental music, having been caught by the said Secretary playing on a fiddle, whereas ‖ his talent [98] and office is only confined to the voice, but this accusation was treated with derision and a horse Laugh.

This night Jealous Spyplot Senr Esqr, Mr Neverout the High Steward, and Mr Secretary Scribble, underwent the penalty of the Gelastic Law, for certain absurdities uttered by them In Club.

At the motion of the Secretary, Mr Theophilus Smirker, ambassador of the Triumvirate, was Created an honorary member,

as also at the motion of Jealous Spyplot Senr Esqr, Capt: Dio Ramble, entertained as a Stranger by the Club, was created an honorary member,

as also, at the motion of Captn Dio Ramble, Captn Prettyman Spyplot, Son of Jealous Spyplot Senr Esqr, was Created an honorary member, having been Entertained by the Club as a Stranger, pursuant to ancient Custom.

Then Jonathan Grog Esqr, master of Ceremonies presented these three Gentlemen, to his honor the President, who Saluted them by manuquassation, and they took their places as honorary members accordingly.

At next Sederunt, which was the 125th, on the 27th of February 1749/50, Jonathan Grog Esqr, being high Steward, the Secretary presented in Club, a letter from Mr Smoothum Sly, in the name of the Eastren Shore Triumvirate, which was read, but not ordered to be recorded or answered.

Then the honorable the President, delivered to the ‖ Secretary a paper, [99] sent to him, by Jonathan Grog Esqr: H:S: which was read, and ordered to be recorded, the tenor of which follows.

To The Truely Honorable, Nasifer Jole Esqr,
President of the Tuesday Club.—an accrostic
To Mr President Jole

This comes dread Sir, in humble manner
Only to advertise your honor,

My Time to serve the Tuesday Club
Returns this night, delightful Job.

themselves unto, when they acted obstinatly and perversly against his Sober Serious and wholsome advice.

After Supper, the king and the Club Toasted, the Conundrums were Called for, and Jonathan Grog Esqr, produced his first Conundrum, vizt:

Club Conundrums

Conundrum 1

> Why is a wanton Lass in bed, like a book Just printed?

After deep Consideration, the Club gave it up, and Jon: Grog Esqr, gave in the following answer.

> ans: Because she is in *Sheets* & wants *Stitching*.

He was declared victor and gave in his Second Conundrum.

Conundrum 2d

> Why is a dancing master Like a Shady tree?

This also being given up, the following answer was delivered.

> ans: Because he is full of *Bows*
> *Boughs*

He being declared victor, the Secretary gave in his first Conundm:

Conundrum 3d

> Why is a wizzard like an Æthiopian?

The Club gave up, and the Secretary gave the following ans:

> ans: Because he is a *Necromancer*
> *Negroe-man-Sir*

Being declared victor, he gave in his Second Conundrum.

Conundrum 4th

> Why is a porter's bum, like a Ladie's page?

To this Jonathan Grog Esqr, answered, because it keeps *behind,* which the Club allowed to be a good answer, the Secretary drank a bumper, and gave in his answer.

> ans: Because they both keep *behind* their owners.

After discussing the Conundrums, and the Club had recovered from

After passing and engrossing of this Law, The Secretary moved the passing of another Law, to place the Sole power of Granting commissions in his honor the president, which, after thrice reading and amendment, passed as follows.

Law XLV. Whereas sundry disputes of a dangerous tendency to the [95] dignity of the Chair, and the presidential Government of this here ancient and honorable Club, have arisen and been fomented, among the Longstanding members, of the said Club, Concerning a power Inherent in the Club to grant Commissions, for remedy whereof, it is prayed that it may be enacted,

And be it enacted, by his honor the President, the State officers and Longstanding members of the Commoners, of this here ancient Club, and by the authority of the same, That from henceforward, the whole and Sole power of granting Commissions, be lodged in his honor the president, and his Successors in the Chair, of this here ancient Club for ever, and, that no member or members, of this here ancient Club, whether State officer, officer of the Commoners, or other Longstanding member of the said Club, either Singly, or Conjointly, shall presume to frame, publish, Issue, bestow, or Grant, any Commission, or Commissions whatsoever, upon any pretext or pretence whatsoever, to any member or members of the said Club, under pain of Incurring his honor's highest displeasure.

Provided always, and it is the true Intent and meaning of this Law, that no new office shall for the future be appointed, unless with the vote and approbation of the Club, any thing in this act to the Contrary notwithstanding.

Thus by moving of these two prerogative Laws, and getting them passed in Club, did the Secretary strengthen the hands of the President merely to spite the Chancellor, but that State officer, regarded this last prerog- || ative Law so little, that he took the first opportunity to break it, [96] for he minded Club Laws, no more than a Great beetle does a Cobweb.

May we not observe here, what great State the Club now take upon them, in adopting the parliamentary Stile, and copying after the procedings of the august Senate of Great Britain; But this, they thought they had a right to do, as being a Club composed of British Subjects, they likewise Considerably added to their State by entertaining Ambassadors, and receiving Embassies from the Eastren Shore triumvirate, and from distant Clubs, as shall be seen, may not this Club then, now be properly called a State Club?

All this, Jealous Spyplot Senr: Esqr, beheld with open, and Indeed with dry eyes, for, why should he lament, for what this Club had brought

[93] Solemn and discerning persons being regular longstanding members of the said Club as his || honor shall think fit to consult and advise with, in any Circumstances of difficulty that may occur, which may require the Immediate deliberation, mature Consideration and expeditious Cogitation, of the said Sage, grave, Solemn and discerning persons, it is prayed that it may be enacted,

I   And be it enacted, by his honor the president, The State officers, and Longstanding members of the Commoners of this here Club Convened, and by the authority of the same, that from henceforth, it shall, and may be lawful, for his honor the president, at any such time as aforesaid, and as often, as he shall think meet and Convenient, at such times, to call together, and Convene at his own house, either by message, or Letter, under his own hand, such, and as many of the members, not exceeding Seven, as to his honor shall seem fit and Convenient, in order to take into their most Grave and mature Consideration, animadversion and Speculation all such momentuous Schemes, devices & proposals, as his honor shall Communicate to them, and give such advice and Council thereon, as may Conduce most to the honor and dignity of the Chair, The Stability and Security of the said ancient Club, and the union and harmony of the Longstanding members.

II   And be it further enacted by the authority aforesd: That the members, so as aforesaid formally met and convened, shall be, and are hereby [94] constituted, appointed, || stiled and denominated his honors most honorable privy Council.

Provided always, and it is the true intent and meaning of this Law, that nothing herein contained shall give his honor the president any power, to constitute and appoint any number of the said members, a Standing fixed and established privy council, as such appointment, might occasion Jealousies, Bickerings, feuds, Janglings, discontents and wranglings, among the other longstanding members of this here ancient Club, but, that the members, so as aforesaid Convened, shall be only a privy Council *pro Ista vice*,[3] and that, as soon as the said meeting is over, they shall return to their former rank and Character, and be absolutely, and to all Intents and purposes *in Statu quo prius*.

Provided also, that any thing that shall be determined by this privy Council or Committee shall, in no ways be binding or restrictory, without the Sanction and approbation of the club next ensuing, any thing in this act, to the contrary notwithstanding.

---

3. "For that time only."

Tunbell: Bowz: The Gelastic Law, the Gelastic Law; ha, ha.

Omn: Haw, Haw, Haw, Haw, hoh, hoh, hoi.

Mr Pres: Sir, I ask you peremtorily, why you laid me under such an Inconvenience, by this piece of misconduct or neglect, had you served Sir, upon the 30th of January, Mr Snap would have served this night, and, I should have been eased of a long Walk, he lying very nigh and convenient to me—answer me that Sir, if you please.

Mr Mus: Hum,—why really and truely Sir, that Circumstance I was unacquainted with, else perhaps, I might for your honor's ease have strained a point upon conscience, but, it was really, as I told you before, a pure point of Conscience, pure Conscience Indeed, Please your honor, I stick to my plea Sir, I must, and will plead conscience.

Chanc: This gentleman talks pritty pertly of conscience and || a fast day. [92] I observed tho, that he eat and laughed as much as any there.

Music: Sir as to my conscience, thank god it is in no person's keeping but my own, and therefore will not grow Rusty, and as to my mirth and eating, I at all times observe the old proverb, *Cum fueris Roma,* you are a Scholar Sir, Interpret me that.

Pres: What does he say, what Gibberish is that, is it Law french?

Music: Please your honor, the English of that is, as I am told do as you see others do, and be good company.

Mr Secret: Will you please to put this case to a vote Gentlemen, whether this Culprit be guilty or not.

Upon taking the vote, he was acquitted by a majority of one.

Music: Gentlemen, it is my opinion that this here Club is a very worthy Just and honorable Club.

This Club trial is pritty much in the Stile and manner of many of the State trials, published in Six or seven volumes in folio, The Reading of which ponderous book, like this Club history, Is, in General, as little amusing as Instructive.

The Secretary, when this trial was ended, having designs and projects in his head, to frustrate the operations of the Chancellor, stood up, and made a motion, for the passing of a Law, to Impower his honor the president, to nominate and appoint a privy Council, upon Important occasions, which, after thrice Reading and amendment, was passed as follows.

Law XLIV. Whereas, our present System of laws, is most woefully deficient, in that there is no Law yet, provided by the Club, To give his honor the president a power, upon occasions of Emergency, to convene, at his own house, between the Intervals of Sederunts, or, when his honor is dolefully afflicted, with Lamentable fits of the Gout, such Sage, grave,

[90] time in Club, as often happens, in grand || Solemn and Sage assemblies, after ceremonies of the like Importance and Significancy. His honor the President, after rolling round his eyes for some time on the members, placed on each Side of him, with great gravity and Composure of Countenance, presented to the high Steward, his new Commission, as Chief musician or protomusicus, and the Chancellor applied the Great Seal to it, after the old Commission, with the virescent melilotian Sigillature was cancelled and destroyed.

Then came on the Tryal of the high Steward for his not serving the Club according to appointment, upon the 30th of January last, which was Carried on, neither by Indictment, bill, plaint or Information, but by way of Interogatory, as follows.

The Chief musician being ordered to stand, at the Lower End of the table, and being there placed.

Mr Præs: Pray Sir, answer me plainly, wherefore did not you serve the Club, upon that day, on which you was appointed to serve as high Steward?

Protom: Why really Sir, if I must declare to your honor the plain truth, It was matter of Conscience, mere matter of Conscience, that day on which I was appointed to serve this here Club, being a fast day ordained by the Church,—The 30th of January, Mr President Sir, is a fast day.

Pres: But good Sir, allow me to Inform you that your time for serving this Club, was not in the day but the evening of the day.

[91] Prot: Mus: Honorable Sir, the Evening and the morning || make the day with me (here Mr Neverout Quoted Scripture)

Pres: But Sir, how a matter of Conscience, what do you mean by a matter of conscience?

Mr Mus: Sir I hope I am not here before a Court of Inquisition.

Chanc: Yea Sir; but you are before a court of Inquiry.

Huff: Snap: It is my humble opinion Sir, that this here Club has nothing to do with conscience.

Chanc: Right, conscience is only my province as Conscience keeper.

Jon: Grog: If this here Club has nothing to do with Conscience, it must of Consequence be an unconscientious Club.

Omn: Ha, Ha, Ha, He, Hi.

Mr Attorn: Spypl: Mr President Sir, I think the Gentleman's excuse is a very reasonable one, for which, Sir, my reasons—(here he was Interrupted)

Huff: Snap: I have observed Sir, that this is the first time that this gentleman has set up for conscience.

Mr Attorn: Sp: Sir,—I Intended to urge a few reasons which—

ing all his fair pretences, in fine, his honor hated the Chancellor, and feared the Secretary.

At Sederunt 124th february 13th, Solo Neverout Esqr being high Steward, Mr Tunbelly Bowzer, admitted a Longstanding member at last Sederunt, was confirmed and Invested with the Club badge, and Solemnly presented to the honorable Mr President Jole, by Jonathan Grog Esqr, master of the Ceremonies, who graciously Saluted him by manuquassation,[1] and he took his Seat accordingly in the Club, as a Confirmed Longstanding member, after having thanked his honor and the Club, in a short Speech.

At this Sederunt, there appeared in Club, Mr Theophilus Smirker, a member of the Eastren Shore triumvirate,[2] sent as Ambassador, from that worshipful Society, to the ancient and honorable Tuesday Club.

This ambassador, rising up, with great Gravity and Solemnity, and making a decent bow, first to his honor the President, and then to the members, according to their dignity and rank, delivered himself to the Chair, as follows.

"Mr President Sir,

I am commissioned by Messrs Lardini Makefun and Sly, Triumvirs of our worshipful eastren Shore Triumvirate, to pay the respects and compliments of the said worshipful Triumvirate, to your honor, and the Longstanding members of this here ancient and honorable Club, which in their name, and by their authority, as their Ambassador and representative, I here execute, in token of which, I make you this Reverend bow, desiring your honor's protection and Countenance, without which they cannot subsist."

To which Speech, the Secretary, standing up in his place made reply.

"Mr Ambassador,

His honor the president, and the Longstanding members of this here Club, are very proud to receive the Compliments of the worshipful the triumvirate, from the mouth of you, their plenipo and Representative, and I, in his honor's name, and in the name of the Club, desire you to deliver, to your worshipful Triumvirate, the compliments of his honor the President and this here Club, and acquaint them that they may rest assured of his honor's gracious favor and protection."

The Secretary then made a low bow to the ambassador and both sat down.

After this Solemn Ceremony, there was a profound Silence for some

---

1. *Manuquassation* is Hamilton's invention for *handshake* (a quassation is a shaking).
2. A Tuesday Club splinter group, founded by the Reverend John Gordon, the Reverend Thomas Bacon, and Robert Morris (see biographical sketches). Hamilton provides an account of its foundation in I, 451–453.

[87] tended, vizt: the good of the common wealth or State. Human Societys, great and small, when rightly considered, are pritty much the same, ‖ being every where fabricated, or made up of members of the same Species, vizt: the human, so, that upon an Impartial Scrutiny, we shall find a great Similitude between Commonwealths and Clubs, therefore, if there be politicians and Statesmen in the first, there must also be a proportionable number of the said Sage and discerning persons in the Latter, an Instance of the verity of this reasoning, is exhibited in the ancient and honorable Tuesday Club, where two expert politicians or Statesmen, vizt: the Chancellor and Secretary, set themselves to Counteract each other's Schemes, and all under a pretence of operating for the General Good, tho' nothing less was Intended by either, their Chief aim (as appears thro' every Step of their following conduct) being each to aggrandize and distinguish himself, the latter of these politicians, began now to look upon the first, with a Jealous and Invidious eye, and, tho' he had been the principal Cause of the Creation of that Great officer, by presenting the Club with a Seal, in expectation of having the office Conferred on himself, in return for his Generosity, yet his dissappointment in this affair, made him become the Chancellor's Secret enimy, and looking upon him as a bar to his promotion in Club, he begun to lay Schemes to render this State officer's projects for establishing the Liberty of the Club Ineffectual, this, he was artful enough to do, not by an open opposition, for while he pretended to be a friend to liberty, and to approve of the Chancellor's Schemes, he Slyly threw Stumbling blocks in his way, by assuming a pretended moderation, which he said was to qualify and mitigate the Chancellor's Impetuosity and violence, this he did by affecting to pay some regard to the lawful power and prerogative of the Chair, which he professed, he could not see invaded, even under pretence of

[88] preserving the Liberties of the club, tho' the latter he owned ‖ was very dear to him, actuated by these motives, when the Chancellor made a party in the club to grant Sir John a commission, to spite the president, as has been related, the Secretary formed another party, which protested against that proceeding, not that he had any real value for the prerogative of the Chair, or was an Enimy to that Commission, but merely to frustrate the Chancellors ambitious projects, whereby he proposed to Ingross all power and Influence to himself, but these two politicians operated in vain and advanced no nearer their ends, notwithstanding all their cunning, for his honor the president looked upon the chancellor now, as an open enimy, and always stood prepared to defend himself against his attacks, and the Secretary he was excessively Jealous of, as thinking him to be made up Intirely of cunning and dissimulation, and worse than an open enimy, notwithstand-

ans: Because too often comes from thence
An empty *Sound* devoid of Sense.

These Conundrums having thrown the Club into a grave humor, by reason of the Intense Study the members exercised to solve them, in order to raise again the flagging Spirits of the Longstanding members, it was proposed that toasts should be drank with epithets, which Epithets should Rhime to the name of the Lady Toasted—This is an exercise of wit, at times much used in polite Companies, for Example, suppose one should drink miss Smart, has gained my heart, or miss Price is cosy and nice, or miss Roe, swift as a doe, and the like, after several toasts of this Sort, miss Hunt was proposed as a toast in Club, at which Laconic Comus Esqr The deputy President said bluntly, in his dry manner, *who?* || *Miss Hunt? it will be no difficult matter to find a rhime to fit her name*—and was Just going to say more, when an universal Laugh broke out among the members, which was so violent and loud, that the like had never yet been heard in Club, even when the Gelastic law was put in execution with the utmost violence and Rigor, or, when Mr Protomusicus exerted his best at a horse Laugh, in short, it was astonishing to hear how they laughed, till the tears gushed out at their Eyes, and they lost their breath, and the poet Laureat, who loved with all his Soul, a Joke of this Sort, laughed till his wig tumbled off of his head, and his bare poll would have equally become a Laurel or an Ivy wreath, had any one Claped it on at that time, but Laconic Comas Esqr, looked very much amazed and said once or twice, *Well! damn it!—what then?—what then?*—Thus merrily ended the Sederunt 123, which was the first Sederunt of the *Conundrums,* and might properly be called the gelastic Sederunt.

[86]

Chapter V

First Embassy of the Eastren Shore Triumvirate, Tryal of Mr Protomusicus, prerogative Laws passed, Club Conundrums, accrostic of the poet Laureat, motion for a Cap of State.

It is a rule with Statesmen and politicians, when they operate each for their own particular advantage and Interest, and they seldom operate on any other motive, to counteract one another, and proceed by methods diametrically opposite, tho' the accomplishment of the same end is pre-

Then he delivered his Second conundrum to this purpose.

Conundrum 2d

> How shall I to myself compare
> The watch which in my fob I wear.

The Club after deep consideration could not answer this Conundrum, and Jonathan Grog Esqr, being declared victor gave in his answer to the following purpose.

> ans: 2d: Because that each of us Contains,
> A great deal more of *Guts* than Brains.

There arose a learned dispute in Club, whether this last was a proper Conundrum or not, as there seemed to be no Clench, or playing upon a word contained in it, at last it was agreed that it was proper.
 Then the Secretary being called upon to produce his Conundrums, he gave in his first to this effect.

Conundrum 3d

> Wits of the Tuesday Club, most critical,
> How does the ancient Law Levitical
> (If any likeness you can see)
> With Jonathan Grog Esqr, agree.

[85]

After deep Consideration, Slyboots Pleasant Esqr made answer, Because they both dealt in *Types,* the Club pronounced it a good answer, and the Secretary, drinking a Bumper to the proseperity of the Club, delivered his own answer to the following purpose.

> ans: The answer's easy, when 'tis found
> They both of them in *Types* abound.

Then he delivered his Second Conundrum to this effect.

Conundrum 4th

> Tell me ye Sages of the Club,
> Why is a pulpit like a Tub.

Jonathan Grog Esqr, made answer to this, because from thence came *Sound,* which was allowed by the club to be a good answer, then, the Secretary drinking another Bumper to the prosperity of the Club, delivered his answer to this purpose.

Club Conundrums Introduced.

[83] to such a noble office and Station, and recommending it to you to support and mantain ‖ the dignity and honor of our ancient and honorable Club, in all times of danger and difficulty, in all attacks and assaults and Incursions of an enimy as might become a Doughty and valorous knight, in token of which, we have caused our Great Seal to be hereunto affixed in full Club, and subscribed our names to these presents, this 30th of January 1749/50.

[Great Seal]   Subscr: pr: order
                                     Loquacious Scribble Secrtry

                   Philo Dogmaticus Cancellarius
Jonathan Grog Mr Cer: Slyboots Pleasant
Solo Neverout P:M: Huffman Snap H:S:
Jealous Spyplot Senr: Prim Timorous
Laconic Comus D:P: Tunbelly Bowser
Jealous Spyplot Junr   Loquacious Scribble Sec:

This Commission was the occasion of much disturbance in the Club, having given great offence, to his honor the president, and was the first Step made by the Chancellor to excite that great Clubical rebellion, which sometime after, threw every thing into Confusion and uproar, and ended at last, in the Lamentable Decathedration of his honor the President.

Supper being ended, and the king and Club Toasted, The Conundrums were Called for according to the order of last Sederunt, when Jonathan Grog Esqr, master of the Ceremonies, with great Gravity, produced in Club his first Conundrum, wrote out upon a Scroll of paper, which was to the following Purpose.

[84] *Club Conundrums*

Conundrum 1st

> To drowsy man, pray how can you Compare
> A garment that is worn till quite thread bare.

After deep Consideration, and handing round the billet among the members, Huffman Snap Esqr gave in answer, Because they both wanted a *nap*, the Club declared it was a good answer, and Jonathan Grog Esqr, drinking a Bumper, to the prosperity of the Club, delivered in another Scroll of paper, wrote upon to this effect.

> ans: 1st: The answer's easie, for we all must grant,
> That Both, and each of them a *nap* does want.

the Tuesday Club   [Book VII] 59

rash proceeding, and, to show, that he durst use the Great Seal, the badge of his office, without consulting his honor the President about the matter, this, he avowedly owned he did, to pull down alittle the presidential pride, and throw light upon his hardened, or darkened conscience, of which Conscience, he Justly reckoned himself the master or keeper.

Against This resolution of the Club however, Laconic Comus Esqr deputy President, Jonathan Grog Esqr, Master of Ceremonies, Slyboots pleasant Esqr L:St:M: and Loquacious Scribble Esqr Secretary, requested to enter their protests, but were overruled and not suffered to do it.

Then the aforsaid members desired that the yeas and nays might be entered, but herein also they were over ruled.

Then the Secretary was ordered Immediatly to draw up a Commission for Sir John, which having done, the great Seal was affixed, all the members present subscribed their names, and the Commission was Solemnly presented to Sir John by the Secretary, in the name of all the members, for which Sir John made a Champion like Compliment & bow, the form of this Commission follows.

THE CLUB'S COMMISSION TO SIR JOHN.   [82]

By the order and Authority of the members of the ancient and honorable Tuesday Club, in full Club Convened, upon the 30th of January, 1749/50.

To our Trusty and well beloved Sir John, The members of the aforesaid ancient and Honorable Tuesday Club send Greeting.

Whereas we place an especial trust and Confidence in you, our trusty and well beloved Sir John, as also upon account of the many good qualities and uncommon talents of which you are possessed, and knowing that our ancient and honorable Tuesday Club cannot any longer be without a Champion to defend them from all perils and dangers, which from time to time Impend over their heads, we therefore, being Sensible of your Achillean Courage and Intrepidity, for our own Safety and defence, and for the Support and protection of our ancient and honorable Tuesday Club, hereby give and grant unto you, the said Sir John, the most noble Title of *Sir John,* knight and Champion of our ancient and honorable Tuesday Club, Creating and Constituting you, a most noble *knight of the Solitary order,* ordaining you to take the Right hand of the Great Presidential Chair, and to be the first great State officer, of our ancient and honorable Tuesday Club, Conferring upon you all the titles honors and dignities appartaining

[80] It was high time for Mr Protomusicus to send such a petition and remonstrance as the above to the Club, for he had now absented himself, ever since the 27th of June last, at Sederunt 108,[a] when he served as high Steward himself, which was an absence of no less than 14 Sederunts, and it is a difficult point to determin whether the Clemency of the Club in forgiving him this trespass or his own Impudence in desiring and petitioning for it, be most || to be admired at, but, it was a principal Ingredient in this Gentlemans Character, never to be disappointed for want of proper assurance, and he made it a constant rule, never to suffer himself to be put out of Countenance at any checks or reproofs he might meet with.

After reading of this Remonstrance, and the Club had Complied with what was therein Requested, Sir John, knight and Champion of the Club, stood up, and made a complaint, That the Understrappers, or Subaltern officers of this here Club, had already received their Commissions from his honor the president, at a Certain Sham Committee, which he hoped the Club would examine into, and, that he, the Chief State officer of the Club, and the next person in dignity to the Chair, the defender and Champion of the liberties and privileges of the Club, the Check and Controuler of arbitrary and despotic power, had been slighted, neglected, and used in an affrontive and Contemptuous manner, having had no Commission as yet, granted or offered to him, by his honor the President, the first, which he had received, with the virescent melilotian Sigillature, having been in an arbitrary and unwarrantable manner cancelled, and rendered of no effect, he therefore requested the Club, if they had any regard for his character and dignity as chief State officer, or any care for their own Safety and liberties, as he was their Champion, to give him Immediatly a Commission, and power to act as knight and Champion of the Club, otherwise, his Sword helmet and Coat of mail, might, for ought he Cared lye bye and rust, and this here ancient club be exposed to Continual assaults and Insults, without his trowbling himself about defending or protecting it.

[81] The Club finding the Justice of these complaints and foreseeing the danger of these terrible threats, entered Seriously upon Consideration of the matter, and, after some warm debates, it was resolved, that a Commission should be drawn up for Sir John under the great Seal, and subscribed by all the members, this was a piece of machinery of the Chancellor's, who finding the terror the Club was in, at the boisterous threats and Stern looks of the Champion, took this opportunity to bring them to consent to this

---

(a) This is numbered Sederunt 107, in the first volume of the History, a mistake copied from the original Record.

pology, the harmony of the heart and affections, is always more engageing and amiable, than that produced by bare Insignificant, or Inarticulate Sounds, whether they arise, from the Inimitable modulations of the *Vox humana,* the flatus of pipes and whistles, the martial Clangor of trumpets, the noble blast of organs, the vibrations of wire, the Scraping on Catgut or the damn'd buzzing of a bagpipe, and tho' some few discords now and then arise, from the Clashing of prerogative and privilege, between the honorable the president and the worthy members, yet, as the Discords, in musical Compositions, when well ranged and Judiciously Introduced, serve to decorate and set off the Harmony, so, these little broils and bickerings serve as a foil to the General Harmony that prevails in your ancient Club's proceedings, and add to them in Inexpressible beauty and elegance.

It is hoped that the honorable the president and the worthy members of your ancient Tuesday Club, will Indulge their humble Supplicant, so far as to wink at, overlook, slur over and forgive his long absence, as he declares it proceeds from no Slight or Contempt, but Solely from the cause above recited.

And, presuming, that it will not appear Impudent and barefaced in the aforesaid Protomusicus, it is furthermore || humbly requested by your Supplicant that you would please to excuse his serving your ancient Club, upon Tuesday next, being the 30th of this Instant January, the day upon which your ancient Club has appointed him to serve, he being then necessarily obliged, to attend upon some Pressing Business of his own, and your Supplicant hereby engages, god willing, to serve your ancient and honorable Club, upon Tuesday the 13th of February next Ensuing, barring Sickness, unforseen accidents, and necessary avocations, whether negotiatory or Eroto-logical,[2] in token of which, your Supplicant, delivers these presents, signed with his own hand this 26th of January, *anno Dom:* 1749/50,

Sig: *Solo Neverout Protomusicus.*

To Loquacious Scribble Esqr, Secretary and Register of the ancient and honorable Tuesday Club, praying that this may be presented and read, to the honorable members in full Club Convened, upon Tuesday the 30th of this Instant January, and also, faithfully Entered and Registered, in your ancient and Learned book of Records, *in perpetuam rei memoriam,*[3]

Sig: *Solo Neverout Protomusicus.*

---

2. Pertaining to the science of love (i.e., whoring).
3. "In perpetual memory of the thing."

To the most honorable The President, the most noble Sir John, knight, the honorable the Chancellor, the worshipful the master of the Ceremonies, the wise directors of the Conundrums, and all the worthy officers and longstanding members of the ancient and honorable Tuesday Club. The petition and Remonstrance of Solo Neverout Esqr Protomusicus, and Chief musician, of the said ancient and honorable Tuesday Club—

Humbly showeth,

[77] That whereas your Supplicant has been for several ‖ months necessarily called away, upon pressing business, which could by no means be delayd or postponed, unless to his great dammage, whereby, he has not only been hindered from duely attending upon your ancient and honorable Club (whereof he has the honor to be a longstanding member, and hopes still so to continue) but, has also, to his great grief and disappointment, been necessarily obliged to absent himself on those nights, upon which he was appointed by your ancient and honorable Club, to serve as high Steward— This is therefore humbly to apologize for his Conduct, which, tho' it might have appeared to some neglectful, and disrespectful, yet flowed from no other cause but necessary business and avocations, and it is hoped, that the honorable president and worthy members, will look upon it in that light, and believe that he is still a member of, and well wisher to your ancient and honorable Club, and that nothing can ever abate his affection to it, or make him prove remiss in his duty to the honorable the president, whose liege Subject he professes himself to be, or in his regard for the worthy members, whose fellowship and conversation he will always esteem as an advantage and honor.

And tho' thro' the absence of the aforesaid Protomusicus or Chief musician, your ancient Club may for some time be deprived of the Solace of vocal music (granting that the honorable the President, with his most exquisite pipe, could not supply his place amply, in that respect as my friend [78] said) yet, there subsists such an exact harmony ‖ 'mongst the worthy members, in every Step of their Conduct, that, as the most exquisite vocal Harmony can never excell it, so, that must Sufficiently(a) —— fill up the Gap; for according to Ethical Sages, and the wisest doctors in Philanthro-

---

(a) Here Solo Neverout Esqr, chief musician, whom every one thought to be at 30 miles distance, came into the Room with great Jack boots on his legs, which caused a general perturbation.

Conge-de lire,[1] directed to Laconic Comas Esqr, dep: Pres: in the same form and words as that of Seder: 99 directed to Jonathan Grog Esqr.

The Deputy presidents commission at this Sederunt was Sealed with black wax, on account of it's being the martyrdom day, of that pious Martyr Charles I of Blessed memory.

Mr Bowzer after admission was presented by the master of Ceremonies to the honorable the deputy, by whom he was Saluted, and afterwards by all the Longstanding members, the Ceremony of his confirmation, being postponed, till the honorable Mr President Jole, should appear in the Club.

Then a letter from the high Steward to Sir John, was produced and Read in Club as follows.

To The Honorable Sir John,
knight of The ancient and honorable Tuesday Club.

Great and Tremenduous Sir John,

As you are sometimes the Great Luminary of our ancient and honorable Tuesday Club (that is, when the honorable the President is not among us, for, in his presence, you must, notwithstanding the high and exalted opinion you have of yourself, be conscious that you appear only, as would the full moon in the Splendor and light of the Sun) I must beg the honor of viewing this evening at my house the fullness and rotundity of your face, where it will appear to the best advantage, without any danger of being obscured by the Superior brightness of our honorable president, whom the envious Gout still holds in chains, and || whose absence is best repaired in point of lustre by your presence, come therefore, Sir John, and shine this night without a rival, and thereby gratify your own boundless ambition, and add to the many obligations already conferr'd upon, Great & magnanimous Sr John,

> Your Honors Most obedt:
> Humb: Servt:
> *Huffman Snap H:S:*

The Secretary, after reading this Sublime Letter, produced in Club a petition and Remonstrance from Solo Neverout Esqr Chief musician, who, having been often accused of non attendance and neglect of serving the Club at these times when he was appointed to serve, in consequence of these repeated accusations and his paying no regard to them, was threatned to be expelld the Club, he thought fit, to prevent this Disgrace, to address the Club in the following manner.

---

1. "Permission to elect."

upon himself, and ten to one but he finds a like or a worse picture there. The Carracatura then Corresponding with his own features, or perhaps not so ridiculous or distorted, will probably, as soon as he perceives it, strike him so as to make him forbear, or at least behave with more Charity and moderation.

We have observed thro' the course of this History when we had occasion to touch upon the Character and actions of the Honorable the President, that his Chief foible was Love of power, and therefore, he used all the methods possible to make himself absolute in the Club, this was the Cause of frequent Brawls between him and the Longstanding members, who were very unwilling to submit to an unreasonable yoke. The late Created Chancellor Philo Dogmaticus, soon discovered this unhappy foible in his honor the President, and took an opportunity to Ingratiate himself with the members, by setting up as an advocate for, and a mantainer of their Liberties and privileges, and being an open free spoken man, and withal positive, and somewhat Rough in his behaviour, he failed not at all times to reprimand his honor the President to his face and || use hard speeches to him, calling him a Tyrant, and an oppressor, as will be seen on many occasions in the Sequel, This State Officer it was, that first spoke boldly and openly to the Chair, and shook the foundations of that Despotic power, which had by degrees so firmly established itself, in this here ancient and honorable Club, but notwithstanding the Chancellors Specious pretences for Clubical liberty, and his professed detestation of Tyranny and arbitrary power, he was himself of such an austere Cast and disposition, that of all men he was the most unfit to be trusted with any degree of power or authority over others; which appeared by his boistrous and Tumultuous behaviour, which many times broke out with ungovernable violence, and, had he ever obtained the Chair, he would Surely have Turned out, a more arbitrary Tyrant than his honor the president, but being partial to himself, like most men, he never perceived that he possessed this foible to a greater degree, than his honor the President, for, to say the truth, when he reprehended his honor on this account, it was neither more nor less, than the pot calling the kettle black-arse according to the old proverb.

At Sederunt 123 January 30th, Huffman Snap Esqr, being high Steward, and Laconic Comas Esqr, Deputy President by Commission, Jealous Spyplot Senr Esqr, acquainted the Club, that Mr Tunbelly Bowzer, was desirous of being admitted a member Thereof, and the Ballots being put round he was unanimously elected, after Reading the Commission of

ordered also, that the Conundrums for each night, with the answers, be recorded under the Title of *Club Conundrums*.

This ancient Club, having now for some time droped the Custom of Set Speech making, and letter writing also, becoming less frequent than usual, on account of his honor the President's not suffering them to see the light, now found, that they wanted || some proper subject to exercise their wit upon, and to Embelish their Records, which for want of such decorations appeared quite naked, and therefore they Resolved to Indulge and encourage a poetical vein, among their members, (as we have seen in the above Epicædion) and also to lay a foundation for some facetious and witty conversation, and a trial of Skill among the members, in resolving dark and obscure questions, for this purpose, they wisely Instituted the Conundrums. And, either entertaining a better opinion of the Secretary and master of Ceremonies as wits, than of the Rest, or proposing to throw the Labouring oar, Intirely upon these two Gentlemen, or thinking such an employment most agreeable to their turn and Genius, they appointed them *Conundrumificators* for the Club, and we shall see many Examples of the acute wit of these gentlemen exhibited in the Sequel of our History.

Chapter IV

Election of a Longstanding member, Sublime letters, Petition and Remonstrance of Mr Protomusicus, Complaint of Sir John, Club Conundrums and Jests.

It is a question that has often been propounded by Philosophers, but never to my knowledge has had a Satisfactory resolution, vizt: whether there be any Remedy in nature to cure men of that Impertinent, Censorious and fault finding humor that prevails among them? It is Certain that every man has a particular failing, peculiar to himself, which he can by no means thorrowly conceal, but it will be ready to break from him on occasions when he is not aware or on his Guard, drunk or Sober, and the reason of this is that every || man gives more attention to his neighbours defects than to his own; and, whatever contributes to render his neighbour's Character Ridiculous, he will paint it out in strong and lively colors, and Censure and Condemn him for it beyond all measure or modesty. To Cure this malignant humor effectually, a man need only with alittle more attention look Inwards

that if upon any contingency the honorable president should ommit, upon his own absence to appoint a deputy, or, in Case the deputy appointed should be absent, then the Chancellor, with the Consent and approbation of the Club, is to take the Chair, or the Club to elect, by a majority of voices, any other member for that purpose.

This law will bear a few observations, the honorable the president had, ever since the unlucky affair of the letter of Cats, showed very little Inclination to appoint deputies by Commission in his own absence, and sometimes with difficulty could be brought even to nominate his deputy, denying at the same time, that the Club had any power to chuse a deputy themselves. This certainly was the President's privilege, by article 1mo of Law 19th, but then, if he should refuse to nominate, that could be no reason why the Club should be Intirely disabled from appointing a deputy of their own, for, this article does not expressly say that he should have the *Sole power;* but notwithstanding, this was a point his honor never would give up, to the Club, and he looks upon all proceedings and laws to be void, which are made under a deputy of the Club's Chusing, and Indeed, as to laws, he denies that the Club has any power to make any, even under a deputy of his own appointment, and therefore, none but his fiat can give them a Sanction, tho' there be no express law of the Club or privilege granted the president to support this Claim, thus we have an Instance of the desire of power Implanted in || great men, so that even the mildest tempers among them are for allowing nothing at all to those that are under their Sway; The Chancellor, by whose direction this Law was made, showd in his conduct here, the desire he had, to curb the overgrown power of the chair, and to acquire privileges and powers to himself, under a notion of operating for the liberty of the Club, but this State officer, being of a much more violent and Impetuous temper, than his honor, the Club were Jealous of his operations, and would not grant him an unlimited privilege to take the Chair on all occasions, but Inserted a Clause in the Law, by which they wisely reserved to Themselves a power of Election.

It was ordered by the Club, that henceforward Jonathan Grog Esqr Master of the Ceremonies, and Loquacious Scribble Esqr Secretary, should prepare each of them a *Conundrum,* to be proposed in Club, Immediatly after the Toasts are drank, and, in case the Club should solve or answer these Conundrums, the aforesaid Jonathan Grog Mr of Cerem: and Loquacious Scribble Secretry, shall, each of them, drink a bumper, to the prosperity of the Club, and in case the members cannot solve or answer the said Conundrums, the abovesaid Gentlemen, are to be declared *Victors,* It was

"Alas, poor Tuesday Club, alas! ⎫
How Sad, and how forlorn your Case, ⎬
Unbless'd with Jole's auspicious face, ⎭
For now with akes and rueful pains
The Cruel gout binds him in Chains."

The Genius of the Club thus spoke,
On which the briny tears forth broke.
The Goddess paus'd a while, & then
Resum'd the Lamentable Strain.
"Bereft of so benign a Chief,
How Just, how dutiful our grief,
No deputy can e'er pretend
To steer with such a steady hand,
And when the pilot fails in Skill,
The foundering bark must bilge & fill.
Avert propitious powers, our fate,
And help, before it be too late,
Long may he live to load his table
With partridge pies and pies of apple,
With good neats tongue & lusty Gammon,
With generous wine and punch of Lemon,
Nor may the Envious Gout again
Invade those precious Limbs, *Amen.*"

[69]

This epicedion was the first effort of the poetical Genius of this ancient and honorable Club, and tho' elegantly performed, yet displeased much his honor the president, and was the first thing that put him out of conceit with calling Club Committees at his own house, he alledging, that it was too gross a piece of flattery, for the Club to mention in these verses, the very dishes with which he had treated them at the Commission committee, and looked, as if they admired him for no other reason, but because he crammed their bellies with dainties, his honor observed also, that they verified the old proverb, vizt: *they could not fare well but they must cry roast meat.*[4]

At the same Sederunt there passed the following Law.

Law XLIII. Passed into a Law, *Nem: Con:* by the President and Club now met, this 16th of January, 1749/50, and by the authority of the same,

[70]

---

4. In other words, they could not enjoy their good fortune without boasting about it. This was a familiar proverb in Hamilton's day, but he is perhaps most immediately recalling Henry Fielding's use of it in *Tom Jones*, bk. 4, chap. 5.

and representative, for us and our ancient Tuesday Club, and do by these our Letters patent Impower and Authorize you, the said Comely Coppernose Esqr, to negotiate, transact and manage all manner of Business and affairs, of what nature and Importance soever, Ecclesiastical, Civil or military, relating to us and our ancient Tuesday Club, in the City of London or elsewhere, within the Dominions of Great Britain, France, Ireland, the mountains of Wales & the Town of Berwick upon Tweed, with the same force and efficacy, as if we ourself, were actually there *In propria persona.*

[Great Seal appended]	Given under our hand and the great Seal
Nasifer Jole	of our ancient Tuesday Club, at our
	Residence in North east Street in the City
	of Annapolis in Maryland, this Day
	of 1749/50, In the 5th year of our
	Presidential Government.

We may Justly remark here the grandure, that this ancient and honorable Club began to take upon themselves, in this Instance of their appointing their agent in a distant part of the world, their affairs now became so diffused, and their fame so extended, that there was a necessity for their establishing also, soon after an agent for A- ‖ merica and the Islands thereunto belonging, as shall be related in its proper place in this history.

The Club Considering, that his honor the president was now much Indisposed with the Gout, which prevented his attendance on his Important office, Concluded, upon this occasion, to send him a Condoling address, as they had done formerly at Sederunt 97th January 17th 1748/9, and having drawn up this address in verse, ordered it to be recorded, and wrote out fair, To be presented by the Secretary to his honor, on the morrow, being Wednesday the 17th Instant, this address was as follows.

> *The Epicædion of the Ancient Tuesday Club,*
> *on the mournful Indisposition of Nasifer Jole Esqr:*
> *Their honorable President—Inspired by the conjoint Muses*
> *of the several Members of the Club,*
> *met at the house of the*
> *Honorable Sir John, Knight.*
>
> Divine Melpomene,[3] The Bard,
> Invokes you in a task that's hard,
> To make such verse as you'll enable
> On this occasion Lamentable.

---

3. The Muse of tragedy.

the Tuesday Club [Book VII] 49

Scribble Esqr Secretarius—with which reasons, your Committee being abundantly satisfied, his honor was then graciously pleased to deliver, in a Solemn and formal manner the following Commissions, vizt: one under the privy Seal at Arms to Philo Dogmaticus Esqr Cancellarius, and two under the Great Seal, to Jonathan Grog Esqr, magister Ceremoniarum, and Loquacious Scribble Esqr, Secretarius, for which these Gentlemen made an humble obeisance, and thanked his honor the president.

Then your Committee and asistants went to Supper, which was in an elegant manner prepared for them by his honor the President, and after handing about the bowl, replete with lemonian punch, they dismissed.

Teste Loquacious Scribble Secretarius.

After reading of this report in Club, the Secretary desired to know if it should be recorded, the members entered into a debate concerning it, It was proposed then to put the Question, Record or not record? but the previous Question was moved by a member, whether this question should be put or not? it Carried 5 against 4, then the first question being put, it carried by the same majority. [66]

The Club however, took under their consideration the nature of this Special Committee, and questioned the Legality of it, upon which, it was concluded, that the matter is afterwards to be examined into, and the Secretary Called to an account.

The Secretary presented in Club, a patent for Captn Comely Coppernose, Impowering him to be agent for the Club at London, which he had drawn up and prepared, according to an order of the Club, and, after the Club had examined and Corrected the same, it was ordered to be entered in the book, and a Copy thereof drawn out fair, and presented to his honor the president, to have the great Seal appended, to be signed by the president, undersigned by the Secretary, and sent to Capt: Coppernose at London, the Tenor of the Patent follows.

PATENT

The Honorable Nasifer Jole Esqr,
President of the Ancient Tuesday Club.

To our Trusty and well beloved Captain Comely Coppernose, greeting.

Whereas we repose an Especial Trust and Confidence ‖ in you, our trusty friend, Comely Coppernose Esqr, be it therefore known to all concerned unto whom these presents shall come, that we do hereby constitute appoint and declare you, the said Comely Coppernose Esqr, agent, Plenipo' [67]

[64] and the head is threatned to be abscinded, there is dan- ‖ ger that there shall be nothing left but a decapitated corps; therefore, as our Club seems at present to be threatned with Epileptic paroxisms, and mortal Syncopes, from the distraction that has happened between the honorable the President and the rebellious members, your presence this night with your helmet, breast plate and broadsword, will be very salutiferous and necessary, as well to prevent the violence of Democratical fury, as to Impede the petulancey and rigor of arbitrary and despotic Sway, but if you cannot come, pray expedite for that purpose the most trusty and valorous Squire you have, and send along with him, the erroneous commission with the virescent melilotian Sigillature, I am,

Janry 2d 1749
Your faithful Squire and
most humble Servt:
Slyboots Pleasant.

In this Letter, Mr Slyboots affects very much the Stile of a Learned man, it being stuffed quite full of terms of art, which technical Phrazes were not altogether agreeable to Sir John, as he found that they were not of a right Clubical Stamp, but seemed rather to be Culled from Quack bills.

The Secretary Informed the Deputy President & Club, that a Special Committee of the Tuesday Club, had met at the house of the honorable Mr President Jole, upon Monday the 15th Instant, for the Sealing and Delivering the new Commissions, the Proceedings of which Committee were read as follows.

Monday January 15th 1749/50

[65] At a Special Committee of the Tuesday Club, held ‖ at the house and by the appointment of his honor the president, in pursuance of law 23d were present

Nasifer Jole Esqr Præs:
Philo Dogmaticus Esqr Cancellarius
Jonathan Grog Esqr Magister Ceremoniarum
Slyboots Pleasant Esqr ⎫
Laconic Comus Esqr ⎬ asistants
Loquacious Scribble Esqr Secretarius

The honorable the president addressed your Committee in a Gracious Speech, setting forth his motives for not delivering the New Commissions at last Sederunt, which his honor declared were founded upon the absence of Philo Dogmaticus Esqr Cancellarius and the misconduct of Loquacious

Chapter III

Report of the Committee for Commissions, patent for an agent in Great Brittain, Epicedion of the Club, Institution of the Conundrums.

That Celebrated mathematician and Philosopher Doctor Whiston, when he prophesied the end of this world approaching, braced and strengthned his argument, by proving the Completion of all the ancient Scriptural Prophesies, and the appearance of several prodigious Phænomena, in these Latter times, such as Comets and the like dreadful meteors.[1] || Were I to Imitate the Example of this great Philomath, I might, upon the like principles prophesy the dissolution of the ancient and honorable Tuesday Club, from the Completion of the old prophesy of Jealous Spyplot Esqr, and from the appearance of several dreadful hubbubs of late, excited between his honor and the members, but, least I should be Called a false prophet, as the said Doctor Whiston has been, a thousand times over, I shall not venture to prophesy any such matters, for whatever State we may have seen already assumed by the ancient and honorable Tuesday Club, and whatever hurly burlys may have as yet happened in the said Club, yet it is all nothing to what we shall find in the Sequel of this History. [63]

At Sederunt 122 Janry 16th 1749/50, The worshipful Sir John being High Steward, and Philo dogmaticus Esqr, Deputy president By Commission, The High Steward produced in Club a letter from the high Steward of last Sederunt, which was read and recorded as follows.

To The Honorable Sir John Oldcastle,
Knight of the Tuesday Club.

Invincible Sir John,

When perils and dangers Superimpend, so as to periclitate[2] the body politic, when the members of the said body, are in a morbific Idiosyncrasy

---

1. William Whiston (1667–1752), English theologian and mathematician, was expelled from Cambridge in 1710 for his Arian views, which he elaborated upon in *Primitive Christianity Revived* (London, 1711–1712). Hamilton is referring, however, to Whiston's *A New Theory of the Earth, from Its Original, to the Consummation of All Things* (London, 1696), especially chap. 5, "Phaenomena Relating to the General Conflagration: With Conjectures Pertaining to the Same, and to the Succeeding Period, till the Consummation of All Things."
2. To imperil or endanger.

since he applies to it the title *venerable,* the Proper Epithet of the ancient Tuesday (or whin bush Club) of Lanneric.

Another Letter from Sir John to the Secretary, with a Certain billet Inclosed, Sealed and directed to a Certain Sir John Oldcastle, was produced, read and Recorded as follows.

To Doctor Loquacious Scribble,
Secretary to the most honorable Tuesday Club.
Sir,

I Just Received the Inclosed, as by direction I find it is not for me, I have sent it to you, as Secretary, that, if you know any Oldcastle, in our most worthy Tuesday Club, I request the favor of you, as I am Ill, and can't attend, to deliver it to the Honorable Sir John Oldcastle.

Pray Sir, make my compliments to the honorable the president, to the keeper of his honor's C—— to the high Steward, and to all the worthy members, as well to these understrappers of officers, as to those out of office.

I'll say no more, for I dare say you'll find it a hard matter to pick out what I have said, so conclude with tender of my best Services, am Grandee Sir, yours &ct:

*Sir John: Knight of the
Tuesday Club.*

In the beginning of this letter Sir John exhibits a delicate piece of Banter, on the person who addresses him with his cast off title. At the Close of the letter, his ‖ using a blank after the letter C—— would seem as if he Intended to put a dowble Entendre on the Club, who had not as yet forgot his after Supper toast, for which he had been Indicted, the conclusion of the letter bears a great Show of modesty and politeness.

As it was necessary to pacify his honor the president for the bad usage he was supposed to have received, in the proceedings of last Sederunt, the whole misconduct was laid at the Secretary's door, who was now become the General bear-blame of all the mischief that happened in the Club, The matter was fully considered by the Club & after mature deliberation thereupon, the Secretary was found Guilty of Concealing the proceedings of Sederunt 95th, where the Sole power of appointing Club officers was Granted to his honor the president—and upon the Club's proposing to Inflict a Censure upon him, he prudently submitted, owned his fault, and the Honorable the president was pleased to Grant him a pardon for all past offences.

a prerogative granted him at Sederunt 95th, which was, the Sole power of appointing Club officers, and mantained that this was an affair which the Club had nothing to do with. This occasioned very hot and high debates in the Club, for at least two hours, and the members were spurred on by the Chancellor, who droped a word now and then, which, like a firebrand rekindled the flame, as often as it began to abate. The members indeed were Conscious, and it appeared from the face of the Record, that they had Inconsiderately granted the president this power and wanted to have that grant Revoked; but in vain; his honor, like all, or most men in power, would take as much as they pleased to grant him, but never || would give [60] back again what he had once got; at last, Mr Spyplot the High Steward, had the Skill to allay this Club tumult, but his honor the president declared all these Commissions, delivered at that Sederunt to be void, and ordained that they should be Renewd in another form, that is, leaving out the words *By order of the Club*.

At Sederunt 121, Slyboots Pleasant Esqr, being high Steward, the Secretary, after his honor had taken the chair, got up as usual to read the proceedings of last Sederunt, and he had no sooner pronounced, Sederunt 119 (so entered in the book by mistake for Sed: 120) Than Jonathan Grog Esqr, said, Interrupting him, That he hoped the proceeding of that Sederunt was not so long as the 119th Psalm, for then the President and Club would not have time to hear it read over. The Longstanding members Laughed at this flash of wit of the poet Laureat, and the Secretary proceeded with great gravity to read the proceedings.

A Letter was produced by the honorable the President from the high Steward, which was read in Club as follows.

To The Right Honorable Nasifer Jole Esqr,
President of the Tuesday Club.

Honorable Sir,

I have this night the honor to entertain your ancient and venerable Society, and, as you must be Conscious how agreeable your Company will be to every member of the Club, I flatter myself you will not deny so great a Satisfaction, which is most earnestly desired by,

Your Honor's most obedt: &
faithful Servt:
Slyboots Pleasant H:S:

By the Stile at the beginning of this Letter, it appears that The writer [61] of it was not unacquainted with the ancient History of this honorable Club,

[58] many good qualities and uncommon Talents of which you are possessed, grant unto you, our ‖ trusty and well beloved, Loquacious Scribble Esqr, by this our commission, and these our Letters patent, under our hand, and the great Signet of our ancient Tuesday Club, the distinguished title of *Secretary,* and *Registarius ab archivis* to us, and our ancient Tuesday Club, hereby creating you our Chief Clerk, and Register, and Granting you all the privileges, honors, titles, dignities and perquisites appertaining to such a distinguished office, and Constituting you the next person in dignity to our respectful Protomusicus or chief musician, the third and Lowest officer of our Commoners, *that is to say,* to take your place, at the Lower end of the table opposite to our great presidential Chair of State, and to be a Correct and accurate Register, and recorder of the dignity of our Chair, and Setter forth & mantainer of our Authority, as also an Elegant Scribe to our ancient Tuesday Club, in every Case and Emergency, as might become a faithful and Correct Secretary.

[Great Seal]	Witness ourself at our Dwelling in N:E:
Nasifer Jole	Street in Annapolis, this 2d Day of
	January, 1749, in the 5th year of our
	Presidential Governt:

Sig: pr: order *Philo Dogmaticus Cancellarius.*

These were the Commissions as delivered at Sederunt 120, as for the Date of the Second of January, which was after this Sederunt, It was occasioned by the said Commissions then being cancelled and renewed, on account of a dispute and variance in Club, between his honor and the members.

[59] As for Sir John the Champion's Commission, as it differed ‖ from the others in form, at the time of the Renewal, I defer giving a copy of it, till I come to that particular part of our History, but what occasioned the cancelling and renewing of these Commissions was a dispute in Club concerning them, which happened as follows.

By consent and order of the Club, there was an addition made to these Commissions, vizt: after *Nasifer Jole Præses,* were added these words, *By order of the Club,* and at the Bottom, before the Secretaries name, *Signed pr: order of the Club,* This, it was thought was done at the Instance and Suggestion of Philo Dogmaticus the Chancellor, who, tho yet scarce warm in his Seat, began to strike at the power and prerogative of the Chair and endeavor to make his honor the president pull in his horns alittle.

This Incensed the honorable president very much, and he declared in a passion, and with much vehemence that he never would consent to give up

thority, as also, a performer of the honors of our ancient Tuesday Club, in every Case and Emergency, as might become a worshipful master of the Ceremonies.

[Great Seal] Witness ourself at our dwelling in North
Nasifer Jole east Street in Annapolis, this 2d day of
Janry, 1749, in the 5th year of our
Presidential Government.

Sig: pr: Order *Loquacious Scribble Secry*

CHIEF MUSICIAN'S COMMISSION

Nasifer Jole Præses

To our Trusty and well beloved, Solo Neverout Esqr, greeting.

We, of our particular grace and favor, as also in Consideration of the many Good qualities and uncommon talents ‖ of which you are possessed, [57] grant unto you, our trusty & well beloved Solo Neverout Esqr, by this our Commission, and these our Letters patent, under our hand and the Great Signet of our ancient Tuesday Club, the Respectful title of *Musicus con voce*, to us and our ancient Tuesday Club, hereby creating you, our vocal musician, and prime Choirister, and granting you all the privileges, honors, titles, dignities and perquisites appertaining to such a respectful degree and office, and constituting you, the next person in dignity, to our Worshipful Master of the Ceremonies, Second officer of our Commoners, *that is to say,* to take your place at the left hand, next our Chancellor and keeper, and to be a Clear, melodious and Tuneful Chanter forth of the dignity of our Chair, and a proclaimer and mantainer of our authority, as also a musical Celebrator of the worth of our ancient Tuesday Club, in every Case and emergency, as might become, a true and well tuned vocal musician.

[Great Seal] Witness ourself at our dwelling in N:E:
Nasifer Jole Street in Annapolis, this 2d of January
1749, in the 5th year of our Presidentl:
Governt:

Sig: pr: order *Loquacious Scribble Secr:*

SECRETARIE'S COMMISSION

Nasifer Jole Præses

To our Trusty and well beloved Loquacious Scribble Esqr, greeting.
We of our particular grace and favor, as also in Consideration of the

hereby creating you, a Judge of equity in all Cases, that may come before us and our ancient Tuesday Club, and granting you all the privileges, honors, titles, dignities and perquisites, appertaining to such an honorable degree and office, and constituting you, the next person in dignity to our noble Champion and privy Councellor Sir John, Second State officer to the Chair, *That is to say,* to take your place at our left hand, next to our great presidential Chair, and to be a Just and equitable Judge in all Cases that come before us and our ancient Tuesday Club, a Supporter of the dignity of our Chair, and a mantainer of our authority, as also a defender of the Liberties and privileges of our ancient Tuesday Club, in every case & Emergency, as may become an honorable and equitable Chancellor.

[Privy Seal]   Witness ourself at our dwelling in North
Nasifer Jole   east Street in Annapolis, This 2d Day of
   Janry 1749, in the 5th year of our
   Presidential Government.

Signd pr: Order *Loquacious Scribble Secrtry*

MASTER OF CEREMONIES'S COMMISSION

Nasifer Jole Præses

To our Trusty and well beloved Jonathan Grog Esqr, Greeting.

We, of our particular grace and favor, as also in consideration of the many good Qualities and uncom- || mon talents of which you are possessed, grant unto you, our trusty and well beloved Jonathan Grog Esqr, by this our Commission, and these our letters patent, under our hand and the Great Signet of our ancient Tuesday Club, The Worshipful Title of *Master of Ceremonies* for us and our ancient Tuesday Club, hereby creating you a polite and expert Sir Clement Cotterel,[2] and granting you all the privileges, honors, titles, dignities and perquisites appertaining to such a worshipful degree and office, and Constituting you, the next person in dignity to our honorable Chancellor, first officer of our Commoners, *that is to say,* to take your place at the Right hand, next to our noble knight and Champion Sir John, as the next in office to our Honorable Chancellor, and to be a polite and Ceremonious Master of our Ceremonies, and a mantainer of our au-

---

2. By Hamilton's day the name Sir Clement Cotterell was virtually synonymous with the master of ceremonies. The original Sir Clement Cotterell of Wylsford, Lincolnshire, was groom-porter to James I and muster-master of Buckinghamshire by 1616. Like his ancestor, the Sir Clement Cotterell who flourished in the early 18th century was master of ceremonies and a noted antiquarian besides.

that it is the will and pleasure of the honorable the President and Club, that the Die should be sent by the first fair opportunity to Annapolis.

I shall send you further advice, together with the patent, when the Badges come in. In the mean time I must Inform you, that the honorable the president and Club have created you an honorary member, even in your absence, in acknowledgement of the obligations they lye under to you, a favor, never as yet bestowed upon any person, which, I hope, will serve to evidence and demonstrate, their gratitude, I am, in the name of the honorable the President and Club,

Decr: 19, 1749	Your most Devoted
being club night	humble Servt:
	Loquacious Scribble.

After Reading this Letter, the Secretary was ordered to dispatch it with the first opportunity for Lon- || don. Then his honor the President delivered to the Secretary, five Commissions, vizt: one for Sir John, one for the Chancellor, one for the Master of Ceremonies, one for the Chief musician, and one for the Secretary, and having read the Chancellor's Commission, he presented it to him, together with the other Commissions, which he read to the particular persons to whom they were directed, and then applying the Great Seal to them delivered them to Sir John, the Master of Ceremonies, and the Secretary, Mr Protomusicus Neverout, not being present, the Sealing and delivering of his commission was postponed to another Sederunt, the Chancellor's Commission, was under his honors privy Seal at arms, Sealed in red wax, the others were under the great Seal of the Club, Sealed in Green, which Sir John affirmed, was nothing but melilot plaister, which the Secretary had used for that purpose, and therefore, these first Commissions, were called the Melilotian Commissions. [54]

These Commissions Run in the following form.

CHANCELLOR'S COMMISSION

Nasifer Jole Præses

To our trusty and well beloved Philo Dogmaticus Esqr, greeting.

We, of our particular grace and favor, as also in Consideration of the many good qualities and uncommon talents, of which you are possessed, grant unto you, our trusty and well beloved Philo Dogmaticus Esqr, by this our Commission, and these our letters patent, under our hand, and privy Seal at arms, the hon- || orable title of *Chancellor,* and keeper of the great Seal of our ancient Tuesday Club, as also, keeper of our political conscience, [55]

Repent,[1] The first because they are wise men, and the last, because they are fools, from this maxim, if true, we may Justly observe || and conclude, that both his honor the president, and Mr Secretary Scribble were wise men, for we shall find his honor very soon repenting his act, in suffering a chancellor to be created in the Club, since that officer proved the greatest check to his projects for arbitrary power, therefore, as he is found capable of Repentance in this single instance, he is proved to be no fool, again the Secretary, at the Creation of this new state officer, tho' he began to despair of his ever ariving himself at that dignity, yet was far from despairing at climbing to some other office of State in the Club, and therefore is to be esteemed no fool, according to the above maxim, and if these two be no fools, then *concludendum est,* according to the Rules of Logic, They were both wise men, since the learned hold no mean between folly and wisdom.

At Sederunt 120, Decemb: 19th, Jealous Spyplot Esqr being high Steward, the Secretary Reported to his honor and the Club, that a committee had met, according to appointment on Saturday the 16th of December 1749, at the house of Huffman Snap Esqr, to draw up the commissions and the patent, the first of which were compleated, but the Patent was postponed to a farther day.

Then the Secretary Read a letter of thanks to Capt: Comely Coppernose, which he had prepared, according to an order of the Club, a Copy of which from the Record follows.

To Capt: Comely Coppernose.

Dear Sir,
Yours of the date of June 24th came safe to hand, Together with the great Seal of the Club, which was pre- || sented to the honorable the president and Club, and very much approved of.

I am appointed by the honorable the president & Club, to return you their hearty thanks for your diligence in executing their Commissions, which they have reason to believe, will be as Elegantly performed in the badges as in the great Seal, the last, in their opinion, being a compleat and handsom piece of work.

The honorable the President and Club have granted your desire, and Intend to prepare a patent, and affix the great Seal to it, to constitute you Sole agent for the Tuesday Club in London. I am desired to acquaint you,

---

1. John Henley (1692–1756), or Orator Henley, contributed to the *Spectator* as "Dr. Quir" and published numerous works on oratory, theology, and grammar. This passage does not appear in his best-known work, *A Course of Academical Lectures on Various Subjects* . . . (London, 1731).

Dong ding
May the king
Ding dong
Live Long.

2d, that Quaint and Laconic advertisement, put up by a doctor on the Street door of the house where he Lodg'd.

In this place
Lives Doctor Case.[72]

The Tavern Inscription got the Landlord much Custom and the Parson Guzzled his pots of Beer Gratis, 'till like most parsons he waxed very fat and unwieldy, as for Doctor Case, The Singularity of his advertisement, much augmented his practise. [51]

There are two Sorts of these posies, vizt: posies for wedding rings, and posies for Ladies Garters, Examples of both follow.

Ring Posies	*Garter Posies*
By Love	Love ever Join
I move.	Your heart and mine.
At heart	Who views your eyes
I smart.	Most Surely dies.
To you	Give me one kiss
I bow.	And Crown my bliss.

Many Examples might be given of posies, but these are Sufficient, to give the Reader a taste. And now having finished this Important Chapter, whose length I suppose, will the less Chagrin the reader, when he considers that this extensive Subject has been discussed in so small a Compass, I have nothing now to do, but to proceed with our History.

Chapter II

Solemn Delivery of the Commissions, Disputes thereupon—Club letters.

It is an observation of the Celebrated Mr Orator Henly and several other Ingenious and witty men, *That Wise Men never despair, and fools never*

---

72. The bearer of that sign is John Case (fl. 1680–1700), an astrologer who eventually styled himself M.D. and is mentioned by Addison, Pope, and others.

> Pity me Celestial fair,
> Or I quickly shall dispair,
> Oh let love and pity Join,
> Love and pity make you mine.

The foregoing accrostic, you'll easily find, is Intended for one Miss Mary Pool, by the Initial letters of the lines, and is exactly in the moderen taste of love Sonnets, the dowble accrostic stands thus.

All ye Cupids,	Alle ye Graces,
Nymphs so fair and	Neat, whose faces,
Ne'er by fair	Naids were outdone,
Ever bright	Even as the Sun,
Do not once	Dare to compare,
Unto my	Unequal'd fair,
For you'll ever	Fail to pass,
For Beauties	'Fore my matchless Lass.

[50] This accrostic you see is made on one miss Anne Duff, the letters of whose name lace down the beginning and middle of the piece, as for the etymology of accrostic, it may be said to be quasi *a Cross Stick,* the Initial letters of the name being stuck like a Stick accross the piece; If any one quarrels with this Etymology, let him find a better, I have here done my best. I shall only mention with honor, before I have done with this article, that Ingenious moderen who composed, the acrostical arguments to Plautus's comedies,[71] were that ancient now alive to peruse these quaint pieces, he'd Surely think they Contained a greater Comedy than any in his book.

The last piece of moderen wit which I shall Consider, is the posie, which may be called a dwarfish Sort of poetry, the lines being short, and consisting of few words, because these performances must be crammed into a small Space, that is, into a wedding ring or a pair of Garters, tho' there has been Instances of this kind of poetry upon Tavern Signs, and advertisements, two Remarkable ones of this Sort, are 1st That Ingenious Posie, which was Composed by a Certain Parson, at the Instance of a Tavern keeper, at the Sign of the Bell, at whose house he often Tossed off a Can of good beer, The Landlord desiring that the Inscription upon his Sign post might be a Loyal one, and also have some relation to the bell, the Parson composed the following Ingenious Rhime to be wrote under the Bell.

---

71. Both an acrostic argument and a nonacrostic argument are prefixed to some of Plautus's comedies. Formerly, the acrostic arguments were thought to be post-Plautine, or "modern"; now both acrostic and nonacrostic are so thought.

Chronogram

Da	1	a 1	This is a french prophesy, said to have been made by a Jesuit at Paris, the Sense of the words, and the addition of the figures arising in that order from the vowels, are Certainly to give us a peace in the year, 1745.
pacem	12	e 2	
domine	432	i 3	
in	3	o 4	
diebus	325	u 5	
nostris	43		
quia	531	angl: give	This is a pritty extraordinary Invention and much admired by the Curious here in England, as they say, not less firmly believed and relied on, by great numbers in France, as the author is said to have made several other predictions, which have really proved true—Thus far the observator—The Invention Indeed is very Ingenious, and worthy a wit of the 14th Century, but the Prophet happens to be a small matter out of time, vizt: four Years, for the peace was not Concluded with France, till the year 1749.[70]
non	4	peace in	
est	2	our time	
alius	135	O lord,	
qui	53	because	
pugnet	52	there is	
pro	4	no other	
nobis	43	that	
nisi	33	fighteth	
tu	5	for us,	
deus	25	but only	
noster	42	thou, our	
	1745	God.	

We come next to the acrostic, which is a trial of Skill, different from all the others, this is a poetical performance, which is most commonly exercised upon the fair Sex, and, I cannot say, I ever knew it applied to any male Subject but one, which was upon the honorable Mr President Jole, by Jonathan Grog Esqr, which we shall exhibit in it's proper place in our History; There are two Sorts of the Acrostic, the Simple and Compound, or Rather, the Single and dowble, in the first, the Initial Letters of the Lines begin with the Letters of the Ladie's name, as they stand in their proper order, so that the name may be read from above downwards, in the Second, or dowble acrostic, the said letters are not only placed at the beginning of the lines, but Run down the middle of the piece, I here give an example of Both kinds. [49]

> Mighty love has pierc'd my heart,
> And has made me feel Sweet Smart,
> Restless all the night I rove,
> Young and fair's the Nymph I love.

---

70. Hamilton has accurately transcribed the entry but has added the portion beginning with "Thus far the observator. . . ."

Anagrammatized thus, supposing the first person to be a rogue and the latter a whore.

Jasper Goswall	Mary Carrier
anagram	anagram
A Gallows I press.	I marry Care.

These anagrams are of the Satyrical kind, but some are of the panegyrical Stamp, such as authors may compose for their patrons, and lovers for their mistresses, I shall give two examples of this Sort, the first passing a Compliment on a patron, the latter expressing a lover's Suffering for his mistress.

Robert Boonight	Elmira Damahoy
anagram	anagram
Right noble root.	Oh! I am realy mad!

And this is enough to show the nature of this kind of Ingenuity.

[48] The Chronogram comes next under our consideration, which is a piece of Ingenuity, that expresses any number of years, or the present year of the Christian Æra, by culling out certain letters of a proper name, of any person, place or town, and making them in a gigantic manner to outgrow and overtop their fellow letters, in the same word, Thus, if I had a mind, to express the year of God 1506, in the name Lodovicus Magnus,[68] I should do it thus, first transpose the two words, by the figure υστερον προτερον,[69] and then write the name thus, Magnus, loDoVIcus, which in Roman Numbers makes M.D.V.I. Another kind of Chronogram there is, which is done by the five vowels a.e.i.o.u. and calling them according to their order as they stand, 1,2,3,4,5, any number or term of years may be signified, one example of this Sort of chronogram I shall give, that was published some years agoe in the *Maryland Gazette,* No 18, vizt: in august 1745 during the time of the late french war, with the observation there made on it.

---

68. Lodovicus Magnus may be a play on the name of the Italian poet Lodovico Ariosto (*magnus* [great] is roughly the Latin equivalent of the Greek *ariosto* [best]), who was alive in 1506.

69. "Last thing first"; "hysteron proteron" is a rhetorical term for inverted sequence of terms or events.

much as to say an art, which describes any one name or thing by an aggregate of many things, or simply *by things, ars Explicativa Rei alicujus, Rebus.*⁶⁵

The moderens have also used the Rebus in the manner of the ancients, a remarkable Specimen of which, I once had occasion to see in an epistle wrote by that Ingenious poet Allan Ramsay Esqr, Poet Laureat of the Whin bush Club, to a friend of his,⁶⁶ the letter was of a Considerable length and not above half a dozen words in it wrote in the Common manner, and these only conjunctives, adjunctives and expletives e:g: *as, and, or, for, thus, the* &ct: to express which there are not any animals or things to be found, In this Letter, the Ingenious author has occasion to mention a man that was poxed; now this Celebrated distemper in the City of Edinburgh, goes by the name of the Canongate Breeches, so that you understand a man has got the Clap or pox, when you hear it said, that he has got a pair of Canongate Breeches, which is a modest and witty way of expressing the Disease, the Canongate being a Street in the Suburbs of Edinburgh, famous for a great number of bawdy houses, and also for the palaces of the ancient Scots nobility, our celebrated bard, in this learned Epistle of his, describes this distemper by three pictures, vizt: the picture of a Canon a Gate and a pair of breeches, || Thus ⚜ 🚪 👖. The Elegance and beauty of this hiero- [47] glyphical Rebus I can never Sufficiently admire, and think it far excells that of Abel Drugger,⁶⁷ who upon his Sign, to express his name, painted a great capital A, the figure of a 🔔 bell, a Capital D, the picture of a 🪣 rug, and to express *er,* (which I take to be the most Ingenious part of the Rebus) there stood the figure of a 🐕 dog snarling. This Ingenious artist we find, to compleat his design, is obliged to Introduce, two Capital letters, which I take to be two Capital errors in his piece.

I come now to the Anagram, which is only a proper Name transformed, by shifting the letters of it from their natural places to others, by which transposition and transmutation, is framed a word or a Sentence, which expresses some remarkable quality accident or action of the person, whose name is so anagrammatized, for example, let us take a man's name and a womans, such as Jasper Goswall, and Mary Carrier, they might stand

---

65. "An art explicative of any thing by means of things."

66. Allan Ramsay (1686–1758) was a Scottish poet and bookseller noted for his elegies and satires, his collections of old Scottish and English songs (*Tea-table Miscellany* [1724–1732] and *The Ever Green* [1724]), which helped revive vernacular Scottish poetry, and his principal work, *The Gentle Shepherd* (1725), a pastoral drama. I have not found the letter Hamilton is referring to. Ramsay's affiliation with the Whin-Bush Club is also discussed by Hamilton earlier (see I, 59).

67. Abel Drugger is a character in Ben Jonson's *Alchemist*.

Of a high German critic take Volume the first,
And a Creature with dullness & long ears accursd,
A fish that in northeren Seas they do take,
The same cur'd with Salt & then dried on a flake,
A Rabble of houses, built all in a Cluster,
Put them aptly together, a man's name you'll muster.

A Rebus was made by a Celebrated wit upon a Certain old pedantic Schoolmaster, which, as it is a very good one, I shall give as an example of this kind of Composition.

A little word that Couples words,
A plant that cures the Spleen,
A gage that thrice fifteen affords
And half a pair of eyen,
A grain that gives the Boor his bread,
And chears the ploughmen's hearts,
Give name to a pedantic head
Of slender wit and parts.

I need not tell the learned in these matters, that this Ingenious Rebus, properly considered, will give *And Rue ell eye oat,* which words being aptly conjoined, and reduced to proper orthography make up Andrew Elliot.

The verse and the Stile of the above Rebuses, are exactly adapted to our polite Moderen taste in this kind of polite Learning, as you'll find by comparing them with many of the same Sort published in our monthly magazines, by the first rate wits of the age, the humor and elegance of these performances, cannot Sufficiently be admired, and Indeed, the moderens seem to have Improved much upon the learning of the ancients in this particular, nor could any one Imagine, was he to think and ponder for a thousand years, How the names Thomas Codlington, and Andrew Elliot, could be more wittily and elegantly expressed.

As in the Rebus Strict regard is not had to the proper Orthography of names, so the same often happens in the Conundrum, and, in this only circumstance they agree, we have seen in the above Examples, how the orthography is mangled, in the Rebus, and to show how it suffers sometimes in the Conundrum, I shall give one Example in the following, vizt: why is a Cruel Barbarous murder like a Sunday dinner? ans: Because it is *Lamb-on-table,* that is, Lamentable.

As for the name *Rebus,* it seems to be derived from the ablative plural of the Latin noun *Res,* which is Rebus, *with things,* or *by things,* that is, as

I have no knowledge of my own,
Yet Stores of learning I make known,
I oft require a pinch of Snuff,
And often vanish at a puff.

Any one, who has a moderate quantum of brains, may discover that which is Intended by this Ænigma, and therefore I need show him no *Candle* to guide him in his way.

The Rebus is a Species of the Riddle or Ænigma, being a Sort of hieroglyphic, whereby the name of a man, woman, country, Town or City are expressed either by pictures of certain things that have not any real Relation or resemblance to the name Intended, or by a description, commonly in verse, of those things, which being tagged together artificially, frame the Intended name. In the exercise of this Ingenious art, the wit, or artist, needs not confine himself to the proper orthography of the name of the person &ct: which he would describe, but, if the names of the things described resemble in Sound, the Sillables or members of the proper name of that person or name, that is Sufficient, as will appear, by two examples which I shall give below.

The ancients generally framed their Rebus in pieces of Sculpture or painting, or struck it on medals and it went by the Name of Hieroglyphic. The moderen Rebus differs from the Ancient Hieroglyphic in this particular, that it is done by circumlocution, or a prolix description, instead of exhibeting the Pigmata or Iconographia. To give an Instance, suppose a Gentleman, whose name is Thomas Codlington,[64] was to be Hieroglyphized in the ancient, or Rebused in the moderen manner, an ancient operator would do it thus, first, draw the figure of any one volume of a Large book in folio, which makes *Tom*, the first Silla- ‖ ble of the name, only throwing out the (h) a Supernumerary aspiratory letter, then represent the figure of an Ass, which Compleats *Tom as* or Thomas, then after allowing a convenient distance between the figures to distinguish the Christen'd name from the Sirname, represent the figure of a Cod fish, then the said fish salted, dried, and spread out, which is *ling,* and last of all, the picture of a Town, and thus you will have *Cod ling town,* or Codlington, which summed up makes Thomas Codlington; The Moderen method to Rebus this gentleman's name, would be quite different, for a wit of the present age, would employ many words to express only these two, and this he would chuse to do in verse, perhaps in the following manner.

---

64. Hamilton is perhaps making a snide reference to Thomas Codrington (d. 1691?), Catholic divine and chaplain to James II.

mance of wit which has two extremes, but never a mean, or middle part, and these two extremes are distorted, or turned the wrong way, so that to find a mean, or meaning for it, and turn the distorted parts into their proper situation or posture, is a trial of Skill in the person that resolves the Conundrum, this figure, might *ad libitum,* be depicted, either with a gelastic grin, or with a grave countenance, according to the Species of wit couched under the Conundrum, some Subjects being grave & Solemn, and others light and merry, and, as the Bushy beard, was a Symbol of wisdom among the Ancients, some may think it proper to paint this figure with a voluminous beard, but I think it would be more proper, and more *a la Moderne,* to delineate it with a large Bushy full bottom'd wig, the moderen Signature of wisdom and Sagacity, as the beard in our times, Conveys no such Idea as that of wisdom in the wearer, this latter dress will answer well for the Hieroglyphic of your graver sort of conundrums, and the fool's Cap, as in the prefixed figure, will be proper for those of a lighter nature, as for any other Significant matters expressed by this hieroglyphic, I mention them not here, that the critics of Succeeding times may have some Scope to work upon, for probably these Gentlemen, may discover certain Mysteries in it, which I, the Inventor, never once thought of, like many of our moderen Antiquaries, and medal Historians, who find out meanings ‖ in medals and old Inscriptions, which the Inventors never Intended.

Every old woman and School-boy knows what a riddle is, that being an usual entertainment by a winter's fire, a proper place for framing of Riddles and solving of them, so that it will be needless for me to give a definition of it here, these have been exhibited to the public, by our wits both in prose and verse, and the late Ingenious Dean Swift has given Specimens of his great Skill in this kind of Composition, in his poetical *Miscellanies,*[63] which, as they are in every bodies hands, I shall make no excerpts from them, but shall here give my readers a Riddle of my own framing, as an example, to let them see wherein this piece of wit differs from the pun & Conundrum.

Riddle

My head is wavering and light,
And yet I serve to guide aright
All travellers that walk by night,

---

63. Probably a reference to *Miscellanies in Prose and Verse,* 5 vols. (London, 1727–1735), of which the first volume has a preface signed by Swift and Pope, and the fifth has some titled riddles in it in verse like Hamilton is showing here (p. 87).

Etymology of the word in the foregoing part of our History,[62] and have little more to add concerning it here. As to its definition, it may properly be called a Pun involved, I might here give examples of several Celebrated conundrums Invented by the wits of our times, but I shall wave that for brevitys Sake, as I shall have occasion in this history to exhibit many of the Tuesday Club Conundrums, which, for elegance and propriety, excell all others, that have been Invented before or since; In fine, as a Conundrum, is a Species of the Riddle or Ænigma, because it is something Involved, that Requires an Evolution, or Explication, I think it would be proper, that the Moderens, who are the true Inventors of the Conundrum (for I cannot find, that this Species of wit was at all known to the ancients) should Represent it, by some Sort of Hieroglyphical painting, as the Ancients have represented their Ænigma by a Sphynx, which, if I mistake not was a Creature with the Body of a Lyon, and the Head and Breasts of a woman. This Creature, as fabulous History Informs us, was killed by Oedipus, but, as we are not in these christian and || enlightened times, to believe there was [40] ever any such creature alive, we are only to suppose that Oedipus was a famous Solver of Riddles, and therefore was said to kill the Sphynx, but, to the point, if I may be allowed to give my advice, in this Important affair, I think some such figure as the following, would be a proper representation

of the moderen Conundrum, which is a human head placed upon a large brawny pair of buttocks, this truely represents a Conundrum as a || perfor- [41]

62. See I, 218.

Satyrs with horns, long ears, and Cloven hoofs, as we moderens paint the devil, Chariots drawn by doves, pigeons Peacocks and Eagles, and a thousand other devices of the like kind; The moderen Inventions of this kind Indeed, consist more in productions of the fancy of a more abstract nature, and not comeing directly under the Cognisance of the Sculptor and painter, Such are these prodigious productions of human wit, called puns, Conundrums, Riddles, Rebuses, Anagrams, Chronograms, accrostics & posies, all which, I Intend to treat of in order as they stand.

    A pun is properly the evolution of a Conundrum, as a Conundrum is the Involution of a pun, but this definition, like many others, would need a Comment or Explication, and, as the best way of explaining, is by giving examples, I shall here exhibit a pun and a Conundrum in their proper Shapes. A gentleman in a Tavern, speaking of a table, round which the Company sat, said: *This is not a Tavern Table,*—why so? said one of the Company,—because said he, there is never a *drawer* in it, The Table being without that convenience,—This is a genuine and proper pun, but, if the same || gentleman had said, *Why are some tables like Taverns?* and any one had answered, because they have got *drawers* in them, this would have been a proper conundrum, or the aforesaid pun Involved. Again, if a punster should say to a Soldier, *Whatever harm is done you, you always have red-dress,* tis a right pun, but should the same pun be involved, The Question would run thus, *Why has a Soldier the best Justice done him?* the answer would turn out, Because he has *red-dress.* In fine, the Art of punning, consists Solely in being master of a multitude of words, simular in Sound, but differing in Sense or meaning, and using these words in such a manner, as to excite admiration and mirth, and sometimes Indignation in the hearers. There are many different Sorts of puns, which I have not time here to explain, examples of all Sorts will be exhibited in the Sequel of this our History, Invented and uttered by the wits of the Tuesday Club, and particularly by that Ingenious moderen wit Jonathan Grog Esqr. A Certain Celebrated English university, was, for a great while famous for this art of punning, but, since the Marshe on which it stood has been drained, that facetious humor is Intirely lost,[60] however, many of these Ingenious puns, are still preserved, in these learned and Curious || collections, entituled the *Oxford* and *Cambridge Jests.*[61]

    I have Sufficiently Enlarged upon the Conundrum with regard to the

---

    60. Hamilton is probably referring to Cambridge.
    61. Hamilton is referring to two separate jestbooks here: Capt. William Hickes, *Oxford Jests, Refined and Enlarged,* 3d ed. (London, 1671); and *Cambridge Jests; or, Witty Alarums for Melancholy Spirits* (London, 1674), by "a Lover of Ha, Ha, He."

Sir Richard Blackmore Informs us very Gravely, and more like a Physician or Philosopher than a poet, That "Wit proceeds from a Concurrence of regular and exalted ferments, and an affluence of animal Spirits, rectified and refined to a degree of purity."[59]

Tho it does not become me to criticise upon great poets and Philosophers, being myself but an understrapper, yet I may modestly differ from them, and therefore, I reject the preceeding definitions as faulty, and shall give you one of my own framing.

Wit then, is a certain faculty, actuated by the fancy, which can out of Chaos bring order, and again reduce order to a Chaos, the materials it works upon, being the brain furniture of a poet or Critic of the Celebrated academy of Grubstreet, which Chamber and furniture exactly resembles a Lumber Garret, and its Miscellaneous contents, The operator *Fancy*, putting the broken pieces together, consistently or Inconsistently as she pleases, by which she always excites Gelastic motions in the Landlord of the said Garret or the wit himself, and sometimes in others, but more frequently in these others produces ‖ furious contorsions of the countenance, scornful frowns, and contemptuous grins and Sneers, this garret lumber being often full of spikes Snags, and crooked rusty nails, which being hursled about in a violent manner by the fantastical operator Fancy, are apt to gall, prick, fret and wound whenever they touch tender parts. This Fancy is a very Ingenious artist, and a fit Inhabitant for such a Lumber Garret, as a poet's or critic's Skull, for she has the knack of bringing together and uniting things that bear no relation or afinity to each other, things that are even directly opposite and contradictory one to the other, and thereby Creates such forms and monstruous Structures as are fit to frighten children, vizt: Chymeras, Sphynxes, Harpies and Centaurs; abundance of her freaks this way may be seen in the ancient Theology and mythology, and more glaringly in the productions of our moderen wits; In the first, are still to be seen, upon Stones and medals, dowble faced Januses, men and boys with wings and plumage, Serpents with human heads, women with Snaky tresses, and Castles for head attire, Gyants with a hundred arms and hands, Shep- ‖ herds with a hundred eyes, River gods, with iceicle beards and Sedgey locks,

---

definition of wit . . . is only this: That it is a propriety of thoughts and words; or, in other terms, thoughts and words elegantly adapted to the subject."

59. The entire passage appears in *An Essay upon Wit* as follows: "Wit owes its Production to an extraordinary and peculiar Temperament in the Constitution of the Possessors of it, in which is found a Concurrence of regular and exalted Ferments, and an Affluence of Animal Spirits refin'd and rectify'd to a great degree of Purity; whence being endow'd with Vivacity, Brightness and Celerity, as well in their Reflections as direct Motions, they become proper Instruments for the sprightly Operations of the Mind" (*Essays upon Several Subjects* [London, 1716], 193).

about St James's, which properly are the *Membres Basses*, of this antic Gothic fabric.

The pulpit, which poured forth Streams of excellent paragrammatical, or pragmatical wit, in those halcyon days, and sounded forth deep Mysteries, in a beautiful Ænigmatical Stile, is now turned into a rostrum, whence nothing is to be heard but dry morality. When, oh when, shall we again hear Paradise Called a *pair of dice*, all houses, *Ale houses*, Divines, *Dry vines*, & matrimony a *matter of money*, from that Learned Chair of truth; when shall another pious divine, such as the Good Mr Flawel, Spiritualize navigation and husbandry,[56] when again, shall these blessed times return, when Ingenious punsters shall be promoted according to their merit, to places of honor and profit? when again shall our ‖ Theatrical performances overflow with that quaint punning, with which they teemed in the days of Shakespear and Ben Johnson. Heaven restore that happy time, when the true Paragrama shall again raise her head, and banish what is called Simple Nature, with her plain fanatic puritanical Dress, but, that I may not digress too much and run away from my Subject, I shall now proceed to the Critical part of this history of wit and humor.

The Species of wit, which is my proper Subject at present, is what I call true Sheer wit, and, as it is usual for Learned authors to define their Subject, before they enter fairly upon it, I shall here take some pains, to define that Sort of wit which is here treated of.

Mr Locke, Mr Dryden, and Sir Richard Blackmore, have all of them defined wit differently, and, as it is common for wits to differ, as much as Doctors, I (tho a puny wit) shall beg leave to differ from them all.

Mr Locke says, that "wit consists in an assemblage of Ideas, and Joining such of them together as have any fitness or congruity, with such variety and Quickness as to excite agreeable visions and pleasant pictures in the fancy."[57]

Mr Dryden Tells us that "wit is a propriety of words, and thoughts, adapted to the Subject,"[58] and

---

56. John Flavel (1630?–1691) was an English Presbyterian clergyman and author of *Husbandry Spiritualised* (London, 1669).

57. Locke's famous definition of wit appears in *An Essay concerning Human Understanding* (1690) as follows: "Men who have a great deal of Wit, and prompt Memories, have not always the clearest Judgment, or deepest Reason. For *Wit* lying most in the assemblage of *Ideas*, and putting those together with quickness and variety, wherein can be found any resemblance or congruity, thereby to make up pleasant Pictures, and agreeable Visions in the Fancy: *Judgment*, on the contrary, lies quite on the other side, in separating carefully, one from another, *Ideas*, wherein can be found the least difference" (ed. Peter H. Nidditch [Oxford, 1975], 156).

58. This quotation appears as follows in "The Author's Apology for Heroic Poetry and Poetic Licence," Dryden's preface to *The State of Innocence, and Fall of Man* (1677): "The

Coxcombs, (some of whom had almost been committed to the flames for Heresy,) would not let this Glorious model of Literature stand, but pulling it to pieces, in order to Scrutinize and examin every part, like a parcel of Inquisitive pragmatical puppies, as they were, it exceeded their Skill to set the noble Gothic fabric up again in it's pristine form, and so, in its place, they erected a foolish and Simple Structure of their own in the false taste, as much Inferior to the former, as is the famous St Stephens wall brook,⁵⁴ or the Celebrated Cathedral of St Pauls is to Westminster abbey, which they tell the world, is founded upon nature and Common Sense, but let it be ‖ founded on what you will, it is so common that every fool may understand and comprehend it at first Sight, and therefore, as there is no mystery in it so there can be but little learning or true Philosophy.   [32]

But tho this Curious Gothic fabric has been pulled to pieces, and it's members scattered abroad, so as not readily to be found and replaced, yet there is enough of it still standing upon the old Foundations, to show what it has once been; No latter, than in the Reign of King James I, of Learned memory, a great part of this Glorious fabric stood fair to the view, Several Columns, pilasters, Chapitres, arches, Niches, porticos and Bass reliefs curiously adorned and Interwoven with puns, Conundrums, Quaint Saws and Clenches, were to be discerned fair in that monarch's reign, upon the Higher parts of this ruined pile, which are now very much wore out, and to be discerned now only upon the lower members of it, by the Invidious attrition and Corrosion (not of time but) of some of our late Virtuosi, who have passed for men of Good taste and literature, The prodigious puns to be met with in the Sermons of Bishop Andrews,⁵⁵ and the writings of many of the authors of those times ‖ both in prose and verse, demonstrate the truth of what I now say, which alas! are now as much forgot, as if they had never been, and Indeed, the only remains of them, are to be found scattered about in Ale-houses, Bawdy houses, Chop houses, Bethlehem Hospital, and among the black Guard boys, water men, porters, in the precincts of Wapping, the Garrets of Grubstreet, and among people of Quality in and   [33]

---

instauratae progymnasmata (1602–1603), sought a compromise between the Ptolemaic and Copernican systems, suggesting that the earth was stationary but that the five planets revolved around the sun. Roger Bacon (1214?–1294), the English philosopher and alchemist, settled at Oxford as a Franciscan monk. Lord Verulam is Francis Bacon (1561–1626), the famous English philosopher and author. John Tillotson (1630–1694) was a Cambridge Latitudinarian who became archbishop of Canterbury. Benjamin Hoadly (1676–1761) was an English bishop famous as the initiator of the Bangorian Controversy, an attempt to reduce church authority.

54. Hamilton is apparently referring to a famous brook at St. Stephen's Chapel, Westminster, where the House of Commons sat until the building was destroyed by fire in 1834.

55. Lancelot Andrewes (1555–1626) was an English bishop famous for his theological works, including his hand in the King James Bible.

attempting even to create animals by the Instruction of their grand master Paracelsus, in the middle of this hurly burly, and stumbling over one another in the dark, they light upon several chance discoveries, which they

[30] never thought of or looked after, some of which turned out for || use, others for no use, and others for nothing but mere mischief, Such were printing, gun powder, the Mariners Compass, furnace Glass, Clocks and watches, Phosphorus, Savealls, extinguishers, violins, violoncellos, Harpsicords, Bagpipes, French horns, Church organs, Saddles and Stirrup leathers, Snuff, tea, Coffee, Coaches, Jack Boots, operas, Routs, Drums, Masquerades, Ridottos, tweezer Cases, wigs, walking Canes and picktooths,[52] from this mass of moderen Ingenuity and Learning, in process of time sprung up, Conundrums, Riddles, Rebus's, accrostics, posies, anagrams and Chronograms.

Thus have we gone thro' our Historical Enquiry into the Origin of moderen wit, and after all this, can we Sufficiently admire at the Impudence and absurdity of those, who argue for the great Superiority the ancients have over the moderens, in respect of wit and Invention—In this Glorious State, was the Learned world, not above a Couple of Centuries agoe and might probably have continued, going on and Improving in this exquisite kind of Literature, both Civil and religious, had not a parcel of wrong headed fellows step'd in, and put all their System into Confusion and over-

[31] set this curious Structure, which had Cost || so much time, pains and Study to erect, These fellows among the Divines were Luther, Zwinglius, Calvin, Knox and Buchanan, to whom we may Join Cervetus, among the astronomers, Copernicus, Galilæo and Tycho Brache, among the Philosophers and mathematicians, Fryar Bacon, Erasmus, and of a Later date Lord Verulam, Sir Isaac Newton, Lord Shaftesbury, Mr Locke & Mr Addison, among the poets, Buchanan, Pope, Dryden, Shakespear, Milton, Voltaire, and Lastly among the Bishops Archbp: Tillotson and Dr Hoadly;[53] These meddling

---

52. In this context, a *saveall* is a type of candle holder; a *rout* is a fashionable gathering or assembly, evening party or reception, popular in the 18th century; a *drum* is also an assembly, especially of fashionable people at a private house; a *ridotto* is a social gathering consisting of music and dancing.

53. Ulrich Zwingli (1484–1531) was a famous Swiss divine who established the Reformation in Zurich (1523). John Knox (1505–1572), generally considered the leader of the Protestant Reformation in Scotland, was author of the *Treatise on Predestination* (1560) and the *History of the Reformation of Religion within the Realme of Scotland* (1587). George Buchanan (1506–1582), a Scottish historian, scholar, and poet, published *Detectio Mariae Reginae* (1571), a violent attack on Mary, Queen of Scots, *Rerum scoticarum historia* (1582), long regarded as a standard source of Scottish history, some tragedies, and some good elegiac and occasional poetry. Michael Servetus (1511–1553) was a Spanish theologian, physician, and astrologer who opposed the doctrine of the Trinity in *De trinitatis erroribus* (1531) and in *Christianismi restitutio* (1553), for which he was eventually imprisoned in Geneva at Calvin's request and burned at the stake as a heretic. Tycho Brahe (1546–1601) was a Danish astronomer whose principal work, *Astronomiae*

ate, who opened a vast budget of mighty profound learning, concerning *Substantial forms, entities, Identities, occult qualities, Soporific, Scientific, prolific, Drastic, elastic, Plastic and Gelastic powers, Gover-* || *ning, regulating, prognosticating and Influencing Stars, and Constellations, Symbolical, parabolical, Hyperbolical and Diabolical Incantations and Charms, mystical, cabalistical, papistical and Sylogistical propositions and problems, Hypothetical, prophetical magnetical and heretical maxims, political, Critical, hypocritical, and Analytical Theorems and axioms.* [29]

These wonderful Sages ascended up into the heavens, and conversed with the Stars, and made them reveal what Secrets they pleased, descended into hell, and turned the Devils out of house and home, settled a Colony of witches in Lapland, and made a mere Jack ass or beast of burden of old Beelzebub, while the Chymists followed, the useful and Instructive tract of the transmutation of metals, and enquired Diligently into the Discovery of the grand Elixir, or the *Lapis Philosophorum,* Introducing a new mysterious Language, concerning the Seven Planets, and the Signs of the Zodiac, and

---

(fl. 9th century), was an Arabian physician, philosopher, astronomer, and astrologer who abridged or commented on all of Aristotle's works and proposed medical remedies based on the harmony of music. Johann Joachim Becher (1635–1682) was a German chemist, economist, and physician who wrote *Institutiones chymicae, seu manuductio ad philosophiam hermeticam* (1662), *The Universal Character* (1661), an attempt to construct a universal language, *Magnalia Naturae; or, The Philosophers-Stone* . . . (1680), and numerous other works. Johann Wier (1515–1588) was a Belgian physician who challenged the popular belief in witchcraft. Georgius is probably George de Trebizonde (1396–1486), famous professor of Greek in Venice who translated into Latin the *Problems* of Aristotle (spurious) and the *Almagest* of Ptolemy, providing an introduction to the latter. Tholosan was the pseudonym of René Milleran (b. 1665), a French grammarian known during the 18th century for his compilation of imaginary words and names, *Lettres familieres et galantes, et autres sur toutes sortes du sujets,* 6th ed. (La Haye, 1705). Bernardinus de Bastes is probably Edward Bernard (1638–1696), English critic and astronomer affiliated with Bath. Robert Gaguin (1433?–1501) was a French priest and scholar known for his *De puritate conceptionis bearae Mariae Virginis* (1498) and for a history of France from 1200 to 1500, the *Compendium super francorum gestis* (1497), which Hamilton is perhaps recalling for its many references to miracles and prodigies. Guntrum is probably Edmund Gunter (1581–1626), the English mathematician and professor of astronomy. For Olaus Magnus, see 27n, above. Martin Biermann (fl. 16th century) was a German physician and natural philosopher whose *De magicis actionibus exetasis succincta* (1590) argued against some of Bodin's extreme opinions on the occult. Cornelius Gemma (1535–1577), of Louvain, was a professor of medicine, astrologist, mathematician, and author of *De naturae divinis characterismis* . . . (1575) and *De prodigiosa specie naturaque cometae* . . . (1578). Johann Godelmann (fl. late 16th century) was a German Protestant who, in *Malleus,* moderately insisted on normal judicial procedure in cases of enchantment and strongly believed in witchcraft and demonology. Damahoderius is possibly Josse de Damhouder (1507–1581), Flemish legal expert, scholar, and author of *Patrocinium pupillorum* (1580). Goclerius is probably Rudolf Göckel (1547–1628), German logician and philosopher whose works include the *Cosmographia* (1597), *Astrologia generalis* (1611), and other works on astrology and astronomy. Sir Christopher Heydon (d. 1623) was an English writer on astrology who was suspected of complicity in the Essex uprising (1601); his chief work was *Defence of Judiciall Astrologie* (1603).

24 [Book VII]   The History of

who it is said studied Physics under the Learned Professor Beelzebub, at the College of Pandæmonium, In these glorious and enlightened times it was, that the following great unparallelled philosophers and wits appeared, and made Incredible Improvements in the occult Sciences, vizt: Albertus Magnus, Cardan, Dandiuses, Pompanacius, Andræus, Victorellus, Lodovicus de la Cerdu, Martinus Capella, Joannes Duns Scotus Philosophus Subtilis, Joannes Secundus Poæta, Zantius, Bodinus, Spodanus, Bombastus Paracelsus, Sandyvogius, Zozymus, Rosincrucius, Faustus and his airy Councellor Mephistophylus, Messahala, Leal, Alkindus, Alhandal, Becherus, Wierus, Georgius, Tholosanus, Bernardinus de Bastes, Robertus Gaguinus, Guntrum, Olaus Magnus, Biarmannus, Gornelius Gemma M:D: Godelmannus, Damahoderius, Goclerius, Sir Christopher Heydon, Agaberta Maga,[51] and a mighty Cloud of others too tedious here to ennumer-

---

51. Of this list, the following can be identified with some degree of certainty. For Albertus Magnus, see 21n, above. Cardan, or Geronimo Cardano (1501–1576) was an Italian mathematician, physician, and astrologer, whose works include *De subtilitate rerum* (1551), *De rerum varietate* (1557), and numerous works on astronomy, astrology, rhetoric, and medicine. Pompanacius is Pietro Pomponazzi (1462–1525), Italian philosopher and author of the anti-Thomistic *De immortalitate animi* (1516) and *Secretum secretorum* (1508), concerning his experiments on minerals and metals in quest of the philosopher's stone. Andreus is probably Johann Valentin Andreä (1586–1654), German Protestant theologian and likely fabricator of the whole Rosicrucian idea, including the *Chymische Hochzeit* of Christian Rosenkreutz (1616) and other works on the Rosicrucians. Lodovicus de la Cerdu most probably is Joannes Ludovicus de la Cerda (ca. 1560–1643), a Spanish Jesuit who wrote *Adversaria sacra* (1626), *De excellentia coelestium spirituum* (1631), and commentaries on the works of Tertullian. Martianus Capella (Martin the Chaplain) was a Carthaginian writer of the 5th century whose chief work was an allegory in prose and verse, *Satyricon*, or *De nuptiis Mercurii et Philologiae et de septem artibus liberalibus*, constituting a quirky encyclopedia of contemporary knowledge. For Duns Scotus, see 20n, above. Johannes Secundus was the pen name of Jan Everaerts (1511–1536), Dutch poet noted for his Latin lyrics, elegies, and other works, including *Basia*. Zantius probably refers to Jean Zanti (fl. 16th century), French litterateur and astronomer who wrote several obscure works on astronomy. Jean Bodin (1530–1596) was a French political philosopher and economist whose *Six livres de la république* (1576) was the foundation of French political science, and whose *Démonomanie des sorciers* (1580) denounces all those who disbelieve in sorcery and urges the burning of witches and wizards. Spodanus is probably Henri de Sponde (1568–1643), bishop and author of *Annales ecclesiastici* (1613), *De coemeteriis sacris* (1638), and *Annales sacri . . . a mundi creatione ad ejusdem reparationem* (1639). Paracelsus (1493–1541) was a famous Swiss physician, alchemist, and astrologer. Michael Sendivogius (1566–1646) was a Polish chemist who sought for the philosopher's stone and contributed to a collection of treatises known as *Novum lumen chymicum* (1608). Zosimos (late 3d century or early 4th century A.D.) was an Egyptian alchemist who composed an encyclopedic work on chemistry in at least 28 books, parts of which still survive. Christian Rosenkreutz was the reputed 15th-century founder of the alchemistical Rosicrucian Society, but probably the creation of Johann Valentin Andreä (see above). Johann Faust (1480?–1540?) was the famous German magician, astrologer, and soothsayer who supposedly performed miracles with the help of a devil (Mephistopheles). Messahala is Macha-Allah (late 8th century A.D.), Arabian astronomer and astrologer whose works on astronomy were much in vogue in the 14th century. Leal presumably is Leal Lealis (fl. 17th century), Spanish author of *De partibus semen conficientibus* (Padua, 1726). Alkendi, or Kendi

a hundred other voluminous pieces, equally witty amusing and Instructive. These were the Heroical Histories of the times. There were also the amorous Histories of *Cassandra, Cleopatra, Clelia,* & *Almahyde,*[49] all adapted to excite amorous and tender passions, particularly among the readers of the fair Sex, The ancient Kingdom of France was very productive of Inventions of this kind, naturally flowing from the volatile and sprightly Humor of that Gay people.

To Natural Philosophy and Physics Considerable additions were also made, Alchymie, or the Spagyric art, as they Called it, began now to make her appearance, and her votaries, stiled Philosophers by way of eminence, would allow that name to none but themselves, new terms of art were Invented by those Sages, never before uttered or heard of, such as || *alcohol, alcahest, alhandel, Bismuth, Cohobation, amalgama, amalgamization, Gas, colcothar,* and a hundred other Strange uncouth sounding words. [27]

Judicial astrology began at this time also to Increase and prosper, and multitudes of Technical terms from that quarter, poured in upon the learned world, such as *Alchorodon, Geniture, ascendant, nocturnal, Culminate, trine, quartile, platique, Hyleg, Seatille, Horoscope,* and the like.

In Lapland too, the magical Doctors began to outwit the Devil himself, their perpetual Grand master, and to make him play Gambols and tricks against his will, by pronouncing some Strange words, and drawing stranger figures, among these Dæmoniacal Doctors appeared a new Sort of merchants or Traffickers, who bargained for Winds, that is, bought and sold them, and used to make considerable profits in their dealings with Mariners, bound to different quarters of the world, Olaus Magnus says, that Eric, king of Norway, had a Cap of four Corners, by which he could shift the winds at any time by twirling it round on his head.[50]

About this time Navigation too was Considerably Improved, tho' the use of the Compass was not as yet discovered, for a method was found out to || navigate in eggshells and make Sails and rigging of Cobwebs, by Certain venerable and Diabolical Philosophers called witches and wizzards, [28]

Cabral, a chivalric novel, or *Palmerín de Oliva* (1513), also a chivalric novel, involving the exploits of a Palmerin who eventually becomes emperor of Constantinople.

49. The first two titles were written by Gauthier de Costes de La Calprenède (1614–1663), French author of several lengthy romances. *Cassandre* (1644–1650) concerns the daughter of Darius and wife of Alexander; *Cléopâtre* (1647–1656) involves a supposed daughter of Antony's Cleopatra. The last two titles were written by Madeleine de Scudéry (1607–1701), prolific author of French romances. *Clélie* (1654–1660) concerns the Clelia who escaped the power of Porsenna by swimming the Tiber; *Almahide* (1660) is a story of the Moors in Spain.

50. Olaus Magnus (1490–1558) was a Swedish ecclesiastic and historian best known in English for *A Compendious History of the Goths, Swedes, and Vandals, and Other Northern Nations* (London, 1658), which includes the chapter "Of the Magical Art of Ericus [king of Sweden, not Norway] with His Windy Cap, and of Others" (pp. 45–46).

he recommended, was laughd at, by his bretheren Physicians—"whatever you may now think, gentlemen, of this my practice, however you may please to redicule it, yet I know it will prevail and be in vogue, when all our heads are laid."[44]

Rhime and Jingle in poetry, became so universal at this time, that it was constantly used by the monks in their latin verses, both in the Heroic and Epigrammatic manner, a Certain Monk, (whose name I find not upon Record) had such a Luxuriant Genius this way, that he translated several books of Virgil's *Ænead* into Rhime and Jingle, and affirmed, that that performance only wanted Rhime, to render it a perfect poem;[45] and Mr Dryden affirms the same, in a long preface of his, with relation to our english Tragedy,[46] a Specimen of the latin epigrammatic poetry of the latter times you have in the following little piece.

> *Gallus Galinaceus,*
> *Est animal Insigne,*
> *Et sepe prestat homini*
> *Officiis benigne.*[47]

[26]   History likewise, in these enlightened times, received additions and Improvements which it never before had, and was dressed up in very fine and Gaudy trappings, to the Immortal Geniuses of that age, we owe, the new and rare Invention of Romance writing, a kind of History, altogether Novel, (hence some kinds of Romances are called *Novels*) and hitherto unknown, from these great Historians, came the Prodigious Histories of *Amadis De Gaul, Amadis de Grece, Don Bellianis, Esplandian, Palermin,*[48] and

---

44. Thomas Sydenham (1624–1689), "the English Hippocrates," introduced new methods of treating smallpox, agues, and other maladies as a result of clinical observation rather than theory. In the preface to *The Whole Works of That Excellent Practical Physician Dr. Thomas Sydenham* (London, 1696), Sydenham anticipates the negative responses his observations will draw, but not in the words Hamilton attributes to him.

45. Hamilton is probably recalling Gawin Douglas (1474–1522), the Scottish poet and bishop of Dunkeld who translated the first nine books of the *Aeneid* into heroic couplets.

46. Hamilton is probably referring to Dryden's preface to *The Conquest of Granada,* "Of Heroique Playes: An Essay," where he says of earlier poets, those "who have written worst in it [Rhyme], would have written worse without it" (*The Works of John Dryden,* ed. Edward Niles Hooker *et al.* [Berkeley, Calif., 1956–], XI, 8). Note also Dryden's dedication to his translation of the *Aeneid* (1697), where he elaborates upon his decision to complete the rhyme and verse of Vergil's hemistiches, "not being willing to imitate *Virgil* to a Fault" (*ibid.,* V, 333).

47. "The ordinary chicken cock / Is an outstanding animal / And often shows man his duties / In a kindly fashion" (not classical).

48. Amadis de Gaul is the chivalric hero of *Amadís de Gaula,* a 15th-century Spanish or Portuguese romance; *Amadís de Grecia* (1530) is a Spanish sequel to it by Feliciano da Silva and *Las sergas de Esplandián* (1510) was another sequel. By *Don Bellianis* Hamilton probably means *The Honour of Chivalrie* (1598), the story of Prince Don Bellianis and his love for the Princess Florisbella. By *Palermin* he means either *Palmerim da Inglaterra* (1544) by Francisco de Morães

Which words, are so contrived and placed in a Square, that you'll observe, you may read them from Right to left, in the manner of the hebrews, from left to Right in the manner of the Greeks and Romans, from top to bottom, in the manner of the Chinese, and from Bottom to Top, and yet you still find the same words, and the same order; this little Ingenious conceit, was Certainly || the first hint towards our moderen Acrostic, both Simple and Compound. [24]

Poetry too, at this time, began to raise her mortified head, from among the Rubbish of Ignorance & barbarism, and was so overjoyed, that she began at once to carrol it, in pleasant jingle, and delectable Rhime, which jingle, she has been so fond of ever since, that she has never quitted it, and has been much admired and Cherished in these Jingling trappings By some of the most considerable of our moderen Bards, vizt: Tasso, Ariosto, Boileau,[40] Voltaire, Chaucer, Spencer, Pope and Dryden, and, tho some old fashioned fellows, such as Milton and Shakespear among the English, have dizened her up, in her ancient plain Stole of the Blank Rithmos, yet she still most affects the company and conversation of our Jingle Jangle men, and soft Sweet Rhimers, this attire, which she has of late appeared in, is utterly moderen, true indeed some of the ancients attempted, but *Invita Minerva*,[41] to put her in this dress, and were laugh'd at for their pains, particularly Cicero, when he took it in his head to turn poet, composed an admirable Jingling line so often quoted since his time, as an instance of his Strong genius for Poetry,

O Fortunatam, natam me Consule Romam,[42]

and also Homer, that most venerable Bard, did at times, as is supposed when he put on his night cap, fall into this Jingling Humor in many Instances, one of the most remarkable of which follows. [25]

εςπετε νυν μοι μουςαι ολυμπια δοματ εχουςαι.[43]

But Cicero, in the above recited instance, might have said the same, as the renownd Doctor Sydenham said, when a certain mode of practice, which

---

40. Torquato Tasso (1544–1595) was the Italian author of *Jerusalem Delivered* (1581), the romantic epic *Rinaldo* (1562), and the tragedy *Torrismondo* (1586). Lodovico Ariosto (1474–1533) was the Italian author of *Orlando furioso,* the greatest of Italian romantic epics, which portrays the struggle between Saracens and Christians for European dominance, with the Christian Orlando emerging victorious over the Saracen Agramante. Nicolas Boileau (-Despréaux) (1636–1711) was a French poet, critic, and literary arbiter whose *Art poétique* (1674) lays out his maxims and displays his remarkable sense of discrimination and good taste.

41. "Even though Minerva was unwilling" (Horace, *Ars poetica* 385). Cicero interprets the phrase as "contrary or repugnant to nature" (*De officiis* 1.31.10).

42. "O lucky Rome, born when I was consul!" (quoted in Quintilian, *Institutes* 9.4.41, for its bad scansion, and 11.1.24, for its immodest sentiment).

43. "Tell me now, Muses that have homes on Olympus" (*Iliad* 2.484).

unknown, such as how to know another man's thoughts, how to see into futu- ‖ rity, how to make yourself loved or hated by any person, man or woman, how to prevent an evil eye, how to dream whatever you pleased, how to avoid witchcraft and fascination, how to exorcise the devil, and how to charm away distempers and cure them by repeating of certain words, an Instance of which we have in the Ingenious Invention of a Sage of those times,[39] which is a Charm of words to drive away a quartan ague, vizt:

a b r a c a d a b r a
a b r a c a d a b r
a b r a c a d a b
a b r a c a d a
a b r a c a d
a b r a c a
a b r a c
a b r a
a b r
a b
a.

This admirable Charm, has, as we are told been used with Success for a thousand times, but some how or other, in these our degenerate days, has lost it's efficacy, probably from some necessary Circumstance being ommitted in the use of the Charm, such, perhaps, as repeating it in ‖ a certain hour of the day or night, or fasting, or in a particular posture of body, or dressed in a particular attire, or with two Stockings on one leg, or with a Jacket wrong Side outwards, or with one's face towards the east, west, South or North, the ommission of any the least part of which ceremonies, would render the Charm of no effect.

Among these Charms, there is another handed down to us, the Author and design of which, to the great dammage of posterity are both Irretrievably lost; but, for it's antiquity and curious Structure and contrivance, is thought worthy of a place here.

S a t o r
a r e p o
t e n e t
o p e r a
r o t a s

39. *Abracadabra* is a cabalistic charm, supposedly derived from the initials of the Hebrew words *Ab* ("Father"), *Ben* ("Son"), and *Ruach Acadsch* ("Holy Spirit") and formerly used as an antidote against ague and other maladies.

a Sort of Learning, very Intricate and obscure, which dealt chiefly in *abstracted notions, Entities, Identities, quiddities, Substantialities, consubstantialities, Transubstantialities, Spiritualities, materialities,* and a hundred other Sesquipedalian terms, then was Introduced the *Ars dialectica,* together with

> *Barbara, Celarunt, Darii, ferio, Baralipton,*[35]

and other such Barbarous terms, which sounded in vulgar ears like the names of so many Infernal Devils. By this art, a man could in a Sylogistical way prove very clearly, that *a man was no horse* or *a horse no man,* and vice versa, *a man was a horse* and *a horse a man,* this Celebrated Science has since been of Singular use both in ‖ the pulpit and at the bar,—Then was Introduced also the *Ars metaphysica,* which could reduce nothing to something, and something to nothing, create many an *Ens rationis,*[36] and draw a parallel between abstracted Ideas and Substantial forms, making them walk hand in hand together by analogy, so as either to force your assent, or altogether deprive you of your Senses. [21]

By the Sages of these Bright Illuminated times, many dark matters, or arcana of nature were discovered, Magic, that ancient art, was revived and new modelled, and, Instead of being conversant in the motions and revolutions of the heavenly bodies, and geometrical problems, as in the Days of Abraham, Zoroaster, Hermes and Ptolomy,[37] it consisted in drawing Circles, erecting Strange figures, Invoking certain devils by new Invented names, and putting the Body into antic dresses and postures, from this sprung the Subaltern arts of Legerdemain, Chyromancy, Physiognomy and Judicial astrology. Then many elaborate Tracts were wrote *de Secretis naturæ,* after the Stile and manner of the great Albertus Magnus, who, in those days composed an Ingenious tract, *De Secretis mulierum,*[38] in these profound writings were displayed many great arcana and Secrets, hitherto utterly

---

35. These words, nonsense in themselves, are a Scholastic mnemonic for teaching the patterns of syllogisms.

36. "Thing of the mind"; a Scholastic term, probably from Duns Scotus, meaning "something that exists only in the mind," as opposed to an *ens reale.*

37. Zoroaster, Greek name for Zarathustra (a figure of Aryan legend known to the Greeks as early as the 5th century B.C.), was credited with an immense number of works dealing with theology, astrology, and magic. Hermes Trismegistus, the name given to the Egyptian god "Thoth the very great," was the reputed author of philosophical-religious treatises and various works on astrology, magic, and alchemy. Ptolemy (fl. A.D. 127–148) was a celebrated mathematician, geographer, and astronomer whose major work, the *Almagest,* is a complete textbook of astronomy as the Greeks understood it.

38. Albertus Magnus (1192?–1280) was a German Dominican friar and great Scholastic philosopher (nicknamed Doctor Universalis) skilled in mathematics, chemistry, and mechanics and known as a wizard, although he was not a professed alchemist; of his many works on chemistry and philosophy, the ones Hamilton cites are spurious.

turn, and humor more adapted for your hum-drum Clubs, tho as much a droll as the first. Heraclitus too, in his character seems to have had a mixture of the burlesque, for, I cannot help thinking, that it was a droll humor in him to cry at these very follies and frailties, which the other laughed at, under the notion of buffooneries, Solemn triffles, Serious Jests, pompous farces, and Merry Andrew Gambols,[33] which everlastingly appear in the lives and actions of all degrees of men; But of all the droll fellows that ever appeared among these Philosophers, that Sage, (whose name I cannot now recollect)[(a)] in my eye, seems the most whimsical and burlesque, who, when he was Caught in the act of leudness with his doxy in the Streets of the City of Sparta, || being reproved for it, was (as he pretended) very much Surprized at the Insolence of his reprovers, seeing (as he said) that he was employed about a very Laudable work, for the good and advantage of Society and posterity, vizt: *The planting of men.*

Having thus cursorily traveled thro antiquity and given a slight Scetch of the State of wit among our ancestors, I should now take a Survey of the moderen State of wit, which I shall do in as brief a manner as I possibly can.

The Gothic Incursions had for some centuries, buried polite Learning and Arts, in a huge Chaos of Barbarism, Stupidity and Ignorance, so, that there was not to be seen or found in any place, not even in the Cells and Cloisters of the monks, where the small remains of learning and wit, fled at first for refuge, the least Sign of a Genius for any Sort of wit or Ingenuity. Those who devoted themselves to a monastic life, a State of Leisure and Inactivity, Instead of Bestowing their leisure time, of which they enjoyed a great deal, in useful Studies, did nothing but eat, drink, whore, loll, saunter, sleep, and mutter over a rabble of unintelligible prayers. In this State of Torpor was the drowsy world for a Considerable Time, till Mahomet the Great took and sacked the City of Constan- || tinople, then a Swarm of Greek monks poured in upon Europe, and bringing along with them, such of the writings of the ancients, as were saved from the fury of war, fire and desolation, curiosity prompted some to pry into and study these writings, upon this, wit began again to raise her disconsolate head, and the first grand task she applied herself to, was commenting and expatiating upon the writings of that Great Philosopher Aristotle, this was for a great while the labor of Duns Scotus and the Schoolmen,[34] who were the broachers of

(a) This is told of Diogenes.

33. Merry Andrew is a buffoon or attendant on a quack doctor, said to derive from Andrew Boorde (ca. 1490–1549), who was physician to Henry VIII and noted for his eccentricity.

34. John Duns Scotus (1265?–1308?), known as Doctor Subtilis, was one of the great medieval Scholastic theologians.

Aristotle in his *Rhetoric,* takes notice of the noble art of punning, and describes several Sorts of puns which he || Justly classes among the beauties of Rhetoric, and calls them *paragrams,* giving several examples of them, out of the oldest and best greek writers.[29]

Pliny the Younger was certainly an admirer of puns, Quirps and clenches, and esteemed them among the exquisite and uncommon flashes of wit, for he writes to his friend Tiro in these words, *adhibe Solatia, sed nova aliqua, sed fortia, quæ audierim nunquam, legerim nunquam, nam quæ audivi, quæ legi, omnia tanto dolore Superantur,* "afford me Solace and entertainment altogether new, and of a Strong and effectual Nature, such as I have never heard or read of before, for what I have before heard or read, will be rendered Ineffectual, by this mighty grief that now hangs over me."[30]—And what other kind of Solace could this new Solace be, but the Cracking of quaint puns and conundrums, since every pun or Conundrum, may with great propriety, be called a Stroke of wit, never once before thought of, and therefore affording still what is new.

Lucian, the prime droll, and most extravagant wit among our ancient writers, Relates a Story of one Passus, a painter and wit, who being desired by a Customer of his, to paint him a horse rolling on his back, with his heels upwards, drew that animal *passant* (as the heralds term it) the fellow, on seeing it, was angry, and swore, that the picture was not done according to his desire, Passus on this, turned the Tablature upside down, which showing the horse in the reverse posture, || the man went away very well satisfied. This Passus had certainly an excellent punning Genius.[31]

Petronius Arbiter, in his *Satyricon,*[32] abounds with Clubical wit puns and repartees, scattered up and down, not only in the prosaical, but poetical parts of that performance.

Democritus and Diogenes, Both Philosophers of ancient Greece, seem to have been persons of a Strong turn towards Drollery, and Clubical wit, tho of opposite characters, The first being a merry, facetious and good humored companion and a hearty Laugher, the latter of a more Solemn

---

replacing it with an idealized but actual countryside. The passage means: "Who was it that first invented horrible swords? / How savage he was; in fact, how steely" (Tibullus 1.10.1).

29. See Aristotle, *Rhetoric* 3.2.1412a.

30. More literally, "Bring me comforts, but new ones, strong ones, such as I have never heard, never read; for what I have heard, what I have read, all are conquered by this great grief" (*Epistulae* 1.12.13).

31. Lucian (ca. 120–ca. 200) was a Greek satirist and reputed author of *In Praise of Demosthenes,* which contains this story of Pausias, a Greek painter of the 4th century B.C. (chap. 24).

32. Petronius Arbiter (fl. 1st century A.D.) was a Roman author at Nero's court, best remembered for the *Satyricon,* a prose satirical romance interspersed with verse and probably intended as a parody of contemporary Greek novels.

cepted) of all the Latin poets. An Instance of the wit of the last mentioned poet, will not come in Improperly here with an Ingenious translation of it, by a young Student, applying it, to one Doctor Fell,[25] his Pedagogue, or master, who it seems was a person, not much loved by his pupils.

> *Non amo te, Sabidi, nec possum dicere quare,*
> *Hoc tantum, possum dicere, non amo te.*
>   Translated
> I love you not Doctor Fell,
> And why, I cannot tell,
> I only this can tell,
> I love you not Doctor Fell.

[16] The Greek epigrammatists have many of them shown a Luxuriant genius for punning, and have dealt very much in that curious study, which indefatigably explores the Similitude of words in Sound, which have a different Signification. Horace, the famous Latin Lyric poet, in some degree, applied himself to this art, and Isocrates,[26] Plato and Cicero sometimes take pleasure In diverting their Readers and hearers in this manner, and the latter has given Specimens of several quaint and witty Sayings, which are in every respect perfect puns.

Triphiodorus,[27] among the ancient Greek poets that are lost, was an Eminent wit in his particular way, he showed, as we are told, his contempt, for all the letters in the alphabet one after another, and made it evident to the world, That he could compleat an heroic poem without their aid, This appeared in his *Odyssæ*, the first book of which, had not a single α in't, the Second not a β, the third not a γ, and so on, thro the whole Alphabet.

Tibullus, a Roman Poet, shows a mighty Inclination to pun, in the beginning of one of his moral observations thus.

> *Quis fuit horrendos primus Qui protulit ensis*
> *Quam ferus et vere ferreus ille fuit &ct:*[28]

---

25. Dr. John Fell (1625–1686) was bishop of Oxford and promoter of the Oxford University Press. Although much respected in his day, modern readers remember him most as the butt of Thomas Brown's poem. Fell, dean of Christ Church, had expelled Brown but said he would remit the sentence if Brown could translate Martial's 23d epigram (first book). The translation Hamilton provides is roughly the same as Brown's ("Dr. Fell" replaces "Sabidius" in both instances).

26. Isocrates (436–338 B.C.) was an Athenian orator and teacher of rhetoric who took his own life when the Greeks were defeated by Philip of Macedon at Chaeronea.

27. Triphiodorus was an epic poet from Egypt; he composed a mediocre poem on the capture of Troy in 691 hexameters at the beginning of the 3d or 4th century A.D. and the leipogrammatic *Odyssey* to which Hamilton is referring.

28. Tibullus (ca. 60–19 B.C.) was a Roman poet whose elegies celebrate love and reject myth,

Another Instance there is in Anacreon, where that Ancient poet, in a manner truely moderen, represents the Sun, the Moon, the Earth, the Sea and trees, in the Shape of a drunken Club, tossing off their Cups, which ode, tho' elegantly translated by our English Cowley,[22] yet I reject that translation as not truely Clubical, and shall present another, the performance of a Clubical Bard.

Ode from Anacreon

Nature, in perpetual round,
Drinks apace, the thirsty ground
Drinks the Rain, and every tree
Drinks the ground. The Spacious Sea
Quaffs the air, the Sun again
Greedily sucks up the main,
And, when fuddled with his Cup,
Sister Phæbe drinks him up,
Tell me, Carping Com'rads, why
Should all nature drink, but I.

The prince of poets Homer, who has been Called with great propriety the father of Poetry, shows himself || to have been a compleat master of the Gelosophia,[23] (if I may be allowed the term) in his characters of Thersites the Buffoon, and Vulcan the Blacksmith, as also, in his history of the amours of Mars and Venus, and in the Conduct and actions of Irus, where the true Burlesque is exactly followed up, and seems much the same with that used at this day, by our Moderen Grubstreet Bards, and in our Club Conversations, Virgil also, that Incomparable Roman poet, gives us a Specimen of his taste for this Sort of Clubical wit, in his Story of Monætes, who, after having been thrown overboard, is represented drying himself on a rock in a very Comical manner, and attitude.[24] Ovid, thro' all his works, abounds with genuine paragrammatical, or Rather *pragmatical* wit, and seems to have had the rarest knack at it, (Martial the Epigrammatist ex-

[15]

---

praise. Waller's poem "On a Girdle," in which he is joyfully reminded of all the pleasures associated with his mistress by wearing her sash around his head, was one of his earliest and least auspicious performances.

22. "Drinking," in *Anacreon Done into English*, 38–39. Though "elegantly" translated, Cowley's version is tedious. Hamilton's more "clubical" rendition is exactly half the length of Cowley's and consequently a good deal livelier.

23. *Gelosophia* is Hamilton's invention for "the art of laughter." *Gelastic*, meaning "risible," stems from the Greek "to laugh."

24. Vergil relates the story of Menoetes in the *Aeneid* (5.160–182).

ment of the Letters of any name, which Ideas, the bare name itself, could never have excited.

Anacreon, one of the most ancient of the Greek Poets, Surely had a mighty turn for the pun and Dowble Entendre, and for Introducing Similitudes and allusions, much in the manner, as is now done, by many of our late moderen Lyric poets and amorous Rhimers, as the following Specimen will show, faithfully translated from one of his Odes, by a Clubical Bard.

[13] *Ode from Anacreon*[20]

But I a looking glass would be,
Still to be look'd upon by thee,
Or I, my love, would be thy Gown,
By thee to be worn up and down,
Or a pure well, full to the Brims,
That I might wash thy purer limbs,
Or I'd be precious Balm, to 'noint,
With Choicest care, each Choicest Joint,
Or, if I might, I would be fain,
About thy neck the Happy Chain,
Or, would it were my blessed hap,
To be the Lawn o'er thy fair pap,
Or would I were thy Shoe to be
Daily trod upon by thee.

Here observe the excellent, and truely Clubical wit of this ancient Poet, in the extravagant novelty of the thoughts contained in this Ode, he wishes himself a looking Glass, a gown, a well, an ointment, a Chain, a piece of Lawn and an old Shoe, and all for the Sake of his mistresse's touch, supposing at the same time, in order to make his piece || somewhat consistent, that these parts of his mistresse's dress and things, applied to her body, were beings Capable of Sensation; our moderen Poet Waller, has Imitated this kind of wit pritty well, in his little poem upon his mistresse's girdle.[21]

[14]

20. This poem appears as "The Wish to His Mistress" in Abraham Cowley's (1618–1667) translation, in *Anacreon Done into English out of the Original Greek* (Oxford, 1683), 39–41, which Hamilton refers to in the paragraph preceding the next Anacreon poem below. Hamilton's translation is shorter and sweeter.

21. Edmund Waller (1606–1687) was a member of Parliament who, by turns, opposed and supported Charles I, Oliver Cromwell, and Charles II; he headed a plot (1643) to seize London for Charles I, for which Cromwell banished him. A precocious poet, he early wrote a complimentary piece, "His Majesty's Escape at St. Andere," one of the first poems in English literature to employ the heroic couplet, and numerous other poems that gained him Dryden's

fellow, His Successor Killigrew[16] In the Reign of K: Charles I, was a very noted Punster, for one day, talking of Dr Laud,[17] who was ArchBishop of Canterbury, and a man of small limbs || and diminutive Stature, said, wittily enough, as he said Grace at the kings table, *Great Laud to God, and little Laud to the Devil,* in Xenophon's *Sympos:* we find one Philip, a buffoon or Jester, brought in to make Sport.[18] [11]

We learn from Herodotus, and other ancient Historians, that the Ægyptians of old dealt very much in Hieroglyphics,[19] which were certain figures of animals and things cut upon obelisks and Stones, by which, they expressed not only the passions, virtues and vices, but whole Sentences and discourses were thereby signified, to such readers as studied and understood this Sort of orthography, this I take to be the Origin of the *Rebus,* an exercise of wit, much in use among the moderens, and much relished by people of the best fashion and taste. Among the Ancient Romans, C: Julius Cæsar, and Marcus Tullius Cicero, have both left behind them, Specimens of their Skill in the Hieroglyphical Rebus; The first, because it was expressly against a Roman Law, for any private man to stamp his Image upon the public money, struck an Elephant on the money which he Coined, the Word *Cæsar* in the punic Language signifying that animal; The latter to express his name Caused Marcus Tullius, and the figure of a Vetch to be Cut upon a monument, *Cicer* in Latin, signifying a Vetch.

Among the ancient Greek poets, we find a Species of wit prevalent, which bears a distant resemblance to our moderen acrostic, many curious pieces of this Sort have been transmitted to posterity for upwards of two thousand years, modelled in the Ingenious figures, of altars, axes, eggs, wings and Shepherd's pipes; The cutting, Shaping & paring of Sillables, words and letters, to make an aggregate of verses resemble those things, discovers an exquisite fancy, and exhibits, not only an extraordinary genius, for Pyndaric poetry, resembling pritty much the Dutch Taste of shaping ever greens in Gardens into the forms of Gyants and wild beasts, but shows a quaint turn for designing. Our Moderen Accrostic and anagram, bear some Sort of resemblance to this ancient humor, these modelling men and womens names Into variety of different Shapes, and forms, and exciting new Ideas, by creating words and Sentences, out of the different arrange- [12]

---

16. Thomas Killigrew (1611–1682) was a playwright, master of revels, and the famous court fool known as "King Charles's jester."

17. William Laud (1573–1645) was archbishop of Canterbury (1633), supported Charles I in his struggle with the Commons, and enforced uniformity in the Church of England before being impeached for high treason in 1640 and beheaded in 1645.

18. See Xenophon, *Symposium* 1.11, for the entrance of Philip.

19. See Herodotus 2.106.

piece of humor in the Sage, afforded matter of laughter and wonder for nine days at least, to all the young Smarts and rakes of these times; Even Socrates himself, the Gravest, and most Sedate of all the Athenians, a person who had the divine testimony of the Delphian Oracle for his wisdom, condescended at times to mix in the Company of Strollers & Comedians, to drink off his glass with roaring Companions, and in frolicksome Clubs, to write fables, and tell witty tales. The known Story, of the Scurvey usage this Philosopher met with from Xantippe his wife, the most perplexing termagant and Vixen, that ever Contended for the Breeches, evinces this wise man's Strong turn for wit and humor; after he had received, as an Eplogue to a Smart Scolding bout, from the hands of that Invincible virago, the discharge of a well replenished pispot right on his head, he said pleasantly, wiping and stroaking || down his head, face, hoary beard and garments, and shaking his reverend ears, that nothing was more common, after fierce winds, and loud Claps of thunder, than heavy Showrs of Rain.[11]

The Spartans of old seem to have been a very merry and facetious people, and to have taken much pleasure in Jocular conversation, with which, doubtless, punning, or the paragrama was blended, for we find, that they were Instructed, even by their Law giver Lycurgus to pay worship and offer Sacrifice to the God of Laughter,[12] and were taught to exercise their wit in tricking of and stealing from their neighbours, and it is a very ancient Saying

Risum divum atq3 hominum Æterna Voluptas.[13]

The Romans at their feasts and entertainments used Jesters, and Drolls, for Sueton tells us, Cap: 61, *in deliciis habuit Tiberius Scurras & adulatores,*[14] which mode was but of late observed by some of our British Monarchs, no Longer agoe than the Reign of K: James I. who kept a Buffoon called Archie,[15] (as is thought) on account of his being a very arch

---

11. Hamilton is probably recalling the account by Diogenes Laertius of Xanthippe's argument with Socrates, in which, after she scolds him, then drenches him with water (not urine), he wisely informs his companions that he knew her thunder would end in rain (*Socrates* 2.35).

12. Plutarch, in his life of Lycurgus, relates the story of how Lycurgus (probably fl. 9th century B.C.), the traditional founder of Sparta's constitution and the "good order" it created, dedicated a statue to the god of laughter.

13. "Mirth of the gods, and the eternal pleasure of men." Hamilton's Latin appears to be purposely elliptical or garbled, redolent of Lucretius 1.1.

14. Suetonius (ca. 70–ca. 160) was a Roman historian and author of *De viris illustribus* (biographies of Roman authors, including Terence, Horace, and Lucian) and of *De vita Caesarum* (the lives of the Caesars from Julius to Domitian). The passage that Hamilton attributes to him, meaning "Tiberius had buffoons and flatterers among his favorites," does not appear in *De vita Caesarum*, although a story about taking a jester's advice does.

15. Archie Armstrong (d. 1672) was a jester in the court of James I.

of those Sort of Slips and mistakes, commonly laid to the charge of our moderen Hibernians, while the Great Cyrus solaced himself, with laughing at these facetious Stories, a certain morose fellow, among his Colonells, named Aglaitadus, who did not relish such Club Jokes, asked Cyrus with a Sneer, if he believed these Stories for Truths,—why not answered the prince? what temptation can there be for Inventing them?—none other replied the Cynic, but to make you, their prince laugh and be merry, and, in this they flatter you, and show themselves to be a vain ostentatious Sort of fellows ‖ and sempiternal coxcombs.—Not so fast Sir, replied Cyrus, dont call these good humored people ostentatious, there is no ostentation at all in good humor, the Character is only applicable to such as set themselves up for wiser and richer than nature and fortune has made them, by which they propose to reap to themselves some advantage, but, as for such merry fellows as endeavor to excite laughter and mirth in others, without any view of gain to themselves, or design of detriment to others, I see no reason, why these may not with greater propriety be called Civil and facetious Companions,[9]—Thus did the Great Cyrus approve of mirth and merry Companions, such as are to be met with in our well Constituted Clubs. [8]

Athens, which was of old, a celebrated Seat of the Muses, brought up, like an Alma mater, several Celebrated punsters, Riddle-me-ree men and repartee masters, The Learning of the Sceptics, (who had a Considerable School there) consisted chiefly in clenching and playing upon words, nor could their arguments, such as they were, finely spun, and nicely wove, (much like those of our moderen Metaphysicians,) be Successfully Carried on, without frequent use of the dubious and dowble meaning, and the quaint quibble, and the Signal of victory, was to turn the Laugh upon their adversaries, which was effected by short Significant Saws, and Subtile traps ‖ in discourse,—to Learn this art, among other quaint and humorous accomplishments, Xenocrates shut himself up for several years, in this famous nursery of arts & Sciences, and returned again into the world an accomplished wit; a notable Instance of humor and drollery he exhibited, by getting to bed for one whole night with Lais, the famous Corinthian Courtezan, after whom, all the world, at that time ran mad for Love, or rather lust, and got up from her in the morning fresh and fasting, and, as Good a maid (as he affirmed himself) as when he went to bed with her;[10] this odd [9]

---

9. This story appears as Hamilton tells it in Xenophon's *Cyropaedia* 2.2.11–13.

10. Xenocrates of Chalcedon, a disciple of Plato and head of the Academy from 339 to 314 B.C., was known for his austerity and self-control. Lais was the name of at least two celebrated courtesans of Corinth and, eventually, a generic name for courtesan. Among Hamilton's sources for the story are probably Valerius Maximus (4.3.3), where she is identified as Phryne, and Diogenes Laertius (4.2), who identifies her as Phryne in some accounts, Lais in others.

[6] Immediatly after the General flood, we find Ham, exercising his wit upon his Sire Noe, passing Scurvy Jokes on his drunkeness and Nakedness, for which the old fellow, who seems not to have understood railery, bestowed a hearty curse on him and his posterity. There are many Instances in the Sacred archives, of great feats done by wit and Ingenious finnesse, Jacob tricked his brother Esau out of his birthright, Imposed upon his father Isaac, so as to get the blessing from his elder Brother, but herein he was asisted by the wit and Subtilty of a woman, ‖ vizt: his mother Rebecca, and, we often find, that the artifice and wit of a woman, excells all other, except only, that of the Old Serpent himself,—The same Jacob we find afterwards tricking his uncle Laban out of his cattle, by a quaint device, and Joseph, one of his Sons, ammassed a great fortune in Ægypt, by Interpreting of dreams and Riddles, many more Instances might be mentioned of the like nature, but for brevity's Sake, I pass them over, only, I cannot help mentioning one more, and that is, of Sampson, Judge of Israel, whom we find puzzling the Philistines with a riddle, to answer which he allowed them Seven days, but all their wit could not unriddle it, 'till they were privatly Informed of it by his wife, who had wormed the explication out of her husband, under a promise (as is supposed) of Secrecy, and, which the Silly Husband, putting too much Confidence in that promised Secrecy, explained to her, merely to satisfy her curiosity, a passion very Strong in most, if not all of the fair Sex, the Philistines, by the help of this explication, to the no small astonishment of the Riddle maker, explain the Riddle, upon which, Sampson turns punster, and tells them, that if they had not ploughed with his heifer, they never could have expounded his riddle, this

[7] shows us the great antiquity of Riddles and puns, and from thence ‖ we may draw this conclusion, that women in all ages of the world, were bad Secret keepers.[8]

Having given that preference, which is due to Sacred History, I now proceed to exhibit some Specimens of wit, out of profane writers, to wit, Poets, Philosophers, and Historians.

Xenophon, one of the oldest greek Historians, in his *Cyro-pædia*, Introduces a dialogue, or conversation, between Cyrus and Hystaspes, one of his officers, which seems to be exactly after the humor and genius of our moderen Club Conversations; there a humorous account is given, of several enormous blunders, committed by a good natured fellow, out of an overreadiness to please, and obey Command, which blunders savor very much

---

8. Hamilton's biblical allusions are to Gen. 9:22–25 (Ham); Gen. 25:29–34, 27, 30:31–43 (Jacob); Gen. 41 (Joseph); and Judg. 14:12–18 (Samson).

The works of mortal men, as well as mortal men themselves, are subject to the universal ravager Time, metal, Stone, Bricks, wax, Barks of trees, parchment and paper, upon which Substances, men have, by certain Characters communicated their thoughts to one another and transmitted them to posterity, are liable to be changed into other Substances, and pass thro' certain Transmutations by the Irresistable operations of fire, water, air and the worm, hence it is, that many valuable works of an- ‖ tiquity are now irrecoverably lost, it would therefore be a fruitless labor in any Historian, to pretend to give a distinct, accurate and full account of such Transactions and occurrences as would properly come under the purview of History in the Earliest ages of the world, the most that can be done therefore, in this case, is, to gather as much as we can from Traditions, and fragments of writings, accidentally preserved, and deliver them as such, without attempting, as many Romantic Historians have done, to create forms of our own fancy, to fill up the blanks, and thereby palm upon the world, a hideous collection of fables, without either meaning or moral. [4]

In this short history of wit, therefore, I shall not pretend to gull my readers, or Impose upon their understanding, by presenting them with a circumstantial account, as a true and Genuine one of the State of wit, before the General Deluge, or for many centuries after it.

The first, and most ancient wit that we hear of Indeed is the Devil, who outwitted mother Eve, and persuaded her by certain quibbling Speeches and dowble entendres, to eat that Cursed *Apple* (as some call it) which empoisoned her whole posterity with Sin and misery. The admirable Milton, who has given us a beautiful and finished poem upon this very Subject, Introduces this ancient Rebel and deceiver, very much in Character, by making him an expert punster, we find him Calling gun powder in the act of Explosion, *Terms of Composition,* a breast work ‖ of cannon, *an open front,* [5] and the confusion of the opposite Squadrons upon their discharge, he calls *a quick result to these terms.*—This is as plain punning as can be, and (if true) the most ancient Instance that is extant of it; In answer to these puns, Belial, his brother Devil, produces a whole String of them, he calls the Shot, or Bullets, *terms of weight of hard contents,* which being *urged home stumbled many,* and those who receive them right, *had need to understand well from head to foot,* and, if not well understood, they serve *to show when the enemy does not walk upright;*[7] These ancient diabolical puns (with all reverence be it spoken to our Celebrated Poet,) would pass exceeding well, among our greatest Club wits and punsters in Christendom.

---

7. *Paradise Lost,* 6.611–627.

witness the celebrated Tom Brown,[2] that prime Bard of Grubstreet, and that yet unparallelled paragon, Mr Ward, author of that Ingenious, smart and elegant piece, Intituled the *London Spy,* and those Inimitable poems ycleped *Matrimonial Dialogues,*[3] where the *Basse Meurs* of mankind, or rather the *Bathos* of the mobile, are wonderfully display'd and exposed, in a Manner highly picturesque—as also the Inimitable Tom Durfey, the Learned and Anonymous author of *Laugh and be fat,*[4] and a hundred others of the same Class and kidney—and let us not forget that most Solemn and Sublime Bard Sir Richard Blackmore, Singularly favored by his patron Apollo, in the arts of Medicine and poetry, stiled by some, the British Homer, author of a poem, which, had it had Justice done it, ought to have been called the *Arthuriad,*—who wrote an Ingenious Satyr on wit;[5]

[3] But not one of all these famous Grubeans, tho very || equal to the task, has deigned to give us a detail historical and critical, of that distinguishing faculty of human Nature. I therefore, tho altogether unqualified, for so arduous an undertaking, and only a Star of the Second or third magnitude, among these Illustrious sons of Hesperus, shall humbly presume to lead the way, and open a door for abler heads, and Sharper pens, to treat this curious and new Subject.

That wit and humor must be as ancient as mankind is a truth, which I believe none will Impugn, since it is allowed by all, that these are the very faculties, which, in a most conspicuous manner, distinguish man as a reasonable animal, from animals of an Inferior class, to whom Philosophers, out of their very deep penetration into the *mens Brutorum,*[6] have not been pleased to allow the least Scantling of Reason, but have represented them, as actuated by a certain *Je ne sçai quoi,* Sort of Impulse or Instinct, or rather moved, by a necessary and Irresistable Impetus, like Automotory Machines.

2. Thomas Brown (1663–1704) was an English satirist and author of the famous "I do not love thee, Dr. Fell" (see below) and *Amusements Serious and Comical* (London, 1700), humorous sketches of London life.

3. Edward "Ned" Ward (1667–1731) was an English author of Hudibrastic doggerel verse and coarse, humorous prose, including *The London Spy* (London, 1698–1703), the observations of a countryman in London, *Hudibras Redivivus* (1705–1707), and the *Marriage Dialogues* (1709), expanded in 1710 into *Nuptial Dialogues and Debates.*

4. D'Urfey (1653–1723) was an English author of numerous songs, satires, and farces, remembered most for his comedies, *The Campaigners* (1698), *Madame Fickle* (1677), and *The Virtuous Wife* (1680), and for his collection of songs and ballads, *Wit and Mirth; or, Pills to Purge Melancholy* (London, 1719–1720). *Laugh and Be Fat* (ca. 1625) was the work of John Taylor, the Water Poet.

5. Blackmore (d. 1729) was physician to Queen Anne and author of several lengthy poems and essays, including *Creation: A Philosophical Poem Demonstrating the Existence and Providence of God* (1712), *Prince Arthur: An Heroick Poem* (1695), and *An Essay on Wit* (1716).

6. "The mind of brute beasts."

The History of the Ancient and Honorable Tuesday Club

[1]

Book VII

From the Creation of the Chancellor &ct: To the Introduction of the Conundrums, and the Chancellor's trial.

Chapter I

General History of Conundrums, Puns, Riddles, Rebuses, Anagrams, Chronograms, Posies and Acrostics.

Upon my entry into the Second Volume of this most prodigious History, methinks I am like one embarked, and ready to lose himself in a vast and Boundless Ocean, where I shall be tumbled about and carried to and fro, over restless and rolling waves, and scarce find any landing place, or the least prospect of *terra firma,* or land mark, whereon to fix my roving view. I am now to engage in a very Intricate and difficult task, That is, to give a short and summary History of wit and Humor, short and summary, I say, because I shall only skim the Surface, and take the Cream as I go along.

An accurate history of wit is what has been much wanted in the republic of letters, for, after Indefatigable Searches, and diligent Scrutinies, I cannot find any single author of our Clubical Class, that has treated this Subject in an historical manner, Some Indeed among the moderens, particularly the celebrated Mr Addison, has but Just transiently handled the Subject, and treated on Clubs *en passant,*[1] giving a few Specimens of the humors and Conceits of these nocturnal assemblies, others more on the Clubical lay have exhibited curious collections of witty Sayings and Jests,

[2]

---

1. Hamilton is alluding especially to *Spectators* 9, 34, and 89.

	Orator, appointment of a Rustic Club, poetical Entry of the Laureat 415	
Chapter VI.	The Genearchy of the Club, Records mutilated and defaced, Letter from the agent in Great Brittain, remonstrance of the Laureat against Colley Cibber 432	
Chapter VII.	Arguments In Club against the Genearchy, Club Search warrants Issued, Speech of the Orator, New Club Song Composed by Crinkum Crankum Esqr . . 446	
Chapter VIII.	Death of Sir Hugh Maccarty Esqr, and the Mutilation of the Frontinbrassian articles .455	

Book X

From the Death of Sir Hugh Maccarty Esqr, & the mutilation of the Frontinbrassian Articles, to the End of the Chancellors Rebellion, and Civil wars concerning the Great Seal.

Chapter I.	Dissertation on Civil Commotions and Rebellions, their Causes & effects, & the way of preventing them 464
Chapter II.	Beginning of the Chancellor's Rebellion, and the Great Commotions and uproars in Club 480
Chapter III.	Effects of the Commotions and uproars in the Club, and the decathedration of his Lordship 488
Chapter IV.	Clubical Interregnum, usurpation of the Chancellor, Eclipse of the Club, *Carmen Seculare,* and alteration of the Calendar by the Club 496
Chapter V.	Mournful Ditty of the Club to the Tune of Chevy Chace, concerning the great Clubical Rebellion, enquiry into the Defacing of the Club Records 509
Chapter VI.	Special Embassy of pacification from the Longstanding members to his Lordship, and the Conference that happened thereupon 520
Chapter VII.	Heroic Episode by the poet Laureat on his Lordship's displeasure, and other, trivial matters 528
Chapter VIII.	Happy Conclusion of the Great Rebellion, his Lordships happy restoration, and his cession of the Title of Lord president 536

	homony by the Orator, History and Character of Coney Pimp Front-in-brass Esqr, account of Sir Hugh Mccarty Esqr 274
Chapter IX.	Sublime Letters of Coney Pimp Front-in-brass Esqr, to his honor the President, Disputes in Club, the Frontinbrassian Articles drawn up and assented to, new titles conferd on the president, Creation of a Serjeant at arms, Coney Pimp Frontinbrass Esqr made agent and Plenipo for the Club in America 286
Chapter X.	Coney Pimp frontinbrass Esqr, his patent Sealed and delivered, *Lugubris Cantus* by the Club, dispute upon Law 2d not determined 299
Chapter XI.	Sublime poetical Letter by Mr Attorney Spyplot, Tryal and Condemnation of Jonathan Grog Esqr, Heroic Letter of Sir John, Speech upon Noses by the orator, Grand Ceremony of the Capation 308

Book IX

From the grand Ceremony of the Capation, to the death of Sir Hugh Mccarty Esqr, and the Mutilation of the Frontinbrassian Articles.

Chapter I.	Of the Importance and Significancy of ensigns and Symbols of authority and State, and a dissertation concerning the Balance of power 333
Chapter II.	Usurpation of the Chair, by Mr Protomusicus, disputes in Club, Speech of the Orator to his Lordship the president, Celebration of the Sixth Anniversary, Aniversary Speech and Ode, Music by Signior Lardini 349
Chapter III.	Special Club, by order of his Lordship, the President, Fourth Embassy of the Triumvirate, Commissions granted to the Triumvirate, poetical address of the Triumvirate 391
Chapter IV.	Florish of Mr Protomusicus, neglect of the Secretary, Speech of the Orator, congratulating his Lordships escape from an Imminent danger 400
Chapter V.	A heroic poem by the Laureat on his Lordship's miraculous Escape, Eulogium on the Chancellor by the

Contents 3

Chapter VIII. Admission of a Longstanding member, Deputy Chancellors Commission, Rustic Club, Seizure of the Great Seal, disputes concerning it, Impeachment & acquittal of the Chancellor 163

Book VIII

From the Impeachment and acquittal of the Chancellor, to the Grand Ceremony of the Capation.

Chapter I. A modest proposal for the new modelling and Improvement of our Modern Theatre 181

Chapter II. Club Conundrums, letter to the agent in Great Brittain, Conundrum on the Chancellor by Mr Comus, Tryal of the Secretary, a new Record Book ordered, more Club Conundrums 202

Chapter III. State Questions resolved in Club, new Record book delivered by the master of Ceremonies, Secretaries Conundrum Condemnd 219

Chapter IV. Extraordinary Club held by his honor the president's Special Order, third Embassy of the Triumvirate, election of a Triumvir, Eulogium on a Triumvir Deceased, Club Conundrums, Opinion of Doctor Rhubarb on the Secretaries Conundrum, abolition and expulsion of the Conundrums, Sublime Speech by the Secretary, the Secretary Created Club Orator 230

Chapter V. Tryal of Mr Attorney Spyplot, Tryal of Tunbelly Bowser Esqr, General Search for the Great Seal, repeal of the order of Sederunt 132 245

Chapter VI. Speech of thanks to his honor the president Delivered by the orator, abuse of the great Seal, Specimen of the Clubs regard for religion & charity, Tryal of the Secretary 255

Chapter VII. Spurious Letter from the Agent in Great Brittain, Commencement of the History of Box No 1. and the Delivery of the Cap of State, with a Speech by the Orator, address to the Chancellor by the Orator 264

Chapter VIII. Disputes Concerning the Cap of State, Speech on

Contents of the History of the Ancient and honorable Tuesday Club

Volume II

Book VII

From the Creation of the Chancellor, to the Introduction of the Conundrums, and the Chancellor's tryal.

Chapter I.	General History of Conundrums, puns, Riddles, Rebuses, Anagrams, posies and accrosticks	1
Chapter II.	Solemn delivery of the Commissions, hot disputes thereupon, Club Letters	51
Chapter III.	Report of the Committee for Commissions, patent for an agent in Great Britain, Epicædion of the Club, Institution of the Conundrums	62
Chapter IV.	Election of a Longstanding member, Sublime Letters, petition and remonstrance of Mr Protomusicus, Complaint of Sir John, Club Conundrums and Jests	72
Chapter V.	First Embassy of the Eastren Shore Triumvirate, tryal of Mr Protomusicus, prerogative Laws passed, Club Conundrums, accrostic by the poet Laureat, motion for a Cap of State	86
Chapter VI.	Poetical Epistle from Mr Protomusicus, fatal Comusian Conundrum, Commotions in Club, remonstrance of the protesting members burnt, several Club Conundrums, Second Embassy of the Triumvirate	102
Chapter VII.	Arrival of the Club medals, Celebration of the 5th Anniversary, Ode and Speech on that occasion, Anniversary Music by Signior Lardini	123

History of The Ancient and Honorable Tuesday Club

From The earliest ages Down to the present times.

Volume II

Containing the Transactions of that Society from Sederunt 120, to Sederunt 178, Inclusive, with all the dialogues, Speeches, poems, addresses, Embassies, altercations and battles that occurred in that Course of time.

Autor Noster, Ita describit heroas Clubicos, ut Incertus hæreat Lector, an eruditi magis, fortesve Essent, Corporisque potius aut animi viribus pollerent.

Written in the year 1755

FRONTISPIECE

General Congregation of Caps. vid. pag: 264

The History of the Tuesday Club

Volume II

LIST OF MUSIC

Anniversary Ode for 1750 107
    Air for His Honor 108
    Minuet for His Honor 108
Anniversary Ode for 1751 278
    Club March against Sir Hugh Maccarty 289
Minuet for Sir John 293

LIST OF ILLUSTRATIONS

Frontispiece xii
Club Conundrums Introduced 61
Club Squabble concerning Sir John's Commission 81
The Tuesday Club Medal 93
The Second Grand Anniversary Procession 98
Division of the Theatre 147
The Honorable Nasifer Jole Esqr Wears the Cap of State 202
Coneius Pimpeius Frontinbrass the Great 211
Private Conference of Frontinbrass with the Honorable Nasifer
    Jole Esqr 216
Prim Timorous Esqr, Serjeant at Arms to the Tuesday Club 223
The Genius of the Tuesday Club Appearing to the Longstanding
    Members 230
Jonathan Grog Esqr under Custody of the Serjeant at Arms 238
Grand Ceremony of the Capation 246
Third Grand Anniversary Procession 267
Grand Rehearsal of the Anniversary Ode 269
Signior Lardini, Musician *Con Stromenti* to the Tuesday Club 277
Narrow Escape of the Secretary 298
The Tragical Night Adventure in His Lordship's Bedchamber 307
Genearchy of the Club 326
His Lordship Encounters Sir Hugh Maccarty's Coffin 343
Deputation of the Club to His Lordship 386
A List of the Present Members of the Ancient and Honorable
    Tuesday Club of Annapolis, and Their Order of Serving 399

CONTENTS

List of Illustrations viii
List of Music ix

The History of the Ancient and Honorable Tuesday Club, VOLUME II

    Contents 2
    Book VII 7
    Book VIII 137
    Book IX 251
    Book X 347
    Index 401

Publication of these volumes was made possible by a grant from a fund established by DeWitt Wallace, founder of Reader's Digest.

The Institute of Early American History and Culture
is sponsored jointly by the
College of William and Mary and the
Colonial Williamsburg Foundation.

© 1990 The University of North Carolina Press
All rights reserved
Manufactured in the United States of America

The paper in this book meets the guidelines for permanence
and durability of the Committee on Production Guidelines
for Book Longevity of the Council on Library Resources.

Printed in the United States of America

94 93 92 91 90   5 4 3 2 1

Library of Congress Cataloging-in-Publication Data

Hamilton, Alexander, 1712–1756.
    The history of the ancient and honorable Tuesday Club / by
Alexander Hamilton; edited by Robert Micklus.
        p.   cm.
    "Published for the Institute of Early American History and
Culture, Williamsburg, Virginia."
    Includes index.
    ISBN 0-8078-1851-8 (set: alk. paper)
    1. Annapolis (Md.)—History—Colonial period, ca. 1600–1775—
Fiction. 2. Tuesday Club (Annapolis, Md.)—History—18th century—
Fiction. 3. Maryland—History—Colonial period, ca. 1600–1775—
Fiction. I. Micklus, Robert. II. Institute of Early American
History and Culture (Williamsburg, Va.) III. Title.
PS763.H35H57 1990
813'.1—dc20   89-30768
                                                                        CIP

The History of the Ancient and Honorable Tuesday Club

BY DR. ALEXANDER HAMILTON

VOLUME II

Edited by Robert Micklus

PUBLISHED FOR THE INSTITUTE
OF EARLY AMERICAN HISTORY AND CULTURE
WILLIAMSBURG, VIRGINIA

BY THE UNIVERSITY OF NORTH CAROLINA PRESS
CHAPEL HILL AND LONDON

The History of the Tuesday Club

OHIO UNIVERSITY LIBRARY

Please return this book as soon as you have finished with it.

method of admitting members	58
Whitefield (George) effects of his preaching on female hearers	28
distinguished by his action	241
Whitehall palace, Converted to Stables	115
Whores, of Quality, dangerous to Jest with	505
Wig (old) despicable	23
William (conqueror) how he acquired the Crown of England	47
Wisely, (Oldham) made an honorary member	197
his Speech in Club	394
Will with the wisp, a Club worthy	132
Wines, (deep red,) their effects	39
Wisdom, a Speech on it by the president of the Tuesday Club	270
Wits, modern	463
Wit, an active principle	286
must have a crust to Chaw	ibid
Women, Superannuated, despis'd	23
Woman, falling from her horse, a Story of one	482
Women haters in the Tuesday Club	145
Worship, paid by Certain priests to Certain nuns	116
Words, their pronounciation by people of Rank	271
Worthies (clubical) neglected by historians	129
Wood (Benjamin) draws the Club badges	359
Wranglers, enimies to Clubs	72

X

Xenophon, Compared to the author of the history of the tuesday Club	5

Y

Yule, or Jule, the Scots name for Christenmass	253

Z

Zeno, his doctrine of motion	468
Zeuxis, an ancient painter	21
Zoroaster, an ancient astronomer	224

Index

deprive the honorary members of
their votes 506
dispute about abdicating the chair 514
Lose their Master of Ceremonies &
dep: Secretary 515
reject the Secretaries proposal to
write their history 530
write to the Eastren Shore
Triumvirate Ibid
Expell the Extraneous regular
members 537
Introduce hieroglyphical
Characters 539
Receive their Great Seal 545
Create a Chancellor 565
become a State Club 567
Turbulent Spirits, their means of
rising 497
Turlupin, a french droll 218, 470
reviver of punning ibid
Turlupinade, a club term 218
Turkish Empire, its ensign 259
Twopenny ale, its virtues 44
Tythes, of divine authority 138

U

Ugly Club, described 117
Qualifications of its members ibid
Club room described 119
members, ragged philosophers 120
Their officers 122
first president ibid
Characters of their principal
members 123
their Records lost 122
Mode of Conversation 126
Dissolution 127
Universe, comparatively a triffle 299
Urim and Thummim, what 561

V

Vanity, Ingrafted in man 238
how apparent ibid
Chief amusement 298
Varnish (Major) member of the
Redhouse & ugly Clubs 120
Verses, (ancient ones,) repeated at the
admission of members of the
whin bush Club 59

Verses on a baltimore bard 187
Verses on the backward beauties of
the fair Sex by Bavius 189
Viar (St) a Club worthy 136
Vices, favorite ones, no Jesting with
them 505
Virtue, the best blazoning 559
Virtuosi, tenets of upstart ones 455
Etymon of the word 271
Vices of parents, affect the character
of their children 484
Vision, how accounted for of old 26
Virginia knights, a modern order 260
Vulvaris (St) a Club Saint 136

W

Walpolize, what 433
Wants, Imaginary, created by Luxury 234
Warble (Ignotus) made an honorary
member 197
Summond by the badge
Committee 258
Speech to the Club on
Chearfulness 250
Introduces the toast of the king
and Club 447
Warburton (Doctor) compared to
the author of the history of the
Tues: Club 24
We[alt]h, it's Importance 7
Wel[sh], an ancient people 16
Wh[ig Son]g in the whin bush Club 54
Whi[gs, s]trict ones in the Tuesday
Club 173
Whig and tory toasts 488
Whin bush Club, Its history 43
Their Records Lost ibid
Number of its members ibid
Traditions concerning it ibid
Their Liquors drank in Club 44
their Total Eclipse 47
Records recovered ibid
Qualities necessary to procure
admission into it 48
how Governed 51
Time and place of meeting changed 54
Members whigs ibid
at the battle of Bothwell Bridge 53
meet in the whin bushes ibid

Luxury of Dress Introduced	224	Improve their Epistolary Stile	355
make a ball for the Ladies	225	Celebrate their Third Anniversary	358
Conference between the president & Secretary	ibid	Dissentions at it	359
		petition against the box	363
Taxed to raise a fund for Charity	236	dispute thereon	366
bad policy in taxing the honorary members	ibid	General protest	367
		Dissentions	ibid
President made Chief treasurer	237	vote out the Box	368
pass the first penal law	238	meet in the Room of the Ugly Club	ibid
Speech making Introduced	242		
bestow two more privileges on the president	251	give up their power of electing officers	375
first Anniversary Committee	256	Their Inconstant temper	378
first Anniversary Celebrated	ibid	yield the privilege of *Conge-de lire* to the presid:	385
not more triffling than other Societies	300		
		Elect 4 Long Standing members	386
badges Instituted	258	Confirmation Ceremony	406
Badge Law passed	ibid	give up the power of electing Longstanding members	407
Their Imprudent Conduct	ibid		
members make Congratulatory Speeches to one another	273	allow the president the title of Lord	418
create a Champion	273	apply for an act of Grace	ibid
Resolve to exclude Speech making	274	Cause of their Declension	420
Create a Master of Ceremonies	273	Silver badges & Seal appointed	421
Their Bacchinalian dance	275	blank commissions printed	426
discord concerning the Scots rebellion	ibid	allow their president the title of most Illustrious	424
compard to a Ship	277	Create a poet Laureat	426
Bold Stroke against the Club box	278	become subject to bribery and Corruption	420
Create a Speaker	279		
and a musician	283	Create an Orator	430
Introduce Epistolary writing	286	printed ballots Introduced	428
adopt the title of high Steward	288	Second Anniversary Committee	438
Celebrate their Second Anniversary	293	Celebrate their fourth anniversary	447
		first Anniversary Ode	449
first grand anniversary procession	ibid	Compared to the ancient Greeks	452
Saluted by Coll: Bumbasto	ibid	first power over the American Clubs	453
Second penal Law passd	317		
Preposterous proceeding	319	disputes concerning the toast of the King & Club	488
Letter of thanks to Merry Makefun Hon: memb:	326	Reject the Scheme of a box	493
		allow the president the title of Right honorable and highness	494
Indict and try Mr Protomusicus	331		
dispute about a punch ladle	337		
dispute about the Treasurer	340	Spirit of Liberty appears	496
dispute about serving at the anniversary	341	abolish the office of Speaker	ibid
		discover the Secretarys plots and policy	499
Compared to the Thessalonians	343		
Their Slavish State	348	a dreadful hubbub in club	ibid
give their president a badge of State	351	exclude dowble entries	503

Index 441

Arts and Sciences rendered
    obscure by them   ibid
Temple of Solomon, a den of Thieves   114
Temperance, heroic, an Instance of it   148
Terms of art, used by Gypsies   215
    by courtiers   ibid
Theologues, use terms for what   211
This here Club (the Stile explaind)   217
Thoughtless (Capt: Giddy) a Satirist   190
Timber Countenance, what   230
Time, Idly squandered   viii
Time killers, what   ix
Time, compard to a glutton   31
    to an Anthropophagite
    To a camelion
    To a Salamander   } ibid
    to an ostridge
    wasted in triffles   viii
Timerous (Prim) a member of the
    Redhouse Club   102
    admitted to the Tues: Club   387
    his character   388
    Introduces Hieroglyphics   539
    his Secrets of State with the
        president   ibid
Titles, their Importance   7, 488
Toasts, polite bawdy ones   105
    Test Toasts   488
Tobacco, its qualities   44
Tomlinson (Luke,) president of the
    whin bush Club, deposd   51
Tongue, a member much concerned
    in clubs   556
    cousin german to the ear   457
    a mischief maker   457
    betrays the follies of its owner   ibid
    a Spout of Scandal   459
    raiser of discord   ibid
    destructive of Clubs   ibid
Toys, a Curious arrangement of   158
Tramontane knights of Virginia   261
Tradesmans Club, antidiluvian   37
    Their first president   Ibid
Treasury of the whin bush Club,
    how Collected   53
Triffles, often amuse the Great   298
    vanity, a Synonom for triffle   ibid
    Enumeration of them   299
    a Superlative triffle   ibid
Truth, the Best Guide to Historians   iv
Trullus, who   133
Trumpery, religious   212
Tubal Cain, the Sound of his hammers,
    first hint towards Instrumental
    music   29
    president of an Antidiluvian Club   37
Tuesday Club, as old as time   7
    To be traced in a direct line from
        the Deluge   40
    It's constitution endangered by
        Luxury   55
    its first Settlement and Institution
        in America   141
    is the whin Bush Club translated
        to America   ibid
    first planters of it in America   141
    its first Sederunt at Annapolis in
        Maryland   ibid
    first Laws there   142
    modelled on the plan of the whin
        bush   ibid
    its Simplicity & happiness at its
        first Institution in Annapolis   143
    passes the Gelastic Law   151
    Introduces Balloting   168
    Introduces punning   170
    Expells the Batchellor's Cheese   171
    Loyalty of its members   173
    Cause of their prosperity and
        Stability   ibid
    their amorous disposition   174
    seized with a *furor poeticus*   175
    encounter the Baltimore Bards   176
    Their Compositions Compared to
        excrements by Bard Bavius   183
    poetical Genius on the Decline   190
    danger of their becoming a State
        Club   194
    purchase a leaden Tobacco box of
        Nasifer Jole Esqr   195
    pass the exclusion Law   196
    number of Regular members
        limited   ibid
    honorary members Indefinite   ibid
    pass the Catch law   196
    meet once a fort night   197
    give up their liberty and for what   202
    Chuse a perpetual president   204
    List of members regular and
        honorary, in 1745   208

appears in his robes	285
his political motion	284
his office abolished in Club	430
Spectacles, an Impediment to vocal music	162
Speech making, Itch of, flowing from vanity	239
public places for it	ibid
why not at first prejudicial to the Tuesday Club	266
Speech, on the passions by Serious Social	265
from the Chair, destructive of the balance of power in the Club	269
of Sir John at his trial	412
Speeches, Congratulatory, Set ones	273
expelld the Tues: Club, except on particular occasions	274
Spirit, Inward, what	28
Subtile	ibid
gross	ibid
Spiritous liquors, their effect in Clubs	ibid
Spit boxes, used in the Tu: Club	146
Spyplot (Jealous) a member of the red house club	102
of the Tuesday Do:	128
his Speech of Statesmen and State Clubs	194
presents the Club with a money box	238
a Club orator	265
accuses the Secretary of State plots	283
pleads for Sir John at his tryal	413
Thanks the Secretary for his anniversary Speech	447
is chairman of a box Commtee:	491
his proposals relating to the orator's office	495
his prophesy accomplished	567
Spyplot (Jealous Junr:) his admission to the Tues: Club	385
Criticism on his letter to the president	517
Spruce (Capt: Seemly) a good Clubsman	141
first deputy president of the Tuesday Club	243
his Eulogium	509

States, compard to the Hydra	116
Stage, Itinerant orators	239
Stars & garters, badges of honor	259
Stentor Snuffysnout, summond to the Tuesday Club	328
gives evidence against protomusicus	332
Steward family, their hereditary Indefeasible right to the Crown of Great Britain proved	47, 79
Stiffrump (Aminadab) a Story of him	27
Strong liquors, excite religious disputes	350
Stiles (John,) a Club worthy	30
Stile, carless and Jantee, an example of it	493
Stuttering boy, a Story of one	479
Stylphon, the Philosopher, a Story of him	466
Subordination in human Society, a wise provision	543
Superstitious people, enimies to Clubs	70
Surly people, ditto	ibid
Swash (Joshua,) member of the ugly Club	125
his character	ibid
Swarthy (Capt:) member of ditto	120
Swagbelly (Swillum) made an hon: member of the Tues: Club	316
Swallowbeak (Dr Samuel) Taster of the Redhouse Club	106
Sycophants, persevering ones	554
Sylvius (Capt: Samuel) by a Speech lays a hubbub in the Tuesday Club	500
Sympathetic power in Clubs	26
Syllabub Club, its description	85
Consists of female members	86

T

Table Conversation, Impertinent	149
wisdom of the Tues: Club in excluding it	148
Tantarabobus, a Club worthy	134
Taxes, why Imposed	234
Technical terms, an Impediment to learned Studies	209
their origin uncertain	210

Index

his answer to the triumvirates letter	ibid	of the Commission Committee	567
his eulogium on the Triumvirate	533	Sneers of the Secretary	437
is suspected of Jacobitism	540	Snuff taking, it's use	104
Turns Sycophant	544	Social (Serious, Capt:) a good Clubs man	141
his Speech at the delivery of the great Seal	558	a Club Orator	265
		Leads a Bacchinalian dance	275
proposes to elect a chancellor in the Club	563	Leaves the Club & why	327
		his character	ibid
Sederunt, a Club term, Explained	217	Society, Improves the Rational faculties	551
Selden, a Story quoted from him	138	& arts and Sciences	ibid
Self love, a reasonable one	556	a Type of heaven	ibid
Senses, given for good purposes	455	Socrates, compared to Solo neverout Esqr	251
Serjeant at arms in a Club, his qualities	222	acts the part of a droll	342
Severus (Empr:) a Story of him	167	equivalent to many triffles	298
Severus (Alexander) fond of whelps & pigs	167	Classed with Clubical worthies	311
		His tale to Phædras	ibid
Shakespear, (Quoted)	301	a Comedian	342, 465
Shuttlecock (game) likened to Satyr	504	a rider of hobby horses	ibid
Shields and Scutcheons, their use	261	ridiculed by Alcibiades	Ibid
Shoes (old) despicable	23	Solitary people, Enimies to Clubs	69
Signs (Adam and Eve Conversed by them)	30	Song, a Scots one sung by Mr Sly	192
Silenus, a Club Companion	41	by Capt: Social	196
Skeletons, Illustrious ones	263	by Mr Neverout	281
Slavery, Caused by Luxury	56	by ditto	314, 315
Sleep, caused by Club orations	259	favorite one by Mr Comus	423
by want of a Stock of Ideas	ix	by the Musician	360
by dedicators	vi	by the president	340
Sleepers (Seven) obscure worthies	137	Sophist, a Story of one	468
Sloan (Sir Hans) an admirer of bawbles	159	Sorray (Abbe) a poor poet	476
		Souls, some think women have none	164
Sly (Smoothum) his Character	128	Sourface (Surly) member of the Red house Club	102
Infected with the poetical itch	175	Spaniards, an ancient people	16
becomes a Club orator	249	why fond of duelling and cock fighting	13
Characterised in the presidents Speech	272	Their Tawny hue, whence	39
made Master of Ceremonies	273	Spanish women, why fair	ibid
first high Steward of the Tuesday Club	288	Spartan Commonwealth, its character	10
Congratulatory Speech to the Secretary	313	Speakers of the house of Commons, an Establishd Custom among them	204
his deputy presidentship disputed	374	Speaker of the Tues: Club, created	279
Leaves the Club	430	his privileges	ibid
writes to the Club	437	resigns his office	280
his Speech at the anniversary 4th	451	resumes it	281
Snap (Huffman) admitted to the Tuesday Club	385	made a State officer	284

Satiety of power, not in nature	234	his Second anniversary Speech	294
of Riches Ditto	ibid	accuses the musician	314
Satyrs, members of ancient Clubs	33	first Corruptor of Epistolary	
Satire, false, what	462	writing in Club	329
true, what	ibid	is council for Protomusicus at his	
Compard to a game at Shuttlecock	504	trial	322
Scald miserables, (fraternity of) their		Third anniversary Speech	360
Solemn procession	255	accused with his deputy of a misdemeanor	393
Sceptics, enimies to Clubs	72	his trial and acquittal	403
modern, their doctrines	566	his Speech at Sir John's Trial	414
Scots arms, an Interpretation of their motto	257	his protest	ibid
Scipio, a merry fellow	342	gives the president the title of Lord	418
Scholastic doctors, how Employed in the times of Ignorance	469	undergoes the penalty of the gelastic Law	ibid
Scriptural passage, explain	96	his policy and turn for corruption	420
Scots, an ancient people	16	offers to present the Club with a Seal	421
why fond of leaving their Country	83	moves for Silver Club badges	ibid
Scribble (Loquacious) a member of the ugly Club	126	promotes bribery and Corruption	433
of the Tuesday Ditto	128	prompts a Satyrical motion	437
Infected with the poetical itch	175	sneers at his honor the president & Prim Timorous Esqr	ibid
made Secretary of the Tuesday Club	191	his Speech of thanks to the president	448
his character	ibid	his answer to Smoothum Sly's Speech	452
Vide Secretary		his fourth Anniversary Speech	443
Seal (great) of the Tuesday Club, arrives	545	His Speech on the Box	482
it's uses	562	his ambition frustrated	495
Seceding Bretheren in Scotland, their Synodical Clubs	40	Compard to a Turkish Janisar Aga	497
excommunicate one another	ibid	to the dog in the fable	ibid
Secret Services, what	234, 269	his Machiavallian policy	ibid
Secretaries (Clubical) their qualities	222	moves for an asistant in his office	498
Secretary of the Tuesday Club, the first Speech maker	242	his designs therein	ibid
his character	ibid	excites a dreadful Club hubbub	499
his first Speech to the Club	244	Specimen of his Skill in Oratory	521
is gravelled & how	ibid	made honorary orator of the East: Shore Triumvirate	522
his Speech on Clubs, at the first anniversary	258	his Speech on Mr Muddy's leaving the Club	527
quarrels with the president	275	Turns plagiary	372
Conference with the president on a ball cake	225	his designs on the Chair	373
his eulogium on Drawlum Quaint	278	accused for it	408
resigns his office	280	his answer	ibid
resumes it	281	moves for writing the Clubs history	530
his vindication	284	is Refused	ibid

his character	ibid	Rendezvous, private places of	239
verses wrote under his picture	432	Renitency, necessary in Civil Governments & Clubs	267
his Speech of thanks to Jonathan Grog	434	Repeating watches of the times	307
Do: to the President & Secrety	ibid	Resentment, a Clubical one	508
his Speech to the Chair	502	Riches, their advantages	22
made deputy Secretary	503	never satisfy the possessor	234
Intends to hold Club in the School Room	511	Robin Goodfellow, a Club worthy	133
		Roe (Richard) a Club worthy	131
Cleans it out and writes the Letter of Cats	512	Romances, what	4
		Roman Republic, its fate	11
Resolves to resign his places & leave the Club	513	Rome (city) why holy	15
		Romans, Ruin'd by Luxury & ambition	57, 419
Leaves the Club	515	Roman Empire, its ensign	259
		Round (Broadface) made an honorary member	225

R

		his Speech on Charity	250
Ramsay (Allan) poet Laureat to the whin bush Club	59	Routs, polite modern assemblies, excluded from the Class of Clubs	85
Rational Nature, what distinguishes it from the brutal	ix	governed by the Ladies	ibid
		their amusements	461
Rawhead & bloody bones, vide Hobgoblin		Royalist Clubs in Annapolis	87
Reading and Study, mental food	3	extinct	100
Reason, founded on Law, not always current	514	Royalists, a Club party	94
		arguments against the Levellers	ibid
Records of the Tuesday Club, end of the first book	324	Rulers, their Imitation of Inferiors, politic and popular	103
proposal to burn them	501	Rumbo, it's effects	350
Rejected	ibid	Rump Committee, examine the Records of the whin bush Club	47
Red house Club, it's rise and Constitution	100	Rural Deities, their origin	33
governed by presidents	101	Rural Clubs, very ancient	ibid
Its first meeting	102		
Laws	Ibid	## S	
Eating, drinking and Snufftaking	103		
a bad name on that account	104	Sanctity, emblems of it	264
Conversation	ibid	Sancho (Brother to the king of Navarre) a Story of him	88
disputes on Religion	105		
method of talking bawdy	ibid	Sages, Clubical, Compard to Socrates	342
Tolerates all Religions	106		
Seat of Goverment changd	108	Saints, rags of their apparel valuable	22
dissolution	112	Their Images made of the same materials with those of the pagan deities	114
Club house turnd to a Nunnery	114		
Religion, to be altered by degrees	121		
misplac'd In Idle rites & ceremonies	212	obscure ones	135
Lucrative to priests	211	prejudicial to physicians and apothecaries	136
productive of more Sects than any other thing	252	Their Days encourage Idleness	252

Protomusicus of the Tues: Club,
    Created   281
    his privileges   282
    an air vender   312
    rewarded with air   ibid
    accused by the Secretary   ibid
    In danger of losing his place   319
    his character   ibid
    criticises on Sir John Oldcastles letter   322
    disputes with the Mr of Ceremonies   323
    Information Lodg'd against him   325
    an Indictment ordered agt him   327
    plays the fool & how   330
    Is Indicted by the Speaker   ibid
    Sentence & Condemnation   333
    his vindication from principles of natural philosophy   334
    accused by the Speaker   338
    Condemn'd & punished   ibid
    muddles the president with Strong beer   339
    contends with the Secretary about the chair   348
    suspected of Jacobitism   361
    his method of arguing by a horse laugh   366
    protests against a resolve of the Club   370
    sleeps in the Presidential Chair   378
    his sleepy disposition in Club   380
    master of the modern polite Phraze   494
    promotes discordant Sounds   500
    Characterized by the Eastren Shore Triumvirate   520
    a parallel between him and the president   ibid
Psalter of Cashel, an Irish legend   17
Public Judgement of Courtiers   341
Puffendorst (Don Fart-in-hando) his essay on farting   30
Pun, Cousin German to Conundrum   218
Punning, first Introduced into the Tuesday Club   170
    (modern,) the Rise of it   469
    advances men to high offices   476
Punch Ladle, a dispute Concerning one   337
Punch, its effects & Character   44
Puzzlementation, a Club term   216
Puzzlementationful, a derivative from it   i
Pythagoras, the first who assumed the name of Philosopher   304

Q

Quacks, their motives for Speech making   239
    obliged to Mr Jack pudding   240
Quaint (Drawlum) admitted to the Tuesday Club   153
    his amorous Disposition and Strange adventure   174
    Turns Satyrist   190
    Becomes a Club Orator   246
    his Speech in Club   ibid
    is voted a dead member   247
    provokes the president   250
    Chairman to a Sham Committee   275
    made Speaker of the Club   279
    an air vender   312
    rewarded with air   ibid
    accused by the Secretary   ibid
    Congratulates the Mr of Ceremonies   313
    his Stile Imitated by the Secretary   330
    Congratulated by the Secretary   353
    his Speech Concerning the box   368
    Leaves the Club   373
    vide Speaker of the T: club
Quakers, how Inspired in their Silent meetings   27
Quaker, a Story of one   ibid
    distinguished by action   241
Quality, (persons of), not distinguished by nature from other men   263
    Compared to pigmies, Skeletons and Dwarfs   ibid
    who apt to be mistaken for such   263
    their alterations of the common pronounciation of words   271
Qualities of great men   ii
Queries concerning Swan necks   186
Quirpum Comic, admitted to the Tuesday Club   385
    made Mr of Ceremonies   431

Index

attends the 3d anniversary	359
Physical terms, fit to conjure the devil	214
Physicians, great users of obscure terms	213
why they use them	215
Pickle herring, Serviceable to quacks	240
Pigmies, Illustrious ones, who	263
Pineal Gland, the Seat of memory	147
Pimps (noble ones) not to be Jested with	505
Plagiarism, of the pulpit	239
of the Stage	ibid
Planetary System, Comparatively a triffle	299
Plato's man, what	466
Pleasant, (Slyboots) admitted to the Tuesday Club	153
contributes largely to the box	272
studies the Gelastic Law	367
is angry with the president	ibid
his Character	399
acts out of Character	ibid
Poet Laureat of the whin bush Club, his office	53
Poetæ minorum Gentium, their Scribble destructive of the peace of Society	184
Poets, Chang'd to grasshoppers	311
Poet, Clubical, a Translation by one	342
Poets, the better for being kept poor	426
Poetical Jargon, its mischievous effects	177, 184
Poetasters, described	177
Polyhistor (Dr) admitted an honorary member	168
Politicians, (State ones)	194
Polypharmacus (Dr) his cure for the poetical itch	182
Poor Scholar, a Story of one	480
Pope of Rome, why he antecedes all the Rom: Catholic princes	14
a witty Saying of one	480
pox'd by the whore of babylon	485
dangerous to Jest on him	505
excommunicates the K: of Spain once a year	525
Pope (Alexander, poet) of a remarkable make	77
Stories of him	477, 478
Popish Religion, whence	529
Posture of an orator, described	247
Portico Clubs, what	41
Power, not to be supported without friends	234
Praise, a tribute due to the Great	542
Presbyterians, how they Celebrate Christenmass	253
how they Commemorate the martyrdom	254
Clubical disputes Concerning them	350
Presbyterian maxims	480, 485
Presidents of Clubs, when first elected	33
President of the Tuesday Club, Compar'd to Apollo	34
President, Synonoms of that office	34
whether originally *Jure divino*	ibid
Tyrants	35
Their arguments for Tyranny	36
Likened to gods	ibid
Privy councellors to the Devil	ibid
Dangerous to Jest with them	505
President of the Tuesday Club, his character, as a pres:	519
Compared to the Sun	i
Presidential, a Club term	216
Preachers, female ones, distinguished by their action	241
Priests, how enriched & supported	22
Devotees	116
Privy Councellors to the devil, who	36
Princes (theatrical orators)	239
Privilege, a new one given to the Chair in the Tues: Club	237
Procession, 1st grand Anniversary one	293
Prodigy, conjectures Concerning one	109
seen before the dissolution of the red house Club	110
Their portentous nature disputed	111
Prologues, (modern) little Connected with the pieces to which affixed	518
Prophesy, an old one	115
Proposition, a Self evident one	125
Propositions and political maxims at Court, what	341

assumes the Chair at the 2d Anniversary	294
his extreme complaisance	344
Dangerous precedent set by him	ibid
not Imitated	ibid
opposes the Chair	344
gives up the title of Oldcastle and why	361
speaks against the box	367
Compared to Hercules	369
his character	376
his obscene toast in Club	378
Indicted for the same	414
Indicted for drinking the first toast after Supper	409
Speech at his trial	412
Bullies the president and Club	417
drinks again his obscene toast	ibid
Speech concerning the Canopy of the Club Chair	429
advises the Burning of the Records	501
Political Conference with the president	540
Old woman, an emblem or hieroglyphic	109
how saved from Lightning	108
Old women, contemptible	23
Old Standing member, a Club term, whence derived	217
Orations, the greatest difficulty in framing them	222
Orator of a Club, his qualities	ibid
Orators, Lucrative ones	239
Orators of Clubs, prompted by vanity	240
Orators, why dangerous in a public & in Clubs	266
Chang'd to Grasshoppers	311
Orator, Created in the Tues: Club	430
Duties of his office	436
Orator Comus, becomes a Creature of the Chair	490
Embassy sent him from the Club	492
his cunning and policy	ibid
operates Secretly to Introduce a Club box	492
Resigns his office in Club	495
appointed to Resign his office every Club night	525
compared to the Pope and Doge of Venice	ibid
Orators office, dropd in the T: Club	496
Orators of Tyburn	240
Orthography of great men	271, 363

P

Pan, a Club Companion	33
Panegyric, a difficult province	3
Panthæon at Rome, Transform'd	114
Papists, their effrontery	255
(Presbyterian)	54
Paracelsus and followers, rise from a fog	470
Parallel between Emperors and presidents of Clubs	302
Parsons, good Drinkers	89
Passions, gelastic, not to be Commanded by others	206
Pasquelino De Marzis, master of Ceremonies to the whin bush Club	50
Patric (St:) a Club worthy	135
Patrons, (noble ones) esteemed unerring Judges	320
not exempt from the fury of Critics	321
Partiality to ones own profession, an Instance of it	246
Pedantius, member of the ugly Club, his Character	123
Penal Law, the first one passed in the Tues: Club	238
Petticoat interest, it's great power	49
Petticoat pensioners	484
Petition, female one to the President of the Tuesday Club	523
Petition against the Club box	363
Petty princes or heads of Clans, who Compard to butchers	12 ibid
Peripatetic Philosopher's observation	542
Philalethes (Dr) publishes a Nostrum	180
Philosopher, whence the name and by whom first assumed	304
Philosophy, true, what	305
Phraze (Coll: Courtly) made an honorary member	173
His panegyric on the Ladies	ibid

Index 433

Musician of a Club, his qualifications 220
Musicians, changed to Grasshoppers 311
Mysteries, ancient, like our modern
    free masons 41

N

Nations, contend for antiquity 45
    ancient & modern disputants 8
    how aggrandized 9
Natural & nincompoop, their
    difference 520
Negroes, whence they derive their
    color 38
Neilson (George) a description of his
    person 76
    his dress 77
    principles 78
    Religion 79
    Learning 80
    Skill in music 81
    narrowly escapes a drowning 83
    place of Birth uncertain ibid
    Reason of his coming to America 84
    sets about reforming the Clubical
        Constitutions in Annapolis 90
    sends out Scouts 91
    conjectures concerning his
        behaviour 92
    his great prudence & patience ibid
    Compard to Achilles 93
    raises the Spirit of party in the
        Annapolitan Clubs ibid
    espouses the party of the Levellers 97
    his Sufferings for Clubical liberty 98
    his Battle with the Royalists ibid
    is thrown in the kennel 99
    besieges the Club house ibid
    raises the Seige ibid
    Neilsonists named from him ibid
    hotly persecuted by the royalists 100
    founds the Redhouse Club 102
    Chuses a privy Council ibid
    erects the presidential
        Government ibid
    his policy ibid
    First president of the Red house ibid
    takes Snuff to help contemplation 103
    his death foretold by prodigies 109

    his death 111
    his eulogium ibid
Neverout (Solo) his admission to the
    Tuesday Club 195
    his turn for poetry 175
    his Sophism borrowed from Isaac
        Bickerstaff Esqr 247
    his Genius to Rhime & Satyr 248
    Becomes a Club orator 249
    Compared to Socrates 251
    is chairman to the badge
        Committee 256
    is made Chief musician of the
        Tuesday Club 283
    vide protomusicus
Newton (Sir Isaac) an observation of
    his 25
Neutrum Quid, a remedy for the
    poetical Itch 182
Nincompoop, what 520
Nimrod, president of a Club 39
Nine (the number) unlucky 549
Noe, president of a Club 37
Nonsense, set off with a proper
    action, taking 241
Nokes (John) a Club worthy 30
Novels, what 4
Nuns, a particular Sort 114
Nunneries in England, turned into
    bawdy houses 114

O

Oaths, used in the Redhouse club 107
    of Prim Timerous 389
Ocularis, a Club Saint 136
Ode, anniversary 449
Offices, high ones, filled with fools 220
    Their punctual execution, not
        necessary in a public ibid
    Low ones, best executed 221
    necessary in Clubs 219
Officers, high, compar'd to low 220
    necessary in Clubs ibid
    of State, danger of multiplying
        them in Clubs 277
    addicted to Ceremony 314
    tenacious of precedence ibid
Oldcastle (Sir John) his privileges 274

Maryland Gazette, Lampoons the baltimore bards	173
Master of Ceremonies, his proper badge of office	222
Created in the Tues: Club	273
The duties of his office	435
Maxim, a true one	234
false ones	ii
Mayor, (Lord) of London's Anniversary	255
Mean fellows, who	460
honorably promoted	ibid
Mechanic arts, Subservient to virtue	559
Medals of the Tuesday Club, struck at London	538
Members of Clubs, Communicative, and how	26
Members of the Tuesday Club, not philosophers	198
Philogasters	ibid
Members of note, who	219
Members of parliament, their motives for Speech making	239
Members, list of them in the Tuesday Club may 14, 1745	128
list of Regular & honorary members, 26th Novr 1745	208
List of do: in may 26th 1747	296
List of do: in may 16, 1749	454
List of do: in decemb: 5th —49	568
Members of the Tues: Club, their Character	519
Memoirs of persons of quality, flatulent Diet	4
Men, Superannuated, dispised	23
Mentularis, a Club Saint	136
Merry Andrew, of use to Quacks	240
Methodist preachers, distinguishd by their action	241
Mevius, a Baltimore bard	176
his Epigram on Swan necks	185
Mecromegas, his Lubberly book of Philosophy	310
Mind, the human, an active principle	ix
Ministers of State, their methods of Corruption	234
Miracle, an Irish one	135
Miracles, by what means wrought	22
Mirth, the best physic	72
the Nepenthe of Homer, Venus's cestis and Helen's bowl	342
not repugnant to Philosophy	ibid
worshiped by the Spartans	343
Misunderstanding In Clubs, what	40
Mites in Cheese, might Claim honor from antiquity of family	20
Mobile, it's unruly nature	456
Modern maxims of philosophy	ibid
amusements	461
Mohock Club, like the Ancient bacchinalians	41
Monarchies, great machines	220
Moral Conversation, Inconsistent with modern politeness	461
Moral qualities, compared to accidental, and natural ones	7
Moral virtues, Insufficient to support the grandure of States and empires	10
Morality, depreciated by priests	212
necessary to make a good Xtian	485
Moors, why expelld Spain	39
Motely (Prattle) member of the Ugly Club	120
his character	124
first Secretary of the T: Club	152
his amorous disposition	174
Infected with the poetical Itch	173
Gelastic Law first executed on him	152
goes to England	191
Muddy (Roundhead) admitted to the Tuesday Club	489
Confirmed	491
his Speech to the Club	490
Ditto	492
a Loud Talker	491
Desires to be struck out of the list of the members	508
Speech at leaving the Club	526
made a Longstanding member non-resident	528
suspects the Secretary of Jacobitism	540
speaks against Law 42d	542
Has the Gelastic Law Executed upon	ibid
Music, it's antiquity proved	29
Musical Club (antidiluvian)	37

Index

from Slyboots pleasant to the pres: 397
from Huffman Snap to do: 399
from do: to Sir John 401
from Quirpum Comic to the
    president 424
From the President to the
    Secretary 425
From Laconic Comus to the
    anniversary Committee 440
from the anniversary Committee
    to the President 439
From Do: To Laconic Comus ibid
From Protomusicus to the
    President 493
From Roundhead Muddy to the
    President 494
From Jealous Spyplot Sen: to
    Ditto 506
From Sir John to Ditto 508
From Jon: Grog to Ditto 510
From Jealous Spyplot Junr To
    ditto 516
From the Eastren Shore
    Triumvirate to the Club 517
From the Club to the Eastren Shore
    Triumvirate 530
From Huffman Snap to the
    President 536
From ditto to Sir John 537
From Prim Timorous to the
    President 538
From Capt: Comely Copper nose
    to the Secretary 545
From the Secretry to the pres: 548
From do: to Sir John 550
Levellers, a Club party 94
    Their arguments against the
    Loyalists ibid
Liberty, Bartered for triffles 199
Lyes, a good home Staple 484
Lightning, method to avoid it 109
Limberloins (Spruce,) Secretary to
    the ugly Club 122
Literary kitchens 4
    food ibid
Little Breeches, who 248
Long (Thomas) member of the ugly
    club 120
Long robe (Gentlemen of) their
    motives for Speech making 239

Longstanding member, a Club term 51
    whence derived ibid
    false derivation of it ibid
Lord, the advantage of being made
    one 484
    dangerous to Jest with 505
Love ditties, flatulent food 4
Love and lovers, a Club Speech on
    them 249
Low Club party 36
Lottery, Philadelphian, swallows up
    the Tues: Club box 370
Lubentia Dea, by whom worshiped 343
Lumber, Aristotelian, what 470
Luxury, its first rise in the T: Club 224
    crepd in by degrees there 143
    methods taken by the Club to
        prevent it 142, 147
    pernicious effects of it in eating
        and drinking 149, 150
    a Theatrical description of it 170
    not to be supported without
        means 234
Liars, enimies to Clubs 72
    not to be believed when speaking
        truth 487
Lycurgus, a doating Lawgiver 10

M

Maccarty (Sir Hugh Esqr) a Club
    worthy, and president of a great
    Imaginary Club 140
Macdonals, (Scots family) their
    antiquity 18
Machiavalian maxims 497
Macfun, (Mungo) a member of the
    Redhous Club 100
    a Club droll 106
Machiavalian politics 93
Mahometanism, it's rise 528
Makefun (Merry) made an honorary
    member 291
    makes the Club a present of
        English beer 324
    The Club's Letter of thanks to him 326
    a triumvir 518
Mammillaris, a Club Saint 136
Mankind, to be led not driven 121
Mares, Impregnated by the wind 18

K

Keating (Doctr) an Irish historian	16
Kentish men, and men of Kent, their difference	153
King of Spain, formerly excommunicated yearly by the Pope	525
Kingdoms, compar'd to the Hydra	116
King and Club, a toast	447
Kings of Clubs, first made by Conquest	87
Kings, first movers in monarchical machines	220
dangerous to Jest with	505
Knighthood, (orders of) their ensigns	259
Knights of the Garter, their origin	26
Knights (virginian) of the horse Shoe	261
Knight of the Tues: Club, created for burning the Records	274, 501
his political conference with the president	540
Knights (ancient) who	551
(modern) who	ibid
Knight of the T: Club, reviver of ancient chivalry	552
Knowledge of ones Self, how gained	306
Knowledge of mankind, ditto	ibid

L

Laconic (Prim) made Hon: member	316
Ladies, disputes for precedency among them, not yet decided	99
Epithets applied to them in Club toasts	106
Express themselves by contrarieties	117
The first toasted after Supper in the Tues: Club	145
Great Regard paid them by the Tuesday Club	ibid
In the turk's Seraglio, fond of Cats	167
ancient manner of entertaining them	226
Their favors, how gained	483
Lambs wool, the drink of the Junto of wits at Batchellor's hall	186
Lamech, president of a Club	37
Language, Cause of its fluctuation	271
Lælius, a merry fellow	342
Lardini (Signior), admitted an honorary member	208
Performs a piece of music at the 2d anniversary	295
Laughing, preferable to Sneezing	72
Cheaper than drinking	186
Law, Gelastic	151
Law, founded on reason	514
Law (common) why an Intricate Study	264
Lawyers, seldom plead *in forma pauperis*	131
much addicted to obscure terms	213
conceal the mysteries of their profession from the vulgar	215
compared to merchants	485
Orators at Westminster hall	240
Learning (human) triffling	299
Leatherlungs (Vocifer) orator of the ugly Club	122
Letter to the City of Annapolis by bard Bavius	182
Letter-writing, Introduced into the Tuesday Club	286
Letter from the Bards at Batchellors hall to Roughby Ranter	187
Letters, Clubical, from the president to Smoothum Sly	288
from ditto to the Secretary	287
from ditto to the Speaker	291
from ditto to Laconic Comus	292
from Sir Jno: to the President	321
from the master of Ceremonies to the president	323
From the Club to Merry Makefun	326
from the Secretary to the presd:	328
from the president to Smoothum Sly	346
from Jonathan Grog to the Pres:	349
from the Secret: to the pres:	354
from ditto to Sir John	356
from Sir Jno: to the Presid:	362
from the Secr: to the pres:	371
from Jon: Grog to ditto	370
from Sir Jno: to protomusicus	377
Condolatory, from the Club to the president	379
From Jonath: Grog to ditto	391

Index 429

Extolls Mr Broadface Rounds
   Speech on Charity & why ibid
is privileged to serve always on the
   Club Anniversary 251
has two more privileges granted
   him ibid
becomes a club orator 270
his eloquence dangerous 268
delivers a Speech from the Chair 270
agrees with Doctor South 271
follows the modern mode of
   altering the common
   pronounciation of words ibid
Quarrells with the Secretary and
   Club 275
is Suspicious of the Secretry 279
has another privilege given 285
Introduces Epistolary writing in
   the Club 287
Creates the title of high Steward 288
his motives for it 289
Thinks himself above Club law 316
procures a law to augment the box 317
his notions of Charity 326
his Indulgence to the Club 336
Contributes for a punch ladle 337
is muddled with Strong beer 339
His generosity 341
Compard to Scipio & Lælius 343
Compard to Lycurgus ibid
made Sole treasurer 344
objects to the validity of Law 36th 348
has a presidential badge given him 351
Rejects the box petition 363
is afraid of Sir John 367
delivers up the Box 368
discovers the designs of the
   Secretary 373
gains the privilege of electing
   officers 375
Secrets authentic papers 376
Retains but one State officer ibid
Receives a condolatory epistle
   from the Club 379
appoints his deputy by Special
   Commission 381
gives Commissions of *Conge-d'elire* 383
and appropriates that privilege to
   himself 384
sends orders to the Club 386

his Speech to the new members 406
seizes the whole power of electing
   Long Standing members 407
acquires the title of Lord 418
Refuses an act of grace to the
   members ibid
takes the title of most Illustrious 424
receives a message from the
   anniversary Committee 439
answers the Committee's message 440
Enforces the toast of the king and
   Club 488
orders dowble entries 490
appoints a box Committee ibid
Takes the title of right honorable
   and highness 494
prevents the burning the records 501
is guilty of a breach of Law 508
appears in a mourning badge 509
objects to the Club's being held in
   the School room 511
Is angry with the letter of Cats 512
swears to leave the Club ibid
recants 513
Refuses to send a deputation Ibid
grants the petition of the Single
   females 523
gets a new privilege 525
Specimen of his eloquence 532, 533
political Conference wt Sr John 540
settles the Toast of the K: & Club 547
Compar'd to a cornucopia 548
Creates a Club Chancellor 565
Jolliday, anniversary, what 252
Ireland, settled before the flood 16
saved from the General deluge
   and how 17
The Island of Saints ibid
Irish, a very ancient people 16
fond of overgrown bulls 13
Chronology exceeds all 16
Italy, Inhabited by a mungrel people 45
Jubal, Inventor of music 29
president of a club 37
Judgematical, a club Term vi
Jule, the Scots name for Christenmass,
   derived from Julius Cæsar 253
Jugglers, (modern) their diet 95
Justice, how soonest procured in
   courts of Law & equity 485

Jehoiakim Jerkum, an advertiser	183	Inclination to the fair Sex	ibid
Jerusalem, why in the first rank of Cities	13	Esteem & generosity to Cats	ibid
		His way of educating them	165
Jestor and Jestee	504	Instance of his compassion	ibid
Jests, not to be particularly pointed	462	discipline of his cats	ibid
when offensive	504	apology for him	166
Tragical effects from them	505	a friend to mankind	167
Jew (Wandering) a Club worthy	136	of a Suspicious temper	ibid
Inanimate beings, valued for their antiquity	21	Introduces Luxury into the Tues: Club	168
undervalued for Ditto	23	His first Step towards the presidential Chair	172
Indictments, Clubical, against Mr Protomusicus	331	Introduces rack punch in Club	171
1st against Sir John	409	Introduces the Catch of the *Great bell of Lincoln*	196
2d against ditto	414		
Innovations, dangerous	121	Introduces an Iced Cake	198
Injuries, repayd with Injuries, unchristian	486	Compared to Julius Cæsar	201
		His elegant entertainment and Club Supper described	ibid
Joan (pope) a Club worthy	139	his Cathedration	204
Jocke Frizzle, parson, a Story of him	482	His eulogium as President	202
John (Prester) a Club worthy	137	Tenacious of prerogative	ibid
Jole (Nasifer) prime of presidents	41	privileges granted him	205
admitted to the Tues: Club	153	Remarks on them	ibid
place of his birth	ibid	odd occurrens at his Cathedration	207
Education	ibid	ascends first the presidential chair in a high dress	223
Skill in mercantile affairs	154		
his character of a merchant and pedlar	ibid	likened to a Comet	224
		his clubical Character	228
Master of several arts	155	his foibles, ambition and love of power	ibid
his weak Side	ibid		
Taste in houshold affairs	156	positive & dogmatical	229
Skill in Gardening	ibid	Satyrical and Sharp	ibid
fond of nosegays	ibid	Inattentive	ibid
Taste in cutting out patterns for Sempstresses	157	fond of punctillios, ceremonies and badges of honor	230
Taste in setting a table for an entertainment	158	precise in his proceedings	ibid
		vanity his Chief foible	230
arraingement of his Shop toys	ibid	uneasy and dissatisfied when in highest power	ibid
Taste in dress	159		
military valour	ibid	his familiar way of talking of his club officers	231
his cure for the gout	160		
Iconography of his person	ibid	of a forgiving temper and patient	231
knack at Story telling	ibid	Industry and application to please the club	252
his religion	ibid		
Skill in music & divinity	161	made chief treasurer of the club	237
his collection of Sermons	ibid	Condemns Smoothum Slys Speech on popular liberty	249
an enimy to awkward punning	162		
his favorite Song	ibid	leaves the chair in a passion, & resumes it	250
Taste for antiquities	163		
fondness for old times	164		

Index

Heads, (empty ones) best adapted for
    drinking bouts   88
Hebrew (high priest) his Symbols   561
Heaven, the way to it mistaken   211
Heidagger (Mr) Compared to the
    Devil   47
Heralds office, a modern Institution   560
Heresy, a Species of it   470
Hermes, an ancient astronomer   224
Hieroglyphic, explained   539
    Introduced in the T: Club letters   ibid
High Steward, first appointed in the
    Tues: Club   288
    a cement between the State officers
        & officers of the commons   290
High Club men, a Sect   96
Hint, a delicate one   521
History, best kind of writing   I
    why it abounds wt falsities   ii
    a nourishing dish   3
    Compared to a Sirloin of beef   ibid
    how made Improving   xii
    Fictitious, a bad diet   4
    of the Tuesday Club, it's Character   4
    what uses it may be put to   74
    for what Sort of readers adapted   147
    Subject of it a farce   x
    not an uncommon one   ibid
    not more triffling than othr
        Histories   298
    Compard to other Histories   97
Histories, dry ones   47
    of Clubs and nations, parallel drawn
        between them   xii
Historians, useful writers   I
    Truth, their surest guide   iv
    Good ones scarce and why   2
    led by false maxims   ii, 42
    in their varying one from anothr
        compard to Irish evidences   iii
    Their faults   Ibid, 2
Hoadly (Bishop) a Story of him   481
Hobby horse Song   310
Hobby horse, used by Socrates   342
Hobgoblin, a Club worthy   134
Holy, the term, why applied to
    buildings & Inanimate things,
    not easily accounted for   14
Hollidays, what   252
Homer, his Intimacy with the Gods   34
    Imitated by the author of the History
        of the Tues: Club   92
Honesty, a Club Speech on it   246
    a rare thing   ibid
Honorary members, first made in the
    Tues: Club   144
    Taxed by the club   236
Honor, the Speediest way to procure
    it   483
    on what founded   548
Hope, an universal passion   553
    a flattering power   ibid
    destroy'd by despair   ibid
    often deceived   ibid
Horse Shoe, knights of Virginia   261
Horses, valued on account of
    antiquity of family or Stock   18
Horse, a consul of Rome   167
Horse Laugh, a Clubical method of
    arguing   366
Houses of office, beholden to
    Romance writers   6
Hubbub, a dreadful one in the T:
    Club   499
Human puppies & kittens, who   ix
Humdrum Clubs, what   26, 334
    in Moorfields   ibid
Humor, fitted for clubs, examples of
    it from antiquity   464
Hunters Club, antideluvian   37
    Lamech, first president   ibid
Hurly burly, description of a Clubical
    one   499

I

Jack with the Lanthorn, a Club
    worthy   132
Jack pudding, a quack orator   240
Jailors, necessary officers in a public   220
James I (King) Reigned by a party   93
    Story of him and his fool   473
    an enimy to tobacco   45
Ibrahim, an arab, antiquity of his
    horses family   18
Iced Cake, Introduced into the T:
    Club   198
Ideas, false association of them   328
    of Mr Pope   478
Jealousies, excited in the T: Club   235

Getula, vide Robin Goodfellow	
G——n (J—n) Secretary & privy councellor to the Sillabub Club	86
Glass, a few rounds of it an enlivener of wit	463
Globe of Earth, Comparatively a triffle	299
Goddess of mirth, worshiped by the Spartans	343
Government (forms of,) gradually to be alterd and Introduced	121
Government of the Tongue, a Subject much handled	458
Great Bell of Lincoln, a Club Catch	169
Grandees, above the duties of office	294
Greasing, (political) what	234
Great men, their forms to save appearances	204
supposed to have short memories	205
often of a peculiar make	77
subject to the ear itch	460
how to obtain their favor	483
Their favors, of what productive	484
familiarity with them dangerous	486
Their resentment compared to gunpowder pent up	515
To be given way to	516
Greatness of Capacity and greatness of office, distinct things	323
Great Seal of the Tues: Club, arrives	545
Greece, (modern) Inhabited by a mungrel people	15
Greeks, ruined by Luxury	56
Grecian Laws, compard to those of the Tuesday Club	452
Greenland Sentences, what	499
Grocers, beholden to the Authors of Romances	6
Grog (Jonathan) his collection of learned papers	133
his admission into the Tues: Club	344
his character and Iconographical description of his person	345
founder of the Grogorian Sect	ibid
promoter of Clubific felicity	346
his speech to the Chair	352
Compard to Rossius the Roman actor	354
his explication of S.S.C. on the South Sea coin	378
is the first commissioned deputy president	381
his Speech of thanks to the Secretary	421
his distich on the Club badge	426
his epigram on a gate	427
is made poet Laureat of the Tuesday Club	426
his uncommon genius for Doggerel verse	427
prints the Blank Commissions	426
proposes to print Ballots	428
His Stories and apothegms	479, 487
His witty devices	524
His poetical panegyric on the presidents entertainment	547
Draws a Scheme for a Club box	491
his first anniversary ode	449
made Master of Ceremonies	541
Confirms Philo-Dogmaticus	557
his poetical Speech to the Secretary	563
Grogorian, a Club term	216
Grogorians, a modern Sect	ibid
Groping Chair, used at the Installment of the popes	139
Grubstreet Rhimers, Serviceable to Tyburn Orators	240
Grumblings in the Tues: Club	235
Gundiguts (Dumpling) admitted to the Tues: Club	153
Compard to a Chair in a Country Dance	361
leaves the club	ibid
Gunpowder treason anniversary	355
Gyants, whence sprung	37
Gypsies, their terms of art	215

H

Haberdashers, beholden to Romance writers	6
Handicraft employments, vilified	12
Hangman, a necessary officer in a public	220
Harvey (Doctor) his opposers	38
Hasty (Joggle) admitted to the Tuesday Club	153
disputes with Capt: Spruce	175
leaves the Club	197

Index

Empires, their Rise . . . 11
  Compard to the Hydra . . . 116
  Compard to Clubs . . . 301
Englishman, the advantage of being born one . . . 50
Epictetus, a maxim of his . . . xiv
Epicurean Philosophers, the L: Standing members of The T: Club none . . . 198
Epicurus, his doctrines mistaken . . . 198
Epigram, on Swan necks . . . 185
  on a gate . . . 427
  Critic on the first . . . 185
  Critic on the 2d . . . 427
Epistolary writing, Introduced into the Tuesday Club . . . 286
Esteron (monsieur) his Strange food . . . 98
Eulogium, the best one in the mouth of fame . . . 559
European Nations, not ancient . . . 16
Excess in eating & drinking, cause of diseases . . . 199
Example of great men, its Influence . . . 103

F

Fabulous history, whence . . . 42
Faculties of the mind, given for good purposes . . . 455
Fame, the love of it in authors . . . 5
Families, how honor'd by Antiquity . . . 11
  how they become ancient . . . 12
  Great ones, how distinguished . . . 261
Farting (a Treatise of) . . . 30
Fairy tales, flatulent food . . . 4
Fasts and feasts, encourage Idleness . . . 255
Fat peer, a Story of one . . . 481
Favors of the great, produce fulsome compliments . . . 484
Female Charms, triffles . . . 299
Females (Single) their petition . . . 523
Ferithar, President of the whin bush Club, noted for a great brose eater . . . 43
Fethelmach, president of the whin bush Club . . . 44
  killd by Kenneth II k: of Scotland ibid
  Inventor of the Dishes of Cock a leekie & dads & blads ibid
Flattery, gains on all men . . . 155
and falshood, always Companions . . . 209
it's effects on great men . . . 2, 374
Fluter (Joshua) made an hon: memb: . . . 197
Foliot, vide Hobgoblin
Folio (Tom) a Club worthy . . . 139
Fools, put near the persons of princes . . . 472
  their use as advisers . . . ibid
  powerful ones, not to be Jested with . . . 505
Fool, a Story of one belonging to the K: of France . . . 473
  of one belonging to K: James I. . . . 473
  —Belong: to Bajazet I. . . . 472
Fool (natural), a Smart Saying of one . . . 474
Folly day (what) . . . 253
Fortune (bad) a term often used for Indiscretion . . . 554
Free masons, their Society eludes the Jaws of time . . . 11
  an ubiquitarian Club . . . 32
  Their mysteries misunderstood by the women . . . 51
  Their public anniversary processions exploded . . . 255
  Cause of their antiquity . . . 11
French Authors, like their Cooks . . . 4
Frizzle (Jockey) the parson, a Story of him . . . 482
Fuddle cap Societies, their origin . . . 57
Fulsom Compliments, Compard to fætid Stools . . . 484
Fundamental eructations, musical . . . 30
Furor poeticus in Baltimore, stopd by Jehoiakim Jerkum . . . 183

G

Gammon law in the Tues: Club . . . 142
Gate, an epigram on one . . . 427
  Critic on it . . . ibid
Gelastic law of the Tuesday Club . . . 151
Genius, an original one . . . 427
George (St) patron of England, a person of uncertain existence . . . 135
George a Green, a proverbial worthy . . . 241
Gew-gaws in religion, what . . . 396
Gesticulation in oratory . . . 241
George II, K: a Story of him . . . 474

Index

Demosthenes, the athenian orator,
    his qualities of an Orator   241
    a Story of him   ibid
    Ditto   266, 468
    how he Corrected an Impediment
        in his Speech   157
Deputy presidents of the Tues: Club   243
    form of their Commission   382, 390
Despair, enimy to hope   553
Devil, possesses beer Sots   334
    in a fools coat   470
    a general bear-blame   ibid
    a Stage buffoon   ibid
    master buffoon   471
    his office as such   ibid
    master of the Revels   ibid
    struts in buskins   ibid
    Ladies become familiar with him   ibid
Dictionary words among people of
    Quality   263
Diet, a Strange one   95
    Serious   461
Dignities, their Importance   7
Dioclesian (Empr:) turns Gardiner   158
Diogenes, a Solemn droll   464
    a Story of him   465
Discourse, Subjects of it wore out   460
Disputes, Clubical, their Importance   151
Disputers, enimies to Clubs   72, 151
Divines, compard to merchants   485
Doctrines, Good ones the worse for
    being put in practice   486
Doe (John) a Club worthy, his
    Character & history   131
Doge of Venice, his ceremony of
    marrying the Adriatic Sea   526
Dogmaticus (Philo) his observation on
    Mr Muddy   527
    his petition to the T: Club   554
    admitted to the club   557
    Receives the manuquassation   ibid
    is confirmed   ibid
    his congratulatory Speech to the
        president & Club   558
    made Chancellor, keeper of the great
        Seal, of the presidents political
        Conscience, State officer and
        privy councellor to the Chair   565
Domestic animals, the antiquity of their
    families   19

Domitian (Empr:) a fly catcher   159
Dont know howish, a Club term   426
Dottle (Anthony) choaked with
    Cheese in the whin bush Club   54
Drinking, more Costly than
    laughing   486
Droll, the Character, when
    dangerous   470
Drums, modern assembli[es],
    excluded from the Class of Clubs   25
    governed by the Ladies   85
    their amusements   461
Duelling, by whom Introduced   13
Dunciad, a prose one by Bard Bavius   182
Dwarfs (Illustrious)   263

E

Ear, a member much Concerned in
    Clubs   457
    nighly related to the tongue   457
    often suffers for its trips   458
    Loves to be tickled   459
    open to Scandal & the Secrets of
        othrs   ibid
Easter, a moveable feast, not yet
    settled in Christendom   253
    Cause of much bloodshed   254
Eastren Shore Triumvirate, whence
    derived   144
    first founded   453
    a centumvirate   529
    write to the tuesday Club   517
    answer to their letter   530
    Its great Increase   529
    Its praises of the president and
        Club Justly applied   543
Ecchoes of the times   307
Edinburg, by whom founded   481
Effluvium, a Subtile one in Clubs   26
Election, of presidents in Clubs,
    how old uncertain   33
    of Representatives   200
    swayd by Corruption & venality   ib[id]
Electricity, great discoveries relating
    to Clubs expected from it   27
Emperors and presidents, compard   300
    not safe to Jest with   505
Emulation of females, productive of
    Luxury   56

Index 423

moves for a Club box	490	Courtly (Curious) made an Hon:	
Vide Orator		memb:	316
Colley Cibber, his love of fame	5	Coxco]mbs (modern) their	
Colledge Club, described	89	Lear[nin]g and qualifications	307
Constables, necessary officers in a		[Creed], (Athanasian) an excellent	
public	220	Composition	160
Companions, three, a Story of them	482	[Crit]ic, on the president's Speech	271
Companion, a merry one, better		on Sir Jno: Oldcastles Letter	322
than a Song	342	[Cr]itics of the Tues: Club, Combine	
like a waggon to a tir'd traveller	ibid	against the Baltimore Bards	177
Company, enlivens the mind	519	[Cri]tics, their Impudence to great	
Commissions under the great Seal,		men	320
ordered in the Tues: Club	567	[Cri]tics on the Times, enimies to	
Common law, a voluminous and		Clubs	70
Intricate Study	537	Excluded the Clubical Commonw:	71
Common place of wit, modern	463	[Cri]tics, Clubical, Compared to dried	
Contradictors, banished the Clubical		gourds, Smoked Gammons &	
Commonwealth	71	blank blotted Scrolls	310
Confirmation, form of	406	[Cra]pe, Gentlemen of, their motives	
Connoiseurs of Quality, their		for Speech making	239
doctrines	455	[Cr]omwell (Oliver) disperses the	
Conversation, Clubical, how to		whin bush Club and seizes	
divert it from mischief	461	their Records	47
Commonwealth, Clubical	71	Cruisards, their ensign	259
Conundrum, its Etymon	218, 219	Curses, Christian ones, against	
Cousin german to pun	218	whom vented	254
Etymon of its derivatives	219	Custard, a Standing dish at a Lord	
Committee, first anniversary one	256	Mayor's feast	387
Second ditto	438	Customs, new ones Introduced thro	
Sham ditto	438	caprice or humor	487
Box ditto	490	Cyrus the Great, an Inscription on	
Coppernose (Capt: Comely)		his Tomb	300
Employed by the T: Club at			
London	422	**D**	
made an honorary member	567	Dance, Bacchinalian, of the T: Club	275
patent granted him	567	Dedications, Impropriety of their	
Cork (Jno:) member of the ugly		Stile	ii
Club	120	[D]edicators, by what maxims	
Counterblast, a royal performance,		Conducted	ibid
quoted	45	their false characters	ii
County Clerkship, a Conscientious		Deformities of the body, less than	
office	126	those of the mind	118
Corruption, Introduced by degrees		not a Subject of ridicule	505
into the Tues: Club	234	Deities (Heathen) changed into	
Courtiers, use Cant words	215	Saints	114, 529
Thorro' paced ones have no		Demetrius the Grammarian, a Story	
private Judgement	341	of him	306
Their propositions and political		Democritus, why he laughd	310
Maxims	ibid	his doctrines	465

Index

[Clu]bs, their badges of office	222
[Chara]cters, Hieroglyphical	561
express the moral virtues	ibid
more ancient than Heraldry	560
[Charity] Box in the Tues: Club	235
[Chari]ty, a Club discourse on it	
[de]livered by Mr Broadface	
Round	250
[th]e presidents nice notions of it	326
[Char]les I. (King) his Martyrdom, how Celebrated by opposite parties	254
Cheary (Chantum) made Hony: memb:	291
Chearfulness, a discourse on it by Ignotus warble	250
Cheese law in the Tuesd: Club, abrogated	171
arguments against it	172
Cheyne (Doct:) Imitated by the author of the Hist: of the Tu: Club	27
Chip in porridge Conversation	x, 461
Chop houses in Change alley, by whom frequented	58
Christenmass, dissentions about it	253
Called a holiday, a Jollyday and a follyday	ibid
of Christian Institution	ibid
of pagan original	ibid
Julius Cæsar's birth day	ibid
Strange medley at its Celebration	ibid
Chronological Table of the Tuesday Club	62
Church, it's Independance on the State prov'd by Dr Warburton	104
Churches, why Sanctuaries for Villains	14
Cicero, a merry fellow	342
Civil Government, a Club Speech on it by Smoothum Sly	249
why Compared to Clock work	267
Clans, nations divided into them	12
whence derive their honor	ibid
Clergy, not to be Intrusted with power	89
Clergy-men, distinguished from the laity, more by their habit than manners	264
why they practise not what they preach	486
Cloak of St Alban, Canonized	136
Cloths (old) despicable	23
Club, ubiquitarian one	32
female one described	87
wars	88
Conversation	26
Catches	143
disputes	151
Terms of art	216
Club (Tuesday) becomes a State Club	567
Clubbing, natural to mankind	31
Clubical, a Club Term	216
missapplied	307
Clubific, a club term	216
Clubified, ditto	ibid
Clubs, whence derive their antiquity	30
defind	25
formd by the power of attraction	ibid
as ancient as the world	26
originally what	25, 32
Etymon of their name	32
ancient place of meeting	33
first civilizers of men	ibid
Theocratical	36
antidiluvian	37
In Annapolis	85
a Speech on them by the Secretary	258
Soporific effects of it	ibid
Coats of arms, family badges, their Origin	261
Congallus de Rutherin, president of the whin bush Club	43
Comus, (Laconic) a good Clubs man	141
Congratulated on his return to the Tuesday Club	290
disputes with Smoothum Sly	350
is muddled at Club	ibid
a master of the pathos	423
moves for a punch ladle	336
his character	ibid
is chosen orator & State officer	430
accuses the Secretary	489
Receives a message from the anniversary Committee	439
answers it	440
His Speech at the Anniversary	442

Index

applied to them	396
Blockheads (wealthy) dangerous to Jest with	505
Bloody Cross, a Christian ensign	259
Bodies in Nature, Sympathize	25
Bodily deformities, Improper Subjects of Ridicule	505
Bona dea (mysteries of) like our modern Gossipings	41
Box (money box) in the T: Club	236
Box law, hot dispute on it	246
Box, extraordinary liberality to it	272
first and last disbursment from it	325
Compared to a mortmain	362
Box petition	363
Box, delivered up	368
proposals to revive it	490
rejected	492
Bribery, caused by Luxury	56
Bribes, when necessary	234
British, why fond of Bear baiting & cock fighting	13
Brutes, derive honor from Antiquity	18
Brutal nature, how distinguished from the Rational	ix
Bulls, (Irish) overgrown ones	13
Bull dogs (political)	12
Bully Blunt (Capt:) a good Clubs man	141
Infected with the poetical itch	175
his Speech and behavior at the Cathedration	203
Created knight and Champion of the Tues: Club	273
Vide Oldcastle	
Bumbasto (Coll:) Salutes the grand Anniversary procession	293
Bumbailiffs, necessary in a public	220
Bumpers, drank in the Red house Club	106
Bumper (Abraham) made an honorary member	144
Butchers (political)	12
Bunter, a cant word us'd at Court	215

C

Cain, founder of Edinburgh in Scotland	481
Calanus, the Indian Philosophers advice to Alexander the Great	467
Calves head feast, when used	254
Cameron's Congregation, their place of meeting	54
Canopy of State, fixed to the presidential Chair	429
Cap (old) despicable	23
Capation, a Club term	216
Card meetings, excluded from the Class of Clubs	25
Cards (games of) Indifferent amusements	461
Card billet Stile	493
Cardinals, temporal titles Improperly applied to them	396
C——r (Mris A—) Chief of the female Sillabub Club	87
Cathedration, a Club term	216
of Nasifer Jole Esqr	207
Cato, turns Cook	158
a merry fellow	342
a punster	467
Cashel, (psalter of) an Irish legend	17
Castle Building, practis'd in Clubs	40
Cats, Docile Creatures	165
one buried like a Christian	ibid
(letter of,) gives offence	510
Catches, Club ones	143, 144
Censor of the whin bush Club	52
Certain man, history of one	49
Ceremony, a theatrical Image of it	171
Ceremonies, the Shadow of religion	211, 396
Ceremonies (master of) in the Tues: Club	274
his privileges of office	ibid
Confirmed	317
duties of office	435
Speech att the Confirmation of members	406
[Chines]e, very ancient	8
Chronology, fabulous	ibid
[Chancel]lor, Created in the Tuesday Club	566
his character	ibid
[of] Republican principles	ibid
[Chancel]lors and Champions of	

Index

Arms (coats of) whence derived 261
Artful men, how they become
   popular 201
Arts and Sciences, obscurd with
   terms 210
Asiatic Nations, not ancient 15
Association of Ideas (false) an
   Instance of it in Mr Pope 478
Athens, why now Infamous 14
Athenians, their wisdom 199
Athenian State, its fate 11
Attention, its effect on the body 245
Author of the history of the Tues:
   Club, Compard to othr authors xi
   vindicated x
   compard to Colley Cibber 5
Authors, Literary Cooks 3
   use an Improper Stile in their
   Dedications 260
Authority, presidential, how
   augmented in the Tues: Club 235

B

Babel (Tower of) a Club house 40
Babylon (city) turned into dens for
   wild beasts 114
Bacchinalian Dance of the T: Club 275
Bacchus, a Club Companion 41
Badge Committee, summons Ignotus
   Warble 258
Badge, presidential, it's Institution 351
   renewd and altered 540
Badges, of the Tuesday Club 258, 358
   of State, their use 221
   used by empires & nations 259
   of honor, real ones 262
   useful to religious orders 264
   To Physicians ibid
Badges of the Tues: Club, Improv'd 359
Bagnios, monasteries and Nunneries
   become such 114
Bajazet I, king of the Turks, a Story
   of him and his fool 472
Balance of power, how destroyed in
   the Tues: Club 269
Ball, made by the Tuesday Club 227
Ball Cake conference 226
Baltimore County, a poetical
   Contagion propagated there 176
Baltimore Bards, their History 176
   Cruelly hunted 180
Baltimore Belles, a Celebrated poem 179
   Critic on it 181
Baltimore Critics, their Sentiments
   of the Bards 179
Baltimore muses, their Death 189
Banditti, licenced ones xii, 9
Bards, an Instance of their fondness
   for their own performances 179
Bard Bavius, his *methodus medendi* 182
Baristers, their helps to discourse 216
Baronets, knights, their origin 289
   fill up a gap 290
Bassoon, its Strange effects 81
Bastard of a Lord and Cobler, equally
   base born 484
Batchellors, Indulged by the T: Club 147
Batchellor's Cheese law ibid
Batchellor's Cheese, Expell'd 171
Batchellor's hall, a meeting of Bards
   & Critics there 186
Bath, (Earl of) his conduct in the
   house of peers 97
Bathos, a remarkable Instance of it 182
Bavius, a Baltimore Bard, his
   character 178
   cured of a *furor poeticus* 181
   advertised as a run away 183
Bawdy, well wrap'd in the Red house
   Club 105
   a favorite topic of discourse ibid
Beauty of women, not to be
   Questioned 505
Beaus, their origin 33
Beer, it's effects 334
   a present of it made to the T: Club 324
Beer Clubs, compard to Swine 334
Beer Sots, possessed ibid
   Translated to Bedlam ibid
Beer, many a Genius Solely Inspired
   by it 521
Benecarlo wine, it's effects 38
Bickerings in the Tues: Club 235
Biography, its Subject 1, 75
Birth, noble, Its Importance 7
Bishop, fond of Childrens plays 159
Bishops, temporal titles Improperly

Index of the Contents of this Volume

A	Page

Abbe le Boe, his account of horses	18
Abbe Soray, a ragged poet, his adventure with a proud marquis	476
Abdication, a dispute in the Tuesd: Club on the word	514
Abuse, much used in controversy	95
Action, Graceful in Oratory	241
Adrian IV (pope) a Story of him	87
Adrian (Empr:) his affection to dogs and horses	166
Adriatic Sea, married by the Doge of Venice	526
Advice to Club Companions	72
Ægyptians, their use of hieroglyphics	561
Æsop, a Statue erected to him	559
Æthiopians of Afric, best Claim to Antiquity	17
Affectation, described	118
a real deformity	ibid
Deviation from nature	ibid
Agapestor, a Story of him	467
Aidan, president of the whin bush Club, Inventor of the bagpipe drone	43
Alban (St) the martyr	136
Alexander the Great, president of a Club	41
Alicant wine, its effects	39
Ambition, a passion of the Great	223
it's effects	ibid
a laudable one	419
American Indians, very ancient	17
why they smear with bears Grease	109
Amphibolus (St) a Club worthy	136
Amusements (Triffling)	x, 8, 308
Annapolitans, given to Clubbing	85
Anniversary Committees	258
Anniversaries, Celebrated universally	252
Cause of disputes in Christendom	ibid
of less note	254
of Clubs	255
Anniversary, I of the Tues: Club	258
II of ditto	293
Procession	ibid
III of the Tues: Club	359
Committee, 2d	438
IV of the Tues: Club	442
Speech	443
ode	449
Answer to the Critics on this history	74
Anticlubarian, a Club term	216
Anticlubarians, (who)	304
Confuted	ibid
Antipathy (perfect) not in nature	25
Antiquity, regard paid to it	7
on what grounded	9
exceptions to the Gen: rule	13
Appuleius, compared to Jonathan Grog Esqr	343
made a laughing Stock in Thessaly	ibid
Apollo, president of a Club	41
Arabians, their esteem for horses	18
Archie, fool to K: James I, a Story of him	473
Archbishop of Canterbury, why he takes place of all the English peers	14
Arguefication, a Club term	216
Aristotle, a Story of him	467
Aristotelian Lanthorn, lost in a fog	470

A List of the members Regular and Honorary of the Ancient and honorable Tuesday Club, from the 16th of may 1749 to the 5th of December, the same year.

Regular members	Honorary members
The Hon: Nasifer Jole Esqr, præs:	Mr Abraham Bumper
Sir John, knight and Champn	Doctor Polyhistor
Philo dogmaticus Esqr Cancell:	Mr Oldham wisely
Laconic Comus Esqr, Orator	Mr Joshua fluter
Jonathan Grog Esqr, P:L:M:C:	Mr Ignotus warble
Solo Neverout Esqr Proto-mus:	Signior Lardini
Loquacious Scribble Esqr Secrty	Mr Broadface round
Quirpum Comic Esqr dep: Secr:	Mr Merry Makefun
Slyboots pleasant ⎫	Mr Chantum Cheary
Capt: Seemly Spruce ⎪	Coll: Courtly Phraze
Jealous Spyplot Senr ⎪	Mr Curious Courtly
Jealous Spyplot Junr: ⎬ Esqrs	Mr Swillum Swagbelly
Huffman Snap ⎪	Mr Prim Laconic
Prim Timorous ⎪	Revd Mr Smoothum Sly
Roundhead Muddy ⎭	Revd Mr Roundhead Muddy
	Capt: Comely Coppernose

Club during these grand transactions, but this is nothing at all, to the State, pomp, pageantry and lofty titles, which this here Club and it's president took upon themselves, a short while after, which shall be minutely and circumstantially related in the following Books.

End of the 6th Book & of Volume I.

very night, in which he was admitted a Longstanding member, without so much as applying or making Interest for it, which is a sign of either the great personal merit and Capacity of this gentleman, or at least, of the great opinion, his honor the president and Club had of his abilities and parts, but be that as it will, his honor never was so much mistaken in his man as now, ever since he was a president, for he thought he had now got a firm friend to the prerogative and power of the Chair, but in a little time found himself most woefully baulked, for Mr Dogmaticus turned out to be a Zealous Republican, and a Stiff advocate for, and mantainer of Clubical liberty, and, we shall find this State officer, in the Sequel of our History, giving many a bold check to the petulence of the Chair, and occasioning many heartburns, broils, dissentions and Contentions, between his honor & the Longstanding members, and the principal author, exciter and fomenter of a great, dangerous & bloody rebellion, which broke out in the Club, as in due time shall be related.

The Secretary, by this remarkable occurrence, was now for ever deprived of all his hopes of becoming a State member of the Club, which he still expected some time or other to be, by his stepping into the orator's Chair, for tho he sometime after Indeed, procured that office and title, yet he did not become thereby a State officer, || the Chancellor taking the [567] precedence of him in that quality, neither did he by his office of orator enjoy the degree of Chief officer of the Commons long, for a new officer was created, under the name of his honor's Attorney General, who took place of all the other Commoners.

The Club ordered at the same Sederunt, that Commissions should be made out for the worshipful Sir John, and the other officers, under the Great Seal, and that a patent should be granted under the said Seal, to Capt: Comely Coppernose, to be agent for the Club at London, and also, that the said Capt: Comely Coppernose, should be entered and enrolled among the honorary members of this Club.

Ordered also, that a Letter of thanks be drawn up to Capt: Comely Coppernose, with the patent and Commissions, by Huffman Snap Esqr, and the Secretary, a Committee of two for that purpose, and laid before the Club at next Sederunt.

Thus, we find this ancient Club now taking great State upon itself, and the prophesy of Jealous Spyplot Senr Esqr, in a great measure accomplished, with regard to the Club's becoming a state Club, for now indeed it was a State Club with a witness, tho' not thro' the operation or Means of Mr Protomusicus Neverout, who was for the most part absent from the

414 [Book VI]　　　　　　　　　　　　　　　　　The History of

Philo Dogmaticus Esqr. Chancellor of the U: C:

[facing page 563]

They speak by me, my Words their Sense express,
My Lays are pregnant with their Thankfulness,
Accept our grateful thanks, this Seal you give,
Will make our Club to distant ages live,
The Sculptors art, displays to future times
The worth of virtue and the Guilt of Crimes,
This art, or praise or Satyr speaks as Strong
As painters Coloring, or the poet's Song,
These types (c) the virtue of our Club declare,
Here hand Joins hand, while but one heart we share.
Posterity shall see, and shall admire,
How pure amongst us Glows the Social fire.
A Social Club our Sons shall have in view,
And all the bright example shall pursue.
   If this bright Seal, our Club shall Eternize,
No mean one, bounteous Sir, shall be your prize,
Your Generous name shall live, our grateful page
Shall sound your name to every distant age,
And if these humble lays a place may Claim
In Records Sage, 'twill swell the poet's fame,
And you, and I, and every Social Soul
Immortal praise shall share with Noble Jole.

   This poetical Speech had the applause of the whole Club, and Jonathan Grog Esqr, making a reverend bow to the honorable president and Club, sat down.

   Then the Club proceeded to chuse a Chancellor, and keeper of the great Seal, and the Revd: Mr Philo dogmaticus, by a great majority was elected for that Important office, and the great Seal being Solemnly delivered to him by Jonathan Grog Esqr, master of Ceremonies, he in a handsom manner gave Thanks for the great and Important trust Committed to him, of Chancellor and keeper of the honorable the Presidents Clubical Conscience, solemnly promising a faithful execution of it, and then took his place appointed by the Club, on the left hand of his honor's Chair of State, in quality of a State officer, and privy Councellor to the Chair, the wonted place of the Orator and Speaker, before these offices were taken away and quite discontinued in Club.

   Thus we find, in a most Surprizing and astonishing || manner, this gentleman promoted to a great and new office of trust in the Club, on the

---

(c) Showing the Impression in wax.

[563] president and Club, to which writings, I humbly request, that this Seal, may be for the time to come ‖ a Sanction and Corroboration, and, that some trusty person, from among the members of this worthy Society, not already dignified with an office, may be chosen *Chancellor,* or keeper of this great Seal, to affix it to such writings, as the honorable the president and Club shall Command, and, if this my present is chearfully accepted by the honorable the president and worthy members, and it is put upon Record, that this was the gift of their faithful Secretary, I shall esteem myself, dowbly and Trebly rewarded, for any little Expence or trowble it may have cost me."

The Secretary having thus spoke, presented the Seal and Impression, to the honorable the president & Club, who were pleased to give their approbation.

Then Jonathan Grog Esqr, Master of Ceremonies, being Commanded by his honor the President, to return thanks to the Secretary for his present, stood up and addressed himself to this purpose.

> Whilst the Club's thanks my task is to rehearse,
> I leave Dull prose for my beloved verse,
> For great must be the wit that can Compose,
> Fine florid Speeches in Phlegmatic prose,
> My Rhiming Genius, therefore fixes here,
> Plain thoughts in Rhime will better please your ear.
>   While your Indulgent Smiles great Sir,[a] Inspire,
> I slight Apollo, and his virgin Choir,
[564]
> While propd by thy bold Courage O Sir John,
> I need no Pegasus to ride upon,
> While this rare punch, is on the table brought,
> The Streams of Helicon to me are nought,
> Cheer'd by your Smiles,[a] by this rich liquor warmd,
> 'Gainst Critics and the Bathos I am armd,
> Th'obsequious bard, your orders then obeys,
> And thus proclaims our Secretaries praise.
>   For this rich present, Generous Sir, to you[b]
> The thanks I pay, which Justly are your due,
> Illustrious Jole Commands, and I obey,
> He and the Club, assent to what I say,

(a) To the president.
(a) To the members of the Club.
(b) To the Secretary, with the Seal and Impression in hand.

the Symbols wore by the magistrates and priests, which notified or Implied some peculiar virtue or excellency, were I to ennumerate the things of this Sort, used even by the Jewish priesthood, such as the Urim and Thummum, the Seraphs and Cherubs, the Ephods and Candlesticks and lavers &ct: by which, I might like some learned historians derive this mode even from divine Institution, I doubt I should become not only too refined, but abundantly too tedious and prolix, and keep your honor, and these here Gentlemen, the Longstanding members, if you had a mind to hear me out, sitting here till Christenmass, which is now pritty nigh at hand.

Therefore, since it appears, to have been a prevailing custom in all ages, for certain men, and Societies of men, to adopt particular marks and Signatures, by which they desire to be known, and distinguished, which often, if not always, are expressive of some virtues or excellencies, peculiar to the Society to which they belong, it seems highly Just and reasonable, that this worthy Society, the ancient and honorable Tuesday Club, whose honorable President and Longstanding members, have now, for some years distinguished themselves in this present age, and, in this City wherein they live, by exhibiting an example of good fellowship, and a friendly and Sociable disposition, should in conformity with so many || worthy patterns of antiquity, who have florished in former ages, and lived in greater Cities, Invent and Design for themselves, some Laudable and Ingenious device expressive of that amity and Sociable Spirit, which prevails among them, this Indeed has been done, in an elegant and well contrived, tho Simple device, of two hands Joined over a heart, with the Mottos of CONCORDIA RES PARVÆ CRESCUNT, and LIBERTAS ET NATALE SOLUM. This device then Mr President and Gentlemen, formerly delineated upon a fragile Card of no duration or permanency, I, out of the great Regard I have for this worthy Society, and out of Gratitude for the trust they have reposed in me, in honoring me with the office of their Secretary, have caused to be here curiously engraved on Silver, in the form of

a Seal, which Seal, I humbly present to the worthy Society for their use, to be affixed to all Commissions Summons, writings, or Instruments of whatsoever kind, which shall henceforth be Issued in the name of the honorable

Characters, whatever they were. To give an Instance from Antiquity, we find an old Classic Author, saying of the famous Mythologist Æsop.

Æsopo Ingentem Statuam, posuere Attici,
Servumq3 collocarunt Æterno in basi,
Patere honoris, scirent ut cumque viam,
Nec Generi Tribui, sed virtuti Gloriam.

Athens of old, admiring virtuous fame,
A Statue reard, to Æsop's honor'd name,
Him tho a Slave, in Lasting brass they plac'd,
His Image, tho deformd, their City grac'd,
Thus Deemd they birth and Sounding titles nought,
Since virtue only lasting Glory brought.[2]

[560] Now Sir, as I flatter myself, that this worthy Society the || ancient Tuesday Club, is not in a mean degree possessed of some great virtues and excellencies in which true Intrinsic worth and merit essentially consist, so, I hope this worthy Club, may assume to themselves that privilege, which other associations and Corporations have taken before them, that is to devise and invent for themselves, Certain Significant Characters or Hieroglyphics, which being engraved or Cut upon Stone, Metal, or such like durable Substances, may be expressive or significant of certain virtues, peculiar to that ancient, honorable and worthy Society, such as, amity, concord, benevolence, Generosity, Good fellowship, and the like, and thus not only Inform the present generation, and their contemporaries, how well disposed the members of this worthy Club are, but also, leave a lasting and permanent Character behind them by which posterity may be put in mind, that such a worthy Society once florished, and by this means the Succeeding generations may be prompted to follow so fair an example.

Gentlemen,

We may go farther back, than the History or records of the Heralds office, an Institution at best but modern and Gothic, we may take an earlier date than even the oldest order of knighthood, now extant in Christendome, In searching for Authorities from antiquity, when particular Societies of men, first Invented for themselves Certain marks and Signatures, by which they were distinguished and known from other Societies, were I to
[561] Instance || The many Signatures and hieroglyphics used by ancient Ægypt,

---

2. More literally, "The men of Attica erected a great statue to Aesop; / They placed this slave on an eternal pedestal / That they might know the road of honor was always open, / And that glory was given to virtue, not family" (Phaedrus, *Fabulae,* II, epilogue).

"Honorable Mr President,
Honored Knight,
and all ye other worshipful officers, and,
Worthy members of the ancient & honorable Tuesday Club,

I Joyfully acknowledge the honor you have done me by my admission into your most noble Society, for which I return you my most grateful thanks, from a heart that shall always be devoted to the promoting of the honor and benefit of this Club in opposition to all Envious Rivals, and malicious Enimies, who can distinguish themselves only by reviling or detracting from that worth, which they must for ever despair of equalling.

May the ancient and honorable Tuesday Club, subsist and flourish, while the Sun and moon Endures, and you my honored Superiors, and other worthy fellow members of it *Macti virtuti, omnique Genere foelicitatis estote,*[1] *Amen* and *Amen.*"

Mr Dogmaticus, having thus finished his gratulatory Speech, was Saluted by all round as a member, and took his Seat in Club accordingly.

Then the Secretary rising up, Informed the Club, that he had received the Great Seal, sent by Captain Comely Copper Nose, and that he had further Intelligence from the said Gentleman, that the Club medals were already struck at London, and would very soon be sent over, then putting his Countenance in a proper order, he delivered the following Speech.

"Mr President Sir,

It is a Certain truth, which will be granted by every man of plain Sense and understanding, as well as your professed Sage or Philosopher, that the noblest and most eminent ‖ marks or Signatures, which can dignify or decorate men or distinguish human Societies, are Virtue, honor and Integrity, since these more effectually recommend men to the regard of their Contemporaries, to the esteem of posterity, and form a more eloquent Eulogium in the mouth of fame, than all the blazoning of the Herald's office, or the utmost Skill of the Sculptor or engraver, tho exercised upon the most durable Substances of Stone and metal, hence it is, that many Societies have made these mechanic arts, only Subservient, to the above-named excellent virtues, but using them to fabricate Certain material monuments, and Significant designs, by which either the effigies of great and virtuous men, or particular virtues and qualities peculiar to themselves, were preserved and signified to posterity, and remained legible in these

---

1. "Be honored with virtue and every kind of happiness" (first phrase echoes Horace, *Satirae* 1.2.31).

have also shared in, thro' that generosity, which has once and again Invited and admitted me, a Stranger among you, to the honor and pleasure of being a witness and partaker of your most ravishing Conversation, I humbly beg and petition, the honorable the president, the honored Sir John, knight, and the other worshipful officers, and all the Respectful worthy members of the ancient Tuesday Club, to perfect the honor they have already done me, by admitting me a member of it, and, however unworthy I may be at present, your noble examples, and Improving Conversation, will I hope, render me by degrees more worthy of such an honor, and lay under an Infinite obligation,

Your most Loving, Devoted and
Obedient humble Servant
Philo Dogmaticus.

[557] This petition being read, the ballots of yeas & nays were put round, and, the Reverend Mr Philo dog- || maticus being unanimously elected a member of the Tuesday Club, Jonathan Grog Esqr, Master of Ceremonies and the Secretary, waited upon him in the next Room, acquainting him that he was elected a member, upon which they conducted him into the Club Room, where the honorable the president met him at the Door, and Saluted him with a hearty manuquassation, an honor, which was never done to any longstanding member, either before or since, and a happy Presage, or pompous prelude, to the great honors, that were soon to be heaped upon him.

Then Jonathan Grog Esqr, Master of Ceremonies, placeing him nigh the presidential Chair, confirmed him in the following manner.

"Sir,

I as master of Ceremonies to our ancient and honorable Tuesday Club, with all the Ceremony I am master of, which mastery in Ceremonies, I acknowledge to be conveyd to me, by the authority of our honorable President, do Inaugurate, constitute and confirm you, Philo Dogmaticus Esqr, a good firm and Longstanding member of the Commoners, of this our ancient and honorable Tuesday Club, in token of which, I Invest you, with this the Club's badge, and here Solemnly present you, to the honorable the president, recommending it to you, to make your acknowledgements to the honorable the president and Club, in the handsomest and best Speech you can devise, upon this Important, and honorable occasion."

Then Mr Dogmaticus, standing in a proper posture and attitude, addressed the honorable the president and Club as follows.

places and titles of honor, have them, I know not how, pop suddenly into their mouths to the great Surprize and astonishment of every one, who cannot comprehend how they came to have such good Luck, these are such as have been born with a Silver Spoon in their mouths, or a Cawl on their heads, as the proverb goes; a remarkable Instance of this, we shall find in the case of the Reverend Mr Philo Dogmaticus, who, at one and the same Instant, as it were, was made a Long Standing member of this Club, Chancellor, State officer and privy Councellor to the Honorable The Chair, as also, keeper of his honors political Conscience, which transaction shall presently be related.

On the aforesaid Sederunt 118 the Secretary presented to the Honorable the president and Club, a petition from the Reverend Mr Philo Dogmaticus, who being desired to withdraw into an adjoining Chamber, it was read as follows.

To the honorable Nasifer Jole Esqr President, || The honored Sir John knight, and the other worshipful officers, and worthy members of the ancient and honorable Tuesday Club. [555]

Gentlemen,

As without Society, man would be the most wretched Creature upon earth, so to this he owes, tho' not his rational powers and faculties, yet the use and Improvement of them, arts Sciences, and all the advantages and pleasures of life flow from this fountain, which alone renders it more secure, and Comfortable, than the Condition of the Irrational tribes, for without this, even reason it self would avail us very little, our nobler powers would Languish and perhaps be employed in mutual destruction, but Society, founded upon principles of right reason, directed by Just Laws, Impartially executed, under the administration of wise and virtuous Rulers, what a glorious Idea is it! what heart can conceive a greater blessing upon Earth! it is the very prelude, or rather type of heaven, where nothing is to be found but order, peace, love and all happy enjoyments worthy of the rational nature.

Wherever such well Constituted Societies are || to be met with upon Earth, be they more public or more private, formed for more General advantage or the Comforts of a more private life, what wonder is it that men should wish and endeavour, to be members of such Societies, who, being prompted by a natural and reasonable Self love, wish themselves happy. [556]

Moved by this principle, and the fame of this ancient, honorable and worthy Society of the Tuesday Club, the pleasures and benefits of which, I

request the honor of your magnanimous presence this night, in the name of the Ancient Tuesday Club, to which is high Steward, under favor of the honorable the president, most magnanimous Sir John,

Decr 5th 1749
                                  Your worships most humble
                                  Servt: and faithful Squire
                                  Loquacious Scribble.

The other great and Important transactions of this most memorable Sederunt, are reserved as the Subject of the following Chapter, to which we refer the reader if he desires to know them.

Chapter VIII

Admission of Philo Dogmaticus Esqr, Speeches in prose and verse at the Delivery of the Great Seal, Creation of the Chancellor, and an account of the Club Medals being struck at London.

Hope is a passion by which all mankind are buoy'd up, be their Circumstance what it will, prosperous, or adverse, this Strange Phantom still haunts and attends them, thro all the windings and turnings of this foolish life as the Philosophers call it; if they enjoy good fortune Hope still promises a better, if they Labor under distresses and difficulties, Hope whispers them, that they shall sometime or other be relieved; In fine this flattering power is still in view, unless when despair takes place, for this latter, being her mortal and sworn Enimy, she always takes flight at the Sight of his horrid front, as a beautiful modest and Coy virgin would fly at the Sight of a Rude rake or ravisher, and yet some people have as little ground or reason for Entertaining this flattering Phantome, as those who hope for the Millennium, have a chance to live to see those halcyon days, or those who fear the Sky will fall and smother the Larks, run a risk to be smothered and Crushed in their Company.

But tho this vain propensity, may often present us golden Scenes at a distance, and promise us relief in our greatest distresses and difficulties, ‖ yet such is the caprice of Lady fortune In human affairs, or, to speak more Intelligibly, such is the Indiscretion and Imprudence of the bulk of mankind, that ten to one, those that hope for, and desire most, enjoy the Least of the good things of life, and many, who scarce ever hoped or expected a better fortune, than that they are at present possesed of, or ever longed after

To The worshipful Sir John,
knight of the Noble order of the Tuesday Club, These.

Most undaunted and magnanimous knight,

It would be Impertinent and Idle to tell a man of your understanding, and knowledge in Chronology, how ancient the order of knighthood is, and for || what purpose instituted, the worthy knights of old were defenders and champions of virtue, and friends to the fair Sex, and mighty princes have not thought it beneath them, to gird the Sword of Justice upon their manly thighs, to protect the Innocent and relieve the oppressed, but alas, this Noble order is now degenerated, into I dont know what kind of a farce, and our moderen pigmy knights, Instead of Swords, helmets, and coats of mail, the ponderous and manly badges of heroes, wear delicate soft silks, velvets, Ribbons, garters, Stars, Jewels, Golden fleeces, crosses and other gewgaws, Just enough emblems of their Softness, effeminacy and cowardice, and, instead of the noble feats of arms in the fields of Mars, and defending the oppressed and mantaining the Cause of the fair, they storm bawdy houses, kick poor whores, bilk hackney Coach men, break windows, knock down the watch, Cudgel drunken Constables, smoke Coblers, dance, fiddle, sing, shuffle Cards, rattle dice, make fantastical legs and foppish grimaces at the Ladies, and make a figure no where but at bagnios, masquerades, Ridottos, Italian operas, Drums, routs, taverens, gaming Tables, cock pits, horse races and Broughtons Amphitheatre.[2] This would almost tempt one to think that the long expected *Annus mirabilis,* was nigh at hand, when the women shall put on breeches and armor, and the men step into Smokes and petticoats.

Observing this degeneracy, in the ancient and noble order of knighthood, I should long ago have given up all for lost, and Imagined, that true Valor || and courage was banished out of the world, did I not find that there is yet extant, one valiant and tremendous knight, of courage right Steel'd and tried bravery, even Sir John, (heretofore Oldcastle) the renownd and Invincible Champion of the Ancient Tuesday Club, under whose puisant arm, the longstanding members sit in Safety, and, by whose brave presence and Influence, The honorable president is stuck fast and Immoveable in his Chair, and hugs himself, secure from all violent assaults, both from within doors, and from without, your worship being therefore so necessary a person, upon whom we depend for Safety, and in whom we place our Confidence, the only remaining type of the true and ancient chivalry, I must

---

2. The British prizefighter John Broughton established a theater for boxing in 1743 (John Ford, *Prizefighting: The Age of Regency Boximania* [New York, 1972]).

have been dizened out, with the Tinsel badges of Titulary Honor, have appeared in this age, in that age, and In every age, mere fools, knaves, Scoundrells and Coxcombs, whilst men, who are placed in a lower rank, as the world esteems it, such as the honest Presidents of ancient and worthy Clubs, like this here Club of ours, have in effect been men of more Intrinsic honor, and more noble principles.

I have the pleasure here to observe, that, as I had the honor to be Steward (not high Steward) of that auspicious Club, in which your honor was created president, and ascended our stately Chair, vizt: the memorable 26th of November, 1745, so, by some propitious fate and good fortune, it has so fallen out, that I always have been honored with your honor's presence, for these eight successive times, which I have since served, sometimes Steward, and sometimes as high Steward, this time is now the 9th, in which I solicit and apply for the same favor, Some augurs have observed, that nine is an unlucky number, I pray it may not prove so in this Instance, so as to deprive me of your honor's company this night (tho' if it should, I have less reason to complain, than any other Longstanding member of our ancient Club) If it happens otherwise, I shall have a meaner opinion than ever I yet had of these idle and Super- || stitious maxims, and it will more and more oblige, Honorable Sir,

Decr: 5th 1749   Your honor's obsequious Servant
and faithful H:S: and Secretary
Loquacious Scribble.

In this Letter, we find the Secretary very much upon the flattering and cajoling Strain, and it must be observed here, that this officer, after he found that he could not obtain his darling preferment, by violent methods and by exciting tumults and hubbubs in the Club, had recourse to this Smoothing method with his honor and Sir John, but his machinery still proved insufficient, for these two great politic and wise men, easily saw thro' his designs, and would by no means make themselves Gudgeons, to be Entraped in his Subtile Snares, however, the Secretary did not turn flatterer on the same grounds as the Eastren Shore Triumvirate and Jonathan Grog Esqr did, for he was still a dependant and hanger on, so, that he might properly be classed among those Sempiternal Sycophants, mentioned in the beginning of this Chapter.

Another Letter was presented in Club, by the worshipful Sir John, writ to him by the same High Steward.

And for fine feasting and the Sparkling bowl,
First thank the Gods, and then Illustrious Jole.

This Sublime poetical Speech met with great applause from all the Longstanding members, and the poet Laureat having delivered it, took a hearty pull at the bowl & sat down.

His honor having drank the king and the Club after Supper, some of the members murmured at his giving the preference to that foolish Toast as they Called it, upon which, his honor, after his usual peremptory way declared That none of the Longstanding members had any right to dictate to him, in these matters, or pretend to direct him in his choice of a toast, and therefore his honor expressly ordered from the Chair, that this toast of the king and the Club, should henceforth be the || first toast proposed after [548] Supper, The longstanding members on this were silent, and said no more, perceiving that his honor had assumed his peremptory face, and could not brook Contradiction.

At Sederunt 118 December 5th 1749, Mr Secretary Scribble being high Steward, his honor produced in Club the following Letter from the high Steward.

To The Honorable Nasifer Jole Esqr
President of the Tuesday Club, These.

Honorable Sir,

The title with which I address your honor, is undoubtedly your Due upon many accounts too prolix here to ennumerate, but plainly Conspicuous to every member of our ancient Club, who observes with what Impartial Justice, with what mild and Gentle moderation, with what modesty and tender humanity, with what regard to merit and Just abhorrence of Iniquity you moderate and regulate all affairs, relating to your humble Subjects, the members of the Ancient Tuesday Club, how like an exuberant Cornu-copia, you plentifully and magnificently entertain and regale them, how like a kind father, you administer to all their wants, and wink at and pass over all their Infirmities, and, how like a humane and mild ruler, you comply with all their proposals and demands, tho sometimes bordering upon extravagance.

These great qualities and Enduements, In my humble opinion, give a Juster Claim to the titles of *your honor* and *honorable Sir,* than all the foppery of Stars and gar- || ters, golden fleeces, Georges, St Andrews crosses, This- [549] tles, and such like farcical trash and Trumpery, nay even than the Royal patents, where these good qualities are wanting, for, it is certain, that many peers of noble blood and ancient extract, and also, many new upstarts who

[546] will weigh each very near one onz ½ of Silver, and it must be quite pure, for fear of hurting the Dye, so, that ‖ had you dowble the number, they would still be Cheaper, I shall have them in my possession, so that any number may be supplied on proper notice, I would send them to you, but they would not be Serviceable, as you have no engine to strike them with, the Engraver would not engrave them for Less than ten Shillings a piece. The great Seal comes by the bearer, and, I hope you'll think it well done, and not dear, the medals will be done in about 6 weeks, and come by another opportunity that will then offer.

If I please the worthy Gentlemen of the Club, in this commission, I hope to be favored with a patent under the great Seal, as agent for the Club in London, you'll do me the favor of presenting my duty to the honorable the President, and my humble Service to all the gentlemen of the Club and believe me, Dear Sir,

Your most humble Servant
Comely Coppernose.

This Letter was well received by his honor and the Club, and the Secretary was ordered to prepare a proper answer to it, and dispatch it with the first opportunity.

His honor at this Sederunt, having as it was usual with him, given the Club a very elegant entertainment, Jonathan Grog Esqr, Master of Ceremonies and Poet Laureat, after Supper, when his honor had resumed the Chair, stood up & delivered himself as follows.

[547]
> The President our Lofty chair has grac'd,
> The Brimming bowls in decent order plac'd,
> We all have tasted rich delicious Cheer,
> Sure nothing but good humor can be here.
> Come, fellow members, let the bowl go round,[a]
> Let this grand hall with Songs and Jokes resound,
> Sure, from Joves board, Ambrosial Cates we share,
> And heavenly nectar flows to sooth our Care,
> Such Cates as these, Celestial feasts may grace,
> And this rich punch of nectar take the place,
> To you, Great Sir, our humble Thanks we pay,
> Who spare no pains or cost to make us gay,
> We, in our turn, our wits shall exercise,
> To tell the world, you're Noble Generous, wise,

---

[a] Here the poet Laureat took the bowl in his hand.

exhibit, upon the Supper given by him to the Club, but, when they Consider, that the Eastren Shore Triumvirate, owed it's rise, Increase and Glory, to the ancient and hon- ‖ orable Tuesday Club, even granting that the members of that Triumvirate were as good, by family birth and titles, and as wise men as the members of the ancient and honorable Tuesday Club; when they Consider also that Jonathan Grog Esqr, was lately promoted, by his honor's grace and favor, to the high office of Master of the Ceremonies, tho' the said Jonathan Grog Esqr, might be a man of a more ancient family, a readier wit, quicker genius, and a greater poet, than his honor the president or any other of his Longstanding members, they will Surely agree with me, that those praises and panegyrics, were properly and Justly enough applied to both the President and the Club, by that there Triumvirate, and this here poet Laureat, and were not altogether so ill placed and premature as the fulsome praises and flattery of some Impudent, Indefatigable and persevering Sycophants, who extoll their foolish or wicked patrons, at the expence of truth, candor and Sincerity, e'er they have received either promises or favors, but continue in the uncertain and hungry State of expecters and hangers on. [544]

At Sederunt 117, Novr 21 1749, The honorable Mr President Jole being high Steward, a Letter from Capt: Comely Coppernose to the Secretary was produced after Supper, read, and ordered to be recorded, the tenor of which follows.

To Doctor Loquacious Scribble, Annapolis. [545]

Dear Sir,   London June 24th 1749

I have your kind favor, the 11th of april via Ireland, I am extremely obliged to you and all my good friends for your kind wishes, I believe they had a good effect, for we had a charming passage.

The honorable the president, the principal officers, and worthy members of the Club, do me a very great honor in Laying their further Commands on me, I shall execute them to the best of my power, but I am afraid to tell you what they will cost, I consulted most of the workmen in what manner such a thing must be done, I had but two Choices, to have a dye cut, and so have them struck, or to have them engraved, the Latter would look very plain and ordinary, and come very near the price of the first method, vizt: struck, and this will look bold and Handsom, and be a beautiful medal, I have agreed to have the Dye cut for Six Guineas and a half, the other expences will come to about two and Sixpence a piece, besides the Gilding, what that will Cost, I cannot tell, suppose about 2/ or 2/6, They

could by no means annull the entry of Sederunt 113, after some dispute on the point, the Subject was waved till a more full meeting.

Upon the Honorable The President's giving the Signal, the gelastic Law was put in execution against the Reverend Mr Muddy, who talked alittle more upon this ungrateful Subject, than came to his Share, but the Gentleman bore this Severe Club punishment, with great patience and Resignation, and was utterly silent upon the argument, not pretending to say one word more to the point, either by himself, or his learned Councel.

Chapter VII

Eulogium of the poet Laureat on his honor the President's Entertainment, arrival of the Great Seal, more Sublime Club Letters.

It was well observed by a certain Peripatetic Philosopher, that Praise is a tribute due to the great, whether they Justly deserve it or not,[1] wherefore we find, that all Inferiors think themselves obliged to pay a deference or respect to their Superiors, and this respect they express both by words and gestures, and for once that they apply their praise and panegyric Justly, they ten times strain it too high, and carry it to a pitch beyond all reason and truth, thus have I seen many a Sage and grave Philosopher, uncover his Sagacious head to an arrant blockhead, whom capricious fortune has in the eye of the world raised above him, with regard to birth titles and possessions; I have seen also a grey headed venerable and worthy elder, bow to the grownd, when he came in the presence of a foolish princely greenheaded puppy; but as this is, and has constantly been, the way of the world, and providence, for the good order of human Society, has wisely ordained Subordinations among men, we must submit to it, however absurd it may appear at first view to wise men.

Some may perhaps Incline to apply this observation to the Eastren Shore Triumvirate, and To Jonathan Grog Esqr, poet Laureat, when they examin into the Conduct of both, and may condemn the first for writing in such a flattering strain to the Club, and the latter for smoothing up his honor the president, in a Set of fustian verses, which we shall presently

---

1. Hamilton is playfully referring to Aristotle, who says exactly the opposite in the *Nicomachean Ethics* 1.12.2 ("we praise just men and brave men . . . because of their actions and the results they produce").

The honorable The President appointed Jonathan Grog Esqr Master of Ceremonies for the night, who in a decent and proper manner, Invested his honor with his new badge, then Jonathan Grog Esqr, was ordered by his honor to return thanks to the Secretary, for his diligence in preparing the presidential badge, which he did in an Elegant and Succinct manner.

The Honorable The President this night expressed some concern, that the high Steward had not wrote him a Letter, according to the usual Custom, by which the Records for this Sederunt would appear Imperfect, but he declared to the Club, that the H:S: had made him amends for that neglect, by waiting upon him in person, upon which the Club was satisfied, there seemed at this Sederunt, to be a more than Common Intimacy and Cordiality, between his honor the president and Sir John, they sitting by the fire || face to face, and foot to foot, smiling upon each other for a considerable time, but the conversation of these two great men, consisted more in political nods, winks and Shrugs than in a flow of words, which made the Club suspect, that some grand design was *in petto*.

It was moved by the Secretary, that the ancient Custom of this Club, relating to a Side board, and a gammon of bacon, or any other one dish of dressed vittles, should be revived, and Strictly adhered to, or, that at least, if there was to be a table in form, and a Cloth laid, no person, except his honor the President, who is privileged, should exceed one dish of roast or boiled, for the Club Supper, and that under high penalty, but this Salutary motion was set aside, under pretence that there was not a full Club, mark here the Clubs disregard to a Law, that was not as yet repealed.

Jonathan Grog Esqr, applied to his honor the president and Club, to be permitted to lay down four of his five P offices, retaining only that of the Poet Laureat, which request was granted, then he applied to be created Master of Ceremonies, and the honble: the President and Club, finding him a person Sufficiently qualified, and the potent objection of the five Ps removed, he was accordingly created Mr of Ceremonies, *Quam diu bene se gesserit*,[6] the honorable the president taking him by the hand in token of approbation, at the same time always reserving to himself, the privilege granted at Sederunt 113, thus were the five Ps, of || Jonathan Grog Esqr, converted into P.L.M.C. That is to say, *Poeta Laureatus, Magister Ceremoniarum*.

After Supper, Mr Roundhead Muddy spoke against the Law passed at Sederunt 114 and showed by his councel, Mr Secretary Scribble, that that Law was not balloted according to form, and therefore was of no force, and

---

6. "So long as he behaves himself well."

there cannot be any thing more conduceive, to the Satisfaction of the ||
whole Club, than to see you placed in the great Chair, hope we shall not be dissappointed, I remain your honor's

Most obedient humble Servant
Prim Timerous.

(a)

For an explication of the Cypher or hieroglyphic at the end of this Letter, we must refer, to his honor the president's original Copy, tho' some presume to say, upon what grounds, I cannot tell, that these mystical Characters contain a Club Secret of State, between the high steward and his honor, not fit for all the members to be let into, but, the explication given in the note below, if genuine, seems to point at no such Secret, and as it speaks in the third person, seems not to have been penned by the high Steward himself, at least, If penned by him, he talks, as well as writes in mysteries after the manner of the Celebrated Bishop Atterbury,[5] and his political Correspondents, but this is only the first Introduction of hieroglyphical Characters Into the Club writings and Letters, we shall find one more Instance of it in the Sequel of this History, which has not as yet, nor I believe ever will be explained, unless Mr Protomusicus Neverout, the Ingenious author and Inventor of that particular way of Cyphering, gives us a key to it.

At Sederunt 116, Novr 7th 1749, Laconic Comus Esqr being high Steward, the Secretary, according to an order of Last Sederunt, presented to his honor the President || and the club, the presidential badge, properly adorned and lettered, with a variation from the former Inscription, tho the form of the Card was still retained, viz: *Nasifer Jole Armiger, Societatis Annapolitanæ,* THE TUESDAY CLUB *dictæ Præses.* The Secretary, when he presented this addressed himself to his Honor the President, and the Club, in a Speech proper upon the occasion, but so loaded with hard, obselete and new Coined words, That some present, who did not comprehend his meaning, particularly the Reverend Mr Roundhead Muddy, thought it was a rebellious Jacobitish harangue.

(a) The meaning of this is conjectured, by the most Skillful decypherers, to be— Signior ―――― would not Let me write this Letter, he Intends to leave you this night, God bless the president, so says the Parson.

5. Francis Atterbury (1662–1732), bishop of Rochester, frequently engaged in the political and theological disputes of the day and was imprisoned in 1720 for allegedly plotting to restore the Stuarts to power; he was a strong supporter of the Church of England and the author of numerous political pieces.

him much of that verbosity and prolixity of Stile, peculiar to those gentlemen, his brethern by profession, who study that voluminous and perplexed Science called the *Common Law of England*.

After reading and recording the above Letters, the Club passed the following Law.

Law XLII. Resolved by the president and Club, that no person whatsoever, that does not reside in the place, and attend the Club regularly at its meetings, or serve in his turn as high Steward, shall be a regular member of this Club, therefore, the entry of last Sederunt, concerning the Reverend Mr Roundhead Muddy, is hereby annulled, as also all other such entries, if such there be, granting the like privilege to any other person, and he and they, are henceforth to be deemed only honorary members of this Club.

This law was procured, at the Instance and desire of his honor the president, who being Jealous and tenacious of the prerogative of the Chair, was afraid of its being Infringed or Impaired, by the Increase of the number of extraneous regular || members, who all had a title to vote in Club, and who being non residents were not so Immediatly under his eye, as those regular members who remained on the Spot, and therefore he got them Reduced to the Station and degree of honorary members, who, by a preceeding law, had no vote in Club. [538]

At Sederunt 115 octor: 24, 1749, Prim Timorous Esqr being high Steward, the Secretary reported in Club, that he had dispatched the Answer to the Triumvirate's Letter, and delivered a copy of the same to his honor the president.

Then the Club took it under their Serious consideration, that the badge Card of the honorable the President was so gone to decay, and out of Repair, that the Letters were scarce legible, and the ornaments were become dim, and their Lusture faded, it was therefore resolved, that there should be a new Badge Card prepared for his honor, that the grandure and dignity of the Chair in this Club, may duely be kept up, and the Secretary was ordered to prepare the same, and produce it at next Sederunt.

A Letter from the high Steward to his honor the president was produced in Club, the tenor of which Follows.

To The honorable Nasifer Jole Esqr,
President of the Tuesday Club in Annapolis.

Sir,

This being my time to serve as high Steward of the Tuesday Club, think it my duty to acquaint your honor therewith, and, as I am convinced,

dent, who smiled all the time, I shall leave to nicer physiognomists than I to determin; as for Jonathan Grog Esqr, he heard with great composure and Sedateness, and a taciturnity becoming a free Mason, the Conjecture made Concerning him in your postscript, and, when I had Just finished reading your Letter, he took it in his hand, gravely perused the postscript to himself, returned it to me, with a half Smile, rolled his chaw over his tongue, to the other corner of his mouth, and Clasping his two hands together over his belly, sat in a Settled posture, appearing no more moved, than if he had been the corner Stone of a great Cathedral. *L:S:*

The Secretary was ordered to dispatch the above letter to the Reverend Mr Sly, by the first opportunity, delivering a copy of the same to the honorable the president.

After Supper, two Letters from the high Steward, to the honorable the president, and to the worshipful Sir John, were presented, and read in Club, vizt:

To the Honorable Nasifer Jole Esqr,
President of the Tuesday Club.

Most worthy President,

Having the honor of serving as high Steward to the ancient Tuesday Club this Evening at my house, I trowble you with this Scrowl by way of notice, and humbly request the gracious favor of your presence, I am, most worthy Sir,

10th octor, 1749   Your honors most obedient &
                            Most humble Servt:
                            Huffman Snap.

To the most magnanimous Sir John.

Sir John,

As have the honor of serving as high Steward to the Ancient and worthy Tuesday Club this evening, it becomes my duty, as well as Inclination, to request your presence amongst us at my house; I am, Sir John,

10th octor 1749   Your worships most obedient
                            Humble Servant
                            Huffman Snap.

These Laconic letters show how much this Gentleman's conversation with the club, had Improved him since his admission into it, having striped

Ah! can the worshipful Triumvirate, ever Sufficiently caress, so valuable and so accomplished a penman? and *Proh dolor!*³ can the ancient Tuesday Club ever enough bewail, the being deprived of so facetious and Erudite a member.

> *Quis desiderio sit pudor, aut modus*
> *Tam Cari Capitis?*⁴

I am commissioned to return to your worshipful Triumvirate, the Compliments of the honorable the President, and the members of our ancient Tuesday Club, and upon all occasions, we shall never fail to express that true and sincere regard, which with so much Justice we profess for the worthy gentlemen ‖ of the triumvirate, all of whom, the honorable president esteems as his own Children, and the members of the ancient Tuesday Club, look upon them as their brethren, they being all members of that ancient and worthy Society, as for the abstract of the Clubs history, which you mentioned to me in another Letter, the thing has not as yet been laid before the honorable the president with proper form and ceremony, so that his Consent is yet wanting, and his Superlative prudence will not permit him to give his consent to any proposition suddenly, let it appear ever so Simple or plain, but there must be mature Consideration upon the matter, before the Determining *fiat* be pronounced from the Chair, there is also as yet wanting, a proper and able Historiographer, to connect and form into an uniform Rhapsody affairs and facts of such Singular Importance, but so soon as these weighty points are discussed, I shall give you further notice, in the mean time, permit me, in the name of the honorable the president and members of our ancient Tuesday Club, to subscribe myself Sir,

Octor: 10th 1749   Your most Devoted and obedient
                                     Humble Servant
                                     Loquacious Scribble Secr:

P:S: Some observed, during the reading of your letter, tho I will not vouch it for a truth, because my eyes were fixed another way, that the worshipful Sir John, knight of the Tuesday Club, wore an austere frown upon his countenance, but whether ‖ it was that he thought himself slighted in not being mentioned respectfully or so much as taken notice of in your Letter, or, because he often delights to act a Counterpart to his honor the presi-

---

3. "For sorrow!"
4. "What shame or restraint should there be for the mourning of so dear a head?" (Horace, *Carmina* 1.24.1).

however, if there appears any excellence in the Phraze, or Stile, I must not take all the glory to myself, but frankly ascribe the largest half to the honorable president's accurate pen, for his honor was pleased to Revise the Letter, before it was sent away, he refined and interlined it, and added some touches of Inexpressible elegance, and that particular passage, which you Quote, vizt: *Please tell Mr Makefun in Particular, if ever he makes another present of English beer to the Club &ct:* was Inserted by his express Command, || which, I agree with you comprehends so much wit and archness in a few words, that the author of that short sentence, whoever he be, might well pass in the eyes of the world for an original.

[533]

Gratitude obliges us here to take notice of the elegancies of your Letter, since you did us the honor, to touch somewhat largely on what you are pleased to call most beautiful flowers of Rhetoric, and a wonderful Group of fine Images in ours. Your whole Letter is such a fluent and finished piece of the true Sublime, that the honorable president and Club cannot Sufficiently recompense the author, for giving them an opportunity to adorn and decorate their archives, with such a masterpiece of wit and eloquence, where, among the many Elegant touches, that shine in the body of the work, the divine art of punning stands in the most conspicous view, what a beautiful and Striking pun is couched under these words, *Short in the Instrument—al way,* what a master Stroke is there in *Some who pretend to see as far into a Stone as a free Mason,* what an elegant and Succinct Definition of a *Nincompoop,* have we got in these words, *Artifice, Artifice all,* what a droll but Just Contrast Is Introduced betwixt the said *Nincompoop* and a *Natural,* what an apt Simile is that of a *Cat's purring alittle in time and tune,* and in fine, what a Consistent group of fine tropes and touches, is there in the honorable President's *Thrilling notes, Commanding our Souls, stilling our passions, and at the same time forceing us to laugh* || *when we had a great mind to appear grave,* there are besides these Inimitable beauties, the *Quantums* & *Quales,* the *quas humana parum Cavit natura,* the *macti este virtuti,* elegant, and I may safely say, Classical ejaculations, which shine in the body of your elaborate epistle like Splendid and precious Sapphires set in Gold, and which, as they are wrote in Large text Characters in our book of Records, will recommend us all to posterity as very Learned men, and most profound Scholars; Oh! how can we recompense or retalliate such a profusion of Learned bounty and benevolence? when shall the ancient Tuesday Club have a Secretary of such erudition, as to make equal returns or answers to such elaborate and Superlative Sketches of Learning and wit? and can we ever put too great a value upon such a learned friend and Correspondent?

[534]

To The Revd: Mr Smoothum Sly, Talbot County.

Sir,

Your Letter in the name of the worshipful Eastren || Shore triumvirate [531] was read in Club, upon Tuesday the 26th *ultimo;* I had the honor to read it, and did it with a *bon grace,* and a Stentorian voice, it was received with Infinite Satisfaction and respect by the whole Society, and in a particular manner by the most honorable the president, who wore upon his countenance, during the whole time of the lecture, a most gracious and Serene Smile, which added a peculiar Grace and Comliness to the Corrigations of his countenance, among the rest of the members, (I mean the Commoners) the effect was of a rougher, or more unpolished Cast, for my voice, loud as it was, several times was drowned with *Grandes eclats de rire,*[2] notwithstanding our Laughter Master general, Mr Musician Neverout happened not to be in Club, and it was more the pity that he missed the opportunity of hearing himself Justly enough pictured out, tho' not to any great advantage.

The honorable president and Club, were all very well pleased with your opinion of the musician, & think it exactly Just, but some of our Stricter politicians took somewhat in bad part your opinion of the Club, concerning their Conduct In my unhappy affair of the Orator, as for my own part, modesty forbids me to say so much of the matter, Tis like, the honorable president & Club, who are competent Judges in affairs of this Nature, might see some Ineptitude in me, for that dignified office, which the worshipful Triumvirate, from the abundance of their good nature and humanity might overlook, or not readily perceive, but one motive, I am Sure Influenced our honorable pre- || sident and Club, which was this, that I was [532] already Secretary and Chief Clerk of the Club, and therefore they were unwilling to Load me with another Charge, lest I should be negligent in my office, as Secretary, which office they esteemed more essential and necessary in the Club than that of orator.

I am mightily obliged to the worshipful Triumvirate for the honor they have done me, in appointing me their honorary Orator, a dignified place, in which, I am afraid my slender abilities, will not enable me Conspicuously to shine, however, I shall to the utmost of my power endeavor to deserve it, by a most bombast and Sonorous Oration, to be delivered, the first time I am so happy as to visit your parts.

As for your high Compliments upon the Rhetorical touches in my Letter, it is not for me to take much notice of them, or to Insist much on the affair, one way or other, lest I should unwarily betray some vanity,

---

2. "Great bursts of laughter."

upon Paganism & Xtianity, and tho' the Slip has overgrown the Stock so as quite to kill the Christian Scyon, yet the pagan Stock and the Graft are now so Incorporated, that you cannot distinguish the one from the other, and they have both become as it were one religion, only changing the names of the objects of worship, vizt: those of the ancient heathen Deities for those of Saints, for a Confirmation of which Consult Doctor Conyers Middletons *Letter from Rome,*[1] 3d, the Eastren Shore Triumvirate, at first a small Society, founded upon the policy, and springing from the bowels of the ancient and honorable Tuesday Club, consisting at first only of three members called Triumvirs, has now, as it were become a centumvirate, spreading itself all over the Spacious Territory of Talbot county, and part of Queen Annes, on the Eastren main, whereas, its parent, the Tuesday Club, is Confined to the narrow Limits of the City of Annapolis, and a Scattering of a few honorary members, in the Counties of both Shores.

This Triumvirate was now become so great and numerous, that they began to assume to themselves pompous names and titles, and like the free masons, stile their Society the *Worshipful* and *right Worshipful*, and had wrote, (as we have seen) by ‖ their Secretary, a Long letter to the ancient and honorable Tuesday Club, which was there read.

At Sederunt 114 October 10th 1749, Huffman Snap Esqr, being high Steward, the Secretary produced an answer to the triumvirates Letter, drawn up by him, according to the order of Last Sederunt, but before he read it to the Club, he made the following motion, at the Instance, (as he said) of the Worshipful Triumvirate.

"That an exact and accurate History of the ancient and honorable Tuesday Club, should be undertaken and penned, from its first foundation, to this present time, and, that an able Historiographer, should be appointed to compose and Collect the same."

To which motion the Honorable the President and the Club, gave a Categorical answer in the negative and would by no means Consent, that any such History should be compiled, this repulse very much chagrined the Secretary, as he expected to be employed, in this great work, being the only proper person for it, as keeper of the Records, for he promised himself not only great Profits, as the Club's Historiographer, but also flattered his vanity, that he should make a very great figure in the Republic of Letters, In quality of an Historian.

The answer to the Triumvirates Letter was read as follows.

---

1. Hamilton is referring especially to chapter 4, "Worship of Images," in which Middleton argues that the Catholic Church has simply replaced the gods of the Pantheon with idols of its own.

Mr Muddy having thus spoke, sat down, and the Reverend Mr Philo Dogmaticus (entertained this night as a Stranger by the Club, according to their ancient custom of Civility to Strangers) for whom this Compliment was Intended, made a Low bow to the Speaker, and observed to the Club, that it was pity this Gentleman was going to leave the Club, for that he would make an excellent Club orator.

The Secretary then rising up spoke as follows, directing his discourse to Mr Muddy.

"Sir,

Our honorable president, and the Longstanding members of this here Club, are very Sensible of their loss, in being deprived of so worthy a member, as you, and nothing could so well compensate, or make a mends for this Incident, as their being assured that it is for your advantage, in many respects, ‖ that you leave this parish to take the charge of a better, tho' you will scarce find, that you leave this here Club to become a member of a better, as a better than this is no where to be found, this, together with the expectation that we shall not utterly be deprived of your Company, and, that when you are called to this place, you will visit us *en passant,* contributes to alleviate our Concern, for being deprived of so agreeable a member."

It was then Decreed, that the Reverend Mr Roundhead Muddy, should still continue a regular member of this Club, tho a non-resident.

Chapter VI

Proposal for writing the History of the Club rejected, Hierogliphical Characters Introduced into the Club Letters, Jonathan Grog Esqr, created Master of Ceremonies.

As Slips will often overgrow the Stocks on which they are grafted, so, some Societies, that rise out of the bowels of others, will overgrow their parent Society, and some religions will outstrip in number of professors their parent Religion, this is evident in three particular Cases which I shall name, vizt: two Religious and one Civil Case, 1st Mahometanism, was Grafted upon Judaism and Christianity, and now has far out grown them Both, having overspread almost all Asia, and a great part of Europe and Afric, whereas the others are only scattered in very small ‖ parcells here and there, in Europe and America, and some other bye corners of the world; 2d The popish Religion, which is called the Catholic Church, was Engrafted

> For, if his holiness would thump
> His reverend bum 'gainst horses rump,
> He might b'equipp'd from his own Stable
> With one as white and eke more able.

Some may alledge Indeed, that his holyness the pope has a very good lucrative reason for keeping up this form, whereas, we do not find, that his honor the president, or indeed any body else, made any gain ‖ or profit by Mr Comus's resuming or resigning his office every Club night, but, to silence all objections and Cavils of this Sort, does not the Doge of Venice yearly sail out in a Gondola, and formally wed the Adriatic Sea, by throwing into it a gold ring, that very Significant Symbol of matrimony.[8] If then this powerful high priest, and that magnificent Duke or Doge, observe these Superfluous ceremonies, why may not Laconic Comus Esqr do the same.

The Reverend Mr Roundhead Muddy after Supper, stood up, and addressed himself to his honor the president and Club as follows.

"Right Honorable Mr President,

And you most worthy Longstanding members, of this august and ancient Tuesday Club,

After I have in a grateful manner, acknowledged the many great favors, I have received from your honor, and this right worthy Society, I am to tell you with regret, that I am now obliged to leave it, the nature of my affairs so requiring it, that I must remove to a distant place, I should have thought myself happy always to have enjoyed the pleasure of your good company, and conversation, and to have continued a Constant and assiduous member of this here ancient and honorable Tuesday Club, but as this cannot be, I must now take my leave of your honor and these here Longstanding members, I only ask this favor, which I hope your honor and these worthy gentlemen will readily grant, ‖ that I may still be continued a regular member of this here Society, and as often as I am in the place when the Club meets, I shall always do myself the pleasure of waiting upon your honor and these worthy members, this Satisfaction I have however, upon my leaving the place, that I have left in my Room a worthy Gentleman, of established good Character, so that the people, not only of this parish, but, the Long Standing members of this here Club, (as I suppose the Gentleman will soon become one of our Society) have made a very advantageous exchange."

---

8. In 1177 Pope Alexander III gave the Doge, or chief magistrate of Venice, a gold ring in honor of the Venetian victory at Istria over Frederick Barbarossa; in annual commemoration of this event, the Doge threw a similar ring into the Adriatic, saying, "We wed thee, O sea, in token of perpetual domination."

people stare and laugh, he had a curious punch bowl, Japaned exactly like China, which was not frangible, which he would often let drop out of his hand, as he gave it to his fellow, which excited both Surprize and fear in the Standers by, but he always took Special Care that almost all the Grog or Rumbo was evacuated before he put this Joke in practise, that there might be as little loss as possible, he had a small piece of Glass Cylender, which looked like Sealing wax, with which he duped many, by making them hold it to the candle, to melt it till they burnt their fingers, he had in his Chaw box, a small piece of the tail of a pig, which he gave to several persons who asked a Chaw of him, but they might have tugged, till they pulld out their teeth, but could not bite it, or make it separate. With these merry Jokes, this bard used often to divert himself.

Mr Protomusicus Neverout, having been absent, ever since the 27th of June Last when he was high Steward, It was disputed whether or not he had forfeited his Seat as a member, by the tenor of Law 13th, but it was made appear, that he had sent an excuse, upon the 22d of || august, when [525] Jonathan Grog Esqr served as high Steward, which the Secretary had ommitted to enter.

The place of Master of Ceremonies being now vacant, it was disputed, who should next fill that office, and was at last determined, that it should be a privilege of the Chair, to nominate or appoint, a master of Ceremonies for the night, when necessity should require, thus, the longstanding members not considering the consequences, still kept heaping of new privileges on the Chair.

It was also thought expedient, that Laconic Comus Esqr, should formally resign his office of orator every Club night, Some may think this a very absurd resolution of the Club, but not so fast, there can be a very good precedent given for it, dont we all know, that his holiness the pope, who is Infallible, as we are told, for an old Grudge, formally excommunicates his Catholic majesty of Spain, sometime about Easter, once a year, and his catholic majesty, in order to get clear of that heavy Sentence, presents his holiness, with a fine milk white mare of the best breed, as our Ingenious English Lyric poet has observed.[7]

> As once a twelvemonth, to the priest,
> Holy at Rome, here anti-christ,
> The Spanish king presents a Gennet,
> To show his love, that's all that's in it,

---

7. Hamilton has accurately quoted the opening lines of Matthew Prior's lengthy "Epistle to Fleetwood Shephard, Esq."

388 [Book VI]

[523]

To this Letter the Secretary was ordered to prepare an answer, and lay it before the Club, next Sederunt.

After Supper a petition was presented, to the honorable the president, from the Single Ladies of Annapolis, which was read, and ordered to be entered, the tenor of which follows.

To The Honorable Nasifer Jole Esqr, President of the worshipful and ancient Tuesday Club, the petition and remonstrance, of sundry of the Single females of Annapolis.

Showeth,

That whereas it has been observed by sundry persons as well as your petitioners, that a Singular and Surprizing Success, has all along attended such happy females, as your honor has been pleased to pitch upon, as the toasts of the honorable Chair, every one of whom in a short time, after having been thus adopted by your honor, has Successfully and happily been provided, with a much more Eligible State, than that of a Single Life,

Your petitioners therefore, earnestly pray, that your honor, instead of conferring your favors in so partial a manner, would, in Commiseration of our desperate Situation, Include us all in the circle of your favor, that the benign Influence of your honor's maritiferous notice, may henceforth equally shine upon us all, which benevolent Condescention of your honor, will have a tendency to multiply the Inhabitants of this City, as well as to better our present forlorn Situation.

And your petitioners shall ever pray &ct:

The honorable the president was pleased to declare that he would grant this petition as far as lay in his power.

[524]

I must not here omitt an arch Joke of Jonathan Grog Esqr, passed upon Jealous Spyplot Senr, the Latter was making a bowl of Rumbo, and wanted some nutmeg to grate upon it, when the facetious poet, put into his hand a pig nut, as hard as a pebble Stone, exactly of the Shape and colour of a nutmeg, at which he might have rubbed and scrubbed till dooms day, even upon a file, and not have procured a Democritic atom from it, so that the worthy Mr Spyplot was for one quarter of an hour at least *occupatus nihil agendo*,[6] and furnishing matter of laughter for the Club. The Ingenious Laureat, had several Jokes of this kind by which he used to make

---

6. "Occupied doing nothing"; above, Hamilton is alluding to the atomic theory of Democritus (born ca. 460–457 B.C.), the famous "laughing philosopher" and the greatest of the Greek physical philosophers.

he should ever make another present of English beer to the Club, to be Sure to Commit it to more trusty hands than Mr Musician Neverout's"—what a rare collection of the most beautiful flowers of Rhetoric, and how wonderful a group of the finest Images is here, such as *Please!—another present!—English beer!—The Club!—Trusty hands!*—we think we might fairly challenge any orator, either ancient or modern, to muster up such a delightful knot of Rhetorical florishes, within so small a compass, besides, what a delicate hint is here given, to Mr Makefun, to make another present of English beer to the Club, In fine Sir, the beauties of this passage, could be owing to nothing less than the Inspiration of English beer, which Butler says has Inspired many,[4] and, as we doubt not you excell as much in the declamatory, as in the petitory way, so, we think you exceedingly well ‖ qualified for the office of [522] an orator, this we thought proper for your Sake to remark *en passant,* as it may serve for a hint to the worthy Society, to consider better of your merit, and prefer you to the office you are so ambitious of, be that as it will, we have, upon this admirable Specimen of your abilities, constituted you honorary Orator of our Triumvirate, vizt: Mr Makefun, Signior Lardini & myself.

We have the honor to send our dutiful Compliments to the Illustrious and Serene President, and our best respects to the worthy Society, as well State as Common officers, not forgetting our honorary Orator, this, in the Name of the above Triumvirate, be pleased to represent from Sir,

Talbot County	Your most humble Servant
August 31st 1749	*Smoothum Sly.*

P:S: We Sincerely condole the Death of Capt: Seemly Spruce, and doubt not, but the Eulogium Mr Jonathan Grog[(a)] made upon him, was Intended both to do Justice to his memory, and to pay a Compliment to the Club, tho' some that pretend to see, as far into a Stone as a *free Mason*[5] are of opinion that it was owing to his being a Gentleman born & bred in New England—S:S:

(a) Vide *Maryland Gazette* No 223.

4. In *Hudibras* Samuel Butler invokes the nameless muse who ". . . with Ale, or viler Liquors, / Didst inspire *Withers, Pryn,* and *Vickars,* / And force them, though it were in spight / Of nature and their stars, to write" (*Hudibras,* ed. John Wilders [Oxford, 1967], 1.1.639–642).

5. Again, Hamilton seems to have applied an old proverb in a new way. To "see as far into a stone as any other man" is the typical use of this proverb (see, e.g., Dryden's "I am a fool, . . . but yet I can see as far into a Mill-stone as the best of you" [*Amphitryon* V.i.]). Hamilton has adapted the proverb to the Freemasons, who were known for their secrecy, or in this case, for their ability to penetrate mysteries.

prosper, may your Society be lasting, and it's happiness equal to your wishes.

[520]   Certain it is, tho I know not how it happens, that the mind is more Sprightly and active in company, than alone, the Images crowd in faster, and humor flows in a freer vein, || perhaps it may be owing to the Sight of our friends, and I doubt not, the toasting of the Ladies, gives a brisk and agreeable motion to the Spirits, and by that means enlivens conversation and calls forth every humorous Sentiment, this made Mr Makefun Signior Lardini and myself, resolve to erect a Club in our neighborhood, tho' we are sorry to tell you, that we have not as yet been able to accomplish our design, if we had, we were determined fully, to copy after your original as near as possible.

    Mr Musician Neverout's rude behavior upon many occasions, to the honorable the president, besides, the flemmish account he has made of the English beer, Sufficiently recommends him to Mr Makefun, but above all his Impudently disputing the prize with the honorable president, in Singing, provokes our resentment, and raises our Indignation, in a word, we look upon the one to be a natural, the other to be a mere Nincompoop in vocal music, that is to say, the honorable the President is by nature furnished with these gifts, that are requisite to form a good Singer, whereas the other is nothing but an Artifice, artifice all, we have frequently heard Mr Musicians made tunes and unnatural Notes, to the great disquiet of our ears, and the no less danger of a headake, on the other hand, the proper tunes, thrilling notes and captivating Sounds of the honorable president, have frequently stilld our passions, commanded our Souls, and forced us to laugh, when we had a mind to appear grave, in short, when we hold up the musician to the light of the honorable the president, he is Intirely eclipsed, and we can only compare him to a Cat, that can pur alittle In time and tune, so that he seems to us to be as Imperfect in the vocal, as he has been deem'd short in the Instrument—al ways.

[521]   Tis with the utmost concern Sir, that we differ in any thing with your worthy Society, but their rejecting your offer as orator, is a piece of conduct, that we cannot altogether reconcile ourselves to, especially, as you generously set yourself up as a candidate for that office, which motion, we understand, was not so much as seconded—This we take to be a procedure, by no means equal to the Judgement of the ancient Tuesday Club, or the merit of their faithful Secretary, for, from a passage in your letter, it appears to us, that your abilities as an orator, are far from being Inconsiderable. The passage is as follows, *"Sir, Please to tell Mr Makefun, in particular, that in case*

that Society, would have Indeed been too heavy for me to support, had not a reflection, upon the uncommon Candor of your August Club, on the one hand, and the Remarkable good nature of the Gentlemen on the other, come Seasonably in to my relief, but, to convince you, that I urge not this as a plea, for Indolence or Laziness, I assure you Sir, that after having Invoked Genius, eloquence and Learning to asist me, and being Inspired with some of Bacchus's richest Gifts in the hospitable house of the Generous Mr Makefun, I attempted to execute the Commands of the honorable the president, and the worthy members of the ancient Tuesday Club, in the handsomest and most polite manner, in the kindest and most expressive terms, I was able, the Message was received by the Gentlemen with the profoundest respect, and the most grateful acknowledgements, especially to the President, the *Grand Original,* of honor and Ex- || cellence, that adds a [519] dignity to, and spreads a Lusture over your society; a president, of whose body and mind, we are far from being able to describe the *Quantums* and the *Quales,* and indeed, in our opinion, the Sublimest panegyric, and the finest picture, must come far short of the *Original,* the Solemnity of his countenance prognosticates his wisdom, and his air of Insinuating address, a deep penetration, his good breeding is enough to polish a province, and his humor and facetious disposition to Charm the most Intelligent Club, his conversation is universally acknowledged to be the Standard of Sheer wit, and his picquant reflections to be big with the Sharpest and Justest Satir,—The humble and quiet member, might ever find a safe retreat, under the Shadow of his Eyebrows, and be covered with the wings of his authority, in a word, we may, without the Imputation of flattery, pronounce him a mantainer of the Dignity of the Chair, a friend to prerogative, and an enimy to false patriotism and faction. What a delightful figure must such a president make, at the head of a Club, Composed of members, in whose generous bosoms dwell the noble and disinterested friendship, the melting love, the humane benevolent Sentiment, the ardent Gratitude, the soft compassion, and the Candid opinion,[(a)] notwithstanding some little blemishes, *Quas humana parum Cavit Natura*[(b)], *macti este virtuti,* go on and

(a) Vide Fielding's *History of Tom Jones.*[2]
(b) Horace quoted by Fielding, *History of Tom Jones.*[3]

2. This passage is typical of the many panegyrical speeches in *Tom Jones,* such as the one Tom delivers on Nightingale's wife in bk. 14, chap. 7.
3. "Which human nature has failed to avoid, be honored for virtue" (Horace, *Ars poetica,* line 353; *Satirae* 1.2.31). The first passage appears twice in *Tom Jones,* at the end of bk. 10, chap. 1, and in bk. 11, chap. 1.

To the Honorable Nasifer Jole Esqr,
President of the Tuesday Club.

Honorable Sir, Septr 26th 1749

The Club, according to the appointment of the last meeting, is to be at my Father's house this night, where I have the honor of serving as high Steward, therefore Sir, according to the usual and Just manner, of the wise and worthy members, of our ancient || and well constituted Society, I (by this) desire the honor and favor of your auspicious presence, the want of which seemed to *boad,* a dissolution of our happiness and unanimity.

I hope, by this nights Chearfulness, every thing that is past and unpleasant will be erased and forgot, I am, Honored Sir,

Your obedient & humble Servt:
Jealous Spyplot Junr:

What the penman of this Letter (which seems to be wrote in a concise and elegant Stile of Language) means by every thing that was passed being erazed and forgot, must be left for future Criticks to find out, for, it exceeds my ability to explain the passage, unless you will admit, (which I am very loath to do) that this gentleman bore a Spite and animosity to all the Club Records, and therefore wished, that every thing that was passed should be erazed; As for his wishing that things unpleasant should be forgot & erazed, I think that no Strange wish in any good natured man.

Then the Secretary produced in Club, a letter from the Reverend Mr Smoothum Sly, in the name of the Eastren Shore triumvirate, In answer to one, which he had been ordered to write by the club, on Sederunt 110th, the Transcript of which Letter follows.

To Loquacious Scribble Esqr, at Annapolis, These.

Sir,

Next to my acknowledging the receit of your Second || (tho the first to me), I cannot forbear remarking, that the preamble or prologue of it, differs from most other modern prologues in this, vizt: whereas these have little or no connexion with the pieces they stand before, yours on the contrary is a very pertinent Introduction to the Letter it is prefixed to, and the whole production is a manifest proof to me, how well you are qualified for sustaining the office of Orator in the ancient Tuesday Club, in which, however, I am sorry to understand, you were lately disappointed.

The arduous Task of returning to Messrs Makefun and Lardini, the compliments of the honorable the President and worthy members of the ancient Tuesday Club, in a manner suited to the Dignity and excellence of

accommodate matters to the Satisfaction of his honor the president, which the high Steward wisely foresaw was Impossible to be done without making a Sacrifice of him, for the good of the Common weal, and therefore like a wise and politic Statesman, he stood up with great gravity in his countenance, mixed with a small degree of Gelasticity, and declared His Intention to leave the Club, on account of the Great Inconvenience and trowble it was to him, to serve in his turn as H:S: he being a Single man, possessed of no house of his own, in which with Decency, to entertain his honor and the Club, and begged the members to Indulge him so far, as to take this his proposal in Good part; The members willingly & chearfully agreed to it, professing, That by their Constitution they were a free Society, and every man was at liberty to go and come at pleasure. Thus by this Impolitic Step, the Club lost a deputy Secretary & Master of Ceremonies at one blow.

Chapter V

More Sublime Club Letters, Petition to his honor the President from the Single females, several Club Speeches.

The resentments of Great men, must at all events be gratified, and suffered at first eruption to have their full Spring, for, should the Inferiour powers, || That is, the *profanum vulgus,*[1] endeavor to confine it, like a Spark among gun powder pent up and rammd down, it produces a violent explosion, which tears and rends and drives every thing before it, with an Inexpressible and Irresistable fury, whereas, if it has free air, and is left to its Self, it will either Spontaneously die away, or go off with a puff, this politic maxim, the Longstanding members of this ancient and honorable Club seemed not to be Ignorant of, when to save their constitution, now In danger of a Lapse, they at Sederunt 113 Septr 26th, 1749, Jealous Spyplot Junr Esqr, being high Steward, gave way to the earnest desire of his honor the president, to have the Letters of the Late high Steward, which had given such offence, read, and Condemned to perpetual oblivion, a Just fate to all fomenters of mischief. [516]

A letter from the High Steward, to his honor the President was read and entered as follows.

1. "Vulgar mob" (see, e.g., Horace, *Carmina* 3.1.1).

either to come himself to Club, or send a deputation, but it was too late, for his honor, being Implacable at that time would do neither, Therefore, the members understanding the Cause of offence, was that Ill Contrived letter of Cats, as above related, they advised the high Steward to write a Submissive Letter to his honor, requesting him to come to Club, which advice he followed, and the Letter was sent to his honor, by a Special messenger, from the Club, but still to no purpose, his honor remained Inflexible, then a dispute arose among the members present, whether this meeting was a Club or not, as there was no Deputy appointed, and if it was not a Club, whether or not his honor the president, had not voluntarily and of his own

[514] ‖ free will and accord, abdicated the Chair, in this dispute some doubts were started, whether the word *abdicated* was proper, as were in a very wise and august assembly at Westminster, in the year —88, but this appearing to be a dangerous argument to Insist upon, no determination was made thereon.

This was the first time, that his honor the president refused to send a deputation in his own absence, which obliged the Club afterwards for the Security of the Constitution, to pass a Law, whereby they took to themselves the power of electing a deputy, in case of his honor's refusing himself to appoint one, but his honor, to this day with some Show of Reason, (at least reason founded upon Law, which I think does not always come up to the Sterling Stamp, for tho we are told by Certain Grave Dons, that the Law is founded upon reason, yet Philosophers will not agree, that reason derived from Law is every where Current) Questions their power to make any such Law, as it plainly encroaches upon, and is contradictory to the presidential prerogative, which he is obliged Strictly to mantain against all attempts, for his own Sake, and that of his Successors in the Chair, thus, we see, how this ancient and honorable Club, by rashly giving too much to his honor the president, have entangled themselves in an Everlasting Labyrinth of Cavils, and disputes about prerogative and privilege, like some other Sagacious and politic Societies and States, who, bewitched by the Jargon of a Set of Quibbling Gownmen, Chuse rather to be Governed by rules and orders of their own Invention, than submit themselves to the direction and dictates of common Sense and reason.

[515] After Supper, Mr Secretary Scribble came into the Club & reported to the members, from the honorable the president, (with whom he had been for some hours in private Conference) his high displeasure at the high Stewards Letter, for which the members expressed their concern and Sorrow, and resolved to consider on ways and means, against next Sederunt, to

ture, I should be loath to say, that it was mere caprice, or out of some picque he had conceived at the high Steward, but be that as it will, Quirpum Comic Esqr, the high Steward, In order to please his honor *If possible,* had the room Cleaned, well sweeped and scrubbed, with mops, brushes, dusting Cloths brooms and Rubbers, and all in decent order for the Reception of the Club, which it had not been, for 50 years before, at least not in the memory of any body then Living, This Possibly might have brought his ‖ honor in some measure to comply, had the high Steward [512] gone no farther, but he being in some degree nettled by his honor's unreasonable and uncivil behavior, could not restrain his rash and unadvised hand, but wrote his honor a Satyrical letter, which I cannot call by a more proper name than the *letter of Cats,* this letter was not suffered to be recorded, but the passage in it that gave offence, was nearly to this purpose, "That he [the high Steward] Intended to hold his Club in the School room, and, that his honor might have no objection to it, on account of the nastiness of the room, he had swept it clean, and taken care to whip out all *Cats* and dogs, Cats especially, as being a vermin mighty apt to breed fleas, and to piss about, and excite a very disagreeable perfume." This was the pinch, not only talking in such a Slighting manner of Cats, his honors favorites, but besides, there was a Sting in the tail of this observation, which was contained in the Implication, that his honors rooms were nasty, and perfumed with a disagreeable Odor, as he kept always a great number of these domestic animals about him, and also, that his honor's taste in this particular was ridiculous and weak, in making such mighty favorites of those brutes, this raised his honors Spleen and resentment to such a height, that he was heard to swear in his wrath, that he never would come nigh the Club again, or be any way concerned in it, and had his honor kept to this rash vow, here would have been an end and final Dissolution of this ancient and honorable Club, The frame and Consti- ‖ tution of which, was now so [513] Interwoven with his honor's presence and countenance, that it could no ways subsist or exist without him, but the destinies had decreed otherwise, and his honor, as we shall see, was soon reconciled, tho the high Steward thought it his best prudence and policy to leave the Club, to evade the furious blow that threatened him from his honor's Just resentment, tho' like all great men, when they give up their offices and places, he pretended that his departure from the Club was voluntary, as we shall presently see.

At the same Sederunt, a few of the Longstanding members met (not at the School room as was Intended but) at the house of Prim Timerous Esqr; The high Steward having given up his purpose of meeting in the School room, in order, *if possible,* to be reconciled to his honor, and Induce him,

[510] At Sederunt 111, augst 22d, Jonathan Grog Esqr being high Steward, his Honor the president pro- ‖ duced a Letter from the high Steward, which was read and recorded, the Tenor of which follows.

To Nasifer Jole Esqr,
President of the Tuesday Club,
at his Mansion house in North East Street, Annapolis.

Honorable Sir,

This short Epistle is a Messenger to acquaint you, that the Tuesday Club, of which you are most deservedly the head, is to meet at my house in Charles Street this evening, being the twenty Second of the month, where I hope you will honor me with your *august* presence, as without that the entertainment will be tastless and Insipid to the members, but especially Great Sir to

> Your much devoted
> Very humble Servant & H:S:
> *Jonathan Grog.*

I come now to relate a transaction, seemingly triffling in itself, which notwithstanding, occasioned such a difference between his honor the president and the Club, as that it had well nigh ended in a final dissolution of this ancient and honorable Society, it was a Letter wrote to his honor the President by the high Steward Mr Quirpum Comic, at Sederunt 112, September 5th 1749, which was Intended for a Jest, but not being properly [511] Seasoned with discretion, or applied to a proper person, proved ‖ a mischievous Jest, Mr Comic being a Single man, and no house keeper, intended to hold his Club in the School Room, the ancient place of meeting of the ugly Club as has been mentioned elsewhere, in this history, his honor had an objection to this, alledging that a place where School boys met, was not at all proper for such wise men as the Longstanding members of the Tuesday Club to assemble in; besides, he objected to the place, on account of its Nastiness, and professed publicly and openly, that if the Club was held there, he would neither come himself, nor appoint a deputy, what his honor's reason could be, for objecting to this place of meeting, at this particular Juncture, (when it appears, he made no manner of objection to it at Sederunt 87, when the Club met there and his honor was there present himself at the drawing up the articles for the Delivery of the Club box; and also at Sederunt 101, when the said Mr Comic was high Steward and kept His Club in that place, when his honor tho not present show'd his approbation by appointing Laconic Comus Esqr his Deputy,) we can by no means conjec-

eraze his name from the list. This astonished some of the Longstanding members very much, and they did not know which most to admire at, the caprice of his honor the president, in refusing such a legal and reasonable demand, or the thin Skin of Mr Muddy in resenting such a triffle, tho many believed that Mr Muddy was not in earnest, and that his resentment of this, was nothing but a Clubical resentment.

At Sederunt 110 augst: 8, 1749, The worshipful Sir John being high Steward, The Club took into their Serious consideration, the Rev^d Mr Muddy's request to the Secretary as it stood upon the Record of last Sederunt, vizt: whether It should be complied with or not, but before they had proceeded far in the argument, the Revd Mr Muddy, came and took his Seat in Club, which determined, or put an end to the dispute.

His Honor the president produced a letter from the High Steward, which was read and recorded as follows.

To the Honorable Nasifer Jole Esqr,
President of the Honorable Tuesday Club.

Sir,

I am to have the pleasure of Entertaining The most worthy Tuesday Club, this night at my ‖ house, *whare* I hope you will give me the honor of your good company, which is, not only to night, but at all times acceptable to, *grate* Sir, your Honor's

From my Castle	Most humble &
August the 8th, 1749	Most obedient Servant to Command
	Sir John, knight of the Most honble:
	Tuesday Club.

His honor the president sung the Catch called the *Great bell of Lincoln*, this night, on account of the admission of the Reverend Mr Muddy into the Club, we find in the records of this Sederunt the following entry.

"This night The honorable Mr President Jole, appeared in a mourning badge Ribbon, on account of the Death of Capt: Seemly Spruce, late a worthy regular member of this Club, and one of the oldest members, having been of the Club, since the time of it's first Institution, a Gentleman, whose humane and benevolent Character, whose friendly and Sociable disposition, procured him so much the esteem and affection of every one that knew him, in his life time, that his Death is most Justly and most Sincerely Lamented, and in a particular manner, by the members of this Club, who, out of regard and affection for his memory, have ordered their Secretary to enter this short, tho' Just eulogium in their Book of records."

This Law was passed on occasion of the general Clamor and hurly burly, at last Sederunt. Against it Sir John Entered his protest, declaring that he was for an unlimited liberty of Speech in Club, and for his part would always use that Liberty—none durst contradict him.

Law XLI. Resolved *Nem: Con:* and passed into a Law by the President and Club now met, that for the future no honorary member shall be allowed to vote in any dispute whatsoever.

His Honor the President produced a letter from the high Steward, which was read and recorded as follows.

To Nasifer Jole Esqr,
President of the Tuesday Club.

Sir,

This night being the Tuesday Club, whereon it comes to my turn to serve, as Steward, *Custome* has made it necessary, not only so, but Instituted it Into a Law, for every Steward in his turn to serve ‖ to acquaint the President therewith, it therefore becomes a duty in me, so to do; I hope you'll favor me with your presence this evening at the Club, at my house, which shall esteem as a great honor Conferrd upon me, by a person of your exalted merit, I have the honor of being with great respect Sir,

July 25th 1749

Your most obedient
Most obsequious and
Most humble Servant
Jealous Spyplot Senr:

This Letter is wrote in a plain honest and manly Stile, and, (except a little florish at the Conclusion) exactly in Character, for this Longstanding member was none of those that dealt in high sounding titles, such as, *your honor, your highness* and such like, tho' we shall find the force of bad example in this Club to be such, as to Corrupt the plain Simplicity and bluntness of even this very Gentleman, who grossly deviates from his usual manner in a Letter which he wrote sometime after this to his honor the president, tho' some suspect that letter to be none of his own Inditing, but his setting his hand to such fustian throws a Cloud over his wonted Sincerity.

It was moved this night, that the *Great bell of Lincoln* should be sung, in honor of the Admission of the Reverend Mr Roundhead Muddy, but, upon account of its having been too late, when the motion was made, his honor the president deferred that ceremony till another night, upon which Mr Muddy, with too ‖ much precipitation and warmth declared That he was no more a member of this here Club, and desired The Secretary to

nature, would occasion abundance of Enmity and ill blood, and even outragious quarrels and blows both wet and dry, where the Shuttle Cock, (to Carry on our metaphor,) lighted upon a tender Skin or an Inflammed or excoriated part, or in a word galled an old Sore.

This makes it necessary, that in passing Joke or Jest, the quality of the Jester and the quality and temper of the Jested, or to speake in the manner of our Learned Lawyers, the *Jestor* and *Jestee,* must always be maturely weighed and Considered, In order to evade an ensuing mischief; The Disposition of the But must be known, whether he be a person, that understands raillery, and also the nature and texture of the Jest it self,—Should the Jestor, for Instance, be a man of a Low degree, and the Jestee a Grandee, should the Jestor be a young Smart, and the Jestee an old Coxcomb or Choleric Don, should the Jestor || be a poor fellow, and the Jestee rich, [505] should the Jestor be a reputed wit, and the Jestee an arrant dunce, it is by no means safe for the Jestor to exercise his talents upon these occasions, and in these cases, again, should the Jest touch some favorite or acquired vice, or natural failing, or expose some folly, or bodily deformity in the Jested, should it strike at any of the favorite maxims of politics or religion, of any party or person, should it affect the beauty, virtue or reputation of any woman, tho ugly as Hecate and leud as Messalene, it is in itself extremely dangerous, and by all means for peaces Sake to be avoided, for history abounds with Instances of the woeful and tragical effects, of such Jests, such as families ruined, Cities burnt and Razed, provinces laid waste, multitudes of men, women and Innocent babes put to the Sword, virgins and modest matrons Ravished &ct: &ct: &ct:

Hence I conclude, that it is a very rash, and Inconsiderate thing, to pass Jests upon Emperors, kings, popes, Lords, proud prelates, powerful fools, noble pimps, wealthy blockheads, Whores and presidents of Clubs. The mischievous and almost fatal effects of an unlucky Jest, to this here ancient and honorable Club, the occasion of this preamble, shall be related in its proper place in this very Chapter.

At Sederund 109, July 25th 1749, Jealous Spyplot Esqr, being high Steward, the following Laws were passed.

Law XL. Resolved and passed into a Law, by the president and Club [506] now met, this 25th of July 1749, that no member shall speak above once in a dispute, and that not above Six minutes, the person who first made the motion may reply, not exceeding the said limited time, and, in case two or three or more members rise up to speak at once, they are to be Called to order, and deliver their opinions one after another as nominated by his honor the president.

account of an Interpolation, added to your honor's Commission of deputation to Slyboots Pleasant Esqr, had not your honor graciously Interposed and overlooked the trespass, which made me again lay down, this unthankful office, yet to show your honor, and these here longstanding members, that I bear no Spite or animosity, to this here turbulent officer, and that I have a Sincere regard, for the peace and wellfare of this here ancient and honorable Club, I freely, and of my own accord offer my Service to act as his deputy with your honor's and the Club's permission, which— ‖ hum— hum—It is my duty to pay a regard to, and thus put a Stop to all his noise and Complaints for the future—hum—hum."

When Mr Comic had thus addressed himself, he sat down, and his honor the President was pleased to confirm him in the office of Deputy Secretary according to his request, then the Secretary desired the President to return him the Record book, which his honor refused first to do, 'till he should make some Submission, and own to the Club, that he had been in the wrong, which, he obstinately refusing to do, by the advice of the Club, to prevent another uproar, which was Just ready to break out, the record book was Solemnly delivered into his hands, by the honorable the president, without any other condition of Reacceptance, but that of his being allowed an asistant in his office.

Then the Club ordered for the greater ease of the Secretary, that Dowble Entries and letters, are henceforth not to be permitted in recording, except the Latter, by a particular order from the President and Club.

Chapter IV

Sublime Club Letters, Eulogium on a Longstanding member deceased, Letter of Cats, danger of a dissolution of the Club, The Master of Ceremonies leaves the Club.

Tho Jesting and Joaking, is often a very pritty Innocent and entertaining amusement, when Introduced ‖ with proper prudence and discretion, as we have somewhere else observed, being like a game at Shuttle Cock, where the volatile and feathered witicism is bandied about from hand to hand, with great Glee, vivacity and agility, which alighting upon any of the bye standers or players, by reason of its light Substance, being Compounded only of Cork and feathers, neither hurts nor bruises, yet have I often known that a Joke or Jest, tho' volatile and light enough in it's own

During this hurly burly, and general Club hubbub and Scuffle, Capt: Nathaniel Sylvius, a plain honest and Simple Gentleman, Invited that night to the Club as a Stranger, according to ancient Custom, endeavored to stand mediator, between his honor & the members, and starting up from his Seat, in the middle of this Club altercation, cried out with great earnestness, expanding his arms, and separating the long Standing members one from another, as one passing thro' a marshe or Swamp, does the reeds or Sedges, "Pray Gentlemen,—good Gentlemen—good Sir President—Sweet Sir President,—pray be quiet—for Gods Sake be easy—Pray good Sir—I beseech you Sir President—gi' me leave Dear Sir—Psha forbear!—avast ho!—Stand aloof,—Let them alone pray—luff luff—port, port—Let them alone, theyll come too presently, the Storm ∥ will blow over." Thus did this [501] good man, with these short and pithy ejaculations, endeavor to make peace between his honor and the Longstanding members, and the Storm was laid by degrees.

When the general clamor was hushed, some proposed that his honor should appoint a Committee, to burn the book, and not only destroy all the Records of the Club hitherto made, but keep no more for the future, this procedure some were of opinion, would tend to the final dissolution of the Club, and therefore it was warmly opposed, and his honor the President, foreseeing, that by this one rash resolve, if he should unadvisedly give in to it, at the Instance of his privy Councellor and right hand man Sir John, who was warm for this motion's taking place, he should lose all the Security he had for his prerogative and authority, notwithstanding that his resentment would have prompted him to do any thing to thwart the Secretary, declared himself openly against this proceeding, and, by his honor's prudence and moderation, the precious book of records, was thus snatched from the devouring flames, and the memorable transactions of this ancient and honorable Club, from eternal oblivion, which, had they been lost, would have been an Irretrievable Dammage to posterity, and have occasioned a Lamentable Chasm or blank, in the Journal De Sçavants, or Republic of Letters.

At Last Quirpum Comic Esqr, Master of the Ceremonies stood up [502] with a grave Staid and Serio-Gelastic countenance, and adjusting his wig, and stroaking down his face and Chin, addressed his honor as follows.

"Mr President, Sir,—hem—

Tho I have heretofore, at the risque of my ears—hum—hum—served your honor's turbulent and ungrateful Secretary, in quality of his deputy without commission or order from your honor or this here Club, and had like to have been drawn by his means Into a premunire, at Sederunt 98, on

374 [Book VI]   The History of

Club Hubbub, concerning the Records.

[facing page 500]

alledged That his was, of all offices in the Club the most trowblesome, especially, since he had been obliged, by an order of the honorable Chair, to make dowble entries, that he had served the Club now almost four years, in quality of Secretary, and that since by all his care and pains, he could not become *Emeritus*, yet he hoped, his honor and the Club would Indulge him at least as much as they had done Mr Orator Comus, whose office and place, was not attended with nigh so much trowble & pains, neither had he served the Club, in any office so long. Upon this, the Secretary delivered the book of Records to his honor the President, declaring That he would not receive it again, till his request was granted.

In making this motion, the Secretary had two ends in view, first to put the Club Into an uproar and confusion, and then to force them, as it were || by this Surrendry of his place to chuse another Secretary, and by some means to get the orators office revived in Club, so, that having removed the objection of his Enjoying a multiplicity of offices, he might the more easily step himself into that honorable place, but the Club made a timely discovery of his policy in this affair, and would by no means Listen to his proposals, however, the motion that he made, so far answered his purpose, as to excite a very hot dispute in Club, some taking one part, and some another, a terrible noise, Clamor, and vociferation arose among the Long standing members, all spoke at once, and all stood up at once, The Reverend Mr Muddy, who was gifted with a mighty Stentorian voice, was heard above all the rest, and his honor the president was not heard at all, it being only known that he spoke by the quick motion of his lips, his turning his face first to the right then to the left of the Chair, and his waving the book of records up and down, which he grasped in both hands, it was for sometime a Confused medley of broken Sentences and words, like those heard in Groenland upon the coming of a General thaw, as Pray Sir—nay Sir—I say Sir—by your leave Sir—what!—must I Con- —no by G—therefore—pox on it—patience alittle—here Club—Judgematic—holla!—damn the book —burn the—hey, hey!—and such like unintelligible Jargon, while the Secretary like a Sly bitch, sat silent all the time Laughing in his Sleeve, and expecting || what the Issue of this general confusion would be, in short, it seemed, as if the Longstanding members would go from words to blows, while the Loud laugh of Mr Protomusicus Neverout, Joined with the hoarse and Stentorian bass of the Revd Mr Roundhead Muddy, and the mingled Clamor of the other members, made the most horrid discord that ever was heard, a thing very unbecoming this musical Gentleman, whose business it was to promote and Improve concord and harmony In Sounds at least, if not in actions and behaviour.

of Club orator, yet that officer was ever after only Classed among the officers of the Commons.

Chapter III

Commotions in Club, the Records In danger of being burnt, Confirmation of a deputy Secretary.

Turbulent and ambitious Spirits, when they cannot by open practices and mere compulsion obtain their ends, often employ cunning and artifice, and place their whole Confidence in that Cursed Machiavelian maxim, *Divide et Impera;* Thus, some wicked politicians, who pretend to act for the good of the public, keeping still a Steddy eye, upon one little pitiful, diminutive point, vizt: their own private Interest and advancement, will clear their way, thro all difficulties and rubs, by exciting the fury of party and faction, among those whom they Intend to make their fools or gulls, and like the dog in the fable, pick up the bone, while their fellow Curs are a fighting,[1] or like a Turkish Janisar Aga, mount the breach of preferment, upon heaps of the Carcases of his own Asapi, or base Soldiery, thrown down by thousands for that purpose alone.

Thus, the Secretary, that ambitious, restless, and turbulent Club officer, still aiming at the Dignity of a State member, which he seemed resolved to procure at any rate Cost what it would, after having by his cunning practices, and fustian orations against the box, undermined and overset Mr Orator Comus, and in a manner wheedled him, into the Surrendry of his honorable || office, made long strides to get into that dignified place himself, and because his cunning and artifice failed him at that Juncture, as we shall see in the relation of what follows, he endeavored all he could to set his honor the president and the Club together by the Ears, in order to try if he could not succeed by that means.

At Sederunt 108, after Mr Orator Comus had made a Surrendry of his office, the Secretary moved to the Club, when he found that his ambitious expectations were quite frustrated, by the Club's proceeding, in abolishing the offices of Orator and Speaker, into one of which he expected to be promoted, That he should have an asistant in his office allowed him, for he

---

1. Hamilton is recalling Swift's "Republick of Dogs," in *The Battle of the Books* (*Prose Works of Swift*, ed. Davis, I, 141–142).

secret, tho' it is conjectured by some, who reckon themselves well skilled in the designs and Secrets of politicians, that it was on account of his bad Success in the attempt made by him to re-establish the Club box; Pray'd his honor the president and Club, that he might lay down his office of Orator, after some dispute, whether he should be Indulged in this Strange request, his honor demanded the Reasons why he should give up his place, but Mr Orator declined giving any reasons, alledging that he was not obliged to do so.

This proposal much pleased the Secretary, whose ambition could stop no where, but at the degree of a State officer, to which dignified Station, he had now for a Long time been endeavoring to climb, and no sooner had he gaind two or three rounds of the Ladder, than he met with a repulse, in spite of all his artifice and Cunning, we shall see how his expectations were here again frustrated, for, tho' this place was given up by Mr Comus, the Secretary was baulkd in his expectations of succeeding him, the Club at last granted Mr Comus's request, and the Orator's Chair being thus vacant, it was next to be considered, who was to succeed in that office, but before the Club could proceed to determin this, Jealous Spyplot Esqr Senr: made the following proposition, That Mr Comus should be Indulged so far, as to have his office as a Sinecure, and be excused from officiating as orator || in consideration, that he was naturally a man of very few words, and of but an Indifferent action and delivery, but, that still retaining the dignity honors and profits, (if any should accrue) he should have leave given him to appoint Deputies to Officiate for him, which proposal Mr Comus Declined, and Insisted upon giving up, place, titles, honors, profits, and every thing belonging to it, which request was most graciously granted him by his honor the President, and Consented to by the Club.

[496]

Then the Question was put, vizt: whether there should be any such officer as a Club Orator or not? it was Caried in the Negative, 7 nays against 4 yeas, this show'd a spirit of Liberty in the Longstanding members, who found that the Chair grew too Strong and powerful with two State officers, and at the same time, their determination in this point, did not displease his honor the president, for he was too Jealous of the other members, to trust them with such an office, particularly the Secretary.

Another Question was then proposed, whether or not there should be any such officer in the Club as a Speaker, the ballots were put round, and it Carried in the negative, Six nays against five yeas, and thus this great office and title in Club, droped, and was extinct, and tho' sometime after this, the title was revived, and the Secretary procured at last by his devices the office

out being high Steward, his honor the president produced a Letter, which was read in Club, and ordered to be recorded as follows.

To the Honorable Nasifer Jole Esqr,
President of The Tuesday Club.

Sir,

    I confess that I had like to have forgot, that I have the honor to serve as high Steward, to your ancient and worthy Club, and therefore Intreat the favor of your most august company.

    But, if Sir, I am to be deprived of that happiness, please to let me know, whom you Intend the honor of representing you, and you'll much oblige Sir,

June 27th 1749	Your most humble Servt:
	Solo Neverout H:S: of the
	Tuesday Club.

[494] This epistle is wrote in the true careless stile and jantee taste, much like that of the Card billets of these our polite times, which shows that Mr Protomusicus was well versed in the Modish Phrazeology.

At the following Sederunt July 11th, the Reverend Mr Roundhead Muddy being high Steward, his honor produced in Club, a Letter from the high Steward as follows.

To The right Honorable Nasifer Jole Esqr,
President of the Tuesday Club.

Sir,

    I expect your *precedential* highness, will honor me with your company, this evening, and tho' I cannot subscribe myself your Honor's high Steward, yet will take it as a favor, if you will accept of such a Chair, as my Lodgings affords, I am, with the most profound respect, your honors

Tuesday evening July the 11th 1749,	Most dutiful &
given at my Lodgings	Most obliged humble Servt:
	Roundhead Muddy.

What a high Strain do we now see the Long Standing members running into, in their compliments to his honor the president, they now address him with the pompous titles of *Right Honorable,* and *highness,* one would think they would stop here, but we shall find it otherwise.

[495]   At this Sederunt Mr Orator Comus, for what ‖ reasons remains a

together with a Scheme for setting on foot a Club box, drawn up by Jonathan Grog Esqr, a member of the said Committee, and his honor delivered them to the Secretary, who read them to the Club.

A Letter under the hand of the Revd Mr Smoothum Sly, was presented in Club by Sir John, containing the Compliments of the Eastren-shore triumvirate to his honor and the Club, Then Quirpum Comic Esqr, the Master of Ceremonies, confirmed the Revd Mr Roundhead Muddy, a Longstanding member of the commoners of the ancient & honorable Tuesday Club, according to the usual form.

Then the Reverend Mr Muddy, addressed with a Loud voice his Honor and the Club as follows.

"Most honorable Mr President, most magnanimous Sir John, most musical Mr Protomusicus, most polite Master of the Ceremonies, most Sublime Poet Laureat, most worthy Mr Secretary, and all ye Gentlemen Longstanding members of this here ancient and honorable Club, I thank you for the favor you have done me."—Then Mr Muddy sat down, and by this concise Speech we may understand, that Mr Orator Comus, was not in Club this night, as Indeed he was not, for an Embassy was dispatched to him by two officers of the Club, vizt: the Secretary and master of ceremonies, to require his attendance, but this Cunning State officer, excused himself to the Club, not caring, as is thought, to appear openly in the affair of the box, tho he operated in a conceald manner, to promote that mischievous Scheme. [492]

The Secretary, in place of Mr Orator Comus, by appointment of the Committee, delivered a Speech to the Chair, concerning the box, now proposed to be set on foot, in which he set forth both the advantages and disadvantages, that might arise from having a Club box, and shut up his argument, by declaring his opinion, that this box should be admitted or rejected by the Club, as the one or the other prevailed.

Then the Club entered into the Consideration of the box, and, the first question proposed was, whether || it should pass by a majority or unanimity, it was Carried by Six against five, that it should pass by a majority, then the first report of the Committee was again read, vizt: That "your Committee are humbly of opinion, that It should be proposed to his honor the president and the Club, that there should be a Club box, set on foot." The Question was put, a box or no box, upon putting round the Ballots, it Carried in the negative, Seven nays against four yeas, thus was this pestilent Scheme knocked on the head for ever. [493]

On the next Sederunt, which was the 107th, Mr Protomusicus Never-

member of the Tuesday Club, upon wednesday, In which Argument Mr Orator Comus held out very stiffly, it was resolved, that the ballots should be put about, after Mr Muddys consent was asked.

Upon putting about the ballots, the Election was unanimous, and Mr Muddy was Saluted by his honor the president and the Club, as a Longstanding Member, and then addressing himself to the honorable the Chair, and to the Club, he spoke as follows with a Strong and loud voice.

[490] "Most honorable Mr President, most worshipful Sir John, Most Noble Mr Orator, and you Gentlemen, the other worthy Longstanding members of this here ancient and Honorable Club, I return you thanks for the honor you have done me."—Then Mr Roundhead sat down and as a member of the Club, took his place accordingly, his confirmation, on account of the absence of the master of Ceremonies, being defferred till another time.

Mr Orator Comus, Lately created by his office a State member, we shall find now begin to truckle to the Chair, and become Intirely a creature to his honor the president, In such a manner, as to presume to Introduce again a Club box, for, at this Sederunt, It was moved by this State officer, that that pestilent fomenter of mischief in the Club, the Box, should again be set on foot, this he plainly did to curry favor with the Chair, the motion occasioned pritty warm disputes in Club, at last his honor the president appointed the Reverend Mr Roundhead Muddy, Jealous Spyplot Senior and Jonathan Grog Esqrs, a Committee to draw up proposals for establishing a box, to be reported to the Club at next Sederunt.

Then, his honor being Jealous of some Slippery tricks from the Secretary, gave orders from the Chair, that all the minutes of the Club proceedings, should be henceforth roughly drawn upon a waste piece of paper, and laid before the Club, before they were entered in the book, to prevent [491] errors, Interpolations || erazures and Interlineations, that might otherwise be practised, and, that after the Club had examined and ammended this rough draught, it should thus ammended be entered verbatim in the book of records, without adding or deminishing one title, and not afterwards altered upon any pretence whatsoever.

Accordingly at Sederunt 106 June 13th, 1749, Slyboots pleasant Esqr, being high Steward, the proceedings were produced upon a piece of waste paper, and being read, were corrected by the club, and Entered in the Record book.

Jealous Spyplot Esqr, Chairman of the Committee for drawing up proposals for establishing a Club box, which sat upon the 9th Instant, presented to his honor the president, the report of the said Committee,

or fancy, and often the spirit of opposition, which has had force enough at times to 'stablish the most absurd customs that ever were Broached, for, once oppose or thwart, any particular fancy, or any particular maxim or opinion, and use endeavors to suppress them, they shall soon find numberless defenders and grow to a prodigious Size, however Inconsistent and absurd they may be in them- ‖ selves, and however repugnant to the common sense and reason of mankind; this we see abundantly exemplified in many Sects and maxims both religious and political.

[488]

We find here at this period, an instance of the thing in this our History, it had been established long agoe, by a Law of this Club, that the Ladies should be first toasted after Supper, but all of a Sudden, an odd and whimsical Toast of the King and the Club, starts up, and takes the precedence, which toast was accidentaly Introduced by an honorary member, upon the Anniversary Night, vizt: Mr Ignotus Warble, who happening to toast the king and the Club, met with great opposition from the Long standing members, some affirming that this toast was not Clubical, and that it ought to be the *King of Clubs,* to make it more in Stile, others asserting that It should be the Club and the king, among whom was Sir John, who was for placing the Club before every thing, and the reason given for this was, the example of our high Church partizans, who in their toasts drink the Church and king, and not the king and Church, as the Phanatic whigs puritans and such low vermin do, a third party in the Club were of opinion, that the toast was too whiggish, and seemed to call in question the Loyalty of the Longstanding members, as if some among them were suspected of Jacobitism, and therefore declared against all such abominable test toasts. These disputes and Cavils, it is thought, Incenced his honor the president, to such a degree, who was not only ‖ a high churchman, but a strenuous whig, (two extremes that seldom meet in one Character) that ever after, In opposition to these libertine principles, in the Longstanding members, he made the King and Club the first toast after Supper, but, as all earthly things are transitory, so this famous toast had it's time, and gave way at last, as we shall find to the High Stewards health.

[489]

At Sederunt 105 May 31, 1749, Mr Secretary Scribble being high Steward, an accusation was exhibited against the high Steward, by some of the members, for Irregularly adjourning the Club to an unusual Day (being wednesday) on account of a public ball, but the prosecution of this affair was postpon'd, till other business was dispatched.

The Reverend Mr Roundhead Muddy, attended the Club, at this Sederunt, in order for his admission, and Mr Secretary moved the thing to the Club, after some dispute, whether Mr Muddy could be duely elected a

16 He was firmly of opinion, that to return Injury for Injury, and affront for affront, was expressly contrary to the Spirit of Christianity, and the same as if you should spue in my porridge, because I had pissed in your drink.

17 If it should cost us as little to Drink as to laugh, said he pleasantly and Smilingly smacking his lips, we should have plenty of good grog for nothing.

18 Beware quoth he of too great familiarty with great men, if you sit too nigh a rousing Christenmass fire, you may chance to burn or blister your Shins.

19 He asserted that if a number of books upon Shelves, could make a man a Scholar, sleeping in a pew at Church would make him a very good Christian.

20 As good Cloths are always the worse for wearing, so, said he, good doctrines, are the worse for being put in practice, the reason why our prim Clergy, who are as careful of their doctrines, as they are of their beavers, bands, Gouns and Cassocks, dont care much to practise what they preach, this also he spoke as a presbyterian.

21 He was fond of Honoring the names of ancient worthies, by converting them into puns, for with him a pun was the quintessence of wit, for example, if you asked a Chaw of tobacco of him, he would hand you his box, and say pleas- ‖ antly "That's good old *Chaw-Sir*," meaning thereby to honor the name and memory of our ancient english bard.

22 Finally, he used to say of one Pandragoras, much addicted to lying when Sober, who one day in his cups said, with a Sigh, *All men are mortal,*—I know not how to believe you said his cousin Sobrio.

These Stories and apothegms, we reckon Sufficient to give a Specimen of the acute genius of our Club Bard.

Chapter II

Introduction of the Toast called the king and Club, Proposals for reviving the Box rejected, the orator lays down his office, abolition of that office in Club.

It is wonderful to observe, how old customs will be exploded, and new ones Introduced in their place; while no one can give better reasons for those odd Incidents, when they occurr in History, than that of blind caprice

taken off by the Sulphurous Steams and Stinking mephites, of these Subterranean dark Caverns.

6 Lies he often affirmed proved a very good home Staple, but seldom or never yielded much at a foreign market, hence the small regard that is usually paid, to the overgrown Lies of Travellers.

7 It was his custom to observe, that many devoured the favors of the great, like Luscious dishes, which being well digested, produced fulsom and Ill applied compliments, very much resembling the fætid Stools of an epicure or glutton.

8 He affirmed that he knew many men, that lived as if they were never to die, and died as if they had never lived.

9 It was a maxim of his that in case a man's father had been a thief, and his mother a whore, their vices, (tho' he had nothing to do with them) would be laid at his door, and thrown in his teeth from Generation to generation everlastingly, unless he could have the good luck to get himself created a peer.

10 He would affirm with a minc'd oath, for he seldom swore round ones, that as Sure as two and two made four, so Sure a Lords bastard, was base born, as much as the bastard of a Cobler.

11 He confidently asserted it for a truth, in Spite of the Sceptics of the age, That all men were mortal, that black and white, day and night were opposites and quite different things, that a Stool was a Stool, a table a table and a gun a gun, and not an Idle notion or Idea, as some would persuade us, and finally that there was no such thing as being a good man, or in other words a good Christian, without morality. [485]

12 He mantained that a man never was to be Cock Sure of having Strict Justice done him, in any human court either of Law or equity, unless he was furnished with a very ponderous purse.

13 He affirmed that the Pope of Rome had been poxed, above a thousand years agoe by the whore of Babylon, as appeared by his Blueboars, which boars the Ignorant vulgar believed to be bulls, with blue Leaden hoofs, like the bulls of Ireland, because the lying priests told them so, this he spoke in the Spirit of a Presbyterian, for he was a true blue one.

14 He said that our Lawyers and divines differed very little from our merchants, since they made trade and traffic of Justice and religion, and the small difference was this, that they could not like the merchants suffer by Shipwreck, since they never sent their wares over Seas.

15 He affirmed, that it was as absurd to stile Bishops my Lord, your Grace, and Right Reverend father in God, as to call the Emperor of China the Vicar of || Bray, this he spoke also in the Spirit of a Presbyterian. [486]

to God Almighty, said the parson—The very best curate you could have pitched upon replied the other.

One Story more of this celebrated Club wit, and then I have done,—A woman once riding along the road, tumbled from her horse, and turning head over heels, discovered some Arcana, which the whole Sex are very Solicitous about concealing, when she got up, and had rectified her petticoats, she spied a fellow passing by, & could not forbear exclaiming, in Surprize and Confusion, Did you ever see the like!—yes by God, said the fellow, a hundred and a hundred times over, my wife has got Just such another.

With numberless such delectable and merry tales and Stories, this Celebrated Club Bard used to abound, and by his good natured and Comical way of relating them, was often very Serviceable, in keeping up a proper Club conversation, and preventing the members, from entering upon mischievous topics of discourse.

I shall now mention some of the favorite maxims of this celebrated Club wit, and with them Conclude this long Introductory Chapter.

1 He used to say, that if one would gain a Ladie's affections, he ought to persevere, and stand stiffly to it without shrinking. This was a good Standing Joke, and fit for a Longstanding member, but not altogether consistent with Monsieur What d'ye call 'um's rules of decency in his reflections on ridicule.[29]

2 He would say sometimes, that if a man's Conscience lay heavy on his hands, he might put it out to Interest.

3 He declared often, that the Surest way to procure honor, and the General esteem of mankind, was to get rich any how, taking care, in your voyage, towards the Regions of Dis or Pluto, to keep but a very little, or Just touch and go, as they call it, to the windward of the Gallows, pillory and whiping post.

4 He often affirmed it to be his opinion, that a man must by all means acquire a mean Sneaking behavior, before he can step into the favor and good graces of the great, and also that eves-droppers and Tale bearers, or (when he had a mind to pun) *Tail* bearers, were very useful and necessary members of some political States, whether under Male-administration, or petticoat government.

5 He often said, that your petticoat pensioners were like the Miners in the west Indies, always digging and poaking in dark holes and Caverns, for little bits of gold and Silver, yet never lived to reach the bottom, being

---

29. Abbé Jean-Baptiste Morvan de Bellegarde (1648–1734) was the author of *Réflexions sur le ridicule, et sur les moyens de l'éviter* (Paris, 1696).

consist—In what your honor pleases good Sir—Nay, pray be particular Sir—as particular as your honor pleases Sir—do you understand any of the Learned Languages,—what Learned Languages Good Sir,—why, the greek, latin, hebrew, Chaldee or the oriental tongues,—Not a word of any of them Sir—are you a proficient in the Mathematics, algebra Arithmetic, or any of the arts or Sciences,—I never heard of such things 'till this minute, and like your honor—Can you read or write,—Never could in my life Good Sir—very well friend, heres half a Crown for you,—you are in every respect the poorest Scholar I ever yet met with.

If I mistake not, I have heard him tell a humorous Story, of the Great and learned Bishop Hoadly,[28] who one day coming out of the parliament house, when it rained, looked round him, and asked, with an earnest voice, Where is my fellow?—I gad my Lord says a wag that stood near him, he is not to be found in all England.

One of the like nature, I think, was a favorite of this Club wit,—a fat peer one day in parliament time, meeting a lean commoner, who had a mind to pry into the Secrets of his house, asked his Lordship,—My Lord said he, what are you about now,—Just three yards if you measure the round of my belly answered his Lordship.

He used to give a curious, yet comical account of the foundation of the Ancient City of Edinburg in the kingdom of Scotland. Cain said he, after he had murdered his brother, went to the Land of Nod, which could be no other than Scotland ($\sigma\kappa o\tau\iota\alpha$) in the Greek Idiom signifying darkness, and a dark corner is The most likely to make one Nod, or go to sleep, and there he built a City, which could be no other than Edinburg corruptly, anciently Eden-burg; tho not named In Sacred writ, for Cain Called it Edenburg, in honor of the Garden of Eden, from which place his parents had been lately expelld.

But one arch Story in particular, I remember to have heard Mr Grog often tell, It was of three companions riding the road together, and passing a place where were many unripe blackberries a growing, one said, Lord! how red these blackberries are—you fool, says another, who ever heard of red-blackberries; you're both fools alike said the third, for blackberries are always red, when they're green.

Another Jest he used often to tell of a Simple Country parson, nick-named Jockey Frizzle, who had a very Large parish, one asked him what he did with his flock, in the extreme parts of his parish—I e'en leave them

---

28. Benjamin Hoadly (1676–1761) was an English bishop famous as the initiator of the Bangorian Controversy, an attempt to reduce church authority.

association of Ideas, as Mr Locke Calls it,[26] in making Ignorance an Inseparable companion of foppery, for this young man explained the passage, and convinced the whole Club of wits, that the difficulty arose only from an error in the press, in the ommitting of a point of Interrogation.—Pray Sir, says Mr Pope with a Sneer, Do you know what a point of Interrogation is?—yes Sir.—what ‖ is it pray?—why 'tis a little crooked thing that asks questions. This repartee effectually turned the laugh upon Mr Pope and silenced him, for he was a man of a slender small body, and had a little hump upon one of his Shoulders.

But now, since we talk of poets, we must not ommit our celebrated Poet Laureat of the ancient & honorable Tuesday Club, vizt: Jonathan Grog Esqr, who, I may safely say, is as well stocked with Jests, quaint Stories, puns, conundrums, and other such conceits, as any wit, either ancient or moderen, that ever was heard of, to recount all the Witticisms of this bard, would be an endless Labor, and would require a huge ponderous volume, therefore, a few specimens will serve to show the acute wit and lively Imagination, of this moderen Club Bard.

His favorite Story was of a Stuttering boy, who was sent with a present of a Roasting pig in a basket, to his master's friend, the basket was covered, in which the pig was, which (to speak in the Stile of the Learned Doctor Lister in his *Journey thro' Paris*)[27] was to prevent I suppose the pig's escaping, the boy had occasion to step behind a hedge on his way, and deposited the basket 'till he had dispatched a certain necessary business, a fellow passing by in the mean time, stole the pig, and Clap'd a puppy in its place, and Covered up the basket again, the boy not perceiving this, Carried it to the Gentleman, for whom the present ‖ was Intended, and leisurly uncovering the basket said Sis-Sis-Sis-Sis-Sir, m-m-my ma-ma-master has se-se-sent you a ro-ro-roasting P-P-P-P-P-uppy by God!—and so out Jumped the puppy.

Another Story, that this Ingenious Gentleman told, was of a poor Scholar—A Gentleman, whose Charity was chiefly bestowed upon poor Scholars, had a visit paid him one day by a fellow in a very ragged Condition, having opened his chamber door to him, he asked him who he was,—a poor Scholar Sir, replied he,—'Tis well Sir, pray walk in said the Gentleman,—well, you say you are a poor Scholar, in what does your Scholar-craft

---

26. Locke discusses the dangers arising from a false association of ideas in *An Essay concerning Human Understanding* (1690), chap. 33, sec. 9.

27. Martin Lister (1638?–1712), English zoologist, physician, and fellow of the Royal Society, published an account of his journey to Paris in 1698 with the earl of Portland, who was ambassador there.

pocket to hire a coach, went under a pent house to screen himself, a proud Marquis Riding that way in his Chariot, happened to spy this Ragged Bard, and having a mind to make himself merry at his expence, without the least design to bestow a dinner upon him, sent his lacquai to ask him in what battle he had received that terrible Gash or wound in his hat, the Servant did as he was ordered, saying, that monsieur the marquis had sent his compliments, and desired to know in what || battle he had received that [477] dreadful wound in his hat, on which the Abbe elevated his cane, and letting full drive at the fellows head made answer, at the Battle of *Cane-y* you Rascal. The poor Lacquai went back with his bloody crown, and complain'd to his master, who, Jumping out of the Chariot, went boldly up to the Ragged Son of Apollo, and asked him how he durst use the Servant of a man of his quality in such a rude manner,—Because he was Saucy said the Abbe,—Saucy says the marquis, pray Sir, do you know who I am—yes replied the Bard—and who am I pray, said the marquis—you're a fool said the poet, and so the Marquis mounted his Chariot again, hanging an Arse, being afraid that if he should carry the conference any further, the poets cane would know no difference between the master and valet,—Thus we see how dangerous a thing it is to meddle with poets, or hungry sharp set wits, but even poets will sometimes meet with their matches, as the following instances will show.

Alexander Pope Esqr, our Celebrated English Poet, being lighted home by a link boy, gave him a Sixpenny piece—bless your honor said the boy, I have gone a great way with your honor, and hope your honor will give me more,—God mend me boy, said Pope, his usual oath,—nay Sir, said the boy Interrupting him, God had better make nine others than mend such an odd figure as you. || Mr Pope was so pleased with this smart [478] repartee that he gave the boy half a Crown.

It did not however turn out so well with the said Mr Pope on another occasion, who being once in a Coffee house, surrounded by a Club of Town wits, who were his most humble Servants and submitted to his Judgement and decision in every thing, they were looking over a passage in Anacreon the greek poet, which puzzled the whole Junto, none of them being able to find out the meaning of it, a young Smart, Just fresh from the University, dawbed over with lace, and decked with a Sword and Cockade, as having Just entered into the army, beg'd leave to look at the book, Mr Pope handed it to him, and leerd on him with great contempt, thinking it much out of Character that such a foppish figure, should pretend to Learning of any Sort, but the event soon Convinced him, that he trusted too much to a false

the word of God was a preaching,—Ah! Good Sir, said the Idiot, had I not been a fool, I should have been asleep too.

Many such Instances might be produced, of the Smart and witty Sayings of both fools and wise men, which shone forth by degrees, brighter and brighter, after the Revival of Learning in Europe, but I shall trowble you with no other examples of these times, but that of a certain Pope who was no fool. At the Installment of these holy fathers, there used to be a net laid upon a large table, instead of a Cloth, at which his holiness is to eat, as he represents Peter the poor fisherman, his predecessor, this Pope, after he found he had secured the Main Chance, or the papal Chair, coming into the Room, where this farcical net had been laid out, desired the waiters to Take away the Net, and lay a Cloth, for the fish was already caught.

About the beginning of the 16th Century, this kind of wit and Drollery, was much on the Increase, then was the Republic of letters blessed with a Rabelais, and a Verveille,[23] whose Instructive and witty writings have been of such General Service to Church and State, and have been carefully Common placed || by all our Succeeding Jesters, by the Celebrated Tom Brown, that comic Star of Grubstreet, by the Celebrated Mr Ward,[24] author of the *London Spy*, and even by the Incomparable Dean Swift, that delicate and modest writer, who has brought the art of Jesting and Buffonery, and writing huge essays upon nothing, to a greater perfection than any man ever did before or since.

In the wise and politic reign of King James I, This useful art was in great perfection at the English Court, and a good pun, Conundrum or Jest, would then recommend a man to a fat Bishoprick, or to any great office in Church or State.

There is a good Jest told of one Abbe Soray,[25] a poor poet, who, one day walking the Streets in a ragged habit, having a great hole or Chasm in the Crown of his hat, was taken in a Shower, and having no Money in his

---

23. François Béroalde de Verville (1558–1612) was a French mathematician, scientist, and author whose works include a poor imitation of *Utopia* called *Idée de la république* (1583), *Appréhensions spirituelles* (1583), *Le Cabinet de Minerve* (1601), and *Moyen de parvenir,* or *Salmigondes* (1610), a collection of licentious tales.

24. Thomas Brown (1663–1704) was an English satirist and author of the famous "I do not love thee, Dr. Fell" and *Amusements Serious and Comical* (London, 1700), humorous sketches of London life. Edward "Ned" Ward (1667–1731) was an English author of Hudibrastic doggerel verse and coarse, humorous prose, including *The London Spy* (London, 1698–1703), the observations of a country man in London, and *Hudibras Redivivus* (1705–1707).

25. Probably Nicholas Soret (fl. 17th century), a French priest and poet, whose works include *La Céciliade; ou, Martyre sanglant de Saincte-Cécile, patrone des musiciens* (1606), a five-act tragedy in verse.

his majesties wise head, as some think, not Improperly, the master being thought by many more a fool by nature than the man,—How now Archie said the king, what's this for—For sending the prince your Son to Spain, replied the fool—what then, said the king, I hope he'll return safe—Then Nunkle, said Archie, I'll send mine nown Cap to the king of Spain, and he shall wear it.

A fool of this Sort, who belonged to one of the kings of France, having a small Spite at the master huntsman, was resolved to be revenged on him, and, one day, as he attempted to ford a river with his pack of hounds, being doubtful of the depth of the Channel, he asked this fool, if he might safely pass, who assured him he might, but the poor man and his horse were first mired, and then drowned in attempting it, while the fool stood by, Laughing all the ‖ while, a complaint of this being brought to the king, the fool was asked why he had done this mischief, he replied That he was not at all to blame, for he had seen his majesties Geese pass the River at that very place, not ten minutes before, and Surely a man on horseback might wade where a parcel of geese did, on this the fool was excused, because he gave advice to the best of his knowledge, and the huntsman blamed, because he trusted too much to the advice of a fool.

A very recent example of this Sort, happened, in a question, put to his present Britannic majesty, by a certain Nobleman, who, tho' no fool by profession, yet in this Instance assumed the Character of a Jester or Buffoon, his majesty being much Incensed, with his Scots Subjects, on account of a rebellious Insurrection of the mob at Edinburgh, who had in an outragious manner hanged Capt: Porteous,[22] was asked by this Nobleman, at the time that the General Assembly of the kirk was about to meet there, who his majesty would please to nominate for his commissioner to represent him, in this assembly,—The Devil, replied the king in a huff,—The nobleman after some pause, asked his majesty how he would please to have the Devil addressed, if in the usual form, *To our Trusty and well beloved Cousin and Councellor.*

But the most remarkable quaint Saying, that I have yet met with, which was the more so, as it came from the mouth of a Natural fool, was the foll- ‖ owing. A dull parson, once holding forth in his pulpit, the whole congregation, except this natural, fell fast asleep, upon which the preacher reproved them Smartly, and rousing them, with half a dozen Smart Cushion thumps, bid them take example by that fool, who did not sleep while

---

22. John Porteous (d. 1736), captain of the Edinburgh city guard, fired on a crowd gathered to rescue a popular smuggler and was later hanged by an armed group in disguise.

the Celebrated Mr Heydagger,[19] late regulator of the Masquerades and Ridottos.

When Signior Devil had thus served his apprintiship, and assumed a higher part, the office of Jesting was put into the hands of certain arch [472] fellows, who had more Cunning than their neigh- ‖ bours, and were placed near the persons of great princes, under the title and Character of Fools, tho in fact they were nothing less, these fellows were very useful in their way, for they often gave advice, and wholesome Councel with Impunity, to the hot headed Tyrants their Masters, when none else, not even those of the greatest Sagacity and prudence among their Subjects durst open their mouths.

It is recorded of one of these fellows, belonging to the Tyrant Bajazet I king of the Turks,[20] that one day, his master being determined to put all his Kadilisquers or Judges to death, for accepting bribes in Causes that were brought before them, this fool dress'd himself up in the garb of an ambassador, and appeared with a very grave countenance before the Sultan his master, who asking what he meant by this device? replied that he came to solicit him to be sent Ambassador To the Emperor of Constantinople,— For what? said the Tyrant—To bring to court a posse of his grave monks and friars, replied the fool—and what then?—To supply the places of these venerable Judges, whom your majesty Intends to hang, said the fool—may not I supply their places from among my own Subjects said the Sultan—Ay, but these monks and friars will do very well replied the fool, on account of their grave and demure Countenances, since men of an adequate knowledge in the Laws, to these miserable Condemned Judges, are not to be found [473] among all your majestie's ‖ Subjects. This made the Tyrant think alittle, and turning to one Alis Bassa of his privy Council, he told him that the fool was very right, and asked him what he had best do, the Bassa advised Bajazet to pardon and replace these Judges, and allow them Sufficient Sallaries, whereby they should be above Corruption, which the Tyrant accordingly did.

It is told of James I, that Royal Virtuoso, & reputed Solomon of the age in which he lived, that he kept nigh his person a fellow Called Archie,[21] to divert him with his Jests at times, this Archie, or rather Arch fellow, one day, while the king was at dinner, clapt his fools cap, bells and all, upon

---

19. John James Heidegger (1659?–1749) was the English theater manager of the Italian opera at Haymarket for the Royal Academy of Music from 1720 to 1728.

20. As ruler of the Ottomans (1389–1402), Bajazet I besieged Constantinople but was defeated and taken prisoner by Tamerlane.

21. Archie Armstrong (d. 1672) was a jester in the court of James I.

ter of drolls, being afraid of fire and faggot, the reward of heresy, for every thing was damnable heresy, that differed in the least from the Jargon of the Schools, and a parcel of aristotelian Lumber, They made the poor devil, who with reason they esteemed fire proof, stand between them and all harm, by cloathing him in a motely fool's coat, for men were at all times very ready to roll the blame upon the Devil's back, and to clear their hands of guilt, therefore this venerable old Don the Devil, was always brought upon the Stage, whenever any piece of Drollery, mirth or Buffonery was to be performed, and accordingly we find this ancient Sinner brought in like an antic in several comic farces, where he diverts the audience, either by his blunders or his Sufferings. Thus, in a representation of the Story of David and Abigail where the Devil is made Lacquai to Nabal, the latter goes to sheer his Sheep, and the Devil In Imitation of his master, falls tooth and nail to the Sheering of a great overgrown hog, which makes a dreadful vociferation and horrid Screaming, under Signior Satano's paws, and much diverts the Spectators, hence the old proverb, *Great cry and little wool as || the devil said when he shore his Hogs.*[17]   [471]

The Devil for a considerable Time held the honorable place of general Droll, and master buffoon, being often brought on the Stage as a but or Subject of Laughter, his task being often to dance in a circle of witches, with a candle in his fundament, to ride long Journeys thro' the air on broomsticks, to make long voyages in eggshells, to say prayers backwards in a Short Cloak & high Crownd hat, while the candles burnt wonderfully blue, and other such foolish amusements fit for his devilship, 'till at last, having performed his parts with general approbation, he was advanced to the honorable office of master of the revells, and appeared on the Stage in a higher Character, as for instance, in the famous pantomime, of Harlequin Doctor Faustus,[18] where he performs the majestic and dignified part, of Soveraign monarch of hell, and struts in buskins, then the Ladies became so familiar with his devilship, that they could look him in the face with the same Indifference, as if he had been any mortal man of a course feature like

---

17. Hamilton appears to be the first author to associate this proverb with the devil (see Apperson, *English Proverbs and Proverbial Phrases,* 432, where pre-19th-century uses typically read "Much cry and little wool, as one said . . . " or "as a man said"). Since the devil is not known for shearing hogs in the Bible, it seems evident that Hamilton has applied an old proverb to a contemporary farce in which the devil does perform such shenanigans. What is curious about the proverb as Hamilton has patched it together, however, is that it did become popular as he uses it, in the 19th century.

18. *Harlequin Doctor Faustus* (1723), which established the tradition that Harlequin must play someone other than himself, was written by John Thurmond, an 18th-century actor who invented many profitable pantomimes for Drury Lane.

other, *Ergo,* there is no such thing as motion;[15] while this argument was going on, a certain Comical Crabbed fellow, stood in a corner of the School, at some distance from the Learned Lecturer. And when he had finished his argument, he advanced Gravely towards him, and gave him a Smart box on the ear, with his dowbled fist, and then returned to his place,—The Sophister asked him ‖ why he used him in such a rough manner?—It was not I Sir, replied he,—How says the other, did I not see you come from that corner where you are to this corner where I am and strike me?—That could never be Good Sir replied the Droll, since you and I are two bodies, and These corners two distant places, and, as no body can move either in its place, or out of it's place, I never could have moved from this corner to that to give you a box on the ear. This was a Solid and hard argument and a Sophism *ad hominem* as our Logicians call it.

But enough of ancient examples of this kind, I come now nigher our moderen times.

After the Gothic Barbarism had overclouded the face of Europe, the Intire abolition of Learning was followed by a still calm of Dullness, the Solemn and Subtile Doctors among the Schoolmen, groped thro' this Dusky Gloom, under the guidance of Aristotles Lanthorn, and consumed all their oil, and spent all their Labour, in refining and Commenting upon words and abstract notions, yawning over a vacuum, analysing of farts, unravelling of Cobwebs, distilling the moonshine, and the like useful and Curious operations, from whose Indefatigable brain work, it is thought, that curious moderen art of punning first took its rise, while this Laborious Scrutiny was going on, none had leisure to apply themselves to any other Study, and therefore, the progress of Quaint Stories, Sage apothegms, and Smart repartees, was at a stand till some early wits of the 15th Century, about the time of the Sacking of Constantinople by the Turk, ‖ of whom the famous french Philosopher Turlupin[16] was one, began to break out like the morning Star from a black horizontal Cloud, and threw some faint rays of wit and humor, over the Darkened face of Europe, then began the light of the Aristotelian Lanthorn to fade, & was at last lost in a certain fog, no body knows where or how, from which murky fog arose the celebrated Paracelsus and others, his followers, searchers after the Philosopher's Stone. But, as none durst in these bigotted times appear barefacedly in the Charac-

---

15. Born ca. 490 B.C., Zeno studied under Parmenides, employed his teacher's monistic principles to argue against motion, and according to Aristotle, invented the dialectic. Zeno's argument about the paradoxical laws of motion appears in Aristotle's *Physics* 239, B5.

16. On Turlupin, see p. 218n, above.

them, for, getting a small pitcher, he put his withered right leg into it, and ordered that every man in the Company should do the same, while he tossed off his bumper, the whole company, like a parcel of fools, attempted to do it, but in vain, so Agapestor laugh'd in his turn and they drank kelty.[12]

Cato seeing two Ambassadors sent from Rome to a foreign State, one of whom had a very small head, like an owl, the other so lame, that he could not walk without Crutches, said very archly, and much like one of our moderen punsters, here's an Embassy that has neither head nor tail.[13]

The Philosopher Aristotle, being once teized with the Impertinence of a talkative fellow, who at every period would ask him, Is not this very Strange, Aristotle?—no Indeed says the Philosopher, but I think it very Strange that one who has Legs to run away, should stand to hear your Idle Stories; and the same Philosopher being asked once by a fellow, who had been several hours in telling him a tale of a tub, If he had not tired his patience—By my troth no, replied the Sage, for I have not heard one single word you said.

A Certain Indian Philosopher, Calanus by || name, an enimy to talk- [468] ing, showed Alexander the great, who consulted him about where he should fix the Seat of his Empire, a very Significant emblem of the nature of Civil Government, by throwing a dry raw hide on the ground and treading upon it all round the edges, by which the other Side still tilted up, but at last clapping his foot right in the middle of the hide, it lay flat and even.[14] One need be no conjurer to find out what Lesson the conqueror gathered by this example.

The Companions of Demosthenes, In his Embassy to Philip king of Macedon, commended that prince for his beauty, eloquence, and for his being a good toaper—These elogiums said the Orator, are more applicable to a woman, an advocate and a Spunge than to a king.

Zeno, a Certain Philosopher among the Sophists, once Lecturing in his School, argued thus against motion,—If a body moves at all, it must move either in it's place, or out of it's place; but in its place it cannot move, because the Idea of motion Implies a Constant Change of place, neither can it move out of its place, because a body must always possess some place or

---

12. Agamestor was an Academic philosopher, called Agapestor in Plutarch, *Quaestiones convivales* 1.4.3., the source of this anecdote.

13. The Cato story is loosely derived from Plutarch's life of Cato.

14. Calanus's (fl. 4th century B.C.) real name was Sphines, but he was wont to say *Cale,* the Indian form of salutation, so the Greeks called him Calanus. He acted as counselor to Alexander, who greatly mourned him after his death. The Calanus story appears in Plutarch's life of Alexander.

as great a fool as any, since he publicly ownd and proclaimed it, that he was an Ignoramus, for he only knew one thing, and that was, *that he knew Nothing,* and, in this very opinion Tully long after agreed with him, expressly saying, *Stulte et Incaute omnia agi video.*[8]

Ille Sinistrorsum hic dextrorsum, unus utrique,
Error, sed variis illudit partibus omnes.

One Reels to this, another to that wall,
'Tis the same error that deludes them all.[9]

Robertus Burton

The Divine Plato, having defined a man to be *Animal bipes Implume facie Erecta,* or an unfledgd two legd animal,[10] a wag one day strip'd a cock of all his feathers and drove him into a School, where Philosophical Lectures were held, according to the Sect of the Platonists, and on being asked, what he meant by that conceit, he told them that he had sent them *Plato's man.*

When Demetrius took Megara he asked Stylphon a Philosopher, if he had lost any thing,—Not I Sir Indeed replied he, I carry nothing about me, which you can make prey of or take from me, that is of any value, This Philosopher esteeming nothing of such value, as to be reckoned wealth or riches or real possessions but the Moral virtues, upon the same conqueror's leaving the City, he told the same Philosopher, that he quitted the City to him in an Intire State of freedom,—Very true Sir (replied || Stylphon) for once you and your dragoons are departed there will not be so much as one Slave left among us.[11]

One Agapestor, a cripple in his right leg, being at a merry making, the company in ridicule ordered that every man should stand on his right leg and drink off his Glass, when it came to his turn to Command he matched

---

8. "I see all things being done foolishly and without caution" (Cicero, *Epistulae ad Atticum* 7.10.10). Socrates appears as a caricature Sophist in Aristophanes' *Clouds;* in Plato's *Apology,* 19C, Socrates invites the court to compare the caricature with the reality. The allusion to his knowing nothing appears in Plato's *Apology* 21–23.

9. More literally, "That one to the left, this one to the right; either way, / One error deludes all in their various directions" (Horace, *Satirae* 2.3.50).

10. Literally, "unfeathered, biped animal, his face upright." The "wag" who plays the joke on Plato is Diogenes the Cynic (see Diogenes Laertius, 6.40).

11. Demetrius I (336–283 B.C.) of Macedonia established control over Greece but lacked wisdom as a ruler. Stilpon (ca. 380–300 B.C.) was a Megarian philosopher who strongly influenced Zeno the Stoic and maintained the monism characteristic of the Megarian school, denying the Platonic distinction between universals and individuals. This story appears in Plutarch's life of Demetrius.

on this great earthly stage, by his fellow Mortals, this Philosopher used to teach, that the whole course of human life was only matter of Laughter, all men he said were a kind of two leg'd asses, monkies, or rather wild beasts of a more fierce nature, that Reasoned, Philosophized squabbled quarrelled and destroyed one another, about things that were In themselves triffles, and that there was no difference between men of a mature age and Children, excepting this trivial one, that the latter diverted themselves, with babies made up of rags and Remnants, and the first with Bawbles, composed of more costly Stuff, tho' alike perishable and vain.

There is a stale Story of Diogenes the Cynic, which I have sometimes seen curiously done on Japand tables and || cupboards, he had no other house than an old hogshead or wine cask, and no other cup but the hollow of his hand, and was one of your Sneering Solemn drolls, whom I esteem the most Gelastic and entertaining; of him it is said, that being one day asked by Alexander, the Macedonian Conqueror; what it was in his power to do for him? bidding him only declare and it should Immediatly be granted.—He replied with a Cynical grin, and a very gelastic contorsion of Countenance, tho' he did not Intend to make a laughing matter of it—Tis in your power said he to bestow upon me many triffles, on which, as I want them not, I set no value, but prithee take not that from me which thou canst not give, get you from between me and the Sun, for I dispise even your Shadow. [465]

The same Diogenes, as he one day sat in his tub, scranching[7] of turnips like a Hog, a certain Smart fellow passing by had a mind to be arch with the philosopher, and told him That if he would only learn the art of flattery, he might convert his tub into a palace, and his nasty roots into delicate viands,—And you vain Glorious Coxcomb (replied the Sage) if you could learn to be contented with this wholesome and homely fare, need never study and practice the fawning arts of a Spaniel.

Socrates, the famous Athenian Sage, tho' he was reckoned the wisest man of the age in which he lived, yet, when Aristophanes the Comedian introduced him upon the Stage, in a ridiculous Character, to promote the Jest, and at the same time, to disarm the Satyrist, mounted the public Theatre, and acted that very part himself, and when the same Socrates had taken abundance of pains to find out one wise man, conversing for that purpose with || men of all degrees and professions, from the philosopher to the Clown; he at length concluded that all were fools alike, and he himself [466]

---

7. Crunching. The first story about Diogenes the Cynic appears in Diogenes Laertius 6.38. The second story is an adaptation of Diogenes Laertius 6.58.

rounds of the glass, which effectually brightens up our Clubical geniuses, that are naturally more slow and heavy, besides, there are the famous Collections of the Oxford, Cambridge, and London Jests, and the Curious Collection of Jests and Jokes, published by that Learned and Ingenious Gentleman Mr Joseph Miller, under the title of *Joe Miller's Jests*,[5] to which bright Constellation of Grubstreet, I must own it is matter of Surprize to me that the Royal Society have not shown some respect, in Dubbing him a brother or F.R.S. or at least bestowing upon him one of their annual medals, or that neither of our famous Universities have yet conferrd upon him the degree of Doctor, since it is notoriously known, that these learned bodies have heaped their favors and honors of Late, on geniuses far Inferior to his.—There is also the late Collections and publications of Conundrums, Composed for the entertainment of persons of quality,[6] which may all be purchased for the value of five Shillings (a small præmium for such an exhaustless fund of wit) and are abundantly Sufficient to stock any Gentleman, tho' naturally never so dull, with a never failing magazine, if he has only memory enough to con half a doz- ‖ en Stories or conundrums every club night, and if he be one whose genius does not enable him to enter so far Into the Spirit of a Joke, as to tell it with a proper Emphasis and Grace, the Joke by this means is Improved upon, and becomes rather more Clubical, there being an additional Joke in the way of telling it.

I now proceed to give Instances both from ancient and moderen history of this kind of wit and humor, so Serviceable to, and so much fitted for the Genius of Clubs, and at the same time so effectual a Remedy against the epidemical distemper of Idle and mischievous conversation.

I shall begin with that Celebrated Ancient Droll Democritus of Abdera, who, tho' a profound Philosopher, was esteemed mad by his fellow Citizens, this notion they conceived of him, from his often breaking into violent fits of Laughter, when no body knew for what, little dreaming that he laughed at the Sempiternal Comedy, which he saw acted from day to day

---

5. *Oxford Jests, Refined and Enlarged*, 3d ed. (London, 1671), by Capt. William Hickes, was in its 14th edition by 1740. *Cambridge Jests; or, Witty Alarums for Melancholy Spirits* (London, 1674), by "a Lover of Ha, Ha, He," was reprinted in 1742. *London Jests; or, A Collection of the Choisest Joques and Repartees, Out of the Most Celebrated Authors, Ancient and Modern* (London, 1684) was in its 3d edition by 1740. *Joe Miller's Jests; or, The Wits Vade-Mecum* (London, 1739) was actually compiled by John Mottley under a pseudonym. Mottley (1692–1750) was the author of two dull tragedies, a few comedies, and lives of Peter the Great and Catherine I. Joseph Miller (1684–1738) was a Drury Lane actor and a reputed humorist.

6. Hamilton is referring to *The Witling: Being a Compleat Collection of the Most Celebrated Conundrums Now in Vogue among People of High Taste* (London, 1749) and *A Key to the Witling: Being Proper Answers to . . . the Conundrums* (London, 1750).

cerned, the Innocent tho' triffling amusements of those polite assemblies called Routs and Drums; There are also, the humorous games of Cross purposes, hunt the whistle, Break the friar's neck, and what is it like,[4] adapted to the humor and Capacity of the younger Class of persons of condition of both Sexes.

I grant you, that these conceits and Inventions are very well adapted for this purpose, where mixed assemblies of both Sexes are concerned, being to a tea suited to the humor and taste of our polite young Gentlemen and Ladies, who do not in the least understand Subjects of a more perplexed and abstruse nature, but, they will by no means answer the purpose of those assemblies Called || Clubs, which are of a more Solid and Philosophical turn, and therefore, the remedy I would propose to prevent mischievous Conversation in these nocturnal meetings is this, Let them exercise themselves in merry Jests, Smart Sayings, pithy and Concise apothegms, quaint Repartees, Ingenious puns, and knotty conundrums, which has been the practice of many wise and politic Clubs, both in ancient and Moderen times, of which I Intend presently to give examples, but, I would by the bye put in this caution, that their Jests, Smart Sayings, apothegms, Repartees, puns and Conundrums, be not particularly pointed at any one in the Company, or his friend, or dipt in Gall or wormwood, else they will Surely give offence, and Instead of bearing the true Character and Spirit of Satyr, which always ought to be generally placed, and rather seem to laugh in a pleasant manner, than grin with a Sneer, they will deservedly come under the name and Imputation of Scandal or Invective and personal abuse. If they be generally placed, and the Chief Seasoning or Ingredient be of the Comic Sort, they will never fail to please, with such as have any humor at all, and afford a very agreeable and Sprightly conversation, well Seasoned with mirth and Laughter. This I take to be an effectual preservative against the abuse of the ear and tongue in Clubs; but here I may be told, that every member of a Club is not qualified for this Sort of Conversation, it requiring a lively Imagination, and quick turn of thought, I grant you this, but allow me || to affirm at the same time, that there are few Clubs that consist of ten or a dozen members, where there are not at least one or two, that have a genius for this kind of Conversation, and this is Sufficient to enliven and furbish up all the rest and set them in motion, as a small quantity of yest does a huge barrell full of Small beer wort; and especially after five or Six

---

4. *Cross purposes* is a parlor game in which a ludicrous effect is produced by connecting questions and answers that have nothing to do with one another; in *hunt the whistle* the seeker is blindfolded and has a whistle fastened to him, which the other players blow at intervals; *what is it like* is perhaps Hamilton's phrase for charades.

would have thought it indissoluble, let all Clubs then beware how they admit or entertain such members, who have this depraved or Simple turn of mind, who cannot lay the least constraint upon that little member the tongue.

[460] The ear again is a small organ, which in most people likes to be tickled, there is a Sort of Tentigo (as the Physicians call it) to which it is very subject ‖ and nothing to which it is more open than Scandal, or the Secrets of others, this has been particularly remarked as a distemper peculiar to great men and rulers, a *tentigo auricularis,* or ear itch, whence it happens, that certain mean fellows, whose trade it is to pick up foolish Stories, and whisper them to such great men, their patrons, find mighty favor and countenance with them, and are promoted to places and honorable employments, for which neither their natural or acquired parts have by any means qualified them, and therefore, their only merit is this pitiful and depraved quality; those who have curious ears to draw in the worst and basest filth of conversation disgorged by these pitiful Scavengers, have also been of great hurt to Societies and Clubs of all kinds, and have often been very Instrumental in separating of those who have thought themselves happy, in being united in the Sacred bands of friendship.

Now, I question not, but I shall be told, that all this discourse is mighty good, and wonderfully grave and Satirical, and what we well knew before, but for what purpose, or to what end, such Sage, such pointed lectures? we are perswaded that mens ears and tongues, are very often ill Emploied, and what signifies our knowing all this unless we could find a certain remedy for it, useful and Instructing Subjects of discourse are now [461] become so stale, that people of all ‖ ranks begin to be tired of them. A man cannot always be philosophizing, moralizing, praying, singing of Psalms and Sacred hymns, hearing of Sermons, and leading a life of mortification, such as is prescribed by the reverend & pious Mr Law, in his rules for the life of a Christian.[3] These rules are now become altogether inconsistent with true politeness. To speak metaphorically, human nature cannot subsist with this Sort of Serious diet alone, the far greatest part of it must consist of Sauce compounded of triffles, to make the Serious relish the better; hence our moderen virtuosi, to keep men out of mischief, have Invented a Sort of Chip in porridge Conversation, which is in itself Indifferent, Importing neither good nor bad, is neither beneficial nor altogether useless, Such are these Sorts of pastimes and amusements, in which cards are con-

---

3. William Law (1686–1761) was a famous English spiritual leader and author of *A Practical Treatise upon Christian Perfection* (London, 1726) and *A Serious Call to a Devout and Holy Life* (London, 1729).

other, so as that they may properly be called cousin Germans, being in such a nigh ‖ Neighbourhood, that the anatomists tell us, the roots of the first [458] have a connexion or communication with the membranes and ligaments of the Latter, so that the first seldom wags, but the latter fixes itself into a listening posture, and often suffers Smartly for its Slips and trespasses, being not only liable on that Score, to many Dry drubs and boxes, but sometimes to the vindictive incision of the keen knife of Justice, by which one or both of these externall excrescencies, are shaved smack and smooth with the pericranium.

The first of these little members, has been reckoned by philosophers in all ages a very mischievous tool when not kept within a proper and decent compass, and so many books and treatises have been wrote upon the due Government of it, as might serve a man of leisure, who has a mind to collect them, to read and ponder upon all his life long, and therefore it will be needless for me to enlarge upon this trite Subject, since it is Impossible to say any thing upon it, which has not already been amply discussed by much better pens than mine, I shall therefore only say in General, that this little member, is very often apt to display the Ignorance, folly, Simplicity and wickedness of it's owner; for, as we are told somewhere in the Sacred Archives, *Out of the fullness of the heart the tongue speaketh,*[2] so when a fool, or Ignorant fellow, is stocked with a multitude of Silly, Idle, Impertinent, and pedantic Ideas, his tongue, if his natural Stupidity does not constrain it, (for his natural wisdom never can) will soon betray him ‖ for a rank coxcomb, and altogether unfit for Solid or Sensible conversation, again, when [459] an envious or Ill natured mortal, has not this Impertinent member under proper Governance, it becomes a mere conduit or Spout, of Scandal Invective and abuse, and the Innocent as well as guilty are smeared over with its poisonous ejections—If a busy meddling fellow, who minds other peoples affairs more than his own, cannot restrain this voluble member, the whole neighbourhood where he lives, are Sure to be set together by the ears, and quarrells will tread upon the heels of Quarrells, every triffling occurrence, and private piece of history or Lousy family transaction, supplying fresh fewell to feed the fire of discord, 'till every Individual in the Society, becomes an Inveterate enimy, either Conceal'd or open, one to another.

These foolish, Invidious and meddling people, who cannot keep this nimble member under a Strict guard, have by this means been the destruction of many an amicable Club, and dissolved that Strong band of Society and friendship, which, at it's first Institution was so firm that every one

---

2. See Luke 6:45.

Honor, Justice, equity, Candor, temperance, Charity, piety and the like, in such a Slighting and Sarcastical manner, declaring them absolutely to be no other than Insignificant names, Invented by the more politic and Cunning Class of mankind, To keep the vulgar herd, or Ignorant mobile in awe, in so far as that is necessary to preserve decorum and Order in Society[1]—Tho' these wise Dons in my opinion here only beg the Question, while they grant the necessity of preserving order in Society, and yet sneer at the means of doing it, at least they act very Impoliticly, in publishing and mantaining these their new Coind philosophical Dogmas, for, should this many headed beast the vulgar or mobile, once give credit to these novell fine spun maxims, and be Convinced right or wrong, that they are true, the broachers must rack their Invention to discover some new devices, to keep them in order; since, if the abovenamed virtues (as they are called) are once strip'd of their value and Significancy, and || the prospect of all future rewards and punishments is struck off, it will not be halters, gibbets, Swords, axes, whips, racks, fire, faggot, and all the tormenting inventions of cruelty, that will keep this giddy multitude in awe, for they will Surely gratify their Lusts for the time present, at the Expence of the public, and every private Interest but their own, and to the ruin and Subversion of the whole civil oeconomy, and laugh at the most exquisite punishments, as if they were only flea bites.

But some may properly enough ask here, why this grave Moral dissertation in a Club History? does it become a Club Historian to turn a Lecturer in Ethics? I beseech you Gentlemen, to have a little patience, 'till you see the drift of my Introducing this book and Chapter with so grave a disquisition, and then I hope, you will neither wonder at nor condemn me.

Tho' it would seem by this preamble, that I Intended to discant, upon the use and abuse of the Senses and faculties, yet, I must here, before I go farther, let you know, my good discerning readers, that I purpose only to Insist alittle upon the use and abuse of the ear, or Sense of hearing, and the use and abuse of the tongue, or faculty of Speech, as these two members are chiefly concerned in Clubs, where various topics of conversation are carried on, and many things heard, as well as said, both consistent with, and repugnant to decency and good manners.

The Tongue and ear are two members pritty nighly related to each

---

1. Hamilton is alluding particularly to the libertine principles espoused by John Wilmot, earl of Rochester (1647–1680), and his circle of friends, and to the rather cynical social and moral views advanced by Mandeville in the early 18th century. For a good discussion of Epicurean philosophy in early-18th-century England, see Thomas Franklin Mayo, *Epicurus in England, 1650–1725* (Dallas, Tex., 1934), 165–216; see also James G. Turner, "The Properties of Libertinism," *Eighteenth-Century Life*, n.s., IX, no. 3 (1985), 75–87.

History of The Ancient and honorable Tuesday Club

[455]

Book VI

From the foundation of the eastren-Shore Triumvirate, to the Creation of the Chancellor, and Striking of the Club Medals at London.

Chapter I

Of the Witty Sayings, apothegms and Jests of Jonathan Grog Esqr, and other Ingenious men.

None of our Senses were given us but for good purposes, our faculties also were originally Intended to be exercised upon worthy objects and pursuits, by which we daily contribute to our own quiet and happiness, and to the benefit of the Society in which we have been plac'd—This is a doctrine, which has been preached up by Philosophers & Moralists, ever since the beginning of time, and I believe has never been either doubted or denied, 'till of late Certain upstart virtuosi, and Connoiseurs of Quality, who pretend to have made certain very useful discoveries for the ease of the looser part of mankind, and picque themselves in mantaining of, and dogmatizing upon || certain new coined libertine principles and maxims, have [456] taken it into their heads to assert, That our chief happiness consists in giving a full Swing to Sensual pleasures, and Indulging every craving and Idle appetite in this life, seeing the wisdom of this age has lately discovered, that we have little or no hope, or probability (notwithstanding the fine Speeches of Divines and Philosophers) of enjoying any future being, therefore a short life and a merry is the best—If this be not the doctrine of some deep headed modern Sceptics, what do they mean by treating the terms,

A List of the members Regular and Honorary of the Ancient and honorable Tuesday Club, from the 9th of June 1747 to the 16th of May 1749.

Regular members	Honorary members
The Hon: Nasifer Jole Esqr Præs:	Mr Abraham Bumper
Sir John Knight & Champion	Doctor Polyhistor
Laconic Comus Esqr Orator	Mr Oldham Wisely
Solo Neverout Esqr, protomusicus	Mr Joshua fluter
	Mr Ignotus warble
Jonathan Grog Esqr P:P:P:P:P:	Signr: Lardini
Loquacious Scribble Esqr, Secretry	Revd Mr Broadface round
	Mr Merry Makefun
Drawlum Quaint Esqr Speaker left the club novr 8, 1748	Mr Chantum Cheary
	Coll: Courtly Phraze
Revd Mr Smoothum Sly Mr of Cer: left the club, april 11, 1749	Mr Curious Courtly
	Mr Swillum Swagbelly
	Mr Prim Laconic
Quirpum Comic Esqr, Mr of Cer:	Revd Mr Smoothum Sly
Jealous Spyplot Esqr Senr:	
Jealous Spyplot Esqr Junr	
Capt: Seemly Spruce	
Capt: Serious Social left the Club Octor: 13, 1747	
Slyboots Pleasant Esqr	
Huffman Snap Esqr	
Prim Timorous Esqr	

standing member, and the Club determined to proceed to his election at next Sederunt, then Jealous Spyplot Senr Esqr, made some motions with regard to regulating the Succession to the Chair, In case of the demise or removal of the honorable the president, which were dissagreeable to his honor & the Club, and therefore not seconded, the *Great Bell of Lincoln* was sung, the king and Ladies toasted after Supper, and every thing was transacted with || that gaiety, vivacity, good humor and decorum, becoming the great and Solemn occasion, thus finished the fourth Anniversary, and thus I conclude the fifth book of our history.

Then the Reverend Mr Smoothum Sly, late a regular, and now an honorary member of the Club, standing up, spoke as follows.

"Mr President, Sir,

I am to Inform your honor, that there is a Club now a forming upon the Eastren Shorc, of which I have the honor to be a member, this Club is yet in its Infancy and is not as yet perfectly modelled, but we hope || that in time we shall bring it to bear, and I am Commissioned from the Gentlemen of that Club, Sir, to pay their respects to your honor, and the Longstanding members of this here ancient and honorable Club, for, as you have acquired a great name far and near, by your wise and Just Conduct in that there Chair, as president of this here worthy Club, so, they having heard of your fame and Character, have a Just respect for you, and beg you would kindly receive their compliments, from my mouth, and Covet much your acquaintance and Correspondence, and to be regulated by your advice and direction." [452]

To this the honorable the President made reply That he was mightily obliged to the Gentlemen for the honor they did him, and desired Mr Sly to Compliment them in his and the Club's name.

Then the Secretary standing up, remarked as follows.

"Mr President Sir,

I think the gentlemen pay this here Club, a piece of respect which they highly deserve, nor ought we to be remiss in returning their compliments, and we hope, as our Laws are allowed to be well framed and penned, and our constitution settled on a firm basis, that these Gentlemen, of that there other Club, will not think it beneath them, to consult our body of Laws, in order, the better to form a plan for theirs, as the Republic of Rome of old did that of Greece, when they sent for the tables of || the grecian Laws, tho' I would not have you Inferr from this, that either they are as great as were the ancient Romans, or we as wise as the ancient Greeks." [453]

At the close of the Secretaries Speech, Sir John, frowned and said—"Sir!—Sir!—I make bold to affirm, that we of this here Club, are as great, and as wise as any body, not excepting either Greeks or Trojans."

This was the first foundation of the worshipful the Eastren Shore triumvirate, a Society, which we shall find in the Sequel, intirely dependant upon, and subjected to the honorable Mr President Jole, and his ancient and honorable Tuesday Club, and thus began the power Influence and Jurisdiction of this great and Illustrious President and Club, over the other presidents and Clubs in British America.

The Secretary then Informed the Club, that the Reverend Mr Roundhead Muddy, the new parson of the parish, desired to be admitted a long-

Air

>Whene're we meet
>With bowl replete,
>The Loyal healths go round,
>>And in each toast
>>We all can boast
>We're honest, hearty Sound.

Recitativo

The Ladies too, with whom the President,
Their Constant friend and hero first begins,
In bumpers round the Spacious room are sent,
But no one yet his Sole affection wins.

Air

Long live the Tuesday Club, so wisely fram'd,
That 'mongst all those great Addison has nam'd,
Not one so great, Long may the members stand,
And still mantain their badge of hand in hand.

Chorus

Our president we honor and revere,
Who most deserv'dly fills our Stately Chair.

When the poet Laureat had read this ode, the Club approved of it, and the Chorus was only sung by Mr Protomusicus, who by the help of Mr Ignotus Warble, an honorary member, set a tune to it, the performance ∥ of the rest of the ode being defferred, 'till the Club can procure their band of Instrumental music, and some asistance from that Ingenious composer Signior Lardini.

It was moved, that Jonathan Grog Esqr, poet Laureat should have the thanks of the Club, for composing this Elegant ode, and Mr Ignotus Warble, being ordered to deliver the thanks of the Club, spoke to the following purpose.

"Mr Poet Laureat, Sir,

I return you thanks, in the name of his honor the president and Club, for taking the pains to compose this elegant ode upon this occasion, in which the brightness of your poetical genius, and your great regard for the honorable the president and Club at the same time appear." To which Jonathan Grog Esqr, made answer,

"Mr Warble, Sir,

I thank you for your odd thanks for my ode"—In this Laconic Speech appears the poet Laureat's great propensity to punning.

the Tuesday Club [Book V] 341

Then the Master of Ceremonies moved, that thanks should be returned for these thanks delivered by the Secretary, which was done in a Succinct manner by the Master of Ceremonies himself.

Then it was moved that thanks should be returned to Mr Orator Comus, for appointing so fit a person as the Secretary, to open the Anniversary Solemnity with a Speech, which was also done in a very Succinct manner, by the Master of ceremonies.

Then the Anniversary Ode, Composed by Jonathan Grog Esqr, Poet Laureat, was called for, and ordered || to be read, and after some dispute, [449] whether the Secretary or the author should read it, 'twas determined that it should be read by the author, or poet Laureat of the Club, upon which Jonathan Grog Esqr, standing up, drank first a draught of punch, wiped his mouth, clear'd his pipes & read distinctly as follows.

An Anniversary Ode on the Tuesday Club

By Jonathan Grog Esqr Poet Laureat

Recitativo
The Tuesday Club, let the sweet music sound,
Whose fame is spread from east to westren Clime,
Honor'd in future Annals shall be found,
And Jole's Great name endure to th'end of time.
Air
Her wholesome laws contriv'd and penn'd so well,
Shall ages hence her Solid wisdom tell,
To after Clubs a pattern she shall stand,
With that most beauteous badge of hand in hand.
Chorus
Our President we honor and revere,
Who most deserv'dly fills our Stately Chair.
Air
He, oer the Judge and Advocate,
The Doctor, Gentleman beside,
With wisdom and with Judgment great
Does by one General choice preside.
Recitativo [450]
Had other Clubs so great and good a head
As this, they need no dissolution dread.

moisten his desiccated pipes, Mr Ignotus Warble, an honorary member pledged him, drinking a new fangled toast, which he called the King and the Club.]

After the Secretary had delivered this Speech, it was moved, that thanks should be returned for the same, and the Master of Ceremonies was called upon to perform this office, but he declining it, Jealous Spyplot Senr Esqr, stood up, and in a handsom manner returned thanks to the Secretary, observing, that his Speech was devised in a very good method, first, being complimentary to the president and Club, and then monitory, or expressing some good advice, how they should behave themselves upon this occasion—To which thanks delivered by Mr Spyplot, the Secretary returned this compliment, saying That he took Mr Spyplot's Civility so much the more kindly, as that he had done it Spontaneously or undesired, whereas others whose proper business it was, and who had been appointed to compliment him, upon the occasion, had declined it, from a consciousness as he suppos'd of personal unfitness or dissability.

After Supper, which was served up in a very elegant manner and consisted of several curious dishes nicely prepared, there was a motion made, that thanks should be returned to his honor the president for his elegant entertainment, and the Secretary being desired to officiate stood up, and after setting his countenance in a proper order and trim, addressd his honor as follows.

"Mr President Sir,

I return thanks to your honor in the name of this here Club, for your most Sumptous and elegant entertainment, with which you have regaled them, upon this occasion of the Anniversary, the Club find Sir, that you not only exert yourself Strenuously to govern them well, by exhibiting and executing good and wholesome Laws, to keep them in decent order, but also, you study how to exalt and exhilirate their Spirits, by feeding them with rich and nourishing viands & cordial drinks, and therefore I may be allow'd on this occasion to quote a Certain witty and Celebrated poet,[1] *a propos* to the present case.

> Who fed them for the public weal,
> With marrow pudding many a meal,
> And Cram'd them 'till their guts did ake
> With Candle Custard and plum cake."

---

1. The author of these lines is Jonas Green, Tuesday Club poet laureate.

the president's high merit and deserts, must prompt you to exert your powers and talents to the utmost for the Support, defence and honor of his chair and dignity.

Sir Clement Cotterell,
Mr Protomusicus[a] and
Mr Poet Laureat,

This occasion affords each of you an opportunity of putting your best foot foremost, the first in setting every thing in order, that might, without his care be misplaced, the next in warbling forth melodious and melliflous notes, to Charm our ears, and captivate our Senses, and our Sublime Son of the Muses may now pindarize it, in praise of the honble: the President & Club.

Gentlemen, [446]

This present meeting Commences the fifth year of the Æra of our Society, and I hope, as it has hitherto florished and Increased, it will still continue so to do, not only for five years, but for fifty times five, that the name and being of so worthy and polite a Club, as this of ours, may not be lost to posterity, and unknown to future ages—In fine,

Mr President and Gentlemen,

This is not a time to speak much, but to act well and as becomes us upon this occasion, without many more words then, in order that our meeting here, may be as agreeable as the occasion Requires, permit me to make this motion, that our discourse and conversation be regular, orderly, free, humorous and Jocose, without reflection, without passion, without reserve, without Clamor, without noise, and also that this Speech and Motion of mine, may have your kind and Candid reception, as it proceeds from a heart full of good will and benevolence to the Society, and to conclude, let our Songs be in tune, our puns and repartees *a propos,* and not too poignant or Satyrical, our toasts loyal and Amorous, our Stomachs keen, to relish the elegant fare prepared for us by his honor the president, on this Joyful occasion, and our punch bowls always replete, with fragrant and nectarious liquor, for this Cordial Juice, taken with temperance and moderation [here the Secretary took the punch bowl in his hand,] lightens the Spirits, enlivens the wit, and will conduce not only to make me a more fluent orator, but you more Jolly and benevolent Long standing members [then the Secretary made ‖ some profound bows, first a grand bow to his honor the president, [447] then to all the members round, and drank a Stout pull of the punch to

---

(a) The compliments adapted to the musician, were not delivered by the Secretary, he not being in club, when this Speech was pronounced, tho' he came in afterwards.

Gentlemen,

It would be vanity and presumption in me, by arguments from personal weakness, and Inability, to disqualify myself from properly complimenting, the honorable the president and you, upon this Solemn occasion of ‖ rejoicing, since that would be the same as calling Mr Orator's judgement in question.

I grant then I am fit gentlemen, and I hope without Imputation of vanity, since Mr Orator, and the worthy Committee have esteemed me fit, for the discharge of this grand task, their consenting that I should be called to this dignity silences me and leaves me without excuse, I must therefore acquiesce in their Commands, and shall acquit myself to the best of my ability.

Mr President Sir,

Not only myself, but all these here Longstanding members who now hear me, I shall be bold to speak for them and in their name, have a Singular pleasure and Satisfaction in seeing your honor possessed, of that there dignified Seat and office in this here Club, we have found by experience, Sir, that our Constitution has hitherto flourished and prospered under your honor's benign management and oeconomy, for we all know, and must own that your honor's administration has more of the Sweet than the bitter in it, and has all along been carried on, with that even temper and Steadiness as to preserve an equal balance, between too rigid a Severity on the one hand, and a Supine mildness and Indifference on the other. Neither can we accuse your honor of partiality or respect of persons, for some of our first rate grandees, have found the resentment of the Chair, when Just cause was given, as effectually, as the most Inconsiderable of our commoners,— we have continued now Sir, for four years, a regular, harmonious and polite Society, under your honor's discreet conduct and direction, and, as we are all conscious that you are the fittest person among us to possess that there Chair of State, and exercise the office of Supreme Governor ‖ of this here Club, so we wish you may long sit there, and Continue to bless us for many anniversaries to come with your wholesome and mild government.

Worshipful Sir John, knight of the order of the Tuesday Club,

Most Dignified and eloquent Mr Orator Comus,

I address you both in particular, as dignified State officers of this here Club, and the main props and Supporters of the honorable Chair.

It would be Impudence in me, to pretend to advise gentlemen of your rank and dignity, that Innate Generosity, that Inbred Spark of virtue and honor, which qualifies you for the high offices you hold in this here Club, together with the opinion you cannot but Justly entertain of the honorable

in a quarter of an hour, and they also resolved not to Invest themselves with their badges 'till they came to the President's gate.

At Seven o'Clock in the evening, the members proceeded accordingly, to meet his honor the president, and were Joined in the way by Prim Timorous Esqr; The honorable the president graciously advanced to meet them about ten paces from his own gate, and did each member the honor of a Salute by manuquassation. The members, before they entered the president's gate, Invested themselves with their badges, and walked in decent order to his honor's back yard, the way being strow'd with flowers, and the Club flag display'd, after sometime staying in the yard, they removed into his honor's great Saloon, and the honorable the president mounted the Chair.

Then Silence being commanded, by the Master of Ceremonies, Mr Orator Comus, was called upon to deliver a harangue to the Chair, upon this occasion, on which Mr Orator, rising up gravely, made a profound obeisance to the Chair, and pulling out a written paper, put on his Spectacles, and read as follows.

"Mr President, Sir,

Eight days agoe, there was a Committee of the Club held at the Secretaries house, which Committee sent a message to me, under the hand of Mr Secretary, ac- ‖ quainting me, that they desired to know whether I Intended to officiate upon the Anniversary, by delivering a Speech to the Chair, and, at the same time, Informing me, that Mr Huffman Snap, who I Intended should officiate for me, was not at the Club's committee, and declined serving me upon this occasion; I therefore sent an answer to the Committee, that I appointed Mr Secretary Scribble, to officiate for me on the anniversary day, by delivering a Speech to the Club, and, as I have not heard that Mr Secretary has refused, so I hope he will proceed, with your honor's and the Club's permission to perform that ceremony in my stead."

[443]

Mr Orator having thus delivered himself sat down, and after some debate, whether the Secretary should be permitted to deliver any Speech, it was concluded that he should, and he rising up, made a profound obeisance to the Chair, and delivered the following oration.

Anniversary Speech, delivered by the Secretary

Mr President, Sir,

I have the honor to be appointed by Mr Orator Comus, to perform the Ceremony of congratulating your honor, and the longstanding members of this here ancient and honorable Club, upon this agreeable occasion of the Anniversary.

able to any other place," and therefore the Committee, in obedience to his honors commands, acquiesce.

Mr Orator Comus, sent for answer to the Committees message, the following short billet.

Gentlemen,

As you apprehend that Mr Snap will not supply the office of orator, I desire Mr Secretary Scribble may officiate, and am yours &ct:

From my bed chamber *Laconic Comus.*

In pursuance of these answers from the President and orator, the Committee Resolved as follows.

[441] 1mo That the anniversary Solemnity shall be Celebrated at the house of the honorable Mr President Jole, upon Tuesday the 16th Day of may.

2do That Mr Secretary Scribble open the Solemnity of the Anniversary with a Speech.

3tio That the members shall convene at the secretarie's house upon Tuesday, the 16th Day of may, at half an hour after Six in the Evening precisely, bringing their badges with them.

4to That the members after they are convened, shall send his honor the president notice of their coming to meet him a quarter of an hour before they proceed.

5to That the members shall wear their badges at the grand anniversary procession, when they go forth to meet the president.

6to That the Secretary shall give timely notice to all the members of the time and place of meeting.

After entering these Resolves, Jonathan Grog Esqr, Chairman, produced to the Committee, the ode, prepared to be sung at the Anniversary, according to an order passed at Sederunt 101, March 21, which Ode, tho' not yet quite finished, the Committee approved of, and ordered it to be set to music in two parts, ordered also, that the proceedings of this Committee be sent to his honor the president to morrow morning.

Signed,
Jonathan Grog, Chairman.

Pursuant to the order of the Committee, the Secretary sent a Copy of the proceedings to his honor the president at the time appointed.

[442] The members convened at the Secretarie's house upon the 16th, according to the appointment of the Committee, and dispatched a message to the honorable Nasifer Jole Esqr, that they Intended to proceed to meet him

To the honorable Nasifer Jole Esqr,
president of the Tuesday Club.

Honorable Sir,

Your Committee being now met, and having Elected Jonathan Grog Esqr, Chairman, we hope your honor will approve of our choice.

We only wait your honor's further orders, before we proceed to business, and, if your honor has any matters to recommend to our Consideration, besides what was appointed to be deliberated upon, last meeting of the Club, we request that your honor would let us know what it is, we are certainly Informed that there will be a great meeting of the members honorary and regular, at the Anniversary, vizt: upwards of twenty, and therefore, as Mr Quaint, late a worthy member of the Club, has made us a kind offer of a house where there are large rooms, we desire to know your honors mind, whether or not for the better conveniency of the Club, you will accept of that offer, and we shall appoint the meeting there accordingly.

Sig: per order,
Loquacious Scribble Clk: Com:

After dispatching this message, the Committee sent another to Mr Orator Comus, in the following words.

To Laconic Comus Esqr,
Orator of the Tuesday Club.

Sir,

The Committee desire to know, if you are to open ‖ the anniversary [440] solemnity with a speech, if so, you are to send no answer, but, if you appoint another person, you are to let the committee know who it is you appoint, you cannot appoint Mr Huffman Snap, he not being present at this committee, if you fix on any other, please to notify it, for the committee must know this night.

Sig: per order
Loquacious Scribble Clk: Com:

Upon the Return of the Gentlemen from the honorable the president, this answer was delivered, "That the Committee should proceed to the business appointed them to consider of at last Club, and also to appoint the place, where all the members are to meet, before they are to go in procession to attend the president, and as to the place for holding the anniversary, his honor acquaints the Committee that he Chuses his own house, prefer-

certifying him of the time of Solemnizing the Anniversary, and Returning the Club's compliments to him.

The Solemnity of the Anniversary was appointed to be held, upon Tuesday, the 16th Day of May next, at the house of the honorable Mr President Jole, and a Committee was appointed to meet at the house of Mr Secretary Scribble, upon the 9th of May next, being the Tuesday Immediatly preceeding the anniversary day, to consider of things preparatory for this great Solemnity, and this Committee was ordered, and instructed by the honorable the chair to consider of no other affairs, but such as were relative to the anniversary, The president by this Instruction showd his Jealousy of encroachments on his prerogative and power, not || having yet forgot, the affair of the Sham Committee, of which Drawlum Quaint Esqr, had been Chairman, which proceeded without Instructions. The Gentlemen named by his honor for this Committee were Mess: Jonathan Grog, Prim Timorous, Jealous Spyplot Senr, Huffman Snap, Slyboots Pleasant, and Loquacious Scribble, or any three of them Exclusive of the Secretary, who was to act as Clerk to the Committee, and they were ordered to transmit a Copy of their proceedings to the honorable Mr President Jole, the next day after their sitting.

Chapter XI

Celebration of the fourth Anniversary, Speeches on that Occasion, by the Orator and Secretary, Anniversary Ode, foundation of the Eastren-shore Triumvirate.

This ancient and honorable Club, having now arrived at its greatest pitch of glory, grandure, and magnificence, very grand preparations began to be made for Solemnizing the ensuing anniversary, that every proceeding might be transacted with that dignity and State, becoming so noble a president, such noble State officers and noble Commoners and Longstanding members.

The Committee for the Anniversary, met upon the 9th of may 1749, at the Secretarie's house according to appointment, and having Elected Jonathan Grog Esqr Chairman, they dispatched the following message, to the honorable the president, by Mr Protomusicus Never- || out and Slyboots Pleasant Esqr, two of their members, vizt:

As to the duties of the orators office, they remain the same as those of the Speakers, as expressed below, only the Club think fit, that when Speeches are made in || Club, Mr President only, and no other officer or [436] member, shall be addressed, any Law passed, at Sederunt 46th to the contrary notwithstanding, so that now, it is resolved, to be no part of the orator's privileges, as formerly it was the Speakers, to be addressed to, when any motion is made in Club, but the Orators duties are as follow.

1mo He is, as formerly the Speaker did, to sum up the whole of any argument or dispute, and report it to the Chair.

2do He is to be a privy councellor to the honorable the Chair, in conjunction with Sir John, knight of the Club, and to demean and behave himself, like a State officer of the Club.

3tio He is to moderate and regulate all disputes in Club, and call to order, when too much discord or noise arises in any dispute, and, in Case of disobedience, the Gelastic law is to be executed.

4to He is to command the Master of Ceremonies to return thanks to any member or Gentleman, whom the Club shall think worthy of the same.

5to He is to open the Solemnity of each Anniversary with a congratulatory Speech, to the president and Club, or in case he declines doing it himself, he shall have the power of commanding any other longstanding member properly qualified to do the same for him, giving him notice of the same, the Club or Committee, Imediatly preceeding the Anniversary.

6to He shall have power to order the Clerk, to draw up Indictments, when gross trespasses are Committed in Club, that is, he is to exercise the office of prosecutor in the Club.

A member moved for the alteration of Law Second, and that two dishes of vittles should be allowed for Supper at || the Club Suppers, but his [437] motion was only faintly seconded and not complied with, this Satyrical motion was prompted by the Secretary, and done by way of Sneer on his honor and some of the members, particularly, Prim Timorous Esqr, who never paid any Regard to that frugal Law.

At Sederunt 103 April 25th 1749, Mr Orator Comus being high Steward, the worshipful Sir John produced in Club, a letter from the Reverend Mr Smoothum Sly, late an old Standing member and Master of Ceremonies of this Club, presenting his compliments to the honorable the president and the members, and declaring his Intention to come to the ensuing Anniversary, together with Signior Lardini, a worthy honorary member, provided the honorable the president should Celebrate that Solemnity himself, and he should be advertised of the time of its Celebration, upon which, the Secretary was ordered to write an answer to the Reverend Mr Sly,

them, in procuring or Causing to be made, this magnificent canopy, as an Ornament for your honor's Chair."

After which Speech his honor the president bowed to the master of ceremonies, but some of the Longstanding members, believed, and that with some reason, that this Speech verified the proverb, *Thank you for nothing says the Gallipot*,[6]—the master of Ceremonies then proceeded addressing himself to the Secretary.

"Mr Secretary Sir,

I return you most hearty thanks, in the name of the most honorable the president and Club, for your honoring the || presidential Chair, with this most gorgeous and Splendid Canopy of State"—To which the Secretary replied

"Sir, The honor the Club does me, in returning thanks by the mouth of a person of your Consequence, & learning, is more than Sufficient recompense for any small trowble I may have taken in the way of my duty."

Then the Master of Ceremonies, after all this Ceremony taking his place, enquired of the Secretary, what were the duties of his office, "for Sir said he, I know not but in what I have Just now done, I have exceeded my Commission," to which the Secretary replied, and it stood as a rule for the future

1mo   That he is to Invest the president, as often as he ascends the Chair, with his proper badges of State, and affix the Canopy of State, as often as required so to do.

2do   That he is to present such Gentlemen Strangers as shall be entertained, according to ancient custom of the Club, To his honor the President, Sir John, the Orator, and the Longstanding members, recommending them to their favor.

3tio   That he is to Invest all new admitted members at their Inauguration, or confirmation, with the Club's badge, and deliver to them, the Master of Ceremonies form of confirmation, as recorded in the proceedings of Sederunt 99th—it is also expressed to be the mind of the Club that—

4to   He is to deliver the thanks, congratulations, or Compliments, of the honorable the president and Club, to any member or Gentleman, whom the Club shall think deserving of the same.

---

6. The phrase "thank you for nothing" appears in the works of several authors with whom Hamilton would have been familiar, but the only one that even remotely resembles the gallipot proverb appears in Thomas Shadwell's *The Sullen Lovers* (1668) as follows: "One . . . promised Jupiter a silver cup. Jupiter thanked him for nothing" (act 5, sc. 3). Hamilton has perhaps misremembered these lines and is confusing a gallipot (a small earthen cup) with the silver cup.

honor and the Club, and proper application made to the Secretary, who is the only person, with whom the book of Records ought to be trusted.

After Supper, Mr Orator Comus, repeated the same Question, which had been started by Sir John, before Supper, with regard to the Canopy of State affixed to the Chair, demanding by whose authority and orders it had been made? To which the Secretary made answer, that he had some considerable time agoe, received some money of his honor the president to be applied to the use of ornamenting the Chair, and that by means of this money, and a small addition of his own, he caused that canopy to be made and prepared, with which answer, Sir John, the orator, and the Club seemed satisfied. Thus we see this ambitious officer erecting his batteries on all hands, but a little while since, he attempted to corrupt the Club, by offering to make them a present of a Seal, and now is endeavoring to corrupt his honor, by covering his venerable head with a Canopy of State, we shall find this longstanding member barefacedly Walpolizing it in this here Club, that is promoting and establishing bribery and corruption.

Jonathan Grog Esqr, produced at this Sederunt, a Set of new ballots, done in the form of little oblong books, according to his promise last meeting, which the Club accepted of, and they were committed to the care and keeping of the Secretary.

The master of ceremonies moved in Club, that thanks should be returned to Jonathan Grog Esqr for providing || these ballots, for the use of the Club, and, the said Master of Cerimonies being required to do the same, he spoke to the following purpose. [434]

"Mr Jonathan Grog, Sir,

I am commanded by his honor and the Club to return you thanks, for presenting them with a neat Set of Ballots, and accordingly I comply with their commands, and, In the name of the honorable the President and Club, I thank you Sir, I thank you heartily and kindly for this favor."

To which Jonathan Grog Esqr Replied, that this was but a small token of his grateful Sense of the Clubs favors towards him.

Then the master of Ceremonies moved in Club, that there should be thanks returned to the honorable the President, and to the Secretary, for their procuring and causing to be made, a Stately canopy of State for the presidential Chair, upon which the Club appointed the said Master of Ceremonies, to return thanks to the honorable the president and Secretary, which he did as follows.

"Mr President Sir,

This here ancient and honorable Club, by means of me, your Honor's Master of ceremonies, return your honor thanks for your honors favor to

it will be proper in this place, to give a short Sketch of his person and Character.

Quirpum Comic Esqr, is of a middle Stature, and wears on his Countenance a remarkable droll Cast or turn, altogether undescribable by words, there being as it were a Jest in the very turn of his features, posture of his mouth, mold of his nose, and cast of his eye, || his disposition is comico-serious, or rather Serio-comical, having more of the Grave than Gelastic in his air, for he is seldom or never seen to laugh, tho' he has a Surprizing power, or faculty of setting every body else a laughing, which he does by his Superlative grave air, and *Judgematical countenance* that he puts on when talking of the most trivial or rather Clubical matters, and the queer Clubish gestures, which he uses while he speaks, which by the bye is but seldom, for he is not very fluent of tongue, he never speaks in Club, but it is much to the purpose, that is, his discourse is exactly adapted to the true turn and Nature of Clubical conversation, and always excites gelastic Commotions, in the muscles of every face but his own, for he never was but once observed to laugh in Club, and that was at the extravagant Speech and gestures of Mr Protomusicus Neverout, attempting to talk greek, in a Cause which he pled, in quality of Attorney General, to the Club, when the over exercised faculty of Risibility, had like to have made one half of the Longstanding members expire, to sum up the Character of this Club worthy, I shall give here, the four latin verses that were wrote under his picture, when the portraitures of the members were drawn.

> *Longostati corum Sociorum cerne Cremorem,*
> *Qui nos per noctes sepe delectat Jocis.*
> *Comici Ingenii Juvenis, tua verba per aures,*
> *Vadentia risum, Cachinnamque cient.*[5]

The Club at this Sederunt, having observed, that the book of Records, was too much bandied and tossed about, by certain overcurious and Inquisitive members, to the great hindrance of the Secretary in his office of reading the proceedings, and entering the minutes of the Club, and to the stirring up || and encouraging needless disputes, and objections concerning the Laws; it was therefore resolved, that at next Sederunt, the Club should take some method to prevent this abuse for the future, that the book shall not be thus thumbed and looked Into, upon all occasions, by every member at his own pleasure, while the Club is sitting, without leave given by his

---

5. "Behold the cream of the longstanding members, / Who often delights us with jokes through the night. / Young man of comic genius, your words through our ears / Passing, stir up humor and laughter."

Laconicus Comus Esqr, orator of the Tuesday Club.

[facing page 429]

[430] Sure || I am, that I, tho a person of rank and consequence, in this here club, was neither consulted, advised with, nor Concerned, in preparing, ordering and erecting this seemingly Superflous ornament."

Before his honor could make any reply to this bold harangue of the knight's, the Secretary politicly moved, that the Club should proceed to business of more Importance, and the enquiry went no farther at this Juncture.

The Reverend Mr Smoothum Sly, late Master of the Ceremonies, and an old Standing member of this Club, having departed the City, the office of Master of Ceremonies by his leaving the Club, became vacant. These two Important offices, of Speaker, and Master of Ceremonies, being therefore, at this time vacant, the Club resolved at this Sederunt to elect new officers to fill their places, but when the Club was proceeding to this Election, a question was started, whether the title of Speaker, should be changed for that of orator, yea or nay, and, the ballots being put round, it was carried in the affirmative, eight yeas & three Nays.

Then Laconic Comus, Huffman Snap, and Jealous Spyplot Senr: Esqrs, were set up as Candidates for the office of orator, and the Election was carried in favor of Laconic Comus Esqr, who, accordingly, after Supper, took his place at the left hand of the Chair, as Orator and State officer of the Club, and privy Councellor to the Chair.

The Club then proceeded to the election of a master of the Ceremonies, and two questions were put, after the following Gentlemen were pro-
[431] posed, as Candidates || for the office, vizt: Jealous Spyplot Junior, Jonathan Grog, and Quirpum Comic Esqrs, The first question proposed, was, whether Jonathan Grog Esqr, as already enjoying several offices and titles in the Club, vizt: Poet, punster, Printer, Punchmaker general and Purveyor, properly expressed by 5 Capital P's, after the manner of the old Romans, Thus, Jonathan Grog Esqr P.P.P.P.P. was to be burdened with any other offices in Club, or was a proper person to stand Candidate for another office, yea or nay, the ballots were put about, and, it passed in the negative, nine Nays, and two Yeas; upon which the Club by balloting, Chose Quirpum Comic Esqr, master of Ceremonies, who took his place accordingly, at the right hand of Sir John, after the Club had been long delay'd in their proceedings in this Election, by a dispute upon some nice distinctions, fomented by Mr Protomusicus Neverout, a gentleman remarkable for raising objections, where no body else could find any.

As Quirpum Comic Esqr, will at times make a Considerable figure in this Club History, both in the Quality of an officer and private Member,

badges, for in that instance, the ballots at the first taking were not all unanimous, there being one Nay, but this Cunning officer, pretending there had been a mistake made, got the Club to ballot again, and the whole were Yeas, and it was even suspected, that at this Second balloting he by some Slight or Legerdemain had contrived to remove a nay from the hat, and put a yea in its place; the other law passed at this Sederunt was as follows.

Law XXXIX. Passed into a Law, by the President and Club now met, this 21 of March 1748/9, that no Law for the future shall be passed in Club, unless two thirds, at least, of the members be present.

After passing these Laws, Jonathan Grog Esqr proposed to prepare for the Club, Ballots made in such a manner, as that they might be thrown into the hat, without any person's discovering what was put in, a Nay or yea, which the Club accepted of.

At Sederunt 102, april 11th 1749, Prim Timorous Esqr, being high Steward, a magnificent Canopy appeared fixed upon the presidential Chair, in the Shape and model of a large Scallop Shell, and upon the forepart of it, was erected an oval Shi- || eld, with the proper devices and mottos of the Club, curiously delineated there- upon, of which the figure in minature is here in the margin annexed; this too was a contri- vance of that plodding officer, the Secretary, and designed by him to promote mischief in the Club, for we shall soon find, this very de- vice, triffling as it was, raise con- tentions, and hot disputes which were not easily quell'd.

Sir John, after having taken his Seat as usual, at the right hand of the Chair, and deposited a na- ked Sword upon the Club table *in terrorem*, casting a fierce eye upon this new Canopy, with a frown in his countenance, addressed the president, and spoke as follows.

"Mr President,

I cannot help taking notice of some Innovations here, which I pre- sume, have been contrived and Introduced, without advice or consent of the Club, pray Sir, may I presume to ask, by whose authority, advice and expence, this Sumptous and noble canopy, has been affixed to the Chair, for

no other being found to match it among all our ancient or moderen bards, in short, his Compositions had something in them peculiar to themselves and altogether Inimitable, they were pointed & edged, as one might say *I dont know howish,* or as the ‖ french express it, they had a *Je ne sçai quoi* of a Salt or relish in them, which cannot well be expressed any other way, but by perusing Specimens of his performances, of which follows one, wrote in the epigrammatic Stile, upon a Subject so barren in itself, that one would be Surprized, how this keen wit could make any thing of it; it is upon a Gentleman's erecting a gate in an out o' the way place or Corner.

Epigram, by Jonathan Grog Esqr

Between these Sticks
This gate to fix
Was Esquire Bl——n's[4] fancy,
But why it was done
I'm Son of Gun,
If I at all can see.

The doggrell is here punctually observed and followed, and there is something of a delicate burlesque turn in the epigram, this Specimen alone will show how well qualified this Gentleman was for a Club poet.

At this Sederunt, there was an amendment made on Law 36th, vizt: after these words in the Law, *Excepting only the election of members,* the following words are to be added, *and matters of expence,* then the two following laws were passed in Club, vizt:

Law XXXVIII. Passed into a law, by the president and Club now met, this 21 of March 1748/9, that from henceforth, when the ballots are to be put round upon any Question, the Secretary is to give all the members present warning, before he destributes the Ballots, and propose the Question in plain and Intelligible terms, and then ‖ destribute the ballots, and, after once going round, whatever the result be, they are to be put round no more upon the same question, during that Sederunt, and for three Succeeding Sederunts after that, and, that all the ballots, both yeas and nays, shall be taken in by two different persons, before those that the Secretary takes be examined.

This law was made, on a Suspicion the members had of some Juggling practises of the Secretary at Sederunt 100, when he procured by flattery and other artifices the consent of the Club, to his proposals concerning the

---

4. Hamilton's draft has Bladen, probably a reference to Thomas Bladen; see biographical sketch.

We find his honor the president as yet complaisant enough, to agree to what the Club had resolved in his absence, but we shall not always find it so, for by the machinations & practises of Sir John, and the plots of the Secretary, he became at last so Jealous and Suspicious, that he absolutely refused to give a Sanction, to the veriest triffles that were transacted in Club without him.

The Secretary reported to the Club, that he had this day delivered their Commissions concerning the badges and Seal to Captain Comely Coppernose, who is to have them done at London, and further, that he ordered them to be Cast with fine pinchbeck mettle, Instead of Silver according to the order of the Club, that mettle being fitter for gilding in Case the gilding should in time wear off, which orders of the Secretarie's the Club approved of.

Then the Secretary gave Jonathan Grog Esqr, thanks for his diligence, in printing 26 blank Commissions, for the use of his honor the president and Club, and Jonathan Grog Esqr, returned a very civil compliment, in answer to the Secretary.

This evening was produced, a curious distich, wrote upon the envelope of the Club's badge, sent to the high Steward by Jonathan Grog Esqr, to the following purpose.

To Mr ⌘

Inclos'd I've sent your Tuesday badge,
To night, you'll see, how well 'twill fadge.[3]

The Club approved so much of this distich, that they Immediatly Created Jonathan Grog Esqr *Poet Laureat of the Club,* and thus made a new officer, yet, by this addition the Club fund was by no means Impaired, that having been long agoe, Intirely swallowed up in the Philadelphian lottery, and, had there been any Club fund now In being, it would not have been affected by the Creation of this officer, for the Club wisely Judged, in not allowing him any Sallary, knowing he would Rhime the better, the poorer he was kept, like all his brethern bards, whose geniuses are only Clogged and Clouded, by too much pampering and Cramming, after his Creation, the Club ordered him to prepare an ode proper for the next anniversary Solemnity, to be sung by Mr Proto-musicus.

The turn, or Genius of Jonathan Grog Esqr, in his poetical performances, was so uncommon, that it might well be called an original Genius,

---

3. How well it will suit you, or agree with you.

well Constituted Society, I find myself not only unable to equal the meanest of their performances in this way, but even utterly unstock'd with a choice of thoughts and diction, in any degree worthy of your honor's attention, and therefore, not to detain your honor Longer, or occasion any further loss of those precious moments, that are constantly employed by your honor, in promoting the grandure and well being of this your honor's Ancient Tuesday Club, I, an unworthy member thereof, humbly take the Liberty to acquaint your honor, that this evening, being especially appointed, for the meeting of this most honorable Society, I propose to officiate in duty of high Steward at the free School, and am in hopes your honor will favor the Club with your presence, I am your honor's

From my lodging in	Most obedient
Tabernacle Street	Most obliged
21, March 1748	Most devoted and
	Most humble Servt: & Subject
	Quirpum Comic.

We may observe from the tenor of this letter, what gradual Steps, the members of this ancient and honorable Club took in raising up great titles for their President, since he is here addressed by the title of *Most Illustrious Sir,* a title never once thought of, or applied to him in Speeches or letters before this time, (If we only except the Secretaries Stile in the Indictments against Sir John) these Imprudent steps in the members of this Club, screwd up the pride of the Chair, to such an extravagant pitch, that it became at last quite Intollerable, and a burden too heavy for them to support, so that the Constitution of the Club, shook and Cracked under it.

The Secretary having wrote to his honor the President, Concerning the proposals of last Sederunt, he had the following answer.

To Loquacious Scribble Esqr,
Secretary of the Tuesday Club, These.

Sir,

I approve of the proposals, and have sent you the Commission, which please to deliver according to directions Immediatly after the Clubs meeting, you have also the high Stewards letter, and as it well deserves a place in our book of records, desire it may be forthwith recorded, either by yourself or Chief Clerk, I am Sir,

March 21, 1748/9	Your humble Servant
	Nasifer Jole.

to sing these Songs, besides which the deputy Complimented the Club with a Voluntaire Song, which as it was a favorite of his we shall here give a Copy of.

Club Song, sung by Laconic Comus Esqr D:P:[2]

She tells me, with Claret, she cannot agree,
And she thinks of a hogshead, whene'er she sees me,
For I smell like a beast, and therefore must I,
Resolve to forsake her, or Claret deny.

Must I Leave my dear bottle that was always my friend,
And I hope will Continue so, to my life's end,
Must I leave it for her, 'tis a very hard task,
Let her go to the Devil, bring 'tother full flask.

Had she found out my Chloris, up two pair of Stairs,
I had baulk'd her and gone to Saint James's to prayers,
Had she tax'd me with gaming, and bid me forbear,
Tis a thousand to one, I had lent her an ear.

Had she bid me read homilies, three times a day,
Perhaps she'd been humor'd, with little to say,
But at night to deny me, my dear flask of red,
Let her go to the Devil, there's no more to be said.

The honorable deputy sung this Song very pathetically, passion appearing in the twist of his features and glare of his eyes, especially, when he pronounced these words, *let her go to the Devil,* by which his hearers might easily know, that he was himself a dear lover of his bottle, and this was really the Case, for Mr Comus, tho he would talk but very little upon any Subject, yet, when the bowl or bottle came to be the Topic of discourse, he held forth very emphatically.

A letter from the high Steward, to his honor the presi- ‖ dent was produced in Club as follows, vizt:

To the honorable Nasifer Jole Esqr,
President of the Tuesday Club, Annapolis.

Most Illustrious Sir,

It is with the deepest concern, that being sat down to address your honor, agreeable to the practise of your honor's worthy members of this

---

2. This song appears as "The Jolly Toaper" in D'Urfey, *Wit and Mirth,* and in John Sadler, *The Muses Delight* (Liverpool, 1754), 165.

mitting the Care of the same to Capt: Comely Coppernose, (this evening entertained as a Stranger by the Club, according to ancient Custom) who in a little time Intended to go for England.

Jonathan Grog Esqr, was ordered by his honor the deputy and the Club, to deliver the thanks of the Club to the Secretary, for this generous proffer, which he did in the following form.

"Mr Secretary Sir,

Not only in obedience to the commands of the honorable the deputy president and Club, but of my own frank and free Inclination, I return you hearty thanks, in the name of the honorable the deputy and Club, for your Generous offer to make us a present of a Silver Seal for the Club's use, and in token that I do this Sincerely I drink your health" [then he took a hearty pull of the bowl]

Then the Secretary moved the Club, that there should be badges of Silver, prepared for each Regular member of the Club, weighing half an ounce each, dowble gilt, with the proper Signatures and mottos of the Club Imbossed, or raised thereupon, to be fixed upon ribbons, instead of the Card badges now used, and that the || said badges, should be ordered to be prepar'd and done at London, upon this motion of the Secretarie's, the yeas and nays were put round, and it was unanimously agreed to; the Secretary then received orders to commit the Care of this to Capt: Comely Coppernose, who undertook to have it done in the cheapest and the neatest manner, at the Common expence of the Regular members of the Club, The Secretary moved next, that blank Commissions should be printed, for the use of his honor the president, which was agreed to, and the Club, ordered Jonathan Grog Esqr, to print the same.

At the time of making these motions by the Secretary, the Club did not forsee the designs of this politic officer, in broaching them, but, the violent heats and disputes, which the Seal, these Badges, and these Commissions occasioned afterwards in Club, made them Sorely repent that ever they had agreed to these motions.

On Sederunt 101, Quirpum Comic Esqr being high Steward, and Laconic Comus Esqr deputy president by Commission, the Club met again in the School room, the ancient place of meeting of the Ugly Club, and the Songs of, *Stand Around my brave boys,* and *Bumpers 'Squire Jones,*[1] were sung by the deputy, at the express Injunction and Command of his honor the President, who had made it a Condition at the bottom of his Commission,

---

1. Handel's "Stand Round My Brave Boys" was published in the *London Magazine* (November 1745), 560–561. "Bumpers Squire Jones" appears in *Calliope, or English Harmony* and was also published in the *Gentleman's Magazine* (November 1744), 612.

heroic action, as well as Club, on this noble and virtuous emulation (tho at first but mere banditti and Ruffians) the ancient Romans, laid the foundation of their great empire, which rose at last to such a height, as to outbrave every enimy but Luxury avarice and ambition, under the Insatiable Tyranny of which last, it fell and never rose again.

When the Ancient and honorable Tuesday Club, kept within decent bounds, as to expence, pageantry, Show, and presidential power, when they exercised their learning and bright parts in making of Speeches, penning of Letters, and striving, who should excell in this Laudable exercise, evading flattery and bombast in their Compositions of this Sort, they flourished, prospered, and grew up to that pitch of Grandure, in which they appeared at this very period, but when the power of the Chair was streched to an extraordinary extent, and the longstanding members strove one among another, who should have most favor and Influence with the honorable Chair, || then the glory power and Character of the Club began to decline. But the prime cause of this declension of the grandure of the Club, was the emulation and contention among the State officers, and the officers of the Commons about precedency, which, like the Contentions between the Patricians and Tribunes of the people at Rome, laid the first foundation for Tyranny and Arbitrary power, and, the Secretary, an ambitious and turbulent officer of the Commons, was one of the Chief fomenters and promoters of this mischief, for, when he found that he could not advance himself in the Club, or gain the favor of the honorable Chair, by flattering Speeches, Orations, and fustian bombast letters, he went to work another way, and tried what might be done, by making great and valuable Presents to the Club, Introducing certain Seals, Medals, Canopies of State, Shields or Scutcheons, caps of State, Conundrums, and the like tinsel trumpery, which, we shall find in the Sequel raised great disturbance in the Club, set his honor the president, his State officers, and longstanding members together by the ears, and, this politic officer, at last compassed his ends, in a great measure, by picking up and securing to himself, whatever he could snatch, in these General hubbubs and Club hurly-burlys.

At Sederunt 100 March 4th 1748/9, Jealous Spyplot Junr Esqr being high Steward, and Huffman Snap Esqr, by commission, deputy president, the Secretary || offered to make the Club a present of a Seal, cut in Silver, expressing the proper design and motto of the Club, to be used by the honorable the president, in the Sealing of Commissions &ct: which the Club accepted of, and the Secretary undertook and promised accordingly, to have this Seal done and finished at London, as soon as could be, com-

Club, and tho' the members blamed Coney pimp Frontinbrass Esqr, long after this for foisting this title upon them, yet, this makes it clear, that the Secretary first Introduced it.

The Secretary again protested against the proceedings of the Club, in their quashing the Second Indictment, and being taken up short, by his honor, and some of the Longstanding members, was attempting to speak farther in his own defense, when the Gelastic Law was put in execution against him in an Illegal tumultuous and Clamorous manner, without any Signal given by the honorable the president, this conduct the Secretary begged leave to enter as a riot or trespass and humbly craved that Indictments might be drawn up against the particular offenders, which he beg'd his honor the president to Issue his orders for, from henceforth resolving and protesting, that for his part, as Secretary of the Club, he never would draw up any more Indictments, without particular orders and authority from the honorable the president, as also, declaring, that it was his opinion, that the worshipful Sir John, knight of this Club, is less, (if at all) dissaffected to the Chair, than some pretended loyal long Standing members.

Some members, at this Sederunt, being conscious, that they had been guilty of certain trespasses, and fearing that Indictments might be ordered against them, applied to his honor for an act of Grace, forgiving all past offences, but the honorable the president declined granting it, observe here the Servile disposition of the Club.

Chapter X

Grand proposals in Club by the Secretary, Creation of a poet Laureat, Canopy of State added to the Chair, Speech of Sir John on that occasion, The master of ceremonies leaves the Club, election of a new master of Ceremonies, election of a Club Orator.

[419] An honest Emulation for precedency in learning or virtue, is always commendable (I say an honest || emulation, because I would make a distinction between learning and virtue, and what are frequently mistaken for them, Pedantry and Hypocrisy, by which many rogues have Imposed upon the world,) and an ambition to excell in such excellent things, as are worth excelling in, is a glory to him that possesses it, 'tis *Ingeniorum Cos,* the whetstone of wit, and has been the cause of the rise and grouth of many a

able the president, or his deputy, Solemnly sitting and sleeping in the presidential Chair, and in the presence and hearing of several of your fellow members, then and there met, with force and arms, rautously and riotously, did take into your hands, a certain punch bowl, of the value of 4 Shillings, charged with a certain Liquor called punch, and drank the following execrable, abominable, detestable, horrible, dreadful, Immodest, contumelious and damnable [here Sir John with great violence exclaimed *ha! ha!*] toast, which you, the said Sir John, otherwise Called Sir John Oldcastle knight of the Tuesday Club, expressed in the following English words, viz: *To the pious memory of Sally Salisbury's* —— against your aleidgeance due to our Lord the president, and setting a bad and pernicious example to your fellow members to be guilty of the same, and against the peace of our said Lord the president his Chair and dignity. What say you Sir John, are you Guilty &ct:

After reading this Indictment, and Sir John not pleading, the case was argued for sometime and very learnedly handled by Mr Attorney Spyplot, but Sir John, having procured, by certain political devices, a very Strong party in the Club, this Indictment, to the Surprize of many, was also quashed, and Copies of both were Solemnly delivered to the Honorable Mr President Jole, to be reposited in his Store of Clubical archives, after some argumentation in the Club, whether or not they should be burnt or destroyed.

Sir John then addressed himself to the President and said "as to this last Indictment Sir, 'tis a parcell of damnd Stuff,—but as to the first, I protest, that had I not promoted drinking toasts In the Club, the whole members, as well as the deputy president, would have fell fast asleep."

It is plain from the management of these trials, that Sir John bullied and Intimidated both his honor the president and the Club; and that they were much struck with a pannic fear at the bellicose Countenance of this Club heroe, which probably would not have happened, had there been a Speaker in the Club, to manage the cause against Sir John, of equal Genius with Drawlum Quaint Esqr, the want of which able officer, the Club now felt in a particular manner, and to verify this observation, I must not ommit this circumstance, that Sir John after quashing the second Indictment, filled a bumper, and In the face of his honor and the Club, drank again, *viva voce*, the same filthy toast, for which he had been but Just Indicted, he also had his broadsword in Club this night.

It will be worth while to observe here, that in these Indictments || his honor the president has the title of *Lord* given him for the first time in the

Indictamentum IIdum

Tuesday Club Ss⁹

Socii societat⁹, diei mart⁹ Annapolitan⁹ anglice *The Annapolis Tuesday Club,* super honor⁹ suam present⁹ quod dom⁹ Joannes eques Societat⁹ alias dom⁹ Joannes Oldcastellius, eques Societat⁹, anglice *Sir John knight of the* ‖ *Club, otherwise called Sir John Oldcastle knight of the Club,* nuper de civitat⁹ Annapol⁹ in Comitat⁹ Annarund⁹ homo pernicios⁹ et Seditios⁹ prave⁹ ment⁹ et turbulent⁹ disposition⁹, timorem dom⁹ nostri presid⁹ in ment⁹ non habens vi et armis, rautose et riotose, Decimo, Septimo die mensis Januarii anno domination⁹ dom⁹ nostri presid⁹ quarto apud aul⁹ Baccalaur⁹ anglice *Batchellor's Hall,* in civitat et comitat prædict, coram ipso dom⁹ presid, Solenniter sedent⁹ et dormient⁹ in Cathedr⁹ presidential⁹ et in present⁹ diversor⁹ nostror⁹ Socicior⁹ adtunc et Ibid⁹ present⁹, et existent⁹ Certam Crater⁹ anglice *A punch Bowl,* pretii quatuor Solidor⁹ replet⁹ certo liquore, anglice *Punch,* manu tenens, Toastam Sequentem exicrabilem, abominabilem, detestabilem, horribolem, horrisonam, Immodestam, contumeliosam et damnabilem, Societati proposuit, hisce scil⁹ verbis anglican⁹ *To the pious memory of Sally Salisbury's* —— Contra Ligeantiam debitam, in malu⁹ et perniciosu⁹ exemplu⁹ omniu⁹ alioru⁹ in tali casu delinquend⁹ et contra pacem dict⁹ dom⁹ presid, cathedr⁹ et dignitat⁹.

To which Indictment Sir John said "Pish and phogh! prithee ha' done, there's too much of this Stuff, this is worse than the other, by Jupiter."

The Secretary then read the English Indictment as follows.

Indictment II

Sir John, you stand Indicted by the name of Sir John, ‖ otherwise called, Sir John Oldcastle, of the parish of St Annes in the County of Annarundel, knight of the Tuesday Club, for that you, as a pernicious, Seditious, depraved and turbulent knight, not in your heart having the reverence due, to our most Illustrious and Serene Nasifer, president of the said Club, but, led by your own wicked and devlish Inclination, in utter contempt of the Laws of the said Club, and the authority of the said Serene President, you, the said Sir John, otherwise called Sir John Oldcastle, knight of the said Tuesday Club, upon the 17th day of January, in the 4th year of the dominion, of our said honorable president, in the parish and County aforesaid, at a place called Batchellors hall; before the said honor-

Mr Attorney Spyplot Long Stand. Memb: of the T. C.

*Maximus Eloquio, en, pollens flumine linguæ
Eloquium Docti qui Ciceronis Habet.
Quæ sit enim culti fucundia sensimus oris
Clubica pro trepidis cum tulit arma reis.*

[Greatest in eloquence, behold! powerful in the flow of his speech
Who has the eloquence of learned Cicero;
For what was the readiness of his well trained mouth we knew
When he bore the Clubical arms on the occasion of alarming events.]

[facing page 409]

say further, Sir, that you need not be Surprized if the Chair should suffer a violent Shake, since you permit the underminers and Sappers to approach so nigh your own foundations, by digging under my props."—Then Sir John frowened & was silent.

The Indictment being read, and Sir John refusing to plead, Mr Attorney Spyplot, council for Sir John, stood up and spoke as follows.

"Mr President Sir, (here he took a pinch of Snuff)

I should be sorry—humph—That Mr Secretary should be allowed to prefer Indictments, in this here Club, Just when and how he pleases, and desire to know Sir by whose authority, and by whose advice and Instigation, this here Indictment, or rather libel Sir, has been trumpd up; for Sir, If we do not enquire into this, it is my opinion Sir—ah hey ho, [here Mr Attorney youned] it will be a dangerous affair, and I humbly Conceive, Mr President Sir, It concerns us a—a haunch—a—a haunch—a—a haunch [here he sneezd thrice] all Sir, for Sir, if Sir John, a Noble and State officer of this here Club, is laid open to these attacks libels and Insults, none of us, Longstanding members of the commoners, can reckon ourselves safe, ‖ and gi' me leave to say, Mr President, Sir that your honor's Chair may be in danger, for which Mr President Sir I should be very sorry"—here Mr Attorney Spyplot sat down.

Then Sir John deigned to arise from his seat, shifted his Chaw, and declared, that he was Surprized that any one could be so audacious, as to draw up such scandalous libels against the Champion and protector of the Club.

Upon enquiry made, the Club found, that the Secretary had no authority to draw up this first Indictment, and therefore it was quashed.

Mr Secretary against this proceeding Solemnly protested, because he affirmed That he had express orders from the Club of the 17th of January last to draw up the said Indictment, to prove which he called upon Jonathan Grog Esqr, who was present and asisting at that Club, to which Jonathan Grog Esqr, made reply, that he very well remembered such orders, then his honor the president asked the Secretary if he had orders from the deputy of the Chair for that night, To which the Secretary answered That he had not, and how could he, since Solo Neverout Esqr, then deputy president, was at the time fast asleep in the Chair, to which his honor replied, that this argument was little to the purpose.

The Secretary then read the Latin Copy of the Second Indictment as follows.

the County aforesaid, at a place called Batchellors hall, before the said President, in the person of his deputy, Solemnly sitting and sleeping in the presidential Chair, and in the presence of several of the Liege members of the said Club, with force and arms, wickedly made an open assault, upon the Chair honor and person of the said president, in open Contempt of the Laws of this here Club, then and there, taking into your hands a Certain punch bowl, of the value of four Shillings, and most Impudently, audaciously and Insolently, the said punch bowl, charged with a certain liquor called punch, to your mouth uplifting, drank the first toast after Supper, against an express Law of this here Club, which has given that privilege, of drinking the first toast after Supper || to the honorable the president alone, [412] and this contempt and open assault, you, the said Sir John, otherwise called Sir John Oldcastle, knight of the tuesday Club, with force and arms, rautously and riotously, Impudently, audaciously and Insolently, hast perpetrated, against the aleigeance, due to the honorable the President, and setting a bad example to your fellow members, to commit the same Insolence, and against the peace of his said honor the president, his Chair and dignity. What say you Sir John, are you guilty of the matter wherewith you stand Charged or not Guilty.

Sir John would not plead, but looked very Sour and Surly first at the Secretary, then at his honor the president and then at all the Longstanding members round him, every one of whom remained mute, as it is thought thro fear.

The Champion however was not altogether silent during the reading of the Indictment, for, at the words, *Late a State officer of the said Club,* he Interrupted the Secretary and without rising from his Seat spoke to the following purpose.

"*Late a State officer!*—pray Sir, why *Late a State officer?*—Mr President Sir,—I have the honor to sit here at your right hand—I say Sir at your right hand in quality of a State officer, of this here Club, and, I beg leave to affirm Sir, that I was not only late a State officer, but also actually *Now a State officer,* and permit me also to take notice Sir, that it is altogether Irregular, nay Illegal Sir, to proceed against the nobles by way of Indictment, but, had I been guilty of any crime Sir, I ought to have been Impeached, and here I boldly appear Sir, and || claim the privilege of my [413] peerage, being, I assure you, not alittle Surprized, that you should countenance such Illegal and audacious proceedings, against a person who has the honor to be Champion of this here Club [here Sir John laid his hand upon the hilt of his broad Sword] and prop of the Chair, and must beg leave to

rebellion, contra dict, dom, presidem, Decimo Septimo die Janrii, annoq3 domination, dom, nost, presid, quarto, in aulo Baccalaur, anglice *Batchelor's hall* in civitat et comitat predict, ‖ coram ipso dom, pres, solenniter sedent, et dormient, in Cathedr, presidential, et in presentia diversor, nostror Socior, adtunc et Ibid, present, et existent, vi et armis, rautose et riotose, assaultation, fecit exicrabilem, in Cathed, et honor, dict, dom, presid, Craterum Certam, anglice *A Punch Bowl* pretii quatuor Solidar, in manu tenens Impudenter audacter, et Insolenter, crater, dict, ori suo admovens, primam post ceniam Compotavit tostam contra Leges hujus Societat, quæ Confirmant dom, nost, presid, hanc privilegiam compotand, prim, post Ceniam tostam, et hanc contumeliam perpetravit, et assaultation, fecit predict, dom, Joannes eques Oldcastellius, anglice *Sir John Knight otherwise Oldcastle* vi et armis, rautose et riotose, Insolenter Impudenter et audacter, contra Ligeantiam debitam, in malu^9 et pernicosu^9 Exemplu^9 omniu^9 alioru^9 in tali casu delinquand^9, et contra pacem dict^9 dom^9 presid^9 cathedr^9 et dignitat^9.

After Reading this Indictment, Sir John said, "Hum, Hum, a fine Rigmeroll indeed! who the devil understands one word of all this Stuff"— Then the Secretary read the English Indictment as follows.

Indictment I

Sir John, You stand Indicted by the name of Sir John, otherwise Called Sir John Oldcastle, in the parish of St Anne in the County of Annarundel, knight of the Tuesday Club, for that you, as a false traitor, against the most Illustrious and Serene Nasifer, President of the said Tuesday ‖ Club, due reverence to the said Illustrious and Serene Nasifer In your heart not having, nor weighing your duty towards his august Chair, but being moved and seduced by your own wicked Instigation, and due obedience to the said Illustrious and Serene Nasifer, utterly withdrawing, and endeavoring and Intending with all your might, the peace and Common tranquillity of this our Tuesday Club to disturb, and the Laws of the same established to overthrow, and to pull down and bring into Contempt, our said Serene president and his Chair, and the said honorable Chair, wickedly, maliciously and devillishly to usurp, you, the said Sir John, otherwise Called Sir John Oldcastle, knight of the Tuesday Club, and late a State officer of the said Club, on the 17th day of January, in the fourth year of the Dominion of our said Illustrious and Serene Nasifer, in the parish of St Annes aforesaid, in

put a power into his honor the presidents hands, which he neither expected nor applied for, vizt: no less than the Sole power of electing members into the Club, it is true, they did not annex this power to the Chair, by any express law or rule, but his honor, tenacious of all powers and prerogatives given him, would never a- ‖ gain give up this power, alledging, that none [408] could be a longstanding member of the Club, without going thro' this ceremony of confirmation, which occasioned abundance of disputes and wranglings between his honor the president and the Longstanding members, in a famous case, which will appear in it's proper place in this history.

After these Ceremonies were over, the Secretary was accused by some of the members, of the Interpolation mentioned at last Sederunt, and was called upon to answer for that misdemeanor, which he flatly denied, alledging, that the addition of *præs:* to his honor's name, was not in his hand writing, but this accusation and proceeding was discountenanced by his honor the president, who expressed his displeasure at the forwardness and petulancy of some members, in finding fault, with his manner of Signing, alledging that it was a thing entirely at his own choise, to sign all Commissions and all Clubical Instruments and papers whatsoever, Just in what manner and form he pleased, without taking Instructions or directions from the Club.

The Secretary then, delivered to his honor and the Club, two Indictments against Sir John, knight of the Club, which he was ordered to read aloud, upon which Sir John, stood up, and with a bold and Intrepid countenance said that he was ready ‖ and prepared, to give a categorical answer [409] to all Indictments, and Libels whatsoever, which Mr Secretary or the Club should bring against him. Then the Secretary proceeded to read the first Indictment in Law latin.

Indictamentum Imum

Tuesday Club Ss:

Socii Societat, Annapolit, diei martis, anglice *The Annapolis Tuesday Club* super honorem suam present, quod dom, Joannes, eques Societat, alias, domd, Joannes Oldcastellius eques Societat, anglice dict *Sir John knight of the Club, otherwise Sir John Oldcastle knight of the Club,* nuper de Civitat, Annapol, in Comitat, predict, homo pernicios, et Seditios, pravæ mentis, et turbulent, disposition, machinans et Intendens contra honor, et dignitat, domin, presidis, Socios hujus Societat ad odium et vituperation anglice *Dislike,* person, dict, dom, presid, et gubernation, Stabilat, in fra dict, dom, presid, perturbare et incitare, et movere Sedition, et

Follows the form of the master of Ceremonies his Speech, to each of the new members, when he Invested him with the Club badge, and presented him to his honor the president.

"Sir,

I as master of ceremonies of our tuesday Club, with all the Ceremony I am master of, which mastery in ceremonies, I acknowledge to be conveyd to me by the authority of our honorable president, do Inaugurate, constitute and confirm you,

Huffman Snap
Jealous Spyplot Junrs proxy } Esqr
Quirpum Comic
Prim Timorous

a good firm Longstanding member, of the Commoners in this our Tuesday Club, in token of which, I Invest you with this the Club's badge, and here Solemnly present you, to the honorable the president, recommending it to you, to make your acknowledgements to the honorable the president and Club, in the handsomest and best Speech you can devise."

Upon which the gentlemen tacitly assented to do so, and after the Ceremony each new member and the proxy made a low bow to the Chair, and his honor took each of them by the hand, giving them a Clubical manuquassation.

Then the honorable the president addressing himself to the new Confirmed members spoke to the following purpose.

"Gentlemen,

I had the misfortune to be under great pain, being Indisposed with the gout that night in which || you were admitted, or elected into the Club, and nothing gave me greater concern, than my being thus prevented from giving attendance to your admission, in which I do assure you, I should have had not alittle pleasure, but, however, tho I had not the Satisfaction to be present at your admission, the news of your Election, contributed much to my health and recovery, and I veryly believe, you will prove very worthy members of this our Club, and therefore I heartily congratulate you, upon your admission, and am very Glad we have got such agreeable members, wishing you all the Satisfaction in the thing that you can desire."

This polite Speech ended, the gentlemen made another low bow to the honorable Chair, and resumed their Seats accordingly, Invested with the proper badges of the Club.

We must observe, in the course of these ceremonies, and transactions that the longstanding members, without the least foresight or reflection,

North East Street Ss:

Whereas it has been reported to us, by the Reverend Mr Smoothum Sly, our Master of Ceremonies, and Loquacious Scribble Esqr our Clerk, Commissioners deputed by the Tuesday Club, in the Name, and by the authority of said Club, met at the house of Capt: Seemly Spruce our then high Steward upon Tuesday the 31 *ultimo,* Jonathan Grog Esqr being our deputy president, that the said President and Club, then and there, Solemnly met, by a Special Commission, under our hand and privy Seal at Arms, did proceed to the election of the following Gentlemen, vizt: Messrs Huffman Snap, Jealous Spyplot Junior, Quirpum Comic and Prim Timorous, by balloting, according to a rule of said Club, for that Intent made and provided, and that the said election was carried unanimously, for the said several Gentlemen abovenamed; *Be it therefore known,* by these presents, to all herein Concerned, that *we*(a) Confirm, strengthen, stabilitate, Corroborate, make valid and perpetuate, by our authority the above election, in such manner, as it shall be for ever good || firm and uncontrovertable, Sufficient, valid and effectual, whatever objections may be brought to the contrary notwithstanding, and accordingly, *by these presents,* which we hereby command our clerk to enter in our book of records, *in perpetuam Rei memoriam,*[3] the above named Gentlemen, viz: Messrs Huffman Snap, Jealous Spyplot Junior, Quirpum Comic and Prim Timorous, are declared, avowed, pronounced, appointed, affirmed and Confirmed to be rightful, Lawful, effectual, firm, regular, and duely elected Standing members of the Commoners of our 'foresaid Tuesday Club, from this day forth and for ever.

[405]

To Loquacious Scribble Esqr, Clerk of our Tuesday Club	Given under our hand and Seal, this 28 day of february, in the 4th year of our presidential Government. *Nasifer Jole.* [Seal]

As the Secretary named the Gentlemen at the Conclusion of the above form, the master of Ceremonies confirmed them, one after another, by Investing them with the Club's badge, and Solemnly presenting them to the honorable the president, who Graciously took each of them by the right hand, giving them a Gentle Clubical Squeeze.

(a) Here Sir John observed, that the particle or pronoun *We,* was Improperly applied, because when this form was drawn, he was neither present, concerned, nor Consulted.

3. "In perpetual memory of the thing."

nius like yours, for what knight I say, what emblazon'd Champion, either ancient or moderen, had ever such Subjects to exercise his valor upon and act in defence of, as the honorable the president, and longstanding members of the ancient and honorable Tuesday Club! for, such an honorable president and such longstanding members, I believe, never were heard of, seen or known, either to antiquity or these baser and Latter times, neither do I believe, shall Expecting posterity, ever be so happy as to behold such a president, such members, and above all, such a magnanimous, epouvantable and Invincible knight.

After this well adapted prelimination, I am next to sollicit you, most Invincible and heroic Sir John, to do me the honor and dignity of your knightly presence this evening, at the house of our honorable President, where I am to have the Glory of officiating for the first time as high Steward, and I doubt not but your magnanimous presence, will Inspire into me that courage and undaunted Spirit, which will be necessary, when I stand before the honorable presi- ‖ dents august chair, to be Inaugurated and confirmed a perpetual Standing member, of our Ancient Tuesday Club, I am the more bold in demanding this of you, as I know you glory, in being the valiant champion of our Tuesday Club, and the protector, of not only the whole bod thereof under the honorable the president, to whom good manners and duty require me to give the first place, but also of every particular member, and especially of persons timerous and untaught like myself, and, as I hope your magnanimity will Indulge me so far, I am, Most Invincible and Tremendous Sir John,

Annap: 28 febr: 1748   Your worship's most humble
　　　　　　　　　　　 Servant and dutiful Squire
　　　　　　　　　　　 Huffman Snap.

This Letter is upon the right Clubical Bombast Stile, and savors pritty much of many Dedications wrote by certain finical puppies of authors, to patrons of very little merit and Significancy, at least, patrons of far less worth and Importance, than the worshipful Sir John knight and Champion of the Ancient and honorable Tuesday Club.

After Reading these letters, and Committing them Into the Secretarie's hands to be registered in the book, the Reverend Mr Sly, Master of Ceremonies, called upon the late admitted members, to stand round the presidential Chair in order for their confirmation, and they accordingly stood up, Jealous Spyplot Senr Esqr, standing ‖ proxy for his Son Jealous Spyplot Junr Esqr necessarily absent.

Then the Secretary read aloud the form of Confirmation as follows.

your honor and the Club, will humanly overlook, and not attribute my trips to design, rudeness, or Ill manners.

I design this evening, to do myself the honor and pleasure, of attending your honor's commands, at your honor's house, to serve as your honors willing and Chearful, tho unworthy and unqualified high Steward, where, when that Solemn minute approaches, when I shall stand with my other fellow novices, before your honors august Chair, to be, as it were Inaugurated, confirmed and consecrated, an effectual and true Standing member of your || honor's ancient and honorable Tuesday Club, I earnestly beg your honor, to give Command to your honor's Master of Ceremonies, to Instruct me particularly in every Circumstance, relating to the deportment and carriage to be observed, when in this Solemn and awful Situation, that I may not, to the dissatisfaction and disgust of your honorable and ancient Club, and my own Shame and Confusion, be guilty of faults or blunders, or any Sort of misbehavior, thro' Ignorance or Simplicity, and, by this gracious Condecention, a permanent, and never to be forgotten obligation, will be conferrd upon, Honorable Sir, [401]

Anap: 28 febr: 1748

Your honors most humble
Most obedient, and
Most dutiful Servant & H:S:
Huffman Snap.

After Reading of this very polite and high strained letter to his honor the president, another to the worshipful Sir John, from the same hand was produced and read.

To the Most Redoutable Sir John, knight of the Tuesday Club.

Most puisant and Invincible Sir John,

Dreadful and horrendous have been the feats and atchievements, performed by the magnanimous knights of old, who, by their unparalleled Chivalry, shook mountains, burst rocks in twain, knocked down Dragons and Griffins, and made mere popets of Gyants, and all for the Sake of some fine fair Lady, whom perhaps they never saw— || those atchievements were most heroic, marvellous and epouvantable, as any one must know, who but peeps into our Gotheric Romances.—But oh! ye Sempiternal astripotents! what a more Sublime field and excellent foundation, has a knight of such a Society as our tuesday Club to work upon, what an Infinite number of heroic actions and Glorious Exploits, must spring from such a groundwork, such an excellent foundation, when operated upon by a magnanimous ge- [402]

[399] ‖ me leave with all possible veneration, to subscribe myself, May it please your honor,

>Your honor's most obedient and
>Devoted Servant
>*Slyboots Pleasant*.

The Stile of this letter, is rather too far screwd up to the tip top Strain of Complaisance, and seems to abound with too many Superflous repetitions of *your honor*, & *your honor*, The whole of it Contains only some Sheer compliments in the form of puff paste, and an accusation of Sir John and the Secretary, and, I must own, I can by no means account for the virulence of this epistle, from either the Ambition, or ill nature of the Author, for that Gentleman seemed all along, to be the least ambitious, and was bles'd with the mildest and most complacent temper of any of the members of the Club, in short, the only account I can give of this conduct in this Longstanding member, so much out of Character, is that he had a mind to promote a Squabble, between his honor, Sir John, and the Secretary merely for fun.

The Letter from the high Steward to his honor the President, was to this effect.

To the Honorable Nasifer Jole Esqr
President of the Tuesday Club.

Most Honorable Sir,

Unpractised in that polite art and Demeanor, so natural to the mem-
[400] bers of your honor's Tuesday Club, ‖ and utterly unlettered and untaught in the ornate diction and peculiar Nitidity of Stile, conspicōus, in the Epistolary and congratulatory compositions, addressed to your honor upon occasions like this which is the motive of my now writing, It may seem to your honor somewhat bold and assuming in me, to presume addressing your honor, upon this occasion, and in this manner, especially before having passed thro' your honor's Solemn Ceremony of Confirmation, and consecration (if I may with propriety use that Sacred word) and also, by a diligent application and Study in writings of the like nature, plentifully scattered about in your honor's erudite book of Records, Sufficiently Instructed myself, so as to be capable to write, what is worthy your honor's perusal, the hearing and approbation of your ancient and honorable Club, and the dignified degree of a spare Corner, in your honor's learned, Elaborate and ancient archives, but, seeing I am as yet a novice, and an unconfirmed member, I hope, if I make any blunder, in Stile, or propriety of address,

dents head, so, that he began now, not to know, which end of him was uppermost, for, at Sederunt 99th, Huffman Snap Esqr, being high Steward, the following letters to his honor were read in Club.

To the Honorable Nasifer Jole Esqr,
President of the Tuesday Club.

Honorable Sir, March[a] 28, 1748

    I Return your honor, the Commission your honor was pleased to favor me with, and permit me to Express to your honor, the grateful Sense I have, of that Signal Instance of your honor's favor, in promoting me to the Great and Important trust of Representing your Honor, in a Station of such eminent and exalted dignity, the good opinion your honor is pleased to express of my prudence and abilities, and, in consequence of that opinion, your honor's advancing me to an office, in its nature so elevated, and in it's execution so arduous and difficile, could not fail to excite in my breast, the most lively emotions of || Joy and gratitude, but, I have the great mortification to acquaint your honor, that, notwithstanding the utmost efforts of my prudence and abilities, to maintain the honor and dignity of your honor's Chair, in as great perfection as if your honor's Self had been present, a most enormous and detestable crime was perpetrated by some member, or members dissaffected to your honor's government, a crime, of so Insolent and audacious a nature, as Calls upon your honor, for the most vigorous exercise of your honor's authority, as this affair is very fully to be seen, in the records of last Club, I shall not presume to trowble your honor, with a particular recital of it here, nor shall I Insinuate to your honor, the person I suspect of this high Misdemeanor, any further, than by saying that I wish the Secretary may give your honor some better proofs of his Innocence, than barefac'd denyal, but this, I doubt all his dexterity at quibbling and Sophistry, will not enable him to do, upon as Strict an enquiry into the matter, as the Importance of it requires, I make no doubt but Sir John will be found to be at the bottom of it, notwithstanding his absence, which I must confess, is a very artful Contrivance, to prevent your honor's Suspicion of his Guilt, and, when your honor comes to reflect, upon the captious, and fractious, and Snarling disposition of the said knight, ever since the memorable dissappointment of his ill fated ambition, I dare say, your honor, will Join with me, in saying, that it is at least highly probable, that the person, who committed the above mentioned enormity, was nothing more than an humble Instrument, in the hands of this aspiring knight; give

[398]

(a) A mistake of the month, which ought to have been february.

Contents himself with few, and those moderate titles of honor, when the State officers do their duty, and exceed not their Commission, when the officers of the commons stand up Strenuously for Clubical liberty, when Club Law is duely executed, and Justice done Strictly on offenders, and matters of expence do not run too high, then all goes smoothly and Swimmingly on, and the Society flourishes, but, when the Chair aims at great power, and assumes great and Sonorous titles, such as *My Lord, Lord president, Lord presidential, your Honor, Honorable,* and *right Honorable,* titles, which Venerable presidents of Clubs ‖ have no more business with than our Reverend Bishops and Cardinals, now a days, who Call themselves the Successors of a parcel of poor and needy fishermen, have with *your Eminence, your Grace* and *your Lordship,*—when the State officers prove loose, dissolute and obscene in their conversation, and set themselves above punishment and the Laws, when the Longstanding members quietly submitt to oppression, and unwarrantable power, when enormous crimes and trespasses are slur'd over, and all Sort of Luxury and extravagance encouraged and countenanced, when pimps in office, are flatterd and Cajoled, by worse pimps out of office, then *Actum est,*[1] the Clubical State may for a little time make a great noise and Show, but suddenly, like a fair blossoming tree upon the Coming of a blast or frost, all its pride and Glory tumbles to the Ground.

This we shall soon find to be pritty much the case with this here ancient and honorable Club, which, now in its highest glory, strained to be higher, and thus, breaking the strings, Sinews or nerves of the Constitution, every thing ran precipitatly to decay, and, tho' a dissolution did not Immediatly Happen, yet, was the beauty, order and Strength of it much Impaired, by means of Superflous ceremonies Introduced, high sounding titles, badges of honor, Seals, medals, Caps of State, Canopies of State, and the like useless trumpery, which, like the Gewgaws used in the Ceremonials of Religious worship, that divert the attention of the populace, or great mobile, from the Substance to the Shadow, ‖ so these farcical, clubical conceits, divert the minds of the members from more rational pursuits, and set them on the hunt after pitiful bawbles. The first Remarkable appearance of this Clubical madness, broke out, in the Stile of some letters to his honor the president, wrote in so extraordinary a Sublime (such I am Sure, as Longinus never delivered any rules for)[2] that they quite turned the presi-

---

1. "That does it!" (a phrase typical of Seneca).
2. Longinus (ca. 213–273) was a rhetorician and philosopher who taught at Athens. He was generally considered to have been the author of the literary treatise *On the Sublime* until 19th-century scholars more accurately traced its authorship to the 1st century A.D.

polation, or high misdemeanor, and after a great many arguments and warm Speeches || upon the Subject Mr Oldham Wisely, a worthy honorary member, stood up after Supper in his place, and gravely pulling his pipe from his mouth, and streching out his left hand towards the Company, objected in the following terms against preferring an Indictment against the Secretary. [394]

"Mr President, Sir,

It is with Concern what I am going to say, that I think it is not altogether equitable, to prefer an Indictment against the Chief Secretary for this trespass, as there was no such term as *Præs:* mentioned by the said Secretary, when he read the commission, to this here Club, but only *Simple Nasifer Jole*, without any additional term or designation whatsoever, therefore, I would humbly advise the Club, against such an Iniquitous proceeding."

Mr Wisely upon this sat down, and Collecting himself in his Seat, with great composure and gravity resumed his pipe, and began again to emitt Clouds of Smoke from his mouth, while the Club took his objection under their Serious consideration, and after some fine spun reasoning on the point, It was rejected.

After some Quibbling arguments used by the Secretary and his deputy, in their defence, the said Mr Wisely being asked, by the Club, what opinion he had now of the said Secretary and his deputy, as to their Innocence of the matter they were charged with, he pulld his pipe from his mouth, emitted the Smoke, spit, and made answer, that he thought worse and worse of the said Secretaries.

Chapter IX [395]

Sublime Club Letters, Ceremonies of Confirmation, The tryal and acquittal of Sir John, the Gelastic Law executed on the Secretary.

Musical Instruments, we are told, may be tuned up to a certain pitch, to which being kept, they have a pleasant and agreeable effect, but beyond this they occasion a discordant Jarring, and become highly offensive and grating to the ear, and the Strings at last start and fly. So in Clubs, the Constitution is capable of being exalted to a certain pitch, and no farther, without being unable to support it's own weight, and at last tumbling to pieces. When the presidential power is kept within Certain bounds, and he

Oldham Wisely Esqr. Delivering a Speech in Club.

[facing page 394]

from the pleasure of seeing you there yourself to grace the club in the presidential Chair, but I now Sir, return it you, with a multitude of thanks, for the Singular favor then done me, the most unworthy of all the members for such a dignified Station, as that of deputy president, however Sir, as it was your will and pleasure, I did every thing as far as my ability permitted, according to the directions therein to me given, and can with pleasure acquaint you, (tho this I suppose, our worthy Secretary has already done) that no affront, or any thing like it, was offered the Chair, nor any Irregularity or Misdemeanor Committed except, that one of the extraordinary members (by whom I mean an officer) happened to *Nod,* and let his *pipe fall,* which, had yourself been there, I know you would have had Clemency enough to *Wink at,* and pass over, especially, as it was Involuntary, and the same Gentleman afterwards, *Raised his pipes* and performed with the approbation and applause not only of myself, but other Good Judges. In pursuance of your Instructions to me, Messrs: Huffman Snap, Jealous Spyplot Junr: Quirpum Comic, and Prim Timorous, were, (agreeable to the law for that purpose made and provided,) all unanimously admitted, as members of the Tuesday Club, each and every of whom, I, as deputy President, in the name and behalf of the President in Chief, took by the right hand, and bid welcome || in the club, as did afterwards the other old standing & long-standing members, but the grand point of Confirmation, which cannot be performed by any so well as yourself, is postponed, 'till your health, which I earnestly wish for, will admitt of your attendance, and which, I flatter myself, as it is fine weather, will be this evening, when, to serve in quality of high Steward to your honor's ancient and honorable Tuesday Club, falls to the pleasing lot of, Honorable Sir,

[393]

Charles Street	Your much obliged
Valentine's day	Greatly devoted
1748,9	Very humble Servant
	Jonathan Grog.

After Reading the Commission directed to Slyboots Pleasant Esqr, as deputy president, it was found, that the said Commission was subscribed *Nasifer Jole,* without any designation, or title, to the presidents Name, but after the said Commission was delivered by the Deputy President, to be minuted, or entered in the Club book, there appeared the term *Præs:* annexed to the president's name, which false addition, or Interpolation, was ordered to be the Subject of enquiry at a following Club, but, upon this very matter, arose a hot dispute in Club, for, it was moved, that the Secretary, or his deputy Mr Quirpum Comic, should be Indicted for this Inter-

302 [Book V]

sion, the deputys Commission was read in Club, which, as it differs from that of the preceeding Sederunt, both in Stile and form, and is exactly according to the Stile and form of all the Subsequent Commissions, for the Deputies of the Chair, I shall here, once for all give the form of it.

COMMISSION

To our Trusty and well beloved Slyboots Pleasant Esqr.

Not doubting of your prudence and abilities for the office of Deputy President, and that you deserve to fill our Chair in our absence, we have appointed you, Slyboots Pleasant Esqr, deputy president of our Tuesday Club, this 14th day of February, 1748/9, for which this is your authority, and, we hope, you will behave yourself, with due decorum and decency in your office, not admitting any Irregularities, or indecencies || to be committed in Club, nor suffering any affront to be passed upon our Chair, nor any of our Laws to be openly and audaciously violated, that we have no Complaint, nor cause of complaint, nor criminal prosecution, and this behavior, you shall Carefully observe, as you shall be answerable therefore, and so we bid you heartily farewell.

[Seal] Given under our hand and Seal, at our dwelling in North east Street, this 14th day of february, in the fourth year of our Presidential Government *annoque domini*, 1748/9.
Nasifer Jole.

Slyboots Pleasant Esqr, by virtue of the above Commission, having taken the Chair, a Letter was produced In Club by the Secretary, wrote by Jonathan Grog Esqr high Steward, to his honor the President, which was read in Club, the tenor of which follows.

To Nasifer Jole Esqr,
President of the Tuesday Club,
at his dwelling house in Northeast Street, Annapolis.

Honorable Sir,

My having been one of the late Grand Jurors, and, since that, having had a pritty deal of business, of one kind or other, has, till now, prevented my returning you the Commission, which you was pleased to honor me with at the last assembling of the Club, at the house of || Seemly Spruce Esqr, then high steward thereof, when your Indisposition prevented us

and merry company, tho' he never attempted to be Jocular and witty himself, yet, he had this Singular good quality, that he could bear a Joke passed upon himself with great good nature, and was by no means one of that morose Set, who, because they cannot be witty or arch upon others themselves, will not bear a Jest from others, but are perpetually taking offence, looking grim, and Surly, upon the least Smart repartee or bob, which they think is pointed at themselves, Mr Timorous could bear very well to be plaid upon, and would Join heartily in the Laugh, when the Jest hit him full in the teeth, and his Laugh had something peculiar in it, his ha, ha, has, measuring such equal time || as he breath'd them forth, as do the clicks of a [389] short pendulum Clock, being at equal Intervals one from another, and while he laughed in this manner, he would Clap his hands & stamp with his feet, regularly at every ha, ha, like one beating time to music, which afforded much pleasure and mirth to the company; he was very tender mouthed, when he adventured at any time to talk Smutty, and seemed to mince his words in such a manner, as if he was afraid to utter them, for which reason, he never could find in his heart, to pronounce Certain naughty english words, and paultry monosyllabs, that are used as toasts by our moderen rakes, and that in the politest companies, and are commonly wrote on the walls of houses in large Characters with Chalk Stone by our English School boys; but would always express his meaning in a Circumlocutory way, tho' no man loved better than he to hear bawdy discourse, and at all times, when such discourse happened to be Introduced, he would listen to it with all his ears, and laugh at it in his Solemn way, he was so grave and Sedate in his carriage & behavior, that many of his companions called him by the name of parson Timorous, downright swearing he was averse to, and would never venture farther than some small minced Oaths, such as *figs, ods bobs, by George,—as God shall Judge me! God!—Bless the king, the Lord proprietary and all the rest of the Royal family, may I die upon this Spot alive!*—and the like, and even these forms of Swearing, he never would use, unless taken at unawares, and, as it were Surprized into them, he was timorous both by name and nature, and much || addicted to superstition, [390] having great faith in the doctrine of Witches, Ghosts, apparitions, fairies, and Devils Incarnate, now kick'd out of doors and laugh'd at, by our moderen wise men and philosophers; Mr Timorous, was, to sum up all, a good naturd peaceable Companion, neither giving offence to any body, nor taking offence at any thing, and none better qualified than he, to take him in a lump, for a good Club's man.

 At Sederunt 98, February 14th 1748/9, Jonathan Grog Esqr, being high Steward, and Slyboots Pleasant Esqr deputy president, by Special Commis-

sengers, having brought along with them, Mr Prim Timorous, Solemnly delivered to the Deputy president and Club, after Supper, his honor's orders, and Mr Prim Timorous, being unanimously ‖ elected by the Ballot, took his Seat accordingly, the further orders were punctually performed by Mr Protomusicus, after some trivial and Insignificant arguments upon the matter, and this was no sooner done, by this musical Gentleman, than he fell fast asleep in Club, as was his usual custom, with his pipe in his mouth, which at last he dropt and broke to pieces.

Capt: Seemly Spruce, the high Steward, it was thought, Considered Jonathan Grog Esqr, by reason of his grand commission from his honor, in the light of a Lord Mayor of London at a City feast, for he solicited and pressed him very much to eat one Custard after another at Supper, 'till he made him swallow about half a dozen pritty large ones, after having eat pritty heartily of other things, which he washed down with a proper Quantum of good punch.

The Catch of the *Old bell of Lincoln,* usually sung upon the Admission of new members, by the honorable the president, as also the confirmation of these new elected members, of which the Secretary was appointed to draw up a new form, were deferred, till his honor the president should be present in Club.

The Secretary reported to the Club, that according to an order of Last Sederunt, he had wrote out a fair Copy of a letter, ordered to be sent to his honor the President, & sent it to him accordingly upon Wednesday the 18th of this Instant January, and his honor was pleased to return for Answer, *That he was obliged to the Club, thanked them for their Compliment, and that he was something better.*

As Mr Prim Timorous, now admitted a long Standing ‖ member of this ancient and honorable Club, was heretofore a member of the red house Club of Annapolis, under the Celebrated Mr George Neilson, of whom, and of this Club of his erecting, we have given a particular account, in the Second book of our history, and, as the same Gentleman will be seen, holding a Considerable office, in this here ancient and honorable Club, vizt: that of Serjeant at arms, to the Right Honorable the Lord President Jole, (as he was at that time stiled) it will be proper in this place, to give a short Scetch of his Character.

Mr Prim Timorous was a person of a middle Stature, Inclinable to a slender make, of a mild Complacent Countenance, much given to smile, tho for the most part he carried in his look, a Sedate and Stayd gravity. He was by no means of a Loquacious disposition, for he loved better to hear others speak, than to hold discourse himself, he was always fond of Jocular

always supposed to have Conveyd to him by that appointment, the whole powers and authority of the Chief president, during the time ‖ that he held [385] his office, so that there was no necessity to grant any further particular Commissions, to Impower him to act, in the election of Longstanding members, or any other Clubical proceeding; the Club however, at this time, did not dispute the Legality of this proceeding of the president's, for fear it should have obstructed this election, but acquiesced in it, tho' sometime after this they called this power of his in question, and acted directly Contrary to it in the Election of Mr Crinkum Crankum, and Doctor Jeronimo Jaunter, now longstanding members of the Club, at the present time of my writing this history, but his honor did then, and does still assert and mantain his right to give a *Congé d'elire,* in every Case, where he is not himself present, which evinces the danger of allowing such bad precedents to be Introduced into any constitution, potentates and Presidents being always Inclined to hold fast, every privilege they have granted or conceded to them, however much the Subject may suffer, by such an exorbitant Streech of power.

The above Commission being read, the deputy president ordered the Ballots to be prepared, by the Secretary, which being done, they were elected in the following order, vizt: Mr Huffman Snap, Jealous Spyplot Junr, and Mr Quirpum Comic, and the elections were unanimous, the above Gentlemen being congratulated by all the longstanding members, and their healths respectively drank ‖ about, they took their Seats in Club [386] accordingly.

Then Mr Huffman Snap, moved the Club, that if the honorable the president's Commission had not been confined to the above Gentlemen, he would humbly propose to the Club, another Gentleman, viz: Mr Prim Timorous, who was desirous of being admitted a member at this Sederunt, upon which, the Club not presuming to proceed farther (a dangerous piece of Complaisance) without the consent of the honorable Mr President Jole, dispatched to him two Special messengers, vizt: the Reverend Mr Sly Master of Ceremonies, and Mr Secretary Scribble, with a written request from the Deputy president and Club, to Indulge them so far as to suffer them to proceed in his election, which, the honorable Mr President Jole, Readily Granted, with this further message, to be delivered to the deputy president of the Club, to drink the healths of all the new Elected members, singly, in these particular words, vizt: *That each one might be a longstanding member of the Club,* and betwixt each health, Mr Protomusicus was ordered to sing a new Song, exerting upon the occasion, his musical faculties to the utmost.

Pursuant to this Embassy and these orders, the two Gentlemen mes-

plurals of the same; *We* & *Our,* being made use of, as more adapted to the presidential dignity.

Jonathan Grog Esqr, by virtue of the above Commission, having ascended the Chair, the Reverend Mr Sly, Master of Ceremonies, moved the Club, that the following Gentlemen, vizt: Mr Huffman Snap, Jealous Spyplot Junior, & Mr Quirpum Comic, should be admitted longstanding members of this here ancient and honorable Club, They having themselves made proper application, upon which motion, Mr Deputy President presented the Secretary with a Special Commission from the honorable Mr President Jole, to authorise and Enable him, to proceed and act, with full power in this election, which the Secretary read to the Club, in manner and form as follows.

North east Street, Annapolis Ss:

We hereby Authorize and Command you, our deputy Chairman for the Tuesday Club, met at the house of Capt: Seemly Spruce, our high Steward for the time being; this 31 day of January, 1748/9, In the fourth year of our presidential Government, In case Messieurs Huffman Snap, Jealous Spyplot Junior, and Quirpum Comic, should apply, to be made longstanding members of our Society, || to admit of their request, and of the request of none others, at this Sederunt, so far, as to proceed to election by balloting, according to the Rules and Constitution of our Club, and to proceed in that election, with the same power, authority and efficacy, as if we ourself were present, and sitting in the Chair, and let our Clerk be ordered to remitt us an account, of the Issue of the Election, and, for so doing, this shall be your authority and warrant.

To Jonathan Grog Esqr,	Given under our hand and Seal, this 31
Deputy president of our	day of January, 1748/9, in the fourth year
Tuesday Club.	of our presidential Government.
	Nasifer Jole. [Seal]

We may observe, in the form of this commission, that his honor alters his Stile, adopting now the plural Number, and Instead of the pronouns *I* and *My,* using their plurals *We* and *Our,* a Stile much more adapted to his Station and dignity as a president, and what is daily used by all princes and great men; but we must also here remark, that the president seems to assume to himself a privilege, which we find no where granted to him by the Club, and that is, a power of Granting a *Congé d'elire.*[4] It is true, he had granted him a privilege of appointing his own deputy, and this deputy was

---

4. "Permission to elect."

The Secretary was ordered to copy this letter fair, and present it to his honor upon the morrow, being Wednesday the 18th Instant.

The following Sederunt, being the 97th Janry 31, 1748/9, Capt: Seemly Spruce being high Steward, and Jonathan Grog Esqr, by special Commission, deputy president, was one of the most Remarkable that ever happened in this here Club, for election of members, Ceremony and pomp.

His honor the president, having already perceived in Jonathan Grog Esqr, that extraordinary acumen and vivacity of Genius, with which nature had liberally endued that Gentleman, sent him a Special Commission, *Sub Sigillo et Syngrapho*,[2] appointing him deputy president, at this memorable Sederunt, as Judging him most qualified, of all the other Long-standing members, to perform the ceremonies and honors of the Club, upon this remarkable occasion, and, we must observe here, that this Ingenious person, was the first Longstanding member who || was honored with a special [382] commission, under his honor the president's hand and Seal, the Commission run as follows.

COMMISSION

To Jonathan Grog Esquire.

Not doubting of your prudence and abilities, for the office of deputy president, and, that you deserve to fill my Chair in my absence, I have appointed you Jonathan Grog Esqr, to be deputy president of the Club, this 31 of January 1748/9, for which this is your authority, and, I hope you will behave yourself, with due decorum and decency in your office, not admitting any Irregularities or Indecencies, to be committed in the Club, nor suffering any affront to be passed, upon the Chair, nor any of my Laws to be openly and audaciously violated, that I may have no complaint, or cause of complaint, or Criminal prosecutions, and this behavior, you shall carefully observe, as you shall be answerable therefore.

[Seal][3]   Subscribed *Nasifer Jole*.

We may observe, that this Commission runs in the humble Stile, his honor expressing himself in the Singular number, using the pronouns || *I* [383] and *My*, which in the following Commissions we shall find changed for the

---

2. "Under seal and sign."

3. Here and throughout the *History*, Hamilton did not insert the actual seals that were originally used in club documents. He simply wrote *seal, privy seal*, or *great seal* within a fancy circle to indicate that those seals appeared in the original papers. Here and in the following pages I have placed the words he used within brackets to indicate the same thing.

the Club, this was done in prose, as the poetical Genius of the Club, had not as yet broke out in its full Glory, but, on all the following occasions of the like nature, this Condolatory address was penned in verse, this Epistle Run as follows.

By order of the Deputy President and Club, January 17th 1748/9.

To the Honorable Nasifer Jole Esqr,
President of the Tuesday Club.

Honorable Sir,

It is with regret that we address your honor upon this lamentable occasion, an Occasion which || affords more pain than pleasure, as the Subject is disagreeable.

That gratitude and respect, which is due from us to your honor, as our most worthy president, obliges us to express some marks of concern, for your honor's Indisposition, and therefore we have ordered our Secretary to write you this our Epistle of our proper Inditing and framing, by which, we mean to Intimate our good wishes for your honor's speedy recovery, and our Sincere concern, since that, by reason of Sickness, we reap not the advantage, of your Gracious and precious presence & direction.

Our Club is now, as it were in a State of Anarchy, the rudder wants a skillful pilot to steer this our Clubical vessel in a right course, the deputy president falls fast asleep in the Chair, Sir John, the Champion looks like a *Mope in the Moonshine,* the Ladies are but faintly toasted; music and Song are quite mute, mirth and laughter are no more, our eye-sight turns dim in the glimmering of the candles, so, that we may say, with a certain great and wise preacher, *those that look out at the windows are darkened, and all the daughters of Music are brought low.*[1]

We have only one thing left to Comfort us, which is, that the Indisposition your honor Labors under is not of so malignant and mortal a nature as to extinguish our hopes of again partaking and enjoying your honorable presence, and benign Influence, || which, that it may speedily happen, is the earnest desire, and ardent prayer of, Honorable Sir,

From the Club Room,	Your most affectionate and dutiful
Jan: 17th 1748/9	members of your ancient and dignified
	Tuesday Club
	Signed p: order of,
	and in the name of the Club,
	Loquacious Scribble Secrtry

1. Hamilton has patched together two lines from Eccles. 12:3, 4; the persona of Ecclesiastes is repeatedly referred to as "the preacher."

The misbehaviour of Sir John.

[facing page 378]

[378] After Supper, Sir John, taking the precedence of || the chair, took upon himself to stand up with a Settled Countenance, and drink the first toast, expressly contrary to the Rules of the Club; and not only so, but proposed a nauseous fowl mouthd and beastly toast, repugnant to modesty and good manners, drinking in plain English words, while he held a replenishd bowl of punch in his right hand, *To the pious memory of Sally Salisbury's* ———.[3] Against this toast the Revd Mr Sly, master of ceremonies protested, and the Sense of it, Jonathan Grog Esqr, most devilishly wrested, asserting that the letters S.S.C. on the South Sea Shillings, did not stand for the words mentioned in Sir John's toast, but meant neither more nor less than *South Sea company,* during this whole Smutty transaction Mr Protomusicus the Deputy sat fast asleep in the Chair, and was thought not to have heard a single word that passed, thus executing his office of deputy president in such a careless manner, as if it had not been worth a pinch of Snuff, since it would have cost him no more to have kept himself awake.

Chapter VIII

A Letter of Condolance wrote to his honor the President, Election of four Longstanding members, Disputes in Club, Speech of Oldham Wisely Esqr, Honorary member, and other trivial matters.

It was with this ancient and honorable Club, as it is with humorsome Children, to whom they say have your Cake and eat your Cake, or some ||
[379] fractious people, to whom is applied the Scotch proverb, *you'll neither dance, nor hold the candle;* so, this Club seemed never to know when they were well, either with, or without the honorable the president, for, when he was present, it was nothing but contention, wrangling, Jangling and brangling, about prerogative and privilege, presidential authority, and Clubical Liberty, and when he was absent it was nothing but pining, whining and declining. It was now the Season of the year for his honor to be laid up with the gout, which Calamity occasioned his absence from Club at Sederunt 96th, therefore, the Club, before breaking up, ordered the Secretary, to write a condolatory epistle to his honor, upon that occasion, in the name of

---

3. Sally Salisbury (or Sally of Salisbury) is the alias of Mrs. Sarah Priddon, a fictional whore and the central character of Capt. Charles Walker's *Authentick Memoirs of the Life, Intrigues, and Adventures of the Celebrated Sally Salisbury* (London, 1723). Hamilton's draft, which reads "To the pious memory of Sally Salisbury's C—t," is a bit more explicit.

eral of the most authentic Clubical papers, and prevented the recording of them, that he might the more easily gull the longstanding members of this here Club, out of that little Scantling of liberty they had still left, it was a very politic Step in his honor also, not to appoint another State officer, by suffering the Creation of a new Speaker, the Conduct of that State officer, with regard to the Club box, being still fresh in his mind, he now found, that one officer of State and privy councellor, vizt: The worshipful Sir John, knight of the Club, was enough for him to manage, and afforded him always his handsful, as that great man, was of a restless, bustling, unsteady and ambitious temper, and a great check, to the arbitrary proceedings of the Chair.

At Sederunt 96th January 17th 1748/9, The worshipful Sir John being high Steward, and Solo Neverout Esqr Deputy President, for which he had a letter of attestation, directed and writ to him by the worshipful || the high [377] steward, in a pithy, concise and heroic Stile, worthy the Champion of a club, as follows.

To Solo Neverout Esqr, This.

Grate Sir,

Mr President Jole

desired me to acquaint you, he expects you, Sir, to do him the honor of representing him, the said President, in the *said* presidential Chair, this night, at my Castle.

And so, I hereby acquaint you *grate* Sir, accordingly, under my hand this 17th of January 1748/9.

> *Sir John,*
> Of the said Tuesday Club, and always on the right hand of the said Chair, *and that's what I say.*

We may observe a peculiar elegance of Stile, manner of expression and uncommon Orthography, in all the Clubical letters of this great Champion, and in none more than in that Just now transcribed.

Sir John moved to the Club, that a Gentleman of Annapolis, was desirous to be made a member of this here Club,[2] upon which the Secretary was ordered to prepare the ballots, or *Yeas* and *Nays,* and, upon their being put round and examined, it was carried in the negative, there being two nays and four yeas.

---

2. See biographical sketch for John Raitt.

At Sederunt 95th Janry 3d 1748, Jealous Spyplot Esqr being high Steward, Smoothum Sly Esqr, having ascended the Chair as deputy president, by virtue of a verbal Commission, from his honor Mr President Jole, unable thro Indisposition to attend himself, Sir John objected to that proceeding, and some others of the long Standing Members, refusing him the honors due to that place, forbid the Secretary to read the proceedings of the former Sederunt, till the dispute was determined and this very Important affair settled, which was to be done, by waiting the Return of a Special messenger

[375] ‖ sent by the Club, to the honorable the Chief president, accordingly, upon the return of this messenger, he was Solemnly asked by the Secretary in the hearing of the Club, *Who the honorable the President had appointed for his deputy?* and, upon answering, that he had appointed Smoothum Sly Esqr, the said Gentleman ascended the presidential Chair, accordingly, and the proceedings of last Sederunt were read according to the usual form, by this it appears, how little Confidence the Club had in the word of Mr Sly, who having of late exercised himself so much in the art of flattery, would often deviate from truth, the temper of Sir John also appears in this transaction, who was like the Dog in the manger, for he would neither take the Chair in quality of deputy himself, nor could he bear to see any other longstanding member, possessed of that honor.

Some proposals having been made at this Sederunt with regard to the Election of a Speaker, Mr deputy President declined proceeding in that affair because of the absence of Mr President Jole, and so, tho' the votes were taken, and the Election passed in favor of Jealous Spyplot Esqr, against Mr Protomusicus Neverout, the Election was Looked upon as Irregular, and the affair dropt till another meeting, thus, we find the Longstanding members, as it were, Spontaneously, without the least force or constraint, giving up the Sole power of electing and appointing of Club officers, into the hands of the honorable the president, a privilege, which he was not originally possessed of, but, once he had got it in his hands, by

[376] the carelessness and overcomplaisance of the Longstanding ‖ members, he grasped it so hard, that it could never be wrested from him again, nay, he even prevailed so far upon the Club, as to make them pass two Strict Laws, to secure this valuable privilege, to him and his Successors in the Chair for ever.

It was resolved at this Sederunt, that the honorable Mr President Jole, should be addressed, to bring in the Copies of several letters, wrote to him by the High Stewards of the Club, not already given in, in order that they might be duely registred in the Club book; by this we see that his honor was now riding post haste towards Arbitrary power, and had Secreted sev-

was done without Consulting his honor and the Club, was cancelled, || for, [373] the honorable the Speaker, that useful, and eminent officer, having left the Club, for reasons best known to himself, but not out of any disgust, occasioned great uneasiness and Concern to his honor and the long Standing members, they being Sensible, that the Club would suffer greatly, by the want of that State officer; The Secretary took upon him, by an ill devised entry in the book of Records, to put the Master of Ceremonies Into that honorable place, to officiate as Speaker *pro tempore,* till another Speaker should be chosen by the Club, which Chagrined his honor the president much, and the entry was cancelled, or struck out, the Secretary in doing this had a design against the Chair, The power of which, he thought had now grown to too great a head, and Imagined, that by putting in Mr Smoothum Sly, a longstanding member of an officious disposition and uncommon turn to flattery and adulation, he might, by degrees, so poison the principles of his honor the president (the common effect that flattering arts have upon great men) that he would be guilty of some arbitrary procedure, which would necessaryly give a finishing stroke to that exorbitant power, the chair was now possessed of; but this finnesse of the Secretaries would not answer his purpose, his machinations, one after another being discovered by the Sagacity and penetration of his honor, who looked still with Jealous and hawks eyes, upon this designing officer. After the cancelling of this false entry a hot || dispute arose, concerning who should succeed as Speaker to [374] the Club, it being thought a difficult matter to cull out from among the longstanding members, a person of that Staid gravity Solemnity, prudence and elocution, equal to the gentleman who but lately possessed that honorable office, and indeed it is my opinion, that his equal was not to be found in the Club. Several of the Longstanding members, and particularly the Secretary showd a great desire to be advanced to that eminent place, but his honor was so Chagrined at the Secretarie's Imprudent conduct, that he absolutely refused putting any of the longstanding members into that office, and so it remained a great while vacant; In the midst of these disputes and wranglings, Sir John, to put the Club in a good humor (being happily in good humor himself, which was but seldom) sung the celebrated old Song of the *Hundreds of Drury,*[1] with a very comic air, Chawing the Trolloll Chorus of that ditty in such an antic manner, as set the members of the Club into a hearty laugh.

1. This tune was originally called "The Bowman Priggs' Farewell." Harold Gene Moss includes a copy of the tune dated 1750 in "Ballad Opera Songs: A Record of Ideas Set to Music, 1728–1733" (Ph.D. diss., University of Michigan, 1970), IV, 72–73.

of serving as high Steward, I am, Mr President, with profound respect, and all due deference,

From my dwelling house in	Your most obedient
Charles Street	Greatly Devoted
August the 30th 1748	Very humble Servant
	Jonathan Grog H:S:

In this letter, we may perceive, the great genius of Jonathan Grog Esqr, shining forth in a well formed pun, in the very beginning of it, and that gentleman's great Abilities in that excellent Clubical Art, will appear in many Instances thro the course of our History.

At Sederunt 92d, November 8, 1748, Mr Secretary Scribble being high Steward, the following letter from him to the President was produced in Club.

To the Honorable Nasifer Jole Esqr,
President of the Tuesday Club, These.

Honorable Sir,

As there is no body whatsoever, either natural or politic, that is good for any thing, without || the head, that eminent regulator and Instructor of the members, so, the members of any Society (and those of our Club among others) must, of consequence, be very torpid and paralytic, if not altogether dead and useless, when deprived of this necessary and dignified Superintendent.

It is for this Important Reason, Honorable Sir, that I would request your honor's gracious presence, this evening, at my house, where the members of our Tuesday Club, are to meet and discuss some affairs of Importance, which I am afraid they will want power and Spirits to do, unless Invigorated and Inspired, by your honor's awful countenance and presence, which too, will very much oblige and honor, Honorable Sir,

Novr 8th 1748	Your honor's diligent and faithfull
	Secretary & high Steward
	Loquacious Scribble.

In the very beginning of this letter, the Secretary plainly acts the plagiary, having borrowed or rather stole, that fine metaphor of the head, from a letter of the Ingenious Jonathan Grog Esqr, wrote to his honor the president upon a paralell occasion, which the reader may see, if he has not perceived it already, by only turning back to the preceeding page.

At this same Sederunt, an entry was made by the Secretary, which, as it

discord and dissention, hubbub and hurly burly, in this here ancient and honorable Club, totally, and finally overcome, and mortally knocked on the head, by the heroic Longstanding members; The Invincible Sir John, the Hercules and leader of the Club, being the head and Champion of this bold Clubical Enterprize.

At Sederunt 88 August 30, Jonathan Grog Esqr being high Steward, the Club box, as pestilent a box as that of Pandora, in which was five Pounds || fifteen Shillings and Sixpence, was Solemnly delivered by his honor the president, to the Reverend Mr Smoothum Sly master of Ceremonies, to be disposed of by him according as his honor and the longstanding members should direct, which money was afterwards laid out on lottery tickets, contrary to his honor's Intention.

Solo Neverout Esqr, chief musician, protested against a resolve of the Club; "That the Speech he made at Sederunt 86th concerning the box petition, was void, and of no effect in Clubical Law, because he did not sing it," as he alledged, that he was not obliged by any law of the Club, to sing his motions and speeches, as may be seen by an Entry of Sederunt 49th Decemb: 9th 1746, beginning "Solo Neverout Esqr upon account of &ct:" but the Club still agreed to support the president and Club's protest, against the proceeding of Sederunt 86th, and Mr Protomusicus's Speech, to support the same, as the said Speech, whether sung or said, is now thought by the Club, to have been at that time unseasonable, assuming and unpolite, wherefore he, the said Solo neverout Esqr, had the Gelastic Law put in execution against him, the whole company Joining in a most vociferous and roaring Laugh, in which protomusicus himself Joined, with most prodigious force of Lungs.

A letter was produced in Club, by his honor the President, sent to him by the high Steward as follows.

To Nasifer Jole Esqr,
President of the Tuesday Club,
at his dwelling in North east Street, Annapolis.

Mr President,
This Evening, being the 30th of the month, I am to || have the honor of Entertaining the *August Tuesday Club,* and, as that, as well as every thing else, looks odd and Imperfect, without a head, I hope Sir, you who have so long, and so worthily been the head of that Club, will then Be pleased to grace it with your presence, which is an honor I am anxious to be dignified with, as it has never yet been conferred on me, when I have had the honor

At Sederunt 87, August 16th 1748, Smoothum Sly Esqr, being high Steward, the Club met in the school room, the ancient place of meeting of the ugly Club, of which we have given a particular description in the Second book of this history, and Mr Speaker Quaint, in a very elegant Speech opened to the president, the affair of the Box, entered upon at last meeting, and his honor seeing the Impending ruin that threatned the Club, if he should persist in obstinately refusing their demands, was graciously pleased to consent, that the money in the box should be disposed of, in the following manner, the Conditions being drawn up by Mr Speaker Quaint, that is to say,

"Ordered that the money now in the box, be delivered next Club Night, to the Reverend Mr Sly, by him to be disposed of as follows, that his honor the president first, and every other member of the Club afterwards, may give orders under their hands, for the disposal of their proportional parts, into the hands of such person or persons, as each member for himself shall think fit, being a resident in town & not otherwise."

As to the entry of last Sederunt, concerning the order for delivering up the Club box, it being made after Club hour, and Mr Protomusicus Neverout, not singing his motion, as he ought to have done, it was protested against and cancelled by his honor the president and the Longstanding members.

Thus his honor the president at last yielded up his darling, thinking that he had done it on tollerable terms, since he believed, he had by the above Condition, effectually prevented the money's being laid out, in Lottery tickets (for he professed himself an enimy to all Sorts of gaming) but we shall see in the Sequel, how this money was dissipated.

Chapter VII

Solemn Surrendry of the Club box, and disposal of the Treasury, Club letters, the honorable the Speaker leaves the Club, disputes about who should succeed him, misbehavior of Sir John.

Hercules's Labors, tho' painful and difficult, were by constancy, courage, and Indefatigable perseverance, accomplished at last, and the Heroe crowned with victory and Success, in the same manner, by constancy and perseverance, was this monster of the Club-box, the cause of so much

gentlemans custom, & Indeed, whatever melody there was in his voice, there was none at all in this laugh of his, for the tintimarre of it struck thro one's head like a dart, as his honor the president was pleased often to say, In this dispute, Slyboots Pleasant Esqr, a Longstanding member, of a very mild and pacific disposition, and very little given to making of Speeches or talking in Club, ‖ (making the gelastic Law his main Study, tho he never laughed in such a noisy manner as Mr Protomusicus) was so provoked, at the obstinacy and unreasonableness of his honor the president, that he showed some Signs of anger and resentment, a thing extremely rare and uncommon with him, for he was a man of a very mild temper. [367]

The Club, by preferring this petition, it is thought, did not so much want the money, to purchase Lottery tickets, tho' that was used as a pretence, they wanted in short, to knock up the box, altogether, and remove out of the way, that pestilent bone of contention, that had now been, for upwards of two years, a breaker of the peace and harmony of the Club, and Sir John, owned so much to his honor's face, as he sat in the Chair, telling him "that, that there Damn'd box, was the cause of more noise and racket than it was worth, and I wish to God, (says he) that it was at the Devil, or in hell, or some such place." At wch his honor bridled up, and looked with great displeasure on Sir John, but said nothing, for that undaunted Champion, had his honor been but in the least Snappish with him, would have knocked the Chair to pieces and sent his honor a packing, nor Indeed did this valiant knight, and his bold 'Squire Mr Protomusicus, desist 'till they had quite compassed their ends, in demolishing this terrible monster the box.

Upon the honorable the presidents denyal of the request in the petition, the members in generall protested against this arbitrary proceeding, and a great revolt from the Club was threatned, several of the Stanch old Standing members professing that they would Immediatly leave the Club; they voted however, that the money, now in the box, (excepting the Quota Contributed by his honor himself,) should be drawn out for the use above mentioned, vizt: to purchase Lottery tickets, upon which the ‖ Secretary, by order from the Club desired his honor the president to see the box forth coming, upon Tuesday the 16th of this Instant august, at next Sederunt of the Club, this Order met with no other reply from his honor, but a Stern frown; this was the boldest Stroke for Clubical liberty that ever was struck by the longstanding members of this here ancient and honorable Club, and it is thought, that the authority of the Chair, met with such a Shake upon this occasion, that it was a long time before it recovered again its wonted vigor. [368]

[365] tions ground the reasonableness of their present Remonstrance, and petition ‖ to your honor, vizt: that this here box, is the Indisputable property of this here Club, being established and set on foot, by the consent and approbation of the members, and therefore, Secondly, it ought to be disposed of according to the pleasure of the Club, or the majority of the same, as appointed by Law 36th, & according to the meaning and Intent of the words of Law 20th, vizt: for Charity, or such other good purposes, as the majority of the Club shall see proper.

As your honor then, has been entrusted with the abovesaid box and money, it is to be hoped, that you will not refuse the Request of all the members under written, who earnestly require and sollicit, that the money now Remaining in the box, may be aplied to purchase tickets in the Philadelphia Lottery now on foot, by which means a public benifit or good will be promoted, one of the noblest, one of the best and greatest works of charity, as it regards not a few Individuals, but the whole community and is by no means confind to private benefits, and like wise, our Stock probably may be Increased, at least, at the worst, we can be no great losers, there being at present, according to the Secretaries account, only five pounds Seventeen Shillings and Sixpence Currency in the box, after deducting your honors Share, which your honor may Chuse to dispose of as you please, a Sum so Inconsiderable, that it cannot be applied to any use of consequence,

[366] and scarce ‖ deserves the name of a treasury, and therefor cannot confer the dignified title of treasurer to its keeper, this, we earnestly desire your honor maturely to consider, and must Insist on being satisfied in our demands, and your Orators shall ever pray &ct:

Signed. Sir John
Drawlum Quaint Spkr: Jealous Spyplot
Smoothum Sly Mr of Cer: Cap: Seemly Spruce
Solo Neverout Protomus: Laconic Comas
Loquacious Scribble Secret: Jonathan Grog
Sly Boots Pleasant

This petition was presented by Mr Protomusicus and recommended to his honor's consideration, by that Gentleman, in a very pathetic harangue, which done he put it into the Secretarie's hands, who read it in Club, his honor the president, absolutely refused, to grant the request therein contained, which occasioned for some time in Club, very loud vociferation and noisy dispute, in which, Mr Protomusicus was heard above all the other members, sometimes bawling Insufferably loud, at other times answering the arguments of his honor, with a great horse laugh, as was often this

health, but, as it so hap- ‖ pening, I flatter myself, that you, and the rest [363] of the *worthey* members, have goodness enough to overlook what may be amiss.

However, Sir, I hope to have the pleasure of your good Compe: which will outshine any thing that could *possably* be in my power to do, even in the best of times, I am, Sir, with *grate* respect

19th July 1748   Your Most humble Servant
                                          Sir John.

In this letter, Sir John follows the example of many great men, who eminently distinguish themselves from vulgar writers, by deviating from the Common Orthography, in many of their words.

On the following Sederunt August 2d, Captain Seemly Spruce being high Steward, a petition signed by all the longstanding members, was presented and read in Club as follows.

To the honorable the President of the Tuesday Club, the humble Remonstrance, and petition of the Longstanding members of the said Club.

May it please the president,

Whereas, at a Sederunt of this here Club, held at the house of Capt: Serious Social, late a worthy longstanding member of this Society, upon the 14th of ‖ January 1745, there was established and set on foot, a money box, [364] to be applied to such uses as the Club should see proper, according to the Laws made for that purpose, vizt: the Laws 20, 21, 22, 23, and particularly by Law 36, passed february the 16th 1747/8 at a Sederunt held at the house of Mr Speaker Quaint, where the money in this box, is ordained to be disposed of by a majority of voices. *Furthermore,* at the above said Sederunt, in January 14th 1745, The Club appointed your honor, treasurer, giving you the privilege of keeping the box, and one key thereof, while the Secretary had the trust of the other key, and lastly at a Sederunt, held at the house of Sir John Oldcastle (as then stiled) the Second day of febry 1747/8, your honor was confirmed in the title of Sole Treasurer, the Secretary being only stiled key keeper, The members here underwritten, unanimously acknowledge, that it was from the opinion they conceived of your honor's merit, and great Integrity that they bestowed upon you, this trust, and honor, and hope they shall have no cause to alter their mind, or change that good opinion which they have so Justly conceived of their Honorable Chairman, an opinion so necessary to support and Continue your honor, in the said trust.

The members underwritten therefore upon the two following posi-

Who would set it up again,
Huzza! Huzza! Huzza!

Some Longstanding members, who were either too strait laced in their whiggish principles, or were at bottom, no true friends to our happy constitution, alledged that this was a Jacobite Song, but the Club and Mr Protomusicus laughed at their Ignorance and presumption.

Mr Dumpling Gundiguts, having been absent from the Club, ever since the 16th of february last, and having offered no excuse, was, by the tenor of Law 13th, excluded the Club, and, as he was a longstanding member of very little Significancy, or Importance, serving only, like a Chair in a country dance, to fill up a void Space, neither his honor the president, nor the Club, were sorry for it.

At Sederunt 83d June 18th, Jealous Spyplot Esqr being high Steward, the title of Oldcastle, was taken from Sir John, at his own earnest request; because (said he) he was Informed, that one, of the title of Sir John Oldcastle was hanged, in the reign of Henry V, for being a Lollard, and he would bear no titles, on which the least mark of Infamy had been laid, whatever the Crime was, treason, heresy or felony, and besides it was his opinion, that these borrowed names and || titles, were beneath the dignity of the knight and Champion of this here ancient and honorable Club, who, if he had any title at all, it was very fit that he should have one peculiar to himself and none other.

At Sederunt 84, June 28, 1748, a contribution was raised among the Longstanding members for Mr Benjamin Wood, who had wrote out the New Club badges, and the money delivered to Jonathan Grog Esqr, to be paid to the said Wood, it is Surprizing to see the Stupidity and Infatuation of the members of this here Club, in this here very instance, to suffer themselves to be taxed in this here manner, when there was now upwards of Six pounds cash in the Club box, in the hands of his honor the president, but this had hitherto been a Sort of Mortmain, or bottomless gulph, into which, whatever was thrown, could never be brought out again.

On the following Sederunt, a letter from Sir John to the president, was produced and read in Club as follows.

To Nasifer Jole Esqr,
President of the Tuesday Club.

Sir,

Notwithstanding I am *fare,* from being well, that the Club may not *waite* any longer on me, I *entend* to entertain them this evening, in the best manner I can, tho' not so well as I could wish, were I in a better State of

assembled In the Great Saloon in the house of the Honorable Mr President Jole, then high Steward, and Invested themselves in their badges, and the honorable the Speaker, and several of the members made congratulatory Speeches to his Honor the President upon this Solemn occasion, several loyal healths were drank after Supper, || and the entertainment as usual was very Sumptous and elegant.

[360]

Some little contests arose at this time among the long standing members, concerning the publication of an article of news in the weekly Journal of Jonathan Grog Esqr, relative to the Club's Anniversary,[3] which in some measure broke and Interrupted the mirth and Jollity of the night, the Secretary and Master of Ceremonies looked much askew at one another, Sir John Oldcastle put on first his Spectacles, and then his blusterous countenance to examine the devoted paragraph Intended for the press, and deeply Grumbling with Indignation, took pen and Ink, and blotted out Interlined and refined as he thought proper, Laconic Comus Esqr, mumbled and Grumbled, and was heard to swear *by God,* and *God damn it* several times, between his teeth as it were, chawing the Stem of his pipe, the Roman Catholics and Jacobites were mightily run down, and abused by some in the Club, and by others defended, in short, there had like to have happened a lamentable brawl, but this variance was in a great measure mitigated, by an humorous Speech, delivered after Supper by the Secretary, which, not having been recorded, is now Irrecoverably lost, and at last, they were thorro'ly recovered from their doleful dumps, by the vivacity and musical voice of Mr Protomusicus, who Concluded the Solemnity with the following trumpet Song.

Trumpet Air, sung by Mr Protomusicus[4]

The kings health, the kings health,
   Let the trumpet sound,
   And the glass go round,
   Huzza! Huzza! Huzza!

To the downfall of usurpation,
   And I Long to see the day,
   Confusion to him

[361]

---

3. Having caused such a lamentable hubbub, this article announcing the club's anniversary was never published in the *Md. Gaz.*

4. A variation of this toast appears in Thomas D'Urfey's *Wit and Mirth; or, Pills to Purge Melancholy,* 6 vols. (London, 1719–1720), II, 83–85.

Gentleman had for the Bumbast. In this Strain of writing he held for some considerable time, and Infected with it some of the Longstanding members that after this came into the Club, nay even the wise grave and Sagacious Jealous Spyplot Esqr, and the plain spoken Mr Laconic Comus did not escape this Contagion; till at Last he mixed the Sublime with the bathos, in a very burlesque manner, by || affecting to blend this puffed up Stile, with some Strokes of Jonathan Grog Esqr's punnish and Conundrumish expletives and tropes.

The honorable the President mounted the Chair this night with his new badge card, which made a very resplendent Show, and was cut or fashioned in the Shape of a Star curiously Gilt painted and Spangled, of which a figure or representation is here exhibited in the margin.

As the Anniversary of the Clubs Institution was now fast approaching, matters were to be put all in Decent order, for the Celebration of that most grand and Solemn festival, and his honour the president had been constantly Employed night and day, watching, working and running about, for at least the Space of three weeks, that every thing might be put in decent rank and file, or (as the Saying is) *in gynger bread order* for this Grand feast.

The Club badges now almost wore out were renewed, and had an Improvement made upon them (which was curiously drawn by Mr Benjamin Wood) this was the figure of two hands Joined over a heart, very expressive of that cordiality, that reigns, or ought to reign among the members of the same Club; and Indeed among the members of any Society, great or small, that desires to last and prosper. The figure of this new badge card is represented in the annexed draught.

Upon the 81t Sederunt, being Tuesday the 17th Day of May, 1748, was Celebrated the third Anniversary of the Club, when all the Longstanding members, and four of the Honorary members, vizt: Collonel Courtly Phraze, Mr Oldham Wisely, Mr Abraham Bumper and Mr Joshua Fluter,

The tenor of the Letter to Sir John Oldcastle was, as follows. [356]

To the Right Worshipful, Sir John Oldcastle
knight of the Tuesday Club.

Superlatively Worshipful & dignified Sir John,

I being most extatically elevated with the propinquity of the occasion, when I shall be dignified with the ministerial dignity of high Steward, to our most Stupendous and august Society, cannot forbear, in the midst of my accumulated Raptures, writing to the honorable the president, and your Equestrian dignity, the honor of his presence, I question not, but I shall participate, but the Splendor of the grand Consistory will be Incompleat, unless your worship deigns to confer your presence, and then Indeed, O then! we shall shine with Irresistable Splendor, and magnificence, and dispell every cloud that may threaten to hang over our Significant heads, excepting only that of tobacco, the dear Specific condensator of political and Sage conceptions.

I have sent to the honorable the president his badge of office, a most Splendid Glittering ornament, made in the form of a periphery, so begilt and bespangled, as that it looks like the planetary System in minature, elucesscent in full Glory, a Just type of the Nitor[2] and harmony of our homogene Society, of which his honor the president himself, may be said to be the Solar Center, your worship that kindly planet the moon, ‖ who [357] reflects the light she receives from the former, less constant and vigorous indeed, but milder and more benign, the rest of our officers, according to their talents may be accounted the Smaller planets, and our Commoners are Second rate Stars or Satellites, that move round the Greater or more Splendid orbs, pray excuse this poetical excursion, and if possible, let us have the honor of your worship's worshipful company, this will not only oblige the whole Junto, but, in a particular manner, Most worshipful and dignified Sir John,

Die martis	The humblest of your
April 26th 1748	humble Servants
	Loquacious Scribble H: Std:

At this same Sederunt it was agreed, that there should be no procession at the Subsequent Anniversary, but the members were appointed to meet at the honorable the presidents and there Invest themselves with their badges.

The above letters of Mr Secretary Scribble's show the turn which that

---

2. Brightness, brilliance.

continued still to Increase, ever since that happy Epocha, as will appear in the Sequel.

The first thing they Improved in, was their Epistolary writing, for, at Sederunt 80, April 26th 1748, Mr Secretary Scribble being high Steward, we find two Sublime letters wrote to his honor the president, and the worshipful Sir John Oldcastle, by the Secretary, and, as this Gentleman was the first Introducer of Set Speeches in the Club, so he was the first Improver of Epistolary writing, the Letters stand upon Record as follows.

To the Honorable Nasifer Jole Esqr,
president of The Tuesday Club, These.

Most Honorable Sir,

It being my good fortune to serve as high Steward to your honor and the worthy Club this night, your presence, to grace the Chair, and enliven the Society, would considerably add, to the pleasure I enjoy, in being honored with that Sublime office, the return of every opportunity of this kind, to serve your honor, and the worthy Club, gives me no small Satisfaction, to serve the Club to be Sure is a pleasure, whether your honor be absent or present, but I think your presence, reflects a particular dignity upon the high Steward, which as it is not || in the power of even the magnanimous Sir John Oldcastle himself, to communicate in such an eminent degree as your honor, so, far less, can there be any such Innate dignity, in a deputy president, or Inferior officer,—I hope then, your honor, will be so benign & benevolent, as to do me that honor, upon which I deservedly set so high a value.

I have sent the presidential Badge, adorned and finished in such a manner, as I hope will please your honor, it is fixed upon my own badge Ribbon, to show the way, in which it is to be adapted, I could wish your honor would wear it this night, according to the Law of Sederunt 78, to decorate our Club, but that I must leave to your honor's determination, whether you will wear it this night, or deferr your appearance in it to the Grand Anniversary parade; please send back my badge Ribban, as I shall have occasion to use it this night.

I have wrote to the worshipful Sir John Oldcastle in a Sublime and exalted Stile, adapted to his dignity and office, and, I believe, he will Considerably add to the Splendor and Dignity of our Society, by his attendance, I have therefore prepared for him a magnificent Chair of State, at your honor's right hand, & am, with all due respect,—most honorable Sir,

Die martis
April 26th 1748

Your faithful high Steward and
trusty Secretary
Loquacious Scribble.

Sociable and agreeable, and besides I find that we eat and drink well in this here Club, hence must flow good humor, and as a consequence of that we must sleep well—and this here Society seems to be settled upon so firm a basis, that nothing but Death can separate the members of it one from another."

Having delivered this Speech, Jonathan Grog Esqr, bowed low to the honorable the Chair, and then to the members all round, and sat down, wearing on his face an open and pleasant Smile, while he renewd again || his chaw of tobacco, which he had deposited when he rose up to speak; [353] we shall observe here, that this is the first Set Speech to the Chair, that stands upon Record, and, In its Structure and Composition, some Scattering Sparks of the authors Ingenuity and vivacity of Imagination break forth, the lively corruscations of which, we shall find abounding in all his Club Compositions.

The Speaker being desired to deliver the thanks of the Club to Mr Grog for his speech, requested the Secretary to do that office for him, which he did, and the Secretary having finished this Speech to Mr Grog, addressed Mr Speaker Quaint in a congratulatory manner, upon the occasion of his late marriage, for which he had the thanks of Mr Speaker, delivered in a very ornate and polite Stile.

Chapter VI

Clubical Letters, Celebration of the Third Anniversary, Improvement made on the Club badges; the title of Oldcastle resigned by Sir John, the Success of the Box petition.

When Roscius[1] the Actor florished at Rome, which was much about the time of the Augustine age, all Sorts of Learning and arts, were in their full perfection, the Imperial Court was crouded with polite Authors of all Sorts, Poets, Historians, Philosophers, orators and Letter writers, Such were Virgil, Horace, Livy, Tully; Just so was it at this very period, in the ancient and || honorable Tuesday Club, when Jonathan Grog Esqr, that [354] Celebrated Comic poet, began to florish there, the wit and genius of several of the Longstanding members shone out with a Conspicuous Lustre, and

---

1. Gallus Roscius (fl. 1st century B.C.) was a famous Roman actor whose name became synonymous with the consummate artist.

being high Steward, the regulation of the next Anniversary procession was agreed in Club to be referred to the consideration of a more full meeting, and the Catch of the *Great bell of Lincoln* was sung by his honor the president, in honor of the Admission of Jonathan Grog Esqr.

[351] At Sederunt 78 March 29th 1748, Laconic Comus Esqr being high Steward, the following Law was passed.

Law XXXVII. That the president shall appear every Club Night with his badge, with the following additional Inscription upon a Square Card, to distinguish his, from the badges of the high Steward & other Members, vizt: NASIFER JOLE *armiger, Societatis Annapolitanæ, Diei martis* (THE ANNAPOLIS TUESDAY CLUB) *uti vocatur Præfectus.*[5]

Accordingly, Jonathan Grog Esqr, was ordered to prepare and produce this Card to the Club at next Sederunt, pursuant to which order, at the following Sederunt, Mr Speaker Quaint, being high Steward, the Card was produced in Club, which, upon examination, was committed to the hands of Jonathan Grog Esqr, to receive some additional alterations and Improvements.

Thus we see, that this ancient and honorable Club, not satisfied with the honors and dignities, which they had already Conferred upon his honor the president, proceeded still to heap more of these upon him, we shall find that they did not stop here, and shall also see what thanks and grateful returns they had from his honor, for taking all this pains, which I hope, will be a lesson to all Clubs, to be cautious how they go too far, in bestowing marks of honor and dignity upon their presidents.

[352] At this Sederunt, Jonathan Grog Esqr, delivered a || congratulatory speech to his honor the President, upon the occasion of his admission, and rising from his Seat he first bowed to the Chair, and then to the Club, and with a pleasant Smile on his countenance, spoke as follows.

"Mr President, Sir,

I here stand up, in quality of a Longstanding member, of this here ancient and honorable Club, to make my grateful acknowledgements of the obligations I lie under to your honor, and the Longstanding members of this here Club, in doing me the honor, to admit me a longstanding member of their honorable Society; an honor I set a great value upon, and shall always endeavor to behave myself in such a manner, as that your honor and these here longstanding members, shall never have reason to repent your having conferrd this honor upon me, I have the best reasons in the world to be satisfied with this here good Society, as I find every thing in it that is

---

5. "Nasifer Jole, arms-bearer of the Annapolis Tuesday Club, where he is called Prefect."

tlemen, should appear first in Club ‖ should take the Chair, as deputy. The Secretary appearing first, took that honorable Seat, but Mr Protomusicus entering the Club room soon after, attempted in a violent manner to pull the Secretary out of the Chair, and would have mastered him by superior Strength, but was prevented by the Interposition of the Longstanding Members.

A very Complaisant Letter, sent by the high Steward to his honor the president, was produced in Club, and being read by the Revd Mr Sly, deputy Secretary, was ordered to be entered upon record as follows.

To Nasifer Jole Esqr,
President of the Tuesday Club,
at his dwelling house in North east Street Annapolis.

Honorable Sir,   St Davids day A:M: 1747/8

Your absence from the Club at their last meeting, on Tuesday night, the 16th of february, prevented my having an opportunity then, of returning my thanks to you, for my admittance, into that worthy and honorable Society, over which you so deservedly preside, however Sir, I hope, you will now be pleased to accept of my hearty and Grateful acknowledgements of the favor, I have heard with great regret, some few days agoe, that you were Indisposed with the Gout, but, I flatter myself, that you are now ‖ better, and hope you will dignify the Club this evening with your presence at the house of, Honorable Sir,

> Your much obliged
> Greatly Devoted
> Very humble Servant
> *Jonathan Grog, high Steward.*

Before the Club broke up, a hot dispute happened between the deputy Secretary, and Mr Laconic Comus, concerning the Presbyterians, to which sect, the last mentioned Gentleman had a rooted aversion, and on this occasion Mr Comus was observed to talk more copiously & fluently, than he had ever done at any time before in Club, or ever since, which some naturalists would attribute to the power and virtue of the High Steward's Rumbo, the fumes of which, had ascended so copiously into Mr Comus's cranium, that the deputy president, and deputy Secretary, found great difficulty that night, to carry him home safe, this was a glaring instance of the truth of that maxim, that men are most apt to slide into Religious controversy, when flustered with Strong liquor.

At the following Sederunt, on the 15th of March, Capt: Seemly spruce

Then the following Law was passed, vizt:

Law XXXVI. Whereas several contests and disputes have happened in Club, concerning a Clause in Law 27th appointing the money in the Club's box to be disposed of only by unanimous consent, to prevent therefore such disputes for the future; Be it ordained & passed into a Law, by the president and Club now met, this 16th Day of february 1747/8, and by the authority of the same, that all resolves whatsoever, and all points which come under the consideration of the Club, shall be settled and determined by a majority of voices, excepting only the election of members, any law, rule or order of this here Club, to the contrary notwithstanding.

In this Law we find the Club, first adopting the enacting Stile, and looking upon themselves as a Solemn Legislative power, which we shall find, sometime after this they carried still farther, for their Stile and diction became at last quite parliamentary; The Club found themselves under a necessity to make such a Law as this, in order to extract the money out of the box, for such purposes as they saw proper, since no arguments, perswasions or methods of any Sort, could bring his honor the president to part with one single farthing of it, except for such || purposes as were pleasing or agreeable to himself, but this law was of little or no Significancy or use, for his honor the president afterwards objected to it, as being passed in his absence, hence we see, what a fine kettle of fish this here Club had Cooked for themselves, in granting so much power to the Chair, and 'tis Lamentable to think to what a state of Slavery their rash concessions had already reduced them, but we shall soon see a flame burst out in the Club, concerning this box, which had well nigh consumed the Club it self, and compleated its dissolution, but, by the prudence and good management of the Speaker, tho' a Stanch courtier, the mischief was prevented and the affair ended in the destruction of this pestilent box, and here we may observe, that tho' the breath of the honorable Speaker, was not hot enough to kindle an unextinguishable flame in the Club, upon another occasion, yet on this exigency, the frigidity of the said flatus was such that it quickly extinguished the fire.

At Sederunt 76th March 1, 1747/8, The Club was held for the first time by Jonathan Grog Esqr, as high Steward, Mr Secretary Scribble, being by his honor's appointment deputy in the Chair, and the Revd Smoothum Sly Esqr, Deputy Secretary.

There happened at this Sederund, a kind of civil Commotion in the Club, a furious brawl having arisen between Mr Protomusicus, and the Deputy President, about the Presidential Chair, his honor the president having sent orders to the high Steward, that which ever of those two Gen-

the Tuesday Club [Book V] 275

been once seen to frown; his body is thick and well set, and for one of his make and Stature he has a good Sizeable belly, into which he loves much to convey the best vittles and drink, being a good clean knife and forks man, tho' no Glutton, and his favorite Dish is Roast turkey with oisters, and his darling liquor of late is Grog, he professing himself to be of the moderen Sect of the Grogorians, and as some think the patron and founder of that Sect in Annapolis, which we shall have occasion to describe somewhere in this history, he is a very great admirer, Improver and encourager of wit, humor and drollery, and is fond of that Sort of poetry which is called Doggrell, in which he is himself a very great proficient, and Confines his genius chiefly to it, tho sometimes he cannot help emitting some flashes of the true Sublime, in his Club Compositions; puns, Conundrums || merry [346] tales and Jests, are the favorite Subjects, on which he Chuses to exercise his wit and talents, and we shall find him affording abundance of mirth to the Club, in his compositions of this Sort, in fine, to sum up all he is really a good humored, smooth tempered, merry, Jocose, and Innofensive companion, a man of the most happy Clubical Genius that ever was known, and a Great promoter Improver and encourager of Clubific felicity, for were there 50 Clubs in the place, he'd be a member of every one of them; he is a passionate admirer of natural Curiosities, and certain little knick knacks, produced by the whimsical Inventions of art, of which he has a valuable Collection by him, some of which we may have occasion to mention in this history.

At the following Sederunt, which was held on the 16th of february, Smoothum Sly Esqr, being high Steward, and Laconic Comus Esqr, deputy in the Chair, Mr Jonathan Grog made his first appearance in the Club, and being Civily Saluted and welcomed, by all the longstanding members, he took his Seat in Club, as a Longstanding member. A Letter from his honor the president to the high Steward, was produced in Club, and read as follows.

To the Revd: Smoothum Sly,
high Steward of the Tuesday Club, These.

Sir,

As I shall not be at the Club this night, be pleased to acquaint the Gentlemen, that I have appointed Mr Comus to take the Chair in my room, and, as I || hope the most *Importand* affairs have been debated, your present [347] meeting will be attended with good harmony and agreement, I am, Sir,

Feb: 16th 1747   Your most humble Servant
                                           Nasifer Jole.

[Hamilton's translation on back of drawing]

Behold of Clubic Bards the prime
Who sings thee, Cole, in pleasant Rhime,
And whilst his rhime is read, thy fame,
Shall live, so shall our poets name.

[facing page 343]

the Tuesday Club [Book V] 273

than Grog Esqr, as the Thessalonians did of Appuleius, and, of the admission of this facetious Gentleman, we are now going to give an account.

On Sederunt 74th February 2d 1747/8, the Club assembled at the house of the worshipful Sir John Oldcastle high Steward, who, Invested with the Clubs badge in a Courteous, civil and Champion like manner, ‖ complimented the honorable president, by meeting and Saluting him ten paces from the door; this was a piece of complaisance in Sir John, which it was feared would Introduce a bad custom, among the members, and occasion an additional trowble to the high Stewards, but, great as the personage was, who set the first example, it never was since Imitated by any of the Succeeding high Stewards. [344]

The dispute carried on in Club at last Sederunt concerning the Secretaries claim, to the title and office of deputy treasurer, which was then left undetermined, now came again upon the tapis, and was at this Sederunt, determined, settled, and Concluded, by the eloquence and Arguments of Mr Speaker Quaint, who confuted all the Strenous arguments brought against him by Sir John Oldcastle, and Mr Protomusicus, and thereupon, it was ordained, by a majority of voices, that the honorable the president should be Sole Treasurer, and that the Secretary should only have the title of key keeper; a great baulk to that ambitious and aspiring Secretary, who had been still aiming at advancement, and a multiplicity of offices in the Club, but was not able as yet, to compass his ends, tho' we shall find that he had better Success in the Sequel.

Upon a motion made by the Master of ceremonies, to Elect Mr Jonathan Grog of Annapolis, a member of the Club, he having made application, for the same to several of the members, the ballots, or Yeas and Nays were put Round by the Secretary, pursuant to the tenor of Law 9th, and being found all Yeas, the Secretary was ordered to acquaint the said Mr Jonathan Grog of this, by writing, desiring his attendance ‖ at next Sederunt. As this gentleman, will in the Succeeding part of our History, make a very considerable appearance, as a longstanding member of this ancient and honorable Club, holding no less than five offices at one and the same time, vizt: those of purveyor, punster, punchmaker General, Printer and poet, which were signified, for brevity's Sake, by five capital P's thus, Jonathan Grog Esqr, P.P.P.P.P. it will not be amiss here, to give an Iconographical description of his person, and a Scetch of his Character. [345]

This Gentleman is of a middle Stature, Inclinable to fat, round faced, small lively eyes, from which, as from two oriental portals, Incessantly dart the dawning rays of wit and humor, with a considerable mixture of the amorous leer, in his countenance he wears a constant Smile, having never

so, many a grinning Lubber may presume, if they please to laugh at our Clubical Sages, tho' not half so wise as they; and Horace says of Scipio and Lælius,

> *Qui, ubi se a vulgo et Scena in Secreta remorant,*
> *Virtus Scipiades, et mitis Sapientia Læli,*
> *Nugari cum Illo, et discincti ludere donec*
> *De coqueretur olus, soliti—*

Which passage I find thus translated by an old Clubical bard.

> Valorous Scipio, and Gentle Lælius,
> Removed from the Scene, and rout so Clamorous,
> Were wont to recreate themselves, their robes laid by,
> Whilst Supper by the cook was getting ready.[3]
>
> *Robertus Burton,*
> *Oxon: poeta Clubicus*

[343] And this was often the very case with the grave, the wise the ancient and honorable Tuesday Club, and particularly the honorable the president, who used to lay bye his robes like Scipio and Lælius, and Bestirr himself vigorously, backwards and forewards, in a blue Silk Jacket, whilst Supper was getting ready in the kitchen. The old greeks had their *Lubentiam Deam,* their Goddess of mirth, and the Spartans, Instructed by their Lawgiver Lycurgus, did *Deo Risui sacrificare,* sacrifise to the God of Laughter, after their wars especially, and in times of peace, which was practised in Thessaly, as appears by Appuleius Book 2d of the *Golden Ass,*[4] who was himself made the Instrument of their laughter, why therefore might not the ancient and honorable Tuesday Club, after their hot disputes, and In their Calmer Intervals, by the Instruction of the honorable Nasifer Jole Esqr, their wise president and Lawgiver, make themselves merry, be Jocose, and execute their great gelastic Law, one upon another? And this we shall find they often effectually did, making use for an Instrument on these occasions, of Jona-

---

ingly contrasts paganism and Christianity. Valerius Maximus (fl. 1st century A.D.) was a sententious and sometimes bombastic Roman historian; the passage that Hamilton attributes to him, which literally means "Placing a hobby-horse on his shin, playing with his children, he was mocked by Alcibiades," does appear in bk. 8, chap. 8, ext. 1 of Valerius Maximus's works.

3. Scipio is identified above (see p. 10n); his close friend Gaius Laelius shared in Scipio's African campaign (204–202 B.C.) and became proconsul in Gaul (189 B.C.). More literally, the passage translated by "Robertus Burton" (probably Hamilton) reads: "In the secret places where they removed themselves from the crowd and the stage, / Courageous Scipio and mildly wise Laelius / Were wont to joke with him [Lucilius], and to play unbelted / While supper was cooking" (Horace, *Satirae* 2.1.71).

4. Apuleius (born ca. 123) was a poet, philosopher, and rhetorician whose *Metamorphoses* (better known as *The Golden Ass*) is the only complete Latin novel extant.

white, day is night, two and two make five, while they, and all the world besides, are Conscious of the falsity of these propositions, and political maxims.

On the same Sederunt, a debate arose in Club about who should serve upon the Anniversary of the Club next ensuing, vizt: the 14 of may 1748, whether the member in Course, or the honorable Mr President Jole, Several of the members, particularly, Jealous Spyplot Esqr, high Steward, and Sir John Oldcastle, set up in Competition for the honor, and Mr Secretary, to whose turn it fell of Course, by a Just Calculation, pleading his right, his honor generously determined the dispute, by taking it upon himself, which, as it conduced most to the honor of the Society, and the Importance of the occasion, so it was unanimously Consented to by the whole Club.

Chapter V

Election and admission of Jonathan Grog Esqr, into the Club, more Club letters, Institution of the presidential Star and badge, Speech of Jonathan Grog Esqr, to the Chair.

Magninus says, that a merry Companion is better than a Song, and, as the old proverb goes, *Comes Jucundus* || *in via pro vehiculo*, a Jocular fellow to a man in the moaps is as a waggon to a Jaded foot travellar,[1] for mirth may be said to be the Nepenthe of Homer, Hellen's bowl and Venuse's girdle or Cestis, nor is mirth In my opinion at all repugnant to true philosophy, seeing the gravest and most philosophical dons, have been at times extravagantly merry, The wise Socrates would be merry by fits, would sing, dance and drink his glass, or Theodoret Damnably belies him, so would Cato, and even Tully by his own confession, in his familiar Epistles book 7th Xenophon describes Socrates as a very droll old fellow, taking on himself the Character of an Actor or comedian, and Valerius Maximus Cap: 8, lib: 8 says of him, *Interposita Arundine cruribus, suis cum filiis ludens, ab Alcibiade risus est*; he would ride hobby horses with his children, and was laugh'd at for this by Alcibiades, who was not by half so wise a man as he,[2]

[342]

---

1. Jean-Chrysostome Magnen (fl. 17th century), a French physician and philosopher, was the author of *Democritus reviviscens* (1646), to which Hamilton is referring. The passage literally means "an agreeable companion is like a cart on the road."
2. Theodoret (ca. 393–466), a monk, was bishop of Cyrrhus, Syria (from 423), and author of the *Church History* (spanning the period from Constantine to 428), the *Religious History*, and the *Graecarum affectionum curatio* (to which Hamilton is probably referring), which painstak-

> What if I Lay you down, my pritty maid?
> Why then you must cover me, Sir she said,
> I thank you kindly my pritty maid,
> Your Kindly welcome, Sir she said.
>
> But should I get you with Child my pritty maid?
> Why then you must father it, Sir she said,
> I thank you kindly, my pritty maid,
> Your kindly welcome Sir, she said.
>
> But I will not marry you, my pritty maid,
> I never desird you, Sir she said,
> I thank you kindly my pritty maid,
> Your kindly welcome Sir she said.

The Justness of the measure, the uniformity of the Rhime and the unity or Sameness of the Sentiment or thought, (for Indeed there is but one thought runs thro the whole, tho not a very modest one,) show not only the excellence of this Song, but the great propriety of his honor's taste in chusing it to entertain the Longstanding members.

At the following Sederunt, which was the 73d, on the 5th of January, 1747/8, Jealous Spyplot Esqr being high Steward, a dispute arose in Club concerning a Claim the Secretary put in, of being deputy treasurer, under the honorable the president, as being entrusted with one key of the box; The honorable the president Claiming himself the title of sole treasurer, after many arguments pro and con, the high Steward, and the Master of Ceremonies standing up, on the part of his honor the president, and Sir John Oldcastle, and Mr Protomusicus, on the part of the Secretary, In which dispute, Mr Musician Neverout, in the opinion of the majority of the Club, made several bold and Strenous Speeches in the defence of Clubical Liberty, and in the opinion of his honor the president, and the gentlemen on the other Side of the argument, arogant and assuming ‖ speeches, the affair was left undetermined, till Mr Speaker Quaint should be present in Club, to regulate and settle the dispute, this gentleman having now gained such a great character in the Club, for pleading and arguing, that they Implicitly submitted all to his decisions, but, he being a state officer, it was no difficult matter to guess, on which Side he would declare whenever the honorable Chair was concerned in the dispute, a common way with thorro' paced Courtiers, who have no opinion or private Judgement of their own, but act by a kind of public Judgement, founded upon the will and pleasure, or rather the caprice of their patrons, lords and masters, hence it is, we often find those gentlemen, gravely and confidently asserting that black is

which it was established, but great men, as well as little men ought always to Remember to be consistent with themselves at all times in arguments of this nature, for had his honor reflected on this rule, he would not have gravely proposed, a few Sederunts after this, to buy with the box money a Club table Cloth and Club Napkins, of some very fine diaper, which he had in his own Store for Sale; I would only ask, what Sort of Charity this was, after this dispute, the Club broke up in a bad humor.

At the next Sederunt, Mr Protomusicus Neverout being high Steward, this gentleman was again accused by the Speaker, for a breach of Law 30, for not wearing the Club badge, and after some arguments pro and con, he was condemn'd to drink off a bumper, which he complied with, and drank to the long continuance of the Club, and to the good agreement of the upper and lower houses of Assembly now sitting, and then, Investing himself with the Club badge, he began to ply his honor the president with bumpers of Strong beer, and dealt it so liberally about among the Longstanding members, that the whole remainder of the nine bottles, left in his hands, was soon sucked up, this shows, that he had but little regard to the health of the Longstanding members, as has been hinted above, tho' this gentleman's friends do not stick to || say, that he did this to punish the Club for their scurvy usage of him, and allowed them to swallow so much Strong liquor on purpose, that, feeling the bad effects of it, they might never again, make such another racket about Strong beer on a like occasion, should it ever happen, his honor the president however, by this profuseness of the high Steward at other people's expence, got so bungy,[5] as the phraze is, that after having outsung Mr Protomusicus, and beat him at his own weapons, in the Celebrated Club Song of *When Cloe we ply,* he sung a favorite Song of his own to the Club, with great humor and Glee, together with many others, which he had in a book that he usually Carried about with him in his pocket.

[339]

A favorite Club Song, sung by his honor the President[6]
Where are you going my pritty maid?
I'm going a milking, Sir, she said,
Shall I go with you, my pritty maid?
You're kindly welcome Sir, she said.

---

5. *Bungy* means "puffed out" or "protuberant"; here, "bloated from too much drinking."
6. I have not located a contemporary copy of this tune, though apparently it was a popular tune indeed, since another version of it later appears as "Young Donald, of Edinborough Town" in *The Universal Songster; or, Museum of Mirth* (London, 1828), III, 102.

At the following Sederunt, Slyboots Pleasant Esqr being high Steward, his honor the president paid to the Secretary out of the box, the Sum of ten Shillings in consideration of his having furnished the Club, with a new book of Records.

And at this same Sederunt, Mr Laconic Comus, made a motion in Club, to the Surprize of many, for he was a man of very few words, vizt: That a voluntary Contribution should be raised to purchase a handsom Silver punch Ladle, for the use of the Club—This motion came naturally enough from Mr Comus, of whom it might well be said, *mens in patinis,*[4] for the greatest part of his Cogitation ran upon punch and its appurtenances, such as bowls, || ladles and strainers; this motion however, excited a very warm dispute, the Secretary and some others opposing the motion with all their might, alledging That there was no necessity for taxing the Club for any such thing, as there was money enough in the box, wherewith to procure any thing of that Sort, which was wanted, for the use of the Club. This objection did not at all please his honor the president, who said That it would be contradictory to the original design of the box, which was allotted for charity, to lay out that fund upon punch Ladles, or any such triffles. The Secretary upon this boldly replied That he saw no occasion for the Longstanding members being taxed to purchase triffles—at which words his honor the president frowned tremendous from the Chair, but that tremendous frown availed nothing, The Secretary harangued still and spoke very loud, and the whole Club fell into a general uproar, while Mr Comus laying down his pipe with great Indignation, rubd his forehead nose and Chin with the palm of his right hand, and often threw in the pithy Interjections, of *by God & God damn it—damn the box—send it to hell!* and such like, Some of the members Indeed contributed towards purchasing of this triffle, and that very Largely, and among others his honor the president himself, in order to keep the box shut, opened his purse strings, others kept their pockets shut, and were Inexorable on that Score, among whom was the Secretary, at this proceeding Mr Comus was much chagrined, To find his first, and Indeed his last motion in Club (for he never after this made another) thus Crushed and quashed, his honor the president was also much Incensed, || not for being dissappointed of this Club ladle, for he declared afterwards, that he looked upon it as a bawble, but because an open atack had been made upon the box, the pillaging of which he could not bear to hear of, as it would be as he said, Intirely frustrating the Charitable end for

---

4. "His mind is on the dishes."

> ——*Nil spissius illa,*
> *Dum bibitur, nil clarius est dum mingitur, unde,*
> *Constat quod multas fæces in corpore linquat.*

That is to say—

> Nothing goes in so thick,
> Nothing comes out so thin,
> It must needs follow then,
> The Dregs are left within.[3]
>
> Robertus Burton a Club bard

And therefore, allowing the arguments of these philosophers, Mr Protomusicus was not so much to blame in this affair as some may Imagin, but we shall see by and bye, whether this chief musician, really intended good to the Club, in an Instance of his conduct, with regard to the use to which he applied this very beer.

At Sederunt 70th Novr 24th 1747, Mr Secretary Scribble being high Steward, the following law was passed, at the Motion of the Master of Ceremonies.

Law XXXV. That henceforth from this day there shall be no disputes whatsoever, or Judicial trials carried on, or negotiated upon that night, in which the honorable the president is high Steward, or upon the anniversary of this club.

This law was procured at the Instance and ‖ desire of his honor the [336] president, whose good humor and Complaisance was such, that he chose not to have the Quiet and pleasure of the Club Interrupted or marr'd upon that night on which he entertained, a very great Indulgence this, that his honor would rather suffer the Guilty to escape (a thing that he was by no means at other times fond of) or delay their punishment, than Interrupt the pleasure the Club had in enjoying his most elegant entertainments, where the choicest dainties were always produced according to ancient custom. Yet some thought that his honors true motive for procuring this Law, was because these trials and disputes, confined him too much to the Chair, so that he had not full Liberty of trotting to and from the kitchen, to see how the Club Cookery went foreward.

---

of whose teachings appear in Galen's works (which probably contain this passage meaning "coarse food generates blood").

3. More literally, "Nothing is thicker than it / When it is drunk, nothing clearer when pissed; hence / It is plain that it leaves many dregs behind in the body." The more refined translation by "Robertus Burton" is probably Hamilton's.

gravity, and the solemnity of the occasion, could not forbear letting his face first expand it self, into a gelastic grin, and then burst out a laughing, most Immoderatly in the Chair, at last It came to high words and loud Swearing, between the evidence and the criminal, but the Speaker behaved with that profound gravity and decency which became his office.

However, at last, the Club Inclining to favor him, determined that he was not guilty of converting the beer to his own use, but guilty of retaining it in his hands for his own service night, for which he was reprimanded in a very Solemn and Serious manner by his honor the president from the Chair.

This Criminal trial was the first that occurred in this ancient and honorable Club, since its Institution, and was carried on with great decency and [334] Solemnity, except now and then a horse laugh, and a loud ex- || clamation from the Criminal, with two or three full mouthed Oaths from Mr Stentor Snuffysnout the evidence, who rapt out several *God Dammes* with great vehemence, and as they said swore thro' a plough Share.

Many people, deeply versed in physical causes, asserted, that the club acted wrong, in making such an uproar about this beer, for, said they, it is notorious, that the compotation of beer, very much deadens and flattens the animal Spirits, and, being a Sleepy Phlematic Guzzle, it brings on a hebetude and dullness, or a Stupidity peculiar to those hum-drum Clubs, in the neighbourhood of Moorfields, who, Immerged in beer and tobacco, sit whole nights and days together in a State of torpor or perfect Inactivity, and cannot communicate their Ideas, either by Speech or action, being only remarkable for their Swagbellies, broad faces, carbuncle noses and muddy eyes, till at last, these beer Sots losing all the little wit and Senses they had, the Devil finds an empty tenement, in their earthly tabernacles, a fit dwelling for him, and entering upon the premises, as he did of old into the herd of Swine, they become possessed, and by an easie transition, go into the neighbouring hospital of Bethelem, where ten to one they spend the remainder of their Days.

It was therefore asserted by these Ingenious naturalists, that Mr Protomusicus Neverout, consulted the Interest of the Club in what he did, and really, if we take the word of learned men for it, this assertion of theirs [335] seems to be grounded upon very good reasons; for || Henricus Ayrerus, a famous Physician, in advising an hypochondriac patient, condemns the use of beer, as also does Crato, saying *Crassum generat Sanguinem*,[2] and to confirm this, there is the old latin Sentence.

---

2. Perhaps a reference to Georg Heinrich Ayrer's (1702–1774) *De limitum praescriptione* (Göttingen, [1746]). Crato is probably Crito, physician at Trajan's court (ca. 100), fragments

Whereupon, at Sederunt 69th Novr 10th 1747, The honorable the President being high Steward, he was, in the face of the Club, Indicted by Mr Speaker Quaint as follows.

"Solo Neverout Esqr, musician of the Tuesday Club, stands Indicted by the said Club, that he, the said Solo Neverout Esqr, being unworthily dignified with the title of musician, did, on the third day of august last, unjustly, willfully, maliciously, and with a bad Intention, censure a most elegant letter, wrote by Sir John Oldcastle to his honor the president, and that he the said Solo Neverout Esqr, on the 27th day of october last, did willfully and Insolently absent himself, from a Club, held at the house of Mr Speaker Quaint, without sending a line of || excuse before noon to the said Mr Quaint, the high Steward, contrary to an act of this here Club, in that case made and provided, and, that he, the said Solo Neverout Esqr being Intrusted, with nine bottles of English beer, presented by Mr Merry Makefun, an honorary member, to this Society, did, unjustly willfully and pitifully, deprive the said Society thereof, and convert the same to his own use, contrary to right Justice and Inconsistent with the honor of this honorable Society, and the dignity conferred upon him, the said Solo Neverout Esqr, by the said Society." [332]

To all which three charges, Jointly and Severally, Mr Protomusicus Neverout, pleaded not guilty, in manner and form as aforesaid, and had allowed him for council, Mr Secretary Scribble, by whose eloquence and acuteness, the die turned up in his favor, as to the two first articles of accusation, tho the evidence was pritty Strong against him.

Upon the third Article, Mr Stentor Snuffysnout, who attended the Club at this Sederunt, was called upon to deliver his evidence, which he did in a distinct and peremptory manner, declaring in a Strong pithy voice, uttered in a loud key as high as *G Sol re in alt,* and with a particular Emphasis, That Mr Merry Makefun, had sent to Mr Neverout, and to him, (the evidence,) a large parcell of English beer, and that he had ordered one dozen and a half bottles of the same, to be de- || livered for the use of this here ancient and honorable Club, the moiety of which, vizt: nine bottles, had been delivered into the hands of Mr Neverout, and the other moiety he, the evidence had already delivered himself to this ancient and honorable Club. [333]

This peremptory evidence gravelled Mr Protomusicus's Learned council, for, it was so plain against the Culprit, that he knew not how to quibble him out of this premunire or puzzlement, as he called it, which put Mr Neverout in a Sort of huff-gruff humor, and made his council faulter in his discourse; on which, his honor the president notwithstanding his great

so much, that at last he would not suffer one Clubical letter directed to him to be entered upon record.

The parallell at the conclusion of this letter of the Secretarie's, is an Imitation of the elegant Phraseology || of the honorable Speaker himself, in a speech he made to a young Lady, who refused, upon her being desired to sing, which was to this purpose, "Surely Miss, you cannot but sing well, if your *Inward voice* is as harmonious, as the beauty of your *Outward form* is uncommon."

Chapter IV

Trial of the Chief musician, disputes concerning a punch Ladle, accusation and Condemnation of Mr Proto-musicus, more disputes of little Significancy.

Delirant Reges, plectuntur Achivi, says a Certain celebrated poet,[1] whom perhaps you may be more thoroly acquainted with than I, and if not, 'tis not a farthing's matter, for our present purpose; as I only use this Adage, to apply it to the circumstances of the ancient and honorable Tuesday Club, at this Juncture, by the preposterous conduct of Mr Protomusicus Neverout, the meaning of the Saying is, "That when kings or great men lose their wits, or play the fool, the people must smart for it," but how is this applicable, you'll say, to Mr Protomusicus or the Club? why thus, Mr Protomusicus as a great man, or Club officer, tho' not a State officer, must be looked upon as a ruler in the Club, the next query will be, how this Club officer came to play the fool? and how by his playing the fool, the Club became Sufferers? The State of the case is shortly thus, || the long standing members had an opportunity, of soaking their noses for one night at least in good Strong English beer, presented them by Merry Makefun Esqr, honorary member, which would have been a good and comfortable thing for them, but they were unjustly baulked of this refined pleasure, by means of Mr Neverout's secreting and keeping back that beer, in which conduct, that officer may Justly be said to have plaid the fool, for he drew upon himself thereby, the Indignation of his honor the president, the wrath of the Club, and had a Standing Joke fixed upon him, which has been kept up to this very day, and it is thought that he will never hear the last of it.

1. "When kings go crazy, the Achaeans are punished" (Horace, *Epistulae*, 1.2.14).

absent from the Club at this Sederunt, tho' in town, and not sending a letter of Excuse to the high Steward, according to the tenor of Law 33d, it was ordered also that Mr Stentor Snuffybeak, be Summoned by the Secretary to attend the Club at next Sederunt, to give in his evidence against Solo Neverout Esqr.

His honor the president presented in Club, a letter from the Secretary, which was read as follows.

To Nasifer Jole Esqr,
president of the Tuesday Club, These.

Honorable Sir,

Being prevented by Indisposition, I shall not have the pleasure of attending the Club this night, at Mr Quaint's. This therefore is to Inform your honor and the Club, that I have, according to your order of the 10th Instant, dispatched the Societie's letter of thanks to Mr Merry Makefun, writ and devised in the same form and tenor, as was then read to the Club, and as is now entered in our book of minutes,—I have farther to Inform your honor and the Club, that I have, according to your Instructions, provided a new register book, for the use of the Society, which I Intended to have produced at this night's meeting, but shall be obliged to defer that ceremony to the Subsequent meeting of the Club, upon ‖ the 10th of [329] november next, when your honor serves as high Steward, and I hope then to be able to wait upon you with that duty and decency requisite upon such a Solemn occasion. In the mean time, I heartily desire to be remembered to all our worthy members, and hope, they will be most elegantly and pompously entertained by Mr Speaker Quaint, high Steward for this night, and in this, I Surely cannot be mistaken, if Mr Speaker's *Outward apparatus,* and *Decoration,* at feasts of this nature, be as *Elegant* and *Harmonic,* as his *Inward Rhetoric* and *Eloquence,* at the Club and bar, is uncommon, I am, Honorable Sir,

Octor the 27th 1747
Your most humble Servant and
Trusty Secretary
Loquacious Scribble.

This is the first letter upon record of the Secretarie's proper inditing, where it may be remarked the Stile is tollerably plain and easie, having little or nothing of that Clubical Bombast and pallaber, abundance of which will be found in the Subsequent letters wrote by that officer, who, by his pernicious example, also led the way to the other Longstanding members, to Imitate the same ridiculous Stile, which disgusted his honor the president

To Mr Merry Makefun, Merchant at Oxford.

Sir,

I am enjoined and ordered by the honorable Mr President Jole, and the longstanding members of the Ancient and honorable Tuesday Club, in his and their names, to return you their thanks, and grateful acknowledgements, for the favor you lately did us, in making a present to the Club of a Sortment of English beer, by the hands of Mr Stentor Snuffybeak, in which we have more than once drank your health, and paid you that deference due to a worthy honorary member, whom we esteem an ornament to our Society.

I therefore in their name, and by their authority make due acknowledgement of the favor, being Sensible that your generosity is prompted by a Sincere esteem for our Society, so wishing you all || health and happiness, we profess ourselves to be

Octor 13th 1747   Your Sincere friends and fellow members,
Signed pr: Order
Loquacious Scribble Secrtry

At this Sederunt Capt: Serious Social, a worthy long Standing member, voluntarily left the Club, not thro' any disgust, for he was a person of a thorro' clubical disposition, and had a true taste for the bowl, pipe and chat, but thro' age, and bodily Infirmity, he was unable now to attend these nocturnal meetings, an entry of this occurrence is found on the book to this purpose.

"Capt: Serious Social, having been 4 nights absent from the Club, without giving any reasons, is hereby excluded the Club, according to the tenor of Law 13th."

At the following Sederunt, Octor 27th, Mr Speaker Quaint being high Steward, the said high Steward represented to the Club, that in pursuance of an order, from Mr Merry Makefun of Oxford, to Mr Protomusicus Neverout, to deliver nine bottles of English beer to the ancient and honorable Tuesday Club, of Annapolis, he had sent to him, the said Neverout, for some of the said beer, for the use of the Club, and he, the said Neverout, returned for answer that he had no beer for the said Club. The Society taking offence at this rude answer, passed an order, that Mr Speaker Quaint, draw up an Indictment, against the said Solo Neverout Esqr, for this, and other misdemeanors || charged upon him at some of the preceeding Sederunts, particularly, his censuring of Sir John Oldcastles letter to his honor the president, dated the 3d of august last, unjustly, as also, his being

requesting his honor the president and club to consider of ways and means to procure a new one, in order to Carry on regularly, the minutes of this Club. This was a very laudable care in the Secretary, and tended to preserve these valuable Records for the use of posterity, which, as there was not a full meeting of the members, it was postponed to another Sederunt.

Mr Merry Makefun, an honorary member, having sent a present of English beer to the Club, and entrusted a parcel of it with Mr Protomusicus Neverout, the Secretary was ordered by his honor the president and Club, to draw up a letter of thanks, to the said Mr Makefun, to be laid before the Club at next sederunt, to receive proper corrections and ammendments.

An Information was brought at this Sederunt against Mr Protomusicus Neverout, for not acquainting the Club with an order he had from Mr Merry Makefun, to present the Club with some English beer, for which he is ordered to be Indicted next meeting by Mr Speaker Quaint. [325]

This is the first Instance of an order for a Criminal trial, to be carried on in this ancient and honorable Club, and the Chief Musician is the first delinquent, or Culprit, we shall have occasion to relate several others in the course of this history, and this very gentleman, we shall find more than once, under the vindictive Claws of Clubical Justice.

At Sederunt 67, Octor 13, 1747, after a long adjournment, on account of birth days and horse races, the Club met at the house of Dumpling Gundiguts Esqr, high Steward, and after mature consideration, with regard to the book of Records, it was ordered, That ten Shillings Currency be paid by his honor the president, out of the box, to the Secretary, who for this Sum undertakes to provide a record book for the use of the Club; this is the first disbursment from the treasury that we find upon record, in this ancient and honorable Club, and, I believe the only one, that ever was made, from the foundation, to the final evacuation of the box, which shows how far the charitable Intentions of the box were put in practice; but, his honor the president, being Sole Judge in this affair, we need not be Surprized that none of the Clubs money had as yet been laid out on Charitable purposes, his honor being very || nice and hard to please, with regard to such as were proper objects of charity, not chusing, like many, who would be thought very good christians, to bestow charity, or have any the least compassion upon such as he thought unworthy objects. [326]

The Secretary produced at this Sederunt a copy of a Letter of thanks to Mr Merry Makefun, drawn up by him, according to an order of the preceeding Sederunt, of which a transcript follows.

By this Law, we may perceive, the Jealousy that had now grown in the Club, of the Secretaries makeing false entries, tho' some are of opinion that this Law was procured by the vociferation and Clamor of Mr Protomusi- [323] cus, who Imagined himself Ill used in || the entry of last Sederunt, concerning his censuring of Sir John Oldcastle's letter, but this entry in fact was made by the Revd Mr Sly, then deputy Secretary, the Chief Secretary being absent, and concerning this very affair, some hot disputes happened in Club at this Sederunt, between the Revd Mr Sly, master of Ceremonies and Mr Protomusicus Neverout, which begun with noise and ended in nothing as many disputes do, and they were left undetermined, till Mr Speaker Quaint appears in Club, to determin and put a finishing Stroke to these Controversies, being Informed in nothing relating to the said Controversies, this seems to be putting a very great Confidence in the Speaker's Judgement and penetration, supposing him to be able to determin a controversy of which he knew not the least circumstance, an Instance of that Implicit trust, which understrappers, are apt to put in the Judgement and decision of great men, which proceeds from a false association of Ideas, too prevalent among the vulgar, in Joining greatness of capacity & Judgement with greatness and dignity of office.

At the next Sederunt, which was September 1st, The Revd Smoothum Sly Esqr, being high Steward, the president produced In Club a Letter from the High Steward, vizt:

To Nasifer Jole Esqr,
president of the Tuesday Club.

Sir,

[324]   As high steward of the Tuesday Club, which meets || this night, in pursuance of last appointment, I think it my duty to give you this Notice, and to desire the honor of your company to preside at the said meeting to be held at the house of Slyboots Pleasant Esqr, I am with regard, Honorable Sir,

Septr 1, 1747   Your most humble Servant and
                                            very dutiful high Steward
                                            Smoothum Sly.

[*Here endeth the first book of the Club records.*]

At Sederunt 66th Septr 15th 1747, Laconic Comus Esqr, being high steward, a letter was produced from the Secretary to his honor the president, Intimating that the book of Records of the Club was filled up, and

great, Lordly and unerring Judges, notwithstanding their lofty titles, high birth and ponderous purses, which last enables them to give many a poor poet, and many a starving author a dinner, are not altogether exempt, from the || attacks and sneers of the critics, when these carping and fault finding gentry, have a mind to fall foul of their works. [321]

A glaring instance of this appeared in the reception, that a letter wrote by no less a person than the Worshipful Sir John Oldcastle, principle State officer of this ancient and honorable Club, and of his honors most honorable privy council, met with when presented and read in Club, which I shall relate, as the matter stands in the book of Records.

At Sederunt 63d August 4th 1747, The worshipful Sir John Oldcastle being high Steward, his honor the president produced to the Club a Letter, sent him by the worshipful, the high Steward, which being, in his honor's opinion (for great men are apt to compliment one another mightily, even on very Slight and triffling occasions) a *very respectful letter,* he desired the same might be read, and recorded in the book as follows.

To the Honorable The President of the Tuesday Club.

Sir,

I am to acquaint you, I have the pleasure of the worthy Club at my house, where I hope to have the honor of your good company, mean time am with due respect

August 3d   Your most humble Servant
                                                    Oldcastle.

This Letter was in a very warm manner objected to by Mr Protomusi- [322]
cus Neverout, as being wanting in due respect, but as his objections were Inconsistent with the respect due to his honor the president, the worshipful the high Steward, and the Club, he was gently reprimanded for the present, by the honorable the president from the Chair, but it was hoped, that this rude behavior of his, would be Sufficiently chastised by Mr Speaker Quaint, at next meeting.

At the following Sederunt, which was the 18th of August, Capt: Seemly Spruce being high Steward, there was a Law passed in Club, vizt:

Law XXXIV. That every entry, relating to particular members, or censures passed upon particular members, by this Club, as also the form and tenor of Laws, be read by the Secretary to the Club, before they are entered at Large into the book of records, that they may undergo such corrections, additions or Improvements, as the Club shall think proper, and that, notwithstanding this first reading, they shall be read as usual, at the opening of the following Club after registration.

ard, the Secretary reported to his honor and the Club, that the old record book was almost filled, and proposed to the Society, that his honor the president, or Sir John Oldcastle should Contribute for a new book, for the use of the Club, and, it being put to the vote, it was carried, that his honor the president should present the Society with a new record book, to which Resolve his honor tacitly dissented, and Indeed, this was a foolish proceeding, in the Club, being a presumption, that the taxed, had a power to tax, their tax master, who had the club treasury in his power, and therefore would be no such fool, as to part with his own private property, so long as he had the public funds in his hands.

It was moved in Club, at this same Sederunt, that Mr Protomusicus Neverout, on account of his non attendance, should be deprived of his office, and Mr Laconic Comas put in his place, but, upon it's being put to the vote, it was determined, that he should first have a hearing, and that, in case of his absence at next meeting, the Club should proceed Judicially against him.

We shall find thro' the whole course of this Club History, this Longstanding member, and officer of the Commons, the most Irregular of any of the others in his attendance on the Club, The most Inconsistent in his proceedings and Speeches in club, the most Clamorous and noisy at times against the preroga- || tive of the chair, and at other times the most busy in arguing for it, the most Incessant Laugher and vociferator, and yet by a peculiar good luck, that attends many people, which is not of their own Seeking, this Longstanding member escaped at all times that Just censure and punishment, which ought to have been Inflicted upon him, by his honor and the Club, many wondered how this could be, but, in short, we can only account for it thus, that he audaciously laughed in their faces, and carried off even the most Serious matters, fairly with a Joke.

Chapter III

Sir John Oldcastle's Letter censured, Club's letter to Mr Makefun, an honorary Member, other Clubical letters of no great Importance.

Tho' the Learned generally pitch upon Great and Illustrious men, that is, men of high birth and titles for their patrons, supposing them to be perfect and unerring Judges, in all Sorts of Learning whatsoever, and Intirely acquiesce in their Judgement and opinion, yet we find, that those

thought that it was by Salutation, and Manuquassation,[4] and after long dispute, the following Law was passed.

Law XXXIII. That every member of the Club, who is, or shall be honored with an office in it, provided he be in town, shall attend the Club at meetings punctually, or send his excuse in writing, to the high Steward for the time being, on the Club day, by twelve o Clock at noon, or to forfeit half a crown currency, to be paid into the hands of the honorable the president as chief treasurer, which money, is to be laid out upon rack, or other Liquors, to be agreed upon by the Society at their meeting, preceeding the Anniversary of the Club, to be used on that occasion.

The cause of passing this law, it was said, was the remissness of several of the Longstanding members, in their attendance on the Club meetings, particularly Mr Protomusicus, who very often absented, and would either give no reason for his doing so, or very triffling ones, but this seems only to be a pretence, to cover a worse design, In short, it was a Scheme to enrich the box, his honor the president's darling, to do which all methods, direct or Indirect were taken in Club, || and now we find, that by the express tenor of the above law, the fund in this box, is partly allotted to support the Luxury of the Club, in purchasing rack, and other expensive Liquors, and the original purpose of Charity is no more talked of, but we shall find by and bye, that those Schemes did not take, for, tho' the said protomusicus and other Club officers, often transgressed this Law, yet it is no where to be found upon record, that they ever paid the penalty into the box, tho often desired by his honor the president.

However, against this Law, the worshipful Sir John Oldcastle entered his protest; Because he said it was partially penal, making only the officers liable to the fine, and omitting the longstanding members of the Commoners.

After some warm dispute in Club at this Sederunt, concerning State officers, and officers of the Commons, it was Resolved, that the master of ceremonies, Musician and Secretary, are not State officers, but officers of the Commons, and that Sir John Oldcastle, and the honorable the Speaker, are State officers, and of his honor's honorable privy council of State.

'Tis strange to see, how soon pride, vanity, ambition and love of power, took place in this here ancient and honorable Club, in spite of all the opposition of that wise and foreseeing Longstanding member, Jealous Spyplot Esqr.

At Sederunt 62d July 27, 1747, Capt: Serious || Social being high Stew-

---

4. *Manuquassation* is Hamilton's invention for *handshake* (a quassation is a shaking).

by as it were comparing him to the great Pluto, king of hell, but likewise made an excellent elogium on himself as a musician, by likening himself to Orpheus, the other Song was to this purpose.

Club Song, sung by Mr Protomusicus[3]

Save women and wine, there is nothing in life
   Can bribe honest Souls to endure it,
When the heart is tormented with care & with Strife,
     Dear women and wine,
     Sweet women and wine,
   Dear women and wine only cure it.

Come on my brave boys, we'll have women and wine,
   And wisely to purpose employ them,
He's a fool that refuses such blessings divine
     As women and wine,
     Sweet women and wine,
   Who has vigor and health to enjoy them.

Our wine shall be old, and so my dear Jack
   To heighten our amorous fire,
Our Girls plump and Sound, they will kiss with a Smack,
     Our bottles will Crack,
     Our Lasses will smack,
   And gratify every desire.

The Club was so well pleased with these Songs, and Mr Protomusicus's performance, that they granted him the privilege of asking any member of the Club to sing, after having first sung himself, not even excepting his honor the President, who, notwithstanding in this case, as indeed in all others questioned the power which the Club assumed to themselves, in giving any Longstanding member an Authority over him, for it always was, and is now his fixed opinion, that as president, he is above all Club law, and is at no time obliged to give reasons for his conduct, to the Club. At this Sederunt, Mr Curious Courtly, Mr Swillum Swagbelly, and Mr Prim Laconic, were made honorary members.

At Sederunt 61, July 7th 1747, Jealous Spyplot Esqr being high Steward, the Master of ceremonies was Confirmed in his office by his honor the president, but, by what particular ceremony, is not left on record, tho' it is

---

3. "The Pleasures of Life," or "Save Women and Wine," appears in *Calliope, or English Harmony,* I, 147.

congratulatory Speech, in a nervous and elegant Stile, which was at all times quite natural to that Gentleman.

Thus did these polite longstanding members mutually compliment and congratulate each other, after the ceremonious manner of ambassadors, plenipo's and great councellors of State, who, when they assemble, which is but very seldom, pass off the greatest part of the time in compliment and Ceremony, but, notwithstanding, when the precedence comes to be disputed for, are loth to yeild it one to another.

At Sederunt 60, June 23d, 1747, Slyboots Pleasant Esqr, being high Steward, the Secretary vented his Spleen against the Chief musician, by accusing him of negligence in his office, as he had done the Speaker on the preceeding Sederunt, but the Club acquitted him, on account of his good performances, at other times, and as an acknowledgement of the favor, he entertained the Club, with two excellent new Songs, the one Solo, the other In company with another voice, the Songs were as follows.

New Song, sung by Mr Protomusicus Neverout[2]

When Orpheus went down to the regions below,
   Which men are forbidden to see,
He tun'd up his lyre, as old histories show,
   To set his Euridice free—To set &ct:

All hell was Surpriz'd, that a person so wise
   Should rashly endanger his life;
But, O ye good gods! how vast their Surprize,
   When they knew that he came for his wife.

To find out a punishment fit for his fault,
   Old Pluto had puzzl'd his brain,
But hell had not Torments Sufficient he thought,
   So he gave him his wife back again.

But pity succeeding, soon vanquish'd his heart,
   Being pleas'd with his playing so well,
He took her again, in reward of his art,
   Such power had music in hell.

It would seem by the above song, sung on such an occasion, that Mr Protomusicus Intended, not only to cox and sooth his honor the president,

---

2. "Orpheus and Euridice" appears in *Calliope, or English Harmony* and in *Universal Harmony; or, The Gentleman and Ladie's Social Companion* (London, 1745), 34.

membering this tale of Socrates or some other such antiquated tale, thought, that their Orator, vizt: the honorable Mr Speaker Quaint, and their musician, the good Mr Proto-musicus Neverout, were like these ancient musicians and Orators, whom Jupiter turned into grasshoppers, that is, that the diet fittest for them was air, and that they had no occasion for meat and drink, for as they vended nothing but air to the Club, in their vociferations, when the one sung and the other declaimed, so they had nothing but air in return for their Labor, that is Sound, of which air is the medium, excited either by loud laughing, or clapping of hands, by way of applause. As for other rewards, they had not so much as the value of one single farthing, to help, as the Saying is to keep life and Soul together, this cold Comfort surely, together with the notion of their being very great Club officers, and above doing their duty, made them negligent and remiss in their respective offices, so that it was now a very rare thing, to hear either a Speech from the honorable the Speaker, or a Song from the tuneful Mr Proto-musicus; which attracted the hawks eyes of that cunning and politic officer the Secretary, and gave ground for an accusation brought against these two eminent Club officers by him at two several Sederunts for negligence and remissness in their respective offices, but these accusations were

[313] little || regarded by the Club, and in a manner slured over, the reason of which probably was, that his honor the president was Suspicious, (as he constantly professed to be) of the Secretaries designs, Imagining, and perhaps with some reason, that this Cunning menial Club officer, wanted one or other of these great Club officers to be degraded, that he might step into his place, as this is the common practice of great Statesmen and officers, who generally envy one another, and the understrappers among them are always on the Gape, for the places of those above them, wishing and praying daily with great fervency, that they may either be displaced, die, or go to the Devil, the Secretary probably might have some such designs in his Noddle, but then, it must have been the honorable the Speaker's place he aimed at, for, he was by nature so unfit for the other, that he knew as little how to sing, as a bull-frog or a goose, and far less than a Swan, Cricket or Grasshopper.

At Sederunt 59th June 9th 1747, Solo Neverout Esqr, being high Steward, several Congratulatory Speeches, were made in Club to the Secretary, on occasion of his late Marriage, The Reverend Mr Sly, in particular, complimented him upon that occasion, and, when he was done speaking, the honorable Mr Speaker Quaint, rising up, with that gravity, Solemnity and action, which was his peculiar talent on all such occasions, discoursed but

[314] little upon that Subject, delivering chiefly an || encomium upon Mr Sly's

world, and like a flitch of Smoked bacon, whose Salt is soaked out, you go out of it, dry, dead, musty, Insipid and Sapless, having never in your lives enjoyed the Sweets and delights of clubical humors and recreations, without which life is not worth enjoying, but is a *tabula rasa,* or a *Cart Blanch,* or rather a blotted Scroll or Scutcheon, in which nothing of Sense or Significancy can be read or discerned, like that great lubberly book sent by Micromegas the Siryan Philosopher to ‖ the Accademie des Sçiences,[15] out of which, the aged, purblind and Learned Secretary could not read one single Sillable or Letter, and so, in a christian like manner, I bid you for ever farewell.

Chapter II

The accusation of the Speaker and Chief musician, several Congratulatory Speeches, the Master of Ceremonies confirmed, and some other triffling occurrences.

Socrates the Athenian philosopher, (of whom perhaps, some of my readers may only have heard the bare name, which is enough for their purpose and mine too, since it ranks him in the Class of Clubical worthies) being one day standing, or walking, or Lying or sitting, (it matters not how, or where,) under a plane tree, with the beautiful Phædrus,[1] in a Sultry Summer's day, when the Sun shone bright, and the plains and the mountains and the fountains smoked again, while the Cattle stood under the Shady trees, and hung down their heads and ears, and switched their Sides with their tails to keep off the flies, and the Grasshopers Chirruped and sung, he took that opportunity to tell him a tale, how Grasshopers were once musicians, orators and poets, before the muses were born, and lived without meat and drink (as god knows many poor poets do now at this very day) and for that cause were turned by Jupiter into Grasshoppers, ‖ which is a creature, that like the Camelion, is said to live upon pure air.

It is very probable, that the honorable Mr President Jole, and the Longstanding members of the ancient and honorable Tuesday Club, re-

---

15. A philosopher from the star Sirius is the central character of Voltaire's *Micromégas* (1752), a Gulliverian tale about the relativity of all dimensions and the insignificance of mankind. At the close of the tale Micromégas leaves his teachings, a ponderous volume full of blank pages, to the Académie des Sciences.

1. Plato's friend and the central figure of his famous dialogue *The Phaedrus.*

Rubbers, the lurch, Size Cinque, Seven's the main, mattadores, the Vol, Codille,[12] Race horses, hounds, Spaniels, pointers, laced Jackets, powdered wigs, of Signior Lampuni, Madam Albinoni,[13] opera airs, farces, pantomimes, Routs, Drums, masquerades, Ridottos, Vauxhall and Ranelaw, Garric and his play mates, a few paltry Authors of the same foppish turn with yourselves, and all this by rote? Phogh! ye blind puppies, you are fit for nothing else but to be carried to the kennell and drowned! but no; we will preserve you for this use at least,—to afford matter of fun and Gelastic mirth, for our wise and facetious Clubs.

But I shall leave you here, ye Incorrigible Anticlubarians, ye cutters out and fashioners, of what you are pleased to call decency and decorum; ye danglers after a Sort of fools whom you call people of fashion, ye critics upon letters, words, points, Commas, colons & crotchets,[14] ye Shapers of fantastical plans and patterns for greater fools than yourselves to walk by, ye Eternal trifflers, I shall bid you an eternal Adieu in this very place, and henceforth take no more notice of you than if you were not in being, or never had been hatched, which, had things really turned out so, ‖ would not have been a farthing's matter, either of profit or Loss to the world, and we should never have had occasion to sing the old Song,

Wail a day! and wo be our lot!
For oh! for oh! the hobby horse is forgot.

Let me only conclude with this condolatory exclamation; Oh how I pity you, for your want of the true taste of life; for the want of that blessed humor, which set Democritus a Laughing, and Heraclitus a crying, That quickning Spirit, that divine Automoton, that rational principle, that prompts wise men, to Democritise and Heraclitize, for, ye dry withered Stocks of human Society, Ye Statues and poppets in human form, you can neither laugh nor Cry in earnest, nature has absolutely denied you the power of both, and like a parcel of upstart mushroms, ye come into the

---

12. *Rubbers* is the deciding match (of three) in a card game; *lurch* was originally a 16th-century game resembling backgammon, but here it probably refers to that stage in a card game where one player is enormously ahead of another; *size cinque* is a variant of *sice cinque* ("to set at cinque and sice" is to take great risks; here, to be reckless at playing cards); the *main* is the number called (from five to nine) in a card game by the caster before the dice are thrown (here, seven's the main); *mattadores* is a name applied to certain principal cards in games such as quadrille or ombre; *vol* is presumably a variant of *vole*, "a deal at cards that wins all the tricks"; *codille* is a term used in ombre or quadrille when the game is lost by the challenger.

13. On Lampuni (probably Lampugnani), see p. 57n, above. Tommaso Albinoni (1674–1745) was an Italian violinist and composer from whom Bach borrowed; perhaps Madam Albinoni was a relation of his.

14. A *crotchet* is the symbol for a note half the value of a minim.

certain ceremonies forms and proceedings, nonsensical Stupid, Silly and *Clubical* indeed (which elegant term by the bye you Improperly use as an expression of contempt) while you are too dull, and too Stupidly Solem to understand, compass or comprehend, any thing at all of the true Spirit and Significancy of these gelastic mysteries, are ye not a parcel of pragmatical, foppish, strait laced Coxcombs, who Imagining you have all the Learning and Philosophy yourselves, condem every body else, who do not Imitate and follow your formal Band-box humors and precise decisions, as Simpletons fools, asses and Idiots.

What does your humor consist in, is it any thing in the world but a dull form and precise Starchness, which you contract by an uniform stupid habit, like the Idiot, who continued to tell the Clock by force of custom, even when the Clock was no more, are you any thing else but the ecchoes or repeating watches of the leading fops and finicals of the times? do you || employ your time in any thing, but the dull, tiresome and Impertinent [308] circle of ceremony and Grimace, do you know any thing more than to make a jantee bow, a Scrape with the leg and foot, to pull off your hats to your betters, and strut by your equals without taking notice, to make formal and Starched Speeches, to fringe scollop, shape and proportion your words and actions, like a Taylor, or a pastry Cook at work, who have patterns for every mode and fashion that their Cloth and paste are to be cut and molded into, to learn to come into a room by Geometry, to drink by hydraulics, cough fart, and sneeze by pneumatics, and to pay compliments and make speeches by Gunter's scale,[10] to put on demure faces for a Show of wisdom, while your Sculls are as empty as dried Gourds, and, for all the world, like Retorts set in Snow where they may remain till the Greek Kalends,[11] before any volatile Spirit will Sublime, or produce any thing that one may smell to. Does not your conversation, consist chiefly of trite thread bare observations, or cut & dry compliments coned by heart from your bretheren Coxcombs, or in censuring of triffles that are not worth censuring, or praising greater triffles that never deserved any praise; does the Sublimest pitch of your mirth, go beyond an affected horse laugh, the tribute which you pay to the stupid Sayings of some great person of Quality or fashion; does your Conversation || ever run higher for the most part than the ace of Spades, [309] and the knave of Clubs, can you talk of any thing to the purpose, but the

---

10. A flat rule, two feet long, marked on one side with scales of equal parts and on the other side with scales of the logarithms of those parts; it was named after its inventor, Edmund Gunter (1581–1626), the distinguished English mathematician.

11. The "Greek Kalends" is Hamilton's humorous expression for "never," since the Greeks used no calends in reckoning time.

Benevolent and free: Hypocrisy,
She scorns, and Starch Screwd up formality,
The boast of fools, and haters of mankind.

The true mark of wisdom, is a lively and Constant Chearfulness, it is *Baracco* and *Baralypton*,[6] and such like pestilent Stuff of the Schools, 'tis an affected primness preciseness and Ceremony, the darlings of triffling fops, which renders some pretended philosophers, (not Philosophy) so base and Contemptible. Those that place true || philosophy then in such triffles, know no more concerning her, than what they know by hearsay, her Sole end, is to render a man more happy, in making him more wise, and what can make a man more wise than the knowledge of himself and his own species? what can conduce more to that than his going abroad in the world, and frequenting of Clubs; *Ergo*, Clubs, as they Conduce to make a man more wise, will Surely make him more happy. Q:E:D:

It is said of Demetrius the Grammarian,[7] that one day, popping into the Temple of Delphos, he spied there a Club of philosophers in a very merry vein, Chating, Laughing and cracking of Jokes. Gentlemen said he (putting on a precise look) I am either very much deceived, or finding you in such a giggling disposition, you seem to converse on nothing but triffles, unbecoming wise men and profound Sages, To whom Heracleus the Megarian[8] made answer, It is the business of those, (you meddling fool) who employ their whole time in enquiring, whether the future of the Verb $\beta\alpha\lambda\lambda\omega$ be wrote with a dowble λ and whence the Comparatives $\chi\epsilon\iota\rho\text{o}\nu$ and $\beta\epsilon\lambda\tau\iota\text{o}\nu$[9] are derived, to those I say, it belongs to be dull finical and stupid in Conversation, but philosophers in their Discourse, are accustomed rather to be merry and Sprightly, than precise and formal, this Demetrius was Surely in his time, a thick skulld || morose clubical critic and anticlubarian, and these wise philosophers were Stanch and true Clubists.

But once more, ye perverse anticlubarians, pray who set you up for modelers of manners, and for absolute regulators of Societies? have you any right to Censure or Callumniate any thing but what is in itself really Immoral and wicked? by what authority do you set yourselves up for men of taste and wisdom above all others? what malignant Spirit moves you to call

---

6. These words, nonsense in themselves, are a Scholastic mnemonic for teaching the patterns of syllogisms.

7. Probably Demetrius Ixion (fl. 2d century B.C.), who disputed Aristarchan textual principles and compiled an Atticist lexicon.

8. The Megarians, members of a philosophical school founded by Euclid, or Eucleides (450–380 B.C.), were noted for their vehement disputations. Surely the irony of the "merry and Sprightly" pose of this particular Megarian did not escape Hamilton.

9. The verb *to throw;* the comparatives *worse* and *better.*

recreations? do you never whore? do you never game? do you never swear? do you never lie? do you never flatter? do you never Idle your time away in insipid flat, childish and unprofitable Conversation? || among fops like yourselves? If so, you are rational creatures Indeed, if otherwise, you are as far to seek in point of Rationality, as the rankest Clubist that ever breathed. Wise men indeed! pray who made you wise men? on what ground do you claim that title to yourselves? is it on account of your knowledge? is it on account of your Learning? your knowledge is nothing, when compared to your vanity and Self conceit, and your Learning is Collected from broken Scraps of plays, Romances, Lewd authors,[4] title pages and hearsay, do you pretend to know more than Socrates, who, tho' the wisest of the Athenians,—of the greeks, and consequently of the whole world in his time, yet declared that *he knew nothing,* yet was pronounced a wise man by the Oracle, it will be a lying Oracle Surely that declares you any other than Self conceited fools, since you differ so much from the said Socrates in conceiving a great opinion of your own knowledge, and condemning all Sorts of Clubical and Gelastic pastimes, of which that philosopher was often very fond. You wise men I say again! are you wiser than Pythagoras the Samian Sage, who thinking that the term wise men, or Sages, was a title too assuming for the Connoiseurs and virtuosi of his age, took another in it's place, by which he made it known, that he thought it not altogether so proper to arrogate to himself the actual possession of wisdom, being only an humble Enquirer after it, and therefore, he took to himself the appellation of || philosopher, or lover of Science, or wisdom, a name ever since given, to those that make natural Science and morality their Study. But if you persist still, and say these Low clubical humors are Inconsistent with philosophy, pray what do you take Philosophy to be? do you think it is consistent with Philosophy, to be demure, finical, pragmatical, chagrin, foppish, fantastical and Coxcombish? Such philosophy, I believe, may suit the humor of certain Starched up fellows, such as you; I tell you ye dunces, that there is nothing more gay, more frolicksome and (if I may so speak) more Jocose than Philosophy, and I think, Mr Jonathan Grog's Anonymous poet, gives a Just description of true Philosophy under the name of virtue in the following Lines.[5]

> True virtue seldom haunts the Cynic Cell,
> Morosely wise, she wears eternal Smiles,
> The face of Innocence, is social still,

---

4. Unlettered, or untaught, authors.

5. These lines, part of the lengthy poem "To the Ladies" (signed by "Eumolpus"), appeared in the *Md. Gaz.*, Dec. 24, 1745.

But take me along with you, ye conceited Sophisters, ye paultry reasoners of this world, Pray does not an Emperor eat, drink and sleep as much as a president; does he not stink at times as hideously as a president? does he not prevaricate, swear, cheat and lie as grossly as a president? does he not tyrannize, oppress, fornicate, whore, kill and massacre as much, nay more than any president? and finally, does he not die and rot after and often rot before he dies as well as a president? Is he not subject to weaknesses, passions, foibles and distempers as much as a president? Is he not a Sinfull man as well as a president? may he not be poxed as well as a president? may he not have the plague, the hyppo, the palsey, the Rheumatism, the gout, the fistula in Ano, the Ripples, the whiffles, nay the Itch as well as a president?[3] Nay, may he not play the fool as much as a president? what then is the difference between an Emperor and a president, and in what does it consist, a triffle, believe me, a very triffle, and not worth Contending for.

Again, is not an Empire bounded as well as a Club? has it not a beginning as well as a Club, has it not a rise decay and end as well as a club? are there not wicked men, fools, knaves, pimps, flatterers and Idiots in it as well as in clubs? is it not subject to the vices of Luxury || effeminacy and corruption as well as clubs? what then is the great difference between Empires and Clubs? a triffle, a pitiful triffle, nothing at all, but as a drop to the bucket, or a dust to the balance good friend Sophister.

I question not, but I shall be asked, why I should fall into this odd Rhapsody, this rant, which they'll say looks as if it had been hatched in Bedlam? but let me tell you my grave, Serious friends, (whom I shall take the liberty to call by no worse name than Anticlubarians,) that your ridiculous, Silly, and Idle remarks, uttered with a grave tho unmeaning face, and an Empty head, against the Lawful recreations of Innocent mirth, and Inoffensive drollery, has been the occasion of all this rant, so, if I have Committed any mortal Sin, at your doors I lay it, ye Impertinent, precise, Stiff, Starch'd up, Cynical Logerheads.

I know you'll say, ye good for nothing wiseacres, ye mock critics, and bungling molders of modes and manners, that such Clubical pastime is beneath the dignity of rational creatures, and wise men; but tell me, ye pragmatical dunces, If you call yourselves rational creatures, (which grand epithet by the bye, many foolish puppies such as you, irrationally assume to themselves) are you never Employed about amusements less becoming a rational nature, than these droll, facetious, gelastic and harmless Clubical

---

3. *Hyppo* is an obsolete abbreviation for *hypochondria; ripples* refers to a weakness in the back accompanied with shooting pains; *whiffles* refers to an attack either of bragging or of farting, probably the latter.

Memoirs of the Characters and lives of mighty Emperors, kings, Generals and Commanders of armies.

Will you have the Impudence to say, that Julius Cæsar was a greater man than Nasifer Jole Esqr, because the first was Emperor over great territories, and the latter only President of a little paltry Club; Surely no, consider the Inscription, which Cyrus the great ordered to be put upon his tomb, and you'll find no difference between great Emperors and presidents of Clubs, The Inscription runs thus, *"O Man, whosoever thou art, and from whence soever thou comest, for I know thou wilt come, I am Cyrus, the founder of the great persian Empire, do not envy me this little portion of earth that covers my body,"* and pray does not an emperor take as small a portion of the Earth to lye in, as a president of a Club, notwithstanding, his Spacious palaces.

> *Tu Secanda marmora*
> *Locas sub ipsum funus; et Sepulchri*
> *Immemor Struis domos. Horat:*[1]

Our famous dramatic poet also observes of Alexander the Great, "that he died, was buried, returned to dust, dust is earth, of earth is made Lome, with lome we stop a beer barrell." Pray can any president be reduced lower than this mighty Alexander; and then that Inimitable bard subjoins

> Imperial Cæsar, dead and turn'd to clay,
> Might stop a hole to keep the wind away,
> Oh! that that earth, which kept the world in awe,
> Should patch a wall, t'expell the winter's flaw![2]

Again, will you pretend to assert with a grave composed countenance, (that is, in Sober earnest, without laughing) that the Roman, or the Russian, or the Turkish or the Persian or the Chinese Empires, are greater than this here Club, because they are Empires, & this here Club only a Club? Surely no,— and why pray? Why thus,—Is there any difference but in Size or Magnitude? are not the parts of a mite, as perfect as those of an Elephant, tho smaller? has not a mite its Sinews, nerves, arteries, veins, muscles, brain, heart, Lungs, Stomach, Intestines, genitals, legs, feet, toes, hair, Skin &ct: as well as an Elephant, and wherein do they differ but in magnitude of body? Has not the Tuesday club, it's president, State officers, officers of the Commons, Longstanding members, honorary members, and an Empire or kingdom, it's Emperor or king, prime || ministers, rulers, nobles, commons &ct: and wherein I pray do they differ but in bulk.

---

1. "You gather the marble for cutting / Right at the edge of your grave, and, / Mindless of the tomb, build a palace" (Horace, *Carmina* 2.18.18).
2. *Hamlet*, act 5, sc. 1, lines 208–212, 213–216.

But, to particularize alittle, what did Cæsar Conquer for? a Triffle; What did Brutus kill him for? a triffle; a Shadow, as he owns himself, what was the Grandure of the Roman Empire? a triffle a vapor, an evanescent Smoke; what was Cato's virtue? a morose triffle, what was Lucretias Chastity? a Squeamish triffle; what was Messilene's Lewdness, an Impudent triffle, what Cleopatra's pride and Luxury? a haughty puffd up triffle, I ask you, was not Socrates, tho a poor hard favored fellow, of more weight and Significancy, than all these triffles put in a bundle together; again, I ask you what is the learning and wisdom of philosophers? a triffle; what is the Splendor, equipage and pomp of great princes? a triffle; what are Crowns, triple Crowns, Coronets, mitres, Scepters, pikes, maces, truncheons, Stars and Garters? all transitory, vain, perishing || triffles, bawbles, toys, in which the great babies of this world delight; What is a great man, attended by his Levee of pimps, liars, flatterers, Sycophants, parasites and hungry dependants? a damnd Superlative, unequalled unparalelled triffle, a paragon of triffles, the Sum Substance, essence and cause efficient of all the other evanescent triffles about him, since he contains them all, and they him, since they think by him, act by him, live by him, move by him, breath by him, and by him they have their being, not as rational men, which god made them, before they mangled god's work—but as fools, prigs and Coxcombs, which their foolish patron molded them into, for him they adore, and him they worship, more than they do God, their Creator. What are all human Enquiries, learned discourses, Dissertations, explications, comments, paraphrases and Annotations? Triffles! Triffles! the mockery of Learning, and the very Image of Ignorance. What are all the Charms of the fair Sex, all their allurements, all their Smiles, all their blandishments, all the pleasures in the lump, which they are able to afford? perfect, paultry perishing, good for nothing triffles. To sum up all, what is this Globe and all its Contents, compared to the General System of nature? an atom, a triffle, a thing of nothing; what the General System of Nature compared to endless space? a Spec, a triffle, a grain of dust; and what are all these to the Supreme Essence? more than a triffle, and less than nothing if possible.

Say then, ye wise men of Gotham, ye round heads of this world, with what face of Impudence can you || assert, that this here History of ours, is a triffling History and this here Club a triffling Club, comparatively speaking, since there is not an ace difference between what you call Serious, Solid and rational, and all the triffles that you can ransac and cull out, in this our history, and in the Characters of these the heroes of our Club, which In fact are not more arrant triffles, than these other triffles that are to be met with in the histories of great Empires kingdoms, commonwealths, and in the

The History of the Ancient and honorable Tuesday Club

Book V

From the first grand Anniversary procession, to the foundation of the Eastren Shore Triumvirate.

Chapter I

A Chapter of triffles, and concerning Clubical Critics and Anticlubarians.

Were it not for triffles, says a certain philosopher, (which I know only by hearsay) the world would be but very scurvily entertained, and life would hang on us like a heavy Clog, and our time be a burden, whoever doubts of this doctrine, let him read the works of Solomon, that Royal preacher, whom I look upon to be a philosopher of no mean degree, that knew well the nature of triffles and vanities, among which he Classes all Sublunary enjoyments, after having himself had a taste of all.

Triffles and vanities are but Synonomous terms, and therefore, all that passes in this transitory life, this petty ‖ scantling of time, which we have allotted us to peregrinate thro' this absurd worldly wilderness, and to rant our Comical, or (as some are pleased to call it) tragical parts out upon this terrestrial Stage, is but of a triffling nature, why should any saucy, pert, demure, pricise, finical coxcomb of a Clubical Critic, to say no worse of him, nay, any Chuckleheaded, unexperienced, raw, Saucy Jackanapes pretend to say, that this our famous History, is more triffling than any other history, or this our ancient and honorable Club more triffling in it's constitution, government, model, form and Conversation, than any other Society whatsoever, great or small, be it Empire kingdom, Commonwealth corporation or Club.

A list of the members Regular and Honorary, of the ancient and honorable Tuesday Club, from the 26th of November 1745 to the 26th of May 1747.

Regular members	Honorary members
The Hon: Nasifer Jole Esqr præs:	Mr Abraham Bumper
Sir John Oldcastle knight	Dr Polyhistor
Drawlum Quaint Esqr Speaker	Mr Oldham wisely
Solo Neverout Esqr, Protomusicus	Mr Joshua Fluter
Loquacious Scribble Esqr Secretry	Capt: Huffbluff Surly
Revd Mr Smoothum Sly Mr of Cerem:	Mr Ignotus warble
Jealous Spyplot Esqr	Signr: Lardini
Capt: Seemly Spruce	Revd Mr Broadface Round
Laconic Comas Esqr	Mr Merry Makefun
Capt: Serious Social	Mr Chantum Cheary
Dumpling Gundiguts Esqr	Coll: Courtly Phraze
Slyboots pleasant Esqr	

much astonished, as the mob is at a coronation procession, or any such Idle pageantry, This was called the first grand anniversary procession, and the only one, ever honord, with the presidents presence.

[294] Having come into the great hall, where they were to sit, his honor ordered Sir John Oldcastle to take the Chair while he looked after the Supper and Entertainment, in this his honor showed his great humility and earnest desire and willingness to oblige and serve the Club.

The honorable the Speaker, was desired by the Secretary, in the name of his honor the president and Club, to open this grand Anniversary meeting with a Speech proper upon the occasion, but Mr Speaker, not being in the humor of Speech making, like many other grandees, who are either above doing the duty of their office, or utterly unqualified for it, desired to be excused, and requested the Secretary to officiate for him, which the Secretary did, directing his discourse to Sir John Oldcastle in the Chair, and to the other members of the Club, and then in particular, to the Speaker and Chief musician, congratulating the Club, on it's entry on the third year of it's Institution; to this Speech, the honorable the Speaker returned a short answer of thanks. By these opportunities, of exercising his elocution, the Secretary found means of making himself a considerable person in the Club, and at last, acquired such a knack at making speeches, that in spite of opposition, he worked himself into the office of orator to the Club, and became thereby the author and Instigator of much mischief and discord in the Club, as will be made appear in the course of our History.

[295] The members at this anniversary, were all in high dress, Sir John Oldcastle being dizened up in a fine Spencer wig, and a wastcoat with massy gold lace, and Mr Protomusicus Neverout, having a Jacket dawbed over with Silver lace, an Instance of the Luxury of the times.

After Supper, which was very elegant, and all served up in China, his honor the president resummed his place in the Chair, and Sir John Oldcastle, descended to his proper place at the right hand, putting on a very grim look.

The honorable Mr Speaker made a handsom Encomium on the elegance of the Club Supper and entertainment, and there was performed after Supper a Cantata of music, by a violin, violoncello, and two voices, which met with great approbation, the performers on the Instruments were Merry Makefun, Violino, Signior Lardini Violoncello, and protomusicus and another voice accompanied the Instruments. Thus did this grand Anniversary finish, in mirth & Jolity among the members, and thus I finish this fourth book of our history.

End of the fourth Book.

The first grand anniversary Procession

[292]   At the following Sederunt, april 21, 1747, Capt: Serious Social being deputy president, and Laconic Comas Esqr high Steward, the Club received the following epistle from his honor to the high Steward.

To Laconic Comas Esqr,
high Steward to the Tuesday Club—These.

Mr Comas, April 21, 1747

    I Just received yours, and some days ago, on a considerable appearance of ammendment, I flattered my self with hopes of being at your Club this evening, but my obstinate gout has returned again, and I now, in as great pain as ever; That I am sorry to acquaint you and the other members of the Society, that I cannot Join with you in company this night, so appoint Capt: Social to take the Chair, in my room, or in his absence, to make choice of any other member, by majority of voices. I should always be very glad to see you, and am sorry for your Indisposition, which you say has prevented it, please communicate the above Contents to the Club, to whom I give my Service, in which you'll oblige Sir,

Your Humble Servant
Nasifer Jole.

[293]   As the Anniversary of the Clubs Institution, happened upon thursday the 14th day of may next ensuing, the Club adjourn'd it self to that Day, no an- || niversary committee being appointed, but, the honorable the president, whose privilege and turn it was to serve on that day, thought fit to adjourn farther 'till Tuesday the 26th of may, when his honor said, probably Green peas and Gooseberries would be in Season, which would be a great addition to the Anniversary Supper; It was accordingly celebrated on that day, being Sederunt 58th, with abundance of pomp and Solemnity, the Regular members, and four of the Honorary members, vizt: the Revd Messrs Broadface Round, and Lardini, Mr Merry Makefun and Capt: Huffbluff Surly, waited upon his honor the president, at his own house, ornamented with their badges and Ribbans, and went with his honor in Solemn procession, marching two and two, his honor and Sir John Oldcastle leading up the Van, and Mr Protomusicus Neverout, and Secretary Scribble, closing the rear, to the house of the honorable Mr Speaker Quaint, where the Anniversary feast was kept, his honor and his longstanding members, thus marching along, Received a very Low bow from the Great Collonel Bumbasto, then accidentally passing by, which they returned in good order, keeping their Ranks, they were Sufficiently stared at, as they passed, by persons of all Ranks and degrees, who seemed to be as

The custom of Epistolary writing Introduced by his honor, soon began to spread and take among the long-standing members, and Mr Speaker Quaint as a State officer, was the first Longstanding member, after his honor, that put it in practice, the Club receiving a polite letter of apology from that State officer for nonattendance, at Sederunt 54th March 10th 1746/7, Dumpling Gundiguts Esqr, being high Steward, which letter to the great dammage of posterity is irrecoverably lost.

At Sederunt 55th March 24th, 1746/7, Mr Secretary Scribble being high steward, Mr Laconic Comas, a worthy Longstanding member, who had been absent from the Club several months, upon a voyage to England, appeared in Club, and was Joyfully received and Saluted by all the Longstanding members, and, the honorable the Speaker being absent, the Secretary was ordered to congratulate him upon this occasion, which he did with approbation, he also congratulated, the Reverend Mr || Broadface Round, an honorary member, upon his appearance in Club, after a long absence, but notwithstanding the said Speeches of congratulation, the Club saved to themselves a Speech from the honorable Mr Speaker Quaint upon this occasion, which Speech by the bye was never yet delivered.

At the following Sederunt, which was April 7th 1747, Jealous Spyplot Esqr, being deputy president and the honorable Mr Speaker Quaint high Steward, Mr Chantum Cheary of Philadelphia, and Mr Merry Makefun of Oxford were made honorary members, the latter of which Gentlemen, makes no small figure in this history, at the same Sederunt, a letter from his honor the president to the high Steward, was read in Club as follows.

To Drawlum Quaint Esqr,
High Steward and Speaker of the Tuesday Club, These.

Sir,   April the 7th 1747

 I am very ill in bed with the gout [which^(a)] prevents my being at the Club this night, for which am very sorry, so name Mr Spyplot to take my Seat in the Chair, and on his absence or refusal, then to chuse any other Gentleman by majority of voices, pray, my Service to all the Gentlemen, and am Sir,

             Your Humble Servant
             Nasifer Jole.

P:S: I would have been more particular in writing had I not been very ill.
             N:J:

(a) This word [which] not in the original letter, but subjoined by the Secretary to compleat the Sense.

To the Revd: Mr Smoothum Sly,
high Steward of The Tuesday Club, These.

Sir, Febr: 24th 1746/7
I Just now received your message, per the Negro Man, and, in answer to it's contents, as I cannot be at the Club this night, have wrote to Mr Secretary Scribble, To signify the same to you and the other Gentlemen at meeting of the Club, and am, Sir,

Your humble Servant
Nasifer Jole.

[289] After reading these Club letters, the Secretary, according to his honor's desire, made a congratulatory Speech to the Revd: Signior Lardini, on his appearance in Club, Mr Speaker Quaint being absent.

The Stile of these letters is so peculiarly neat and elegant, that we cannot ommit transcribing in this history all letters from his honor, that are now upon record relating to the Club, since the ommission of this would be an Irreparable loss to posterity, who must certainly profit, by this patteren of stile and politeness. The terms in these letters—*have appointed,* for I have appointed,—*as have heard,* for, as I have heard—*per the negro man,* for by the negroe man, show plainly that Mr Jole had studied the mercantile Stile, and made himself perfect in that elegant and ornate manner of writing.

We find now how his honor established the title of high Steward in this ancient and honorable Club, a title which remained ever afterwards, and Surely, his honor, as president and Sovereign of the Club, had, located in himself, a power to create as many new titles as he pleased, and bestow them on his Subjects the longstanding members, for the same Reason as king James I. that politic prince so deeply versed in King-craft, had an inherent power of creating knights Baronets, an Inferior Class of nobility, or rather a rank, which makes a cement, or fills up a gap, between the lowest of the nobility and highest of the Gentry, tho' his honor had a
[290] different motive for acting thus, than that ‖ prince, his honor's motive being a generous ambition for Clubical power and grandure; whereas that Shitten Monarch's motive was sordid avarice, and a desire to fill his coffers, and support his extravagance, by means of the fees, which certain Rich fools gave him for these caps and feathers, and, as his honor the president's motive was more noble and heroic, so the thing answered the same good purpose, as the other device did, the title of high Steward, being as it were a cement between the State officers, or the nobility, and the officers of the commons, or gentry of this ancient & honorable Club.

chew, and accordingly we find the humor of Epistolary writing take place among the members of the Club, it is ‖ uncertain who first began this epistolary correspondence, the dispute lies between his honor the president, and the worshipful Sir John Oldcastle, some giving the merit of the Invention to the first, and some to the Latter, it is certain that Sir John wrote a letter of excuse to the Club, for his not attending it at Sederunt 44th, Septr 30, 1746, Mr Speaker Quaint being Steward, and another, in answer to one of Mr Secretary Scribble, at Sederunt 46th octor: 28, the said Secretary being Steward, on which Mr Speaker Quaint made some remarks, but, as neither these letters, nor the remarks are recorded in the Club-book, and his honor's letters, wrote soon after, are all fairly registered, we cannot help giving his honor the preference to Sir John Oldcastle, as to this Ingenious Invention.

The first essay of this kind from his honor, was at Sederunt 53 February 24th 1746/7, Dumpling Gundiguts Esqr, being deputy president, and Smoothum Sly Esqr high Steward, (the first who bore that title) when a letter directed to the Secretary, from his honor, and another to Mr Sly giving him the title of high Steward, were produced and read in Club.

To Loquacious Scribble Esqr,
Secretary to the Tuesday Club, These,

To be opened, and read to the Gentlemen when they are all met.

Gentlemen,

As I cannot be at the Club this night, have appointed Mr Spyplot to take my place in the Chair, ‖ not doubting but my choice will be agreeable to you all, and as I understand some of the members, will not be able to come, it's probable you'll postpone the resolves of the last Club to our next meeting, and if the Reverend Signr: Lardini, one of our worthy honorary members, be with you, as have heard he will, Mr Speaker being absent, must desire the favour of Mr Secretary to make my compliments of congratulation on his appearance in Club, after so long an absence—I wish you very merry, and hope you'll meet with nothing to obstruct it, I respectfully Salute you, and am Gentlemen,

Your most humble Servant
Nasifer Jole.

P:S: I understand that Mr Spyplot is not in town, so, if he does not come in time, have appointed Mr Gundiguts to take the Chair in his room.

The Letter to the High Steward was as follows.

ard, the honorable the speaker appeared in the Club very late (having been detained by some matters of Gallantry) with his badges of office, for the first time, (and Indeed for the last time, for he never once wore them afterwards,) vizt: a long flowing black Gown and a band, but we do not find, that these right reverend ensigns, or Signatures of gravity and Learning, in the least brightened up the Genius of this Club orator, for he made no speeches at this Sederunt, tho' they added somewhat to the awfulness and Solemnity of his person and presence.

It was agreed in Club, at this same Sederunt, that his honor the president should have the privilege of drinking the first toast after supper, and it was observed, that the happy fair one, whom his honor chose for his toast, (for he constantly kept to one) had the good luck soon after, to be provided in a husband, which made his honor so famous among the Girls, that they petitioned him for the precedence, as we shall relate in it's proper place, in the course of this history.

Chapter VIII

The laudable custom of epistolary writing Introduced into the Club, the title of high Steward, and the first grand Anniversary procession.

Human wit (if I may be allowed the expression,) is an active and restless principle, it can never be kept quiet or still, but will always be nibbling, if any of my readers object to this proposition and these terms of art, in stiling wit a principle, I shall only tell them, that they must even take the proposition and terms as they stand; I never having had leisure enough to study Logic or Metaphysics; but as I endeavor, never to use reflections foreign to my purpose, so, I think I have brought in this short apothegm, much *a propos,* in this particular part of the history, for we now find the epidemical distemper of Speech making and declaiming, thrust out of doors by the members, and the whole Quantum left of that *Cacoethes*[1] lodged in the honorable the speaker, who at times was very sparing of it, and dealt it out in small parcells to the members as occasion served. What then must take place of this declaiming humor, now ceased among the members of this ancient and honorable Club? for, it cannot be supposed, that their wit can lie fallow or Idle, no, it must have something to nibble at, or a crust to

---

1. Evil habit.

the Secretary had no hand in proposing this entry, and therefore clears himself of all allegations of political designs, which may hereafter be brought against him, by any wrangling or dangling members whatsoever."

The reason of putting in this *Nota bene* in the record was this, that the Secretary intended thereby to clear himself of all blame that might be thrown upon him by posterity, relating to this matter in particular, of creating another Great officer in the Club, as he had, at a former Sederunt been severely taken to task, by Mr Serjeant Spyplot, for attempting to make a state Club of this ancient and honorable Society, by promoting and encouraging the creation of the Speaker, who || at Sederunt 49th Decemb: 9th [284] 1746, Jealous Spyplot Esqr, being steward, was exalted to the dignity of a state officer, and took the left hand of the Chair, the Champion and he, being henceforth stiled, his honor the president's council of state. But, at this Sederunt, the Secretary was absent, for the first time since the Institution of the Club, Therefore, whatever reasons Mr Serjeant Spyplot had for blaming the Secretary, for procuring the creation of this Club officer, he could have not the least color to accuse him of causing that gentleman to be made an officer of state, Mr Neverout, had the title of *Protomusicus,* or *Musico-con voce* given him, and at Sederunt 60 June 23d 1747, Slyboots Pleasant Esqr, being high Steward, (for then that pompous title was Introduced) had this privilege granted him, which is the only one he ever had, or is ever likely to have as Musician, of ordering any other member of the Club, to sing, after he had sung himself.

At Sederunt 49th Decemb: 9th 1746, Jealous Spyplot Esqr, being Steward, the following remarkable entry is found upon the Club book, made by Mr Smoothum Sly deputy Secretary.

"Upon reading the entry of last meeting, appointing Mr Neverout to sing his vote, Mr Speaker Quaint moved, that the said Mr Neverout, chief musician, should not only sing his Votes, but likewise every motion he should make in the Society, which was rejected, as the Chief musician declined it."

This was a more politic motion, than perhaps the Club apprehended at the time of making it, since it || had a tendency, if the order had taken place, [285] to restrain the Chief musician from making many speeches and motions, for the support of the Liberty and privileges of the Club, for which this Gentleman had always been a strong friend and stickler, till he was taken off, by being made attorney general, and, of consequence, a state officer, this motion came naturally enough from the honorable Speaker, as he was now become a mere creature of the Chair.

At Sederunt 50th January 13th 1746/7, Capt: Serious Social being Stew-

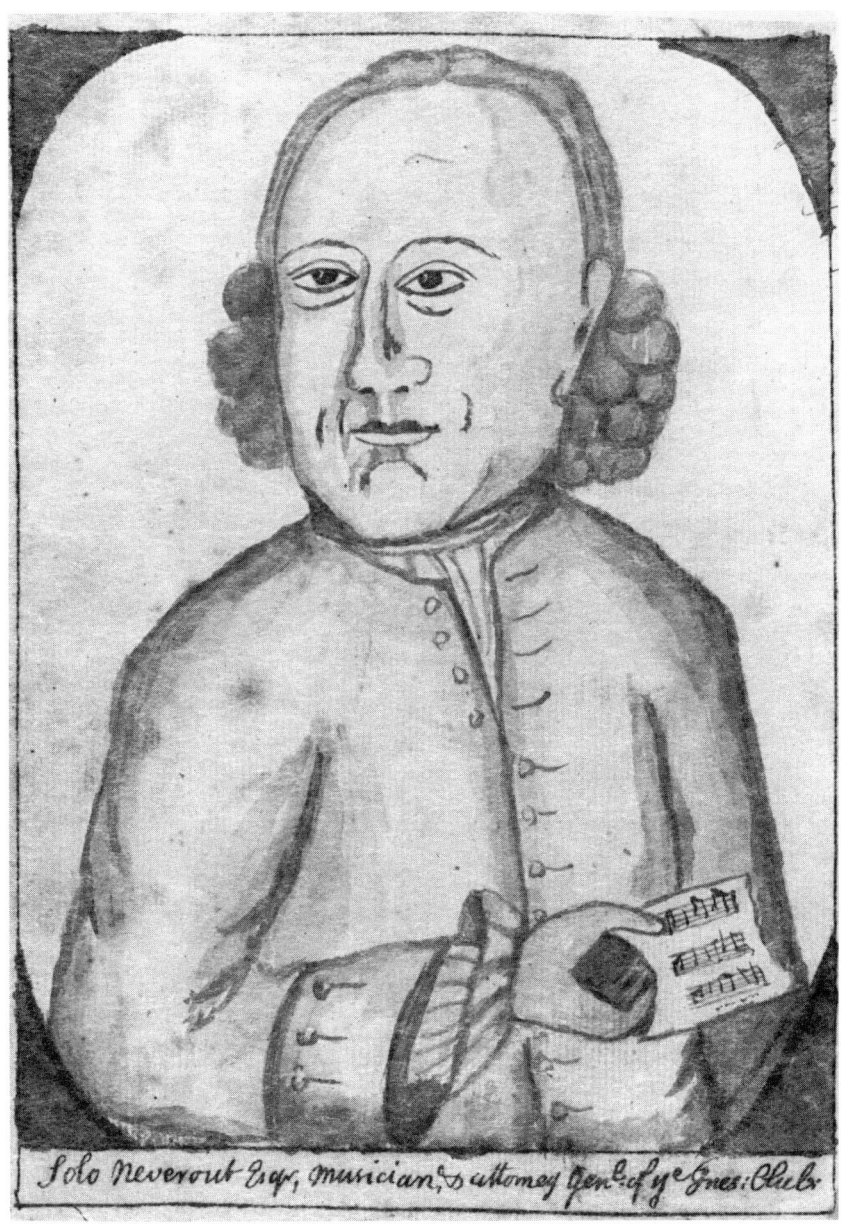

[facing page 283]

> Her Eyes do our hearts so enthrall.
>   But 'tis for her pelf,
>   And not for herself,
> 'Tis artifice, artifice all, all, all,
> 'Tis artifice, artifice all.
>
> The maidens are coy,
>   They'll pish, and they'll fie
> And swear if you're rude they will bawl,
>   But they whisper so low,
>   By which you may know
> 'Tis artifice, artifice all, all, all,
> 'Tis artifice, artifice all.
>
> The wives they will cry
>   My dear, if you die,
> To marry again, I ne'er shall,
>   But less than a year
>   Will make it appear,
> 'Tis artifice, artifice all, all, all,
> 'Tis artifice, artifice all.
>
> In matters of State
>   And party debate
> For Church and for Justice they'll bawl,
>   But if you'll attend,
>   You'll find in the end
> 'Tis artifice, artifice all, all, all,
> Tis artifice, artifice all.

This song Mr Neverout performed, so much to the satisfaction of the Club, that they determined according to the following entry, which appears upon record.

"Solo Neverout Esqr: on account of his uncommon talent at Singing, is, by unanimous consent, appointed Chief Musician *con voce* of the Club, and, that, as often as he votes, he is to sing it in a musical manner, else his vote to go for nothing.

N:B: That as Mr Neverout's qualifications in Instrumental music are unknown, to the Club, he is not to perform upon any instrument, but his modulation and melody is to be confined to the voice only, and also, that this entry is not a state Entry, any objections to be brought against it by members now absent, to the contrary notwithstanding, and, finally, that

ject the records do not mention or explain, however, the result was, that the Speaker and Secretary both resigned their places, and refused to officiate, the Speaker's reason for resigning, is thought to have been some opposition from the Chair, to his being addressed by the speaking member, the Secretarie's reason stands upon record, vizt: that he was accused of some artful practises against the dignity of the Chair, and tho' this accusation might have been grounded upon plausible circumstances, considering the Character of that Sly officer, yet he took it so much in Snuff, that he contemptously threw down his office, and delivered up the book of Records to the Club, but was so far dissappointed in this his rash procedure, that the honorable the Chair took no manner of notice, nor seemed to be in the least moved about the matter.

[281] At the following Sederunt however, which was || the 47, on the 11th of November, 1746, Solo Neverout Esqr being Steward, both these officers got into so good a humor, that they again resumed their proper offices, this Strange Change in two such resolute officers, could be attributed to no better cause, than this, that his honor and the Club took no manner of notice of their being out of humor.

At Sederunt 48 Novr: 25th, 1746, Slyboots Pleasant Esqr, being Steward, Mr Ignotus Warble, an honorary member appeared in the Club, who having been Summoned by the last anniversary committee, to appear, to answer to some charges, that were to be urged against him, had refused to obey that Summons, therefore was liable to a Severe censure, but his trial was put off, on account of the absence of Mr Speaker Quaint, and it happened luckily for that Delinquent, that it never afterwards came on, by which means, he escaped a condign punishment, which probably might have been Inflicted upon him.

At the same Sederunt, Solo Neverout Esqr, being gifted with an excellent musical voice, entertained the Club with a Song, which, as it became the Subject of frequent contests and trials of Skill, between his honor the president and him, which should sing it most musically, and apply the best air to the words, we shall here give a transcript of it.

Club Song, sung by Mr Neverout[1]

When Cloe we ply,
We swear we shall die,

---

1. "When Chloe we ply" appears in Ramsay's *Tea-table Miscellany* (II, 63–64) almost exactly as Hamilton has it. It also appears in *Calliope, or English Harmony* and in Watts, *Musical Miscellany*, III, 81.

the Club, upon Sederunt 45 octor: 14th 1746, desired to be excused from the same, upon account of multiplicity of business, and after a formal apology, he was accordingly excused, till another opportunity.

Upon which, the Secretary, in the place of Mr Quaint, delivered an extempore speech, which chiefly consisted in Encomiums upon Mr Quaint as a Speaker, of which Speech the Club approved, and he had the thanks of the same delivered from the mouth of Mr Quaint.

Hereupon, Drawlum Quaint Esqr, In consideration of his uncommon Talent at Speech making, was unanimously constituted and appointed, honorable Speaker of the Club, by his honor the president; this piece of mischief, the Secretary was principally concerned in, and we shall always find this petty officer, in the sequel of this history busying himself in mischief, and contriving schemes and projects, to set his honor the president and his Longstanding members together by the ears. He was a cunning, Sly and conceal'd operator, for advancing the Authority of the Chair, and, tho the honorable the president, always took him for an enimy to, and an underminer of his prerogative and privileges, yet, it will appear in the course of this history, that all his actions, designs and plots (under a mistaken policy to advance himself) had a tendency to establish a tyrannical power in the Club.

At Sederunt 46, octor 28, 1746, Mr Secretary Scribble, being Steward, the following Laws were passed.

Law XXXI. That no disputes relating to the business of the Club, shall be entered upon when strangers are Present.

Law XXXII. That the honorable Speaker of the Club shall be addressed, when any Speech is made in Club, and that it shall be a part of his office, to sum up the argument, to the honorable Chair, when the member has done speaking.

By this last law we see, how considerable a person the Speaker is made in Club, and it may seem to some, that this privilege granted him, of being addressed by || the speaking member, Jars, or Interferes with the privilege 5to of his honor the president, where, it is expressly said, that when any motion is made, "the president is to be first addressed by the moving member, giving him his proper title," and this very thing, occasioned some dispute, in the trial of Mr Serjeant Spyplot, which shall be related in it's place, but there is really no such privilege given to the Speaker, great as it seems to be, for the Law does not say, that he shall be first addressed, but only addressed, which supposes still that his honor the president is first addressed by the Speaking member, who, after that necessary ceremony, directs the rest of his discourse and argument to the Speaker.

Some warm disputes happened at this Sederunt, but, upon what Sub-

[277] uneasy Sensation in the Suffering persons, much like that occa- ‖ sioned by the application of causticks in Surgery, and therefore they have the same reason to call out, no more of this, we feel the Smart of it too much already; One would think, that the ancient and honorable Tuesday Club, had already Sufficiently smarted, by the late proceedings of the chair, in creating two great officers, and had very good reason to exclaim, No more officers, good Mr President; but not a word of complaint on the matter, they were too much benumned and stupified, to feel the twinge that was given them, and Instead of exerting themselves to put a Stop to these proceedings, they allowed another state officer, and another officer of the Commons to be palmed upon them, so that it was likely that in a short time, the whole club would become State officers, and officers of the commons, and so all the Crew, being Quarterdeck men, as the Saying is, there would be no hands left to heave out the long boat, and therefore, the Ship of this Clubical common wealth, must of Consequence soon founder, or become a wreck, none exclaimed so much against these proceedings in Club, as Mr Serjeant Spyplot, who foresaw all the mischiefs and Inconveniencies that threatned the Club, from this wrong headed policy, but his wise councels and wholesome advice, were not regarded, till it was too late.

At Sederunt 45th October 14th 1746, The honorable the President being Steward, the payment into the box was again put off till next meeting, as it had been at the preceeding Sederunt, in the Stewardship of Drawlum Quaint Esqr, under pretence of there not being a full meeting of the [278] members, but the truth was, ‖ that the members were tired of this tax, when they found that his honor the president held fast whatever he got, and never would suffer a farthing of this fund to be applied, but for such uses, as he only, in his presidential wisdom thought proper, and, accordingly, we find, for six Sederunts following, this payment was still shifted off, when, at Sederunt 52d febry 10th 1746/7, Capt: Spruce being Steward, we find on the book of records this remarkable Entry, vizt:

"Some warm disputes arose in Club, concerning the box, which ended in this general Result of the members of the Club, (except his honor the president, who refused his assent) that the payment into the box, ought to be voluntary, and at the pleasure of each member, and not by Constraint, or at appointed times, and also, that no more disputes concerning the box, should be brought upon the Carpet."

This bold Stroke of the long standing members, gave the first mortal blow to the box, and we shall soon find this bone of contention, Intirely abolished and swallowed up, in the voracious maw of a philadelphian Lottery.

Drawlum Quaint Esqr, having been appointed to deliver a discourse to

of a committee held at the Secretarie's house, upon monday the 21st Instant, read the proceedings of the said Committee to his honor the president & Club, which were declared void, because the committee was not appointed by his honor the president.

What was the business before this Committee cannot now certainly be known, because their proceedings were cancelled, but it is conjectured, that there was therein a plan or method, proposed to the Club, for Celebrating rejoicings, on account of some news lately arived, of the pretender's being defeated and taken, and the rebel army routed, by the king's troops, concerning which very matter, his honor the president, tho' a loyal and true blue whig, differed outragiously with the Secretary, in which Scuffle, the Secretary (as his honor alledged) robbed his honor of some political Club letters, and papers, snatching them away by force. In this dispute his honor opposed with all his might || the design of the Club's rejoicing on that [276] occasion, which gave the Club so violent a Shoke, as had like to have ended in it's dissolution, from this transaction we may observe to what an enormous height the presidential power had already grown in this here Club; since the members, who before had a full power of forming themselves Into Committees, now saw themselves utterly divested of that power, and rendered Incapable to proceed in that manner, without his honor's express consent and appointment.

There was a meeting appointed to be held at the Steward's (Capt: Social) house, upon Saturday the 26th Instant, but the Squabble between his honor and the Secretary prevented it. Nothing material happened after this, till Sederunt 45th, except a neglect of the then members of paying their quarterly dues into the box, but these transactions are reserved for the following Chapter.

Chapter VII

The Creation of the Speaker of the Club, & his privileges, and also of the Chief musician and his privileges.

No more blue Stone good Doctor, is an old proverb, of which, I was never able to learn the first broacher, but waving such enquiries, my design in Introducing it here, is only for the Sake of the application, when any proceeding or piece of conduct, has been found hurtful to those who have practised it, or to those upon whom it has been practised, there follows an

gloom of his warlike countenance, some Satisfaction and Joy, at this unlooked for promotion, but pretended at the same time not to be satisfied, and refused to take his place, unless ushered in a proper manner, upon this, his honor Immediatly nominated and Created the Reverd: Mr Smoothum Sly, Master of Ceremonies, or Sir Clement Cotterell, to the ancient and honorable Tuesday Club, who Instantly rose from his Seat, || took the Worshipful Sir John Oldcastle by the right hand, and placed him upon the right of the presidential Chair, The worshipful the knight, was stiled a state officer, and had afterwards, at Sederunt 39th July 22d 1746, Capt: Serious Social being Steward, the privilege of dispensing with the Law of one dish, as well as his honor the president, this was Indeed a mere farcical privilege, for this law was long agoe become a mock law, and disregarded by all the members; The Master of Ceremonies was stiled chief officer of the commons, and made the honors of the Club to strangers, ornamented his honor the president with his proper badges of State, and confirmed new members; Thus did this Club, Inconsideratly permit the raising of great officers among themselves, and putting them above law, and hereby were Instrumental in establishing an Intollerable Tyranny over the long standing members, by strengthning the already overgrown power of the Chair, which occasioned a deal of trowble and perplexity, to this here ancient and honorable Club, as was wisely forseen and foretold by Jealous Spyplot Esqr, a Sagacious Oldstanding member, who always opposed these mad proceedings, and seldom Judged wrong in these cases.

[274]

His honor's Speech from the Chair, so far excelled all others, that, at the same Sederunt, a resolve of the Club was made, that there should be no more Set Speeches delivered in Club, unless upon the nights of quarterly payment into the box, and upon the Anniversary of the Club's Institution, and, the first article of this order was punctually observed, for, as there were no more quarterly payments into the box, which soon after this Intirely || dropt, so, were there no more set speeches made by the members, unless, upon the anniversary days of the Club, which were pronounced generally by the Speaker or Secretary, and latterly by the officer stiled the Orator.

[275]

Drawlum Quaint Esqr, however was appointed to deliver a Speech on the 14th day of October next, being the day of Quarterly payments into the box, we shall soon see how punctually this payment was made, and that Speech delivered, before this Sederunt broke up, the Joy of the Club appeared to rise to an excess, by their dancing in a ring round the Club table, like a parcell of Ancient Bacchinalians, Captn Serious Social, leading up the dance to an old Scots Song.

At Sederunt 39th July 22d Drawlum Quaint Esqr, appointed Chairman

Sir John Oldcastle Knight, Champion of the Tuesd: Club

[facing page 265]

members, viz: the Rev: Mr Smoothum Sly, whom he described as a person born far North, very much skilled in the art of palaber, smooth coaxing and flattering Speeches, but this Severity of his honor, was so far from Injuring that member, that it rather, in his honor's opinion, recommended him to a dignified office in the Club, which was accordingly Conferr'd upon him at that very Sederunt, hence we may observe, that when great men condescend so far as to take notice of little men, or to make them the Subject of their discourse, whatever Stile these great men use, pangyrical or Satyrical, it bodes good fortune to the little man, and is a Sure forerunner of their promotion, hence some have affirmed, that these great men are swayd by fear, others by Caprice.

After the delivery of this speech, the Secretary, in the best terms he could, by order of the Club, returned thanks to his honor the president, for his Gracious Speech from the Chair, and his honor, willing to preserve all forms of state, pulling his papers from under the Chair again, where he had deposited them, made a reply to the Club in form, thanking them for their civilities.

The first Symptoms of Joy, that broke out among the members, upon this gracious condecention of his honor, appeared in their Extraordinary liberalities to the box, which looked like the Largesses of a British parliament to the Crown, after a most gracious Speech from the throne, among others, Slyboots pleasant Esqr, contributed one pistole, the || secretary four Shillings and Sixpence, and the Sum now in the box, amounted to five pounds, three Shillings and Sixpence, an Immense Sum, to be collected in so short a space as half a year.

The next thing the Club went upon, was the making of short congratulatory Speeches to one another, in which Drawlum Quaint Esqr, outshone every one else; he, in the most Sublime manner, and with all his natural grace of action, at the command of his honor the President, thanking Slyboots Pleasant Esqr, for his liberality to the Club Box, and Mr Secretary Scribble for his constant attendance on the Club, he having not been absent one Sederunt, since it's first Institution.

At these proceedings Capt: Blunt, seemed to grumble and be uneasy; being, as he said, Justly alarmed, at the growing power of the Chair, on which, his honor the president, having some reason to be afraid of the Influence of this Old Standing member, Saluted him, by the title of knight, and Champion of the Club, under the name of The worshipful *Sir John Oldcastle,* knight of the Ancient and honorable Tuesday Club, and ordained, as a principal privilege of his noble office, that he should sit at the right hand of the Chair; Sir John, could not help showing, thro' the wonted

The hon:ble Mr Presidole delivering a Speech in Club.

[facing page 271]

the papers he put them in order, and looking round him for a little while, he fixed himself in a proper posture in the Chair of State, and, while two of the long standing members, vizt: the Secretary and Mr Neverout, held a candle to him on his right and left, behind the great chair, he, with great Solemnity, and a Clear distinct voice, without much action excepting only alittle nodding of the head, pronounced an elegant oration, of about half an hour in Length, the Subject of which was wisdom; the Stile of this oration was much like that of a Sermon, and some censorious people did not stick to say, that the very marrow and Substance of it, was taken from a Sermon composed by one Doctor South,[1] but this much might be urged in vindication of his honor the president, whom I would be loath to accuse of plagiarism, without better grounds, that it is a very common thing, for Great and Sublime Geniuses to agree in Sentiments, so far, as even to use the same [271] words, when writing or speaking on the same || Subject, and therefore, from this very reasonable Supposition we may conclude, that his honor, and the aforesaid Doctor South, expressed themselves in the same manner on the same Subject, without the least Intercourse, or Communication one with the other, but what gave a Colour for this malicious Insinuation, were some seeming Slips his honor made, in pronouncing of some words used by the said Doctor South, such as *Chous* for *Chaos,* which made some rashly conclude, that his honor the president, did not understand the meaning of these words, but how Silly and groundless is this Insinuation, seeing it has always been customary, for great Geniuses to alter not only the Common Orthography, but also the Common pronounciation of words, Just as they please, which being Imitated by persons of small Genius, has for ever been the principal cause of the Instability and fluctuation of our Language, and pray, where is the great occasion to make a pother about *Chous* for *Chaos,* when it is known, that our politest people, and persons of the first fashion and Quality and taste, use, Instead of *Anatomy, Otomy,* for *Encyclopædia, In sickly pay day,* for *positive pos,* for *paltry paw,* for *Reputation Rep',* for *Incognito Incog',* for *plenipotentiary plenipo,* for *taste Vertu* (hence vertuoso for a man of taste) and many other Instances might be given of the caprice of great and distinguished wits, in the new modeling of old words, that are [272] too hard to be pron- || ounced, by most of the present lisping and toothless Generation.

It was remarked, that his honor the president, in this Celebrated Speech, was remarkably Severe and Satirical upon one of the old Standing

---

1. Hamilton is alluding to "For the Wisdom of This World, Is Foolishness with God" (1 Cor. 3:19), sermon 9 in Robert South's *Twelve Sermons Preached upon Several Occasions* (London, 1692).

person of great Qualifications that way, to enslave them more and more; for, as he had formerly, by his natural Civility, Complaisance and Innate politeness, Introduced Luxury in eating, drinking and dress into the Club, so now by his Silver tongued eloquence, he lulled the members into such an Insensibility, that like as if they had been all asleep, they permitted him, without the least resistance, to create two great and powerful officers in one night, vizt: a knight or Champion of the Club, and a Master of Ceremonies, by the first promotion, the Club had a Standing army established upon them, and besides, lost a powerful || advocate for their liberty and a strong rival to the Chair, by the other, the Chair procured an assiduous flatterer, who not only vindicated, but even praised and extolled every act and proceeding, flowing from that fountain of power, tho never so arbitrary and oppressive, and thus was the balance of power almost unhinged, in this here ancient and honorable Club by means of a fine fustian Speech from the Chair, tho' it is suspected by some, that the force of Eloquence was not Solely Concerned in this Infatuation, but that certain Corrupt practices were used to silence some clamorous members, which were charged to the treasury in an article of Secret Services, and that hush money had been set to work at this time is almost Certain, for upon rendering an account of the treasury to the Club, the Sum in the box, fell short one Shilling and Sixpence; and his honor as box keeper, thought fit to throw the blame on Dumpling Gundiguts Esqr, with whom the box had been left for some days, tho' the Club thought, and with some reason, that the said Gundiguts was the person bribed by his honor, as he was the person of the most corrupt principles in the Club. [269]

It has been already mentioned, how at Sederunt 34 The anniversary Committee, addressed his honor the president, that he would Graciously be pleased to deliver a discourse from the Chair, upon what Subject his honor pleased, and with this request, his honor wisely forseeing what advantages would thence accrue to the Chair, wisely complied.

And accordingly, at Sederunt 38, July the 8, 1746, Jealous Spyplot Esqr being Steward, his honor in a high presidential dress, ascended the Chair, and it being very || warm weather, he first of all pulled off a voluminous fair wig, which covered two thirds of his face, and laying it Carefully, together with his hat and gloves under the Seat of the Chair, he drew from his pocket, a fair, clean, white Linnen night cap, which with profound gravity, he drew over his pericranium and ears, then pulling out a large Roll of paper in folio, and a pair of temple Spectacles, he wiped the latter with a fair Cambric handkerchef, first breathing on the Glasses to clean them, and then he saddled his nose with that catoptrical machine, and turning over [270]

these declamators, has not broke out with any violence in the Club, except a small Spark, excited on occasion of that political Speech made by the Reverend Mr Sly, which was Blown up alittle by the Breath of Mr Councellor Quaint, ‖ but the breath of Mr Quaint, not being vigorous enough to kindle it into a blaze, it soon went out, being smothered by the Submission and complaisance of the long-standing members. The true reason of the Inoffensiveness of this custome of Speech making, at it's first Introduction Into this ancient and honorable Club, is, it's being destributed into the hands of so many members, for almost the whole Club became orators and declaimers, at that time, and each of them pulling different ways, (as every member Intended to advance himself in particular) there arose a sort of Renitency in the body politic, which preserved the constitution from falling to pieces, and from receiving any violent Shocks, as the Springs weights and balances do in a piece of Clock work, hence I observe, with what propriety and fitness, some learned writers have compared forms of civil government to pieces of clock work, there being always in these, even when most despotic and arbitrary, some kind of renitency and Counterpulling, between the Governing and the governed; but after this general humor of Speech making droped or ceased in this ancient and honorable Club, which it soon did, the practice became more confined, and therefore more dangerous to the Clubical constitution, an officer being appointed, first, under the name of Speaker, who quickly rendered himself a person of Influence and Importance in the Club, and after that, a politic, Sly, designing, ambitious, and mischief making member of the Club, was promoted to that office, and was called Orator, who proved the exciter of much wrangling, noise, disturbance, hubbub and hurly burly in this here Club, as shall be shown in the Sequel. ‖ If then it is clear, that speech making and declaiming is a dangerous thing in Clubs, when exercised by one, two or more of the members of common rank or degree, in these Clubs, how much more dangerous must it be, when practised by an officer, or officers of rank power and Influence, and what pen can describe, or tongue express, the mighty mischiefs it is capable of effecting, when exercised by the chief officer, or president himself.

Yet notwithstanding that the Longstanding members of this ancient and honorable Club, were wise enough to know and forsee, the mischiefs necessarily arising from Introducing these oratorial perorations in the Club, and had Indeed once found the Smart of it, yet O unaccountable Infatuation, or rather Stupidity! they Inconsideratly addressed the honorable the president himself, requesting him to assume the office of an Orator, by which they rashly put it in the power of the honorable Nasifer Jole Esqr, a

Law XXIX. That the proceedings of the former Sederunt shall be read at every Subsequent meeting.

Law XXX. That the Steward for the time being shall wear the Badge of the Club.

At this Sederunt also, Jealous spyplot Esqr, delivered a discourse upon trade and traffic, which was approved of.

At Sederunt 37th June 23d 1746, Solo Neverout Esqr being Steward, Capt: Serious Social, delivered an Elegant discourse to the Club upon prudence, in which he gave a fine description of the irascible and Concupiscible passions, incident to human nature, which was the more applauded, in so far, as it was known to every one, that this gentleman never was much addicted to speech making.

Chapter VI

The Creation of Sir John Oldcastle knight of the Club, and the privileges thereunto annexed, & the appointment of the master of Ceremonies.

It has been observed by wise and Cunning politicians || that orators [266] and speech makers are a very dangerous Sort of people in a commonwealth, since being great masters of the pathos, they can work upon the passions of the Mobile, and set them into violent Commotions; the truth of this observation is very much confirmed by a Story of Demosthenes, a Celebrated Athenian Orator, who being told that a certain man, one of his hearers, at a public oration which he delivered, being asked what he thought of the orator, protested on his conscience, that he thought him a most dangerous pestilent fellow, to the Athenian State, and as such, ought to be banished the Republic. To which the Sagacious orator replied, without the least chagrin; that he was very glad to find one man at least in Athens at that time o' day, who had a true and Just notion, of the ancient Athenian Liberty.

If then it be allowed, that these orators and Speech makers, are a dangerous crew in a common wealth or State, it must follow of consequence, that they are alike dangerous in Clubs, seeing they have the same opportunity of practising upon the passions of the members, and setting the whole Society in an uproar. We have seen several of the Longstanding members of this ancient and honorable Club, exercising the office of orators and Speech makers, but indeed, hitherto, the mischief flowing from

rather artful terms, for want of something else to say; Again, as nature now a days, does not distinguish our nobility and Gentry, from the common Rascallion herd of men, by any remarkable perfection of mind body or limbs, they being now Generally an Ignorant, degenerate, puny, pigmy race, it is absolutely necessary, that these Illustrious pigmies, Skeletons and dwarfs, should have their arms and badges of honor, painted upon their coaches and equipage, that they may be known for what they really are, according to their noble titles, vizt: such a Duke, such a Lord, such a Bishop, such an Earl, such a marquis, such a Baron, such a Baronet, such a Squire, such a Squiret, and such a Squirt, and not || be mistaken for pages, powder monkies, Ghosts or Inhabitants of the Realms of Pluto, or stewd wretches Just come from a fluxing in an hospital.

These badges of distinction are also very Significant and useful in Religious orders, and Communities, as well as in Civil Societies, a Mitre, a crosier, a pair of Lawn Sleeves, a red hat, a broad brimd beaver or Castor with a large twist of black Ribbon called with great propriety a rose, a starched band, a black gown, a white Surplice, a rope, a Cowl, a Cassock, are certain marks and emblems of Sanctity, as they are appropriated to the holy ministers of the Church, and Successors of the apostles thro' out christendom, who seldom possess any thing more than these Symbols, properly apertaining to their holy function and character, to distinguish them from the prophane and profligate Lares,[10] and it is known to all, how much Indebted our grave and deeply learned Judges are, to that particular antic, or rather Comical Dress, which they wear on the bench in Westminster hall, which exhibits a badge or Symbol of their profound knowledge in the Law, one of the most perplexed and Intricate Sciences, that ever yet was hatched, Thanks to the great plenty of Rogues, in all professions we are blest with, by such outward Signatures too a regular Physician, or Learned fellow of the Colledge, may be distinguished from a Quack, the former always appearing in a grave Sable dress, and the latter in a gaudy Suit of Scarlet, or some other || lively and stricking colour, daubed over with lace.

The Ancient and honorable Tuesday Club, in Imitation of these honorable, pious, wise, learned and politic bodies or Societies, thought fit, as we have related, to distinguish themselves from others, by a badge, peculiar to the members of that Club, and to none else.

At Sederunt 35th May 27, 1746, Mr Secretary Scribble being Steward, The following laws were passed.

---

10. In Roman mythology, the Lares were spirits who guarded the dwellings they once inhabited.

Nunc arma Defunctumque bella,
*Clypeum hæc paries habebit,*⁹

and was an expressive history, in hierogliphic, of the warlike exploits of the family to which this ancient and battered Shield belonged, Yet now a days, very few of these ancient gothic heroical badges remain, the old families || being almost all Cut off, by the natural ferocity, and barbarousness of these violent times of heroism; The heralds office, however, discovering that this would turn out to be a profitable trade, as all trades are which flatter human pride and vanity, have fallen upon a way, by the force of fancy and Invention, to bestow promiscously for a fee or reward, these honorable ensigns, whether the persons deserve them or not, hence we find that many taylors, Shoemakers and weavers, who never used any other warlike or missile tools, but a needle, an awl and a Shuttle, (the first of which heroes by his mortal Steel, has destroyed many a backbiter and bloodsucker, and the Second has boldly peirced many a tough hide) have by means of a few pence, procured for their Illustrious families, the ensigns and Shields of bravery and heroism.

[262]

Now, the use of these badges is evident, they being absolutely necessary, to distinguish and render conspicous, certain families and persons, who have no other quality in nature, (except sometimes the pretended, and rarely the real merit of their ancestry) to distinguish or render them conspicuous; the above said merit, by some philosophers, being reckoned of no real value, as being not so easily transferable, as money lands and mannors, and therefore in it self only chimerical, and also, it is well known, that very few families or heads of families, are furnished with these eminent Substantial, and distinguishing badges of honor, which are called by the said Philosophers, magnanimity, Justice, Charity, gratitude, temperance, honesty, Integrity || and many other such like obselete qualities, which qualities with our *people of Quality,* have now become only dictionary words, of no certain Signification, but serve only to enable knaves to gull fools more easily, that is to say, such fools as believe that there is any signification at all in these words, and indeed, if these words were ever in use among persons of the first rank and fashion, they served for nothing more than Sound and expletives of discourse, as Insignificant and unmeaning as oaths among persons of Quality, or fal lal de ral in the Chorus of a Song, but now they seem to be Intirely obselete, and not of any Emolument or advantage to our families of note, tho' a Set of Idle fellows called authors, in their Epistles Dedicatory to Noble patrons, will make use of these very words, and terms of art, or

[263]

---

9. "Now that he is discharged from arms and war, / This wall will bear his shield" (after Horace, *Carmina* 3.26.4).

that were founded about 30 or 40 years agoe, and I know not but may still subsist; His majesties ancient colony of Virginia is stocked with Inhabitants, which Consist of two Classes, the Grandees and the Common people, the first Class are fond of pomp Show and extravagance, and make a Shift to cast a fine dash in dress and equipage, without any certain estates to support it, as for the plebs, we only observe that they are very poor and very miserable, and therefore highly dispised by the Grandees, these Grandees being fond of some particular badge of distinction, Instituted, as I have said, some years agoe, an order of knighthood among themselves, of which, since I have not learnt the true name, I shall venture to call them by that of the Tra- || montane knights, or the knights of the horse Shoe,[6] their badge being a bit of Gold in the form of a horse Shoe, with this Inscription, *Juvat transcendere montes*,[7] for these Cavalier adventurers had exhibited a Specimen of heroism and true Courage, by travelling over the mountains, and having viewed a large tract of a wild uncultivated country, returned home again, all Safe and Sound from this dangerous expedition.

The herald's office shows how fond even families are of badges and marks of distinction, all great families, and even almost all little families, and late upstarts, having some badge or Symbol, which they call their *Coat of arms*, and which they wear upon their furniture coaches and equipage, with which they adorn their houses by way of picture, and which they engrave upon their plate, tho' this custom is originally gothic, and took its rise first in the days of Chivalry, when every Soldier in the field of battle, wore a Mark to distinguish him, least, his vizor being down, he should be mistaken by a friend for a foe, and afterwards this depicted Shield, like Horaces lyre, was hung up for a badge of honor, so that *mutatis mutandis*[8] it might be said by these Gothic heroes,

---

6. Hamilton is referring to the surveying expedition Gov. Alexander Spotswood of Virginia led to the Blue Ridge Mountains in 1716. The nickname Knights of the Golden Horseshoe stems from Spotswood's having given each man in the company a small golden horseshoe as a souvenir. See Edward P. Alexander, "An Indian Vocabulary from Fort Christanna, 1716," *VMHB*, LXXIX (1971), 303–313, and his edition of *The Journal of John Fontaine: An Irish Huguenot Son in Spain and Virginia, 1710–1719* (Williamsburg, Va., 1972), 13–19, 101–109. In both works, Alexander states that the romanticization of the Spotswood expedition began in 1845 with William Alexander Caruthers's *The Knights of the Horseshoe: A Traditionary Tale of the Cocked Hat Gentry in the Old Dominion*, but Hamilton's remarks show that a romantic tradition surrounding the Tramontane Knights had already developed, if only in a minor way, more than a century before Caruthers's novel. Before Hamilton, too, the Reverend George Seagood had printed the English translation of Arthur Blackamore's *Expeditio ultramontana* in the *Maryland Gazette*, June 17 and 24, 1729 (reprinted by Earl G. Swem, Richmond, Va., 1960).

7. "It is pleasant to cross mountains."

8. "Given the necessary changes."

Club records, it is now Irrecoverably lost, whether there was something flat or unentertaining in this Speech, or something unintelligible, as that Club orator affected a learned Stile, peculiar to himself, or some fault in the manner of delivering it, he having used notes, we || cannot now positively [259] determin, but, it was observed, that some Gentlemen, Invited that night to the Club, fell fast asleep, while the Secretary held forth, and with some difficulty were roused by pinching and hunching, one passage in it bordered alittle on the Gelastic, for one of the members, vizt: Mr Dumpling Gundiguts, a Gentleman of a Clumpish Genius, and not at all of a risible disposition, was observed to laugh.

We have in the foregoing part of our History, observed upon the use and Significancy of Badges, and we shall observe here, that this ancient and honorable Club, showed their wisdom and Sagacity, in Inventing and using a badge, for the members of their Society, to distinguish themselves from those of other societies.

Badges have been used by great Empires and nations, and by armies in warlike expeditions, the badge of the Roman Empire was a spread Eagle, and as this is a royal bird, it was a proper type of the grandure and dignity of that vast empire, and its being spread, was a proper figure of its extent; The Turkish Empire uses a crescent, to signify, that it is still upon the growing hand, and this ensign also, shows the great Regard the Mahomedans, pay to their feasts of the new moon, The Crusards, when they went out to extirpate the Infidels, wore a red cross, to signify that they were christian Soldiers, and that they delighted in the blood of those that were enimies to the Cross.

Several Illustrious orders of knighthood, wear badges proper to their order, The Stars and Garters of England, are now, and have been for many years noble ensigns of honor and family, we all know the origin of the || most noble order of the knights of the garter, and the rise of their badge [260] and motto; the first being no other than the garter of a Lady of Quality, which she dropt, in dancing with that brave and heroic prince Edward III, at a ball, and she, suspecting some waggish Intention in that monarch, when she felt his hands fumbling about the Skirts of her petticoats, as he stooped to pick it up, took offence, after the manner of women, at this seeming Insult upon her modesty, on which that Gallant prince exclaimed *Hon'y soit qui mal y pense,* which Sentence of old french, signifies no more than, Shame be to him who evil thinks, and these words have ever since become the Motto of this Noble and Illustrious order, with which many of our European princes have been Invested. I cannot help here taking notice, (as America is the Scene of our History) of an order of Virginian knights

216 [Book IV]   The History of

of latin, trite or common enough for their motto and Inscription, and such was the plainness and Simplicity of the whin bush Club, that they had none in any language whatsoever, tho their badge might have born such a motto, as the Scots Thistle, vizt: *Nemo me Impune lacesset,*[5] seeing furz is rather more beset with prickles than the thistle, but the Reason why this ancient and venerable Society, rejected any such pompuous motto, was, as I conjecture, this, they were Jealous, that some acute wits, would clap to it some foolish or Impertinent Interpretation, or Comment, as they did to the other, that is *None shall scratch me without paying dear for their familiarity, or Catching the itch,* which is a distemper, to which it is said the Scots Nation, are extremly liable, and for that reason, have become the Just ridicule of some Smarts, who perfectly know when ridicule is Justly and appositely placed; and from this rare Joke only has proceeded an Infinite flow of delicate wit and Satir.

[258]   It will be proper here, to give a figure of this Simple badge, as it appeared, at its first Invention and Institution, for some time after it had several additions and alterations made upon it, the Simple Card being converted to a resplendent medal of Silver dowble Gilt, and some other Ingenious devices added to it, an exact description of which we shall exhibit, in its proper place.

This Badge Committee issued their Summons for Mr Ignotus warble, an honorary member, to appear before the Club, at next Sederunt, to answer what should then and there be laid to his Charge, which he refused to obey, they also humbly addressed his honor the president, that he would be pleased to deliver a Speech from the Chair, upon Tuesday the 27th of this Instant May, His honour so far complied, as to promise to deliver a discourse from the chair, which he did on the 8th of July following, as we shall relate in the Sequel.

The Secretary at this anniversary delivered a discourse to the members upon Clubs, in which he gave a succinct General History of these Illustrious Societies, their antiquity, Importance, frame, constitution and government, which speech met with approbation, but not being entered in the

---

5. "Nobody provokes me with impunity."

other, and ever since, that Right worshipful fraternity || have left the street [256] clear, for their mock bretheren the Scald miserables, and make their processions in a more private manner, Round the Great hall, where they hold their general Communications.

The Ancient and honorable Tuesday Club, In Imitation of this ancient and universal Custom of Celebrating anniversaries, Thought fit, at Sederunt 34th May 14th, 1746, The Honorable Mr President Jole being Steward, to Celebrate the anniversary of the Club's Institution, by holding a great feast, and wearing badges, the feast was prepared and given by the honorable the president, and was managed in a very polite and elegant manner; at this first anniversary Indeed, there was no procession, only two of the Long-standing members, vizt: Capt: Blunt, and Solo Neverout Esqr, marched forth, with their badge ribbons, to meet his honor the president, as he came from his own house to that of Capt: Seemly Spruce, where the Anniversary was celebrated.

These badges, by order of the committee, which met at the Secretaries house, and of which Solo Neverout Esqr was Chairman, and the Reverend Mr Smoothum Sly, and Drawlum Quaint Esqr, longstanding members, and the Reverend Mr Broadface Round, and Mr Ignotus Warble, honorary members, were the Committee appointed, and Mr Secretary Scribble Clerk Comttee: The Committee Issued an order, which was Solemnly presented to his honor the president, in full Club, by Solo Neverout Esqr, Chairman, with which the Club Concurred and passed into a Law, vizt:

Law XXVIII. Ordered by the Committee, that to morrow, being wednesday, the 14th Instant May, the anniversary of the Institution of this here Club, each || member shall wear a badge, fastened to a belt of yellow Rib- [257] ban, which badge, shall be a piece of card, cut into a round form, in the Center of which, shall be writ in large characters THE TUESDAY CLUB, and underneath *Libertas et natale Solum,*[3] 1746, and upon a label round the edge of the Card, the proper motto of the Club, *Concordia res parvæ crescunt,*[4] and that this badge shall be wore, by every regular, and every honorary member, that shall attend the Club meetings on the Anniversary, from this time forth, so long as the Club is in being.

This badge, we find at first was very simple, and here the Club Imitated the great example, of the Ancient and Venerable Tuesday (or whin bush) Club of Lanneric; whose badge as we observed before is only a Sprig of furz, but they differed from them in this, that they adopted a few Scrapes

---

3. "Liberty and native soil."
4. "Small endeavors flourish through unity" (Sallust, *Jurguitha* 10.6).

time, but let us see how the high flowen presbyterians celebrate this anniversary, do they not demean themselves with the same Christian Spirit wisdom and Sagacity with their bretheren of the other Side, when out of a pious Spite and resentment, they, as it were openly, take the guilt of the Death of this Royal Martyr, (as he is called) upon themselves, by Ironically and Impudently, dressing, preparing and eating, a *calves head*, on that very day.

Other Anniversaries there are of less note, that is, where particular Cities, corporations, Societies or Clubs are only Concerned; Such are the anniversaries of the Birth or Coronation of princes, which are celebrated commonly by || firing of great guns, by exhibiting of Squibs, crackers, fireworks, Skyrockets, Illuminations, bonfires, compotations and balls; The Anniversary of the gunpowder treason is yet, and I hope ever will be kept, in Brittain, Ireland and British America, In commemoration of that Singular delivery from a horrid and bloody popish plot, tho' the Roman Catholics, according to their wonted assurance, deny that there ever was such a plot; There is also the Grand Anniversary of the Lord Mayor of London, on which the worshipful aldermen observe the Ancient Custom of eating a great quantity of Custard, and the moderen mode of devouring mighty loads of Turtle, for which luscious dish we are Indebted to the west Indies, and also swallow down floods of Burgundy Champain, Claret and other outlandish liquors (instead of the Stout beer of old England,) with which it is said they often before the evening of that Joyful day get as drunk as Emperors and Lords.

Clubs also have their Anniversaries, which they Celebrate by solemn processions and feasts, the Anniversary of Saint John Baptist, is a great and Jolly day, with the ancient and honorable Club of free and accepted Masons, who used to strut in grand procession, with all their ornaments, Jewels, badges and ensigns on that day, Till the Burlesque fraternity of Scald Miserables,[1] Instituted a comic procession, in Imitation of them; ornamented with riders on asses Arsy-versy, dungcarts, mops, broomsticks, dishclouts, and Soot-bags, much in the Nature and humor of a Skimmington procession,[2] which Gelastic pomp and pegeantry, put a stop to the

---

1. The Scald Miserables were early-18th-century mock Freemasons, who rode on donkeys through the streets of London escorting a hearse, in which a tattered ragamuffin represented the Grand Master, followed by a bawling troop carrying columns and waving Masonic symbols.

2. An old custom in rural parts of England and Scotland, whereby nagging wives and unfaithful husbands were publicly ridiculed in effigy by a procession of their neighbors; the origin of the name is uncertain.

have not some called it a holy-day and some with great propriety a folly-day; have not some said it was of Christian, and apostolic Institution, and some of pagan original, which they prove from the old Scots name *Yule,* or *Jule,* derived, as they say from Julius Cæsar, a pagan Roman Emperor, whose birth day they confidently affirm it was, dont even the most Zealous observers of it, spend it in a fantastical medley of devotion and mirth; do they not one day attend divine Service, Sacraments and Sermons, and another frolicks tricks, and what they call Christenmass gambols, and dont some fanaticks (as they are called) celebrate it in ridicule, by a Sort of mock feast, in which the principal dish is a goose pye; Is it not a time of Idleness, drunkeness and debauchery among most of the Common people, and of frolic and foolish pleasantry among many of the better Sort, In fine, the enimies of this Sacred Institution, do not stick to say, that the wicked priests of the Second or third century of the Christian æra, Instituted it as an Indulgence to their poor Slaves the people, allowing them a certain time in which to be as Idle and Intemperate as they pleased, to appease or Check the Clamours raised against their Sacred brotherhood, who had assumed to themselves the liberty of Indulging in Idleness and Luxury all the year round, thereby Imitating the example and policy of Mahomet their brother Cheat and Imposture, who to appease certain clamours against his own Incontinency, allowed his disciples the privilege of having four wives at once & as many concubines as they could mantain; There is also the anniversary of Easter, which is not fixed to this day, nor is it determined by Christendom in general, upon what day it shall be kept, being one of those Sorts of comical feasts of the Church called moveable feasts, and thus, different churches keep it on || different days, what fury, what rage, what [254] bloodshed, massacre & murder has not been exhibited in the Christian world, about fixing of this very anniversary, But to descend to particulars & come nigher home to our own country and Religion, with what Solemn mourning and humiliation, doth the Church of England now, celebrate the Anniversary of the Martyrdom of that most pious Saint and Martyr king Charles I. who Surely deserved to be Canonized as much as the Holy Archbishop Thomas Becket, since he was as great a champion, for that Idol of his family *Arbitrary power,* in civil matters, as the latter was for that Idol of the Roman See, absolute and uncontrouled Sway, both in Civil and Ecclesiastical affairs; How, upon this Solemn occasion does the nation then mourn for the Sins and trespasses of the nation, what grief, what contrition is not expressed, what holy Lessons and prayers are not read on the occasion, and, what volleys of christian like Curses and terms of abuse, are not thrown upon the wicked presbyterians, by the Zealous preachers at this

212 [Book IV]

At this Sederunt, a Committee was appointed to prepare matters for Solemnizing the Club anniversary now at hand, this Committee was ordained to meet upon tuesday the 13th of May, the day Immediatly preceeding wednesday the 14th, and the honorable the president was privileged to serve always on this Anniversary day, the Club dispensing not only on this, but on all other occasions of his honor's serving, with the Law of one dish, which was only a matter of form, since he did not wait for such dispensation, but broke thro' that law long before he mounted the Chair, these two privileges more were now added to the Chair, by which the Longstanding members flattered his honor's vanity, and encouraged and countenanced his turn for Luxury.

[252] ## Chapter V

The Celebration of the Club Anniversary, for the first time, The Institution of the Club badges, and other significant matters.

The custom of Celebrating Anniversaries, has been practised and kept up in all ages, by all civilized nations and people, whether Jews, christians, pagans, or Mahometans, but to go no farther than the christian countries, who have Indeed been the fondest of any, in observing this ancient and universal Custom, we find so many anniversaries of Saints, anniversary fasts, and anniversary feasts, that in some Countrys, particularly Spain, whose Inhabitants are the best catholics in Christendom, above two thirds of the year is taken up by these Anniversaries, by some called holidays, these holidays are days of liberty, or rather Licentiousness, like the ancient Saturnalia at Rome, and every one is at full freedom, to bestow his time as he pleases, (excepting only, that they are debard working at their lawful Calling or trade) either in devotion drunkenness or debauchery, and tho' there be but few who chuse the first, and most of these few hipocrites and bigots, yet all pretend, that it is a religious regard to those anniversary holidays, feasts, and fasts, that makes them observe and keep them so strictly, and, as religion is a Subject, about which men have differed more widely and split into more numerous factions and Sects, than any thing else, so the disputes, wrangles and brawls have been carried to an excessive height among Christians, about these anniversaries. What differences have
[253] there not been about christenmass || the grand anniversary of christendom; have not some been for the celebration and observation of it and some not,

raising some small dispute in Club, between his honor and the Longstanding mem- || bers, Mr Councellor Quaint, growing warm in the argument, [250] told his honor, That all power rested in the Club, for, as they had placed his honor in *that there* Chair, so they could displace him again, whenever they pleased, a wicked whiggish maxim, absurdly mantained by such as are enimies to the Sacred and Indelible Character of presidents; His honor took great offence at this, and threatned to resign the Chair, getting out of it with great precipitation, but, at the entreaty of some of the members, was prevailed upon to resume that honorable Seat, tho' many thought that these entreaties were needless, as his honor, upon Second thoughts, would have done the same without them.

It was ordered that the Revd Mr Broadface Round, and Mr Abraham Bumper, honorary members, should each of them prepare a discourse to be delivered in Club, and also, that Mr Secretary Scribble, should prepare a Speech to be delivered at next Sederunt, the Subjects of these discourses, being left to their own Choice.

At next Sederunt, which was the 33d on the 29th of April, the same year, Drawlum Quaint Esqr, being Steward, the Revd Mr Broadface Round, delivered a discourse upon Charity, which had very great approbation from the honorable Chair, upon this account chiefly, as it seemed to favor and promote the Scheme of the box, of which his honor was passionatly fond, for certain political Reasons above mentioned, and his honor never failed to extoll every thing, that squared with the Interest of the Chair.

Mr Ignotus warble, an honorary member, delivered also a discourse upon cheerfullness, in which he Introduced, a very pritty Comparison || or [251] parallel, between Mr Neverout and Socrates, This Comparison was striking, being entirely new, and what none else would have thought of, it was built upon Mr Neverout's being a batchellor, and of an amorous complexion, both which circumstances were Socrates's case, before this, the Club never found out any such Similitude, between this moderen batchellor and that Ancient philosopher, and were conscious of no other, than that asperity of countenance, or hardness of favor, as some call it, peculiar to them both, the Secretary excused himself at this Sederunt, as not yet being prepared to deliver his discourse, and requested longer time, which was easily Granted him.

Thus did these Club orators, shine, each in his particular sphere, in declaiming or speech making, but Drawlum Quaint Esqr outshone them all, still excepting his honor the President who would not (Indeed should not) yield to any in Clubical Qualifications, and, whom we shall soon see acting the Orator in Club, in a most Surprizing manner.

and poetical Strain, but never compleated any more than one Couplet, which he made in Club, and was as follows.

> Whilst at the window, stood two prying pimps,
> Scratching and wishing, for the Buxom Nymphs.

This, we may say, was the last effort, made by the muse of this Ingenious Gentleman, the first we have given an account of in the preceeding book, we shall Indeed find in this History two other poetical performances, which he pretended to pass off for his own, but one is plainly borrowed from the Celebrated Rabelais, the other, excepting five or Six lines, was Composed by some other members of the Club.

These two great geniuses for sometime contended together with weapons of wit, and, we must own, that Councellor Quaint at last got the better, for, he gave the first provocation and had the last word to himself, this noted oration of his intirely silencing his antagonist.

[249] At Sederunt 31, April 1, 1746, Slyboots Pleasant Esqr, being deputy in the Chair, and the Revd Mr Smoothum Sly Steward, Mr Solo Neverout, according to an order of last Sederunt, delivered a discourse of Love and Lovers, he used Notes, and had such a graceful action and delivery, and withal handled the Subject in so elegant and polite a manner, not making one single Slip, (unless you reckon his pronouncing the word *Phystologists*,[8] *Phigiogolists,* according to the modish accent and pronounciation, was a *lapsus Linguæ* as the learned term it) that the Club was Intirely satisfied with his performance, requesting him to deliver it over again, which he did very Complacently, and with a Singular good grace; There was not one single touch at Satyr in the whole piece, tho many Imagined that he would have taken this opportunity, to pay off Scores with Mr Councellor Quaint.

The Reverend Mr Smoothum Sly, and Mr Ignotus Warble, an honorary member, were ordered to prepare discourses to be delivered in Club, the Subjects *ad libitum.*

At Sederunt 32, April 15th 1746, Dumpling Gundiguts Esqr being Steward, the following Law was made.

Law XXVII. That all Cases, excepting that of the admission of members, and the disposal of the money in the Club-box, shall be determined by a majority of voices.

Mr Smoothum Sly, at this Sederunt, delivered his discourse, which was upon civil government, and had the approbation of the Club in general, excepting his honor the president, who alledged he spoke too much in favor of popular liberty, to the hurt of prerogative and power in rulers, this

---

8. Perhaps *phytologist,* a botanist.

partial with regard to the Gentlemen of the Law (the orator being himself a ‖ Lawyer) this longstanding member had a peculiar action when he spoke, which attracted the Eyes of the audience, and fixed their attention as much as the Subject on which he harangued, he kept his body still and motionless, his head and Shoulders stooping forwards, extending his neck to a considerable length, his right arm streched out, with alittle bend of the elbow, the forefinger of his right hand in a pointing posture, wch he moved gently up and down, his chin, when he made a pause, dropping down on his breast, his left hand under the waste band of his breeches, and, when he had occasion to stop in his discourse, (which was pritty often) to consider of what he was next to say, he would like many orators spit or hawk, or Cough, or yawn, and, for these excellent qualities in oratorial action, as well as for his elegant Stile and phrase of *this here* and *that there,* he was soon after promoted, to the honorable place of Speaker to the Club, as we shall relate in the Sequel, the Satyr of this Discourse was chiefly pointed at Mr Neverout, then Sheriff of the County, who, at a preceeding Sederunt, undertook to prove that Mr Quaint was Dead, which argument he managed so artfully and Sophistically, that he seemed to Convince the Club that he really was a dead member, and they actually voted him such, Mr Neverout, the same night Elevated with his Skill in argumentation, tho' Indeed, he had borrowed most of his reasoning from the Celebrated Isaac Bickerstaff Esqr, in his famous controversy with Mr Patridge,[7] Student in Physic and astrology, thought he could ‖ go farther in displaying his great abilities, and exhibit a Specimen of his poetical Genius, the occasion was this, Mr Quaint had wrote a Satyr on him and some others, which he entituled the *Reverend Scout,* In which was a relation of an adventure of Solo Neverout Esqr, Mr Secretary Scribble, and Mr Slyboots pleasant, who had one night a Set meeting with some Celebrated Nymphs of the town, at one of these polite assemblies, called twopenny hops, which was held at the house of Mr George Downie Musicioner, these Gallants and their Nymphs were observed from a low window in the Street, by two Scouts or spies, who, having Informed Councellor Quaint therewith, he wrote the aforesaid Satyr, In which he distinguishes Mr Neverout, by the name of *Littlebreeches;* Neverout still resenting this, was resolved to answer it in the same Satyrical

---

7. Hamilton is alluding to Jonathan Swift's "A Vindication of Isaac Bickerstaff Esq; Against What Is Objected to Him by Mr. Partridge, in His Almanack for the Present Year 1709," especially the passage beginning: "Without entering into Criticisms of *Chronology* about the Hour of his Death; I shall only prove, that Mr. Partrige is not alive" (*The Prose Works of Jonathan Swift,* ed. Herbert Davis [Oxford, 1939–1968], II, 162).

Franklum Quaint Esqr, delivering a Speech in Club

to say on the Subject, so finding himself at a Stand, and that he could by no means recover himself, he stoped short for some time, and had recourse to his papers.

The Club seemed to approve of this Speech, at least they did not condemn it, and they so well liked of this custom Introduced by the Secretary, that they ordered Mr Drawlum Quaint, to prepare a Speech to entertain the Club at next Sederunt, and to chuse his Subject, and we shall soon find some other members excelling this way, vizt: Mr Solo Neverout, Capt: Serious Social, Mr Jealous spyplot & Mr Smoothum Sly, and even his honor the president himself in a remarkable manner, display'd his Rhetorical and oratorial learning, in an elegant Speech that he delivered to the Club, which we shall relate in it's proper place.

At Sederunt 28th Febr: 11, 1745–6, Slyboots Pleasant Esqr being Steward, a hot dispute arose in Club concerning the Club Box, and the honorary members, vizt: whether the money in the box, should be disposed of, at the discretion of his honor the president, by the direction of the Club or by both conjointly, and, whether the Club had any power to tax the honorary members, and oblige them to || contribute to this box, many violent and warm Speeches were made on both Sides of the argument, for five Sederunts successively, there was abundance of bawling, Sharp railing, invective, repartee, alittle Swearing, and much taking of Snuff, both in a literal, and metaphorical Sense, at last, it was determined at Sederunt 32d April 15th 1746, Dumpling Gundiguts Esqr being Steward [246]

Law XXVI. That the Box shall continue, according to it's primitive Institution (vid: Law 20, 21, 22, 23.)

Thus we see in part, the prophesy of Jealous Spyplot Esqr come to pass, with regard to this box, heats and dissentions already arising in Club about it, tho' as yet, there was not above 40 Shillings in the treasury, a strong Instance of that propensity in human nature, to wrangle and differ, about the veriest triffles where Interest is concerned, a Specimen also, of the ambition of presidents, who struggle and Contend, still for an addition to their power and Influence, they, never being satisfied, with the quantum of power allotted them, let it be ever so great.

At Sederunt 30th March 11th 1745–6, the Revd Mr Smoothum Sly being deputy in the Chair, and Capt: Seemly Spruce Steward; Drawlum Quaint Esqr, Delivered a long Speech to the Club, the Subject of which was honesty, this Speech was delivered without notes, but was very sarcastical and Severe, the Gentleman took almost all professions, offices and callings to task, allowing a very small portion of honesty to any Station in life, particularly to Sheriffs and other public officers, tho he seemed to be very

Mr Secretary Scribble delivering a Speech in Club

and advantage, where it did not Interfere or clash with his own, or stand in the way of his ambitious Schemes, to advance his own Influence in the Club, and make himself a person of weight and Importance, and in this indeed he resembled many other Secretaries and politicians, who, In Indifferent matters can give very good advice, but whenever Self is to be served, that must of necessity be done, tho every body else should go to the devil.

At Sederunt 29th febr: 25th 1745/6,[6] Capt: Seemly Spruce being first deputy in the Chair, and Capt: Bully Blunt Steward, || the Secretary stood up and Informed the Club that he had a discourse or Speech to deliver, and craved permission to deliver it; this Speech we must observe, had been prepared of his own head, without orders from the Club, to which he was in all probability prompted by his vanity, having surely this opinion of himself, that he had an excellent knack at Speech making, and that the Club could not otherwise than be mightily entertained and Instructed, with this Sort of Exercise, he had leave given him to deliver this discourse, tho' not without some grumblings from Capt: Blunt the Steward; who said he was for no Innovations of this Sort, Damn the Speeches says he, we meet together in this here Club to smoke, Chat, and put about the bowl, and not to hear and make Speeches, however, being permitted to deliver this Speech, he put himself into a proper attitude for it, and Imagining that he had Cond it by heart, did not use his papers, but began to repeat it with a tollerable good grace; his Subject was the advantages reaped from Society, and some encomiums on Clubs, a thread bare and trite Subject, but put together in a tollerable Stile, The Secretary had gone thro' one half of this oration, smoothly enough, without hesitating, and the Longstanding members had given a close attention to it, when an odd Circumstance happened, which made the orator stop short all of a Sudden, and obliged him to fumble in his pockets for his papers, which, having pulled out, he read very distinctly the remaining part of it, the occurrence was this, Drawlum Quaint Esqr, a Longstanding member, was more attentive than any one else to this harangue, and the better to swallow what was delivered by the Secretary sat || with his neck streeched out, his mouth wide open, motionless, every limb of his body remaining as still, as if he had been a piece of Sculpture, and, in his right hand he grasped his tobacco pipe, the extremity of the Stem about two Inches from his mouth, in the very same altitude as it was, when he pulled it from his lips, this figure struck the Secretary, (happening to turn his eyes that way) in such a manner, that it obliterated at once, from his memory, all that he had been saying, and all that he had yet

[244]

[245]

---

6. Hamilton apparently was well aware that he had reversed Sederunts 28 and 29.

The Secretary executed the Laborious part of his office tollerably well, by entering all the proceedings of the Club in the book of records, but then, his natural vanity, or opinion of his own self Sufficiency appeared glaringly even in this the execution of his office, for he often would, without the advice of his honor the president, or the Club, enter matters, in what manner and form he pleased, which was often the Cause of great disgust and heart burnings betwixt his honor & the Longstanding members, since the president often urged and mantained, that the Secretary had no business to enter any thing there, but by his order and direction, and, that nothing relating to what the members did or said, had any title to a place in these Records, but his Actions and his Sayings alone should be entered, while on the other hand, the members thought, that their proceedings, debates and determinations, had as good a title to a place in the records, as the acts and Sayings of his honor the president; Thus the Club and the President differed among themselves, and both with the Secretary, who, notwithstanding the many grave and Sharp rebukes, which he had from the honorable Chair, and checks and threatnings from the Club, went on in his usual way and would still enter matters as he pleased, an Instance of perverse obstinacy as well as of vanity and Self conceit, and Indeed, a positive and wayward humor, was none of the least failings || which this club officer could be charged with, by which he often Introduced confusion into the Government of this here Club, thereby drawing the Indignation of his honor the president upon himself and the members; This Secretary was also of a Scheming, plotting, Restless disposition, and his plots and Schemes, tho generally carried on, under pretence of doing honor to the President, and for the advantage of the Club, yet, for the most part, terminated in mischievous purposes and attempts, either to make tools of the Longstanding members, or to derogate from the honor and prerogative of the honorable Chair, at least, this Gentleman was much belied by his honor and the Longstanding members, if he was not a Sly, cunning, Insinuating, deceitful, mischief making member, the continual Author and promoter of Brawls, wrangles, Jealousies, Grumblings, heartburnings, hubbubs and hurly burlys in this here ancient and honorable Club, and it will appear in the Sequel, when we give an account of the *Cap of State,* and the *Box No 1,* that these allegations against the Secretary were not grounded on Suspicion only; Some indeed affirmed that the Secretary was a deep politician, but his honor the president was always angry when this was mentioned and spoke of him as a person only skilled in what is called *Low Craft,* however, this may be said in his commendation, that he was a very constant and punctual attendant on the Club, and spared no pains to do every thing for its interest

Loquacious Scribble Esqr
Secretary & orator of the anc^t & hon: Tuesd: Club

Nostri ab archivis consortii, aspice Scribam
Qui tua verba Jole, Stylo perenni arat,
nec non facta tua, lepido Sermone renovat,
Nestora quem lingua vincere posses putes.

[From the archives of our club, look upon the Scribe
Who plows out your words, O Jole! with eternal pen,
And also recites your deeds in elegant style,
Whom you consider able to defeat Nestor at talking.]

[facing page 241]

thought of or delivered, and which penitential orations are often Cryd about by the hawkers in their own hearing, before the cart has left them pendulous between heaven and earth, or the Inexorable hempen noose with cruel gripe has stop'd the volley of oaths and curses proceeding from their Inebriated throats.

But these orators that hold forth in Clubs are prompted and spur'd on Solely by vanity, and they can Surely have no other motive but this, seeing it is out of a desire to Instruct and Inform their fellow members (which supposes a Superiority of understanding in the said Club orators) that they take upon themselves the character and office of declaimers.

[241] The desire to show a graceful action in the delivery of an Oration, may be an Incentive to many to become Speech makers; especially if we consider, that many orators have such barren fancies, that they cannot find matter enough, to frame a discourse of any Length, and would make but a very Silly figure, without some graceful action or gesture of body. And indeed, we often find stark nonsense, go much better off, with a proper and violent gesticulation, than the most finished good sense with none at all, this is so true a proposition, that Demosthenes, the famous Athenian Orator, being asked, what was the principal qualification of a declaimer? answered, Action.—what the Second?—replied action.—what the third?—still action, and so on to Infinity,[5] and thus, we find clearly exemplified in these our days, in our Itinerant preachers, and holders forth, The Reverend Mr Whitefield, the New light men and Methodists, and also in many of our Quaker (particularly female) preachers, who, tho' there is nothing at all in any thing they say, yet never fail to surprize and move their hearers, by the strength of their action, and bodily gesture alone.

It is more than probable, that the members of this ancient and honorable Club, were, at this time actuated by this Vanity only, which made them feel an Invincible propensity to speech making, for, it could not be from any prospect of gain or reward, that they were prompted to become orators, since they were so far from receiving or even expecting any reward or præmium or perquisite for it that I do not understand, that any one member, who set up for a Club declaimer, earn'd so much as thanks for his trowble.

[242] The first long standing member that was seized with this pestilent itch of speech making, was the Secretary, who was one, not the least stocked with vanity, in this here Club, as I promised before, to give the Character of this Club officer, I think it will come well in this place.

---

5. This story appears in Cicero, *De oratore* 3.213.

desire of pecuniary Rewards, offices of honor, places of profit, titles, and what we call a comfortable livelihood or a Glorious exit, Some of these orators, tho they seem to perorate powerfully for hire, yet they use the words of other men, to whom nature has been more liberal in the gifts of wit and Invention, than to the orators themselves, many of our pulpit orators for Instance, only Deliver the words of one Doctor Tillotson, one Doctor Smallridge, one Dr Clerk, one Dr Barrow and one Dr South,[1] with very few additions or Interpolations of their own, which makes it differ from the form, in which it was delivered from the mouths of the original authors, only as a hash, or Second hand dish does from the whole meat of which it is Compounded, being cut and slash'd and mash'd, and divided in a very curious manner, with the addition of a Sophisticated Sauce to disguise the true relish of the meat, our Theatrical declaimers Indeed are Intirely Indebted for their matter, to a Certain Shakespear, a certain Row,[2] a certain Congreve & others; || our orators at Westminster hall, whether [240] parliamentary or bar Declaimers, have Inexhaustible funds of discourse, from the printed proceedings and debates of parliament, and from the huge and ponderous volumes of Reports Entries, and Law Cases and precedents from time Immemorial. Our Stage Itinerants are Indebted much to the Ingenious composers of Quack bills,[3] of which numberless Specimens may be collected from the news papers, to suit all cases, and also to the facetious Elocution of that famous and Ingenious Gentleman ycleped Merry Andrew, Jack pudding, or Pickle herring,[4] and the worthies of Tyburn, to the learned Geniuses of Grubstreet, who often pen for their use last Speeches and dying words, which Speeches or words they never once

---

1. John Tillotson (1630–1694) was a Cambridge Latitudinarian who became archbishop of Canterbury. George Smalridge (1663–1719) was bishop of Bristol whose character Addison praised and whose sermons Samuel Johnson placed in the first class of those preached by English divines. Samuel Clarke (1675–1729), an English divine generally regarded as the first of English metaphysicians after Locke's death in 1704, published numerous sermons and treatises. Isaac Barrow (1630–1677), professor of Greek, geometry, and mathematics at Cambridge, was the author of *Exposition of the Creed, Decalogue, and Sacraments* (London, 1669), *Euclidis Elementa* (London, 1655), and *A Treatise of the Pope's Supremacy* (London, 1680). Robert South (1634–1716), a great court preacher favored by Charles II, was known for his humorous, pithy sermons.

2. Nicholas Rowe (1674–1718), a popular playwright, was the author of *Tamerlane* (1702), *The Fair Penitent* (1703), and numerous other plays, including *Lady Jane Grey* (1715).

3. Hamilton's burlesque of quack advertisements appeared in the *Md. Gaz.*, Apr. 12, 1749.

4. Merry Andrew, a buffoon or attendant on a quack doctor, was said to derive from Andrew Boorde (ca. 1490–1549), physician to Henry VIII noted for his eccentricity. Jack Pudding was a clown or mountebank who may have performed tricks such as swallowing large quantities of black pudding. Pickle-herring, the German term for a clown or buffoon, derived from a humorous character of that name in an early-17th-century play.

as well as at Set Clubs, at this same Sederunt also, the two following Laws were passed.

Law XXIV. That the book of minutes shall always be Lodged in the hands of the Secretary, any law to the contrary notwithstanding, who is to produce it to the Club as often as it is called for.

[238]

Law XXV. That whoever stays with the Steward after the hour of eleven, the penalty of one Shilling current money shall be paid by each and every member so transgressing, into the box, at the ensuing meeting of the Club.

This is the first penal law passed in the Club, and it is plainly Intended to promote the Scheme of the box, but we shall soon find what regard was paid to it and every other Law of this Club.

At the following Sederunt on January 28, Solo Neverout Esqr, being Steward, Jealous Spyplot Esqr, presented to the Club, a curious box of black walnut, for which he had the thanks of the Club, formally delivered to him by the Secretary, and his honor the president took Immediate possession of this box, generously putting ten Shillings into it, to show a good example to the Long-standing members, his honor kept one of the keys of this box, and the Secretary the other.

Chapter IV

The Introduction of set Speeches into the Club, and the members that made the Greatest figure that way.

So Inherent is vanity in human nature, that it seems to be Inextricably Incorporated and Ingrained with it, so as that it cannot be separated or Extracted, by the most Subtile Chemistry, wash'd away by the strongest Suds or purged off by the purifying fire of purgatory itself.

This Inherent principle of vanity appears in nothing more, than the great desire most men have to Speech ‖ making, and engrossing to themselves a great share of the talk in all places of rendezvous, such as Coffee houses, Taverens, Teatables, but more particularly in Clubs; as for those who hold forth in public assemblies, such as the members of both houses of parliament, the Gentlemen of the long Robe and of the Crape; The Theatrical Emperors, kings, Princes, heros and heroins, the Celebrated quacks of the Age; and the Tyburn Heroes and worthies, there may be other motives besides that of vanity to tempt those licenced holders forth, such as the

[239]

be the cause of wrangling and Discord in the Club, and here indeed he proved a true prophet, as he was also in some other cases. Then was passed the following Law.

Law XX. That in order to raise a fund for Charity, or such other good uses as the Club shall see proper, Sixpence every club night, shall be contributed by every regular member, the payment to be made quarterly, and also, to promote this fund, every honorary member shall contribute five Shillings, at his first admission, and the same Sum yearly afterwards, so long as he continues in the Club, this fund to be disposed of, as the majority of the Club shall determin.

Thus we find by this law, a tax of Sixpence each Sederunt Laid upon the members, and Charity made use of as a pretext, a very bad precedent, and a dangerous Stroke to the liberties of the Club. We shall see in the Sequel how far this fund was applied towards charity, I cannot but observe here, that this here Club took alittle too much upon them, in taxing the honorary members without their own consent; but, I suppose it was thought that they were bound to pay something, for the honor of being called honorary members of this ancient and honorable Club.

Law XXI. That every quarter day, or day of payment, the Contents of the box shall be made known to the members of the Club, and every member shall have a note of the Sum then contained in it delivered to him by the Secretary.

Law XXII. That there shall be two locks and keys to the box, the one to be kept by the president, the other by the Secretary, and the Secretary is to keep the accounts and present the State of them quarterly to the Club. [237]

Law XXIII. That the president shall have a power of calling together the members, at any time when necessity requires, in order to dispose of the charity, and that the fund is to be paid into the Secretary's hands and lodged with the president.

This is an exact transcript from the records of the Laws made on account of the box, we shall find in the Sequel, how strictly they were put in execution, and what all this fracas about charity ended in, after having occasioned a mighty hurly burly and hubbub in the Club, between his honor the president and the long standing members.

By the last recited Law, a new privilege is added to the Chair, vizt: that of calling the members together at pleasure, to dispose of the charity, we shall find this privilege soon extended farther, and a power given to his honor to call the members together by Summons, when, and as often as he pleased, which Indeed, they never had reason to take amiss, for even on the occasions of private Committees, his honor always treated very handsomly

hands, of consequence, their friendship can neither be gained nor preserved without political greasing as it is called, or in plain terms tipping the Bribe, but whence are the funds to be procured to carry on this game, the answer is natural, we find that ministers of State, and those at the head of affairs, commonly have recourse to taxes upon the poor people, to supply themselves with moneys to be laid out in Secret Services, as they are called, it is Just the same in Clubs, where exorbitant power gains footing, those who have raised themselves to that power, will naturally study and practise ways and means to support and augment it, for it is a true maxim Confirmed by the experience of many ages, that no determined quantum of either power or riches, creates a Satiety, and Indeed it never was known, that either a great Emperor, or a very rich man, declared positively, that they had [235] enough of either, or wanted no more; and we shall soon || see those very practices take place in this here Club, and certain great officers created to support the authority and power of the Chair, and promote its dignity and grandure, but this was done by degrees, and Inch by Inch as it were, and, the members were first of all taxed, under a pretence of raising a fund for Charity, while the manager of that fund, thought of nothing less, in consequence of this, a treasurer was to be created in the Club, who would be an officer useful to the Chair, and a firm friend to the presidential prerogative, and Interest; and, it could not happen otherwise, since the President himself Grasped at, and actually obtained that office of trust, and, in spite of the Sophistry and Subtilety of logicians and metaphysicians; none sure could be a firmer friend to himself, than his very Identical Self, and, the Notion of the Clubs treasury or property, being Intirely in his honor's possession, and at his honor's disposal, when or how he pleased, raised among the members, first Jealousies and fears, then Grumblings, mumblings and discontents, and, last of all dreadful dissentions and bickerings, which had like to have ended in the utter ruin and final dissolution of the Club, but I shall open this Scene by degrees, and display the whole proceedings of the Chair, with regard to the treasury and the creation of great officers, as they follow one another in the order and course of our History.

It was at Sederunt 26th Janry 14th 1745–6, Capt: Serious Social being Steward, that a motion was made in Club by a member (Influenced and prompted, as is supposed, by his honor the president, who always showed an extreme desire to have the purport of this motion established into a Law) that there should be a Club box set on foot, for charity, and other [236] Laudable purposes, this carried || by unanimity, every one at last consenting to it, tho' Jealous Spyplot esqr, an old standing member showed some reluctance, and did not come easily into the thing, fortelling that it would

Services of the Club, often has he neglected his own affairs, for the affairs of the Club, and has lost many a night's rest, and wore out his Spectacles in perusing and examining Letters, commissions, petitions, remonstrances, Songs, poems, odes, Summons, epigrams, accrostics, Club conundrums, and other Clubical papers of great || Importance and Significancy, to the [233] danger of his eyesight health and understanding, often has he with great modesty declined being flattered and cajoled by the longstanding members, and Sincerely professed, that, as to power he desired no more of it, than what was Just necessary for the good and wellfare of the Club, and this, he has often declared from the Chair, with the same Sincerity as some of our princes of the Steward family declared from the throne to their obstreporous parliaments. Often has he, with great Complacency and good nature, sung and warbled Sweetly from the Chair, (for he had an excellent small musical pipe,) love ditties and witty Songs, for the entertainment of the long Standing members, tho some were Ill natured enough to say, that he did this out of emulation to Excell Solo Neverout Esqr, Chief musician, in short, his good qualities were so many, that he was the admiration of all members, and all Clubs, and were we to lose, this great and worthy president, heaven only knows when or where we could procure such another.

Chapter III

Of the Introduction of the Club box, and other Important matters.

"Ye Gods! what havoc does ambition make among your works!"—says the Celebrated Mr Addison in the first Scene of his Tragedy of Cato,[1] and, I Introduce this pathetic exclamation, at the beginning of this Chapter very || much *a propos,* as it will be a seasonable preparative to my readers, and [234] prevent their being overmuch Surprized at the dreadful Havoc made by ambition, in this here ancient and honorable Club.

We have seen how Luxury has been Introduced into this here club, and gained now a Strong footing in it, but Luxury is not to be supported without means, there must be wherewithal to supply the Idle and Imaginary wants which it creates, neither can power be supported without friends, and these faithful friends being Slaves to Luxury, must have wherewithal to supply their many wants both real and Imaginary, put into their

---

1. Quoted accurately from Portius's opening speech in Addison's *Cato* (1713).

only amused him with a false show, in setting him in a chair of state, and bestowing certain Sham titles and privileges upon him; for that still, notwithstanding all this pomp and ceremony, he looked upon himself as a president and no president, seeing the members would not be ruled entirely by his will, but still acted by their own, tho sometimes his honor would forget this ungrateful Subject, and would in a pleasant humor, compare himself to the King, his State officers to the Nobles or peers, and the other members to the commons, whom he regarded as people of little or no account or Signification, then indeed, would his honor, with a Sweet Smile in his countenance, talk very pleasantly, of our Chancellor, our knight and Champion, our Protomusicus, our attorney General, our Master of Ceremonies, our poet Laureat, our Secretary &ct: for both in his conversation and writing, he assumed the royal Stile of we us and our.

But this worthy and honorable Gentleman, if like other mortal men, he had his little foibles, he was at the same time endued with very great qualities, of which, his forgiveness, long Suffering, and Surprizing patience were none of the least; often has he been Insulted, and affronted even in the Chair, by petulent and Saucy long standing members, and as often has he bore it with heroic resolution, and Surprizing composure of mind; once was he dragged out of it, pulled about the room, tossed and hursled from corner to corner, his ruffles tore, his ensigns of State threatned to be burnt, he himself called a traitor, a tyrant, nay even an old || fool, yet after all this, could this great man forget and forgive; Often has he showd an extreme Solicitude to humor and please the Club, and to provide every thing handsom and Genteel for them, while he has had little thanks for the same, some maliciously alledging, that he did this more out of a vain desire of making a Show, than any other motive. Many a week has he spent, in preparations for Anniversary solemnities, and even ordinary times of serving, he has traversed the whole town twice or thrice in a day, after the Butchers, Tallow Chandlers, and Tobacco pipe merchants, appearing often, notwithstanding the dignity of his office, with troops of these Sort of cattle about him, and would often deign, to carry himself thro' the street, bundles of tobacco pipes, and other such provision for the Club, many a day, and many a night, has he spent and watched in his kitchen, amidst Steam grease and Slush, sweating over the fire, cutting, sliceing, kneading, seasoning, boiling, roasting, stewing, baking and preparing delicacies for the entertainment of the Club, often, while he was racked with the excruciating pains of the gout, has he walked, trotted and run about in great anguish to serve the club, often has he Immerged his feet in cold water, to the great peril of his life, merely to overcome the attacks of the gout, that he might be able to do the

which made him often scratch, where he did not itch, make wry faces, and sit uneasy in Club.

He was extremely Inattentive, or affected so to be, for the most part, when any member was speaking, or delivering his opinion in Club, particularly, if that Speech or opinion, was not altogether according to his own notions, and, by the bye, his notions and conceptions of things, almost always differed from those of the Club, this Strange inattention he showed, by holding a conversation in whisper, with those who sat next him, while a member was delivering himself to the Chair, nay often, when a member or Stranger drank to him, he would not advert or take any notice, tho' they bawld 'till their throats were sore, and hunchd him 'till their elbows aked, many thought this was only an air of grandure and State, it being peculiar to some Great men to be Inattentive, while address'd by their Inferiors.

He was very fond of punctillios Ceremonies, and distinguishing badges of honor, thinking they contained in themselves something very edifying, expressive and Significant, and the long Standing members soon finding out this weakness, in a Course of a few years, loaded him with ceremonies, and ornamented him with a superfluity of pompous accoutrements, till at last they effectually cured him of this malady, for he smelt a rat, and grew sick and tired of these farces as will appear in the Sequel. [230]

He was precise to the utmost nicety in all his proceedings relating to the Club, both in and out of the Chair, and would be uneasy if a pin was stuck in a wrong place, or any thing out of rank and file in the Club room, or upon the Club table.

Vanity was none of the least of his foibles, and it was thought he had some opinion of the Elegance of his form and features, for, he generally chose, when in the Chair, to sit opposite to a large looking Glass, and to turn and wriggle his body into different attitudes, in order to show himself to himself to the best advantage, to stroke down his face and beard, adjust the foretop of his wig, and to affect a complacent Smile and Smirk of the countenance, tho' at times, when Speeches were made that displeased him, or Snappish replies or retorsions were given him by the Chancellor, there followed an elongation of countenance, and a droping of the Lower Jaw, which some of the members called his timber Countenance, which would have afforded no uncommon hint to the famous Hogarth.

Even when he was in his highest Zenith of power in the Club, and ordered, and did Just as he pleased, he still expressed a Sort of uneasiness and dissatisfaction, that ‖ his power and authority was not greater, which made him often exclaim in conversation, that the members of the Club, had [231]

to the milky way, and telling them, that he hoped, most of the young Ladies in the Ring, were travelling fast, towards that same Galaxy or milky way, ‖ [228] and abundance of other droll witty and facetious repartees, puns, dowble entendres, and gallant Sarcasms passed, 'till that Gentleman, being called upon, by a lady to dance; he pretended to step aside alittle for his hat and gloves, but took care to abscond, and not make his appearance again that night upon the dancing Stage. In fine, every thing was conducted with great elegance, and mirth prevailed in the company, nothing being wanting to compleat all, but the presence of his honor the president, who, by his absenting that night, showed that he was not altogether pleased, with this piece of Gallantry.

As we have given in a preceeding part of this history, the private Character of his honor the president, we shall here give a small Sketch, of what we may call, his clubical Character.

The President, tho' he possessed many good qualities, yet, like other mortal men, on this Side the grave, he had his particular foibles, which I, as his historian, am obliged faithfully to recount, out of the great Regard I have for truth, and I shall promise, to be as little sparing to the other Longstanding members, and even to myself, in that way, as to his honor.

His chief foible was ambition and love of power, a fault peculiar to great men and heroes, this appeared by his extreme desire to grasp as much of that, as he possibly could, by his endeavoring to have all matters transacted in the Club, Solely by his own authority and Influence; by his enforcing and procuring Laws, to lodge the whole governing and managing authority in his own hands; by his extreme tenaciousness of the privileges already granted him, and vehement desire to have more added to them; by his Jealousy of the other members who had any privileges which he was ‖ [229] apt groundlessly to Imagine, Jarred or Interfered with his own, this will appear in his future conduct, with regard to the Chancellor, a high officer of the Club, who he thought was a grandee of too great power and Influence, and therefore, he used all means and methods to render him, his office and great Seal, of no effect or Significancy.

He was also very positive, and not to be convinced, by the clearest arguments, where he had the least Suspicion, that these arguments had a tendency to subtract from his Clubical authority, and the dignity of his office.

He was at times very sharp and satirical, while in the Chair, against those who offended him, by any thing they said or did in Club, and the Secretary in particular, felt the poignancy of his Satyr upon many occasions,

bent upon the thing, but had they taken his advice, which they ought to have done, considering his station and dignity, he would have advised them to a much more gentile and polite way of treating the Ladies, than that common and thread bare method of giving a ball. The Secretary Intreated his honor to declare how that was to have been done. After some Sort of reluctancy his honor told him "That it was thus, in the manner of the Christenmass gifts of old times, for, in my notion of things (said he) the old methods, are much the Gentilest and prettiest, and, had it been ordered thus, I should have condescended to make the cake with my own hands, but now, as it is, I shall not concern myself with it, but thus it is," and so he proceeded see-sawing, and rolling up his handcerchef on his knee, for this great man was very apt to do so while he was discoursing or telling of a Story, "in my Grandmothers time, who was a very notable woman, and understood ceremonies as well as any, it was customary to send a Slice of cake, and half a pint of canary or sack, at christenmass, upon a neat Silver ‖ Salver, to every lady in the neighbourhood, and this method I would have had the Club to take to treat the Ladies, instead of that foolish way of giving a ball." The Secretary listened to this with great attention, and breaking Silence, owned that the method was very pritty and Genteel,—but then, honorable Sir, said he, we should have occasion for at least twenty or thirty half pint decanters, or Cruets, for so many Ladies are there in the place, who ought, and will expect to be treated,—That difficulty is soon Removed, Replied the president, for, I could have furnished the Club with twice as many decanters or cruets, if wanted, from my store, at half a crown a piece—upon this the conversation ended, and the Secretary made his leg and took his leave, being Sufficiently convinced, as I believe every one else, who reads this, will be of the reasons his honor had, for dissapproving the ball, and advising the other way of entertaining.

[227]

 The ball then was held at the time appointed, which happened to be an extreme cold night, and therefore the better for dancing, there were a great many Ladies and Gentlemen, and most of the members of the Club attended, the Cake was froze, but the wine and punch retained their Liquidity, the Longstanding members that chose to dance, danced; and those that chose not, looked on, and drank a bumper now and then to expand the Animal Spirits, by the frigid air drove to the Centre, there were danced many minuets, country dances & Jiggs, and, there was as much bowing, cringing, complimenting, Curtsying, oggling, flurting and Smart repartees, as is usual on such occasions, and the Reverend Mr Sly, tho the gravity of his Cloth, would not permit him to dance, yet he made by much the Smartest figure, in Squiring the Ladies, comparing them, as they stood in a row,

the brim, long beards, banyans and greasy wrappers, in laudable Imitation, of their worthy predecessors of the Ugly Club, now we shall find, turning beaus, and Indulging themselves in all the extravagance of dress and finery, appearing in regimental Suits, long flowing black gowns, bands, and full bottomd wigs.

[225] The extravagance of the members went so far at this Sederunt, being extremely elevated at seeing their honorable president exalted for the first time in his Chair of State, as that the following order was made, vizt:

"That on Tuesday, the 31 of December instant, there shall be a ball held at the Stadt house, for the entertainment of the Ladies, at the common expence of the Club, and the president is pleased to appoint the Secretary, to prepare the same against the time appointed."

O Luxury! O excess! whether wilt thou arive at last, wilt thou not, now thou hast begun, go on in an unwearied round, 'till thou hast utterly ruined and anihilated this ancient and honorable Club?

At this Sederunt the Reverend Mr Broadface Round, and Doctor Hereum Thereum, were made honorary members of the Club.

Against the approaching time of the Ball, the Secretary applied all his diligence to make proper preparations, and, as there was to be a cake provided for the Ladies, and having little or no Judgement in the Structure of a cake himself, he went pensively along one morning, $βη$ $δε$ $ακεε$ $παρα$ $θινα$,³ to consult his honor the president concerning this cake, as a person thorro'ly skilled in that nice part of pastry; and found him sitting in his Saloon in a dishabille, with some of the Club papers before him, which showed the care that this great man took, about every thing relating to the Club, he made his obeisance, which the president was graciously pleased to return, and being permitted to sit down, he opened to his honor, the [226] business, about which he came, vizt: the Ball ‖ cake, concerning the confabrication of which, he humbly desired his honor, would be pleased to give him his advice.

His honor seemed to wave the Subject, by saying he did not chuse to be concerned in the affair, at which the Secretary seemed to be not alittle astonished, as he discovered by this behaviour a secret, before unknown to him, and this was that his honor was not pleased with the order of the Ball, which Indeed, after some pause, his honor frankly owned to this officer, thus confirming his suspicion, and said, at the same time that out of complaisance to the club, he did not care to Interpose his authority in that affair, but allowed them to proceed in it unmolested, as he found they were

---

3. "He went silently along the shore of the loud-roaring sea" (*Iliad* 1.34).

The Hon: Nas: Ide Esqr, first mounts the Prendential Chair of State

[facing page 223]

Rhetorician; he had begun, alas, with too great Success, to Introduce excess and Luxury in matters of eating and drinking into this here Club, and it would have been well, had he stopped there. Had he gone no farther, than rack punch, iced cake, plumb pudding, custard, Sillabub, apple pie, partridge pye, Ragoos, fricassees, hashes and venison pasties, things might have gone tollerably well. But, at Sederunt 25th Decr: 10th 1745, The Club being held at the house of Jealous Spyplot Esqr, Steward, The Chair of State being prepared as ordered at last Sederunt, and set forth, at the head of the Club Table, the Honorable Nasifer Jole Esqr made his appearance, in a flamming Suit of Scarlet, a magnificent hat, bound round with massy Scolloped Silver lace, a fine large and full fair wig, white kid Gloves, with a gold headed cane, and I cannot be certain whether or not he had a Silver hilted Sword, with a beautiful Sword knot of Ribbons, white Silk Stockings rolld, large Shining Silver Shoe buckles, his coat and vest edged round with gold twist, the buttons gold & gilt Spangles, || the button holes trimmed with gold and several brilliant rings upon his fingers, his Shoes shining like a looking glass, his beard close shaved, and his nails close pared, in this luxury of dress did he ascend the chair of state, and looked like a flaming comet in his perihelion, the laced hat resembling the resplendent body of the Star, the flaxen wig the tail, and the other sparkling parts of his dress, the Shining constellations surrounding it, so that had Hermes, Zoroaster, or Ptolomy,[2] or any of the ancient Astronomers have seen him, when it was usual to translate Heroes to the Skies, and make constellations of them, they probably would have alloted this Clubical hero, a place in the heavens, and he would have decked the Celestial Sphere, under the name of *Præses Jolæus,* and might have sat there in State in the *Cathedra Cassiopæa,* as he sits now in State in the Grand Cathedra of the ancient and honorable Tuesday Club.

Thus did this great man, Inconsideratly Introduce the Luxury of dress, into this here ancient and honorable Club, and we shall soon find some of the Longstanding Members Imitating him in this, and, such as never knew before, any other than a Simple plain dress, members wont to come to club *sans ceremonie,* with night caps not over clean, Slouch hats, ragged round

---

2. Hermes Trismegistus, the name given to the Egyptian god "Thoth the very great," was the reputed author of philosophical-religious treatises and various works on astrology, magic, and alchemy. Zoroaster, the Greek name for Zarathustra (a figure of Aryan legend known to the Greeks as early as the 5th century B.C.), was credited with an immense number of works dealing with theology, astrology, and magic. Ptolemy (fl. A.D. 127–148) was a celebrated mathematician, geographer, and astronomer whose major work, the *Almagest,* is a complete textbook of astronomy as the Greeks understood it.

ments in minature, there is a necessity for a president or head, who, in order to qualify him- ‖ self better than nature has done for his high office, must have certain marks and Symbols of State and dignity, such as a chair of State, a cap of State, a badge of state, a canopy of State; these are all absolutely necessary to equip a President of a Club, in order to Inspire a proper and decent awe into the Subordinate members; His officers of State, and Superior officers, such as chancellor, champion, Mr of Ceremonies, must likewise have their ensigns of honor, as a Seal, a Sword, a fan, or some such flurting[8] Instrument, and their particular privileges. As for his Inferior officers, such as his musician, orator, Secretary and Serjeant at arms, it is only requisite the first two be endued with a clear voice, the next have a quick and Stiff pen, and the last should be a Strong fisted resolute fellow, to qualify each of them for their respective offices, and to keep the Longstanding members in that awe and Subjection, which their duty requires of them, all these great qualifications, we shall find in the respective officers of the Ancient and honorable Tuesday Club, and thus, having briefly discussed this Important Subject, I now proceed with our History.

Chapter II

Of a great Club Ball, and matters of Gallantry, with the Clubical Character, of Nasifer Jole Esqr.

I have heard it said of a certain orator and Rhetorician, who used in his time to mount the rostrum with a *bon grace,* and hold forth with a *grand eclat,* that what puzzled him more than any thing else, in his oratorial and Rhetorical compositions, and exercises, ‖ was how to make a good conclusion, or ending, for, as to the exordium, or beginning of an oration, it was as easy as to whistle, and he could flourish it away in that part after a very Sublime manner, but how to end or conclude, or indeed where properly to stop, without making many an Impertinent circumbendibus, was the difficulty, *hic labor, hoc opus;*[1] that is, it required the art of hocus pocus.

The Honorable Nasifer Jole Esqr, now president of the ancient and honorable Tuesday Club, was just in the same Situation as this orator and

---

8. Derived from *flurted* (flowered, figured) or *fleuret,* an ornament shaped like a small flower.

1. Hamilton has purposely botched the passage from Vergil noted above (p. 213).

sary to the public, tho' of a baser metal. Now, as to the necessity of these offices and officers, I believe none will question it, but, as to the offices being well executed, and the officers properly qualified to execute their functions, it is to be supposed all will grant, that is not so absolutely necessary, and that especially in the very highest offices and first rank of officers, else why should we often find, a Savage and Inhuman brute, in human Shape, a bitter Enimy to every other Creature in human Shape, a murderer ravisher, plunderer, and oppressor sitting at the helm, and yet the Ship of the Common wealth, steering a smooth course, why do we so often observe, fools, boys and Changelings, sitting in Councils of State, and yet matters pritty well managed, blockheads fill Judicial Chairs, and yet the affairs of Justice go Swimingly on; Cowards lead Armies, and yet victory pop into our mouths, Covetous and rapacious men entrusted with the public treasure, and yet the fund very carefully managed, and fair accounts rendered of it; But in most cases, the Lower Class of officers, must of necessity be men well qualified, that is, they must be Sly cunning, Strong fisted || rugged fellows, else they never could cleverly catch their fellow rogues or keep them when cought, or even whip or hang them with any decency or good grace, hence, I doubt not, some will conclude, that your catchpoles, Bum-bayliffs, Jaylors and hangmen, are the most worthy and meritorious persons in office, in a kingdom or state, being always persons of great qualifications and abilities for the Important offices they hold and are entrusted with, whereas, your high and dignified officers, are often children, fools, Ignoramuses, pimps, knaves, cowards, covetous and Cruel fellows, which qualities render them, not quite so fit for their exalted offices, as their bretheren of the Lower class are for theirs, to whom many of these very qualities are of Singular Service.

Indeed, where certain qualities, called by many, necessary qualities, are wanting in Superior officers, these are very well supplied, by Certain badges of State, which have a mighty power and virtue to Influence and awe the herd of mankind; such as Seats called thrones, and chairs of State, canopies, maces, mitres, Crowns, triple Crowns, caps of State, full bottomd wigs, white Staves, ribbons, Stars, garters, truncheons, Swords and the like,[a] which being exposed to the view of the populace, or carried in procession, (tho' really in the nature of things no better than a fools cap and bells, with a bladder full of peas on a pole) Inspire a mighty awe and reverence for the proprietors & possessors of them.

As it is in Civil governments, so is it in Clubs, which are civil govern-

(a) Vide the frontispiece.

ished in the 15th Century, and Invented, or rather Improved very much the Science of dowble Entendre; (a Science much cultivated since his time by the Jesuits) and used in a droll and waggish Sense, some words of an ambigous meaning, or simular Sound, and therefore, punning, since his time has been Called by the French *Turlupinader;* but to find the true Etymology of *Conundrum,* will be no such easy matter, however, to satisfy the Curious, I shall here deliver what I know Concerning it, tho' to me, the derivation seems to be somewhat strained and far fetched.

Every one, who understands the french Language, knows what is meant by the word *Con,* which, for fear of offence to modest ears, I shall not translate into English, it is derived then, says my author, from this french || word *con,* and two english words added to it, vizt: the words *under* and *him,* but the two last words for the ease of our polite pronouncers and writers have been contracted thus, *und'r'um,* and the whole Joined together make *Conund'r'um,* which without the break and apostrophæs, make the plain word *Conundrum;* why the word should be analysed in this awkward manner, I cannot tell, unless the Imagination and wit is as much exercised by a new broached conundrum, as the limbs and members are, at the broaching of a new maidenhead, but least I offend the modest, I shall have done. [219]

As for the derivatives of this celebrated word used in our Club stile, I shall now knock them off, as fast as peas, *Conundrumify,* I assert, is as proper as Shipify, *Conundrumification,* as recapitulation; *Conundrumatic,* as problematic, *Conundrumatical,* as fanatical; *Conundrumish,* as funnish, punnish (which last too, is a Club phrase) rummish or rammish, *conundrumation,* as modulation, or 'Nation, which some people use for Damnation, and thus have I explained, and accounted for these words, Introduced into the Club, by members of note, and Called Club Stile.

And now, since I talk of members of note, it will be proper, before I conclude this Chapter, to say something of high Club offices and dignified officers.

Offices and officers, are alike necessary in Civil Government, as in Clubs, the last being a Consequence of the first, for an officer cannot exist without an office, no more than an office without an officer, || But which of them had the prior existence, or if they existed at first Synchronously, I shall not here determin, leaving that nice enquiry to your Subtle metaphysicians; Thus, in a kingdom or monarchy, there must be a King, or Supreme magistrate to govern in Chief, and under him, must be his ministers, and Subordinate magistrates, to support the head and first mover of the great political Machine, these are great officers, and under them are smaller fry, such as Constables, bum bayliffs, Catchpoles, Jailors and Hangmen, equally neces- [220]

are often used, as beautiful expletives of discourse, and serve much better to fill up a gap, than coughing, Spitting, wiping ones face or mouth with a fine Cambric handkerchef, rubbing ones forehead, shifting ones wig and screwing ones mouth into a political grin, taking a pinch of Snuff, or a quid of tobacco, which are all practised to perfection by orators, when they are at a loss what to say next; now, *this here Club Sir*, and *that there Club Sir*, pronounced in a slow deliberate and drawling manner, as they are only words of Course, that require no attention, flowing out as it were mechanically, may give the orator an opportunity, to rake out from among the rubbish and Lumber of his fancy, what he is next to say.

As to *Longstanding members*, I have said enough of that in the last Chapter of the first book, where I have clearly show'd the Significancy of the term, and its origin; *Old Standing members* are those who were of the Club at its first Institution, and I think it a very proper term, cavil at it who will.

But they'll say, why *Presidential*; I shall only answer why Substantial, circumstantial, and many other derivatives of the like nature.

Again, who ever before heard of *Cathedration*, very true, 'tis a new Coind clubical term, and pray is it not as good as Castration, damnation, consideration &ct:

As for *Sederunt,* it is a latin word, and signifies they sat, being used much in the Journals of the Scots parliaments, and the number annexed expresses the number of Sittings, the Club has sat, vizt: Sederunt 20th or Sed: 24: this arose from the whin bush club.

[218]   As to the rest, take them in the lump, I think that *Clubical* is as proper as comical; *Clubific,* as pacific; *Clubified,* as horrified; *capation,* as coronation; *puzzlementation,* as fermentation; *arguefication,* as qualification; *Anticlubarian,* as antitrinitarian; *Grogorian,* as historian; but as for *Conundrum* and it's derivatives, I must beg leave to enlarge alittle upon it.

It is uncertain whence the word *conundrum* it self is derived,[6] it seems to be a word of an odd Sound, and conveys a Sort of Burlesque Idea; (if I may so speak) being much of the same nature with the french *Turlupinade,* tho' that by the Bye signifies a pun; but as puns and Conundrums are cousin germans, or brother and Sister's Children, we may look upon the two words, as pritty much alike; Turlupin[7] was a famous Droll, who flour-

---

6. The origin of *conundrum* is, as Hamilton suggests, uncertain; it is referred to as an Oxonian term, having possibly originated in an Oxford joke.

7. Turlupin was the stage name of Henri Legrand (d. 1637), one of a trio of French actors who performed at the Hôtel de Bourgogne in Paris in the early 17th century (not the 15th, as Hamilton suggests) and delighted the public with their coarse popular farces.

and Improvement of our Language, for, from whence, if not from this pure fountain, came these elegant words, now much in use at court, vizt: *Bully, cully, bite, bamboozle, bumbaisd, humbug, fun, queer, Bunter,*[5] and many such like elegant terms and epithets. It is commonly urged, by the learned professors of law and physic, that the great and cheif design of their terms of art, is to conceal the mysteries of their particular crafts from the vulgar, and to humor a Sort of foolish people, of whom there are a considerable number, in all places, who think there is nothing extraordinary in plain language and common phrazes, and I know not but our Theologues and Gypsies, may have the same use for their particular terms of art.

Is it then to be wondered at, that Clubs, and particularly the ancient and honorable Tuesday Club, should have a stile and terms of art peculiar to themselves, since all Societies, learned and unlearned, have had their technical terms and favorite stile. [216]

Let none of our Readers then, stare gape and be astonished, when they meet in the course of this club History, with such as these following terms and Phrazes, vizt: *Sederunt, Cathedration, puzzlementation, this here Club, that there Club, long standing members, old standing members, Presidential, Clubical, Clubific, Clubified, conundrum,* and its derivatives, *conundrumify, conundrumification, Conundrumatic, conundrumatical, conundrumish, conundrumation, capation, arguefication, anticlubarian, Grogorian,* and some others of less note, but let them be assured that they are all very proper, Significant and elegant Club phrazes, and proper Club stile, coined and Introduced, by certain of the members of greatest note and Eminence.

But to recapitulate, they'll say, why *this here Club,* and *that there Club,* might not *this Club* and *that Club* do as well; I grant it might, with regard to speaking of this Club, and that Club in General, but then it does not so clearly express this club at present sitting, or that Club at present sitting, for, the particles *here* and *there,* point out emphatically, something *here* present, or *there* existing, whereas, the other way of Speaking, does not at all define the Club *Congregatim,* or existing as a Club, This I think is Sufficient to Justify the expression, not to mention the Example of people of rank and quality, who use this expletive much even in their Common discourse, the Phrazes *this here* and *that there,* being favorites at St James's ‖ and in the army, the two British accademies of politeness and propriety of Stile, there is besides to be considered the weight authority and example of many of our great orators and barristers, for by them, *this here* and *that there* [217]

---

5. A *bully* is the protector of a prostitute; a *cully* is a dupe; a *bite* is a sharper or swindler; to *bumbaze* is to perplex or bamboozle; to *fun* is to cheat or hoax; a *bunter* is a low, vulgar woman.

that he meant and Intended, *one's nighest relation, in ones own wrong, Division, Barring all delays & excuses, to hear and determin, you shall Cause to be done, you shall Cause to be known, a warrant, a murder, a raut, a riot, I forbid prosecution, he shall not leave the province or kingdom, a true bill*, and *we know nothing at all of the matter.*

In Physic again, we shall often hear, a Learned Gentleman in a full bottom wig, black coat, with a Snuff box in his hand, and a cane dangling at his wrist, ‖ enveloped in a large Scarlet Rockela,[4] outward marks, ensigns and Symbols of learning and Philosophy, holding forth, concerning *Symptoms, prophylaxis, Idiosyncrasy, Gruma, coagulum, Phlebotomy, venesection, cathartics, eccoprotics, emetics, Juleps, pills, troches, ecclegmas, decoctions, apozems, incision, unguents, liniments, Embrocation &ct:* which an Intelligent man at first hearing would Imagin to be words framed on purpose to conjure up the Devil, and the Devil himself, were he conjured up, unless he understood latin greek and arabic, would never discover that this Learned don, meant by these Phrases, only *Signs of a distemper, method of cure, disposition or tendency, curd like matter, Blood letting, a purge, a vomit, a mixture of Sugar and distilled waters, little round balls to swallow, small flat things in various Shapes, or Tablets, thick mixtures of honey, Sugar and oil, broths made of herbs, cutting the flesh, ointments,* and *greasing the Skin with them.*

This fantastical Custom, has not only prevailed among the Learned, but also among the Ignorant, vulgar, and that even the lowest, tho' I dare not say the most vicious or wicked class of mankind, vizt: Gypsies, Theives, pickpockets and vagrant beggars, who have Invented terms of art, and framed a Language of their own, which Indeed excells the learned Jargon in this particular circumstance, that they are not Indebted to other Languages for their terms of art, but Invent them whenever they have occasion.

Thus, they call an Ale house, a *bouzing ken.* a beggar born and bred, a *Clapperdudgeon.* a pretended Dumb man, a *Dummerer.* a Shuffling Impostor, a *Crank;* Strong liquor, *Hum.* Money *Lour.* Virgins *Dells.* Strumpets, *Doxies.* Beggars, *Maunders.* Hats, *Nab Cheats.* Hands, *Fambles.* Staves, *Filches.* to steal *Filsh.* Rayment, *Back cheat.* Food, *Belly Cheat.* Good words *Ben whids.* Stand on your Guard, *Fumbumbus.* a man *Cove.* Beaten, *Lumb'd.* a pot of ale, *Gag of ben house.* Rogues *Claws.* Hedges, *Ruffmans.* To lie with a maid, *Twang a Dell.* Pigs, *Grunting Cheats.* Chickens, *cackling Cheats.* Hens *margery praters.* to steal a buck of Cloaths, *mill a Lag of duds.* And several of these cant words as they are called, have in our days been adopted, by persons of quality, rank and politeness, to the great decoration

---

4. A *roquelaure* is a knee-length cloak.

This profitable trade and cunning Science, under the Specious title of [212] Christianity and religion, as bad wares are commonly vended, by having fine outlandish names given them, has, in all ages gained much ground among frail Sinful men, because it points out to them, as they foolishly believe, a streight, wide and direct road, whereby they may go speedily to heaven, and yet fornicate, adulterize, Gormandize, tipple, rob, steal, swear, forswear, and Cut throats all the way as they go along, and fare never the worse for it, be never an ace the less christians, and Surely hit the mark at last, remembering to pay the priests and holy church their perquisites, else all this pegeantry turns out good for nothing, and the same, as if you should rub your arse with a brick bat.

What a lamentable thing is it, that thus a plain and easie matter is rendered difficult and Intricate by such far fetched technical terms and confounded Trumpery, what occasion have they, but for the greed of filthy Lucre, to perplex with difficulties, and involve in terms, such as *transubstantiation, Consubstantiation, reprobation, Sanctification, regeneration, predestination, Supererogation, free grace, adoption &ct*: a matter, which consists only in, *fear God, love your neighbour, and honour the king,*—and above all, *do as you would be done by*—this, I suppose, every man may understand at first hearing, or reading of a certain book Called the new testament (condemned from the perusal of the vulgar, by certain cunning priests, as containing ‖ dangerous doctrine,) without being at the trowble to rummage the Fathers, [213] or Commentators for a nice explication of it, for this would be like descending into deep and dark Caverens, to explore the light of the Glorious sun, or rather, as the famous Sir Rowland that mad peer of France did, like sending their wits and Senses a gadding to the moon,[2] that they might know where to look for them, should they ever have occasion to use them.

The learned gentlemen of the Law and Physic have been guilty of this absurdity to a very Scandalous degree, and to undertake the Study of either has now become a labor, almost Insurmountable, *Hoc opus hic labor est*, as the poet tells us;[3] we shall hear a Gentleman, of the first of these learned professions, talk of *Prochain amy, en son tort, apportionment, Essoin, oyer* and *terminer, fieri facias, scire facias, Warrantum, murderium, rautum, riotum, nolo presequi, ne exeat Regnum, billa vera, Ignoramus,* and a thousand other such cramp terms, by which no well meaning Christian could once Imagin,

---

2. Roland was the famous paladin who was defeated by the Spanish at Roncesvalles (778) and later became a legendary hero in French literature. Hamilton is referring, however, to the humorous account of Roland's efforts to recover his senses in Lodovico Ariosto's *Orlando furioso*, 34.66–71.

3. "This is the task, this is the work" (Vergil, *Aeneid* 6.129).

such words cannot be found, how much easier, how much shorter would his task have been.

Whether an enthusiastic reverence for the Superior abilities of the ancients, who surely were the first Inventors, or a Supine Indulgence and remissness in the moderens, was the cause of these latter, not taking the trowble to alter those terms of art, and adapt them to the particular languages of the Countries where they were received, is not my business here to enquire, but, I shall be bold to make a few observations on this General Corruption, that in these latter centuries has overspread Europe, and prevailed so far, as to gain footing even in Clubs.

This Idle piece of foppery, has extended it Self so far, as to Infect not only the professors of Science and literature, but has taken place even among mechanics and tradesmen, who too have their particular terms of art, and uncouth names and designations, which extend even to their tools, and the materials upon which they work. Nay, Divinity, or Theology, as some are pleased to call it, because they would have both a greek ‖ and latin term, which in plain english, is nothing but a discourse or doctrine Concerning God, his nature and attributes, in which, all mankind, for the Sake of their own happiness and good are so nearly concerned, has been hampered Cramped, obscured, and rendered mysterious, I may say unintelligible, by a parcell of Lucrative, covetous and designing Schoolmen and priests, who, Instead of the practice of piety and morality, the main purpose and design of Religion and revelation, have crammed up the heads of the Ignorant and Superstitious mob (for I account all those gentlemen mob, who take things Implicitly and depend upon the say so of others, without exercising their own reason and Judgement) with Idle Stuff, concerning orthodoxy and hetrodoxy, heresy and heritics, Ceremonies, rites, Songs, riddles, rebuses and fiddlesticks, and perswaded them, that they may go to heaven by Legerdemain, or Slight of hand as it were, climbing up on piles and mountains of Mitres, Copes, Surplices, Chalices, crosiers, hoods, Cowls, cassocks, bagpipes, fiddles, Crucifixes, pictures, tinckling bells, pixes,[1] Consecrated wafers, triple Crowns, bunches of keys, altars, hour glasses, folio books, bells, bell ropes and cats o' nine tails, which last, are for alittle good Christian-like Jerking & Scourging, with a penny or two by the bye for the poor priests, to Indulge in Gluttony letchery and Idleness, and also to enable the chast nuns, to pray for the Souls of the Dead, who never once thanked them for it, to deliver Sinners out of purgatory, and commit Iniquity in their Cloysters.

1. A *pyx* is the vessel containing the Host, or consecrated bread of the Sacrament.

The History of the Ancient and Honorable Tuesday Club

Book IV

From the Cathedration of the honorable Nasifer Jole Esqr, president, to the first grand Anniversary procession.

Chapter I

Of Club stile, and Clubical terms, necessary for the understanding of this history, as also of Great Club-offices and officers, their nature, dignity and privileges.

For some Centuries past, at least, since the Æra of the Gothic Ignorance, when Learning Arts Clubs, and every thing that had a tendency to humanize and civilize mankind, were almost totally extinguished, and nothing prevailed but a Savage ferocity and rude use of arms, it has been the Custom among our moderen Literati, and Cultivators of arts and Sciences, to clog and Encumber these arts and Sciences, with certain uncouth and Cramp terms, called Technical terms, borrowed and compiled, from either dead or outlandish Languages, such as the Greek, latin, old French and Arabic, to the no small hindrance and discouragement, of the painful, laborious, poring and brain beating Student, who, before he can understand aright, || The Substance or marrow of any art or Science, must spend half his life in exploring the meaning of these terms used in that art or Science, this necessarily forces him to the drudgery of learning many other Languages besides his mother tongue, and he must spend much of his precious time, in the dry and tedious toil of turning over many of these (too often) Impertinent and voluminous compositions called Dictionaries, whereas, had these terms been expressed, in the vernacular or vulgate tongues, either by words of the same Signification, or a Circumlocutory description, when

List of the members Regular and honorary, of the Ancient and Honorable Tuesday Club, that were in the Club, between the 14th of May & the 26th of November 1745.

Regular members	Honorary members
Loquacious Scribble M:D: Secr:	Mr Abraham Bumper
Prattle Motely Esqr Secr:	Doctor Polyhistor
Revd: Smoothum Sly	Mr Oldham Wisely
Jealous Spyplot Esqr	Mr Joshua Fluter
Capt: Bully Blunt	Capt: Huffbluff Surly
Capt: Seemly Spruce	Mr Ignotus warble
Mr Laconic Comas	Signior Lardini
Capt: Serious Social	Coll: Courtly Phraze
The Hon: Nasifer Jole Esqr pres:	
Mr Dumpling Gundiguts	
Drawlum Quaint Esqr	
Mr Slyboots pleasant	
Mr Joggle Hasty	
Mr Solo neverout	

hastily up, the Chair was overset, and, to the Surprize of every body, there Tumbled out a Close Stool pan, which as good luck would have it, had none of its proper contents in it, thereupon, Capt: Blunt, observed with a Sneer, That the President had made a Shitten entry into his office, and he hoped he would make the like exit.

Thus, was this great man exalted to the office of perpetual president of this ancient and honorable Club, and to this day, has kept his Seat Steadily in that Chair, and we shall now see him make a considerable figure thro' the Course of this History, sometimes ruling in peace and quietness, sometimes in the midst of disturbance and hurly burly, sometimes exalted, sometimes depress'd, by his Inconstant and unruly Longstanding members. The Club ordered Jealous Spyplot Esqr, to prepare a proper chair, for the president, against the next meeting of the Club.

[208] At this Sederunt, Signior Lardini was made an honorary member; This gentleman, we shall find, making a considerable figure as musician *Con stromenti,* and musical Composer to the Club, as also, Chief Triumvir of the worshipful Eastren Shore Triumvirate.

Thus, this ancient and honorable Club, by creating a perpetual president, came nigher to the model of the ancient and venerable Tuesday, (or whin bush) Club of Lanneric, but deviated from that excellent ancient constitution, in this Important circumstance, that they gave a much greater power and more privileges to the Honorable Nasifer Jole Esqr, than any Venerable president, of that ancient and venerable Club ever had, in the memory of man.

End of the third book.

The unlucky adventure at the Cathedration of the Honorable Carlo Nauger Jole Esqr

vote, but the first part of it entirely annulls the wise law of unanimous consent, in electing members and making new Laws, some Sederunts before this so warmly Disputed, and Grants a greater privilege than any president ever yet had, by striking at the root of a fundamental and constitutional Law.

4to That the president shall alone have the power of Judging, when the Gelastic Law ought to be put in Execution by making some Signal for executing the same.

This is another unwarrantable privilege, and seems quite preposterous, and contrary to the Law of nature, nay even to the Law of nations and Clubs, that any President shall take upon him to direct me, when, or how to laugh, or cry, or Grin, whensoever he pleases; I believe I may safely affirm that Laughing, or crying or grinning, must come naturally, and cannot be forced, and I should laugh at any man Indeed be he a president or not, that would take upon him to Command the muscles of my face, whensoever he thought fit; In fine, this seems to be a villanous privilege, because it makes of the members a parcel of momuses, histrios or Commedians, or rather poppets, subject to the caprice and will of the president.

5to That if any motion is made in Club, the president is to be first addressed by the moving member, giving him his proper title.

This, I grant, is a very Just privilege, and what all presidents as moderators of Clubs ought to have, tho' the Club afterwards pretended to rescind it, and order the address to be directed to the Speaker, on account of the Presidents Strange in attention in such cases.

6to That at the common expence of the Club there || shall be procured a chair for the president, raised one Step above the other Seats or chairs in the Room.

This privilege several of the members grumbled at, particularly Jealous Spyplot esqr, who always thought that every member there ought to be on a Level.

Then it was Resolved, that in case other privileges should be thought proper, to be conferrd upon his honor the President, they should be considered and argued, at some of the Subsequent Sederunts of the Club.

Mr President seemed, with great reluctance and modesty, to accept of these valuable privileges, but afterwards, like all men in power, proved very tenacious, not only of them, but of some others that were since given him.

Then was he led by two members, vizt: Mr Smoothum Sly, and Mr Secretary Scribble, to a Semicircular Smoking Chair, which happened to be in the Room, and set down in it with his back to the door, which Capt: Blunt perceiving, Invidiously thrust open the door, and, his honor getting

procedure, it being Customary, for the honorable, the Speaker or Chairman of the House of Commons, to profess himself insufficient at his election, and humbly desire, that a man of Greater Abilities may be put in the Chair, as soon as this election was over, it was entered in the book of Records

"That Nasifer Jole Esqr, upon account of the Elegant entertainments given by him to the Club, and his known abilities, was voted perpetual president, or Chairman of the Club, and had Immediatly the following privileges granted him."

Law XIX. 1mo That the President shall have the Sole power to nominate his own Deputy, in case of necessary absence.

Here it must be observed, that the Club Inconsideratly gave up all power inherent in them, to appoint deputy presidents, and they soon felt the bad consequences of this, for at several times, the president refused absolutely to name or Commission his deputy, and therefore, by a following law, they took to themselves, a power of chusing a *deputatus Electus,* but the president never would give up this valuable privilege, and says that this here other Law, is no Law at all, till they revoke the first, which they never can do; for, as he is a perpetual president, the Law, which gives him his privileges, must necessarily be a perpetual Law, This ought to be a Seasonable warning to all free Clubs, how they part with their power of election, to any president whatsoever, because, they put it in the power of that president to throw the constitution into Disorder, whenever he pleases, by depriving it of a proper head or ruler.

2do That upon every Club night, the Steward for the time being, shall acquaint the president of the time and place of meeting, that he may know the appointed Deputy, In case the President cannot attend, and to acquaint the Club when met, of the person named to take the Chair.

This I observe was giving the Steward a deal of trowble to very little purpose, and is only a needless piece of State or form, which absolutely supposes great men or grandees to have shorter memories than other people. Why could not the president, as well as any other member, know and remember the stated times of meeting every fortnight, and send his orders to the Secretary, concerning his Deputy, whose propper office it was, (and not the Steward's) to deliver it to the Club.

3tio That the President shall have the privilege of taking out one single nay, if at any time such shall happen in balloting, the other being all the Contrary part, or yeas, and in Cases where a majority carries in Club, he shall have the Casting vote where there happens a parity.

The last part of this privilege, I think is not to be objected to, because it is the undoubted right of all presidents and Chair men to have the casting

It happened then, upon the memorable 26th of November, 1745 O:S: at Sederunt 24th, Mr Secretary Scribble being Steward, that the Club resolved to Chuse a perpetual president or Chairman, and The Illustrious Nasifer Jole Esqr, was proposed || by Mr Smoothum Sly, as a proper person for the presidential Chair, But, Capt: Bully Blunt stood up, and opposed it, telling the Club That he did not know that Nasifer Jole Esqr, or any esquire whatsoever, had any Juster claim to the Chair, than any other member or Esquire, That, he humbly conceived, without the least grain of Vanity, that, he himself being also an Esquire, deserved as much that eminent place and office, as any Longstanding member in this here Club, and therefore hoped that this here Club, would do him the Justice to elect him president, and so put in his claim, To this a member made reply—That if corpulency and enormous Size of body was a qualification for the Chair, Captain Blunt in that respect only was Sufficiently qualified; but really if this here Club, was to Chuse a president, for that qualification alone, they might as well pitch upon Mr Spyplots great Dog Mars, and place him in that honorable Seat. It was also observed by the same member, after alittle pause, That Captain Blunt, was not at all in a proper dress, for such a Solemn ceremony, as that of being elected a president, for, granting that he was every other way worthy of the place, yet, the Dirty night cap, the long beard, and the greasy banyian, was by no means a propper apparel, in which to ascend a presidential Chair. Upon this, Captain Blunt Retired, and, in a few minutes after, to the Great Surprize of all the members, appeared, dressed out in his regimentals, as fine as || if he had Just been taken out of a band box; with a fair Ramilee wig, a clean Shaved beard, a clean Ruffled Shirt, a Laced wastcoat and Sword, but all this fracas prov'd in vain; for, on putting about the vote, the members gave their voices for Nasifer Jole Esqr, and Captn Blunt had no other vote but his own, and Nasifer's, who modestly gave him his. Upon this Nasifer Jole Esqr, with great modesty declared to the Club, his Insufficiency for this high and dignified office, and Solemnly protested that it was a thing he by no means desired, and wished it had pleased the members to bestow it upon a person more Qualified for and worthy of the place. But this was only like Cæsar's putting aside the Crown faintly, when offered him by Mark Anthony, and Indeed, these professions with most of the members passed for words of course, and bare formal and complimentary Speeches, as is usual with great men on such occasions, when they are promoted or advanced, who, to save appearances at least, and keep up a state or form, pretend Insufficiency and want of merit, tho' neither themselves nor hearers believe these expressions and terms of humiliation to be true in fact, but this Illustrious president had a good Precedent, for this

*It may be well observed here, how artful men will gain upon the opinion and affections of a people, when they observe a mild, easie deportment and behavior towards them, and when they heap benefits and favors upon them unasked. This was the very case with Nasifer Jole Esqr, and the long standing members of the ancient and honorable Tuesday Club; This gentleman wore a complacent and mild countenance, always adorned with a Smile, and like Cæsar of old, flattered the people, that by gaining the ascendant over their affections, he might the more easily seize the Tyranny into his own hands, and govern their persons as he thought fit, neither did he spare any bounty in the way of entertaining, for, at the very first time of his being Steward, he Introduced into the Club that expensive Liquor called rack, (so bewitching to our Refined palats, because it is so far fetched) as has been Related above, and had a large table in the next Room, elegantly spread, the cloth and napkins nicely pinched, and perfumed Sweetly with Lavander and roses, and several elegant dishes of meat, were curiously Ranged on this Table, the passage, between the Club room and Supper room beautifully Illuminated, with Sconces nicely disposed, in the figures of diamonds, triangles, Stars and circles, at the second time of his serving Steward, which was Sederunt 23d, he added an Iced cake to the entertainment, which was dealt about in Luncheons || to the members, curiously wrap'd up in clean white paper, this Cake, this fatal Cake, Compleated the Catastrophe of the Clubs liberty, and, as Esau sold his birthright to Jacob, for fair words and a mess of porridge, so this unhappy Club, bartered their Liberty to Nasifer Jole Esqr, for an old Song, Rack punch, plumb pudding, four pound of Candles, and an Iced Cake!

But tho I condemn the conduct of the Club in this affair, yet, that I may do Strict Justice to that great and Illustrious personage, Nasifer Jole Esqr, I am Sincerely of opinion that the Club could not have pitched upon a milder or more Complacent governor than he, for, at all times, he has shown himself benign, gentle and easie to be entreated, and, excepting only in that nice point of giving up the least article or particle, of his valuable prerogative and privileges, of which he is Justly tenacious, he has spared no pains to humor the Club, in every thing they desired, as will be plainly seen in the Sequel of this History. But what tho' the Club be in a great measure happy and easie, under the government of this polite and accomplished *Archon,* yet, it cannot with any Certainty be expected, that it will always remain so under that of his Successors, who, not minding his example, may turn out to be bloody and Cruel Tyrants.

[202]

(*) Vide anniversary oration 9th, almost verbatim the same with this and the following paragraph.

Magister artium, Ingeniique largitor venter.[11]

Smooth Language and cunning coaxing too go a great way in driving this Scurvey bargain. Therefore, it was a wise provision in the Athenians, of old, who were under ‖ a democratical government, like that of this here Club at it's first establishment, to take off their great men, so soon as they became popular, nothing conducing more to Introduce an absolute Tyranny, than the popularity of one man, we see the Sad effects of this corruption and venality, at our Elections for burgesses and Representatives; the man who treats best & gives most Cyder and punch, and makes the most Coaxing, wheedling and pallabering Speeches, being always returned by the Giddy constituents, tho' perhaps less qualified for the trust than another, who either could not, or would not be so lavish of his money and words.

I shall here observe also, how prone all men are to flatter and cajole those, from whom they have already received and yet expect to receive favors; it is presumtously said in the above entry "That elegance and mirth were promoted, without transgressing the Rules of the Club," but I may with Confidence aver, that the fact was not so, for, the one dish or gammon Law, was most audaciously violated, and trampled under foot, there having been, that very night, a formal laid out table, garnished with boiled and roast, pies, tarts and Custards, besides, the needless apparatus of a table Cloth, napkins, knives, forks, and two or three removes of plates, all in decent order, hence we see, that when people go about flattering of Great men, they will not stick to put even the most palpable untruths upon Record, *O tempora, O mores!*[12] and thus I conclude this Long Chapter.

Chapter VIII

The Election and Cathedration, of the Honorable Nasifer Jole Esqr, President.

We are now come to that period, where we must bid adieu to Clubical Liberty, for, as the end of the Roman Li- ‖ berty, was at the time of their admitting a perpetual Dictator, so, the period of the Liberty of the ancient and honorable tuesday Club, was, at their election of a perpetual President.

11. "Generous queen"; "it is the teacher of arts and the fertile womb of genius" (Persius, *Satires,* prologomena, 11).
12. "Oh the times, oh the customs!" (Cicero, *In Catilinam,* speech 1, sec. 1).

It is therefore the opinion of this Club, that some Signal mark of honor, or distinction, be conferr'd upon the Steward, in reward of the honor he has done the Society, as soon as may be."

I shall beg leave to make a Reflexion or two upon this transaction and these entries.

Some people may rashly conclude, upon reading the above entry, that the Longstanding members of this here Club, were Epicurean Philosophers, but soft and fair, let us before we draw rash conclusions, beware of swerving from truth and Justice, in matters of this weight and consequence, let us neither allow too much merit to these Longstanding members, nor detract too much from the Character of that worthy ancient Philosopher Epicurus; In the first place, I deny that the members of this here Club were in the least degree Philosophers in this particular circumstance, or lovers of Science, but, were more properly Philogasters, or Lovers of their Belly, For I never yet heard that Luscious eating and drinking, was any one of the Seven liberal arts and Sciences, but rather one of the many beastly appetites or lusts, that men are subject to, *ergo,* in whatever case these Longstanding members were Philosophers, || they were none in this. As to Epicurus, some [199] fools have entertained a notion of him, that he affected tippling and Gormandizing, loved to lie in down beds, to cloth in Silk, to keep his concubines, and take his afternoon's nap, but I believe nothing at all of the matter, being persuaded that he was a Sedate, temperate, and Sober Sage, who thought that the greatest happiness consisted in an absence of bodily pain, and the Enjoyment of mental pleasure, by the practice of virtue and Temperance; but, how Idle it is to think, that Luscious eating and drinking, soft lying, Laziness, and an excessive Indulgence of venereal pleasures, could be Ingredients in this Philosophers System of happiness must appear, when we reflect, that he knew as well as we do, that these excesses constantly bring with them, gouts, Rheumatisms, Sciaticas, gravels, Scurvies, poxes, toothakes, colics, boils, blotches, Scabs, and all the plagues of Pandora's box, which are accompanied with pain, rack and torment Inexpressible.

We may see by this transaction, with what cunning and gaining methods, men of an ambitious turn will attempt, to raise themselves, we may also see, how liable to corruption human nature is, and, how men will be Induced to barter liberty, and every other valuable possession, for a little good belly timber, or what we call Eatables and drinkables, and if many do not exchange their liberty directly for that consideration, yet they truck it for money, which is the *Alma Regina,* and procures all these Gimcracks.

Jog hooly good man or the bed'ill fa',
The bed, it's tied at head and feet
With Simmer won hay and thats right Sweet,
And In comes the Crummie Cow she eats it a,
Jog hooly Good man or the bed'ill fa'.

[197] At Sederunt 17th 10th September 1745, Capt: Bully Blunt being Steward, Mr Joshua Fluter was admitted an honorary member, and Mr Joggle hasty forfeited his Seat in Club, by transgressing of Law 13th.

At Sederunt 18th Septr: 17th, Capt: Seemly Spruce being Steward, it was ordained

Law XVI. That no mention shall be made, by any member of the Society, of any person whatever, desirous to be admitted, before such person appears himself in the Society, and desires the same.

Law XVII. That the Secretary Ingross the rules and Laws of the Club, at the end of the book of Records, in the same order as they are passed.

Upon Sederunt 20th October 1st, Mr Laconic Comas being Steward, Mr Oldham wisely, was admitted an honorary member of the Club.

And upon the following Sederunt October 15th, Drawlum Quaint Esqr, being Steward, Capt: Huffbluff Surly, and Mr Ignotus Warble, were created honorary members.

At Sederunt 23 Novr 12th, Nasifer Jole Esqr, being Steward, the following Law was passed.

Law XVIII. That the meeting of this Society shall be once a fortnight, any Law to the contrary notwithstanding, and that as usual, on tuesday evening.

Thus we find already the effects of Luxury and unnecessary expence in this Club, that Society, which before, met amicably once a week, and enjoyed themselves over a bowl, pipe and Gammon or cheese, now find, that by reason of the unnecessary expence of Set Suppers, introduced of late into the Club, it was Inconvenient to all, or most of the members, to have such frequent meetings, we shall likewise find more of it's pernicious effects pre-

[198] ‖ sently taking place, and that is, settling an arbitrary and despotic power in the Club, for, Nasifer Jole Esqr, at this Sederunt, so far outdid all the other members at entertaining, having now Introduced an Iced Cake, which was dealt about in large lunceons to the members, we find an entry at this Sederunt upon the Book of Records to this purpose.

"The whole Society this night express their Satisfaction at being entertained in a very agreeable manner, by the Steward, elegance and mirth being promoted effectually, without transgressing the rules of the Society.

that he was one of the greatest opposers to the creating of such in the Club, when exorbitant power, and boundless ambition had gained the ascendant there, 'till he was created an officer of State himself, by the honorable the president, and then, like other politicians, who have compassed their ends, by having their mouths stop'd, he became utterly silent on that point, tho abundantly clamorous and noisy on others.

At Sederunt 13th August 6th, Mr Slyboots Pleasant being Steward, it was resolved

Law XII. That no member for the future shall be admitted into this Society, without his personal appearance antecedent to his admission.

This, and Law 16th was occasioned by some gentlemen applying to be admitted into the Club, and afterwards retracting.

At Sederunt 14th August 12th, Mr Secretary Scribble being Steward, the Club purchased a leaden tobacco box, painted and gilt, of Nasifer Jole Esqr, price eighteen Shillings, and Solo Neverout Esqr, an Eminent Long Standing member took his Seat in Club, at this same Sederunt, In Consequence of his election at Sederunt 12th.

At Sederunt 15th, August 20th, Mr Secretary || Scribble being deputy [196] Steward, for Jealous Spyplot Esqr, The following Laws were made.

Law XIII. That if any member be absent four nights successively, from the Club, and gives no reason for his absence, or offers no plausible excuse, he is *ipso facto* excluded from the Society.

Law XIV. That the full number of Regular members of the Club be fifteen, but the number of the honorary members Indefinite.

Law XV. That at the admission of every new Member, the Catch called the *Great Bell of Lincoln,* shall be sung by Nasifer Jole Esqr.

At this Sederunt Mr Jole sung the abovementioned Catch so well, that it was the cause of passing the above Law, the members being willing to make as many occasions as possible, to have the opportunity of hearing the fine well tuned voice of that gentleman, Capt: Serious Social too, at this Sederunt, exercised his musical talent, in singing the following song, which became ever since a favorite Club air.

Club air, sung by Cap: Serious Social

Jog hooly good man, or the bed'il fa,
Jog hooly good man or the bed'ill fa,
The bed is made of rotten timmer,
And if it fas it'l smoor our good Mither,
And she'll Cry out and shame us a'.

> When she comes hame, she lays at the Lads,
> And Ca's the lasses baith bitches and Jades,
> And me my sell, an auld Cockold cairlie,[10]
> Oh! If my wife would drink hooly and fairly.
> *Chorus* Hooly and fairly, hooly and fairly,
> Oh! If my wife would drink hooly and fairly.

At this Sederunt it was moved by Drawlum Quaint Esqr, That Mr Solo Neverout, should be admitted a member of this here Club, which motion raised a very warm and obstinate dispute, Jealous Spyplot Esqr alledging that the said Neverout had too much of the States man, and politician in him to make an agreeable member, and tho it was evident, by the laws and constitution of this here Club, that politics and State matters were alltogether excluded as being triffling Subjects below its dignity & Importance, yet, he found, some Longstanding members,(a) who had assurance enough to attempt making a breach in so excellent and wise a constitution, by proposing the said Neverout as a member, therefore, since the said Neverout, was known to converse daily with States men, and politicians, and, assuming the character and air of a politician and States man himself, to enter into the Cabinet councils of great men, mimicking their Stiff formalities, feignd friendship, horse Laughs, and empty promises and protestations, it was a very dangerous and rash proceeding to admit the said Neverout, as a member of this here Club, as by that means probably, the Longstanding members, would not only be in danger of contracting some of these absurd and fantastical habits, but, these great men and politicians, the said Neverout's associates, would foist themselves into the Club, by his Interest, and thereby this here Club, would become a State Club, which Metamorphosis, would assuredly work its ruin and downfall.

As Mr Spyplot was looked upon, to be a long standing member of a deep and Solid understanding, this objection had great weight with many of the members, and some had no regard at all to it, who thought that Mr Spyplot was no wiser than his neighbours, tho' one of the privy council of the celebrated Mr George Neilson, yet, it had like to have obstructed Intirely, the gentleman's election into the Club, but, after a great deal of dispute, and abundance of altercation, Mr Solo Neverout was unanimously admitted a member by the Ballot, and we shall see in the Sequel of this history, that this gentleman, was so far from Introducing state members,

---

(a) This was the first time the term *Longstanding members* was Introduced Into the club.

10. "Cuckolded pipsqueak."

duct; he had a considerable Share of vanity, for he lov'd on all Occasions when haranguing the Club as orator, to tire out their patience with long quotations from obselete Authors, that wrote in the dead Languages.

Tho' there passed abundance of dispute at this Sederunt, concerning law 4th, which many were for altering or rescinding, yet, the members were in a very merry vein, and Mr Smoothum Sly, sung the following Scots Song.

Club Song, sung by Mr Smoothum Sly[4]

> Down in yon meadow a Couple did ta-ry,
> The wife she'd drink nathing but Sack or Canary,
> The Husband Complaind to her friends very early,
> O If my wife would Drink hooly and fairly.[5]
> *Chorus* Hooly and fairly, hooly and fairly,
>   Oh! if my wife would drink hooly & fairly.
>
> A logg with her cummers[6] I would her allow,
> But when she has mair, shes apt to get fou,
> And when she's fou, she's unco Gamstary,[7]
> Oh! if my wife would drink hooly & fairly.
> *Chorus* Hooly &ct:
>
> She drank her Stockings, she drank her Shoon,
> And next, she drank her bran new Gown,
> And eke the Smoke that Civer'd her early,
> Oh! if my wife would drink hooly & fairly.
> *Chorus* Hooly &ct:
>
> First she drank Crummie & then she drank Glairie,[8]
> Next she drank my bonny gray Marie
> That Carried me ay thro' the dubs & the Lairie,[9]
> Oh! gin my wife would drink hooly and fairly.
> *Chorus* Hooly &ct:

---

4. The earliest known version of this song, including several additional verses, appeared as "The Drunken Wife of Gallowa" in *Yair's Charmer* (Edinburgh, 1751). It is included with an introduction in James Johnson, ed., *The Scots Musical Museum*, 6 vols. (Hatboro, Pa., 1962; orig. publ. Edinburgh, 1787–1803), II, 180–182.
5. "Gently and cautiously."
6. "A pint with her female friends."
7. "Very unruly."
8. "She drank the cow and then the whites of the eggs."
9. "Muddy pools and the swamp."

Rank fools you appear by your billingsgate Sheets,
And your Poems, shall soon be b—s—t.

Soon after, the Junto of Bards and Critics at Batchellor's hall, having nothing left to exercise their wit upon, broke up, but yet the Spirit of poetry still remained among the members of the ancient and honorable Tuesday Club, and we shall see it often breaking out, with vigorous coruscations in the Sequel of this History, till at last the whole force of it, like a collected *Ignis* [191] *fatuus,* which before was diffuse || and erratic, centered in the most Sublime Genius of Mr Jonathan Grog, now poet Laureat to the ancient and honorable Tuesday Club.

I come now to a remarkable part of our History, but before I enter upon it, I shall discuss some matters of Lesser consequence; as I Intend to ommit nothing, which relates to the Laws and Rules of this Club, and the execution of them, nor Indeed, the least title relative to their Sports, pastimes and Recreations, as I look upon this here Club, to be a pattern for all other Clubs, that are now, or shall be in after ages.

At Sederunt 12th July the 30th 1745, Joggle Hasty Esqr, being Steward, Mr Secretary Motely having taken his departure for England, Loquacious Scribble M:D: was appointed Secretary to the Club, and had the book of Records delivered to him, and that Gentleman, will in the course of this history, make a considerable appearance, not only as Secretary and Record keeper, but as Orator of this here Ancient and honorable Club, in both which offices, he has distinguished himself in a very remarkable manner, sometimes highly pleasing, and at other times much disgusting his honor the president, and the Long standing members of the Club, and, it must be owned Indeed, that his Clubical Character, was always dark and Mysterious, and never could be thorro'ly understood by most of the Members, which made his honor the President extremely Jealous of him, and these Jealousies were much Increased, by the Suggestions of some Longstanding [192] Members, particularly Capt: Blunt, || afterwards Sir John Oldcastle, tho' some alledge, that this was only a political fetch in Sir John, to render his honor uneasy in his Chair, to which Seat of honor, he, the said Sir John, ambitiously aspired, for many reckoned the Secretary a main pillar of the Club, and the Ingenious artist, by whom the whole Clubical machinery was set and kept in motion, tho' it must be owned, that he was of a positive fractious and fiery temper, and often excited Commotions and disputes in Club, by making absurd and Phantastical motions, under pretence of checking the grouth of Luxury, and arbitrary power in the Club, for he was always a Strenuous Stickler for the one dish law, and an opposer of the box, which first gave his honor the president cause to take offence at his con-

A Ladie's neck no more is like a Swan,
Than you ye monster's like an apish man.

The above fragment was snatched out of the hands of an Ignorant Clown, [190] who was Lighting his pipe with the only remaining copy of this excellent piece, and the words wrote down, are what remained unburnt; I shall here give one entire Song, of the Satyrical kind, wrote by the Junto upon these bards, which has been accidentally preserved from the rage of time.

Song on the Baltimore Bards, by the Junto at Batchelor's hall

1
Ye Baltimore Bards, while your fame we reherse,
   The muses we cannot Invoke,
Since we ne'er should expect they would dictate our verse
   While singing so arrant a Joke.

2
This too would resemble some Clerks of our day,
   Who act as absurdly as think,
In the morning on Sundays they preach & they pray,
   In the evening they sing and they drink.

3
Say wonderful bards, how your muse is Inspir'd?
   By what magic power does she sing,
By the Demon of Moorfields,[3] or punch is she fir'd,
   For she drinks not the Helicon Spring.

4
Say, does she not soar to a wonderful height
   In Clubs of our Raking gallants,
When o'er punch and Tobacco on Sundays at night
   The Cuckold and Cuckoo she Chants.

5
To the Tune of the Cuckold, pray Chant it no more,
   For on this I will venture my oath,
Your Slut of a muse will turn out Common whore
   And shortly will Cuckold you both.

6
As Cuckolds are hooted and scoff'd in the Streets
   For their horns, so may you for your wit.

---

3. Bethlem Royal Hospital, popularly known as Bedlam, was at one time located in Moorfields, an outlying section of London.

[189]   *Verses to the Bard on the Ladies backward beauties*
By a Baltimore Bard

veniam petimus, dabimusque vicissem. Hor: de art: poet:[2]

The lovely Sex, my friend, are charms all o'er,
And strike behind as powerful as before.
In H—n—s—n's Shape is seen as fine a grace,
As that which shines in H—mm—nd's Smiling face,
Bright as the Sun, they shine from every part,
Charm every Eye, and ravish every heart,
If thy cold heart no beauty can delight,
Tis not for want of Charms, but want of Sight,
Then friend be wise, your ill plac'd Jeers give oer,
Who sees no Charms behind, sees none before.

Thus melodiously did Bard Bavius sing, nor did his mellifluous muse desist, 'till the reiterated provocations of the Junto of Bards and Critics at Batchellors hall, had put him into a violent rage, in the midst of which Frenzy he wrote his dirty Epistle to the City of Annapolis, much about the time that the Learned Doctor Polypharmacus had him in the powdering tub, and there flagrantly acted, contrary to his own maxim, vizt: He that writes Ill natur'd must write ill. At last Jehoiakim Jerkum silenced him for ever—and thus the Baltimorian muses gave up the Ghost. But the Bards and Critics of Annapolis did not here desist but Emploied their Genius in Satyr. Mongst These Drawlum Quaint Esqr, a Longstanding member, and afterwards Speaker of the ancient and honorable Tuesday Club, made a most considerable figure, having Composed two Satyrs, one Entituled the *Reverend Scout,* and another the *Spiritual Rake,* both now in the Custody of the Reverend Mr Smoothum Sly, among these Satyrists appeared the Ingenious Capt: Giddy Thoughtless, who, one evening over a bowl of punch, composed a Satyr on Bard Bavius, of which we have only a fragment left, which we give here as a Specimen of what the rest must have been, and pity it is that so excellent an original should be lost.

  ✲✲✲ me ✲✲✲✲✲ Lord.
  ✲✲✲✲✲✲✲ one single Turd
  ✲✲✲✲ for ✲✲✲✲✲ flat
  ✲✲✲✲✲✲✲✲ a nine taild cat.

---

2. "We seek pardon, and give it in our turn" (paraphrased from Horace's *Ars poetica*, chap. 11).

For if thus with your verses you play fast and loose,
Instead of a Swan, we shall think you a goose,
And thus, you at last will be left in the Lurch
And bring a disgrace on the Cloth & the Church.

After these Clubical poets had thus Indulged and let loose their genius, against this devoted Baltimore Bard, they Commissioned one of their number, to Inclose the original Epigram with the Queries and annotations annexed, and the above answer to it, to Mr Roughby Ranter of Baltimore county, whom they pitched upon as their Mecenas, being a great encourager of such Sort of Gelastic, and Jocular Learning, the letter wrote to this Gentleman, was to the following purpose.

Sir,

One of your Baltimore Bards, (for we hear you have many) has pritty much diverted our Town Connoiseurs, by Comparing the necks of some of our Annapolitan Ladies to those of Swans, in an Epigram Composed by him in Church, || seated behind those Ladies, to hear the as yet unheard of doctrines of the famous Mr Whitefield, our Illustrious american apostle, an able Critic has subjoined his remarks, and one of our Bards (for with us also, the Spurious Sons of Apollo abound) has wrote a reply to it. You have the whole Inclosed, and we leave it to your Judgement to determin, whether the Streams of Helicon run purer in Baltimore than with us in Annapolis, we cannot at all forgive your bard for that thought, (tho altogether new) of seeing the most powerful Charms of the Ladies behind, and therefore, from this argument *a posteriori,* we Conclude, that, as the Gentleman has the honor to be of the Clergy, he ought to beware, how he broaches such novel Doctrines, Least thereby the Interest and power of the Clergy should be Impaired, which would necessarily be attended with some fatal Consequences to the Church. We are Sir,

To Mr Roughby Your most obsequious Servants
Ranter, *These* *Mevius Philo-Bavius*
  Martinus Scriblerus.

The Contents of this letter were exposed to the view of Bard Bavius, and maturely considered, and pondered by him, and, soon after, appeared, in the hands of many, a copy of finished and elegant verses, by him Composed, which were sent under Cover to a Gentleman of Rank and Eminence in the City of Annapolis,[1] they are as follows.

1. Probably Jonas Green, editor of the *Md. Gaz.,* who never published these verses.

162 [Book III]   The History of

The drinking of Lambswool at Batchellors Hall

[facing page 188]

the Tuesday Club   [Book III] 161

annexed to it some Critical remarks, annotations and Queries, to the following purpose.

Quere. Where were the Author, the Ladies, and Mr Whitefield at the [186] time of composing these verses? probably in Church.

Quere. Whether nonsense be any part of Rhetoric?

Quere. Whether Canting harmony be a proper term in music? unless the author, or somebody else, bore a part of the Chorus or Song with Mr Whitefield, harmony being a term only applicable to two or more voices or Instruments, singing or playing in concert?

Quere. Whether the Ladie's necks resembled those of Swans by their extraordinary Length, whiteness, or both?

Quere. Whether or not the bard kissed the Ladies, and if so, where? Probably in church.

This Clubical Critic or observator, at the end of these queries takes notice, that the author of this epigram is not to be forgiven for that thought, tho altogether new, of placing the most powerful Charms of the fair Sex behind, or *a posteriori,* by which great Injustice is done to their Sunny eyes, ruby lips, rosy cheeks, Ivory forehead, and pearly teeth, as also to their Snowy breasts and alabaster arms as our moderen bards stile them.

This notable Composition, with these annotations anexed, having come into the hands of some of the members of the Ancient and honorable Tuesday Club, vizt: Messrs Blunt, Sly, Motely and Scribble, they with some others, had a Set meeting, at a place called Batchellor's hall, and having called a few more bright geniuses to their asistance, there took the matter into their Serious consideration, over a large Tankard of Lamb's wool, a reviving Liquor, the pierian Spring of the moderen muses, compounded of white wine, Sugar and roasted apples, and, when the generous liquor had furbished up their wit, they began to make learned observations on the backward beauties of the fair Sex, which they committed to writing, and among other productions || their conjoint muses hammered out the follow- [187] ing piece.

Verses on the Baltimore Bard

A Parson in Church, with some Swan necks before him ⎫
To kiss and to touch, he hardly forbore'um,   ⎬
Being Check'd by the awe of the *Sanctum Sanctorum,*   ⎭
Had they and the poet been but in the Dark,
He'd have thrown off the parson, and put on the Spark,
And now, Mr Parson, If we may advise,
Pray pick up your swans under other disguise,

cured that pestiferous *furor poeticus,* which had for some time raged in Baltimore, and set many people a quarrelling, and as many a Laughing, and, the members of the ancient and honorable Tuesday Club, that were concerned in this conflict and victory, valued themselves much upon it, as having largely Contributed to the peace and quiet of the public, nothing being more destructive to the good order of Society and private families, than the Scribble of the *Poetæ Minorum Gentium,*[12] whether Panegyrical or Satyrical, handed about either in Manuscript, or from the press.

Chapter VII

The drinking of Lamb's wool at Batchellor's hall, and the Danger of the Clubs being converted into a State Club.

Those who have read the beginning of the preceeding Chapter of this history, will remember, that it was there said, that Bard Mevius Composed an elegant epigram upon some Ladies in Church, while the Reverend Mr Whitefield was holding forth from the pulpit, a true Copy of that masterly piece here follows.

> *On The two Miss ******'* as they sat before me,*
> *hearing of Mr Whitefield—An Extempore Epigram.*
>
> Plac'd as I was, such charms within my view,
> Say, Whitefield, what could all thy Rhet'ric do?
> In vain the nonsense trickl'd from thy tongue,
> In vain with canting harmony you sung;
> Their blooming beauties more perswasive prov'd,
> My heart with greater energy they mov'd,
> Their Swan-like necks my ravish'd eyes did bliss,
> Courted the touch, and tempted me to kiss.
>
> *Mevius*

This epigram was first handed about, in the Author's own hand writing, without any Annotations critical or explanatory, but it was not long before a certain Critic, thought to be a member of the Ancient and honorable Tuesday Club, and afterwards Secretary and orator to the said Club,

---

12. "Lower-class poets."

and knowledge in Chemistry, by absolutely pronouncing Doctor Polypharmacus a dunce, for using the term *Neutrum quid,* which he says is in it Self Stark nonsense, as Intending something that is only chip in porridge, or neither Chalk nor Cheese, then he slides into a Learned Enquiry into the nature of Ordure and excrement, to which he elegantly compars the works and compositions of his Antagonist Bards.

This Learned Epistle made some noise for a time among the wits and critics, particularly of Annapolis, and produced several learned criticisms, dissertations and essays; and certain critical and Explanatory Notes were wrote upon it in the names of Martinus Scriblerus & Hurlothrumbo,[10] the first in a grave, the other in a Burlesque Stile, all which learned papers, paraphrazes and Commentaries, are they not to be seen laid up in the Musæum, of the Curious and Ingenious Mr Jonathan Grog, even at this Day.

Bard Bavius, the only person now aimed at (since his associate Mevius, had altogether retired and absconded,) was also attacked by another wit, who appeared in the *Maryland Gazette* No 47, under the Character of an advertiser;[11] This wit assumes to himself, the name of Jehoiakim Jerkum, and is thought to have been personated, by one or more of the Longstanding members, of the ancient and honorable Tuesday Club, takeing upon them the Character of a Master advertising his run away Servant; Bard Bavius is mentioned || in this advertisement, under the names of Bard & Bavius, he is described as a fellow disordered in his Senses, wearing a String of Bells about his neck, carrying with him several Stollen materials from the works of Pope & Prior, together with abundance of Trash of his own. A nasty Fellow, whose discourse turns chiefly on excrementitious Subjects, of uncertain parentage, and therefore, in himself an original, praising for the Sake of praise, and Censuring for the Sake of censure, apt to bewray himself in company, thro' a relaxation of the *Sphincter ani,* and then lay the blame on others, an Enimy to the Presbyterians, tho' himself a Muggletonian, the profit of his poems for one hundred years to come, is offered to those who go on the *Chace* after him, and apprehend him, as it appears to be a difficult thing so to do, besides what the Law allows in such cases.

[184]

This Burlesque advertisement, utterly silenced Bard Bavius, and consequently, the other Baltimore Bard, whose Champion he was, and effectually

---

10. Martinus Scriblerus was a pseudonym sometimes used by Pope (the *Memoirs of Martinus Scriblerus,* a prose satire against false learning, was published in the second edition of Pope's works [1741]). *Hurlothrumbo* was the title of a popular burlesque (1729) by Samuel Johnson, a Manchester dancing master.

11. Hamilton is referring to a notice in the *Md. Gaz.,* no. 47 (Mar. 18, 1746), 4 (see Appendix 3).

158 [Book III]   The History of

The Phrensy of a Baltimore Bard

[facing page 183]

> Let Venus hail her for the wife of Jove,
> And Juno take her for the queen of Love,
> Let Pallas frowning &ct:

Upon this the Doctor applies cupping Glasses, as he says, to his head, and gives him a large dose of hellebore, which procures a copious and fætid Stool, after which the Bard exclaims

> Maria sings, now bid the Muses hear
> Or Call Apollo from the Crystal Sphere.

Polypharmacus on this, suspects a calenture, plies him with cooling Glysters to Relieve the encephalon, and Claps Sinapisms to his feet, and soon after, he breaks out thus.

> See, Lovely Risteau![7] happy, hapless Maid!—
> Happy the man whom this fair Maiden loves,
> O happiest he, whom this fair maid approves,
> Great is her worth, yet useless and unknown,
> Or useful to her charming Self alone.

This last, the Physician observes, is a most remarkable Instance of the Bathos, and by this, he percieved that the Violence of the Distemper abated, and gives him his famous remedy, which he calls his *Neutrum quid*,[8] the Composition of which may be seen in the said *Gazette* No 41, if now to be found.

Soon after this Bard Bavius wrote his celebrated Letter to the City of Annapolis, which he Intends as a kind of prose Dunciad, Introducing all his critics and opponent Bards in some Ridiculous Character or other, here he learnedly criticises on the term *Neutrum Quid*, and, assuming the Character of a Physician himself, he proposes a Remedy, or *Methodus Medendi*,[9] so very much out of the common road, that never any thing like it was seen either before or since, nor, I believe, ever will be, in this transient world, the piece it self being Inimitable, and extraneously extravagant, in short, to cure those frantic poets, as he calls them, Mr Jonathan Grog, (to whose name we shall have occasion soon, to clap with propriety the title of *'Squire*) was to put them into his press or typographical machine, and, an operator with a Spatula ‖ was to extract excrementitious matter from their fundament, while Parson Sly was to sing a Psalm, to Comfort them under the operation; in this prophylactic dissertation our Bard displays his profound skill

---

7. Catherine Risteau was the wife of Thomas Cradock (see biographical sketch for Cradock).
8. "Something that is neither of the two."
9. "Method of healing."

decoy, Bard Mevius, was prevailed upon to own that he had a great hand in it, but nevertheless he confessed, he was much obliged to his friend Bard Bavius, who shared the most considerable part of it, for the whole Excellent plan, Invention and Machinery was his; and as for his own part, he had only asisted in some degree in the versification and Rhime, so soon as the critics were Informed of this, they set up a furious cry against these Illustrious Bards, and, like a pack of blood hounds, hunted them in such a manner, as to allow them no Sort of repose or rest. Bard Bavius stood out, with great Intrepidity against them, bawling, railing, scolding, reviling and cursing in as loud a key as they, but Bard Mevius, was obliged, from his natural Timidity, to look out for lurking holes, and skulk from the violence and rage of these furious critics.

The news of this soon reached the Clubical Bards and Critics at Annapolis, together with a copy of the composition it Self, who set about it, tooth and nail, and gave it no quarter. One, under the name of Doctor Philalethes, published in the *Gazette* No 34 an Infallible receipt to cure the Epidemical and afflicting distempers of Love and the poetical Itch.[4] Soon after, another Learned Physician, who stiles himself Doctor Polypharmacus, in *Gazette* No 41 publishes another recipe,[5] and seems to be diffident of the efficacy of the former, according to the humor of great Physicians, who commonly prefer their own Nostrums, to those of all the faculty besides, this Learned Gentleman, describes Bard Bavius, under a violent delirium or *furor poeticus,* excited by a *febris Amatoria,*[6] which he cautions us not to mistake for the Chlorosis or green Sickness, in his fits of raving he repeats severall passages of the celebrated piece of the *Baltimore Belles,* on the Doctor's first feeling his pulse, he exclaims thus.

> A well turn'd praise requires the nicest Skill,
> And he who writes ill natur'd must write ill.

And again, upon being asked how he did, he bawls out

> Then let the Muse her tuneful numbers raise
> And praise the beauties for the Sake of praise.

Soon after he accosts the Doctor thus.

> In every charm, some glorious goddess place,
> And let the Charm the glorious Goddess grace,

---

4. Hamilton is referring to a notice that appeared in the *Md. Gaz.,* no. 34 (Dec. 17, 1745), 3–4 (see Appendix 1).
5. This notice appeared in the *Md. Gaz.,* no. 41 (Feb. 4, 1746), 4 (see Appendix 2).
6. "Amorous fever."

and timorous, since he was much asisted thereby, in bearing the violence and fury of the Attacks made upon him, by his professd foes, the Critics and Bards of the Tuesday Club.

This Gygantic auxiliary Bard, mustering up all his force and straining the Sublime of his genius to the utmost, advised the other, to show the dignity of his muse, by outsoaring all those pitiful bards and Critics, that set up against him, and, that he should have his asistance, in whatever Subject he undertook, it was then resolved, by these two eminent Baltimore Bards, over a bowl of punch and a pipe of tobacco, to pen a Sublime panegyric on || the celebrated toasts and beauties of their county, under the title of *The Baltimore Belles*. This piece was then Immediatly set about, and the Muses Invoked, and being finished by these rapid Geniuses in a few hours, was carefully revised, corrected, and wrote out fair, It was read by Bard Bavius, in a Sonorous and theatrical tone of voice, much approved of by both bards, and after a Second third and fourth reading, was left lying on the table for further perusal and consideration, or, rather to be exposed to the eye of the public, that it might meet with the applause it so Justly deserved; being such a specimen of the Sublime, as exceeded the execution of all Bards whatsoever, either ancient or moderen, since the days of Pindar. [179]

This piece then, Lieing on the table in a tavern, soon had readers enough of all capacities, from the Scholar to the dunce, from the Gentleman to the Clown, and various were the opinions that were given of it, Some shook their heads at it and pronounced it to be damn'd Stuff, others attempted to read it, but stammered and blundered so, that they threw it down with seeming Indignation and disdain, before they had mumbled out three lines, some said that the Rhime was Good, and the verse smooth enough, but the Sense past their Comprehension, these were the Sentiments of the Baltimore Connoiseurs concerning it, and the bards all this time Lay perdue, expecting to have their opinion asked thereupon, which hapened to their wish, and accordingly, they pronounced it an excellent piece, and declared, that if Pope had been alive and In America, they should have Judged it to be of his composition, a remarkable Instance this, of the fondness and tender Indulgence of Bards towards their own performances, who, like fond parents, always Imagine, that their own brats, are the handsomest, best, Sweetest, comliest of any in the world, but, their soun- || ding the praises of this composition so extravagantly, soon made the Critics smell a rat; for, they being a sagacious discerning Sort of people, Immediatly took the Scent, and discovered the piece to be a production of these very bards who extolld it so much, & they clenched the discovery in this cunning manner, they heartily Joined with them in praising the piece, and, by this [180]

preconceived of our Bard; the critics were in an uproar against it, they took this poor Bards performance all to pieces, as is the custom with Critics in these our degenerate days, and discried more blunders and Inaccuracies in it than there were words, Some of the Longstanding members of the Ancient and honorable Tuesday Club were among these Critics, particularly Messieurs Blunt, Sly, Quaint and Scribble, who exercised the acuteness of wit and Genius pritty Smartly upon this unfortunate Bard, and were Joined by others, both bards and Critics in Baltimore and Elsewhere, from Criticising in prose, they went to Satyrizing and Lampooning in Rhime, So the Baltimore Bards & the Critics of the Tuesday Club strenuously contended who should outrhime, and who should outcriticise each other, there was nothing but paquets, papers and Scrowls handed about, stuffed with abundance of repartee and railery, as is usual in these cases, and some who thought them wiser than themselves admired much their wit, while others who had no opinion of their wisdom laughed at their folly and assurance, and condemned them much, as Idle and mischievous, in trowbling people that thought no harm with such poetical Jargon, which set many tongues a wagging in a Scandalous manner, and prompted many peaceable || christians to quarrel and fall out one with another who before lived in perfect amity, not to mention the Idle habit some contracted by it, in squandering their time in Composing of Silly rhimes, vainly Imagining that they had a poetical turn, tho they found themselves at last miserably mistaken, and were obliged to bear the Laugh of the public with patience, seeing they had drawn it upon themselves, by their own folly and vanity.

It came at last to that pitch, that even the weekly Journal of Mr Jonathan Grog, entituled the *Maryland Gazette,* was stuffed with comments, Reflections and Satyrs on this unfortunate Bard and his performances,[3] so, that it is thought he must Infallibly have sunk under the pressure, of this formidable hostile power of Critics, had not an Invulnerable Champion, stood up in his defence, vizt: the tremendous Bard Bavius, who was reckoned by many the compleatest bard of the two, and Indeed, the most extraordinary bard, that was to be found, far or near, and not to be daunted, or put out of countenance, by the conjoint forces of all the Critics put together.

This Illustrious Bard, was of a stern, Severe countenance, whose Severity and Sterness, was of great use to the other, naturally mild, modest

---

3. Although Hamilton says the *Maryland Gazette* was "stuffed" with remarks concerning this battle between the Baltimore Bards and the members of the Tuesday Club, I have not located any comments other than those he specifically mentions later in this chapter.

was so Infected as to break all at once into blank verse, and with great violence and vociferation, exclaimed to the Surprize of all present,

> With dowble Lustre, Beckie's beauties shine.

And when he was desired to proceed farther, and make a Couplet of it, he bawld out in a furious manner,

> Rise Jupiter, and snuff the moon!—

Upon which the company thinking he was crazed left him || to himself, and urged no more questions, since which his muse has been altogether silent, having overshot herself at her first setting out, except one faint Essay in Rhime which she made, but we shall relate that in its proper place.

We have reason to believe, that this poetical Contagion took its rise first in the north, and therefore was of the frigid Sort, for, in the county of Baltimore, there appeared two Celebrated Bards, vizt: Bard Bavius, and Bard Mevius,[2] who, having broke out into most violent fits of Rhiming and versifying, Infected many people around them with the same distemper, the first essay, which the conjoint Muses of these two Northeren Bards produced, was an original piece called the *Baltimore Belles,* of which performance we shall say something in its proper place, intending first, to discuss other matters, in which these bards were concerned, more particularly relating to the Club.

The first bold Stroke that appeared of this kind was from the celebrated Bard Mevius, who, one day being In church, hearing the Reverend and pious Mr George Whitefield hold forth, was diverted in his attention to the Sweet words of that Inspired Saint, by some Ladies, who sat in a pew Just before him, with the whiteness and beautiful Length of whose Necks, or perhaps both, he was so miraculously Charmed, that, Intirely forgetting where he was, he fell directly to Composing of verses on this delightful Subject, and hammered out a very pritty epigram of eight lines, the Stile and turn of which was so peculiar, that it is yet unequalled by any bard that has since appeared, and is really an original, || having never been paralelled in former ages, by any of the Bards of Antiquity.

Immediatly, upon the appearance of this amorous epigram, which was Industriously handed about in manuscript both by the friends and foes of the Bard, the first to praise and extoll his lofty genius, the latter to ridicule his pertness and vanity, each acting according to the opinion they had

---

2. On Bavius, see p. 153n. Mevius was another poetaster who incurred Horace's and Vergil's wrath. Here, the names synonymous with bad poetry are pseudonyms for Thomas Chase and Thomas Cradock (see biographical sketches).

resolved not to return, till he had blunted the edge of his desires, with some Gentle and kind Nymph, but, his resolution did not carry him thro' thick and thin, for, he was so terrified, at the Sight of a Superannuated female, who, upon his knocking opened her door to him, that all his tender Ideas vanished like Smoke, and taking to his heels, as if the Devil had been after him, he run faster back than he went forth, and took his Seat again in Club, quite out of breath.

It was not so with Laconic Comas Esqr, and Mr Secretary Motely, two Stanch Longstanding members, the first a widower, the other a batchellor, who, after the dismissing of the Club, went in pursuit of some fair Nymphs, who that night were assembled at a dance, and carried the Steward with them, but what their adventures and exploits were, we shall not relate here, as having nothing to do with the History of the Club, which is of too grave and Solid a nature, to admit of the detail and relation of amours, these triffles, properly belonging to Romances and Novels, and therefore cannot be any credit to True histories such as this.

At this Sederunt, the Hon: Col: Courtly Phraze was admitted an honorary member of the Club.

Chapter VI

Some of the Members seized with a furor poeticus, and some account of the Baltimore Bards.

Much about this time, appeared an epidemical distemper in the Club, which broke out, no body can tell how, it was what Physicians might properly call a κακο-ηθεια or μανιας ποιητικης,[1] *malignitas poetica,* or *Furor poeticus,* several of the members having been taken in an unaccountable manner, with fits of Rhiming, and writing of Rhimes, those that seemed to be most affected with it were Messiurs Sly, Motely, Blunt, Quaint and Scribble, tho' none were writers but the two last, however, the whole Club was in some measure touched with this malignity, so that they could scarce speak to one another, but in Rhime and Jingle, and even Mr Solo Neverout, sometime after, admitted a Member of the Club, who had never before shown the least genius or turn to Rhiming or versification, nay even made a Jest of it in his laughing way, and ridiculed all poets and poetasters,

---

1. "Poetical wickedness or madness."

Pepperell,[2] || drank several loyal toasts, such as Success to his majestie's arms [173] by sea and land. Generall Pepperel. Commodore Warren. The several Land and Sea officers. The brave Soldiers and Sailors. the perpetual possession of cape Breton to the English. Prosperity to all his Majesties Plantations. Governor Shirly.[3] The Colony of new England, and the like. By these loyal and well affected toasts, this ancient and honorable Club, showed their firm and Steady attachment, to the present happy Establishment, and, there being no opposition in Club, to any of these toasts, we may pritty surely conclude from thence, that all the Longstanding members were Stanch whigs, and averse to all Jacobitish principles and maxims, a happy Circumstance, and what has contributed much, among other Concurring causes, to the prosperity and Stability of this ancient and honorable Club, we have all of us reason to pray, that this noble Spirit of Liberty, may grow and Continue among us, and, that no bribery, corruption and Luxury, may gain footing so far, as to extinguish so noble, heroic and generous a disposition.

While these matters were transacting in Club, the members had a visit from the Hon: Coll: Courtly Phraze, who made his appearance so suddenly, that none present could certainly tell, in what manner he came into the Room, tho' many affirmed, that he seemed to them to enter back foremost; and turning his face to the Company, made a most profound bow, passed some polite compliments, and sitting down gravely, told the members that he had Just now left the Company of the Ladies, those dear angelical creatures! for the Colonell, was always a person || noted for his [174] courtly polite behaviour and address to the fair Sex, the Collonels discourse concerning the Ladies, put the members of the Club into an amorous vein, and there was not one there excepting Mr Jole, but resolved to have his Girl that very night; Drawlum Quaint Esqr, the Steward seemed to be more agitated by this amorous enthusiasm, than any of the other members, for, he went out of Club, attended by Loquacious Scribble M:D: and was

2. Sir Peter Warren (1703–1752), a British naval officer, helped capture the French fortress of Louisburg on Cape Breton Island (1745) and helped defeat the French off Cape Finisterre (1747). Sir William Pepperell (1696–1759), an American general, assisted the British in capturing Louisburg, was created baronet (the first American so honored, 1746), served in the French and Indian War, and was promoted to lieutenant general in 1759.

3. William Shirley (1694–1771), colonial governor of Massachusetts (1741–1749, 1753–1756), planned the expedition against the French at Louisburg, served on a commission in Paris to determine the boundary between New England and French North America (while visiting England, 1749–1753), and was appointed major general (1755) at the outbreak of the French and Indian War. On the great joy and sense of achievement with which the conquest of Louisburg was received in the American colonies, see Nathan O. Hatch, "The Origins of Civil Millennialism in America: New England Clergymen, War with France, and the Revolution," *William and Mary Quarterly*, 3d Ser., XXXI (1974), especially 417–422.

that the batchellor's Cheese was Expelled the Club, by an express Law, in which it was declared

Law XI. That Cheese shall no more be deemed a dish of vittles, and therefore the use of it as such in the Club is forbid.

The Chief moover for this Law, was Nasifer Jole Esqr, whom we shall find afterwards by gradual Steps Introducing high relished dishes and dainties into the Club, he began first with rack punch, here madam Luxury first pop'd her head from behind the curtain, with her far fetched commodities, presently after this, come the bowl and tobacco pipe procession, then her adjutant Ceremony followed her beck; then an Iced cake makes it's appearance, as we shall relate in its place, and thence Mr Jole proceeded gradually in his Schemes, and slap dash, there followed a whole troop of frecassees, ‖ ragous, hashes, soups, pasties, pies, puddings, dumplings, tarts, Gellies and Syllabubs, and it is thought, that it was by these artful Steps, that this politic gentleman raised himself to the presidential Chair, and advanced one Step, or Six inches above the other Longstanding members.

The Chief argument that was brought against the Cheese Law, was, the absurdity of it, when compared with a preceeding law, which allows a gammon of bacon, or any other one Dish of Dressd Vittles, now this law of the Cheese said they annulls of course the law of the Gammon, or dressed Vittles, for, it never once was Imagined, by any man in his right Senses, that cheese is a dish of dress'd vittles, but rather a relisher or desert, therefore they asserted *a priori,* that this law of the Cheese was in itself void, as being absurd and nonsensical, and also directly repugnant to Clubical liberty, for which reason the Cheese was expelled as a nauseous, Stinking and Clownish mess, but it is not the first time, that good Laws, ordained for the establishment of frugality and temperance, have been annulled upon the like Specious pretences, and Luxury and Epicurism, have met with Strenuous advocats to support their Cause, and vindicate the practice of these effeminate Vices, whoever doubts of this, needs only read, the Learned and Ingenious Doctor Mandeville, his *Fable of the bees,* where I think, it is seemingly made out, beyond all question, if you will take the Doctor's own word for it, that private vice is public emolument.[1]

On the same Sederunt, the Club having news of the taking of Cape Breton, from the french, by the Sea and land forces under Warren and

---

1. Bernard Mandeville's (1670–1733) *The Fable of the Bees* (London, 1714), designed to illustrate the essential vileness of human nature, was at the heart of the controversy over luxury that Hamilton satirizes in the *History*. Mandeville argued that the taste for luxury in a populace stimulates the economy in general, providing benefits to all; virtuous frugality, on the other hand, is the ruin of active commerce.

which arose upon this || Question, vizt: whether or not a man, born and bred a taylor and understanding no other craft, either of head or hand, might be qualified to take holy orders, and become a parson of a parish? The first asserted that the transition was natural, for, as his first employ was to make up breeches, to cover his customer's bums, so his second occupation, would be to make up breaches among his flock; but the other took this In Snuff, and would not assent to the argument, so this great point of the breeches and breaches, still remains undetermined, this was the first time that punning took place in this ancient and honorable Club, which Ingenious art, received great Improvements afterwards, from the facetious Jonathan Grog Esqr, poet Laureat of the Club. [170]

Chapter V

The expulsion of the Batchellor's Cheese, and the Signal Loyalty of the Longstanding members, with an Instance of their amorous disposition.

We have now discussed the primitive, Simple times of this ancient and honorable Club, and must bid farewell in a little Space, to that virtuous and heroic frugality, which prevailed in it at it's first Institution, for now Luxury[a] began to peep from behind the Scene, and prepare for her pompous entry upon this Clubical Stage, and, Indeed, to carry on our metaphor, this bold actress took one great Stride at her first advance, and proceeded afterwards, with a *grand pas,* to expell Simplicity and plainness from the Club, and to Introduce, pomp show and || extravagance, her constant pages and attendants, while another, her companion and coactor, with the like buskined pride, plaid the part of a momus or mimic, this was no less a person than Ceremony, as much a beau, as the other is a belle, whom we shall soon see also, showing his pragmatical front, upon the most conspicuous part of the Scene, and Introducing certain fantastical punctillios, forms and modes, by which he so disguised and poisoned the manners and behavior of the longstanding members, of this here ancient and honorable Club (as indeed he does those of all mankind, especially such as are in higher life, for he is never seen among beggars & Clowns,) that they did in no manner seem to be the same persons they were at their first Institution. [171]

It was at Sederunt 10th July 18, Drawlum Quaint Esqr, being Steward,

---

[a] Vide 9th anniversary Speech, almost verbatim the same wt the following.

The Tobacco-pipe procession.

[facing page 168]

Law X. That the book of Rules belonging to the Society, and likewise the Ballot boxes, be Lodged with the Steward, and by him be delivered to his Successor in that office.

At the same Sederunt, Doctor Polyhistor, was made an honorary member, and the *Great bell of Lincoln* was sung for the first time by Nasifer Jole Esqr, a large bowl of Rack punch, being carried in procession Round the great table, typically representing the great bell, while the members followed it in Regular order, shouldering tobacco pipes, this was the first appearance of pomp and pegeantry, in this ancient and honorable Club. The Catch called the *Great Bell,* as it is often mentioned in this history, I shall give a Copy of as follows.

The Great Bell of Lincoln, sung by Nasifer Jole Esqr

> The great Bell of Lincoln
> It rings once a year,
> But we're not for Lincoln
> While this Bell rings here. (a)

Chorus There are five men to raise her (b)
> And at whitsontide rings,
> Then turn the bell over
> And see how she rings. (c)

> Now the bell is turnd over
> And has lost her old Strings,
> And she must be mended
> Before she will ring.

> New frame, new wheel,
> New Clapper, new Strings,
> Then turn the bell over
> And see how she rings.

Chorus Drink right, or else your wrong,
> Poor Tom is dead and gone.
> To—m, To—m

At this Sederunt there passed abundance of Learned discourse, between Capt: Seemly Spruce, and Mr Joggle hasty, two long Standing members,

---

(a) Here they sound upon the bowl with a tobacco pipe.
(b) Here 5 take hold of the bowl, and raise it up high in the air.
(c) Here they drink.

and about twenty thousand ring doves and pigeons in cages, Alexander Severus was often pleased to play with whelps and young pigs, The famous Montaigne, speaks feelingly of his favorite puss,[17] and, the great Ladies in the great Turks Seraglio, at this very day, keep a great many cats, to pass away the time, not to mention our best and politest Ladies of quality in England, who converse much with monkies, Lapdogs, parrots and Squirrells, where then is the Great wounder, that our Clubical heroe should keep about him some 40 or 50 Cats, for his amusement and recreation.

Carlo Nasifer Jole, tho' he had no great communication with mankind, was thought to be a friend to human nature and a well wisher to Society, for, he always expressed a great aversion and hatred to thieves, rogues and villains, in such a manner, that, whenever he heard of any wretches accused of theft, robbery or murder, he was for tucking them up, without the ceremony of a trial, Some Indeed said, that this proceeded from a rigid temper and cruel disposition, and therefore pronounced him a Mysanthrope, but I must beg leave to be of a contrary opinion.

In fine, Mr Jole was of a very Suspicious temper, cared not to trust any body, and was exceeding fond of power and authority, of which we shall see many Instances, in the Sequel of this History.

[168] Having said thus much of our heroe, in order to prepare our readers, for encountering him in his Clubical Character, thro' the following history, I now proceed to the thread of my narration.

After the admission of the abovenamed Gentlemen, into this ancient and honorable Club, it was agreed at Sederunt 8th

Law IX. That members shall be admitted for the future, by way of balloting, as also the passing or making of any new rule or Law.

At Sederunt 9th July the 9th 1745, Dumpling Gundiguts Esqr, being Steward, 26 ballots, marked N & Y. were produced in Club, by Mr Secretary Motely, according to the Law for that Intent, made and provided, and at Sederunt 11th (the 10th I purposely omitt here) July 23, Nasifer Jole Esqr, being Steward, the following law passed.

---

17. Aelius Lampridius (fl. early 4th century A.D.) was a Roman historian and one of the collaborators in the *Historia Augusta* (Aelius Spartianus, however, wrote the chapter on the Roman emperor Severus [A.D. 145/146–211], which does not mention his affection for birds, nor do any of the other allusions to Severus in the *Historia*. Severus Alexander (A.D. 208/209–235) was adopted by Heliogabalus and made emperor at age 13 when the latter was murdered. Montaigne writes particularly of his fondness for animals in the two essays "Of Cruelty" and the "Apology for Raimond Sebond." Hamilton is probably referring to a passage in "Of Cruelty," where Montaigne remarks: "When I play with my cat, who knows but that she regards me more as a play thing than I do her? (We amuse each other with our respective monkey-tricks; if I have my moments for beginning and refusing, so she has hers)" (*The Essays of Montaigne*, trans. E. J. Trechmann [New York, 1946], 444).

upon his back and belly, while he stroked one, patted another, tickled a third, and tossed another gently away from him, tho' they, like Saucy favorites, would sometimes make too familiar with their patron and protector, and oblige him at times to use a small Switch, with which hed gently scourge them out of the room, in fine the Great Nasifer, in the midst of his cats, looked like the Grand Signior in the midst of his Seraglio, and by means of his good discipline and advice, they were all so modest and well bred that when he entertained Company of the human Species, not one of those brutes would dare so much || as to appear, or even to peep, but all retired to their proper Chambers, and appartments allotted for them. [166]

Some may think it very Strange, that Mr Jole, a Gentleman born and bred in a christian land, should pay so much deference and respect, to these brute creatures, Indeed, had he been a Turk, they'll say, whose religion enjoins a respect to dogs and cats, and such like brute animals, and whose enthusiasm prompts them to build hospitals for them: had he professed himself a Pythagorean philosopher, or an Indian Santon, who believe that the Souls of their grandfathers are lodged in these brutes, and transmigrate from Animal to Animal: had he been an ancient Ægyptian, who made divinities of these creatures and paid them divine honors: In fine, had he been a persian Dervis, who understood thorro-ly the Language of brutes, there might be some plausible reason for his amusing himself in this manner; but as he is an old Englishman, and a protestant, and Christian of the Church of England, as by Law established, there is no other way they'll say, for accounting for this odd humor, but by ascribing it to mere whim and fancy, but, granting it was no other but this last, have we not the example of many ancient great worthies, who were delighted with the same Sort of amusements, does not Homer tell us, that Hector was very familiar with and held several Grave Conversations and conferences with his horses; are we not told that Toby had a dog that followed him when he went forth, does not Spartian Inform us that Adrian the Emperor, was so Enamoured with dogs and horses, that he bestowed Sumptuous monuments and tombs on them, and buried them decently || in graves;[16] dont we find that Caligula [167] had such an opinion of his horse's abilities, that he created him Consul of Rome, and dressed him in purple like a wise Senator, Lampridius affirms, that the Emperor Severus kept tame Pheasants, ducks, partridges, peacocks,

---

16. Hector exhorts his horses in the *Iliad*, bk. 8, 224–239. Tobias's dog is noted above (see p. 20n). Aelius Spartianus (fl. 3d century A.D.) was one of the principal authors of the *Historia Augusta* (for the story of the Roman emperor Hadrian's affection for his dogs and horses, see *The Lives of the Later Caesars* [London, 1967], 80).

Single, having been, as it is thought, ever averse to the Clog of a wife, and a man of too much prudence and Solidity ever to keep a concubine, for this reason the world is not likely to be much entertained with his amours, and the transactions of his life would therefore afford very unfit materials for a novel; It being a question whether he ever permitted a woman to come nigher to him than arms Length, or a modest and decent distance, so as to hold Indifferent discourse, for, tho' he never showed any affection to the Sex, yet, he would deign to converse with them as rational Creatures, which showed, that he was too much of a christian to believe with some Philosophers, that women had no Souls,[15] but then he would behave himself with the same Indifferent coldness, as one man does to another, or as one maid would accost another.

Yet, as man is a Sociable animal, and the most Savage and retired have at times their Darling companions, so, this celebrated Gentleman, Judging his own Species, unworthy to make constant companions and Intimates of, chose a Society of Cats for his friends, fellows and playmates, both at bed and board, and so far did his extra- || ordinary charity and benevolence extend to those Cats, that he would deign to converse with them in the most familiar manner, giving some of them a christian like education, for he had some that he taught to sit erect, and clap their fore feet or paws together in a praying or begging like posture, he would stroke down their soft Skins, apply their mouths to his, give the females, Silk and velvet beds, in which to lie in, or deposit their kittins, and when, for fear of their multiplying too much, he would order some kittens to be drowned or buried alive, he was so tender hearted, that he would not see the execution, but shut himself up, and grieve for some time, as a tender mother does for her babes; nay, it is said, that he once buried a favorite Cat, with great form and ceremony, like a christian, he gave her a band box for a Coffin, and had an epitaph wrote upon her tombstone, it would delight your eyes to see the great benevolence of this good Gentleman to these domestic brutes, for you could never step into the house, but you would find all these his favorites great and little, about their kind benefactor, some upon his Shoulders, others on his head and neck, some on his knees and others crawling up

---

15. Hamilton is alluding to the traditional Turkish belief that had become commonplace in 18th-century England. In the famous opening lines of his *Epistle to a Lady,* for example, Pope writes: "Nothing so true as what you once let fall, / 'Most Women have no Characters at all'" (*The Twickenham Edition of the Poems of Alexander Pope,* vol. III, pt. ii, ed. F. W. Bateson [London, 1951]); see also Samuel Butler's "Women": "The Soules of women are so small / That Some believe th' have none at all" (*Satires and Miscellaneous Poetry and Prose,* ed. René Lamar [Cambridge, 1928], 220).

hand, Some of these verses are in themselves very Sublime and poetical, one of which, for its beauty and Singularity, I cannot ommit here quoting.

> Here there lies Interr'd a Squire
> Underneath this marble Stone,
> Who for Loving did expire,
> And he never Lov'd but one.

This verse in particular Mr Jole would sing with so lamentable a voice, as to draw tears from the eyes of the most flinty hearted, tho many affirmed that these tears flowed not from Commiseration, but from a certain gelastic conquassation.[13]

This Illustrious gentleman has a very pritty taste for antiquities, of which he keeps a curious collection by him, now to show, to all Connoiseurs who are desirous of seeing them, these are petticoats, Scarfs and Caps that belonged to his grandmother, hats, nightcaps and ruffs of his great grandfather, the little Spoon, with which his grandfather was fed when a child, his own baby Cloths, in which his mother dressed him, with the Stains of the Slabber carefully preserved on the bibs to this very day, and several other Curiosities and Nicknacks, on which the old Gentleman can exhibit a whole afternoon's lecture, in a very pleasant and Delectable manner, and elegantly expatiate upon the Superexcellency of all ancient things, and how vastly they exceed every thing of a moderen date, for, he is an enthusiastic admirer of antiquity, posi- ‖ tively asserting that all old [164] things are best, tho' it is doubted whether he will have the assent of the fair sex, for the truth of this general proposition, however, Mr Jole's taste in this is not Singular, for we find several Learned universities, fond of keeping antique remains in their musæums, such as, the pen of Duns Scotus, with which he wrote his Subtile Philosophy, the bonnet or cap of Aristotle, the Inkhorn and Candlestick of John Knox, the Skull of Buchanan &ct:[14] which shews that there is a real value in these ancient reliques.

As I talked but Just now of the fair Sex, it will be proper here to enquire, how far Mr Jole was ever engaged with them, he has lived always

---

13. Severe shaking caused by laughter.
14. John Duns Scotus (1265?–1308?), known as Doctor Subtilis, was one of the great medieval Scholastic theologians. Knox (1505–1572), generally considered the leader of the Protestant Reformation in Scotland, was the author of the *Treatise on Predestination* (1560) and the *History of the Reformation of Religion within the Realme of Scotland* (1587). George Buchanan (1506–1582), a Scottish historian, scholar, and poet, published *Detectio Mariae Reginae* (1571), a violent attack on Mary, Queen of Scots, *Rerum scoticarum historia* (1582), long regarded as a standard source of Scottish history, the tragedies *Baptistes, Medea, Jephthes,* and *Alcestis,* and some good elegiac and occasional poetry.

[162] heads ought to observe, vizt: to encourage and promote all Ingenious and Learned men. For this reason Chiefly Mr Jole admires these Quaint Sermons, affirming that there ‖ were no such sermons to be met with now a days, which every one will frankly own to be true, yet, fond as he is of this Sort of learning, and quaint Sententious writing, there is nothing he detests more than awkward Imitations of it, as appears in his displeasure with, and opposition to the Club Conundrums, and the dislike he expressed to that pestilent and assuming humor of punning in Jonathan Grog Esqr, a Longstanding member and poet Laureat of the Club.

His knowledge in music, he has merely by the force of Genius, having never been taught, and his talent this way lies in vocal execution, he having a number of old Songs by him, to the words of which, he affirms, he never is at a loss to find a tune, and Indeed, give him words at any time, and he'll Immediatly clap a tune to them, with so Sweet and small a voice, and so delicate a trill, that some people have doubted whether or not he has in his youth been Italianized, but, be that as it will, (tho it may be said of him, as it was of *Aurelius Philippus Paracelsus Theophrastus Bombastus de Hohenheim, Testimonium virilitatis prebet rigida barba*)[10] he has a most exquisite pipe, and, were he not obliged sometimes to wear his Spectacles, to read the words of the Song, when he sings by book, his voice would be quite clear, and without asperity, but this nasal machine, will sometimes in the high notes, occasion a Snuffling, which a nice ear will easily excuse, seeing the cause is known to proceed from no natural defect, among many other favorite Songs, which shall afterwards be mentioned, Mr Jole had one of the amorous kind, entituled, *Whilst I gaze on Cloe trembling*,[11] which Song in the printed editions, wants about twelve or 15 Stanzas, which Mr Jole [163] used to sing to the tune,[12] ‖ this Induced some to believe, tho' Mr Jole never showed it, or seemed to be vain of it, that he had a poetical Genius, and had added several verses to that ancient Song with his own accurate

---

10. Full name of Paracelsus (1493–1541), a famous Swiss physician, alchemist, and astrologer. The quotation about him—the source of which is uncertain—means "A stiff beard bears witness of virility." Not surprisingly, Jole is never depicted wearing a beard.

11. "Whilst I gaze on Chloe trembling" appears in Ramsay's *Tea-table Miscellany* (II, 5) in only 4 stanzas. That Jole, a man who has no passion for the ladies, would invent another 12 or 15 stanzas about the raging passion of a frustrated lover is humorous indeed. This song also appears in *Calliope, or English Harmony*, in Charles Coffey's ballad opera *The Devil to Pay* (1731), which was performed in Annapolis in 1752, and as "The Lukewarm Lover" in John Watts's *The Musical Miscellany*, 6 vols. (London, 1729–1731), II, 76.

12. Hamilton's sentence breaks off here without telling us what Mr. Jole was singing to the tune of (although it hardly matters, since Jole was probably warbling off-key anyhow). *To the tune* perhaps simply means "accordingly" or "appropriately."

Auld Rob Morris, I ken him fou well,
His arse it sticks out like ony peet creel.⁹

His presence is grand and majestic, especially when he ascends the Club Chair, and sits erect in it, his walk is stately and upright, tho' alittle on the hobble, which is not natural but from a gouty weakness in his feet, but he has contracted a habit of Seesawing often when he sits, especially if he be telling of a Story, at which he has a particular genius or knack, and tho' he be somewhat circumstantial or prolix, yet, he seldom fails to fix the attention of his hearers, and affords them abundance of Instruction and agreeable amusement.

As to his religion, he values himself much upon being of the Church of England, as by Law established, which he declares he thinks is the only true Church in the world, he has a profound regard for all Creeds received by that Church, particularly the Athanasian Creed, which he esteems a most excellent composition, || and to be believed by every true and Sincere christian, on pain of eternal Damnation, as that admirable and excellent *Symbolum,* expressly bears in it self; he is Intirely wedded to the Strict observation of the fasts, feasts and hollidays of the Church; and accounts all those to be heretical Presbyterians (for whom he has a very high Contempt, not only as foolish fanatics, but most of them lousy Scotsmen) who neglect them, especially the Martyrdom of that most pious martyr Charles I, of Savory memory, whom those hellish presbyterians (as some say) butchered in a most Inhuman manner; he carries his observation of feasts so far, as even to regulate his diet by them, Pancakes for example he looks upon to be profane and Insipid food, at any other time of the year but Shrovetide, tho never so well relished with wine and Sugar, and he also esteems it highly absurd, to eat plumb porridge or minced pies, except at christenmass and the hollidays.

The chief of Mr Joles Learning, besides that of cookery pastry, and other parts of housewifery, consists in divinity and music, his knowledge in the first he picked up, from a Curious collection of old books of Sermons, bound In parchment and many of them printed in a black character, with learned marginal notes, which Sermons were chiefly preached, by Learned Divines, in the Halcyon days of K: James I. when punning and quaint Sayings were very much in vogue, and diligently practised, encouraged and rewarded, by that wise monarch and his Sententious courtiers, when it was usual for men of bright Geniuses to pun themselves into bishopricks and places at court, a noble example this, and what all great princes & crowned

---

9. Peat basket.

Even in his Dress Nasifer showed a peculiar elegance of taste, he always went clean, and neat, tho never tawdry, he wore a large full flaxen wig, sometimes too a laced hat, his favorite color was red, for he often wore a Scarlet Coat, edged round with gold galloon, and ornamented with gold buttons and button holes, but this was properly his military dress, he being Leutenant General of the Independent foot Company of Annapolis, and had formerly been ensign thereof, but was promoted, in reward of his brave behaviour in the Dangerous expedition of that warlike Corps, against the Nanticock Indians, whom they took prisoners to the number of about 30, out of a boat at Wapping dock at Annapolis, and Conducted them safe to the City prison, without stricking one blow, or sheding one drop of Christian blood.[7]

Carlo Nasifer Jole was exactly, and to a title, as genteel in his undress, as in his high military dress, he wore a red or green velvet cap, a large blue wrapper, Girt about with a red ‖ military sash, a blue Silk Jacket with Silver mounting, and a genteel clouded cane; which last, vanity did not prompt him to Carry, but necessity obliged, being at times much afflicted with the gout, for the violent pains of which, his most effectual cure was Immerging his legs in Cold water.

Our heroes person, which in general was genteel and well made, sett off his dress, rather more than his dress his person, he is of a fair complexion, long and Sharp visage; somewhat Inclinable to a Square countenance, his nose aqueline, his chin of a Considerable length and prominent, in short, he is what many call in their vulgar Stile somewhat hatchet faced; his body is thick and well built, of a middle Stature and every way proportional except a little (tho' not disagreeable) *prominentia chīnium,* resembling somewhat the description of Rob Morris in the old Scots Song,[8] who is described in the following distich thus.

Suetonius, *The Twelve Caesars,* sec. 83 of "Augustus"). Sloane (1660–1753), president of the Royal Society (1727–1741) and president of the College of Physicians (1719–1735), was a noted naturalist with a penchant for collecting the kinds of curiosities Hamilton pokes fun at.

7. In 1742 the Nanticokes briefly participated in a revolt against the English settlers on the Eastern Shore of Maryland. While the Nanticokes and other tribes on the Eastern Shore were engaged in a war dance, a Choptank Indian exposed the plot and the revolt came to an abrupt end. The Nanticokes were severely reprimanded by the Maryland Assembly for their part in the uprising, and by 1744 the Nanticokes removed themselves from the province to live among the Six Nations. For a good discussion of this and other disputes concerning the Nanticokes, see Frank W. Porter III, "A Century of Accommodation: The Nanticoke Indians in Colonial Maryland," *Maryland Historical Magazine,* LXXIV (1979), 175–192.

8. "Auld Rob Morris" appears in Ramsay's *Tea-table Miscellany* (I, 59–60) and in *Calliope, or English Harmony,* 2 vols. (London, 1739, 1746). The comparison between Jole and Rob Morris is none too flattering. In the song, a girl's parents try to coerce her into marrying Morris, and she swears she would rather die than marry such a poor excuse for a man.

of Nasifer Jole Esqr, with little looking Glasses, bugles, Spangles, Isinglass and tinsel.

Some Cynical Mortals, may probably object here to these particulars in the character of this great man, and with a Sneer say, Well, what then? is this your Club hero? what is all this but triffling, and a Silly fancy or taste for bawbles and toys? but, in answer to those morose remarkers, I shall only produce some instances from history, of certain great men, who amused themselves with things rather more trivial and Insignificant, and shall give one recent example of the moderen taste this way.

Dioclesian the Emperor, gave up his Sceptre and turned Gardiner; Constantine wrote 40 books of husbandry; the austere Cato was an excellent cook, and wrote a Great book on the art of Cookery, Lysander, when ambassadors came to him talked || of nothing but his orchard; what shall I say of Cincinatus, Tully and many others, who delighted in pruning, planting and Grafting, nay Domitian the Emperor was mightily pleased with fly catching. Augustus was entertained playing with nuts among little Children, and a Certain Right Reverend and Learned french Bishop, whose name I have forgot, used to shut himself up in his chamber, and spin tops, and ride Hobby horses with a favorite child, his pupil, or probably his nephew, Sir Hans Sloan, that noted Physician and Philosopher, with many learned members of the Royal Society, took great pleasure in handling and tumbling over, little pieces of metal, with the pictures and heads of a great many Rogues of Antiquity, stamp'd upon them, and also, used often to divert themselves, with placing in regular order, Shells, feathers, flies, Cobwebs, and such like toys, and exercise their great and profound learning, in making florid lectures on them.[6]

[159]

6. Diocletian (A.D. 245–316), Roman emperor who ruled during a period of extreme difficulty, resigned the emperorship in 305 and turned to tending his cabbages. Constantine (ca. A.D. 285–337) was the Roman emperor who restored the empire to its former strength and converted to Christianity (Hamilton is perhaps recalling Constantine's *Liber de agricultura*). Cato (95–46 B.C.) was the famous Roman praetor noted for his Stoicism and adherence to old Roman principles (Cato concludes his *De agricultura* with some recipes, especially for preserving, but he did not produce a book solely on cooking). Lysander (d. 395 B.C.), Spartan general and statesman who destroyed the Athenian navy at Aegospotami, was noted for his impolite reception of his guests (see the section on him in Plutarch's *Lives*). Cincinnatus was a model of integrity and frugality who, according to Roman tradition, was called from the plow in 458 B.C. and appointed dictator to free Minucius from the Aequians, then returned to his farm beyond the Tiber. Domitian (A.D. 51–96), Roman emperor noted for his strict enforcement of public morality and his attempt to impose Greek refinement on the Romans, was also known for his extreme cruelty and is said to have spent hours each day in strictest privacy, catching flies and piercing them with a sharp instrument. Augustus (63 B.C.–14 A.D.), the great Roman emperor, often amused himself by playing at dice, marbles, or nuts with little boys (see

often used perfumes, such as musk, ambergrise, Civet, Bergamot, and the like, tho others affirm, that his design in that (and those were such as thought he was little attracted by the vanities of the fair Sex) was to conceal or Improve a perfume of a Ranker nature, which he contracted by keeping a number of favorite brutes about him, called by the greeks γαλαι,[5] of which we shall speak by and bye, and, if he used these perfumes for this purpose, he Surely is as Justifiable, as was Demosthenes the Athenian Orator, who held in his mouth at all times when he declaimed in public, a parcell of small pebble Stones to correct the natural uncouthness of his Speech & pronounciation.

He had a curious and elegant taste in cutting out patterns of work for Sempstresses, and would save a deal of trowble to these gentle Nymphs by cutting out all his own Shirts, and nightcaps, and Instructing them how to work them up, and some of his patterns I have seen, so beautifully Scolloped, and Jagged round the edges, that it was even delectable and wonderful to behold, and excited grand Ideas of the Sublimity of his Imagination, and fertility of his Invention, nay more, sometimes this Ingenious gentleman, would use the needle himself, and dern and patch to the admiration of all that saw his work.

[158] In setting out a table for an Entertainment, it was ‖ delightful to behold in what elegant order and Symmetry the table furniture was disposed, how charmingly the cloth was plaited, and pinched with regular figures in many places, how the plates, knives, forks, dishes, Salts, boats, cruets, casters &ct: were ranged in beautiful order, and how curiously the napkins were folded, and how delightfully perfumed.

Mr Jole in short, showed a delicacy of taste in every thing he had about him, both as to cleanliness and order, even in the disposition and arangement of the toys in his Shop, in which he dealt, to the great emolument of the Children of the place where he lived, who purchased of him at a good living price; those toys were piled up in pyramids, prisms, cylenders and Cones, and other Geometrical figures on the Shelves (which showed his Skill in the Mathematics) so as to attract the eyes of all passengers, particularly the longing and admiring eyes of Children and Schoolboys; they shining with as great Resplendency and Lustre, as does the throne of the great Mogol, Thick sown with diamonds, pearls, rubies, emeralds, Sapphires, topazes, and other precious Stones, in this manner shone the Shop

---

5. Mr. Jole keeps a bevy of cats about him, for which he is sometimes chided by other club members; it is probably no coincidence, then, that Hamilton has used the Greek word for *weasles* in referring to Jole's cats.

Clothing, drinking, air, Soil, Language and Commodities of Old England, in short, with him old England was all in all, but if this was an Infirmity in Mr Jole, it is an Infirmity generally Incident to human nature, in which, there is Ingrafted, such a Luxuriant Slip of vanity, that the wisest man that ever stept on two legs, may be cajoled or managed in this manner, if any artful Sycophant or flatterer, is lucky enough to hit upon, and humor his natural foibles, in fine, among all men, let their professions be what you will, it is the same now a days, as it was in the days of Tully, when || in his epistle to Atticus he says, *Nemo unquam poeta aut Orator, qui quenquam se meliorem arbitraretur,*[4] some may apply this to the present case, by using the words *Coquus* and *Culinarius,* instead of *poeta* and *Orator.*

Carlo Jole had a very elegant taste, in most things relative to houshold affairs, which he acquired by long and painful experience and application, during the many years that he spent in a Single life; he understood perfectly well how to set out a mantle piece or bofett, with plate, Glass and China, in the neatest and most Showy order; how, and in what places to dispose of flowers in the season, how to paper candlesticks and adorn glass Sconces, how to hang pictures, filigrams and pettipoints, and such like ornaments in a room, how to cut papers for decoying the flies from the hangings and Valence of beds, and how in the most charming and elegant taste to dress up a nosegay, for which he always kept a choice Collection of flowers in his Garden, that looked like a pleasant thicket or grove, shaded over with trees, bearing variety of fruits, such as apples, peaches, cherries, and Covered below, with all Sorts of kitchen Stuff, vizt: Cabbage, coleworts, Spinage, beets, carrots &ct: and Indeed, this curious gentleman showd the elegance of his taste, as much in the disposition and order of his Garden, as in any other knick-knack that he had about him, and, as to nosegays, which we but Just now mentioned, it was his practice in Spring, Summer and fall, never to go to bed, without at least half a dozen of these about him, vizt: one at his head, one stuck in his mouth, one in each hand and one on his breast, and at all times, when he went to Church, he wore one in his buttonhole, so beautifully decked, that it attracted the eyes of all the Congregation, || particularly those of the Ladies, while he kept twirling a Charming pink Iris, Jonquille, or Ænemonie betwixt his finger and thumb, and often applying it to his nose, which was of no moderate Size, some suspected, as Mr Jole was a Batchellor, that he Intended thus to lay traps, or attract the Regards of the fair Sex; for this purpose, it is thought also, he

---

4. "There was never a poet or orator who considered anybody better than himself" (Cicero, *Epistulae ad Atticum* 14.20.3.8).

purchased them at) to the prejudice of the Reputable merchant, he would prove very clearly, by unanswerable arguments, that 300 per cent, tended more to the public good, (vizt: the good of the merchants or Storekeepers, who were of public Service) than 50 per cent, because, said he, 300 per cent, is a living price, and enables the merchant to carry on trade and commerce, with vigor and life, whereas, any thing under that is a pitiful peddling price, and occasions trade, (vizt: Storekeeping) to languish and decay, that high prizes for goods in the retale way, was what Chiefly made the nation (vizt: the Storekeepers and merchants) flourish, but low prizes were the ruin and bane of Society, i:e: The Society of Storekeepers or merchants. He would often endeavor to Inculcate this doctrine to Ignorant people, who could not comprehend how this could be, and endeavored to perswade them, that it was much more for their advantage and Interest to give a reputable merchant half a crown a yard, for any kind of Stuff, than to buy the same Stuff of a Scots pedlar for one & Sixpence, the wares of the first being good, those of the latter trash, but, I never heard that he made any proselytes to this way of thinking, not only because this doctrine was *gratis dictum*,[3] as the Logicians term it, but because the Sordid Love of money is so generally prevalent, that people would still buy where they could at the Cheapest rate, which made Mr Jole very much admire at their Stupidity and Ignorance in thus preferring Scots pedlars, to merchants of repute & Character.

Mr Jole had a great part of his education on board a man of war, where he had learned many useful arts, particularly that of Cookery, and he was such a proficient in that noble Science, that he understood as well as any notable husiff, how to stew a frecassée, or ragout, mix, compound, boil or bake a pudding, or raise a pasty, and he knew his own Skill in these Important operations so well, that with reason he picqued himself upon it, and people approved of, and acquiesced in his Judgement herein so far, that they often eat of his dishes with high relish and pleasure, Indeed, his fondness for these niceities, and desire of applause on that Score, might Justly be called his weak side; for, tho' he was a person pritty tenacious of his property, yet, he would spare no expence in making a Show with such delicacies, and dainties, and any hungry fellow or abandon'd Epicure, might get a good meal out of him, as often as he pleased, by only praising his Cookery, and saying that it put one in mind of *Old England;* for he was so passionatly fond of Old England, as we have said, and every thing belonging to it, that nothing in the world was to be compared to the manners, customs, eating,

---

3. "Freely asserted."

The Honorable Carlo Nasifer Jole Esqr. President of the Ancient & honorable Tuesday Club

Prandum flos, alta infixus ecce Cathedra
Consortii nostri et decus, et gloria..
Cedito, o Hugo, tu Cognominate Maccarte
Vestrum nam caput, nostra tiara temnit.

[Hamilton's translation on back of drawing]

Behold of Presidents the prime prick'd up in lofty Chair
Who of our Club the Glory is, and ornament Right fair.
Yeild then to us, O haughty Hugh, who Sirnam'd art Maccarty
Since that your Cap is by our head, held in Contempt right hearty.

[facing page 153]

[153] its top to its bottom, from the highest of the || Sublime, to the lowest of the bathos; from Virgil to Bavius, from Milton to Pryn and Wythers, from Cervantes and his follower Henry Fielding Esqr, to the Reverend Mr Gazeteer Eachard & the Celebrated Mr John Bunyian.[1]

Upon the celebrated 2d of July, O:S: in the year 1745, a day ever to be remembered by the ancient and honorable Tuesday Club, at Sederunt 8, Mr Secretary Motely being Steward, were admitted to the Club several members, vizt: Messieurs Nasifer Jole, Dumpling Gundiguts, Drawlum Quaint, Slyboots Pleasant, and Joggle Hasty; The first of these Gentlemen is the Subject of this dignified and distinguished Chapter, and Indeed, will be the Chief heroe of our Succeeding History, as for the others, we shall mention them only occasionally as we go along, according to the Station they hold, and figure they make in the Club.

Mr Nasifer Jole, otherwise Carlo Nasifer Jole, was a native of old England, and the County of Kent claims the honor of his birth, he often Justly values himself on his being born an Englishman, and is not alittle fond of letting it be known, that he is a man of Kent, sprung of a race of ancient heroes and true british blood, not a kentish man,[2] who is only the mungerell Issue of the Roman, Saxon, Norman, Dane, Scot, pict, and a hundred other mixed foreign Nations, that gained footing in England but of late.

He was educated in the mercantile way, and made such progress in the Science of traffic and trucking, that he could tell at his fingers ends, all the noble Ingredients that Compound the Character of a reputable merchant, or storekeeper, & could distinguish such from a Scots pedlar at a miles distance without the help of a perspective glass, his chief Characteristic of a [154] merchant, was one that bought very Cheap, and || sold at a living price, as he called it, which golden rule he followed himself, as much as in him lay, and his distinguishing mark of a pedlar, was a fellow, that presumed to vend his wares at a low, or what some call a reasonable rate, (whatever price he

---

1. Bavius (fl. 1st century B.C.), a Roman poetaster, was rescued from oblivion only by Vergil's contempt. William Prynne (1600–1669), a Puritan pamphleteer, wrote against Arminianism and endeavored to reform the manners of the age, for which he was confined to the Tower of London. George Wither (1588–1667), an English author, was noted for his satires (*Abuses Stript and Whipt* [London, 1613]), his pastorals, including *The Shepherds Hunting* (London, 1615), and his *Hymnes and Songs of the Church* (London, 1623), written after he became a devout Puritan. John Eachard (ca. 1636–1697) was an English divine and satirical writer whose works include *The Grounds and Occasions of the Contempt of the Clergy and Religion Enquired Into* (London, 1670) and two dialogues ridiculing Hobbes's philosophy (1672, 1673).

2. A man of Kent is one born east of the Medway; these men went out with green boughs to meet William the Conqueror and consequently obtained a confirmation of their ancient privileges from the new king. A Kentish man is a resident of the western part of the county.

This sage Club therefore, considering how dreadfully fatal the consequences might be, if such Subtile disputes were suffered to take place in their Society, thought of a method to prevent this mischief, and fell upon the most effectual remedy, which shows their deep Judgement and Sagacity; they pitched upon ridicule, as the most effectual way to Cure it, and Indeed, we find it to be true, that men are much sooner laughed out of their follies and faults, than cured of them by grave admonition and advice, they therefore at Sederunt 6th, June 18, passed the following law.

Law VII. That if any Subject of what nature soever, be discussed, that levels at party matters, or the administration of the Government of this Province, or be disagreeable to the Club, no answer shall be given thereto, but after such discourse is ended, the Society shall laugh at the member offending, in order to divert the discourse.

This Law was called the *gelastic Law*, and, in its Substance and Structure, shows the wisdom and Sagacity of the Longstanding members, of this ancient and honorable Club, as much as any Law framed by them, either before or since, and, we shall find in the Sequel, this Law put in execution, against several offending members, sometimes with effect, and sometimes with none at all, which shows us, how difficult a task it is, for even the utmost Strech of human wisdom, to frame a Law or Laws, that cannot be evaded, at the same Sederunt there passed another rule, vizt: [152]

Law VIII. That Mr Prattle Motely, shall be Secretary of the Club during pleasure.

At the next Sederunt, (Mr Laconic Comas being Steward) two Gentlemen were proposed by the Reverend Mr Smoothum Sly, to be admitted members of the Club, vizt: Mr Nasifer Jole, of whom we shall have a great deal to say in the next chapter, and Mr Dumpling Gundiguts, of whom we shall say all in this place that can be said of him, that is, that he was only noted for his being a very fat unwieldy man, and a vociferous Singer in Club, making more noise than music, at this Sederunt the Gelastic Law, was the first time put in execution, against Mr Secretary Motely, who entered into a prolix harangue concerning the Consciences of Lawyers.

Chapter IV

The private Character of Nasifer Jole Esqr, and other prodigious matters.

I am now entering upon a chapter in this History, in which I shall have occasion for the asistance of all the muses, which Inhabit Parnassus, from

occasions, have I not given a Specimen of it, is it any thing but mere balderdash, so confused, and so noisy, that I defy the wisest head in Christendom to methodize it, and, after all Impediments are removed, and the Club forms itself again round the great table, how dull, how sleepy are the members, when their Stomachs are overcharged, how flat, how low the Conversation, what yawning, what gaping, what Streching of limbs, what Nodding, what Sleeping, what Snoring, or rather driving of hogs! Oh! Oh! Tis Lamentable to behold, how much better is it to spend the time, in witty conversation, such as punning, framing quaint Conundrums, cracking Sly Jokes, telling comical Stories, singing old catches, or composing extempore Rhimes, but alas! all this is only preaching to the wind, and beating the air in vain, for one may preach to eternity, and never reform the manners of Clubs, nay more, the manners of mankind in General, till the example of great men and presidents shows them the way.

[151] I come now to relate a transaction, which shows in a very conspicuous Light, the wisdom of this ancient and honorable Club; It is a truth not to be disputed, that the greatest pest of Clubs, and the most common disturber of the peace of those || Societies, is that violent propensity in human nature to dispute, every one thinking himself the wisest and most learned person in company, and therefore not obliged to yield one ace to the opinion or Judgement of another. This has been the cause of the dissolution of many Clubs, and, where disputes have arisen about such Important matters, as what is the right, and what the wrong end of a black pudding, at what end one shall break an egg, with most ease and conveniency to eat it, which is the most amicable, or familiar way of Saluting a friend, to shake him by the hand, or clap him on the Shoulder, what is to be reckoned among men of nice honor, the greatest affront, a twitch o' the nose, or a kick o' the breech, the consequences of these learned disputes, have been fatal to those Clubs, where they have been fomented or encouraged, have entirely broke them up, and rendered those who were before, good Club Companions and friends, bitter enimies to one another, to the great hurt and Dammage, of that Social Clubical disposition, which nature has been so careful to Implant in mankind.

Complete Body of Practical Divinity (London, 1723). Like most divines, Dod and Doolittle frequently admonish their readers against the dangers of excessive eating and drinking, but I suspect that Hamilton is especially recalling their treatises on the Lord's Supper. In *A Briefe Dialogue, concerning Preparation for the Worthy Receiving of the Lords Supper* (London, 1627), Dod discusses the dangers of excessive eating and drinking in his section on the sins against the Fourth Commandment; in *A Treatise concerning the Lords Supper* (London, 1667), Doolittle writes: "It is an hainous sin that those that are reeling in the street, . . . rather than degrading themselves below the rank of men" and "reducing them[selves] to the Primitive Institution, . . . should be seen kneeling at the Sacrament" (p. 3).

Simple frugality of the Golden age was this, and how different from that luxury and profuseness that prevails in most of our moderen Clubs, where, the whole apparatus of a formal table is Introduced, the Club room is pestered with the passing and repassing of Servants, the hobnails of whose Shoes, make a miserable Clamping over the planks, and, when this is over ‖ it proves only a prologue to the confusion and Superfluous Ceremony that [149] succeeds, for, as soon as the Steward gives the Signal that Supper waits, there is hawling of Chairs, crossing over, Casting off, figuring in, right and left, like so many people at a Country dance, There is—pray Gentlemen take your places—as the Steward's prologue,—there is grace to be said, of which not one word can be heard, for talking and laughing, then follow Sharp reproofs from the Chaplain, and grumblings from the offending members; next it is—pray take a Seat—Pray Sir sit here—here's room enough—excuse me Sir, I eat no Suppers—I seldom sup a nights Sir—for my part, I never sup Sir. Then comes the table conversation—Here boy, some bread—Pray shift that Dish this way—who carves best?—what do you chuse Sir?—pray gi' me leave to help you—Shall I help you to this pray good Sir?—Shall I help you to that—Sir, your most humble—pray Sir help yourself,—hold good Sir—here's enough—dont you chuse Sauce—please to hand me that mustard,—pray shove the vinegar cruet this way—a clean plate there—This is fine veal, that's delicious mutton—these apples are well baked, these cheese cakes are not done,—of all things commend me to pudding—do you love Cold pudding Sir—no good Sir, my love is settled,—pray Sir eat 'tother Custard,—boy, some Small beer—a glass of wine you—Sir, my humble Service—Sir your health—yours Sir,—and yours Sir,—and yours Sir—your most obedient humble Servant—pledge you Sir—fill me a glass of Claret there ho—avast you Son of a bitch, none of your bumpers damn you!—well, come away, let's have at this turkey and oysters,—my Stars and garters what a twist of the under Jaw you have got,—I play a good knife ‖ and fork, thanks be praised—here take away,—and so [150] they get up one by one, and fall to picking their teeth, sauntering about the Room, or standing with their bums to the fire; I would ask what pleasure there can be in all this, except only that of eating and drinking, which, as it is a pleasure we enjoy in Common with the brute, and often employ to baser purposes, the destruction of health and constitution, we ought to glory but little in, as the pious Mr Dods, the Reverend Mr Dolittle, and several other learned Divines tell us,[2] as for the table conversation on these

2. Probably John Dod (1549?–1645), Puritan divine known as "Decalogue Dod" for his exposition of the Ten Commandments (1604). Thomas Doolittle (1632?–1707) was a Nonconformist tutor and preacher who published several volumes of religious writings, including *A*

of nurses children and Shallow wits by a winters fire, but have adapted it to the taste of the learned & Ingenious, by Interlarding the narration of facts In several places, with proper and apposite observations and remarks, and these, my readers are to expect to meet with, wherever the nature of the Subject will permit, and, if any Slender wits happen to be among my readers, I advise them, for their own ease, to pass over these learned Remarks, as being above their capacity and understanding, but, I hope all my learned Readers will esteem them the very marrow and Cream of this history, and therefore read them over with attention and Carefully store them up in their Intellectual warehouses and magazines, which, as the learned Descartes says, is in the middle Ventricle of the brain, near the pineal Gland, where memory keeps her court.[1]

This virtuous and frugal Club, Imagining that they were still too lavish in allowing a Gammon of bacon, or one dish of dress'd vittles for Supper, passed at Sederunt 5th June 11, the following Law, viz:

Law VI. That such as are batchelor members of the Club may have a Cheese upon one Side board, instead of dress'd vittles.

This not only exhibited, a Singular Instance of frugality and moderation, but also, a high degree of Indulgence to those batchelor members, who, not always having cooks at home, and for the most part, little or nothing for Cooks to lick their fingers upon, must be at abundance more trowble in providing, than such of the members as were matirmonized, they likewise showed in this an Instance of heroic temperance and moderation, much like that of a certain Roman General; who, when foreign ambassadors came to have audience of him, was busied in boiling a turnip for his own Dinner.

(*)Happy then was it with the members of this ancient and honorable Club, for, without Interruption, let or molestation, they could sit with their legs across, loll upon the table or an Elbow chair, smoke their pipes, kiss the Glass or bowl, in their turns, converse upon Clubical matters, either grave or facetious, drink toasts either loyal or amorous, crack Jokes, frame puns or conundrums, and, should their Stomachs call for a whet, without Ceremony or trowble to themselves or fellow members, they might rise up, go to the Side board, and after having taken their Slice of cheese or Sliver of Gammon standing, return again to their compotation, Jocosity, and Clubical conversation, how charming, how regular, and how much like the

---

(*) Vide anniversary Speech in 1754, almost verbatim the same with this paragraph.

1. Hamilton is probably recalling Descartes's 1664 *Essay on Man* (*Traité de l'homme*), in which Descartes explains that memory is located in the pineal gland (see *Oeuvres de Descartes*, ed. Charles Adam and Paul Tannery [Paris, 1897–1910], XI, 177–178).

when any thing that looks like Satyr || or accrimination is laid at the door of [146] a member, for tho' a regard to truth, obliges me as an historian to mention every circumstance, yet, a regard to my own quiet, and the good will of others, constrains me to forbear naming of names upon all occasions, and therefore, I shall leave my Judicious Readers to guess, who I mean in this particular, and in many other particulars of the like nature, which may occur in the course of this History.

And, now, since I am upon the Subject of the Club's regard for the fair Sex, I must not omitt an order that passed at this Sederunt, which, somehow or other, by the fault of the Clerk or Secretary, was not entered in the book of records; and that was the Introduction of certain utensils into the Club, these were Sand boxes to spit in, as most of the members smoked, and some Chawed, this contrivance was fallen upon to prevent abusing and soiling the floors of the rooms where the Club sat, and these conveniencies were carried about with great pomp and Solemnity, from one Stewards house to another, every time the Club met, but cleanly and useful as they were, and contrived for the ease of Servants and neat house wives, whose chief ambition and Care of life, is to make their plank floors shine like glass, yet, were they soon dismissed, because, it was thought, that the married men of the Club, were afraid of falling under the Ridicule of the Batchellors, by showing in this, a more than Common care and Sollicitude, about Incurring the displeasure of their wives.

Chapter III

The Introduction of the Batchellor's Cheese into the Club, the passing The Gelastic law, and other matters of Importance.

We shall meet with some Histories, where there is nothing || but a dry [147] relation of facts, without any useful reflections, or observations interspersed, which are Indeed the Salt of History, and afford it a Savor which makes it agreeable to the palat of every Judicious reader, without this, it would look like the York-shire Squire's Story of himself and his friend, which consisted chiefly of—and so quoth he, and so quoth I, and so we agreed on this, and so we differed on that, and so I went there, and so he came here, and so—and so—and so &ct:

Whoever reads this history, must not expect to find any such trumpery in it's structure and composition; I never Intended it for the entertainment

honorary member of this ancient and honorable Club; These honorary members, of whom we shall find many admitted in the course of our History, had a right to attend the Club meetings as often as they were in the place, and were not obliged to serve the Club at any time as Stewards, an excellent policy in the Club, to Increase and add to their Strength and Importance, and to spread their fame abroad, without much expence or trowble, from these honorary members, arose, in process of time, a considerable Society, Called the *Eastren Shore Triumvirate,* depending upon this ancient and Honorable Club, as shall be related in its proper place.

Before this Sederunt broke up, the Steward, Capt: Serious Social, being in a very gay and pleasant humor, took up the punch bowl, and with a musical voice, sung the following Catch, which went round the members.

Club Catch sung by Capt: Serious Social

There was a man of very great fame,
Signior Domingo was his name.
He was a man not given to quarrel,
But now and then, with a Sma' beer barrel,
And, when he died, he was so kind,
As to leave this very bowl for us behind.

The next meeting or Sederunt of the Club, was at Capt: Bully Blunt's, which was on the 4th of June, when the Club passed another Law, vizt:

Law V. That Immediatly after supper, the Ladies shall be toasted, before any other healths go round.

This Law stood in force for a great while, but at last gave place to the King and the Club, and even that submitted to the high Steward's health, as he was stiled.

This Law shows the great regard, that this ancient and Honorable Club had for the Ladies, and, there will appear in the Sequel of this History, more marks of honor and respect, which this Club conferrd upon this amiable Sex, tho' it must be owned, that there were in the Club at that time, two longstanding members, that were remarkable for their disregard to, (I will not say, utter Indifference for) the Sex, for, one of these gentlemen, loved a piece of old hat very well (as the Saying is) but his humor led him to partake of it in a hugger mugger way, as for the other, he was a Sort of apathy, had not the least Inclination for that Sort of amusement, and Indeed, never much affected being In the company of the Ladies, If my readers have a Curiosity to know, who these members were by name, I must beg to be excused, not thinking it proper, to mention names in this history,

Law I. That the meeting of the Club be weekly, at the members houses, by turns, thro' out the year, upon Tuesday evening.

Law II. The Steward for the time being, shall provide a gammon of bacon, or any other one dish of dressed vittles and no more.

Law III. No Liquor shall be made, prepared or produced after eleven o clock at night, and every Member shall be at liberty to retire at pleasure.

Law IV. No members shall be admitted without the concurring consent, of the whole Club, and after such admission, the member shall serve as Steward next meeting.

Having passed these laws with great wisdom and Sagacity, they betook themselves again to their punch and pipes, and then, the Gammon, according to Rule, appeared on a Side-board, with some plates in a heap, and knives and forks, there not being so much as the formality of a Cloth laid, and every member at pleasure arose from his Seat and helped himself, without taking up time in Saying of Grace, setting Chairs, passing compliments, about taking place at table, or trowbling themselves about shifting of dishes, handing of plates Spoons, cruets mustard pots &ct: and Servants running over one another, which not only wastes much time, but creates more noise than is needful.

Happy, O happy had it been for this ancient and honorable Club, had they always kept to this golden mean of frugality and temperance, but the mode soon changed, and Luxury crept in by degrees, as we shall find in the Sequel.

This first Sederunt was finished in a gay and Jovial manner, by the Singing of several ancient Catches, at which Capt: Serious Social was a good hand, and sung the following, holding up a large punch bowl well Replenished, which I think worthy of a place in this history, because it became afterwards a Constant Club Catch.

Club Catch sung by Capt: Serious Social

Merry meet, and merry part,
Here's to thee with all my heart.
One bowl in hand, and another in store,
Enough's enough, and we'll have one more.

Nothing more, worth remarking passed at this first Sederunt.

At Sederunt Second, May 21, which was held by Jealous Spyplot Esqr, the Evening passed in putting round the bowl and Smoking; but, on the 28 of may, when the Club was held by Capt: Serious Social, the order of honorary members was established, and Mr Abraham Bumper was made an

First Sederunt of the ancient and honorable Tuesday Club.

[facing page 142]

Chapter II

[141]

The first Sederunt of the Ancient and honorable Tuesday Club, and the wise Laws then framed.

Such of my readers, as have perused the last chapter of the preceeding book, if their memory be not very short, will Remember, that Messiurs Prattle Motely and Loquacious Scribble M:D: the residue of the Ugly Club, called to their asistance Jealous Spyplot Esqr, Serjeant at Law, and the Reverend Mr Smoothum Sly, parson of the parish, in order to form a new Club, and fix it upon a better and more lasting foundation, than any of the Clubs hitherto erected, They presently got four more to Join them, vizt: Captn: Seemly Spruce, a Jolly boon companion, and no early Starter, being one who usually wore his Sitting breeches at a nights compotation, Captn: Serious Social, of the same kidney, and noted for Singing of old Club Catches, Mr Laconic Comus, a Jolly old cock, of Surly aspect and few words, but gifted with an excellent musical voice, and a Sincere lover of the Bowl and tobacco pipe, these had formerly been members of the Red house Club; and Captn: Bully Blunt, a person of a very happy turn to the Burlesque, which made him an exceeding good Clubs man.

These Gentlemen then, meeting upon Tuesday the 14th day of May, in the Year 1745, the same month and day on which the Red house Club met under Mr George Neilson Sixteen years before, formed and erected themselves into a club, which they called by the name of the *Tuesday Club;* they met first at the Lodging of || Doctor Loquacious Scribble, who first exercised the office of Steward, and Chairman to the Club; and the Candles being lit, the punch made, and the pipes fairly set a going, after two or three rounds of the punch bowl, they applied themselves to make and pass some wholesome Laws, for the good government and regulation of the Society, In which, they did not trust so much to their own Judgement, and Invention, as some vain people are apt to do, but took for a pattern, the regulations and laws of other Clubs, particularly those of the ancient and venerable Tuesday, (or whin bush) Club of Lanneric, of which, they reckoned themselves a direct continuation, on the same line, and, upon this position they assumed the name of the *Ancient and honorable Tuesday Club, of Annapolis in Maryland,* and thus having fixed their ancient and honorable title, they, at their first Sederunt established the following Laws.

[142]

Since we cannot certainly tell what Sort of people those worthies abovementioned were, I think, to fix the matter, and In some measure to satisfy posterity, we may take upon us to pronounce, with great verisimilitude, that ‖ they were all once on a time, members of certain Clubs, and by that means, their names have been handed down, in winter Evening Stories, Legends, Law papers, proverbs and the like, tho' their actions have been most of them buried in oblivion, thro' the Neglect of Clubical Historians and Secretaries.

I shall mention but one other worthy before I conclude this Chapter, by Name, Sir Hugh Mccarty Esqr, an Illustrious person, whose name has spread far and near within these two or three years, being the Honorable the President, of the Ancient and Right honorable Monday Club of New York,[30] as it has been called; but still one Strange peculiarity attends this great man and his Club, that tho' both be of very moderen date, yet not one Soul, far or near, can be found, that can upon oath or honor declare, that they ever saw that Illustrious personage, or ever were once in his Club, or heard any thing at all of it in the City of New York, where it was said to meet, tho he, and his Club were both very famous in several places at a distance, from that City, like the new Island lately Discovered by Admiral Anson's Crew,[31] known every where, but in the very place where it lies, and for this reason, I have Introduced him and his Club, in the Catalogue of these worthies merely nominal, and as I shall have occasion to say a great deal of this noble personage, in the Sequel of this history, I shall drop him here, together with his club, and, flattering myself, that my labor and pains, will preserve the worthies, of the ancient and honorable Tuesday Club, (of which I may Justly say, I am the faithful Secretary,) from that misfortune, of having little else but their bare names known to posterity, I with pleasure pursue the thread of my history.

Faber as the "chief Workman, containing the fruitfulness of generations and Seeds, as it were the internal efficient cause," and suggests that in the "*Archeusses* of the bowels . . . the planetary Spirits do most shine forth, even as also, in the whole influous *Archeus*" (*Van Helmont's Works* [London, 1664], 35–36). A Tom Fool is a clumsy fool, fond of practical jokes.

30. Sir Hugh (or Colonel Morris, as Hamilton calls him in the "Record") and his Monday Club remain a mystery. Carl Bridenbaugh alludes to the Monday Club in *Cities in Revolt: Urban Life in America, 1743–1776* (New York, 1955), 163, but he has borrowed his information from Hamilton.

31. George Anson, Lord Anson (1697–1762) was an English admiral who commanded a squadron in the Pacific, inflicted damage upon the Spanish, and circumnavigated the world (1740–1744).

Church, at a small distance from the altar, upon this the Archbishop, Solemnly called him by his name to appear, and lo, the priest rose from his grave also; The Archbishop urged him to absolve the lord, which he did, and this Lord quietly retired to his rest again, within the rail of the Altar. The Archbishop would fain have persuaded the priest to stay on earth, to make Converts, with regard to paying of the tythes, but he also retired to his grave, positively refusing to grant the good Archbishop this boon, as having no personal Interest in the thing, however, upon this miracle, the Lord, with whom the Archbishop had the dispute, quietly payd the tythes ever after"—let our prophane denyers of the divine right of tythes read this Story and tremble, be convinced and converted.

There is but one pope, whom I shall mention among these nominal worthies, and it is Pope Joan,[27] who is said to have been a female pope, and put an arch trick upon the wise Cardinals of the Conclave, there is nothing more known of this pope or popess, but this piece of waggery, this Story is denied by all true and Stanch catholics, who say, it is only a Scandalous lie, Invented by the Heretics, to throw a Slur upon holy Church, but, I would ask them, for what reason the Cardinals now use a Groping Chair at the Installment of the popes? is it not to be certain of the virility of the Candidate, and, that they may never again have such another trick playd them. [139]

Tom Folio[28] is another worthy of this class, who is often mentioned, in conversation, it is uncertain when and where he lived, but we have reason to believe, that he was a profound Critic in title pages, and had treasured up in his head a voluminous catalogue of books, since it is a common appellation, bestowed upon all such (since his time) as talk much of books which they have never read, dipt into or understood, such people being properly stiled Tom Folios.

Many others besides these I have mentioned might be Introduced among the nominal worthies, such as messiurs Jack-a-napes, Jack-a-Dandy, Joannes ad oppositum, The man in the moon, Archæus Faber, and Tom Fool,[29] but let those I have already exhibited serve as a Specimen of the great worth and dignity of these obscure heroes.

---

27. The mythical female pope who supposedly succeeded Leo IV (855); she disguised herself as a monk so that she could gain admission to her lover, the monk Folda. After being elected pope, she was discovered when she gave birth during her enthronement.

28. Thomas Rawlinson (1681–1725), an English book collector, was satirized by Joseph Addison in the *Tatler* (no. 158) as "Tom Folio," but Hamilton may be referring to a more mythical figure.

29. A Jackanapes is a pert, apish little fellow (originally, the name probably signified a tame monkey [*Jack*] from Naples). A Jack-a-dandy is a smart, bright little fellow. For variations of the man in the moon myth, see *Brewer's Dictionary of Phrase and Fable*. Jan Baptista van Helmont (1577–1644) in chap. 5 of his *Oriatrike, or Physick Refined* (1662) defines the Archaeus

Circumstance alone, I think, is Sufficient to convince all prophane cavillers at the divine right of tythes, but, as this age has come to such a gross degree of Infidelity, as to give little or no credit to quotations from Scripture, and the pious and Learned labors of the Revd Mr Commissary Henderson, on that Subject,[24] for even our nobles of the English Nation, (witness the late learned Henry Saintjohn Lord Bolingbroke, in his letters against the Authenticity of Sacred History)[25] have run much into that Strain, we shall to reclaim them (tho we have reason to think it will be as much in vain, as foreign to our present purpose) relate a miracle, which is quoted by the Learned Selden, in his book upon tythes.[26]

"It happened on a time, that Saint Austin, the famous Archbishop of Canterbury, in the time of the Saxons, had a dispute with some Lord concerning the tythes, he refusing to pay them, upon this, the Archbishop, on a Solemn day, at Church, pronounced a curse upon all those who refused to pay the tythes, forbidding them to come within the rail of the altar; he had no sooner pronounced this Interdict, than the Corps of a man, that lay enterred within that rail, miraculously rose from the grave, and very gravely walked out of the Church; the Archbishop calling him back, asked him who he was, and what was the reason of his rising out of his grave; he replied that he had Layn buried there 170 years, and, that he was in his life time Lord of the Mannor, and had refused to pay the tythes, upon which the priest of the parish excommunicated him, and, upon the Archbishops pronouncing the Curse, he was obliged to rise from his grave, and quit that holy ground, where he lay enterred, the Archbishop asked him if he knew who, or where that priest was, he answered that he lay buried in the same

---

24. Jacob Henderson (d. 1751) was born in Ireland, ordained in 1710 and licensed to Virginia, appointed commissary for the Western Shore of Maryland in 1715, and then reappointed commissary for the whole colony in 1729. Henderson was embroiled in a dispute over ministers' salaries, and Hamilton is probably alluding especially to Henderson's *The Case of the Clergy of Maryland* ([London, 1729]); see J. A. Leo Lemay, *Men of Letters in Colonial Maryland* (Knoxville, Tenn., 1972), 120–121.

25. Henry Saint John, Viscount Bolingbroke (1678–1751) was an English statesman who supported Robert Harley and the Tory party, managed the peace negotiations at Utrecht (1713), acted as James the Pretender's secretary of state and drew up his declaration for invasion, and after returning to England, retired and wrote numerous political tracts. Hamilton is referring to Bolingbroke's *Letters on the Study and Use of History* (London, 1752), in which Bolingbroke argues against the credibility of miracles.

26. John Selden (1584–1654) was an eminent lawyer of the Inner Temple whose *Historie of Tithes* ([London], 1618) offended the clergy and was suppressed; he was noted also for his treatise *De diis Syris* (London, 1617), which established his reputation as an Orientalist. The passage on Augustine appears in the *Historie of Tithes* (see the tale of Augustine and the lord of Cometon, chap. 10, pp. 272–274), but Hamilton has loosely paraphrased the story and added the derogatory remarks. (Selden does not say, for instance, that the priest refused to stay on earth because he had "no personal Interest in the thing.")

laris, Saint Vulvaris,[19] and so forth. These Saints have done Infinite dammage to Physicians and Apothecaries, and conveyd thousands of pounds out of their pockets into those of the priests, by means of a certain latent virtue they have of Curing distempers in all parts of the body, such as headakes, toothakes, Pleurisies, Colics, and even the venereal Distemper, which has been of such vast Emolument, for this Century past, to certain obscure doctors of Physic.

There is a person, whether a Saint or a hermit, or both, I cannot be certain, nor Indeed is he known by any other name but that of the Wandering Jew,[20] this person is said to have been strolling from place to place, like a Scotsh pedlar, for upwards of Seventeen hundred years, Several persons of great || credulity and moderate credit, have affirmed that they have seen him, and, it is believed by many, that he will persevere in this Strolling way, to the end of the world, or at least, to the long, and longer yet to be wished for Millennium. [137]

As for the Seven Sleepers[21] and their dog, who sleeped in a Cave for 500 years, we need not wonder that nothing is known of them but this Sleeping bout, since Sleep is a State of torpor or Inactivity, in which the only thing we can be Employed about is dreaming, an employment, which several people exercise, to as great perfection when broad awake, as others do when fast asleep.

Prester John[22] is another obscure worthy, whose place of Residence and proper office is not yet fixed, many believe him to be an Emperor, a king, a great prince; but all agree in this, that he is a priest, but if so, he is a priest of whom we know as little as of the Ancient Melhisedec,[23] who is mentioned only by Name in Sacred History, and all that we know of him, is that Abraham paid him the tythes of the Spoils taken in battle, which

---

19. These are all invented names (for different parts of the body) except Saint Januarius, the bishop of Beneventum who was beheaded during the Diocletian persecution in 305.
20. A widespread medieval legend concerned a Jew who refused Christ comfort while Christ was bearing his cross to Calvary and who was therefore condemned to wander over the face of the earth until the end of the world.
21. The seven noble Christian youths of Ephesus who fled the persecution of Decius (250) and concealed themselves in a mountain cave, which Decius ordered to be walled up; they slept for around 200 years, and after awakening and telling their story, they died.
22. Legendary Christian priest and king who is alleged to have reigned both in Asia and in Africa in the 12th century.
23. Melchizedec was the high priest of Salem "who met Abraham returning from the slaughter of the kings" and received a "tenth of the spoils" (Heb. 7:1–4). The proximity of this allusion to the Selden allusion below suggests that Hamilton is recalling the story of Melchizedek and Abraham related in the first chapter of Selden's *History of Tythes* (see p. 137n, below).

the bye, this George a Green, tho we have no documents of his ever having been Canonized, yet he must have been a person of excellent qualifications, for ever since his time, his name has been used in a proverbial Comparison, vizt: *were you as good as George a Green;* but what this worthy was really good for, cannot now be known from any records extant.

Saint Patrick, the Irish Saint is another, of whom we have but very Imperfect accounts, but the most remarkable thing related of him, is his swimming a river, after his head was struck off, with that very Identical head in his teeth, a genuine Irish miracle.

Were I to mention all the Saints named in the Calendar, of whom nothing but their bare names is known, I should compose a whole volume or Index of names, and therefore, I shall take notice of only a few more, The most remarkable of these obscure Saints is Saint Viar, mentioned with honor, by Doctor Conyers Middleton in || his *Letter from Rome,*[17] who has not left behind him one single circumstance to make him famous, it is said indeed that he was *PræfectuS. VIARum* under some of the twelve Cæsars, and that is Indeed all we know of him, besides the Circumstance of his being a Saint.

There is also Saint Amphibolus, who lived in the time of Saint Alban,[18] the british martyr, the only circumstance we know of him, is, that he was the Cloak of the said St Alban, and was Sainted, because he suffered martyrdom in company with him, Tho some have gone so far, as to assert, that this holy Cloak was Bishop of the Isle of Man, and consequently, was very moderate in his principles, doing neither good nor harm.

Several other Saints there are likewise, of whom we have nothing but their names, of whom Saint Januarius is the most Eminent, and besides there are Saint Ocularis, Saint Auricularis, Saint Mammillaris, Saint Mentu-

---

17. Middleton (1683–1750) was educated at Trinity College, Cambridge; his chief works include the *Life of Cicero* (London, 1741) and the latitudinarian *Free Inquiry into Miracles* (London, 1748), which aroused much controversy by concluding that postapostolic miracles were unreal. Hamilton is purposefully misconstruing Middleton's *Letter from Rome*, 2d ed. (London, 1729), in which the story of Saint Viar is used to point out the ridiculous nature of idolatry. In the *Letter,* Viar is a Spaniard whose sainthood is demonstrated when his people produce a sacred stone with *S. Viar* on it; antiquaries, however, prove the stone to be only a fragment of an old Roman inscription in memory of a Praefectus Viarum, or overseer of the highways.

18. Amphibalus was the cleric who supposedly converted Saint Alban and whose name was invented by Geoffrey of Monmouth from the cleric's cloak (*amphibalus*) used by Saint Alban to conceal his identity. Saint Alban (d. ca. 304), the first British martyr, was put to death during the Diocletian persecution. A layman, he sacrificed his life to save the life of a priest by disguising himself in the priest's cloak.

with a Strange uncouth Countenance, as if he had the dry belly ake, this account Cardan gives of him Libro 16. *De rerum varietate*,[10] he appears to be one of these Sorts of people that are *occupati nihil agendo,* and that make a mighty pother *de lana Caprina*,[11] as the Learned express it.

I shall but Just mention that famous ancient Gentleman Called Tantarabobus,[12] of whom nothing is said, but *that he lived till he Died,* wherefore he has become a worthy pattern, to those Sort of Philosophers among the Vulgar, who never think of any thing but the present time, their concise Philosophy prompting them to use this worthys name in a proverb, viz: "I care not, let the world wag, for I shall live as long as Tantarabobus, and he lived till he Died," happy would it have been, for multitudes of poor wretches in this world, had Alexander the Great, Julius Cæsar, Hannibal, and Kouli Can,[13] mighty men at arms, and Saint Athanasius, St Ambrose, Saint Cyryl,[14] and other Zealous Christian Saints, followed the example of this Indolent worthy Tantarabobus, who as he never was the au- ‖ thor of [135] any good during his long life, so none can lay any bloodshed or mischief at his door.

I come now to speak of some Saints, priests and popes, of whom we know little more than their bare names, the Seven Champions of Christendom[15] are all Saints of this Class, one of the principal of them is Saint George, the English Champion, we know little more of him, than that he killd a monstrous dragon, it is true, Spencer has given him a whole Legend in his poem of the fairy Queen, but, as that is Intirely allegory and fiction, the Incidents are as applicable to George a Green[16] as to St George; and by

---

10. Cardan, or Geronimo Cardano (1501–1576), was an Italian mathematician, physician, and astrologer whose writings include *De subtilitate rerum* (1551) and numerous works on astronomy, astrology, rhetoric, and medicine. Hamilton's allusion is to book 16 of Cardan's *De rerum varietate* (1557), "On the different kinds of liver."

11. "Busy doing nothing"; "over goat's wool," or "over trifles" (Horace, *Epistulae* 1.18.15).

12. Perhaps Hamilton's invention, a combination of *tantara* (fanfare, or trumpet flourish) and *bobus,* or *bogus,* meaning "a counterfeit sound," or in this case, "a counterfeit name."

13. Kublai Khan (1216–1294) was the founder of the Mongol dynasty in China.

14. Saint Athanasius (ca. 295–373), the theologian who played an influential part at the Council of Nicea, was the leader in the fight against Arianism. Saint Ambrose (ca. 339–397), the bishop of Milan whose teachings influenced Augustine, also opposed Arianism and supported strict orthodoxy in general. Saint Cyril (376–444), the Alexandrian archbishop, defended orthodoxy and persecuted the Novations, the Jews, and the Nestorians.

15. The patron saints of England, Scotland, Wales, Ireland, France, Spain, and Italy (Saint George, Saint Andrew, Saint David, Saint Patrick, Saint Denis, Saint James, and Saint Anthony).

16. The poundmaster of Wakefield, Yorkshire, who single-handedly resisted the attempted trespass of Robin Hood and his men; to be "as good as George a Green" is therefore to be resolute and dutiful.

new light, and treats his followers in the same manner, as the Reverd: and pious Mr George Whitefield A:B: used to do his disciples, giving them first a Glimmering of the road or path, and then leaving them as much in the dark as ever. He will sometimes go on board Ships among Sailors; (*In Navigiorum Summitatibus ascendit,* saith Eusebius)[6] and wantonly climb to the mast head, but these cattle love his company, and always make him welcome, because, loving to keep out of danger, he always comes at the end of a Storm.

The next remarkable worthy, is he who goes under the Name of Robin Goodfellow,[7] he has always been esteemed a very courteous civil and obliging Gentleman, he would at any time condescend, for a mess of milk, to grind Corn, cut wood, scour peuter, empty piss pots, or do any other kind of drudgery work in a family, Thelosanus lib: 7 Cap: 14, calls this ancient worthy by the name of Trullus and Getulus, and says that in his time he travelled to France, and learned the fashions, and has appeared heretofore in the highlands of Scotland in the form of a hairy man, and used to take great delight in drawing water dressing meat, and sweeping the hearths Clean.[8]

[134] Another obscure Gentleman of renown, is he whom the Italians Call Foliot, the English Hob Goblin, known in our Nurseries by the name of Raw head and bloody bones,[9] He generally loves to frequent old forlorn houses, and ruinous castles; he will make Strange noises in the night, howl sometimes pitifully, and then laugh again, cause great flames and sudden lights, fling Stones, rattle Chains, shave men, open doors, flap them to again with great Clapping & Jarring of rusty hinges, fling about plates, Stools, Chests, bedsteads and tables, and look out at windows, grinning

---

character who is supposed to be invisible to the clown and to Pantaloon and who rivals the clown for the affections of Columbine.

6. Eusebius (ca. 260–340) was a historian and theologian whose thought was inspired by the transformation of the Roman Empire into a Christian kingdom under Constantine and who tried to demonstrate the superiority of the Bible over pagan philosophy. This passage, in which Eusebius is criticizing pagan superstition, means "he climbed in the tops of ships" (*Contra philosophos,* chap. 48).

7. A merry domestic fairy, famous for his mischievous pranks and practical jokes; also known as Puck.

8. Tholosan was the pseudonym of René Milleran (b. 1665), a French grammarian known during the 18th century for his compilation of imaginary words and names, *Lettres familieres et galantes, et autres sur toutes sortes de sujets,* 6th ed. (La Haye, 1705).

9. A hobgoblin was an impish, ugly sprite (a variant of Rob-Goblin, or the goblin Robin). In the *Anatomy of Melancholy* Burton refers to a kind of hobgoblin that "frequent[s] forlorn houses, which the Italians call *foliots*" (I, II, i, 2) and uses Cardan as his authority (see following note). Rawhead and Bloody-Bones were famous bogies who were the terror of children.

makes me conclude, that not only their Credit must be very great, but they must be Gentlemen of distinguished humanity, generosity and good nature, seeing they run so many risques, for persons to whom they are utter Strangers, and yet, there is one very Surprizing circumstance in the traditions concerning them, that is, tho those gentlemen never ask any Questions, concerning the circumstances of those people, for whom they || become [132] engaged, yet I never yet could find that they lost one farthing by their becoming Surities or pledges, but, at the same time, with regard to their Pledgees, the balance between them is exactly even, for, if they never lost a penny, they never gained any thing by it, nay, I am told, not so much as thanks, for people were in time so habituated to those pledgors that it is thought as absurd to thank them for their favors, as to thank a chair for supporting one's bum, a razor for shaving one, or a pair of Gloves for keeping ones fingers from the Cold; for certain it is, where no distinction is made in bestowing of favors, they lose the name of favors, tho' some profane people have a very loose and Improper way of Speaking, such as, I a'nt Cold, thank these Gloves, and this Great Coat, I am Clean Shaved, thank this razor; I sit easie, thank this elbow Chair &ct: these expressions are every whit as extravagant, as if one at Law should say, I have good Pledges, thank John Doe and Richard Roe.

Another Eminent person whom I shall mention is Jeck with the Lanthorn or Will with the wisp as some Call him, by the Ancients called Mr Ignis Fatuus.[4] This Gentleman was supposed to be of a melancholy turn, and therefore a constant night walker, having never once been known to make his appearance in the day, which is a Strong proof that he is a frequenter of some humdrum Clubs, and is seen a nights either going to, or coming from some such Club or Clubs, he loves a rural retirement, and is very famous among the Country people, having never once been seen in great Cities, he affects walking thro marshes and bogs, and by this means has misled many who have attempted to follow him, and made them run into Ditches and || quagmires, to the great danger of their lives and dammage of their Cloaths; it is said, he sometimes will make so free with Travellers on horseback, as to vault upon the horses mane & ride merrily before them; but he seldom keeps his Seat long, Jumping and skipping about like any Harlequin,[5] as to his Religion, he is Inclinable to that of the [133]

---

4. Jack-o'-lantern and will-o'-the-wisp were two of the many names for ignis fatuus (see p. 116n, above).

5. In Italian commedia dell'arte, Harlequin is one of several stock characters along with Columbine, Pierrot, Pantaloon, and others. In English pantomime, which was derived from the Italian commedia and to which Hamilton is probably referring, Harlequin is a mute

always go together, by the Name of John-a-Nokes and John-a-Stiles;[1] these we often hear mentioned in bargains, conveyances, deeds, testaments, bonds, declarations &ct: and very often we find them going to Law together, a mischievous practice, used for many ages, both among friends and foes; It is so uncertain at what time these Illustrious personages lived, that several people have doubted, whether there were such men ever alive, tho' others alledge they came in with William the Conqueror, and were properly called, de Nokes and de Stiles; and Consequently their Descendents, if any remain, are of as ancient a family as any in England. I make no doubt of their having once flourished, and that they were very eminent men, but, as to their Country, parentage and birth, these must for ever remain in the Dark, unless some Casual medal or Tombstone not yet ploughed or dug up, or some ancient manuscript, not yet found should agreeably Instruct us. There seems to be something Inconsistent and contradictory, in the traditions handed down concerning them, for, sometimes, we find John a Nokes, conveying great Estates to John a Stiles, and sometimes John a Stiles is exercising the same Generosity to John a Nokes, sometimes Nokes is prosecuting Stiles in the most violent manner, || and at other times Stiles becomes plaintiff and Nokes defendant, Nokes often makes his will in favor of Stiles, and bequeaths him Immense estates and possessions, again Stiles bestows very great legacies upon Nokes; Stiles often beats Nokes and abuses him with very Scurrilous and oprobrious language, and again Nokes uses Stiles in the same rude and Rascally manner. But for these Inconsistencies in the transactions of these great men, we must Intirely blame the carelessness of historians. The only certain thing that is known of them, is, that they were good friends to the Gentlemen of the Law or long robe, helping them out at a dead lift upon all occasions, and filling up many blanks and deficiencies in their pleadings, for, as these gentlemen, never transact business, or plead without a fee or reward, being professed Enimies to all Causes *in forma pauperis*,[2] and, as we find these two worthies oftner named in their briefs, than any other Clients, we Judge from that, that they must have feed their Lawyers handsomly.

The two whom I shall next name, are John Doe and Richard Roe,[3] who Surely were, and are now, for aught I know, men of great credit and Character, for, in all our Courts of Justice, we shall find them named, as pledges and Surities for the appearance of plaintiff and defendant, which

---

1. Names formerly given to fictitious persons in an action at law.
2. Literally, "in pauper's form"; referring to cases in which the court allows an indigent petitioner to plead without paying court costs.
3. Names signifying any plaintiff and defendant in an action of ejectment.

The History of the Ancient and honorable Tuesday Club

[129]

Book III

From the first Sederunt of the Ancient and honorable Tuesday Club, to the Cathedration of the Honorable Nasifer Jole Esqr President.

Chapter I

Of Great and Illustrious personages, whose names only have been transmitted to posterity.

It has so happened, to the great hurt and Dammage of Posterity, that several Eminent Clubical heroes, and Illustrious personages, have very unjustly, and undeservedly been deprived of that Reward, which is for ever due to Clubical merit and virtue, by an entire ommission, of all their famous actions, which have perished in oblivion, by means of the woeful and Lamentable neglect of Club Historiographers, and Secretaries, and we know no more of them, but their bare names, their lives, in all other respects being one entire blank or Chasm.

Several of these worthies I shall here mention, || of whom it is uncertain who they were, tho' we may probably conjecture that they were members of some Certain Clubs, that have been long obselete, and the last of my roll, shall be a very famous and Illustrious moderen Clubical Worthy, who was President of a great Club, but what seems most strange, it is a matter of mighty doubt, among the Learned in Club History, whether this hero or his Club had ever any real existence.

[130]

The two first which shall appear upon my list are famous persons, who

Members of the Ancient & honorable Tuesday Club,
at its first Sederunt.

Loquacious Scribble M:D: Capt: Serious Social
The Revd Mr Smoothum Sly Capt: Bully Blunt
Prattle Motely Esqr: Capt: Seemly Spruce
Jealous Spyplot Esqr Mr Laconic Comas

tain, They being as ancient as the ancient and Venerable Tuesday, (or whin-bush) Club of Lanneric, of which we have given a short history in the preceeding Sheets, and now proceed to Scenes of greater action and Importance in the following Books.

End of the Second Book.

However, the wrangles, debates and disputes of these two Gentlemen, and the turbulent Disposition of Prattle Motely Esqr, led this Club into parties, and then every thing turned uproar and Confusion, which produced much cursing and Swearing, and hence accrued fines (for they had Laws in this Club, which Imposed fines upon certain trespasses) this soured the members at one another, and all Sort of Clubical cordiality and friendship, began to decrease, and at last was quite extinguished, so that the Members drop'd off one by one, and from a numerous Club, it dwindled to nothing, and at last expired. [127]

After the Decease of this Club, which Indeed could not be of long Continuance, having no such able Genius as Mr Neilson's to support it, out of its remains sprung a Club, which since has made the most Shining figure of any that have yet appeared in America, vizt: the ancient and Honorable Tuesday Club of Annapolis, in the frame and Constitution of which, In process of time, arose the real likeness and Image, of the Ancient and Venerable Tuesday (or whin bush) Club of Lanneric, being nothing but that very Club It Self, translated to America, the effecting of this, was what the Great Mr Neilson aimed at, with all his might, but the Inexorable Destinies, cut the thread of his life, before he had half accomplished his Laudable design, however, he had the honor to lay the foundation of this great Superstructure, tho he enjoyed not the pleasure of seeing it perfected.

This happy lot fell upon persons much less conspicuous than he, viz: Prattle Motely Esqr, and Loquacious Scribble M:D: who were the only two members of the Late Ugly Club that stuck together and Strenuously operated to keep alive || the taste for Clubbing in Annapolis, for which purpose they called to their asistance two very able politicians, vizt: Jealous Spyplot Esqr, Serjeant at Law, and the Revd Mr Smoothum Sly parson of the parish, the first had been a companion of the Great Mr Neilson in his trowbles, came to America with him, and was also of his privy council in the Red house Club, he was a Gentleman of great discernment, and could see into men's breasts and fortell Events at a distance, as well as any Conjurer of the Age. The latter was a Gentleman very well adapted for Clubs, being of a free airy disposition, full of compliment and panegyric to all, and of a Jocose turn, much given to quaint Repartee, dowble Entendre, & withal a hearty & loud laugher, these four gentlemen having procured four more to be of their party, whom we shall afterwards mention, laid the first foundation of that famous Club, whose History I now write, but, I would not have my readers here to misunderstand me, they were not so much the founders of the Ancient and honorable Tuesday Club, as the Settlers and revivers of that Club in America, for the time of their foundation is uncer- [128]

only Reckoned as words of Course; he Indeed had an unlucky ambition to rule the roast in all Companies, and his chief talent lay in Exercising the office of a Sir Clement Cotterell.[3]

Joshua Swash Esqr, was by profession a Lawyer, and had the honor to possess the place of Prosecutor for the County, he was a man of very few words, and loved much the circulation of the Bowl, so that it was thought he was for the most part muddled and often fuddled; The most that he said was *here's to ye again*, or *Herefordshire kindness*,[4] he had the best title of any of the members to be of this Club, by reason of his ragged appearance and his settled Philosophical Countenance; once when it was his turn to sit in the Chair as President, he wore a great Jockey ‖ coat, and standing up with profound gravity and awful Solemnity to give some orders, or directions to the members, this Surtout fell open, and discovered the tattered State of those garments which it covered, which put me somewhat in mind of robes of state. He had little or no regard or passion for the fair Sex, tho' he was no woman hater, therefore the Ladies declared him a very handsom fellow, and often toasted him, which procured his admission into this Club.

I was myself a member of this worthy Club, some time before it's dissolution, but, as I had no office in it, but that of an ordinary member, I shall not here Characterize myself, but defer that, till the time, when I shall appear in this History, a degree above the Rank of Common members, In the ancient and honorable Tuesday Club, In the Quality of their Orator and Secretary.

Their Chief employment in this Club, was to argue and debate upon various Subjects, and to discuss points of a knotty and abstruse nature, they often also, exercised themselves in law pleadings, and argued cases and pled causes, with great elegance, distinctness and perspicuity, in this Sort of Declamation, Messrs: Limberloins, and Leatherlungs exercised themselves much, and had almost all the talk to themselves, by this means each Improved his talent to admiration, for they Learned how to wrest a meaning, to Quibble and play upon words, prevaricate, and make the best of a bad Cause, and both turned out afterwards, very Eminent Lawyers, tho the first soon gave up his practise for a County Clerkship, which he Thought was a more Conscientious Calling.

3. By Hamilton's day the name Sir Clement Cotterell was virtually synonymous with the master of ceremonies. The original Sir Clement Cotterell of Wylsford, Lincolnshire, was groom-porter to James I and muster-master of Buckinghamshire by 1616. Like his ancestor, the Sir Clement Cotterell who flourished in the early 18th century was master of ceremonies and a noted antiquarian besides.

4. Roughly, "and here's to you"; the people of Herefordshire were renowned for toasting those who toasted them.

twice a year, vizt: at Christenmass and Lammas, which || gave him a Just [124] claim to be a member of this Club, he understood *Qui Genus,* and *propria Quæ maribus* perfectly well, and could repeat *As in presenti,*[1] from begining to end, without Stammering or hesitating, with a delectable and musical tone of voice, in the Right Recitativo taste, he was an Hybernian by birth, and was pritty well stocked in that Sort of modest assurance, which is reckoned peculiar to that Nation. He had a particular turn to Mechanics, and made such great Strides towards the discovery of the *perpetuam mobile* and the Longitude, that it is thought, by many competent Judges, had his Means or purse been Sufficient, he would have effected them both. Like others of his profession he was positive dogmatic and Imperious, treating all persons, as if they were his pupils or Schoolboys, much given to dispute, and always Sure he was in the Right, and Commonly used to get the better of the Argument, by quoting greek and latin Authors, which few or none of the Club understood.

Prattle Motely Esqr, had studied the Law in his younger days, which had given him a habit of perpetual dictating, wrangling and Disputing, he had pritty much of the Misanthrop in him, and was too apt to entertain a bad opinion of mankind In General, believing and asserting, that most men were either fools or knaves, when he conversed in Club, he seldom or never kept to one Subject a minute together, but would Ramble up and down from topic to topic, abuse people in Superior Stations, with the names of Pimps || and Bunters,[2] and conclude all with a hearty pinch of snuff, and [125] half a Dozen round Oaths. He affirmed often, that he was much skilled in Secret History, and in the Heraldry and Genealogy of families, and often would assure the Company, that he could tell such Stories, of such and such persons, as would make their blood boil, and their hair stand on end, and when he had thus raised their Curiosity to a great pitch, with such Rodomontade expressions, he'd either leave them on the rack, or allow them to guess, if they could, what these pieces of Secret History were, or, if they got it out of him, it proved either some stale Story they had heard before, or some piece of buffonery, which excited laughter more than admiration, horror, or resentment; nevertheless, he was a very good Club member, and Contributed much, by his facetious Conversation, to promote the Mirth and good humor of the Company, for his Sarcasms, and nicknames, were

---

1. "What genus," or "what kind"; "belongings which by sea"; "as at present" (legal terminology).

2. *Bunter* is a cant word for a woman who picks up rags from the street, which is used, by way of contempt, for any low, vulgar woman.

surer, Orator and Secretary; The treasurers was a Circulating office, he continuing only for a stated time, and the Club was also Governed by a Rotation of Presidents, a new Chairman being elected at the end of every two months, the Honorable Major Vaunter was first president, the offices of orator and Secretary were permanent, and the persons best qualified were put into these places. Vocifer Leatherlungs Esqr was Orator, a man of Good action and Gesticulation, of easie fluent and Copious Speech, and a loud Clear delivery; he used some very elegant expressions in his Orations, which were afterwards adopted by Succeeding Orators, in the ancient and honorable Tuesday Club, These were *This here Club, That there argument, These here laws,* and so forth.

The Secretary was Mr Spruce Limberloins, a person of great abilities and uncommon understanding, being very well versed in the common Law, he very Carefully entered the proceedings of the Club into a folio book, which record would have been exceeding valuable, and of Great use In Compiling this History, but It was unfortunately burnt, with many other useful papers and books belonging to that Learned Gentleman; the Secretary did not always || Strictly confine himself to his office, but sometimes would make excursions and encroach upon the Orators province, which laid the first foundation for the Dissolution of this Club, for, these two great men becoming Jealous of one another (as great men often do) Strenuously contending for the palm of victory in the oratorial way, it grew at last to hot and violent disputes, and wrangling, and Ended in hatred and aversion to one another, as we shall show presently, this is no uncommon thing in human Society, there being often two or more men of an aspiring Genius in a Club or Neighbourhood, who get together by the ears, and like a couple of prize fighters or wrestlers, striving who shall be uppermost, each draws his faction after him, there arises a division of parties, the fabric of the constitution receives such violent Shokes, that at last, it tumbles about our ears, and lies in ruinous heaps, never again to be repaired.

I shall mention three more extraordinary Geniuses, Members of this Club, who made no Contemptible figure in it, either as notable Slovens or queer fellows, vizt: Mr Pedantius, Mr Prattle Motely, and Joshua Swash Esqr.

The first was a man of Letters, having for some time exercised the office of Schoolmaster In the City of Annapolis, and exerted himself to admiration, in that conspicuous Station, he was remarkable for wearing dirty Linnen nightcaps in Summer, and Greasy worsted Ditto in winter, and for having long nails, and he used to wash his face and hands duely

Cork, Thomas Long, Mr Prattle Motely, Mr Pedantius, Mr Spruce Limberloins, Captain Swarthy, Mr Vocifer Leatherlungs, and Mr Loquacious Scribble.

I shall now proceed to give an account of their Constitution and government, and the Cause of their Dissolution.

Chapter VIII [121]

An account of the Constitution and Government of the Ugly Club, Its dissolution, and the first Scheme for erecting the Ancient & Honorable Tuesday Club of Annapolis in Maryland.

Tho Mr Neilson, when he first founded the Red house Club, did not model that Society exactly after the plan, of the ancient and venerable Tuesday (or whin bush) Club of Lanneric, yet he Intended to have done it by degrees, and was proceeding very Successfully in that Laudable Scheme, when death, the Confounder of all human projects Interrupted him; It may be asked by some short sighted persons, unacquainted with human nature, and therefore Ignorant of the humor, and disposition of Clubs, why did he not do it at once? to which we need only answer, that such sudden Innovations, are dangerous and destructive to Schemes, let them be never so laudable, that great man did more, than half a dozen others could have effected, by lessening the Character of the Royalist Clubs, setting up a presidential government, and establishing a Society on an opposite footing. Had he at first, slap dash, adventured, to Introduce Baylies, Censors, Masters of Cerimonies, and such like State officers, into Clubs, his project in all probability had failed, and his party entirely deserted him, for, it is a true observation, that men are to be wrought upon by degrees, when any new model or form of Government Religion or Clubs is proposed, they must be soothed, flattered, Cajoled, cozened and hoodwinked, as being most obstreperous animals, that may Slyly be led, but never forcibly drove.

The founders of the Ugly Club, being some of the most Judicious and politic members of the Red house Club, and having been of Mr Neilson's privy council, were hearty favorers of his Schemes, & therefore, set off with a full purpose, to model this new Constitution, according to the plan of that great Club politician, they therefore made the best use of their commission from him, and appointed in this Club several officers, vizt: a Trea- [122]

Squint eyes, deep pock fretting or a nose set awry, or a good many of those pimples called by some courage bumps, these were not objected to when any person proposed himself as a member; Some peculiarities in dress also, qualified people to be members of this Club, such as a Stocking slackly gartered, or put on all of one Side, full of derns or holes; Greasy leather breeches, Codpiece unbuttoned, with Shirt hanging out, a Shoe down at heel and buttoned the reverse way, ragged ruffles, Slouch hat, wig uncombed and uncurld, dirty hands & face, long beard and the like; a certain Slovenly Stile in discourse too was reckoned a qualification, such as Coarse homespun Similies, gross metaphors and allusions, pronounced with a harsh tone of voice and a horse laugh.

But what Chiefly gave this Society the name of the Ugly Club, was the Squalidness of the Room where they sat, and held their meetings, it being a large Ghastly apartment, of an old Building, made use of for a School Room, the plaister of the walls and Ceiling was much decayed, and cracked, moldy, dirty, and in several places fallen off, around the walls were many names engraved and done with Ink Chalk and marking Stone, and some human faces and figures of a Strange wild fancy, with monstrous noses, unconscionable mouths, and horrid Staring eyes, the Cieling was Smoked In several places with a Candle, || and very much garnished with cobwebs, and the Clay Nests of worms and wasps, many panes of Glass in the windows were broke and Cracked, the window Sills and Shelves covered with dust, which had been collecting there for half a century. The floor was Squalid, full of Spots, and plaistered in many places with dawbs of dirt, collected from Chaws of tobacco, and such like plastic Substances, which having been trod upon, adhered, and in a manner Grew to the plank, the furniture of the Room, consisted of a parcell of old forms and desks, which served the members of the Club to sit and loll upon, there was only one antiquated elbow Chair, which was set apart for the president of the Club.[2]

Thus was it Solely upon account of the Slovenliness of the members (who looked when met like a parcel of ragged philosophers) their affectation of odd gestures, and the dirtiness and unseemliness of the Club room, that this Society had the name of the Ugly Club; and not from any bodily deformity in the members themselves, for, in that respect, some of them were proper enough men, and tollerably well made.

Their Chief members were Major Vaunter, Joshua Swash Esqr, John

---

2. According to Charlotte Fletcher, the Ugly Club met in the King William's schoolroom ("An Endowed King William's School Plans to Become a College," *Maryland Historical Magazine*, LXXX [1985], 160–161).

[facing page 118]

members, like another Club of that name described by the *Spectator*,[1] it was not at all necessary, that a man should be hard favored, crooked, or hunch backed, to qualify him to be a member of this Club, it was Sufficient for him Sincerely to profess and believe that he was not handsom, till he was declared to be a monstrous ugly fellow by the Ladies in public company, for then, as that Sex are perfect Judges of beauty, propriety of feature and proportion of body in the other, and, as it is their constant custom, when on this Subject, to express themselves Contrary to what they think, all those declared ugly by them were Reckoned unqualified to be members of this Club, and all declared handsom, by the same fair Judges, perfectly qualified to be admitted to it. A man was to show his Sincerity in this opinion of himself, by assuming a certain Slovenliness and peculiarity in his dress, by never throwing away his time at a looking Glass, and diligently evading all foppish and finical airs and || affectation either in his gesture of body, Speaking or gait in walking, but, if he ever observed any oddity of Gesture, affected by another man, such as a wink, a cast of the Eye, a sudden toss of the head, to one Side or other, or wry twist of the mouth, or knitting of the brows, a sudden turning round upon the heel, while he is spoke to by another, these he was Strictly to Imitate, and perfect himself in, as being real deformities and deviations from nature in a much higher degree than bodily distortions and blemishes, which the members of this Club, did not think Carried in them so much deformity, as to entitle their possessors to a Seat in their Society, this kind of affectation Mr Spruce Limberloins, a distinguished member, being Secretary to this club, was perfect in, having set for his pattern and example, a certain eminent Squire, under whose direction and precepts, he had been brought up, Some will object here, I suppose, to our excluding the beaus and pritty Gentlemen, who are as much given to affectation, and deviate from nature as widely as any Set of men whatsoever, but, let it be remembered, that the fopperies and affectation of these gentlemen, are original, and not Imitated, besides, they are much ridiculed (that is praised) by the Ladies, who being perfect Judges of what is handsom and pritty, the antics of these fops, beaus and pritty Gentlemen, cannot be Classed with such things as are termed ugly.

Nevertheless, there were some particular bodily blemi- || shes and defects, which a man might possess, that no ways disqualified him from being a member of this Club, such as a remarkable Scar on the face, freckles,

---

1. The Ugly Club is mentioned in nos. 17, 48, 52, 78, 87, and 553 of the *Spectator*, but the most extended account of the club—and the one to which Hamilton is probably referring—appears in no. 32.

But Sixteen hundred, forty three,
    Who'eer shall see that day,
Will nothing find within that court,
    But only grass and hay.

These nuns It is said, resembled the Roman vestals in one thing, that they fed and kept up a perpetual fire, and were ‖ visited every night, by many of the priests and votaries of Venus, who seldom went away from them, without carrying some of that same Sacred fire, or rather *Ignis fatuus*,[2] concealed in their Breeches, these priests payd divine honors to these Nuns or vestals, and worshiped them with great devotion, for, they seldom or never went In their presence, but they fell down upon their knees, and seemed moved and agitated with great extasies, fetching deep Sighs, and earnest groans, but we shall leave these nuns and priests, to carry on their pious frauds, and proceed with our Clubical History.

Chapter VII

The Rise of the Ugly Club, from the Ruins of the Red house Club.

As Empires, kingdoms and States may be compared to the Hydra, new ones springing up continually from the Downfal of the old, so it is the same with Clubs, for no sooner is one of these nocturnal assemblies dissolved, or dissipated, but Immediatly another Rises up in its place, as is plainly exemplified here in our History, for scarce was the Red-house Club, a branch of the ancient and venerable Tuesday (or whin bush) Club of Lanneric, at a period, but Immediatly sprung up from it's remains, like the Phoenix from its own ashes, a Club Called the *Ugly Club,* a description of which we are now to give.

A residue of the members of the Red house Club, vizt: Major Vaunter, Mr Prim Timorous, and some others, after their dissolution, laying their heads together, laid out the first plan for forming of this club, which they agreed should be called the Ugly Club.

My Readers are not here to Imagin, that they assumed that appellation, upon account of ugliness of feature, or deformity of body in the

---

2. As Hamilton was no doubt aware, *ignis fatuus* literally means "foolish fire" (a flamelike phosphorescence produced over marshes by the spontaneous combustion of decayed vegetable matter, which eludes those who attempt to follow it).

these old Deities ever had, and a preferable adoration, since this is offered by Christian, whereas that was paid by pagan devotees; Indeed, as for the Materials, of which these christian Deities are made, the difference is little, they being the Self same Stones and blocks of wood, of which the pagan Divinities were Confabricated; We have it from Scripture history, that the Temple of Solomon, which was a consecrated Ædifice, set apart for divine worship, at last became a den of thieves; The ancient City of Babylon, Inhabited by magnificent monarchs, and a polite people, was turned into dens for Lyons, tygers, panthers, and all manner of wild beasts, The Nunneries and Monasteries in England, In the Reign of Henry VIII, were found to be Surprizingly metamorphosed, from the habitations of holy men and women, professing Celebacy and Chastity, into brothwells, bawdy houses and bagnios, The City of Rome, once the habitation of men of the Sword, is now a dwelling for holy and peaceable men of the Gown, and, it is scarce yet out of the memory of our Grand- || fathers, that the Royal palace of Whitehall, was in the time of the Rump and roundheads, converted into Stables and apartments for Grooms, of which event, there was an old prophesy, concerning an ass, whose master(a) was hanged Drawn and quartered, in the wise Reign of James I, for this ass, it seems brayd in a treasonable manner, against that Second Solomon and his Courtiers, the Prophesy runs thus.

> Some seven years since, Christ rid to court,
>   And there he left his ass.
> The Courtiers kick'd him out of doors,
>   Because they had no grass.(*)   (*)Grace
>
> The ass went mourning up and down,
>   And thus I heard him bray,
> If that they could not give me grass,
>   They might have given me hay.

(a) Mr Williams, a councellor of the temple, and a Roman Catholic, who was executed at Tyburn for publishing a Satyrical book against the King and ministry entituled *Balaam's Ass*. Howels *Familiar Letters*.[1]

1. The story of Balaam's ass seems to have aroused considerable theological controversy and satirical retort during the 17th century. The verses Hamilton transcribes appeared in James Howell's (popular author and friend of Ben Jonson) *Epistolae Ho-Elianae: Familiar Letters*, 2d ed. (London, 1650; see vol. III, letter XXII, "To Dr. W. Turner," 35–36). In his note to the poem, Howell says that *Balaam's Ass* was "compos'd [more than 20 years ago] by one Mr Williams a Counsellor of the Temple, but a Roman Catholic, who was hang'd drawn and quarter'd at Charing Cross for it" (p. 35).

As it is usual for historians to make some Sage reflexions, on the persons of great men after their Death, It will be proper here to bestow a word or two on our Club heroe.

Mr Neilson was like all other Illustrious men, he had blemishes blended with his excellencies, Imperfections Interwoven with his perfections, but the quantum of the first bore so small a proportion to that of the latter, that he may Justly be Classed among the most perfect Clubical worthies, that have decorated Clubical History, we shall weigh and examine his perfections and defects, both of body and mind.

If Mr Neilson was of a hasty passionate temper, he was at the same time placable, and his passion like a flash || broke out and disappeared in an Instant, if he was opinionative dogmatic and positive, in any thing he asserted, he had at the same time such a clear Judgement and understanding, that he was seldom or never in the wrong box; if he was profuse and extravagant, he was also of a genteel and polite taste, and withal, Generous to an excess; If he was refractory and ungovernable in Company, he was also a Loyal Subject, to such as he thought had an Indefeasible hereditary right to reign over him; if he had some little Irregularities in his life, and was too much given to women, we must remember, that he was quite orthodox in his religious principles, having copied these from the perfect pattern of the Celebrated University of Oxford, tho he was not educated there, if he was at times given to prophane Swearing, he was at other times much addicted to fervent devotion and prayer.

Again, if his visage was long, his forehead was high, If his nose was crooked, his eyes were lively, if his chin was peaked, his complexion was good, if his body was slender, it was at the same time streight and well proportioned, if his legs were Comically made, his feet were small and neat, If his walk was hobbling, yet he danced to the admiration of all that beheld him, and if he was of a small Stature he was well built, and thus, having exactly balanced his perfections and Imperfections, I here leave this Illustrious Clubical heroe, to sleep in peace with his fathers.

After the breaking up of this Club, the house was converted to a nunnery, several females fixing their habitation in it, who afterwards were dignified with the name || of nuns; It will perhaps seem strange to some how this should have happened, but Instances of the like nature may be produced from history both ancient and moderen; That famous ancient Rotunda, the Panthæon at Rome, which was originally appropriated for the habitation of the heathen Deities, is now converted to a christian chapel, under the name of the Church of all Saints, and is Inhabited by a great number of holy Saints, who have now as much adoration paid them, as

shift its place of meeting, seeing the house by this accident became ruinous, and unfit alike for Clubs as tennents.

It was reported that some great prodigies were seen alittle before this happened, such as meteors like blazing Stars with long tails, which appeared and vanished again in a Second of time, and also, Strange noises were heard, of Screech owls, crickets, dismall howlings of dogs, and crowing of cocks at midnight, these unusual appearances, it was said, portended this event, others affirmed that these were prodigious forerunners of Mr [111] Neilson's Death, which happened about ‖ four years after, and quoted examples from History of various Phênomena of the like nature, before the death of great men, many believed this, and marvelled much thereat, tho' there were not wanting some prophane atheistical persons, who laughed at all this, and affirmed that there was nothing in it, these being only natural appearances, that the Shooting Stars, (as they are Called) happened always either in Clear hot weather, or in Clear, frosty nights, and that owls hooted and screamed, dogs howled and barked, and Crickets chirrup'd at all times, and even Cocks, before and after the Great and Solemn feast of Christenmass, were observed to crow Incessantly all night long, and would still continue to do so, even tho' there was no such Club as the Red-house Club, or no such man as Mr Neilson,—but these foolish arguments we reckon only *Gratis dictu*.

This Club then, changed its place of meeting to a large house near Bloomsbery Square, where were many Spacious apartments, but one of these they pitched upon, in particular, for the Club to sit in, where, for a considerable time, in great peace and tranquillity, they smoked their pipes, took their Snuff, drank their punch, eat their gammon and bread and Cheese, and carried on a Clubical conversation, concerning various Subjects.

In this happy State were they, when the death of Mr George Neilson, [112] put an end to all their Glory by ‖ putting an end to their peace and quiet, which is a lesson to men in prosperity and easy circumstances not to be too vain or secure, for adversity and distress may suddenly come upon them, e're they are aware; In short, after the Death of their founder and leader, they split into factions and parties, every one aspiring to the management of affairs, and showing a desire to rule the roast, but none being of capacity or wisdom equal, or even nigh to their Illustrious founder, they bilged upon this Sandbank, and like a mouldering wreck, gradually separated one from another, till at last from a numerous Club, they became nothing, and from their ruins Immediatly after, there sprung up another Club, which we shall describe in it's proper place.

nothing, not even Clubs, tho well Constituted, are exempt from this mutability, the Seat of Government, or place of meeting in this club was Changed in the year 1732, which happened thus.

The house where they met was struck with Lightning, and was thereby shattered in such a woeful manner, that it became unhabitable, all that were In it at that time were stunned or knocked down, excepting one old woman, who happened to be in the Cellar making candles, who was not hurt, which lucky escape, has since been ascribed by many, to the tallow with which she was besmeared all over, from head to foot, and tallow, wax, rozin and such like, being non electrics, || the elementary fire only Glanced upon the Surface of the old womans Skin and Cloaths, but did not penetrate her body, by which means she escaped, if this should be true, it would be prudent for those who are afraid of Lightning, to have a Slush bucket always at hand, to besmear themselves with, which I think would be an easier preservative against it, and less expensive, than fixing iron rods and wires upon houses, for, this Method will preserve people from it out of doors, as well as within, and, perhaps this may be the reason, why the native Indians of America, (a quarter of the world very subject to violent thunder gusts) smear their bodies all over with bears grease. [109]

Some people skilled in omens and prodigies, affirmed, that this prodigy foretold an utter dissolution of the Club, others more truely prophetical, said, that it did not portend a dissolution, but only a translation of the Club, from one place of meeting to another, which they affirmed they discovered, by the circumstance of the old Woman, and they explain it thus, Age say they is a State which is approximated to that translation called Death, which, tho' it shifts the place, or rather habitation of the Soul, yet does not destroy it's entity or existence, therefore, the Circumstance of the old woman, showed that the Club was to shift its place, but not to lose Its entity or existence, but these Gentlemen have two difficulties to get over, e'er they establish their argument, first they must prove, that Spirit || can be said to possess or shift a place as matter does, and Secondly, they must answer all the learned arguments, that our moderen Smarts have urged against the Immortality of the Soul, and a future State, else their argument falls to the Ground, *with these objections, or Reasons under it* as Mr Drawlum Quaint used to say, in his Speeches to the ancient and honorable Tuesday Club, when honored with the office of Speaker there. However, this prediction was reckoned by some, a very cunning and wise one, but some critics who pretended to see farther, alledged that it was a very easy and natural prediction, and, that those who were no prophets, might make a hundred such in half an hour, for, what could be more plain, than that the Club must [110]

[107] || free cost, which he liked very well, for he loved good liquor dearly, but loved his money Infinitely better, if this Gentleman said it was Sad Stuff, they then drank but sparingly, and he got a larger share for himself, but, if he smacked his lips and declared that it was good, and only wanted alittle more powder, then it went down their throats with force Sufficient to drive a mill.

They were very cautious about Swearing in Club, tho' some modest oaths upon particular occasions, they would not scruple to use, which oaths were pronounced with great Solemnity and composure of countenance, When the truth of any thing was to be urged, admiration expressed, or abhorrence declared. These were Commonly, *as God shall Judge me—as I am a living Soul—god save the king, the Lord proprietary, and all the rest of the Royal family,—I wish I may die on this Spot alive,* and the like modest oaths and exclamations, which were particularly used by Mr Prim Timorous, a worthy member of this Club, and afterwards a Longstanding member of the ancient and honorable Tuesday Club of Annapolis, which shall be shown in its proper place.

These were the Chief customs of this worthy Club, which was ruled in a mild and gentle manner by Mr Neilson, as often as he had the presidential power in his hands, and, as all the other members followed his example, they were Continually blessed, with a mild and Easy goverment, there being no such thing as one tyrant to be found, among their presidents, from their first Institution, to their dissolution.

[108] # Chapter VI

The translation of the Seat of Government in the Red house Club, the Cause of its dissolution, and the place of meeting converted to a Nunnery.

This Club was for some considerable time governed by a Rotation of presidents, and, we do not find, that there were any Subaltern officers in the Club, excepting only the taster, it does not appear that they had even a Secretary or kept Records, or, if there were any Records they are lost, for, what is here delivered, is collected only from oral tradition, for the Greatest part of which we have been obliged to Mr Prim Timorous, a member of that Club, and since Serjeant at Arms to the honorable Nasifer Jole Esqr, president of the ancient and honorable Tuesday Club.

But, as there is a Constant fluctuation among Sublunary things, and

lute decrees, propitiatory Sacrifices, lay baptism, and such like profound and Ingenious topics, but, in points of this Sort, they agreed perfectly well, understanding little more than the bare words; there being a toleration in this Club, for all Sorts of Religions, which was a very wise and politic provision, and contributed much to its growth and Interest, preventing Infinite wrangles and disputes.

Bawdy they did not often touch upon, and when they did it was very cleanly wrapt, so that it scarce would have tickled the ears of a vestal, and, that was Generally, when it grew late, and they had drank so liberally, that Bacchus began to Introduce Venus by toasting the Ladies all round, which was an established custom of the Club, the worst discourse of that Sort, that passed among them, was such a Lady, and such a Gentleman mounted upon her, the B:C:J:C:[2] the mother of all Saints, the universal Chymist, and sometimes, when merrier than ordinary, they would say here's ——t's health, and such like, which are favorite toasts to this very day among our politest and best bred people.

When they drank the Ladies after Supper, they || would often use epithets, answerable to the Initial letters of the Ladies name that was toasted; thus, suppose the Initial letters to be B:R: It might be beautiful and rich Miss B:R: or Buxom and Rompish Miss B:R: or Bold and Rattling Miss B:R: &ct: which display'd in a very elegant manner, the wit, learning and humor of the members; But, if any member used a word, which his fellow had used before him, he was condemned to drink kelty in a bumper, and, that was the greatest excess, that ever this Club came to in drinking, they often also told comical and delectable Stories, by which the whole Club would be set in a roar of Laughter, their Greatest Genius at this, was the Celebrated Mr Samuel Minskie, alias Mungo Macfun, by birth a high German.

Sometimes they would converse upon the price of tobacco, the fineness or badness of the weather, the Scarcity of news, the dearness of goods, of this much and that much percent advance and deduction, and sometimes for half a night together, it would be heres to you,—and heres to you—and thank you Sir,—and pledge you Sir, but this only happened when conversation run low, which generally was when the liquor was not good, and this was always determined by the opinion of an Ingenious Gentleman, vizt: Doctor Samuel Swallowbeak, who was taster to the Club, and Indeed to all the Clubs in this place, by which office he enjoyed the benefit of drinking at

[106]

---

2. This abbreviation means the "bad character" (the mark formerly set on a soldier guilty of misconduct) of someone or something whose initials were J. C.

Mr Neilson taking Snuff with the Redhouse Club.

excellent piece of policy, which all rulers ought to observe, for nothing gains the hearts of a people more, than their Rulers Imitating them, tho' in triffles, Mr Neilson has been closely Imitated in this very thing by the Honorable Nasifer Jole Esqr, who, it must be owned, has copied from this eminent personage, many of his amiable qualities.

Taking of Snuff also, prevailed very much in this Club, according to the example of their founder, tho few or none of the members took it before, which shows how apt Inferiors are to Imitate their Superiors, in every thing they do, and this ought to be an Incitement to great men, governors and presidents, to give those beneath them good example, which would contribute more to reform mankind, than the preaching of a hundred thousand parsons, Indeed, some have thought that the taking of Snuff in this Club, grew to a vice, tho Mr Neilson took it for a good purpose, to wit, to help contemplation, and Philosophical Cogitation, || to which he [104] was much addicted, as also to promote the consumption of the Staple Tobacco, yet others took it only In Imitation of him, and went to that excess, that you might have swept at least a large boxfull of Snuff, from the breasts and lappets of the members coats on a Club night, and they stuffed their nostrills with it to such a degree, that many of them Snuffled, which made some Ill natured people out of doors, reflect upon the members, and wickedly assert, that most of them were far gone in a distemper, which, for modesty and decencie's Sake, I shall not here mention or name.

The Conversation of this Club, was of a mixed kind, Sometimes they would dip into politics, and examin with great candour and moderation, the merits of the Cause upon both Sides of the Question, but they were very Cautious how they argued against the *Jure Divinoship* of kings, Indefeasible hereditary right, and the Independancy of the Church upon the State, the last of which, the Reverend and Learned Doctor Warburton, has in an elaborate and voluminous tract, proved as clearly as it ever can or will be proved;[1] knowing that these were Sacred points, which Mr Neilson would not suffer them to profane or Jest with, and therefore, when they entered upon these Solemn topics, they seldom durst go any farther than Significant nods winks and Shrugs.

Sometimes they would talk of Religion, and were || permitted to de- [105] clare their opinion freely, in the great points of predestination, free will, the lawfulness and unlawfulness of eating black pudding, the Sacred and divine Institution of tythes, passive obedience, non resistance, reprobation, abso-

---

1. Hamilton is probably referring to Warburton's tract *The Alliance between Church and State; or, The Necessity and Equity of an Established Religion and a Test-Law Demonstrated* (London, 1736).

adverse and prosperous fortune. The names of the principal of them were as follows, Mr Jealous Spyplot, Attorney at Law, Mr Andrew Vapor, Mr Surly Sourface, Capt: Serious Social and Mr Mungo Macfun.

The names of the Chief of the others, who had made a Secession from the Royalist Clubs, were Capt: Seemly Spruce, Major Vaunter, and Mr Prim Timorous. These were of Mr Neilsons privy council.

At the first meeting of this Clubical Council, on the first of April (commonly called fools day) in the year 1729, Mr Neilson proposed Erecting a government by presidents, which was agreed to, but being a man of Great foresight, wisdom and penetration, he Judged that it would not be proper, In the Infancy of this Club, to propose appointing any person perpetual president, by Seniority or personal merit, according to the excellent ancient constitution of the whin bush Club of Lan- || neric, revived, or rather continued since, in the ancient and honorable Tuesday Club of Annapolis; least it should be thought, that he Intended to seize the tyranny into his own hands, and make himself absolute, especially, as he knew it was suspected, that his Jacobitish principles, made him a favorer of Arbitrary power, it was therefore agreed, that this Club should be Governed by a rotation of presidents, and each should have the Chair in his turn.

This Club had it's first Regular meeting upon the 14th Day of May, in the year 1729, and Mr Neilson being Reckoned the person of Greatest ability, and the Chief founder of the Club, was, by unanimous voice appointed first Archon or president, to continue in place for the Space of two months, which was reckoned a Sufficient time, to model and form aright, the constitution of the Club.

They were appointed to meet once a week, at the Red house in Market Street, at Six o'clock in the evening, their laws and Regulations were few and Simple, and tended Chiefly to exclude luxury and excess in eatables and drinkables, to prevent wranglings and disputes and all disorders of that Sort, an example worthy the Imitation of all Clubs, which, if duely observed, would settle them upon a firm and lasting foundation.

As to eatables in this Club, they at first seldom went higher than Bread and Cheese, Smoked gammon, or roasted oysters, punch was their Chief liquor, and sometimes in cold || nights used warm flip. Some of the Club members smoked tobacco, and some not, Mr Neilson himself only using tobacco in the form of Snuff, of which he sucked up a vast quantity, he would Indeed handle a clean pipe, twisting it about, and turning it first one way, and then another, and often putting it to his mouth, as if he was a smoking, this he did in Complaisance to the other members, that smoked, that he might seem at least to accompany them, and appear Sociable, an

fousted, and Scabarabused,[7] and had the most unmerciful thumps on the back, and blows on the breech bestowed upon them, and withall, had their Crowns most miserably Clapperclaw'd, so that when they came abroad they || seemed most pitiful Spectacles, being all over bumps, bruises and [100] Scratches. This Inhuman persecution, naturally raised pity and Compassion, in the breasts of many, and being daily Joined by fresh numbers, they unanimously pitched upon Mr Neilson for their leader, upon this, an Intire Separation was made from the Royalists, and Mr Neilson Conveen'd his adherents in a house in Market Street, which was painted red, where having harangued them in a very Learned manner, he proposed, that they should Erect themselves into a Club, under different regulations from the Royalist Clubs, which Regulations he should propose to them, then pulling some papers from his pocket, among which was his Commission under the Venerable Mr Neal Gilpin's hand and privy Seal, and a Scheme or plan of a Club, he read both with a Clear and audible voice, and they unanimously agreed to form themselves into a Society, under the name of the *Red house Club*, the constitution and Government of which, we shall give a Succinct account of, in the following Chapter.

Chapter V

Description of the Red-house Club, it's Customs, Oeconomy and Government.

Our hero having thus drawn his party together, they began daily to Increase, and the other, vizt: that of the Royalist Clubs, to decline, so that in the space of one || or two years there was not the least trace of the latter [101] left, this Great Revolution happened In the beginning of March, in the year 1728.

The Red house Club being once established and set on foot, Mr Neilson applied himself Intirely to the forming of it's constitution and Government, for which Reason he Chose to himself a privy Council, from among the members. The Chief of these Councellors, were such Gentlemen, his countrymen, who had bore a Share, and gone Snacks with him in both his

---

7. *Pica-fousted* seems to be Hamilton's invention, deriving from the Spanish *picar* ("to pierce") and the obsolete *foutch* ("sword"); *scabarabused*, another invention, obviously means "abused by striking with a scabbard," or "scabbarded."

Mr Neilson's battle with the royalist Club

[facing page 98]

It is Inconceivable what hardships, abuses, and Scurrilous usage, this great personage suffered and went thro' to bring about this laudable Scheme, for clubical liberty. They would call him a hundred abusive names in half an hour, such as lousy scabby scot, poor rascally pedlar, Itchified Son of a bitch, Scoundrel, knave, fool, ass, Goose, blockhead, ugly beetle browd, squint eyed, Lenteren Jaw'd, Jacobitish, Skip kennel Scrub, nasty, blewbellied, blanket ars'd, hip-shotten, maggot eaten, round about, Snuff besmeard, flyblown Son of a whore, and conclude all, with the epithet of bloodthirsty traitor and Rebel and No-nation Spawn of Vexation. This, for some time, Mr Neilson bore with christian like patience, notwithstanding the natural heat and Impetuosity of his temper, but at last, an Accident happened, which brought about the great end, that he and his asociates had been for a long time plotting, and it was thus.

One Evening, Mr Neilson being at one of these Royalist Clubs, upon a dispute arising concerning Clubical Government, The king called him a Gallows fac'd Rebel; Mr Neilson, who was alittle warmed with liquor, and not brooking this harsh apellation, hastily drew upon his majesty, and in a trice overset him and his throne, Immediatly all was in an uproar, decanters, Glasses, and Tobacco pipes flew about like hail, his majesties guards at last seized upon Mr Neilson, tore his tye wig and neckcloth, stuffed his mouth full of tallow and Candle wick, wrung his nose, || broke his Sword, and tossed his whole box or mull of Snuff in his Eyes, and taking him by the legs and arms, carried him out of doors, and threw him headlong into a puddle, so that he was the most woefull Spectacle ever was beheld by the eyes of any Christian, and leaving him there, in a most miserable nasty pickle, his Scouts soon had Intelligence of it, and, coming to his asistance, they beset, begirt and besieged the Club house; but it was too late, the enimy had secured the Doors, and fortified the place, so strongly, that they found the fort Impregnable, and resolved to turn the Siege into a blockade; but being much annoyed with Stink-pots from the besieged, they were obliged to raise the Siege and march off.

Immediatly after this tumult, the Club Royalists, who found that several of their members had a warm Side towards Mr Neilson, and his party, in order to put a stop to this Scism and division, raised a hot persecution against the Neilsonists, the most cruel punishments were Invented, for those, whose consciences would not allow them, to toss off the bowl to be made king, the whole quantum of punch was poured upon their heads, which made them look like drowned rats, they were condemned to be pica-

---

government; requested to form his own government, Pulteney refused and became a comparatively silent member of the House of Lords.

were branded with the usual names of Atheist, Infidel, Reprobate, and such like; the Advocates for the Bowl, who were reckoned the High-Club party in this dispute, alledging that the opposite party or Low-Club Gentlemen, denied the authority of Revelation, because in Scripture it is said that Noe planted a vinyard, and drank liberally of the Juice thereof, that wine chears the heart of man, and oil maketh his face to shine, and finaly somewhere we find the following passage, *drink wine for thy Stomach's Sake,*[5] and some learned comentators think that the most authentic manuscripts have it, *Drink punch,* and that the word οινω, *wine,* has been Surreptitiously put into the text, by some Ignorant ammanuensis, instead of πυνσιω, either thro' design or Ignorance, for if they suppose the π or Initial letter to have been erased in a copy, and the υ made pritty nigh to meet at the top, so as to resemble an ο, and also the σ obliterated, it would stand thus, υνιω, which by an easy transposition of the ι before the ν, makes οινω, and thus this error might have crept in, but others more probably conjecture that this corruption of the text was made by the priests, who wanted an authority from Scripture, for drinking all the wine themselves, & giving the laity, nothing but a dry wafer, or Crust.

[97] Mr Neilson and his emissaries, espoused the party of the levellers upon this occasion, as the fittest persons to bring about their purpose, as Cromwell and his Independants, espoused the party of the Presbyterians to bring about their Designs upon the Royalists, but this conduct was expressly contrary to his own political maxims, for in other State controversies, he and his followers showed themselves always to be Strenuous Royalists and Cavaliers, arguing loudly and boisterously for the *Jure divinoship* of kings, and hereditary indefeasable right, and non resistance, and passive obedience in the Subject, and such like favorite topics, and damning to the Infernal pit, all Revolutioners, whigs, presbyterians, Hanoverians, and sneaking low churchmen, but this is no novelty, for we shall find the wisest men sometimes shifting sides, and taking that party which suits their Interest best, according to the doctrine of our Moderen polite philosophers, who think that right and wrong, truth and falshood, do not really exist in the nature of things, but are only Specious terms to be made use of by politicians and Statesmen, hence we see, the now Earl of Bath, heretofore Mr Poultney, a wise Statesman and politician, who, has of late from a Clamorous patriot, in the house of Commons, become a very complaisant, moderate, and I may say, silent peer in the house of Lords.[6]

---

5. 1 Tim. 5:23.
6. William Pulteney (1684–1764) was a Whig political leader and member of Parliament who served as secretary at war (1714–1717) before contributing to the downfall of Robert Walpole's

makers of their throats, Stomachs and heads, they could by no means either Increase or deminish their capacity, width or Strength, They therefore thought it would be expedient, and for the Interest of the whole Club, to lay aside that barbarous way of electing kings, and to allow each member to take it by turns, each having a certain time allotted him to reign, as king over his fellows, and, that every member might be suffered to drink as much or as little as he pleased. The other party argued, that custom was a Second nature, that it was extremely dangerous to the State, to alter old established customs, and, that a man by a Steady perseverance, might bring himself to any thing, and to confirm this, they very learnedly quoted ancient authors, and historians, whose authority they held to be as Sacred and Valid, as many of our divines do that of the fathers, such as Polybius Livy Herodotus ‖ and Xenophon, who says the persians eat once a week, and stoold once a month,[3] they also gave Instances of men, who, by force of custom, lived Intirely upon cable ropes and candles ends, and eat flint Stones, without Receiving any hurt, as old Saturn once devoured a Stone, and for aught we know, digested it well enough, and Mithridates, king of Pontus made poison his common diet, and numberless moderen examples they give of Jugglers eating fire, pitch, tar, knives, Swords, hatchets, halberts, pikes, poakers and the like indigestable materials, and yet were as healthy as other men, nay, they Instanced several frenchmen, that would eat Carrion, and one in particular called Monsieur Esteron, who flourished in the beginning of this present Century, who could make a Comfortable male of a Sir reverence,[4] provided it was of such a Solid consistence, as to admit of Chawing.

[95]

These disputes and Cavils, gave Mr Neilson and his Scouts an opportunity to carry on their laudable Schemes, with all the Success they could wish, their business was to blow the coals, and spread the flames of party, so that in a little time, the Disputants from Serious, grave and Learned arguments, came to abuse, as is very usual in political, as well as religious controversy, particularly the latter. Ignoramus, blockhead, dunce, rogue, liar, knave and fool, were Common ‖ appellations, among them, and some

[96]

---

3. Since the Persians were notorious for their heavy eating, it is doubtful that Xenophon made this claim about them.

4. Even though the name "Esteron" is apparently not an invention (the French doctor Pierre d'Estiron flourished in the 14th century and other Frenchmen surely had the same name), it is doubtful that one existed at the beginning of the 18th century who could dine comfortably on human excrement. Rather, it seems likely that here and throughout this paragraph Hamilton is simply poking fun at the 18th-century preoccupation with scatology, in this case at the expense of the French.

fun of him, that he was seen to lay his hand on the hilt of his Sword, but, his Philosophy, overcoming his passion, he quickly retracted it again, and composed his countenance.

I might on this occasion, to decorate this history have Introduced the Goddess Philosophy, in a beautiful Similitude, pulling Mr Neilson, by one of the ties of his wig ‖ to restrain his heroic fury, as Homer has Introduced Minerva, pulling the yellow Locks of Achilles, upon a paralell occasion,[1] but I purposely evade these Similies and allusions, for fear this history should exceed the Size of a portable volume.

Mr Neilson and his Scouts, having at last discovered by Indefatigable application and Industry, the Disposition and bent of these Club members, and finding that like other men they were mightily Inclined to party, upon this ground they laid their plan of Reformation, and set upon erecting a new Club on a different model, by strictly observing, that known Machiavelian maxim *Divide et Impera*,[2] Imitating therein, the glorious example, of their Illustrious and Royal Countryman King James VI of Scotland & I of England, who first set on foot, the two famous and Irreconcileable parties of whig and Tory, which names they adopted, about the time of the Infamous and Scandalous revolution, which has sapped the foundation of true Church, established Presbytery and Phanaticism, Introduced the toleration act, and brought the Nation most damnably in debt, these two prevailing parties, have shone with great Glory in their particular Spheres, ever since the time of that learned wise and Cunning Monarch, and their Contentions have Cost one of that monarch's Sons his head, and his Grandson his Crown, and perhaps these parties and disputes, may last as long as the English can say they are a free people, and when that ceases, probably all parties will be swallowed up in one.

The two parties that contended in these Clubs I shall Call The royalists and the Levellers; the royalists were those that stood up for the kingly government, in the Shape in which it now existed, these were your Stout toapers, who made no bones of tossing off a gallon bowl at a draught, and procure for themselves the regal crown at any time, The levellers were those, whose Swallows were not so wide, nor Stomachs so capacious, or, whose heads were not so Strong, those argued, that it was unjust to measure a man's merit by such a criterion, that, as they were not themselves the

---

1. See Homer, *Iliad* 1.261–268.
2. This maxim—"divide and conquer"—has been attributed to Machiavelli, although he actually argues against the sense of it in his *Discourses* (see bk. 2, no. 25, "To Attack a Divided City in the Hope That Its Divisions Will Facilitate the Conquest of It Is Bad Policy").

Mr Neilsons anger restrained by Philosophy

having an ample Commission in his pocket, under the Privy Seal of the Venerable Mr Neal Gilpin, Impowering him to erect Clubs ‖ in any of his majestie's plantations in America, he made the best use of the power conveyd to him by that commission.

His first business was, like all other wise and long headed politicians, to hear all and say nothing, for which Reason, he, in the beginning, attended these Clubs like a Pythagorean Philosopher, resolving with himself to keep a Strict Silence, till such time as he should discover the bent and Genius of these Clubs and the humours of the members, at the same time, he constantly had his Scouts out, to make observation, and bring him due Intelligence, these were some Ingenious persons, his own countrymen, who perhaps may make, some of them, a conspicuous figure in this history; they frequented these Clubs themselves, drank with them, roard with them, laughd with them, fought and squabbled with them, and were Crowned kings with them; but they carried their policy farther in making cunning enquiries into the particular private Characters of the members, by frequently visiting the matrons and old women of the City, where Certain Gossoping Clubs of females, Informed themselves carefully of every private occurrence in families, and as carefully divulged them again, sometimes by way of Secret, and sometimes with openness and frankness free of all reserve.

Upon account of this silent, reserved, and politic behavior, Mr Neilson passed among these people, for either a bashful Sheepish fellow, or a morose Sullen com- ‖ panion, and some Imagined he was melancholly mad, others, that he was in love, and, if he had not constantly drank his bumper in his turn, and tossed off the Bowl, and suffered himself to be crowned king by the Club, without saying a word, they would have expelld him from their Clubs as an useless member.

Mr Neilson, by this behaviour, put a very great constraint upon himself, for he was naturally of an airy and volatile disposition, much adicted to talking and fond of displaying his Learning and parts, besides, being of a hasty and passionate temper, it Cost him many a hard Struggle to contain himself, when any of these Club wits passed their Jokes upon him, and made him the but of the company, which they were very apt to do, upon the account of the oddity of his appearance, vizt: his oblong Sharp visage, his peaked Chin, his Snuff besmeard countenance, his large wig and his long Sword, Sometimes his passion would so ferment and fret within his breast, that his color, would come and go in his face, now turning pale as chalk, and then as red as a turkey Cock, and, it is said, he was once screwd up to such a pitch, by their running their rig, and making their game and

The only Club among these, that was distinguished by a particular name, I find to be that called the College Club; but for what reason this Club was so called I cannot conjecture, unless it was this, that one of their members was a parson, and had had a College education. This parson had the honor to be crowned king of the Club, much oftner than any other member, he having a very Strong (I dare not say an empty or a hard) head, like most of his cloth, so that it was not a small quantity of Liquor that would knock him down; This Club was soon dissolved, and Mr Neilson gave a very Learned and Ingenious reason for it, which was this, that they Indiscreetly Intrusted the Clergy, with too much power, and suffered the priesthood to meddle too much in State affairs, which conduct, will at last Surely prove the ruin of every kingdom, State, commonwealth and Club, since the Gentlemen of the crape, once they are exalted to power, always prove the most Cruel and oppressive Tyrants, and, he gave a glaring example to support this learned argument, which was, the calamities and hardships the Christian princes labored under, for several centuries, by rashly clapping no less than three crowns at once, upon the head of a certain old doating parson at Rome, ‖ who at last grasped so much power, that he [90] made many wise men teach, and fools believe the doctrine, that he had a full and unlimited power to depose kings, and kill them at his pleasure, an Instance of the Truth of this gentleman's observations, we may have occasion to exhibit, in the History of the Ancient and Honorable Tuesday Club.

How Mr Neilson disliked the Regal government in Clubs, and how he, with much pains, labor and perswasion, established the presidential Government in it's place, and Erected a Club near upon the plan of the Ancient and Venerable Tuesday (or whin bush) Club of Lanneric, by virtue of a Special commission, from the venerable Mr Neal Gilpin, we shall show in the Sequel.

Chapter IV

The first Institution and foundation of the Red-house Club of Annapolis, by Mr George Neilson and other Illustrious personages.

Mr George Neilson, after his arrival in Annapolis, Took some time to look about him, and having maturely considered, the wretched and Confused condition, that the Clubical constitutions were under in that City, he set himself Strenuously about working a Reformation in these Clubs, and,

The Royalist Club.

[facing page 87]

erned by kings, and were called the Royalist Clubs, they were therefore, so many distinct monarchies, as Ireland was, before the English conquest, but then, the Reigns of these monarchs were Commonly very short, for, they might perhaps hold up an hour or two, and then be fairly knocked under the table, they acquired their Royalty by conquest, he who could drink off a large bowl of punch at a draught, being Immediatly Crowned king of the Club, and he held his place, till another drank off a larger, so that, in one night, you might see all the members of one of these Clubs, crowned king, each in his turn, and each in his turn fall flat under the Table, This method of Conquest was easier, than that enjoined by Pope Adrian IV, who, thinking that he had ample authority, to dispose of all the kingdoms in the world, very || generously gave unto Sancho, Brother to the king of Arragon, the Land of Ægypt, then in the possession of the Sarazens, and he should have it, if he would take the pains to conquer it, and accordingly proclaimed him king of Ægypt, Sancho Informed of this, would not be behind hand with his holiness in curtesies, and so, he gravely proclaimed the pope Caliph of Bandas, which he might conquer and possess if he pleased;[5] I say, these Club Conquests of the Bowl, were much easier accomplished, than the Conquests proposed by this pope, for to effect these last, men, money, a wise head and good conduct were requisite, whereas the first might be affected with a wide Swallow, Long breath, and no further conduct was necessary, than to conduct the bowl to the head, which, in this case, proved so much the better, the less brains or wisdom it contained, as there was thereby a Greater vacuum in the Skull to receive the Intoxicating fumes.

In these Clubs, the king had an absolute power to command any of his Subjects, to drink as often and as much as he pleased, but then he was obliged to pledge him in a Cup of an equal Capacity.

When they went to war in these Clubs, (and their wars were generally civil or Intestine) it was only with offensive arms, and generally did not break out, till it grew very Late, and several monarchs, one after another, had mounted the throne, and one after another fallen prostrate or Supine under the table, these offensive weapons were bottles, de- || canters, candlesticks, glasses, and sometimes, when they used great ordenance or heavy artillery, Chairs and Stools, till at last, O tragic Scene! the floor was strowed with the Slain, and much good christian liquor was shed, and flowed about, blended with the frothy Spewings of the knocked down Combatants.

---

5. Adrian IV, or Nicholas Breakspear (1100?–1159), the only Englishman ever to become pope (1154–1159), was especially famous for giving Ireland to Henry II. Sancho VI (d. 1194) was king of Navarre (1150–1194) whose war with Aragon and Castile (1173–1180) was terminated by an alliance with Aragon.

negus Clubs, Syder Clubs, Rum Clubs, Bub Clubs, and Syllabub Clubs, The last of which were all female Clubs, tho' some Sorts of beaus and pritty fellows were admitted to them, who, in their mein and address approached nighly to the Feminine Gender.

To describe every one of these in Particular, would take up too much time, and consume a world || of paper and Ink, I shall therefore only say, that the main Intent and purpose of the meeting of these Clubs, was to drink and be merry, and among them all, it was hail fellow, well met, there being little or no distinction, tho the wine Clubs punch Clubs and bub Clubs were reckoned in the first rank, as also the Syllabub Clubs, and the Secret negus and Bishop Clubs, which were composed of Ladies, The Rumbo Clubs, Lambs wool and Flup Clubs were reckoned the Second degree, and the Cyder and Rum Clubs of the Lowest Class.

The favorite liquor in the female Clubs, as I have said, was Syllabub, which they drank avowedly and publicly, they had, tis true, other liquors, which they used in their privy councils, of a more diuretic nature, such as Bishop and Negus, which they were unwilling should be used at any time, but when shut up in the Conclave, least it should be thought by the men, (O horrid!) that they were adicted to strong liquors, which all fine Ladies must Surely abominate, or seem to abominate, by keeping these shut up in their Closets, only to look at, or smell at when vaporish, and Indeed they Chose not to let any of the Males see them tipple these liquors except Mr J—n G—bs—n,[3] who was their Secretary and privy Councellor, on all occasions, and is said, used to get so far Into their councils and Confidence, as to be permitted to hold the ——, while some of them —— but this being a piece of Secret History, my readers must excuse me, if I do not speak plain, therefore, as to the above breaks and dashes, I leave all my wise politic and discerning readers || to fill them up with what words they please. The Reverend and Pious Mris A—— C——,[4] who had more of the Coquette than the prude in her Character, was Leader and directress of these female Clubs, sometimes Indeed, this wise Lady would Graciously condescend to permit them to drink this Negus and Bishop in a more open manner, but always with this proviso, that, upon the approach of any of the Male Sex, except the aforesaid Mr J—n G—bs—n, who was by some thought to be of the doubtful Gender, they should Clap the bowl or tankard under their petticoats, so soon as the adversarry came in Sight, and keep them snug in the same manner as the dutch frows do their Stoves.

Such of these Clubs as were Composed of Male members, were Gov-

---

3. John Gibson (see biographical sketch).
4. Perhaps Ann Carter (see biographical sketch).

remainder of his life, with others of that Loyal party, to retale rum & punch & to found Clubs.

Chapter III

Of the turn and genius of the Annapolitans to Clubbing, at, and after the arival of Mr George Neilson in America.

At the time when this great personage arrived in America, with many of his countrymen, equally concerned with him, in the same loyal and honorable undertaking, the Annapolitans were very || much addicted to Clubbing, so that I shall speak within Compass, If I say, that there were then at least 40 clubs in that City.¹ Since then, I must own, that the Clubbing humor is much abated among them, there being now at this day, not above four or five Clubs, and, to make up this number, we must reckon the Free masons and Routs, which by many connoiseurs, are not in a strict sense reckoned Clubs, the first, dealing in mysteries, which they keep Intirely to themselves, and submitting to a great number of Rulers, such as Grand masters, Deputy Grand masters, masters and pass masters, the latter are governed and managed Intirely by the Ladies, being mixed assemblies of male and female, and among these last, the disputes for Precedency, are not as yet, nor ever can be adjusted, the first of these Societies, for want of proper presidents, cannot be called Clubical, the latter, on account of their modern Institution, deserve not the name of Clubs.

[85]

The Clubs that prevailed at this time In Annapolis, were all bouzing or toaping Clubs, there were wine Clubs, punch Clubs, Rumbo Clubs (for Grog was not yet invented) Flup Clubs,² Lambs wool Clubs, Bishop Clubs,

---

1. Hamilton may be exaggerating a bit, but there certainly were a good many clubs in colonial Maryland. Another Marylander, Henry Darnall, observed that in Maryland "there are settled Clubs in every County, where they talk over Affairs" (*A Just and Impartial Account of the Transactions of the Merchants in London, for the Advancement of the Price of Tobacco* [Annapolis, Md. (1729)], 12). Given the relish with which Marylanders apparently approached clubbing, perhaps some of the clubs Hamilton mentions in the *History* actually existed (e.g., the College Club, the Red-House Club, the Ugly Club, the Eastern Shore Triumvirate, the Hiccory Hill Club, the Saturday Club, and the club at Charles Town in Cecil County). However, the standard works on colonial culture, including Richard Beale Davis, *Intellectual Life in the Colonial South, 1585–1763*, 3 vols. (Knoxville, Tenn., 1978), do not include any information on the clubs, nor does the *Maryland Gazette* or the indexes of the *Maryland Historical Magazine* and the *Virginia Magazine of History and Biography*.

2. Here and in the next paragraph, Hamilton uses *flup* for *flip*, a mixture of beer and liquor sweetened with sugar and heated with a hot iron.

powder, or kiss cold Iron. These excursions or flights passed upon many simple people, and they submitted to the prowess of his Invincible Arm, but Mr Neilson sometimes met with undaunted heroes, who were not to be Intimidated by these methods, and once in particular, a Gygantic Champion, clapped him in a hamper, with his tie wig, Sword, and other warlike Accoutrements about him, and throwing him headlong into the river, he narrowly escaped a drowning, and after he was draggd out of the water, he Remained as mute as a fish, and made no more words of the matter.

It will be expected here, that I should give an account of our heroe's parentage and place of birth, but as both are uncertain, I shall only say, that he was born in the Lowlands of Scotland, either in the City of Edinburgh, or that of Air, which is only conjectured from his dialect or Speech, and so leaving these two ancient Cities, to contend for the Honor of this great man's birth, as Seven Grecian Cities did for the birth of Homer,[8] I shall Conclude this Chapter, with an account of the reason of his coming to America.

The general reason that is given for the Scots leaving their own country, is, that it is a place where they have but very cold comfort; The Climate, tho healthy, being unkindly and uncomfortable, the country poor, Generally barren, and badly stocked in provisions, and that the || natives, being of a bustling, pushing disposition, cannot rest at home, where nothing is to be got, but range about to all parts of the world, Improve their fortunes, hence it is, that in all quarters of the Earth, many Scots men are to be found. This I grant may be the case with many of that nation, but it was by no means the case with our heroe, whose departure from his native country, we have reason to believe was Involuntary.

The Case then with Mr Neilson was this, being a Loyal and hearty espouser of the cause of the Steward family, in the year —15, he took the field, with many other valiant and hardy Champions, who then made a bold attempt, to set James VIII, as they called him, upon the British Throne, and after many Skirmishes, and one decisive battle at Sherrifmuir,[9] where much blood was spilt, and many bones broke to no purpose, our heroe fled, among the rest of the vanquished Rout, and being unluckily taken, luckily escaped a hanging, and was sent over Seas to America, to plot out the

---

8. Hamilton is probably drawing his information from the discussion of Homer's life in Pope's preface to his edition of the *Iliad*, where he states that Salamis, Ithaca, Colophon, Io, Colony, Smyrna, and Chios all claimed to be Homer's birthplace (see *The Poems of Alexander Pope*, ed. Maynard Mack [New Haven, Conn., 1951–1969], VII, 43–45).

9. An engagement during the Fifteen rebellion (Nov. 13, 1715), between 10,000 Jacobite rebels under the earl of Mar and 3,300 loyalist Scots under the duke of Argyll. After an indecisive confrontation, Mar retreated and his rising collapsed.

He liv'd, 'till this his dissolution,
In Sanguine hopes of revolution,
He liv'd in hopes of better days,
But Grew Impatient with delays,
And still he would have liv'd, no doubt,
Poor man, but that his Rum was out,
And all he left behind they tell you,
Was an old plaid Nightgown & his Nelly.(a)

Now, as to Mr Neilson's moral Character, he was reckoned one of those people whom the world Calls good natured men, being apt to let his Substance go out faster ‖ than it came in, of a free liberal and open disposition, for which many wise men esteemed him a fool, and those who profited by his lavishness, never once gave him thanks for his favors, but after the manner of the world, used to receive as fast as he gave, and then laugh in their Sleeves, he was esteemed a man of great veracity, except only in two points, and these were, when he talked either of his family or travels, on both which topics many Imagined that he shot flying,[6] for, on the first, he would fall into Rhapsodies, of great Princes, dukes and Earls of the Name of Neilson, the Progenitors and Chiefs of his family, on the latter he dealt much in the marvelous, as many Great travellers do, among the other prodigies he had seen in his travels, he would talk of Churches twenty miles Long, of Spiders as large as a Sheep, of men 15 or 20 feet high, of Scots Lairds worth 20000 lib Sterling a year, and among his own exploits, he used to relate, how he once spited[7] 24 woodcocks on the wing, at one Shot upon the ramrod of his Gun, and strung them all exactly thro' the Eyes, and such like Stories, he was of such a noble and elevated Spirit, that he would never stoop to ask favors of any body, tho' he sometimes stood in need of the asistance of others, and some say, that his virtue in this particular, carried him so far, that he died in very great want and extreme necessity, yet his Inate Spark of heroism, made him desirous that the world should believe, he was in very opulent Circumstances.

Mr Neilson was a man of very warm passions and stood much upon points of honor, very apt to be highly provoked at Slight affronts, and upon all occasions of this Sort, out flew the Spado, or pistol, & his common expressions ‖ on these occasions, were to desire his adversary, to smell

(a) Mr Neilsons housekeeper.

6. As J. A. Leo Lemay suggests, *shooting flying,* or *shooting a bird on the wing,* had become synonymous by Hamilton's time with telling a tall tale ("The Tall Tales of a Colonial Frontiersman," *Western Pennsylvania Historical Magazine,* LXIV [1981], 46n).

7. *To spit* is to string together (needles) by passing a wire through the eyes.

His Learning was of a mixed kind, having a Spice of every thing, it is said he understood the languages, being thought a critic in Erse, Low dutch and Law french, the first he acquired in the highlands of Scotland, being led to converse much there, by reason of his political principles, the Second he learned among the Dutch Regiments quartered in Scotland, and the last by his diligent application to the common law, which last, (a Strange unaccountable taste) he studied more for pleasure than profit, as to latin and greek, he was always shy of showing his knowledge in either, and therefore it cannot be ascertained how deep a Clerk he was in these languages; True Indeed, it is said of him, that being asked the English of *Sancta Maria,* he made answer, he did not know, but he might possibly say so on purpose, to discourage the opinion that prevailed, of his being a Roman Catholic, we cannot certainly affirm, that he was versed in any of the Oriental tongues, such as the persic, turcic, Arabic, Syriac or Coptic, tho' some alledged that he spoke all these fluently, but I am rather apt to think, that it was a very broad Scots dialect, which he spoke with great volubility, especially when in a passion.

Having thus dispatched the Languages, we next remark on his Skill in the liberal Arts and Sciences, he was a bold musician, and could play in a very extraordinary || manner upon several Instruments, such as the violin, Bass viol, flute, Hautboy and Bassoon, and some say that he handled the Jews Harp with great dexterity; but the Bassoon excelled all his other performances, for by means of this Solemn Instrument, he used to draw many of the Rustics about his door, who flocked to the Sound, as the Stones and trees did of old to the Sound of Orpheus's Harp,[4] with this difference, that, as the harp of the latter used to animate Inanimate beings, so *vice versa,* the Bassoon of the first, used to Inanimate animated beings, or Convert human Shapes into Stocks and Stones.

In other things also, he was Profoundly versed, such as Physiognomy, palmistry, Judicial astrology, Cookery, Pastry, Chemistry, Pharmacy, and many other accomplishments, which we cannot here Ennumerate, In fine, he was such an extraordinary Genius, in his way, that a Certain Poet wrote an Epitaph on him,[5] which for its Justness and Singularity I shall here transcribe.

Poor Neilson's gone, a warlike Scot,
What was he, and what was he not?

---

4. The most popular version of this myth appears in Ovid, *Metamorphoses* 6.86–109; see also Vergil, *Georgics* 4.494.

5. If Hamilton himself was not responsible for this doggerel, the author was probably the club poet laureate, Jonas Green, who would have taken this occasion to exercise his genius.

Canvassed; That they had an Indefeasible hereditary right to their Dominions, provided they were true kings, and not usurpers, and Creatures of popular formation; That they were accountable to no earthly power; That the Steuart family had the only Indefeasible and Indisputable title and Right to the Crown of Great Brittain France and Ireland, and were the only True Defenders of the faith; and that all and every person or persons, who secluded them from that Claim and right, were *Ipso facto,* Usurpers, traitors and Rebels, If any one contradicted him in these tenets, by alledging that the hereditary right of the line of British kings was Interrupted by three Illustrious bastards, viz: William of Normandy, Called the Conqueror, the Son of a base mechanic; The Issue of John of Gaunt, Duke of Lancaster, by his concubine Catharine Swynford, from whom sprung Henry VII, in a direct line; and Robert Steuart, || the first of that name, had a bastard by Elizabeth More, who succeeded, by a Scotch act of parliament, his lawful Issue by his queen being excluded; he would either answer them by drawing his Sword, and bidding them encounter cold Iron, or presenting his pistols, and daring them to smell powder, but when he had a mind to be more moderate, he would convince them by this Silencing argument, by which he proved beyond dispute, the uninterrupted legitimacy, of the royal line of those princes, vizt: that they possessed the miraculous power of curing the king's evil by the touch, a power, which neither the House of Orange, nor that of Hanover, could ever pretend to.

As to Mr Neilsons Religion, I can say but very little, he having never been very communicative on this point, Some however, have Imagined he was a nonjuror, others, a high flown Episcopalian, others a Roman Catholic, and there have not been wanting some, who have maliciously asserted that he was a Presbyterian, an Anabaptist, Seventh Day man, Quaker, and even a muggletonian,[3] nay some have suspected him for a Jew, and of the Seed of Abraham, because forsooth he did not love pork, and was thought to be circumcised, but, as for the first, it is a food, which many Scots men detest, and yet are no Jews, and as for the other, we all know, that their are some Circumstances, a man may be under, that may oblige him to part with a Slice of his foreskin, and when that is the case, there is so small a difference between the Scar, made by the priests knife and the Surgeons, that they cannot easily || be distinguished, but, as this affair is at best uncertain, I shall leave it where I found it.

---

3. A member of a sect founded in 1651 by Lodowicke Muggleton (1609–1698) and John Reeve (1608–1658), who claimed to be the "two witnesses" of Rev. 11:3–6; Muggleton, a journeyman tailor, was imprisoned and fined for blasphemy.

alittle peaked, his eyes lively and full of motion, he was neither bandy legg'd nor battle Ham'd, nor Spla footed, as it is said most Scotsmen are, but he had, I know not what Sort of peculiarity about his legs, which I cannot otherwise describe, but that it did not resemble || that of any other person, but, we often find, that great and Illustrious men, have had Certain peculiarities in their make, Thus, Alexander the great had a wry neck, Ptolomy Physcon, king of Ægypt was pot Bellied, Julius Cæsar was bald, Cicero had an excressence like a vetch on his Eyebrow, Hannibal was cock eyed, Monsieur Scarron was made like the letter Z, Monsieur St Evermond had a bottle nose, and a large bump on his forehead, The Duke of Luxemburg was Hump backed, and Alexander Pope Esqr, had a crump Shoulder.[2]

Having given this short description of his person, I shall next delineat his dress, he wore one of your large Revolution hats, tho in principle, he was an Antirevolutioner, under that, a very voluminous tye wig, which covered two thirds of his face, and hung down before half way to his pocket holes, and the bob behind depended to within two Inches of his loins; Round his neck, he usually wore a large twisted neck cloth, which was drawn thro' the fourth or fifth button hole of his upper coat, which was commonly very much daubed with Snuff, that he took, from out of a large Mull, that he Carried with him as his constant fellow traveller, his loins were girt with a leatheren belt, at which hung a small Sword, of the length and Size of a Spanish Spado, with which he used to defend himself on all occasions against Insults. As to his other aparrel, there was nothing re- || markable, that differed from that of other men, only, when he went a horseback he was commonly armed with pistols.

I shall now give a detail of his political principles, and learning, and wind up the whole with a catalogue of his virtues and vices.

Mr Neilson was in principle a Jacobite, having Imbibed in his tender years, before the maturity of his Judgement, (as indeed most Jacobites do) the heroic tenets and maxims of that Illustrious party. He firmly believed that kings were *Jure Divino,* and God's vicegerents upon Earth, and therefore, their actions of what nature soever were not to be enquired into or

---

2. Ptolemy VII (184?–116 B.C., nicknamed Physcon, or "fat paunch") was a friend of culture but extremely vicious and dissolute. Paul Scarron (1610–1660) was a French burlesque dramatist and novelist who was deformed and paralyzed in his lower limbs. Charles de Saint-Denis, sieur de Saint-Évremond (1613–1703), was a French exile who spent most of his later years in England, associating with the wits and courtiers of the day and writing essays on a variety of literary and philosophical topics. François Henri de Montmorency-Bouteville, duc de Luxembourg (1628–1695), was a French soldier who served in wars against Spain and Holland and was created marshal of France in 1675.

Mr George Neilson

[facing page 76]

Nasutus sis quisque licet, sis denique Nasus,
Non potes in nugas dicere plura meis,
Ipse ego quam dixi.[18]

And thus, having Called whore first, I go off with flying colors.

Chapter II

The History and Character of Mr George Neilson, and the Cause of his coming to America.

It is the Indispensable duty of all Historiographers, and Biographers, to collect and compile, in the most Impartial, Candid, and unprejudiced manner, the Glorious actions atchieved by great men, and faithfully to transmitt them to posterity.

The lives of great princes, Generals, poets, Philosophers, orators, and founders of Clubs, hold the first Rank in Biography, and shine like the Stars of the first magnitude among those of Physicians, Logicians, magitians, arithmeticians, musicians, Lawyers, Divines, mechanics and Almanac makers, which may be Compared to the fainter constellations.

Micat Inter Ignes
Luna minores. Horat:[1]

The Illustrious person, of whose life I am now going to give some account, as being the founder of a Club, Immediatly derived from, and established upon the constitution, and police of the Ancient and venerable Tuesday (or whin bush) Club of Lanneric, stands therefore in the foremost rank of such worthies as have decorated Biography.

As the public is generally curious, to know the Stature, dimension, features, dress and air of Great and Illustrious men, I shall here present my readers with the portraiture of our Hero, and finish it off as well as I can.

Master George Neilson then, was a man of a small Stature, about four feet eight Inches high, of which he Cared not to lose one quarter of an Inch, for he strutted in his walk, and stood bolt upright like a pike, he was of a slender make, long visage, nose Inclinable to the aqueline, his chin

---

18. "You can turn up your nose if you please, and turn into one finally; / You can't say more against my nonsense / Than I have said myself" (Martial, *Epigrams* 13.2.1).

1. "The moon shines out among the lesser fires" (Horace, *Carmina* 1.12.46).

wit, learning. Raw, rude, crude, harsh, fantastical, absurd, Insolent, Indiscreet, vain, Scurrile, Indigested, idle, Silly, dull and dry—and what care I? all this I confess, and freely own that I affect it, and all of you together cannot say worse of me, than I do of myself, unless you prove this to be a History of lies, which I defy you to do. Like other Authors, I pilfer out of old books, stuff up new comments, scrape Ennius's dunghills, and drink from Democritus's well,[15] I contribute my Quota, to stuff our Libraries full of putrid papers, and also to furnish every close stool and Jakes, *Scribo carmina quæ legunt cacantes,*[16] they'll serve also to put under Christenmass pies, wrap up Spice and tobacco, and keep roast meat from burning; and tho' the perusal of them may keep some fools Idle, yet it will keep them out of mischief; I grant you, these Lucubrations are not worth reading, therefore lose no time, I pray you, in perusing this vain Subject, as I have in writing on it, all the Apology I shall make is that I have precedents for it, an apology which Sure may serve me, a Simple Scribbler, since it has heretofore served The wisdom of the British Nations In Parliament assembled, || and the profound wisdom of our grave Judges and Lawyers; who have [75] taken precedents for their Rule, in matters every whit as exceptionable, by the Standard of right reason, *Uno absurdo dato mille sequuntur, perfugium iis qui peccant,* others as absurd, vain, Idle, Illiterate, *non nulli alii Idem fecerunt,* so that of me or you, it cannot be said as a certain old Author said of a very great man, *Oinom, Duonorum, pleorumei virom Illom optimom esse Consentiunt,* perhaps you yourselves have acted as absurdly as I, *novimus et qui te &ct:* we have all of us our faults and blind Sides, *scimus et hanc veniam &ct:* Thou Censurest me, so have I done others, and may do thee, *nam dubito multos lectores hic fore stultos, cedimus inque vicem &ct:* is *lex talionis* and *quid pro Quo,* go on now censure, criticise, scoff, rail.[17]

---

15. Ennius (239–169 B.C.), one of the founders of Latin literature, was famous for his influence on subsequent Roman writers, all of whom borrowed from him. Vergil in particular admitted that "he gathered gold from Ennius's dung heap." The Democritus referred to here is again Robert Burton, who signed himself Democritus Junior and who borrowed lavishly from earlier authors. Burton himself reflected on plagiarism, comparing authors to apothecaries, who make new mixtures by pouring from one vessel into another.

16. "I write poems that they read while shitting" (Martial, *Epigrams* 12.61.10).

17. "Given one absurdity, a thousand follow: a refuge for those who go wrong"; "certain others have done the same"; "of the good men, a great many agree that he was the best man"; "we who know you"; "we know, and pardon this"; "for we concede that many readers here will doubtless be fools, and vice versa"; "this is the law of retaliation and quid pro quo." The "certain old Author" could refer to almost anyone, but it is most likely Isocrates. The Greek version of the passage appears in Engelbert Drerup, *Isocratis opera omnia* . . . (Leipzig, 1906–), I, 143.

preferable to Sneezing) and enlivener of the fancy, there is no Science, no wisdom, mirth is the life and Quintessence of Physic; medicine and ‖ whatever is applied to prolong the life of man, without this, is dull and dead, and of no force, *dum fata sinunt vivite læti,* says Seneca the Philosopher, ὁ βιοσ βραχους, says Hippocrates the Physician,[10] and I say, be merry, be merry.

>Would you shun Charon the ferryman,
>Consult Doctor Diet, Doctor Quiet and Doctor Merriman.

It was Tiresias the prophets councel to Menippus, that travelled all the world over, even down to hell itself to seek content, and his last farewell to him to be merry, Contemn the world, (sayth he) and count it and its vanities and toys, Trash, lumber, trumpery and Rubbish, this only covet all your life long, be not curious in other men's affairs, or ever Solicitous in any thing, place not your happiness in what is Intirely in the power of another, but with a well composed and contented estate, enjoy yourself within yourself, and above all things, and by all means be merry, and keep a constant Sunshine and Clear weather, within the precincts of your pericranium, thus will you enjoy peace and Quiet and pleasure to yourself, and communicate Satisfaction, and delight to your neighbour.[11]

And now, ye Learned Dons of the Critical tribe, ye Myrmidons of Billingsgate, ye Sons of Erynnis[12] and Spawn of Medusa, ye empoisoned Snakes that lurk in the flowery herbage of literature, It is evident, I have excluded you together with the aforesaid Humdrum fellows from our Clubical Commonwealth, I know well what Sentence you will pronounce upon me, but snarl, revile, cavil, carp and oppose what you will.

>*Allatres licet usque, nos et usque,*
>*Et gannitibus Improbis lacessas.*[13]

I know what you'll say, *aperto ore,*[14] you'll blame my Doric Dialect, unpolished Stile, tautology, apish Imitation, a Rhapsody of rags raked together from dunghills, excrements of authors, fopperies, toys, tumbled and Jumbled and Crumbled higglede-pigglede, without Invention, art, Judgement,

---

10. "While the fates permit, live happily"; "life is short."

11. Tiresias was the legendary blind Theban seer. Menippus (fl. 3d century B.C.) was the originator of the seriocomic style in literature.

12. *Erinyes* was the Greek name for the Furies (the avenging deities, Alecto, Megaera, and Tisiphone).

13. "However much you will rail at us / And provoke us with your constant snarling" (Martial, *Epigrams* 5.60.2).

14. "Openmouthed," i.e., with a big mouth.

become mouldy, musty and worm eaten, with a pack of Lazy, loitering Idle monks, Hermits and Anchorites, and, to pass thro' the world silently, without leaving any the least trace or tract or path behind them, as a Ship in the wide ocean, or a bird in the air.

There is also a Set of fellows, of a Grum, Sullen, boisterous, Surly, Growling, captious disposition, who cannot bear a Jest, quirp, pun, conundrum or witty repartee, but Immediatly upon such being vented put on a threatning, passionate, furious countenance and are for nothing but Swords, daggers, pistols, blood, fire and destruction, *Sevit atrox Volscens,*[6] these are not fit to be on the face of the Earth, and therefore *a priori,* not qualified or adapted to be in Clubs (since all Clubs are earthly) where good humor and plasantry, should rule the roast, and appear in every countenance.

Having excluded these, and many others, whom it is needless to enlarge upon, such as your eternal wranglers, disputers, contradictors, falsifiers, Sceptical Doubters &ct: from our Clubical Commonwealth, I will now assert and mantain, that none but your merry, droll, facetious, Jocose, good humored, risible companions, punsters, comical Story tellers, and *Conundrumifiers,* ought to be members of those nocturnal assemblies, called Clubs, for the Quintessence, marrow and main fulcrum of Clubs consists in gayiety, Jollity, pleasantry and Jocosity.

What shall I then say, to every true Clubical genius but this.

Utere conviviis, non tristibus utere Amicis,
Quos Nugæ et risus et Joca salsa Juvant,[7]

and, as Marselius Ficinus, winds up his epistle, to Bernard Canisianus,[8] so will I conclude this learned Chapter, with an advice to all free, honest, open Club Companions, and lastly, bestow a mild word or two on the Criticks.

Live merry my friends, void of care, perplexity, anguish, grief, live merrily, *lætitiæ Cælum vos creavit,*[9] again, and again I request you to be merry, if any thing trowbles your head, or frets your guts, neglect it, let it pass, and this I enjoin you, not only as a Philosopher, but as a Physician, for, without this mirth, which is a Clearer of the head, (for laughing is

---

6. "Savage Volscen rages" (Vergil, *Aeneid* 9.420).

7. "Indulge in banquets, cultivate friends who are not sad, / Who are delighted by trifles, laughter, and spicy jokes."

8. Marsilio Ficino (1433–1499) was a learned Italian philosopher who revived Platonic philosophy and is best remembered for his translations of Plato and Plotinus. Hamilton is referring to Ficino's *Epistolarium familiarum* (1495), but he has faithfully lifted Ficino's advice—and the Tiresias story immediately following it—from Burton's chapter "Mirth and Merry Company" in the *Anatomy of Melancholy.*

9. "Heaven made you for joy."

[70] cloud, rising from the dirty blustering South east, saturated with || hollow murmuring Smouldering blasts, sending before it grumbling, tumbling, Jumbling thunder, and Infectious puffs of pestilential Steams, darkening the face of the fair day with polluted murky and Stiffling vapors, exhalations and damps, saturated, loaded, Impregnated and overcharged, with morbific Sulphureous atoms, bursting from the mouth of Tartarus it self.

———*Corpus onustum*
Histernis vitiis, animum quæque pergravat una. Horat:[4]

This disposition, according to Lemmius, *Institut, ad vitam optimam* Cap: 26, causes dryness of the brain, frenzy, dotage, and makes the body Dry, lean, hard and ugly to behold, the humors become a dust, the Eyes sunk in the head, the nose turns Sharp, the Jaws fall, Choler is Increased, and the whole body inflamm'd.[5]

These fellows ought never to be concerned in Clubs, compotations, merry meetings, Jovial frolicks, delectable Sports, or Juvenile Entertainments, for, they mar, spoil, disturb, destroy, contaminate, confuse and Interrupt all mirth and good humor.

Your Insipid, havy dull drivelling moralizers, Criticisers and Censors on the times, I do veryly think, also, are not at all fitted to be members of free, frolicksome, gay and Gamesome Clubs, those who will draw a moral [71] Conclusion, out of a decayd turnip, or rotten Cheese, and gravely || infer from thence, that all flesh is grass; make a bad omen of two Straws accross, a Salt Seller overset, a Jacket buttoned awry, or a Coffin, as they call it, in the candle, or a Stocking wrong side out, or the glowing of ones face, or the Itching of ones elbow, or the noise of the worm Called the Death watch, are as little fit to make Companions of, and therefore, I would have all such fellows banished from our Clubical, as Plato banished Poets and musicians from his Philosophical Commonwealth, for they are fit for nothing but to be shut up in Solitary desolate caves or celles, and there to

---

4. "A body loaded with yesterday's vices, any one of which crushes the soul" (Horace, *Sermones* 2.2.77).

5. Levinus Lemnius (1505–1568) was a Dutch physician and author of *The Touchstone of Complexions* (London, 1565), *An Herbal for the Bible* (London, 1587), and *The Sanctuarie of Salvation, Helmet of Health, and Mirrour of Modestie and Good Maners* (London, 1592). Hamilton is referring to Lemnius's "How to Lead a Life That Shall Be Most Excellent," the supplement to his popular *The Secret Miracles of Nature* (London, 1658). In chap. 26, "Moderation in Sleeping and Waking," Lemnius writes: "Immoderate watching is hurtful for all ages, but most hurtfull for old age, as is also fasting, for both those dry the brain, and besides that they make men frantick and doting, they dry the whole body, and make it lean and starved" (p. 341). Hamilton embellishes the passage and yanks it out of context, which has nothing to do with misanthropy.

History of the Ancient and Honorable Tuesday Club

Book II

From the transmigration of the Club to America, To the first Sederunt of the Ancient and honorable Tuesday Club of Annapolis in Maryland.

Chapter I

A learned Dissertation, in the Stile and manner of the Ingenious Mr Robert Burton.[1]

Those Solitary, moaping, morose, humdrum fellows, who evade, shun, run and fly, from all company, hate the Sight of men, as if they were Tygers, bears, Serpents, hobgoblins, Rhinoceroses and Panthers, and of the fair Sex, as if they were no better than Basilisks, cocatrices, harpies and Crocadiles, *Lemures Nocturni, mentulæque tersores,*[2] are mortal and Irreconcileable enimies to all Clubs, Jovial meetings, and humerous Conversations.

When I see a fellow of this Stamp, with his Clouded brows, and Lowring countenance, *monstrum deforme Ingens,*[3] I Imagine I behold a black

---

1. Burton (1577–1640) was vicar of Saint Thomas's in Oxford, rector of the parish of Seagrave, Leicestershire, and author of *The Anatomy of Melancholy* (Oxford, 1621). The influence of Burton's *Anatomy* appears throughout the *History,* not just in this chapter. Hamilton frequently parodies Burton's inflated rhetoric and pilfers passages from the *Anatomy,* and he dubiously honors Burton by signing his own translations of Latin doggerel "Robertus Burtonus." Hamilton clearly intended to set forth an anatomy of humor at Burton's expense, and nowhere does he parody Burton more effectively than in this chapter (pp. 74–75, for instance, are lifted almost verbatim from Burton's preface, "Democritus Junior to the Reader").

2. "Night demons and penis purgers" (similar to Horace, *Epistulae* 2.2.109).

3. "Unnatural, deformed monster" (similar to Vergil's description of Polyphemus, *Aeneid* 3.658).

the Tuesday Club [Book I] 67

A:C:	Treasurers	Masters of Ceremonies	Poets Laureat	Secretaries
1713	Gilbert Farqhar in 1716, George Neilson a member of this Club was transported to America for his Loyalty to the pretender	Moses Mcguire ob: 1714 Succ: by Donald Braidie	Joseph Dallas ob: 1715 Suc: by Tory Rory killd the same year in the battle of Shereifmoor and Succ: by	James Mccaupie ob: 1714 Succ: by Laughlan McIntosh M:D:
1728	Gilbert Farqhar ob: 1730 Succ: by Archb: Halyburton	Donald Brade ob: 1735 Suc: by Signr: Pasquelino de Marzis who plays the violoncello, and is now master of Ceremonies	Peter Birnie ob: 1728 Succ: by Allan Ramsay who wrote his elegy and is now poet Laureat of this Club	Laughlan Mcintosh M:D: ob: 1733 Succ: by the Learned and Ingenious Mr John Duncan now Secretary
1736	Arch: Halyburton ob: 1737 Succ: by Daniel Bradie now Treasurer			

8. I have not been able positively to identify many of the names and pseudonyms of the Red-House Club and Ugly Club members. The only extant portion of Hamilton's draft of volume I (in which he provides actual surnames rather than the pseudonyms in the *History*) does not concern these precursors of the Tuesday Club, though occasionally I have managed to identify a pseudonym by comparing the index for the draft with that for volume I. Regrettably, then, Mr. Pedantius, Surly Sourface, Captain Swarthy, Andrew Vapor, and Major Vaunter remain a mystery. However, Hamilton does identify Mungo Macfun as Samuel Minskie (p. 106); the administration bond for Minskie reveals that he lived in Anne Arundel County with his wife Catherine and that he died in 1739 (Box 42, No. 1, Maryland State Archives, Annapolis). This bond was signed by Joshua Hopkinson (Joshua Swash in the *History*; Hamilton sketches his character on pp. 125–126), confirming that he and Minskie were indeed close friends. Moreover, either Spruce Limberloins or Vocifer Leatherlungs is the John Euens in the index to the draft, possibly John Evans (d. ca. 1766), a planter who lived in Prince George's County with his wife Eleanor (Wills, Md. State Arch.). Thomas Long was perhaps Thomas Long of Frederick County; the inventory of Long's possessions (Box 11, No. 34, Md. State Arch.) indicates that he died by 1781, that his wife's name was Jane, and that he was a friend of John Gibson's (see p. 86n, below). George Neilson (d. 1736) was the founder of the Red-House Club. A native of Scotland who joined the Jacobite rebellion in 1715 and was taken prisoner at Sheriffmuir, Neilson arrived in Virginia in 1716 as a Jacobite prisoner and was purchased by Charles Digges of Calvert County, Maryland. After serving his time, Neilson moved to Annapolis, where he began to brew and sell beer and then became a tavern keeper; his inn was used at least once as a meeting place for the Provincial Council in 1727 and for various business meetings (J. Thomas Scharf, *History of Maryland from the Earliest Period to the Present Day*, 3 vols. [Baltimore, 1897], I, 355, 388; William Hand Browne et al., eds., *Archives of Maryland* [Baltimore, 1883–], XXV, 487, 501). Neilson was, indeed, a disputatious and tenacious fellow. In 1722 he initiated a grievance against William Digges and Charles Carroll over a large quantity of malt that they had agreed to provide him; he continued the grievance until 1733, when it was finally settled in their favor (No. 5, Chancery Court I.R.2, pp. 487–503, 631, Md. State Arch.).

A:C:	Presidents	Baylies	Censors
1713	The venerable *Sir John Kirkaldie* sirnamed *Cruikshanks* præs: 14 years	*Joseph Affleck* ob: 1715 Succ: by *Dugal Patullo* *Gavin Prue*	*Diego Trelawny* ob: 1718 Succ: by *Thomas Waughop*
1728	The venerable *Mas: James Gillespie* præs: 7 years, in his time, 1732, this club settled a Colony in America	*Gavin Prue* ob: 1729 Suc: by *Duncan Gordon* *Dougal Patullo* ob: 1736 Succ: by *Andrew Gutterie*	*Thomas Waughop* In 1728 *George Neilson* a member of this club founded the Red house Club in Annapolis in Maryland
1736	The venerable *Mr Neal Gilpin* now in the Chair	*Duncan Gordon* *Andrew Gutterie* now baylies	*Thomas Waughop* ob: 1739 Succ: by *Sawny Mccawl* now Censor

anno

1728	Erection of the Red house Club of Annapolis in Maryland, by Mr George Neilson, a Standing member of the ancient and venerable Tuesday (or whin bush) Club of Lanneric, this Club was Governed by a Rotation of Presidents, first President Mr George Neilson.
1732	Translation of the Seat of Government in the Red house Club.
1736	Death of Mr Geo: Neilson & dissolution of the Red-house Club.
1739	Foundation of the Ugly Club, by a residue of the members, of the Red house Club, this Club Governed by a rotation of Presidents, Mr Spruce Limberloins Secretary, Mr Vocifer Leatherlungs Orator.[8]
1744	Dissolution of the Ugly Club.
1745	The Revival or Settlement of the ancient and honorable Tuesday Club in America, by a residue of the members of the Ugly Club, this at first Governed by a rotation of Stewards, till the Election of the Honorable Nasifer Jole Esqr perpetual president, in November the same year, whom God preserve long in the Chair.

the Tuesday Club [Book I] 65

A:C:	Treasurers	Masters of Ceremonies	Poets Laureat	Secretaries
1619	Mathew Paisly went beyond Sea 1620 Succ: by Josh Murhead	John Auchtermoughtie	Thomas Jolly	Malcolm Purdie ob: 1621 Succ: by Joseph Aikenhead
1630	Josh Murhead ob: 1639 Succ: by Donald Duncaster	Jno Auchtermoughtie ob: 1632 Succ: by Duff Murdock	Thomas Jolly, deposed for composing doggrell Rhimes, 1631 Succ: by Simon Mavis	Joseph Aikenhead hang'd for atheism, 1640 Succ: by David Crighton
1649	John Muirhead ob: 1650 Succ: by Duncan Strang	John Murdoch ob: 1652 Succ: by Ringan Fairy	Simon Mavis ob: 1650 Succ: by Zachary Boyd who translated the Bible into elegant verse	David Crighton ob: 1650 Succ: by Neal Mclaster
1659	Duncan Strang ob: 1672 Succ: by Harbottle Grimston	Ringan Fairy ob: 1663 Succ: by Godfrey Purdie	Zachary Boyd ob: 1660, and left a legacy to the college of Glasgow, to print his Sacred pindarics Succ: by Simon Goldie	Neal Mclaster ob: 1669 Succ: by Joseph Irwin
1675	Harbottle Grimston ob: 1692 Succ: by Daniel Waigle	Godfrey Purdie ob: 1694 Succ: by Moses Mcguire	Simon Goldie ob: 1676 Succ: by Duncan Mcgregor owtlawd	Joseph Irwin
1696	Daniel Waigle Died drunk 1705 Succ: by Gilbert Farqhar	Moses Mcguire	Duncan Mcgregor owtlawd & killd in a duel 1697 Succ: by Joseph Dallas	Jos: Irwin ob: 1697 Succ: by James Mccaupie

[67]

64 [Book I]   The History of

A:C:	Presidents	Baylies	Censors
1619	The venerable *Tobias Hodge* præs: 10 years	*Const: Abercrombie Giles Breckendrige* ob: 1620 Succ: by *Anthony Dottle*	*Dermot Mcleod* ob: 1623 Succ: by *Robert Restlerig*
1630	The venerable *Zachary Auchmoutie* Præs: 18 years	*Const: Abercrombie* ob: 1631 Succ: by *Jasper Tough Anthony Dottle*	*Robert Restlerig* ob: 1633 Succ: by *Donald McNash*
[66] 1649	The venerable *Jeremiah Majoribanks* præs: 9 years	*Jasper Tough Anthony Dottle* ob: 1650 being choaked with Cheese in Club Suc: by *Simon Spindle*	*Daniel McIntosh* went beyond Sea 1651 Succ: by *James Gorie*
1659	The venerable *Praisegod Maccarty* Præs: 15 years	*Jasper Tough* ob: 1660 Succ: by *Thomas Tubbs Simon Spindle*	*James Gorie*
1675	The venerable *Theophilus Petticrue* præs: 20 years	*Thomas Tubs* ob: 1681 Succ: by *Joseph Affleck Simon Spindle*	*James Gorie* obiit 1676 Succ: by *Ambrose Peezle*
1696	The venerable *Rowland Mcpherson* Præs: 16 years	*Simon Spindle* ob: 1699 aged 90 Succ: by *Gavin Prue Joseph Affleck*	*Ambrose Peezle* ob: 1698 Succ: by *Diego Trelawny*

the Tuesday Club   [Book I] 63

A:C:	Treasurers	Masters of Ceremonies	Poets Laureat	Secretaries	
1535	David Killigrew ob: 1539 Succ: by Geo: Montgomery	Laughlan Mclean	David Lindsey	Constant: Forbes ob: 1539 Succ: by John Trotter	
1547	George Montgomery ob: 1553 Succ: by Giles Borlin	Laughlan Mclean deposed for whoring 1552 Succ: by Jervais Fuckater	David Lindsey ob: 1548 Succ: by Obadiah Mowat	John Trotter	[65]
1566	Giles Borlin ob: 1569 Succ: by Daniel Hog	Jervais Fuckater killd by an Irishman for excessive farting and belching in Company, 1572 Succ: by Duncan Tweedie	Obadiah Mowat ob: 1569 Succ: by Adam Thacker	John Trotter ob: 1567 Succ: by Willm: Mclatchy A:M:	
1574	Daniel Hog, expelld the Club, for perpetual Sleeping and loud Snoring 1677 Succ: by Mungo Strachan	Duncan Tweedie ob: 1594 Succ: by Adam Bell	Adam Thacker ob: 1593 Succ: by Jasper Bamph	Wm Mclatchy A:M: ob: 1585 Succ: by Obadiah Primrose	
1596	Mungo Strachan ob: 1598 Succeed: by Neal Craig	Adam Bell	Jasper Bamph ob: 1599 Succ: by Tobias Mowbray	Obadiah Primrose ob: 1603 Succ: by Malcolm Purdie	
1610	Neal Craig ob: 1610 Succ: by Mathew Paisly	Adam Bell ob: 1612 Succ: by John Auchtermoughty	Tobias Mowbray ob: 1613 Succ: by Thomas Jolly	Malcolm Purdie	

62 [Book I]   The History of

	A:C:	Presidents	Baylies	Censors
	1535	The venerable *Gustavus Ockletree* The great præs: 11 years	*Darby Yare* ob: 1537 Succ: by *Andrew Dalziel Andrew Jolly* ob: 1539 Succ: by *Thomas Pintleridge*	*Doctor Pengueasel* ob: 1536 Succ: by *Donald McLaurie*
[64]	1547	The venerable *Alexander Kilspindie* Præs: 18 years	*Andrew Dalziel* ob: 1563 Succ: by *John Short Thomas Pintleridge*	*Donald Mclaurie* ob: 1551 Succ: by *Thomas Troop*
	1566	The venerable *Mathew Pendragon* the Great of the Race of Arthur king of Britain præs: 7 years	*John Short Thomas Pintleridge* ob: 1567 Succ: by *Robert Cameron*	*Thomas Troop* ob: 1571 Succ: by *Jervais Bogie*
	1574	The venerable *Arthur Kilbuckie* præs: 21 years	*Robert Cameron John Short*, expelled the club for blasphemously saying, he knew many priests that were damnd rogues 1567 Succ: by *Robert Drumore*	*Jervais Bogie* ob: 1595 Succ: by *Ringan Dobson*
	1596	The venerable *Giles Punton* præs: 13 years	*Rob: Drumore Rob: Cameron* ob: 1603 Succ: by *Giles Breckendridge*	*Ringan Dobson* ob: 1608 Succ: by *Ezekiel Orum*
	1610	The venerable *Sir Walter Wadle* Pres: 8 years	*Robert Drumore* ob: 1611 Succ: by *Constantine Abercrombie Giles Breckendridge*	*Ezekiel Orum* ob: 1612 Succ: by *Dermot McLeod*

A:C:	Treasurers	Masters of Ceremonies	Poets Laureat	Secretaries
1440	Gundy Galbreath	Alexr: Maccarty obiit 1443 Succeeded by Jodocus Gundy	Godfrey Connor an Irish bard	Gustavus Coulter obiit 1448 Succeeded by Joannes Duns Scotus, Grandson to the Philosophus Subtilis
1457	Gundy Galbreath ob: 1463 Succ: by Jervais Dalgleish	Jodocus Gundy	Godfrey Connor ob: 1465 Succ: by Sylvester Fulk	Joan: Duns Scotus ob:1467 Succ: by Archibaldus Petrie
1470	Jervis Dalgleish deposed for profane Swearing anno 1487 Succed: by Jonas Bogle	Jodocus Gundy obiit 1483 aged 95 Succ: by Andrew Logie	Sylvester Fulk ob: 1484 Succ: by Luke Fodry	Archibald: Petrie obiit 1485 Succ: by Robertus Kirk
1486	Jonas Bogle	Andrew Logie	Luke Fodry	Robertus Kirk
1496	Jonas Bogle ob: 1501 Succ: by Mungo Mcafferty	Andrew Logie	Luke Fodry	Robertus Kirk
1502	Mungo Macafferty ob: 1512 Succ: by Michael Dougharty ob: 1526 Succ: by David Killigrew	Andrew Logie ob: 1506 Succ: by Geofry Tough expelld for drunkenness 1534 Succ: by Laughlan Mclean	Luke Fodry ob: 1510 Succ: by Laughlan McIntosh ob: 1526 Succ: by David Lindsey	Robertus Kirk ob: 1519 Succ: by Constantine Forbes

60 [Book I]

[62]	A:C:	Presidents	Baylies	Censors
	1440	The venerable *Congallus de Rutherin* uncertain when he tooke the Chair, the records being lost before this year, pres: after this 16 years	*Godofredus Gallatly* *Gustavus De Bruce* obiit 1449 Succeeded by *Gawen Macclewraith*	*Jordanus Crie* obiit 1452 Succeeded by *Ebenezer McLeash*
	1457	The venerable *Donough deagh Deagha* lineally descended of the monarchs of Ireland Presid: 12 years	*Godofridus Gallatly* ob: 1460 Succeed: by *Duncan Davis* *Gawen Macclewraith*	*Ebenezer Mcleash*
	1470	The venerable *Dongallus Auchtermughty* Præs: 15 years	*Duncan Davis* *Gawen Macclewraith* ob: 1482 Succ: by *Oneal Norton*	*Ebenezer McLeash* obiit 1477 Succed: by *Jacob Craigie*
	1486	The venerable *Duncan Fairlie* præs: 9 years	*Duncan Davis* ob: 1489 Succ: by *Job Drumlanridge* *Oneal Norton*	*Jacob Craigie*
	1496	The venerable *Luke Tomlinsonus* præs: 6 years, and was deposed for being a Lollard, eating roast beef on Good friday and other heretical practises	*Job Drumlanridge* ob: 1498 Succ: by *Jervis Dennison* *Oneal Norton*	*Jacob Craigie*
	1502	The venerable *Alexander Pujolas* pres: 32 years aged 96	*Jervis Dennison* ob: 1518 Succ: by *Darby Yare* *Oneal Norton* ob: 1508 Succ: by *Andrew Jolly*	*Jacob Craigie* ob: 1503 Succ: by *Fulk Dallas* ob: 1529 Succ: by *Doctor Pengueasel*

A Chronological Table

of the

Ancient and Honorable Tuesday Club

of Annapolis in Maryland

from the year 1440
Down to this present time[7]

---

7. In the following chronology, Hamilton apparently has invented a good many of the Whin-Bush Club names (e.g., Donough deagh Deagha and Jervais Fuckater are obvious inventions), or he is having fun with the family names of his contemporaries and friends (e.g., Craigie, Dalgleish, Abercrombie, Strachan, Murdoch, and even Majoribanks are all Scottish surnames, though none of those I have located has the given name Hamilton provides). Indeed, I would suspect the entire table of being a fabrication except that at least four of the characters named—three of them poets laureate—did exist. For Allan Ramsay, see p. 59n, above. David Lindsey was possibly Sir David Lindsay (1490–1555; Hamilton shortens his life seven years), a popular poet of great influence in his day, noted for satirizing the vices of the clergy and exposing the disorders of church and state. Zachary Boyd was probably the Reverend Zachary Boyd (1585–1653; Hamilton grants him another seven years), rector of Glasgow University (1634–1635, 1645), who wrote *The Last Battell of the Soule in Death* (Edinburgh, 1629), "Zion's Flowers" (MS at Glasgow University Library), and many other devotional works in verse. Harbottle Grimston (1603–1685; Hamilton adds seven years—he apparently did not think anyone would be silly enough to check these dates), was a member of Parliament, and I suspect that Hamilton may be toying with the names of other members of Parliament as well.

Tho these verses at first hearing, seemed to me alittle upon the hobbling order, yet in my opinion they Contain an excellent Sentiment, and a most beautiful metaphor and Similie.

[60]   Having thus delivered some anecdotes relating to the constitution of this venerable Club, which I think Sufficient to show, that it was the ancient and venerable Tuesday Club, and, that the Ancient and Honorable Tuesday Club of Annapolis in Maryland, is no other than the same Club transmigrated to America, In order to preserve the thread of this history Intire, I shall here give you, the Lineal Succession of the Presidents and respective officers of this venerable Club, from the year 1440 (for the Records go no further back, all before that period being lost) in a kind of Chronological table, with which I shall close the first book of this History.

The Whin Bush Club, admitting a member.

latter allowing all for the back, and little or nothing for the belly, devour their poor threepenny meals, amidst poorer conversation, and leave Devil a Scrap for their fellow Dogs to feed upon—But to return to our history—

As all Societies, have certain mysterious Ceremonies, at the admission of members, so this venerable whin bush Club, have proper rites which they use on this occasion, and, which I shall here mention, that we may afterwards compare them with the ceremonies used by the ancient and honorable Tuesday Club of Annapolis, on the like occasion, and see how nighly they agree.

When I was admitted a member of that venerable Club, which was in the year 1737, In the Presidentship of the present venerable Mr Neal Gilpin, I was conducted into a private Room, by Mr Secretary Duncan, and two other Standing members of that venerable Club, They first asked me my age, to which having answered, they asked me where I was born, and receiving a proper reply, they demanded next where my Father and Grand-[59] fathers were born, and these last being born In Clydsdale, they Clap'd || a hat upon my head, stuck a bunch of furz into my button hole, (here I cannot but remark the great Simplicity of the badge of this venerable Club) made me subscribe the book of Rules, pay a fee to the Secretary, and conducting me with great State into the Club room, delivered me over to Signior Pasquelino De Marzis, master of Ceremonies, who first presented me to the venerable Mr Neal Gilpin, the President, and in a Set form of words, proclaimed me a Standing member, of the ancient and venerable whin bush Club of Lanneric. The venerable President took me most graciously by the hand, to whom I made a Complimentary Speech, and drank a bumper, or Quaff full of twopenny ale, and had a Clean pipe and tobacco presented to me, then these verses were Solemnly pronounced, by Mr Allan Ramsay, Poet Laureat.[6]

> As this furz is ever green,
> And this pipe streight white & clean,
> May your virtue still remain,
> Unchang'd, chast, pure, without a Stain,
> Which, if it does, then you we dub,
> A Standing member of this Club.

---

6. Ramsay (1686–1758) was a Scottish poet and bookseller noted for his elegies and satires, his collections of old Scottish and English songs (*Tea-table Miscellany* [1724–1732] and *The Ever Green* [1724]), which helped revive vernacular Scottish poetry, and his principal work, *The Gentle Shepherd* (1725), a pastoral drama. I have not found these verses in Ramsay's works.

Romans, or do they Resemble them in the least feature? No. They are a parcel of Singers, dancers, fidlers, pipers, effeminate catamites, Silly eunuchs and Idle Sauntering priests. Where now are their Scipios, Cæsars, Pompeys, Luculluses, Catos, Ciceros, Virgils, Horaces and Lucretias?[4] are they not sunk into these pigmy mortals, called by the soft and languishing names of Signior Corelli, Vivaldi, Tessarini, Torelli, Martini, Geminiani, Alberti, Valentini, Lampugnani, Senesino, Farinello, Bonancini, Beneditto, and Seniora or Madona Auretti, Violante, Berberini &ct:[5] we may thence see & beware of the danger of admitting luxury into any Society, and, tho wise Societies and nations, have embraced this Cockatrice, yet that does not at all prove, that there is any good to be had of her, and tho' the ancient and honorable Tuesday Club, of Annapolis, be one of the wisest Clubs that ever yet appeared, yet she may see the time, when her constitution will feel the Smart of admitting Luxury to gain ground among her longstanding members, when she may receive such a Shake, as she may never be able to recover, and, tho she may not thereby be quite extinguished, yet may she sink from her || present grandure excellence and conspicuity, to the obscure [58] degree of an Infamous ale-house Club, like those that are held in your Chop-houses at the back of Change alley, where poor poets, and poorer military officers, the first mantained on Short commons by the muses, the

---

4. Lucullus (probably fl. ca. 75 B.C.) was a Roman soldier, administrator, and patron of the arts. Lucretia, the wife of Tarquinius Collatinus, was raped by Sextus, son of Tarquinius Superbus, then took her own life.

5. Arcangelo Corelli (1653–1713) was an Italian violinist and composer of sonatas especially distinguished for his dance movements. Antonio Vivaldi (1675?–1741), Italian violinist and composer of operas and sonatas, greatly influenced the development of violin concertos. Carlo Tessarini (1690–1765) was an Italian violinist who established the form of the violin sonata with three movements. Giuseppe Torelli (1658–1709) was an Italian violinist and composer who established the concerto form as used by George Frederick Handel, Corelli, and others. Giovanni Battista Martini (1706–1784) was an Italian monk, composer, and music theorist who wrote the *Storia della musica*, 3 vols. (Bologna, 1757–1781). Francesco Geminiani (1687–1762) was an Italian violinist and composer noted for his concertos and sonatas. Domenico Alberti (ca. 1700–1740) was an Italian musician and composer of sonatas remembered for the device now known as the Alberti Bass. Valentini could be either Pier Francesco Valentini (d. 1654), an Italian composer of madrigals and of a canon with more than 2,000 musical combinations, Giuseppe Valentini (b. 1681), composer of violin and bass solos, or Giovanni Valentini (fl. 17th century), composer of madrigals, masses, and sonatas. Giovanni Battista Lampugnani (b. ca. 1706), an Italian conductor and composer of operas, was in London in 1743. Francesco Bernardi Senesino (ca. 1680–ca. 1750) was an Italian male mezzo-soprano who performed in many of Handel's operas from 1720 to 1733. Carlo Farinelli (1705–1782) was an Italian male soprano who performed operas in London in 1734 and was famous throughout Europe for his extraordinary range. Bonancini is probably Giovanni Battista Bononcini (1670–ca. 1750), an Italian composer and an associate of Handel's in England. Beneditto is probably Benedetti, an Italian singer who appeared in London around 1720. The three women were probably also Italian singers who appeared in London in the 18th century.

covenanters, anticovenanters, whigs, tories, Revolutioners, Jacobites, so, this venerable Club, from their late place of meeting, took the name of the whin bush, changing for it the ancient name of the Tuesday Club of Lanneric, which ancient name is now kept up and preserved, only by the Ancient and honorable Tuesday Club of Annapolis, which proceeds in a direct line, from the Ancient and Venerable Tuesday (or whin bush) Club of Lanneric, and is indeed the Self same Club, as shall presently be made appear, by the most authentic historical proofs.

Having but Just now mentioned bread & cheese, It will be proper to take notice in this place, that this ancient and venerable Club, had a Standing law, that nothing was to be admitted of eatables but this, which was only to give a relish to their Liquor, formal Suppers taking up too much time, and occasioning too much Ceremony and Confusion in the Club, this Law, the ancient and Honorable Tuesday Club of Annapolis at first adopted, in Laudable Imitation of their patrons of the whin bush, but Luxury by degrees crept in among them, and they now Indulge themselves In sumptuous Suppers, which some have ‖ attributed to the custom established by that Club, of Celebrating their anniversary, at which time, the honorable Mr President Jole, out of the overflowings of his generosity and respect to the club, always provides them in a most elegant entertainment, and the longstanding members, (as it is natural for the Inferior class of mankind to ape those above them) in Imitation of his honor, try who shall outdo one another, in pomp and elegance of Club Suppers, and this is not alittle promoted, by the ambition and Emulation of the females, related to the Club, to shine & be remarkable in this particular.

This circumstance will admitt of a few grave reflexions; all allow, that Luxury is a destructive thing, and sooner or later fatal to every society or Community that once admits of it; as having a tendency to Introduce abject Slavery, by means of its being a promoter of bribery and Corruption, yet, we have Instances of the wisest Societies, that have, sometime or other fallen into her traps; Did not the Greeks, a wise and warlike Nation, after having for several ages, mantained their honor and dignity, in arts and arms, and Integrity of Morals, sink by degrees into Softness and effeminacy, by which, the persians overcame them, after they had subdued the persians by their arms and warlike prowess; and what are they now? how degenerated from their ancient honor and bravery, are they any better than a parcell of Quacking, pedling, rope dancing Juggling ‖ knaves, and withal, abandoned Slaves to the Law and government of Mahomet; what now are the Romans? once a wise honorable and warlike people, who ruled the world, and grasped the Globe at a handful, are they any wise like the Ancient

night, and, by the very old records we find, that this venerable Club, went by the name of the Tuesday Club of Lanneric, but, in the Presidentship of the venerable Mr President Majoribanks, the day of meeting of this Club was changed into Friday, for what Reasons is not known, unless it was upon account of the Turbulent times of persecution, which broke out sometime after the happy restoration, when so much countenance and favor was shown to papists and high Church Caviliers, that Sober discrete moderate whigs could not sleep in a Sound Skin. It is thought, that then, the members of this venerable Club, being all true blue whigs, and many of them concerned in the battle of Bothwell Bridge,[2] in Clydsdale, they were obliged to abscond and skulk, and || met under the shelter of the whin or furz bushes (like Mr Cameron's congregation,[3] which met under the Canopy of the heavens) that they might not be discovered and routed by the blood thirsty Caveliers, who were on the Scent after them, so, being constrained to assume the Sham name of true Catholics, for their own Safety, they absconded on fridays, pretending to be fasting and praying, while all the time they were soaking their noses in twopenny ale, smoking tobacco, and devouring bread & cheese, this food they were particularly fond of, and one of their Baylies, vizt: Anthony Dottle, choaked, while he was voraciously swallowing a great mouthful of Cheese in Club, in the year 1650; This custom they continued for some time, lurking in the fields among the furz and broom, 'till the times began to relax in their Severity, then they betook themselves to a taveren, which hung out for a Sign a whin bush, (hence their moderen name of whin bush Club) in honor of this club; their day of meeting still continued to be friday, and their meetings were very private (this was in the presidentship of the venerable Praise-god Maccartie) 'till the happy revolution, at the coming over of King William of Glorious memory, and, in the presidentship of the venerable Theophilus Petticrue, then they sung whig Songs with all the Jollity and freedom Imaginable, mounting a large table, clapping each his wig under his right foot, holding a pipe of tobacco in one hand and a || bumper of punch in the other. From that time the Club has continued to meet on fridays, and, as the different Sects and parties in politics and religion, at that time, were fond of taking new names, and laying aside the old, as the Cameronians,

[54]

[55]

---

2. In the battle fought on June 22, 1679, the rebel Covenanters of southwest Scotland were defeated by 10,000 men under the duke of Monmouth. Of about 4,000 rebels perhaps 200 to 400 were killed and 1,200 captured.

3. Richard Cameron (d. 1680) was a Scottish Covenanter and field preacher who formally renounced allegiance to Charles II and whose followers, the Cameronians, later constituted a sect of Reformed Presbyterians in Scotland.

niority, the oldest member of the Club, always holding it, but in case there was a parity of age, that person who was the member of the longest Standing, took that place of honor, from whence we derive the title of *Longstanding member,* in the ancient and honorable Tuesday Club of Annapolis, the members of that Club, taking to themselves that title, from a certain noble emulation and ambition, sometime or other to ascend the chair, each in his turn, and not from any Waggish Entendre, as some Imagine was Intended by Jealous Spyplot Esqr, when he Revived that Significant term, in the ancient and honorable Tuesday Club. In case two or three members, were of equal age, and of equal *Long standing* (I desire none may misinterpret my words in the manner that some evil minded females, have done the mysteries of the Free Masons) then, and then only, the Chair was elective || and the Club determined the affair by a majority of voices. Under this president were several officers, vizt: a Senior and Junior Baylie, a censor, a Treasurer, a master of Ceremonies, a poet Laureat, and a Secretary, who, all, but the Master of Ceremonies, Poet and Secretary, were appointed and Commissioned by the president, the last three being chosen by the Club, the first were called State officers, the other officers of the commons, The Senior and Junior Baylies, sat at the Right and left hand of the Chair, The Censor was an officer of Great authority, and it was his business to remark and bring to a trial, all trespasses and misdemeanors committed in Club, before the worshipful the Baylies, as also, to take into custody all offending members, and them to keep without bail or Redemption, till the Issue of the Cause was tried, I do not find by the Records that they ever had any Champion, or military discipline in this Club, their Constitution was so pacific, that they had no occasion for one, neither had they a chancellor or great Seal, the Presidents own privy seal, serving all Clubical Commissions and Instruments of writing, it was the Secretaries business to enter the proceedings in the book of Records, (and nothing was entered there, without the Presidents consent,) to draw up Indictments Impeachments, declarations, and Informations against offenders, The treasurer kept the Club box, and the fund was || collected, by every present member's clubbing one penny at each Sederunt, and by fines; the master of Ceremonies Introduced Strangers, Installed new members, and performed the honors of the Club, to the venerable the President, The poet Laureat, on particular occasions, exercised his genius in praise of the venerable the president and Club, and Repeated certain ancient Clubical verses at the admission of new members.

As to the Laws of this venerable Club, they were few and Simple, one Law was, that the Club should meet once a week upon Tuesday Evening, at the Hour of Six, Summer and winter, and not to exceed eleven o clock at

qualities to recommend him) would certainly all his life time have been a beggar.⁷

As for Signior Pasquelino de Marzis, now master of Ceremonies to this venerable Club, tho' a native of Italy, yet he being grandson to Mathew Paisly (which name was Italianized into Pasquelino) who was Censor in the Presidentship of the venerable Sir Walter Wadle, and the Venerable Tobias Hodge, he had a good title to be admitted a member.

I must observe here, after what I have mentioned above, that it is a mighty great advantage for a man to be born in some particular places, how happy for instance, were those born in Clydsdale, upon this single privilege, of being qualified to be Members, of this ancient and venerable Club, happy were they also, whose fathers and grandfathers were born in that Shire before them, happy, for a simular reason, are all those who are true born Englishmen, being by that circumstance alone, bless'd with liberty, the quiet enjoyment of property, and absolute exemption from popery, Slavery, pagan Idolatry, Mahometan Superstition, bribery and corruption. O Glorious Nation! whose natives surpass all mankind besides in Courage comeliness and vigor! who wallow in the delights of good eating and drinking! who know not what it is to live upon scraps, dry crusts, and Soup meagres, like the Raw bon'd French and Spaniard! but abound all the days of your lives in lusty beef, Glorious pudding, and Invigorating ale!

Chapter VI

A Succinct account of the Ancient and Venerable Tuesday (or whin bush) Club of Lanneric, in the kingdom of Scotland.

The ancient and venerable Tuesday (or whin bush) Club of Lanneric, was time out of mind governed by a president, who, once he had attained the Chair, continued *durante vita,* or *quam diu bene se Gesserit,*¹ for we have an Instance of one being deposed, vizt: the Venerable Luke Tomlinson, who was degraded in 1502 for heresy, and eating roast beef on Good fridays. This place was neither elective nor hereditary, but was possessed by se-

---

7. Hamilton is apparently referring to one of the more dubious affairs in the life of the profligate Frederick Calvert (1731–1771), sixth Lord Baltimore and proprietor of Maryland from 1751 until his death.

1. "During his lifetime," or "so long as he behaves himself well."

John Duncan, who was then, and is now, for aught I know, Secretary of that ancient and venerable Club, who was so kind as to communicate to me, some anecdotes, relating to the government and policy of that ancient and venerable Club, which I shall give to my readers in the thread of this History, in proper places, where they will naturally occurr.

In order to be admitted a member of this venerable Club, it was necessary, among other notable qualifications, for a man to be of the Shire of Clydsdale, either by his own birth, or that of his father or Grandfather, and some, upon proving that their great grandfather was of that Shire, or that their cousin germans or Cousins once removed, were natives of that Shire, were Indulged so far as to be admitted, provided, that they were men of a truly Clubical Genius or Disposition, that is, could drink a bumper, smoke a pipe, crack a Joke, or tell a waggish Story, nay, I remember one Instance of a Gentleman's being admitted who was a native of the Town of Sanquhar in the north, || whose ancestors, time out of mind, had been born there, upon a Supposition, that his grandfather had once travelled thro' Clydsdale, in his way to Galloway, and had a new heel Clapped to his boot, by a Clydsdale Cobler, but in fact, the Chief merit on which he was admitted, was, his having married a Daughter of the Late Sir John Norris,[6] admiral of England, with whom he had a world of money, and Indeed, we find, that thro' petticoat Interest, many men have had very honorable promotions, and have been entrusted with Employments of the greatest profit and emolument, not from any personal qualifications of their own, but, by the transmitted excellencies of their wives, Sisters and daughters, who, from their extreme handsomness, or some other equivalent property, become the prime favorites of great men, and I must here observe, that it is no extraordinary thing to see men admitted members of venerable and honorable Clubs upon female merit alone, since by that ladder, some have Climbed to the highest Titular honors, and procured to themselves, Principalities, Dukedoms, Lordships, Papacy, Cardinal-hats and Bisho-pricks, not to mention numberless places of an Inferior rank, procured Solely, by the Influence of certain commodities, in the possession only of the fair Sex; I myself know a certain man, who, for certain reasons, shall be nameless, who now lives in a certain City, whose wife at a Certain time, found out a method to please a certain Lord, which procured for her husband, a certain handsom yearly Income, who, had it || not been for that (he having no certain good

---

6. Norris (1547?–1597) was an English military commander who fought under Essex against the Irish (1573) and, with Sir Francis Drake, commanded the fleet that ravaged the coasts of Spain and Portugal in 1589.

The advocates for punch, from these learned passages prove, that this venerable Club, was stupified by the fumes of Tobacco, for, say they, this Learned and Royal Author Clearly demonstrates, that these Stinking fumes, moisten the brain, and Create Clouds there, so as to obscure the understanding or Sensorium; for, according to Dryden, a Celebrated poet, ‖ great wits are nighly related to madmen, and according to Sir Richard Blackmore, a noted Poet, a Learned Physician, and withal a knight Baronet, the brains of all madmen are very dry and parched,[5] therefore the brains of great wits are in a degree of temperature, between those of madmen and heavy dull fellows, that is, they are temperatly dry, but, as the fumes of tobacco moisten the brains, they must necessarily render men heavy and dull. *Q:E:D:*

This venerable Club was under a total eclipse, during the Cromwellian usurpation, in the presidentship of the venerable Zachary Auchmoutie the great, and part of the time of the Venerable Jeremiah Majoribanks, for Oliver Imagining that they were a Cabal a plotting against the common wealth, seized their Records, and dispers'd them, but, upon these being examined, by a learned Committee of the *Rump,* there appeared nothing of politics or State matters in them, but only Simple facts, relating to fines and forfeitures, and drinking of toasts in bumpers &ct:

But, in the Presidentship of the venerable Rowland Macpherson, on the happy restoration of the Steuart family, who, to be sure, had an Indefeasible hereditary right to the British crown, derived in a curve line, direct, Indirect and collateral, from William the Bastard of Normandy, who, acquired it partly by conquest, Sword in hand, and partly by an Authentic last will and testament of Edward the Confessor, those valuable records were again restored, to this venerable club, when most ‖ of the other national records were lost, a lucky Incident, and what at this day will give us great Insight into the history of the ancient and honorable Tuesday Club of Annapolis.

These circumstances I deliver as authentic, having the honor to be myself, a standing member of that venerable Club of the whin bush of Lanneric, and have a hundred and a hundred times over seen and perused their Records, during the Secretaryship of the learned and Ingenious Mr

---

5. Hamilton is alluding to the following lines from *Absalom and Achitophel*: "Great Wits are sure to Madness near ally'd; / And thin Partitions do their Bounds divide" (*The Works of John Dryden*, ed. Edward Niles Hooker *et al.* [Berkeley, Calif., 1956–], II, 10, lines 163–164). Blackmore (d. 1729) was physician to Queen Anne and author of several lengthy poems and essays, including *Creation: A Philosophical Poem Demonstrating the Existence and Providence of God* (1712).

this hebetude of humour, in that venerable Club, was at all produced by the fumes of that glorious Liquor, but rather by the thick and gross steams of Tobacco, and, to support this argument, they quote a book of great authority, composed by a royal author, entituled the *Counterblast*,[3] which being bound up in a large, learned and ponderous volume of his other works in Folio, which is now scarce to be seen, for the benefit of my readers, I shall here quote these passages.

"Shall we, I say, that have been so long civil and wealthy in peace, famous and Invincible in war, fortunate in both,—shall we, I say, without blushing, abase ourselves so far, as to Imitate those beastly Indians, Slaves to the Spaniards, refuse to the world, and as yet Aliens to the holy covenant of God; It seems a miracle to me, how a custom, springing from so vile a ground, and brought in by a Father[(a)] so generally hated, should be welcomed upon so slender a warrant, it was neither brought in by king great conqueror,[(b)] or learned Doctor of Physic,— ‖ and that the suffumigation thereof cannot have a drying quality, it needs no further probation than that it is a Smoke, all Smoke and vapor being of it self humid as drawing near to the nature of the air, easie to be resolved again into water, whereof there needs no further proof but the Meteors, which being bred of nothing else but the vapours and exhalations, sucked up by the Sun, out of the Earth the sea and waters, yet are the same Smoaky vapours, transformed into rains, dews, Snows, hoar frosts, and such like watery meteors, as by the contrary, the rainy clouds, are transformed and evaporated into blustering winds—This Stinking Smoke then, being sucked up by the nose, and Imprisoned in the cold and moist brains, is by their Cold and wet faculty, cast forth again, in watery distillations, and so are you made free and purged of nothing, but that wherewith you willfully burdened yourselves—a Custom loathsome to the eye, hateful to the nose, harmful to the brain, dangerous to the Lungs, and, in the black Stinking fumes thereof, nearest resembling the Stygian Smoke, of the pit that is bottomless."

(a) Sir Walter Rauleigh, who was a father of learning and a brave Soldier, and therefore hated by Gondemar,[4] the Spanish Ambassador, and his creature king James, which was the same as to be universally hated, at least in that corrupt and Sycophantish court.

(b) Here his majesty tells a gross lie.

3. Hamilton is referring to James I's *A Counterblaste to Tobacco* (London, 1604), a serious, carefully reasoned treatise against smoking. For the most part, Hamilton accurately transcribes King James's text, although in the original text "it was neither brought in by king great conqueror, or learned Doctor of Physic" precedes "It seems a miracle to me...." Hamilton's derogatory notes and his patching together of snippets of King James's prose make the argument against tobacco seem a good deal sillier than the original.

4. The count of Gondomar, Diego Sarmiento de Acuña (1567–1626), as Spanish ambassador to England (1613–1618, 1619–1622), successfully prevented James from aiding Spain's enemies.

told at Christenmass meetings, of this ancient and venerable Club, long before this period, as that the venerable Aidan was president, at the time of the coming of Fergus I from Ireland, when Coyl was king of the Britons, he was famous for playing on the bagpipes, and added the Drone pipe to that Instrument, which before Consisted of one single treble pipe only, The venerable Ferithar was president in the time of Fergus II king of Scotland, and was only remarkable for his being a very great || devourer of Brose, a [44] dish, made of the fat Skimmings of Salt beef broth and oatmeal; The venerable Fethelmach was a noble Pict, and was Killed by king Kenneth II and his Clan at the extirpation of that Nation, he is famed for having Invented the high Relished Dish of Cock-a-leekie, and the Comfortable Soup called Dads and Blads.²

What Sort of Liquor that ancient Club drank in these early times is not mentioned in their Records, but, since the latter part of the Reign of Elizabeth of England of Glorious, and the beginning of the Reign of James the Sixth of Scotland of Shitten memory, in the Presidentship of the venerable Sir Walter Wadle, we are pretty certain, that they drank twopenny ale and smoked tobacco, for punch was not as yet received among them till after the restauration, when the manufacture of the Sugar Islands began to prosper and Increase; whether this same punch, which has been much extoll'd, by many of our moderen Bowzers, as a most beatific liquor, and exactly like the Nectar of the Gods, furbished up and Improved the wit and humor of this venerable Club, does not appear by the Records of the same, they rather seem to me, to have flagged in their conversation, since the use of this compound guzzle, for, before this time, when Simple twopenny ale was their drink, some lively Sparks of wit and humor passed amongst them, at every Se- || derunt, but since the use of tobacco and punch, we find nothing [45] in these records, but "James such a one, fined one penny for coming *Sero*, or late to Club, Robert such a one fined four pence for absence, without being able to render a satisfactory reason, and Andrew such a one, fined Sixpence for Swearing." But the advocates for punch will not allow, that

---

2. The club presidents, Congallus de Rutheren, Ferithar, and Fethelmach, appear to be Hamilton's inventions. The British kings, however, are real. Aidan (d. 606) was the king of the Scottish kingdom of Dalriada, but after announcing his intention to govern it as an independent kingdom, he was defeated by Ethelfrith, the king of Northumbria. Fergus I was the legendary king of Scotland who came from Ireland ca. 330 B.C. to assist the Scots against the Picts and Britons. Fergus II (d. 501) was the first Dalriad king in Scotland. Kenneth II (d. 995) was a Scottish-Pictish king who tried to consolidate the warring territories of Scotland. By "Coyl" Hamilton is perhaps recalling Coilus, British king of the first century A.D., referred to in Geoffrey of Monmouth's *History of the Kings of Britain*. For other information on the Whin-Bush Club members, see p. 60n, below.

[An antique marble bas-relief dug up from the rubbish dumps of an old monastery near Drumlanridge.]

[facing page 43]

try to tack together fragments, and broken hints of history, to produce a Chimêra, or monstruous birth, which seems to every Judicious Reader, altogether Inconsistent in it self, ridiculous, and Indeed Incredible, hence we have, what are called the fabulous accounts of the Poets, the Stages and periods of the Golden, Silver, Brazen & Iron ages, which, in themselves, duely perpended & considered, contain as much of the Legend, as the famous books of knight Errantry, or the accounts of the Miracles, done by the Saints of holy Catholic Church.

That I may evade splitting upon this dangerous rock, I shall lay aside all disquisitions and Dissertations, concerning ancient times, enveloped In obscurity, and at once making a skip, shall trace in a direct line, our ancient and honorable Tuesday Club of Annapolis, from a Celebrated Club, called the ancient and venerable Tuesday (or whin bush) Club of Laneric,[1] in the ancient kingdom of Scotland, which was in its highest Glory, about two centuries before the usurpation of Oliver Cromwel, In the Presidentship of the venerable Congallus de Rutheren, consequently, about the middle of the Reign of Henry VI of England, It is found, by the ancient Records of that Club, now remaining, for all before that time were lost, by means of the national feuds subsisting in that unhappy kingdom, that there were then 350 Living members in the Club, Some few Traditional Stories, are yet

[43]

---

1. While probably exaggerated, most of what Hamilton says about the Whin-Bush Club is based upon fact. His reference to the club's association with Clydesdale, for instance (see p. 48), is verified by Allan Ramsay (see p. 59n, below). In "A Petition to the Whinbush Club" Ramsay offers himself to the club as a

> Native of *Clydsdale's* upper Ward
> Bred Fifteen Summers there,
> Tho, to my Loss I'm no a Laird
> By Birth, my Title's fair
>   To bend wi' ye and spend wi' ye
>   An Evening, and gaffaw,
>   If Merit and Spirit
>   Be found without a Flaw.

In an explanatory note to the poem, Ramsay further observes: "This Club consists of *Clydsdale*-Shire Gentlemen, who frequently meet at a diverting Hour, and keep up a good Understanding amongst themselves over a friendly Botle. And from a charitable Principle, easily collect into their Treasurer's Box a small Fond, which has many a Time relieved the Distresses on indigent Persons of that Shire" (*The Works of Allan Ramsay,* ed. Burns Martin and John W. Oliver [Edinburgh, (1951)–1974], I, 210–211). For verification of Hamilton's membership in the Whin-Bush Club, see his letter to his brother Gavin, where Hamilton implores him to "be so good as Remember me to all the Members of the whin-bush Club, especially to the Right honourable, the Lord Provost, and other magistrates and officers of that ancient and honourable society, inform them that every friday, I fancy myself with them, drinking twopenny ale, and smoking tobacco" (June 13, 1739, Dulany Papers, MS. 1265, Maryland Historical Society, Baltimore).

Pythagoras &ct: down to those famous moderen Architects, Inigo Jones, and Sir Christopher Wren,[13] so, I say, might I follow the tract of Clubs, from those famous presidents Apollo, Bacchus, Silenus, Alexander the Great, &ct: down to the Honorable Nasifer Jole Esqr, the prime and paragon of moderen Presidents, but I leave that to the Reverend Doctor Warburton, and others more versed in antiquities and Critical learning, and also, for another weighty reason I ommit it, that is, least I should make this work too voluminous and bulky.

I shall therefore hasten towards the main point of my Subject, and omitting the Clubs of ancient greek Philosophers, who used to assemble in the porticos (the same to them as our Coffee-houses are to us at this Day) as also the private assemblies, of those that were Concerned in the Mysteries, which were properly the Ancient Lodges of Masons, and the meetings of the Bacchinals, which were mad Clubs, like our late moderen Mohooks, and the Celebrated Hellfire Society;[14] The mysteries of the Bona Dea,[15] which were || female Clubs, resembling much our moderen Gossopings, after a lying in, and a thousand others of the like nature; in the following Chapter, I design to proceed to the more Immediate Spring and origin of the Ancient and honorable Tuesday Club of Annapolis in Maryland.

Chapter V

The more Immediate origin and rise of the Ancient and honorable Tuesday Club, of Annapolis in Maryland.

It has been the misfortune of most Historians, while they grope, fumble and blunder in the dark, among the Rubbish of Antiquity, and vainly

---

13. Jones (1573–1652) was the English architect who designed settings for court masques by Ben Jonson and others. Wren (1632–1723) was the famous English architect best remembered for designing the Pembroke College chapel and Saint Paul's Cathedral in London.

14. The Mohock Club was one of the more frolicsome, blasphemous, and rakish clubs that thrived in England around 1712 (see Robert J. Allen, *The Clubs of Augustan London* [Cambridge, Mass., 1933], 105–119). Hamilton may have heard of Boston's Hellfire Club, a group of wits who contributed to James Franklin's *New-England Courant* in the 1720s (see Shunsuke Kamei, "Cultural Clubs in Colonial America, 1720–1750," *Studies in English Literature* [English Literary Society of Japan], English Number [1963], 40). However, given the context, Hamilton is probably referring to the rakish Hell-Fire Clubs (there were actually three) that flourished in England in the 1720s (see Allen, 119–124).

15. The Bona Dea was a Roman goddess of unknown name, probably an earth spirit protective of women. Rites in her honor were celebrated annually in December and were attended only by women.

in the plain of Sinaar, and erected a most Stupenduous tower, ‖ which they [40] probably Intended for a Club house, and with which they thought to overtop the Clouds, but their conversation becoming confused and Irregular, they could not understand one another, and so were obliged to disperse, and form themselves into various Clubs, this has been the fate of many Clubs since, and even at this day, where it frequently happens, that while the members are vainly building Castles in the air, they either do not, or will not understand each other, and thus, a misunderstanding, as it is called, arising among them, they separate, and become members of other Clubs, for that of Clubbing, is so natural to mankind, that every man must necessarily be in some Club or other, a remarkable Instance of this, happened lately in the Synod of the Seceding bretheren among the Clergy in Scotland, who not understanding one another in point of Doctrine, or Rather in point of ambition for popularity, separated Into many Clubs or Synods, and very Solemnly declared each other heretics, pronouncing the dreadful Sentence of excommunication, against each other, then the Reverend Mr Ralph Erskin, excommunicated the Reverend Mr Fisher and his Synod, the Reverend Mr Fisher excommunicated the Reverend Mr Wilson and his Synod, and the Anathemas flew about as thick as hops.[11]

I might, since I have dip'd so far into the Subject of ancient clubs, trace the origin of the ancient and honorable Tuesday Club of Annapolis In Maryland, from the uninterrupted Succession of Clubs thro the first ages, after the General Deluge, down to the present times, still finding, as ‖ I [41] went along, some Club or other, that met on Tuesday, and this I might do with the same propriety, as the ancient & honorable fraternity of Free and accepted Masons, do, by their printed constitutions (of which many fair Editions are now extant and may be had for money of the booksellers) trace their Society from Noe, Tubal Cain, king Solomon, king Hiram of Tyre,[12]

---

11. Ralph Erskine (1685–1752) was a Scottish seceding divine and religious poet whose preaching was remarkable for its pathos, and the author of *Faith No Fancy* (Edinburgh, 1745), a repudiation of the image of Christ as man. James Fisher (1697–1775) was one of the founders of the Scottish secession church and primary author of *The Assembly's Shorter Catechism Explained by Way of Question and Answer,* 2 parts (Glasgow, 1753–1760), long regarded as the standard manual for catechismal instruction in the secession church. William Wilson (1690–1741) was a Scottish seceding divine who sided with Erskine and Fisher and published *A Defence of the Reformation Principles of the Church of Scotland* (Edinburgh, 1739) and several other collections of sermons. These three men seem to have been opposed more to the general assembly of Scotland than divided among themselves. They were all in agreement, at least, about the fundamental issue behind their secession: each regarded the congregational right of appointing clergy as sacred and opposed the general assembly's act allowing that right only to the heritors and elders of the church.

12. Hiram, king of Tyre (970–936 B.C.), befriended Solomon and David and helped erect Solomon's temple and David's palace.

from the Royal Society, and to be entered a member of that learned body, as the smallest recompense for my Study and application in making this Important discovery; I may meet with some, perhaps, who may treat me, as his contemporary Physicians treated Doctor Harvey, when he first discovered the Circulation of the blood,[8] who mantained that Hippocrates, Galen, and many others, were the first discoverers of it, They may attribute this my discovery to Pythagoras, Aristotle, or some other ancient Philosopher, but they must quote a better authority for it than that of το σωμα κυκλος εστι,[9] for, I will undertake to make it plain, either by fair disputation *viva voce,* or in writing, that none ever thought of this before me; The Short and the Long of it is no more than this, Some of Noe's Jolly family, probably Ham, drank 'till he became || black in the face, goggle eyed, flat nosed and blubber liped, and thus his posterity have remained ever since, hence we may conclude, that it was of some deep coloured wine they Drank, such as the Alicant and Benecarlo, that are made In old Spain, and what confirms this, is that the Spaniards, by even the moderate use of this wine, (for they are reputed a very Sober and temperate people) are generally of a dusky Swarthy complexion, tho' some have erroneously attributed that color in the Spaniard, to a mixture of the Moorish blood, which cannot be, for these abominable Infidels were murdered massacred and expelld by them, in the very same manner as the Indians of South America were, to promote the good christian cause of Holy catholic Church, some Centuries agoe, which, as it originally took root from the blood of the Saints, so it needs to water and nourish it plenty of worthless Infidel blood, and besides, had this been the case, that tawny cast must have been now wore out, from among our moderen Spaniards, also, if this is to be attributed to the Moorish blood, why are not the Spanish ladies, noted for their fair complexion, of the same hue with the men; the reason is plain, the women there are kept so Strictly to rules, that they are not suffered, by their austere lords and masters, to Indulge in the Rites of either Bacchus or Venus.

Soon after the flood, we find Nimrod at the head of a Club of warriors and hunters, and also we read of a Great Club, or assembly of bold adventurers (as that learned Cosmographer Heylen calls them,)[10] that assembled

---

8. William Harvey (1578–1657) was the famous English physician who in 1616 proposed his theory on the circulation of the blood.

9. Literally, "the body is a wheel."

10. Peter Heylyn (1600–1662) was the English author of works on ecclesiastical history and of *Microcosmus, or a Little Description of the Great World* (Oxford, 1621; enlarged and reissued as *Cosmographie* in 1652). Heylyn relates the story of Babel and refers to its founders as "the first *Adventurers*" in his introduction to the *Cosmographie* (see pp. 7–9 of the 1658 edition).

lor in the Court of the said Jupiter, but it is the opinion of many Learned men (for I here as I hinted above wave giving my own opinion) that most of these wicked presidents, may more properly be stiled representatives of, and privy councellors to the Devil, and their Government truely Diabolical, but this by the way of digression, let us thence draw this reflexion, ‖ O [37] thrice happy, ancient and honorable Tuesday Club of Annapolis! for thou flourishest under the benign Sway of the Gentle, the pacific, the mild, the merciful and the Honorable Nasifer Jole Esqr, thy Illustrious president, whom heaven preserve for ever-more, *Amen.*

We have no certain accounts of any particular Clubs before the general Deluge, tho' doubtless there were such Societies among the Antidiluvians, we meet with a dark hint of the sons of God cohabiting with the daughters of men, from whence sprung a Club or Association of Gyants, the same as is supposed, who, according to the poets attempted to dethrone Jupiter, but this account being very obscure, I leave it Just where I found it. Some Ingenious Historians have alledged, with some Show of probability, that there was an Antidiluvian Tradesman's Club, of which Tubal Cain was president, who is said to have first formed a regular Lodge of Free masons, that there was also a Club of Musicians, of which Jubal was Chief, and a Club of Bowmen and hunters over which Lamech presided.[6]

Immediatly after the Deluge, we find Noe given to Clubbing, for he plants a vinyard and drinks the Juice of the grape with his bon-companions, and gets fuddled, and this, for aught we can find from Scraps and fragments of ancient History, was the first origin of our Fuddling Clubs, and it is said, that some members drank so hard, at the first Institution of these fuddlecap Societies, that their countenances ‖ turned first florid, then purple, and at [38] last they plied it so hard, that many became black in the face with mere force of Drinking, and this, I think, more naturally accounts for the origin of the Moors and Negroes, than any other fine spun reasons that have been delivered to the Accademie Royal de Sciences,[7] or any other learned Society on Earth, who have proffered very great Rewards to the literati, to account reasonably for this strange phænomenon; and, as I look upon myself, to be the Author of this very useful Discovery, I hope the Republic of letters will allot me a handsome reward, suitable to my merit, at least I expect a medal

---

6. For a good discussion of the longstanding confusion between Jubal and Tubal-Cain and the respective clubs they founded (with passing references to Lamech as well), see volume 2 of Paul E. Beichner, *The Medieval Representative of Music, Jubal or Tubalcain?* (Notre Dame, Ind., 1954).

7. I have searched in vain for any reference to the origins of Moors and Negroes in the *Histoire de l'Académie Royale des Sciences*. However, Pierre Barrere (d. 1755), a French physician, did publish *Dissertation sur la cause physique de la couleur des Nègres* (Paris, 1741).

the above mentioned Apollo, who was none of your *Diiminorum gentium*,[4] but one of the privy Councellors of Jupiter *optimus maximus*, others laugh'd at this Assertion, and mantain that the said Apollo never trowbled his head about it, having other guess'[5] fish to fry, much Learning has been display'd in this controversy, and the parties are not yet agreed, nor never will while the world stands, as it is none of my business to dip into disputes, I shall leave every man at liberty to think of it as he pleases, nor, shall I declare my own opinion in the affair, least I should, by the opposite party be thought a very Silly fellow, and this my history be thrown aside by them, as wretched Stuff and not worth reading.

It appears that these presidents were Invested with great power and authority, and some, from ambitious views of extending that power, have tyraniz'd it in a most astonishing manner, so as to excite grumblings, discontents, Seditions, rebellions, and Infinite mischiefs in their respective Clubs, it is Inconceivable to think what havoc has been made, and what hub-bubs have been occasioned among the members of many Clubs, by the Tyrrannical and arbitrary proceedings of presidents in all ages, if any one gives himself the trowble to turn over ancient Clubical History, he will be Surprized to find the number of broken heads, bruised noses, black Eyes, dislocated Jaw bones, and bloody teeth, of many valiant members of Clubs, who have gloriously stood up, and shed their precious blood In defence of Clubical Liberty, against the Tyranny of arbitrary ‖ presidents, he will stand amazed at the number of broken Glasses, bottles, decanters, candlesticks, mugs, Juggs, platters, tobacco pipes, bowls, Sticks, cudgels, truncheons and Clubs, that have been exhibited on these melancholly occasions, not to mention the tearing of numberless coats, Jackets, Shirts and the burning of wigs.

Thus, we find, tho civil power and authority was first established for good and wise purposes, in Clubs, yet there have not been wanting wicked presidents who have abused that power, by grasping at more than what was their due, while they and their adherents, have had the Assurance to affirm, that being above Clubical Law, they were accountable to none, but were at liberty to perpetrate all manner of vilanies, and to commit all Sorts of Crimes unpunished, and all upon the Strength of their *Jure Divinoship*, derived, as they assert from the aforesaid Apollo, by which they absurdly conclude, that the Constitution of all Clubs, is theocratical, and all Presidents gods, and privy Councellors to Jupiter *optimus maximus*, because Apollo's parnassean Club was a Theocracy, and he himself a privy councel-

---

4. "Lesser gods."
5. Here and throughout the *History*, Hamilton uses *guess* in the same sense as "kind of."

probably Jolly drunken Club Companions, but this was before the Cultivation of arts and Sciences, when men were barbarous and unpolished, and, by these Clubs, it is thought, they were first Civilized, and taught the use of arts and Arms, Love, dress and the bottle, hence the members of these early Clubs were deified, and those Satyrs, were nothing but the first beaus, that appeared in wigs, with long rolld Cues, wearing also full bottomd manes, Smart Cock'd hats with feathers, high heeld Shoes &ct: &ct:—hence, the Ignorance of the age, and the wild fancy of Succeeding poets painted them like Devils, with long hair, monstrous ears, tails and Cloven feet.

We cannot possibly ascertain the time when it became customary to elect presidents in Clubs, but probably it was very early, since we find Apollo, a Celebrated ancient beau, distinguished by the Ladies for his excellent voice, in Singing of love Songs and opera airs, and also for his playing on the fiddle and flute, he had a Smattering too in Physic, having read Colepeppers *Midwifery*[2] Six times over, which art he also taught his Sister Lucina,[3] remarkable for his dexterity in handling the curling tongs, powder puff and perfume box, of an exquisite taste in || the choice of fans, necklaces, [34] tweezer cases, and other ornaments of dress, in many of which accomplishments, the present honorable president of the ancient and honorable Tuesday Club, has remarkably distinguished himself, we find, I say, this same Apollo, presiding over a female Club of Nine Muses, who met on the top of a Mountain Called Parnassus, of which Apollo, Homer and Hesiod, poets that lived nigh two thousand years agoe, talk as familiarly, as if they had been his Intimate acquaintance, tho we have reason to believe, that the said Apollo, flourished many Centuries before their time.

But, in all probability, Clubs in ancient times, when they found the Conversation become disorderly, noisy, or quarellsome, or when they observed some ambitious Spirits, grasping at power and precedence, and Inclinable to oppress and distress the members, saw it fit to chuse from among their members, some wise, discreet, venerable and awful person, to moderate in the Club, and to keep them in order, this person was distinguished by the title of *APXON, Præses, Dux,* President, and appellations of the like Signification according to the difference of Languages and Idioms. Whether these presidents from the beginning were *Jure Divino,* or by Civil Institution or appointment, has been the Subject of much dispute, the advocates for the first, have urged the divine Authority or Command || of [35]

---

2. Nicholas Culpeper (1616–1654) was the English author of numerous works on astrology and medicine, including *A Directory for Midwives* (London, [1651]).
3. The Roman goddess who presided over childbirth.

And thus having settled this great and Important point, I proceed to the next Chapter.

Chapter IV

Some Scraps of Ancient History relating to Clubs.

[32] The Cruelty of time is such, that nothing can move his pity, nothing excite his compassion, he is an universal glutton, a gormandizer of all things, he is an Anthropo-phagite or cannibal, feeding as freely upon human flesh as any thing, he is a Camelion, for he lives on the fleeting air, a Salamander, for he consumes even fire it self, that universal consumer, which he ‖ does by short snaps, as may be proved by many new experiments of electricity; nay he is an Ostridge, for he devours Iron, he is in short,— what not? and among the numberless things of which he makes garbage and waste, Empires, kingdoms, Cities, Republics, noble families, and, *O lamentabile dictu*,[1] even Clubs themselves are not exempt from his Iron teeth, for, many of these have flourished for a time and made a great Show, 'till he thought fit to gulp them up into his horrid Maw, and then were they no more heard of or mentioned, that Club, which has eluded his rage at all Seasons, is not now in being, tho' the ancient and honorable Fraternity of the Free and accepted Masons, which is a kind of ubiquitarian Club, affirm, that they have found means, from the very beginning of things, to elude his traps; but whether it really be so, is their business to prove, and none of mine to deny; my task being to rake out from the ruinous Remains of hoary antiquity, the first origin of the ancient and honorable Tuesday Club of Annapolis in Maryland, of which I have, (I hope not rashly) undertaken to pen the history.

[33] In the earliest ages of the world, it is supposed, that Clubs consisted as they do now, of Certain Select knots of men (hence the name Club, as these knock-down weapons are most commonly made of the most knotty part of the tree) ‖ that met together, either in the field, or under covert of a tent or house. It may be conjectured with some Show of probability, that the first societies of this sort, assembled in some Cave or grotto, or in some thicket or grove, hence we may derive the origin of the ancient Rural or Sylvan Deities, of Pan, the Satyrs, Bacchus, Silenus, and their followers, who were

---

1. "O sad to say."

his anvil, there follows a *reductio ad absurdum*, as the Logicians term it, for how in the name of wonder could Tubal's hammers become musical before Jubal taught them, but to cut short this Ingenious Enquiry, in order to establish this learned authors assertion for an undenyable truth, it will be necessary to suppose, that neither men, birds nor beasts, had throats, or vocal organs before Jubal's time, nor had they the power of framing Sounds, either articulate or Inarticulate, emitted up- || wards thro' the throat, or downwards thro' the anus, since some nice ears have discovered a kind of music even in the fundamental eructations, as may be seen in a learned treatise concerning the practice and theory of farting, by that Ingenious Philosopher, Don Fartinhando puffendorst.[10] Consequently, that curious Supposition, that the Language of Adam and Eve in paradise was hebrew, must fall to the ground, for, granting this Author's assertion to be true, they must have conversed only by signs, it is also necessary to suppose, that bodies before Jubals time, were not Sonorous, therefore, when struck against one another, they yielded no Sound, or at least, that Sound was not varied, so that it was the same thing to strike a bell or a drum, as if you had thumped a cushion, the emission of Sound from both, was one and the same, till Jubal gave each of them their particular and proper tone. [30]

Were I to trace the origin of these Societies called Clubs, in the same manner, as this Ingenious Author, has done that of music, I should bring myself under the same dilemma, for example, should I affirm, that Cain, by building a City in the land of Nod, was the first erector of Clubs, because, it is in towns and Cities, that those Societies are commonly held, I might in the opinion of many Superficial Critics, talk very plausibly, but to cut the matter short, and clear away all Rubs, Stumbling blocks and cavils, I will venture to say that Clubs and Clubbing, began as soon as the first men were || created, and therefore are certainly as ancient as mankind & very nigh as ancient as the Globe it self, therefore, I think, that Clubs may cope with any thing in nature for antiquity, and, were I disposed to be tedious and Impertinent to my readers, I could prove the uninterrupted Succession of Clubs, from the very beginning, down to the ancient and honorable Tuesday Club of Annapolis in Maryland, now the Club of Clubs, and the only true ancient Club upon Earth, as plainly and perspicuously, as some Roman Catholics and Nonjuring Clerks of the Church of England, have proved the uninterrupted Succession of Bishops, from the time of the Apostles, down to the hierarchy of both these Churches, which, as they both affirm, are the only true christian catholic Churches in the world. [31]

10. *The Benefit of Farting . . . Explained by Don Fartinando Puff-indorst* (London, 1722) is attributed to Jonathan Swift.

such a large Share, that he often throws his female hearers into fits, by the copious emissions thereof, which flow from him when he preaches.

The grosser Sort consists of the Spirit of wine and brandy, of Rum, Whisky and such liquors, which very often gives a philip to the former, and asists the Saints very much in their Devotions, this is what is always used in those assemblies called Clubs, and when it first rises to the Alembic of the head, it Surprizingly produces good humour, makes the dumb to talk, the morose good natured and merry, the mistuned musical, the enimy a friend, hence we find frequently after Cracking of the Second bottle in Clubs, abundance of friendship professed, a profusion of cordiality, hearty embraces, and Shakings by the hand, musical vociferations and Singing of catches, with loud peals of laughter, but when the gross fumes begin to rise, by augmenting the fire, that is, when the empty bottles are piled up by dozens, then they gradually go into Disputes, brawls, Scuffles, quarrels, 'tis *bella, horrida bella*,[8] and thence ensue broken heads, bruised bones & horrid bloody noses.

[29] Of these Societies called Clubs, there are numberless kinds, which I shall not pretend to treat of par- || ticularly, other Authors having done that before me, to much better purpose, than I, with all my Clubical learning can pretend to, and therefore, I shall directly proceed to say alittle, concerning the great antiquity of these Societies.

I have heard of a certain author, who took abundance of pains to prove the antiquity of music, and very learnedly traced it from Jubal,[9] its reputed Inventor, who, according to the Mosaic chronology, must have been born some centuries after the creation. Of consequence, for that space of time, vizt: between the Creation and the birth of Jubal at least, every thing in nature must have been mistuned, the birds could not warble or modulate, till the same Jubal taught them, or set them proper lessons, there was no melody or regular cadence in the human voice, till Jubal formed and Instituted it, even the divine Plato's harmony of the Spheres was nothing but discord till Jubal regulated their Chorus, how then will you say could Jubal discover this art of music, or from what hint, if it is affirmed that it was from the well timed Strokes and Chimings of Tubal Cain's hammers upon

---

8. "Wars, frightening wars" (Vergil, *Aeneid* 6.86).

9. Hamilton is referring to his friend Alexander Malcolm's *A Treatise of Musick, Speculative, Practical, and Historical* (Edinburgh, 1721). In chap. 14, "Of the Ancient Musick," Malcolm claims that "of all human Arts *Musick* has justest Pretences to the Honour of *Antiquity.*" Malcolm traces instrumental music back to Jubal, but, he writes, "we have sufficient Reason to believe that *Musick* was an Art long before [Jubal's] Time; since it is rational to think that *vocal Musick* was known long before *Instrumental*" (pp. 463–464). Hamilton is being intentionally difficult in interpreting his friend's argument.

pipe, with that of another, to account for this Strange, tho' true Circumstance, let us suppose, that there is some very Subtile Effluvium, or Aura, that goes from one member to another, and Communicates a titulation or pleasure to the nerves, by || setting the animal Spirits in a sort of undulatory motion, which has puzzled our Physiologists so much to account for; If any body should object to this my hypothesis, let them consider, that here I follow the example of the learned and Ingenious Doctor Cheyne, in his Elaborate treatise of health and long life,[5]—it is to be hoped tho' that the late Ingenious experiments on electricity, will give some light into this dark phênomenon, and confirm this my new hypothesis.[6] [27]

To this Invisible aura, perhaps it may be owing, that the Quakers, and those that are gifted with the Inward Spirit, feel the most violent emotions of that Spirit, when congregated in their silent meetings, especially, when the Sisters are assembled with them, for, I have by repeated observation found, that the effluvium is more pervading and active, when males and females are together, than when one or other of the Sexes, meet in separate Clubs.

I have heard a Story of a Quaker, named Aminadab Stiffrump, who was asked by a high Churchman (of consequence no friend to his Sect) how it came to pass, that the Spirit seldom or never operated so vigorously, as to set the friends to preaching and vociferating, but when they were assembled in their meetings? To which Aminadab answered and said, Verily Friend thou knowest, that one fire coal by itself will never make a fire, but put two or three together and they will burn briskly. Just so it is with the friends when separate and Congregated.

Now since I talk of the Spirit, it will be worth while to say a word or two concerning it.

It may be divided into two sorts, the Subtile and the gross, the Subtile Spirit is that exalted aura, that moves and agitates the Saints in their congregations, of this Sort, the Zealous and pious Mr George Whitefield[7] has [28]

---

5. George Cheyne (1671–1743) was a Scottish physician and mathematician whose works include *An Essay of Health and Long Life* (London, 1724; 9th ed. 1745) and *The English Malady; or, A Treatise of Nervous Diseases of All Kinds* (London, 1733).

6. A good contemporary account of the experiments of Jean Antoine Nollet, Benjamin Franklin, and others appears in *Histoire de l'Académie Royale des Sciences* (Paris, 1753), 6–39. Hamilton may also be referring to the medical applications of electricity proposed by Ebenezer Kinnersley, a club visitor (see J. A. Leo Lemay, *Ebenezer Kinnersley: Franklin's Friend* [Philadelphia, 1964], 72).

7. Whitefield (1714–1770) was an English evangelist whose dynamic oratorical style and religious zeal made him the leader of the Methodists in England and a great reviver of religious sentiment in America during the Great Awakening.

these Philosophers, the power of attraction, which we find prevails and governs very much, among men and other Animals, and occasions that great propensity in human nature, to unite and form into Clubs.

[26] In these Clubs, formed thus, by one Individual attracting another, we find that the several members are apt to ‖ communicate to each other, their own faculties and dispositions, their own sentiments and particular turn of thought, whether this is done by the perpetual flying off of thin Surfaces from one member to another, as the old philosophers used to account for vision,[3] before the discovery of optics, or, by the communication of some Imperceptible Sympathetic qualities, to speak in the clear Style of the Schools, I cannot take upon me to resolve, this being a more Intricate and difficult enquiry than perhaps most men may Imagine; I am only certain that the fact is so, that there is a particular Sympathetic Social quality in Mankind, that makes them fond of Clubbing, whether they be adapted for conversation or not; this may be undenyably proved, from the example of many moderen Clubs, which have consisted of members, who had little or no turn or talent for that Sort of conversation, that is carried on by Language or speech, or, at least, if they used Speech, it was to no better purpose, than one that says *Bo to a goose,* their whole dialogue consisting in, you've baulk'd your glass—you drink kelty[4]—put about the bowl—fill tother pipe—here's to you—pledge you—and such like short Sentences.

Is it not probable then, that the whole and Sole pleasure of such humdrum Clubs, consists in barely looking at one another, in successively kissing the Glass or bowl, or benevolently Intermixing the Smoke of one

---

the laws of universal gravitation, but certainly Newtonianism underlay much of the 18th-century commentary on the subject. If Hamilton is indeed making a specific reference to Newton, he could be recalling the passage that concludes Newton's *Principia* (1687), where Newton remarks that there is "a certain most subtle spirit which pervades . . . all gross bodies; by the force and action of which spirit the particles of bodies attract one another . . . and cohere" (*Sir Isaac Newton's Mathematical Principles,* trans. Florian Cajori [Berkeley, Calif., 1946], 547).

3. The "old philosophers" are Democritus and all the Atomists. The prevailing Scholastic view before the 18th century had been that visual perception occurred as a result of the transmission of minute bodies from the object to the eye. Aside from theories of idealism, like the Platonic, this was the only kind of explanation of sense knowledge before the understanding arose that the reflection of light was the necessary medium of vision. A good discussion of this topic is Gordon Keith Chalmers, "Effluvia, the History of a Metaphor," Modern Language Association, *Publications,* LII (1937), 1031–1050. According to Chalmers, by the 17th century the Atomists' notion of effluvia had become useful not only as an explanation of sense perception but also, as Hamilton humorously applies it in the following paragraph, "as an explanation of any action without apparent corporeal contact" (p. 1034).

4. *Bo to a goose* is a proverbial saying meaning "opening one's mouth," or, in this context, "babbling"; *kelty* is a term denoting the complete draining of a glass of liquor.

in his *Divine Legation* and other writings,[14] thro' an Infinity of windings, turnings and perplexed arguments, and a great and pompous display of historical and critical Learning, come within Sight of my point at last, but this being a copious subject, I reserve it for another Chapter, as the above named Reverend and Learned Author, has reserved the conclusion of his great and ponderous argument, for another volume or volumes, which, pray God, may come out sometime or other, to the Confusion of all Deists and freethinkers, as bulky voluminous, and verbose as the former, else we shall be most woefully left in the lurch.

Chapter III

[25]

Of Clubs in general, and their Antiquity.

By *Clubs* I mean those societies, which generally meet of an evening, either at some taveren or private house, to converse, or look at one another, smoke a pipe, drink a toast, be politic or dull, lively or frolicksome, to philosophize or triffle, argue or debate, talk over Religion, News, Scandal or bawdy, or spend the time in any other Sort of Clubical amusement. Out of this definition I expressly exclude, all your card matches and meetings, those properly belonging to the celebrated moderen assemblies called Routs and Drums,[1] which are many degrees Inferior to Clubs, as being less ancient.

It has been observed by some ancient philosophers, particularly one Sir Isaac Newton, that there exists a certain affection or fellow feeling, between all bodies in nature, by which they have a strong tendency, to approach, one towards another, to Join, and even to Incorporate, and that a perfect antipathy is never, a partial one seldom to be met with;[2] This has been called by

---

14. William Warburton (1698–1779), bishop of Gloucester, frequently engaged in theological controversy. His writings include *The Divine Legation of Moses Demonstrated* (London, 1738–1741), which argues that Moses' divine mission is implied by the very absence in Mosaic law of any reference to future life.

1. A *rout* is a fashionable gathering or assembly, evening party or reception, much in vogue in the 18th century; a *drum* is also an assembly, especially of fashionable people at a private house.

2. The analogy between the attractive power of gravitation, which governs the behavior of physical bodies, and the attractive power of love and sociability generally, which governs human conduct, was frequently drawn in the 18th century (see, e.g., George Berkeley's essay in the *Guardian*, no. 126, Aug. 5, 1713). The roots of the idea antedate Isaac Newton's discovery of

convey wealth into the treasury of Holy Church, and supply Sufficient means to mantain and support a great number of holy pamper'd priests and prelates, who take infinite pains for the Salvation of Souls, and while they Indulge in plenty, ease and Luxury (for they follow no hard labor, or any Sort of Craft or trade, by which the community might be enriched, it being expressly contrary to the wise rules of their respective orders, and Incompatible with that pious and devout life, to which they dedicate themselves, the Community being obliged to enrich them) they, out of pious fatherly love and Charity to their poor, needy, close shorn and Starving flock, put themselves in the Station of Drones in a hive, and while they devour the best honey, and the fruits of the painful labor of others, lead a lazy loitering life, for the good and Salvation of Souls, Charitably exposing themselves to

[23] damnation & perdition, like the Epicure, who enjoyed all || his good things in this life, and had his portion of bad things in the next, can any thing be more brotherly and charitable than this, and all is brought about by the virtue of these antiquated rags, and lumber & other such venerable trumpery, which a man to look at, would think worthy of nothing but the dunghill, but having once heard their virtues explained, must be rapt in admiration at the wonderful power of antiquity.

Things animate and Inanimate, that derive no manner of merit from their antiquity, are Superannuated men and women, monkeys, Cats, and such like animals, who, the more ancient they grow, are looked upon with greater contempt, nay, sometimes with hatred and abhorrence, how many deplorable Instances have we in history of old cats, old women, and old men, being looked upon as Infernal witches and Wizards, and familiars of Satan, and have therefore deservedly been delivered up to temporal tormentors, and exalted on Gibbets, drowned in water, and Consumed by raging fire.

As for Inanimate things that bear the Stamp of antiquity, an old Coat, wig, cap, Shoes, provided they do not exceed the compass of a century or

[24] two, or have never belonged to any pious Saint or eminent || Hero, they are so far from possessing any merit on account of their antiquity, that they are reckoned absolutely Infamous, and convey Shame and Contempt to their wearers and owners.

Why this should be, and for what reasons, will require more learning and Philosophy, than I am master of to determin, and therefore, I think it best to say nothing at all on the Subject, but leave it to abler pens.

I should now proceed to speak of the antiquity of Clubs, having, like the most Reverend, most learned, and most Ingenious Doctor Warburton,

ten thousand times their weight in diamonds and Gold dust, a Statue of Praxateles, a Scetch or design of Apelles, Zeuxis or Protogenes, a piece of engraving of Tubal Cain, a musical Composition of Jubal's,[12] will at any time bring an estate to the happy possessor, and pour in heaps of that Earthly Mammon, so much Coveted by Men in owr times, since by this, great honors, and all the favorite Luxuries and delecacies of life are procured, and not only so, but the man who has the good fortune to possess a *quantum Sufficit* of it, need never puzzle his brains to procure a character, by ap- || plying himself to the practice of any single virtue, or species of Industry, for this lucky circumstance alone, without the aid of qualifications mental or corporeal, will make him seemingly esteemed, respected, and really followed, flattered, caressed, and often couzened, by multitudes of his good friends, and hangers on, who get the Scent of his golden piles; Tho a Villain, he will be Called an honest and an honorable Gentleman; tho' Graceless they'll say *please your grace,* tho a blockhead and Illiterate, he'll be made to believe he is a profound Scholar, and dub'd a patron or Mecenas to the Muses, tho' ugly he will be an Adonis, and all his faults and deformities will be patterns for Imitation; In fine tho' he may deserve the gallows, he will be as safe from that quarter, as if he had the Innocence of a Lamb, while poor rogues must hang and be Damn'd for want of that same precious metal, to salve their knavery and Crimes withal, but to evade digressions and come to the point. [21]

We come now to old rotten rags, worm eaten Chips and pieces of wood, rusty nails, Jaw bones and Shank bones, perhaps honeycombed by the pox, teeth, beards, whiskers, parings of nails, Smoak tails[13] and the like, which, when once they have procured the character of having once been part || of the aparrel or body of some ancient Saint or Anchorite, Immediatly have a Superlative virtue and veneration annexed to them, have the power of working miracles, that is, of curing Incurable distempers, and even raising the dead to life, and (which is the most essential quality they possess, without which, all the rest would be good for nothing) they can [22]

---

12. Praxiteles (fl. 4th century B.C.) was an Athenian sculptor noted for his ability to depict various types of emotion. Apelles (fl. 4th century B.C.) was a famous Greek painter whose portraits included Philip, Alexander, and their circle. Zeuxis (fl. early 5th century B.C.), the Greek painter best remembered for his portrait of Helen of Troy, was said to have died laughing at his painting of an old woman. Protogenes (fl. late 4th century B.C.) was a Greek painter and sculptor whose works are characterized by their excessive elaboration. Tubal-Cain was the son of Lamech and Zillah and the "instructor of every artificer in brass and iron" (Gen. 4:22). Jubal was the son of Lamech and Adah and the "father of all such as handle the harp and organ" (Gen. 4:19–21).

13. A *smock tail* is a woman's undergarment, shift, or chemise.

the westerly wind, or any other wind you please, we should not only have a glorious breed, of gay, airy volatile fellows, and most accomplished beaus and belles, but we should find few of the fair Sex, willing to run ‖ the risque of the thraldom of matrimony, where it is Commonly reported, the Husband Carries the Sway, and rules the roast, tho' I believe in many cases, it happens Just the reverse.

There is a relation given by a Certain Arabian writer, of a horse, that belonged to one Ibrahim, an Arab, whose genealogy was traced all the way back to the Removal of Abraham and his family to Canaan,[9] having sprung in a direct line, from a Sprightly Courser in that Caravan, but, as to the qualities of this horse, good or bad, nothing is said, therefore it will now be a hard matter to determin, whether he was the better or worse as to his morals, by reason of the great antiquity of his family, and I shall not dip into this Inquiry, since my Arabian Author is Intirely silent upon that point.

The above named Abbe le Boe, tells us of a horse of the same Illustrious family, whose lineal Genealogy was traced by authentic records, for at least 500 years back.[10]

Much might be said of the antiquity of the families of monkeys, parrots, cats, dogs, hawks, and other tameable and domestic animals, but this I shall wave, having no purpose or design to swell these my observations into a bulky Volume, but only to mention Just as much as may serve my purpose, in these matters, tho' by the bye, if any of the posterity of Tobit's Dog, ‖ whose proper name has not been transmitted to us by His historiographers, or Ulysses's Dog, mentioned In the *Odyssy*,[11] could be found at this day, these two canine families would be very Ancient, and Indeed, when the honor and dignity of a family, flows from nothing else but it's antiquity, I, for my part, cannot see, why the families of Dogs, and even mites and maggots in Cheese (could records of them be handed down) might not with equal Justice claim honor on that Score, as the families of Certain rational Animals called Men.

As to Inanimate beings, it is well known, what a value they receive from their antiquity, the rust of an ancient medal, the mold of an old Stone, the powder of an old worm eaten post, are often much more valued, than

---

9. Ibrahim Pasha (fl. 16th century) was grand vizier of Turkey and a favorite of Suleiman the Magnificent, but I have not located an account of this allusion to his horse. It seems reasonable to assume, however, that Hamilton has not invented the story, since some of the most famous thoroughbreds have been named Ibrahim.

10. *Critical Reflections on Poetry, Painting, and Music*, II, 398.

11. A dog accompanies Tobias, the son of Tobit, and the angel Raphael on their journey to Ecbatana, narrated in the book of Tobit in the Apocrypha; Ulysses' dog, Argos, is mentioned with honor in the *Odyssey*, bk. 17.

learned Composers of that Authentic and Canonical Record, the *Psalter of Cashel*,⁽ᵃ⁾ ever Imagined, that any human Creature but Noe and his small family, weathered that disaster, notwithstanding the great learning, veracity, and Consistency of these Irish Poets and Historians, I am humbly of opinion, that the Indian natives of America, and the Æthiopians of Afric, tho not quite so civilized and learned a people as the ancient Irish, nor such great Saints, bid the fairest for being the most ancient and unmixed people now in the known world, and therefore have on that Score the Justest claim to honor & precedence.

It is well known, that families at all times have picqued themselves much upon their antiquity and || on that score alone have taken precedence of others, in many respects not a whit Inferior to them, the Macdonalds of Scotland, are now accounted the most ancient family there, and for that reason alone are to be honored and esteemed, by all true Scotsmen and lovers of their Country. [18]

Having thus considered the merit which those of the human Species derive from antiquity, I think it proper now to bestow a word or two upon the brute creation, who have been much valued upon this very account, we are Informed by many Authors, and among others, the Abbe le Boe, that Horses are much more valued among the Arabians, for their being of an ancient Stock or family than for many other qualities, whether it be their being adapted for the Chace, course, battle, Saddle or draught,[7] we have an account somewhere (I forget where) of certain very ancient Mares, that were Impregnated by the westerly wind, and brought forth Colts, remarkable for their Swiftness,[8] this ancient Stock was highly valued, and, let me remark by the bye, that if our women were to be so Impregnated, that is, by

---

(a) An old foolish legend, on which some Irish historians lay great Stress.[6]

6. In his history of Ireland, Keating often refers to this ancient compilation of historical, genealogical, and legal subjects, traditionally ascribed to Cormac mac Cuilenan, who died at the beginning of the 10th century; the work supposedly was lost or was carried off by the Danes (see *History of Ireland*, ed. Comyn, IV, 422; *The History of Ireland*, trans. John O'Mahony [New York, 1857], lxxiv, n. 3).

7. Jean-Baptiste (Abbé) Dubos (1670–1742) was a French historian and the author of the *Histoire critique de l'établissement de la monarchie française* (Paris, 1734) and *Réflexions critiques sur la poésie et sur la peinture* (Paris, 1719–1733), which argues that poetry can be judged only by the emotions it produces, not by fixed rules and principles. For Dubos's remarks concerning Arabians and their horses, see *Critical Reflections on Poetry, Painting, and Music*, trans. Thomas Nugent (London, 1748), II, 396–399.

8. According to Homer, Achilles' horses, Xanthus and Balius, were the offspring of Zephyrus (the west wind) and Podargé (one of the Harpies); Homer also mentions other divine horses, bred by the north wind on mortal mares grazing in the meadows before Troy (*Iliad*, bks. 16 and 20).

[16] claim to antiquity any farther back, than the Incursions of the Goths, Vandals, Tartars, Huns, Lombards and Sarazens into these countries, Greece and Italy are now Inhabited by a mungrell people Intirely || differing in language and manners, from their ancient Inhabitants, heroes and worthies, as consisting now chiefly of Slaves, peasants, Dervises, Fiddlers, rope dancers, pantomimes, Singers and Idle overgrown loitering priests, much the same may be said of Germany, France and Spain, &ct: The Islanders to the westward, or the Irish, Scots highlanders and Welsh, are those who have the best claim for Antiquity among the Europeans, and they picque themselves much on their antiquity, and the great honor and dignity they derive therefrom, and Surely it is a very honorable thing and what they have great reason to be proud of; But the Irish excell all in their Chronology, for, it appears from their Authors, transcribed faithfully, by that accurate and Learned Historian, Doctor Keating, that a colony settled in that ancient Island, long before the General Deluge, for two of Cains Daughters landed there, of whom a certain Irish poet of great Credit and authority sings thus.[5]

> Tri hingiona Chaid hin Chain mar aon
>   is Seth Mac Adhaimh,
> Ad chonaire Banba ar uus as
>   Meabhair liom aniom thus.

> The two fair Daughters of the Cursed Cain
> And Seth the Son of Adam first beheld
> The Isle of Banba.(*)   (*)Ireland

[17] Some other Antidiluvian Settlers in that ancient Island, it is said, had the luck to escape that great calamity of the General Deluge, which is most wonderful, and can be accounted for no other way than thus; as that Island has been called, time out of mind, the Island of Saints, probably these were such Saints as could by their Sanctity save that Island from the general disaster, as a few Saints, according to holy writ, could have saved the Cities of Sodom and Gomorrah, from being consumed by fire, however, I believe none, but the aforesaid Authors of the Ingenious Doctor Keating, and the

---

5. Geoffrey Keating (1570?–1644?) was an Irish writer and priest whose most important work was a history of Ireland from the earliest times to the English invasion, *Foras feasa ar Eirinn* (Foundation of knowledge on Ireland [1629]), which was written in the Irish language and borrowed heavily from popular Irish folklore and poetry. Hamilton loosely transcribes and translates Keating's Gaelic, which more literally means: "Three virgin daughters of Cain, / With Seth, son of Adam, / They first saw Banbha, / I remember their adventure" (*The History of Ireland,* ed. David Comyn [London, 1902–1914], I, 138–139).

The City of Jerusalem, which we may reckon the most ancient city now in being, (as Babylon is no more) unless we admit the monstrous Chronology of the Chinese, is not only venerable for its antiquity, but is to be reckoned in the foremost rank, as being a holy City, which sets it in a point of view above all others, for holy ‖ things as well as holy men, (I mean men of the holy Cloth) are always to have the preference, else whence comes it that Churches and Chapels are made Sanctuaries for knaves and Villains and assasins, but because they are Sacred Ædifices and the ground on which they stand is holy, in the same manner we find that his holiness the pope, is exalted one or two degrees above human nature, nay often equaled to Almighty God, and takes place of all Catholic princes on Earth, and even in England, a reformed Country, his grace the Archbishop of Canterbury, tho' he gives place to the king out of mere Civility, yet takes the Right hand and precedence of all the peers in England—Therefore it is, that Jerusalem, an ancient holy City, has cost such Seas of Christian and Infidel blood, for as to wealth, magnificence or extent, it is not to be named among Cities of the fifth or Sixth Class. The Epithet holy adds a Character and lustre to many things as well as to Cities; but how Cities, Stone walls, bricks, planks, or any other kind of dead matter, can with any propriety be stiled holy, is not my business to enquire, I leave that therefore to our Learned Divines. [14]

The City of Athens, which retains it's name & pritty nigh its ancient place to this day, is now notwithstanding its great antiquity, sunk into obscurity, and is of no note or character, being Inhabited by a parcel of Servile drudges, and Ignorant peasants, Infinitely ‖ short of the Spirit, learning and valor of its ancient Inhabitants. [15]

The City of Rome, of old, the mistress of the world, Tho it was founded by a parcel of Banditti, and Inhabited by the valiant cutthroats of all the nations round her, yet, is venerable, and honorable, on account of her antiquity, and is now also classed among the holy Cities, as being the Residence of our holy father the Pope, and many other holy prelates and priests, who enjoy great wealth in a spiritual capacity, who share the patrimony of the poor fisherman among them, who understand good living perfectly well, and how to carry on their Spiritual merchandize, and bring it to the best market, as to their knowledge and abilities in other matters, belonging to their holy function, it is none of my business here to dwell upon them, being Intirely foreign to my Subject.

Many nations have laid a great Stress upon their antiquity, and reckoned it a badge of honour, there are none of our Nations now on the European Continent Southward of Lapland and Greenland, or in the Greatest part of Asia westward of mount Taurus or Imaus, That can lay

(who perhaps know nothing of the matter) that, the main Excellence of their Constitution, and principal Cause of their Antiquity rests on their admirable Talent at keeping a Secret.

[12] Now, permit me a word or two relating to the honor conveyd to families by antiquity. We find the || scots, welsh, Irish and Spaniards, the most noted people for antiquity of families, and every one knows, who has read their Histories, that they were anciently divided into families and Clans, and over each Clan, there reigned an absolute petty prince, called the Chief of the Clan, poor enough in every thing but honor & Ancient pedigree, who was by trade a Butcher, and his Subjects or vassals, might properly be called his bull dogs, (I must here be understood metaphorically, for those princes had too much honor and Noble blood in them, to apply their thoughts or diligence, to any low mechanic Craft) these warlike Clans, used to pelt one another continually, and every butcher, and every bull dog, had a greater or smaller proportion of honor, according to the numbers he had worried or butchered. Those families then, that escaped total extirpation, during this general hurly-burly, stood the most ancient in the heralds list, and, as their antiquity exhibited a glaring proof of their Superior Valor, and military Skill, it must necessarily follow, that as they centered all honor, in this Sort of butchering trade, These surviving ancient families were with great reason esteemed the most honorable, hence, we find, in these our degenerate days, that the great Representatives of these ancient families,

[13] always take the right hand, the door the wall || and the road, of our upstarts of a Later date, tho' loaded with more dignified titles, and hence, we find, that these honorable people the Spaniards, are to this day so fond of Bull fighting and assasinating, the British of Bull and bear baiting, Stage and Cock fighting, and the Irish of your great overgrown bulls. Duelling is indeed a more polite and Gentleman like manner of Butchering, Introduced by our Beaus and petti maitres of the last Century.

II As for exceptions to this general rule, which is the Second part of this enquiry, they shall be cleared up as I go along.

If these above delivered, be not the true reasons why antiquity, has given precedence to Nations, Cities, tribes, families and Clubs, I must own, I can give no better to satisfy those who may question their validity; this reason only I have still in reserve, which they may accept or reject as they please, vizt: that they are of greater antiquity than others, and therefore are Justly entituled to the preference.

History, see Robert Micklus, "The Secret Fall of Freemasonry in Dr. Alexander Hamilton's *The History of the Tuesday Club,*" in *Deism, Masonry, and the Enlightenment: Essays Honoring Alfred Owen Aldridge,* ed. J. A. Leo Lemay (Newark, Del., 1987), 127–136.

to themselves glory, and to found great Empires and states, on the Ruins, calamities and distresses of little petty kingdoms, which Empires and states in time, became very ancient, and therefore very honorable and venerable. We find few or none of these great states and Empires, laying the foundation of their fame and honor, upon the aforesaid stale props called the moral virtues, Some small Inconsiderable States indeed, we find setting a Value upon these, the Spartan common wealth rested for a few Centuries upon such weak Supports, bequeathed, and as it were palm'd upon them by an old doating Lawgiver called Licurgus,[3] but finding that by the virtue of these wise Laws, as some called them, they could not subdue Greece and were at the same time forced to resist the temptation of amassing riches by hostile Spoils, they violated their Sanguinary Law against such as should possess gold or Silver money, and finding they could follow this Laudable practice with Impunity, the old foolish regulations were kick'd out of doors, their little political fabric fell to the ground, and having changed their ponderous and Cumbersome Iron money, for precious Gold and Silver, they at the same time bartered their temperance for excess, their Integrity and Simplicity for cunning and fraud, Their Justice for oppression and Iniquity, their plainness and humility for Luxury and pride, and by these laudable pursuits, became at last Ill- || ustrious slaves to Philip of Macedon, [11] and his mad-cap Son Alexander, called the Great, and Succeeding Eminent Tyrants; The same fate had the Athenian State, the same had the Roman Republic; They all found these supports too weak, and therefore had recourse to more Certain ways, and means, such as cutting of throats, burning, plundering, slaying, masacring and extirpating whole Nations, proscribing their own Citizens, and killing them up, like Sheep in a pen, by hundreds and by thousands, whereby the Strongest was at last Sure of engrossing all the power to themselves, amassing great treasure, and from this opulence sprung their permanency, Grandure, power and honor.

As for Clubs, the honor which they derive from Antiquity, evidently arises from this; that their Constitution and oeconomy must be founded upon very Solid and Sound maxims, rules and Laws, by which only they have preserved their being thro' a long tract of time, and enjoyed an uninterrupted Succession of presidents, a glaring Instance of which, I hope, soon to make appear, in the course of this our History. As for that ancient and honorable Club, the Free and Accepted Masons,[4] many are of opinion,

---

3. Lycurgus was the traditional founder (probably fl. 9th century B.C.) of Sparta's constitution and social and military systems, and consequently of the "good order" they created.

4. Hamilton was Grand Master of the Annapolis Freemasons, and other club members also belonged. Many of his apparent jibes at the Freemasons throughout the *History* are obviously more affectionate than malicious. For a discussion of Hamilton's use of Freemasonry in the

the first confining themselves to the narrow Compass of the Mosaic history, the last restricting themselves to no Compass at all.

Now, since it is generally agreed, that antiquity Carries with it a certain dignity and excellence, it will be worth while to enquire

I Upon what this Dignity and excellence is founded, and

II To consider, whether or not there be some exceptions to this general rule, that antiquity Carries honor and Dignity along with it. That is, if [9] there are not some || beings in nature both of the animate and Inanimate Class, that are rather depreciated by their antiquity, and therefore neglected scorned and undervalued.

I As to our first enquiry, upon what the merit and Dignity of Antiquity is founded, we may say, that antiquity claims, or rather exacts respect, on account of its hoary and venerable aspect. Ancient Nations, Clubs and families are respectable, because they could not thro' so many centuries have mantained an uninterrupted Succession, from father to Son, from president to president, and from Generation to generation, unless they possessed in themselves some Glaring excellencies by which they outshone and at last eclipsed other Nations Clubs and families, or were concerned in some great and heroic actions, which spread their name abroad, and handed down their glory to Succeeding ages. But let us examine alittle of what nature these actions were, upon which this merit was founded. We find many ancient nations, supporting and aggrandizing themselves, by the bold and valorous actions of their Heroes and warlike Spirits, these Illustrious Banditti, used to range the face of this globe without controul, plundering, knocking on the head, burning, hewing to pieces and extirpating, the helpless and forlorn of their own Species, what Glory, what renown, was not acquired by our Cyruses, Alexanders, Cæsars, Pompeys, Scipios, [10] Annibals, || Tameralanes, Osman's, Solyman's[2] and a hundred others, who made it their constant practice to scour the earth, Sword in hand, to acquire

---

History of China, Containing a Description of the Most Considerable Particulars of That Vast Empire (London, 1688); see especially chap. 3, "Of the Antiquity of the Kingdom of China, and What a High Opinion the Chineses Have of It." Hamilton is perhaps recalling this account, which establishes the precedence of Chinese antiquity, but he is apparently directly referring to a more contemporary account that I have not located.

2. Cyrus the Great (ca. 600–529 B.C.) was the founder of the Persian empire. Scipio Africanus (236–184/183 B.C.) was a great Roman general who helped establish Rome's domination in Spain, Africa, and the Hellenistic East. Hannibal (247–183 B.C.) was the great Carthaginian general. Tamerlane, or Timur-Leng ("Timur the Lame"), ca. 1336–1405, the famous descendant of Genghis Khan, ruled by terror and desolation over parts of Turkestan, Siberia, Persia, and India. Osman I (1259–1326), the founder of the Ottoman Empire, conquered northwestern Asia Minor and assumed the title of emir (ca. 1299). Suleiman I, the Magnificent (1494–1566), was a Turkish ruler who reformed the administration of his country and added Belgrade, Budapest, Baghdad, Algiers, and other territories to his empire.

Itch, would vellicate in a dreadful manner, the Tender plicæ of the Rectum, where it terminates in the anus; and here I shall terminate this Chapter, lest I vellicate the ears of my reader by talking too much in my own praise.

Chapter II

Of Antiquity, It's dignity and Importance.

[7]

 Among other things of great value and Significancy, to which my brethren Historians, by general Consent have given the preference, as communicating a Certain lusture and Dignity, to Nations, persons and things, to which they are accidentally annexed, that of Antiquity holds the foremost Rank.

 From this position, which certainly no man in his senses will presume to deny, may be clearly prov'd, the Dignity, grandure, worth and excellency of that Club, of which I now Compile the History, since it can be made evident, by authentic Records, that it is as ancient as Time itself.

 Wealth, a royal or noble birth, offices of honor, titles and dignities, in all polite Societies have a Certain fixed value, and may be called excellencies of the first Class; Honesty, truth, Candor, Charity, Humanity, Piety, and such other Scholastic terms, which your Venders of Ethics call moral virtues, are of a fluctuating nature, having sometimes a modicum of worth, at other times no worth at all Annexed to them, according as they tally or Correspond with the prevailing modes of the times in || which they make their appearance, these are of the Second Class, their Intrinsic worth being very hard to be ascertained by our polite modern Connoiseurs.

[8]

 But still at all times and in all Circumstances, Antiquity Carries with it a certain value, and takes place of every thing else, being an Inestimable prize, for which Historians in all ages have eagerly contended, each aledging and mantaining that his own Nation has the Justest claim to it. Among the Ancients, the Ægyptians and Scithians Contended long for the precedence in point of Antiquity, and I cannot find that the Dispute was ever determined in favor of either party; the Chief modern disputants on this point, are the Irish, British and Spaniards of Old Castile, Aragon and Leon, but the Chinese Chronology, lately struck in, and outdid them all,[1]

---

1. Travel accounts of China were plentiful in the latter 17th and early 18th centuries, but the one that most thoroughly discusses Chinese chronology is Gabriel de Magaillans, *A New*

Pindar, Æschylus, Virgil and other ancient poets, there being in this work, abundance of poetical flowers, and noble flights, which by the bye, I must honestly own, to be Sprouts of the Luxuriant Genius of Jonathan Grog Esqr, poet Laureat to that ancient and honorable Club, of which I now Collect the History. These great, these Invaluable advantages, I shall Enjoy, as being Historiographer, to the most Honorable Mr President Jole, some degrees I hope, above those celebrated authors, who have penned the Histories of *Tom Thumb, Jack and the Gyants* & || *the wise men of Gotham,*[4] and a hundred degrees above our moderen french Romance compilers, to read whose works, is enough to give any Christian the Spleen, such as the Authors of the *Grand Cyrus, Clelia, Almahyde, Amadis de Gaul, Amadis de Grece, Don Bellianis, Cassandra, Cleopatra*[5] and a hundred other such voluminous writers, to whom not (to say) only the Tobacconists and spice Shops, but even the Houses of office, have been of late years so Infinitely Indebted, who, had they not been supplied from these vast piles of waste paper, would have been at a Sad loss how to wrap up their grocery and haberdashery, and besides, many honest well meaning Christians, must have run the risque of befowling their fingers, in using the tender leaves of vegetables, which are not of so tough a nature, as that same other Historical Stuff is, besides the risque they must have run, of getting that most grievous distemper called the piles, by means of the Corrosive down that often abounds upon the leaves of the said vegetables, which like so much low

---

35 B.C.) was the Roman senator and historian especially remembered for his history of the conspiracy of Catiline. Livy (59 B.C.–A.D. 17) was the Roman historian whose massive history of Rome ranges from the foundation of the city to the death of Drusus in 9 B.C.

4. Although Hamilton was surely aware of Henry Fielding's burlesque play, *Tom Thumb, a Tragedy* (1730), the context here suggests that he is referring to the famous nursery tale. *Jack the Giant-killer* is another famous nursery tale. By "the wise men of Gotham" Hamilton is probably referring to the *Merrie Tales of the Mad Men of Gotam by A. B.* (possibly Andrew Boorde [ca. 1490–1549], a physician). This collection of tales concerns Gotham, a village in Nottinghamshire, whose inhabitants acquired a reputation for folly, perhaps as a result of an actual incident in which they feigned idiocy to prevent King John's displeasure.

5. The first three titles were written by Madeleine de Scudéry (1607–1701), prolific author of French romances. *Artamène; ou, Le grand Cyrus* (1649–1653) deals with the love of Cyrus, grandson to the king of Media, for Mandane; *Clélie* (1654–1660) concerns the Clelia who escaped the power of Porsenna by swimming the Tiber; and *Almahide* (1660) is a story of the Moors in Spain. For *Amadís de Gaula,* see p. iin, above; *Amadís de Grecia* (1530), by Feliciano da Silva (fl. 16th century), is a Spanish sequel to *Amadís de Gaula;* and *Don Bellianis* (which Hamilton later refers to as Don Bellianis of Greece) is probably a reference to *The Honour of Chivalrie* (1598), the story of Prince Don Bellianis and his love for the Princess Florisbella. *Cassandre* and *Cléopâtre* were written by Gauthier de Costes de La Calprenède (1614–1663), French author of several lengthy romances. *Cassandre* (1644–1650) concerns the daughter of Darius and wife of Alexander; *Cléopâtre* (1647–1656) involves a supposed daughter of Antony's Cleopatra.

Ragoos, fricassies, anduilles, amulets, Solomongundies,¹ and the like. The first kind of Cookery breeds as many crudities in the Intellect of the readers, as the other does in the Stomachs and habits of the eaters.

The History which I am now about to present to your worships, is none of your vamped up Frenchified pieces of Cookery, it is a Solid and Serious performance, plain and homely, and withal true, every article thereof, being copied exactly from nature and the life, and yet, Simple and true as it is, I shall be bold to affirm, that it contains as great a variety, and as many Surprizing and unaccountable events, as any true history that ever yet appeared, and, the Characters of the eminent persons therein concerned, are so nicely ‖ touched, as to strike at first view, and excite in the mind of [5] the Reader, the Idea of a well executed piece of painting, in it self so highly picturesque, as to force the attention and admiration of all that view it.

While I am penning these prologomena, to this most excellent history, my genius and parts, are not alittle furbished up, sharpened and exalted, by the delightful prospect, of procuring to myself thereby Immortal fame, and a lasting Character, to be transmitted to future ages,(a) and Indeed it gives me no small pleasure to reflect, that a thousand years hence, I shall share the same rank of honor, with Herodotus, Diodorus Siculus, and Halicarnasseus, Xenophon, Plutarch, Justin, Trogus, Polybius, Cæsar, Tacitus, Salust and Livy,³ as also I shall stand in the same degree with Homer, Hesiod,

---

(a) Vide, *Life of Colley Cibber*, written by himself.²

1. *Andouilles* are hog's guts stuffed with other entrails, cut into small pieces, and seasoned with pepper and salt; *salmagundies* are composed of chopped meat, anchovies, eggs, onions, oil, and condiments.

2. Hamilton is probably alluding to the following remarks Cibber addresses to Alexander Pope: "You may ask me, why I give myself all this Trouble? Is it for Fame or Profit to myself, or Use or Delight to others? For all these Considerations I have neither Fondness nor Indifference" (*An Apology for the Life of Colley Cibber*, ed. B.R.S. Fone [Ann Arbor, Mich., 1968], 6–7).

3. Herodotus (ca. 480–ca. 425 B.C.) was the famous Greek historian known as the "Father of History." Diodorus Siculus was a Roman historian who flourished under Caesar and Augustus until at least 21 B.C. and wrote a world history in 40 books, from the beginnings of history to Caesar's Gallic War. Dionysius of Halicarnassus (fl. ca. 25 B.C.) was a Greek literary critic and historian who lived in Rome during Augustus's reign. Xenophon (ca. 427/428–ca. 354 B.C.) was the Greek philosopher and historian remembered as one of the most prolific writers of antiquity. Plutarch (before A.D. 50–after 120) was the Greek biographer and moral philosopher especially remembered for his *Lives* of 46 Greeks and Romans. Pompeius Trogus was the Augustan historian noted for a universal history, *Historiae philippicae*, coming down to us only in the abridgment of Marcus Junianus Justinus of the 3d century. Polybius (ca. 200–after 118 B.C.) was the Greek historian of the rise of Rome to world power. Tacitus (ca. A.D. 56–ca. 117) was the Roman historian best remembered for his *Germania*, a description of the Germanic peoples and their origins, *Agricola*, an account of the Roman conquest of Britain, and *Annals*, a review of the period from the death of Augustus to the death of Nero. Sallust (probably 86–

and like Slovenly cooks neglect the proper and decent seasoning of apposite remarks and observations, others Indulge too great a Luxuriance of Stile, and stepping out of their rank, turn poets, some will be too Superstitious and credulous, others too Sceptical, and in fine the far greatest part, if not the whole herd, will have a wicked or rather Senseless byass to a party.

I am not now to dwell upon Historical writings in the Stile of a panegyrist; That, as I apprehend, being not only foreign to my purpose, but a task for which I am by no means equal, tho honored at present, with the office of Orator, to that ancient ‖ and honorable Club, of which I am now to collect the history. I may perhaps be allowed, without vanity, some small talent in declaiming, in praise of Illustrious personages, as the Honorable Nasifer Jole Esqr, president of the aforesaid ancient and honorable Club, but to expatiate in praise of history, or any such extensive, and Complicated Subject, is beyond my province.

As good eating and drinking serve to nourish the body, so good reading and study Invigorate the mind. Among the various viands, which are cooked in our Literary kitchens, where Learned authors are the Cooks, I take History to be a dish, when dressed clean and plain, of all others the most Substantial and nourishing, and can be compar'd to nothing so aptly as to a Sirloin of Good Roast beef, served up in it's own gravie, with a plain pudding, if you please, but without any addition of pickles, or adulterated and Sophisticated Sauces, which confound and spoil the natural relish of the meat, and rob it of its nutritive and Salutary Virtues, allow me here to compare the gravie and pudding to useful and Solid reflections, and the pickles and Sophisticated Sauces, to party Scurrilities, palpable falshoods, mean Subterfuges, and poetical bumbast or Impertinent fustian, relished only by vitiated palats.

Histories founded upon truth, and wrote in a plain, easie and natural Stile, are Sirloins of beef plainly dressed, wholesome, hearty and nourishing ‖ to a robust and healthy Stomach, but those erected upon fiction, and stuffed with Bombast and fustian phrazes, are vapid, windy, unwholsom and adulterated with your damn'd sauces and pickles, fitted only for crazy and luxurious apetites, which require a Spur to excite them to a proper pitch, and are apt to breed worms, maggots and monstruous Crudities, in the brains and Intelects of such students as feed upon them. Such are Romances, novels, fairy tales, Love adventures, private, or Secret memoirs of Courts, and persons of Quality of both Sexes, and other such verbose trumpery, with which the french Artists have crouded our Libraries, as their Cooks have confounded our kitchens and loaded our tables, with Devilish

The History of the Ancient and Honorable Tuesday Club

[1]

Book I

From the earliest ages, to the Transmigration of the Club to America, and the foundation of the Red-house Club, of Annapolis in Maryland.

Chapter I

Of History and Historians.

History has always been classed among the most useful and Instructive writing. Hence Historians, among the numerous herd of writers, are deservedly honored and esteemed.

Various are the Subjects of History, The transactions of Empires, kingdoms, Republics and *Clubs,* yield an Inexhaustible fund of matter, not to mention the atchievments of great men and Presidents, a Sort of History Called Biography, in which many incidents relative to the public are Interwoven.

Yet notwithstanding this great variety of Subjects, and redundancy of matter, which the various Scenes around us afford for History, we find that good Historians are very thinly sown; which I cannot account for in a more plausible manner, than that the talents necessary to produce a good Historian, are so many and so great, that it is a rare thing to find one man possessed of them all, or even a moderate portion of them. Some wanting Judgement and Invention of their own, copy too Slavishly from others & are not masters of a proper stile and expression, some confide too much in common rumor, others are too strictly attached to what they call truth and demonstration, some are only dry drivelling narraters of Incidents and facts,

[2]

to Season the following history with such apposite observations and remarks, upon such Incidents, as were worth observing and remarking upon, so, that I hope, my Readers, if any there be, may Gather some Instructions from them, if so, my reward is Sufficient, but if none will be at the pains to read these historical Collections, which may be the case for aught I know, I am satisfied, and quite easy about the matter, they may, and will do, Just as they please, nay, even should they apply these Labored papers, to wipe a part wch decency forbids me to name, I shall not Care one single farthing, and nevertheless, shall sleep as Sound as usual, Remembering that golden Maxim of Epictetus, never to make myself, over Solicitous or uneasy, about matters that are Intirely in the power of another, and altogether out of my own reach or command.[8]

---

8. See Epictetus, *Moral Discourses,* bk. 1, chap. 1, "Of the Things Which Are, and of Those Which Are Not, in Our Power."

The Preface

cannot plead its own Cause, it deserves no advocate, every trevat ought ‖ to [xii] stand upon its own legs, and every tub upon its own bottom, if this History has no bottom or legs to stand upon, e'en let it tumble down a gods name.

 Histories are no farther Instructive, than as they display to us human nature in a true picture, & as a picture is not compleat, without the Coloring and Shading, to fill up the design or outlines, so history is not compleat, without proper observations remarks and reflections, Interspersed or Interlarded with the bare Narration of facts, which last I take to be the Outlines or Sketch of the historical picture, and the other the Shading or coloring, which raises and Emboldens it, and makes it more forceibly strike the eye, the more then of these observations and remarks are disseminated in a historical piece, the more Instructing it becomes to the understanding of the reader, and Indeed, as to the bare narration of facts and occurrences, there is really but a trifling difference between the histories of the smallest Clubs, and those of the greatest Empires and kingdoms, we find in the latter, a parcel of mortals, denominated Emperors, kings, potentates and princes, contending and scrambling, about little parcels and portions of this terrestrial ball, we find State politicians racking their Invention to bring about Certain Schemes, and still, like a parcel of earth moles, Countermining and undermining one another, we find generals, or rather licenced banditti, leading forth great armies, pillaging & laying ‖ waste vast coun- [xiii] tries, burning towns and cutting throats, and all to acquire for themselves or masters, a certain perishing power, eminence and grandure, or Certain Sonorous titles, we find grand and grave councils and Senats in deep Consultation, about things that are as plain and Self evident, as that two and two make four, and In fine we find the whole world in an uproar, about certain matters in themselves, abstractedly of a very mean Consideration, and of a perishing transitory Nature, can any thing worse be said of these trivial Transactions, that are to be met with in Clubs, whose members being men, (tho esteemed in a Lower rank in life) have the very same affections and passions, with those mortals called the great, and go upon pursuits and Schemes of a parallel and like Insignificant and ridiculous Nature, for the bringing about purposes equally vain and transitory, tho under a different Class and denomination.

 If Histories of Nations and kingdoms then, are only capable to Instruct, in so far as they Justly point out the passions Incident to human Nature, and their effects, and exhibit a general Character of Mankind, and, in so far as they are Salted and Seasoned, with useful Remarks and observations, I hope the same may be allowed to the Histories of Clubs, ‖ which [xiv] are composed of men, as well as greater Societies, I have done my utmost,

Rational, Intellectual and Gelastic[4] faculties, when you, and twenty other such Loggerheads as you, who pretend to call me to account for it, have been exercising the keenest acumen of your obtuse thoughts upon a game at whist, piquet, Cribbage, put or all fours,[5] and stocking the *Sensorium Commune* with a rabble of black and Red Spots, called Spades, Clubs, harts and Diamonds, while you have been gazing and gaping at a Sign post, bawling at a boxing match or Cock pit, sotting in an alehouse or Tavern, over trite Sophisticated and Stupifying Conversation, and more Sophisticated and Stupifying liquor, while you have been nodding over a Silly news paper, funking abominable mundungus,[6] scalding your guts with politic Coffee, or Listening to hawkers ballad, while you have been fumbling and tumbling a whore in a bagnio, gaping at Henlys Nonsense,[7] or taking an afternoons nap, after having spent two hours more than what was necessary in beastly cramming, while you have been talking away the precious hours, about fiddlers, fools and farces, handing about the bumpers, drinking of [xia] bawdy || toasts, and singing obscene Songs, while you have been reading of smutty books, and luscious ballads, triffling at a tea table, or playing the fool at a great man's levee, or, if you Employ any thought at all about these, your paltry amusements and pastimes, 'tis perhaps how to dress and deck out your mortal Clay, to entrap the Ladies, how to ensnare the virtue and Innocence of some Simple girl, how to erect a character upon the ruins of your neighbour's, how to live upon and get drunk at other peoples expence, how to tell a plausible lie to promote your own Interest, and how, for the same noble and generous view, to circumvent your neighbour, in a bargain, or in short any other Idle or vicious occupation, which requires a deal of low Cunning, but little thought. Now, I would Seriously ask you, which of us have been employed to the best purpose, you, in these triffling pastimes, and wicked and pernicious Schemes, which, upon a Strict examination, you'll find, Consume much the greatest part of your time, or I, in writing this (as you call it) Silly history; I believe upon a due Scrutiny I shall have the advantage of you, as my employment has been in it Self at least Indifferent and harmless, whereas yours must turn out to be prejudicial both to yourselves and others.

As to this History, it needs no apology, let it speak for it self, if it

---

4. *Gelastic,* meaning "risible," stems from the Greek "to laugh."

5. *Put* is a card game for two, three, or four players, resembling Nap, three cards being dealt to each player; *All Fours* is a card game for two players, and so named from the four particulars by which it is reckoned (High, Low, Jack, and Game).

6. *Funking abominable mundungus* means "smoking raunchy tobacco."

7. John Henley (1692–1756), or Orator Henley, contributed to the *Spectator* as "Dr. Quir" and published numerous works on oratory, theology, and grammar.

The Preface

chip in porridge² amusements, should be Invented and Introduced, to keep at least three fourths, of what we presume to call the rational world awake, and the Remaining fourth out of mischief.

Some people, who may find time enough to throw away in reading of this, will undoubtedly exclaim, Well! and what the Deuce is the meaning of these grave observations? I'll tell them In short what they mean; Many, I am satisfied, will either be mightily astonished, or pretend to be so, that any Mortal Wight, could waste, as they Call it, so much precious time, besides paper and ink, in compiling and Collecting, the History of, (as it may seem to them) a Ridiculous Club, whose chief pastime (they'll say) appears from the face of the History it self, and from the Grotesque Stile of its Idle Author, to have been the carrying on, a Silly, Stupid and unmeaning farce. Very well, my good friends, what if I should grant you all this, since you are pleased to assert it, the Subject of this History is a farce, and a very Silly one too, since you will needs have it so, I will not Indeed so easily grant you that it is an unmeaning one, since it bears an exact resemblance to many other farces in human life, esteemed (tho they are not really so) of a more Serious nature, I will grant you too, that I the Compiler, am more Silly if possible in collecting the history of this arrant farce, than any of the members of that ridiculous and foolish Club, (as you esteem it,) in acting of it, and I have squandered a deal of precious time, Ink and paper, besides fire and Candle, in the Compiling of it, *Iamque opus exegi nugosum, oleumq3 perdidi*,³ Now, when all this is granted, Let us examine how I, the Compiler, of this here farcical history, differ from other men, with regard to the Importance and utility of my painful Labors to others and myself, and, how this, as a history, differs from other Histories, with regard to its Subject and Contents. [xi]

If I have laid out much time in writing of these triffles, as you call them, pray, have not you and many others as wise as either you or I, that is, in their own Conceit, laid out an equivalent of time, upon equivalent, if not greater triffles, only with this difference, that this triffling Scribble of mine, required some thought and application, and your triffling Occupations require no thought at all, at least none worthy of a rational being, for the very pursuit of them is directly repugnant to thought and reflec- tion, and proceeds originally from a privation of both. Have I not been poring reading studying and turning over Ancient Authors, and modern wits, in the composition of this History, to the great Solace and Improvement of my [xa]

---

2. A *chip in porridge* is a matter of no importance; here, trivial amusements.
3. "Now I have performed a trifling work, and wasted my oil."

[viii] # The Preface

Nothing more Common in every man's mouth than That time is precious, and therefore ought to be well husbanded, and yet, precious as this time is, we meet with but few, who are nigh so careful about saving it, as about saving their money, since we see it often squandered away, in foolish, vapid, tasteless, foppish and Impertinent conversation, and, that even among such people, as have the Assurance to call themselves men of taste, we find it also lavished, in Silly unimproving and Childish diversions and amusements.—How many for Instance, sleep one half of their time and dream the other half? how many follow Chimerical and Romantic pursuits, and gallop full Speed after a Shifting Cloud, how many plod and plod on from day to day, and do nothing but build Castles in the Air, how many are Entertained with a tooth pick, a Shuttle cock and battle door,[1] a pair of dice, a Cup and ball, a game Cock, a pair of Cudgels and foiles, a Race horse, a fiddle, a bagpipe, a french horn, a ring of bells and a pack of Cards, [ix] for much the ‖ greatest part of their time, and triffle thro' a triffling life, in a promiscuous multitude and medley of triffles,—But 'tis well we have these toys to amuse the great Babies of the Age, and keep them out of mischief, to which it is the nature of children to be prone,—These serve to keep our human puppies and kittens in play, for, were it not for these curious Inventions, very properly called time killers, they would, after running alittle round and Round in pursuit of their own tails, or perhaps the tails of others, drop asleep, for want of a proper Stock of Consistent Ideas, to employ the mind, which being a very busy and active principle, cannot be a moment without some Subject to work upon, for, should it ever be in this Idle Situation, it Immediatly drops its clog the body, for a space, and retires to the Inner chambers of the brain, hence, we find, all such Animals, as have not their Intellectual Chambers well furnished, pass a very large portion of their time in Sleep, this is a Sure Criterion, by which we may know to what degree of propinquity, the Rational approaches to the brutal nature, for all Philosophers have allowed the latter but a small Stock of Ideas, and these [x] very Simple, it was therefore highly ‖ expedient, that many bawbles and

---

1. A *battledore* is the racket used in badminton.

same honest open Candid and pure Stile as I talk of his honor the President and his Longstanding members in the Subsequent History, It is true, I might, had I thought || fit, have Ennumerated your good qualities as an attorney General, profoundly versed in the *Corpus Juris Clubicalis,* might have Extolld your gravity, Depth of Judgement, eloquence, Elocution, Erudition, probity and undaunted perseverance, in doing the duties of Your great and honorable office, to this I *dares* to say you would have had no *Animosity,* and it would have done all very well, and perhaps a Couple of pages of this Stuff, tho *Judgematically* executed, might have lulled every reader (except you and I) asleep, for, it is to be supposed, that Self love, natural to us both, as creatures of the human Species, might have Counteracted the Hypnotic quality of the Stuff; But then Good Sir let me ask you Seriously, if I should not by this means have brought myself upon a *Precipe?* for would it have been fair dealing with the world to paint out all your excellencies and good qualities, in a Clubical Capacity, without also giving an Impartial Account, and putting you in mind of a few little foibles (I mean Clubical ones) which all who know you, allow you to be possessed of, and I am Confident, you know yourself so well, that you'll allow what I say to be true. In fine, should I have mentioned your good Qualities, without || glancing by the way at a few of your foibles, I should have made of you but a very Sorry picture, all light and no Shade, and Just in the ridiculous taste of our Dedication painters, who make such Tawdry things, such be-bugled, be-spangled and be-tinseled Images of their patrons, that they serve for nothing but the public to stare gape and laugh at; it stands to reason then, that if I do you and the public Strict Justice, I ought also at the end of the list of your accomplishments & perfections, to have summed up your failings, which to be Sure, you as a reasonable man, a Philosopher, and a Lawyer, can never deny you have, unless you would make yourself a monster in nature, which a Character absolutely perfect must absolutely be— But I think it is now high time to drop, both your perfections, and Imperfections here, and (after heartily wishing that you may still be Reforming and Improving every day in your life,) to subscribe myself, Learned Sir,

From my Study Your most Humble Servant
Septr the 9th 1754 *The Author.*

[iv] live, whence the Circumstances || and facts are so mashed and broken, so mangled and obscured, by this foolish method of proceeding, that they are rendered utterly Incorrigible, and, Instead of being bettered, by the Historians of the Succeeding age, who often Labor under the Disease of a bad memory and worse Judgement, the whole mass turns out to be a hodge podge, almost unintelligible, and quite Irreconcilable to Nature and Common Sense.

Conscious of these evils, flowing from too Strict an observation, of these above mentioned Impertinent and foolish maxims, I have not either in quality of a Dedicator or Historian, allowed myself to be guided by them, but have all along had a Strict regard to truth and Nature, and whatever the truth is, or wheresoever she is to be found, I bring her out to fair View, without any regard to foppish forms and Ceremonies, and I care not a fig who takes offence at it, nor Indeed, would I entertain so Slight a regard for that Amiable Goddess, (who the Ancient Mythologists tell us, is hid in a well)[4] as to deviate from her in the least title either for fear or favor, hence you'll find, if you take the trowble to read the following history, that I have therein given every one his due, without partiality, favor or affection, there, all comes out to open light, be it what it will, good or bad, and I hope, nay am assured, that I have been as little Partial to myself as to others, however, as the Saying is, the proof of the pudding is in the eating, so, the [v] proof of what I here write, will be elucidated || by reading what I have there wrote, but, as I apprehend, You will not give yourself the trowble to read such a prolix Rhapsody, as is the following history from end to end, having, it is likely, things of greater Importance, or at least, things which you believe to be of greater Importance, whereon to bestow your precious moments, I shall only refer you to this here Dedication, which I now address to your Learned worship, which, as it is none of the Longest, I hope you will take the trowble to peruse, both for my Sake and your own, that is, to vindicate the Conduct of both to the present times and also to futurity in this here affair; you will find in this Epistle Dedicatory, an eikon or Image of the History it self in minature, and therefore I put it to your Conscience, as a Learned man, and Clubical Lawyer, to Judge with equity and declare with Candor whether I have acted herein like the Common herd of Dedicators, who load their patrons with so many fine Qualities, and so many transcendent perfections, that they can scarce see themselves for Sunshine, such a prodigious glare of light is thrown about them. No Sir, I hope I have talked to you, in a plain easie and natural manner, in the

---

4. This expression has been attributed to Heraclitus and other ancients.

observe, who, Carried away, either by the power of Flattery, or, by their pestilent Inclination to party, or pusilanimous fear of the anger and resentment of men in power, vent in their Compositions, ten falshoods for one truth, hence it is that the public is loaded with such a quantity of lies and Rodomontades, and Impudent barefaced Gasconades, that little or no Confidence can be put, either in dedicatory or historical writings, so, that it may, to our Shame be said, that the History of *Amadis de Gaul* or *Esplandian*[3] afford as much Genuine truth, as do our Modern Histories, of England, France, Spain, &ct: and one may as well go to the Devil, the father of Liars, for the Gospel of truth, as to these Dedicators for a genuine Character of a Great man, or to these Historians for a fair Impartial and true Narration of facts, our herd of Dedicators, for example, observing exactly, the above Silly and Impertinent maxims, will Impudently load their patrons in the face of the discerning world, who well know the Contrary, with Eulogiums and praises, which they never merited, tho' Ignorant as children and Idiots, they must be called learned, tho' Stupid & dull || as [iii] owls, they must be lively and facetious, tho' ugly as Swine, they must be handsome & well made, tho wicked and worthless as the Devil, they must be decked and adorned with all the Moral Virtues. Again they must Surely be descended from noble and Illustrious progenitors, tho' this present generation can well Remember their Grandsires peddling and hawking, and mumping about the Streets, this Romantic Ancestry must also be virtuous, brave & honorable, tho' many an honest man knows, and will swear to it, that there never was a pack of arranter Rascals unhang'd than they.

If it be not from a superstitious regard to the above absurd maxims, suggested by party zeal, pusilanimity, and a mean turn for flattery, and productive of an utter disregard for truth, whence does it arise, that we shall find a couple of grave historians, giving opposite Characters to one and the same person? whence comes it, that what the one calls white, the other pronounces black? whence does it proceed that they are still in different Stories, like two Suborned Irish evidences, one giving it this way another that, in such a manner, that the bewildered reader, does not know, or cannot determin, which of them is the greatest liar? Is it not also, from the fear of disobliging, and drawing down upon themselves, the resentments of great men and Illustrious families, that no Historian dares honestly Compile the genuine memoirs and transactions of those very times in which we

---

3. Amadis de Gaul is the chivalric hero of *Amadís de Gaula*, a 15th-century Spanish or Portuguese romance. Esplandian, the son of Amadis de Gaul, is a valorous knight who battles the Turks and eventually marries the daughter of a Greek emperor. *Las sergas de Esplandían* (1510) was a sequel to *Amadís de Gaula*.

[i] # Dedication

To the Most Learned, the Attorney General of the Ancient and honorable Tuesday Club,[1] and his Successors.

Learned Sir,
    As it is more than probable that the Honorable the President, and the Longstanding members of the ancient & Honorable Tuesday Club, in their profound wisdom and Sagacity, will pitch upon you, and your Learned Successors, as keepers of their Valuable archives and historical Chronicles, as well as of their *Corpus Juris* or body of Laws, so I, their humble historiographer am of opinion, that I cannot dedicate these my Labors to a fitter person than to your most erudite and Learned worship (to speak in Clubic Stile), and to your Successors in that Eminent laborious, and *Puzzlementationful* office, which you have the honor to possess in our Ancient and honorable Club, under the kindly and benign Influences, and Cherishing beams of his honor the president, whose Smiles and prolific Aspect, produces Learned Ideas, as plentifully and thick, In your Worship's Capacious Cranium, as the Sun breeds Insects on a dunghill, Pardon, dear Sir, the allusion.

[ii]   There are two maxims often made use of in Common discourse, and generally received as true ones, || tho' for my part, I think them at best but paltry Stuff, & if not absolutely false, yet nighly border on falshood, vizt: 1st That the truth ought not to be spoken at all times, and 2d, that we ought to be tender of the Characters of the dead.[2] These maxims may be esteemed good rules for some Dedicators and historians (nay Indeed for most,) to

---

    1. William Thornton (see biographical sketch).
    2. According to G. L. Apperson, *English Proverbs and Proverbial Phrases* (London, 1929), the following passage appears in Sir Roger L'Estrange's translation of Seneca's *Moral Essays* (ca. 1680): "The thing was true; but all truths are not to be spoken at all times" ("On the Happy Life," chap. 7), but I have not located this passage in any of the first three editions of L'Estrange's translation (1679, 1682, 1685), or in the original "De vita beata." In any event, Hamilton is perhaps recalling John Gay's remark that "Truth should not always be reveal'd" (*Fables,* 1st Ser., no. 18 [1727; rpt. Los Angeles, Calif., 1967], line 24). The second maxim has been attributed to Chilon, one of the Seven Sages of Greece, although Plutarch gives Solon the credit for it.

Chapter VII.	Eulogium of the poet Laureat upon his honor the presidents entertainment, arrival of the Great Seal, more Sublime Club Letters	542
Chapter VIII.	Admission of Philo Dogmaticus Esqr, Speeches in prose and verse at the Delivery of the Great Seal, Creation of the Chancellor, and an account of the Club medals being struck at London	553

Chapter IX.	Sublime Club Letters, the trial and aquittal of Sir John, Gelastic Law executed on the Secretary, Ceremonies of Confirmation	395
Chapter X.	Grand proposals in Club by the Secretary, Creation of Jon: Grog Esqr poet Laureat, Canopy of State added to the Chair, Speech of Sir John on that occasion, the master of Ceremonies leaves the Club, Election of a new master of Ceremonies, election of an Orator in place of Speaker	418
Chapter XI.	Celebration of the fourth anniversary, Speeches on that occasion, anniversary ode, foundation of the Eastren Shore Triumvirate	438

Book VI

From the foundation of the Eastren Shore triumvirate, To the Creation of the Chancellor, and Striking of the Club Medals at London.

Chapter I.	Of the witty Sayings, apothegms and Jests of Jonathan Grog Esqr, and other Ingenious Men	455
Chapter II.	Introduction of the toast Called the king and Club, proposals for reviving the box rejected, the Orator Lays down his office, abolition of that office in Club	487
Chapter III.	Commotions in Club, the Records in danger of being burnt, Confirmation of a deputy Secretary	497
Chapter IV.	Sublime Club Letters, Eulogium on a Longstanding member deceas'd, Letter of Cats, danger of a dissolution of the Club, the Master of Ceremonies leaves the Club	503
Chapter V.	More Sublime Club letters, petition to his honor the president from the Single females, several Club Speeches	515
Chapter VI.	Proposals for writing the history of the Club rejected, hieroglyphical Characters Introduced into the Club Letters, Jonathan Grog Esqr made master of Ceremonies	528

Contents

Chapter VIII. The Laudable Custom of Epistolary writing, introduced into the Club, The title of high Steward Instituted, and the first Grand Anniversary procession 286

Book V

From the first grand Anniversary procession, to the foundation of the Eastren Shore Triumvirate.

Chapter I. A Chapter of Triffles, concerning Clubical Critics and Anticlubarians 297
Chapter II. The accusation of the Speaker and Chief Musician, several Congratulatory Speeches, the master of Ceremonies confirmed, and some other triffling occurrences 311
Chapter III. Sir John Oldcastle's letter censured, Club's letter to Mr Makefun, an honorary member, other Clubical Letters of no great Importance 320
Chapter IV. Trial of the Chief musician, disputes in Club concerning a punch Ladle, accusation and condemnation of Mr Protomusicus, more disputes of little Significancy 330
Chapter V. The election and admission of Jonathan Grog Esqr, more Club Letters, Institution of the Presidential Star and badge, Speech of Jonathan Grog Esqr, to the Chair 341
Chapter VI. Clubical letters, the Celebration of the Third Anniversary, an Improvement made on the Club badges, the title of Oldcastle resigned by Sir John, the Success of the box petition 352
Chapter VII. Solemn Surrendry of the Club box and disposal of the treasury, Club Letters, the honorable the Speaker leaves the Club, disputes about who should succeed him, misbehaviour of Sir John 369
Chapter VIII. A Letter of Condolance wrote to his honor the president, admission of four long Standing members, disputes in Club, the Speech of Oldham Wisely Esqr, honorary Member, and other Trivial matters 378

Chapter IV.	The private Character of Nasifer Jole Esqr, and other prodigious matters	152
Chapter V.	The expulsion of the Batchellor's Cheese, The Signal Loyalty of the Longstanding members, and an instance of their amorous Disposition	170
Chapter VI.	Some of the members seized with a *furor poeticus,* and some account of the Baltimore Bards	175
Chapter VII.	The drinking of Lamb's wool in batchellors hall, and the danger of the Club's being converted to a State Club	185
Chapter VIII.	The Election and cathedration of the Honorable Nasifer Jole Esqr President	200

Book IV

From the Cathedration of the Honorable Nasifer Jole Esqr President, to the first grand anniversary procession.

Chapter I.	Of Club Stile, and Clubical terms necessary for the understanding of this History, and also of great Club officers and offices, their nature, Dignity and privileges	209
Chapter II.	Of a great Club ball, and matters of Gallantry, with the Clubical Character of Nasifer Jole Esqr	222
Chapter III.	The Introduction of the Club box, and other Important matters	233
Chapter IV.	The Introduction of Set Speeches into the Club, and the members that made The greatest figure that way	238
Chapter V.	The Celebration of the first Anniversary, the Institution of the Club badges, and other significant matters	252
Chapter VI.	The Creation of Sir John Oldcastle knight of the Club, and the privileges thereunto Annexed, & the appointment of the master of ceremonies	265
Chapter VII.	The Creation of the Speaker of the Club and his privileges, as also of the Chief musician and his privileges	276

Book II

From the transmigration of the Club to America, to the first Sederunt of the ancient and honorable Tuesday Club of Annapolis in Maryland.

Chapter I.	A Learned dissertation in the Stile and manner of the Ingenious Mr Robert Burton	69
Chapter II.	The History and Character of Mr George Neilson, and the Cause of his coming to America	75
Chapter III.	Of the turn and Genius of the Annapolitans to Clubbing, at and after the arrival of Mr G: Neilson in America	84
Chapter IV.	The first Institution and foundation of the Red house Club of Annapolis, by Mr Geor: Neilson and other Illustrious personages	90
Chapter V.	Description of the Redhouse Club, its Customs, oeconomy and Government	100
Chapter VI.	The translation of the Seat of Government in the Red house Club, the Cause of its dissolution, and the place of meeting converted to a Nunnery	108
Chapter VII.	The Rise of the Ugly Club, on the ruins of the red house Club	116
Chapter VIII.	An account of the Constitution and government of the ugly Club, it's Dissolution, and the first Scheme for erecting the Ancient and honorable Tuesday Club of Annapolis in Maryland	121

Book III

From the first Sederunt of the ancient and Honorable Tuesday Club, to the Cathedration of the Honorable Nasifer Jole Esqr President.

Chapter I.	Of Great and Illustrious personages, whose Names only have been transmitted to posterity	129
Chapter II.	Of the first Sederunt of the ancient and honorable Tuesday Club, and the wise Laws then framed	141
Chapter III.	Introduction of the Bachellors Cheese into the Club, the passing of the Gelastic Law, and other matters of Importance	146

Contents of the History of the Ancient and honorable Tuesday Club

Volume I

Dedication i
Preface viii

Book I

From the earliest ages, to the Transmigration of the Club to America, and the foundation of the Red house Club of Annapolis In Maryland 1

    Chapter I.   Of History and Historians . . . . ibid
    Chapter II. Of Antiquity, its dignity and Importance 7
   Chapter III. Of Clubs in general, and their antiquity 25
   Chapter IV. Some Scraps of ancient History relating to Clubs 31
    Chapter V. The more Immediate origin and rise of the ancient and Honorable Tuesday Club, of Annapolis in Maryland 42
   Chapter VI. A Succinct account of the ancient and venerable Tuesday (or whin bush) Club of Lanneric in the Kingdome of Scotland 51
Chronological Table of the ancient and honorable Tuesday Club 61

The History of the Ancient and Honorable Tuesday Club

From the earliest ages down to this present year.

Volume I

Autor Noster, ita describit Heroas Clubicos, ut Incertus hæreat Lector, an eruditi magis fortesve essent, corporisque potius aut animi viribus pollerent.[1]

---

1. "Our author so describes the Clubical heroes, that the reader remains uncertain, whether they are more erudite or brave, and whether they are more powerful in strength of body or of mind."

[Hamilton's drawings are reproduced in this edition courtesy of the John Work Garrett Library of the Milton S. Eisenhower Library at the Johns Hopkins University. The location of each drawing in the manuscript is indicated in brackets following the illustration.]

The History of the Tuesday Club

Volume I

some mercantile business; member of Lower House, Annapolis, 1757–1758. He was associated with Stephen Bordley (q.v.) and left his land and houses—one of which may have served as the meeting place for the Tuesday Club—to his wife (Wills, 1761, vol. 31, pp. 465–467). Woodward's obituary reads: "Saturday Night last, Died, at his Plantation near Town, after a short Illness, in the 28th Year of his Age, Mr. HENRY WOODWARD, a few Years since one of the Representatives for this City. He has left an inconsolable Widow, and Four young Children, to lament an affectionate Husband and tender Father" (*MG,* Sept. 24, 1761).

Woolf, Garrett. Associate.

Born in Germany and naturalized by an act of the Maryland General Assembly in 1727 (William Hand Browne *et al.,* eds., *Archives of Maryland* [Baltimore, 1883–], XXXVIII, 406–407); as Hamilton indicates, he was a cordwainer in Annapolis (Test. Procs.).

Interr'd, Mr. WILLIAM WILKINS, who was for a great Number of Years Prosecutor in our Mayor's Court, and a very useful Clerk to many Committees in the Lower House of Assembly" (*MG,* Mar. 5, 1761).

Wollaston, John (fl. 1736–1767). "Squeak Grumbleton." Visitor.

Portrait painter; probably the son of John Woolaston, London artist of the early eighteenth century; came to America in 1749 and remained nearly ten years, producing over three hundred portraits from New York to Virginia (including portraits of Maryland's most prominent families); influenced Gustavus Hesselius and probably his son John Hesselius (q.v.); according to George C. Groce, outside of New England Wollaston's influence on colonial painting was "greater than that of any English artist . . . prior to the Revolutionary War" ("John Wollaston [fl. 1736–1767]: A Cosmopolitan Painter in the British Colonies," *Art Quarterly,* XV [1952], 133).

Wolstenholme, Daniel (d. 1795). "Giovanni Precisio." Visitor.

Immigrated to Maryland from England; resident in Annapolis by 1750; husband of Deborah (d. 1807); Anglican; merchant, planter; member of Lower House, St. Mary's County, 1765–1766, 1768–1770; a Loyalist, Wolstenholme in 1775 refused to sign the Association of Freemen of Maryland.

Wood, Benjamin (1715–1753). Associate.

Wood's obituary reads: "Last Friday died, after a very long and lingering Illness, at the House of *Jonas Green,* where he had lived upwards of Eleven Years . . . Mr. BENJAMIN WOOD, Printer, aged *38,* born at *Tattershall* in *Lincolnshire:* He had a good Education, well understood the learned Languages, and was an ingenious and skilful Artist" (*MG,* Aug. 2, 1753).

Wood, Samuel (d. by 1759). "Nathaniel Sylvius." Visitor.

Resident of St. Mary's County; he left his few possessions to his daughter Ann and sons Samuel and Jonathan (Wills, 1758, vol. 30, p. 527; Accounts, 1759, vol. 43, p. 354).

Woodward, Mr.   Associate.

This might be any number of Woodwards, but I suspect it is either Abraham Woodward of Anne Arundel County, whose will was witnessed by William Rogers (q.v.) (Wills, 1744, vol. 24, pp. 7–8), or, more probably, Henry Woodward (1733–1761). He was a native Marylander; son of Amos Woodward (d. ca. 1735) and Achsah Dorsey (ca. 1704–1741); married Mary Young in 1755; Anglican; Gent., 1756, and Esq., 1759; planter, engaged in

London (probably for the first time); he served as curate to the Reverend Thomas Bacon (q.v.) at St. Peter's, Talbot County, until he was appointed to Port Tobacco Parish in 1762; in 1779 he and his wife Mary were living in Kent County (Inventories, 1779, Box 34, No. 5); sometime prior to 1785 he moved to Virginia, where he held parishes until his death.

Thornton, William (d. 1769). "Solo Neverout," "Protomusicus." Longstanding Member (admitted 1745), Chief Musician, and Attorney General.
Merchant and shipowner (*MG,* Nov. 11, 1746, Jan. 16, 1751); Thornton owned land in Prince George's and Anne Arundel counties and apparently moved from Annapolis to Baltimore County before his death; he was the brother of Thomas Thornton (q.v.) and left most of his possessions to his son William (born to Sarah Heigh) (Wills, 1769, Box 37, No. 80). Thornton's obituary reads: "On Friday last died, at BALTIMORE-TOWN, Mr. WILLIAM THORNTON, formerly Sheriff of this County [Anne Arundel].—A Gentleman much respected by his Friends and Acquaintance" (*MG,* Feb. 9, 1769).

Tilghman, Edward (1713–1785). "Prim Laconic." Honorary Member (admitted 1747).
Native Marylander; son of Richard Tilghman (1672/1673–1738/1739) and Anna Maria Lloyd (1677–1748); married Anna Maria Turbutt ca. 1738, Elizabeth Chew (1720–1759) in 1749, and Juliana Carroll (b. 1729) in 1759; Anglican; Gent., 1737, and Esq., 1740; colonel by 1755; member of Lower House, Queen Anne's County, 1745/1746–1748; died a wealthy landowner.

Troy, John. "Capt. Furbisher." Visitor.
Notices in the *MG* show that a Capt. John Troy commanded the snow *Polly,* and that he, Lancelot Jacques (q.v.), and William Thornton (q.v.) apparently dealt in the slave trade (June 14, 21, 1753).

Wallace, Charles (1727–1812). Visitor.
Native Marylander; son of John and Anne Wallace; married Catherine (ca. 1731–1795), then Mary Bull Rankin (ca. 1747–1834); Anglican; Gent., by 1757, Esq., by 1776; staymaker, tavern keeper, land developer, and merchant.

Wilkins, William (1700–1761). "Spatterdash Wouldbe." Visitor.
Resident of Annapolis; husband of Deborah and father of five children (Wills, 1761, Box W, No. 73). Wilkins's obituary reads: "Saturday last Died here, after a long Indisposition, Aged 61 Years, and on Tuesday was decently

while living in America, and many of his pieces appeared in the *MG*. Sterling's obituary says that for his "uncommon Abilities and extensive Learning, particularly in all the Branches of polite Literature, [he stood] unrival'd in this Part of the World" (Lemay, *Men of Letters*, 257–312; *MG*, Nov. 17, 1763).

Steward, John. Visitor.
A John Stewart of London advertised in the *MG* for Sept. 26, 1750, as a merchant. This is possibly the same John Stewart who opened a store in Anne Arundel County in partnership with William Lux of Baltimore (q.v.) (*BDML*, s.v. "Lux, William").

Stewart, Mr. "Mr. Boniface." Visitor.
This could be any number of Stewarts, but it is possibly John Stewart or Anthony Stewart, business associate of Thomas Richardson (q.v.) in the rum trade (Inventories, Box 80, No. 16).

Stringar, Samuel (d. 1747). "Samuel Swallowbeak." Mentioned.
Anne Arundel County physician; husband of Lydia Warfield (Admin. Bonds, Box 47, No. 49); Stringar's obituary reads: "Last Wednesday died, much lamented, at *Elk-Ridge*, in this County, Dr. *Samuel Stringar*, formerly Mayor of this City" (*MG*, Aug. 25, 1747).

Swan, Robert (1720–1764). "Stentor Snuffysnout (Snuffybeak)." Visitor.
Affluent Annapolis merchant, of Scottish ancestry; he apparently died childless, leaving everything to his nephews (Inventories, 1765, Box 72, No. 29; Wills, 1764, Box S, No. 107). Swan also "carrie[d] on the Business of Tanning, and Currying of Leather, and Shoemaking" (*MG*, May 7, 1752). Swan's obituary reads: "Friday last Died here, in the 44th Year of his Age, Mr. ROBERT SWAN, Merchant, one of the Common-Council of this City: And on Sunday his Remains were very decently Interr'd" (*MG*, May 10, 1764).

Thompson, John. "Joannes Tomlinsonus." Visitor.
Annapolis merchant (see, e.g., *MG*, May 30, 1750, Mar. 5, 1752).

Thornton, Thomas (d. 1791). "Nolens Volens." Visitor.
Thornton was licensed for Maryland in 1754; the *MG* for Apr. 24, 1755, notes that the Reverend Mr. Thomas Thornton had lately arrived from

Snowden, Richard (1687–1763). "Oldham Wisely." Honorary Member (admitted 1745).

Resident of Anne Arundel County; husband of Elizabeth and father of three sons (Inventories, 1766, Box 73, No. 32). Snowden's obituary reads:

> Yesterday Morning Died, at his Seat on *Patuxent* River, near his Iron-Works, in the 76th Year of his Age, the venerable Mr. RICHARD SNOWDEN, a Gentleman universally and deservedly Esteem'd, who has left a sorrowful Widow, numerous Offspring . . . and Acquaintance, to lament a most tender Husband . . . and agreeable Companion. He was of a most benevolent and humane Disposition, remarkably Hospitable and Generous in his Entertainment of Strangers, as well as his intimate Acquaintance. By a diligent Application to the extensive Business which he was a long Time engag'd in, he acquired an affluent Fortune, with a fair unblemish'd Character; and led the Life of a Christian truly worthy of Imitation. . . . *Mark the perfect Man, and behold the Upright, for the End of that Man is Peace.* Psal. xxxvii. 37 (*MG,* Jan. 27, 1763).

Snowden also seems to have held some trade as a tobacco dealer (*MG,* July 31, 1751).

Spencer, Archibald (1698–1760). "Dr. Rhubarb." Visitor.

Physician, lecturer on experimental philosophy, and apparently a deist who was nevertheless ordained a minister and licensed for Virginia in 1749; rector of All Hallows Parish, Anne Arundel County (from September 1751), where he remained until his death (J. A. Leo Lemay, "Franklin's 'Dr. Spence': The Reverend Archibald Spencer [1698?–1760], M.D.," *MHM,* LIX [1964], 199–216). Spencer's obituary states that "while he seemed in good Health, . . . he declared, with great Indifference, his Expectation of a speedy Death, and afterwards met his Fate with a singular Constancy and Resignation" (*MG,* Jan. 17, 1760).

Sterling, James (1701–1763). "Rev. Rodomantus." Visitor.

Born in Ireland; matriculated at Trinity College in 1716; immigrated to America in 1737, having already established himself in Dublin and London as a poet and playwright; inducted into All Hallows Parish, Anne Arundel County, where he remained until his resignation in 1739, when he was appointed rector of St. Anne's, Annapolis; resigned from St. Anne's in 1740 to accept a more lucrative position at St. Paul's, Kent County, where he remained until his death; continued to write poetry—mostly occasional—

beth Ross, the wealthy daughter of John Ross, Esq. (*MG,* Sept. 9, 1756); he died a modestly wealthy physician (Admin. Bonds, 1814, Box 112, No. 14; Wills, Box S, No. 20). Scott's glowing obituary appeared as follows.

> Departed this life, on Wednesday evening the 23d ult, at the advanced age of 90 years, Dr. UPTON SCOTT, a native of Ireland, but for more than 60 years a most distinguished inhabitant of this City.
>
> Society seldom mourns the loss of a more excellent and valuable member, than the venerable man whose decease we now record. Through the course of a life, protracted far beyond the ordinary span of human existence, his career has been one unbroken tenor of virtue, dignity, and usefulness. Pure in his principles, discerning in his judgment, unshaken in his attachments, he has been the hereditary counsellor and friend of many generations, and has enjoyed the successive confidence and affection of grandsire, son and father, who have been successively enlightened by his wisdom, and enobled by his friendship.
>
> Bred among heroes, whom history delights to honour, and in scenes which though at present dimly seen "through the long vista of departed years," have not yet lost their interest, his soul was of that lofty cast which befitted the chosen friend of Wolfe, while the treasures of his mind, enriched by the constant accumulations of experience, and the elevated and endearing qualities of his heart, rendered him the oracular adviser of the young, the boast and ornament of the aged.
>
> A Gracious Providence lengthened to him not merely "the frail tenure of a feverish being," but the diviner bounty of moral and intellectual pleasures; and at a period of life when most men, despoiled by time of the feelings and faculties which make life a blessing, seem but as melancholy mementos of mortality, the vigour of his understanding, and the unchilled ardour of his affections, rendered this venerable man the soul of an extensive circle of family friends and connections, in whom as in a common centre, their affections and enjoyments converged and were united (*MG,* Mar. 3, 1814).

Sedgewick, John. Visitor.
Anne Arundel County mariner; husband of Sarah Gaither (b. 1726) (Wills, 1753, vol. 30, p. 511; Newman, *Anne Arundel Gentry,* 90, 447). Sedgewick appears in the *MG* as commander of the ship *Friendship* (May 2, 9, 1750).

House (served several terms); died a wealthy landowner. Ridout's obituary reads:

> On Friday the 6th instant, at his house in the city of Annapolis, after a short illness, departed this life John Ridout, Esquire, in the 66th year of his age. In the amiable character of this useful and worthy member of society were uniformly and eminently displayed soundness of judgment, evenness of temper, benevolence of heart, integrity and prudence in conduct. A kind and affectionate husband, a tender and discreet father. . . . Sensible, polite and social in his manners, obliging, beneficent and unassuming in his deportment, his loss is deeply regretted by his friends and neighbours (*MG*, Oct. 12, 1797).

Rogers, William (1699–1749). "Seemly Spruce." Oldstanding Member (admitted 1745).

Born in New England; resident in Annapolis by 1720; husband of Mary Townley (d. by 1725); chief clerk and register of the Prerogative Court, 1736–1749 (*BDML*, s.v. "Rogers, John"). Rogers's obituary reads: "Last Saturday Morning died here, very much lamented, after a long and lingering Indisposition, in the Fiftieth Year of his Age, and on Sunday Evening was decently interred, WILLIAM ROGERS, Esq; a Gentleman born and bred in *New-England*, but had long been a worthy Inhabitant of this Place; where he was greatly belov'd and esteem'd. He enjoyed many Posts of Honour and Trust, which he discharged with Judgment and Fidelity; and has left a sorrowful Widow and three Children" (*MG*, Aug. 2, 1749).

Scott, Andrew (d. 1766). Visitor.

Prince George's County physician and surgeon; husband of Mary Abington. After ending an extremely unhappy marriage, Scott left Maryland in the early 1750s and settled in New Bern, North Carolina, where he continued to practice medicine until his death (George F. Frick, James L. Reveal, C. Rose Broome, and Melvin L. Brown, "The Practice of Dr. Andrew Scott of Maryland and North Carolina," *MHM*, LXXXII [1987], 123–141).

Scott, Upton (1724–1814). "Jeronimo Jaunter." Longstanding Member (admitted 1754).

Scott came to America from Glasgow in 1753, bringing a letter of introduction from his teacher, Dr. Robert Hamilton, Alexander Hamilton's cousin (Lemay, *Men of Letters*, 244); in September 1756, he married Eliza-

[Beale] *Bordley*'s, near the Stadt House in *Annapolis,*" then "removed from the House over against Mr. *Bordley*'s in *North East* Street, to the House where Mr. *Ashbury Sutton* lately lived, near the Dock in *Annapolis*" (*MG,* June 15, Dec. 7, 1748). He left bequests of £1,000 to each of his five children (Newman, *Anne Arundel Gentry,* 264). Raitt's obituary reads: "On Thursday last died here, after a short Indisposition, greatly Lamented by his Family and Friends, and on Friday was decently Interred, Mr. JOHN RAITT, a Merchant in this City, and late Sheriff of *Anne-Arundel* County, which Trust he Discharged to the intire Satisfaction of all with whom he had any Concerns" (*MG,* July 6, 1758).

Richard, James. "Roughby Ranter." Associate.
Sheriff of Baltimore County. Richard's defense of his reputation against what he considered the slanderous attacks of Richard Chase and others (including Thomas Chase [q.v.]) appeared in the *MG* for July 28, 1747; Richard was vindicated in court in his dispute with the Chases (see Lemay, *Men of Letters,* 200, and Rosamond Randall Beirne, "The Reverend Thomas Chase: Pugnacious Parson," *MHM,* LIX [1964], 7). Other notices in the *MG* indicate that Richard was a wealthy landowner (see, e.g., Sept. 30, 1746), and unless there were two James Richards, he was also an Annapolis merchant (*MG,* Nov. 18, 1746, May 19, 1747).

Richardson, Thomas (d. 1768). Visitor.
Probably born in Scotland; Annapolis merchant and business associate of Anthony Stewart (q.v.) in the rum trade (Wills, 1768, vol. 36, pp. 478–479; Inventories, Box 80, No. 16). Richardson's obituary reads: "On the Evening of Friday last, Mr. THOMAS RICHARDSON, late of this City, Merchant, was instantly kill'd by a Flash of Lightning, which melted his Watch, Shoe, and Knee Buckles.—He was sitting in a Room at Mr. ADAIR's, in BALTIMORE-TOWN, with another Person, at a small Distance, who was struck down, but soon recovered. . . . Mr. RICHARDSON was a young Man, in the Prime of Life, and possess'd many good Qualities, which justly entitled him to the Esteem of a numerous Acquaintance" (*MG,* June 23, 1768).

Ridout, John (1732–1797). Visitor.
Immigrated to Maryland from England in 1753; son of George Ridout (1702–1779) and Mary Hallett; husband of Mary Ogle (1746–1808); Anglican; Esq., 1753; protégé of Horatio Sharpe (1718–1790) and served as his secretary during Sharpe's term as governor; planter; member of Upper

apprehensive of any Danger . . . unfortunately gave the Signal for firing, whilst the Boat was aside of the Ship. . . . The Wadding of the first Gun pass'd near the Head of Mr. *James Dickenson,* who sat by Mr. *Morris;* and that of the third did the Mischief. The Breechings were indiscreetly left under the Guns, and the Ship had a heel to the Side next the Boat; otherwise this sad Accident could not have happened. . . .

The Bone of his Arm was broke a little above the Elbow, and a large Wound and Contusion was made in the Flesh.—The Wound began to mortify the next Day, but by the Skill and Assiduity of the Surgeons who attended him, the Mortification was stopped, and there was good Hopes of saving both his Life and Arm, until Wednesday Evening, when he was seiz'd with a violent Fever, which carried him off next Afternoon (July 18, 1750).

The rest of the obituary confirms Banning's high opinion of Morris.

North, Benjamin (d. by 1761). Visitor.
The inventory of North's personal effects, witnessed by William Rogers (q.v.) and William Lux of Annapolis (q.v.), indicates that North was a mariner who lived in Baltimore County and owned very little (Inventories, 1761, Box 15, No. 13).

North, Robert (d. by 1751). "Huffbluff Surly." Honorary Member (admitted 1745).
Resident of Baltimore County; son of Thomas and Ellen North of Whittington, Lancashire, England (Newman, *To Maryland from Overseas,* 130); father of three children; wealthy landowner (Wills, 1749, Box 8, No. 2; Accounts, 1751, vol. 30, p. 141).

Pickering, Stephen (d. by 1765). "Gasperus Pickeringtonus." Visitor.
Anne Arundel County merchant; sued by Sarah Gresham (q.v.) and bailed out by the Reverend Charles Lake (q.v.); his will, witnessed by Lake and the Reverend Archibald Spencer (q.v.), indicates that he was a gentleman with apparently little property; he had no children (Inventories, Box 72, No. 56; Wills, 1753, Box P, No. 41; Accounts, 1765, vol. 53, p. 309).

Raitt, John (d. 1758). Visitor.
Native of Scotland; husband of Ann (Admin. Bonds, Box 60, No. 7); wealthy merchant. Raitt first sold his goods "at his Store over against Mr.

cal Society, *Collections,* 1st Ser., VII [1801], 171–200), and as Sir William Johnson's secretary for Indian affairs (Lemay, *Men of Letters,* 246).

Middleton, Samuel (d. 1770). "Mr. Leidemont." Host.
Husband of Anne and father of three sons and one daughter (Wills, Box M, No. 55). He owned and operated Middleton's Tavern and the ferry at Annapolis; Middleton's Tavern is still standing and still thriving.

Mitchelson, [Samuel?]. "Mr. Lisper." Visitor.
Since Mr. Mitchelson is given a dubious character in the *History,* perhaps he is the Samuel Mitchelson who was convicted for stealing, and then convicted for prison breaking (see *MG,* Dec. 25, 1751).

Morris, Robert (d. 1750). "Merry Makefun." Honorary Member (admitted 1747) and member of Eastern Shore Triumvirate.
Born in Liverpool; son of Andrew Morris, mariner, and his wife Mauldin (Newman, *To Maryland from Overseas,* 125). In the "Narrative of the Principal Incidents in the Life of Jeremiah Banning" (1793), Banning writes: "As a mercantile genius it was thought he [Morris] had not his equal in the land. As a companion and bon vivant he was incomparable. . . . He gave birth to the inspection law on tobacco and carried it through though opposed by a powerful majority. He was the first who introduced the mode of keeping accounts in money. . . . At repartee he bore down all before him. Mr. Morris was father to the present Robert Morris, . . . the most distinguished merchant of his time in America" (in William F. Boogher, *Miscellaneous Americana: A Collection of History, Biography, and Genealogy* [Washington, D.C., 1895]). Morris's obituary, relating the unusual nature of his death, appeared as follows in the *MG.*

> On Thursday last died at his House in *Oxford,* Mr. ROBERT MORRIS, Merchant, Agent and Factor of *Foster Cunliffe,* Esq; of *Liverpool.* He received his Death by a Gunshot Wound in his Right Arm, which melancholy and unfortunate Accident happened in this Manner:—The Friday before his Death, upon the Arrival of the *Liverpool Merchant,* a Ship of Mr. *Cunliffe's,* he went on board her with some Company; and, after a small Stay there, went into the Boat to come ashore; at which Time the Captain was about paying him the usual Compliment with his Guns. Mr. *Morris . . .* being under an unusual Apprehension of Mischief, desired the Guns might not be fir'd 'til he was astern of the Ship: But the Captain, not

the Stamp Act controversy, 1765, and was one of the organizers of the Baltimore Sons of Liberty, 1766.

Lyon, William. Visitor.
Probably Queen Anne's County physician (Inventories, 1767, vol. 93, p. 59, 1770, vol. 104, p. 351); notices in the *MG* also imply that he was a druggist who sold his wares at his shop in Baltimore (Nov. 4, 1746, June 19, 1755).

McPherson, Alexander (d. 1776). Visitor.
Resident of Charles County; husband of Elizabeth and father of five children; tobacco planter and modestly wealthy landowner (Wills, 1775, vol. 40, p. 488; Inventories, 1776, vol. 122, p. 387).

Malcolm, Alexander (d. 1763). "Philo Dogmaticus." Longstanding Member (admitted 1749), Chancellor, then Honorary Member.
After meeting Hamilton in Massachusetts, Malcolm was inducted into St. Anne's, Annapolis, in 1749 when Andrew Lendrum (q.v.) resigned; he was inducted into St. Paul's, Queen Anne's County, in 1753, and in 1755 became master of the Queen Anne's County school, from which he was forced to resign. His obituary calls him "a Gentleman who has obliged the World with several learned Performances on the Mathematics, Music, and Grammar" (*MG*, June 30, 1763); his *New Treatise of Arithmetick and Bookkeeping* (Edinburgh, 1718), which had reached several editions by his death, was assessed as "the best in English and perhaps any other Language" (*New Hampshire Gazette* [Portsmouth], July 22, 1763). For further information on Malcolm's career, see James R. Heintze, "Alexander Malcolm: Musician, Clergyman, and Schoolmaster," *MHM*, LXXIII (1978), 226–235. According to Heintze, Malcolm's *A Treatise of Musick, Speculative, Practical, and Historical* (Edinburgh, 1721) established him as "the most significant music theorist to have immigrated to the colonies during the eighteenth century" (p. 226).

Marshe, Witham (d. 1765). "Prattle Motely." Oldstanding Member (admitted 1745), Secretary, then Honorary Member.
Marshe is best remembered as secretary to the Maryland Commissioners at the treaty of Lancaster in 1744 with the Six Indian Nations (and author of the "Journal of the Treaty Held with the Six Nations by the Commissioners of Maryland, and Other Provinces," Massachusetts Histori-

ish, in the room of the Reverend and Ingenious Mr. JOHN GORDON, who is Removed, to the great Grief of his Parishioners, to *St. Michael*'s Parish in *Talbot* County" (Apr. 5, 1749).

Lloyd, Edward (1711–1770). "Courtly Phraze." Honorary Member (admitted 1745).

Native Marylander; son of Edward Lloyd (1670–1718/1719) and his wife Sarah (1683–1755); married Anne Rousby (1721–1769) in 1739, then a second wife (name unknown); Anglican; colonel by 1741; Esq., 1747; planter, merchant; member of Lower House, Talbot County, 1738, 1739–1741, and Upper House (served several terms); died a wealthy landowner. Lloyd's obituary reads: "Lately died at his Seat, on *Wye* River, in *Talbot* County, greatly lamented, EDWARD LLOYD, Esq; formerly one of his Lordship's Council of State, and Agent and Receiver General for this Province: He was a tender and affectionate Parent . . . and a polite and agreeable Companion. As he was possessed of great Wealth, so was he remarkable for his Hospitality to Strangers, and Benevolence to real Objects of Compassion" (*MG*, Feb. 8, 1770).

Lomas, John (d. 1757). "Laconic Comas (Comus)." Oldstanding Member (admitted 1745) and Orator.

Lomas lived in Annapolis with his wife Margaret (*MHM*, X [1915], 128). Various advertisements in the *MG* show that Lomas was an Annapolis merchant and owned a plantation near South River, and that he left for London in 1749 and returned in 1750 (the time of his absence from the Tuesday Club) (Apr. 7, 1747, Mar. 8, 1749, Aug. 30, 1749, June 20, 1750). Lomas moved to Glasgow by 1754 and died in Liverpool (*MHM*, IV [1909], 196–197; *MG*, June 30, 1757).

Lux, William, of Annapolis. "Crinkum Crankum." Longstanding Member (admitted 1753).

Native Marylander; Annapolis merchant; advertised goods for sale in *MG* (see, e.g., Sept. 4, 1751). He left his entire estate to his "dearest friend and relation," William Lux of Baltimore (q.v.) (Wills, 1772, vol. 38, p. 824).

Lux, William, of Baltimore (1730–1778). Visitor.

Native Marylander; son of Darby Lux (ca. 1698–1750) and Ann Sanders (ca. 1705–1785); married Agnes Walker (1731–1783) in 1752; Anglican; Gent., 1752, and Esq., 1778; wealthy merchant and land speculator; participated in

mented by all his Friends, and the Loss to his Family is truly deplorable, being snatched from them in the very Prime of Life, aged no more than 42 Years" (*MG,* June 2, 1763).

Key, Philip (1696/1697–1764). "Signior Phrazeobundus." Visitor.
Immigrated to Maryland from England ca. 1720; married Susannah Gardiner (d. 1717), then Theodosia Lawrence (d. 1772); Anglican; Gent., 1738, and Esq., 1750; merchant, planter, lawyer; member of Lower House, St. Mary's County, 1728–1731, 1734/1735–1737, and Upper House, 1763; died a wealthy landowner. Key's obituary reads: "On Monday the 20th of this Instant, Died, at his Seat in *St. Mary's* County, in the LXVIIIth Year of his Age, the Honble PHILIP KEY, Esq; one of the Council of this Province. He was a truly pious and devout Christian, an affectionate and tender Husband, an indulgent and fond Parent, a humane Master, a warm Friend, a friendly Neighbour, and a most agreeable and chearful Companion. His Death is sincerely lamented by his Family, and all his numerous Friends and Acquaintance" (*MG,* Aug. 30, 1764).

King, Thomas (d. by 1761). Associate.
Resident of Anne Arundel County; husband of Rachel (Admin. Bonds, Box 54, No. 35); King's advertisements as a shoemaker, such as the following notice, frequently appeared in the *MG:* "Notice is hereby given, That *Thomas* King, Shoemaker, who formerly kept his Shop at the Gate-House of the City of *Annapolis,* now keeps his Shop at the Old Prison" (Sept. 22, 1747).

Lake, Charles (d. 1764). "Rev. Whiner." Associate.
Rector of St. Anne's, Annapolis, from 1740 to 1743, and of St. James's, Herring Creek, from 1749 until his death; proposals for the Reverend Lake's system of divinity, the *Florilegia Sacra,* were advertised in the *MG* for Nov. 14 through Dec. 5, 1750.

Lendrum, Andrew (d. 1769). "Roundhead Muddy." Longstanding Member (admitted 1749), then Honorary Member.
Possibly A.B., Trinity College, Dublin, 1739; inducted into St. Anne's, Annapolis, in 1749 and resigned shortly thereafter to become rector of St. George's, Baltimore County, where he remained until his death; the notice of his induction into St. Anne's appeared as follows in the *MG:* "Wednesday last the Reverend Mr. ANDREW LENDRUM was Inducted into this Par-

(see George T. Hollyday, "Biographical Memoirs of James Hollyday," *Pennsylvania Magazine of History and Biography,* VII [1883], 426–447).

Jacques, Lancelot (1709–1791). Frequent visitor.
A French Huguenot who came to America as a refugee and sought to develop the country by starting iron furnaces, constructing and operating the Catoctin Furnace in Frederick County (T. J. C. Williams and Folger McKinsey, *History of Frederick County, Maryland,* 2 vols. [Frederick, Md., 1910], I, 106); numerous advertisements in the *MG* further indicate that he was a merchant "at his Store fronting the Court House" in Annapolis (June 14, 1749).

Jennings, Catherine. "Madonna Swashgut." Associate.
Annapolis storekeeper whose house was such a familiar spot that an advertiser in the *MG* directed his friends to his new dwelling "near the widow Jenning's" (Dec. 6, 1753; see also Nov. 20, 1751, Feb. 27, 1752). Jennings moved to Frederick Town, Frederick County, where her will was probated in 1765 (Wills, vol. 33, pp. 250–251).

Jennings, Thomas (d. 1759). "Prim Timorous." Longstanding Member (admitted 1749) and Sergeant at Arms.
Resident of Anne Arundel County; husband of Rebecca and father of Elizabeth and Ann (Admin. Bonds, Box 61, No. 37); he was a judge and a modestly wealthy landowner (*MG,* Jan. 3, Mar. 21, 1750). Jennings's obituary reads: "Sunday last Died here, after a tedious and lingering Indisposition, Mr. *Thomas Jennings,* Chief Clerk of the Land-Office, and for a great many Years in the Commission of the Peace for this County; by whose Death his Family has lost a tender Husband, indulgent Father, and kind Master; and the Community, a very useful, honest, and inoffensive Member" (*MG,* Aug. 30, 1759).

Johns, Kensey (d. 1763). Visitor.
Probably the son of Aquila Johns (*MG,* Mar. 13, 1751); husband of Susannah (Admin. Bonds, Box 66, No. 40); commander of the *Rumney* and the *Long* (*MG,* Apr. 13, 1748, Apr. 4, 1750, Mar. 6, 1751). Johns's obituary reads: "On Thursday last Died at his House at *West-River,* KENSEY JOHNS, Esq; High Sheriff of this County [Anne Arundel]. He was a tender Husband, affectionate Father, sincere Friend, upright Magistrate, humane Officer, kind Neighbour, and chearful Companion: His Death is sincerely la-

in Upper-Marlborough, in the 65th year of his age, JOHN HEPBURN, Esq; for many years one of the judges of the provincial court, which important trust, he executed with the fidelity and uprightness becoming a good magistrate—in private life, he approved himself the tender husband, the affectionate and indulgent parent, the humane master, the beneficent neighbour, the faithful friend, the polite companion, and the man of nice honour, and unshaken integrity" (*MG,* Aug. 24, 1775).

Hesselius, John (1728–1778). "Signior Sehesslius." Visitor.

Probably a native Marylander; son of Gustavus Hesselius, a native of Sweden naturalized by the Maryland General Assembly in 1721, and his wife Lydia; married Mary Woodward (1763); church warden and vestryman, St. Anne's, Annapolis, 1763–1764; portrait painter and one of the most prolific painters of the pre-Revolutionary period (see Newman, *To Maryland from Overseas,* 92; Theodore Bolton and George C. Groce, Jr., "John Hesselius: An Account of His Life and the First Catalogue of His Portraits," *Art Quarterly,* II [1939], 77–91; and Richard K. Doud, "John Hesselius, Maryland Limner," *Winterthur Portfolio,* V [1969], 129–153).

Hill, Richard, Jr. (d. 1755). "Chantum Cheary." Honorary Member (admitted 1747).

Hamilton calls him Richard Hill "of Philadelphia," probably because Hill was born and raised in Philadelphia at the home of his father, Richard Hill (1673–1729; see *Dictionary of American Biography*); Hill had established residency in Anne Arundel County by 1735; his connection with Samuel Stringar (q.v.), a fellow surgeon (Test. Procs., vol. 30, p. 27), suggests that this is the Hill to whom Hamilton is referring, and probably the same Hill whose death notice appeared in the *MG,* May 15, 1755.

Holliday, Robert (d. by 1748). "Hereum Thereum." Honorary Member (admitted 1745) and member of Eastern Shore Triumvirate.

Baltimore County physician; husband of Achsah (Wills, 1747, Box 7, No. 46; Inventories, 1748, Box 11, No. 44).

Hollyday, James (1722–1786). "Joshua Fluter." Honorary Member (admitted 1745).

Native Marylander; son of James Hollyday (1696–1747) and Sarah Covington (1683–1765); never married; Anglican; admitted to the Middle Temple in 1754 and returned to Maryland in 1758 to practice law; member of Lower House, Queen Anne's County, at various intervals from 1751 to 1770

Gresham, Sarah (d. 1756). Associate.

Widow of John Gresham (d. 1752); Annapolis merchant and owner of a plantation near South River Church (*MG,* Jan. 23, 1752, Nov. 28, 1754, Oct. 28, 1756); her will, which was witnessed by Jonas Green, indicates that she was probably well-to-do, leaving her son Richard properties in Gravesend and Northfleet, England (Wills, Box G, No. 72).

Hamilton, Dr. John (1697–1768). "Dr. Polyhistor." Honorary Member (admitted 1745).

Older brother of Alexander Hamilton; married Mary Scott in 1722 (*BDML,* 390); also a physician, John preceded his brother in coming to America and establishing a medical practice; he resided in Calvert County, owned a water mill, and left everything to his grandchildren (Wills, vol. 36, pp. 461–464). His obituary reads: "He has left, few, very few Equals, and none superior to him, in the Character of a skilful, and able Physician, and of an honest, humane, benevolent Man" (*MG,* Mar. 31, 1768).

Hamilton, Rev. John (d. 1773). "Broadface Round." Honorary Member (admitted 1745) and member of Eastern Shore Triumvirate.

Immigrated from Ireland and was inducted into St. Mary Anne's, Cecil County, in 1746; married Lettice Short, then Jane Peck (1757); active in the formation of the Corporation for the Relief of Widows and Orphans (see Wills, vol. 39, pp. 373–374).

Hart, Samuel. "Ignotus Warble." Honorary Member (admitted 1745). Married Catherin Gardner (1742) and apparently resided in Anne Arundel County (St. Margaret's Parish Register, MHS).

Henderson, Captain. Visitor.

The *MG* for Dec. 4, 1751, notes that Captain Henderson of the *Nancy* supplied Daniel Wolstenholme (q.v.)—and probably other merchants associated with the Tuesday Club—with fresh goods.

Hepburn, John (1710–1775). Visitor.

Resident of Prince George's County; survived by his son Samuel Chew Hepburn and his daughter Ann Leeke (Wills, Box 12, No. 11); appointed one of the judges of assize, on the Western Shore, in place of William Rogers (q.v.) (*MG,* Aug. 9, 1749); several notices in the *MG* suggest that he was a wealthy landowner (see, e.g., May 30, 1754; see also his will). Hepburn's obituary reads: "On Monday the 14th instant, died at his house

throughout the Revolution until his death (see Newman, *To Maryland from Overseas*, 79, and Mary M. Starin, "The Reverend John Gordon, 1717–1790," *MHM*, LXXV [1980], 167–191).

Gordon, Robert (ca. 1676–1753). "Serious Social." Oldstanding Member (admitted 1745).

Immigrated ca. 1719 (probably from Scotland) and settled in Annapolis; husband of Agnes (see *MG*, Nov. 8, 1753); Anglican; captain by 1723 and Esq. by 1724; merchant and officeholder; member of Lower House, Annapolis, 1725–1752; his obituary reads:

> On Sunday Evening last died, of the Gout in his Lungs, in the 77th Year of his Age, ROBERT GORDON, Esq; who was for many Years a very reputable Inhabitant of this City, one of the Aldermen . . . as also, one of the Judges of the Provincial Court, and one of the Commissioners of the Loan Office: He executed his public Trusts with Diligence and Integrity: In private Life he constantly maintain'd the Character of an honest Man, a quiet inoffensive Neighbour . . . and a pleasant and agreeable Companion . . . and on Tuesday last in the Evening his Remains were honourably interr'd, the Funeral Sermon being delivered by the Rev. Mr. BACON, and Persons of all Ranks accompanying his Corps to the Grave (*MG*, Sept. 13, 1753).

Green, Jonas (1712–1767). "Jonathan Grog." Longstanding Member (admitted 1748), P.P.P.P.P. (Purveyor, Punster, Punchmaker General, Printer, and Poet), then P.L.M.C. (Poet Laureate and Master of Ceremonies).

Descended from a family of printers, including his father, Timothy, public printer of Connecticut; probably moved to Maryland shortly after his marriage to Anne Catherine Hoof in Philadelphia (1738); public printer of Maryland from 1738 until his death, publisher of the *MG* from 1745 to 1767, poet, and alderman of Annapolis (Lemay, *Men of Letters*, 193–212; see also Lawrence C. Wroth, *A History of Printing in Colonial Maryland, 1686–1776* [Baltimore, 1922], 75–95). Green's obituary reads: "On Saturday Evening last died . . . Mr. JONAS GREEN, for Twenty-eight Years Printer to this Province, and Twenty-one Years Printer and Publisher of the MARYLAND GAZETTE: He was one of the Aldermen of this City. It would be the highest Indiscretion in us, to attempt giving the Character he justly deserved, only we have Reason to regret the Loss of him, in the various Stations of Husband, Parent, Master, and Companion" (*MG*, Apr. 16, 1767).

Washington and Thomas Sim Lee (1745–1819); fought in French and Indian War and became a wealthy landowner.

Forty, John (d. by 1765). Visitor.
Resident of Baltimore County; he apparently left little property and had no relations in Maryland (Wills, 1753, Box F, No. 33; Inventories, 1765, Box 17, No. 16).

Franklin, Benjamin. "Electro Vitrifrice." Visitor.
The *MG* for Jan. 17, 1754, states that Franklin had "arrived in Town, to regulate and settle the Affairs of the Post Offices"; Franklin's affiliation with Annapolis is discussed in Robert R. Hare, "Electro Vitrifrico in Annapolis: Mr. Franklin Visits the Tuesday Club," *MHM*, LVIII (1963), 62–66.

George, Sidney (d. 1774). "Dormer Goggle." Visitor.
Native Marylander; son of Joshua George (ca. 1695–1748) and Allice Docwray; Protestant; Gent., 1749; attorney; member of Lower House, Cecil County, 1751–1754.

Gibson, John (d. 1790). Associate.
Native Marylander; son of Woolman Gibson, Gent. (ca. 1695–1742), and Elizabeth Dawson; husband of Elizabeth (d. 1797); Anglican; Gent., 1777, and Esq. at death; planter; member of Lower House, Talbot County, 1777–1782.

Gibson, Mark. "Dumpling Gundiguts." Longstanding Member (admitted 1745).
Gibson's advertisement in the *MG* for Feb. 18, 1746, reads: "At the Subscriber's Brewing-Office in *Annapolis,* any Person may be supplied with the best Sorts of Malt Liquor, at reasonable Prices."

Gordon, John (1717–1790). "Smoothum Sly." Oldstanding Member (admitted 1745), Master of Ceremonies, then Honorary Member and member of Eastern Shore Triumvirate.
Born in Aberdeen, Scotland; inducted into St. Anne's, Annapolis, in 1745, where he preached against the Rebellion of 1745 (including his "On Occasion of the Suppression of the Unnatural Rebellion, in Scotland," which was advertised in the *MG,* Oct. 14, 1746); became rector of St. Michael's, Talbot County, where his whig principles permitted him to function

Dulany, Dennis (1730–1779). "Dio Ramble." Honorary Member (admitted 1750).

Native Marylander; son of Daniel Dulany and Rebecca Smith, and brother of Daniel Dulany (q.v.) and Walter Dulany (q.v.); entered the British navy in 1743 and remained in the service for several years; clerk of Kent County from 1754 to 1777; died without issue (*BDML*, 285; *Maryland Journal* (Baltimore), Dec. 21, 1779; see also Land, *Dulanys of Maryland*).

Dulany, Walter (d. 1773). "Slyboots Pleasant." Longstanding Member (admitted 1745).

Native Marylander; son of Daniel Dulany and Rebecca Smith, and brother of Daniel Dulany (q.v.) and Dennis Dulany (q.v.); married Mary Grafton ca. 1745; Anglican; Gent., 1747, and Esq., 1764; merchant, investor, naval officer, contractor, landowner, and officeholder (see Land, *Dulanys of Maryland*). His obituary states that he was "one of the Lord Proprietary's Council of State, Commissary General of this province, and one of the aldermen of this city" (*MG*, Sept. 23, 1773).

Earle, Michael (1722–1787). "Jocifer Bluechin." Honorary Member (admitted 1754).

Native Marylander; son of James Earle, Jr. (ca. 1694–1739), and Mary Tilghman (1702–ca. 1736); husband of Mary Carroll; Anglican; Gent., 1749; commander of a merchant ship, 1744, and merchant by 1753; member of Lower House, Cecil County, 1751–1763.

Ellis, John (d. 1747). "Giddy Thoughtless." Visitor.

Ellis's obituary reads: "The Ship *Montague*, Capt. *John Ellis* late Commander, is arrived in *James* River, *Virginia*, from *London,* but last from *Gibraltar;* Capt. *Ellis* died on the Passage; he often loaded in this Province, was a worthy honest Commander, and is lamented here by all that knew him" (*MG*, Sept. 1, 1747).

Fitzhugh, William (ca. 1722–1798). "Comico Butman." Honorary Member (admitted 1753).

Native Virginian, moved to Maryland ca. 1752 and resided there until his death; son of George Fitzhugh (ca. 1690–1722) and Mary Mason (ca. 1697–1728); married George Turberville's widow (née Lee), then Ann Frisby (1727–1793); Anglican; Esq. and colonel by 1752; planter, owner of a grist mill, fulling mills, and a distillery by 1783; member of Lower House, Calvert County, 1754–1761, and Upper House, 1769–1774; close friend of George

Dickinson, James (ca. 1726–1787). "Theophilus Smirker." Honorary Member (admitted 1750) and member of Eastern Shore Triumvirate.

Immigrated, possibly from Cumberland County, England, and resided in Talbot County, Maryland; married Rachel Taylor (1748); Anglican; Gent., 1750, and Esq., 1754; merchant; member of Lower House, Talbot County, 1768–1770; freed six slaves (1781) and ordered in his will that his nephew John Singleton (1750–1819) free all of his remaining slaves.

Dorsey, Edward (1718–1760). "Drawlum Quaint." Longstanding Member (admitted 1745) and Speaker.

Native Marylander; son of Caleb Dorsey, Gent. (1683–1743), and Elinor Warfield (1683–1752); married Henrietta Maria Chew (ca. 1704–1736/1737), stepdaughter of Daniel Dulany, the Elder, in 1748; Anglican; Esq., 1753; lawyer; member of Lower House, Frederick County, 1757–1760.

Dorsey, Richard (1714–1760). "Tunbelly Bowzer." Longstanding Member (admitted 1750).

Brother of Edward Dorsey (q.v.); married Elizabeth Beale, widow of William Nicholson, and resided in Anne Arundel County (Admin. Bonds, Box 62, No. 40); his obituary reads: "Early on Tuesday Morning last [Sept. 2], Died at his Plantation near Town, of the Gout in his Stomach, Head and Bowels, Mr. RICHARD DORSEY, aged 47 Years, Clerk of the Paper Currency Office, and for about 20 Years past, a very worthy Magistrate of this County" (*MG*, Sept. 11, 1760).

Downie, George (d. 1750). Associate.

Husband of Mary; Annapolis "Musitioner" (Wills, 1750, vol. 27, p. 405; Test. Procs., 1750, Box 50, No. 39); possibly the same George Downey who frequently advertised as a soapmaker in the *MG* (see, e.g., May 23, 1750).

Dulany, Daniel, Jr. (1722–1797). Frequent visitor.

Native Marylander; son of Daniel Dulany (1685–1753) and Rebecca Smith (ca. 1695–1737); husband of Rebecca Tasker (1724–1822); completed Eton in 1738 and entered Middle Temple in 1742 (called to the bar in 1746, a form of recognition rarely accorded a colonist); lawyer until 1763, then a planter; member of Lower House, Frederick County, 1749–1757, and Upper House, 1757–1774; argued against Stamp Act but opposed Sons of Liberty and advocated neutrality during the Revolution (see Land, *Dulanys of Maryland*).

until his death; author of numerous sermons, a translation of the Psalms, and the "Maryland Eclogues in Imitation of Virgil's" (see David Curtis Skaggs, "Thomas Cradock and the Chesapeake Golden Age," *William and Mary Quarterly*, 3d Ser., XXX [1973], 93–116).

Cumming, Alexander (1721–1774). "Prettyman Spyplot." Honorary Member (admitted 1750).
Native Marylander and resident of Baltimore County (Wills, Box 15, No. 19); son of William Cumming (q.v.) and Elizabeth Coursey; petitioned Maryland legislature for damages suffered while quartering the king's forces in his father's house in Annapolis (1754), but was denied payment (*BDML*, 246). Cumming's name often appeared in the *MG*, but only to indicate that he had returned from abroad.

Cumming, Thomas (d. 1774). "Coney Pimp Frontinbrass." Honorary Member (admitted 1750) and Agent for the Club in America.
Native of Scotland and a printer in Cork, Ireland; a "sensible Quaker" merchant who was living in New York by 1750–1751, when he visited Philadelphia, met Benjamin Franklin, and then traveled to Maryland and Virginia, where he acquired many friends and business associates. Established in London by 1754, Cumming made a trading voyage to the east coast of Africa, securing a trade agreement from a native ruler; following his return to England, he proposed to Pitt an expedition that led to the capture of the French Fort Louis at Senegal in 1758 (*The Papers of Benjamin Franklin*, ed. Leonard W. Labaree *et al.* [New Haven, Conn., 1959–], X, 345n–346n).

Cumming, William, Sr. (ca. 1696–1752). "Jealous Spyplot, Sr." Oldstanding Member (admitted 1745) and Attorney General.
Transported to America after being arrested in England (ca. 1716) as a Jacobite rebel; sold as a servant; married Elizabeth Coursey (1719/1720), then by 1742/1743, Margaret Thomas (d. 1804); Anglican; studied law while servant to Thomas Bordley and became a practicing lawyer in Maryland; member of Lower House, Annapolis, 1732–1734.

Cumming, William, Jr. (1724–1793). "Jealous Spyplot, Jr." Longstanding Member (admitted 1749), then Honorary Member.
Native Marylander; son of William Cumming (q.v.) and Elizabeth Coursey; planter and attorney; fined £25 during the Revolution for allegedly drinking to His Majesty's health (*BDML*, 246).

Whereas a Certain *John Charlett,* hath lately published in the MARY-LAND GAZETTE, No. 176 . . . his Intention of going to *England* . . . and hath, since that Time, absented himself from my service, to whom he is now a Servant, under Contract, at considerable yearly Wages; which contract he hath not performed . . . but left his said service, without giving me the least Warning, to my very great Prejudice and Damage. He is harboured, encouraged, and entertained, by some persons in this Town [Club members?]; to whom I give this Public notice, that if they continue so to do, I shall take such measures both with him and them, as the Law directs (*MG,* Oct. 26, 1748).

Chase, Thomas (1703–1779). "Bard Bavius." Baltimore Bard.

Immigrated to Maryland from England; son of Samuel Chase and Henrietta Catherine Davis; brother of Richard Chase, the Maryland clergyman; married Matilda Walker (1740), then Ann Birch (1763); educated at St. John's College, Cambridge, and at Sidney Sussex, where he studied medicine; ordained in 1739 and inducted into Somerset Parish on the Eastern Shore in 1740; rector of St. Paul's, Baltimore County, from February 1744/1745 until his death (Rosamond Randall Beirne, "The Reverend Thomas Chase: Pugnacious Parson," *MHM,* LIX [1964], 1–14).

Cole, Charles (d. 1757). "Nasifer Jole." Longstanding Member (admitted 1745) and President.

Regrettably little is known of Cole's life. He was appointed warden of St. Anne's, Annapolis, in 1741 (*MHM,* VIII [1913], 355). Cole's will (dated 1753 and revoked in 1757) indicates only that he was an Annapolis merchant (Wills, vol. 30, p. 511, Box C, No. 60). His obituary reads: "Last Tuesday Evening [July 5], Died here in an advanced Age, Mr. CHARLES COLE, Merchant, who had resided in this City above Forty Years, and was formerly a very considerable Trader. This Gentleman was a Batchelor, who, it is said, Repented of nothing in his latter Years, so much as that he had not Married while he was Young" (*MG,* July 7, 1757).

Cradock, Thomas (1718–1770). "Mevius Pumpkin," "Bard Mevius." Baltimore Bard and Honorary Member (admitted 1753).

Immigrated to Maryland from England in 1744; son of Arthur Cradock and Ann Marson; married Catherine Risteau (ca. 1728–1795) in 1746 (*BDML,* s.v. "Risteau, George"); ordained in 1743 and licensed for Maryland; appointed rector at St. Thomas's, Baltimore, in 1745, where he served

sion of the Peace for this County, and Captain of the City Independent Company" (*MG,* Mar. 15, 1764).

Burman, Anne. Associate.
Various advertisements in the *MG* suggest that Hamilton's Burman was Anne Burman, an Annapolis storekeeper (see, e.g., July 28, 1747, Aug. 23, 1753).

Calder, James (ca. 1695–1755). "Abraham Bumper." Honorary Member (admitted 1745).
Immigrated to Maryland ca. 1727; husband of Katherine Murray; Protestant; lawyer and planter; member of Lower House, Kent County, 1739–1744. Calder's obituary states that he long practiced law "with great Repute" and that he was "greatly esteem'd by all who knew him" (*MG,* Apr. 17, 1755).

Carpenter, John (d. 1748). "Giovanni Carpentiro." Associate.
Husband of Elizabeth Plater (Test. Procs., Box 49, No. 27); his obituary reads: "Yesterday died here Capt. *John Carpenter,* who had long been a worthy Inhabitant of this City, and was many Years Commander of a Ship from *London* in the Tobacco-Trade; and who, by a diligent Application and honest Industry, had acquired a considerable Fortune, with a fair Character" (*MG,* Nov. 2, 1748).

Carter, Ann. Associate.
Hamilton might be referring to any number of Annapolis ladies, but Ann Carter, daughter of Robert "King" Carter and wife of Benjamin Harrison (m. 1722), seems as likely a choice as any for the directress of the Syllabub Club (Richard Beale Davis, *Intellectual Life in the Colonial South, 1585–1763,* 3 vols. [Knoxville, Tenn., 1978], III, 1258).

Charlette, John. "Don John Charlotto." Clerk of the Kitchen (appointed 1753).
Husband of Ann; owner of two houses in London (Wills, 1764, Box C, No. 27). Hamilton's humorous treatment of the constant feuding between Charlette and Charles Cole (q.v.) was apparently no joke. The following advertisement, which Cole ran in the *MG* for nearly three months, implies that Charlette had decided to abdicate his position as Clerk of the Kitchen without Cole's permission.

Native Marylander; son of Thomas Bordley (ca. 1683–1726) and Ariana Vanderheyden (d. 1729); married Margaret Chew (d. 1773), then Sarah Fishbourne (1776); studied law under his half brother, Stephen Bordley (q.v.); Anglican; Esq. at death; elected to American Philosophical Society (1783); judge, planter, and agronomist; member of Upper House, 1768–1774; opposed intemperance and slavery; read extensively and published many books, including *A Summary View of the Courses of Crops, in the Husbandry of England and Maryland* (Philadelphia, 1784), *Yellow Fever* ([Philadelphia, 1794?]), *On Monies, Coins, Weights, and Measures, Proposed for the United States of America* (Philadelphia, 1789), and *Essays and Notes on Husbandry and Rural Affairs* (Philadelphia, 1799) (see Elizabeth Bordley Gibson, *Biographical Sketches of the Bordley Family, of Maryland, for Their Descendants* [Philadelphia, 1865]; Olive Moore Gambrill, "John Beale Bordley and the Early Years of the Philadelphia Agricultural Society," *Pennsylvania Magazine of History and Biography*, LXVI [1942], 410–439; and David Hackett Fischer, "John Beale Bordley, Daniel Boorstin, and the American Enlightenment," *Journal of Southern History*, XXVIII [1962], 327–342).

Bordley, Stephen (ca. 1710–1764). "Huffman Snap." Longstanding Member (admitted 1749).

Native Marylander, son of Thomas Bordley and Rachel Beard (d. 1722); never married; attended school in London and was admitted to the Inner Temple in 1729; returned to Maryland in 1733 to practice law; Anglican; Hon. at death; lawyer, naval officer (Annapolis, 1755–1762), attorney general (1756–1763), commissary general (1762–1764); member of Lower House (Annapolis, 1745; Anne Arundel County, 1749–1751; Annapolis, 1754–1756), and Upper House, 1759–1763 (see Elizabeth Bordley Gibson, *Biographical Sketches of the Bordley Family, of Maryland, for Their Descendants* [Philadelphia, 1865], and Joseph C. Morton, "Stephen Bordley of Colonial Annapolis," *Winterthur Portfolio*, V [1969], 1–14).

Bullen, John (d. 1764). "Bully Blunt," "Sir John Oldcastle." Oldstanding Member (admitted 1745) and Club Champion.

Bullen was a modestly wealthy Annapolis landowner; husband of Sarah and father of John (Wills, 1761, Box B, No. 109); elected mayor of Annapolis in 1749 (*MG*, Oct. 4, 1749); his obituary reads: "Monday last [March 12], Died, of a Complication of Disorders, in an advanced Age, JOHN BULLEN, Esq; one of the Commissioners of the Paper Currency Office, an Alderman of this City, and formerly for many Years in the Commis-

Biographical Sketches

Bacon, Thomas (1700?–1768). "Signior Lardini." Honorary Member (admitted 1745) and member of Eastern Shore Triumvirate.

Native of the Isle of Man; in Dublin, he published *A Compleat System of the Revenue of Ireland* (1737), established the *Dublin Mercury* (1741–1742), and edited the *Dublin Gazette* (1742); in 1743 he abandoned his publishing career and in 1745 was ordained and licensed for Maryland; rector of St. Peter's, Talbot County, by 1746; published *Four Sermons, upon the Great and Indispensable Duty of All Christian Masters and Mistresses to Bring Up Their Negro Slaves in the Knowledge and Fear of God* (London, 1750); active in establishing charity schools; compiled *Laws of Maryland at Large* (Annapolis, Md., 1765); accomplished musician and one of colonial Maryland's most prolific authors (Lemay, *Men of Letters*, 313–342; see also William E. Deibert, "Thomas Bacon, Colonial Clergyman," *MHM,* LXXIII [1978], 79–86).

Barnes, Abraham (d. ca. 1778). "Curious Courtly." Honorary Member (admitted 1747).

Immigrated to Virginia from England between 1740 and 1744; married Mary Elizabeth King (1715–1739), then Elizabeth Rousby (by 1743); Anglican; Gent., 1747; colonel by 1756; merchant, land speculator; member of Lower House, St. Mary's County, 1745–1754, although temporarily dismissed in 1749 for using liquor to influence the electorate; Maryland delegate to Albany Congress (1754); supporter of proprietary power.

Belt, Joseph (ca. 1680–1761). Visitor.

Native Marylander; son of Elizabeth and John Belt (d. 1698); married Hester Beale (1706), then Margery Wight (d. 1783); Anglican; Gent., 1726; colonel, 1726; merchant, planter, and modestly wealthy landowner; member of Lower House, Prince George's County, 1725–1737.

Bladen, Thomas (1698–1780). Associate.

Native Marylander; son of William Bladen (1670–1718) and Anne Van Swearingen; married Barbara Janssen (1737); Anglican; Gent., 1720, and Esq., 1744; officeholder and land speculator; governor of Maryland from August 1742 to October 1746, when he was dismissed for being "quarrelsome."

Bordley, John Beale (1726/1727–1804). "Quirpum Comic." Longstanding Member (admitted 1749) and Master of Ceremonies.

Newman, *To Maryland from Overseas*	Harry Wright Newman, *To Maryland from Overseas: A Complete Digest of the Jacobite Loyalists Sold into White Slavery in Maryland, and the British and Continental Background of Approximately 1400 Maryland Settlers from 1634 to the Early Federal Period with Source Documentation* (Annapolis, Md., 1982)

Addison, John (1713–1764). "Swillum Swagbelly." Honorary Member (admitted 1747).

Native Marylander; son of Thomas Addison (1679–1727) and Elinor Smith (1689–1761); husband of Susannah Wilkinson (d. 1774); Anglican; captain by 1747, and colonel by 1760; probably a planter; member of Lower House, Prince George's County, 1745–1757.

Atkinson, George. "Joggle Hasty." Honorary Member (admitted 1745).
Annapolis merchant; his notices in the *MG* show him frequently leaving for England, then returning to Annapolis to sell his goods (see Feb. 7, 1750, Mar. 22, 1751, Sept. 6, 1753).

Bacon, Anthony. "Comely Coppernose." Honorary Member (admitted 1749) and Agent for the Club in London.
Brother of Thomas Bacon (q.v.); received the B.A. from Trinity College, Dublin, in 1739, shortly before leaving for Maryland; began as a tobacco trader in Maryland and eventually became one of England's wealthiest tycoons (Lemay, *Men of Letters*, 188, 313; see also L. B. Namier, "Anthony Bacon, M.P., an Eighteenth-Century Merchant," *Journal of Economics and Business History,* II [1929], 20–70).

Bacon, John (d. 1756). "John Gabble." Honorary Member (admitted 1751).
Son of Thomas Bacon (q.v.); probable author of "A Recruiting Song, for the Maryland Independent Company" (*MG,* Sept. 19, 1754); on Sept. 30, 1754, Lt. John Bacon marched from Annapolis with a party of soldiers; he was later killed and scalped about five miles from Cumberland Fort (Lemay, *Men of Letters,* 300; *MG,* Oct. 3, 1754, Apr. 8, 1756).

BIOGRAPHICAL SKETCHES

Oldstanding (Original) Members, Longstanding (Regular) Members, Honorary Members, Visitors, and Associates

In compiling the sketches of individuals who were members of the legislature and of the clergy, I have relied particularly on Edward C. Papenfuse *et al.*, *A Biographical Dictionary of the Maryland Legislature, 1635–1789*, 2 vols. (Baltimore, 1979–1985) and on Nelson Waite Rightmyer, *Maryland's Established Church* (Baltimore, 1956). Complete bibliographic information is provided below for items cited in abbreviated form in the sketches. All unpublished Maryland records are in the Maryland State Archives, Annapolis.

BDML	Edward C. Papenfuse *et al.*, *A Biographical Dictionary of the Maryland Legislature, 1635–1789*, 2 vols. (Baltimore, 1979–1985)
Land, *Dulanys of Maryland*	Aubrey C. Land, *The Dulanys of Maryland: A Biographical Study of Daniel Dulany, the Elder (1685–1753) and Daniel Dulany, the Younger (1722–1797)* (Baltimore, 1955)
Lemay, *Men of Letters*	J. A. Leo Lemay, *Men of Letters in Colonial Maryland* (Knoxville, Tenn., 1972)
MG	*Maryland Gazette*
MHM	*Maryland Historical Magazine*
MHS	Maryland Historical Society, Baltimore
Newman, *Anne Arundel Gentry*	Harry Wright Newman, *Anne Arundel Gentry: A Genealogical History of Some Early Families of Anne Arundel County, Maryland* (Annapolis, Md., 1970)

Thoughtless, Giddy	John Ellis
Timorous, Prim	Thomas Jennings
Tomlinsonus, Joannes	John Thompson
Vitrifrice, Electro	Benjamin Franklin
Volens, Nolens	Thomas Thornton
Warble, Ignotus	Samuel Hart
Whiner, Rev.	Charles Lake
Wisely, Oldham	Richard Snowden
Wouldbe, Spatterdash	William Wilkins

Maccarty, Sir Hugh (Col. Rormis)	[?] Morris
Makefun, Merry	Robert Morris
Mevius, Bard (Mevius Pumpkin)	Thomas Cradock
Motely, Prattle	Witham Marshe
Muddy, Roundhead	Andrew Lendrum
Neverout, Solo (Mr. Protomusicus)	William Thornton
Philalethes, Dr.	perhaps Dr. John Hamilton
Philo-Bavius, Mevius	probably Jonas Green
Phraze, Courtly	Edward Lloyd
Phrazeobundus, Signior	Philip Key
Pickeringtonus, Gasperus	Stephen Pickering
Pleasant, Slyboots	Walter Dulany
Polyhistor, Dr.	Dr. John Hamilton
Polypharmacus, Dr.	Alexander Hamilton
Precisio, Giovanni	Daniel Wolstenholme
Pyrgos, Dr.	[?] Towers
Quaint, Drawlum	Edward Dorsey
Ramble, Dio	Dennis Dulany
Ranter, Roughby	James Richard
Rhubarb, Dr.	Archibald Spencer
Rodomantus, Rev.	James Sterling
Round, Broadface	Rev. John Hamilton
Scribble, Loquacious	Alexander Hamilton
Scriblerus, Martinus	probably Alexander Hamilton
Sehesslius, Signior	John Hesselius
Sly, Smoothum	John Gordon
Smirker, Theophilus	James Dickinson
Snap, Huffman	Stephen Bordley
Snuffysnout (Snuffybeak), Stentor	Robert Swan
Social, Serious	Robert Gordon
Spruce, Seemly	William Rogers
Spyplot, Jealous, Sr.	William Cumming, Sr.
Spyplot, Jealous, Jr.	William Cumming, Jr.
Spyplot, Prettyman	Alexander Cumming
Surly, Huffbluff	Robert North
Swagbelly, Swillum	John Addison
Swallowbeak, Samuel	Samuel Stringar
Swashgut, Madonna	Catherine Jennings
Sylvius, Nathaniel	Samuel Wood
Thereum, Hereum	Robert Holliday

TUESDAY CLUB PSEUDONYMS

Bavius, Bard	Thomas Chase
Bluechin, Jocifer	Michael Earle
Blunt, Bully (Sir John Oldcastle)	John Bullen
Boniface, Mr.	perhaps John or Anthony Stewart
Bowzer, Tunbelly	Richard Dorsey
Bumbasto, Col.	?
Bumper, Abraham	James Calder
Butman, Comico	William Fitzhugh
Carpentiro, Giovanni	John Carpenter
Charlotto, Don John	John Charlette
Cheary, Chantum	Richard Hill, Jr.
Comas (Comus), Laconic	John Lomas
Comic, Quirpum	John Beale Bordley
Coppernose, Comely	Anthony Bacon
Courtly, Curious	Abraham Barnes
Crankum, Crinkum	William Lux (of Annapolis)
Dogmaticus, Philo	Alexander Malcolm
Fibber, Humbug	?
Fluter, Joshua	James Hollyday
Frontinbrass, Coney Pimp	Thomas Cumming
Furbisher, Capt.	John Troy
Gabble, John	John Bacon
Goggle, Dormer	Sidney George
Grog, Jonathan	Jonas Green
Grumbleton, Squeak	John Wollaston
Gundiguts, Dumpling	Mark Gibson
Hasty, Joggle	George Atkinson
Hop-a-kickie, Mr.	[?] Jennings
Jaunter, Jeronimo	Upton Scott
Jerkum, Jehoiakim	probably Alexander Hamilton
Jole, Nasifer	Charles Cole
Laconic, Prim	Edward Tilghman
Lardini, Signior	Thomas Bacon
Leidemont, Mr.	Samuel Middleton
Lisper, Mr.	perhaps Samuel Mitchelson

lxxv

and the *Dictionary of Artists in America;* for musicians, the *International Cyclopedia of Music and Musicians;* for folklore, the *Standard Dictionary of Folklore* and *Brewer's Dictionary of Phrase and Fable;* for alchemists, the *Bibliotheca Chemica;* for saints, the *Oxford Dictionary of Saints;* and for an occasional event in British history, J. P. Kenyon's *Dictionary of British History.* An invaluable source of information on the songs Hamilton alludes to has been John Barry Talley, *Secular Music in Colonial Annapolis: The Tuesday Club, 1745–56* (Urbana, Ill., 1988).

 I have tried to find sources for all of Hamilton's quotations or secondhand stories. Though it is impossible in many cases to pinpoint the exact edition that Hamilton may have used, for direct quotations (such as the passage from James I's *Counterblaste* on I, 45–46) I have referred to an edition printed prior to his writing the *History;* for indirect quotations, however (such as the allusion to Dryden on I, 47), I have referred to more recently edited texts, since Hamilton has only paraphrased his source anyway. Where Hamilton has referred to a "certain author" who says something profound, I have done my best to track down the author and the quotation. In some cases I have been successful; in others where I have not, I suspect that the "certain author" is sometimes Hamilton himself.

REMARKS ON THE NOTES

All internal references in the notes are to Hamilton's original pagination, which appears in brackets in the margins of this edition.

Rather than insult the reader by providing superfluous notes on commonplace classical, biblical, and historical allusions, I have generally noted only those allusions that the average reader of this edition might not immediately recognize. Similarly, despite Hamilton's sometimes whimsical spellings, nearly all the words he used are comprehensible to modern readers or available in any good dictionary. I have noted only those words that Hamilton coined (e.g., *scabarabused*) or that have become unfamiliar to most readers (e.g., *lcorice*, a variant of *lickerous*, an archaic word meaning "lecherous or greedy").

I have frequently incorporated information from the following reference works into my notes: for biographical information, I have used the *Dictionary of National Biography,* the *Dictionary of American Biography,* the *Encyclopaedia Britannica* (1910–1911 edition), the *Century Cyclopaedia of Names, La Grande Encyclopédie* (1886 edition), and *Webster's Biographical Dictionary;* for literary allusions, the *Oxford Companion to English Literature,* the *Oxford Companion to the Theatre,* the *Oxford Companion to American Literature,* the *Oxford Companion to French Literature,* the *Dictionnaire des Lettres Françaises,* the *Oxford Companion to Spanish Literature,* E. Cobham Brewer's *The Reader's Handbook of Allusions, References, Plots, and Stories,* and, often the most useful of all, Robert Watt's *Bibliotheca Britannica;* for words, maxims, and proverbial phrases, the *Oxford English Dictionary,* the *Century Dictionary and Cyclopedia,* the *English Dialect Dictionary,* the *Scottish National Dictionary,* Eric Partridge's *Dictionary of Slang and Unconventional English* and *Dictionary of the Underworld,* Burton Stevenson's *Home Book of Proverbs, Maxims, and Familiar Phrases,* Brewer's *Dictionary of Phrase and Fable,* G. L. Apperson's *English Proverbs and Proverbial Phrases,* Morris Palmer Tilley's *Dictionary of the Proverbs in England,* Mitford M. Mathews's *Dictionary of Americanisms,* and Bartlett Jere Whiting's *Early American Proverbs and Proverbial Phrases;* and for classical allusions, the *Oxford Classical Dictionary* and *Harper's Dictionary of Classical Literature and Antiquities.* I have also used the following more specialized reference works whenever possible: for identifying artists, Michael Bryan's *Dictionary of Painters and Engravers,* the *Dictionnaire des Peintres, Sculpteurs, Dessinateurs, et Graveurs,*

cation was finally less important to the members than the act of participation. For Hamilton, music was meant to "soften and humanize" mankind (III, 116), to make man more sociable to man. If that meant having to put up with a few snufflings and assorted noises, it was worth it.

Remarks on the Music   lxxi

contributed to their musical performances in one capacity or another. The principal composers were Bacon and Hamilton, in that order of musical ability. Bacon's works, Talley writes, display "considerable structural skill," and Hamilton's melodies are "usually interesting, often expressive, and well formed," although corrections to the 1750 ode show that "someone [probably Bacon] attempted to make musical sense out of some of the stranger passages."[2] The principal musicians were Bacon (violin and viola da gamba), who was appointed musician *con stromenti* to the club, Malcolm (flute and violin), Hamilton (violoncello), Daniel Wolstenholme (flute), Robert Morris (violin), William Lux of Annapolis (organ and harpsichord), and Jonas Green (French horn), who also wrote the words to the odes. Everyone lent their voices, but William Thornton, Protomusicus, outsang them all. Hamilton reports in the *History* that, because of his "uncommon talent at Singing," Thornton was appointed musician *con voce* "by unanimous consent" and that whenever he voted he was required "to sing it in a musical manner, else his vote to go for nothing" (I, 283). Charles Cole, the club's president, also entertained the club with numerous songs. Cole acquired his musical talent, Hamilton says,

> merely by the force of Genius, having never been taught, and his talent this way lies in vocal execution, he having a number of old Songs by him, to the words of which, he affirms, he never is at a loss to find a tune, and Indeed, give him words at any time, and he'll Immediatly clap a tune to them, with so Sweet and small a voice, and so delicate a trill, that some people have doubted whether or not he has in his youth been Italianized, but, be that as it will, . . . he has a most exquisite pipe, and, were he not obliged sometimes to wear his Spectacles, to read the words of the Song, . . . his voice would be quite clear, and without asperity, but this nasal machine, will sometimes in the high notes, occasion a Snuffling, which a nice ear will easily excuse, seeing the cause is known to proceed from no natural defect (I, 162).

Other of the club's members no doubt emitted equally strange noises from time to time, and no doubt they were also forgiven their trespasses. The Tuesday Club's music, Talley rightly argues, demonstrates that "a high level of musical sophistication existed in the American colonies well before the formal establishment of a concert tradition."[3] But the level of sophisti-

---

2. Talley, *Secular Music in Colonial Annapolis*, 114, 116.
3. *Ibid.*, 121.

to print. By darkening all the notes, scales, and words on my copy of the music, cutting out as much of the blank gray area between the scales as possible, and then making a photocopy of my copy on the lightest possible setting, I was able to eliminate most of the gray that had accumulated over time and to make the music itself more legible. I then repeated the entire process a second time. As a result, the music printed in this edition appears almost as it did when the Tuesday Club first passed it about.

Where holes appear in the manuscript pages of the music, I have supplied the missing measures whenever possible with the corresponding measures from the "Record." I have indicated in brackets the few instances where a given measure or line is illegible in either the *History* or the "Record." Only one section was beyond redemption: the "Grand Club Minuet," which appears immediately following the 1751 ode in the *History*. The Tuesday Club must have particularly enjoyed playing that piece and passing it about, for it has virtually crumbled into illegibility. Regrettably, the only copy of the "Grand Club Minuet" is the one in the *History;* had another copy been available in the "Record," I would have restored that selection as well.

For a conjectural reading of the "Grand Club Minuet"—and conjectures on the passages I have indicated as illegible—and for modernized transcriptions of all the musical pieces in the *History,* see John Barry Talley, *Secular Music in Colonial Annapolis: The Tuesday Club, 1745–56* (Urbana, Ill., 1988). Talley has done a remarkable job not only of reconstructing and evaluating the club's original music, but also of researching all the borrowed songs and catches that the members played in club. His transcriptions helped me to decipher some of the more obscure measures in the club's music. Aside from obvious differences in the appearance of our two versions—Talley uses modern equivalents of Hamilton's symbols and standardizes his many backward or upside-down notes, whereas I have reproduced the original, quirks and all—there are various substantive differences between my restorations and Talley's transcriptions. For the most part, our versions agree. But sometimes we have read notes and entire measures differently, and sometimes—as in the "Gavotta Burlesqua" and the "Grand Club Jig"—our versions differ considerably.

In an age that witnessed an "invasion of music by the amateur in search of diversion," an age when almost "every gentleman played the violin, and every lady the flute,"[1] it is likely that all of the Tuesday Club's members

---

1. Homer Ulrich, *Chamber Music* (New York, 1948), 115.

REMARKS ON THE MUSIC

The original music in *The History of the Tuesday Club* includes—in order of appearance—the anniversary ode for 1750, composed primarily by Hamilton (the overture, air and minuet for his honor [the club's president], and pastorale were composed by Thomas Bacon); the anniversary ode for 1751, which includes the "Club March against Sir Hugh Maccarty," both by Bacon; the "Grand Club Minuet *con variatione*" (1751), a "Minuet for Sir John" (1751), and a "Minuet for His Honor" (1752), all by Bacon; the anniversary ode for 1753, which includes a minuet for the chancellor, a minuet and a gavotte for his honor, and a minuet and a march for Sir John, "by several hands" (probably Alexander Malcolm, William Thornton, Charles Cole, and Hamilton, but not Bacon); a "Minuet for the Poet Laureat" (1753), perhaps by Hamilton; a "Grand Club Jig" (1753), by Thornton; an "Overture for His Honor's Entertainment" (an overture for the 1752 anniversary ode, never set to music), which concludes with a "Gavotta Burlesqua for His Honor," both by Bacon; a "Minuet for the Attorney General" (1753), by Bacon; and "The Jurors for the City Bring" (1755), by Cole. Earlier versions of Bacon's pieces in the 1750 ode, the complete 1751 ode, the 1751 "Minuet for Sir John," the 1752 "Minuet for His Honor," and the "Attorney Generals Minuet" appear in the "Tuesday Club Record Book," MS. 854, Maryland Historical Society, Baltimore.

The manuscript pages of the music are in very poor condition. Hamilton wrote the music on both sides of the paper, and over time the ink has bled badly through the pages, creating numerous lines of music that look like indiscernible masses of gray. Moreover, the pages are badly worn and torn in spots, apparently from much thumbing and passing about during the club's meetings. Some pages, particularly in the 1751 ode, contain more holes than music. Fortunately, the copy of the 1751 ode appearing in the "Record" is fairly legible, making it possible to reconstruct much of that ode in the *History*.

Rather than provide modernized transcriptions, I have sought to restore the music as nearly as possible to its original condition so that I could provide readable copies of the original scores for this edition. I began restoring the music in a rudimentary way for my dissertation, but only recently have I found a means of making the original scores legible enough

scenes of great passion, where the illustrator can "supply the imperfection of the reader's imagination, and the deficiency of the description in the author."[13] At their best, Hamilton's illustrations serve precisely that purpose. The many scenes he depicts, such as the "Club Hubbub concerning the Records," serve not merely to ornament the text but to accentuate particularly lively moments therein and to enhance the reader's imaginative participation in those moments. To be sure, Hamilton's drawings are crude, awkward, at times even clumsy. The work of an untrained amateur, they nonetheless indicate a knowledge of contemporary English illustration and a good understanding of how illustrations should relate to the spirit of the text. They serve, moreover, to capture the physical aspects of an important segment of society in colonial Maryland. Most of all, they bring the comic world of the *History* to life. They are a significant contribution to the corpus of American art.

[Editor's Note: Nearly all of Hamilton's drawings (except for his drawing of the modern theater, half of which is missing) have held up well over time and can be reproduced clearly from photographic copies. Hamilton did not live, however, to complete four of the drawings in volume II. (There are no drawings in volume III for the same reason.) Of those four, two—the frontispiece and the "Deputation of the Club to His Lordship"—are very sketchy. It is quite possible that the last thing Hamilton worked on before dying was the central figure in the frontispiece to volume II. The last drawing of any substance in the *History* is the deputation drawing; Hamilton apparently stopped in the middle of that drawing and went back to provide the frontispiece. Shortly before and after the deputation drawing, two blank pages appear in Hamilton's manuscript where he planned to include drawings of the "Great Clubical Battle of the Great Seal" and of "His Lordship Recathedrized." I have omitted those pages; the two pages with sketches, however, do appear in this edition.]

---

13. "Advertisement concerning the Prints," in Jacob Tonson's edition of *Don Quixote* (London, 1742), xxv.

edition of Tobias Smollett's *The Adventures of Roderick Random* (1748); in any event, there are stylistic parallels between Hamilton's drawings and Hayman's illustrations in these works, particularly in their manner of differentiating individuals and capturing everyday details.

Of the dozen portrait painters active in colonial America during the Tuesday Club's lifetime, two were connected with the club.[10] John Hesselius (Signior Sehesslius; 1728–1778) was active in Maryland in 1750 and 1751. At Sederunt 187 (October 10, 1752), he was ordered to paint a portrait of Charles Cole. This commission was apparently never filled, and no explanation is offered in the *History* (III, 117).[11] John Wollaston (Squeak Grumbleton) visited the Tuesday Club on January 23 and May 25, 1753. During his residence in Annapolis, his paintings were publicly exhibited. Dr. Thomas Thornton, another occasional visitor to the club, in 1753 published a poem in the *Maryland Gazette* entitled "Extempore: On Seeing Mr. Wollaston's Pictures in Annapolis."[12] Other members of the Tuesday Club, including Hamilton, must certainly have seen Wollaston's paintings.

Both Hesselius and Wollaston were skillful portrait painters working within a traditional Anglo-American style. As such, their aim was to present the sitter in the most agreeable pose and to minimize any irregularities of facial structure, while using elegant settings and attributes (clothing, books, etc.) to provide a sense of affluence befitting the subject. Although Hamilton clearly was familiar with such portraiture, he did not follow its conventions himself. Instead he used the simpler format of bust-length portraiture and emphasized precisely the physical features of his sitters (long noses, pointed chins) that Hesselius or Wollaston would have minimized. In this manner Hamilton successfully and comically differentiated his subjects.

Arguing against the common perception that illustrations were mere embellishments, Dr. John Oldfield stated in 1742 that they were "capable of answering a higher purpose, by representing and illustrating many things, which cannot be so perfectly expressed by words," particularly during

---

10. Richard H. Saunders and Ellen G. Miles, *American Colonial Portraits, 1700–1776* (Washington, D.C., 1987), 30.

11. See Elaine G. Breslaw, ed., *Records of the Tuesday Club of Annapolis, 1745–56* (Urbana, Ill., 1988), 372. The portrait is not listed in Richard K. Doud, "John Hesselius, Maryland Limner," *Winterthur Portfolio*, V (1969), 129–153.

12. The poem appeared in the *Maryland Gazette,* Mar. 15, 1753. It is attributed to Thornton by J. A. Leo Lemay in *A Calendar of American Poetry in the Colonial Newspapers and Magazines and in the Major English Magazines through 1765* (Worcester, Mass., 1972), 159. The poem is reprinted in George C. Groce, "John Wollaston (fl. 1736–1767): A Cosmopolitan Painter in the British Colonies," *Art Quarterly*, XV (1952), 140.

tained two hundred carefully engraved vignettes illustrating the lyrics.[7] Given Hamilton's interest in music, he was likely aware of this publication. He was probably also familiar with illustrated editions of Shakespeare's plays, particularly Jacob Tonson's edition (1709), illustrated by François Boitard (ca. 1670–ca. 1717), and he may well have been influenced by Boitard's son, Louis Philippe Boitard (d. ca. 1760), who created book illustrations and scenes of London life, and whose engravings, like Hamilton's drawings, are linear, precise, and awkward.

The most prolific and highly regarded engraver in London in the 1730s and 1740s and, according to Hanns Hammelmann, the man most responsible for bringing from France "the vogue of the elegant engraved book of the rococo [and] the notion that a book should not only be pleasant to read, but also attractive to look at and to handle" was Hubert François Burguignon Gravelot (1669–1773). Gravelot's influence extended to other book illustrators including Hogarth and Francis Hayman, with whom he used to "take his evening ale."[8] Among his works for London publishers were illustrations for *The Dramatick Works of John Dryden* (1735), *The Kit-Kat Club* (1735), *The Works of Shakespeare* (1740), and the first French edition of Fielding's *Tom Jones*—all of which Hamilton probably saw. Particularly in *Tom Jones,* Gravelot's delicate French rococo style at times seems out of place in illustrating some of the rougher and more boisterous scenes in the novel. Hamilton's inelegant style, better suited to the content of the *History,* was perhaps a reaction against the delicate style Gravelot sought to introduce in England.

Gravelot's and Hogarth's drinking companion, Francis Hayman (1708?–1776), was also a prolific illustrator as well as a painter of historical subjects, conversation pieces, narrative scenes, and theatrical portraits. He and Gravelot collaborated on the illustrations for Samuel Richardson's *Pamela* (which Hamilton read) and for Thomas Hanmer's edition of Shakespeare's plays (1743–1744). Hammelmann notes that, particularly in his illustrations for *Fables for the Female Sex* (1744), Hayman "introduced a more homely touch of local genre into the French manner, and this steadily increased in the work of later artists."[9] Hamilton was probably familiar with Hayman's illustrations for the *Fables* and his frontispieces to the second

---

7. Hanns A. Hammelmann, *Book Illustrators in Eighteenth-Century England* (New Haven, Conn., 1975), ed. and completed by T. S. R. Boase, 15–16; Nancy R. Davison, "Bickham's *Musical Entertainer* and Other Curiosities," in *Eighteenth-Century Prints in Colonial America: To Educate and Decorate,* ed. Joan D. Dolmetsch (Williamsburg, Va., 1979), 98–122.

8. Hammelmann, *Book Illustrators in Eighteenth-Century England,* 38, 39.

9. *Ibid.,* 5.

stock situations at all is a testament to his invention. Three additional drawings concern the club's anniversaries. The pattern for these occasions was set the first year when the members, regular and honorary, assembled at the home of the president and marched in procession to the meeting place under the admiring gaze of the citizens of Annapolis. Like the proceedings, these drawings resemble carefully staged theatrical scenes: the action is in the foreground and the background is sketchily represented by a few buildings with figures in the windows. "The First Grand Anniversary Procession" is the simplest of the three; the other two are more elaborate. Hamilton's drawings of the anniversary processions and other events reflect the increasing pomp and ceremony in the club's proceedings, but with a simplicity that humorously undercuts his baleful lamentations against the degenerate effects of luxury.

Although his style is distinctive, Hamilton was surely influenced by other eighteenth-century painters and illustrators, particularly William Hogarth (1697–1764). In the *History* Hamilton pays homage to "the genius of the Celebrated Hogarth" (III, 345–346) and further suggests Hogarth's influence in his verbal sketch of President Jole: "when Speeches were made that displeased [Jole]," he writes, "there followed an elongation of countenance, and a droping of the Lower Jaw, which some of the members called his timber Countenance, which would have afforded no uncommon hint to the famous Hogarth" (I, 230). For the most part, Hogarth concerned himself with series of paintings and prints rather than illustrations for books. He did, however, illustrate a number of literary works during the 1720s and 1730s. Hogarth's figures are less slender than those of his contemporaries and his lines more deeply incised on the plates, making the figures emerge from the paper. His abandonment of the pretty faces typical of eighteenth-century illustrators and the robust character of his drawings no doubt afforded an uncommon hint to Hamilton.

Although Hogarth was the most familiar English artist and illustrator, Hamilton may have been acquainted with the drawings of several of Hogarth's contemporaries. The portrait painter John Vanderbank (1694–1739) was also known for his illustrations for the second edition of *A Select Collection of Novels and Histories* (1729) and for Jacob Tonson's edition of *Don Quixote* (1738). Hamilton was perhaps influenced by Vanderbank's manner of focusing attention on the protagonists in any given episode and on their unusual physical characteristics. George Bickham, Sr. (d. 1769), and George Bickham, Jr. (d. 1749), both designed and engraved illustrations for numerous literary works and for *The Musical Entertainer* (1737–1739), which con-

trait, Hamilton's self-portrait—one of the few extant colonial self-portraits[4]—is a direct representation of himself holding a volume labeled "Record of the Tuesday Club." The portrait of Jonathan Grog, poet laureate and master of ceremonies, is curious because of its singular format, which seems derived from an antique coin, cameo, or seal. A profile of Algernon Sidney of somewhat later date is derived from a seal cut by the seventeenth-century die cutter Thomas Simon.[5] Perhaps Hamilton was inspired by a similar source. He was no doubt also familiar with images of Julius Caesar, commonly portrayed with a crown of laurel leaves. John Burdett of Williamsburg, for example, had twelve portraits of the Caesars in his collection.[6] Hamilton obviously meant to bestow a particular dose of flattery on his good friend Jonas Green by portraying him in this manner.

Six other illustrations in volume I depict incidents concerning the Tuesday Club's precursors—the Whin-Bush Club, the Royalist Club, the Red-House Club, and the Ugly Club. Among the more interesting of these is the violent performance depicted in "Mr Neilson's Battle with the Royalist Club," in which the various objects described in the text are seen flying through the air, the punch bowl is overturned, and chairs are used as battering rams. The compactness of this scene, the lack of space between any of the figures, and the omission of any background rivets attention on the action and adds to the immediacy and intensity of the scene. Whereas the introduction of too much detail diminishes the impact of some contemporary English literary illustrations, Hamilton was careful to avoid unnecessary distractions in scenes such as this. He was, however, capable of setting a scene if he considered it appropriate, as in his drawing of the Ugly Club. In this illustration he follows his text closely, including cobwebs in the corner, chalked figures on the wall, and cracked panes in the leaded glass window. When he wished to provide a detailed setting, Hamilton did so with competence.

The remaining illustrations in the *History* depict the club's proceedings or incidents discussed in the club. Four of these concern individuals delivering speeches to the club. That Hamilton was able to differentiate these

---

4. Ann C. Van Devanter, *American Self-Portraits, 1670–1973* (Washington, D.C., 1974) lists only three from the colonial period. No drawings from the colonial period are reproduced in Marvin Sadik and Harold Francis Pfister, comps., *American Portrait Drawings* (Washington, D.C., 1980).

5. Frank H. Sommer III, "Thomas Hollis and the Arts of Dissent," in *Prints in and of America to 1850*, ed. John D. Morse (Charlottesville, Va., 1970), 137.

6. See Joan Dolmetsch, "Prints in Colonial America: Supply and Demand in the Mid-Eighteenth Century," in *Prints in and of America*, ed. Morse, 59.

contained within a rectangle ruled with a pen and iron gall ink, the same used for the writing of the text and for the inscriptions on the drawings. The single graphite sketch in volume II of the manuscript indicates that Hamilton used a pencil to delineate the basic features of the illustrations; the pencil is not dominant, however, in the completed drawings.

Ten of the drawings in volume I and three in volume II are portraits. The first, Congal de Rutherin, was, according to the inscription, copied from "an antique marble bas-relief dug up from the rubbish dumps of an old monastery near Drumlanridge." Hamilton has correctly drawn a facsimile of a relief, as if taken from a funerary monument. Although a fictive portrait, it is realistic, not idealized as were so many funerary portraits. The other portraits in the *History*—of various members of the club—all share the format of bust-length mezzotint portraits popular in England and in the colonies during the first half of the eighteenth century: each portrait is surrounded by an oval frame set into a larger rectangle, with spandrels normally of a different tone than the immediate background of the portrait within the oval. Space below the portrait is reserved for the title and any additional inscription.

In a very economical style, Hamilton captures the salient features of the club's members, occasionally exaggerating certain characteristics. Although his drawings have been called caricatures, most of them correspond to his verbal sketches.[3] Hamilton's lack of drawing expertise renders his attempts awkward, but this is not tantamount to caricature. Several of the portraits do, however, contain a good deal of exaggeration, a prime example of which is the portrait of the club's president, Charles Cole (Nasifer Jole). Hamilton devotes several pages to describing Jole, noting that he was "of a fair complexion, long and Sharp visage; somewhat Inclinable to a Square countenance, his nose aqueline, his chin of a Considerable length and prominent, in short, he is what many call in their vulgar Stile somewhat hatchet faced" (I, 160). Jole's aquiline nose and pointed chin are used to good advantage in the formal portrait and distinguish him from the other members in the group scenes. Since Jole often dressed flamboyantly—red was his favorite color—we can only regret that Hamilton's portraits are not in color.

Two other interesting portraits are of Hamilton himself (Loquacious Scribble) and Jonas Green (Jonathan Grog). Unlike Jole's exaggerated por-

---

3. Anna Wells Rutledge, "A Humorous Artist in Colonial Maryland," *American Collector,* XVI (1947), 15; J. A. Leo Lemay, *Men of Letters in Colonial Maryland* (Knoxville, Tenn., 1972), 253.

REMARKS ON THE DRAWINGS
Georgia Brady Barnhill

By his own admission in *The History of the Tuesday Club,* Hamilton "had a foolish Sort of a Genius for drawing" (III, 118), and among the more intriguing features of this edition are the many drawings he incorporated into his narrative. These illustrations predate any printed literary illustrations for an American text by almost fifty years. The next significant illustrations of American origin appeared when Elkanah Tisdale designed and engraved illustrations for John Trumbull's *M'Fingal* (1794).[1] Because of the uniqueness of Hamilton's drawings, some commentary on them is appropriate here.

The History of the Tuesday Club contains forty-eight completed drawings—thirty in volume I and eighteen in volume II. In addition there are vignettes of the club badge and seal, the presidential badge and cap of state, and the shield on the presidential canopy. Volume II contains an unfinished frontispiece, an unfinished pencil sketch, and two pages with ruled rectangles and titles below intended for illustrations that were never completed. Volumes II and III contain numerous blank leaves that Hamilton apparently left for illustrations he planned to include but never completed. These blank leaves support Robert Micklus's contention that the manuscript was left incomplete at Hamilton's death.[2]

The illustrations are uniform in technique. Hamilton used a combination of pen and black ink and wash applied with a brush. Each drawing is

---

Georgia Brady Barnhill is Andrew W. Mellon Curator of Graphic Arts at the American Antiquarian Society in Worcester, Massachusetts. She wishes to thank the Bibliographical Society of America and the American Philosophical Society for grants that supported the research for this essay, and the American Antiquarian Society for a research leave in 1986.

1. Donald C. O'Brien, "Elkanah Tisdale: Designer, Engraver, and Miniature Painter," *Connecticut Historical Society Bulletin,* XLIX (1984), 83–96.

2. The "Record of the Tuesday Club" (Maryland Historical Society, MS. 854) contains twenty-three of Hamilton's drawings. The Dulany Papers (MS. 1265) contain several additional drawings, three of which pertain to the Royalist Club and two to the Tuesday Club. A second portrait of George Neilson is in the Dulany Papers, and portraits of Beale Bordley, Richard Dorsey, and Walter Dulany are in the "Record" (these portraits are missing from the *History*). The members are given their proper names, although Latinized, in the "Record" drawings and appear wearing their club badges, which Hamilton omitted from the portraits in the *History.* Since Hamilton's technique improved over time, the illustrations in the *History* are better drawn.

SUPERSCRIPTS

Hamilton's practice concerning superscripts was inconsistent. Sometimes he raised, sometimes he raised and underlined, and often he neither raised nor underlined the last letter or letters of abbreviated words and titles (*Secretary*, for instance, appears abbreviated as *Secret^{ry}*, *Secret^{ry}*, and *Secretry*). Since he showed no particular preference in handling superscripts, I have chosen the least distracting method of bringing them all down to the line.

Editorial Method

even to attempt to normalize Hamilton's spelling in these and similar instances. I can only promise the reader that, however odd a particular spelling may at first appear, if one is patient one will find several more just like it.

I have therefore made few spelling changes. If Hamilton spelled a particular word or sound the same way more than once, I have assumed he knew what he was doing. I have been especially wary about changing spellings that likely reflect his Scottish dialect. It hardly seems coincidental, for instance, that he used the spellings *havy* (*heavy*) and *plasantry* (*pleasantry*) only a few paragraphs apart. I have, however, changed obvious misspellings (*hononor*) and less blatant misspellings that one could probably find some justification for retaining, but that arise in ordinary words Hamilton always spelled otherwise (*istead*). I have changed a word that he spelled the same way more than once only when it could be misread to mean something else, and when the change I have made is consistent with his normal usage. It is confusing, for example, to see *they* spelled *the*, so even though Hamilton spelled it that way three times in the *History*, I have spelled it as he normally did hundreds of other times. Since all superscripts have been brought down to the line in this edition, I have also expanded the few words beginning with the thorn to avoid misreadings (*the* for *ye*, for example).

ABBREVIATIONS

Hamilton abbreviated numerous words and phrases in English and in Latin, and he particularly enjoyed mocking law Latin by almost incoherently abbreviating it. The abbreviations are part of the fun of reading the *History*, and I have retained rather than expanded them.

FALSE STARTS

In this edition I have ignored all false starts. (I included them in my dissertation.) Hamilton wrote the *History* so quickly that it would be pointless to note every false start (e.g., *lwrong*) or slip of the pen.

LIGATURES

Hamilton normally wrote *æ* as a ligature, occasionally in such a way that it might easily be mistaken for a double *e*. I have used *æ* for all those ligatures and *ae* for the few instances where he did not write *ae* as a ligature. Hamilton generally did not use the ligature *œ*, but in the few instances where he did I have reproduced it as such.

SEMICOLONS

Wherever one might expect to find a semicolon, it is likely that Hamilton has used a comma instead. I have therefore added no semicolons in this edition. As with periods, I have occasionally changed semicolons to commas when a word or phrase following the semicolon is clearly an afterthought.

QUESTIONABLE ADDITIONS

Hamilton frequently doubled over the final loop of a letter or carried down the tail of a letter in such a way that he appeared to be adding commas without lifting his pen. These types of letters often occur in places where he normally used commas; but they appear equally often where he normally omitted commas, so unless he physically lifted his pen to add a comma, I have treated the loop or tail as part of the word, not as a punctuation mark. If further punctuation is required, I have added it and included it in my list of punctuation changes.

Spacing

Hamilton often lifted his pen while writing compound words and words with prefixes or suffixes (e.g., *common wealth, can not, over grown, there fore*). But he also lifted his pen in writing even the simplest monosyllabic words, so I have not divided a word such as *commonwealth* unless the space between the two words is clearly as great as the space between most of the other words in a given line. I have been especially reluctant to divide words that Hamilton repeatedly separated by a double end-of-line hyphen.

Spelling

Hamilton's multiple spellings of the same words or sounds are not an indication of his carelessness, but rather an indication of the indefinite nature of standard spelling rules at the time he wrote the *History*. It was not unusual, for instance, for him to use a single or double vowel, or a single or double consonant for the same word, sometimes in the same paragraph (*kept* or *keept, Intelect* or *Intellect*). As the spirit moved him, he sometimes dropped a silent *e* (*falshood, wholesom*), added or doubled a short *e* (*Proseperity, moderen; keept, streech*), dropped a short or silent *i* (*necessarly, transcrpt; aganst, villanous*), dropped the *h* in a word ending with *th* (*sevent*), changed a final *t* to *d* (*Sederund*), and so on. It would be foolish

Editorial Method

QUOTATION MARKS

Hamilton punctuated quotations inconsistently. Often he provided other punctuation before and after quotations, but sometimes he simply left extra space to indicate a pause; often he placed commas or periods before the second quotation mark, but sometimes he placed them below or after it; and often he enclosed quoted passages within single quotation marks, but frequently he enclosed them within double quotation marks and sometimes within combinations of both. In the first two cases, I have followed his normal usage, appropriately adding commas or periods before and after quotations and transposing commas or periods following the second quotation mark. But I have departed from Hamilton's normal usage in the third case because evidence suggests that he enclosed the majority of his quotations within single quotation marks in the *History* merely to save time. Throughout his draft and well into the first volume of the *History*, Hamilton used double quotation marks to enclose quoted material. But midway through volume I he began using single and double quotation marks interchangeably, and in volumes II and III he almost exclusively used single quotation marks. He apparently decided that double quotation marks were too much of a bother, not that they were improper for enclosing quotations. I have therefore used single and double quotation marks according to modern practice, and as Hamilton himself normally did in his draft and the first half of volume I.

Hamilton usually followed the eighteenth-century convention of placing quotation marks along the left-hand margin of his paragraphs, but sometimes he placed them only within his paragraphs, and sometimes he did both or combinations of both. I have placed quotation marks only at the beginning and end of direct quotations. Because Hamilton inconsistently added or omitted quotation marks around indirect quotations, I have retained only those around direct quotations to avoid confusion.

ROMAN NUMERALS, ARABIC NUMERALS, AND CAPITAL LETTERS

Hamilton sometimes placed commas, sometimes periods, and sometimes both after roman numerals, arabic numerals, and capital letters. Consequently, the periods in these cases sometimes also function as commas ("Charles I. who deserved . . ."). I have retained his usage in all such instances, supplying punctuation according to the rules established above only when he has omitted it completely.

Indeed, periods sometimes appear in what may seem to modern readers the most unlikely places, creating sentence fragments ("It could be called but a Compliment paid the president, and no Privilege. Which Solo Neverout Esqr, in a long frothy noisy Speech absolutely denied") or separating a series of items ("they call an Ale house, a *bouzing ken*. a beggar born and bred, a *Clapperdudgeon*. a pretended Dumb man, a *Dummerer*."). I have retained Hamilton's usage in these instances and in all instances where a period unmistakably separates two independent sentences.

In general, I have made relatively few changes involving Hamilton's use of periods in this edition. I have replaced periods with commas (but never with semicolons or other punctuation) only when they are followed by an obvious afterthought ("Thus we find . . . Charity made use of as a pretext. a very bad precedent, and a dangerous Stroke to the liberties of the Club"), or when an uncapitalized conjunction or conjunctive adverb, preceded by a period, separates two independent sentences ("[Ceremonies] alone distinguish the high and great from the Low and Inconsiderable. for, as virtue and merit, . . . come not under the Cognizance of the grosser Senses, . . ."). I have changed commas to periods only when the majority of items in a series are separated by periods and the remaining commas create misreadings ("they call . . . Money *Lour*. Virgins *Dells*. Strumpets, *Doxies*, Beggars, *Maunders*. Hats, *Nab Cheats*. Hands, *Fambles*. Staves, *Filches*. to steal *Filsh*. Rayment, *Back cheat*, Food, *Belly Cheat*."). I have added periods when no punctuation appears between two independent sentences and the first word of the second sentence is capitalized ("the president, assumed his Timber Countenance, which was an Infallible Sign, of his being highly displeased[.] The Secretary, to prevent the Rising Storm, . . . offered to read a paper in Club intituled a Remonstrance"). When no punctuation appears between two independent sentences and the first word of the second sentence is not capitalized, however, I have added a comma in keeping with Hamilton's normal usage ("Mr Neilson was like all other Illustrious men[,] he had blemishes blended with his excellencies"). In effect, I have added periods according to Hamilton's normal usage, but never merely to avoid a comma splice.

QUESTION MARKS

Hamilton separated a series of questions with commas, semicolons, question marks, and sometimes with all three; in all such instances, I have retained his usage. Like exclamation points, question marks occasionally have commas instead of periods; as with exclamation points, I have used regular question marks throughout this edition.

Editorial Method

EXCLAMATION POINTS

Hamilton occasionally employed commas instead of periods in exclamation points. It may appear that he used this curious punctuation mark only to separate a string of exclamations, but no such pattern exists. Rather, it whimsically crops up from time to time, and because it is distracting and not consistent with his normal practice, I have used regular exclamation points throughout this edition.

FLOURISHES

Hamilton often placed a flourish after the salutation or at the close of club letters, but he also used commas at these times. I have used commas in place of his flourishes throughout this edition.

PARENTHESES

More often than not, Hamilton placed other punctuation before parentheses, but he adhered to no particular pattern. Sometimes he provided punctuation within parentheses: "Human wit (if I may be allowed the expression,)"; sometimes he provided punctuation before and within parentheses: "These meddling Coxcombs, (some of whom had almost been committed to the flames for Heresy,)"; and sometimes he provided no punctuation at all before or after parentheses: "every thing turned uproar and Confusion, which produced much cursing and swearing, and hence accrued fines (for they had Laws in this Club, which imposed fines upon certain trespasses) this soured the members at one another." Like colons and dashes, parentheses (and brackets) often take the place of other punctuation in the *History*, so it would be a mistake to add a period, for instance, between "trespasses" and "this" in the last example above. I have not added other punctuation before, within, or after Hamilton's parentheses, and I have added parentheses only where he carelessly omitted the first or second one.

PERIODS

It would be easy to assume from reading Hamilton's manuscript that "he did not bother with periods."[1] Sometimes he used no punctuation at all at the end of sentences (most of these instances occur at the end of his manuscript lines), and as I have noted above, often he used commas in place of periods. Yet unmistakable periods appear throughout the *History*.

1. Elaine G. Breslaw, "The Chronicle as Satire: Dr. Hamilton's 'History of the Tuesday Club,'" *Maryland Historical Magazine*, LXX (1975), 135.

all other Illustrious men[,] he had blemishes blended with his excellencies").

Except in the instances noted above, and in a few other restricted cases that require no elaboration (before *vizt:,* for instance, as in "it's members were now chiefly composed of Slaves[,] vizt: the Slaves of the honorable Nasifer Jole"), I have added commas only to prevent ambiguous, sometimes silly readings of particular sentences ("Roundhead Muddy after supper[,] stood up, and addressed himself to his honor"; "A dull parson, once holding forth in his pulpit[,] the whole congregation, except this natural, fell fast asleep"). All of these additions are consistent with Hamilton's normal usage.

I have omitted commas only when the word (or words) following a comma is an obvious afterthought ("I now invest you with our Club badge, medal"; "From a nice observance of these rules, of ceremony"), and occasionally when Hamilton awkwardly separated two words for no apparent reason ("it was a piece of the most notorious, nonsense"; "under which many strange and dreadful mysteries were, couched"). But Hamilton habitually used commas in what may seem to us the most unlikely places—between any subject and verb, before any prepositional phrase or conjunction—so, aside from the exceptions just mentioned, I have not omitted any of his commas.

DASHES

Aside from using dashes as we would to mark an interruption or to emphasize a word or phrase at the end of a sentence, Hamilton frequently used dashes to separate direct or indirect quotations. Where he has failed to do this, I have added and noted the dash ("When Demetrius took Megara he asked Stylphon a Philosopher, if he had lost any thing,[—]Not I sir indeed replied he, I carry nothing about me, which you can make prey of"; "sometimes . . . it would be heres to you,—and heres to you—and thank you Sir,[—]and pledge you Sir"). Often other punctuation precedes a dash ("[they] triffle thro' a triffling life, in a promiscous multitude and medley of triffles,—But 'tis well we have these toys to . . . keep them out of mischief"); in the few instances where Hamilton carelessly added other punctuation *after* a dash, I have omitted the other punctuation and noted it in my list of punctuation changes ("As if Pone was not bread.—, if Pone be not bread, . . . what is it").

5. Before or after transitional words or phrases ("how many for Instance, sleep one half of their time and dream the other half").

To be sure, in these instances Hamilton sometimes employed commas as we would, and occasionally I have added commas in the above situations—especially in cases such as item 3—to avoid exceptionally awkward or ambiguous constructions. But the exceptions are few. Hamilton felt no qualms about omitting commas in these situations, so generally I have maintained his usage in all such instances.

In the following instances, however, it would be equally misleading *not* to supply commas.

1. When a majority of items in a lengthy series are separated by commas and there is no apparent reason other than hastiness for Hamilton's omitting punctuation ("Ignoramus[,] blockhead, dunce, rogue, liar, knave and fool"; "nasty, blewbellied, blanket ars'd, hip-shotten, maggot eaten, round about[,] Snuff besmeard, flyblown Son of a whore").

2. When a subordinate clause follows or interrupts an independent clause ("There are two maxims . . . generally received as true ones[,] tho' for my part, I think them at best but paltry Stuff"; "Certain it is, tho I know not how it happens[,] that the mind is more sprightly and active in company").

3. When a nonrestrictive clause or phrase follows or interrupts an independent clause ("he was called upon to deliver the Copy of that Commission[,] which he did"; "even the punishment of the gelastic Law, which was inflicted on this occasion[,] was nothing to that vociferous heroe").

4. When a clause or phrase other than a prepositional phrase or appositive interrupts the subject and verb of an independent clause ("Some, insensible of either mirth or anger[,] have sunk into soft Repose").

5. When a missing comma before a conjunction joining two independent clauses makes the sentence as a whole awkward to read ("as the saying is, the proof of the pudding is in the eating[,] so, the proof of what I here write, will be elucidated by reading what I have there wrote"). Where no confusion arises, however, I have not added the comma ("Jonathan Grog was declared victor and he drank a toast to the Club").

6. When no punctuation appears between two independent clauses joined by a conjunctive adverb ("the prop of your honor's understanding is crazy, and very much needs repairing[,] therefore, I move to your honor . . .").

7. When no punctuation appears between two independent clauses and the first word of the second clause is not capitalized ("Mr Neilson was like

"it was not at all necessary, that a man should be hard favored . . . , it was Sufficient for him Sincerely to profess and believe that he was not handsom." These and other comma splices in the *History* may initially pose some difficulties for readers, especially when a clause or phrase is ambiguously sandwiched between two independent clauses ("it is a true observation, that men are to be wrought upon by degrees, when any new model or form of Government Religion or Clubs is proposed, they must be soothed, flattered, cajoled, cozened and hoodwinked"). But once we recognize that, in keeping with his digressive writing style, Hamilton usually added subordinate clauses or phrases onto already existing independent clauses, we have little trouble unscrambling sentences of this sort. (In the preceding example, for instance, the break occurs between "proposed" and "they," not between "degrees" and "when.") At other times, Hamilton more unpredictably scattered commas throughout his sentences, and occasionally his sentences require every ounce of the reader's ingenuity to unscramble them. But that is all part of the fun of reading the *History*, and although I have often added and sometimes omitted commas in this edition (for reasons discussed below), nowhere have I replaced Hamilton's commas with other punctuation merely to make his sentences more accessible to modern readers.

Actually, it is less difficult for modern readers to adjust to finding commas in place of other punctuation than to finding no punctuation at all in places where we normally expect to see commas. Yet in certain constructions Hamilton repeatedly omitted commas, especially in the following situations.

1. In a series of verbs, nouns, adjectives, or other parts of speech ("murdered massacred and expelled"; "cough fart, and sneeze"; "Gluttony letchery and Idleness"; "punctillios Ceremonies, and distinguishing badges of honor"; "a nauseous fowl mouthd and beastly toast"; "gay, airy volatile fellows").

2. When couplings of verbs, nouns, adjectives, or other parts of speech appear in a series ("fringe scollop, shape and proportion"; "mollify malax, soften, intreat and request"; "Simpletons fools, asses and Idiots"; "traiterous rebellious, Scandalous and Submissive letters").

3. When a prepositional phrase, preceded by a comma, splits a subject and verb ("titles and dignities, in all polite societies have a certain fixed value").

4. When an appositive, preceded by a comma, splits a subject and verb ("death, the Confounder of all human projects interrupted him").

Editorial Method

words or omitted letters. I have retained his usage, adding or omitting apostrophes only to prevent an occasional misreading (when *well* should be read as *we'll* or, perhaps, *I'll* as *Ill*).

BRACKETS

Occasionally Hamilton used brackets in place of parentheses, but normally they function in the *History* to enclose stage directions or asides during club speeches ("I shall accuse no other babbler [Here Mr Crankum looked about towards his left hand, where Mr Secretary sat,]"). I have added brackets only where Hamilton omitted one or the other bracket, or where he used a parenthesis instead of a second bracket.

COLONS

Hamilton never used colons to separate independent sentences and very rarely to separate a series of parallel clauses or phrases. Rather, he normally reserved colons for abbreviations, and when an abbreviation occurs within or at the end of a sentence, the colon usually doubles for other punctuation ("Jealous Spyplot Junr: Quirpum Comic, and Prim Timorous, were . . . all unanimously admitted"). As in the preceding example, Hamilton often placed colons after abbreviated words ending with superscripts (which have been brought down to the line in this edition); just as often, however, he did not. If Hamilton provided a colon after the superscript, I have kept it; if he did not, I have added colons only to prevent misreadings (e.g., M^r appears as *Mr* and Esqr appears as *Esqr*, but d^o [*ditto*] appears as *do:* rather than *do* and *Proceed^s* [*Proceedings*] appears as *Proceeds:* rather than *Proceeds*). I have also added colons where Hamilton neglected to follow his normal practice with particular abbreviations (e.g., *Dec:* or *vizt:*).

COMMAS

Like other eighteenth-century authors, Hamilton treated the comma as the most protean of punctuation marks. Huge one-sentence paragraphs littered with comma splices appear throughout the *History,* so that commas abound in places where we normally expect to find periods, semicolons, or colons. To Hamilton, the comma obviously signified pauses of various lengths; moreover, the host of comma splices in the *History* are an integral part of his intentionally digressive writing style. Most readers sensitive to the rhythms of Hamilton's prose will quickly adjust to his all-purpose commas and recognize many of the situations in which they commonly occur, as in the following instances where Hamilton used them much as we would use semicolons: "but it was too late, the enimy had secured the Doors";

oaths; I have followed his normal practice and have italicized all such words.

Pagination

Hamilton's pagination is occasionally unreliable, moving, for instance, from page 270 to 171. In such instances, I have silently corrected his errors. When his pagination overlaps, I have added a letter (e.g., a second page 245 becomes 245a).

Punctuation

It would be a waste of time and energy to note every punctuation change I have made in this edition. In his haste to complete the *History* Hamilton often failed to provide punctuation in chapter, letter, or poem headings, and at the end of footnotes, paragraphs, or stanzas of poetry. To keep the *History* from being pointlessly distracting, I have silently added the proper punctuation in these and similar instances that do not affect the rhythms of Hamilton's poetry or prose. I have listed all punctuation changes, however, that I have made within the stanzas of his poetry or the paragraphs of his narrative.

Most of the punctuation changes I have made are additions rather than substitutions or cancellations, and a majority of these additions appear at the end of Hamilton's manuscript lines. His repeated omission of punctuation at the ends of lines suggests not only his haste to move on to the next line, but also his apparent assumption that a break at the end of a line—be it poetry or prose—marks a pause normally signified by a period, comma, or some other form of punctuation. Hamilton's failure to provide end-of-line punctuation is a perfect excuse for an editor to tinker with the rhythms of his prose and verse. But regardless of whether an omission appears at the end of a line or within it, I have added punctuation only in instances where Hamilton's original usage is awkward or ambiguous in ways that he clearly did not intend. For the same reasons I have occasionally substituted or cancelled previously existing punctuation. My policies regarding individual punctuation marks are outlined below.

APOSTROPHES

Hamilton inconsistently used apostrophes to identify possessives (*its* or *it's*, *president's* or *presidents*), plurals (*Cyruses* but *Solyman's, Speciess* but *Rhombus's*), contractions (*don't* or *dont*), and numerous other abbreviated

ated elsewhere within a line (e.g., *long- standing* becomes *long-standing*, but *man- ner* becomes *manner*). Where Hamilton neglected to provide any end-of-line hyphenation, I have spelled the word as it appears elsewhere within a line (e.g., *long standing* remains *long standing,* but *man ner* becomes *manner*). As the above examples suggest, a compound word such as *long-standing* can be spelled three different ways depending on Hamilton's end-of-line hyphenation.

On rare occasions Hamilton placed what appears to be a hyphen at the end of a line when the mark he used is actually simply a line (e.g., "there may be allowed, two dishes of desert, and no more, Butter - [end of line] Cheese, and all Sorts of Garden Stuff, in their proper Seasons, not being Included in the name of deserts"). Hamilton obviously meant "Butter, Cheese," in the preceding example, not "Butter-Cheese." Because the line in cases such as this might be intended to signify a pause, and not merely to take up space, I have added punctuation (in this case a comma) when appropriate.

Greek and Latin Passages

I have spelled all Greek words as they appear in the *History,* except where Hamilton occasionally used eighteenth-century ligatures that cannot be reproduced typographically. I have expanded the ligatures in those instances. Hamilton was not particularly fussy about accents and breathings: sometimes he used them accurately, sometimes inaccurately, but more often than not he did not bother to use them at all. I have therefore left the accents and breathings as they appear in his manuscript.

In Latin passages I have retained the abbreviation ȝ, which Hamilton generally used in place of *-ue* endings (as in *annoqȝ domini*), and the ⁹, which he used to indicate any abbreviated word. (Ordinarily, the ⁹ takes the place of *-us* in eighteenth-century manuscripts, whereas its variant, ȝ, takes the place of *-es, -et,* and *-m* endings, but Hamilton used them more loosely.)

Italics

Hamilton followed no particular system to signify whether a word or phrase should be italicized. Sometimes he used an italic script, sometimes he underlined, and sometimes he did both. I have italicized all underlined words; where a word or phrase appears to be both italicized and underlined, I have simply italicized it. Usually Hamilton italicized foreign words and phrases, titles of books, forms of address, proverbial phrases, and

frequently as the other letters in this group for the simple reason that he apparently found it easier to use *I, J,* and *T,* all of which he normally wrote with a similar single stroke, than to go back and dot his *i*'s or *j*'s and cross his *t*'s. Since it is impossible to determine which of his *I*'s, *J*'s, and *T*'s Hamilton would have changed to lowercase had he published the *History,* I have left them all capitalized.

A second group of capitalized letters in the *History* generally differ only in size from their lowercase letters (*A, C, G, M, N, O, U, V, W, X, Y, Z*). Because the size of Hamilton's script often changes radically from page to page—sometimes from sentence to sentence—I have determined whether or not a given word in this group should be capitalized first by judging whether its first letter is appreciably larger than its remaining letters, then by comparing it with similar words in the first group of letters, where Hamilton's capitalization is beyond question. Although the auxiliary verb *could* or the preposition *of,* for example, sometimes appears to be capitalized, the fact that Hamilton never capitalized *did* or *for* in similar instances suggests that what might appear to be capital letters in the former cases are more a result of haste than design. In such instances I have treated these letters as lowercase in keeping with Hamilton's normal usage. But wherever the possibility exists that he may have intended to capitalize a word in this group, I have left it alone.

The last letter—the capital *S*—poses particular problems for anyone who edits eighteenth-century manuscripts. As with other eighteenth-century authors, Hamilton's *S* looks exactly like his long *s*. The only way to determine whether or not a given word beginning with *s* should be capitalized, therefore, is to compare it to what Hamilton normally did with similar words in the first two groups. If he normally capitalized similar words, I have treated the long *s* as a capital; if he did not, I have treated it as a lowercase letter.

End-of-Line Hyphenation

Hamilton normally used a double hyphen for end-of-line hyphenation; occasionally, however, he used a single hyphen, and sometimes he carelessly omitted any hyphenation whatsoever. As a rule, he used the double hyphen to indicate that a word should be transcribed without a hyphen (e.g., *man= ner* becomes *manner,* and *long= standing* becomes *longstanding*). Where he used a single hyphen at the end of a line, I have retained the hyphen if the word is hyphenated elsewhere within a line in his manuscript, but I have treated it as a hasty double hyphen if the word is never hyphen-

new page when Hamilton supplied a catchword but neglected to repeat the word at the top of the next page.

Bracketed Material

Hamilton frequently inserted material within brackets, normally to indicate an aside or interruption during club speeches. I have also used brackets when I have supplied a word or phrase that is missing (because of a tear) or obscured in Hamilton's manuscript. Whenever possible, I have traced the word or phrase back to its most immediate source before the *History* (i.e., I have looked first in Hamilton's draft and then in the "Record"). I have therefore rarely needed to guess at missing or obscured letters, but because they are illegible in the *History* itself, I have nevertheless placed them within brackets.

Capitalization

Hamilton's capitalization habits were inconsistent. To be sure, he capitalized certain parts of speech more often than others (nouns more often than verbs, adjectives more often than adverbs, and so on) and certain types of words more often than others (e.g., he was especially fond of capitalizing a whole slew of mock-heroic adjectives such as *Glorious, Heroic, Illustrious,* and *Remarkable*). But it was not unusual for him to capitalize the same words in one sentence that he left uncapitalized in the next. Since he followed no particular system of capitalization, I have retained his original usage with only a few exceptions.

I have capitalized the first word in any sentence, paragraph, or line of poetry. For proper names and place-names, I have closely followed Hamilton's normal usage—meaning not only what he did 90 percent of the time, but also what he did in that 10 percent that might at first appear unusual. For instance, Hamilton usually capitalized both halves of place-names or proper names such as Wapping Dock and Slyboots Pleasant. But it was not unusual for him to capitalize only half of a place-name (Wapping dock, cape Breton) and only the first half of a proper name (Slyboots pleasant, Ignotus warble). I have therefore retained his capitalization in these cases, and in the handful of instances where he neglected to capitalize either half, I have capitalized only one, not both.

I have capitalized all words beginning with uppercase letters that differ in shape from their lowercase letters (*B, D, E, F, H, I, J, K, L, P, Q, R, T*). Hamilton capitalized three of these letters—*I, J,* and *T*—at least twice as

itself does not possess, but to maintain its inconsistencies and, at the same time, to keep Hamilton's prose from appearing silly or cumbersome in ways he clearly did not intend. The specific policies I have followed in making changes are outlined below.

The length of Hamilton's manuscript has made the task of normalizing the *History* initially exasperating but ultimately rewarding. There is little guesswork involved in editing a manuscript of this size, for pattern after pattern unmistakably emerges. The initial temptation (and I fell) is to compile chart after chart of what Hamilton did 90 percent of the time in any given case, and to suppose that, after having pinned down his "normal" usage for virtually every spelling quirk, punctuation mark, or capitalized word, one then has the license to change the 10 percent that does not fit the pattern. So one changes the 10 percent that does not fit here and there until eventually one realizes that the 10 percent that does not fit is part of the pattern, too, and that the infernal itch to tinker with that 10 percent is the editor's obsession, not the author's. The ultimate advantage of editing a manuscript the size of the *History*, then, is that it naggingly reminds an editor that the inconsistencies are also normal, that there are patterns to the inconsistencies as well as to the consistencies, and that the only way to maintain an author's normal usage is to leave his text as unmolested as possible. That is what I have sought to do in this edition. To do otherwise, I think, is to have an author—particularly an eighteenth-century author such as Hamilton—speak in a language he did not use. For better or worse, the voice that emerges from the pages of this text is Hamilton's.

Additions, Cancellations, Overwritings, and Repetitions

Having written about the Tuesday Club in three previous forms, Hamilton had a good idea of what he wanted to include in the *History* by the time he sat down to write it. His cancellations and overwritings are therefore few and insignificant (anyone interested in them should consult my dissertation). I have, of course, included all his additions.

I have added words to Hamilton's text (and included them in my list of substantive changes) only when they are absolutely necessary to make sense of a given sentence. But where I suspect that Hamilton intended to omit a word, I have retained his original usage. (In one of his speeches, for example, President Jole, whose mercantile style of speaking is characterized by his frequent omission of subjects in his sentences, says, "as I know, that is not so good a musician as Poet." Jole obviously means "that he is not," but I have retained the original.) I have also silently added the first word on a

EDITORIAL METHOD

For my doctoral dissertation I prepared a literal transcription of *The History of the Tuesday Club;* since then, I have become convinced that a dissertation is the only place suitable for an exact reproduction of Hamilton's manuscript, and that to publish a literal transcription of the *History* would be a disservice to him. Hamilton was a superb prose stylist, but he did not live long enough even to complete volume III of the *History,* let alone to proofread the entire manuscript. His inability to add the finishing touches to his manuscript shows in many ways: in the missing page references for the index of volume II; in the increasingly sketchy nature of the drawings toward the end of that volume; and in his misspellings, his sometimes careless capitalization, and his often peculiar lack of punctuation throughout the *History.* To be sure, like other eighteenth-century authors, Hamilton's composition habits were consistent mainly in their inconsistency. Still, he did observe certain rules of spelling, punctuation, and capitalization. To ignore those rules for the sake of presenting an exact transcription of the *History* would serve only to display an editor's, not Hamilton's, ignorance of them.

I have therefore made some changes in this edition in spelling, capitalization, and punctuation according to Hamilton's normal practice. Given the length of Hamilton's manuscript and its unfinished state, the changes that I have made are relatively few, and on the whole this edition remains as untidy as the original. One need only compare the punctuation in Hamilton's draft with that in the corresponding pages of volume I of the *History* to discover that he was not an exceptionally tidy author. With no particular consistency, he omitted or added punctuation marks in the *History* that were present or absent in the draft. (His spelling and capitalization also fluctuate inconsistently from one version to the next.) So even though it would be a simple matter to tidy up the *History,* I have made changes only in instances that I am certain are unintentionally awkward, ambiguous, or distracting. Where none of these problems arise, I have retained Hamilton's original usage, even though his normal usage might justify making a change. (He normally placed commas between all compound sentences joined by conjunctions, for instance, but to add commas in every instance where he failed to do so would be, as he would say, an act of supererogation.) In short, my intention has not been to lend the *History* a consistency that the manuscript

Maryland Heritage News, I (1983), 12–14; Robert Micklus, entries on Thomas Bacon, Jonas Green, and Alexander Hamilton in Emory Elliott, ed., *Dictionary of Literary Biography: American Colonial Writers, 1735–1781* (Detroit, Mich., 1984), XXXI, 19–22, 96–98, 101–107; and Micklus, "The Secret Fall of Freemasonry in Dr. Alexander Hamilton's *The History of the Tuesday Club,*" in *Deism, Masonry, and the Enlightenment: Essays Honoring Alfred Owen Aldridge,* ed. J. A. Leo Lemay (Newark, Del., 1987), 127–136.

Two editions of the Tuesday Club's minutes and music are available: Elaine G. Breslaw, ed., *Records of the Tuesday Club of Annapolis, 1745–56* (Urbana, Ill., 1988); and John Barry Talley, *Secular Music in Colonial Annapolis: The Tuesday Club, 1745–56* (Urbana, Ill., 1988).

of Annapolis, in Maryland, 1649–1887 (Annapolis, Md., 1887), 131–136; Lawrence C. Wroth, *A History of Printing in Colonial Maryland, 1686–1776* (Baltimore, 1922), 75–95; Walter B. Norris, *Annapolis: Its Colonial and Naval Story* (New York, 1925), 62–66; Joseph Towne Wheeler, "Reading and Other Recreations of Marylanders, 1700–1776," *MHM*, XXXVIII (1943), 37–55, 167–180; Wheeler, "Literary Culture in Eighteenth-Century Maryland, 1700–1776," *ibid.*, 273–276; Sarah Elizabeth Freeman, "The Tuesday Club Medal," *Numismatist*, LVIII (1945), 1313–1322; Anna Wells Rutledge, "Portraits in Varied Media in the Collections of the Maryland Historical Society," *MHM*, XLI (1946), 282–326; Rutledge, "A Humorous Artist in Colonial Maryland," *American Collector*, XVI (1947), 8–9, 14–15; David Hackett Fischer, "John Beale Bordley, Daniel Boorstin, and the American Enlightenment," *Journal of Southern History*, XXVIII (1962), 327–342; Robert R. Hare, "Electro Vitrifrico in Annapolis: Mr. Franklin Visits the Tuesday Club," *MHM*, LVIII (1963), 62–66; Shunsuke Kamei, "Cultural Clubs in Colonial America, 1720–1750," *Studies in English Literature* (English Literary Society of Japan), English Number (1963), 37–70; Rosamond Randall Beirne, "The Reverend Thomas Chase: Pugnacious Parson," *MHM*, LIX (1964), 1–14; Joseph C. Morton, "Stephen Bordley of Colonial Annapolis," *Winterthur Portfolio*, V (1969), 1–14; Richard Beale Davis, "The Intellectual Golden Age in the Colonial Chesapeake Bay Country," *Virginia Magazine of History and Biography*, LXXVIII (1970), 131–143; J. A. Leo Lemay, "Franklin's 'Dr. Spence': The Reverend Archibald Spencer (1698?–1760), M.D.," *MHM*, LIX (1964), 199–216; Lemay, "Hamilton's Literary History of the *Maryland Gazette*," *WMQ*, 3d Ser., XXIII (1966), 273–285; the chapters on Jonas Green, James Sterling, and Thomas Bacon in Lemay, *Men of Letters*, 187–212, 257–312, 313–342; David Curtis Skaggs, "Thomas Cradock and the Chesapeake Golden Age," *WMQ*, 3d Ser., XXX (1973), 93–116; Skaggs, *The Poetic Writings of Thomas Cradock, 1718–1770* (Newark, Del., 1983); William E. Deibert, "Thomas Bacon, Colonial Clergyman," *MHM*, LXXIII (1978), 79–86; James R. Heintze, "Alexander Malcolm: Musician, Clergyman, and Schoolmaster," *ibid.*, 226–235; Mary M. Starin, "The Reverend Doctor John Gordon, 1717–1790," *ibid.*, LXXV (1980), 167–191; Aubrey C. Land, *The Dulanys of Maryland: A Biographical Study of Daniel Dulany, the Elder (1685–1753) and Daniel Dulany, the Younger (1722–1797)* (Baltimore, 1955); Land, *Colonial Maryland: A History* (Millwood, N.Y., 1981), 179–205; Elaine G. Breslaw, "Merrymaking in Old Annapolis: The Tuesday Club," *Baltimore Sun Magazine*, Mar. 24, 1974, 22, 24, and 33; Breslaw, "A Dismal Tragedy: Drs. Alexander and John Hamilton Comment on Braddock's Defeat," *MHM*, LXXV (1980), 118–144; Breslaw, "The Tuesday Club of Annapolis,"

BIBLIOGRAPHICAL NOTE

Only three chapters of *The History of the Tuesday Club* have previously appeared in print: a modernized version of book 10, chapter 3, concerning the "decathedration" of Nasifer Jole (printed anonymously, but probably by the editor, Dr. William Hand Browne, in the first volume of the *Maryland Historical Magazine* [1906], 59–65); Elaine G. Breslaw's transcription of book 13, chapter 4, concerning the celebration of the club's ninth anniversary (in "The Chronicle as Satire: Dr. Hamilton's 'History of the Tuesday Club,'" *MHM*, LXX [1975], 129–148); and my own transcription of book 8, chapter 1, concerning Hamilton's burlesque of the eighteenth-century conception of tragicomedy (in "Dr. Alexander Hamilton's 'Modest Proposal,'" *Early American Literature*, XVI [1981], 107–132).

Hamilton and *The History of the Tuesday Club* have been only passingly mentioned—when mentioned at all—in general studies of colonial literature and culture (but see Richard Beale Davis, *Intellectual Life in the Colonial South, 1585–1763*, 3 vols. [Knoxville, Tenn., 1978], III, 1383–1390). The most complete study of Hamilton and his works is Robert Micklus, *The Comic Genius of Dr. Alexander Hamilton* (Knoxville, Tenn., 1990). J. A. Leo Lemay provides an excellent chapter on Hamilton in *Men of Letters in Colonial Maryland* (Knoxville, Tenn., 1972), 213–256. Elaine G. Breslaw, "Dr. Alexander Hamilton and the Enlightenment in Maryland" (Ph.D. diss., University of Maryland, 1973); Breslaw, "Wit, Whimsy, and Politics: The Uses of Satire by the Tuesday Club of Annapolis, 1744 to 1756," *William and Mary Quarterly*, 3d Ser., XXXII (1975), 295–306; and Breslaw, "The Chronicle as Satire: Dr. Hamilton's 'History of the Tuesday Club,'" *MHM*, LXX (1975), 129–148, provide informative discussions of Hamilton's social and intellectual milieu and of the political satire in the *History*. The only other essays dealing with the *History*'s value as literature are Robert Micklus, "Dr. Alexander Hamilton's 'Modest Proposal,'" *Early Am. Lit.*, XVI (1981), 107–132, and Micklus, "'The History of the Tuesday Club': A Mock-Jeremiad of the Colonial South," *WMQ*, 3d Ser., XL (1983), 42–61.

Numerous books and articles provide additional insights into the Tuesday Club and its members, including (chronologically) [John G. Morris], "History of the Annapolis 'Tuesday Club,'" *American Historical Record*, II (1873), 149–155; Frank B. Mayer, "Old Maryland Manners," *Scribner's Monthly*, XVII (1878), 315–331; Elihu S. Riley, *"The Ancient City": A History*

PROVENANCE

Alexander Hamilton's widow, Margaret Dulany, gave his manuscripts (including "Man," a lost poem in blank verse) to his old friend and Tuesday Club associate Dr. Upton Scott. The sole surviving club member, Scott kept the manuscripts in his possession until 1809, when at age eighty-five he lent *The History of the Tuesday Club* to the Baltimore Library. Scott presented the library with three volumes of the *History,* two of which were already bound, and requested that they bind the third. Because he considered pages 503–564 (and whatever else there may have been) of volume III as part of an unfinished fourth volume, I suspect that Scott kept those pages in his own possession, which possibly accounts for the different locations of the manuscripts today. Judge George W. Dobbin later acquired the *History* (minus pages 503–564 of volume III), which was then purchased by the Johns Hopkins University in 1905, where it is presently housed in the John Work Garrett Collections of the Milton S. Eisenhower Library (Upton Scott to unidentified person, August 28, 1809, Howard Family Papers, MS. 469, Maryland Historical Society, Baltimore; Scott to unidentified person, August 28, 1809, "Record of the Tuesday Club," MS. 854, MHS; Sarah Elizabeth Freeman, "The Tuesday Club Medal," *Numismatist,* LVIII [1945], 1314).

XI and eight more to Book XII. As he was writing Book XII, however, he divided it into three books—making a total of fourteen in all—and added two more chapters to Book XIV not listed in the table of contents. Hamilton initially intended the final version of the *History,* like the draft, to contain only two volumes and twelve books. But to take his mind off his illness he continued writing up until his death, and the twelve books swelled to fourteen and the two volumes to three. Before dying he wrote "vol. 3d" in the text at Book XI and mistakenly placed "Volume III" alongside the heading for Book X in the table of contents. Since Hamilton did not have the chance to provide a title page to volume III or to change the book and chapter headings in the table of contents to accurately reflect the expansion of volume III, I have done both for him. I have also finished numbering his table of contents and have provided page numbers for his index to volume II.

the drafted text [containing pp. 465–700 of volume I and the index to that volume] appears at the end of volume III of the manuscript of the *History*. The table of contents has been mistakenly placed at the front of the "Record"). Hamilton states in the *History* that he "began to Collect and Compile the History of the Club" in the fall of 1752 (III, 118); he probably stopped working on the draft around January 22, 1754, the date of the last event (Quirpum Comic's trial) listed in the table of contents. The table of contents is divided into twelve books but not into volumes. However, the last page of the extant portion of the draft says "End of the first volume" (Book VI, p. 700); the index, too, has "Contents of The first Volume" placed at the top, suggesting that after he finished all twelve books and the table of contents Hamilton decided to divide the draft into two volumes of equal size. He then numbered the first seven hundred pages and provided an index to volume I. That he provided page numbers for only the first six books in the table of contents suggests that he probably stopped working on the draft after indexing volume I. Rather than spend his time numbering the pages of volume II and indexing that volume, he turned to the final version of the *History*. For a transcription of the draft, see Robert Micklus, "Dr. Alexander Hamilton's *The History of the Tuesday Club*" (Ph.D. diss., University of Delaware, 1980), IV, 1475–1721.

4. *The History of the Tuesday Club*, volumes I–III (John Work Garrett Collections, The Milton S. Eisenhower Library, The Johns Hopkins University, Baltimore, Maryland; pages 503–564 of volume III are in the Dulany Papers, MS. 1265, Box 3, Maryland Historical Society, Baltimore; sections of volume III are missing [pp. 301–332, 455–502, and the final pages; I provide transcriptions from the "Record" for those portions of the narrative]; a draft of the dedication and the first two pages of a draft of the preface have been mistakenly placed at the front of the "Record"; the remaining portion of Hamilton's draft of the preface is also in the Dulany Papers). Hamilton probably began writing the final version of the *History* around September 9, 1754, the date of the dedication. The title page to volume II states that that volume was written in 1755, and the eyewitness account of Dr. Upton Scott, Hamilton's good friend and fellow Tuesday Club member, indicates that Hamilton continued writing the *History* up until his death in May 1756 (letter dated Aug. 28, 1809, Howard Family Papers, MS. 469, Maryland Historical Society). Hamilton numbered all the pages of the *History*, but he did not have time before dying to finish numbering the table of contents or the index to volume II. (I doubt that he ever completed an index to volume III.) Hamilton had simply copied the table of contents from his draft, adding only one more chapter heading to Book

COMPOSITION

Four separate stages of composition went into the making of *The History of the Tuesday Club*. As the club's secretary, Hamilton first kept its minutes from 1745 to 1756; during that time, he also prepared a fair copy of the minutes, the "Record of the Tuesday Club"; he then drafted the *History*, a fictionalized account of the club's proceedings; and finally he rewrote the *History* from first page to last, replacing the names of the club's members with pseudonyms and further embellishing the narrative. The following paragraphs summarize my conjectures about the probable dates of composition of these four stages. (Locations of the manuscript holdings are provided in parentheses.)

1. Minutes of the Tuesday Club, volumes I and II (John Work Garrett Collections, The Milton S. Eisenhower Library, The Johns Hopkins University, Baltimore, Maryland; Peter Force Collection, Series 8D, Item 170, Library of Congress). These are the actual minutes of the club (written in several hands, but mainly Hamilton's), composed at or shortly after each meeting from May 14, 1745, to February 11, 1756. The first volume runs from May 14, 1745, to February 25, 1755; the second volume, from May 27, 1755, to February 11, 1756. The second volume contains only thirty-seven pages of minutes, eight of which are missing (pp. 9–16, or most of Sederunt 241).

2. "Record of the Tuesday Club" (MS. 854, Maryland Historical Society, Baltimore). This is a careful revision of the minutes, covering the period from May 14, 1745, to April 22, 1755. It includes club drawings and music. Although Hamilton indiscriminately referred to this revision and to the original minutes as "record books," I use "Record" to refer only to the volume of revised minutes. (Hamilton himself titled this volume "Record of the Tuesday Club.") It is uncertain when Hamilton began revising the minutes, but it was probably no later than 1750. Elaine G. Breslaw's edition, *Records of the Tuesday Club of Annapolis, 1745–56* (Urbana, Ill., 1988), includes the "Record" and the second volume of minutes.[1]

3. Draft of the *History*, volumes I and II. (The only extant portion of

---

[1]. Breslaw suggests in her edition that Hamilton possibly began revising the minutes in 1755, but that seems unlikely. By fall 1752, he had begun working on the *History* itself. Although he continued to revise the minutes beyond that date, it seems unlikely that he would have begun the formidable task of revising them at the same time that he was devoting so much energy to the *History*.

dity," Hamilton wonders, "without Laughing Immoderatly, either with Democritus, or any other Gelastic Philosopher; and who can blame the members of the . . . Tuesday Club, for Laughing at all the world, as well as at themselves, and furnishing a fund of Laughter to all those who have a turn for the Gelastic humor" (III, 351). *The History of the Tuesday Club* will appeal to many readers of many different interests, but most of all to those interested in exercising and improving their gelastic faculties. I want to welcome those readers to the world of the Tuesday Club. "Begin in the middle of the Book & read backwards" if you like, "then forwards & skip about; I think now & then you will find something that will set you a roaring."[35]

---

35. In a letter dated May 4, 1824, James Carroll addressed these remarks to a member of the Baltimore Library Company upon presenting him with his copy of the "Record of the Tuesday Club." Carroll's remarks, like the rest of his delightful letter, apply equally well to the *History*. The entire letter appears in Elaine G. Breslaw, ed., *Records of the Tuesday Club of Annapolis, 1745–56* (Urbana, Ill., 1988), xxxiv.

> I would Seriously ask you, which of us have been employed to the best purpose, you, in these triffling pastimes, . . . or I, in writing this (as you call it) Silly history (I, x–xia).

According to Hamilton, life is a comedy full of trifles—great and small, to be sure, but, regardless of the size, still trifles—and the most trifling figure of all is the critic who cannot enjoy the human comedy. "All that passes in this . . . petty scantling of time," he says, "which we have allotted us to peregrinate thro' this absurd worldly wilderness, and to rant our Comical . . . parts out upon this terrestrial Stage, is but of a triffling nature" (I, 297–298). Why, then,

> should any . . . finical coxcomb of a Clubical Critic, . . . pretend to say, that this our famous History, is more triffling than any other history, or this our ancient and honorable Club more triffling in it's constitution, . . . than any other Society whatsoever, great or small. . . . Pray does not an Emperor eat, drink and sleep as much as a [club] president; does he not stink at times as hideously as a president? . . . may he not be poxed as well as a president? may he not have the plague, . . . the Ripples, the whiffles, nay the Itch as well as a president? Nay, may he not play the fool as much as a president? what then is the difference between an Emperor and a president, . . . a triffle, believe me, a very triffle, and not worth Contending for (I, 298, 302).

"Oh how I pity you," Hamilton concludes his tirade against these "perverse anticlubarians,"

> for the want of that blessed humor, which set Democritus a Laughing, and Heraclitus a crying, . . . for, ye dry withered Stocks of human Society, . . . you can neither laugh nor Cry in earnest, . . . [but] like a flitch of Smoked bacon, . . . you go out of [the world], dry, dead, musty, Insipid and Sapless, having never in your lives enjoyed the Sweets and delights of clubical humors and recreations, without which life is not worth enjoying, but is a *tabula rasa* . . . in which nothing of Sense or Significancy can be read or discerned (I, 307, 310).

The History of the Tuesday Club is not designed for, nor can it hope to reform these "Incorrigible Anticlubarians" (I, 309); it is designed for those who, like Hamilton's favorite authority, Democritus, know how to laugh good humoredly at the "Sempiternal Comedy . . . acted from day to day on this great earthly stage" (I, 464). Who can observe "this medley of absur-

digressively whittling it away to nothing. Some readers, Hamilton is aware, will deplore his trifling methods and his trifling preoccupation with club history. After circuitously haranguing his readers on the importance of not wasting time in the opening paragraph of his preface, he acknowledges that

> some people, who may find time enough to throw away in reading of this, will undoubtedly exclaim, Well! and what the Deuce is the meaning of these grave observations? . . . Many, I am satisfied, will either be mightily astonished, or pretend to be so, that any Mortal Wight, could waste, as they Call it, so much precious time, besides paper and ink, in compiling and Collecting, the History of, (as it may seem to them) a Ridiculous Club, whose chief pastime (they'll say) appears from the face of the History it self, and from the Grotesque Stile of its Idle Author, to have been the carrying on, a Silly, Stupid and unmeaning farce. Very well, my good friends, what if I should grant you all this, . . . the Subject of this History is a farce, and a very Silly one too, since you will needs have it so, . . . I will not Indeed so easily grant you that it is an unmeaning one, since it bears an exact resemblance to many other farces in human life, esteemed (tho they are not really so) of a more Serious nature (I, x–xi).

Hamilton allows, too, that he might have spent his time more profitably than by composing this silly—though not unmeaning—farce; he will not concede, however, that he has spent his time any more foolishly than the critic who would take him to task for his foolishness. "If I have laid out much time in writing of these triffles, as you call them, pray," he argues,

> have not you and many others as wise as either you or I, that is, in their own Conceit, laid out an equivalent of time, upon equivalent, if not greater triffles, only with this difference, that this triffling Scribble of mine, required some thought and application, and your triffling Occupations require no thought at all. . . . Have I not been poring reading studying and turning over Ancient Authors, and modern wits, in the composition of this History, to the great Solace and Improvement of my Rational, Intellectual and Gelastic faculties, when you, and twenty other such Loggerheads as you, who pretend to call me to account for it, have been exercising the keenest acumen of your obtuse thoughts upon a game at whist, . . . bawling at a boxing match or Cock pit, . . . fumbling and tumbling a whore in a bagnio, . . . or taking an afternoons nap, after having spent two hours more than what was necessary in beastly cramming. . . . Now,

providing one irreverent account after another of the antiquity of ancient nations and families, and finally of the antiquity of "old rotten rags, . . . rusty nails, Jaw bones and Shank bones, perhaps honeycombed by the pox, teeth, beards, whiskers, parings of nails, Smoak tails and the like" (I, 21). Hamilton's digressive account of the dignity of antiquity undercuts the very notion that antiquity carries any particular dignity, just as his digressive narrative itself undercuts the grandiose declarations of authors who take themselves and their works too seriously. His most bombastic digressions, similes, or allusions typically end, of course, with his soberly observing that he values brevity at all costs "for fear this history should exceed the Size of a portable volume" (I, 93). But that does not prevent him from swelling his narrative to three volumes, or from creating one of the most bombastic characters in eighteenth-century literature to play his role as secretary in the *History,* Loquacious Scribble. "Such a Surprize and astonishment as possessed the old hoary and Squalid anarch Chaos," Scribble informs President Jole at the start of one of his anniversary speeches,

> when he was waked out of his eternal Slumbers, by the elucidation of the Celestial lights, when Creation first sprung, such a Surprize, I say, Honorable Sir, must at this Instant possess my Sensorium when I behold the members of this here ancient Club, Incumbent over those capacious bowls, replete with precious punch, most Splendidly elucescent, with those Glittering and Lumeniferous badges, like so many oriental and bright planets, Rising upon the watery deep, and adorning the azure Expance with their Immortal Irradiations! whilst you, Great Sir! like the Solar Center of this grand Clubicular System, dispence Inexhaustible Lustre to all, and, from your fountain undeminished, the whole emanation of light proceeds, the Splendor of our Longstanding members being nothing else, but the reflected glory of your honor, our most honorable president (II, 136).

Scribble continues in this vein, also praising the club's champion, Sir John, in this manner, when Jole interrupts him, saying "I think we have [had] enough of this Stuff" (II, 137). And if it's not Jole interrupting him, it's Sir John saying "Hoh! why so much Fiddle come farts about nothing?" (II, 304) or "Phogh! damn the fustian" (III, 212).

These are hardly the markings of a "Solid and Serious performance" written in a "plain and homely" manner. Rather, they are the markings of an author who loves nothing better than to deflate the customary grandeur of any topic or occasion by bombastically inflating it beyond recognition or

Hamilton felt, were "too strictly attached to what they call truth and demonstration," and others were "only dry drivelling narraters of Incidents and facts" (I, 2). For Hamilton, as for Fielding, the "true historian" sought not simply to present facts accurately but to frame those facts with "the proper and decent seasoning of apposite remarks and observations" (I, 2); to create characters who were combinations of "light" and "shade" rather than one-dimensional (I, vii); and most of all to copy Nature in all its fullness (I, 4). What both authors were attempting to define as "true histories" we now call novels.

In his opening chapter, "Of History and Historians," Hamilton, much like Fielding in his "Bill of Fare to the Feast" in *Tom Jones,* invites the judicious reader to partake of his historical feast and to keep in mind the distinction between his learned labors and the more dubious labors of romance writers or novelists. "Histories founded upon truth, and wrote in a plain, easie and natural Stile," he says,

> are Sirloins of beef plainly dressed, wholesome, hearty and nourishing to a robust and healthy Stomach, but those erected upon fiction, and stuffed with Bombast and fustian phrazes, are vapid, windy, unwholsom and adulterated with your damn'd sauces and pickles, fitted only for crazy and luxurious apetites, which require a Spur to excite them to a proper pitch, and are apt to breed worms, maggots and monstruous Crudities, in the brains and Intelects of such students as feed upon them. Such are Romances, novels, fairy tales, Love adventures, . . . and other such verbose trumpery, with which the french Artists have crouded our Libraries, as their Cooks have confounded our kitchens and loaded our tables, with Devilish Ragoos, fricassies, anduilles, amulets, Solomongundies, and the like. The first kind of Cookery breeds as many crudities in the Intellect of the readers, as the other does in the Stomachs and habits of the eaters (I, 3–4).

"The History which I am now about to present to [the reader]," Hamilton asserts, "is none of your vamped up Frenchified pieces of Cookery, it is a Solid and Serious performance, plain and homely, and withal true, every article thereof, being copied exactly from nature and the life" (I, 4).

Hamilton's declaration of intent is in part a serious attempt to distinguish his narrative from previous narratives and in part an ironic pose designed to fool no one. Immediately after establishing his high seriousness he discusses the "dignity and Importance" of antiquity, first stating that of all things men revere "Antiquity holds the foremost Rank" (I, 7), then

Writers such as Hamilton and Fielding therefore turned not toward the "novel" or "romance" in defining their narratives but toward "history," the most respected prose genre in the eighteenth century.[32] By the end of the seventeenth century the conception of history as a genre had become blurred by European writers who called their romances "histories" simply because their narratives were based on real characters. "In these enlightened times," Hamilton facetiously observes, history

> received additions and Improvements which it never before had, and was dressed up in very fine and Gaudy trappings, to the Immortal Geniuses of that age, we owe, the new and rare Invention of Romance writing, a kind of History, altogether Novel, (hence some kinds of Romances are called *Novels*) and hitherto unknown, from these great Historians, came the Prodigious Histories of *Amadis De Gaul, Amadis de Grece, Don Bellianis, Esplandian, Palmerin,* and a hundred other voluminous pieces, equally witty amusing and Instructive. These were the Heroical Histories of the times. There were also the amorous Histories of *Cassandra, Cleopatra, Clelia,* & *Almahyde,* all adapted to excite amorous and tender passions, particularly among the readers of the fair Sex (II, 26).

Hamilton's complaints about "Romantic Historians" who have "palm[ed] upon the world, a hideous collection of fables" (II, 4) are typical of the eighteenth-century attempt to restore the factuality of history and to establish factuality as the foundation of any good prose narrative.

Rather than associate himself with these romantic historians, Hamilton, like Fielding in *Joseph Andrews,* defines his narrative as a "true history."[33] By doing so he meant not only to indicate that his narrative was rooted in fact but also, like Fielding, to distinguish between "a naively empiricist and a more 'imaginative' species of belief."[34] Some historians,

---

32. As H. Trevor Colbourn observes, by midcentury "the testimonial on history's behalf was overwhelming" (*The Lamp of Experience: Whig History and the Intellectual Origins of the American Revolution* [Chapel Hill, N.C., 1965], 5). History was so respected that, as Jerry C. Beasley points out, the 1740s witnessed the "elevation of private experience to the status of public history," and private experience accordingly became the substance of narrative "histories" during this period (*Novels of the 1740s* [Athens, Ga., 1982], 43). Hamilton also plays upon what his contemporaries would have perceived as the double meaning of "history" and "historian": as not only a narrative of actual events but also a narrated story or *histoire* told by a *histor* who shapes and interprets events (Leopold Damrosch, Jr., argues this point well in *God's Plot and Man's Stories: Studies in the Fictional Imagination from Milton to Fielding* [Chicago, 1985], 273).

33. Hamilton's conception of "true history" and the distinctions he draws between history and romance are very similar to Fielding's remarks in *Joseph Andrews,* bk. 3, chap. 1, bk. 9, chap. 1, and *Tom Jones,* bk. 4, chap. 1.

34. McKeon, *Origins of the English Novel,* 404.

and the anatomy are not, however, mutually exclusive; indeed, particularly during the eighteenth century they frequently converged in the same work. "It was Sterne," Frye says, "who combined them with greatest success. *Tristram Shandy* may be . . . a novel, but the digressing narrative, the catalogues, the stylizing of character along 'humor' lines, . . . the symposium discussions, and the constant ridicule of philosophers and pedantic critics are all features that belong to the anatomy."[29] Much the same can be said of *The History of the Tuesday Club*. It is a comic novel whose narrative centers around the social behavior of a humorous cast of characters, but at the same time one whose narrator provides a comic anatomy of eighteenth-century society and ideas.

Hamilton himself, of course, did everything possible to disassociate himself from the common herd of "novel" writers. Like Fielding and other eighteenth-century novelists, he chose to call his narrative a "history" and would not have been flattered had anyone in his day called *The History of the Tuesday Club* a novel any more than Fielding would have been flattered had anyone called *The History of Tom Jones* a novel. The reason is clear from their remarks concerning novels and romances throughout their works. Lennard J. Davis argues that there was "a profound rupture, a discursive chasm between these two forms" in eighteenth-century England, and so "the romance is not usefully seen as a forebear of, a relative of, or an influence on the novel."[30] Davis's observation is at once insightful and misleading. There *was* a sharp break between the romance and what we *now perceive* as the novel as it was emerging in the works of novelists such as Fielding by midcentury. But at the time they were writing their novels, "novel" and "romance" were virtually synonymous and equally pejorative terms: both were perceived as being overly concerned with the past, with impossible situations, and with idealized characters. During an empirical age that valued factual observation and expected writers to focus their narratives on daily life, most authors consciously avoided associating their narratives with either genre.[31]

---

29. *Anatomy of Criticism*, 311, 312.

30. *Factual Fictions: The Origins of the English Novel* (New York, 1983), 25. Davis presents a strong argument for the influence of contemporary news and journalism, rather than popular romances, upon 18th-century fiction, but he overstates his case, I think, when he claims that by midcentury most English writers clearly distinguished romances from novels (pp. 103–104).

31. The best study of the movement toward historicity in narrative during the early 18th century is Michael McKeon, *The Origins of the English Novel, 1660–1740* (Baltimore, 1987). McKeon nicely summarizes the early-18th-century perception of romance and of particular romances that Hamilton mocks (see especially pp. 26–28, 52–64). A good study of Fielding's attitude toward romance is James J. Lynch, *Henry Fielding and the Heliodoran Novel: Romance, Epic, and Fielding's New Province of Writing* (Rutherford, N.J., 1986).

extraordinary attempt to merge various literary, rhetorical, and artistic modes into one narrative—but what, finally, *is* it?

Although Hamilton would have been the last to admit it, *The History of the Tuesday Club* is a comic novel. Written between the publication dates of the two great comic novels of the eighteenth century—Henry Fielding's *Tom Jones* (which Hamilton read and admired) and Laurence Sterne's *Tristram Shandy* (which was published after Hamilton's death)—*The History of the Tuesday Club* in many ways resembles both. Two of its most prominent features—the introductory essays to each of its fourteen books and the dominant voice of its witty, self-dramatizing narrator—owe much to the example Fielding set in *Joseph Andrews* and *Tom Jones*. But Hamilton's narrative is, by design, far more experimental and discursive than the "architectonic" *Tom Jones*.[27] More often than not, the *History*'s loose plot—concerning the rise of the Ancient and Honorable Tuesday Club to its peak of clubific felicity, and its fall as the insidious forces of luxury, ambition, and pride infest its members—is lost behind a maze of digressions. In the end, the plot hardly matters; structurally and thematically, digression is everything. In its intrinsic structural and thematic discursiveness and in the variety of verbal high jinks Hamilton incorporates into his narrative, *The History of the Tuesday Club* anticipates *Tristram Shandy* as much as it imitates *Tom Jones*.

Like *Tristram Shandy*, *The History of the Tuesday Club* is a comic novel that borrows heavily from the "anatomy," a genre particularly popular during the eighteenth century.[28] As Northrop Frye has argued, the "anatomist"—Swift, for instance, in *Gulliver's Travels* or Voltaire in *Candide*—is primarily concerned with "intellectual themes and attitudes" and with "piling up an enormous mass of erudition about his theme or . . . overwhelming his pedantic targets with an avalanche of their own jargon." The novel

---

27. The symmetrical structure of *Tom Jones* is the focus of Robert Alter's chapter "The Architectonic Novel" in *Fielding and the Nature of the Novel* (Cambridge, Mass., 1968).

28. Throughout this paragraph, I use *anatomy* as Northrop Frye defines it in *Anatomy of Criticism: Four Essays* (Princeton, N.J., 1957), 308–314. In Hamilton's day, of course, it would have been used more typically to describe a treatise such as Robert Burton's *Anatomy of Melancholy* (which Hamilton parodies in bk. II, chap. 1) rather than a narrative prose work. Anticipating his critics, Hamilton also refers to the *History* as a "prolix Rhapsody" (I, v), a word that by the 18th century had come to imply a literary work of miscellaneous or disconnected pieces. At one point Loquacious Scribble mentions in a letter that the Tuesday Club has yet to appoint an "able Historiographer, to connect and form [the club's affairs] into an uniform Rhapsody" (I, 535), a notion that would have been recognized as a ludicrous contradiction in terms. Although the *History* resembles—and indeed burlesques—the rhapsody, Hamilton was clearly poking fun at those who might perceive his narrative as nothing more than that.

nor the heart to prepare for publication Hamilton's huge manuscript once his friend was gone, *The History of the Tuesday Club* remained in the hands of a private few following Hamilton's death.

That is unfortunate, for one can only conjecture about the influence that *The History of the Tuesday Club* might have had on colonial literature. Its influence might well have been great, for it is a book that is both rooted in its time and well ahead of its time. It is particularly rooted in its time as a political satire of the proprietary struggles in colonial Maryland,[24] in its rich allusiveness to contemporary political, literary, and scientific developments, and in its humorous treatment of the outcry against luxury, probably "the greatest single social issue" during the 1750s.[25] But above all, the *History* is a splendid gauge of eighteenth-century wit, loaded with pseudo-learned essays and digressions, surprising metaphors and allusions, raillery and repartee, bombastic letters and speeches, doggerel verses and mock trials, brain-teasing riddles and conundrums, delicate and often indelicate puns, even nonsensical hieroglyphics and missing passages—and, of course, a generous dose of scatological humor and "polite smutt."[26] Hamilton's wit runs the gamut of eighteenth-century comedy—from satire to humor to irony to farce—creating a comedic extravaganza matched, perhaps, but unsurpassed in eighteenth-century literature.

But *The History of the Tuesday Club* is more than just a comic microcosm of its times; it is a unique and innovative narrative. It is, to use one of Hamilton's favorite words, a "puzzlementationful" book. Hamilton employs and burlesques so many literary and nonliterary forms that one hardly knows what to call the *History*. In each of its fourteen books, he typically treats the reader first to an opening essay on some grand or trivial subject, then continues his narrative of the club's misadventures, introducing letters, speeches, trials, indictments, commissions, set dramatic pieces, poetry, drawings, and music—anything he can to embellish his narrative. It is an

---

24. For further discussion of the political implications of the *History*, see Elaine G. Breslaw, "Wit, Whimsy, and Politics: The Uses of Satire by the Tuesday Club of Annapolis, 1744–1756," *William and Mary Quarterly*, 3d Ser., XXXII (1975), 295–306, and Breslaw, "The Chronicle as Satire: Dr. Hamilton's 'History of the Tuesday Club,'" *MHM*, LXX (1975), 129–148.

25. John Sekora, *Luxury: The Concept in Western Thought, Eden to Smollett* (Baltimore, 1977), 75, 66. In Hamilton's day *luxury* meant extravagance in one's domestic and political behavior; it therefore implied not only drunkenness, gluttony, lust, avarice, ceremony, vanity, effeminacy, and affectation, but also ambition, pride, enervation, corruption, and subjection. The first set of vices, many feared, inevitably led to the second set. In a humorous way, that is precisely what happens in the *History*. (For further development of this thesis, see Robert Micklus, "'The History of the Tuesday Club': A Mock-Jeremiad of the Colonial South," *WMQ*, 3d Ser., XL [1983], 42–61.)

26. Bridenbaugh, ed., *Gentleman's Progress*, 177.

administered to Hamilton along with his brother John, wrote that Hamilton suffered from "excruciating pains" during his final months:

> His Brother directed the Treatment, & visited him occasionally, whilst it was my melancholy duty daily to watch the progress of his disease, & by my friendly attention render him all the aid & consolation which the Nature of his complaint would admit of. A liberal Use of Opiates was requisite to make life bearable, & when relieved from pain he amused himself by writing this History, indeed the love of whimsicall drollery was so predominant in his constitution, that, a few days before his death, when I called upon him, I found him just finishing a Story that he had been employed in writing, which he read to me with as much Glee & delight as he was wont to do at the Club, laughing at the same time most heartily.[23]

As Scott states in his letter, Hamilton was the "Life & Soul" of the Tuesday Club. Things were not the same without Loquacious Scribble. The club met for the last time on February 10, 1756, even though Hamilton did not die until Tuesday, May 11, 1756, which would have been the club's eleventh anniversary. In the *Maryland Gazette* for May 13, 1756, Hamilton's good friend Jonas Green lamented the passing of the man they had all come to love:

> On Tuesday last in the Morning, Died . . . ALEXANDER HAMILTON, M.D. Aged 44 Years. The Death of this valuable and worthy Gentleman is universally and justly lamented: His medical Abilities, various Knowledge, strictness of Integrity, simplicity of Manners, and extensive Benevolence, having deservedly gained him the Respect and Esteem of all Ranks of Men.—No Man, in his Sphere, has left fewer Enemies, or more Friends.

No man, too, has left behind a more unusual manuscript than *The History of the Tuesday Club*. There are many indications, particularly the numerous references to his "readers" throughout the text, that Hamilton intended to publish the *History*. But whether because of its unfinished state, or because of its reflections on several of the club's still-living members, or because the obvious person to print it, Jonas Green, had neither the time

---

23. Scott's letter (dated Aug. 28, 1809), which attests to Hamilton's "strict honour & integrity" and calls him "the most eminent Physician in Annapolis," is in the Howard Family Papers, MS. 469, MHS. An abridged version of the letter appears at the front of the "Record of the Tuesday Club," MS. 854, MHS.

perform works of *"Charity, benevolence,* and *Brotherly Love."* Freemasonry, Hamilton well understood, was not some mysterious, subversive organization but part of the eighteenth-century club of man.

A few months later, Hamilton published *A Defence of Dr. [Adam] Thomson's Discourse on the Preparation of the Body for the Small Pox, and the Manner of Receiving the Infection* (Philadelphia, 1751), a twenty-seven-page pamphlet in support of his old friend and medical school classmate. Thomson's methods, Hamilton felt, had been impugned by the "ill natured Sneers and rude Reflections" of a pack of "Physical Dunces," one of whom, he claimed, had recently reported to him a

> newly discovered Method of curing dangerous Dysenteries, by Means of a certain pneumatic Operation. He informed me of "a Patient, dangerously ill with a *Bloody Flux,* at the Point of Death, who, finding some Difficulty in Respiration, desired his Servant . . . to apply his Mouth to his, and blow with all his Force into his Lungs, which the good natured Fellow did several Times; and, to the great Surprize of every Body, the seemingly forlorn Patient recovered." Whether such a Whimsical Cure as this be natural, I leave you to judge: For I shall make no Remark upon it; only, I think, the Gentleman might easily make an Improvement on this Discovery by applying his Mouth to a certain Part, through which he might convey his Air or *Flatus* more immediately into the Place, where that Distemper has it's Seat (pp. 3, 4, 16).

It is not known whether this particular *"Guess-Doctor"* took Hamilton's advice, but his satiric attack eventually elicited an apology from Dr. John Kearsley, Thomson's principal detractor.

Hamilton was unable, however, to defend himself against the consumption that had threatened his health since his first summer in Maryland. Although he managed to visit Gen. Edward Braddock's battered army in the summer of 1755, his poor health made it increasingly difficult for him to attend the Tuesday Club with any regularity.[22] On February 11, 1756, he turned the business of recording the club's minutes over to his friend William Lux of Annapolis. But even though he was forced to abdicate his position as record keeper, Hamilton continued to work on *The History of the Tuesday Club* right up until his death. Dr. Upton Scott, a club member who

---

22. Elaine G. Breslaw reproduces Hamilton's lengthy letter concerning Braddock's defeat by the French and evaluates his appraisal of the disaster in "A Dismal Tragedy: Drs. Alexander and John Hamilton Comment on Braddock's Defeat," *MHM,* LXXV (1980), 118–144.

similar brand of "rational piety,"[19] came close enough to Hamilton's own beliefs that, even though he considered some of the church's sacraments foolish, he was able to join in good faith. Two years later he was elected vestryman of St. Anne's, a position he held until March 30, 1752.

Hamilton's marriage also produced significant changes in his financial and political status. Despite his whiggish sentiments (voiced in the letter to his brother Gavin cited earlier), Hamilton's experience as an observer and as a participant in the tumultuous world of Maryland politics had led him to lean increasingly toward moderation and stability, and consequently toward the proprietary camp. With the aid of the Dulanys, in 1753 Hamilton represented the court party in the election for the Lower House seat of his recently deceased club companion and old proprietary faithful, Robert Gordon. Once again, the election was contested, but Hamilton was officially sworn in on October 9, 1753. He served as a member of the Lower House until the Assembly adjourned on July 25, 1754, when he resigned, probably because of poor health.

Hamilton much preferred the convivial world of clubbing, and in 1749 he and several Tuesday Club members founded a Freemason's lodge in Annapolis. So much has been written about the anxieties that Freemasonry caused the church or state and about all the nefarious rituals that Freemasons reputedly conducted behind closed doors[20] that the least sensational but perhaps most essential fact about Freemasonry has often been overlooked: in an age when clubbing was the thing to do, being a Freemason was as much a part of the normal social fabric of eighteenth-century life as being a member of any other club. In his "Discourse Delivered from the Chair, in the Lodge-Room at *Annapolis,* by the Right Worshipful the Master, to the Brethren of the Ancient and Honourable Society of *Free and Accepted* Masons," Hamilton provided the framework by which not just all Freemasons but all enlightened men sought to structure their lives.[21] The "upright man," in control of his passions and guided by the "Lights of Reason" in his pursuit of liberty, was obliged, he concluded by saying, to

---

19. Henry F. May, *The Enlightenment in America* (New York, 1976), 67.

20. The best scholarly analysis of the various controversies that Freemasonry provoked during the 18th century is Margaret C. Jacob, *The Radical Enlightenment: Pantheists, Freemasons, and Republicans* (London, 1981). For the relationship between Freemasonry and Hamilton's *History,* see Robert Micklus, "The Secret Fall of Freemasonry in Dr. Alexander Hamilton's *The History of the Tuesday Club,*" in *Deism, Masonry, and the Enlightenment: Essays Honoring Alfred Owen Aldridge,* ed. J. A. Leo Lemay (Newark, Del., 1987), 127–136.

21. Hamilton's speech appears at the end of the Reverend John Gordon's Masonic sermon, *Brotherly Love Explain'd and Enforc'd* (Annapolis, Md., 1750).

recording and revising the club's minutes, and administering to his patients, Hamilton also found time, on May 29, 1747, to marry Margaret Dulany, daughter of Daniel Dulany the Elder. His marriage to the "vivacious" Miss Dulany was "the social event of the season,"[14] but much lamented by Stephen Bordley, who had hoped that Hamilton would remain, like himself, one of the Tuesday Club's few surviving bachelors:

> Yet in vain was that hope, since I am now obliged to hold out alone against the numerous and powerful host we . . . formerly provoked by our united hostilities,—for poor Hamilton is gone!—not dead, but married, he was the day before yesterday obliged to surrender discretion to throw himself up to the money of Peggy Dulany, and is already become what you would from your knowledge of the lady now suppose him to be, a very grave sober fellow.[15]

As Bordley well knew, Hamilton's marriage to Margaret Dulany could only enhance his fortunes and lift his spirits. Hamilton was glad to be married, and although he and his wife had no children—at least none that survived birth—they apparently enjoyed their life together.[16]

His marriage into the Dulany family produced several changes in Hamilton's life, the first of which was a change in religion from Presbyterianism to Anglicanism. It simply made good sense socially to practice the Anglican faith in a predominantly Anglican colony, and Hamilton was an eminently sensible man socially and religiously. Like his Latitudinarian friend the Reverend Thomas Bacon, Hamilton believed in a rationally ordered universe, one in which the "revealed Law of God" was consistent with the "Law of Nature."[17] For Hamilton, as for Bacon, God was a benevolent deity who "hath been pleased to make all Men . . . dependent one upon the other, and by a mutual Exchange of Service and Assistance, to contribute to the Comfort and Support of each in Particular, as well as the general Benefit of the Whole."[18] The Anglican church, which stressed a

---

14. Land, *Dulanys of Maryland*, 191.
15. Stephen Bordley to Witham Marshe, May 30, 1747, Bordley Letter Book, MHS.
16. Hamilton's mother wrote more than once that she had received letters from him and his wife attesting to their happiness together (see Mary Hamilton to AH, July 15, 1748, Feb. 15, 1749, and Oct. 25, 1749, Hamilton Letter Book). Margaret Dulany remarried in 1757 after Hamilton's death. She and her second husband, William Murdock, had two children, Rebecca and Margaret.
17. Bacon, *Four Sermons, upon the Great and Indispensable Duty of All Christian Masters and Mistresses to Bring Up Their Negro Slaves in the Knowledge and Fear of God* (London, 1750), 1st sermon, p. 35.
18. *Ibid.*, 2d sermon, p. 56.

an almost limitless fund of entertainment. Those members familiar with law—and some not so familiar—entertained the club by conducting numerous mock trials; those with a flair for speechmaking—and some flaired better than others—entertained the club with their rhetorical effusions; and those gifted with musical talents—and some not so gifted—entertained the club by reciting popular songs and performing their own compositions. But the greatest source of entertainment in the club was the wit of its two principal comedians, Hamilton and Jonas Green—Loquacious Scribble and Jonathan Grog. As club orator, Loquacious Scribble took every possible occasion to impress the club with his erudition by haranguing them with numerous bombastic speeches, especially at each of the club's anniversaries, when he annually delivered a learned and lengthy speech commemorating the grandeur of the occasion. At those times his rhetorical talents were complemented by the literary talents of Jonathan Grog, who traditionally delivered his anniversary ode following Scribble's speech. Grog further entertained the club on many other nights with his humorous verses, practical jokes, puns, and conundrums. Together they jointly shared the distinguished post of club "Conundrumificators," but Grog was the indisputable master and the more bawdy of the two. "Why is the king's prick," he asked the club one evening, "in marking down a Sheriff like an Elephant?"—to which Jealous Spyplot, Sr., rightly answered "Because it always *Stands*" (II, 116). "I shall beg leave to observe," Hamilton notes, "lest it should escape the observation of the Reader, that there seems to be an uncommon delicacy and Elegance in most of the Conundrums, composed by Jonathan Grog Esqr, as may be seen in the one Just now mentioned, Concerning *The king's prick*, which is not only a perfect Conundrum, but Contains also a delicate pun, as the word *Prick* may be Interpreted various ways" (II, 117).

Although it might be difficult to tell from a brief sampling of their elegant humor, Hamilton and Green are the best comic team in colonial literature. They further teamed up in the *Maryland Gazette*, which Green began publishing in 1745. From 1746 to 1750 Hamilton contributed various pieces to the *Gazette*, including an essay on the impertinent question "What News?" (Jan. 7, 1746); a cure for distempered authors and a mock advertisement to catch a runaway wit (Feb. 4, Mar. 18, 1746); an essay on curiosity (Jan. 27, 1747); a dream vision on the fate of the contributors to the *Gazette* (June 29, 1748); a tale for melancholic scribblers (Aug. 31, 1748); a piece on odd orthography (Apr. 12, 1749); and a parody of Masonic ceremonies (Jan. 24, 1750). These humorous pieces helped to make the *Maryland Gazette* one of colonial America's most entertaining newspapers.

While writing for the *Maryland Gazette*, serving the Tuesday Club,

dent); William Cumming, Sr. (Jealous Spyplot, Sr., Attorney General); William Cumming, Jr. (Jealous Spyplot, Jr.); Edward Dorsey (Drawlum Quaint, Speaker); Richard Dorsey (Tunbelly Bowzer); Walter Dulany (Slyboots Pleasant); Jonas Green (Jonathan Grog, P.P.P.P.P.—Purveyor, Punster, Punchmaker General, Printer, and Poet—and later P.L.M.C.—Poet Laureate and Master of Ceremonies); Thomas Jennings (Prim Timorous, Sergeant at Arms); John Lomas (Laconic Comas, Orator); Alexander Malcolm (Philo Dogmaticus, Chancellor); William Thornton (Solo Neverout, also Protomusicus, Chief Musician and Attorney General); and, of course, Hamilton himself (Loquacious Scribble, Secretary and Orator). Other longstanding members came and went, but these were the mainstays.

Every other Tuesday for the next eleven years, longstanding members, honorary members (those who could attend whenever in Annapolis without having to entertain the club), and visitors met, normally at the home of the high steward for the night, to share a side of bacon, some bread and cheese, a bowl of punch, but mainly each other's company and conversation. Hamilton establishes the formula for a boon club companion early in *The History of the Tuesday Club,* maintaining that "none but your merry, droll, facetious, Jocose, good humored, risible companions, punsters, comical Story tellers, and *Conundrumifiers,* ought to be members of those nocturnal assemblies, called Clubs, for the Quintessence, marrow and main fulcrum of Clubs consists in gayiety, Jollity, pleasantry and Jocosity" (I, 72). On the other hand,

> Those Solitary, moaping, morose, humdrum fellows, who evade, shun, run and fly, from all company, hate the Sight of men, as if they were Tygers, bears, Serpents, hobgoblins, Rhinoceroses and Panthers, . . . are mortal and Irreconcileable enemies to all Clubs, Jovial meetings, and humerous Conversations.
>
> When I see a fellow of this Stamp, with his Clouded brows, and Lowring countenance, *monstrum deforme Ingens,* I Imagine I behold a black cloud, rising from the dirty blustering South east, saturated with hollow murmuring Smouldering blasts, sending before it grumbling, tumbling, Jumbling thunder, and Infectious puffs of pestilential Steams, darkening the face of the fair day with polluted murky and Stiffling vapors, exhalations and damps, saturated, loaded, Impregnated and overcharged, with morbific Sulphureous atoms, bursting from the mouth of Tartarus it self (I, 69–70).

The Tuesday Club was no place for such humdrum fellows.

The combined talents of the members of the Tuesday Club provided

Shortly following his return to Annapolis, Hamilton helped to form the Tuesday Club, which met for the first time on May 14, 1745. Over the next eleven years almost everyone of some importance in the northern Chesapeake Bay area either joined or visited the Tuesday Club. In the beginning there were seven members besides Hamilton: John Bullen, captain of the Annapolis Independent Company and commissioner of the Paper Currency Office; William Cumming, Sr., a Scot, arrested during the Jacobite rebellion of 1715 and transported to Maryland, where he became a lawyer and a member of the Lower House; the Reverend John Gordon, a Scot, pastor of St. Anne's, Annapolis, and later of St. Michael's, Talbot County; Robert Gordon, a Scot, Annapolis merchant, judge of the Provincial Court, and commissioner of the Loan Office; John Lomas, an Annapolis merchant; Witham Marshe, secretary to the Maryland Commissioners at the treaty of Lancaster in 1744 with the Six Indian Nations and later secretary for Indian affairs; and William Rogers, chief clerk of the Prerogative Court. A varied bunch, but many of them Scots and all of them public servants in one capacity or another.[13]

As the Tuesday Club grew, its lists expanded to include many of colonial Maryland's most distinguished residents and visitors, such as the Reverend Thomas Bacon, clergyman, musician, philanthropist, compiler of the *Laws of Maryland at Large,* and one of colonial Maryland's most prolific authors; John Beale Bordley, judge, member of the Upper House, author, and member of the American Philosophical Society; the Reverend Thomas Cradock, clergyman and author; Jonas Green, public printer of Maryland, poet, and publisher of the *Maryland Gazette;* the Reverend Alexander Malcolm, clergyman, author, and musician; the Reverend James Sterling, clergyman, poet, and playwright; the sons of Daniel Dulany the Elder; and numerous other members and visitors, not the least of whom was Benjamin Franklin. All comers were welcome, and most men of any note who came to Annapolis visited the Tuesday Club.

The regular members—or the "longstanding members," as they liked to boast of themselves—were limited in number to fifteen. In *The History of the Tuesday Club* they appear under pseudonyms typifying their characters and roles in the club: John Beale Bordley (Quirpum Comic, Master of Ceremonies); Stephen Bordley (Huffman Snap); John Bullen (Bully Blunt, also Sir John Oldcastle, Club Champion); Charles Cole (Nasifer Jole, Presi-

---

The Itinerarium of Dr. Alexander Hamilton, 1744 (Chapel Hill, N.C., 1948; repr. Westport, Conn., 1973).

13. For further information on these figures and the ones mentioned in the following paragraph, see the Biographical Sketches, below.

take important responsibilities in the community at large."⁸ Hamilton met his obligations as a gentleman, but Maryland elections were far from gentlemanly.⁹ "There arose such tumults at giving of the votes in the Mayors Court," he wrote his brother Gavin, "that the majority of the Aldermen left the Bench in a passion. . . . In the afternoon the tumult was so high that the partizans went to Cudgelling and breaking of heads, . . . and they have been afraid ever since to proceed upon the Election." Eventually the election was decided in Hamilton's favor. At the time he questioned whether he would ever run for office again. "I doubt I shall stand again," he told Gavin, "for tho I be a Lover of Liberty, and abhor force or oppression of any kind, and especially when they are exercised by an Insolent Government party, yet I like better to be a peace maker, than an Instrument of disturbance in any Shape."¹⁰ Gentleman that he was, he kept his seat as common councilman for the rest of his life.

But Hamilton's greatest concern in 1743 was not the health of the body politic; it was his own health. He was in such a "Low State, with fevers and a bloody Spitting," that by the end of September 1743 he intended to return to Great Britain. Over the next few weeks, however, he began to recuperate. "I am now Considerably better," he told Gavin, "but am followed up with an Incessant cough, which no medicine whatsoever can abate or deminish, this makes me apprehensive that the consequence will be a confirmed Consumption."¹¹ To improve his health, Hamilton spent the following summer away from the muggy Maryland climate touring the northern colonies. On May 30, 1744, he set out on horseback with his black slave Dromo on a four-month journey from Annapolis, Maryland, to York, Maine, and back, a trip totaling 1,624 miles. Upon his return to Annapolis, he compiled a narrative of his travels, the *Itinerarium*. First published in 1907, the *Itinerarium* has been called "the best single portrait of men and manners . . . in colonial America."¹²

---

8. Rhys Isaac, *The Transformation of Virginia, 1740–1790* (Chapel Hill, N.C., 1982), 131.

9. A good study of the turbulent nature of elections in colonial Maryland is Robert J. Dinkin, "Elections in Proprietary Maryland," *MHM*, LXXIII (1978), 129–136.

10. AH to Gavin Hamilton, Oct. 20, 1743, Hamilton Letter Book.

11. *Ibid*. Hamilton announced his intention to leave in a broadside advertisement dated Sept. 29, 1743.

12. J. A. Leo Lemay, *Men of Letters in Colonial Maryland* (Knoxville, Tenn., 1972), 229. For further discussion of the *Itinerarium*, see Robert Micklus, "The Delightful Instruction of Dr. Alexander Hamilton's *Itinerarium*," *American Literature*, LX (1988), 359–384. Two editions of the *Itinerarium* are available: Albert Bushnell Hart, ed., *Hamilton's Itinerarium: Being a Narrative of a Journey from Annapolis, Maryland, through Delaware, Pennsylvania, New York, New Jersey, Connecticut, Rhode Island, Massachusetts, and New Hampshire, from May to September, 1744* (St. Louis, Mo., 1907; repr. New York, 1971); and Carl Bridenbaugh, ed., *Gentleman's Progress:*

ionship of his brother John helped to alleviate Hamilton's homesickness, but what he needed most was a good club.

To help fill this void, Hamilton joined the Ugly Club of Annapolis in 1739. In *The History of the Tuesday Club* he reports that, unlike the Ugly Club made famous by the *Spectator,* membership in the Annapolis Ugly Club was not determined by any physical deformity:

> It was Sufficient for [a member] Sincerely to profess and believe that he was not handsom, till he was declared to be a monstrous ugly fellow by the Ladies in public company. . . . A man was to show his Sincerity in this opinion of himself, by assuming a certain Slovenliness and peculiarity in his dress, by never throwing away his time at a looking Glass, and diligently evading all foppish and finical airs and affectation, . . . but, if he ever observed any oddity of Gesture, affected by another man, such as a wink, a cast of the Eye, a sudden toss of the head, . . . or wry twist of the mouth, . . . these he was Strictly to Imitate, . . . as being real deformities and deviations from nature in a much higher degree than bodily distortions and blemishes (I, 117–118).

From 1739 to 1744, this club met mainly "to argue and debate upon various Subjects, and to discuss points of a knotty and abstruse nature," but some of the members eventually became so contentious that "all Sort of Clubical cordiality and friendship, began to decrease, and at last was quite extinguished, so that the Members drop'd off one by one, and from a numerous Club, it dwindled to nothing, and at last expired" (I, 126–127).

Shortly before the Ugly Club disbanded, Hamilton also entered the contentious world of Maryland politics.[6] In 1743, "at the desire and Request of many of [his] fellow Citizens," he ran for the office of common councilman of Annapolis "in opposition to a certain creature of the Court."[7] Hamilton was not politically ambitious; he was, however, a gentleman, and in his day "the quality that most nearly epitomized what was needed to make a gentleman was 'liberality,'" including "a certain disposition . . . to under-

---

6. The struggles between the proprietary and anti-proprietary (court and country) parties in colonial Maryland have been enlarged upon in numerous works, but see especially Ronald Hoffman, *A Spirit of Dissension: Economics, Politics, and the Revolution in Maryland* (Baltimore, 1973), 44–59; Skaggs, *Roots of Maryland Democracy,* 84–109; Aubrey C. Land, *The Dulanys of Maryland: A Biographical Study of Daniel Dulany, the Elder (1685–1753) and Daniel Dulany, the Younger (1722–1797)* (Baltimore, 1955), 62–75; and Land, *Colonial Maryland: A History* (Millwood, N.Y., 1981), 151–178.

7. AH to Gavin Hamilton, Oct. 20, 1743, Hamilton Letter Book.

in important ways by 1738. Under the influence of the Bordleys, Carrolls, and Dulanys, Annapolis in particular had gone through a period of rapid expansion shortly before Hamilton's arrival.[2] Yet colonial Annapolis still offered newcomers only the scant cultural menu of horse racing, dancing at the local armory, or drinking and dining at one of its many taverns—no university, no circulating library, no theater, and no literary clubs or scientific societies. Hamilton was not impressed. He was used to Edinburgh, and by comparison the majority of the people and the living conditions in Maryland were, he felt, crude. Five years after his arrival, when he referred to Maryland as a "Barbarous and desolate corner of the world,"[3] he was only half joking. Hamilton learned to cope with the crude living conditions in Maryland by laughing at them; more important, he helped to change those conditions so that by the time he died two decades later the idea of culture existing in Maryland was no longer a laughing matter.

Like many colonial physicians, Hamilton worked double time as a physician and apothecary. Good physicians were scarce throughout the colonies, and those with Hamilton's training were much in demand.[4] Most of the time he was too busy to be homesick, but during his leisure hours he keenly missed the society of his friends back home, especially his friends at the Whin-Bush Club in Edinburgh. A few months after his arrival he nostalgically invoked his brother Gavin to "be so good as Remember me to all the Members of the whin-bush Club, . . . Inform them that every friday, I fancy myself with them, drinking twopenny ale, and smoking tobacco, I Long to see those merry days again."[5] Letters from home and the compan-

---

2. Nancy T. Baker discusses the developments that had taken place in Annapolis before Hamilton's arrival in "Annapolis, Maryland, 1695–1730," *Maryland Historical Magazine*, LXXXI (1986), 191–209. Three particularly informative studies of the social and economic changes that Maryland as a whole had undergone are Russell R. Menard, "Population, Economy, and Society in Seventeenth-Century Maryland," *ibid.*, LXXIX (1984), 71–92; Charles Albro Barker, *The Background of the Revolution in Maryland* (New Haven, Conn., 1940), 27–43; and David Curtis Skaggs, *Roots of Maryland Democracy, 1753–1776* (Westport, Conn., 1973), 30–56.

3. AH to Robert Hamilton, Sept. 29, 1743, Hamilton Letter Book, Dulany Papers, MS. 1265, Box 3, Maryland Historical Society, Baltimore.

4. The deplorable state of the medical profession in colonial America has been well examined by Richard Harrison Shryock, *Medicine and Society in America, 1660–1860* (New York, 1960), 1–18; Brooke Hindle, *The Pursuit of Science in Revolutionary America, 1735–1789* (Chapel Hill, N.C., 1956), 36–58; Whitfield J. Bell, Jr., "Medical Practice in Colonial America," *Bulletin of the History of Medicine*, XXXI (1957), 442–453; and Bell, "A Portrait of the Colonial Physician," *ibid.*, XLIV (1970), 497–517. For further information on medicine in the colonial South, see Richard Beale Davis, *Intellectual Life in the Colonial South, 1585–1763*, 3 vols. (Knoxville, Tenn., 1978), II, 906–928.

5. AH to Gavin Hamilton, June 13, 1739, Hamilton Letter Book.

INTRODUCTION

Although Dr. Alexander Hamilton, alias Loquacious Scribble in his comic narrative, *The History of the Tuesday Club,* once came close to losing his nose at the hands of the club's president during a furious clubical skirmish, he should not be confused with, nor was he related to the Alexander Hamilton who lost his life at the hands of Aaron Burr. To be sure, in *The History of the Tuesday Club* Hamilton relates the infamous duel that occurred in the streets of Annapolis on June 19, 1752, when Loquacious Scribble confronted that arrogant fomenter of clubical mischief, Coney Pimp Frontinbrass, during the great clubical Battle of Farce-alia; but at the approach of the formidable Frontinbrass, "mounted on a lofty Chariot . . . drawn by two fiery Steeds" and armed with "a whip of an Enormous Size . . . which he smacked as he drove along," Scribble "did not stay to make him any answer, but ran precipitately into [a] back alley and Immediatly betook himself to flight, to save his bacon" (III, 65–66). No one was shot; no one was even injured. It was just another afternoon's entertainment in the life of the Tuesday Club.

This Alexander Hamilton was born in Edinburgh on September 26, 1712, fifth son of Mary Robertson Hamilton and William Hamilton (professor of divinity and principal at the University of Edinburgh), at a time when Edinburgh was rapidly becoming one of the intellectual centers of Europe. Hamilton attended the University of Edinburgh and received his medical degree from that institution in 1737. Like other eighteenth-century Scots, he left his homeland shortly after receiving his medical degree for "the simple [reason] . . . that Scotland was a poor country in which too many competed for too few resources."[1] Following the lead of his oldest brother, John, who had established a profitable medical practice in Maryland, Hamilton emigrated to Annapolis during the winter of 1738, choosing the better prospects for professional advancement that the colonies offered.

Hamilton arrived in Maryland at the beginning of the period now commonly referred to as the golden age of Chesapeake culture (1740 to 1770), but had anyone called it that in 1738 he probably would have taken his pulse and checked his temperature. Maryland culture had indeed developed

---

1. William R. Brock, *Scotus Americanus: A Survey of the Sources for Links between Scotland and America in the Eighteenth Century* (Edinburgh, 1982), 18. Hamilton offers much the same explanation himself in the *History* (see I, 83–84).

LIST OF MUSIC

Volume II

Anniversary Ode for 1750 107
    Air for His Honor 108
    Minuet for His Honor 108
Anniversary Ode for 1751 278
    Club March against Sir Hugh Maccarty 289
Minuet for Sir John 293

Volume III

Minuet for His Honor 44
Anniversary Ode for 1753 157
    Minuet for the Chancellor 158
    Minuet for His Honor 163
    Gavotte for His Honor 164
    Minuet for Sir John 167
    March for Sir John 167
Minuet for the Poet Laureat 171
Grand Club Jig 172
Overture for His Honor's Entertainment 173
Gavotta Burlesqua for His Honor 174
Minuet for the Attorney General 176
Song of Robin and Jeck 203
The Jurors for the City Bring 346

The Misbehaviour of Sir John 295
Oldham Wisely Esqr Delivering a Speech in Club 304
Mr Attorney Spyplot, Long Standing Member of the Tuesday
　Club 317
Shield on the Presidential Canopy 327
Laconic Comus Esqr, Orator of the Tuesday Club 329
Club Hubbub concerning the Records 374
The Club Seal 411
Philo Dogmaticus Esqr, Chancellor of the Tuesday Club 414

Volume II

Frontispiece xii
Club Conundrums Introduced 61
Club Squabble concerning Sir John's Commission 81
The Tuesday Club Medal 93
The Second Grand Anniversary Procession 98
Division of the Theatre 147
The Honorable Nasifer Jole Esqr Wears the Cap of State 202
Coneius Pimpeius Frontinbrass the Great 211
Private Conference of Frontinbrass with the Honorable Nasifer Jole
　Esqr 216
Prim Timorous Esqr, Serjeant at Arms to the Tuesday Club 223
The Genius of the Tuesday Club Appearing to the Longstanding
　Members 230
Jonathan Grog Esqr under Custody of the Serjeant at Arms 238
Grand Ceremony of the Capation 246
Third Grand Anniversary Procession 267
Grand Rehearsal of the Anniversary Ode 269
Signior Lardini, Musician *Con Stromenti* to the Tuesday Club 277
Narrow Escape of the Secretary 298
The Tragical Night Adventure in His Lordship's Bedchamber 307
Genearchy of the Club 326
His Lordship Encounters Sir Hugh Maccarty's Coffin 343
Deputation of the Club to His Lordship 386
A List of the Present Members of the Ancient and Honorable Tuesday
　Club of Annapolis, and Their Order of Serving 399

LIST OF ILLUSTRATIONS

Volume I

Frontispiece 2
Congal de Rutherin 46
The Whin Bush Club Admitting a Member 57
Mr George Neilson 75
The Royalist Club 84
Mr Neilson's Anger Restrained by Philosophy 87
Mr Neilson's Battle with the Royalist Club 92
Mr Neilson Taking Snuff with the Red House Club 96
The Ugly Club 105
First Sederunt of the Ancient and Honorable Tuesday Club 126
The Honorable Carlo Nasifer Jole Esqr, President of the Ancient and
    Honorable Tuesday Club 135
The Tobacco-Pipe Procession 148
The Phrensy of a Baltimore Bard 158
The Drinking of Lambs Wool at Batchellors Hall 162
The Unlucky Adventure at the Cathedration of the Honorable Carlo
    Nasifer Jole Esqr 177
The Honorable Nasifer Jole Esqr First Mounts the Presidential Chair
    of State 191
Loquacious Scribble Esqr, Secretary and Orator of the Ancient and
    Honorable Tuesday Club 203
Mr Secretary Scribble Delivering a Speech in Club 206
Drawlum Quaint Esqr Delivering a Speech in Club 208
The Club Badge 216
The Honorable Mr President Jole Delivering a Speech in Club . 225
Sir John Oldcastle, Knight and Champion of the Tuesday Club . 227
Solo Neverout Esqr, Musician and Attorney General of the Tuesday
    Club 234
The First Grand Anniversary Procession 241
Jonathan Grog Esqr, Poet Laureat and Master of Ceremonies of the
    Tuesday Club 274
The Presidential Badge 282
The New Club Badge 282

Book VIII 137
Book IX 251
Book X 347
Index 401

Volume III

The History of the Ancient and Honorable Tuesday Club, VOLUME III

    Contents 2
    Book XI 7
    Book XII 127
    Book XIII 217
    Book XIV 305

Appendixes 359

Punctuation Changes 379

Substantive Changes 394

Index to Volumes I–III 399

CONTENTS

Volume I

Acknowledgments vii
List of Illustrations xi
List of Music xiii
Introduction xv
Composition xxxv
Provenance xxxix
Bibliographical Note xli
Editorial Method xlv
Remarks on the Drawings lxi
Remarks on the Music lxix
Remarks on the Notes lxxiii
Tuesday Club Pseudonyms lxxv
Biographical Sketches lxxix

The History of the Ancient and Honorable Tuesday Club, VOLUME I

    Contents 4
    Dedication 10
    Preface 14
    Book I 19
    Book II 69
    Book III 115
    Book IV 181
    Book V 245
    Book VI 347
    Index 419

Volume II

The History of the Ancient and Honorable Tuesday Club, VOLUME II

    Contents 2
    Book VII 7

ACKNOWLEDGMENTS

This edition is dedicated to the man who introduced me to the world of the Tuesday Club, who showed me early on that scholarship is hard and proud work, and whose sound advice and continued support have firmly established him as perpetual president of my club.

My thanks also to the honorary and longstanding members who contributed to this edition: John Hales, H:M:, who deserves a special place among the clubical worthies for having given up the better part of a summer to help me proofread my typescript against Hamilton's manuscript; Gregory Stiverson, H:M:, who provided useful comments on the biographical sketches; Georgia Brady Barnhill, H:M:, whose remarks on Hamilton's illustrations are included in this edition; Norman Fiering, L:S:M:, who guided this edition through its early stages; Daniel Williman, L:S:M:, and Saul Levin, L:S:M:, who provided transcriptions of the Latin and Greek passages and helped to track down many of the classical allusions; Gil Kelly, L:S:M:, who helped to make many a note more noteworthy; and Edward King, L:S:M:, who designed this edition.

I am particularly grateful to the oldstanding member who has helped me through every phase of this project from beginning to end, Cynthia Carter Ayres, a person whose eye for consistency and attention to detail make her an editor's editor. Together we have cared for and corrected this edition as if we were raising a child. We did the best we could; now it's time to send it a-clubbing into, I hope, a hospitable world.

Finally, I want to thank the Tuesday Club itself. Loquacious Scribble, Jonathan Grog, Quirpum Comic, Prim Timorous—you and your companions have taught me much about friendship, trifles, and laughter.

*Publication of these volumes was made possible
by a grant from a fund established by
DeWitt Wallace, founder of* Reader's Digest.

*The editor is grateful to the John Work Garrett Library
of the Milton S. Eisenhower Library at the Johns Hopkins
University and to the Manuscripts Division of the
Maryland Historical Society Library for permission
to publish this edition.*

For J. A. Leo Lemay

The publication of this work was made possible in part through a grant from the Division of Research Programs of the National Endowment for the Humanities, an independent federal agency whose mission is to award grants to support education, scholarship, media programming, libraries, and museums, in order to bring the results of cultural activities to a broad, general public.

The Institute of Early American History and Culture
is sponsored jointly by the
College of William and Mary and the
Colonial Williamsburg Foundation.

© 1990 The University of North Carolina Press
All rights reserved
Manufactured in the United States of America

The paper in this book meets the guidelines for permanence
and durability of the Committee on Production Guidelines
for Book Longevity of the Council on Library Resources.

Printed in the United States of America

94 93 92 91 90   5 4 3 2 1

Library of Congress Cataloging-in-Publication Data

Hamilton, Alexander, 1712–1756.
    The history of the ancient and honorable Tuesday Club / by
Alexander Hamilton; edited by Robert Micklus.
        p.   cm.
    "Published for the Institute of Early American History and
Culture, Williamsburg, Virginia."
    Includes index.
    ISBN 0-8078-1851-8 (set: alk. paper)
    1. Annapolis (Md.)—History—Colonial period, ca. 1600–1775—
Fiction. 2. Tuesday Club (Annapolis, Md.)—History—18th century—
Fiction. 3. Maryland—History—Colonial period, ca. 1600–1775—
Fiction. I. Micklus, Robert. II. Institute of Early American
History and Culture (Williamsburg, Va.) III. Title.
PS763.H35H57   1990
813'.1—dc20   89-30768
                                                                                   CIP

The History of the Ancient and Honorable Tuesday Club

BY DR. ALEXANDER HAMILTON

VOLUME I

Edited by Robert Micklus

PUBLISHED FOR THE INSTITUTE
OF EARLY AMERICAN HISTORY AND CULTURE
WILLIAMSBURG, VIRGINIA

BY THE UNIVERSITY OF NORTH CAROLINA PRESS
CHAPEL HILL AND LONDON

The History of the Tuesday Club